KU-623-007

THE WITCHING HOUR

Demonstrating, once again, her gift for spellbinding storytelling, Anne Rice makes real for us a great dynasty of four centuries of witches—a family given to poetry and incest, murder and philosophy, a family that over the ages is itself haunted by a powerful, dangerous, and seductive being.

He is called Lasher, and throughout the centuries he haunts the Mayfair women, until the inevitable clash occurs. Only then does it become clear whether Rowan, the Mayfair daughter of today, will prove a force of good or evil . . . or which of them is to be more feared.

Moving in time from today's New Orleans and San Francisco to long-ago Amsterdam and the France of Louis XIV, from the coffee plantations of Port-au-Prince to Civil War New Orleans and back to today, Anne Rice has spun a mesmerizing tale that challenges everything we believe in.

Anne Rice

Also by Anne Rice
Published by Ballantine Books:

INTERVIEW WITH THE VAMPIRE
THE FEAST OF ALL SAINTS
CRY TO HEAVEN
THE VAMPIRE LESTAT
THE QUEEN OF THE DAMNED
THE MUMMY

THE WITCHING HOUR

Anne Rice

BALLANTINE BOOKS · NEW YORK

Sale of this book without a front cover may be unauthorized. If this book is coverless, it may have been reported to the publisher as "unsold or destroyed" and neither the author nor the publisher may have received payment for it.

Copyright © 1990 by Anne O'Brien Rice

All rights reserved under International and Pan-American Copyright Conventions. Published in the United States of America by Ballantine Books, a division of Random House, Inc., New York, and simultaneously in Canada by Random House of Canada Limited, Toronto.

Library of Congress Catalog Card Number: 90-53103

ISBN 0-345-37529-7

This edition published by arrangement with Alfred A. Knopf, Inc.

Manufactured in the United States of America

First International Ballantine Books Edition: October 1991

With Love:

FOR
Stan Rice and Christopher Rice

FOR
John Preston

FOR

O'Brien Borchardt, Tamara O'Brien Tinker, Karen O'Brien, and Micki O'Brien Collins

AND FOR
Dorothy Van Bever O'Brien, who bought me my first typewriter 1959, taking the time and trouble to see that it was a good one.

And the rain is brain-colored.
And the thunder sounds like something remembering something.

STAN RICE

från
Pappa till
mig 93-08-27

Bobbo f/l
Piero
mvd 93-08-23
pmm

THE
WITCHING
HOUR

PART ONE

COME
TOGETHER

One

THE DOCTOR WOKE up afraid. He had been dreaming of the old house in New Orleans again. He had seen the woman in the rocker. He'd seen the man with the brown eyes.

And even now in this quiet hotel room above New York City he felt the old alarming disorientation. He'd been talking again with the brown-eyed man. Yes, help her. *No, this is just a dream. I want to get out of it.*

The doctor sat up in bed. No sound but the faint roar of the air conditioner. Why was he thinking about it tonight in a hotel room in the Parker Meridien? For a moment he couldn't shake the feeling of the old house. He saw the woman again—her bent head, her vacant stare. He could almost hear the hum of the insects against the screens of the old porch. And the brown-eyed man was speaking without moving his lips. A waxen dummy infused with life—

No. Stop it.

He got out of bed and padded silently across the carpeted floor until he stood in front of the sheer white curtains, peering out at black sooty rooftops and dim neon signs flickering against brick walls. The early morning light showed behind the clouds above the dull concrete facade opposite. No debilitating heat here. No drowsing scent of roses, of gardenias.

Gradually his head cleared.

He thought of the Englishman at the bar in the lobby again. That's what had brought it all back—the Englishman remarking to the bartender that he'd just come from New Orleans, and that certainly was a *haunted* city. The Englishman, an affable man, a true Old World gentleman it seemed, in a narrow seersucker suit with a gold watch chain fixed to his vest pocket. Where did one see that kind of man these days?—a man with the sharp melodious inflection of a British stage actor, and brilliant, ageless blue eyes.

The doctor had turned to him and said: "Yes, you're right

3

about New Orleans, you certainly are. I saw a ghost myself in New Orleans, and not very long ago—'' Then he had stopped, embarrassed. He had stared at the melted bourbon before him, the sharp refraction of light in the base of the crystal glass.

Hum of flies in summer; smell of medicine. *That much Thorazine? Could there be some mistake?*

But the Englishman had been respectfully curious. He'd invited the doctor to join him for dinner, said he collected such tales. For a moment, the doctor had been tempted. There was a lull in the convention, and he liked this man, felt an immediate trust in him. And the lobby of the Parker Meridien was a nice cheerful place, full of light, movement, people. So far away from that gloomy New Orleans corner, from the sad old city festering with secrets in its perpetual Caribbean heat.

But the doctor could not tell that story.

''If ever you change your mind, do call me,'' the Englishman had said. ''My name is Aaron Lightner.'' He'd given the doctor a card with the name of an organization inscribed on it: ''You might say we collect ghost stories—true ones, that is.''

THE TALAMASCA

We watch
And we are always here.

It was a curious motto.

Yes, that was what had brought it all back. The Englishman and that peculiar calling card with the European phone numbers, the Englishman who was leaving for the Coast tomorrow to see a California man who had lately drowned and been brought back to life. The doctor had read of that case in the New York papers—one of those characters who suffers clinical death and returns after having seen ''the light.''

They had talked about the drowned man together, he and the Englishman. ''He claims now to have psychic powers, you see,'' said the Englishman, ''and that interests us, of course. Seems he sees images when he touches things with his bare hands. We call it psychometry.''

The doctor had been intrigued. He had heard of a few such patients himself, cardiac victims if he rightly recalled, who had come back, one claiming to have seen the future. ''Near Death Experience.'' One saw more and more articles about the phenomenon in the journals.

''Yes,'' Lightner had said, ''the best research on the subject has been done by doctors—by cardiologists.''

4

"Wasn't there a film a few years back," the doctor had asked, "about a woman who returned with the power to heal? Strangely affecting."

"You're open-minded on the subject," the Englishman had said with a delighted smile. "Are you sure you won't tell me about your ghost? I'd so love to hear it. I'm not flying out till tomorrow, sometime before noon. What I wouldn't give to hear your story!"

No, not that story. Not ever.

Alone now in the shadowy hotel room, the doctor felt fear again. The clock ticked in the long dusty hallway in New Orleans. He heard the shuffle of his patient's feet as the nurse "walked" her. He smelled that smell again of a New Orleans house in summer, heat and old wood. The man was talking to him . . .

The doctor had never been inside an antebellum mansion until that spring in New Orleans. And the old house really did have white fluted columns on the front, though the paint was peeling away. Greek Revival style they called it—a long violet-gray town house on a dark shady corner in the Garden District, its front gate guarded it seemed by two enormous oaks. The iron lace railings were made in a rose pattern and much festooned with vines—purple wisteria, the yellow Virginia creeper, and bougainvillea of a dark, incandescent pink.

He liked to pause on the marble steps and look up at the Doric capitals, wreathed as they were by those drowsy fragrant blossoms. The sun came in thin dusty shafts through the twisting branches. Bees sang in the tangle of brilliant green leaves beneath the peeling cornices. Never mind that it was so somber here, so damp.

Even the approach through the deserted streets seduced him. He walked slowly over cracked and uneven sidewalks of herringbone brick or gray flagstone, under an unbroken archway of oak branches, the light eternally dappled, the sky perpetually veiled in green. Always he paused at the largest tree that had lifted the iron fence with its bulbous roots. He could not have gotten his arms around the trunk of it. It reached all the way from the pavement to the house itself, twisted limbs clawing at the shuttered windows beyond the banisters, leaves enmeshed with the flowering vines.

But the decay here troubled him nevertheless. Spiders wove their tiny intricate webs over the iron lace roses. In places the iron had so rusted that it fell away to powder at the touch. And

5

here and there near the railings, the wood of the porches was rotted right through.

Then there was the old swimming pool far beyond the garden—a great long octagon bounded by the flagstones, which had become a swamp unto itself with its black water and wild irises. The smell alone was frightful. Frogs lived there, frogs you could hear at dusk, singing their grinding, ugly song. Sad to see the little fountain jets up one side and down the other still sending their little arching streams into the muck. He longed to drain it, clean it, scrub the sides with his own hands if he had to. Longed to patch the broken balustrade, and rip the weeds from the overgrown urns.

Even the elderly aunts of his patient—Miss Carl, Miss Millie, and Miss Nancy—had an air of staleness and decay. It wasn't a matter of gray hair or wire-rimmed glasses. It was their manner, and the fragrance of camphor that clung to their clothes.

Once he had wandered into the library and taken a book down from the shelf. Tiny black beetles scurried out of the crevice. Alarmed he had put the book back.

If there had been air-conditioning in the place it might have been different. But the old house was too big for that—or so they had said back then. The ceilings soared fourteen feet overhead. And the sluggish breeze carried with it the scent of mold.

His patient was well cared for, however. That he had to admit. A sweet old black nurse named Viola brought his patient out on the screened porch in the morning and took her in at evening.

"She's no trouble at all, Doctor. Now, you come on, Miss Deirdre, walk for the doctor." Viola would lift her out of the chair and push her patiently step by step.

"I've been with her seven years now, Doctor, she's my sweet girl."

Seven years like that. No wonder the woman's feet had started to turn in at the ankles, and her arms to draw close to her chest if the nurse didn't force them down into her lap again.

Viola would walk her round and round the long double parlor, past the harp and the Bösendorfer grand layered with dust. Into the long broad dining room with its faded murals of moss-hung oaks and tilled fields.

Slippered feet shuffling on the worn Aubusson carpet. The woman was forty-one years old, yet she looked both ancient and young—a stooped and pale child, untouched by adult worry or passion. *Deirdre, did you ever have a lover? Did you ever dance in that parlor?*

On the library bookshelves were leather-bound ledgers with old dates marked on the spines in faded purple ink: 1756, 1757,

1758 . . . Each bore the family name of Mayfair in gold lettering.

Ah, these old southern families, how he envied them their heritage. It did not have to lead to this decay. And to think, he did not know the full names of his own great-grandparents or where they had been born.

Mayfair—a vintage colonial clan. There were old paintings on the walls of men and women in eighteenth-century dress, as well as daguerreotypes and tintypes and faded photographs. A yellowed map of Saint-Domingue—did they call it that still?—in a dirty frame in the hallway. And a darkening painting of a great plantation house.

And look at the jewels his patient wore. Heirlooms surely, with those antique settings. What did it mean that they put that kind of jewelry on a woman who hadn't spoken a word or moved of her own volition in over seven years?

The nurse said she never took off the chain with the emerald pendant, not even when she bathed Miss Deirdre.

"Let me tell you a little secret, Doctor, don't you ever touch that!"

"And why not?" he wanted to ask. But he had said nothing. He watched uneasily as the nurse put on the patient's ruby earrings, her diamond ring.

Like dressing a corpse, he thought. And out there the dark oaks wind their limbs towards the dusty window screens. And the garden shimmers in the dull heat.

"And look at her hair," said the nurse lovingly. "Have you ever seen such beautiful hair?"

It was black all right, and thick and curly and long. The nurse loved to brush it, watching the curls roll up as the brush released them. And the patient's eyes, for all their listless stare, were a clear blue. Yet now and then a thin silver line of saliva fell down from the side of her mouth, making a dark circle on the bosom of her white nightgown.

"It's a wonder somebody hasn't tried to steal those things," he said half to himself. "She's so helpless."

The nurse had given him a superior, knowing smile.

"No one who's ever worked in this house would try that."

"But she sits all alone on that side porch by the hour. You can see her from the street."

Laughter.

"Don't worry about that, Doctor. No one around here is fool enough to come in that gate. Old Ronnie mows the lawn, but that's because he always did, done it for thirty years now, but then old Ronnie isn't exactly right in the head."

7

"Nevertheless . . ." But he had stopped himself. What was he doing, talking like this right in front of the silent woman, whose eyes only now and then moved just a little, whose hands lay just where the nurse had placed them, whose feet rested limply on the bare floor. How easy it was to forget oneself, forget to respect this tragic creature. Nobody knew what the woman understood.

"Might get her out in the sun sometime," the doctor said. "Her skin is so white."

But he knew the garden was impossible, even far away from the reek of the pool. The thorny bougainvillea burst in clumps from beneath the wild cherry laurel. Fat little cherubs, streaked with slime, peered out of overgrown lantana like ghosts.

Yet once children had played here.

Some boy or girl had carved the word *Lasher* into the thick trunk of the giant crepe myrtle that grew against the far fence. The deep gashes had weathered so that they gleamed white against the waxy bark. Strange word that. And a wooden swing was still hanging from the branch of the distant oak.

He'd walked back to that lonely tree, and sat down on the swing for a moment, felt the rusted chains creak, then move as he pushed his foot into the crushed grass.

The southern flank of the house looked mammoth and over-whelmingly beautiful to him from this perspective, the flowering vines climbing together all the way up past the green shuttered windows to the twin chimneys above the third floor. The dark bamboo rattled in the breeze against the plastered masonry. The glossy banana trees grew so high and dense they made a jungle clear back to the brick wall.

It was like his patient, this old place—beautiful yet forgotten by time, by urgency.

Her face might be pretty still if it were not so utterly lifeless. Did she see the delicate purple clusters of wisteria, shivering against the screens, the writhing tangle of other blooms? Could she see all the way through the trees to the white columned house across the street?

Once he had ridden upstairs with her and her nurse in the quaint yet powerful little elevator with its brass gate and worn carpet. No change in Deirdre's expression as the little car began to rise. It made him anxious to hear the churning machinery. He could not imagine the motor except as something blackened and sticky and ancient, coated with dust.

Of course he had questioned the old doctor at the sanitarium.

"I remember when I was your age," said the old doctor. "I was going to cure all of them. I was going to reason with the

8

paranoiacs, and bring the schizophrenics back to reality, and make the catatonics wake up. You give her that shot every day, son. There's nothing there anymore. We just do our best to keep her from getting worked up now and then, you know, the agitation.''

Agitation? That was the reason for these powerful drugs? Even if the shots were stopped tomorrow it would be a month before the effects had fully worn off. And the levels used were so high they might have killed another patient. You had to build up to a dosage like that.

How could anyone know the true state of the woman when the medication had gone on for so long? If only he could run an electroencephalogram . . .

He'd been on the case about a month when he sent for the records. It was a routine request. No one noticed. He sat at his desk at the sanitarium all afternoon struggling with the scrawl of dozens of other physicians, the vague and contradictory diagnoses—mania, paranoia, complete exhaustion, delusions, psychotic break, depression, attempted suicide. It went all the way back to the girl's teens apparently. No, even before. Someone had seen her for ''dementia'' when she was ten years old.

What were the specifics behind these abstractions? Somewhere in the mountain of scribble he found that she had borne a girl child at eighteen, given it up, suffered ''severe paranoia.''

Is that why they had given her shock treatments in one place and insulin shock in another? What had she done to the nurses who over and over again quit on account of ''physical attacks''?

She had ''run away'' at one point, been ''forcibly committed'' again. Then pages were missing, whole years uncharted. ''Irreversible brain damage'' was noted in 1976. ''Patient sent home, Thorazine prescribed to prevent palsy, mania.''

It was an ugly document, telling no story, revealing no truth. And it discouraged him, finally. Had a legion of other doctors talked to her the way he did now when he sat beside her on the side porch?

''It's a beautiful day, isn't it, Deirdre?'' Ah, the breeze here, so fragrant. The scent of the gardenias was suddenly overpowering, yet he loved it. Just for a moment, he closed his eyes.

Did she loathe him, laugh at him, even know he was there? There were a few streaks of gray in her hair, he saw that now. Her hand was cold, unpleasant to touch.

The nurse came out with a blue envelope in her hand, a snapshot.

''It's from your daughter, Deirdre. See? She's twenty-four years old now, Deirdre.'' She held the snapshot out for the doc-

9

tor to see too. A blond girl on the deck of a big white yacht, hair blowing in the wind. Pretty, very pretty. "On San Francisco Bay, 1983."

Nothing changed in the woman's face. The nurse brushed the black hair back from her forehead. She thrust the picture at the doctor. "See that girl? That girl's a doctor, too!" She gave him a great superior nod. "She's an intern, going to be a medical doctor just like you some day, that's the truth."

Was it possible? Had the young woman never come home to see to her own mother? He disliked her suddenly. Going to be a medical doctor, indeed.

How long had it been since his patient had worn a dress or a real pair of shoes? He longed to play a radio for her. Maybe she would like music. The nurse had her television soap operas on all afternoon in the back kitchen.

He came to distrust the nurses as he distrusted the aunts.

The tall one who wrote the checks for him—"Miss Carl"— was a lawyer still though she must have been in her seventies. She came and went from her offices on Carondelet Street in a taxicab because she could no longer climb up on the high wooden step of the St. Charles car. For fifty years, she had told him once when he had met her at the gate, she had ridden the St. Charles car.

"Oh, yes," the nurse said one afternoon as she was brushing Deirdre's hair very slowly, very gently. "Miss Carl's the smart one. Works for Judge Fleming. One of the first women ever to graduate from the Loyola School of Law. She was seventeen years old when she went to Loyola. Her father was old Judge McIntyre, and she was ever so proud of him."

Miss Carl never spoke to the patient, not that the doctor had ever seen. It was the portly one, "Miss Nancy," who was mean to her, or so the doctor thought.

"They say Miss Nancy never had much chance for an education," the nurse gossiped. "Always home taking care of the others. There used to be old Miss Belle here too."

There was something sullen and almost common about "Miss Nancy." Dumpy, neglected, always wearing her apron yet speaking to the nurse in that patronizing artificial voice. Miss Nancy had a faint sneer on her lips when she looked at Deirdre.

And then there was Miss Millie, the eldest of them all, who was actually some sort of cousin—a classic in old lady black silk and string shoes. She came and went, never without her worn gloves and her small black straw hat with its veil. She had a cheery smile for the doctor, and a kiss for Deirdre. "That's my poor dear sweetheart," she would say in a tremulous voice.

One afternoon, he had come upon Miss Millie standing on the broken flags by the pool.

"Nowhere to begin anymore, Doctor," she had said sadly.

It was not his place to challenge her, yet something quickened in him to hear this tragedy acknowledged.

"And how Stella loved to swim here,'' the old woman said. "It was Stella who built it, Stella who had so many plans and dreams. Stella put in the elevator, you know. That's just the sort of thing that Stella would do. Stella gave such parties. Why, I remember hundreds in the house, tables over the whole lawn, and the bands that would play. You're too young, Doctor, to remember that lively music. Stella had those draperies made in the double parlor, and now they're too old to be cleaned anymore. That's what they said. They'd fall apart if we tried to clean them now. And it was Stella who had paths of flagstones laid here, all along the pool. You see, like the old flags in the front and along the side . . ." She broke off, pointing down the long side of the house at the distant patio so crowded by weeds. It was as if she couldn't speak any more. Slowly she looked up at the high attic window.

He had wanted to ask, But who is Stella?

"Poor darling Stella."

He had envisioned paper lanterns strung through the trees.

Maybe they were simply too old, these women. And that young one, the intern or whatever she was, two thousand miles away . . .

Miss Nancy bullied the silent Deirdre. She'd watch the nurse walking the patient, then shout in the patient's ear.

"Pick up your feet. You know damn good and well you could walk on your own if you wanted to."

"There's nothing wrong with Miss Deirdre's hearing," the nurse would interrupt her. "Doctor says she can hear and see just fine."

Once he tried to question Miss Nancy as she swept the upstairs hallway, thinking, well, maybe out of anger she'll shed a little light.

"Is there ever the slightest change in her? Does she ever speak . . . even a single word?"

The woman squinted at him for a long moment, the sweat gleaming on her round face, her nose painfully red at the bridge from the weight of her glasses.

"I'll tell you what I want to know!" she said. "Who's going to take care of her when we're no longer here! You think that spoilt daughter out in California is going to take care of her? That girl doesn't even know her mother's name. It's Ellie Mayfair who sends those pictures.'' She snorted. ''Ellie Mayfair hasn't set foot in this house since the day that baby was born and she came to take that baby out of here. All she wanted was that baby because she couldn't have a baby of her own, and she was scared to death her husband would leave her. He's some big lawyer out there. You know what Carl paid Ellie to take that baby? To see to it that girl never came home? Oh, just get her out of here, that was the idea. Made Ellie sign a paper.'' She gave a bitter smile, wiping her hands on her apron. ''Send her to California with Ellie and Graham to live in a fancy house on San Francisco Bay with a big boat and all, that's what happened to Deirdre's daughter.''

Ah, so the young woman did not know, he thought, but he said nothing.

''Let Carl and Nancy stay here and take care of things!'' The woman went on. ''That's the song in this family. Let Carl write the checks and let Nancy cook and scrub. And what the hell has Millie ever done? Millie just goes to church, and prays for us all. Isn't that grand? Aunt Millie's more useless than Aunt Belle ever was. I'll tell you what Aunt Millie can do best. Cut flowers. Aunt Millie cuts those roses now and then, those roses growing wild out there.''

She gave a deep ugly laugh, and went past him into the patient's bedroom, gripping the broom by its greasy handle.

''You know you can't ask a nurse to sweep a floor! Oh, no, they wouldn't stoop to that, now, would they? Would you care to tell me why a nurse cannot sweep a floor?''

The bedroom was clean all right, the master bedroom of the house it appeared to be, a large airy northern room. Ashes in the marble fireplace. And what a bed his patient slept in, one of those massive things made at the end of the last century, with the towering half tester of walnut and tufted silk.

He was glad of the smell of floor wax and fresh linen. But the room was full of dreadful religious artifacts. On the marble dresser stood a statue of the Virgin with the naked red heart on her breast, lurid, and disgusting to look at. A crucifix lay beside it, with a twisting, writhing body of Christ in natural colors even to the dark blood flowing from the nails in his hands. Candles burned in red glasses, beside a bit of withered palm.

''Does she notice these religious things?'' the doctor asked.

''Hell, no,'' Miss Nancy said. Whiffs of camphor rose from the dresser drawers as she straightened their contents. ''Lot of good they do under this roof!''

There were rosaries hung about the carved brass lamps, even through their faded satin shades. And it seemed nothing had

12

been changed here for decades. The yellow lace curtains were stiff and rotted in places. Catching the sun they seemed to hold it, casting their own burnt and somber light.

There was the jewel box on the marble-top bedside table. Open. As if the contents weren't priceless, which of course they were. Even the doctor, with his scant knowledge of such things, knew those jewels were real.

Beside the jewel box stood the snapshot of the pretty blond-haired daughter. And beneath it a much older and faded picture of the same girl, small but even then quite pretty. Scribble at the bottom. He could only make out: "Pacific Heights School, 1966."

When he touched the velvet cover of the jewel box, Miss Nancy had turned and all but screamed at him.

"Don't you touch that, Doctor!"

"Good Lord, woman, you don't think I'm a thief."

"There's a lot you don't know about this house and this patient. Why do you think the shutters are all broken, Doctor? Almost fallen off their hinges? Why do you think the plaster's peeling off the brick?" She shook her head, the soft flesh of her cheeks wobbling, her colorless mouth set. "Just let somebody try to fix those shutters. Just let someone climb a ladder and try to paint this house."

"I don't understand you," said the doctor.

"Don't ever touch her jewels, Doctor, that's what I'm saying. Don't touch a thing around here you don't have to. That swimming pool out there, for instance. All choked with leaves and filth like it is, but those old fountains run into it still, you ever think about that? Just try to turn off those faucets, Doctor!"

"But who—?"

"Leave her jewels alone, Doctor. That's my advice to you."

"Would changing things make her speak?" he asked boldly, impatient with all this, and not afraid of this aunt the way he was of Miss Carl.

The woman laughed. "No, it wouldn't make *her* do anything," Nancy answered with a sneer. She slammed the drawer into the bureau. Glass rosary beads tinkled against a small statue of Jesus. "Now, if you'll excuse me, I have to clean out the bathroom, too."

He looked at the bearded Jesus, the finger pointing to the crown of thorns around his heart.

Maybe they were all crazy. Maybe he would go crazy himself if he didn't get out of this house.

Once, when he was alone in the dining room, he'd seen that word again—Lasher—written in the thick dust on the table. It

13

was done as if by fingertip. Great fancy capital L. Now, what could it possibly mean? It was dusted away when he came the following afternoon, the only time in fact that he had ever seen the dust disturbed there, where the silver tea service on the sideboard was tarnished black. Faded the murals on these walls, yet he could see a plantation scene if he studied them, yes, that same house that was in the painting in the hall. Only after he had studied the chandelier for a long time did he realize it had never been wired for electricity. There was wax still on the candle holders. Ah, such a sadness, the whole place.

At night at home in his modern apartment overlooking the lake, he couldn't stop brooding on his patient. He wondered if her eyes were open as she lay in bed.

"Maybe I have an obligation—" But then what obligation? Her doctor was a reputable psychiatrist. Wouldn't do to question his judgment. Wouldn't do to try anything foolish—like taking her out for a ride in the country, or bringing a radio to the porch. Or *stopping the sedatives to see what would happen*?

Or picking up a phone and contacting that daughter, the intern. *Made Ellie sign a paper.* Twenty-four years old was plenty old enough to be told a few things about one's own mother.

And surely common sense dictated a break in Deirdre's medication once in a while. And what about a complete reevaluation? He had to at least suggest it.

"You just give her the shots," said the old doctor. "Visit with her an hour a day. That's what you're asked to do." Slight coldness this time around. Old fool!

No wonder he was so glad the afternoon he had first seen the man visiting her.

It was early September, and still warm. And as he turned in the gate, he saw the man on the screen porch beside her, obviously talking to her, his arm resting on the back of her chair.

A tall, brown-haired man, rather slender.

The doctor felt a curious possessive feeling. A man he didn't know with his patient. But he was eager to meet him actually. Maybe the man would explain things that the women would not. And surely he was a good friend. There was something intimate in the way he stood so close, the way he inclined towards the silent Deirdre.

But when the doctor came out on the porch there was no visitor. And he could find no one in the front rooms.

"You know, I saw a man here awhile ago," he said to the nurse when she came in. "He was talking to Miss Deirdre."

"I didn't see him," the nurse had said offhandedly.

Miss Nancy, shelling peas in the kitchen when he found her, stared at him for a long moment, then shook her head, her chin jutting. "I didn't hear anybody come in."

Well, isn't that the damnedest thing! But he had to confess, it had only been for an instant—a glimpse through the screens. No, but he *saw* the man there.

"If only you could speak to me," he said to Deirdre when they were alone. He was preparing the injection. "If only you could tell me if you want to have visitors, if it matters . . ." Her arm was so thin. When he glanced at her, the needle ready, she was staring at him!

"Deirdre?"

His heart pounded.

The eyes rolled to the left, and she stared forward, mute and listless as before. And the heat, which the doctor had come to like, seemed suddenly oppressive. The doctor felt light-headed in fact, as though he was about to faint. Beyond the blackened, dusty screen, the lawn seemed to move.

Now, he'd never fainted in his life, and as he thought that over, as he tried to think it over, he realized he'd been talking with the man, yes, the man was here, no, not here now, but just had been. They had been in the middle of a conversation, and now he'd lost the thread, or no, that wasn't it, it was that he suddenly couldn't remember how long they'd been talking, and it was so strange to have been talking all this time together, and not recall how it started!

He was suddenly trying to clear his head, and have a better look at the guy, but what had the man just said? It was all very confusing because there was no one there to talk to, no one but her, but yes, he'd just said to the brown-haired man, "Of course, stop the injections . . ." and the absolute rectitude of his position was beyond doubt, the old doctor—"A fool, yes!" said the brown-haired man—would just have to listen!

This was monstrous all this, and the daughter in California . . .

He shook himself. He stood up on the porch. What had happened? He had fallen asleep in the wicker chair. He had been dreaming. The murmur of the bees grew disconcertingly loud in his ears and the fragrance of the gardenias seemed to drug him suddenly. He looked down over the railing at the patio to his left. Had something moved there?

Only the limbs of the trees beyond as the breeze traveled through them. He'd seen it a thousand times in New Orleans, that graceful dance, as if one tree releases the breeze to another. Such lovely embracing heat. *Stop the injections! She will wake.*

Slowly, awkwardly, a monarch butterfly climbed the screen in front of him. Gorgeous wings. But gradually he focused upon the body of the thing, small and glossy and black. It ceased to be a butterfly and became an insect—loathsome!

"I have to go home," he said aloud to no one. "I don't feel right exactly, I think I should lie down."

The man's name. What was it? He'd known it just a moment ago, such a remarkable name—ah, so that's what the word means, you are— Actually, quite beautiful— But wait. It was happening again. He would not let it!

"Miss Nancy!" He stood up out of the chair.

His patient stared forward, unchanged, the heavy emerald pendant gleaming against her gown. All the world was filled with green light, with shivering leaves, the faint blur of the bougainvillea.

"Yes, the heat," he whispered. "Have I given her the shot?" Good Lord. He had actually dropped the syringe, and it had broken.

"You called for me, Doctor?" said Miss Nancy. There she stood in the parlor door, staring at him, wiping her hands on her apron. The colored woman was there too, and the nurse behind her.

"Nothing, just the heat," he murmured. "I dropped it, the needle. But I have another, of course."

How they looked at him, studied him. *You think I'm going crazy, too?*

It was on the following Friday afternoon that he saw the man again.

The doctor was late, he'd had an emergency at the sanitarium. He was sprinting up First Street in the early fall dusk. He didn't want to disturb the family dinner. He was running by the time he reached the gate.

The man was standing in the shadows of the open front porch. He watched the doctor, his arms folded, his shoulder against the porch column, his eyes dark and rather wide, as though he were lost in contemplation. Tall, slender, clothes beautifully fitted.

"Ah, so there you are," the doctor murmured aloud. Flush of relief. He had his hand out as he came up the steps. "Dr. Petrie is my name, how do you do?"

And—how to describe it? There was simply no man there.

"Now, I know this happened!" he said to Miss Carl in the kitchen. "I saw him on that porch and he vanished into thin air."

"Well, what business is it of ours what you saw, Doctor?" said the woman. Strange choice of words. And she was so hard,

16

this lady. Nothing feeble about her in her old age. She stood very straight in her dark blue gabardine suit, glaring at him through her wire-rimmed glasses, her mouth withered to a thin line.

"Miss Carl, I've seen this man with my patient. Now the patient, as we all know, is a helpless woman. If an unidentified person is coming and going on these premises—"

But the words were unimportant. Either the woman didn't believe him or the woman didn't care. And Miss Nancy, at the kitchen table, never even looked up from her plate as she scraped up the food noisily onto her fork. But the look on Miss Millie's face, ah, now that was something—old Miss Millie so clearly disturbed, her eyes darting from him to Carl and back again.

What a household.

He was irritated as he stepped into the dusty little elevator and pressed the black button in the brass plate.

The velvet drapes were closed and the bedroom was almost dark, the little candles sputtering in their red glasses. The shadow of the Virgin leapt on the wall. He couldn't find the light switch immediately. And when he did, only a single tiny bulb went on in the lamp beside the bed. The open jewel box was right next to it. What a spectacular thing.

When he saw the woman lying there with her eyes open, he felt a catch in his throat. Her black hair was brushed out over the stained pillowcase. There was a flush of unfamiliar color in her cheeks.

Did her lips move?

"Lasher . . ."

A whisper. What had she said? Why, she'd said Lasher, hadn't she? The name he'd seen on the tree trunk and in the dust of the dining table. And he had heard that name spoken somewhere else . . . That's why he knew it was a name. It sent the chills up his back and neck, this catatonic patient actually speaking. But no, he must have been imagining it. It was just the thing he wanted so to happen—the miracle change in her. She lay as ever in her trance. Enough Thorazine to kill somebody else . . .

He set down the bag on the side of the bed. He filled the syringe carefully, thinking as he had several times before, what if you just didn't, just cut it down to half, or a fourth, or none and sat by her and watched and what if— He saw himself suddenly picking her up and taking her out of the house. He saw himself driving her out into the country. They walked hand in hand on a path through the grass until they'd come to the levee above the river. And there she smiled, her hair blowing in the wind—

17

What nonsense. Here it was six thirty, and the shot was long overdue. And the syringe was ready.

Suddenly something pushed him. He was sure of it, though where he had been pushed he couldn't say. He went down, his legs buckling, and the syringe went flying.

When he caught himself he was on his knees in the semidark, staring at motes of dust gathered on the bare floor beneath the bed.

"What the hell—" he'd said aloud before he could catch himself. He couldn't find the hypodermic needle. Then he saw it, yards away, beyond the armoire. It was broken, smashed, as if someone had stepped on it. All the Thorazine had oozed out of the crushed plastic vial onto the bare boards.

"Now, wait a minute!" he whispered. He picked it up and stood holding the ruined thing in his hands. Of course he had other syringes, but this was the second time this sort of thing . . . And he found himself at the bedside again, staring down at the motionless patient, thinking, now how exactly did this—I mean, what in God's name is going on?

He felt a sudden intense heat. Something moved in the room, rattling faintly. Only the rosary beads wound about the brass lamp. He went to wipe his brow. Then he realized, very slowly, even as he stared at Deirdre, that there was a figure standing on the other side of the bed. He saw the dark clothes, a waistcoat, a coat with dark buttons. And then he looked up and saw it was the man.

In a split second his disbelief changed to terror. There was no disorientation now, no dreamlike unreality. The man was there, staring at him. Soft brown eyes staring at him. Then the man was simply gone. The room was cold. A breeze lifted the draperies. The doctor caught himself in the act of shouting. No, screaming, to be perfectly frank.

At ten o'clock that night, he was off the case. The old psychiatrist came all the way out to the lakefront apartment house to tell him in person. They had gone down to the lake together and strolled along the concrete shore.

"These old families, you can't argue with them. And you don't want to tangle with Carlotta Mayfair. The woman knows everybody. You'd be amazed how many people are beholden to her for one thing and another, or to Judge Fleming. And these people own property all over the city, if you only . . ."

"I tell you I saw this!" the doctor found himself saying.

But the old psychiatrist was dismissing him. There was a thinly concealed suspicion in his eyes as they measured the younger

18

doctor up and down, though the agreeable tone of his voice never changed.

"These old families." The doctor was never to go to that house again.

The doctor said nothing more. The truth was, he felt foolish. He wasn't a man who believed in ghosts! And he could not now bring himself to mount any intelligent argument about the woman herself, her condition, the obvious need for some periodic evaluation. No, his confidence had been dashed altogether.

Yet he knew he'd seen that figure. Seen it three times. And he could not forget the afternoon of the hazy, imagined conversation. The man had been there, too, yes, but insubstantial! And he had known the man's name, and yes, it was . . . Lasher!

But even if he discounted the dreamlike conversation—blamed it on the quiet of the place and the infernal heat, and the suggestion of a word carved into a tree trunk—the other times could not be discounted. He had seen a solid, living being there. No one would ever get him to deny it.

As the weeks passed and he failed to distract himself sufficiently with his work at the sanitarium, he began to write about the experience, describe it in detail. The man's brown hair had been slightly wavy. Eyes large. Fair skin like the poor sick woman. The man had been young, no more than twenty-five at best. The man had been without discernible expression. The doctor could even remember the man's hands. Nothing special about them, just nice hands. It struck him that the man, though thin, had been well proportioned. Only the clothes seemed unusual, and not the style of them, which was ordinary enough. It was the texture of the clothing. Unaccountably smooth like the face of the man. As if the whole figure—clothes, flesh, face—were made from the same thing.

One morning, the doctor awoke with the curiously clear thought: the mysterious man hadn't wanted her to have those sedatives! He'd known they were bad. And the woman was defenseless of course; she could not speak in her own behalf. The specter was protecting her!

But who in God's name will ever believe all this? the doctor thought. And he wished he were home, in Maine, working in his father's clinic and not in this damp and alien city. His father would understand. But then, no. His father would only be alarmed.

He tried to "keep busy." But the truth was, the sanitarium was a boring place. He had little to do. The old psychiatrist gave him a few new cases, but they were not challenging. Yet it was

19

essential that the doctor continue, that he erase all suspicion from the old psychiatrist's mind.

As fall turned to winter, the doctor began to dream of Deirdre. And in his dreams, he saw her cured, revitalized, walking swiftly down a city street, her hair blowing in the wind. Now and then when he woke up from such a dream, he found himself wondering if the poor woman hadn't died. That was the more likely thing.

When spring came around, and he had been in the city a full year, he found he had to see the house again. He took the St. Charles car to Jackson Avenue and walked from there as he had always done in the past.

It was all exactly the same, the thorny bougainvillea in full bloom over the porches, the overgrown garden swarming with tiny white winged butterflies, the lantana with its little orange blossoms pushing through the black iron fence.

And Deirdre sitting in the rocker on the side porch behind her veil of rusted screens.

The doctor felt a leaden anguish. He was as troubled, perhaps, as he'd ever been in his life. *Somebody's got to do something for that woman.*

He walked aimlessly after that, emerging finally on a dirty and busy street. A shabby neighborhood tavern caught his eye. He went into it, grateful for the icy air-conditioning and the relative quiet in which only a few old men talked in low voices along the bar. He took his drink to the last wooden table in the back.

The condition of Deirdre Mayfair tortured him. And the mystery of the apparition only made it worse. He thought of that daughter in California. Did he dare to call her? Doctor to doctor . . . But then he did not know the young man's name.

"Besides, you have no right to interfere," he whispered aloud. He drank a little of his beer, savoring the coldness. "Lasher," he whispered. Speaking of names, what sort of name is Lasher? The young California intern would think him a madman! He took another deep drink of the beer.

It seemed to him suddenly that the bar was getting warm. It was as if someone had opened the door on a desert wind. Even the old men talking over their beer bottles seemed to notice it. He saw one of them wipe his face suddenly with a dirty handkerchief, then go on arguing as before.

Then as the doctor lifted his glass, he saw straight in front of him the mysterious man seated at the table near the door to the street.

The same waxen face, brown eyes. The same nondescript

clothes of that unusual texture, so smooth they shone faintly in the subdued light.

Even as the men nearby went on with their conversation, the doctor felt the keening terror he had known in Deirdre Mayfair's darkened room.

The man sat perfectly still gazing at him. Not twenty feet separated him from the doctor. And the white daylight from the front windows of the bar fell quite distinctly over the man's shoulder, illuminating the side of his face.

Really there. The doctor's mouth was filling with water. He was going to be sick. Going to pass out. They'd think he was drunk in this place. God only knew what would happen— He struggled to steady his hand on the glass. He struggled not to panic completely as he had done in Deirdre's room.

Then, without warning, the man appeared to flicker as if he were a projected image, then vanish before the doctor's eyes. A cold breeze swept through the bar.

The bartender turned to keep a soiled napkin from blowing away. A door slammed somewhere. And it seemed the conversation grew louder. The doctor felt a low throbbing in his head.

". . . Going mad!" he whispered.

No power on earth could have persuaded him to pass Deirdre Mayfair's house again.

But the following night, as he was driving home to the lakefront, he saw the man again, standing under a street lamp by the cemeteries on Canal Boulevard, the yellow light shining full upon him against the chalk white graveyard wall.

Just a glimpse but he knew he wasn't mistaken. He began to tremble violently. It seemed for a moment he could not remember how to work the controls of his car, and then he drove it recklessly, stupidly, as if the man were pursuing him. He did not feel safe until he had shut his apartment door.

The following Friday, he saw the man in broad daylight, standing motionless on the grass in Jackson Square. A woman passing turned to glance at the brown-haired figure. Yes, there, as he had been before! The doctor ran through the French Quarter streets. Finding a cab at a hotel door, he ordered the driver to get him out of there, just to take him anywhere, he did not care.

As the days passed, the doctor had ceased to be frightened so much as horrified. He couldn't eat or sleep. He could concentrate on nothing. He moved perpetually in utter gloom. He stared in silent rage at the old psychiatrist whenever their paths crossed.

How in God's name could he communicate to this monstrous thing that he would not come near the miserable woman in the

21

porch rocker? No more needles, no more drugs from him! *I am no longer the enemy, don't you see!*

To ask the help or understanding of anyone he knew was to risk his reputation, even his entire future. A psychiatrist going mad, like his patients. He was desperate. He had to escape this thing. Who knew when it might next appear to him? What if it could come into these very rooms!

Finally on Monday morning, his nerves frayed, his hands shaking, he found himself in the old psychiatrist's office. He had not made up his mind what he would say, only that he could stand the strain no longer. And he soon found himself rattling on about the tropical heat, headaches and sleepless nights, the need for quick acceptance of his resignation.

He drove out of New Orleans that very afternoon.

Only when he was safe in his father's office in Portland, Maine, did he at last reveal the whole story.

"There was never anything menacing in the face," he explained. "On the contrary. It was strangely unlined. It was as bland as the face of Christ in the portrait on the wall of her room. Just staring at me. But it didn't want me to give her the injection! It was trying to scare me."

His father was a patient man. He did not answer at once. Then slowly he began to talk of the strange things he'd witnessed over the years in psychiatric hospitals—doctors seemingly infected with the neuroses and psychoses of their patients. He'd seen a doctor go catatonic one day in the midst of his catatonic patients.

"The important thing, Larry, is that you rest," his father said. "That you let the effects of this whole thing wear off. *And that you don't tell anyone else about it.*"

Years had passed. The doctor's work in Maine had gone well. And gradually he had built a solid private practice independent of his father.

As for the specter, he had left it behind him in New Orleans, along with the memory of Deirdre Mayfair, sitting eternally in that chair.

Yet there remained in him a lingering fear that he might someplace or other see the thing again. There was the lingering fear that if such a thing had happened once, it might happen another time for entirely different reasons. The doctor had tasted real horror in those damp, dark New Orleans days, and his view of the world had never been the same.

Now, as he stood beside the window in the darkened hotel room in New York, he found the whole affair overwhelming him again. And as he had done a thousand times before, he analyzed the strange tale. He searched for its deeper meaning.

Was the thing really stalking him in New Orleans, or had the doctor misunderstood the silent specter?

Maybe the man had not tried to scare him at all. Maybe it had in fact been pleading with him not to forget that woman! Perhaps in some way it was a bizarre projection of the woman's own desperate thoughts, an image sent to him by a mind which knew no other means of communication.

Ah, there was no comfort in such an idea. Too awful to imagine the helpless woman pleading with him through a spectral emissary, who, for reasons never to be known, could not speak, but only appear for brief moments.

But who could interpret these strange elements? Who would venture to say the doctor was right?

Aaron Lightner, the Englishman, the collector of ghost stories, who had given him the card with the word Talamasca? He had said that he wanted to help the drowned man in California: "Maybe he doesn't know that it has happened to others. Maybe I am needed to tell him that others have also come back from the edge of death with such gifts."

Yes, that would help, wouldn't it? To know that others had seen ghosts too?

But that was not the worst of it, seeing a ghost. Something worse than fear had taken him back to that screen porch and to the wan figure of the woman in the rocker. It was guilt, guilt he would bear all his life—that he had not tried harder to help her, that he had never called that daughter out west.

The morning light was just breaking over the city. He watched the change in the sky, the subtle illumination of the soiled walls opposite. Then he went to the closet and removed the Englishman's card from his coat pocket.

THE TALAMASCA

We watch
And we are always here.

He picked up the telephone.

It was an hour in the telling, which surprised him, but all those details had come tumbling back. He had not minded the little tape recorder going, with its tiny red eye blinking. After all he had used no names, no street numbers, not even any dates. New Orleans, an old house, he had said. And on and on he had talked.

23

He realized now that he had never touched his breakfast, except to empty the coffee cup over and over again.

Lightner had proved an excellent listener, responding gently without ever interrupting. But the doctor did not feel better. In fact, he felt foolish when it was over. As he watched Lightner gather up the little recorder and put it in his briefcase, he had half a mind to ask for the tape.

It was Lightner who broke the silence as he laid down several bills over the check.

"There's something I must explain to you," he said. "I think it will ease your mind."

What could possibly do that?

"You remember," Lightner said, "that I told you I collect ghost stories."

"Yes."

"Well, I know of that old house in New Orleans. I've seen it. And I've recorded other stories of people who have seen the man you described."

The doctor was speechless. The words had been said with utter conviction. In fact, they had been spoken with such authority and assurance that the doctor believed them without doubt. He studied Lightner in detail for the first time. The man was older than he seemed on first inspection. Perhaps sixty-five, even seventy. The doctor found himself captivated again by Lightner's expression, so affable and trusting, so inviting of trust in return.

"Others," the doctor whispered. "Are you sure?"

"I've heard other accounts, some very like your own. And I tell you this so you can understand that you didn't imagine it. And so that it doesn't continue to prey on your mind. You couldn't have helped Deirdre Mayfair, by the way. Carlotta Mayfair would never have allowed it. You ought to put the entire incident out of your mind. Don't ever worry about it again."

For a moment the doctor felt relief, as if he'd been in the Catholic confessional and the priest had spoken the words "I absolve." Then the full import of Lightner's revelations struck him.

"You know these people!" he whispered. He felt his face color. This woman had been his patient. He was suddenly and completely confused.

"No. I know of them," Lightner answered. "And I shall keep your account entirely confidential. Please be assured. Remember, we did not use names on the tape recording. We did not even use your name or mine."

24

"Nevertheless, I must ask you for the tape," the doctor said, flustered. "I've broken confidentiality. I had no idea you knew."

At once Lightner removed the small cassette and placed it in the doctor's hand. The man seemed entirely unruffled. "Of course you may have it," he said. "I understand."

The doctor murmured his thanks, the confusion intensifying. Yet the relief was not altogether gone. Others had seen that creature. This man knew it. He wasn't lying. The doctor was not, and had never been, out of his mind. A faint bitterness surfaced inside him, bitterness towards his superiors in New Orleans, towards Carlotta Mayfair, towards that ghastly Miss Nancy . . .

"The important thing," said Lightner, "is that you do not worry about it any more."

"Yes," said the doctor. "Horrible, all of it. That woman, the drugs."

No, don't even . . . He went quiet, staring at the cassette, and then at his empty coffee cup. "The woman, is she still—"

"The same. I was there last year. Miss Nancy died, the one you disliked so much. Miss Millie went some time ago. And now and then I hear from people in the city, and the report is that Deirdre has not changed."

The doctor sighed. "Yes, you do indeed know of them . . . all the names," he said.

"Then please do believe me," Lightner said, "when I tell you others have seen that vision. You weren't mad, not at all. And you mustn't worry foolishly about such things."

Slowly the doctor studied Lightner again. The man was fastening his briefcase. He examined his airline ticket, appeared to find it satisfactory, and then slipped it into his coat.

"Let me say one thing further," said Lightner, "and then I must catch my plane. Don't tell this story to others. They won't believe you. Only those who have seen such things believe in them. It's tragic, but invariably true."

"Yes, I know it is," said the doctor. So much he wanted to ask, yet he could not. "Have you . . . ?" He stopped.

"Yes, I've seen him," said Lightner. "It was frightening, indeed. Just as you described." He rose to go.

"What is he? A spirit? A ghost?"

"I don't know, actually, what he is. All the stories are very similar. Things don't change there. They go on, year after year. But I must go, and again I thank you, and if you should ever wish to talk to me again, you know how to reach me. You have my card." Lightner extended his hand. "Good-bye."

"Wait. The daughter, what became of her? The intern out west?"

"Why, she's a surgeon, now," Lightner said, glancing at his watch. "Neurosurgeon, I believe. Just passed her examinations. Board-certified, is that what they call it? But then I don't know her either, you see. I only hear about her now and then. Our paths did cross once." He broke off, then gave a quick almost formal smile. "Good-bye, Doctor, and thank you again."

The doctor sat there, thinking, for a long time. He did feel better, infinitely better. There was no denying it. He had no regret that he had told the tale. In fact, the entire encounter seemed a gift to him, something sent by fate to lift from his shoulders the worst burden he'd ever borne. Lightner knew and understood the whole case. Lightner knew the daughter in California.

Lightner would tell that young neurosurgeon what she ought to know, that is, if he hadn't done it already. Yes, the burden was lifted. The burden was gone. Whether it weighed upon Lightner didn't matter.

Then the most curious afterthought came to the doctor, something which hadn't occurred to him for years. He'd never been in that big Garden District house during a rainstorm. Why, how lovely it would have been to see rain through those long windows, to hear rain on those porch roofs. Too bad about that, missing such a thing. He'd thought about it often at the time, but he always missed the rain. And rain in New Orleans was so beautiful.

Well, he was letting go of it all, was he not? Again, he found himself responding to Lightner's assurances as if they had been words spoken in the confessional, words with some religious authority. Yes, let it all go.

He signaled the waitress. He was hungry. He would like a breakfast now that he could eat. And without thinking much about it, he took Lightner's card out of his pocket, glanced at the phone numbers—the numbers he might call if he had questions, the numbers he never intended to call—and then he tore the card into little pieces and put them in the ashtray, and then he set them afire with a match.

TWO

NINE P.M. THE room was dark, save for the bluish light of the television. Miss Havisham, was it not, a wraith in a wedding dress from his beloved *Great Expectations*.

Through the clear, unadorned windows he could see the lights of downtown San Francisco when he chose to look—a constellation burning through the thin fog, and just below, the peaked roofs of the smaller Queen Anne houses across Liberty Street. How he loved Liberty Street. His house was the tallest on the block, a mansion once perhaps, now only a beautiful house, rising majestically among humbler cottages, above the noise and the bustle of the Castro.

He had "restored" this house. He knew every nail, every beam, every cornice. Shirtless in the sun, he had laid the tiles of the roof. He had even poured the concrete of the sidewalk.

Now he felt safe in his house, and safe nowhere else. And for four weeks he had not been out of this room, except to enter the small adjacent bathroom.

Hour by hour, he lay in bed, hands hot inside the black leather gloves which he could not and would not take off, staring at the ghostly black-and-white television screen in front of him. He was letting the television shape his dreams through the various videotapes he loved, the videotapes of the movies he'd watched years ago with his mother. They were "the house movies" to him now, because all of them had not only wonderful stories and wonderful people who had become his heroes and heroines, but wonderful houses. *Rebecca* had Manderley. *Great Expectations* had Miss Havisham's ruined mansion. *Gaslight* had the lovely London town house on the square. *The Red Shoes* had the mansion by the sea where the lovely dancer went to hear the news that she would soon be the company's prima ballerina.

Yes, the house movies, the movies of childhood dreams, of characters as great as the houses. He drank beer after beer as he watched. He drifted in and out of sleep. His hands positively hurt in the gloves. He did not answer the phone. He did not answer the door. Aunt Vivian took care of it.

Now and then Aunt Vivian would come into his room. She would give him another beer, or some food. He rarely ate the food. "Michael, please eat," she would say. He would smile. "Later, Aunt Viv."

He would not see or speak to anyone except Dr. Morris, but Dr. Morris couldn't help him. His friends couldn't help him either. And they didn't want to talk to him anymore. They were tired of hearing him talk about being dead for an hour and then coming back. And he certainly did not want to talk to the hundreds who wanted to see a demonstration of his psychic power.

He was sick to death of his psychic power. Didn't anyone understand? It was a parlor trick, this taking off his gloves and touching things and seeing some simple, mundane image. "You got this pencil from a woman in your office yesterday. Her name's Gert," or "This locket. This morning, you took it out and you decided you'd wear it but you didn't really want to. You wanted to wear the pearls, and you couldn't find them."

Just a physical thing, this, an antenna that maybe all human beings had thousands of years ago.

Didn't anyone appreciate the real tragedy? That he could not remember what he saw when he was drowned. "Aunt Viv," he would say, still trying now and then to explain it to her, "I really did see people up there. We were dead. All of us were dead. And I had a choice about coming back. And I was sent back for a purpose."

Pale shadow of his dead mother, Aunt Vivian would only nod her head. "I know, darling. Maybe in time, you'll remember."

In time.

His friends had gotten more harsh at the end. "Michael, you're talking crazy. This happens that people drown and they're brought back. There's no special purpose."

"That's nuthouse talk, Mike."

Therese had cried and cried. "Look, there's no use me being here, Michael. You're not the same person."

No. Not the same person. That person drowned. Over and over he tried to remember the rescue—the woman who had got him up out of the water and brought him around. If only he could talk to her again, if only Dr. Morris would find her . . . He just wanted to hear it from her own lips that he'd said nothing. He just wanted to take off his gloves and hold her hand in his when he asked her. Maybe through her he could remember . . .

Dr. Morris wanted him to come in for further evaluation.

"Leave me alone. Just find that woman. I know you can reach her. You told me she called you. She told you her name."

He was through with hospitals, with brain scans and electro-encephalograms, through with shots and pills.

The beer he understood. He knew how to pace it. And the beer sometimes brought him close to remembering . . .

. . . And it was a realm he'd seen out there. People—so many of them. Now and then it was there again, a great gossamer whole. He saw her . . . *who was she*? She said . . . And then it was gone. "I will, I'll do it. If I die again trying, I'll do it."

Had he really said that to them? How could he have imagined such things, things so very far afield of his own world, which was full of the solid and the real, and why these odd flashes of being far away, back home, in the city of his boyhood?

He didn't know. He didn't know anything that mattered anymore.

He knew he was Michael Curry, that he was forty-eight years old, that he had a couple of million socked away, and property that amounted to almost that, which was a very good thing because his construction company was shut down, cold. He could no longer run it. He'd lost his best carpenters and painters to the other crews around town. He'd lost the big job that had meant so much, the restoration of the old bed-and-breakfast hotel on Union Street.

He knew that if he took off his gloves and started touching anything—the walls, the floor, the beer can, the copy of *David Copperfield* which lay open beside him—he'd start getting these flashes of meaningless information and he'd go crazy. That is, if he wasn't already crazy.

He knew he had been happy before he drowned, not perfectly happy, but happy. His life had been good.

The morning of the big event, he had awakened late, needing a day off, and it was a good time for it. His men were doing just fine out there, and maybe he wouldn't check on them. It was May 1 and the oddest memory came back to him—of a long drive out of New Orleans, and along the Gulf Coast to Florida when he was a boy. It must have been the Easter vacation, but he really didn't know for sure, and all those who would have known—his mother, his father, his grandparents—were dead.

What he remembered was the clear green water on that white beach, and how warm it had been, and that the sand was like sugar under his feet.

They had all gone down to the waves to swim at sunset; not the slightest chill in the air; and though the great orange sun still hung in the blue western sky, there was a half moon shining straight overhead. His mother had pointed it out to him. "Look,

29

Michael." Even his father seemed to love it, his father who never noticed such things had said in a soft voice that it was a beautiful place.

It had hurt him to remember this. The cold in San Francisco was the one thing he powerfully resented, and he could never tell anyone why afterwards—that such a memory of southern warmth had inspired him to go out that day to San Francisco's Ocean Beach. Was there any place colder in all of the Bay Area than Ocean Beach? He had known how drab and forbidding the water would look under the bleached and sullen sky. He had known how the wind would cut through his clothes.

Nevertheless he'd gone. Alone to be at Ocean Beach on this dim, colorless afternoon with visions of southern waters, of driving with the top down on the old Packard convertible through the soft caressing southern wind.

He didn't turn on the car radio as he drove through town. So he didn't hear the high tide warnings. But what if he had? He knew Ocean Beach was dangerous. Every year people were washed out, natives as well as tourists.

Maybe he'd been thinking a little about that when he went out on the rocks just below the Cliff House Restaurant. Treacherous, yes, always, and slippery. But he wasn't much afraid of falling, or of the sea, or of anything. And he was thinking about the south again, about summer evenings in New Orleans when the jasmine was blooming. He was thinking of the smell of the four o'clocks in his grandmother's yard.

The wave must have knocked him unconscious. He had no memory at all of being washed out. Just that distinct recollection of rising into space, of seeing his body out there, tossed on the surf, of seeing people waving and pointing, and others rushing into the restaurant to call for assistance. Yes, he knew what they were doing, all of these people. Seeing them was not really like looking down on people from above. It was like knowing all about them. And how purely buoyant and safe he'd felt up there; why, safe didn't even begin to describe it. He was free, so free he could not comprehend their anxiety, why they were so concerned about his body being tossed about.

. Then the other part began. And that must have been when he was really dead, and all the wonderful things were shown to him, and the other dead were there, and he understood, understood all the simplest and the most complex things, and why he had to go back, yes, the doorway, the promise, shot down suddenly and weightlessly into the body lying on the deck of the ship, the body that had been dead drowned for an hour out there, into the aches and the pains, and come back alive staring up, knowing it all, ready to do exactly what they had wanted of him. All that splendid knowledge!

In those first few seconds, he tried desperately to tell of where he'd been and the things he'd seen, the great long adventure. Surely he had! But all he could remember now was the intensity of the pain in his chest, and in his hands and his feet, and the dim figure of a woman near him. A fragile being with a pale delicate face, all of her hair hidden by a dark cap, her gray eyes flickering for a second like lights in front of him. In a soft voice, she'd told him to be calm, that they would take care of him.

Impossible to think that this little woman had gotten him out of the sea, and pumped the water out of his lungs. But he had not understood that she was his savior at that moment.

Men were lifting him, putting him on a stretcher, and strapping him down, and he was filled with pain. The wind was whipping his face. He couldn't keep his eyes open. The stretcher was rising in the air.

Confusion after that. Had he blacked out again? Had that been the moment of true and total forgetting? No one could confirm or deny, it seemed, what had happened on the flight in. Only that they had rushed him to shore, where the ambulance and the reporters were waiting.

Cameras flashing, that he did recall, people saying his name. The ambulance itself, yes, and someone trying to stick a needle into his vein. He thought he heard his Aunt Vivian's voice. He begged them to stop. He had to sit up. They couldn't strap him down again, no!

"Hold on, Mr. Curry, just hold on. Hey, help me here with this guy!" They *were* strapping him down again. They were treating him as if he were a prisoner. He fought. But it was no use; they'd shot something into his arm, he knew it. He could see the darkness coming.

Then *they* came back, those he had seen out there; they began to talk again. "I understand," he said. "I won't let it happen. I'll go home. I know where it is. I remember . . ."

When he had awakened, it was to bright artificial light. A hospital room. He was hooked to machines. His best friend, Jimmy Barnes, was sitting next to the bed. He tried to speak to Jimmy, but then the nurses and the doctors surrounded him.

They were touching him, his hands, his feet, asking him questions. But he couldn't concentrate on the proper answers. He kept seeing things—fleeting images of nurses, orderlies, hospital hallways. *What is all this?* He knew the doctor's name—Randy Morris—and that he'd kissed his wife, Deenie, before he left home. So what? Things were literally popping into his head. He

31

couldn't stand it. It was like being half awake and half asleep, feverish, worried.

He shuddered, trying to clear his head. "Listen," he said. "I'm trying." After all, he knew what this was all about, the touching, that he'd been drowned and they wanted to see if there had been any brain damage. "But you needn't bother. I'm fine. I'm all right. I've got to get out of here, and get packed. I have to go back home immediately . . ."

Plane reservations, closing the company . . . The doorway, the promise, and his purpose, which was absolutely crucial . . .

But what was it? Why did he have to get back home? There came another flash of images—nurses cleaning this room, somebody wiping the chrome bar of the bed a few hours ago while he'd been asleep. *Stop it!* Have to get back to the point, the whole purpose, the—

Then he realized it. He couldn't remember the purpose! He couldn't remember what he'd seen while he was dead! The whole thing, all of it—the people, the places, all he'd been told—he couldn't remember any of it. No, this couldn't be. It had been wondrously clear. And they were depending on him. They'd said, Michael, you know you do not have to return, you can refuse, and he'd said that he would, that he . . . that he what? It was going to come back in a flash, like a dream you forget and then completely remember!

He had sat up, brushing one of the needles out of his arms and asked for a pen and paper.

"You have to lie still."

"Not now. I have to write it down." But there was nothing to write! He remembered standing on the rock, thinking of that long-ago summer in Florida, of the warm waters . . . Then the wet soaked cold aching thing that he was, on the stretcher.

All of it gone.

He had shut his eyes, trying to ignore the strange warmth in his hands, and the nurse pushing him back against the pillows. Somebody was asking Jimmy to go out of the room. Jimmy didn't want to go. Why was he seeing all these strange irrelevant things—flashes of orderlies again, and the nurse's husband, and these names, why did he know all these names?

"Don't touch me like that," he said. It was the experience out there, over the ocean, that's what mattered!

Suddenly he reached for the pen. "If you'll be very quiet . . ."

Yes, an image when he touched the pen, of the nurse getting it out of the drawer at the hallway station. And the paper, image of a man putting the tablet in a metal locker. And the bedside table? Image of the woman who'd last wiped it clean, with a rag full of germs from another room. And some flash of a man with a radio. Somebody doing something with a radio.

And the bed? The last patient in it, Mrs. Ona Patrick, died at eleven A.M. yesterday, before he'd even decided to go to Ocean Beach. *No. Turn it off!* Flash of her body in the hospital morgue. "I can't stand this!"

"What's wrong, Michael?" said Dr. Morris. "Talk to me." Jimmy was arguing in the hall. He could hear Stacy's voice, Stacy and Jimmy were his best friends.

He was trembling. "Yeah, sure," he whispered to the doctor. "I'll talk to you. Just so long as you don't touch me."

In desperation he had put his hands to his own head, run his fingers through his own hair, and mercifully he felt nothing. He was drifting into sleep again, thinking, well, it will come as it did before, she'll be there and I'll understand. But even as he nodded off, he realized he didn't know who this *she* was.

But he had to go home, yes, home after all these years, these long years in which home had become some sort of fantasy . . .

"Back to where I was born," he whispered. So hard now to talk. So sleepy. "If you give me any more drugs, I swear I'll kill you."

It was his friend, Jimmy, who brought the leather gloves the next day. Michael hadn't thought it would work. But it was worth a try. He was in a state of agitation bordering on madness. And he had been talking too much, to everybody.

When reporters rang the room direct, he told them in a great rush "what was going on." When they pushed their way into the room, he talked on and on, recounting it again and again, repeating "I can't remember!" They gave him things to touch; he told them what he saw. "It doesn't mean anything."

The cameras went off with their myriad shuffling electronic sounds. The hospital staff threw the reporters out. Michael was scared to touch even a fork or a knife. He wouldn't eat. Staff members came from all over the hospital to place objects in his hands.

In the shower, he touched the wall. He saw that woman, that dead woman again. She'd been in this room three weeks. "I don't want to take a shower," she'd said. "I'm sick, don't you understand?" Her daughter-in-law had made her stand there. He had to get out of the stall. He fell down exhausted in the bed, shoving his hands under the pillow.

There had been a few flashes as he first smoothed the tight leather gloves over his fingers. Then he rubbed his hands together slowly, so that everything was a blur, image piling upon image until nothing was distinct, and all the various names tumbling through his mind made a noise—then quiet.

Slowly he reached for the knife on the supper tray. He was seeing something but it was pale, silent, then gone. He lifted the glass, drank the milk. Just a shimmer. All right! These gloves were working. The trick was to be quick about every gesture.

And also to get out of here! But they wouldn't let him. "I don't want a brain scan," he said. "My brain is fine. It's my hands that are driving me crazy."

But they were trying to help—Dr. Morris, the chief resident, and his friends, and his Aunt Vivian who stayed at his side by the hour. At his behest, Dr. Morris had contacted the ambulance men, and the Coast Guard, the Emergency Room people, the skipper of the boat who had revived him before the Coast Guard had been able to find her—anybody who might have remembered his saying something important. After all, a single word might unlock his memory.

But there were no words. Michael had mumbled something when he opened his eyes, the skipper had said, but she hadn't been able to make out a specific word. It began with an L, she thought, a name, maybe. But that was all. The Coast Guard took him up after that. In the ambulance he'd thrown a punch. Had to be subdued.

Still, he wished he could talk to all those people, especially the woman who'd brought him around. He told the press that when they came to question him.

Jimmy and Stacy remained with him late each night. His Aunt Vivian was there each morning. Therese finally came, timid, frightened. She didn't like hospitals. She couldn't be around sick people.

He laughed. Wasn't that California for you, he thought. Imagine saying something like that. And then he did the impulsive thing. He ripped off the glove and grabbed her hand.

Scared, don't like you, you're the center of attention, knock it off all this, I don't believe you drowned out there, ridiculous, I want to get out of here, I, you should have called me.

"Go on home, honey," he said.

Sometime during the silent hours, one of the nurses slipped a silver pen into his hand. He'd been sound asleep. The gloves were on the table.

"Tell me her name," she said.

"I don't get her name. I see a desk."

"Try harder."

"A beautiful mahogany desk with a green blotter on it."

"But the woman who used the pen?"

"Allison."

"Yes. Where is she?"

"I don't know."

"Try again."

"I tell you I don't know. She gave it to you, and you put it in your purse, and this morning, you took it out. It's just images, pictures, I don't know where she is. You're in a cafe, and you're drawing on the napkin with the pen. You're thinking about showing it to me."

"She's dead, isn't she?"

"I don't know, I told you. I don't see it. Allison, that's all I see. She wrote a grocery list with it, for Chrissakes, you want me to tell you what was on the list?"

"You have to see more than that."

"Well, I don't!" He put back on the gloves. Nothing was going to make him take them off again.

He left the hospital the following day.

The next three weeks were an agony. A couple of Coast Guard men called him, so did one of the ambulance drivers, but they had nothing really to tell him that would help. As for the rescue boat, the woman wanted to remain out of it. And Dr. Morris had promised her that she would. Meantime, the Coast Guard admitted to the press that they had failed to record the name of the craft or its registry. One of the newspapers referred to it as an ocean-going cruiser. Maybe it was on the other side of the world.

Michael realized by this time that he had told his story to too many people. Every popular magazine in the country wanted to talk to him. He could not go out at all without a reporter blocking his path and some perfect stranger placing a wallet or photograph in his hand, and the phone wouldn't stop ringing. Mail piled up at the door, and though he kept packing his suitcase to leave, he could not bring himself to do it. Instead he drank—ice-cold beer all day long, then bourbon when the beer did not make him numb.

His friends tried to be loyal. They took turns talking to him, trying to calm him, trying to get him to lay off the drink, but it was no good. Stacy even read to him because he couldn't read himself. He was wearing everybody down and he knew it.

The fact was, his brain was teeming. He was trying to figure things out. If he couldn't remember, he could understand about all this, this earthshaking thing, this awful thing. But he knew he was rambling on and on about "life and death," about what had happened "out there," about the way the barriers between life and death were crumbling in our popular art and in our serious art. Hadn't anybody noticed? Movies and novels always told you what was going on. You just had to study them to see it. Why, he'd seen it before this even happened.

Take Bergman's film *Fanny and Alexander*. Why, the dead just come walking in and talk to the living. And the same thing happened in *Ironweed*. In *Cries and Whispers* didn't the dead just get up and talk? And there was some comedy out now, and when you considered the lighter movies, it was happening with even greater frequency. Take *The Woman in White*, with the little dead girl appearing in the bedroom of the little boy, and there was *Julia* with Mia Farrow being haunted by that dead child in London.

"Michael, you're bashed."

"It isn't only horror movies, don't you see? It's happening in all our art. Take the book *The White Hotel*, any of you read that? Well, it goes on right past the heroine's death into the afterlife. I tell you, something is about to happen. The barrier is breaking down, I myself talked to the dead and I came back, and on some subconscious level we all know the barrier is breaking."

"Michael, you have to calm down. This thing with the hands . . ."

"I don't want to talk about that." But he was bashed, that he had to admit, and he intended to stay bashed. He liked being bashed. He picked up the phone to order another case of beer. No need for Aunt Viv to go out for anything. And then there was all that Glenlivet Scotch he'd stashed away. And more Jack Daniel's. Oh, he could stay drunk till he died. No problem.

By phone he finally shut down the company. When he'd tried to work, his men had told him pointedly to go home. They couldn't get anything done with his constant talking. He was hopping from subject to subject. And then there was the reporter standing there asking him to demonstrate the power for the woman from Sonoma County. And something else was plaguing him, too, which he could not confide to anyone: he was receiving vague emotional impressions from people whether he touched them or not.

A certain free-floating telepathy it seemed; and there were no gloves to shut it off. It wasn't information he received; it was merely strong impressions of like, dislike, truth or falsehood. Sometimes he was so caught up in this, he only saw people's lips moving. He didn't hear their words at all.

This highly charged intimacy, if that was the proper thing to call it, alienated him to the core.

He let the contracts go, transferring everything in the space of an afternoon, making sure all his men got work, and then closing his small shop on Castro which sold vintage Victorian fixtures.

It was OK to go indoors, to lie down, to pull the curtains, and drink. Aunt Viv sang in the kitchen as she cooked for him meals he didn't want to eat. Now and then he tried to read a little of *David Copperfield*, in order to escape from his own mind. At all the worst moments of his life, he had always retired to some remote corner of the world and read *David Copperfield*. It was easier and lighter than *Great Expectations*, his true favorite. But the only reason he could follow the book now was that he knew it practically by heart.

Therese went to visit her brother in Southern California. A lie, he knew, though he had not touched the phone, merely heard the voice through the answering machine. Fine. Good-bye.

When his old girlfriend Elizabeth called from New York, he talked to her until he actually passed out. The next morning she told him he must get psychiatric help. She threatened to drop work and fly out if he didn't agree. He agreed. But he was lying.

He did not want to confide in anybody. He did not want to describe the new intensity of feeling. He certainly didn't want to talk about his hands. All he wanted to talk about were the visions, and nobody wanted to hear about that, nobody wanted to hear him talk about the curtain dropping that separated the living from the dead.

After Aunt Viv went to bed, he experimented just a little with the touching power. He could tell a great deal from an object when he allowed himself to handle it slowly; if he asked questions of his power—that is, tried to direct it—he could receive even more. But he did not like the feel of it, of these images flashing through his head. And if there was a reason he had been given this sensitivity, the reason was forgotten along with the vision, and the sense of purpose regarding his return to life.

Stacy brought him books to read about others who had died and come back. Dr. Morris at the hospital had told him of these works—the classic studies of the "near death experience" by Moody, Rawlings, Sabom, and Ring. Fighting the drunkenness, the agitation, the sheer inability to concentrate for any length of time, he forced himself through some of these accounts.

Yes, he knew this! It was all true. He too had risen out of his body, yes, and it was no dream, yes, but he had not seen a beautiful light; he had not been met by dead loved ones; and there had been no unearthly paradise to which he was admitted, full of flowers and beautiful colors. Something altogether different had happened out there. He had been intercepted as it were, appealed to, made to realize that he must perform a very difficult task, that much depended upon it.

Paradise. The only paradise he had ever known was in the city where he'd grown up, the warm sweet place he'd left when he was seventeen, that old great square of some twenty-five-odd city blocks known in New Orleans as the Garden District.

Yes, back there, where it all started. New Orleans which he hadn't seen since the summer of his seventeenth year. And the funny thing was, that when he considered his life, as drowning men are supposed to do, he thought first and foremost of that long-ago night when, at age six, he had discovered classical music on his grandmother's back porch, listening in the fragrant dusk to an old tube radio. Four o'clocks glowing in the dark. Cicadas grinding in the trees. His grandfather was smoking a cigar on the step, and then that music came into his life, that heavenly music.

Why had he loved that music so much when nobody around him did? Different from the start, that's what he'd been. And his mother's breeding could not account for it. To her all music was noise, she said. Yet he had loved that music so much that he stood there conducting it with a stick, making great sweeping gestures in the dark, humming.

It was in the Irish Channel that they lived, hardworking people, the Currys, and his father was the third generation to inhabit the small double cottage in the long waterfront neighborhood where so many of the Irish had settled. From the great potato famine Michael's ancestors had fled, packed into the emptied cotton ships on their way back from Liverpool to the American South for the more lucrative cargo.

Into the "wet grave" they'd been dumped, these hungry immigrants, some of them dressed in rags, begging for work, and dying by the hundreds from yellow fever, consumption, and cholera. The survivors had dug the city's mosquito-infested canals. They had stoked the boilers of the big steamboats. They had loaded cotton onto ships and worked on the railroads. They had become policemen and firemen.

These were tough people, people from whom Michael had inherited his powerful build, his determination. The love of working with his hands had come from them and finally prevailed in spite of years of education.

He'd grown up hearing tales of those early days, of how the Irish workingmen themselves had built the great parish church of St. Alphonsus, dragging the stones from the river, laying the mortar, collecting for the beautiful statues that came from Eu-

rope. "We had to outdo the Germans, you see, you know ̣
were building St. Mary's right across the street. Nothing on earth
was going to make us go to Mass with each other." And that's
why there were two magnificent parish churches instead of one,
with Masses being said by the very same staff of priests every
morning.

Michael's grandfather had worked as a policeman on the
wharves, where his father had once loaded cotton bales. He took
Michael to see the banana boats come in and the thousands of
bananas disappearing into the warehouse on the conveyor belts,
warning him about the big black snakes that could hide in the
banana stalks right until they hung them up in the markets.

Michael's father was a fire fighter until his death one afternoon
in a fire on Tchoupitoulas Street when Michael was seventeen.
That had been the turning point of Michael's life, for by that
time his grandparents were gone, and his mother had taken him
back with her to the place of her birth, San Francisco.

There was never the slightest doubt in his mind that California
had been good to him. The twentieth century had been good to
him. He was the first of that old clan ever to earn a college
degree, ever to live in the world of books or paintings or fine
houses.

But even if his dad had never died, Michael's life would not
have been a fireman's life. There were things stirring in him that
had not ever stirred at all, it seemed, in his forebears.

It wasn't just the music that summer night. It was the way he
loved books from the time he learned to read, how he gobbled
up Dickens when he was nine years old, and treasured ever after
the novel *Great Expectations*.

Years later in San Francisco he had given his beloved construction company that name: Great Expectations.

He used to fall into *Great Expectations* or *David Copperfield*
in the school library where other boys threw spitballs and
punched him on the arm and threatened to beat him up if he
didn't stop acting "simple," the Irish Channel word for someone who did not have the good sense to be hard, and brutal, and
disdaining of all things that defy immediate definition.

But nobody ever beat up Michael. He had enough healthy
meanness from his father to punish anyone who even tried. Even
as a child he was husky and uncommonly strong, a human being
for whom physical action, even of a violent sort, was fairly natural. He liked to fight too. And the kids learned to leave him
alone, and also he learned to hide his secret soul enough that
they forgave him the few slips and generally liked him.

And the walks, what about those long walks that nobody else

his age ever took? Even his girlfriends later on never understood. Rita Mae Dwyer laughed at him. Marie Louise said he was nuts. "What do you mean, just walk?" But from the earliest years, he liked to walk, to slip across Magazine Street, the great dividing line between the narrow sunbaked streets where he'd been born and the grand quiet streets of the Garden District.

In the Garden District were the oldest uptown mansions of the city, slumbering behind their massive oaks and broad gardens. There he strolled in silence over the brick sidewalks, hands shoved in his pockets, sometimes whistling, thinking that someday he would have a great house here. He would have a house with white columns on the front and flagstone walks. He would have a grand piano, such as those he glimpsed through long floor-length windows. He would have lace curtains and chandeliers. And he would read Dickens all day long in some cool library where the books went to the ceiling and the bloodred azaleas drowsed beyond the porch railings.

He felt like Dickens's hero, the young Pip, glimpsing what he knew he must possess and being so very far from ever having it.

But in this love of walking he was not entirely alone, for his mother had loved to take long walks, too, and perhaps it was one of the few very significant gifts she had given him.

Houses she had understood and loved, just as he always would. And when he was very small, she had brought him to this quiet sanctuary of old homes, pointing out to him her favorite spots, and the great smooth lawns often half concealed by the camellia shrubs. She had taught him to listen to the cry of the birds in the oaks, to the music of hidden fountains.

There was one dark house she dearly loved which he would never forget, a long grim town house affair with a great bougainvillea vine spilling over its side porches. And often when they passed, Michael saw a curious and solitary man standing alone among the high unkempt shrubs, far to the back of the neglected garden. He seemed lost in the tumbling, tangled green, this man, blending with the shadowy foliage so completely that another passerby might not have noticed him.

In fact, Michael and his mother had played a little game in those early years about the man. She would always say that she couldn't see him. "But he's there, Mom," Michael would reply, and she would say, "All right, Michael, tell me what he looks like."

"Well, he has brown hair and brown eyes, and he's very dressed up, as if he's going to a party. But he's watching us, Mom, and I don't think we should stand here and stare at him."

"Michael, there is no man," his mother would say.

"Mom, you're teasing me."

But there had been one occasion on which she had seen that man, for certain, and she hadn't liked him. It wasn't at the house. It wasn't in that ruined garden.

It was at Christmastime when Michael was still very small, and the great crib had just been set up at the side altar of St. Alphonsus Church, with the Baby Jesus in the manger. Michael and his mother had gone up to kneel at the altar rail. How beautiful the life-sized statues of Mary and Joseph; and the Baby Jesus himself, smiling, with his chubby little arms extended. Everywhere it seemed there had been bright lights and the sweet, softening flicker of candles. The church was full of the sound of shuffling feet, of hushed whispers.

Perhaps this had been the first Christmas that Michael could remember. Whatever the case, the man had been there, over in the shadows of the sanctuary, quietly looking on, and when he had seen Michael, he had given him that little smile he always did. His hands were clasped. He wore a suit. His face looked very calm. Altogether he looked the same as he did in the garden on First Street.

"Look, there he is, Mom," Michael said at once. "That man, the one from the garden."

Michael's mother had only glanced at the man and then fearfully away. She'd whispered in Michael's ear, "Well, don't stare at him."

As they left the church, she'd turned to look back once.

"That's the man in the garden, Mom," Michael said.

"Whatever are you talking about?" she'd asked. "What garden?"

The next time they'd walked down First Street again, he had seen the man, and he had tried to tell her. But again, she played the game. She had teased him, saying there was no man.

They had laughed. It was all right. It didn't seem to mean much at the time, though he never forgot it.

Much more significant that Michael and his mother were fast friends, that they always had so much fun together.

In later years, Michael's mother gave him another gift, the movies she took him to see downtown at the Civic Theater. They would take the streetcar on Saturdays to the matinees. Sissy stuff, Mike, his father would say. Nobody was dragging him into those crazy shows.

Michael knew better than to answer, and as time passed he found a way to smile and shrug it off so that his father left him alone, and left his mother alone too, which meant even more to

41

him. And besides, nothing was going to take away those special Saturday afternoons. Because the foreign movies were like portals into another world, and they filled Michael with unspeakable anguish and happiness.

He never forgot *Rebecca* and *The Red Shoes* and *The Tales of Hoffman* and a film from Italy of the opera *Aida*. And then there was the wonderful story of the pianist called *A Song to Remember.* He loved *Caesar and Cleopatra* with Claude Rains and Vivien Leigh. And *The Late George Apley* with Ronald Colman, who had the most beautiful voice Michael ever heard in a man.

It was frustrating that he sometimes couldn't understand these films, that sometimes he couldn't even follow them. The subtitles invariably went by too fast for him to read; and in the British films, the actors spoke too fast for him to understand their crisp accents.

Sometimes his mother explained things on the way home. They rode the streetcar past their stop and all the way uptown to Carrolton Avenue. It was a good place for them to be alone. And there were the palatial houses of that street to see, the later, often gaudier houses built after the Civil War, not as beautiful as the older Garden District homes, but nevertheless sumptuous to behold and endlessly interesting.

Ah, the quiet pain of those leisurely rides, of wanting so much and understanding so little. He caught the crepe myrtle blossoms now and then with his fingers through the open streetcar window. He dreamed of being Maxim de Winter. He wanted to know the names of the classical pieces he heard on the radio and loved, to be able to understand and recall the unintelligible foreign words spoken by the announcers.

And strangely enough, in the old horror films at the dirty Happy Hour Theater on Magazine Street—his own neighborhood—he often glimpsed the same elegant world and people. There were the same paneled libraries, arched fireplaces, and men in smoking jackets, and graceful soft-spoken females—right along with Frankenstein's monster or Dracula's daughter. Dr. Van Helsing was a most elegant guy, and there was the very Claude Rains who had played Caesar at the downtown theater now cackling madly as *The Invisible Man.*

Try as he might not to do it, Michael came to loathe the Irish Channel. He loved his folks. And he liked his friends well enough. But he hated the double houses, twenty to a block, with tiny front yards and low picket fences, the corner bar with the jukebox playing in the back room and the screen door always slamming, and the fat women in their flowered dresses, smacking their children with belts or naked hands on the street.

He loathed the crowds that shopped on Magazine Street in the late Saturday afternoon. It seemed to him the children always had dirty faces and dirty clothes. The salesgirls behind the counter at the dime store were rude. The pavement stank of rotting beer. There was a stench to the old railroad flats above the shops where some of his friends, the most unfortunate, lived. The stench was in the old shoe shops and radio repair shops. It was even in the Happy Hour Theater. The stench of Magazine Street. Carpet on the stairs in these old buildings looked and felt like bandages. A layer of dirt overlaid all. His mother would not go to Magazine Street even for a spool of thread. She walked through the Garden District and caught the St. Charles car on the Avenue and went down to Canal Street.

Michael was ashamed of this hate. He was ashamed as Pip had been ashamed of such a hate of his own in *Great Expectations*. But the more he learned and the more he saw, the more the disdain grew in him.

And it was the people, always the people, who put him off the most. He was ashamed of the harsh accent that marked you as being from the Irish Channel, an accent, they said, which sounded like Brooklyn or Boston or anyplace where the Irish and the Germans settled. "We know you're from Redemptorist School," the uptown kids would say. "We can tell by the way you talk." They meant it contemptuously.

Michael even disliked the nuns, the crude, deep-voiced sisters who smacked the boys whenever they felt like it, who shook them and humiliated them at whim.

In fact, he hated them in particular for something they had done when he was six years old. One little boy, a "troublemaker," was dragged out of the boys' first-grade classroom and taken over to the first-grade teacher in the girls' school. Only later did the class find out that there the boy had been made to stand in the trash basket, crying and red-faced, in front of all the little girls. Over and over the nuns had shoved at him and pushed at him, saying "Get in that trash can; get in it!" The girls had watched and told the boys about it afterwards.

This chilled Michael. He felt a sullen wordless terror that such a thing could happen to him. Because he knew he would never let it happen. He would fight and then his father would whip him, a violence that had always been threatened but never carried out beyond a couple of licks with a strap. In fact, all the violence that he had always sensed simmering around him—in his father, his grandfather, all the men he knew—might rise, like chaos, and drag him down into it. How many times had he seen the kids around him whipped? How many times had he heard his father's cold, ironic jokes about the whippings his own father had given him? Michael feared it with a horrid, paralyzing speechless fear. He feared the vicious catastrophic intimacy of being hit, being beaten.

So in spite of his general physical restlessness and his stubbornness, he became an angel in school long before he realized that he needed to learn in order to fulfill his dreams. He was the quiet boy, the boy who always did his homework. Fear of ignorance, fear of violence, fear of humiliation drove him as surely as his later ambitions.

But why hadn't these elements driven anyone else around him? He never knew, but there was no doubt in retrospect that he was from the start a highly adaptable person. That was the key. He learned from what he saw, and changed accordingly.

Neither of his parents had that flexibility. His mother was patient, yes, and kept in check the disgust she felt for the habits of those around her. But she had no dreams, no great plans, no true creative force to her. She never changed. She never did much of anything.

As for Michael's father, he was a brash and lovable man, a brave fire fighter who won many decorations. He died trying to save lives. That was his nature. But it was his nature, too, to shrink from what he didn't know or understand. A deep vanity made him feel "small" before those with real education.

"Do your lessons," he'd say, because that was what he was supposed to say. He never dreamed that Michael was drawing all he could from the parish school, that in the overcrowded classrooms, with the tired, overworked nuns, Michael was actually acquiring a fine education.

For no matter how abysmal the conditions, the nuns taught the children how to read and write very well. Even if they had to hit them to do it. They gave the children a beautiful handwriting. They taught them how to spell. They taught them their arithmetic tables, and they even taught Latin and history and some literature. They kept order among the toughs. And though Michael never stopped hating them, though he would hate them for years after, he had to admit that now and then they did speak in their own varying simple ways about spiritual things, about living a life that mattered.

When Michael was eleven, three things happened which had a rather dramatic effect upon him. The first was a visit from his Aunt Vivian from San Francisco, and the second was an accidental discovery at the public library.

The visit of Aunt Vivian was brief. His mother's sister came to town on a train. They met her at Union Station. She stayed at the Pontchartrain Hotel on St. Charles, and the evening after her arrival she invited Michael and his mother and father to join her for dinner at the Caribbean Room. This was the fancy dining room in the Pontchartrain Hotel. Michael's father said no. He wasn't going into a place like that. Besides, his suit was at the cleaners.

Michael went, the little man, all dressed up, walking through the Garden District with his mother.

The Caribbean Room quite astonished him. It was a near silent, eerie world of candlelight, white tablecloths, and waiters who looked like ghosts, or better yet, they looked like the vampires in the horror movies, with their black jackets and stiff white shirts.

But the true revelation was that Michael's mother and her sister were entirely at home in this place, laughing softly as they talked, asking the waiter this and that about the turtle soup, the sherry, the white wine they'd have with dinner.

This gave Michael an enhanced respect for his mother. She wasn't a lady who just put on airs. She really was used to that life. And he understood now why she sometimes cried and said she'd like to go home to San Francisco.

After her sister left, she was sick for days. She lay in bed, refusing everything but wine, which she called her medicine. Michael sat by her, reading to her now and then, getting scared when she didn't speak for an hour. She got well. She got up, and then life went on.

But Michael often thought of that dinner, of the easy and natural way the two ladies had been together. Often he walked by the Pontchartrain Hotel. He looked with quiet envy at the well-dressed people who stood outside, under the awning, waiting for their taxis or limousines. Was he just greedy to want to live in their world? Wasn't all that beauty spiritual? He puzzled over so many things. He was bursting with desires to learn, to understand, to possess. Yet he wound up next door in Smith's Drugstore reading the horror comics.

Then came the accidental discovery at the public library. Michael had only recently learned about the library itself, and the accidental discovery came in stages.

Michael was in the children's reading room, roaming about, looking for something easy and fun to read when he suddenly saw, open for display on top of a bookcase, a new stiff-backed book on the game of chess—a book that told one how to play it.

Now, chess had always struck Michael as highly romantic. But how he knew of it he couldn't have told anyone. He'd never seen a chess set in real life. He checked out the book, took it home, and began to read it. His father saw it and laughed. He knew how to play chess, played it all the time, he said, at the firehouse. You couldn't learn it from a book. That was stupid.

Michael said that he could learn it from the book, he was learning it.

"OK, you learn it," his father said, "and I'll play it with you."

This was a great thing. Another person who knew chess. Maybe they would even buy a chessboard. Michael finished the book in less than a week. He knew chess. For an hour he answered every question his father put to him.

"Well, I don't believe this," his father said. "But you know how to play chess. All you need is a chess set." Michael's father went downtown. When he returned home, he had a chess set that surpassed all Michael's visions. It was made up not of symbols—a horse's head, a castle, a bishop's cap—but of fully delineated figures. The knight sat upon his horse with its front feet raised; the bishop held his hands in prayer. The queen had long hair beneath her crown. The rook was a castle riding upon the back of an elephant.

Of course it was made of plastic, this thing. It had come from D. H. Holmes department store. But it was so much finer than anything pictured in the book on chess that Michael was overcome by the sight of it. Never mind that his father called the knight "my horse man." They were playing chess. And thereafter they played often.

But the great accidental discovery was not that Michael's father knew how to play chess, or that he had the kindness in him to buy such a beautiful set. That was all very well and good. And of course playing chess drew father and son together. But the great accidental discovery was that Michael could absorb something more than stories from books . . . that they could lead him to something other than painful dreaming and wanting.

He had learned something from a book which others believed must be learned from doing or practice.

He became more courageous in the library after that. He talked to the librarians at the desk. He learned about the "subjects catalog." And haphazardly and obsessively, he began to research a whole spectrum of subjects.

The first was cars. He found lots of books in the library on cars. He learned all about an engine from the books, and all about makes of cars, and quietly dazzled his father and his grandfather with this knowledge.

Then he looked up fire fighters and fires in the catalog. He read up on the history of the companies that developed in the big cities. He read about the fire engines and ladder trucks and how they were made, and all about great fires in history, such as the Chicago fire, and the Triangle Factory fire, and once again he was able to discuss all this with his father and grandfather.

Michael was thrilled. He felt now that he had great power. And he proceeded to his secret agenda, not confiding this to anyone. Music was his first secret subject.

He chose the most babyfied books at first—this subject was hard—and then he moved on to the illustrated histories for young adults which told him all about the boy genius Mozart, and poor deaf Beethoven, and crazy Paganini who had supposedly sold his soul to the devil. He learned the definitions of symphony and concerto and sonata. He learned about the musical staff, quarter notes, half notes, major and minor key. He learned the names of all the symphonic instruments.

Then Michael went on to houses. And in no time, he came to understand the Greek Revival style and the Italianate style and the late Victorian style, and what distinguished these various types of buildings. He learned to identify Corinthian columns and Doric columns, to pick out side hall houses and raised cottages. With his new knowledge, he roamed the Garden District, his love for the things he saw deeply and quietly intensified.

Ah, he had hit the jackpot with all this. There was no reason to live in confusion anymore. He could "read up" on anything. On Saturday afternoons, he went through dozens of books on art, architecture, Greek mythology, science. He even read books on modern painting, and opera and ballet, which made him ashamed and afraid that his father might sneak up behind him and make fun of him.

The third thing that happened that year was a concert at the Municipal Auditorium. Michael's father, like many firemen, took extra jobs in his time off; and that year he was working the concession stand at the auditorium, selling bottled soda, and Michael went with him one night to help out. It was a school night and he shouldn't have gone at all, but he wanted to go. He wanted to see the Municipal Auditorium and what went on there, so his mother said OK.

During the first half of the program, before the intermission during which Michael would have to help his father, and after which they would pack up and go home, Michael went inside and up to the very top of the auditorium where the seats were empty, and he sat there waiting to see what the concert would be like. It reminded him of the students in *The Red Shoes*, actually, the students in the balcony, waiting up there with such expectation. And sure enough the place began to fill with beautifully dressed people—the uptowners of New Orleans—and the orchestra gathered to tune up in the pit. Even the strange thin man from First Street was there. Michael caught a glimpse of him far below, his face turned upward, as though he could actually see Michael all the way in the top row.

What followed swept Michael away. Isaac Stern, the great violinist, played that night, and it was the Beethoven Concerto for Violin and Orchestra, one of the most violently beautiful and simply eloquent pieces of music Michael had ever heard. Never once did it leave him in confusion. Never once did it leave him out.

Long after the concert was over, he was able to whistle the principal melody, and to remember as he did so the great sweet sensuous sound of the full orchestra and the thin heartbreaking notes that came from Isaac Stern's violin.

But Michael's life was poisoned by the longing created in him by this experience. In fact, he suffered, in the days that followed, possibly the worst dissatisfaction with his world that he had ever experienced. But he did not let anyone know this. He kept it sealed inside of him, just as he kept secret his knowledge of the subjects he studied at the library. He feared the snobbishness growing in himself, the loathing he knew that he could feel for those he loved if he let such a feeling have life.

And Michael couldn't bear not to love his family. He couldn't bear to be ashamed of them. He couldn't bear the pettiness and the ingratitude of such a thing.

He could hate the people down the block. That was fine. But he had to love, and be loyal to, and be in harmony with, those under his own roof.

Reasonably, naturally, he was devoted to his hardworking grandmother who always had cabbage and ham boiling on the stove when he came in. She spent her life it seemed either cooking or ironing or hanging out clothes on backyard lines from a wicker basket.

And he loved his grandfather, a little man with tiny black eyes who was always on the front steps waiting for Michael after school. He had wonderful stories to tell of the old days and Michael never tired of them.

And then there was his father, the fire fighter, the hero. How could Michael not appreciate such a man? Often Michael went over to the firehouse on Washington Avenue to see him. He sat around, just one of the guys, dying to go out with them when an alarm came in, but always forbidden to do it. He loved to see the truck tearing out, to hear the sirens and the bells. Never mind that he lived in dread that he might someday have to be a fireman. A fireman and nothing else. Living in a double shotgun cottage.

How his mother managed to love these people was another story, and one Michael could not entirely understand. He tried day in and day out to mitigate her quiet unhappiness. He was her closest and only friend. But nothing could save his mother, and he knew it. She was a lost soul down there in the Irish Channel, a woman speaking better and dressing better than those around her, begging to go back to work as a sales clerk in a department store, and always being told no; a woman who lived for her paperback novels late at night—books by John Dickson Carr and Daphne Du Maurier and Frances Parkinson Keyes—sitting on the living room couch, dressed only in a slip on account of the heat, when everyone else was asleep, drinking wine slowly and carefully from a bottle wrapped in brown paper.

"Miss San Francisco" Michael's father called her. "My mother does everything for you, you know that?" he'd say to her. He stared at her with utter contempt on the very few occasions when she drank too much wine and her voice became slurry. But he never moved to stop her. After all, she rarely got that bad. It was just the idea—a woman sitting there drinking like a man, from a bottle all evening long. Michael knew that was what his father thought, no one had to tell him.

And maybe Michael's father was afraid she'd leave if he tried to boss her or control her. He was proud of her prettiness, her slender body, and even the nice way that she talked. He even got the wine for her now and then, bottles of port and sherry which he himself detested. "Sticky sweet stuff for women," he said to Michael. But it was also the stuff that winos drank and Michael knew it.

Did his mother hate his father? Michael never really knew for sure. At some point in his childhood, he came to know that his mother was some eight years older than his father. But the difference was not apparent, and his father was a good-looking man and his mother seemed to think so. She was kind to her husband most of the time, but then she was kind to everyone. Yet nothing in the world was going to make her get pregnant again, she often said, and there were quarrels, awful muffled quarrels behind the only closed door in the little shotgun flat, the door to the back bedroom.

There was a story about his mother and father, but Michael never knew if it was true. His aunt told him the story after his mother's death. It was that his parents had fallen in love in San Francisco, near the end of the war, while his father was in the navy, and that his father had looked very handsome in his uniform and had the charm in those days to really get the girls.

"He looked like you, Mike," his aunt said years later. "Black hair and blue eyes and those big arms, just like you. And you remember your father's voice, it was a beautiful voice, kind of deep and smooth. Even with that Irish Channel accent."

And so Michael's mother had "fallen hard" for him, and then when he went overseas again he had written Michael's mother lovely poetic letters, wooing her and breaking her heart. But the letters had not been written by Michael's father. They had been written by his best friend in the service, an educated man on the same ship, who had laid on the metaphors and the quotes from books. And Michael's mother never guessed.

Michael's mother had actually fallen in love with those letters. And when she'd found herself pregnant with Michael, she went south trusting in those letters, and was received at once by the common good-hearted family who prepared for the wedding in St. Alphonsus Church immediately and had it all done right as soon as Michael's father could get leave.

What a shock it must have been to her, the little treeless street, the tiny house with each room opening onto the other, and the mother-in-law who waited hand and foot on the men and never took a chair herself during supper.

Michael's aunt said that Michael's father had one time confessed the story of the letters to his mother when Michael was still a baby, and that Michael's mother had gone wild and tried to kill him and she had burned all the letters in the backyard. But then she'd quieted down and tried to make a go of it. Here she was with a little child. She was past thirty. Her mother and father were dead; she had only her sister and brother out in San Francisco, and she had no choice but to stay with the father of her child, and besides the Currys were not bad people.

Her mother-in-law in particular she had loved for taking her in when she was pregnant. And that part—about the love between the two women—Michael knew had been true, because Michael's mother took care of the old woman during her final illness.

Both his grandparents died the year Michael started high school, his grandmother in the spring and his grandfather two months after. And though many aunts and uncles had died over the years, these were the first funerals that Michael ever attended, and they were to be engraved forever in his memory.

They were absolutely dazzling affairs with all the accoutrements of refinement which Michael loved. In fact, it troubled him deeply that the furnishings of Lonigan and Sons, the funeral parlor, and the limousines with their gray velvet upholstery and even the flowers and the finely dressed pall bearers seemed connected to the atmosphere of the elegant movies Michael so valued. Here were soft-spoken men and women, fine carpets and carved furniture, rich colors and textures, and the perfume of lilies and roses, and people tempering their natural meanness and crude ways.

It was as if when you died you went into the world of *Rebecca* or *The Red Shoes* or *A Song to Remember*. You had beautiful things for a final day or two before they put you in the ground.

It was a connection that intrigued him for hours. When he saw *The Bride of Frankenstein* for a second time at the Happy Hour on Magazine Street, he watched only the great houses in the picture, and he listened to the music of the voices and studied the clothes more than anything else. He wished he could talk about all this to somebody, but when he tried to tell his girlfriend, Marie Louise, she didn't know what he was talking about. She thought it was dumb to go to the library. She wouldn't go to foreign movies.

He saw that same look in her eyes that he had seen so often in his father's eyes. It wasn't fear of the unknown thing. It was disgust. And he didn't want to be disgusting.

Besides, he was in high school now. Everything was changing. Sometimes he was really afraid that maybe now was the time that his dreams were supposed to die and the real world was supposed to get him. Seems other people felt that way. Marie Louise's father, sitting on his front steps, looked at him coldly one night and demanded: "What makes *you* think *you're* going to college? Your daddy got the money for Loyola?" He spat on the pavement, looked Michael up and down. There it was again, the disgust.

Michael had shrugged. There was no state school in those days in New Orleans. "Maybe I'll go to LSU at Baton Rouge," he said. "Maybe I'll get a scholarship."

"Bull Durham!" the guy muttered under his breath. "Why don't you think about being half as good a fireman as your father?"

And maybe they were all in the right, and it was time to think of other things. Michael had grown to almost six feet, a prodigious height for an Irish Channel kid, and a record for his branch of the Curry family. His father bought an old Packard and taught him how to drive in a week's time, and then he got a part-time job delivering flowers for a florist on St. Charles Avenue.

But it was not until his sophomore year that his old ideas began to give way, that he himself began to forget his ambitions.

51

He went out for football, made first string, and suddenly he was out there on the field in the stadium at City Park and the kids were screaming. "Brought down by Michael Curry," they said over the loudspeakers. Marie Louise told him in a swooning voice on the phone that as far as she was concerned he had taken over her will, that with him she would do "anything."

And these were good days for Redemptorist School, the school which had always been the poorest white school in the city of New Orleans. A new principal had come, and she climbed on a bench in the school yard and shouted through a microphone to inflame the kids before the games! She sent huge crowds to City Park to cheer. Soon she had scores of students out collecting quarters to build a gym, and the team was working small miracles. It was winning game after game, by sheer force of will it seemed, just scoring those yards even when the opposition was playing better football.

Michael still hit the books, but the games were the real focus of his emotional life that year. Football was perfect for his aggression, his strength, even his frustration. He was one of the stars at school. He could feel the girls looking at him when he walked up the aisle at eight o'clock Mass every morning.

And then the dream came true. Redemptorist won the City Championship. The underdogs had done it, the kids from the other side of Magazine, the kids who spoke that funny way so that everyone knew they were from the Irish Channel.

Even the *Times-Picayune* was full of ecstatic praise. And the gymnasium drive was in high gear, and Marie Louise and Michael went "all the way" and then suffered agonies waiting to find out if Marie Louise was pregnant.

Michael might have lost it all then. He wanted nothing more than to score touchdowns, be with Marie Louise, and make money so he could take her out in the Packard. On Mardi Gras day, he and Marie Louise dressed as pirates, went down to the French Quarter, drank beer, snuggled and necked on a bench in Jackson Square. As summer came on, she talked more and more about getting married.

Michael didn't know what to do. He felt he belonged with Marie Louise, yet he could not talk to her. She hated the movies he took her to see—*Lust for Life*, or *Marty*, or *On the Waterfront*. And when he talked about college, she told him he was dreaming.

Then came the winter of Michael's senior year. It was bitter cold, and New Orleans experienced its first snowfall in a century. When the schools let out early, Michael went walking alone through the Garden District, its streets beautifully blanketed in white, watching the soft soundless snow descend all around him. He did not want to share this moment with Marie Louise. He shared it instead with the houses and the trees he loved, marveling at the spectacle of the snow-trimmed porches and cast-iron railings.

Kids played in the streets; cars drove slowly on the ice, skidding dangerously at the corners. For hours the lovely carpet of snow stayed on the ground; then Michael finally went home, his hands so cold he could scarcely turn the key in the lock. He found his mother crying.

His dad had been killed in a warehouse fire at three that afternoon; he'd been trying to save another fire fighter.

It was over for Michael and his mother in the Irish Channel. By late May, the house on Annunciation Street was sold. And one hour after Michael received his high school diploma before the altar of St. Alphonsus Church, he and his mother were on a Greyhound bus, headed for California.

Now Michael would get to have "nice things" and go to college and mix with people who spoke good English. All this turned out to be true.

His Aunt Vivian lived in a pretty apartment on Golden Gate Park, full of dark furniture and real oil paintings. They stayed with her until they could get their own place a few blocks away. And Michael at once applied to the state college for the freshman year, his father's insurance money taking care of everything.

Michael loved San Francisco. It was always cold, true, and miserably windy and barren. Nevertheless he loved the somber colors of the city, which struck him as quite particular, ochers and olive greens and dark Roman reds and deep grays. The great ornate Victorian houses reminded him of those beautiful New Orleans mansions.

Taking summer courses at the downtown extension of the state college, to make up for the math and science which he lacked, he had no time to miss home, to think of Marie Louise, or of girls at all. When he wasn't studying, he was busy trying to figure things out—how San Francisco worked, what made it so different from New Orleans.

It seemed the great underclass to which he had belonged in New Orleans did not exist in this city, where even policemen and fire fighters spoke well and dressed well and owned expensive houses. It was impossible to tell from what part of town a person came. The pavements themselves were amazingly clean, and an air of restraint seemed to affect the smallest exchanges between people.

When he went to Golden Gate Park, Michael marveled at the

nature of the crowds, that they seemed to add to the beauty of the dark green landscape, rather than to be invading it. They rode their glamorous foreign bicycles on the paths, picnicked in small groups on the velvet grass, or sat before the band shell listening to the Sunday concert. The museums of the city were a revelation, too, full of real Old Masters, and they were crowded with average people on Sundays, people with children, who seemed to take all this quite for granted.

Michael stole weekend hours from his studies so that he could roam the De Young, and gaze in awe at the great El Greco painting of Saint Francis of Assisi, with its haunted expression and gaunt gray cheeks.

"Is this all of America?" Michael asked. It was as if he'd come from another country into the world he had only glimpsed in motion pictures or television. Not the foreign films of the great houses and the smoking jackets, of course, but the later American films, and television shows, in which everything was neat and civilized.

And here Michael's mother was happy, really happy as he had never seen her, putting money in the bank from her job at I. Magnin where she sold cosmetics as she had years ago, and visiting with her sister on weekends and sometimes her older brother, "Uncle Michael," a genteel drunk who sold "fine china" at Gumps on Post Street.

One weekend night they went to an old-fashioned theater on Geary Street to see a live stage production of *My Fair Lady*. Michael loved it. After that they went often to "little theaters" to see remarkable plays—Albert Camus's *Caligula* and Maxim Gorky's *The Lower Depths* and a peculiar mishmash of soliloquies based on the work of James Joyce called *Ulysses in Nighttown*.

Michael was entranced with all this. Uncle Michael promised him that when the opera season came he would take him to see *La Bohème*. Michael was speechless with gratitude.

It was as if his childhood in New Orleans had never really happened.

He loved the downtown of San Francisco, with its noisy cable cars and overflowing streets, the big dime store on Powell and Market, where he could stand reading at the paperback rack, unnoticed, for hours.

He loved the flower stands which sold bouquets of red roses for almost nothing, and the fancy stores on Union Square. He loved the little foreign movie theaters, of which there were at least a dozen, where he and his mother went to see *Never on Sunday* with Melina Mercouri and *La Dolce Vita* made by Fellini, absolutely the most wonderful film Michael had ever seen. There were also comedies with Alec Guinness, and dark murky philosophical films from Sweden by Ingmar Bergman, and lots of other wonderful films from Japan and from Spain and from France. Many people in San Francisco went to see such movies. There was nothing secret about them at all.

He loved having coffee with other summer students in the big garishly lighted Foster's Restaurant on Sutter Street, talking for the first time in his life with Orientals and Jews from New York, and educated colored people who spoke perfect English, and older men and women who were stealing time from families and jobs to go back to school just for the sheer joy of it.

It was during this period that Michael came to comprehend the little mystery of his mother's family. By bits and pieces he put it together that they had once been very rich, these people. And it was Michael's mother's paternal grandmother who had squandered the entire fortune. Nothing was left from her but one carved chair and three heavily framed landscape paintings. Yet she was spoken of as something beyond wonderful, a goddess one would think, who had traveled the whole world, and ate caviar, and managed to put her son through Harvard before going completely bankrupt.

As for the son—Michael's mother's father—he had drunk himself to death after the loss of his wife, a "beautiful" Irish-American girl, from the Mission District of San Francisco. Nobody wanted to talk about "Mother" and it soon came clear that "Mother" had committed suicide. "Father," who drank unceasingly until he had a fatal stroke, left his three children a small annuity. Michael's mother and her sister Vivian finished their education at the Convent of the Sacred Heart, and went into genteel occupations. Uncle Michael was "the spitting image of dad," they said with a sigh, when he had fallen asleep from his cognac on the sofa.

Uncle Michael was the only salesman that Michael ever knew who could sell people things while he himself was sitting down. He would come back to Gumps, drunk from lunch, and sit there, flushed and exhausted and merely point to the beautiful china, explaining everything from his chair, while the young customers, couples soon to be married, made up their minds. People seemed to find him charming. He did know all about fine china, and he was a terribly nice guy.

This gradual education regarding his mother's family illuminated much for Michael. As time went on he came to see that his mother's values were essentially those of the very rich though she herself did not know it. She went to see foreign films because they were fun, not for cultural enhancement. And she wanted Michael to go to college because that's where he "ought" to be. It was perfectly natural to her to shop at Young Man's Fancy and buy him the crew-neck sweaters and button-down shirts that made him look like a prep-school boy. But of middle-class drive or ambition she and her sister and her brother really knew nothing. Her work appealed to her because I. Magnin was the finest store in town, and she met nice people there. In her leisure hours, she drank her ever increasing amounts of wine, read her novels, visited with friends, and was a happy, satisfied person.

It was the wine that killed her eventually. For as the years passed she became a ladylike drunk, sipping all evening long from a crystal glass behind closed doors, and invariably passing out before bedtime. Finally one night, late, she struck her head in a bathroom fall, put a towel to the wound and went back to sleep, never realizing that she was slowly bleeding to death. She was cold when Michael finally broke down the door. That was in the house on Liberty Street which Michael had bought and restored for his family, though Uncle Michael was gone by then, too, of drink also, though in his case they had called it a stroke.

But in spite of her own lassitude and final indifference to the world at large, Michael's mother was always proud of Michael's ambition. She understood his drive because she understood him, and he was the one thing that had given her own life true meaning.

And Michael's ambition was a raging flame when he finally entered San Francisco State College in the fall as a matriculating freshman.

Here, on an enormous college campus amid full-time students from all walks of life, Michael felt inconspicuous and powerful and ready to start his true education. It was like those old days in the library. Only now he got credit for what he read. He got credit for wanting to understand all the mysteries of life which had so provoked him in years past when he'd hidden his curiosity from those who might ridicule him.

He could not believe his luck. Going from class to class, deliciously anonymous among the great proletarian student body with their backpacks and their brogans, Michael listened, rapt, to the lectures of his professors and the stunningly clever questions asked by the students around him. Peppering his schedules with electives in art, music, current events, comparative literature, and even drama, he gradually acquired a true old-fashioned liberal arts education.

He majored in history finally because he did well in that subject and could write the papers and pass the tests, and because he knew that his latest ambition—to be an architect—was quite beyond him. He could not master the math, no matter how he tried. And in spite of all his efforts, he could not make the grades that would admit him to a School of Architecture for four years of postgraduate study. Also he loved history because it was a social science in which people tried to stand back from the world and figure out how it worked. And this is what Michael had been doing ever since he was a kid in the Irish Channel.

Synthesis, theory, overview—this was utterly natural to him. And because he had come from such an alien and otherworldly place, because he was so astonished by the modern world of California, the perspective of the historian was a comfort to him. He liked above all to read well-written books about cities and centuries—books, that is, which tried to describe places or eras in terms of their origins, their sociological and technological advances, their class struggle, their art and literature.

Michael was more than content. As the insurance money ran out, he went to work part-time with a carpenter who specialized in restoring the beautiful old Victorians of San Francisco. He began to study books on houses again, as he had in the old days.

By the time he received his bachelor's degree, his old friends from New Orleans would not have known him. He had still the football player's build, the massive shoulders and the heavy chest, and the carpentry kept him in fine form. And his black curly hair, his large blue eyes, and the light freckles on his cheeks remained his distinctive features. But he wore dark-rimmed glasses now to read, and his common dress was a cable-knit sweater and Donegal tweed jacket with patches on the elbows. He even smoked a pipe, which he carried always in his right coat pocket.

He was at age twenty-one equally at home hammering away on a wood-frame house or typing rapidly with two fingers a term paper on "The Witchcraft Persecutions in Germany in the 1600s."

Two months after he started his graduate work in history, he began to study, right along with his college work, for the state contractor's examination. He was working as a painter then, and learning also the plastering trade and how to lay ceramic tile—anything in the building trades for which anyone would hire him.

He went on with school because a deep insecurity would not allow him to do otherwise, but he knew by this time that no amount of academic pleasure could ever satisfy his need to work with his hands, to get out in the air, to climb ladders, swing a hammer, and feel at the end of the day that great sublime physical exhaustion. Nothing could ever take the place of his beautiful houses.

He loved to see the results of his work—roofs mended, staircases restored, floors brought back from hopeless grime to a high luster. He loved to strip and lacquer the finely crafted old newel posts, balustrades, and door frames. And always the learner, he studied under every craftsman with whom he worked. He quizzed the architects when he could; he made copies of blueprints for further examination. He pored over books, magazines, and catalogs devoted to restoration and Victoriana.

It seemed to him sometimes that he loved houses more than he loved human beings; he loved them the way that seamen love ships; and he would walk alone after work through the rooms to which he'd given new life, lovingly touching the windowsills, the brass knobs, the silk smooth plaster. He could hear a great house speaking to him.

He finished the master's in history within two years, just as the campuses of America were erupting with student protests against the American war in Vietnam and the use of psychedelic drugs became a fad among the young who were pouring into San Francisco's Haight Ashbury. But well before that he had passed the contractor's examination and formed his own company.

The world of the flower children, of political revolution and personal transformation through drugs, was something he never fully understood, and something which never really touched him. He danced at the Avalon Ballroom to the music of the Rolling Stones; he smoked grass; he burned incense now and then; he played the records of Bismilla Kahn and Ravi Shankar. He even went with a young girlfriend to the great "Be In" in Golden Gate Park where Timothy Leary told his acolytes to "tune in, turn on, and drop out." But all this was only mildly fascinating to him.

The historian in him could not succumb to the shallow, often silly revolutionary rhetoric he heard all around; he could only laugh quietly at the dining table Marxism of his friends who seemed to know nothing personally of the working man. And he watched in horror when those he loved destroyed their peace of mind utterly, if not their very brains, with powerful hallucinogens.

But he learned from all this; he learned as he sought to understand. And the great psychedelic love of color and pattern, of Eastern music and design had its inevitable influence on his esthetics. Years later, he would maintain that the great sixties revolution in consciousness had benefited every person in the nation—that the renovation of old houses, the creation of gorgeous public buildings with flower-filled plazas and parks, the erection even of the modern shopping malls with marble floors, fountains, and flower beds—all this directly stemmed from those crucial years when the hippies of the Haight Ashbury had hung ferns in the windows of their flats and draped their junk furniture with brilliantly colored Indian bedspreads, when the girls had fixed the proverbial flowers in their free-flowing tresses, and the men had discarded their drab clothes for shirts of bright colors and had let their hair grow full and long.

There was never any doubt in his mind that this period of turmoil and mass drug taking and wild music had borne directly on his career. All over the nation young couples turned their backs on the square little houses of the modern suburbs and, with a new love of texture and detail and varied forms, turned their attention to the gracious old homes of the inner city. San Francisco had such houses beyond count.

Michael had perpetually a waiting list of eager customers. Great Expectations could renovate, restore, build from scratch. Soon he had projects going all over town. He loved nothing better than to walk into a broken-down, moldy Victorian on Divisadero Street and say, "Yeah, I can give you a palazzo here in six months." His work won awards. He became famous for the beautiful and detailed drawings he could make. He undertook some projects without architectural guidance at all. All his dreams were coming true.

He was thirty-two when he acquired a vintage town house on Liberty Street, restored it inside and out, providing apartments for his mother and his aunt, and there he lived on the top floor, with a view of the downtown lights, in exactly the style he'd always wanted. The books, the lace curtains, the piano, the fine antiques—he possessed all these things. He built a great hillside deck where he could sit and drink up the fickle northern California sun. The eternal fog of the oceanfront frequently burned off before it reached the hills of his district. And so he had captured—it seemed—not only the luxury and refinement he'd glimpsed those many years ago in the South, but a little of the warmth and sunshine he so fondly remembered.

By the age of thirty-five he was a self-made man and an educated one. He had netted and socked away his first million in a portfolio of municipal bonds. He loved San Francisco because he felt that it had given him everything he ever wanted.

Though Michael had invented himself as many a person has done in California, creating a style perfectly in tune with the style of so many other self-invented people, he was always partly that tough kid from the Irish Channel who had grown up using a piece of bread to push his peas onto his fork.

He never entirely erased his harsh accent, and sometimes when he was dealing with workmen on the job, he would slip back into it entirely. He never lost some of his crude habits or ideas either, and he understood that about himself.

His way of dealing with all this was perfect for California. He simply let it show. After all, it was only part of him. He thought nothing of saying "Where's the meat and potatoes?" when he walked into some fancy nouvelle cuisine restaurant (he did actually like meat and potatoes a lot and ate them whenever it was possible, to the exclusion of other things), or of letting his Camel cigarette hang on his lip when he talked, just the way his father had always done.

And he got along with his liberal friends principally because he did not bother to argue with them, and while they were shouting at each other over pitchers of beer about foreign countries where they had never been and would never go, he was drawing pictures of houses on napkins.

When he did share his ideas, it was in a highly abstract way, from a remove, for he felt like an outsider in California really, an outsider in the American twentieth century. And he wasn't the least bit surprised that nobody paid much attention to him.

But whatever the politics involved, he always connected most truly with those who were passionate as he was—craftsmen, artists, musicians, people who went about in the grip of obsession. And an amazing number of his friends and lovers were Russian-American Jews. They really seemed to understand his overall desire to live a meaningful life, to intervene in the world—even if in a very small way—with his visions. He had dreams of building his own great houses; of transforming whole city blocks, of developing whole enclaves of cafés, bookstores, bed-and-breakfast inns within old San Francisco neighborhoods.

Now and then, especially after his mother died, he'd think about the past in New Orleans, which seemed ever more otherworldly and fantastical. People in California thought they were free, but how conformist they were, he reasoned. Why, everybody coming from Kansas and Detroit and New York just reached for the same liberal ideas, the same styles of thinking, dressing, feeling. In fact, sometimes the conformity was downright laughable. Friends really said things like "Isn't that the one we're boycotting this week?" and "Aren't we supposed to be against that?"

Back home, he had left a city of bigots perhaps, but it was

also a city of characters. He could hear the old Irish Channel storytellers in his head, his grandfather telling about how he'd snuck into the Germans' church once when he was a boy just to hear what German Latin sounded like. And how in the days of Grandma Gelfand Curry—the one German ancestor in the entire tribe—they'd baptized the babies in St. Mary's to make her happy and then snuck them over to St. Alphonsus to be baptized again and right and proper in the Irish church, the same priest presiding patiently at both ceremonies.

What characters his uncles had been, those old men who died one by one as he was growing up. He could still hear them talking about swimming the Mississippi back and forth (which nobody did in Michael's day) and diving off the warehouses when they were drunk, of tying big paddles to the pedals of their bikes to try to make them work in the water.

Everything had been a tale, it seemed. Talk could fill the summer night of Cousin Jamie Joe Curry in Algiers who became such a religious fanatic they had to chain him to a post all day long, and of Uncle Timothy who went nuts from the Linotype ink so that he stuffed all the cracks around the doors and windows with newspapers and spent his time cutting out thousands and thousands of paper dolls.

And what about beautiful Aunt Lelia, who had loved the Italian boy when she was young and never knew till she was old and dried up that her brothers had beaten him up one night and driven him out of the Irish Channel. No dagos for them. All her long life mourning for that boy. She had turned the supper table over in a rage when they told her.

Even some of the nuns had had fabulous stories to tell—old ones like Sister Bridget Marie who had substituted for two weeks when Michael was in the eighth grade, a really sweet little sister who still had an Irish brogue. She didn't teach them a thing. She just told them tales about the Irish Ghost of Petticoat Loose, and witches—witches, can you believe it!—in the Garden District.

And some of the best talk in those times had been merely talk of life itself—of how it was to bottle your own beer, to live with only two oil lamps in a house, and how they'd had to fill the portable bathtub on Friday night so everybody could take a bath before the living room fireplace. Just life. Laundry boiling over a wood fire in the backyard, water from cisterns covered with green moss. Mosquito netting tucked in tight before you went to sleep. Things now probably utterly forgotten.

It would come back to him in the oddest flashes. He'd remember the smell of the linen napkins when his grandmother ironed them before putting them in the deep drawers of the walnut sideboard. He'd remember the taste of crab gumbo with crackers and beer; the scary sound of the drums at the Mardi Gras parades. He'd see the ice man rushing up the back steps, the giant block of ice on his padded shoulder. And over and over those marvelous voices, which had seemed so coarse then, but seemed now to be possessed of a rich vocabulary, a flare for the dramatic phrase, a sheer love of language.

Tales of great fires, and the famous streetcar labor riots, and the cotton loaders who had screwed the bales into the holds of the ships with giant iron screws, singing as they worked, in the days before the cotton compressors.

It seemed a great world in retrospect. Everything was so antiseptic in California sometimes. Same clothes, same cars, same causes. Maybe Michael didn't really belong here. Maybe he never would. Yet surely he didn't belong back there. Why, he hadn't seen the place in all these years . . .

He wished he'd paid more attention to those guys in those days. He'd been too afraid. He wished he could talk to his dad now, sit with him and all those other crazy firemen outside the firehouse on Washington Avenue.

Had the oak trees really been that big? Had they really arched completely over the street so that you gazed down a tunnel of green all the way to the river?

He'd remember the color of twilight as he walked home late after football practice, along Annunciation Street. How beautiful the orange and pink lantana pushing through the little iron fences. Ah, was there a sky so purely incandescent as that sky, changing from pink to violet and then finally to gold over the tops of the shotgun cottages. There could not have been such an unearthly place.

And the Garden District, ah, the Garden District. His memories of it were so ethereal as to be suspect.

Sometimes he dreamed of it—a warm glowing paradise where he found himself walking among splendid palaces, surrounded by ever-blooming flowers, and shimmering green leaves. Then he'd wake and think, Yes, I was back there, walking down First Street. I was home. But it couldn't really be like that, not really, and he'd want to see it all again.

Particular houses would come back to him—the great rambling house on Coliseum and Third, painted pure white even to its cast-iron railings. And the double-galleried side hall houses he had always loved the most, with their four front columns up and down, their long flanks, and high twin chimneys.

He'd remember even people whom he had often glimpsed on his regular walks, old men in seersucker suits and straw hats, ladies with canes, black nurses in crisp blue cotton uniforms pushing white babies in carriages. And that man, that strange, immaculately dressed man whom he so often saw on First Street in that deep overgrown garden.

He wanted to go back to check memory against reality. He wanted to see the little house on Annunciation Street where he had grown up. He wanted to see St. Alphonsus where he'd been an altar boy when he was ten. And St. Mary's across the street with its Gothic arches and wooden saints, where he had also served Mass. Were the murals on the ceiling of St. Alphonsus really so lovely?

Sometimes as he drifted off to sleep, he would imagine himself in that church again on Christmas Eve when it had been packed for Midnight Mass. Candles blazed on the altars. He would hear the euphoric hymn "Adeste Fideles." Christmas Eve, with the rain gusting in the doors, and at home after, the little tree glowing in the corner and the gas heater blazing on the grate. How beautiful those tiny blue flames had been. How beautiful that little tree, with its lights which meant the Light of the World, and its ornaments which meant the gifts of the Wise Men, and its green-smelling branches which meant the promise of the summer to come even in the depth of the winter's cold.

There came to him a memory of a Midnight Mass procession in which the little girls of the first grade had been dressed as angels as they came through the sanctuary and down the main aisle of the church. He could smell the Christmas greens, mingling with the sweetness of the flowers and the burning wax. The little girls had been singing of the Christ Child. He had seen Rita Mae Dwyer and Marie Louise Guidry and his cousin, Patricia Anne Becker, and all the other pesty little girls he knew, but how beautiful they had looked in their little white gowns with stiff cloth wings. Not just little monsters anymore but real angels. That was the magic of Christmas. And when he got home after, all his presents were under the lighted tree.

Processions. There were so many. But the ones to the Virgin Mary he never really loved. She was too confused in his mind with the mean nuns who hurt the boys so much, and he could not feel a great devotion to her, which had saddened him until he was old enough not to care.

But Christmas he never forgot. It was the one remnant of his religion which never left him, for he sensed behind it a great, shimmering history that went back and back through the millennia to dark forests where fires blazed and pagans danced. He loved to remember the crib with the smiling infant, and the

63

solemn moment at midnight when Christ was born into the world again.

In fact, ever after in California, Christmas Eve was the one day Michael held sacred. He always celebrated it as others celebrated New Year's—for it was for him the symbol of a new beginning: of time redeeming you and all your failings so that you might start again. Even when he was alone he sat up with his glass of wine until midnight, the light of the little tree the only illumination in his room. And that last Christmas, there had been snow—of all things, snow—snow falling softly and soundlessly in the wind at the very moment perhaps when his father had gone through the burning warehouse roof on Tchoupitoulas Street.

Somehow or other, Michael never did go home.

He just never got around to it. He was always struggling to complete a job already over deadline. And what little vacation time he had he spent in Europe, or in New York roaming the great monuments and museums. His various lovers wanted it that way over the years. Who wanted to see Mardi Gras in New Orleans when they could go to Rio? Why go to the South of the United States when they could go to the South of France?

But often Michael reflected that he had acquired everything he had ever longed for on those old Garden District walks, and he ought to go back there to take stock, to see whether or not he was deceiving himself. Were there not moments when he felt empty? When he felt as if he were waiting for something, something of extreme importance, and he did not know what that was?

The one thing he had not found was a great and enduring love, but he knew this would come in time, and maybe then he would take his bride with him to visit his home, and he wouldn't be alone as he walked the cemetery paths or the old sidewalks. Who knows? Maybe he could even stay for a while, wandering the old streets.

Michael did have several affairs over the years, and at least two of these were like marriages. Both women were Jewish, of Russian descent, passionate, spiritual, brilliant and independent. And Michael was always painfully proud of these polished and clever ladies. These affairs were born in talk as much as in sensuality. Talk the night long after making love, talk over pizza and beer, talk as the sun came up, that's what Michael had always done with his lovers.

He learned much from these relationships. His egoless openness was highly seductive to these women, and he soaked up whatever they had to teach, rather effortlessly. They loved traveling with him to New York or the Riviera or Greece and seeing his charming enthusiasm and deep feeling for what he beheld. They shared their favorite music with him, their favorite painters, their favorite foods, their ideas about furniture, clothes. Elizabeth instructed him in how to buy a proper Brooks Brothers suit and Paul Stewart shirts. Judith took him to Bullock and Jones for his first Burberry and to fancy salons for proper haircuts, and taught him how to order European wines and how to cook pasta and why baroque music was just as good as the classical music he loved.

He laughed at all this, but he learned it. Both women teased him about his freckles and his heavyweight build, and the way his hair hung in his big blue eyes, and how visiting parents loved him, and about his bad little boy charm, and how splendid he looked in black tie. Elizabeth called him her "tough guy with the heart of gold," and Judith nicknamed him Sluggo. He took them to Golden Glove boxing matches and basketball games and to good bars for drinking beer, and taught them how to appreciate soccer and rugby games in Golden Gate Park on Sundays if they didn't already know it, and even how to street-fight if they wanted to learn. But that was more of a joke than anything serious. He also took them to the opera and to the symphony, which he attended with religious fervor. And they introduced him to Dave Brubeck, Miles Davis, Bill Evans, and the Kronos Quartet.

Michael's receptiveness, and his passion, tended to seduce everybody.

But his meanness charmed his girlfriends too, almost always. He could, when angry, or even slightly threatened, revert to the grim-faced Irish Channel kid in a moment, and when he did this, he did it with great conviction and confidence and a certain unconscious sexuality. Women were impressed by his mechanical skills as well, his talent with the hammer and nails, and by his fearlessness.

Fear of humiliation, yes, that he secretly understood, and there were a few irrational childhood fears which still haunted him. But fear of anything real? As an adult, he did not know the meaning of it. When there was a cry in the night, Michael was the first one down the steps to investigate.

This was not so common among highly educated men. Neither was Michael's characteristically direct and lusting and enthusiastic approach to physical sex. He liked it plain and simple, or fancier if that's what they wanted; and he liked it in the morning when he first woke up as well as at night. This stole hearts for him.

The first breakup—with Elizabeth—was Michael's fault, he felt, because he was just too young and had not remained faithful. Elizabeth got fed up with his other "adventures," though he swore they "didn't mean a thing," and finally packed her bags and left him. He was heartbroken and contrite. He followed her to New York, but it was no good. He came back home to his empty flat and got drunk off and on for six months of mourning. He could not believe it when Elizabeth married a professor at Harvard, and he was jubilant when a year later she got divorced.

He flew to New York to console her, they had a fight in the Metropolitan Museum of Art, and he cried for hours on the flight back. In fact, he looked so sad that the stewardess took him home with her when they landed and took care of him for three whole days.

By the time Elizabeth came the next summer, Judith had already come into Michael's life.

Judith and Michael lived together for almost seven years and no one ever thought they would break up. Then Judith accidentally conceived a child by Michael and, against his wishes, decided not to give birth to it.

It was the worst disappointment Michael had ever experienced, and it destroyed all love between the couple.

Michael didn't contest Judith's right to abort the child. He could not imagine a world in which women did not have such a right. And the historian in him knew that laws against abortion had never been enforceable, because no relationship existed quite like the relationship between a mother and her unborn child.

No, he never quarreled with her right, and would in fact have defended it. But he had never foreseen that a woman living with him in luxury and security, a woman whom he would marry in an instant if she permitted it, would want to abort their child.

Michael begged her not to do it. It was theirs, was it not, and its father wanted it desperately and could not bear the thought that it would miss its chance at life. It didn't have to grow up with them if Judith didn't want it. Michael would arrange everything for its care elsewhere. He had plenty of money. He would visit the child on his own so that Judith never had to know. He had visions of governesses, fine schools, all the things he'd never had. But more significant, it was a living thing, this unborn baby, and it had his blood in its little veins and he couldn't see any good reason for it to die.

These remarks were horrifying to Judith. They cut her to the quick. She did not want to be a mother at this time; she didn't feel that she could do it. She was almost finished with her Ph.D.

at U.C. Berkeley, but she had her dissertation still to write. And her body was not something to be used merely to deliver a child to another person. The great shock of giving birth to that child, of giving it up, was more than she could possibly bear. She would live with that guilt forever. That Michael did not understand her point of view was exquisitely painful to her. She had always counted upon her right to abort an unwanted child. It was her safety net, so to speak. Now her freedom, her dignity, and her sanity were threatened.

Some day they would have a child, she said, when the time was right for both of them, for parenthood was a matter of choice, and no child should be brought into the world who was not loved and wanted by both parents.

None of this made sense to Michael. Death was better than abandonment? How could Judith feel guilt for giving it away, and no guilt at all for merely destroying it? Yes, both parents should want a child. But why should one parent have the right to say that it couldn't come into the world? They weren't poor, they weren't diseased; this wasn't a child of rape. Why, they were practically married and could certainly get married if Judith wanted! They had so much to give this baby. Even if it lived with others, think what they could do for it. Why the hell did the little thing have to perish, and stop saying it wasn't a person, it was on track to be a person, or Judith wouldn't want to be killing it. Was a newborn baby any more a person, for the love of God?

And so they went back and forth, their arguments sharpening, becoming ever more complex, vacillating between the personal and the philosophical with no hope of resolution.

Finally Michael made his last ditch stand. If Judith would only give birth to the child, he would take it away with him. Judith would never see either of them again. And he would do whatever Judith wanted in return. He would give her whatever he had that she might value. He cried as he pleaded with her.

Judith was crushed. Michael had chosen this child over her. He was trying to buy her body, her suffering, the thing growing inside her. She couldn't bear to be in the same house with him. She cursed him for the things he'd said. She cursed his background, his ignorance, and above all his stunning unkindness to her. Did he think it was easy what she meant to do? But every instinct in her told her she must terminate this brutal physical process, she must extinguish this bit of life which was never meant, and which clung to her now, growing against her will, destroying Michael's love for her and their life together.

Michael couldn't look at her. If she wanted to go, she should go. He wanted her to go. He didn't want to know the exact day or hour that their child would be destroyed.

A dread came over him. Everything around him was gray. Nothing tasted good or looked good. It was as if a metallic gloom had gripped his world, and all colors and sensations had paled in it. He knew Judith was in pain, but he couldn't help her. In fact, he couldn't stop himself from hating her.

He thought about those nuns at school, smacking the boys with the flat of their hands; he remembered the grip of a nun's fingers on his arm as she shoved him into the ranks; he remembered thoughtless power, petty brutality. Of course that had nothing to do with this, he told himself. Judith cared; Judith was a good person. She was doing what she thought she had to do. But Michael felt as helpless now as he'd felt back then, when the nuns patrolled the halls, monsters in their black veils, their mannish shoes thudding on the polished wood.

Judith moved out while Michael was at work. The bill for the abortion—Boston hospital and doctor—came a week later. Michael sent his check to the appropriate address. He never saw Judith again.

And after that, for a long time Michael was a loner. Erotic contact had never been something he enjoyed with strangers. But now he had a fear of it, and chose his partners only very occasionally and with great discretion. He was careful to an extreme degree. He wanted no other lost children.

Also, he found himself unable to forget the dead baby, or the dead fetus more properly speaking. It wasn't that he meant to brood on the child—he had nicknamed it Little Chris, but nobody needed to know this—it was that he began to see images of fetuses in the movies he went to see, in the ads for movies which he saw in the papers.

As always movies loomed large in Michael's life. As always they were a major, ongoing part of his education. He fell into a trance in a darkened theater. He felt some visceral connection between what was happening on the screen and his own dreams and subconscious, and with his ongoing efforts to figure out the world in which he lived.

And now he saw this curious thing which no one else around him mentioned: did not the cinematic monsters of this time bear a remarkable resemblance to the children being aborted every day in the nation's clinics?

Take Ridley Scott's *Alien* for instance, where the little monster is born right out of the chest of a man, a squealing fetus who then retains its curious shape, even as it grows large, gorging itself upon human victims.

And what about *Eraserhead*, where the ghastly fetal offspring born to the doomed couple cries continuously.

Why, at one point it seemed to him there were too many horror films with fetuses in them to make a count. There was *The Kindred* and *Ghoulies* and *Leviathan* and those writhing clones being born like fetuses out of the pods in *Invasion of the Body Snatchers*. He could hardly bear to watch that scene when he saw it again at the Castro. He got up and walked out of the theater.

God only knew how many more fetus horror movies there were. Take the remake of *The Fly*. Didn't the hero wind up looking like a fetus? And what about *Fly II*, with its images of birth and rebirth? The never-ending theme, he figured. And then came *Pumpkinhead*, where the great vengeful Appalachian demon grows out of a fetal corpse right before your eyes, and keeps its overblown fetal head throughout its hideous rampages.

What must this mean, Michael tried to figure out. Not that we suffer guilt for what we do, for we believe it is morally right to control the birth of our young, but that we have uneasy dreams of all those little beings washed, unborn, into eternity? Or was it mere fear of the beings themselves who want to claim us—eternally free adolescents—and make us parents. Fetuses from hell! He laughed bitterly at the whole idea in spite of himself.

Look at John Carpenter's *The Thing*, with its screaming fetal heads! And what about the old classic *Rosemary's Baby*, for God's sake, and that silly movie *It's Alive*, about the monster baby who murdered the milk man when it got hungry. The image was inescapable. Babies—fetuses. He saw it everywhere he turned.

He pondered it just as he used to ponder the magnificent houses and elegant persons in old black-and-white horror films of his youth.

No use trying to talk about all this with his friends. They had believed Judith was in the right; and they would never understand the distinctions he was trying to make. Horror movies are our troubled dreams, he thought. And we are obsessed now with birth, and birth gone wrong, and birth turned against us. And back to the Happy Hour Theater he went in his memory. He was watching *The Bride of Frankenstein* again. So science had scared them back then, and even further back when Mary Shelley had written down her inspiring visions.

Oh, well, he couldn't figure out these things. He wasn't really a historian or social scientist. Maybe he wasn't clever enough. He was a contractor by trade. Best to stick to refinishing oak floors and stripping brass faucets.

And besides, he didn't hate women. He didn't. He didn't fear them either. Women were just people, and sometimes they were better people than men, gentler, kinder. He liked their company better than the company of men most of the time. And it had never surprised him that, except for this one issue, they usually understood what he had to say more sympathetically than men did.

When Elizabeth called, eager to kindle the old flame, he was happy, very happy, to get on a plane for New York. Their weekend was bliss together, except for his elaborate precautions against conception, a matter which had now become an obsession. They would make it work again, they both knew it. They were one step from a rare moment of fine excitement. But Elizabeth didn't want to leave the East Coast, and Michael could not imagine Great Expectations in Manhattan. They would write to each other, they would think about it; they would talk long distance. They would wait and see.

As time passed, Michael lost a little faith that he would ever have the love he wanted.

But his was a world in which many adults did not have that love. They had friends, freedom, style, riches, career, but not that love, and this was the condition of modern life and so it was for him, too. And he grew to take this for granted.

He had plenty of comrades on the job, old college buddies, no shortage of female companionship when he wanted it. And as he reached his forty-eighth birthday, he figured there was still time for everything. He felt and looked young, as did the other people his age around him. Why, he still had those damned freckles. And women still gave him the eye, that was certain. In fact, he found it easier to attract them now than when he had been an overeager young man.

Who could say? Maybe his little casual affair with Therese, the young woman he'd recently met at the Symphony, would start to mean something. She was too young, he knew that, he was angry with himself on that score, but then she would call and say: "Michael, I expected to hear from you by this time! You're really manipulating me!" Whatever that meant. And off they would go to supper and her place after that.

But was it only a deep love that he missed? Was there something else? One morning, he woke up and realized in a flash that the summer he had been waiting for all these years was never going to come. And the miserable damp of the place had worked itself into the marrow of his bones. There would never be warm nights full of the smell of jasmine. There would never be warm breezes from the river or the Gulf. But this he had to accept, he told himself. After all, this was his city now. How could he ever go home?

Yet at times it seemed to him that San Francisco was no longer painted in rich colors of ocher and Roman red; that it had become a drab sepia, and that the dull glare of the perpetually gray sky had permanently blunted his spirits.

Even the beautiful houses he restored seemed sometimes no more than stage sets, devoid of real tradition, fancy traps to capture a past that had never existed, to create a feeling of solidity for people who lived moment to moment in a fear of death bordering on hysteria.

Oh, but he was a lucky man, and he knew it. And surely there were good times and good things to come.

So that was Michael's life, a life that for all practical purposes was now over, because he had drowned on May 1 and come back, haunted, obsessed, rambling on and on about the living and the dead, unable to remove the black gloves from his hands, fearful of what he might see—the great inundations of meaningless images—and picking up strong emotional impressions even from those whom he did not touch.

A full three and a half months had passed since that awful day. Therese was gone. His friends were gone. And now he was a prisoner of the house on Liberty Street.

He had changed the number on the phone. He was not answering the mountains of mail he received. Aunt Viv went out by the back door to obtain those few supplies for the house which could not be delivered.

In a sweet, polite voice she fielded the few calls. "No, Michael isn't here anymore."

He laughed every time he heard it. Because it was true. The papers said he had "disappeared." That made him laugh too. About every ten days or so, he called Stacy and Jim, just to say he was alive, then hung up. He couldn't blame them if they didn't care.

Now in the dark, he lay on his bed, watching again on the mute television screen the familiar old images of *Great Expectations*. A ghostly Miss Havisham in her tattered wedding garb talked to the young Pip, played by John Mills, who was just setting off for London.

Why was Michael wasting time? He ought to be setting off for New Orleans. But he was too drunk just now for that. Too drunk even to call for an airline schedule. Besides, there was the hope that Dr. Morris would call him, Dr. Morris, who knew this secret number, Dr. Morris to whom Michael had confided his one and only plan.

71

"If I could get in touch with that woman," he had told Dr. Morris, "you know, the skipper who rescued me. If I could just take off my gloves and hold her hands when I talk to her, well, maybe I could remember something through her. Do you know what I'm talking about?"

"You're drunk, Michael. I can hear it."

"Never mind that just now. That's a given. I'm drunk and I'm going to stay drunk, but listen to what I'm saying. If I could get on that boat again . . ."

"Yes?"

"Well, if I could get down on the deck of the boat, and touch the boards with my bare hands . . . you know, the boards I was lying on . . ."

"Michael, that's insane."

"Dr. Morris, call her. You can get in touch with her. If you won't call her, give me her name."

"What do you mean, call her and tell her you want to crawl around on the deck of her boat, feeling for mental vibrations? Michael, she has a right to be protected from something like that; she may not believe in this psychic power thing."

"But you believe in it! You know it works!"

"I want you to come back to the hospital."

Michael had hung up in a rage. No more needles, no more tests, thank you. Over and over again Dr. Morris had called back, but the telephone messages were all the same: "Michael, come in. We're worried about you. We want to see you."

Then finally, the promise: "Michael, if you sober up, I'll give it a try. I know where the lady can be found."

Sober up; he thought about it now as he lay in the dark. He groped for the nearby cold can of beer, then cracked it open. A beer drunk was the best kind of drunk. And in a way it was being sober because he hadn't poured a slug of vodka or Scotch in the can, had he? Now that was really drinking, that main-line poison, and he ought to know.

Call Dr. Morris. Tell him you're sober, sober as you ever intend to get.

Seems like he'd done that. But maybe he'd dreamed it, maybe he was just drifting off again. Sweet to lie here, sweet to be so drunk you couldn't feel the agitation, the urgency, the pain of not remembering . . .

Aunt Viv said, "Eat some supper."

But he was in New Orleans, walking through those Garden District streets, and it was warm, and oh, the fragrance of the night jasmine. To think that all these years he had not smelled that sweet, heavy scent, and had not seen the sky behind the oaks catch fire, so each tiny leaf was suddenly distinct. The flagstones buckled over the roots of the oaks. The cold wind bit at his naked fingers.

Cold wind. Yes. It was not summer after all, but winter, the sharp, freezing New Orleans winter, and they were rushing through the dark to see the last parade of Mardi Gras night, the Mystic Krewe of Comus.

Such a lovely name, he thought as he dreamed, but way back then he had also thought it wondrous. And far ahead, on St. Charles Avenue, he saw the torches of the parade and heard the drums which always scared him.

"Hurry, Michael," his mother said. She almost pulled him off his feet. How dark the street was, how terrible this cold like the cold of the ocean.

"But look, Mom." He pointed through the iron fence. He tugged on her hand. "There's the man in the garden."

The old game. She would say there was no man there, and they would laugh about it together. But the man was there, all right, just as he'd always been—way back at the edge of the great lawn, standing beneath the bare white limbs of the crepe myrtles. Did he see Michael on that night? Yes, it seemed he did. Surely they had looked at each other.

"Michael, we don't have time for that man."

"But Mom, he's there, he really is . . ."

The Mystic Krewe of Comus. The brass bands played their dark savage music as they marched by, the torches blazing. The crowds surged into the street. From atop the quivering papier-mâché floats, men in glittering satin costumes and masks threw glass necklaces, wooden beads. People fought to catch them. Michael clung to his mother's skirt, hating the sound of the drums. Trinkets landed in the gutter at his feet.

On the long way home, with Mardi Gras dead and done, and the streets littered with trash, and the air so cold that their breath made steam, he had seen the man again, standing as he was before, but this time he had not bothered to say so.

"Got to go home," he whispered now in his sleep. "Got to go back there."

He saw the long iron lace railings of that First Street house, the side porch with its sagging screens. And the man in the garden. So strange that the man never changed. And that last May, on the very last walk that Michael had ever taken through those streets, he had nodded to the man, and the man had lifted his hand and waved.

"Yes, go," he whispered. But wouldn't they give him a sign, the others who had come to him when he was dead? Surely they

73

understood that he couldn't remember now. They'd help him. The barrier is falling away between the living and dead. Come through. But the woman with the black hair said, "Remember, you have a choice."

"But no, I didn't change my mind. I just can't remember."

He sat up. The room was dark. Woman with the black hair. What was that around her neck? He had to pack now. Go to the airport. The doorway. The thirteenth one. I understand.

Aunt Viv sat beyond the living room door, in the glow of a single lamp, sewing.

He drank another swallow of the beer. Then he emptied the can slowly.

"Please help me," he whispered to no one at all. "Please help me."

He was sleeping again. The wind was blowing. The drums of the Mystic Krewe of Comus filled him with fear. Was it a warning? Why don't you jump, said the mean housekeeper to the poor frightened woman at the window in the movie *Rebecca*. Had he changed the tape? He could not remember that. But we are at Manderley now, aren't we? He could have sworn it was Miss Havisham. And then he heard her whisper in Estella's ear, "You can break his heart." Pip heard it too, but still he fell in love with her.

I'll fix up the house, he whispered. Let in the light. Estella, we shall be happy forever. This is not the school yard, not that long hollow hallway that leads to the cafeteria, with Sister Clement coming towards him. "You get back in that line, boy!" If she slaps me the way she slapped Tony Vedros, I'll kill her.

Aunt Viv stood beside him in the dark.

"I'm drunk," he said.

She put the cold beer in his hand, what a darling.

"God, that tastes so good."

"There's someone here to see you."

"Who? Is it a woman?"

"A nice gentleman from England . . ."

"No, Aunt Viv—"

"But he's not a reporter. At least he says he's not. He's a nice gentleman. Mr. Lightner is his name. He says he's come all the way from London. His plane from New York just landed and he came right to the front door."

"Not now. You have to tell him to go away. Aunt Viv, I have to go back. I have to go to New Orleans. I have to call Dr. Morris. Where is the phone?"

He climbed out of the bed, his head spinning, and stood still for a moment until the dizziness passed. But it was no good.

His limbs were leaden. He sank back into the bed, back into the dreams. Walking through Miss Havisham's house. The man in the garden nodded again.

Someone had switched off the television. "Sleep now," Aunt Viv said.

He heard her steps moving away. Was the phone ringing?

"Someone help me," he whispered.

Three

JUST GO BY. Take a little walk across Magazine Street and down First and pass by that grand and dilapidated old house. See for yourself if the glass is broken out of the front windows. See for yourself if Deirdre Mayfair is still sitting on that side porch. You don't have to go up and ask to see Deirdre.

What the hell do you think is going to happen?

Father Mattingly was angry with himself. It was a duty, really, to call on that family before he went back up north. He had been their parish priest once. He had known them all. And it had been well over a year since he'd been south, since he'd seen Miss Carl, since the funeral of Miss Nancy.

A few months ago, one of the young priests had written to say that Deirdre Mayfair had been failing badly. Her arms were drawn up now, close to the chest, with the atrophy that always sets in, in such cases.

And Miss Carl's checks to the parish were coming in as regular as always—one every month now, it seemed—made out for a thousand dollars to the Redemptorist Parish, with no strings attached. Over the years, she had donated a fortune.

Father Mattingly ought to go, really, just to pay his respects and say a personal thank you the way he used to do years ago.

The priests in the rectory these days didn't know the Mayfairs. They didn't know the old stories. They'd never been invited to that house. They had come only in recent years to this sad old parish, with its dwindling congregation, its beautiful churches locked now on account of vandals, the older buildings in ruins.

Father Mattingly could remember when the earliest Masses each day were crowded, when there were weddings and funerals all week long in both St. Mary's and St. Alphonsus. He remembered the May processions and the crowded novenas, Midnight Mass with the church jammed. But the old Irish and German families were gone now. The high school had been closed years ago. The glass was falling right out of the windows.

He was glad that his was only a brief visit, for each return was sadder than the one before it. Like a missionary outpost this was, when you thought about it. He hoped in fact that he would not be coming south again.

But he could not leave without seeing that family.

Yes, go there. You ought to. You ought to look in on Deirdre Mayfair. Was she not a parishioner after all?

And there was nothing wrong with wanting to find out if the gossip was true—that they'd tried to put Deirdre in the sanitarium, and she had gone wild, smashing the glass out of the windows before lapsing back into her catatonia. On August 13 it was supposed to have happened, only two days ago.

Who knows, maybe Miss Carl would welcome a call.

But these were games Father Mattingly played with his mind. Miss Carl didn't want him around any more now than she ever had. It had been years since he was invited in. And Deirdre Mayfair was now and forever "a nice bunch of carrots," as her nurse once put it.

No, he'd be going out of curiosity.

But then how the hell could "a nice bunch of carrots" rise up and break out all the glass in two twelve-foot-high windows? The story didn't make much sense when you thought about it. And why hadn't the men from the sanitarium taken her anyway? Surely they could have put her in a straitjacket. Isn't that what happened at times like that?

Yet Deirdre's nurse had stopped them at the door, screaming for them to get back, saying that Deirdre was staying home and she and Miss Carl would take care of it.

Jerry Lonigan, the undertaker, had told Father the whole story. The ambulance driver for the sanitarium often drove limousines for Lonigan and Sons. Saw it all. Glass crashing out onto the front porch. Sounded like everything in that big front room was being broken. And Deirdre making a terrible noise, a howling. Horrible thing to imagine—like seeing someone rise from the dead.

Well, it wasn't Father Mattingly's business. Or was it?

Dear God, Miss Carl was in her eighties, never mind that she still went to work every day. And she was all alone in that house now with Deirdre and the paid help.

The more he thought about it, Father Mattingly knew he should go, even if he did loathe that house, and loathe Carl and loathe everything he'd ever known of those people. Yes, he should go.

Of course he hadn't always felt that way. Forty-two years ago, when he'd first come from St. Louis to this riverfront parish, he had thought the Mayfair women genteel, even the buxom and grumbling Nancy, and surely sweet Miss Belle and pretty Miss Millie. The house had enchanted him with its bronze clocks and velvet portieres. He had loved the great cloudy mirrors, even, and the portraits of Caribbean ancestors under dimming glass.

He had loved also the obvious intelligence and purpose of Carlotta Mayfair, who served him café au lait in a garden room where they sat in white wicker chairs at a white wicker table, among potted orchids and ferns. They had spent more than one pleasant afternoon talking politics, the weather, and the history of the parish Father Mattingly was trying so hard to understand. Yes, he had liked them.

And he had liked little Deirdre, too, that pretty-faced six-year-old child he had known for so brief a time, who had come to such a tragic pass only twelve years later. Was it in the textbooks now that electric shock could wipe clean the entire memory of a grown woman so that she became the silent shell of herself, staring at the falling rain while a nurse fed her with a silver spoon?

Why had they done it? He had not dared to ask. But he had been told over and over. To cure her of her "delusions," of screaming in an empty room "You did it" to someone who wasn't there, someone she cursed endlessly for the death of the man who had fathered her illegitimate child.

Deirdre. Cry for Deirdre. That Father Mattingly had done, and no one but God would ever know how much or why, though Father Mattingly himself would never forget it. All his days, he'd remember the story that a little child had poured out to him in the hot wooden cell of the confessional, a little girl who was to spend her life rotting away in that vine-shrouded house while the world outside galloped on to its own damnation.

Just go over there. Make the call. Maybe it is some silent memorial to that little girl. Don't try to put it all together. Talk of devils from a small child still echoing in your ears after all this time! *Once you've seen the man, you're done for.*

Father Mattingly made up his mind. He put on his black coat, adjusted his Roman collar and black shirt front, and went out of the air-conditioned rectory onto the hot narrow pavement of Constance Street. He did not look at the weeds eating at the steps of St. Alphonsus. He did not look at the graffiti on the old school walls.

He saw the past if he saw anything as he made his way fast down Josephine Street, and around the corner. And then within two short blocks he'd entered another world. The glaring sun was gone, and with it the dust and the din of the traffic.

Shuttered windows, shady porches. The soft hissing sound of lawn sprinklers beyond ornamental fences. Deep smell of the loam heaped on the roots of carefully tended rose trees.

All right, and what will you say when you get there?

The heat wasn't really so bad today, given that it was August, yet it was just like the young priest from Chicago said: "You start out fine, and then your clothes just get heavier and heavier." He had had to laugh at that.

What did they think of all that ruin, the young ones? No use telling them how it had once been. Ah, but the city itself, and this old neighborhood—they were as beautiful as ever.

He walked on until he saw the stained and peeling side of the Mayfair house looming over the treetops, the high twin chimneys floating against the moving clouds. It seemed the vines were dragging the old structure right into the ground. Were the iron railings rusted more than when he last saw them? Like a jungle, the garden.

He slowed his pace. He slowed because he really didn't want to get there. He didn't want to see up close the garden gone to seed, chinaberry and oleander struggling with grass as high as wheat, and the porches stripped of paint, turning that dull gray that old untended wood turns in the damp climate of Louisiana.

He didn't even want to be in this still, deserted neighborhood. Nothing stirred here but the insects, the birds, the plants themselves slowly swallowing up the light and the blue of the sky. Swamp this must have been once. A breeding place of evil.

But he was out of hand with these thoughts. What had evil to do with God's earth, and the things that grew in it—even the jungle of the Mayfairs' neglected garden.

Yet he could not help but think of all the stories he had ever heard of the Mayfair women. What was voodoo if it wasn't devil worship? And what was the worse sin, murder or suicide? Yes, evil had thrived here. He heard the child Deirdre whispering in his ear. And he could feel evil as he rested his weight against the iron fence, as he looked up into the hard crusty black oak branches, fanning out above him.

He mopped his forehead with his handkerchief. Little Deirdre had told him that she saw the devil! He heard her voice just as clearly now as he had heard it in the confessional decades ago. And he heard her footsteps, too, as she ran from the church, ran from him, ran from his failure to help her.

But it had started before that. It had started on a dreary slow Friday afternoon when a call came from Sister Bridget Marie for a priest to please come quick to the school yard. It was Deirdre Mayfair again.

Father Mattingly had never heard of Deirdre Mayfair. Father Mattingly had only just come south from the seminary in Kirkwood, Missouri.

He found Sister Bridget Marie quickly enough, in an asphalt yard behind the old convent building. How European it had seemed to him then, quaint and sad with its broken walls, and the gnarled tree with the wooden benches built in a square around it.

The shade had felt good to him as he approached. Then he saw that the little girls seated along the bench were crying. Sister Bridget Marie held one pale shivering child by the thin part of her upper arm. The child was white with fear. Yet very pretty she was, her blue eyes too big for her thin face, her black hair in long careful corkscrew curls that shivered against her cheeks, her limbs well proportioned yet delicate.

There were flowers strewn all over the ground—big gladiolus and white lilies and long fronds of green fern and even big beautifully formed red roses. Florist flowers, surely, yet there were so many . . .

"Do you see that, Father?" Sister Bridget Marie exclaimed. "And they have the nerve to tell me it was her invisible friend, the devil himself, that put those flowers here, brought them right into her arms while they watched, the little thieves! They stole those flowers from the very altar of St. Alphonsus—!"

The little girls began to scream. One of them stamped her feet. A chorus of "We did see, we did see!" broke out with alarming fury. They egged each other on with their choking sobs into a regular chorus.

Sister Bridget Marie shouted for silence. She shook the little girl she had been holding by the arm, though the child had said nothing. The child's mouth dropped open in shock, her eyes rolling to Father Mattingly in a silent entreaty.

"Now, Sister, please," Father Mattingly said. He had gently freed the child. She was dazed, utterly pliant. He wanted to pick her up, wipe her face where the tears had smudged it with dirt. But he didn't.

"Her invisible friend," the sister said, "the one that finds everything that's lost, Father. The one that puts the pennies for candy into her pockets! And they all eat it, too, stuffing their mouths with it, stolen pennies, you can be sure of it."

The little girls were wailing even louder. And Father Mattingly realized he was stepping all over the flowers and the silent white-faced child was staring at his shoes, at the white petals crushed beneath them.

"Let the children go in," Father Mattingly had said. It was essential to take command. Only then could he make sense of what Sister Bridget Marie was telling him.

But the story was no less fantastic when he and the sister were alone. The children claimed they saw the flowers flying through the air. They claimed they saw the flowers land in Deirdre's arms. They had been laughing and laughing. Deirdre's magic friend always made them laugh, they said. Deirdre's friend could find your notebook or your pencil if you lost it. You asked Deirdre and he brought it to her. And there it was. And they even claimed to have seen him themselves—a nice man, a man with dark brown hair and eyes, and he would stand for one second right next to Deirdre.

"She's got to be sent home, Father," Sister Bridget Marie had said. "It happens all the time. I call her Great-aunt Carl or her Aunt Nancy, and then it stops for a while. Then it starts up again."

"But you don't believe—"

"Father, I tell you it's six of one, half a dozen of another. Either the devil's in that child, or she's a devil of a liar, and makes them believe her wild tales as if she's got them bewitched. She cannot stay at St. Alphonsus."

Father Mattingly had taken Deirdre home himself, walking slowly, steadily with her through these same streets. Not a word was spoken. Miss Carl had been phoned at her downtown office. She and Miss Millie were waiting on the front steps of the grand house to meet them.

And how lovely it was then, painted a deep violet color with green shutters and the trim all in white and the porch railings painted a shiny black so you could see the cast-iron roses so clearly. The vines had been a graceful etching of leaf and color, not the menacing tangle they had since become.

"Overactive imagination, Father," Miss Carl said without a trace of concern. "Millie what Deirdre needs is a warm bath." And off the child had gone without a word spoken, and Miss Carl had taken Father Mattingly out for the first time into the glass garden room for café au lait at the wicker table. Miss Nancy, sullen and plain, had set out the cups and silver.

Wedgwood china trimmed in gold. And cloth napkins with the letter M embroidered on them. And what a quick-witted woman, this Carl. She had looked prim in her tailored silk suit and ruffled white blouse, her salt and pepper gray hair in a neat twist on the back of her head, her mouth neatly colored with pale pink lipstick. She put him at ease at once with her knowing smile.

"You might say it's the curse of our family, Father, this excess of imagination." She poured the hot milk and the hot coffee from two small silver pitchers. "We dream dreams; we see visions; we should have been poets or painters it seems. Not lawyers, such as I am." She had laughed softly, easily. "Deirdre will be just fine, when she learns to tell fantasy from reality."

Afterwards, she had shown him through the lower rooms. And Miss Millie had joined them. She was such a feminine thing, Miss Millie, her red hair in old-fashioned finger curls around her face, and jeweled rings on her fingers. She'd taken him to the window to wave to old Miss Belle, who had been cutting back the roses with large wooden-handled shears.

Carl explained that Deirdre would be going to the Sacred Heart sisters just as soon as there was a place. She was so sorry for this silly disturbance at St. Alphonsus and of course they'd keep Deirdre home if that was what Sister Bridget Marie wanted.

Father had started to object, but it was all decided. Simple matter to get Deirdre a governess, someone who knew children, why not?

They walked along the deep shaded porches.

"We are an old family, Father," Carl said, as they went back into the double parlor. "We don't even know how old. There is no one now who can identify some of the portraits you see around you." Her voice was half amused, half weary. "We came from the islands, that's what we know for certain—a plantation on Saint-Domingue—and before that from some dim European past that is now completely lost. The house is full of unexplained relics. Sometimes I see it as a great hard snail shell that I must carry on my back."

Her hands passed lightly over the grand piano, over the gilded harp. She had little taste for such things, she said. What an irony that she had become the custodian. Miss Millie had only smiled, nodded.

And now if Father would excuse them, Miss Carl did have to go back downtown. Clients waiting. They walked out to the gate together.

"Thank you so much, Father!"

And so it had all been waved away, and the little white-faced girl with the black curls had left St. Alphonsus.

But in the days that followed it had bothered Father Mattingly, the question of those flowers.

Impossible to imagine a gang of little girls climbing over the

81

communion rail and robbing the altars of an enormous and impressive church like St. Alphonsus. Even the guttersnipes Father Mattingly had known as a boy would not have dared such a thing.

What did Sister Bridget Marie really think had happened? Had the children really stolen the flowers? The small, heavyset round-faced nun studied him a moment before she answered. Then she said no.

"Father, as God is my witness, they're a cursed family, the Mayfairs are. And the grandmother of that very child, Stella she was called, told the very same tales in this very same school yard many a year ago. It was a frightening power Stella Mayfair had over those around her. There were nuns under this very roof who were scared to death to cross her, a witch is what they called her then and now."

"Oh, come now, Sister," he had objected immediately. "We're not on the foggy roads of Tipperary, looking out for the ghost of Petticoat Loose."

"Ah, so you've heard that one, Father." She had laughed.

"From my own Irish mother on the Lower East Side, Sister, a dozen times."

"Well, then, Father, let me tell you this much, that Stella Mayfair once took my hand, and held it like this, she did, and told me secrets of my own that I had never told a living soul this side of the Atlantic. I swear it, Father. It happened to me. There was a keepsake I'd lost at home, a chain with a crucifix on it, and I'd cried and cried as a girl when I'd lost it, and that very same little keepsake Stella Mayfair described to me. 'You want it back, Sister?' she said. And all the time smiling in her sweet way, just like her granddaughter Deirdre can smile at you now, more innocent than cunning. 'I'll get it for you, Sister,' she said. 'Through the power of the devil, you mean, Stella Mayfair,' I answered her. 'I'll have none of it.' But there was many another teaching sister at St. Alphonsus school that took another tack, and that's how she kept her power over those around her, getting her way in one thing and another right up to the day she died."

"Superstition, Sister!" he'd said with great authority. "What about little Deirdre's mother? You're going to tell me she was a witch, too?"

Sister Bridget Marie shook her head. "That was Antha, a lost one, shy, sweet, afraid of her own shadow—not at all like her mother, Stella, until Stella was killed, that is. You should have seen Miss Carlotta's face when they buried Stella. And the same expression on her face twelve years after when they buried Antha. Now, Carl, she was as smart a girl as ever went to Sacred

82

Heart. The backbone of the family she is. But her mother never cared a fig for her. All Mary Beth Mayfair ever cared about was Stella. And old Mr. Julien, that was Mary Beth's uncle, he was the same. Stella, Stella, Stella. But Antha, stark raving mad at the end, they said, and nothing but a girl of twenty when she run up the stairs in the old house and jumped from the attic window and dashed her head on the stones below.''

"So young,'' he'd whispered. He remembered the pale, frightened face of Deirdre Mayfair. How old had she been when the young mother did such a thing?

"They buried Antha in consecrated ground, God have mercy on her soul. For who's to judge the state of mind of such a person? Head split open like a watermelon when she hit the terrace. And baby Deirdre screaming out her lungs in the cradle. But then even Antha was something to fear.''

Father Mattingly was quietly reeling. It was the kind of talk he'd heard all his life at home, however, the endless Irish dramatizing of the morbid, the lusty tribute to the tragic. Truth was it wore him out. He wanted to ask—

But the bell had rung. Children were lining up in proper ranks for the march inside. Sister had to go. Yet suddenly, she turned back.

"Let me tell one story about Antha,'' she said, her voice low on account of the hush in the school yard, "which is the best one that I know. In those days when the sisters sat down to supper at twelve noon, the children were silent in this yard until the Angelus was said and after that the Grace Before Meals. Nobody has such respect for anything in this day and age, but that was the custom then. And on one spring day, during that quiet time, a mean wicked girl name of Jenny Simpson comes up to frighten the poor, shy little Antha with the body of a dead rat she'd found under the hedge. Antha takes one look at the dead rat and lets out a chilling scream, Father, such as you never heard! And we come running from the supper table, as you can imagine, and what do you think we see? That mean wicked Jenny Simpson thrown over on her back, Father, her face bloody and the rat flying out of her hand over that very fence! And do you think it was little Antha did such a thing, Father? A mite of a child, as delicate as her daughter Deirdre is today? Oh, no! 'Twas the selfsame invisible fiend did it, Father, the devil himself, as brought those flowers flying through the air to Deirdre in this yard a week ago.''

"Sister, you think I'm the new boy on the block''—Father Mattingly had laughed—"to believe something like that.''

And she had smiled, it was true, but he knew from past ex-

83

perience that an Irishwoman like that could smile at what she was saying and believe every word of it at the same time.

The Mayfairs fascinated him, as something complex and elegant can fascinate. The tales of Stella and Antha were remote enough to be romantic and nothing more.

The following Sunday he called again on the Mayfairs. He was offered coffee once more and pleasant conversation—it was all so removed from Sister Bridget Marie's tales. The radio played Rudy Vallee in the background. Old Miss Belle watered the drowsing potted orchids. The smell of roast chicken came from the kitchen. An altogether pleasant house.

They even asked him to stay to Sunday dinner—the table was beautifully set with thick linen napkins in silver rings—but he politely declined. Miss Carl wrote out a check for the parish and put it in his hand.

As he was leaving he had glimpsed Deirdre in the garden, a white face peering at him from behind a gnarled old tree. He had waved to her without breaking his stride, yet something bothered him later about the image of her. Was it her curls all tangled? Or the distracted look in her eyes?

Madness, that's what Sister Bridget had described to him, and it disturbed him to think it threatened that wan little girl. There was nothing romantic to Father Mattingly about actual madness. He had long held the belief that the mad lived in a hell of irrelevance. They missed the point of life around them.

But Miss Carlotta was a sensible, modern woman. The child wasn't doomed to follow in the footsteps of a dead mother. She would, on the contrary, have every chance.

A month passed before his view of the Mayfairs changed forever, on the unforgettable Saturday afternoon that Deirdre Mayfair came to confession in St. Alphonsus Church.

It was during the regular hours when all the good Irish and German Catholics could be counted upon to clear their consciences before Mass and Communion on Sunday.

And so he was seated in the ornate wooden house of the confessional in his narrow chair behind a green serge curtain, listening in alternation to the penitents who came to kneel in the small cells to the left and the right of him. These voices and sins he could have heard in Boston or New York City, so similar the accents, the worries, the ideas.

"Three Hail Marys," he would prescribe, or "Three Our Fathers" but seldom more than that to these laboring men and good housewives who came to confess routine peccadillos.

Then a child's voice had caught him off guard, coming rapid and crisp through the dark dusty grille—eloquent of intelligence and precocity. He had not recognized it. After all, Deirdre Mayfair had not spoken one word before in his presence.

"Bless me, Father, for I have sinned. My last confession was weeks and weeks ago. Father, help me please. I cannot fight the devil. I try and I always fail. And I'm going to go to hell for it."

What was this, more of Sister Bridget Marie's influence? But before he could speak, the child went on and he knew that it was Deirdre.

"I didn't tell the devil to go away when he brought the flowers. I wanted to and I know that I should have done it, and Aunt Carl is really, really angry with me. But Father, he only wanted to make us happy. I swear to you, Father, he's never mean to me. And he cries if I don't look at him or listen to him. I didn't know he'd bring the flowers from the altar! Sometimes he does very foolish things like that, Father, things like a little child would do, with even less sense than that. But he doesn't mean to hurt anyone."

"Now, wait a minute, darling, what makes you think the devil himself would trouble a little girl? Don't you want to tell me what really happened?"

"Father, he's not like the Bible says. I swear it. He's not ugly. He's tall and beautiful. Just like a real man. And he doesn't tell lies. He does nice things, always. When I'm afraid he comes and sits by me on the bed and kisses me. He really does. And he frightens away people who try to hurt me!"

"Then why do you say he's the devil, child? Wouldn't it be better to say he's a made-up friend, someone to be with so you'll never be lonely?"

"No, Father, he's the devil." So definite she sounded. "He's not real, and he's not made up either." The little voice had become sad, tired. A little woman in a child's guise struggling with an immense burden, almost in despair. "I know he's there when no one else does, and then I look and look and then everyone can see him!" The voice broke. "Father, I try not to look. I say Jesus, Mary, and Joseph and I try not to look. I know it's a mortal sin. But he's so sad and he cries without making a sound and I can hear him."

"Now, child, have you talked to your Aunt Carl about this?" His voice was calm, but in fact the child's detailed account had begun to alarm him. This was beyond "excess of imagination" or any such excess he'd ever known.

"Father, she knows all about him. All my aunts do. They call him *the man*, but Aunt Carl says he's really the devil. She's the one who says it's a sin, like touching yourself between the legs, like having dirty thoughts. Like when he kisses me and makes me feel chills and things. She's says it's filth to look at the man and let him come under the covers. She says he can kill me. My mother saw him too all her life and that's why she died and went to heaven to get away from him.''

Father Mattingly was aghast. So you can never shock a priest in the confessional, was that the old saying?

"And my mother's mother saw him too," the child went on, the voice rushing, straining. "And *she* was really, really bad, he made her bad, and she died on account of him. But she went to hell probably, instead of heaven, and I might too.''

"Now, wait a minute, child. Who told you this!''

"My Aunt Carl, Father," the child insisted. "She doesn't want me to go to hell like Stella. She told me to pray and drive him away, that I could do it if I only tried, if I said the rosary and didn't look at him. But Father, she gets so angry with me for letting him come—'' The child stopped. She was crying, though obviously trying to muffle her cries. "And Aunt Millie is so afraid. And Aunt Nancy won't look at me. Aunt Nancy says that in our family, once you've seen *the man*, you're as good as done for.''

Father Mattingly was too shocked to speak. Quickly he cleared his throat. "You mean your aunts *say* this thing is real—''

"They've always known about him, Father. And anyone can see him when I let him get strong enough. It's true, Father. Anyone. But you see, I have to make him come. It's not a mortal sin for other people to see him because it's my fault. *My fault.* He couldn't be seen if I didn't let it happen. And Father, I just, I just don't understand how the devil could be so kind to me, and could cry so hard when he's sad and want so badly just to be near me—'' The voice broke off into low sobs.

"Don't cry, Deirdre!'' he'd said, firmly. But this was inconceivable! That sensible, "modern'' woman in her tailored suit telling a child this superstition? And what about the others, for the love of God? Why, they made the likes of Sister Bridget Marie look like Sigmund Freud himself. He tried to see Deirdre through the dim grille. Was she wiping her eyes with her hands?

The crisp little voice went on suddenly in an anguished rush.

"Aunt Carl says it's a mortal sin even to think of him or think of his name. It makes him come immediately, if you say his name! But Father, he stands right beside me when she's talking and he says she's lying, and Father, I know it's terrible to say it, but she is lying sometimes, I know it, even when he's being quiet. But the worst part is when he comes through and scares her. And she threatens him! She says if he doesn't leave me alone she'll hurt me!'' Her voice broke again, the cries barely audible. So small she seemed, so helpless! "But all the time, Father, even when I'm all alone, or even at Mass with everybody there, I know he's right beside me. I can feel him. I can hear him crying and it makes me cry, too."

"Child, now think carefully before you answer. Did your Aunt Carl actually *say* she saw this thing?"

"Oh, yes, Father." So weary! Didn't he believe her? That's what she was begging him to do.

"I'm trying to understand, darling. I want so to understand, but you must help me. Are you certain that your Aunt Carl said she saw him with her own eyes?"

"Father, she saw him when I was a baby and didn't even know I could make him come. She saw him the day my mother died. He was rocking my cradle. And when my grandmother Stella was a little girl, he'd come behind her to the supper table. Father, I'll tell you a terrible secret thing. There's a picture in our house of my mother, and he's in the picture, standing beside her. I know about the picture because he got it and gave it to me, though they had it hidden away. He opened the dresser drawer without even touching it, and then he put the picture in my hand. He does things like that when he's really strong, when I've been with him a long time and been thinking about him all day. That's when everybody knows he's in the house, and Aunt Nancy meets Aunt Carl at the door and whispers, 'The man is here. I just saw him.' And then Aunt Carl gets so mad. It's all my fault, Father! And I'm scared I can't stop him. And they're all so upset!"

Her sobs had gotten louder, echoing against the wooden walls of the little cell. Surely they could hear her outside in the church itself.

And what was he to say to her? His temper was boiling. What craziness went on with these women? Was there no one with a particle of sense in the whole family who could get a psychiatrist to help this girl?

"Darling, listen to me. I want your permission to speak of these things outside the confessional to your Aunt Carl. Will you give me that permission?"

"Oh, no Father, please, you mustn't!"

"Child, I won't, not without your permission. But I tell you, I need to speak to your Aunt Carl about these things. Deirdre, she and I can drive away this thing together."

"Father, she'll never forgive me for telling. Never. It's a mortal sin to ever tell. Aunt Nancy would never forgive me. Even

Aunt Millie would be angry. Father, you can't tell her I told you about him!" She was becoming hysterical.

"I can wipe that mortal sin away, child," he'd explained, "I can give you absolution. From that moment on, your soul is as white as snow, Deirdre. Trust in me, Deirdre. Give me permission to talk to her."

For a tense moment the crying was his only answer. Then, even before he heard her turn the knob of the little wooden door, he knew he'd lost her. Within seconds, he heard her steps running fast down the aisle away from him.

He had said the wrong thing, made the wrong judgment! And now there was nothing he could do, bound as he was by the seal of the confessional. And this secret had come to him from a troubled child who was not even old enough to commit a mortal sin, or benefit from the sacrament she'd been seeking.

He never forgot that moment, sitting helpless, hearing those steps echoing in the vestibule of the church, the closeness and the heat of the confessional suffocating him. *Dear God, what was he going to do?* •

But the torture had only begun for Father Mattingly.

For weeks after, he'd been truly obsessed—those women, that house . . .

But he could not act upon what he had heard any more than he could repeat it. The confessional bound him to secrecy in deed and word.

He did not dare even question Sister Bridget Marie, though she volunteered enough information when he happened to see her on the playground. He felt guilty for listening, but he could not bring himself to move away.

"Sure, they've put Deirdre in the Sacred Heart, they have. But do you think she'll stay there? They expelled her mother, Antha, when she was but eight years old. And from the Ursulines too she was expelled. They found a private school for her finally, one of those crazy places where they let the children stand on their heads. And what an unhappy thing she was as a young girl, always writing poetry and stories and talking to herself and asking questions about how her mother had died. And you know it was murder, don't you, Father, that Stella Mayfair was shot dead by her brother Lionel? And at a fancy dress ball in that house, he did it. Caused a regular stampede. Mirrors, clocks, windows, everything broken by the time the panic was over, and Stella lying dead on the floor."

Father Mattingly only shook his head at the pity of it.

"No wonder Antha went wild after, and not ten years later took up with a painter, no less, who never bothered to marry her, leaving her in a four-story walk-up in Greenwich Village in the middle of winter with no money and little Deirdre to take care of, so that she had to come home in shame. And then to jump from that attic window, poor thing, but what a hellish life it was with her aunts picking on her and watching her every move and locking her up at night, and her running down to the French Quarter and drinking, mind you, at her age, with the poets and the writers and trying to get them to pay attention to her work. I'll tell you a strange secret, Father. For months after she died, letters came for her, and manuscripts of hers came back from the New York people to whom she'd sent them. And what an agony for Miss Carlotta, the postman bringing her a reminder of such pain and suffering when he rang the bell at the gate.''

Father Mattingly said his silent prayer for Deirdre. Let the shadow of evil not touch her.

"There was one of Antha's stories in a magazine, they told me, published in Paris, they said, but it was all in English, and that come too to Miss Carlotta and she took one look at it and locked it away. 'Twas one of the Mayfair cousins told me that part of it, and how they offered to take the baby off her hands— little Deirdre—but she said no, she'd keep it, she owed that to Stella, and to Antha, and to her mother, and to the child itself.''

Father Mattingly stopped in the church on his way back to the rectory. He stood for a long time in the silent chamber of the sacristy looking through the door at the main altar.

For a sordid history he could forgive the Mayfairs easily enough. They were born ignorant into this world like the rest of us. But for warping a little girl with lies of the devil who drove a mother to suicide? But there was nothing, absolutely nothing, Father Mattingly could do but pray for Deirdre as he was praying now.

Deirdre was expelled from St. Margaret's Private Academy near Christmastime and her aunts packed her off to a private school up north.

Some time after that he'd heard she was home again, sickly, studying with a governess, and once after that he did glimpse her at a crowded ten o'clock Mass. She had not come to Communion. But he had seen her seated in the pew with her aunts.

More and more of the Mayfair story came to him in bits and pieces. Seems everybody in the parish knew he'd been to that house. Over a kitchen table, Grandma Lucy O'Hara took his hand. "So I hear Deirdre Mayfair's been sent away, and you've been to that house on her account, is that not so, Father?'' What on earth could he say? And so he listened.

"Now I know that family. Mary Beth, she was the grande dame, she could tell you all about how it had been on the old plantation, born there right after the Civil War, didn't come to New Orleans until the 1880s, though, when her uncle Julien brought her. And such an old southern gentleman he was. I can still remember Mr. Julien riding his horse up St. Charles Avenue; he was the handsomest old man I ever saw. And that was a real grand plantation house at Riverbend, they said, used to be pictures of it in the books even when it was all falling down. Mr. Julien and Miss Mary Beth did everything they could to save it. But you can't stop the river when the river has a mind to take a house.

"Now, she was a real beauty, Mary Beth, dark and wild-looking, not delicate like Stella—or plain like Miss Carlotta—and they said Antha was a beauty though I never did get to see her, or that poor baby Deirdre. But Stella was a real true voodoo queen. Yes, I mean Stella, Father. Stella knew the powders, the potions, the ceremonies. She could read your fortune in the cards. She did it to my grandson, Sean, frightened him half out of his wits with the things she told him. That was at one of those wild parties up there on First Street when they were swilling the bootleg liquor and had a dance band right there in the parlor. That was Stella.

"She liked my Billy, she did." Sudden gesture to the faded photograph on the bureau top. "The one who died in the War. I told him, 'Billy, you listen to me. Don't you go near the Mayfair women.' She liked all the handsome young men. That's how come her brother killed her. On a clear day she could make the sky above you cloud over. That's the God's truth, Father. She used to scare the sisters at St. Alphonsus making storms like that right over the garden. And when she died that night, you should have seen the storm over that house. Why, they said, every window in the place was broken. Rain and wind like a hurricane around that place. Stella made the heavens weep for her."

Speechless, Father Mattingly sat, trying to like the tepid tea full of milk and sugar, but he was remembering every word.

He didn't call on the Mayfairs anymore. He didn't dare. He could not have that child think—if she was there at all—that he meant to tell what he was bound forever to keep secret. He watched for the women at Mass. He seldom saw them. But this was a big parish of course. They could have gone to either church, or to the little chapel for the rich over there in the Garden District.

Miss Carlotta's checks were coming in, however. That he

knew. Father Lafferty, who did the accounts for the parish, showed him the check near Christmastime—it was for two thousand dollars—quietly remarking on how Carlotta Mayfair used her money to keep the world around her nice and quiet.

"They've sent the little niece home from the school in Boston, I suppose you heard that."

Father Mattingly said that he hadn't. He stood in the door of Father Lafferty's office, waiting . . .

"Well, I thought you got on famous with those ladies," Father Lafferty said. Father Lafferty was a plainspoken man, older than his sixty years, not a gossip.

"Only visited once or twice," said Father Mattingly.

"Now they're saying little Deirdre's sickly," Father Lafferty said. He laid the check down on the green blotter of his desk, looked at it. "Can't go to regular school, has to stay home with a private tutor."

"Sad thing."

"So it seems. But nobody's going to question it. Nobody's going to go over and see if that child's really getting a decent education."

"They have money enough . . ."

"Indeed, enough to keep everything quiet, and they always have. They could get away with murder."

"You think so?"

Father Lafferty seemed to be having a little debate with himself. He kept looking at Carlotta Mayfair's check.

"You heard about the shooting, I suppose," he said, "when Lionel Mayfair shot his sister Stella? Never spent a day in prison for it. Miss Carlotta fixed all that. So did Mr. Cortland, Julien's son. Between them those two could have fixed anything. No questions asked here by anyone."

"But how on earth did they . . ."

"The insane asylum of course, and there Lionel took his own life, though how no one knows since he was in a straitjacket."

"You don't mean it."

Father Lafferty nodded. "Of course I do. And again no questions asked. Requiem Mass same as always. And then little Antha, she came here, Stella's daughter, you know—crying, screaming, saying it was Miss Carlotta who made Lionel murder her mother. Told the pastor downstairs in the left parlor. I was there, Father Morgan was there, so was Father Graham, too. We all heard her."

Father Mattingly listened in silence.

"Little Antha said she was afraid to go home. Afraid of Miss Carlotta. She said Miss Carlotta said to Lionel, 'You're no man if you don't put a stop to what's going on,' even gave him the thirty-eight-caliber pistol to shoot Stella. You'd think somebody would have asked a few questions about that, but the pastor didn't. Just picked up the phone and called Miss Carlotta. Few minutes later a big black limousine comes and gets little Antha.''

Father Mattingly stared at the small thin man at the desk. *No questions asked by me either.*

''The pastor said later the child was insane, she'd told the children she could hear people talking through the walls, and she could read their minds. He said she'd calm down, she was just wild over the death of Stella.''

''But she got worse after that?''

''Jumped out of the attic window when she was twenty, that's what she did. No questions asked. She wasn't in her right mind, and besides, she was just a child. Requiem Mass as usual.''

Father Lafferty turned the check over, hit the back of it with the rubber stamp that carried the parish endorsement.

''Are you saying, Father, that I should call on the Mayfairs?''

''No, Father, I'm not. I don't know what I'm saying if you want the truth. But I wish now Miss Carlotta had given that child up, gotten her out of that house. There are too many bad memories under that roof. It's no place for a child now.''

When Father Mattingly heard that Deirdre Mayfair had been sent off to school again—this time in Europe—he decided he had to call. It was spring, well over three years since the haunting confession. He had to make himself go up to that gate, if for no other reason than because he could think of nothing else.

It came as no surprise that Carlotta invited him into the long double parlor and the coffee things were brought in on the silver tray, all quite cordial. He loved that big room. He loved its mirrors facing each other. Miss Millie joined them, then Miss Nancy, though she apologized for her dirty apron, and even old Miss Belle came down by means of an elevator he had not even known was there, hidden as it was behind a great twelve-foot-high door that looked like all the others. Old Miss Belle was deaf, he caught on to that immediately.

Through the veil of small talk, he studied these women, trying to fathom what lay behind their restrained smiles. Nancy was the drudge, Millie the scatterbrain, old Miss Belle almost senile. And Carl? Carl was everything they said she was—the clever one, the business lady, the lawyer. They talked of politics, corruption in the city, of rising prices and changing times. But not on that visit or any other did she speak the names Antha, Stella,

Mary Beth, Lionel. In fact there was no talk anymore of history, and he could not bring himself to broach the subject, not even to ask a simple question about a single object in the room.

Leaving the house, he glanced at the flagstone patio overgrown with weeds. *Head split open like a watermelon.* Going down the street he looked back at the attic windows. All covered with the vines, they were now, shutters askew.

That was his last visit, he told himself. Let Father Lafferty take care of it. Let no one take care of it.

But his sense of failure deepened as the years passed.

When she was ten years old Deirdre Mayfair ran away from home and was found two days later walking along the Bayou St. John in the rain, her clothes soaking wet. Then it was another boarding school somewhere—County Cork, Ireland, and then she was home again. The sisters said she'd had nightmares, walked in her sleep, said strange things.

Then came word that Deirdre was in California. The Mayfairs had cousins out there to look after her. Maybe the change of climate would do some good.

Father Mattingly knew now that he would never get the sound of that child's crying out of his head. Why in God's name had he not tried another tack with her? He prayed she told some wise teacher or doctor the things she'd told him, that somebody somewhere would help her as Father Mattingly had failed to do.

He could never recall hearing when Deirdre came back from California. Only some time in '56, he knew she was in boarding school downtown at St. Rose de Lima's. Then came the gossip she'd been expelled and run away to New York.

Miss Kellerman told Father Lafferty everything on the church steps one afternoon. She'd heard it from her maid who knew the "colored girl" that sometimes helped in that house. Deirdre had found her mother's short stories in a trunk in the attic, "all that nonsense about Greenwich Village." Deirdre had run off to find her father, though nobody knew if the man was alive or dead.

It had ended with her commitment to Bellevue, and Miss Carlotta had flown to New York to bring Deirdre back.

Then one afternoon in the summer of 1959, over a kitchen table, Father Mattingly heard of the "scandal." Deirdre Mayfair was pregnant at eighteen. She had dropped out of classes at a college in Texas. And the father? One of her own professors, would you believe, and a married man and a Protestant too. And he was getting a divorce from his wife of ten years to marry Deirdre!

It seemed the whole parish was talking about it. Miss Carlotta had washed her hands of the whole thing, they said, but Miss Nancy had taken Deirdre to Gus Mayer to buy her a nice pretty dress for the city hall wedding. Deirdre was a beautiful girl now, beautiful as Antha and Stella had been. Beautiful they said as Miss Mary Beth.

Father Mattingly remembered only that frightened, white-faced child. Flowers crushed under foot.

The marriage was never to take place.

When Deirdre was in her fifth month, the father was killed on his way to New Orleans. Car crash on the river road. The tie rod had broken on his old '52 Ford, the car had gone out of control and hit an oak, exploding instantly.

Then wandering through the crowds of the church bazaar on a hot July evening, Father Mattingly was to hear the strangest story of the Mayfairs yet, one that would haunt him in years to come as did the confession.

Lights were strung across the asphalt yard. Parishioners in shirtsleeves and cotton dresses strolled from one wooden booth to another, playing the games of chance. Win a chocolate cake on a nickel bet when the wheel spins. Win a teddy bear. The asphalt was soft in the heat. The beer flowed at the makeshift bar of boards set upon barrels. And it seemed that everywhere Father Mattingly turned he caught some whisper of the goings-on at the Mayfair house.

Gray-headed Red Lonigan, the senior member of the under-taker family, was listening to Dave Collins tell him that they had Deirdre locked up in her room. Father Lafferty sat there staring sullenly over his beer at Dave. Dave said he'd known the May-fairs longer than anybody, even longer than Red.

Father Mattingly got a cold bottle of Jax from the bar and took his place on the bench at the end.

Dave Collins was now in his glory with two priests in the audience.

"I was born in 1901, Father!" he declared, though Father Mattingly did not even look up. "Same year as Stella Mayfair, and I remember when they kicked Stella out of the Ursuline Academy uptown and Miss Mary Beth sent her to school down here."

"Too much gossip about that family," Red said gloomily.

"Stella was a voodoo queen, all right," Dave said. "Everybody knew it. But you can forget about the penny-ante charms and spells. They wasn't for Stella. Stella had a purse of gold coins that was never empty."

Red laughed sadly under his breath. "All she ever had in the end was bad luck."

94

"Well, she crammed in a lot of living before Lionel shot her," Dave said, narrowing his eyes and leaning forward on his right arm, his left hand locked to the beer bottle. "And no sooner was she dead and gone than that purse turned up right beside Antha's bed and no matter where they hid it, it always came back again."

"In a pig's eye," said Red.

"There was coins from all over the world in that purse—Italian coins and French coins and Spanish coins."

"And how would you know?" Red asked.

"Father Lafferty's seen it, ain't you, Father? You've seen them coins. Miss Mary Beth used to throw them in the collection basket every Sunday, you know she done it. And you knew what she always said. 'Spend them fast, Father, get them out of your hands before sundown, because they always come back.' "

"What are you talking about!" Red scoffed.

Father Lafferty said nothing. His small black eyes moved from Dave to Red. Then he glanced at Father Mattingly, who sat opposite him.

"What do you mean, they came back?" Father Mattingly asked.

"Back to her purse is what she meant!" Dave said arching his eyebrows. He took a long pull off his bottle. Nothing but foam left. "She could give them away forever, and they always came back." He laughed hoarsely. There was the sound of phlegm in his voice. "She said the same thing to my mother fifty years ago when she paid her for doing the washing, that's right, the washing—my mother did the washing in a lot of them big houses, and she was never ashamed of it neither, and Miss Mary Beth always paid her in them coins."

"In a pig's eye," Red said.

"And I'll tell you something else too," Dave said, leaning forward on his elbow, his eyes narrow as he peered at Red Lonigan. "The house, the jewels, the purse, it's all connected. Same with the name Mayfair and the way they always keep it, no matter who they marry. Always Mayfair in the end. And you want to know the reason? They're witches, those women! Every one."

Red shook his head. He pushed his full beer bottle towards Dave and watched as Dave wrapped his fingers around it.

"It's the God's truth, I'm telling you. It come down to them through the generations, the power of witchcraft, and back in them days there was plenty talk of it. Miss Mary Beth, she was more powerful than Stella." He took a big swallow of Red's

95

beer. "And smart enough to keep her mouth shut which Stella was not."

"Then how did you hear about it?" Red asked.

Dave took out his little white sack of Bull Durham tobacco and pressed it flat between fingers and thumb.

"You wouldn't have a ready-made, would you, Father?" he asked Father Mattingly.

Red sneered. Father Mattingly gave Dave his pack of Pall Malls.

"Thank you, Father. And now to your question, Red, which I wasn't avoiding. I know because my mother told me the things that Miss Mary Beth told her, back in 1921 when Miss Carlotta had graduated from Loyola and everybody was singing her praises, such a smart woman, being a lawyer and all that. 'She's not the chosen one,' Miss Mary Beth said to my mother, 'It's Stella. Stella's got the gift and she'll get everything when I die.' 'And what's the gift, Miss Mary Beth?' my mother asked her. 'Why, Stella's seen *the man*,' Miss Mary Beth said to my mother. 'And the one who can see the man when she's all alone inherits all.' "

Father Mattingly felt a chill run down his back. It had now been eleven years since he had heard that child's unfinished confession, but he had never forgotten a word of it. *They call him the man* . . .

But Father Lafferty was glowering at Dave.

"Seen the man?" Father Lafferty asked coldly. "Now what in heaven's name could such gibberish mean?"

"Well now, Father I should think a good Irishman like yourself would know the answer to that one. Ain't it a fact that witches call the devil the man? Ain't it fact they call him that when he comes in the middle of the night to tempt them to unspeakable evil!" He gave another of his deep cracking unhealthy laughs, and pulled a filthy snotrag from his pocket to wipe his nose. "Witches, and you know it, Father. That's what they were and that's what they are. It's a legacy of witchcraft. And old Mr. Julien Mayfair, you remember him? I remember him. He knew all about it, that's what my mother told me. You know it's the truth, Father."

"It's a legacy all right," Father Lafferty said angrily. He rose to his feet. "It's a legacy of ignorance and jealousy and mental sickness! Ever hear of those things, Dave Collins? Ever heard of hatred between sisters, and envy, and ruthless ambition!" He turned and walked off through the milling crowd without waiting for the answer.

Father Mattingly felt stunned by Father Lafferty's anger. He wished that Father Lafferty had merely laughed, as Dave Collins was doing.

Dave Collins swallowed the last of Red's beer. "Couldn't spare two bits, now, could you, Red?" he asked, his eyes darting from him to Father Mattingly.

Red sat listless staring at the empty beer bottle. Like a man in a dream he fished a crumpled dollar out of his pants pocket.

On the edge of sleep that night Father Mattingly remembered the books he'd read in the seminary. The tall man, the dark man, the comely man, the incubus who comes by night . . . the giant man who leads the Sabbat! He remembered dim pictures in a book, finely drawn, gruesome. Witches, he said the word as he passed into sleep. *She says he's the devil, Father. That it's a sin even to look at him.*

He awoke some time before dawn, hearing Father Lafferty's angry voice. *Envy, mental sickness.* Was that the truth to read between the lines? It seemed a crucial piece had been fitted into the puzzle. He could almost see the full picture. A house ruled by an iron hand, a house in which beautiful and high-spirited women had met tragedy. And yet something bothered him still . . . *They all see him, Father.* Flowers scattered under foot, big long white gladiolus and delicate fronds of fern. He saw his shoe crushing them.

Deirdre Mayfair gave up her child. It was born at the new Mercy Hospital on the seventh of November, and that very same day, she kissed it and placed it in Father Lafferty's hands and it was he who baptized it and placed it in the care of the cousins from California who were to adopt it.

But it was Deirdre who laid down the law that the child was to have the name Mayfair. Her daughter was never to be given any other last name, or Deirdre wouldn't sign the papers. Her old uncle Cortland Mayfair had stood behind her on that one, and not even Father Lafferty could make her change her mind. She demanded to see it in ink on the baptismal certificate. And poor old Cortland Mayfair—a fine gentleman—was dead by that time, having taken that awful fall down the stairs.

Father Mattingly didn't remember when he'd first heard the word "incurable." She'd gone mad even before she left the hospital. They said she kept talking out loud to nobody at all, saying, "You did it, you killed him." The nurses were afraid to go into her room. She wandered into the chapel in her hospital gown, laughing and talking out loud in the middle of Mass, accusing the empty air of killing her lover, separating her from her child, leaving her alone among "enemies." When the nuns tried to restrain her, she'd gone wild. The orderlies had come and taken her away as she kicked and screamed.

By the time Father Lafferty died in the spring, they had locked her up far away. Nobody even knew where. Rita Lonigan asked her father-in-law, Red, because she wanted so badly to write. But Miss Carl said it would not be good. No letters for Deirdre.

Only prayers for Deirdre. And the years slipped by.

Father Mattingly left the parish. He worked in the foreign missions. He worked in New York. He went so far away that New Orleans was no longer in his thought, except now and then the sudden remembrance and shame: Deirdre Mayfair—the one he had not helped, his lost Deirdre.

Then one afternoon in 1976, when Father Mattingly had come down for a brief stay at the old rectory, he had passed the house and seen a thin, pale young woman sitting in a rocker on the side porch, behind a veil of rusted screen. She seemed no more than a wraith in a white nightgown, but he'd known at once it was Deirdre. He'd recognized those black curls hanging around her shoulders. And as he opened the rusted gate and came up the flagstone walk, he saw that even the expression on the face was the same—yes, it was Deirdre whom he'd brought home to this house almost thirty years ago.

Expressionless she was, behind the screen, which sagged on its light wooden framing. No answer when he whispered: "Deirdre."

Around her neck on a chain was an emerald—a beautiful stone, and on her finger a ruby ring. Were these the jewels he'd heard tell of? How incongruous they looked on this silent woman in her limp white nightgown. She gave no sign that she either heard or saw him.

His visit with Miss Millie and Miss Nancy had been brief, uncomfortable. Carl was downtown at work, of course. And yes, that was Deirdre on the side porch and she was home to stay, but there was no need to whisper.

"The mind's gone," Nancy said with a bitter smile. "The electric shock wiped out her memory first. Then everything. She couldn't get up to save herself if the place was burning down. Every now and then she wrings her hands, tries to speak, but she can't—"

"Don't!" Millie had whispered, with a little shake of the head and twist of her mouth as though it wasn't in good taste to discuss this. She was old now, Miss Millie, old and beautifully gray, dainty as Miss Belle had been, Miss Belle who was now long gone. "Have some more coffee, Father?"

But it was a pretty woman sitting in the chair on the porch.

The shock treatments had not grayed her hair. And her eyes were still a deep blue, though they were utterly empty. Like a statue in church she was. *Father, help me.* The emerald caught the light, exploded like a tiny star.

Father Mattingly did not come south very often after that, and in the following years when he rang the bell, he was not welcome. Miss Nancy's excuses became more abrupt. Sometimes nobody even answered. If Carl was there, the visit was rushed, artificial. No more coffee in the garden room, just a few quick words in that vast dusty parlor. Didn't they ever turn on the lights anymore? The chandeliers were filthy.

Of course the women were getting quite old. Millie died in 1979. The funeral had been enormous, with cousins coming from all over the country.

Then last year Nancy had gone. Father Mattingly had gotten a letter from Red Lonigan. The priest had been in Baton Rouge at the time and he had driven down just for the funeral.

Miss Carl, in her late eighties, was bone thin, hawk-nosed, with white hair and thick glasses that magnified her eyes unpleasantly. Her ankles were swollen over the tops of her black string shoes. She had to sit down on a gravestone during the final words at the cemetery.

The house itself was going down pitifully. Father Mattingly had seen that for himself when he drove past.

Deirdre too had changed, inevitably. He could see that her fragile hothouse beauty had at last been lost. And in spite of the nurses who walked her back and forth, she had grown stooped, and her hands bent down and out at the wrists, like those of an arthritic patient. They said that her head had now fallen permanently to one side, and her mouth was always open.

It was a sad sight to behold even from a distance. And the jewels only made it more sinister. Diamond earrings on a senseless invalid. An emerald big as a thumbnail! And Father Mattingly, who believed above all in the sanctity of human life, thought Deirdre's death would have been a blessing.

The afternoon following Nancy's funeral, as he had paid a silent visit to the old place, he had met an Englishman stopped at the far end of the fence—a very personable man, who introduced himself to the priest as Aaron Lightner.

"Do you know anything about that poor woman?" Lightner had asked quite frankly. "For over ten years I've seen her on that porch. You know, I worry about her."

"I worry myself," Father Mattingly had confessed. "But they say there's nothing anyone can do for her."

"Such a strange family," said the Englishman sympathetically. "It's so very hot. I wonder does she feel the heat? You'd think they'd fix the overhead fan. Do you see? It seems to be broken."

Father Mattingly had taken an immediate liking to the Englishman. Such a forceful, yet polite man. And he was dressed so well in a fine three-piece linen suit. Even carried a walking stick. Made Father Mattingly think of the gentlemen who used to stroll in the evening on St. Charles Avenue. You used to see them on the front porches, wearing their straw hats, watching the traffic pass. Ah, another era.

Father Mattingly found himself chatting easily with the Englishman in a hushed voice under the low-hanging oaks, about all the "known" things with which the man seemed quite familiar—the shock treatments, the sanitariums, the baby daughter long ago adopted out in California. But Father Mattingly would not have dreamed of mentioning old Dave Collins's gossip of Stella or "the man." To repeat such nonsense would be flat-out wrong. And besides, it came too near to those painful secrets Deirdre had confided in him.

He and Lightner had somehow ended up at Commander's Palace for a late lunch at the Englishman's invitation. What a treat for the priest. How long had it been since he dined in a fine New Orleans restaurant like that with tablecloths and linen napkins. And the Englishman had ordered an excellent wine.

The man admitted candidly that he was interested in the history of families like the Mayfairs.

"You know they had a plantation in Haiti when it was still called Saint-Domingue. Maye Faire was the name of the place, I believe. They made a fortune in coffee and sugar in the days before the slave uprising."

"So you know of them that far back," said the priest, amazed.

"Oh, indeed, I do," said Lightner. "It's in the history books, you see. Powerful woman ran that place, Marie Claudette Mayfair Landry, following in the footsteps of her mother, Angélique Mayfair. But they had been there for four generations. It was Charlotte who had come from France in, what was it, the year 1689. Yes, Charlotte. And she gave birth to twins—Peter and Jeanne Louise, and they both lived to be eighty-one."

"You don't say. I've never heard tell of them that far back."

"I believe it's a simple matter of record." The Englishman gave a little shrug. "Even the black rebels didn't dare torch the plantation. Marie Claudette managed to emigrate with a king's ransom in possessions as well as her entire family. Then it was La Victoire at Riverbend below New Orleans. I think they called it simply Riverbend."

"Miss Mary Beth was born there."

"Yes! That's correct. In, let me see, I think it was 1871. It took the river to finally swallow that old house. Such a beauty it was, with columns all around. There were photographs of it in the very old guidebooks to Louisiana."

"I'd like to see those," the priest said.

"They'd built the house on First Street before the Civil War, you know," Lightner went on. "It was actually Katherine Mayfair who built it and later her brothers Julien and Remy Mayfair lived there. And then Mary Beth made it her home. She didn't like the country, Mary Beth. I believe it was Katherine who married the Irish architect, the one who died so young of yellow fever. You know, he built the banks downtown. Yes, the name was Monahan. And after he died, Katherine didn't want to stay at First Street anymore because he had built it and she was so sick at heart."

"Seems I heard a long time ago that Monahan designed that house," said the priest. But he really didn't want to interrupt. "I used to hear about Miss Mary Beth . . ."

"Yes, it was Mary Beth Mayfair who married Judge McIntyre, though he was only a young lawyer then of course, and their daughter Carlotta Mayfair is the head of the house now, it seems . . ."

Father Mattingly was enthralled. It wasn't merely his old and painful curiosity about the Mayfairs, it was the engaging manner of Lightner himself, and the pleasing sound of his British accent. Just history, all this, not gossip, quite innocent. It had been a long time since Father Mattingly had spoken to such a cultivated man. No, this was not gossip when the Englishman told it.

And against his better judgment, the priest found himself telling in a tentative voice the story of the little girl in the school yard and the mysterious flowers. Now, that was not what he'd heard in the confessional, he reminded himself. Yet it was frightening that it should spill out this way, after a half-dozen sips of wine. Father Mattingly was ashamed of himself. Suddenly he couldn't get the confession out of his mind. He lost the thread. He was thinking of Dave Collins and all those strange things he'd said and the way Father Lafferty had gotten so angry that July night at the bazaar, Father Lafferty who'd presided over the adoption of Deirdre's baby.

Had Father Lafferty taken action on account of all Dave Collins's crazy talk? He himself had never been able to do anything.

The Englishman was quite patient with the priest's silent reverie. In fact, the strangest thing had happened. It seemed to Father Mattingly that the man was listening to his thoughts! But that was quite impossible, and if a man could overhear the memory of a confession in that way, just what was a priest supposed to do about it?

How long that afternoon seemed. How pleasant, easeful. Father Mattingly had finally repeated Dave Collins's old tales, and he had even talked of the pictures in the books of "the dark man" and of witches dancing.

And the Englishman had seemed so interested, only moving now and then to pour the wine, or to offer the priest a cigarette, never interrupting.

"Now, what do you make of all that," the priest whispered at last. Had the man said anything back? "You know, old Dave Collins is dead, but Sister Bridget Marie is going to live forever. She's nearing a hundred."

The Englishman smiled. "You mean the sister in the school yard that long-ago day."

Father Mattingly was now drunk on the wine he'd had, that was the plain truth of it. And he kept seeing the yard and the children and the flowers strewn all over the pavement.

"She's out at Mercy Hospital now," the priest said. "I saw her last time I was down. I suppose I'll see her this time. And what nonsense she talks now that she doesn't know who she's talking to. Old Dave Collins died in a bar on Magazine Street. Fitting place. All his friends chipped in for the biggest funeral."

The priest had drifted off again, thinking of Deirdre and the confessional. And the Englishman had touched the back of his hand and whispered: "You mustn't worry about it."

The priest had been startled. Then he'd almost laughed at the idea that someone could read his mind. And that's what Sister Bridget Marie had said about Antha, wasn't it? That she could hear people talking through the walls and read their minds? Had he told the Englishman that part?

"Yes, you did. I want to thank you . . ."

He and the Englishman had said good-bye at six o'clock outside the gates of the Lafayette Cemetery. It had been the golden time of evening when the sun is gone and everything gives back the light it has absorbed all day long. But how forlorn it all was, the old whitewashed walls, and the giant magnolia trees ripping at the pavement.

"You know, they're all buried in there, the Mayfairs," Father Mattingly had said, glancing at the iron gates. "Big aboveground tomb down the center walk to the right, has a little wrought-iron fence around it. Miss Carl keeps it in good repair. You can read all those names you just told me."

The priest would have shown the Englishman himself but it

was time to get back to the rectory, time to go back to Baton Rouge and then up to St. Louis.

Lightner gave him an address in London.

"If you ever hear anything more about that family—anything you feel comfortable passing on—well, would you contact me?"

Of course Father Mattingly had never done that. He'd misplaced the name and address months ago. But he remembered that Englishman kindly, though sometimes he wondered who the man really was, and what he had actually wanted. If all the priests of the world had such a soothing manner as that, what a splendid thing it would be. It was as if that man understood everything.

As he drew nearer the old corner now, Father Mattingly thought again of what the young priest had written: that that Deirdre Mayfair was shriveling up, that she could hardly walk anymore.

Then how could she have gone wild on August 13th, he'd like to know, for the love of heaven? How could she have broken the windows out and scared off men from an asylum?

And Jerry Lonigan said his driver saw things thrown out—books, a clock, all manner of things, just hurling through the air. And the noise she'd made, like an animal howling.

The priest found it hard to believe.

But there it was, the evidence.

As he slowly approached the gate on this warm August afternoon, he saw the white-uniformed window man on the front porch, atop his wooden ladder. Knife in hand, he applied the putty along the new panes. And each one of those tall windows had shining new glass, complete with the tiny brand-name stickers.

Yards away, on the south side of the house, behind her veil of rusted copper screen sat Deirdre, hands twisted out at the wrists, head bent and to the side against the back of the rocker. The emerald pendant on its chain was a tiny spark of green light for an instant.

Ah, what had it been like *for her* to break those windows? To feel the strength coursing through her limbs, to feel herself in possession of such uncommon power? Even to make a sound, why, it must have been magnificent.

But that was a strange thought for him, wasn't it? Yet he felt himself swept up in some vague sadness, some grand melancholy. Ah, Deirdre, poor little Deirdre.

The truth was, he felt sad and bitter as he always did when he saw her. And he knew he would not go up the flagstone path to the front steps. He would not ring the bell only to be told again that Miss Carl wasn't home, or that she could not receive him just now.

This trip had only been Father Mattingly's personal penance. Over forty years ago, he had done the wrong thing on a fateful Saturday afternoon, and a girl's sanity had hung in the balance. And no visit now would ever make the slightest difference.

He stood at the fence for a long moment, listening to the scrape of the window man's knife, curiously clear in the soft tropical quiet around him. He felt the heat penetrate his shoes, his clothes. He let the soft mellow colors of this moist and shady world work on him.

It was a rare place, this. Better for her surely than some sterile hospital room, or vista of close-cropped lawn with no more variation than a synthetic carpet. And what made him think that he could have ever done for her what so many doctors had failed to do? Maybe she had never had a chance. Only God knows.

Suddenly he glimpsed a visitor behind the rusted screens, sitting beside the poor mad woman. Nice young man it seemed—tall, dark-haired, well dressed in spite of the wilting temperature. Maybe one of those cousins from away, from New York City or California.

The young fella must have just come out on the porch from the parlor, because a moment ago he had not been there.

So solicitous, he seemed. It was positively loving the way he inclined towards Deirdre. Just as if he was kissing her cheek. Yes, that was what he was doing. Even in the dense shade, the priest could see it, and it touched him deeply. It made the sadness well in him painfully.

But the window man was finishing now. He was gathering up his ladder. He came down the front steps and went around the flagstone walk and past the screen porch, using his ladder as he went, to drive back the banana trees and the swollen oleander.

The priest was finished too. He had done his penance. He could go home now, back to the hot barren pavements of Constance Street, and the cool confines of the rectory. Slowly he turned and moved towards the corner.

He glanced back only once. The screen porch was empty now save for Deirdre. But surely that nice young man would come back out soon. It had gone right to the priest's heart to see that tender kiss, to know that someone even now still loved that lost soul that he himself had failed to save so long ago.

Four

THERE WAS SOMETHING she had to do tonight. Someone she was supposed to call. And it was important, too. But after fifteen hours on duty—and twelve of them spent in the Operating Room—she could not now remember.

She wasn't Rowan Mayfair yet, with all Rowan's personal griefs and concerns. She was just Dr. Mayfair, empty as a clear pane of glass, sitting here silent in the doctors' coffee room, hands shoved in the pockets of her dirty white coat, her feet on the chair opposite, a Parliament cigarette on her lip, listening to them talk as neurosurgeons always talk, regurgitating in language every exciting moment of the day.

Soft bursts of laughter, voices overlapping on voices, smell of alcohol, rustle of starched clothes, sweet aroma of the cigarettes. Never mind the personal disgrace that almost all of them smoked. It was nice to remain here, comfortable in the glare of the lights on the dirty Formica table, and the dirty linoleum tile, and the dirty beige walls. Nice to be putting off the thinking time, the time when memory would come back to fill her up again and render her heavy and opaque.

In truth, it had been a damn near perfect day, which was why her feet hurt so much. She had been through three emergency surgeries, one following another, from the gunshot wound at six A.M. to the car crash victim brought in four hours ago. And if every day was like this day, her life was going to be just fine. It was going to be perfectly wonderful, actually.

She was aware of that just now, in a relaxed sort of way. After ten years of medical school and internship and residency she was what she had always wanted to be—a doctor, a neurosurgeon, and most specifically the new board-certified Staff Attending in Neurosurgery in a giant university hospital where the Neurological Trauma Center could keep her operating on accident victims almost full-time.

She had to admit she was glorying in it, glorying in her first week as something other than an overworked and critically exhausted chief resident who still had to operate fifty percent of the time under someone else's eye.

Even the inevitable talk today had not been so terrible—the endless running diatribe in the Operating Room, the dictating of the notes after, and finally the lengthy informal coffee room review. She liked these doctors around her, the shiny-faced interns opposite, Dr. Peters and Dr. Blake, who had just begun their rotation and were looking at her as if she were a witch instead of a doctor. And Dr. Simmons, the chief resident, who told her now and then in a heated whisper that she was the finest doctor he'd ever seen in surgery and that the nurses said the same thing, and Dr. Larkin, the beloved chief of neurosurgery, known to his protégées as Lark, who had forced her over and over again today to elaborate—"Explain, Rowan, explain in detail. You have to tell these boys what you're doing. Gentlemen, behold, this is the only neurosurgeon in western civilization who does not like to talk about her work."

Understatement. She hated talking. She was innately suspicious of language because she could "hear" with remarkable accuracy what lay behind it, and also she just didn't know how to talk very well.

Now they were talking about Dr. Larkin's virtuoso performance this afternoon with the meningioma, thank heaven, and she could drift in this delicious exhaustion, savoring the taste of the cigarette, and the awful coffee, and the lovely glare of the light on the beautifully blank walls.

Trouble was, she'd told herself this morning to remember about this personal thing, this call that had to be made, this something that really mattered to her. So what did that mean? It would come back as soon as she stepped out of the building.

And she could do that any time she liked. After all, she was the Attending, and she didn't have to be here longer than fifteen hours, and she never had to sleep in the on-call room again, and nobody expected her to go down to Emergency just to see what was going on, though left to her own devices, perhaps, that is what she would have liked to do.

Two years ago, less than that perhaps, she would have been long gone by this time, headed over the Golden Gate at the speed limit, eager to be Rowan Mayfair again, in the wheelhouse of the *Sweet Christine*, singlehanding her out of Richardson Bay and into the open sea. Only when she had set the autopilot for a great circular course, well out of the way of the channels, would the exhaustion have conquered her. She would have gone down below deck into the cabin where the wood shone as brilliantly as the polished brass, and falling into the double bunk, she would have lost herself in a thin sleep through which all the little sounds of the boat penetrated sweetly.

But that was before the process of working miracles on the operating table had become positively addictive. Research had still now and then beckoned. And Ellie and Graham, her adoptive parents, were still living, and the glass-walled house on the Tiburon shore was not a mausoleum filled with dead people's books, dead people's clothes.

She had to walk through that mausoleum to get to the *Sweet Christine*. She had to see the inevitable mail which still came for Ellie and Graham. And maybe even hear a phone machine message or two from an out-of-town friend who didn't know that Ellie had died of cancer last year, and that Graham had died of "a stroke," to put it simply, two months before Ellie's death. She watered the ferns still in memory of Ellie, who had played music for them. She drove Graham's Jaguar sedan because to sell it would be a nuisance. She had never cleaned out his desk.

Stroke. A dark ugly feeling passed over her. Think not of Graham dying on the kitchen floor but of the day's victories. You saved three lives during the past fifteen hours, when other doctors might have let them die. To other lives in other hands you gave your skillful assistance. And now, safe in the womb of the Intensive Care Unit, three of those patients are sleeping, and they have eyes that can see, and mouths that can shape words, and when you hold their hands, they grip as you tell them to grip.

Yes, she couldn't have asked for more. Would that she could always leave the tissue transplants and the tumors to others. She thrived on crisis. She needed it. She'd go home in a little while only because it was healthy to do so, healthy to rest her eyes and her feet and her brain, of course, and to be someplace besides here for the weekend; to be on the *Sweet Christine*, at sea.

For now, rest in this great ship called the hospital, for that is exactly what it felt like—a submarine, traveling without sound through time. The lights never went out. The temperature never varied. The engines never shut down. And we, the crew, are bonded together, in spite of anger, or resentment, or competition. We are bonded and there is a form of love whether we acknowledge it or not.

"You're looking for a miracle!" the supervisor in Emergency had said to her at six this evening, contemptuously, glaze-eyed with exhaustion. "Wheel this woman over against the wall, and save your juices for somebody you can do something for!"

"I want nothing but miracles," Rowan had answered. "We're

107

going to get the glass and dirt out of her brain, and then we'll take it from there.''

No way to tell him that when she had placed her hands on the woman's shoulders, she had ''listened'' with her diagnostic sense to a thousand little signals; and they had told her, infallibly, that the woman could live. She knew what she'd see when the bone fragments had been carefully lifted out of the fracture and frozen for later replacement, when the torn dura mater had been further slit and the bruised tissue beneath it magnified by the powerful surgical scope. Plenty of living brain, unharmed, functioning, once she'd sucked the blood away from it, and cauterized the tiny ruptured vessels so that the bleeding would stop.

It was the same infallible sense she'd had that day out on the ocean when she'd hoisted the drowned man, Michael Curry, onto the deck with the winch, and touched his cold gray flesh. Yes, there is life in there. Bring him back.

The drowned man. Michael Curry. That was it, of course, that was what she had made a note to remember. Call Curry's doctor. Curry's doctor had left a message for her both at the hospital and on her machine at home.

It had been over three months since that bitter cold evening in May, with the fog blanketing the distant city so that not a single light was visible, and the drowned man on the deck of the *Sweet Christine* had looked as dead as any corpse she'd ever seen.

She stubbed out the cigarette. ''Good night, Doctors,'' she said rising. ''Monday, eight o'clock,'' she said to the interns. ''No, don't stand up.''

Dr. Larkin caught her sleeve between two fingers. When she tried to pull loose, he held tight.

''Don't take that boat out alone, Rowan.''

''Come on, Chief.'' She tried to free herself. Didn't work. ''I've been taking that boat out alone since I was sixteen.''

''Bad news, Rowan, bad news,'' he said. ''Suppose you hit your head out there, fall overboard.''

She gave a soft polite laugh, though she was in fact irritated by this talk, and then she was out the door, heading past the elevators—too slow—and towards the concrete stairs.

Maybe she should take one last look at the three patients in Intensive Care before she made her exit; and suddenly the thought of leaving at all oppressed her. The thought of not coming back until Monday was even worse.

Shoving her hands in her pockets, she hurried up the two flights of stairs to the fourth floor.

The gleaming upper corridors were so quiet, so removed from

the mayhem inevitably going on in Emergency. A lone woman slept on the couch in the darkly carpeted waiting room. The old nurse at the ward station only waved as Rowan passed by. There had been times in her harried intern days when, on call, she had strolled these corridors in the middle of the night rather than try to sleep. Back and forth she'd walked, covering the length of one floor after another, in the belly of the giant submarine, lulled by the faint whisper of countless machines.

Too bad the chief knew about the *Sweet Christine,* she thought now, too bad that desperate and frightened, she'd brought him home with her the afternoon of her adoptive mother's funeral, and taken him out to sit on the deck, drinking wine beneath a blue Tiburon sky. Too bad that in those hollow and metallic moments, she had confessed to Lark that she didn't want to be in the house anymore, that she lived on the boat, and sometimes lived for it, taking it out alone after every shift, no matter how long she'd been on, no matter how tired she was.

Telling people—did it ever make things better? Lark had piled cliché upon cliché as he tried to comfort her. And from then on everybody at the hospital knew about the *Sweet Christine.* And she wasn't just Rowan the silent one, but Rowan the adopted one, the one whose family had died out in less than half a year, who went to sea in the big boat all alone. She had also become Rowan who would not accept Lark's invitations to dinner, when any other single female doctor on the staff might have done so in an instant.

If only they knew the rest of it, she thought, how very mysterious she really was, even unto herself. And what would they have said about the men she liked, the stalwart officers of the law, and the heroes of the fire brigade hook and ladder trucks whom she hunted in noisy wholesome neighborhood bars, picking her partners as much for their roughened hands and their roughened voices as for their heavy chests and powerful arms. Yes, what about that, what about all those couplings in the lower cabin of the *Sweet Christine* with the police-issue .38 revolver in its black leather holster slung over the hook on the wall.

And the conversations after—no, call them monologues—in which these men with the desperate need so similar to that of the neurosurgeon's relived their moments of danger and achievement, of moxie and dexterity. Scent of courage on their pressed uniform shirts. Sing a song of life and death.

Why that kind of man? Graham had once demanded. "You look for them to be dumb, uneducated, thick-necked? What if one of them puts his meaty fist into your face?"

"But that's just it," she'd said coldly, not even bothering to look at him. "They don't do that. They save lives, and that's why I like them. I like heroes."

"That sounds like a fool of a fourteen-year-old girl talking," Graham had replied acidly.

"You've got it wrong," Rowan had answered. "When I was fourteen I thought lawyers like you were the heroes."

Bitter flash of his eyes as he'd turned away from her. Bitter flash of Graham now, over a year after Graham's death. Taste of Graham, smell of Graham, Graham in her bed finally, because Graham would have left before Ellie's death if she hadn't done it.

"Don't tell me you haven't always wanted it," he'd said to her in the deep feather mattress in the bunk of the *Sweet Christine*. "Damn your fire fighters; damn your cops."

Stop arguing with him. Stop thinking about him. Ellie never knew you went to bed with him, or why you thought you had to. So much that Ellie never knew. And you are not in Ellie's house. You're not even on the boat Graham gave you. You're still safe here in the antiseptic quiet of your world, and Graham is dead and buried in the little graveyard in northern California. And never mind how he died, because nobody knows the story on that, either. Don't let him be there in spirit, as they say, when you put the key into the ignition of his car, which you ought to have sold long ago, or when you walk into the damp chilly rooms of his house.

Yet she still talked to him, still carried on the endless case for the defense. His death had prevented forever any real resolution. And so a ghost of him had been created by her hatred and her rage. It was fading, yet it still stalked her, even here in the safe hallways of her own domain.

I'll take the other ones any day, she had wanted so to say to him, I'll take them with their ego and their rambunctiousness, and their ignorance and their rollicking sense of humor; I'll take their roughness, their heated and simple love of women and fear of women, I'll even take their talk, yes, their endless talk, and thank God that, unlike the neurosurgeons, they don't want me to say anything back to them, they don't even want to know who I am or what I am, might as well say rocket scientist, master spy, magician, as say neurosurgeon. "You don't mean you operate on people's brains!"

What did it matter, all this?

The fact is, Rowan understood "the man question" a little better now than in those days when Graham argued with her. She understood the connection between herself and her uniformed heroes—that going into the Operating Room, and slipping on those sterile gloves, and lifting the microcoagulator and the microscalpel, was like going into a burning building, was like going into a family fight with a gun to save the wife and the child.

How many times had she heard neurosurgeons compared to fire fighters? And then the slick criticism, but it's different because *your* life is not at stake. The hell it isn't. Because if you failed in there, if you failed horribly enough and often enough, you'd be destroyed as surely as if the burning roof had come down on you. You survived by being brilliant and courageous and perfect, because there was simply no other way to survive, and every moment in the Operating Room was a mortal test.

Yes, the same courage, the same love of stress and love of danger for a good reason that she saw in the crude men she loved to kiss and stroke and suckle; the men she liked to have on top of her; the men who didn't need for her to talk.

But what was the use of understanding, when it had been months—almost half a year—since she'd invited anyone into her bed. What did the *Sweet Christine* think about it? she sometimes wondered. Was it whispering to her in the dark: "Rowan, where are our men?"

Chase, the yellow-haired olive-skinned palomino cop from Marin, still left messages for her on the answering machine. But she had no time to call him. And he was such a sweet guy, and he did read books, too, and they had talked once, a real conversation, in fact, when she'd made some offhand remark about the Emergency Room, and the woman who'd been shot by her husband. He'd latched onto that at once with his string of shootings and stabbings and pretty soon they were going at them all from two sides. Maybe that was why she hadn't called him back? A possibility.

But on the face of it, the neurosurgeon had for the moment subsumed the woman quite completely, so much so that she wasn't sure why she was even thinking about those men tonight. Unless it was because she wasn't all that tired, or because the last beautiful male she'd lusted after had been Michael Curry, the gorgeous drowned man, gorgeous even when he lay there, wet and pale, black hair plastered to his head, on the deck of her boat.

Yes. He was, in the old school-girl parlance, to die for, a hunk—just an out-and-out adorable guy and her kind of adorable guy completely. His had not been one of those California gymnasium bodies with overdeveloped muscles and phony tans, topped off with dyed hair, but a powerful proletarian specimen, rendered all the more irresistible by the blue eyes and the freckles across his cheeks which made her, in retrospect, want to kiss them.

What an irony to fish from the sea, in a state of tragic helplessness, such a perfect example of the only kind of man she had ever desired.

She stopped. She had reached the doors of the Intensive Care Unit. Entering quietly, she stood still for a moment, surveying this strange, icy-still world of fish tank rooms with emaciated sleepers on display beneath oxygen tent plastic, their fragile limbs and torsos hooked to beeping monitors, amid endless cables and dials.

A switch was suddenly thrown in Rowan's head. Nothing existed outside this ward any more than anything existed outside of an Operating Room.

She approached the desk, her hand out to very lightly touch the shoulder of the nurse who sat hunched over a mass of papers beneath the low fluorescent light.

"Good evening, Laurel," Rowan whispered.

The woman was startled. Then recognizing Rowan, she brightened. "Dr. Mayfair, you're still here."

"Just another look around."

Rowan's manner with nurses was far gentler than ever it was with doctors. She had from the very beginning of her internship courted nurses, going out of her way to alleviate their proverbial resentment of women doctors, and to elicit from them as much enthusiasm as she could. It was a science with her, calculated and refined to the point of ruthlessness, yet as profoundly sincere as any incision made into the tissues of a patient's brain.

As she entered the first room now, pausing beside the high gleaming metal bed—a monstrous rack on wheels, it seemed—she heard the nurse coming behind her, waiting on her, so to speak. The nurse moved to lift the chart from its place at the foot of the bed. Rowan shook her head, no.

Blanched, seemingly lifeless, lay the day's last car crash victim, head enormous in a turban of white bandages, a thin colorless tube running into her nose. The machines evinced the only vitality with their tiny monotonous beeps and jagged neon lines. The glucose flowed through the tiny needle fixed into the pinioned wrist.

Like a corpse coming back to life on an embalming table, the woman beneath the layers of bleached bed linen slowly opened her eyes. "Dr. Mayfair," she whispered.

A lovely ripple of relief passed through Rowan. Again she and the nurse exchanged glances. Rowan smiled. "I'm here, Mrs.

Trent," she said softly. "You're doing well." Gently, she folded her fingers around the woman's right hand. *Yes, very well.*

The woman's eyes closed so slowly they were like flowers closing. No change in the faint song of the machines that surrounded them. Rowan retreated as soundlessly as she had come.

Through the windows of the second room, she gazed at another seemingly unconscious figure, that of an olive-skinned boy, a weed of a kid, actually, who had gone blind suddenly, staggering off the platform into the path of a commuter train.

For four hours she had worked on this one, suturing with the tiny needle the hemorrhaging vessel that had caused his blindness, then repairing the damaged skull. In Recovery he had joked with the circle of doctors around him.

Now, her eyes narrow, her body still, Rowan studied his subtle movements in sleep, the way that his right knee shifted under the covers, the way his hand curled, palm up, as he moved his head to the side. His tongue darted over his dry lips, and he whispered to himself like a man talking to someone in his dreams.

"Doing just fine, Doctor," the nurse whispered beside her.

Rowan nodded. But she knew that within weeks, he would suffer seizures. They would use Dilantin to control it, but he would be an epileptic for the rest of his life. Better than death and blindness surely. She would wait and watch before predicting or explaining. After all, there was always the chance she was wrong.

"And Mrs. Kelly?" she asked. She turned to look into the nurse's eyes, forcing herself to see the woman clearly and completely. This was an efficient and compassionate nurse, a woman she rather liked.

"Mrs. Kelly thinks it's funny that she still has two bullets in her head. 'I feel like a loaded gun,' she told me. She won't let her daughter leave. She wants to know what happened to that 'street punk' that shot her. She wants another pillow. She wants a television and a phone."

Rowan gave the obligatory soft appreciative laugh. Barely a sound in the humming silence. "Well, tomorrow, perhaps," she said.

From where she stood, she could see the spirited Mrs. Kelly through the last pair of windows at the end of the ward. Unable to lift her head from the pillow, Mrs. Kelly gestured easily with her right hand as she talked to her grown daughter, a thin and obviously exhausted woman with drooping eyelids who nevertheless nodded repeatedly as she hung upon her mother's every word.

"She's good for her mother," Rowan whispered. "Let her stay as long as she likes."

The nurse nodded.

"I'm off till Monday, Laurel," said Rowan. "I don't know if I like this new schedule."

The nurse gave a soft laugh. "You deserve the rest, Dr. Mayfair."

"Do I?" Rowan murmured. "Dr. Simmons will call me if there's a problem. You can always ask him to call me, Laurel. You understand?"

Rowan went out the double doors, letting them swish shut softly behind her. Yes, a good day it had been.

And there really was no excuse for staying here any longer, except to make a few notes in the private diary she kept in her office and to check her personal machine for calls. Maybe she would rest for a while on the leather couch. It was so much more luxurious, the office of the official Attending, than the cramped and shabby on-call rooms in which she'd dozed for years.

But she ought to go home, she knew it. Ought to let the shades of Graham and Ellie come and go as they pleased.

And what about Michael Curry? Why, she had forgotten again about Michael Curry, and now it was almost ten o'clock. She had to call Dr. Morris as soon as she could.

Now don't let your heart skip beats over Curry, she thought, as she took her time padding softly down the linoleumed hallway, choosing the cement stairway again rather than the elevator, and plotting a jagged route through the giant slumbering hospital that would take her only eventually to her office door.

But she was eager to hear what Morris had to say, eager for news of the only man in her life at this moment, a man she didn't know and had not seen since that violent interlude of desperate effort and crazed, accidental accomplishment on the turbulent sea almost four months before . . .

She'd been in a near daze that night from exhaustion. A routine shift during the last month of her residency had yielded thirty-six hours of duty on call, during which she'd slept perhaps an hour. But that was fine until she'd spotted a drowned man in the water.

The *Sweet Christine* had been crawling through the rough ocean under the heavy, leaden sky, the wind roaring against the windows of the wheelhouse. No small-craft warnings mattered to this forty-foot twin-engined Dutch-built steel cruiser, her heavy full-displacement hull moving smoothly though slowly without the slightest rise through the choppy waves. She was, strictly speaking, too much for a singlehander. But Rowan had been operating her alone since she was sixteen.

Getting such a boat in and out of the dock is really the tricky part, where another crew member is required. And Rowan had her own channel, dug deep and wide, beside her home in Tiburon, and her own pier and her own slow and methodic system. Once the *Sweet Christine* had been backed out and turned towards San Francisco, one woman on the bridge who knew and understood all the boat's complex electronic whistles and bells was really quite enough.

The *Sweet Christine* was built not for speed but for endurance. She was equipped that day as she always was, for a voyage around the world.

The overcast sky had been killing the daylight that May afternoon even when Rowan passed under the Golden Gate. By the time she was out of sight of it, the long twilight had faded completely.

Darkness was falling with a pure metallic monotony to it; the ocean was merging with the sky. And so cold it was that Rowan wore her woolen gloves and watch cap even in the wheelhouse, drinking cup after cup of steaming coffee, which never fazed her immense exhaustion. Her eyes were focused as always on the shifting sea.

Then came Michael Curry, that speck out there—could that possibly be a man?

On his face in the waves, his arms out loosely, hands floating near his head, and the black hair a mass against the shining gray water, the rest just clothes ballooning ever so slightly over the limp and shapeless form. A belted raincoat, brown heels. Dead-looking.

All that she could tell in those first few moments was that this was no decomposed corpse. Pale as the hands were, they were not waterlogged. He could have fallen overboard from some large vessel only moments before, or hours. The crucial thing was to signal "Pan Pan" immediately and to give her coordinates, and then to try to get him aboard.

As luck would have it the Coast Guard boats were miles from her location; the helicopter rescue teams were completely engaged. There were virtually no small craft in the area on account of the warnings. And the fog was rolling in. Assistance would come as soon as possible and no one could say when that was.

"I'm going to try to get him up out of the water," she said. "I'm alone out here. Just get here as fast as you can."

There was no need to tell them she was a doctor, or to remind them of what they already knew—in these cold waters, drowning

115

victims could survive for incredibly long periods, because the drop in temperature slows the metabolism; the brain slumbers, demanding only a fraction of the usual oxygen and blood. The important thing was to bring him in and start resuscitation.

And that was the tough part because she had never done such a thing alone. She had the equipment for it, however, the harnesses connected to powerful nylon line running through the gasoline-driven winch on the top of the wheelhouse—in other words, sufficient means to get him on board if she could get to him, and that was where she might fail.

At once, she pulled on her rubber gloves and her life jacket, then fastened her own harness, and gathered up the second one for him. She checked the rigging, including the line connected to the dinghy, and found it secure; then she dropped the dinghy over the side of the *Sweet Christine* and headed down the swim ladder towards it, ignoring the tossing sea and the swaying of the ladder and the spray of the cold water in her face.

He was floating towards her as she paddled towards him; but the water was almost swamping the dinghy. For one second, she thought clearly: this is impossible. But she refused to give up. At last, nearly falling out of the small craft, she reached for his hand and caught it, and brought his body head first towards her. Now, how to get the damned harness properly around his chest.

Again the water nearly swamped the dinghy; she nearly flipped it herself. Then a wave lifted her and carried her over the man's body. She lost his hand. She lost him. But he came bobbing up like a cork. She caught his left arm this time and forced the harness over his head and left shoulder, bringing the left arm through it. But it was crucial to get the right arm through as well. The harness had to be well on him if she was to pull him up, heavy as he was, with wet clothing.

And all the while, the diagnostic sense was working as she kept her eyes on the half-submerged face, as she felt the cold flesh of his outstretched hand. *Yes, he's in there, he can come back. Get him on deck.*

One violent wave after another prevented her from doing anything, except holding onto him. Then finally she was able to grasp the right sleeve and tug the arm forward and through the harness, and at once she pulled the harness tight.

The dinghy capsized, pitching her into the sea with him. She swallowed water, then shot to the surface, the breath gone out of her as the freezing cold penetrated her clothes. How many minutes did she have at this temperature before she lost consciousness? But she had him harnessed to the boat now as surely as she was harnessed. If she could make it back to the swim ladder without passing out, she could reel him in. Letting his line go, she pulled herself in hand over hand, refusing to believe she could fail, the broad starboard side of the *Sweet Christine* a white blur disappearing and reappearing as the waves washed over her.

At last she slammed against the side of the boat. The shock jolted her into full alertness. Her gloved fingers refused to flex as she reached for the bottom rung of the swim ladder. But she gave them the order, Close, damn you, close on the rope, and she watched what she could no longer feel as her right hand obeyed. Her left hand went out for the side of the ladder; again she was giving her numbed body orders, and half disbelieving, she found herself climbing up, rung by rung.

For one moment, lying on the deck, she couldn't move. The warm air from the open door of the wheelhouse was steaming like hot breath. Then she began to massage her fingers until feeling returned to them. But there was no time to get warm; no time to do anything but climb to her feet and get to the winch.

Her hands were hurting now. But they were doing what she wanted automatically as she started the motor. The winch groaned and sang as it reeled in the nylon line. Suddenly, she saw the man's body rising above the rail of the deck, the head bowed, the arms spread wide and falling limp over the nylon loop of the harness, water streaming from the heavy colorless clothes. The man fell forward, head first onto the deck.

The winch screamed as it dragged him closer to the wheelhouse, and then jerked him upright again, three feet from the door. She killed the motor. He dropped down, sodden, lifeless, too far from the warm air to do him good.

And she knew she couldn't drag him inside, and there was no time to fool any more with the lines or the winch.

With a great heave, she rolled him over and pumped a good quart of seawater out of his lungs. Then she lifted him, pushing herself under him and flopping him again on his back. She pulled off her gloves because they were hampering her. And then she slid her left hand under his neck, clamped her right fingers on his nose, and breathed into his mouth. Her mind worked with him, envisioning the warm air pumped into him. But it seemed forever that she breathed, and nothing was changing in the inert mass beneath her.

She switched to his chest, pressing down as hard as she could on the breastbone, then releasing the pressure, over and over for fifteen beats. "Come on, breathe!" she said, as if it were a curse. "Damn it, breathe!" Then she went back to mouth-to-mouth.

117

Impossible to know how much time had passed; she was as oblivious to time as she ever was in the Operating Room. She simply went on, alternating between the chest massage and the lung inflation, stopping only now and then to feel the lifeless carotid artery, and to realize that the diagnostic message was the same—*Alive*—before she continued.

His body tossed on the deck under her efforts, the skin gleaming and waxen in its wetness, the heels of his brown leather shoes rolling on the boards.

Once she tried again to drag him into the wheelhouse, but it was useless. And dimly aware that no lights were shining through the fog and no helicopter was roaring overhead, she went on, only pausing suddenly to slap his face and call to him, to tell him that she knew he was in there and she expected him to come back.

"You know you can hear me!" she shouted as she pressed down again on the breastbone. She pictured the heart and the lungs in all their glorious anatomical detail. Then as she made to lift his neck again, his eyes snapped open, and his face suddenly fired with life. His chest gave a heave against her; she felt the breath pour out of him, hot against her face.

"That's it, breathe!" she'd shouted over the wind. And why was she so amazed that he was alive, that he was staring at her, when she had not thought of giving up?

His right hand shot up and took hold of hers. And he said something to her, something murmured, incoherent, something that sounded nevertheless like a proper name.

Again, she slapped his cheek, but only gently. And his breaths came ragged yet rapid, his face knotted with pain. How blue his eyes were, how clearly and certainly alive. It was as if she'd never seen eyes before in a human being, never seen these fierce, brilliant gelatinous orbs staring up at her from a human face.

"Keep it up, breathe, you hear me, I'm going for blankets below deck."

He grabbed her hand again; he began to shiver violently. And as she tried to free herself, she saw him look past her and straight upwards. He lifted his left hand. He was pointing. A light was finally sweeping the deck. And God, the fog was rolling over them, thick as smoke. The helicopter had come just in time; the wind stung her eyes. She could barely see the blades turning up there.

She slumped back, nearly losing consciousness herself, aware of his hand gripping hers. He was trying to speak to her. She patted his hand, and she said, "It's OK, it's fine now, they'll take you in."

Then she was barking orders at the Coast Guard men as they came down the ladder; don't warm him up fast, and for God's sake, don't give him anything hot to drink. This is severe hypothermia. Radio for an ambulance at the dock.

She feared for him as they took him up. But in truth she knew what the doctors would say: no neurological deficit.

By midnight, she had given up on sleep. But she was warm and comfortable again. The *Sweet Christine* rocked like a great cradle on the dark sea, her lights sweeping the fog, her radar on, her autopilot keeping the same broad circular course. Snug in the corner of the wheelhouse bunk, dressed in fresh clothes, Rowan drank her steaming coffee.

She wondered about him, about the look in his eyes. Michael Curry was his name, or so the Coast Guard had told her when she called in. He'd been in the water for at least an hour before she'd spotted him. But it had turned out just as she'd thought. "No neurological problems at all." The press was calling it a miracle.

Unfortunately, he'd gotten disoriented and violent in the ambulance—maybe it was all those reporters at the dock—and they had sedated him (stupid!) and that had fuzzed things a bit for a while (of course!) but he was "just fine" now.

"Don't release my name to anyone," she'd said. "I want my privacy protected."

Understood. The reporters were being a real pain. And to tell the truth, well, her call for help had come at the worst of times, it wasn't properly logged. They didn't have her name or the name of her boat. Would she please give them that info now if she—

"Over and out, and thank you," she said as she cut them off.

The *Sweet Christine* drifted. She pictured Michael Curry lying on the deck, the way his forehead creased when he woke up, the way his eyes had caught the light from the wheelhouse. What was that word he'd said, a name it sounded like. But she couldn't remember, if she had ever distinctly heard it at all.

It seemed almost certain that he would have died if she hadn't spotted him. It didn't comfort her to think of it, of his floating out there in the dark and the fog, of life leaking moment by moment out of his body. Too close.

And such a beauty he was. Even drowned, he'd been something to behold. Mysterious always, the mix of features that renders a man beautiful. His was an Irish face undoubtedly—square, with a short and rather rounded nose, and that can make for a plain individual in many circumstances. But no one would have found him plain. Not with those eyes and that mouth. Not a chance.

But it was not appropriate to think of him in those terms, was it? She wasn't the doctor when she went hunting; she was Rowan wanting the anonymous partner and then sleep afterwards when the door had shut. It was the doctor, Rowan, who worried about him.

And who knew better than she did all the things that might have gone wrong in the chemistry of the brain during that crucial hour?

She called San Francisco General early the next morning when she brought the boat in. Dr. Morris, the chief resident there, was still on duty. "You have my complete sympathy," she'd said, briefly explaining her own position at University. She described the resuscitation, the instructions she'd given the paramedics about the hypothermia. Curry hadn't said anything, just mumbled something, she hadn't caught any distinct syllables. But she'd felt strongly that he was going to be all right.

"He is, he's fine, he's damned lucky," Dr. Morris told her. And yes, this call was doctor to doctor, completely confidential. All those jackals in the hall needed was to know that a lone female brain surgeon had reeled him in. Of course he was a bit out of it psychologically, talking on and on about visions he had out there, and there's something else happening with his hands, kind of extraordinary—

"His hands?"

"No paralysis or anything like that. Look, my beeper is going off."

"I can hear it. Listen, I'm in my last thirty days at University. Call me if you need me. I'll come."

She hung up. What the hell did he mean about hands? She remembered Michael Curry's grip, the way he had hung on, not wanting to let her go, his eyes fixed on hers. "I didn't screw up," she whispered. "There's nothing wrong with that guy's hands."

She understood about the hands the following afternoon when she opened the *Examiner*.

He had had a "mystical experience," he explained. From some place high above he'd seen his own body down there floating in the Pacific. A lot more had happened to him, but he couldn't recall it now and it was driving him out of his mind, this failure to remember.

As for the rumors flying around about his hands, well, yes, that was true, he was wearing black gloves now all the time because he saw images every time he touched things. He couldn't lift a spoon or touch a bar of soap, but that he didn't see some image connected to the last human being who'd handled it.

For the reporter he had touched the crucifix of her rosary, and told her it had been bought at Lourdes in 1939 and passed on to her by her mother.

This was absolutely accurate, the newspaper claimed, but there were now countless people on the staff of San Francisco General who could attest to Curry's new power.

He'd like to get out of the hospital, he really would. And he'd like this thing with his hands to go away, for his memory to come back of what had happened to him out there.

She studied the picture—a large clear black-and-white shot of him sitting up in bed. The proletarian charm was unmistakable. And his smile was simply wonderful. He even wore a little gold chain and cross around his neck, the kind that emphasized the muscularity of his shoulders. Lots of cops and fire fighters wore those kinds of chains. She adored them. Even when the little gold cross or medal, or whatever the hell it was, hung down in her face in bed, brushing her like a kiss on the eyelids.

But the black-gloved hands looked sinister in the picture, resting as they did on the white cover. Was it possible, what the article said? She did not for a moment doubt it. She had seen things stranger than that, oh, yes, much stranger.

Don't go see this guy. He doesn't need you, and you don't need to ask about the hands.

She tore out the story, folded it, and shoved it in her pocket. It was still there the following morning when she staggered into the coffee room after a full night of the Neurological Trauma Center and opened the *Chronicle.*

Curry was on page three, a good head shot, looking a little grimmer than before, perhaps a little less trusting. Dozens of people had now witnessed his strange psychometric power. He wished that people would understand it was nothing but a "parlor trick." He couldn't help them.

All that concerned him now was the forgotten adventure, that is, the realms he'd visited when he was dead. "There was a reason I came back," he said, "I know there was. I had a choice, and I made the decision to return. There was something very important that I had to do. I knew this, I knew the purpose. And it had something to do with a doorway, and a number. But I can't remember the number or what the number meant. Truth is, I can't recall any of it. It's as if the most important experience of my entire life has been wiped out. And I don't know any way to recover it."

They're making him sound crazy, she thought. And it was probably a routine "near death" experience. We know now that people have these all the time. What's wrong with the people around him?

As for his hands, she was a little too fascinated by that part, wasn't she? She perused the various witness accounts. She wished she had five minutes to look at the tests they'd run on him.

She thought again of him lying on the deck, of the firmness of his grip, of the expression on his face.

Had he felt something at that moment through his hand? And what would he feel now, were she to go there, tell him what she remembered about the accident, sit on the bed beside him, and ask him to do his parlor trick—in other words, barter her meager information for what everybody else wanted from him? No.

Repellent that she should make such a demand. Repellent that she, a doctor, should think not of what he might need, but of what she wanted. It was worse than wondering what it would be like to take him to bed, to drink coffee with him at the table in the little cabin at three in the morning.

She'd call Dr. Morris when she had time. See how he was, though when that would be, she couldn't say. She was the walking dead herself right now from lack of sleep, and she was needed right now in Recovery. Maybe she ought to leave Curry entirely alone. Maybe that was the best thing she could do for both of them.

At the end of the week the San Francisco *Chronicle* ran a long feature story on the front page.

WHAT HAPPENED TO MICHAEL CURRY?

He was forty-eight, a contractor by profession, a specialist in renovating old Victorian houses, owner of a company called Great Expectations. Seems he was a legend in San Francisco for turning ruins into mansions, a stickler for authenticity right down to the wooden pegs and square nails. He owned a little shop in the Castro full of claw-foot tubs and pedestal lavatories. His detailed drawings for restorations were famous. In fact, a book of them had been published called *Grand Victorian Inside and Out*. He'd done the award-winning Barbary Coast Bed and Breakfast on Clay Street, and the Jack London Hotel on Buena Vista West.

But he wasn't doing anything now. Great Expectations was temporarily closed. Its owner was too busy trying to remember what had been revealed to him during that crucial hour when he'd been "dead in the water."

"It was no dream," he said. "I know that I talked to people. They explained what they meant for me to do, and I accepted, I asked to come back."

As for the new psychic ability, that had nothing to do with it, he maintained. It seemed to be no more than some accidental side effect. "Look, all I get is a flash—a face, a name. It's totally unreliable."

That night in the hospital coffee room, she caught him on the TV news—the vivid three-dimensional man. There were those unforgettable blue eyes again, and the wholesome smile. Something innocent about him, actually, his simple straightforward gestures indicative of one who has long ago given up on dishonesty, or of trying to fox the complications of the world in any way.

"I've got to go home," he said. Was it a New York accent? "Not home here, I mean, but home where I was born, back in New Orleans." (Ah, so that was the accent!) "I could swear it's got something to do with what happened. I keep getting these flashes of home." Again, he gave a little shrug. He seemed like a damned nice guy.

But nothing had come back to him as yet about the near death visions. The hospital hadn't wanted to release him, but they had to admit that he was physically fit.

"Tell us about the power, Michael."

"I don't want to talk about it." Shrug. He looked at his black-gloved hands. "I want to talk to the people who rescued me—the Coast Guard who brought me, that skipper who picked me up at sea. I wish those people would get in touch. You know that's why I'm doing this interview."

The camera cut away to a pair of studio reporters. Banter about "the power." Both had seen it for themselves.

For a moment Rowan did not move or even think. New Orleans . . . and he was asking for her to contact him. New Orleans . . . Well, that settled it. Rowan had an obligation. She had heard his plea from his own lips. And this question of New Orleans, she had to clarify it. She had to talk to him . . . or write.

As soon as she reached home that night, she went to Graham's old desk, pulled out some stationery, and wrote Curry a letter.

She told him in detail all that she had observed regarding the accident from the moment she spotted him at sea until they took him up on the stretcher. Then, after a moment's hesitation, she added her home phone and address and a little postscript.

123

"Mr. Curry, I too am from New Orleans, though I never lived there. I was adopted the day I was born, and immediately taken away. It is probably no more than a coincidence that you are a southerner, too, but I thought you should know this. On the boat, you held my hand quite tightly and for some time. I would not want your situation confused by some vague telepathic message you received in that instant, something which may not be relevant at all.

"If you need to talk to me," she finished, "call me at University Hospital or at my home phone."

This was mild enough, neutral enough surely. She had only indicated that she believed in his power, and that she was there if he needed her. No more than that, no demand. And she would see to it that she remained responsible, no matter what transpired.

Yet she couldn't get it out of her head—the idea of being able to place her hand in his, of just asking: "I'm going to think about something, something specific that happened once, no, three times in my life; and all I want is that you tell me what you see. Would you do that? I cannot say you owe me this for saving your life . . ."

That's right, you can't. So don't do it!

She sent the letter directly to Dr. Morris, via Federal Express.

Dr. Morris called her the next day. Curry had walked out of the hospital the preceding afternoon, right after a television press conference.

"He's crazy as a loon, Dr. Mayfair, but we had no legal grounds to hold him. I told him what you told me, by the way, that he hadn't said anything. But he's too obsessed to give up on this whole thing. He's determined he's going to remember what he saw out there, you know, the big reason for it all, the secret of the universe, the purpose, the doorway, the number, the jewel. You never heard such stuff. I'll send the letter on to his house, but chances are, it won't get through. The mail's coming in by the sackful."

"This thing with the hands, is it real?"

Silence. "You want to know the truth? It's one hundred percent accurate, as far as I ever saw. If you ever see it for yourself, it will scare the hell out of you."

The story made the supermarket tabloids the following week. Two weeks later variations of it appeared in *People* and *Time*. Rowan clipped the stories and the pictures. Photographers were obviously following Curry wherever he went. They caught him

124

outside his business on Castro Street. They caught him on the steps of his house.

A fierce protective feeling for him was growing in Rowan. They really ought to leave this man alone.

And you have to leave him alone, too, Rowan.

He himself wasn't granting any interviews anymore, that became clear by the first week in June. The tabloids fed off exclusives from the witnesses to his power—"He touched the purse and he told me all about my sister, what she'd said when she gave the purse to me. I was tingling all over, and then he said, 'Your sister is dead.'"

Finally the local CBS channel said Curry was holed up in his house on Liberty Street, incommunicado. Friends were concerned. "He's disillusioned, angry," said one of his old buddies from college. "I think he's just retired from the world." Great Expectations was closed indefinitely. Doctors at San Francisco General had not seen their patient. They were worried as well.

Then in July, the *Examiner* declared that Curry was "missing." He had "disappeared."

A reporter from television "News at Eleven" stood on the steps of a huge Victorian house pointing to a pile of unopened mail flowing from the garbage can by the side gate.

"Is Curry holed up inside the grand Victorian on Liberty Street which he restored himself so lovingly many years ago? Is there a man sitting or lying alone upstairs in the lighted attic room?"

In disgust Rowan snapped off the program. It had made her feel like a voyeur. Simply awful to drag that camera crew to the man's very door.

But what stayed in her mind was that garbage can full of unopened letters. Had her communication gone, inevitably, into that pile? The thought of him locked in that house, afraid of the world, in need of counsel was a little more than she could handle.

Surgeons are men and women of action—people who believe they can do something. That's why they have the moxie to cut into people's bodies. She wanted to do something—go there, pound on the door. But how many other people had done that?

No, he didn't need another visitor, especially not one with a secret agenda of her own.

In the evenings, when she came home from the hospital and took her boat out alone, she invariably thought of him. It was almost warm in the sheltered waters off Tiburon. She took her time before she moved into the colder winds of San Francisco

Bay. Then she hit the violent current of the ocean. It was erotic, that great shift, as she pointed the boat westward, throwing back her head to gaze up as she always did at the soaring pylons of the Golden Gate Bridge. The great heavy cruiser moved slowly but steadily forward, pushing back the indistinct horizon.

So indifferent the great dull rolling Pacific. Impossible to believe in anything but oneself when you looked at the endlessly tessellated surface, heaving and shifting under a colorless sunset where sea met sky in a dazzling haze.

And he believed that he had been sent back for a purpose, did he, this man who restored beautiful dwellings, who drew pictures that were published in books, a man who ought to be too sophisticated to believe in something like that.

But then he had really died, had he not? He had had that experience of which so many had written, of rising upwards, weightless, and gazing down with a sublime detachment at the world below.

No such thing had ever happened to her. But there were other things, things just as strange. And while the whole world knew about Curry's adventure, no one knew the strange secret things that Rowan knew.

But to think there was meaning, a scheme to things, well, that was quite beyond her philosophical reach. She feared as she always had, that all that was ever meant was loneliness, hard work, striving to make a difference when no difference could possibly be made. It was like dipping a stick into the ocean and trying to write something—all the little people of the world spinning out little patterns that lasted no more than a few years, and meant nothing at all. Surgery had seduced her because she got them up and back on their feet and they were alive and they said "Thank you!" and you had served life and driven back death, and that was the only incontrovertible value to which she could give her all. *Doctor, we never thought she'd walk again.*

But a great purpose for living, for being reborn? What could such a thing possibly be? What was the purpose for the woman who died of a stroke on the delivery table while her newborn cried in the doctor's arms? What was the purpose for the man struck by the drunk driver on his way home from church?

There had been a purpose all right for the fetus she had once seen, a living breathing thing, its eyes still sealed shut, its little mouth like that of a fish, wires running in all directions from its horrid oversized head and tiny arms, as it slumbered in the special incubator, waiting for its tissue to be harvested—while it continued to live and breathe, of course—for the transplant recipient who waited two floors upstairs.

But if that was purpose, the discovery that you could, in spite of all laws to the contrary, keep those little aborted things alive in a secret laboratory in the middle of a giant private hospital, slicing them up at will, for the benefit of a Parkinson's disease patient who had already clocked in sixty good years before he started to die of the illness which the fetal tissue transplant could cure, well, she'd take the knife to the gunshot wound fresh up from Emergency any day.

Never would she forget that cold, dark Christmas Eve and Dr. Lemle leading her up through the deserted floors of the Keplinger Institute. "We need you here, Rowan. I could finesse your leaving University. I know what to say to Larkin. I want you here. And now I'm going to show you something you'll appreciate which Larkin would never appreciate, something you will never see at University, something that you will understand."

Ah, but she didn't. Or rather she understood too perfectly the horror of it.

"It isn't viable in the strict sense of the word," he'd explained, this doctor, Karl Lemle, whose brilliance had so enticed her, brilliance and ambition, and vision, yes, that too. "And technically of course it is not even alive. It's dead, quite dead, because its mother aborted it, you see, in the clinic downstairs, and so technically it is a nonperson, a non-human being. So who is to say, Rowan, that we have to shove it in a plastic trash bag when we know that through keeping this tiny body alive, and keeping others like it alive—these little gold mines of unique tissue, so flexible, adaptable, so unlike any other human tissue, swarming with countless tiny extraneous cells which would eventually have been discarded in the normal fetal process—we can make discoveries in the field of neurological transplants that make Shelley's *Frankenstein* read like a bedtime story."

Yes, right on that score, exactly. And there was little doubt that he spoke the truth when he predicted a future of entire brain transplants, when the organ of thought would be lifted safely and completely out of one worn-out body into a young and fresh one, a world in which altogether new brains might be created as tissue was added here and there to supplement nature's work.

"You see, the important thing about fetal tissue is, the recipient doesn't reject it. Now you know that, but have you thought about it, what it really means? One tiny implant of fetal cells into the eye of an adult human, and the eye accepts those cells; the cells continue to develop, adapting themselves to the new tissue. My God, don't you realize this allows us to participate in the evolutionary process? Why, we are only on the verge . . ."

"Not us, Karl. You."

"Rowan, you are the most brilliant surgeon I have ever worked with. If you . . ."

"I will not do this! I will not kill." *And if I don't get out of here, I'll start screaming. I have to. Because I have killed.*

Yes, that was purpose all right, purpose taken, as they say, to the max.

She had not blown the whistle on Lemle, of course. Doctors don't do things like that to other doctors, especially not when they are residents and their enemies are powerful and famous researchers. She had simply backed off.

"And besides," he had said over coffee later before the fire in Tiburon, the Christmas lights reflected in the glass walls around them, "this is going on everywhere, this research with live fetuses. There wouldn't be a law against it if it were not."

No surprise actually. It was too tempting. In fact the strength of the temptation was exactly equal to the strength of her revulsion. What scientist—and a neurologist was most definitely a scientist—had not dreamed such dreams?

Watching *Frankenstein* on the late show she had longed to be the mad scientist. How she would have loved her own mountain laboratory, and yes, she wanted to see what would happen if you only had the nerve to take the living human brain as a laboratory specimen, divorced of all moral—but no, she would not.

What a horrid Christmas present that revelation, and yet her dedication to trauma surgery had redoubled. Seeing that tiny monster gasping for breath in the artificial light, she'd been reborn herself, her life narrowing and gaining inestimable power as she became the miracle worker of University, the one they called when the brains were oozing out on the stretcher, or when the patient blundered in off the street with the ax still lodged in his head.

Maybe the wounded brain was to her the microcosm for all tragedy: life mutilated continuously and haphazardly by life. When Rowan had killed—and killed she had—the act had been just as traumatic: the brain assaulted, its tissue mangled, the way she so often found it now in victims of whom she knew nothing. There had been nothing anyone could do for those she killed.

But it wasn't to argue about purpose that she wanted to see Michael Curry. And it wasn't to drag him into her bed. She wanted the same thing from him everybody else wanted, and that was why she hadn't gone to San Francisco General to see him, to check on his recovery on her own.

She wanted to know about those killings, and not what the autopsies could tell her. She wanted to know what he saw and he felt—if and when she held his hand—while she thought about those deaths. He'd sensed something the first time he touched her. But maybe that too had been stricken from his memory, along with the things he saw when he was dead.

She understood all this. She had understood, at least in the back of her mind, all along. And it wasn't any less repellent to her as the months passed, that she wanted to use Michael Curry for her own ends.

Curry was inside that house on Liberty Street. She knew it. He needed help.

But what would it matter to Curry if she said, I'm a doctor, and I believe in your visions, as well as the power in your hands, because I know myself that there are things such as that, psychic things which no one can explain. I myself have just such an illicit and confusing and sometimes utterly uncontrollable power—the power to kill at will.

Why should he care? He was surrounded by people who believed in what he could do, wasn't he? But that wasn't helping him. He'd died and come back, and he was going crazy. But still, if she told him her story . . . and the idea was now most definitely a full-blown obsession, he might be the one person in the entire world who would believe what she said.

Perhaps it was madness to dream of telling the whole story to anybody. And there were times she tried to convince herself that she was wrong. Sooner or later she was going to talk to someone, she knew it. Sooner or later the silence of her thirty years would be shattered, if she didn't start talking, by a never-ending cry that would blot out all words.

After all, no matter how many heads she patched up she could not forget those three murders. Graham's face as the life bled out of him; the little girl convulsing on the tarmac; the man pitching forward over the wheel of his Jeep.

As soon as she had started her internship, she had managed through official channels to obtain those three autopsy reports. Cerebrovascular accident, subarachnoid hemorrhage, congenital aneurysm. She had read over all the details.

And what it spelled out in the layman's language was a secret weakness in the wall of an artery, which for no discernible reason finally ruptured, causing totally unforeseen and sudden death. No way to predict, in other words, that a six-year-old child would suddenly go into seizures on the playground, a six-year-old who'd been healthy enough to be kicking six-year-old Rowan and pulling her hair only moments before. Nothing anybody could do for the child either, as the blood poured out of her nose and her ears, and her eyes rolled up into her head. On

129

the contrary, they'd protected the other children, shielding their eyes from the spectacle as they took them into the schoolroom.

"Poor Rowan," said the teacher, later. "Darling, I want you to understand it was something in her head that killed her. It was medical. It had nothing to do with the fight."

And that's when Rowan had known, absolutely, what the teacher would never know. She did it. She caused that kid to die.

Now, that you could dismiss easily enough—a child's natural guilt for an accident she didn't understand. But Rowan had felt something when it happened. She had felt something inside herself—a great pervasive sensation which was not unlike sex when she thought about it; it had washed through her and seemingly out of her at the moment the child fell over backwards. And then there had been the diagnostic sense, operative even then, which had told her that the child would die.

Nevertheless, she forgot the incident. Graham and Ellie, in the manner of good California parents, took her to a psychiatrist. She played with his little girl dolls. She said what he wanted her to say. And people died of "strokes" all the time.

Eight years passed before the man got out of his Jeep on that lonely road in the hills of Tiburon and clapped his hand over her mouth and said in that awful intimate and insolent voice: "Now, don't you scream."

Her adoptive parents never made a connection between the little girl and the rapist who had died as Rowan struggled, as the same blazing anger galvanized her, passing into that exquisite sensation which rendered her body suddenly rigid as the man let go of her and fell forward over the wheel.

But she had made the connection. Quietly and certainly she'd made it. Not then, when she had forced open the door of the Jeep and run down the road screaming. No, she had not even known she was safe. But later, as she lay alone in the dark after the Highway Patrol and the homicide detectives had left them, she knew.

Almost a decade and a half had elapsed before it happened with Graham. And Ellie was too sick with cancer by then to think of much of anything. And surely Rowan wasn't going to pull up a chair to her bedside and say, "Mama, I think I killed him. He was cheating on you constantly. He was trying to divorce you. He couldn't wait the bloody goddamned two months it's going to take for you to die."

It was all a pattern, as surely as a spiderweb is a pattern, but a pattern does not imply a purpose. Patterns exist everywhere, and purpose is at its safest when it is spontaneous and short-lived.

You will not do this. You will not take life. It was remembering heresy to remember slapping that little girl, even fighting the man in the Jeep. And it was too perfectly awful to remember the argument with Graham.

"What do you mean you're having her served with the papers! She's dying! You're going to stick it out with me."

He'd grabbed her by the arms, tried to kiss her. "Rowan, I love you, but she isn't the woman I married . . ."

"No? Not the woman you've cheated on for thirty years?"

"She's just a thing in there, I want to remember her the way she used to be . . ."

"You talk that crap to me!"

That had been the instant that his eyes fixed and the expression washed out of his face. People always die with such peaceful countenances. On the brink of rape, the man in the Jeep had just gone blank.

Before the ambulance had come, she had knelt beside Graham, put her stethoscope to his head. There was that sound, so faint that some doctors could not hear it. But she heard it—the sound of a great deal of blood rushing to one spot.

No one ever accused her of anything. How could they? Why, she was a doctor, and she'd been with him when the "awful thing" happened, and God knows, she did everything she could.

Of course everybody knew Graham was a thoroughly second-rate human being—his law partners, his secretaries, even his last mistress, that stupid little Karen Garfield person who had come over wanting some keepsake, everybody knew. Except, that is, Graham's wife. But there wasn't the slightest suspicion. How could there be? It was just death by natural causes when he was about to make away with the fortune made through his wife's inheritance and a twenty-eight-year-old idiot who had already sold her furniture and bought their airline tickets for St. Croix.

But it wasn't death by natural causes.

By this time she knew and understood the diagnostic sense; she'd practiced it and strengthened it. And when she had laid her hand on his shoulder, the diagnostic sense had said: no natural death.

That in itself ought to have been enough. Yet maybe she was mistaken. Maybe it was the great deceptiveness of pattern which we call coincidence. And nothing more than that.

But suppose she met with Michael Curry. Suppose he held her hand as she closed her eyes and thought about those deaths?

Would he see only what she had seen, or would some objective truth be known to him? *You killed them.* It was worth a try.

What she realized tonight, as she wandered slowly and almost aimlessly through the hospital, as she took detours through vast carpeted waiting rooms and down long wards where she was not known, and would never be known, was that she had felt an overwhelming desire just to talk to Michael Curry for a long time. She felt connected to Michael Curry. As much by the accident at sea as by these psychic secrets. She wanted, perhaps for reasons she didn't fully understand, to tell him and him alone what she'd done.

It wasn't easy for her to face this weakness. Absolution for murder came only when she operated. She was at the altar of God when the nurses held out the sterile gown for her, when they held up the sterile gloves.

And all her life she'd been a solitary person, a good listener, but invariably colder than those around her. That special sense, the one that aided her so as a physician, had always made her too keenly aware of what others truly felt.

She'd been ten or twelve years old before she realized other people didn't have it, sometimes not even a particle of it. That her beloved Ellie, for instance, didn't have the slightest idea that Graham did not love her so much as he needed her, and needed to denigrate her and lie to her and to depend on her always being there, and being inferior to him.

Rowan had sometimes wished for that kind of ignorance—not to know when people envied you, or disliked you. Not to know that many people lied all the time. She liked the cops and the fire fighters because they were to some extent perfectly predictable. Or maybe it was simply that their particular brand of dishonesty didn't bother her so much; it seemed harmless compared to the complex, insidious, and endlessly malicious insecurity of more educated men.

Of course diagnostic usefulness had redeemed this special psyche sense completely.

But what could ever redeem the ability to kill at will? To atone was another matter. To what proper use could a telekinetic ability like that ever be put?

And such a power was not beyond scientific possibility, that was the truly terrifying part. Like the psychometric power of Michael Curry, such things might have to do with measurable energy, complex physical talents which might someday be as definable as electricity or microwaves, or high-frequency sounds. Curry was capturing an impression from the objects he handled, and that impression was very likely the product of energy. Very likely every object in existence—every surface, every definable bit of matter—contained such stored "impressions." They existed in a measurable field.

But parapsychology wasn't Rowan's love. She was mesmerized by what could be seen in test tubes, slides, and graphs. She didn't care to test or analyze her own killing power. She wanted only to believe that she had never used it, that maybe there was some other explanation for what had happened, that maybe somehow she was innocent.

And the tragic thing was, maybe nobody could ever tell her what had really occurred with Graham, and the man in the Jeep and the kid on the playground. And all she could hope for was to tell someone, to unburden and exorcise, as everybody else did, through talk.

Talk, talk, talk.

That's exactly what Rowan wanted. She knew.

Only once before had this desire to confide nearly overcome her. And that had been quite an unusual event. In fact, she had almost told a perfect stranger the entire story, and there were times since when she wished that she had done just that.

It was late last year, a full six months after Ellie's death. Rowan was feeling the keenest loneliness she'd ever known. It seemed to her the great pattern called "our family" had been washed away overnight. Their life had been so good before Ellie's illness. Even Graham's affairs couldn't spoil it, because Ellie pretended the affairs weren't happening. And though Graham was not a man whom any human being would have called a good person, he possessed a relentless and infectious personal energy that maintained the family life in high gear.

And how Rowan had depended upon them both.

Her dedication to medicine had pretty much taken her away from her old college cronies. None of them had gone into the sciences. But the family was all that the three of them ever needed. From the time of Rowan's earliest memories, they were an unshakable trio, whether cruising the Caribbean, or skiing in Aspen, or eating a midnight Christmas dinner on a room service table in a suite in the Plaza in New York.

Now the dream house on the Tiburon shore stood empty as a beached shell.

And Rowan had the odd feeling that the *Sweet Christine* did not belong so much to her and her various well-chosen love partners, but rather to the family who had left the more dominant impression over a decade of happy years.

One night after Ellie's death, Rowan had stood alone in the

133

wide living room beneath the high-beamed ceiling, talking aloud to herself, laughing even, thinking there is no one, no one to know, no one to hear. The glass walls were dark and indistinct with reflected carpet, furniture. She couldn't see the tide that lapped ceaselessly at the pilings. The fire was dying out. The eternal chill of the coastal night was moving slowly through the rooms. She had learnt a painful lesson, she thought—that as they die, the ones we love, we lose our witnesses, our watchers, those who know and understand the tiny little meaningless patterns, those words drawn in water with a stick. And there is nothing left but the endless flow.

It was shortly after that that the bizarre moment had come, when she had almost taken hold of this stranger and poured out her tale.

He was an elderly gentleman, white-haired—British, quite obviously from the first words he spoke. And they had met, in of all places, the cemetery where her adoptive parents had been laid to rest.

It was a quaint old graveyard, sprinkled with weathered monuments on the edge of the small northern California town where Graham's family had once lived. These people, not related to her by blood, had been completely unknown to her. She'd gone back several times after Ellie's funeral, though why she wasn't quite sure. On that particular day her reason was simple: the gravestone had finally been completed and she wanted to see that the names and the dates were correct.

It had occurred to her several times on the drive north that this new gravestone would stand as long as she was living, and after that, it would tumble and crack and lie there in the weeds. The relatives of Graham Franklin had not even been notified about his funeral. Ellie's people—far away in the dim South— had not been notified of her death. Even in ten years, no one would know or care then about Graham and Ellie Mayfair Franklin. And by the end of Rowan's life, everyone who had ever known them or even heard of them would be dead.

Spiderwebs broken and torn in a wind that is indifferent to their beauty. Why bother with this at all? But Ellie had wanted her to bother. Ellie had wanted a headstone, flowers. That was the way they did it in New Orleans when Ellie was a little girl. Only on her deathbed had she spoken of her home finally, and to say the strangest things—that they had laid out Stella in the parlor, that people had come to see Stella and kiss her even though her brother had shot her, that Lonigan and Sons had closed up the wound in Stella's head.

"And Stella's face was so beautiful in the coffin. She had such beautiful black hair, all in little waves, you know, and she was as pretty as her picture on the living room wall. I loved Stella! Stella let me hold the necklace. I sat on a chair by the coffin. I was kicking my feet and my Aunt Carlotta said to stop.''

Every word of that strange diatribe was engraved on Rowan's memory. Stella, her brother, Aunt Carlotta. Even the name Lonigan. Because for a precious few seconds there had been a flash of color in the abyss.

These people were related to Rowan. Rowan was in fact Ellie's third cousin. And of these people Rowan knew nothing, and must continue to know nothing, were her promises to Ellie to be kept.

Ellie had remembered herself, even in those painful hours. ''Don't you ever go back there, Rowan. Rowan, remember what you've promised. I burned all the pictures, the letters. Don't go back there, Rowan, this is your home.''

''I know, Ellie. I'll remember.''

And there was no more talk of Stella. Of her brother. Of Aunt Carlotta. Of the picture on the living room wall. Only the shock of the document presented to Rowan after Ellie's death by her executor—a carefully worded pledge, with absolutely no legal validity whatever, that Rowan would never return to the city of New Orleans, never seek to know who her people were.

Yet in those last days, Ellie had spoken of them. Of Stella on the wall.

And because Ellie had talked too of headstones and flowers, of being remembered by her adopted daughter, Rowan had gone north that afternoon to keep that promise, and in the little hillside graveyard, she had met the Englishman with the white hair.

He'd been down on one knee before Ellie's grave as if genuflecting, copying the very names which had only just been cut into the stone.

He seemed a little flustered when she interrupted him, though she had not spoken a word. In fact, for one second he looked at her as if she were a ghost. It had almost made her laugh. After all she was a slightly built woman, in spite of her height, wearing her usual boat clothes—a navy blue peacoat and jeans. And he himself seemed such an anachronism in his elegant three-piece suit of gray tweed.

But that special sense of hers told her he was a man of only good intentions, and when he explained that he had known Ellie's people in New Orleans, she believed him. She felt a great confusion, however. Because she wanted to know these people too.

135

After all, there was no one left in the world for her but those people! And what an ungrateful and disloyal thought that was.

She said nothing to him as he chatted on in a lovely lyrical British fashion about the heat of the sun and the beauty of this little cemetery. Silence was her inveterate response to things, even when it confused others and made them uncomfortable. And so, out of habit, she gave back nothing, no matter what her inner thoughts. *Knew my people? People of my blood?*

"My name is Aaron Lightner," the man said as he placed a small white card in her hand. "If ever you want to know about the Mayfair family in New Orleans, then by all means, please do give me a call. You can reach me in London, if you like. Please do reverse the charges. I'll be happy to tell you what I know about the Mayfair family. Quite a history, you see."

Numbing these words, so unintentionally hurtful in her loneliness, so unexpected on this strange deserted little hill. Had she looked helpless, standing there, unable to answer, unable to give the smallest nod in response? She hoped so. She didn't want to think that she seemed cold or rude.

But it was quite out of the question to explain to him that she'd been adopted, taken away from New Orleans the day she was born. Impossible to explain she'd made a promise never to return there, never to seek the slightest knowledge about the woman who'd given her up. Why, she did not even know her mother's first name. And she'd found herself wondering suddenly, did *he* know it? Know perhaps the identity of the Mayfair who had been pregnant out of wedlock and given away her child?

Best, certainly, not to say anything, lest he carry back with him some gossip. After all, perhaps her real mother had gone on to marry and have seven children. And talk now could only do the woman harm. Over the miles and the years, Rowan felt no malice for this faceless, nameless creature, only a dreary hopeless longing. No, she had not said a word.

He had studied her for a long moment, quite unruffled by her impassive face, her inevitable quiet. When she gave him back the card, he took it graciously, but he held it out tentatively as if he hoped she would take it again.

"I should so like to talk to you," he continued. "I should like to discover how life has been for the transplanted one, so very far from the home soil." He had hesitated, then: "I knew your mother years ago—"

He stopped, as if he sensed the effect of his words. Maybe their sheer impropriety disturbed him. Rowan didn't know. The moment could not have been more excruciating if he had struck

136

her. Yet she hadn't turned away. She had merely remained there motionless, hands shoved in her coat pockets. *Knew my mother?*

How ghastly it had been. And this man with cheerful blue eyes regarding her so patiently, and the silence as it always was, a shroud binding her in. For the truth was, she could not make herself speak.

"I do wish you'd join me for a lunch, or only for a drink if there isn't time for that. I'm really not a dreadful person, you see. There is a long history . . ."

And the special sense told her he was telling the truth!

She had almost accepted his invitation—to everything, to talk about herself, and to ask him all about them. After all, she had not sought him out. He had come to her with his offer of information. And then, at that moment, had come the compulsion to reveal all, even the story of her strange power, as if he were inviting her to do it silently, exerting some force upon her mind so that she would open its innermost chambers. For he really did want to know about her! And that interest, so keenly personal, from one devoid of the slightest malicious taint, had warmed her as surely as a winter fire.

Patterns, witnesses, all her far-flung thoughts of these things flashed suddenly to the fore.

I have killed three people in my life. I can kill with anger. I know that I can. That is what has happened with the transplanted one as you called me. Is there any place in the family history for such a thing?

Had he flinched slightly as he looked at her? Or was it merely the slanting sun in his eyes?

But this could not happen. They were standing over the grave of the woman to whom she'd made the promise. "No, I will never go back to New Orleans. I will never try to find out." The woman who had cared for her and loved her, and given her more perhaps than her real mother ever could. The mood of the sickroom had come back, the sound of soft, near inhuman cries of pain. "Promise me, Rowan, even if they write to you. Never . . . never . . ."

"You are my mother, Ellie, my only mother. How could I ask for more?"

In those last agonizing weeks, she had feared her awful destructive power most keenly, for what if in her rage and grief she turned it on Ellie's weakened body, and thereby ended this stupid, useless suffering once and for all? *I could kill you, Ellie, I could deliver you. I know I could. I can feel it inside me, just waiting to be put to that test.*

What am I? A witch, for the love of God! I am a healer, not a destroyer. I have a choice as all human beings have a choice!

And there the Englishman had stood, studying her as if fascinated, as if she had been speaking when she hadn't been at all. It was almost as if he said I understand. But of course that was only an illusion. He had said nothing.

Tormented, confused, she'd turned on her heel and left him there. He must have thought her hostile, or mad even. But what did it matter? Aaron Lightner. She'd never even glanced at the card before she'd given it back to him. She did not know why she remembered the name, except that she remembered him and the strange things he'd said.

Months had passed since that awful day when she had driven home, opened the wall safe, and taken out the paper which Ellie's executor had had her sign.

"I, Rowan Mayfair, do solemnly swear before God, and in the presence of the undersigned witness, that I shall never return to the city of New Orleans where I was born, that I shall never seek to know the identity of my biological parents, and that I shall eschew all contact with the family called Mayfair should any member approach me for any reason whatsoever, or on any pretext . . ."

On and on it went in that near hysterical language, attempting to cover every foreseeable contingency, so many words to have so little meaning. No wonder Rowan distrusted language. It was Ellie's wish that carried all the weight.

But Rowan had signed it. The lawyer, Milton Kramer, had witnessed it. Into his files the executed copy had gone.

Had Michael Curry's life passed before his eyes like this, Rowan sometimes wondered, the way that my life is passing before my eyes now? Often she had stared at his smiling face, torn from a magazine and pasted to her mirror.

And she knew that if she saw him this dam might surely break. She dreamed of it, talking to Michael Curry, as if it might happen, as if she might bring him home with her to the house in Tiburon, as if they might drink coffee together, as if she might touch his gloved hand.

Ah, such a romantic notion. A tough guy who loved beautiful houses, drew beautiful pictures. Maybe he listened to Vivaldi, this tough guy, maybe he really read Dickens. And what would it be like to have such a man in her bed, naked except for his soft black leather gloves?

Ah, fantasy. Rather like imagining that the fire fighters she brought home would turn out to be poets, that the policemen she had seduced would reveal themselves to be great novelists, that the forest ranger she'd met in the bar in Bolinas was truly a great painter, and that the husky Vietnam veteran who'd taken her to his cabin in the woods was a great motion picture director hiding from a demanding and worshipful world.

She did imagine those things, and they were entirely possible, of course. But it was the body that commanded preeminence—the bulge in the jeans had to be big enough, the neck powerful, the voice deep, and the coarsely shaven chin rough enough to cut her.

But what if?

But what if Curry had gone on to the South where he came from. That was probably exactly what had happened. New Orleans, the one place in all the world that Rowan Mayfair couldn't go.

The phone was ringing when she unlocked her office door.

"Dr. Mayfair?"

"Dr. Morris?"

"Yes, I've been trying to reach you. It's about Michael Curry."

"Yes, I know, Doctor. I got your message. I was just about to call."

"He wants to talk to you."

"Then he's still in San Francisco."

"He's hiding out in his own home on Liberty Street."

"I've seen it on the news."

"But he wants to meet with you. I mean, well, to put it bluntly, he wants to see you in person. He has this idea . . ."

"Yes?"

"Well, you're going to think this madness is communicable, but I'm just relaying the message. Is there any chance you would meet with this guy on your boat—I mean it was your boat you were on the night you rescued him, wasn't it?"

"I'd be glad to take him back on the boat."

"What did you say?"

"I would be glad to see him. And I'll take him out on the boat if he wants to go."

"That is absolutely great of you, Doctor. But I have to explain a few things. I know this sounds absolutely bonkers, but he wants to take his gloves off and touch the boards of the deck where he was lying when you brought him around."

"Of course he can do that. I don't know why I didn't think of that myself."

"You're serious? God, you don't know how relieved I am. And Dr. Mayfair, let me tell you right now, this guy is just one very nice guy."

"I know."

"He is really suffering, this guy. He hit me with this idea last week. I hadn't heard from him in a month! He was drunk when he called. I thought he'd forget about it."

"It's a very good idea, Dr. Morris. You said the power in his hands was real."

"That's right, I did. And it is. And you are a very special doctor, Dr. Mayfair. But do you know what you're getting into? I begged him, I mean really begged him to come back in. Then he calls back last night, demanding I find you right this minute. He has to lay his hands on the boards of the deck, he's going nuts. I told him, 'Sober up, Michael, and I'll give it a shot.' Then he calls twenty minutes ago, right before I called you. 'I won't lie to you,' he says. 'I've drunk a case of beer today, but I haven't touched the vodka or the Scotch. I am as straight as I can possibly get.' "

She laughed softly. "I should weep for his brain cells," she said.

"I hear you. But what I'm getting to is the man is desperate. He isn't getting any better. And I would never ask this of you if he wasn't just one of the nicest—"

"I'll go get him. Can you call him and tell him that I'm on my way?"

"God, that's terrific. Dr. Mayfair, I can't thank you enough."

"No thanks is necessary. I want to see him."

"Look, strike a bargain with him, Doctor. You'll let him play psychic on the boat if he'll come in here and dry out."

"Call him now, Dr. Morris. Within the hour, I'll be at his front door."

She put down the phone and stood quite still staring at it for a moment. Then she removed her name tag, and stripped off her soiled white jacket, and slowly pulled the pins out of her hair.

Five

S O THEY HAD tried to put Dierde Mayfair away again after all these years. With Miss Nancy gone and Miss Carl getting more feeble by the day, it was best. That was the talk, anyway. On August 13, they'd tried. But Deirdre had gone wild, and they had left her alone, and now she was going down badly, just real badly.

When Jerry Lonigan told his wife Rita, she cried.

It had been thirteen years since Deirdre came home from the sanitarium a mindless idiot who couldn't tell you her own name, but that didn't matter to Rita. Rita would never forget the real Deirdre.

Rita and Deirdre were sixteen when they went to boarding school at St. Rose de Lima's. It was an ugly old brick building, on the very edge of the French Quarter. And Rita was sent there because she was "bad," had been out drinking on the riverboat *The President* with boys. Her dad had said St. Ro's would straighten her out. All the girls slept in an attic dormitory. And they went to bed at nine o'clock. Rita had cried herself to sleep down there.

Deirdre Mayfair had been at St. Ro's for a long time. She didn't mind that it was old and gloomy and strict. But she held Rita's hand when Rita cried. She listened when Rita said it was like a prison.

The girls watched "Father Knows Best" on an old television set with a round six-inch screen, swear to God! And the creaky old wooden radio that stood on the floor under the window was no better. You couldn't get to the phonograph. The South American girls always had it, playing that awful "La Cucaracha," and doing those Spanish dances.

"Don't mind them," Deirdre said. She took Rita with her down to the play yard in the late afternoon. They swung on the swings under the pecan trees. You wouldn't think that was much fun for a sixteen-year-old girl, but Rita loved it when she was with Deirdre.

Deirdre sang when they were on the swings—old Irish and

Scotch ballads, she called them. She had a real true soprano voice, delicate and high, and the songs were so sad. It gave Rita chills to hear them. Deirdre loved to stay out until the sun was gone and the sky was a "pure purple" and the cicadas were really going in the trees. Deirdre called it twilight.

Rita had seen that word written out, all right, but she'd never heard anyone really say it. Twilight.

Deirdre took Rita's hand and they walked along the brick wall, right under the pecan trees, so that they had to duck under the low leafy branches. There were places you could stand where you were completely hidden by the trees. It was crazy to describe it, but it had been such a strange and lovely time for Rita—standing there in the half dark with Deirdre, and the trees swaying in the breeze and the tiny leaves showering down on them.

In those days, Deirdre had looked like a real old-fashioned girl from a picture book, with a violet ribbon in her hair and her black curls tumbling down her back. She could have been real sharp if she'd wanted to be. She had the build for it, and new clothes in her locker she never bothered to try on. But it was easy to forget about things like that when you were with Deirdre. Her hair had been so soft. Rita had touched it once. So soft.

They walked in the dusty cloister beside the chapel. They peeped through the wooden gate into the nuns' garden. Secret place, Deirdre said, full of the loveliest flowers.

"I don't ever want to go home," Deirdre explained. "It's so peaceful here."

Peaceful! Alone at night, Rita cried and cried. She could hear the jukebox of the Negro bar across the street, the music rising over the brick walls and all the way up to the fourth-story attic. Sometimes when she thought everybody was asleep, she got up and went out on the iron balcony and looked towards the lights of Canal Street. There was a red glow over Canal Street. All New Orleans was having fun out there, and Rita was locked up, with a nun sleeping behind a curtain at either end of the dormitory. What would she do if she didn't have Deirdre?

Deirdre was different from anybody Rita had ever known. She had such beautifully made things—long white flannel gowns trimmed in lace.

They were the same kind she wore now thirty-four years later on the side screen porch of that house where she sat "like a mindless idiot in a coma."

And she had showed Rita that emerald necklace she always wore now, too, right over the white nightgown. The famous Mayfair emerald necklace, though Rita had not heard of it then.

'Course Deirdre had not worn it at school. You couldn't wear jewelry at all at St. Ro's. And no one would have worn a big old-fashioned necklace like that anyway, except to a Mardi Gras ball perhaps.

It looked just awful now on Deirdre in her nightgown. All wrong, a thing like that on an invalid who just stared and stared through the screens of the porch. But who knows? Maybe somehow Deirdre knew it was there, and Deirdre sure had loved it.

She let Rita touch it when they sat on the side of the bed at St. Ro's. No nuns around to tell them not to rumple the bedspread.

Rita had turned the emerald pendant over in her hands. So heavy, the gold setting. It looked like something was engraved on the back. Rita made out a big capital L. It looked like a name to her.

"Oh, no, don't read it," Deirdre said. "It's a secret!" And she'd looked frightened for a moment, her cheeks suddenly red and her eyes moist, and then she took Rita's hand and squeezed it. You couldn't be mad at Deirdre.

"Is it real?" Rita asked. Must have cost a fortune.

"Oh, yes," Deirdre said. "It came from Europe years and years ago. It belonged to a great-great-great-great-grandmother back then."

They both laughed at all the greats.

It was innocent the way Deirdre said it. She never bragged. It wasn't like that at all. She never hurt anybody's feelings. Everybody loved her.

"My mother left it to me," Deirdre explained. "And someday I'll pass it on, that is . . . if I ever have a daughter." Trouble in her face. Rita put her arm around Deirdre. You just wanted to protect Deirdre. Deirdre brought out that feeling in everybody.

Deirdre said she'd never known her mother. "She died when I was a baby. They say she fell from the upstairs window. And they said her mother died when she was young, too, but they never talk about her. I don't think we're like other people."

Rita was stunned. Nobody she knew said such things.

"But how do you mean, Dee Dee?" she asked.

"Oh, I don't know," Deirdre said. "We feel things, sense things. We know when people don't like us and mean to hurt us."

"Who could ever want to hurt you, Dee Dee?" Rita asked. "You'll live to be a hundred and you'll have ten children."

"I love you, Rita Mae," Deirdre said. "You're pure of heart, that's what you are."

"Oh, Dee Dee, no." Rita Mae shook her head. She thought of her boyfriend from Holy Cross, the things they had done.

And just as if Deirdre had read her mind, she said:

"No, Rita Mae, that doesn't matter. You're good. You never want to hurt anybody, even when you're really unhappy."

"I love you, too," Rita said, though she did not understand all that Deirdre was telling her. And Rita never ever in her whole life told any other woman that she loved her.

Rita almost died when Deirdre was expelled from St. Ro's. But Rita knew it wàs going to happen.

She herself saw a young man with Deirdre in the convent garden. She had seen Deirdre slip out after supper when no one was looking. They were supposed to be taking their baths, setting their hair. That was one thing Rita really thought was funny about St. Ro's. They made you set your hair and wear a little lipstick because Sister Daniel said that was "etiquette." And Deirdre didn't have to set her hair. It hung in perfect curls. All she needed was a ribbon.

Deirdre was always disappearing at that time. She took her bath first and then snuck downstairs, and didn't come back till almost lights out. Always late, always hurrying in for night prayers, her face flushed. But then she'd give Sister Daniel that beautiful innocent smile. And when Deirdre prayed she seemed to mean it.

Rita thought she was the only one who noticed that Deirdre slipped out. She hated it when Deirdre wasn't around. Deirdre was the only one that made her feel all right there.

And one night she'd gone down to look for Deirdre. Maybe Deirdre was swinging on the swings. Winter was over and twilight was coming now after supper. And Rita knew about Deirdre and twilight.

But Rita didn't find Deirdre in the play yard. She went to the open gate of the nuns' garden. It was very dark in there. You could see the Easter lilies in the dark, shining white. The nuns would cut them on Easter Sunday. But Deirdre would never break the rules and go in there.

Yet Rita heard Deirdre's voice. And gradually she made out the figure of Deirdre on the stone bench in the shadows. The pecan trees were as big and low there as they were in the play yard. All Rita could see was the white blouse at first, and then she saw Deirdre's face and even the violet ribbon in her hair, and she saw the tall man seated beside her.

Things were so still. The jukebox of the Negro bar wasn't playing just then. No sound came from the convent. And even

144

the lights in the nuns' refectory looked far away because there were so many trees growing along the cloister.

The man said to Deirdre: "My beloved." It was just a whisper, but Rita heard it. And she heard Deirdre say: "Yes, you're speaking, I can hear you."

"My beloved!" came the whisper again.

Then Deirdre was crying. And she said something else, maybe a name, Rita would never know. It sounded as if she said: "My Lasher."

They kissed, Deirdre's head back, the white of the man's fingers very clear against her dark hair. And the man spoke again:

"Only want to make you happy, my beloved."

"Dear God," Deirdre whispered. And suddenly she got up off the bench and Rita saw her running along the path through the beds of lilies. The man was nowhere in sight. And the wind had come up, sweeping through the pecan trees so that their high branches crashed against the porches of the convent. All the garden was moving suddenly. And Rita was alone there.

Rita turned away ashamed. She shouldn't have been listening. And she, too, ran away, all the way up the four flights of wooden stairs from the basement to the attic.

It was an hour before Deirdre came. Rita was miserable to have spied on her like that.

But late that night when she lay in bed, Rita repeated those words: *My beloved. Only want to make you happy, my beloved.* Oh, to think that a man would say such things to Deirdre.

All Rita had ever known were the boys who wanted to "feel you up," if they got a chance. Clumsy, stupid guys like her boyfriend Terry from Holy Cross, who said, "You know, I think I like you a lot, Rita." Sure, sure. 'Cause I let you "feel me up." You ox.

"You tramp!" Rita's father had said. "You're going to boarding school, that's where you're going. I don't care what it costs."

My beloved. It made her think of beautiful music, of elegant gentlemen in old movies she saw on late night television. Of voices from another time, soft and distinct, the very words like kisses.

And he was so handsome too. She hadn't really seen his face, but she saw he was dark-haired with large eyes, and tall, and he wore fine clothes, beautiful clothes. She'd seen the white cuffs of his shirt and his collar.

Rita would have met him in the garden too, a man like that. Rita would have done anything with him.

Oh, Rita couldn't really figure it out, the feelings it gave her. She cried but it was a sweet, silent kind of crying. She knew she'd remember the moment all her life—the garden under the dark purple twilight sky with the evening stars out already and the man's voice saying those words.

When they accused Deirdre, it was a nightmare. They were in the recreation room and the other girls were made to stay in the dormitory, but everybody could hear it. Deirdre burst into tears, but she wouldn't confess anything.

"I saw the man myself!" Sister Daniel said. "Are you calling me a liar!" Then they took Deirdre down to the convent to talk to old Mother Bernard but even she couldn't do anything with Deirdre.

Rita was broken-hearted when the nuns came to pack up Deirdre's clothes. She saw Sister Daniel take the emerald necklace out of its box and stare at it. Sister Daniel thought it was glass, you could tell by the way she held it. It hurt Rita to see her touch it, to see her snatch up Deirdre's nightgowns and things and stuff them into the suitcase.

And later that week, when the terrible accident happened with Sister Daniel, Rita wasn't sorry. She never meant for the mean old nun to die the way she did, smothered in a closed-up room with a gas heater left on, but so be it.

Rita had other things on her mind than weeping for somebody who'd been mean to Deirdre.

That Saturday she got together all the nickels she could and called and called from the pay phone in the basement. Somebody must know the Mayfairs' phone number. They lived on First Street only five blocks down from Rita's house but it might as well have been across the world. It wasn't the Irish Channel there. It was the Garden District. And the Mayfair house was a mansion.

Then Rita got into a terrible fight with Sandy. Sandy said Deirdre had been crazy. "You know what she did at night? I'll tell what she did. When everybody was asleep she pushed the covers off and she moved her body just like somebody was kissing her! I saw her, she'd open her mouth and she'd move on the bed—you know, *move*—just like, you know, she was really feeling it!"

"Shut your filthy mouth!" Rita screamed. She tried to slap Sandy. Everybody got on Rita. But Liz Conklin took Rita aside and told her to calm down. She said that Deirdre had done worse than meet that man in the garden.

"Rita Mae, she let him into the building. She brought him right upstairs to our floor, I saw him." Liz was whispering, looking over her shoulder as if somebody was going to overhear them.

"I don't believe you," Rita said.

"I wasn't following her around," Liz said. "I didn't want her to get in trouble. I had just gotten up to go to the bathroom. And I saw them by the window of the recreation room—her and him together, Rita Mae—not ten feet from where we were all sleeping."

"What did he look like?" Rita demanded, sure it was a lie. Rita would know because she'd seen him.

But Liz described him all right—tall, brown hair, very "distinguished," Liz said, and he'd been kissing Deirdre and whispering to her.

"Rita Mae, imagine her opening all the locks, bringing him up the stairs. She was just crazy."

"All I know is this," Rita said later to Jerry Lonigan when they were courting. "She was the sweetest girl I ever knew in my life. She was a saint compared with those nuns, I tell you. And when I thought I'd go crazy in that place, she held my hand and told me she knew how I was feeling. I would have done anything for her."

But when the time came to do something for Deirdre Mayfair, Rita hadn't been able to do it.

Over a year had passed. Rita's teenaged life was gone and she never for a second missed it. She had married Jerry Lonigan, who was twelve years older than her and nicer than any boy she'd ever met—a decent and kind man who made a good living from Lonigan and Sons' Funeral Home, one of the oldest in the parish, which he ran with his daddy.

Jerry was the one who gave Rita news about Deirdre. He told her Deirdre was pregnant by a man who'd been killed already in a highway accident, and those aunts of hers, those mean crazy Mayfair women, were going to make her give up her baby.

Rita was going by that house to see Deirdre. She had to. Jerry didn't want her to go.

"What the hell you think you can do about it! Don't you know that aunt of hers, Miss Carlotta, she's a lawyer? She could get Deirdre committed if she didn't give up that baby."

Red Lonigan, Jerry's dad, shook his head. "That's been done plenty a time, Rita," he said. "Deirdre will sign the papers or wind up in the nuthouse. Besides, Father Lafferty's got a hand in this thing. And if there's any priest at St. Alphonsus I trust, it's Tim Lafferty."

But Rita went.

It was the hardest thing she'd ever done, walking up to that enormous house and ringing the bell, but she did it. And naturally it was Miss Carl who came to the door, the one everybody

147

was afraid of. Jerry told her later that if it had been Miss Millie or Miss Nancy it might have been different.

Still Rita walked right in, just sort of pushed past Miss Carl. Well, she had opened the screen door a crack, hadn't she? And Miss Carl really didn't look mean. She just looked businesslike.

"Just want to see her, you know, she was my best friend at St. Ro's . . ."

Every time Miss Carl said no in her polite way, Rita said yes in some other way, talking about how close she'd been to Deirdre.

Then she'd heard Deirdre's voice at the top of the steps.

"Rita Mae!"

Deirdre's face was wet from crying and her hair was all in straggles over her shoulders. She ran down the steps barefoot towards Rita, and Miss Nancy, the heavyset one, came right behind her.

Miss Carl took Rita firmly by the arm and tried to move her towards the front door.

"Wait just a minute!" Rita said.

"Rita Mae, they're going to take my baby!"

Miss Nancy caught Deirdre around the waist and lifted her off her feet on the stairway.

"Rita Mae!" Deirdre screamed. She had something in her hand, a little white card it looked like.

"Rita Mae, call this man. Tell him to help me."

Miss Carl stepped in front of Rita:

"Go home, Rita Mae Lonigan," she said.

But Rita darted right around her. Deirdre was struggling to get free of Miss Nancy, and Miss Nancy was leaning against the banister, off balance. Deirdre tried to throw the little white card to Rita, but it just fluttered down on the stairs. Miss Carl went to get it.

And then it was just like fighting for Mardi Gras trinkets thrown from the parade floats. Rita pushed Miss Carl to the side and snatched the card up, just the way you snatched a junk necklace off the pavement before anybody else could get it.

"Rita Mae, call that man!" Deirdre screamed. "Tell him I need him."

"I will, Dee Dee!"

Miss Nancy was carrying her back up the steps, Deirdre's bare feet swinging out, her hands clawing at Miss Nancy's arm. It was awful, just awful.

And then Miss Carl grabbed Rita's wrist.

"Give me that, Rita Mae Lonigan," said Miss Carl.

Rita pulled loose and ran out of the front door, the little white card clutched in her hand. She heard Miss Carl running across the porch right after her.

Her heart was pounding as she ran down the path. Jesus, Mary, and Joseph, this was a madhouse! And Jerry was going to be so upset. And what would Red say?

Then Rita felt a sharp, ugly pain as her hair was jerked from the back. The woman pulled her almost off her feet.

"Don't you do that to me, you old witch!" Rita said, her teeth clenched. Rita couldn't stand to have her hair pulled.

Miss Carl tried to tear the little white card out of her fingers. This was almost the worst thing that had ever happened to Rita. Miss Carl was twisting and tearing off the corner of the card as Rita held on to it, and with the other hand Miss Carl was still yanking Rita's hair as hard as she could. She was going to pull it out by the roots.

"Stop it!" Rita screamed. "I'm warning you now, I'm warning you!" She got the card away from Miss Carl and she crumpled it in her fist. You just couldn't hit an old lady like this.

But when Miss Carl jerked her hair again, Rita did hit her. She hit Miss Carl across the chest with her right arm, and Miss Carl fell into the chinaberry trees. If there hadn't been so many chinaberry trees, she would have fallen on the ground.

Rita ran out the gate.

A storm was blowing up. The trees were all moving. She could see the big black branches of the oaks swaying in the wind, hear that loud roar that big trees always made. The branches were lashing the house, scratching at the top of the upstairs porch. She heard the sound of breaking glass suddenly.

She stopped and looked back, and she saw a shower of little green leaves falling all over the property. Tiny branches and twigs were falling. It was like a hurricane. Miss Carl was standing on the path staring up at the trees. At least her arm or leg wasn't broken.

Good Lord, the rain would come any minute. Rita was going to be soaked before she even got to Magazine Street—that on top of everything else, her hair torn to pieces and the tears streaming down her face. She was a sight all right.

But there was no rain. She made it back to Lonigan and Sons without getting wet. And when she sat down in Jerry's office, she broke down completely.

"You shouldn't have gone there, you should never have gone!" he said. He had a funeral going on out front. He should have been helping Red out there. "Honey, they could turn everybody against us, old family like that!"

Rita couldn't do anything but cry. Then she looked at the little white card. "But will you look at this, Jerry! Will you look at it!"

It was all mashed and damp from the sweat of her palm. She broke down again.

"I can't read the numbers on it!"

"Now, just a minute, Rita," Jerry said. He was patient as always, just a really good-hearted man the way he'd always been. He stood over her, unfolding the little card on the desk blotter. He got his magnifying glass.

The middle part was clear enough:

THE TALAMASCA

But you couldn't read anything else. The words below that were just tiny little specks of black ink on the pulpy white cardboard. And whatever had been written along the bottom edge was completely ruined. There was just nothing left of it.

"Oh, Dee Dee!" Rita cried.

Jerry pressed it out under two heavy books, but that hadn't helped. His dad came in and took a look. But he couldn't make anything out of it. Name Talamasca didn't mean anything to Red. And Red knew just about everybody and everything. If it had been an old Mardi Gras society, for instance, he would have known it.

"Now look, you can see something here written on the back in ink," Red said. "Look at that."

Aaron Lightner. But there was no phone number. The phone numbers must have been printed on the front. Even pressing the card with a hot iron didn't help matters.

Rita did what she could.

She checked the phone book for Aaron Lightner and the Talamasca, whatever that was. She called information. She begged the operator to tell her if there was an unlisted number. She even ran personals in the *Times-Picayune* and in the *States-Item*.

"The card was old and dirty before you ever got it," Jerry reminded her. Fifty dollars spent on personal ads was enough. Jerry's daddy said he thought she might just as well give up. But one thing she could say for him, he hadn't criticized her for it.

"Darlin', don't go back to that house," Red said. "I'm not scared of Miss Carlotta or anything like that. I just don't want you around those people."

Rita saw Jerry look at his father, and his father look at him. They knew something they weren't saying. Rita knew Lonigan and Sons had buried Deirdre's mother when she fell from that window years ago, she'd heard that much, and she knew Red remembered the grandmother who had "died young" too the way Deirdre told Rita.

But those two were closemouthed the way morticians had to be. And Rita was too miserable now for hearing about the history of that horrible old house and those women.

She cried herself to sleep the way she had at boarding school. Maybe Deirdre had seen the ads in the papers, and knew that Rita had tried to do what she wanted.

Another year passed before Rita saw Deirdre again. The baby was long gone. Some cousins out in California took it. Nice people, everybody said, rich people. The man was a lawyer like Miss Carl. That baby would be looked after.

Sister Bridget Marie at St. Alphonsus told Jerry the nuns at Mercy Hospital said the baby was a beautiful little girl with blond hair. Not like Deirdre's black curls at all. And Father Lafferty had put the baby in Deirdre's arms and said to Deirdre, "Kiss your baby," then taken it away from her.

Gave Rita the shivers. Like people kissing the corpse right before they closed up the coffin. "Kiss your baby," then taking it like that.

No wonder Deirdre had had a complete breakdown. They took her right from Mercy to the sanitarium.

"Not the first time for that family," Red Lonigan said as he shook his head. "That's how Lionel Mayfair died, in a straitjacket."

Rita asked what he meant, but he didn't answer.

"Oh, but they didn't have to do it like that," Rita said. "She's such a sweet thing. She couldn't hurt anybody."

Finally Rita heard Deirdre was home again. And that Sunday Rita decided to go to Mass at the Mother of Perpetual Help Chapel in the Garden District. That's where the rich people went mostly. They didn't come to the big old parish churches—St. Mary's and St. Alphonsus—across Magazine Street.

Rita went up there to the ten o'clock Mass, thinking, Well, I'll just pass by the Mayfair house on the way back. But she didn't have to, because Deirdre was there at Mass, sitting between her great-aunts Miss Belle and Miss Millie. Thank the lord no Miss Carlotta.

Deirdre looked dreadful to Rita, like Banquo's Ghost as Rita's mother would have said. She had dark circles under her eyes and her dress was some old shiny gabardine thing that didn't fit her. Padded shoulders. One of those old women in the house must have given her that.

151

After Mass, as they were going down the marble steps, Rita swallowed, took a deep breath, and ran after Deirdre.

Deirdre at once gave her that beautiful smile. But when she tried to talk, almost nothing came out. Then in a whisper she said: "Rita Mae!"

Rita Mae leaned over to kiss her. She whispered:

"Dee Dee, I tried to do what you asked me. I could never find that man. The card was too ruined."

Deirdre's eyes were wide, vacant. She didn't even remember, did she? At least Miss Millie and Miss Belle didn't notice. They were saying their hellos to everybody passing. And poor old Miss Belle never noticed anything anyway.

Then Deirdre did seem to recall something. "It's OK, Rita Mae," she said. She had the beautiful smile again. She squeezed Rita Mae's hand and leaned forward and kissed her this time, on the cheek. Then her Aunt Millie said, "We should go now, sweetheart."

Now, that was Deirdre Mayfair to Rita. *It's OK, Rita Mae.* The sweetest girl she ever knew.

Deirdre was back at the sanitarium before long. She'd been walking barefoot on Jackson Avenue talking out loud to herself. Then they said she was in a mental hospital in Texas, and after that Rita only heard that Deirdre Mayfair was "incurably ill" and was never coming home again.

When old Miss Belle died, the Mayfairs called Jerry's dad as they'd always done. Maybe Miss Carl didn't even remember the fight with Rita Mae. Mayfairs came from all over for that funeral, but no Deirdre.

Mr. Lonigan hated opening the tomb in Lafayette No. 1. That cemetery had so many ruined graves with rotting coffins plainly visible, even the bones showing. It sickened him to take a funeral there.

"But those Mayfairs have been buried there since 1861," he said. "And they do keep up that tomb, I'll give them that. They have the wrought-iron fence painted every year. And when the tourists come through there? Well, that's one of the graves they always look at—what with all the Mayfairs in there, and those little babies' names, going back to the Civil War. It's just the rest of that place is so sorry. You know they're going to tear that place down someday."

They never did tear down Lafayette No. 1. The tourists liked it too much. And so did the families of the Garden District. Instead they cleaned it up, repaired the whitewashed walls, planted new magnolia trees. But there were still enough broken-down tombs for people to get their peek at the bones. It was a "historical monument."

Mr. Lonigan took Rita through there one afternoon, showing her the famous yellow fever graves where you could read a long list of those who had died within days of each other during the epidemics. He showed her the Mayfair tomb—a big affair with twelve oven-size vaults inside. The little iron fence ran all the way around it, enclosing a tiny strip of grass. And the two marble vases stuck to the front step were full of fresh-cut flowers.

"Why, they keep it up real nice, don't they?" she said. Such beautiful lilies and gladiolus and baby's breath.

Mr. Lonigan stared at the flowers. He didn't answer. Then after he'd cleared his throat, he pointed out the names of those he knew.

"This one here—Antha Marie, died 1941, now that was Deirdre's mother."

"The one who fell from the window," Rita said. Again he didn't answer her.

"And this one here—Stella Louise, died 1929—now that was Antha's mother. And it was this one over here, Lionel, her brother—'died 1929'—who ended up in the straitjacket after he shot and killed Stella."

"Oh, you don't mean he murdered his own sister."

"Oh, yes, I do," Mr. Lonigan said. Then he pointed out the other names going way back. "Miss Mary Beth, now that was the mother of Stella, and of Miss Carl, and now, Miss Millie is actually Rémy Mayfair's daughter. He was Miss Carl's uncle, and he died at First Street, but that was before my time. I remember Julien Mayfair, however. He was what you call unforgettable, Julien was. Till the day he died, he was a fine-looking man. And so was Cortland, his son. You see, Cortland died that year that Deirdre had that little baby. Now I didn't bury Cortland. Cortland's family lived in Metairie. They say it was all that ruckus over the baby that killed Cortland. But that don't matter. You can see that Cortland was eighty years old besides. Old Miss Belle was Miss Carl's older sister. But Miss Nancy, well, she is Antha's sister. It will be Miss Millie next, you mark my words."

Rita didn't care about them. She was remembering Deirdre on that long-ago day at St. Ro's when they sat on the side of the bed together. The emerald necklace had come to her through Stella and Antha.

She told Red about it now, and it didn't surprise him at all. He just nodded, and said, yes, and before that the emerald necklace had belonged to Miss Mary Beth and before that to Miss

153

Katherine who had built the house on First Street, but Miss Katherine was really before his time. Monsieur Julien was as far back as he could recall . . .

"But you know, it's the strangest thing," Rita said. "Them all carrying the Mayfair name. Why don't they take the names of the men they marry?"

"Can't," Mr. Lonigan said. "If they do, then they don't get the Mayfair money. That's the way it was set up long ago. You have to be a Mayfair to get Mayfair money. Cortland Mayfair knew it; knew all about it; he was a fine lawyer; never worked for anybody except the Mayfair family; I remember once he told me. It was legacy, he said."

He was staring at the flowers again.

"What is it, Red?" Rita asked.

"Oh, just an old story they tell around here," he said. "That those vases are never empty."

"Well, it's Miss Carl who orders the flowers, isn't it?" Rita asked.

"Not that I know of," Mr. Lonigan said, "but somebody always puts them there." But then he went quiet again the way he always did. He would never really tell you what he knew.

When he died a year after that, Rita felt as bad as if she'd lost her own father. But she kept wondering what secrets he'd taken with him. He'd always been so good to Rita. Jerry was never the same. He was nervous afterwards whenever he dealt with the old families.

Deirdre came home to the house on First Street in 1976, a mindless idiot, they said, on account of the shock treatments.

Father Mattingly from the parish went by to see her. No brain left at all. Just like a baby, he told Jerry, or a senile old lady.

Rita went to call. It had been years since she and Miss Carlotta had that awful fight. Rita had three children now. She wasn't scared of that old lady. She brought a pretty white silk negligee for Deirdre from D. H. Holmes.

Miss Nancy took her out on the porch. She said to Deirdre: "Look what Rita Mae Lonigan brought, Deirdre."

Just a mindless idiot. And how awful to see that beautiful emerald necklace around her neck. It was like they were making fun of her, to put it on her like that, over her flannel nightgown.

Her feet looked swollen and tender as they rested on the bare boards of the porch. Her head fell to one side as she stared through the screens. But otherwise she was still Deirdre—still pretty, still sweet. Rita had to get out of there.

She never called again. But not a week went by that she didn't

154

walk back First just to stop at the fence and wave to Deirdre. Deirdre didn't even notice her. But Rita did it nevertheless. It seemed to her Deirdre got stooped and thin, that her arms weren't down in her lap anymore, but drawn up, close to her chest. But Rita was never close enough to make certain. That was the virtue of just standing at the fence and waving.

When Miss Nancy died last year, Rita said she was going to the funeral. "It's for Deirdre's sake."

"But honey," Jerry had said, "Deirdre won't know you're doing this." Deirdre hadn't spoken a single syllable in all these years.

But Rita didn't care. Rita was going.

As for Jerry, he didn't want to have anything to do with the Mayfairs. He missed his daddy more than ever.

"Why the hell can't they call some other funeral home?" he had said under his breath. Other people did it now that his daddy was dead and gone. Why didn't the Mayfairs follow suit? He hated the old families.

"Least this is a natural death, or so they tell me," he said.

Now that really startled Rita. "Well, weren't Miss Belle and Miss Millie 'natural deaths'?" she asked.

After he'd finished work that afternoon on Miss Nancy, he told Rita it had been terrible going into that house to get her.

Right out of the old days, the upstairs bedroom with the draperies drawn and two blessed candles burning before a picture of the Mother of Sorrows. The room stank of piss. And Miss Nancy dead for hours in that heat before he got there.

And poor Deirdre on the screen porch like a human pretzel, and the colored nurse holding Deirdre's hand and saying the rosary out loud, as if Deirdre even knew she was there, let alone heard the Hail Marys.

Miss Carlotta didn't want to go into Nancy's room. She stood in the hallway with her arms folded.

"Bruises on her, Miss Carl. On her arms and legs. Did she have a bad tumble?"

"She had the first attack on the stairs, Mr. Lonigan."

But boy, had he wished his dad was still around. His dad had known how to handle the old families.

"Now, you tell me, Rita Mae. Why the hell wasn't she in a hospital? This isn't 1842! This is now. Now I'm asking you."

"Some people want to be at home, Jerry," Rita said. Didn't he have a signed death certificate?

Yes, he did. Of course he did. But he hated these old families.

155

"You never know what they're going to do," he swore. "Not just the Mayfairs, I mean any of the old ones."

Sometimes the relatives trooped into the viewing room and started right in working on the corpse with their own powder and lipstick. Now, nobody with any sense did that kind of thing anymore.

And what about those old Irish guys who'd laugh and joke while they were acting as pallbearers. One would let his end of the coffin go just so his brother would get the full weight of it—prancing around on the graveyard path like it was Mardi Gras.

And the stories the old ones told at the wake could make you sick. Old Sister Bridget Marie the other night downstairs telling about coming over on the boat from Ireland: The mama said to the baby in the bassinet, "If you don't stop crying, I'll throw you overboard." Then she tells her little boy to watch the baby. Little while she comes back. The baby's gone out of the bassinet. The little boy says, "He started crying again. So I threw him overboard."

Now, what kind of a story is that to tell when you're sitting right beside the coffin?

Rita smiled in spite of herself. She had always liked old Sister Bridget Marie.

"The Mayfairs aren't Irish," she said. "They're rich and rich people don't carry on like that."

"Oh, yes they are Irish, Rita Mae. Or Irish enough anyway to be crazy. It was the famous Irish architect Darcy Monahan who built that house, and he was the father of Miss Mary Beth. And Miss Carl is the daughter of Judge McIntyre and he was Irish as they come. Just a real old-timer. Sure they're Irish. As Irish as anybody else around here in this day and age."

She was amazed that her husband was talking this much. The Mayfairs bothered him, that was clear enough, just as they had bothered his daddy, and nobody had ever told Rita the whole story.

Rita went to the Requiem Mass at the chapel for Miss Nancy. She followed the procession in her own car. It went down First Street to pass the old house, out of respect for Deirdre. But there was no sign Deirdre even saw all those black limousines gliding by.

There were so many Mayfairs. Why, where in the world did they come from? Rita recognized New York voices and California voices and even southern voices from Atlanta and Alabama. And then all the ones from New Orleans! She couldn't believe it when she went over the register. Why, there were Mayfairs from uptown and downtown, and Metairie, and across the river.

There was even an Englishman there, a white-haired gentleman in a linen suit who actually carried a walking stick. He hung back with Rita. "My, what a dreadfully warm day this is," he said in his elegant English voice. When Rita had tripped on the path, he'd steadied her arm. Very nice of him.

What did all these people think of that awful old house, she wondered, and of the Lafayette Cemetery with all the moldering vaults. They were crowded all through the narrow aisles, standing on tiptoe trying to see over the high tombs. Mosquitoes in the high grass. And there was one of the tour buses stopped at the gates right now. Those tourists sure loved it, all right. Well, get an eyeful!

But the big shock was the cousin who'd taken Deirdre's baby. For there she was, Ellie Mayfair from California. Jerry pointed her out while the priest was saying the final words. She had signed the register at every funeral for the last thirty years. Tall, dark-haired woman in a sleeveless blue linen dress, with beautiful suntanned skin. She wore a big white hat, like a sunbonnet, and a pair of dark glasses. Looked like a movie star. How they gathered around her. People clasping her hand. Kissing her on her powdered cheek. When they bent real close, were they asking her about Deirdre's daughter?

Rita wiped her eyes. *Rita Mae, they're going to take my baby.* Whatever had she done with that little fragment of white card with the word Talamasca on it? Was probably right here in her prayer book somewhere. She never threw anything away. Maybe she should speak to that woman, just ask her how to get in touch with Deirdre's daughter. Maybe some day that girl ought to know what Rita had to tell. But then what right had she to meddle like that? Yet if Deirdre died before Rita did, and Rita saw that woman again, well, then she'd go and ask. Nothing would stop her.

She had almost broken down right then and there, and imagine, people would have thought she was crying for old Miss Nancy. That was a laugh. She had turned around, trying to hide her face and then she'd seen that Englishman, that gentleman, staring at her. He had a real strange expression on his face, like he was worried about her crying, and then she did cry and she made a little wave to him to say, It's all right. But he came over to her anyway.

He gave her his arm, the way he had before, and helped her to walk just a little ways away and there was one of those benches so she sat down on it. When she looked up, she could have sworn Miss Carl was staring at her and at the Englishman, but

Miss Carl was real far away, and the sun was shining on her glasses. Probably couldn't see them at all.

Then the Englishman had given her a little white card and said he would like to talk to her. Whatever about, she had thought, but she took the card and put it in her pocket.

It was late that night when she found it again. She had been looking for the prayer card from the funeral. And there it was, that little card from the man and there were the same names after all these years—Talamasca and Aaron Lightner.

For a minute Rita Mae thought she was going to faint dead away. Maybe she'd made a big mistake. She hunted through her prayer book for the old card or what was left of it. Sure enough, they were the same, and on this new one, the Englishman had written in ink the name of the Monteleone Hotel downtown and his room number.

Rita found Jerry sitting up late, drinking, at the kitchen table.

"Rita Mae, you can't go talking to that man. You can't tell him anything about that family."

"But Jerry, I have to tell him what happened before, I have to tell him that Deirdre tried to get in touch with him."

"That was years and years ago, Rita Mae. That baby is grown up. She's a doctor, did you know that? She's going to be a surgeon, that's what I heard."

"I don't care, Jerry." Then Rita Mae had broken down, but even through her tears, she was doing a strange thing. She was staring at that card and memorizing everything on it. She memorized the room number of the hotel. She memorized the phone number in London.

And just as she figured, Jerry suddenly took the card and slipped it in his shirt pocket. She didn't say a word. She just kept crying. Jerry was the sweetest man in the world, but he never would understand.

He said, "You did a nice thing, going to the funeral, honey."

Rita said no more about the man. She wasn't going to go against Jerry. Well, at least at this moment her mind was not made up yet.

"But what does that girl out there in California know about her mother?" Rita said. "I mean, does she know Deirdre never wanted to give her up?"

"You have to leave it alone, honey."

There had never been a moment in Rita's life quite like that one years ago in the nuns' garden—hearing Deirdre with that man, hearing two people talk of love like that. Twilight. Rita had told Jerry about it all right, but nobody understood. You had to be there, smelling the lilies and seeing the sky like blue stained glass through the tree branches.

And to think of that girl out there, maybe never knowing what her real mother was like . . .

Jerry shook his head. He filled his glass with bourbon and drank about half of it.

"Honey, if you knew what I knew about those people."

Jerry was drinking too much bourbon all right. Rita saw that. Jerry was no gossip. A good mortician couldn't be a gossip. But he started to talk now and Rita let him.

"Honey," he said, "Deirdre never had a chance in that family. You might say she was cursed when she was born. That's what Daddy said."

Jerry had been just a grade-school kid when Deirdre's mother, Antha, died, in a fall from the porch roof outside the attic window of that house. Her skull had broken open on the patio. Deirdre was a baby then and so was Rita Mae, of course. But Jerry was already working with his daddy.

"I tell you we scraped her brains up off the flagstones. It was terrible. She was only twenty years old, and pretty! She was prettier even than Deirdre got to be. And you should have seen the trees in that yard. Honey, it was like a hurricane was happening just over that house, the way those trees were blowing. Even those stiff magnolia trees were bending and twisting."

"Yeah, I've seen them like that," Rita said, but she was quiet so he would go on talking.

"The worst part was when we got back here and Daddy had a good look at Antha. He said right away, 'See these scratches around her eyes. Now that never happened in the fall. There were no trees under that window.' And then Daddy found out one of the eyes was torn right out of the socket. Now Daddy knew what to do in those situations.

"He got right on the phone to Dr. Fitzroy. He said he thought there ought to be an autopsy. And he stood his ground when Dr. Fitzroy argued with him. Finally Dr. Fitzroy came clean that Antha Mayfair had gone out of her mind and tried to scratch her own eyes out. Miss Carl tried to stop her and that's when Antha had run up to the attic. She fell, all right, but she was clean out of her head when it happened. And Miss Carl had seen the whole thing. And there was no reason in the world for people to be talking about it, for it to get into the newspapers. Hadn't that family had enough pain, what with Stella? Dr. Fitzroy said for Daddy to call over to the priest house at St. Alphonsus and talk to the pastor if he still wasn't sure about it.

" 'Sure doesn't look self-inflicted to me,' Daddy said, 'but if you're willing to sign the death certificate on this one, well, I guess I've done what I can.' And there never was any autopsy. But Daddy knew what he was talking about.

" 'Course he made me swear I'd never tell a living soul about it. I was real close to Daddy then, already a big help to him. He knew he could trust me. And I'm trusting you now, Rita Mae.''

"Oh, what an awful thing," Rita whispered, "to scratch her own eyes out." She prayed Deirdre had never known.

"Well, you haven't heard all of it," Jerry said, taking another drink of his bourbon. "When we went to cleaning her up, we found the emerald necklace on her—the same one Deirdre wears now—the famous Mayfair emerald. The chain was twisted around her neck, and the thing was caught in her hair in back. It was covered with blood and God knows what else was on it. Well, even Daddy was shocked, with all he'd seen in this world, picking the hair and the splinters of bone out of that thing. He said, 'And this is not the first time I've had to clean the blood off this necklace.' The time before that, he'd found it around the neck of Stella Mayfair, Antha's mother.''

Rita remembered the long-ago day at St. Ro's, the necklace in Deirdre's hand. And many years later, Mr. Lonigan showing her Stella's name on the gravestone.

"And Stella was the one shot by her own brother.''

"Yes, and that was a terrible thing, to hear Daddy tell it. Stella was the wild one of that generation. Even before her mother died, she filled that old house with lights, with parties going on night after night, with the bootleg booze flowing and the musicians playing. Lord only knows what Miss Carl and Miss Millie and Miss Belle thought of all that. But when she started bringing her men home, that's when Lionel took matters into his own hands and shot her. Jealous of her is what he was. Right in front of everybody in the parlor, he said, 'I'll kill you before I let *him* have you.' ''

"Now what are you telling me," Rita said. "It was brother and sister going to bed together?''

"Could have been, honey," Jerry said. "Could have been. Nobody ever knew the name of Antha's father. Could have been Lionel for all anybody knew. They even said . . . But Stella didn't care what anybody thought. They said when she was carrying Antha, she invited all her lady friends to come up there for a big party. Never bothered Stella that she had that baby out of wedlock.''

"Well, that's the damnedest thing I ever heard," Rita Mae whispered. "Especially in those days, Jerry.''

"That's the way it was, honey. And it wasn't just from Daddy

I heard about some of those things either. Lionel shot Stella in the head, and everybody in the house went just plain wild, breaking out the windows to the porches to get out of there. Regular panic. And don't you know that little Antha was upstairs, and she came down during all that commotion, and seen her mother lying there dead on the living room floor."

Rita shook her head. What had Deirdre said on that long-ago afternoon? *And they said her mother died when she was young, too, but they never talk about her.*

"Lionel ended up in a straitjacket after he shot Stella. Daddy always said the guilt drove him out of his mind. He kept screaming the devil wouldn't leave him alone, that his sister had been a witch and she'd sent the devil after him. Finally died in a fit, swallowed his own tongue, and no one there to help him. They opened up the padded cell and there he was, dead, and turning black already. But at least that time the corpse came all neatly sewn up from the coroner. It was the scratches on Antha's face twelve years later that always haunted Daddy."

"Poor Dee Dee. She must have known some of it."

"Yeah," Jerry said, "even a little baby knows things. You know they do! And when Daddy and I went to get Antha's body out of that yard, we could hear little Deirdre just wailing away in there as if she could feel it that her mother was dead. And nobody picking up that child, nobody comforting her. I tell you, that little girl was born under a curse. Never had a chance with all the goings-on in that family. That's why they sent her baby daughter out west, to get her away from all that, and if I were you, honey, I wouldn't meddle in it."

Rita thought of Ellie Mayfair, so pretty. Probably on a plane right this minute for San Francisco.

"They say those California people are rich," Jerry said. "Deirdre's nurse told me that. That girl's got her own private yacht out there on San Francisco Bay, tied right up to the front porch of her house on the water. Father's a big lawyer out there, a real mean son-of-a-bitch, but he makes plenty. If there's a curse on the Mayfairs, that girl got away from it."

"Jerry, you don't believe in curses," Rita said, "and you know it."

"Honey, think about the emerald necklace just for a minute. Two times Daddy cleaned the blood off it. And it always sounded to me like Miss Carlotta herself thought there was a curse on it. First time Daddy cleaned it up—when Stella got shot, you know what Miss Carlotta wanted Daddy to do? Put the necklace in the coffin with Stella. Daddy told me that. I know that for a fact. And Daddy refused to do it."

"Well, maybe it's not real, Jerry."

"Hell, Rita Mae, you could buy a block of downtown Canal Street with that emerald. Daddy had Hershman from Magazine Street appraise it. I mean here he was with Miss Carlotta telling him things like 'It is my express wish that you put it in the coffin with my sister.' So he calls Hershman, I mean he and Hershman were always good friends, and Hershman said it was real, all right, the finest emerald he'd ever laid eyes on. Wouldn't even know how to put a price on it. He'd have to take a jewel like that to New York for a real evaluation. He said it was the same with all the Mayfair jewels. He'd cleaned them once for Miss Mary Beth before she even passed them on to Stella. He said jewels like that ended up on display in a museum."

"Well, what did Red say to Miss Carlotta?"

"Told Miss Carlotta no, he wasn't putting any million-dollar emerald in a casket. He cleaned it all off with rubbing alcohol and got a velvet case for it from Hershman and then he took it over to her. Same as we did together years later when Antha fell from the window. Miss Carl didn't ask us to bury it that time. And she didn't demand to have the funeral in the parlor neither."

"In the parlor!"

"Well, that's where Stella was laid out, Rita Mae, right there in that house. They always did that in the old days. Old Julien Mayfair was buried from the parlor and so was Miss Mary Beth and that was 1925. And that's the way that Stella had said it was to be done. She'd left that word in her will, and so they did it. But with Antha nothing like that happened. We brought that necklace back, Daddy and me together. I came in with Daddy and there Miss Carl was in that double parlor with no lights on and it being so dark in there with the porches and the trees and all, and there she was just sitting there, rocking little Deirdre in the cradle beside her. I went in with Daddy and he put the necklace in her hand. And you know what she did? She said, 'Thank you, Red Lonigan.' And she turned and put that jewel case in the cradle with the baby."

"But why did she do that?"

" 'Cause it was Deirdre's, that's why. Miss Carl never had no right to any of those jewels. Miss Mary Beth left them to Stella, and Stella named Antha to get them, and Antha's only daughter was Deirdre. It's always been that way, they all pass to one daughter."

"Well, what if the necklace is cursed," Rita said. Lord, to think of it around Deirdre's neck and Deirdre the way she was now. Oh, Rita could hardly stand to think of it.

"Well, if it's cursed, maybe the house is too," Jerry said, "because the jewels go with the house, and lots of other money."

"You mean to tell me, Jerry Lonigan, that house belongs to Deirdre?"

"Rita, everybody knows that. How come you don't know that?"

"You're telling me that house is hers, and those women lived in it all those years when she was locked up and then they brought her home like that, and she sits there and—"

"Now, don't get hysterical, Rita Mae. But that's what I'm telling you. It's Deirdre's, same as it was Antha's and Stella's. And it will pass to that California daughter when Deirdre dies, unless somebody managed to change all those old papers and I don't think you can change a thing like that. It goes way back, the will—back to times when they had the plantation, and times before that, when they were in the islands, you know, in Haiti, before they ever came here. A legacy is what they call it. And I remember Hershman used to say that Miss Carl started law school when she was a girl just to learn how to crack the legacy. But she never could. Even before Miss Mary Beth died, everybody knew Stella was the heiress."

"But what if that California girl doesn't know about it?"

"It's the law, honey. And Miss Carlotta, no matter whatever else she is, is a good lawyer. Besides, it's tied with the name, Mayfair. You have to go by the name or you can't inherit anything from the legacy. And that girl goes by the name of Mayfair. I heard that when she was born. So does her adopted mother, Ellie Mayfair, the one that came today and signed the register. They know. People always know when they're coming into money. And besides, the other Mayfairs would tell her. Ryan Mayfair would tell her. He's Cortland's grandson and Cortland loved Deirdre; he really did. He was real old by the time Deirdre had to give up the baby, and the way I heard it, he was against it all the way, lot of good it did. I heard he really took on Miss Carlotta about that baby, said it would drive Deirdre crazy to give it up, and Miss Carlotta said Deirdre was already crazy. A lot of good it did."

Jerry finished his bourbon. He poured another glass.

"But Jerry, what if there are other things that Deirdre's daughter doesn't know?" Rita asked. "Why didn't she come down here today? Why didn't she want to see her mother?"

Rita Mae, they're going to take my baby!

Jerry didn't answer. His eyes were bloodshot. He was over the hill with the bourbon.

"Daddy knew a lot more about those people," he said, his

words slurred now. "More than he ever told me. One thing Daddy did say, though, that they were right to take Deirdre's baby away from her and give it to Ellie Mayfair, for the baby's sake. And Daddy told me something else too. Daddy told me Ellie Mayfair couldn't have babies of her own, and her husband was real disappointed over that, and about to leave her when Miss Carl rang her up long distance and asked if they wanted to have Deirdre's baby. 'Don't tell Rita Mae all that,' Daddy said, 'but for everybody it was a blessing. And old Mr. Cortland, God rest his soul, he was wrong.' "

Rita Mae knew what she was going to do. She had never lied to Jerry Lonigan in her life. She just didn't tell him. The next afternoon, she called the Monteleone Hotel. The Englishman had just checked out! But they thought he might still be in the lobby.

Rita Mae's heart was pounding as she waited.

"This is Aaron Lightner. Yes, Mrs. Lonigan. Please take a taxi down and I shall pay the fare. I'll be waiting."

It made her so nervous she was stumbling over her words, forgetting things as she rushed out of the house and having to go back for them. But she was glad she was doing this! Even if Jerry had caught her then, she would have gone on with it.

The Englishman took her round the corner to the Desire Oyster Bar, a pretty place with ceiling fans and big mirrors and doors open along Bourbon Street. It seemed exotic to Rita the way the Quarter always had. She almost never got to go down there.

They sat at a marble-top table, and she had a glass of white wine because that's what the Englishman had and it sounded very nice to her. What a good-looking man he was. With a man like that it didn't matter about his age, he was handsomer than younger men. It made her slightly nervous to sit so close to him. And the way his eyes fixed her, it made her melt as if she was a kid again in high school.

"Talk to me, Mrs. Lonigan," he said. "I'll listen."

She tried to take it slow, but once she started it just came pouring out of her. Soon she was crying, and he probably couldn't understand a word she was saying. She gave him that old, twisted little bit of card. She told about the ads she'd run, and how she'd told Deirdre that she could never find him.

Then came the difficult part. "There are things that girl in California doesn't know! That property's hers, and maybe the lawyers will tell her that, but what about the curse, Mr. Lightner? I'm putting my trust in you, I'm telling you things my husband doesn't want me to tell a living soul. But if Deirdre put her trust in you back then, well, that's enough for me. I'm telling you, the jewels and the house are cursed.''

Finally, she told him everything. She told him all that Jerry had told her. She told him all that Red had ever said. She told him anything and everything she could remember.

And the funny thing was that he was never surprised or shocked. And over and over again, he assured her that he would do his best to get this information to the girl in California.

When it was all said, and she sat there wiping her nose, her white wine untouched, the man asked her if she would keep his card, if she would call him when there was any "change" with Deirdre. If she could not reach him she was to leave a message. The people who answered the phone would understand. She need only say it was in connection with Deirdre Mayfair.

She took her prayer book out of her purse. "Give me those numbers again," she said, and she wrote down the words, "In connection with Deirdre Mayfair."

Only after she had written it all out, did she think to ask, "But tell me, Mr. Lightner, how did you come to know Deirdre?"

"It's a long story, Mrs. Lonigan," he said. "You might say I've been watching that family for years. I have two paintings done by Deirdre's father, Sean Lacy. One of them is of Antha. He was the one who was killed on the highway in New York before Deirdre was born.''

"He was killed on the highway? I never knew.''

"It's doubtful anyone down here ever did," he said. "Quite a painter he was. He did a beautiful portrait of Antha with the famous emerald necklace. I came by it through a New York dealer some years after both of them were dead. Deirdre was probably ten years old by that time. I didn't meet her until she went off to college.''

"That's a funny thing, about Deirdre's father going off the road," she said. "It's just what happened to Deirdre's boyfriend too, the man she was going to marry. Did you know that? That he went off the river road when he was driving down to New Orleans?''

She thought she saw a little change in the Englishman's face then, but she couldn't be sure. Seemed his eyes got smaller for just a second.

"Yes, I did know," he said. He seemed to be thinking about things he didn't want to tell her. Then he started talking again. "Mrs. Lonigan, will you promise me something?''

"What is it, Mr. Lightner?''

"If something should happen, something wholly unexpected, and the daughter from California should come home, please don't try to talk to her. Call me instead. Call me any time day or night, and I promise I shall be here as soon as I can get a plane out of London."

"You mean I shouldn't tell her these things myself, that's what you're saying?"

"Yes," he answered, very serious-like, touching her hand for the first time but in a very gentlemanly way that was completely proper. "Don't go to that house again, especially not if the daughter is there. I promise you that if I cannot come myself, someone else will come, someone else who will accomplish what we want done, someone quite familiar with the whole story."

"Oh, that would be a big load off my mind," Rita said. She sure didn't want to talk to that girl, a total stranger, and try to tell her all these things. But suddenly the whole thing began to puzzle her. For the first time she started wondering—who was this nice man? Was she wrong to trust him?

"You can trust me, Mrs. Lonigan," he said, just as if he knew what she was thinking. "Please be certain of it. And I've met Deirdre's daughter, and I know that she is a rather quiet and—well, shall we say—forbidding individual. Not an easy person to talk to, if you understand. But I think I can explain things to her."

Well, now, that made perfect sense.

"Sure, Mr. Lightner."

He was looking at her. Maybe he knew how confused she was, how strange the whole afternoon seemed, all this talk of curses and things, and dead people and that weird old necklace.

"Yes, they are very strange," he said.

Rita laughed. "It was like you read my mind," she said.

"Don't worry anymore," he said. "I'll see that Rowan Mayfair knows her mother didn't want to give her up; I'll see she knows all that you want her to know. I owe that much to Deirdre, don't you think? I wish I'd been there when she needed me."

Well, that was plenty enough for Rita.

Every Sunday after that, when Rita was at Mass, she flipped to the back of her prayer book and looked at the phone number for the man in London. She read those words "In connection with Deirdre Mayfair." Then she said a prayer for Deirdre, and it didn't seem wrong that it was the prayer for the dead, it seemed to be the right one for the occasion.

"May perpetual light shine upon her, O Lord, and may she rest in peace, Amen."

And now it was over twelve years since Deirdre had taken her place on the porch, over a year since the Englishman had come and gone—and they were talking of putting Deirdre away again. It was her house that was tumbling down all around her in that sad overgrown garden and they were going to lock her away again.

Maybe Rita should call that man. Maybe she should tell him. She just didn't know.

"It's the wise thing, them putting her away," Jerry said, "before Miss Carl is too far gone to make the decision. And the fact is, well, I hate to say it, honey. But Deirdre's going down fast. They say she's dying."

Dying.

She waited till Jerry had gone to work. Then she made the call. She knew it would show on the bill, and she probably would have to say something eventually to Jerry. But it didn't matter. What mattered now was getting the operator to understand that she had to call a number all the way across the ocean.

It was a nice woman who answered over there, and they did reverse the charges just as the Englishman had promised. At first Rita couldn't understand everything the woman said—she spoke so fast—but then it came out that Mr. Lightner was in the United States. He was out in San Francisco. The woman would call him right away. Would Rita care to leave her number?

"Oh, no. I don't want him to call here," she said. "You just tell him this for me. It's real important. That Rita Mae Lonigan called in connection with Deirdre Mayfair. Can you write that down? Tell him that Deirdre Mayfair is very sick; that Deirdre Mayfair is going down fast. That maybe Deirdre Mayfair is dying."

It took the breath out of Rita to say that last word. She couldn't say any more after that. She tried to answer clearly when the woman repeated the message. The woman would call Mr. Lightner right away at the St. Francis Hotel in San Francisco. Rita was in tears when she put down the phone.

That night she dreamed of Deirdre, but she could remember nothing when she woke up, except that Deirdre was there, and it was twilight, and the wind was blowing in the trees behind St. Rose de Lima's. When she opened her eyes, she thought of wind blowing through trees. She heard Jerry tell of how it had been when they went to get the body of Antha. She remembered the storm in the trees that horrible day when she and Miss Carl had fought for the little card that said Talamasca. Wind in the trees in the garden behind St. Rose de Lima's.

Rita got up and went to early Mass. She went to the shrine of the Blessed Virgin and lighted a candle. Please let Mr. Lightner come, she prayed. Please let him talk to Deirdre's daughter.

And she realized as she prayed that it was not the inheritance that worried her, or the curse upon that beautiful emerald necklace. For Rita did not believe Miss Carl had it in her to break the law, no matter how mean Miss Carl was; and Rita did not believe that curses really existed.

What she believed in was the love she felt in her heart of hearts for Deirdre Mayfair.

And she believed a child had a right to know that her mother had once been the sweetest and kindest of creatures, a girl that everybody loved—a beautiful girl in the spring of 1957 when a handsome, elegant man in a twilight garden had called her *My beloved.*

Six

HE STOOD IN the shower ten full minutes, but he was still drunk as hell. Then he cut himself twice with the razor. Nothing major, just a clear indication that he had to play it very careful with this lady who was coming here, this doctor, this mysterious someone who'd pulled him out of the sea.

Aunt Viv helped him with the shirt. He took another quick swallow of the coffee. Tasted awful to him, though it was good coffee, he'd brewed it himself. A beer was what he wanted. Not to have a beer right now was like not breathing. But it was just too great a risk.

"But what are you going to do in New Orleans?" Aunt Viv asked plaintively. Her small blue eyes looked watery, sore. She straightened the lapels of his khaki jacket with her thin, gnarled hands. "Are you sure you don't need a heavier coat?"

"Aunt Viv, it's New Orleans in August." He kissed her forehead. "Don't worry about me," he said. "I'm doing great."

"Michael, I don't understand why . . ."

"Aunt Viv, I am going to call you when I get there, I swear. And you've got the number of the Pontchartrain if you want to call and leave a message before that."

He had asked for that very suite she had had years ago, when he'd been an eleven-year-old boy and he and his mother had gone to see her—that big suite over St. Charles Avenue with the baby grand piano in it. Yes, they knew the suite he wanted. And yes, he could have it. And yes, the baby grand piano was still there.

Then the airline had confirmed him in first class, with an aisle seat, at six A.M. No problem. Just one thing after another falling into place.

And all of it thanks to Dr. Morris, and this mysterious Dr. Mayfair, who was on her way now.

He'd been furious when he first heard she was a doctor. "So that's why the secrecy," he'd said to Morris. "We don't disturb other doctors, do we? We don't give out their home numbers. You know this ought to be a matter of public record, I ought to—"

But Morris had silenced him quickly enough.

"Michael, the lady is driving over to pick you up. She knows you're drunk and she knows you're crazy. Yet she is taking you home with her to Tiburon, and she's going to let you crawl around on her boat."

"All right," he'd said. "I'm grateful, you know I am."

"Then get out of bed, take a shower and shave."

Done! And now nothing was going to stop him from making this journey, that's why he was leaving the lady's house in Tiburon and going straight to the airport where he'd doze in a plastic chair, if he had to, till the plane for New Orleans left.

"But Michael, what is the reason for all this?" Aunt Viv persisted. "That is what I simply cannot understand." She seemed to float against the light from the hallway, a tiny woman in sagging blue silk, her gray hair nothing but wisps now in spite of the neat curls and the pins in it, insubstantial as that spun glass they would put on the Christmas trees in the old days, what they had called angel hair.

"I won't stay long, I promise," he said tenderly. But a sense of foreboding caught him suddenly. He had the distinct awareness—that free-floating telepathy—that he was never going to live in this house again. No, couldn't be accurate. Just the alcohol simmering inside him, making him crazy, and months of pure isolation—why, that was enough to drive anyone insane. He kissed her on her soft cheek.

"I have to check my suitcase," he said. He took another swallow of coffee. He was getting better. He polished his horn-rimmed glasses carefully, put them back on, and checked for the extra pair in his jacket pocket.

"I packed everything," Aunt Viv said, with a little shake of

169

her head. She stood beside him over the open suitcase, one gnarled finger pointing to the neatly folded garments. "Your lightweight suits, both of them, your shaving kit. It's all there. Oh, and your raincoat. Don't forget your raincoat, Michael. It's always raining in New Orleans."

"Got it, Aunt Viv, don't worry." He closed the suitcase and snapped the locks. Didn't bother to tell her the raincoat had been ruined because he drowned in it. The famous Burberry had been made for the wartime trenches, perhaps, but not for drowning. Wool lining a total loss.

He ran his comb through his hair, hating the feel of his gloves. He didn't look drunk, unless of course he was too drunk to see it. He looked at the coffee. Drink the rest of it, you idiot. This woman is making a house call just to humor a crackpot. The least you can do is not fall down your own front steps.

"Was that the doorbell?" He picked up the suitcase. Yes, ready, quite ready to leave here.

And then that foreboding again. What was it, a premonition? He looked at the room—the striped wallpaper, the gleaming woodwork that he had so patiently stripped and then painted, the small fireplace in which he had laid the Spanish tiles himself. He was never going to enjoy any of it again. He would never again lie in that brass bed. Or look out through the pongee curtains on the distant phantom lights of downtown.

He felt a leaden sadness, as if he were in mourning. In fact, it was the very same sadness he had felt after the deaths of those he loved.

Aunt Viv hurried down the hallway, ankles painfully swollen, hand wandering, then catching the button of the intercom and holding it fast.

"May I help you, please."

"This is Dr. Rowan Mayfair. I'm here to see Michael Curry?"

God, it was happening. He was rising from the dead again. "I'll be right there," he said.

"Don't come all the way down with me, Aunt Viv." Once again he kissed her. If only he could shake this foreboding. What would become of her if something happened to him? "I'll be back soon, I promise you." Impulsively he held her tight to him for a long moment before letting her go.

Then he was rushing down the two flights, whistling a little, so good it felt to be moving, to be on his way. He almost opened the door without checking for reporters; then he stopped and peered through a small round faceted crystal set in the middle of the rectangle of stained glass.

A tall gazelle of a woman stood at the foot of the stairway, her profile to him, as she looked off down the street. She had long blue-jean legs and wavy blond pageboy hair blowing softly against the hollow of her cheek.

Young and fresh she looked, and effortlessly seductive in a tightly fitted and tapering navy blue peacoat, the collar of her cable-knit sweater rolled at the neck.

Nobody had to tell him she was Dr. Mayfair. And a sudden warmth rose in his loins and coursed through him, causing his face to burn. He would have found her alluring and interesting to look at, no matter where or when he saw her. But to know she was *the one* overpowered him. He was thankful she wasn't looking up at the door and would not see his shadow perhaps against the glass.

This is the woman who brought me back, he thought, quite literally, vaguely thrilled by the warmth building, by the raw feeling of submissiveness mingling in him with an almost brutal desire to touch, to know, perhaps to possess. The mechanics of the rescue had been described to him numerous times—mouth-to-mouth, alternating with heart massage. He thought of her hands on him now, of her mouth on his mouth. It seemed brutal suddenly that after such intimacy they had been separated for so long. He felt resentment again. But that didn't matter now.

Even in her profile he could see dimly the face he remembered, a face of taut skin and subtle prettiness, with deep-set, faintly luminous gray eyes. And how beguiling her posture seemed, so frankly casual and downright masculine—the way she leaned on the banister, with one foot on the bottom step.

The feeling of helplessness in him grew oddly and surprisingly sharper, and just as strong came the inevitable drive to conquer. No time to analyze it, and frankly he didn't want to. He knew that he was happy suddenly, happy for the first time since the accident.

The searing wind of the sea came back to him, the lights flashing in his face. Coast Guard men coming down the ladder like angels from fog heaven. *No, don't let them take me!* And her voice next to him. "You're going to be all right."

Yes, go out. Talk to her. This is the closest you'll ever get to that moment; this is your chance. And how delicious to be so physically drawn to her, so laid bare by her presence. It was as if an invisible hand were unzipping his pants.

Quickly he glanced up and down the street. No one about but a lone man in a doorway—the man in fact at whom Dr. Mayfair was staring rather fixedly—and surely that could not possibly be a reporter, not that white-haired old fellow in the three-piece tweed, gripping his umbrella as if it were a walking stick.

171

Yet it was odd the way Dr. Mayfair continued to stare at the man, and the way that the man was staring back at her. Both figures were motionless, as if this were perfectly normal when of course it was not.

Something Aunt Viv had said hours ago came back to Michael, something about an Englishman come all the way from London to see him. And that man certainly looked like an Englishman, a very unfortunate one who had made a long journey in vain.

Michael turned the knob. The Englishman made no move to pounce, though he stared at Michael now as intently as ever he'd stared at Dr. Mayfair. Michael stepped out and shut the door.

Then he forgot all about the Englishman. Because Dr. Mayfair turned and a lovely smile illuminated her face. In a flash he recognized the beautifully drawn ash-blond eyebrows and the thick dark lashes that made her eyes seem all the more brilliantly gray.

"Mr. Curry," she said, in a deep, husky, and perfectly gorgeous voice. "So we meet again." She stretched out her long right hand to greet him as he came down the steps towards her. And it seemed perfectly natural the way that she scanned him from head to toe.

"Dr. Mayfair, thank you for coming," he said, squeezing her hand, then letting it go instantly, ashamed of his gloves. "You've resuscitated me again. I was dying up there in that room."

"I know," she said. "And you brought this suitcase because we're going to fall in love and you're going to live with me from now on?"

He laughed. The huskiness of her voice was a trait he adored in women, all too rare, and always magical. And he did not remember that little aspect of it from the deck of the boat.

"Oh, no, I'm sorry, Dr. Mayfair," he said. "I mean I . . . but I have to get to the airport afterwards. I have to make a six A.M. plane to New Orleans. I have to do that. I figured I'd take a cab from there, I mean wherever we're going and, because if I come back here—"

And there it was again; *never live in this house again.* He looked up at the high bay windows, at the gingerbread millwork, so carefully restored. It didn't seem to be his house now, this narrow, forlorn structure, its windows full of the dull gleam of the colorless night.

He felt vague for a moment as though he were losing the thread of things. "I'm sorry," he whispered. He *had* lost the thread. He could have sworn he was in New Orleans just now. He was dizzy. He had been in the midst of something, and there had been a great lovely intensity. And now there was only the dampness here, the thick overhanging sky, and the strong knowledge that all the years of waiting were finished, that something for which he'd been prepared was about to begin.

He realized he was looking at Dr. Mayfair. She was almost as tall as he was, and she was gazing at him steadily, in a wholly unself-conscious way. She was looking at him as if she enjoyed it, found him handsome or interesting, or maybe even both. He smiled, because he liked looking at her too, suddenly, and he was so glad, more glad than he dared tell her, that she had come.

She took his arm.

"Come on, Mr. Curry," she said. She turned long enough to throw a slow and slightly hard glance at the distant Englishman, and then she tugged Michael after her uphill to the door of a dark green Jaguar sedan. She unlocked the door, and taking the suitcase from Michael before he could think to stop her, she heaved it in the backseat.

"Get in," she said. Then she shut the door.

Caramel leather. Beautiful old-fashioned wooden dashboard. He glanced over his shoulder. The Englishman was still watching.

"That's strange," he said.

She had the key in the ignition before her door was closed.

"What's strange? You know him?"

"No, but I think he came here to see me . . . I think he's an Englishman . . . and he never even moved when I came out."

This startled her. She looked puzzled, but it didn't stop her from lurching out of the parking place and into a near impossible U-turn, before she drove past the Englishman with another pointed glance.

Again, Michael felt the passion stirring. There was a tremendous habitual forcefulness in the way she drove. He liked the sight of her long hands on the gear shift and the little leather-clad wheel. The double-breasted coat hugged her tightly and a deep bang of yellow hair had fallen over her right eye.

"I could swear I've seen that man before," she said half under her breath.

He laughed, not at what she'd just said but at the way she was driving as she made a lightning-speed right turn and plummeted down Castro Street through the blowing fog.

It felt like a roller-coaster ride to him. He buckled up his seat belt because he was going to go through the windshield if he didn't and then realized as she roared through the first stop sign that he was getting sick.

"Are you sure you want to go to New Orleans, Mr. Curry?"

she asked. "You don't look like you feel up to it. What time is your plane?"

"I have to go to New Orleans," he said. "I have to go home. I'm sorry, I know I don't make sense. You know it's just these feelings, they come at random. They take possession. I thought it was all the hands, but it isn't. You heard about my hands, Dr. Mayfair? I'm wrecked, I tell you, absolutely wrecked. Look, I want you to do something for me. There's a liquor store up here, on the left, just past Eighteenth Street, would you please stop?"

"Mr. Curry . . ."

"Dr. Mayfair, I'm going to get sick all over your gorgeous car."

She pulled in across from the liquor store. Castro Street was swarming with the usual Friday night crowds, rather cheerful with so many lighted barroom doorways open to the mist.

"You are sick, aren't you?" she asked. She laid her hand on his shoulder, heavily and quietly. Did she feel the raw ripple of sensation passing through him? "If you're drunk they won't let you on the plane."

"Tall cans," he said, "Miller's. One six-pack. I'll space it out. Please?"

"And I'm supposed to go in there and get this poison for you?" She laughed, but it was gentle, not mean. Her deep voice had a nappy velvet feel to it. And her eyes were large and perfectly gray now in the neon light, just like the water out there.

But he was about to die.

"No, of course you're not going to go in there," he said, "I am. I don't know what I'm thinking." He looked at his leather gloves. "I've been hiding from people, my Aunt Viv's been doing things for me. I'm sorry."

"Miller's, six tall cans," she said, opening her door.

"Well, twelve."

"Twelve?"

"Dr. Mayfair, it's only eleven-thirty, the plane doesn't leave till six." He fished in his pocket for his money clip.

She waved that away and strode across the street, dodging a taxi gracefully and then disappearing into the store.

God, the nerve of me to ask her to do this, he thought, defeated. We're off to a dreadful beginning, but that wasn't entirely true. She was being too nice to him, he hadn't destroyed it all yet. And he could taste the beer already. And his stomach wasn't going to quiet down for anything else.

The thudding music from the nearby barrooms sounded too loud suddenly, and the colors of the street too vivid. The young passersby seemed to come much too close to the car. And this is what you get for three and half months of isolation, he was thinking. You're like a guy out of a jail cell.

Why, he didn't even know what today was, except it was Friday because his plane was Saturday, six A.M. He wondered if he could smoke in this car.

As soon as she put the sack in his lap, he opened it.

"That's a fifty-dollar ticket, Mr. Curry," she said, pulling out. "Having an open can of beer in a car."

"Yeah, well, if you get one, I'll pay it." He must have drunk half the can on the first swallow. And now for a moment, he was all right.

She crossed the broad six-way intersection at Market, made an illegal left turn on Seventeenth Street, and zoomed uphill.

"And the beer blunts things, is that it?" she asked.

"No, nothing blunts it," he said. "It's coming at me from everywhere."

"Is it coming at you from me?"

"Well, no. But I want to be with you, you see." He took another drink, hand out to brace himself against the dash as she made the downhill turn towards the Haight. "I'm not a complainer by nature, Dr. Mayfair," he said. "It's just that since the accident I've been living my life without any protective skin on me. I can't concentrate. I can't even read or sleep."

"I understand, Mr. Curry. When I get you home, you can go on the boat, do what you want. But I'd really like it if you'd let me fix you some food."

"It won't do any good, Dr. Mayfair. Let me ask you something, how dead was I when you picked me up?"

"Completely clinically dead, Mr. Curry. No detectable vital signs. Without intervention, irreversible biological death would have soon set in. You didn't get my letter, did you?"

"You wrote me a letter?"

"I should have come to the hospital," she said.

She drove the car like a race driver, he thought, playing out each gear until the engine was screaming before she shifted to the next.

"But I didn't say anything to you, you told that to Dr. Morris . . ."

"You said a name, a word, something, you just murmured it. I couldn't hear syllables. I heard an L sound—"

—An L sound . . . A great hush drowned out the rest of her words. He was falling. He knew on the one hand that he was in the car, that she was speaking to him, and that they had crossed Lincoln Avenue and were burrowing through Golden Gate Park towards Park Presidio Drive, but he wasn't really there. He was on the edge of a dream space where the word beginning with L meant something crucial, and something extremely complex and familiar. A throng of beings surrounded him, pressing close to him and ready to speak. The doorway . . .

He shook his head. Focus. But it was already disintegrating. He felt panic.

When she braked for the stop light at Geary Street, he was flung back against the leather seat.

"You don't operate on people's brains the way you drive this car, do you?" he asked. His face was hot all over.

"Yes, as a matter of fact, I do," she said. She started out from the light a little more slowly.

"I'm sorry," he said again. "I seem full of apologies, I've been apologizing to people since it happened. There's nothing wrong with your driving. It's me. I used to be . . . ordinary before that accident. I mean, just one of those happy people, you know . . ."

Was she nodding?

She appeared distracted when he looked at her, drawn into her own thoughts. She slowed as they approached the tollgate. The fog hung so heavily over the bridge that the traffic seemed to disappear into it.

"You want to talk to me?" she asked, eyes on the traffic vanishing ahead of them. She pulled a dollar bill out of her coat and gave it to the tollgate keeper. "You want to tell me what's been going on?"

He sighed. That seemed an impossible task. But the worst aspect of it was, if he started he wouldn't stop. "The hands, you know, I see things when I touch things, but the visions . . ."

"Tell me about the visions."

"I know what you think. You're a neurologist. You're thinking it's temporal lobe difficulty, some crap like that."

"No, that's not what I think," she said.

She was driving faster. The great ugly shape of a truck appeared ahead, its taillights like beacons. She fell into place safely behind it, pushing to fifty-five, to keep up.

He downed the rest of the beer in three quick swallows, shoved the can in the sack, and then took off his glove. They were off the bridge, and magically the fog had disappeared, as so often happened. The clear bright sky astonished him. The dark hills rose like shoulders nudging them as they climbed the Waldo Grade.

He looked down at his hand. It seemed unappealingly moist and wrinkled. When he rubbed his fingers together, a sensation passed through him which was vaguely pleasant.

176

They were cruising now at sixty miles an hour. He reached for Dr. Mayfair's hand, which rested on the gear-shift knob, long pale fingers relaxed.

She didn't move to resist him. She glanced at him, then back at the traffic ahead as they entered the tunnel. He lifted her hand off the knob and pressed his thumb into her naked palm.

A soft whispering sound enveloped him, and his vision blurred. It was as if her body had disintegrated and then surrounded him, a whirling cloud of particles. *Rowan.* He was afraid for a minute that they were going off the road. But she wasn't the one feeling this, he was, he was feeling her moist warm hand, and this throbbing heartbeat coming through it and this sense of the being at the core of this great airy presence that had enveloped him and was caressing him all over, like falling snow. The erotic arousal was so intense that he could do nothing to curb it.

Then in an obliterating flash he was in a kitchen, a dazzling modern affair with shining gadgets and appliances, and a man lay dying on the floor. Argument, screaming; but that was something that had happened moments before. These intervals of time were sliding over one another, crashing into each other. There was no up or down; no right or left. Michael was in the very middle of it. Rowan, with her stethoscope, knelt beside the dying man. *Hate you.* She closed her eyes, pulled the stethoscope out of her ears. Couldn't believe her luck that he was dying.

Then everything stopped. The traffic was slowing. She'd pulled her hand loose from Michael, and shifted with a hard, efficient motion.

It felt like skating on ice to him, the way they traveled along, turning right and right again, but it didn't matter. It was an illusion that they were in danger, and now the facts came, the things he always knew about these visions, the things that were simply there in his mind now, as if they'd always been, like his address, and his phone number, and the date of his birth.

It had been her adoptive father, and she had despised him, because she feared she was like him—decisive, fundamentally unkind and uncaring. And her life had been founded upon not being like him, but being like her adoptive mother, an easygoing, sentimental creature with a great sense of style, a woman loved by all and respected by no one.

"So what did you see?" she asked. Her face was wondrously smooth in the wash of the passing lights.

"Don't you know?" he said. "God, I wish this power would go away. I wish I had never felt it. I don't want to know these things about people."

"Tell me what did you see?"

"He died on the floor. You were glad. He didn't divorce her. She never knew he was planning to do it. He was six feet two inches tall, born in San Rafael, California, and this was his car." Now where did all that come from? And he could have gone on; he had known from the very first night that he could go on, if he was only willing to do it. "That's what I saw. Does it matter to you? Do you want me to talk about it? Why did you want me to see it, that's what I should be asking you. What good is it that I know it was your kitchen, and that when you got back from the hospital where they took him and coded him which was plain stupid because he was dead on arrival, that you sat down and ate the food he'd cooked before he'd died."

Silence, then:

"I was hungry," she whispered.

He shook himself all over. He cracked open a fresh beer. The delicious malty aroma filled the car.

"And now you don't like me very much, do you?" he asked.

She didn't respond. She was just staring at the traffic.

He was dazed by the headlights looming at him. Thank God they were turning off the main highway onto the narrow road that led into Tiburon.

"I like you a lot," she answered finally. Voice low, purring, husky.

"I'm glad," he said. "I was really afraid . . . I'm just glad. I don't know why I said all those things . . ."

"I asked you what you saw," she said simply.

He laughed, taking a deep drink of the beer.

"We're almost home," she said. "Would you slow down on the beer? It's a doctor asking."

He took another deep drink. Again the kitchen, the smell of roast in the oven, the open red wine, the two glasses.

. . . it seems brutal but there is absolutely no reason for me to subject myself to her dying, and if you choose to stay around and watch a woman die of cancer, well, then you have to ask why you want to subject yourself to that kind of thing, why you love that sort of suffering, what's wrong with you that . . .

Don't hand me that crap, not me!

Something more to it, much more. And all you have to do to see it is to keep thinking about it. *Gave you everything you ever wanted, Rowan. You know you were always the thing holding us together. I would have left a long time ago if it wasn't for you. Did Ellie ever tell you that? She lied to me. She said she could have children. She knew it was a lie. I would have packed it in if it hadn't been for you.*

They made a right turn, west, he figured, into a dark wooded street that climbed a hill and then descended. Flash of the great clear dark sky again, full of distant uninteresting stars, and across the black midnight bay, the great lovely spectacle of Sausalito tumbling down the hills to its crowded little harbor. She didn't have to tell him they were almost there.

"Let me ask you something, Dr. Mayfair."

"Yes?"

"Are you . . . are you afraid of hurting me?"

"Why do you ask that?"

"I just got the strangest idea, that you were trying . . . just now when I held your hand . . . you were trying to throw me a warning."

She didn't answer. He knew he'd shaken her with the statement.

They drove down and onto the shoreline street. Small lawns, pitched roofs barely visible above high fences, Monterey cypress trees cruelly twisted by the relentless western winds. An enclave of millionaire dwellings. He almost never saw such wonderful modern houses.

He could smell the water even more keenly than he had on the Golden Gate.

She pulled into a paved drive, and killed the motor. The lights flooded a great double redwood gate. Then went out. Of the house beyond, he could see nothing but darkness against a paler sky.

"I want something from you," she said. She sat there quietly staring forward. Her hair swung down to veil her profile as she bowed her head.

"Well, I owe you one," he answered without hesitation. He took another deep foamy drink of the beer. "What do you want?" he asked. "That I go in there and I lay my hands on the kitchen floor and tell you what happened when he died, what actually killed him?"

Another jolt. Silence in the dark cockpit of the car. He found himself sharply aware of her nearness, of the sweet clean fragrance of her skin. She turned to face him. The street lamp threw its light in yellow patches through the branches of the tree. First he thought her eyes were lowered, almost closed. Then he realized they were open and looking at him.

"Yes, that's what I want," she said. "That is the sort of thing I want."

"That's fine," he answered. "Bad luck for it to happen during an argument like that. You must have blamed yourself."

Her knee grazed his. Chills again.

"What makes you think so?"

"You can't bear the thought of hurting anyone," he said.

"That's naive."

"I may be crazy, Doctor"—he laughed—"but naive I ain't. The Currys never raised any naive children." He drank the rest of the can of beer in a long swallow. He found himself staring at the pale line of the light on her chin, her soft curling hair. Her lower lip looked full and soft and delicious to kiss . . .

"Then it's something else," she said. "Call it innocence if you like."

He scoffed at that without answering. If only she knew what was in his mind just now as he looked at her mouth, her sweet full mouth.

"And the answer to that question is yes," she said. She got out of the car.

He opened the door and stood up. "What the hell question is that?" he asked. He blushed.

She pulled his suitcase out of the back. "Oh, you know," she said.

"I do not!"

She shrugged as she started towards the gate. "You wanted to know if I would go to bed with you. The answer's yes, as I just told you."

He caught up with her as she went through the gate. A broad cement path led to the black teakwood double doors.

"Well, I wonder why the hell we even bother to talk," he said. He took the suitcase from her as she fumbled for the key.

She looked a little confused again. She gestured for him to go inside. As she took the sack of beer from him, he scarcely noticed.

The house was infinitely more beautiful than he had imagined. Countless old houses he'd known and explored. But this sort of house, this carefully crafted modern masterpiece, was something unfamiliar to him.

What he saw now was a great expanse of broad plank floor, flowing from dining room to living room to game room without division. Glass walls opened on a broad apron of wooden decking to the south and to the west and to the north, a deep roofless porch softly illuminated from above by an occasional dim floodlamp. Beyond, the bay was simply black and invisible. And the small twinkling lights of Sausalito to the west were delicate and intimate compared to the distant splendid southern view of the crowded and violently colored skyline of San Francisco.

The fog was only a thin slash of mist now against the brilliance of the night, thinning and vanishing even as he gazed at it.

He might have looked at the view forever, but the house struck him as similarly miraculous. Letting out a long sigh, he ran his hand along the tongue and groove wall, admiring the same fine inlay of the lofty ceiling beyond its heavy beams which rose steeply to a central point. All wood, beautifully grained wood, pegged and fitted and polished and preserved exquisitely. Wood framed the massive glass doors. Wood furnishings stood here and there, with dim flashes of glass or leather, chair and table legs reflected in the sheen of the floor.

In the eastern corner of the house stood the kitchen he had seen in the early flashing vision—a large alcove of dark wooden cabinets and countertops, and shining copper pots strung from overhead hooks. A kitchen to be looked at as well as worked in. Only a deep stone fireplace, with a high broad hearth—the kind of hearth you could sit on—separated this kitchen from the other rooms.

"I didn't think you'd like it," she said.

"Oh, but it's wonderful." He sighed. "It's made like a ship. I've never seen a new house so finely made."

"Can you feel it moving? It's made to move, with the water."

He walked slowly across the thick carpet of the living room. And only then saw a curving iron stairs behind the fireplace. A soft amber light fell from an open doorway above. He thought of bedrooms at once, of rooms as open as these, of lying in the dark with her and the glimmer of city lights. His face grew hot again.

He glanced at her. Had she caught this thought, the way she claimed to have caught his earlier question? Hell, any woman could have picked up on that.

She stood in the kitchen before an open refrigerator door, and for the first time in the clear white light he really saw her face. Her skin had almost an Asian smoothness, only it was too purely blond to be Asian. The skin was so tight that it made two dimples in her cheeks now when she smiled at him.

He moved towards her, keenly aware of her physical presence again, of the way the light was glancing off her hands, and the glamorous way her hair moved. When women wear their hair that way, so full and short, just sweeping the collar as it sways, it becomes a vital part of every gesture, he figured. You think of them and you think of their pretty hair.

But as she shut the refrigerator door, as the clear white light went out, he realized that through the northern glass wall of the house, far to his left and very near the front door, he could see a mammoth white cabin cruiser at anchor. A weak floodlamp illuminated its immense prow, its numerous portholes, and the dark windows of its wheelhouse.

It seemed monstrously large, an altogether impossible thing—like a whale beached on the site—grotesquely close to the soft furnishings and scattered rugs that surrounded him. A near panic rose in him. A curious dread, as though he had known a terror on the night of his rescue that was part of what he'd forgotten.

Nothing to do but go to it. Nothing to do but lay his hands on the deck. He found himself moving towards the glass doors; then he stopped, confused, and watched as she pulled backed the latch and slid the heavy glass door open.

A gust of cold salty wind struck him. He heard the creaking of the huge boat; and the weak lunar light of the flood seemed grim and distinctly unpleasant to him. Seaworthy, they had said. He could believe it when he looked at this craft. Explorers had crossed the oceans of the world in boats much smaller than that. Again, it appeared grotesque to him, frighteningly out of scale.

He stepped out on the pier, his collar blowing against his cheek, and moved towards the edge. The water was perfectly black down below, and he could smell it, smell the dank odor of inevitable dead things of the sea.

Far across the bay he could just glimpse the Sausalito lights, but the penetrating cold came between him and anything pictur-esque just now, and he realized that all he so hated in this west-ern clime was coalesced in this moment. Never the rugged winter, nor the burning summer; only this eternal chill, this eternal inhospitable harshness.

He was so glad that he would soon be home, so glad that the August heat would be there waiting for him, like a warm blan-ket. Garden District streets, trees swaying in a warm and inof-fensive wind—

But this was the boat, and this was the moment. Now to get on this thing with its portholes and its slippery-looking decks, rocking gently now against the black rubber tires nailed to the long side of the pier. He didn't like it very much, that was for certain. And he was damned glad he had on his gloves.

His life on boats had been limited exclusively to large ones—old river ferries in his boyhood, and the big powerful tourist cruisers that carried hundreds back and forth across San Fran-cisco Bay. When he looked at a boat like this all he thought about was the possibility of falling off.

He moved down the side of the thing until he had reached the back, behind the big hulking wheelhouse, and then he grabbed hold of the railing, leapt up on the side—startled for an instant by the fact that the boat dipped under his weight—and swung himself over as fast as possible onto the back deck.

She came right behind him.

He hated this, the ground moving under him! Christ, how could people stand boats! But the craft seemed stable enough now. The rails around him were high enough to give a feeling of safety. There was even a little shelter from the wind.

He peered for a moment through the glass door of the wheelhouse. Glimmer of dials, gadgets. Might as well have been the cockpit of a jet plane. Maybe a stairs in there to the cabins below deck.

Well, that was of no concern to him. It was the deck itself that mattered, for he had been out here when he was rescued.

The wind off the water was a roar in his ears. He turned and looked at her. Her face was perfectly dark against the distant lights. She took her hand out of the pocket of her coat and pointed to the boards right before her.

"Right here," she said.

"When I opened my eyes? When I breathed for the first time?"

She nodded.

He knelt down. The movement of the boat felt slow now and subtle, the only sound a faint creaking that seemed to come from no specific place. He took off his gloves, stuffed them into his pockets, and flexed his hands.

Then he laid them on the boards. Cold; wet. The flash came as always out of nowhere, severing him from the now. But it wasn't his rescue he saw, only bits and snatches of other people in the very midst of conversation and movement, Dr. Mayfair, then the hated dead man again, and with them a pretty older woman, much loved, a woman named Ellie—but this layer gave way to another, and another, and the voices were noise.

He fell forward on his knees. He was getting dizzy, but he refused to stop touching the boards. He was groping like a blind man. "For Michael," he said. "For Michael!"

And suddenly his anger over all the misery of the long wasted summer rose in him. "For Michael!" he said, while inwardly he pushed the power, he demanded that it sharpen and focus and reach for the images he wanted.

"God, give me the moment when I first breathed," he whispered. But it was like shuffling through volumes to find one simple line. Graham, Ellie, voices rising and crashing against each other. He refused to find words in his head for what he saw; he rejected it. "Give me the moment." He lay out flat with the roughened deck under his cheek.

Quite suddenly the moment seemed to burst around him, as

if the wood beneath him had caught flame. Colder than this, a more violent wind. The boat was tossing. She was bending over him; and he saw himself lying there, a dead man with a white wet face; she was pounding on his chest. "Wake up, damn you, wake up!"

His eyes opened. *Yes, what I saw, her, Rowan, yes. I'm alive, I'm here! Rowan, many things . . .* The pain in his chest had been unbearable. He could not even feel life in his hands and legs. Was that his hand, going up, grabbing her hand?

Must explain, the whole thing before . . .

Before what? He tried to cling to it, go deeper into it. Before what? But there was nothing there but her pale oval face the way he'd seen it that night, hair squashed beneath the watch cap.

Suddenly, in the now, he was pounding his fist on the deck.

"Give me your hand," he shouted.

She knelt down beside him. "Think, think of what happened at that moment when I first breathed."

But he knew already that was no good. He only saw what she saw. Himself, a dead man coming to life. A dead wet thing tossing on the deck under the blows she repeatedly applied to his chest, and then the silver slit between his lids as he opened his eyes.

For a long time he lay still, his breath coming unevenly. He knew he was miserably cold again, though nothing as cold as that terrible night, and that she was standing there, patiently waiting. He would have cried, but he was just too tired for that, too defeated. It was as if the images slammed him around when they came. He wanted just stillness. His hands were rolled into fists. He wasn't moving.

But there was something there, something he'd discovered, some little thing he hadn't known. It was about her, that in those first few seconds he'd known who she was, he'd known about her. He'd known her name was Rowan.

But how could such a conclusion be trusted? God, his soul ached from the effort. He lay defeated, angry, feeling foolish and yet belligerent. He would have cried maybe if she hadn't been there.

"Try it again," she said now.

"It's no good, it's another language. I don't know how to use it."

"Try," she said.

And he did. But he got nothing this time but the others. Flashes of sunny days, rushes of Ellie and then Graham, and others, lots of others, rays of light that would have taken him in this direction or that, the wheelhouse door banging in the wind, a tall man coming up from below, no shirt on, and Rowan. Yes, Rowan, Rowan, Rowan, Rowan there with every figure he had seen, always Rowan, and sometimes a happy Rowan. Nobody had ever been on this boat that Rowan wasn't there, too.

He rose to his knees, more confused by the second effort than the first. The knowledge of having known her on that night was only an illusion, a thin layer of her profound impression on this boat, merely mingling with the other layers through which he'd reached. Knew her maybe because he held her hand, knew her maybe because before he'd been brought back he'd known how it would be done. He would never know for sure.

But the point was he didn't know her now, and he still couldn't remember! And she was just a very patient and understanding woman, and he ought to thank her and go.

He sat up. "Damn it all," he whispered. He pulled on his gloves. He took out his handkerchief and blew his nose and then he pulled his collar up against the wind, but what good did that do with a khaki jacket?

"Come on inside," she said. She took his hand as if he were a little child. It was surprising to him how much he appreciated it. Once they were over the side of the damned wobbly slippery boat and he stood on the pier, he felt better.

"Thanks, Doctor," he said. "It was worth a try, and you let me try, and for that, I can't say thanks enough."

She slipped her arm around him. Her face was very close to his face. "Maybe it will work another time." Sense of knowing her, that below deck was a little cabin in which she often slept with his picture pasted to the mirror. Was he blushing again?

"Come inside," she said again, tugging him along.

The shelter of the house felt good. But he was too sad and tired now to think much about it. He wanted to rest. But he didn't dare. Have to get to the airport, he thought, have to gather up the suitcase and get out there, then sleep in a plastic chair. This had been one road to discovery and now it was cut, and so he was going to take the other road as fast as he could.

Glancing back at the boat, he thought that he wanted to tell *them* again that he hadn't discarded the purpose, it was just that he couldn't remember. He didn't even know if the doorway was a literal doorway. And the number, there had been a number, hadn't there? A very significant number. He leaned against the glass door, pressed his head to the glass.

"I don't want you to go," she whispered.

"No, I don't want to go either," he said, "but I have to. You see, they really do expect something of me. And they told me what it was, and I have to do what I can, and I know that going back is part of it.''

Silence.

"It was good of you to bring me here."

Silence.

"Maybe . . ."

"Maybe what?" He turned around.

She stood with her back to the lights again. She'd taken off her coat, and she looked angular and graceful in the huge cable-knit sweater, and all long legs, magnificent cheekbones, and fine narrow wrists.

"Could it be that you were supposed to forget?" she asked.

That had never occurred to him. For a moment, he didn't answer.

"Do you believe me about the visions?" he asked. "I mean, did you read what they said in the papers? It was true, that part. I mean the papers made me sound stupid, crazy. But the point is there was so much to it, so much, and . . ."

He wished he could see her face just a little better.

"I believe you," she said simply. She paused, then went on. "It's always frightening, a close call, a seeming chance thing that makes a large impact. We like to believe it was meant . . ."

"It *was* meant!"

"I was going to say that in this case the call was very close, because it was almost dark when I saw you out there. Five minutes later I might not have seen you at all, couldn't possibly have seen you."

"You're casting around for explanations, and that's very gracious of you, I really appreciate it, I do. But you see, what I do remember, the impression I mean, it's so strong that nothing like that is necessary to explain it. They were there, Dr. Mayfair. And . . ."

"What is it?"

He shook his head. "Just one of those frissons, those crazy moments when it's as if I do remember, but then it's gone. I got it out there on the deck, too. The knowledge that, yes, when I opened my eyes I did know what had happened . . . and then it was gone . . ."

"The word you spoke, the murmur . . ."

"I didn't catch it. I didn't see myself speak a word. But I'll tell you something. I think I knew your name out there. I knew who you were."

Silence.

"But I'm not sure." He turned around, bewildered. What was

he doing? Where was his suitcase, and he really did have to go, only he was so tired, and he didn't want to.

"I don't want you to go," she said again.

"You mean it? I could stay for a while?" He looked at her, at the dark shadow of her long lean figure against the distant faintly illuminated glass. "Oh, I wish I'd met you before this," he said. "I wish I . . . I like . . . I mean, it's so stupid, but you're very . . ."

He moved forward, the better to see her. Her eyes became visible, seeming very large and long for deep-set eyes, and her mouth so generous and soft. But a strange illusion occurred as he drew closer. Her face in the soft glow from beyond the walls appeared perfectly menacing and malicious. Surely it was a mistake. He wasn't making out any true expression. The figure facing him seemed to have lowered her head, to be peering up at him from beneath the fringe of her straight blond hair, in an attitude of consummate hatred.

He stopped. It had to be a mistake. Yet she stood there, quite still, either unaware of the dread he felt now, or uncaring.

Then she started towards him, moving into the dim light from the northern doorway.

How pretty and sad she looked! How could he have ever made such an error? She was about to cry. In fact, it was simply awful to see the sadness in her face, to see the sudden silent hunger and spill of emotion.

"What is it?" he whispered. He opened his arms. And at once, she pressed herself gently against him. Her breasts were large and soft against his chest. He hugged her close, enfolding her, and ran his gloved fingers up through her hair. "What is it?" he whispered again, but it wasn't really a question. It was more a little reassuring caress of words. He could feel her heart beating, her breath catching. He himself was shaking. The protective feeling aroused in him was hot, alchemizing quickly into passion.

"I don't know," she whispered. "I don't know." And now she was silently crying. She looked up, and then opening her mouth, she moved very gently into kissing him. It was as if she didn't want to do it against his will; she gave him all the time in the world to draw back. And of course he hadn't the slightest intention of doing so.

He was engulfed at once as he'd been in the car when he touched her hand, but this time it was her soft, voluptuous, and all too solid flesh that embraced him. He kissed her over and over, feeding on her neck, her cheeks, her eyes. With his gloved fingers he stroked her cheek, felt her smooth skin beneath the

187

heavy woolen sweater. God, if only he could take off the gloves, but if he took off the gloves, he'd be lost, and all passion would evaporate in that confusion. He was desperate to cling to this, desperate; and she already mistakenly believed, she was already foolishly afraid . . .

"Yes, yes, I do," he said, "how could you think I didn't want to, that I wouldn't . . . how could you believe that? Hold me, Rowan, hold me tighter. I'm here now. I'm with you, yes."

Crying, she collapsed in his arms. Her hand ripped at his belt, at the zipper of his pants, but these were clumsy, unsuccessful gestures. A soft cry came out of her. Pure pain. He couldn't endure it.

He kissed her again, kissed her neck as her head fell back. Then he picked her up and gently carried her across the room and up the iron stairs, walking slowly round curve after curve, and then into a large and dark southern bedroom. They tumbled down into the low bed. He kissed her again, smoothing her hair back, loving the feel of her even through the gloves, looking down at her closed eyes, her helpless half-open lips. As he pulled at the sweater, she struggled to help, and finally ripped it over her head, her hair beautifully tousled by it.

When he saw her breasts through the thin covering of nylon, he kissed them through the cloth, deliberately teasing himself, his tongue touching the dark circle of the nipple before he forced the cloth away. What did it feel like, the black leather touching her skin, caressing her nipples? He lifted her breasts, kissing the hot curve of them underneath—he loved this particular juicy crevice—then he sucked the nipples hard, one after the other, rubbing and gathering the flesh feverishly with the palm of his hand.

She was twisting under him, her body moving helplessly it seemed, her lips grazing his unevenly shaven chin, then all soft and sweet over his mouth, her hands slipping into his shirt and feeling his chest as if she loved the flatness of it.

She pinched his nipples as he suckled hers. He was so hard he was going to spill. He stopped, rose on his hands, and tried to catch his breath, then sank down next to her. He knew she was pulling off her jeans. He brought her close, feeling the smooth flesh of her back, then moving down to the curve of her soft clutchable and kneadable little bottom.

No waiting now, he couldn't. In a rage of impatience he took off his glasses and shoved them on the bedside table. Now she would be a lush soft blur to him, but all the physical details he'd seen were ever present in his mind. He was on top of her. Her hand moved against his crotch, unzipped his pants, and brought out his sex, roughly, slapping it as if to test its hardness—a little gesture that almost brought him over the edge. He felt the prickly curling thatch of pubic hair, the heated inner lips, and finally the tight pulsing sheath itself as he entered.

Maybe he cried out. He didn't know. She rose on the pillow, her mouth on his mouth, her arms pulling him closer to her, her pelvis clamped against him.

"Ride me hard," she whispered. It was like the slap—a sharp goad that sent his pent-up fury to the boiling point. Her fragile form, her tender bruisable flesh—it only incited him. No imagined rape he had ever committed in his secret unaccountable dream soul had ever been more brutal.

Her hips slammed against his; and dimly he saw the red flush in her face and naked breasts as she moaned. Driving into her again and again, he saw her arms flung out, limp, just before he closed his eyes and exploded inside her.

Finally, exhausted, they tumbled apart into the soft flannel sheets. Her hot limbs were tangled under his outstretched arm, his face buried in her fragrant hair. She snuggled close. She drew the loose neglected sheet over them both; she turned towards him and nuzzled into his neck.

Let the plane wait, let his purpose wait. Let the pain go and the agitation. In any other time and place, he would have found her irresistible. But now she was more than that, more than succulent, and hot and full of mystery and seemingly perfect fire. She was something divine, and he needed it so it saddened him.

Her tender silky arm slid up around his neck as he gathered her to himself. He could hear her heart beating against him.

Long moments later, swinging perilously close to deep sleep, he sat up with a start, and groggily stripped off his hot clothes. Then he lay naked with her, except for the gloves, his limbs against her limbs, breathing her warmth and hearing her soft drowsy sigh like a kiss, as he fell to dreaming beside her.

"Rowan," he whispered. Yes, knew all about her, knew her.

They were downstairs. They said, Wake, Michael, come down. They had lighted a great fire in the fireplace. Or was it simply a fire around them, like a forest blazing? He thought he heard the sound of drums. *Michael*. Faint dream or memory of the Comus parade that long-ago winter night, of the bands beating the fierce, dreadful cadence while the flambeaux flickered on the branches of the oak trees. They were there, downstairs, all he had to do was wake up and go down. But for the first time in all

189

these weeks since they'd left him, he didn't want to see them, he didn't want to remember.

He sat up, staring at the pale milky morning sky. He was sweating, and his heart was pounding.

Stillness; too early for the sun. He picked up his glasses and put them on.

There was no one in this house, no drums, no smell of fire. No one at all, except the two of them, but she was no longer in the bed at his side. He could hear the rafters and the pilings singing, but it was only the water making them sing. Then came a deep vibrant sound, more a tremor than a noise at all, and he knew it was the big cruiser rocking in its mooring. That ghastly leviathan saying *I am here*.

He sat for a moment, staring dully at the Spartan furnishings. All well made of the same beautiful fine grain wood he had seen downstairs. Someone lived here who loved fine wood, who loved things put together perfectly. Everything quite low in this room—the bed, the desk, the scattered chairs. Nothing to interrupt the view from the windows that rose all the way to the ceiling.

But he was smelling a fire. Yes, and when he listened carefully he could hear it. And a robe had been set out for him, a nice thick white terry-cloth robe, just the kind he loved.

He put on the robe and went down the stairs in search of her.

The fire was blazing, on that account he'd been right. But no horde of dream beings hovered around it. She sat alone, legs crossed, on the deep stone hearth, in a robe of her own, her thin limbs almost lost in its folds, and again she was shaking and crying.

"I'm sorry, Michael. I'm so sorry," she whispered in that deep velvety voice. Her face was streaked and weary.

"Now, honey, why would you say a thing like that?" he asked. He sat beside her, enfolding her in his arms. "Rowan, what in the world are you sorry for?"

In a rush her words came, spilling so fast he could scarcely follow—that she had placed this immense demand upon him, that she had wanted so to be with him, that the last few months had been the worst of her life, and that her loneliness had been almost unbearable.

Again and again he kissed her cheek.

"I like being with you," he said. "I want to be here. I don't want be any place in the world . . ."

He stopped, he thought of the New Orleans plane. Well, that could wait. And awkwardly he tried to explained that he'd been trapped in the house on Liberty Street.

"I didn't come because I knew this would happen," she said,

"and you were right, I wanted to know, I wanted you to touch my hand with your hands, to touch the kitchen floor, there, where he died, I wanted . . . you see, I'm not what I appear to be . . ."

"I know what you are," he said. "A very strong person for whom any admission of need is a terrible thing."

Silence. She nodded. "If only that were all of it," she said. Tears overflowing.

"Talk to me, tell me the story," he said.

She slipped out of his arms and stood up. She walked barefoot back and forth across the floor, oblivious apparently to its coldness. Again, it came so fast, so many long delicate phrases pouring out with such speed, he strained to listen. To separate the meaning from the beguiling beauty of her voice.

She'd been adopted when she was a day old, she'd been taken away from her home, and did he know that was New Orleans? She'd told him that in the letter he'd never received. And yes, he ought to know that because when he'd wakened, he grabbed her hand and held onto it, as if he didn't want to let her go. And maybe then some mingled crazy idea had come through, some sudden intensity connected to that place. But the thing was, she'd never really been there! Never seen it. Didn't even know her mother's full name.

Did he know there was a paper in the safe, over there, behind the picture there, by the door, a letter she'd signed saying she'd never go back to New Orleans, never seek to find out anything about her family, her real parents? Cut off, ripped out of it, the past cut away like the umbilical cord and no way that she could recapture what had been thrown away. But she'd been thinking about that of late, that awful black gulf and the fact that they were gone, Ellie and Graham, and the paper in the safe, and Ellie had died making her repeat her promise, over and over.

They'd taken her out of New Orleans to Los Angeles on a six o'clock plane the very day she was born. Why, for years she'd been told she was born in Los Angeles. That's what her birth certificate said, one of those phony jobs they concoct for adopted children. Ellie and Graham had told her a thousand times about the little apartment in West Hollywood, and how happy they had been when they brought her home.

But that wasn't the point, the point was they were gone, dead, and with them their whole story, wiped out with a speed and totality that utterly terrified her. And Ellie in such pain. Nobody should have to suffer like that. And theirs had been the great modern life, just great, though it was a selfish, materialistic world, she had to admit. No tie to anyone—family or friend—

ever interrupted their self-centered pursuit of pleasure. And at the bedside, no one but Rowan as Ellie lay screaming for the morphine.

He was nodding, how well he understood. Hadn't his own life become the same thing? A sudden flash of New Orleans struck him, screen door closing, cousins around the kitchen table, red beans and rice, and talk, talk, talk . . .

"I tell you I almost killed her," Rowan said, "I almost ended it. I couldn't . . . I couldn't . . . Nobody could lie to me about it. I know when people are lying. It's not that I can read minds, it's more subtle. It's as if people are talking out loud in black-and-white words on a page, and I'm seeing what they say in colored pictures. I get their thoughts some times, little bits of information. And anyway, I'm a doctor, they didn't try, and I had full access to the information. It was Ellie that was always lying, trying to pretend it wasn't happening. And I knew her feelings, always. I had since I was a little girl. And there was this other thing, this talent for knowing, I call it the diagnostic sense but it's more than that, I laid my hands on her and even when she was in remission, I knew. It's in there, it's coming back. She's got six months at most. And then to come home after it was all over—to this house, this house with every conceivable gadget and convenience and luxury that one could possibly . . ."

"I know," he said softly. "All the toys we have, all the money."

"Yes, and what is this without them now, a shell? I don't belong here! And if I don't belong, nobody does, and I look around me . . . and I'm scared, I tell you. I'm scared. No, wait, don't comfort me. You don't know. I couldn't prevent Ellie's death, that I can accept, but I caused Graham's death. I killed him."

"No, but you didn't do that," he said. "You're a doctor and you know . . ."

"Michael, you are like an angel sent to me. But listen to what I'm telling you. You have a power in your hands, you know it's real. I know it's real. On the drive over you demonstrated that power. Well, I have a power in me that's equally strong. I killed him. I killed two people before that—a stranger, and a little girl years ago, a little girl on a playground. I've read the autopsy reports. I can kill, I tell you! I'm a doctor today because I am trying to deny that power, I have built my life upon compensation for that evil!"

She took a deep breath. She ran her fingers back through her hair. She looked waifish and lost in the big loose robe, cinched tight at the waist, a Ganymede with the soft tumbled pageboy hair. He started to go to her. She gestured for him to stay where he was.

"There's so much. You know I made this fantasy of telling you, you of all people . . ."

"I'm here, I'm listening," he said. "I want you to tell me . . ." How could he put into words that she fascinated him and utterly absorbed him, and how remarkable that was after all these weeks of frenzy and craziness.

She talked in a low voice now of how it had gone with her, of how she had always been in love with science, science was poetry to her. She never thought she'd be a surgeon. It was research that fascinated her, the incredible, almost fantastical advances in neurological science. She wanted to spend her life in the laboratory where she thought the real opportunity for heroism existed; and she had a natural genius for it, take that on faith. She did.

But then had come that awful experience, that terrible Christmas Eve. She had been about to go to the Keplinger Institute to work full-time on methods of intervention in the brain that did not involve surgery—the use of lasers, the gamma knife, miracles she could scarcely describe to the layman. After all, she had never had any easy time with human beings. Didn't she belong in a laboratory?

And take it from her the latest developments were full of the miraculous, but then her mentor, never mind his name—and he was dead now anyway, he'd died of a series of little strokes shortly after that, ironically enough, and all the surgeons in the world hadn't been able to clip and suture those deadly ruptures . . . but she hadn't even found out about that until later. To get back to the story, he had taken her up into the Institute in San Francisco on Christmas Eve because that was the one night of all nights when no one would be there, and he was breaking the rules to show her what they were working on, and it was live fetal research.

"I saw it in the incubator, this little fetus. Do you know what he called it? He called it the abortus. Oh, I hate to tell you this because I know how you feel about Little Chris, I know . . ."

She didn't notice his shock. He had never told her about Little Chris, never told anyone about that pet name, but she seemed quite completely unaware of this, and he sat there silent, just listening to her talk, thinking vaguely of all those films he'd seen with these recurrent and awful fetal images, but he wasn't about to interrupt her. He wanted her to go on.

"And this thing had been sustained, alive," she said, "from

a four-month abortion, and you know he was developing means of live support for even younger fetuses. He was talking of breeding embryos in test tubes and never returning them to the womb at all, but all of this to harvest organs. You should have heard his arguments, that the fetus was playing a vital role in the human life chain, could you believe it, and I'll tell you the horrible part, the really horrible part, it was that it was utterly fascinating, and I loved it. I saw the potential uses he was describing. I knew it would be possible someday to create new and undamaged brains for coma victims. Oh, God, you know all the things that could be done, the things that I, given my talent, could have done!''

He nodded. "I can see it," he said softly. "I can see the horror of it and I can see the lure.''

"Yes, precisely," she responded. "And do you believe me when I tell you I could have had a great career in research, I could have been one of those names in the books. I was born for it, you might say. When I discovered neurology, when I reached it, you might say, after all the preparation, it was like I'd reached the summit of a mountain, and it was home, it was where I belonged.''

The sun was rising. It fell on the floorboards where she stood but she appeared not to see it. She was crying again, softly, the tears just flowing as she wiped at her mouth with the back of her hand.

She explained how she had run from that laboratory, she had run from research altogether, and all that might have been achieved there, she had run from her ruthless lust for power over the little fetal cells with their amazing plasticity. Did he understand how they could be used for transplants wholly unlike other transplants, that they continued to develop, that they did not trigger the usual immune responses of the host, that they were a field of such dazzling promise. "That's what it was, you could see no end to what could be done. And imagine the extent of the raw material, a little nation of nonpersons by the millions. Of course there are laws against it. Do you know what he said? 'There are laws against it because everybody knows it's going on.' ''

"Not surprising," he whispered. "Not surprising at all.''

"I had killed only two people at that point in my life. But I knew, inside, that I had done it. Because you see it's connected to my very character, my capacity to choose to do something, and my refusal to accept defeat. Call it temper in its crudest form. Call it fury at its most dramatic. And in research can you imagine how I could have used that capacity to choose and do and to resist authority, to follow my lights on some totally amoral and even disastrous course? It's not mere will; it's too hot to be called will."

"Determination," he said.

She nodded. "Now a surgeon is an interventionist; he or she is very determined. You go in with the knife and you say, I'm going to chop out half your brain and you're going to be better, and who would have the nerve to do something like that but someone very determined, someone extremely inner-directed, someone very strong."

"Thank God for it," he said.

"Perhaps." She smiled bitterly. "But a surgeon's confidence is nothing compared to what could have been brought out of me in the laboratory. And I want to tell you something else, too, something I think you can understand on account of your hands and the visions, something I would never tell another doctor, because it would be no use.

"When I operate I envision what I'm doing. I mean I hold in my mind a thorough multidimensional image of the effects of my actions. My mind thinks in terms of such detailed pictures. When you were dead on the deck of the boat and I breathed into your mouth, I envisioned your lungs, your heart, the air moving into your lungs. And when I killed the man in the Jeep, when I killed the little girl, I first imagined them punished, I imagined them spitting blood. I didn't have the knowledge then to imagine it any more perfectly than that, but it was the same process, the same thing."

"But they could have been natural deaths, Rowan."

She shook her head. "I did it, Michael. And with the same power guiding me I operate. And with the same power guiding me I saved you."

He said nothing, he was only waiting for her to go on. The last thing he wanted to do was argue with her. God, she was the only person in the world it seemed who really listened to him. And she didn't need anyone to argue with her right now. Yet he wasn't at all sure that she was right.

"No one knows these things," she said. "I've stood in this empty house and cried and talked aloud to no one. Ellie was my closest friend in all the world, but I couldn't have told her. And what have I done? I've tried through surgery to find salvation. I have chosen the most brutal and direct means of intervention. But all the successful operations of the world cannot hide from me what I am capable of. I killed Graham.

"You know, I think that at that moment, when Graham and I were there together, I think . . . I think I actually remembered

195

Mary Jane on the playground, and I think I actually remembered the man in the Jeep, and I believe, I believe I actually intended to use the power, but all I can remember is that I saw the artery. I saw it burst. But you know, I think I deliberately killed him. I wanted him to die so he couldn't hurt Ellie. I made him die.''

She paused as if she wasn't sure of what she'd just said, or as if she'd just realized that it was true. She looked off over the water. It was blue now, in the sunlight, and filled with dazzling light. Countless sails had appeared on the surface. And the whole house was pervaded by the vistas surrounding it, the dark olive hills sprinkled with white buildings, and to Michael, it made her seem all the more alone, lost.

''When I read about the power in your hands,'' she said, ''I knew it was real. I understood. I knew what you were going through. There are these secret things that set us apart. Don't expect other people to believe, though in your case they've seen. In my case no one must ever see, because it must never happen again . . .''

''Is that what you're afraid of, it will happen again?''

''I don't know.'' She looked at him. ''I think of those deaths and the guilt is so terrible, I don't have a purpose or an idea or a plan. It stands between me and life. And yet I live, I live better than anybody I know.'' She laughed softly, bitterly. ''Every day I go into surgery. My life is exciting. But it isn't what it could have been . . .'' Her tears were flowing again; she was looking at him, but seemingly through him. The sunlight was falling full on her, on her yellow hair.

He wanted so to hold her. Her suffering was excruciating to him. He could scarcely stand to see her gray eyes so red and full of tears, and the very tautness of her face made it terrible when the lines of anguish suddenly sharpened and flashed and the tears flowed, and then the face went smooth, as if with shock, again.

''I wanted to tell you these things,'' she said. She was confused, uncertain. Her voice broke. ''I wanted . . . to be with you and tell you. I guess I felt that because I had saved your life, maybe somehow . . .''

This time nothing could have stopped him from going to her. He got up slowly, and took her in his arms. He held her, kissing her silky neck and her tear-stained cheeks, kissing her tears. ''You felt right,'' he said. He drew back, and he pulled off his gloves, impatiently, and tossed them aside. He looked at his hands for a moment, and then he looked at her.

There was a look of vague wonder in her eyes, the tears shimmering in the light from the fire. Then he placed his hands on her head, feeling of her hair, and of her cheeks, and he whispered: "Rowan." He willed all the random crazy images to stop; he willed himself just to see *her* now, through his hands, and there rose again that lovely engulfing sense of her that had come and gone so swiftly in the car, of her surrounding him, and in a sudden violent hum, like the throb of electricity through his veins, he knew her, he knew the honesty of her life, and the intensity of it, and he knew her goodness, her undeniable goodness. The tumbling, shifting images didn't matter. They were true to the whole that he perceived, and it was the whole, and the courage of the whole, that mattered.

He slid his hands into her robe, touching her small, thin body, so hot, so delicious to his naked fingers. He lowered his head and kissed the tops of her breasts. Orphan, alone one, afraid but so strong, so very relentlessly strong. "Rowan," he whispered again. "Let this matter now."

He felt her sigh, and give in, like a broken stem against his chest, and in the mounting heat, all the pain left her.

He lay on the rug, his left arm bent to cradle his head, his right hand idly holding a cigarette over the ashtray, a steaming cup of coffee at his side. It must have been nine o'clock by now. He'd called the airline. They could put him on the noon plane.

But when he thought of leaving her he was filled with anxiety. He liked her. He liked her more than most people he'd ever known in his life, and more to the point perhaps, he was enchanted by her, by her obvious intelligence and her near morbid vulnerability, which continued to bring out in him an exquisite sense of protectiveness, which he enjoyed almost to the point of shame.

They had talked for hours after the second lovemaking.

They talked quietly, without urgency or peaks of emotion, about their lives. She'd told him about growing up in Tiburon, taking out the boat almost every day of her life, what it had been like attending the good schools. She'd talked more about her life in medicine, her early love of research, and dreams of Frankenstein-like discoveries, in a more controlled and detailed way. Then had come the discovery of her talent in the Operating Room. No doubt she was an incredibly good surgeon. She felt no need to brag about it; she simply described it, the excitement of it, the immediate gratification, the near desperation since the death of her parents to be always operating, always walking the wards, always at work. On some days she had actually operated until she could not stand upright any longer. It was as if her mind and her hands and her eyes weren't part of the rest of her.

He had told her briefly, and a little self-deprecatingly, about his own world, answering her questions, warmed by her seeming interest. "Working class," he had said. How curious she had been. What was it like back there in the South? He'd talked about the big families, the big funerals, the narrow little shotgun house with its linoleum floors, the four o'clocks in the postage stamp of a garden. Had it seemed quaint to her? Maybe it did to him too now, though it hurt to think of it, because he wanted to go home so badly. "It isn't just them, and the visions and all. I want to go back there, I want to walk on Annunciation Street too . . ."

"Is that the name of the street where you grew up? That's so beautiful."

He didn't tell her about the weeds in the gutters, the men sitting on the steps with their cans of beer, the smell of boiled cabbage that never went away, the riverfront trains rattling the windows.

Talking about his life here had been a little easier—explaining about Elizabeth and Judith, and the abortion that had destroyed his life with Judith; explaining about the last few years, and their curious emptiness, and the feeling of waiting for something, though he did not know what it was. He told about houses and how he loved them; about the kinds that existed in San Francisco, the big Queen Annes and the Italianates, the bed-and-breakfast hotel he had wanted so badly to do on Union Street, and then he had slipped into talking about the houses he really loved, the houses back there in New Orleans. He understood about ghosts in houses, because houses were more than habitats, and it was no wonder they could steal your soul.

It was an easy exchange, deepening their knowledge of each other, and amplifying the intimacy they'd already felt. He had liked what she said about going out to sea; about being alone on the bridge with the coffee in her hand, the wind howling past the wheelhouse. He didn't like it, but he liked to hear her tell about it. He liked the look in her gray eyes; he liked the simplicity of her easy, languid gestures.

He had even gone into his crazy talk about the movies, and the recurrent images of vengeful babies and children, and the way he felt when he perceived such themes—as though everything around him was talking to him. Maybe one step from the madhouse, but he wondered if some of the people in the madhouse were there because they took the patterns they perceived too literally? What did she think? And death, well, he had a lot of thoughts about death, but first and foremost, this thought had recently struck him, even before the accident, that the death of another person is perhaps the only genuine supernatural event we ever experience.

"I'm not talking about doctors now. I'm talking about ordinary people in the modern world. What I'm saying is, when you look down at that body, and you realize all the life has gone out of it, and you can scream at it, and slap it around, and try to sit it up, and do every trick in the book to it, but it's dead, absolutely unequivocally dead . . ."

"I know what you're saying."

"And you have to remember, for most of us we see that maybe once or twice in twenty years. Maybe never. Why, California in this day and age is a whole civilization of people who never witness a death. They never even see a dead body! Why, they think when they hear somebody's dead that he forgot to eat his health foods, or hadn't been jogging the way he should have been . . ."

She had laughed softly under her breath. "Every goddamned death's a murder. Why you do you think they come after us doctors with their lawyers?"

"Exactly, but it's deeper even than that. They don't believe they're going to die! And when somebody else dies, it's behind closed doors, and the coffin's closed, if the poor slob had the bad taste to even want a coffin and a funeral, which of course he shouldn't have wanted. Better a memorial service in some toney place with sushi and white wine and people refusing to even say out loud why they are there! Why, I have been to California memorial services where nobody even mentioned the dead guy! But if you really see it . . . and you're not a doctor, or a nurse, or an undertaker . . . well, it's a first-class supernatural event, and just probably the only supernatural event you ever get to see."

"Well, let me tell you about one other supernatural event," she'd said, smiling. "It's when you've got one of those dead bodies lying on the deck of your boat, and you're slapping it around and talking to it, and suddenly the eyes do open, and the guy's alive."

She had smiled so beautifully at him then. He had started kissing her, and that was how that particular segment of the conversation had come to an end. But the point was, he hadn't lost her with his crazy rambling. She had never once tuned out on him.

Why did this other thing have to be happening? Why did this feel like stolen time?

Now he lay on the rug, thinking how much he liked her and how much her sadness and her aloneness disturbed him, and how much he didn't want to leave her, and that nevertheless, he had to go.

His head was remarkably clear. He had not been this long without a drink all summer. And he rather liked the feeling of thinking clearly. She had just refilled the coffee for him, and it tasted good. But he'd put back on the gloves, because he was getting all those random stupid images off everything—Graham, Ellie, and men, lots of different men, handsome men, and all Rowan's men, that was abundantly clear. He wished it wasn't.

The sun was burning through the eastern windows and skylights. He could hear her working in the kitchen. He figured he ought to get up and help her no matter what she'd said, but she'd been pretty convincing on the subject: "I like to cook, it's like surgery. Stay exactly where you are."

He was thinking that she was the first thing in all these weeks that really mattered to him, that took his mind off the accident and off himself. And it was such a relief to be thinking of someone other than himself. In fact, when he considered it with this new clarity, he realized he'd been able to concentrate well since he'd been here, concentrate on their conversation and their lovemaking and their knowing of each other; and that was something altogether new, because in all these weeks, his lack of concentration—his inability to read more than a page of a book, or follow more than a few moments of a film—had left him continuously agitated. It had been as bad as the lack of sleep.

He realized that he had never had his knowledge of a human being commence at such a pitch, and plunge so deep so fast. It was like what was supposed to happen with sex, but seldom if ever did. He had entirely lost sight of the fact that she was the woman who'd rescued him; that is, a strong sense of her character had obliterated that vague impersonal excitement he'd felt on first meeting her, and now he was making mad fantasies about her in his head.

How could he continue to know her and maybe even get to love her, and have her, and do this other thing he had to do? And he still had to do this other thing. He still had to go home and he had to determine the purpose.

As for her having been born down south, it had nothing to do with it. His head was full of too many images from his past, and the sense of destiny that united these images was too strong for it to have come from some random reminder of his home through her. Besides, on the deck of the boat last night, he'd caught nothing of that. Knowing her, yes, that was there, but even that was suspect, he still believed, because there was no profound recognition, no "Ah yes," when she told him her story. Only positive fascination. Nothing scientific about this power of his; might be physical, yes, and measurable finally, and even controllable through some numbing drug, but it wasn't scientific. It was more like art or music.

But the point was, he had to leave, and he didn't want to. And it made him sad suddenly, sad and almost desperate, as if they were somehow doomed, he and she.

All these weeks, if only he could have seen her, been with her. And the oddest thought occurred to him. If only that awful accident hadn't happened, and he had found her in some simple ordinary place, and they had begun to talk. But she was part and parcel of what had happened, her strangeness and her strength were part of it. All alone out there in that big awful cruiser right at the moment when darkness fell. Who the hell else would have been there? Who the hell else could have gotten him out of the water? Why, he could easily believe what she said about determination, about her powers.

When she'd been describing the rescue to him in more detail, she had said a strange thing. She had said that a person loses consciousness almost immediately in very cold water. Yet she had been pitched right into it, and she hadn't lost consciousness. She had said only, "I don't know how I reached the ladder, I honestly don't."

"Do you think it was that power?" he asked.

She had reflected for a moment. Then she had said, "Yes, and no. I mean maybe it was just luck."

"Well, it was luck for me, all right," he'd responded, and he had felt an extraordinary sense of well-being when he said it, and he wasn't so sure why.

Maybe she knew because she said, "We're frightened of what makes us different." And he had agreed.

"But lots of people have these powers," she said. "We don't know what they are, or how to measure them; but surely they are part of what goes on between human beings. I see it in the hospital. There are doctors who know things, and they can't tell you how. There are nurses who are the same way. I imagine there are lawyers who know infallibly when someone is guilty; or that the jury is going to vote for or against; and they can't tell you how they know.

"The fact is, for all we learn about ourselves, for all we codify and classify and define, the mysteries remain immense. Take the research into genetics. So much is inherited by a human being—shyness is inherited, the liking for a particular brand of soap may be inherited, the liking for particular given names. But what else is inherited? What invisible powers come down to you? That's why it's so frustrating to me that I don't really know my family. I don't know the first thing about them. Ellie was a third cousin once removed or something like that. Why, hell, that's hardly a cousin . . ."

Yes, he had agreed with all that. He talked a little about his father and his grandfather, and how he was more like them than he cared to admit. "But you have to believe you can change your heredity," he said. "You have to believe that you can work magic on the ingredients. If you can't there's no hope."

"Of course you can," she'd replied. "You've done it, haven't you? I want to believe I've done it. This may sound insane, but I believe that we ought to . . ."

"Tell me . . ."

"We ought to aim to be perfect," she said quietly. "I mean, why not?"

He had laughed but not in ridicule. He had thought of something one of his friends once said to him. The friend had been listening to Michael rattle on one night about history, and how nobody understood it or where we were headed because we didn't know history, and the friend had said, "You are a peculiar talker, Michael," explaining that the phrase was from *Orpheus Descending*, a Tennessee Williams play. He had treasured the compliment. He hoped she would too.

"You're a peculiar talker, Rowan," he had said, and he had explained it as his friend explained it to him.

That had made her laugh, really break up. "Maybe that's why I'm so quiet," she said. "I don't even want to get started. I think you've said it. I'm a peculiar talker and that's why I don't talk at all."

He took a drag off the cigarette now, thinking it all over. It would be lovely to stay with her. If only the feeling would leave him, that he had to go home.

"Put another log on the fire," she said, interrupting his reverie. "Breakfast is ready."

She laid it out on the dining table near the windows. Scrambled eggs, yogurt, fresh sliced oranges sparkling in the sun, bacon and sausage, and hot muffins just out of the oven.

She poured the coffee and the orange juice for them both. And for five minutes solid, without a word, he just ate. He had never been so hungry. For a long moment he stared at the coffee. No, he didn't want a beer, and he wasn't going to drink one. He drank the coffee, and she refilled the cup.

"That was simply wonderful," he said.

"Stick around," she said, "and I'll cook you dinner, and breakfast tomorrow morning too."

He couldn't answer. He studied her for a moment, trying not to see just loveliness and the object of his considerable desire, but what she looked like. A true blonde, he thought, smooth all over, with almost no down on her face or her arms. And lovely dark ashen eyebrows, and dark eyelashes which made her eyes seem all the more gray. A face like a nun, she had, actually. Not a touch of makeup on it, and her long full mouth had a virginal look to it somehow, like the mouths of little girls before they've worn lipstick. He wished he could just sit here with her forever . . .

"But you are going to leave anyway," she said.

He nodded. "Have to," he said.

She was thoughtful. "What about the visions?" she asked. "Do you want to talk about them?"

He hesitated. "Every time I try to describe them, it ends in frustration," he explained, "and also, well, it turns people off."

"It won't turn me off," she said. She seemed quite composed now, her arms folded, her hair prettily mussed, the coffee steaming in front of her. She was more like the resolute and forceful woman he'd first met last night.

He believed what she said. Nevertheless, he had seen the look of incredulity and then indifference in so many faces. He sat back in the chair, staring out for a moment. Every sailing ship in the world was on the bay. And he could see the gulls flying over the harbor of Sausalito like tiny bits of paper.

"I know the whole experience took a long time," he said, "that time itself was impossible to factor into it." He glanced at her. "You know what I mean," he said. "Like in the old days when people would be lured by the Little People. You know, they'd go off and spend one day with the Little People, but when they came back to their villages they discovered they'd been gone for fifty years."

She laughed under her breath. "Is that an Irish story?"

"Yeah, from an old Irish nun, I heard that one," he said. "She used to tell us the damnedest things. She used to tell us there were witches in the Garden District in New Orleans, and that they'd get us if we went walking in those streets . . ." And think how dark those streets were, how darkly beautiful, like the lines from "Ode to a Nightingale," "Darkling I listen . . ." "I'm sorry," he said, "my mind wandered."

She waited.

"There were many people in the visions," he said, "but what I remember most distinctly is a dark-haired woman. I can't see this woman now, but I know that she was as familiar to me as someone I'd known all my life. I knew her name, everything about her. And I know now that I knew about you. I knew your name. But I don't know if that was in the middle of it, or just at the end, you know, before I was rescued, when maybe I knew somehow that the boat was coming and you were there." Yes, that was a real puzzle, he thought.

"Go on."

"I think I could have come back and lived even if I had refused to do what they wanted me to do. But I wanted the mission, so to speak, I wanted to fulfill the purpose. And it seemed . . . it seemed that everything they wanted of me, everything they revealed, well, it was all connected with my past life, who I'd been. It was all-encompassing. Do you follow me?"

"There was a reason they chose you."

"Yes, that's it exactly. I was the one for this, because of who I was. Now, make no mistake. I know this is nuthouse talk again; I'm so damned good at it. This is the talk of schizophrenics who hear voices telling them to save the world, I'm aware of that. There's an old saying about me among my friends."

"What is it?"

He adjusted his glasses and flashed his best smile at her. "Michael isn't as stupid as he looks."

She laughed in the loveliest way. "You don't look stupid," she said. "You just look too good to be true." She tapped the ash off her cigarette. "You know how good-looking you are. I don't have to tell you. What else can you recall?"

He hesitated, positively electrified by that last compliment. Wasn't it time to go to bed again? No, it wasn't. It was almost time to catch a plane.

"Something about a doorway," he said, "I could swear it. But again, I can't see these things now. It's getting thinner all the time. But I know there was a number involved in it. And there was a jewel. A beautiful jewel. I can't even call this recollection now. It's more like faith. But I believe all those things were mixed up with it. And then it's all mixed up with going home, with this sense of having to do something tremendously important, and New Orleans is part of it, and this street where I used to walk when I was a kid."

"A street?"

"First Street. It's a beautiful stretch, from Magazine Street, near where I grew up, to St. Charles Avenue, about five blocks or so, and it's an old old part of town they call the Garden District."

"Where the witches live," she said.

"Oh, yes, right, the witches of the Garden District," he said, smiling. "At least according to Sister Bridget Marie."

"Is it a gloomy witchy place, this neighborhood?" she asked.

"No, not really," he said. "But it is like a dark bit of forest in the middle of the city. Big trees, trees you wouldn't believe. There's nothing comparable to it here. Maybe nowhere in America. And the houses are town houses, you know, close to the sidewalks, but they're so large, and they're not attached, they have gardens around them. And there's this one house, this house I used to pass all the time, a really high narrow house. I used to stop and look at it, at the iron railings. There's a rose pattern in the railings. Well, I keep seeing it now—since the accident— and I keep thinking I have to go back, you know, it's so urgent. Like even now I'm sitting here, but I feel guilty that I'm not on the plane."

A shadow passed over her face. "I want you to stay here for a while," she said. Lovely deep grosgrain voice. "But it isn't just that I want it. You're not in good shape. You need to rest, really rest without the booze."

"You're right, but I can't do it, Rowan. I can't explain this tension I feel. I'll feel it till I get home."

"That's another thing, Michael. Why is that home? You don't know anyone back there."

"Oh, it's home, honey, it is. I know." He laughed. "I've been in exile for too long. I knew it even before the accident. The morning before, it was the funniest thing, I woke up and I was thinking about home. I was thinking about this time we all drove to the Gulf Coast, and it was warm at sundown, positively warm . . ."

"Can you stay off the booze when you leave here?"

He sighed. He deliberately flashed her one of his best smiles— the kind that had always worked in the past—and he winked at her. "Want to hear Irish bullshit, lady, or the truth?"

"Michael . . ." It wasn't just disapproval in her voice, it was disappointment.

"I know, I know," he said. "Everything you're saying is right. Look, you don't know what you've done for me, just getting me out the front door, just listening to me. I want to do what you're telling me to do . . ."

"Tell me more about this house," she said.

He was thoughtful again, before beginning. "It was the Greek Revival style—do you know what that is?—but it was different. It had porches on the front and on the sides, real New Orleans porches. It's hard to describe a house like that to someone who's never been in New Orleans. Have you ever seen pictures—?"

She shook her head. "It was a subject Ellie couldn't talk about," she said.

"That sounds unfair, Rowan."

She shrugged.

"No, but really."

"Ellie wanted to believe I was her own daughter. If I asked about my biological parents, she thought I was unhappy, that she hadn't loved me enough. Useless to try to get those ideas out of her head." She drank a little of the coffee. "Before her last trip to the hospital she burned everything in her desk. I saw her doing it. She burned it all in that fireplace. Photographs, letters, all sorts of things. I didn't realize it was everything. Or maybe I just didn't think about it, one way or the other. She knew she wasn't coming back." She stopped for a minute, then poured a little more coffee in her cup and in Michael's cup.

"Then after she died, I couldn't even find an address for her people down there. Her lawyer didn't have a scrap of information. She'd told him she didn't want anyone down there to be contacted. All her money went to me. Yet she used to visit the people in New Orleans. She used to call them on the phone. I could never quite figure it all out."

"That's too sad, Rowan."

"But we've talked enough about me. About this house again. What is it that makes you remember it now?"

"Oh, houses there aren't like the houses here," he said. "Each house has a personality, a character. And this one, well, it's somber and massive, and sort of splendidly dark. It's built right on the corner, part of it touching the sidewalk of the side street. God knows I loved that house. There was a man who lived there, a man right out of a Dickens novel, I swear it, tall and sort of consummately gentlemanly, if you know what I mean. I used to see him in the garden . . ." He hesitated; something coming so close to him, something so crucial—

"What's the matter?"

"Just that feeling again, that it's all got to do with him and that house." He shuddered as if he were cold, but he wasn't. "I can't figure it out," he said. "But I know the man has something to do with it. I don't think they did mean for me to forget, the people I saw in the visions. I think they meant for me to act fast, because something's going to happen."

"What could that something be?" she asked gently.

"Something in that house," he said.

"Why would they want you to go back to that house?" she asked. Again, the question was gentle, not challenging.

"Because I have a power to do something there; I have a

power to affect something.'' He looked down at his hands, so sinister in the black gloves. ''Again, it was like everything fitted together. Imagine the whole world made up of tiny fragments—and suddenly a great many of those tiny fragments are lights and you see a . . . a . . .''

''Pattern?''

''Yeah, exactly, a pattern. Well, my life has been part of a greater pattern.'' He drank another swallow of the coffee. ''What do you think? Am I insane?''

She shook her head. ''It sounds too special for that.''

''Special?''

''I mean specific.''

He gave a little startled laugh. No one in all these weeks had said anything like that to him.

She crushed out the cigarette.

''Have you thought about that house often, in the past few years?''

''Almost never,'' he said. ''I never forgot it, but I never thought about it much either. Oh, now and then, I suppose whenever I thought about the Garden District, I'd think about it. You could say it was a haunting place.''

''But the obsession didn't begin until the visions.''

''Definitely,'' he said. ''There are other memories of home, but the memory of the house is the most intense.''

''Yet when you think of the visions, you don't remember speaking of the house . . .''

''Nothing so clear as that. Although . . .'' There it was again, the feeling. But he feared the power of suggestion suddenly. It seemed all the misery of the last few months was coming back. Yet it felt good to be believed by her, to be listening to her. And he liked her easy air of command, the first characteristic of her he had noticed the night before.

She was looking at him, looking just as if she was listening still though he had ceased to speak. He thought about these strange vagrant powers, how utterly they confused things, rather than clarifying them.

''So what's wrong with me?'' he asked. ''I mean as a doctor, as a brain doctor, what do you think? What should I do? Why do I keep seeing that house and that man? Why do I feel I ought to be there now?''

She sank into thought, silent, motionless, her gray eyes large and fixed on some point beyond the glass, her long, slender arms again folded. Then she said:

''Well, you should go back there, there's no doubt of that. You aren't going to rest easy till you do. Go look for the house. Who knows? Maybe it's not there. Or you won't have any special feeling when you see it. In any case, you should look. There may be some psychological explanation for this idée fixe, as they call it, but I don't think so. I suspect you saw something all right, you went somewhere. We know many people do that, at least they claim they did when they come back. But you might be putting the wrong interpretation on it.''

''I don't have much to go on,'' he admitted. ''That's true.''

''Do you think they caused the accident?''

''God, I never really thought of that.''

''You didn't?''

''I mean I thought, well, the accident happened, and they were there, and suddenly the opportunity was there. That would be awful, to think they caused it to happen. That would change things, wouldn't it?''

''I don't know. What bothers me is this. If they are powerful, whatever they are, if they could tell you something important with regard to a purpose, if they could keep you alive out there when you should have died, if they could work a rescue into it, well, then why couldn't they have caused the accident, and why couldn't they be causing your memory loss now?''

He was speechless.

''You really never thought of that?''

''It's an awful thought,'' he whispered. She started to speak again, but he asked her with a little polite gesture to wait. He was trying to find the words for what he wanted to say. ''My concept of them is different,'' he said. ''I've trusted that they exist in another realm; and that means spiritually as well as physically. That they are . . .''

''Higher beings?''

''Yes. And that they could only come to me, know of me, care about me, when I was close to them, between life and death. It was mystical, that's what I'm trying to say. But I wish I could find another word for it. It was a communication that happened only because I was physically dead.''

She waited.

''What I mean is, they're another species of being. They couldn't make a man fall off a rock and drown in the sea. Because if they could do such things in the material world, well, why on earth would they need me?''

''I see your point,'' she said. ''Nevertheless . . .''

''What?''

''You're assuming they're higher beings. You speak of them as if they're good. You're assuming that you ought to do what they want of you.''

Again, he was speechless.

"Look, maybe I don't know what I'm talking about," she said.

"No, I think you do," he answered. "And you're right. I have assumed all that. But Rowan, you see, it's a matter of impression. I awoke with the impression that they were good, that I'd come back with the confirmation of their goodness, and that the purpose was something I'd agreed to do. And I haven't questioned those assumptions. And what you're saying is, maybe I should."

"I could be wrong. And maybe I shouldn't say anything. But you know what I've been telling you about surgeons. We go in there swinging, and not with a fist, but with a knife."

He laughed. "You don't know how much it means to me just to talk about it, just to think about it out loud." But then he stopped smiling. Because it was very disturbing to be talking about it like this, and she knew that.

"And there's another thing," she said.

"Which is?"

"Every time you talk about the power in your hands, you say it's not important. You say the visions are what's important. But why aren't they connected? Why don't you believe that the people in the visions gave you the power in your hands?"

"I don't know," he said. "I've thought of that. My friends have even suggested that. But it doesn't feel right. It feels like the power is a distraction. I mean people around me here want me to use the power, and if I were to start doing that, I wouldn't go back."

"I see. And when you see this house, you'll touch it with your hands?"

He thought for a long moment. He had to admit he had not imagined such a thing. He had imagined a more immediate and wonderful clarification of things. "Yeah, I guess I will. I'll touch the gate if I can. I'll go up the steps and I'll touch the door."

Why did that frighten him? Seeing the house meant something wonderful, but touching things . . . He shook his head, and folded his arms as he sat back in the chair. Touch the gate. Touch the door. Of course they might have given him the power, but why did he think that they hadn't? Especially if it was all of a piece . . .

She was quiet, obviously puzzled, maybe even worried. He watched her for a long moment, thinking how much he hated to leave.

"Don't go so soon, Michael," she said suddenly.

"Rowan, let me ask you something," he said. "This paper

209

you signed, this pledge never to go to New Orleans. Do you believe in that sort of thing, I mean, the validity of this promise to Ellie, to a person who's dead?''

"Of course I do," she answered dully, almost sadly. "You believe in that sort of thing, too.''

"I do?"

"I mean you're an honorable person. You're what we call, with great significance, a nice guy.''

"OK. I hope I am. And I put my question wrong. I mean, what about your desire to see the place where you were born? But I'm lying to you now, you know, because what I want to say is, is there any chance you'll come back there with me? And I guess a nice guy doesn't tell lies.''

Silence.

"I know that sounds presumptuous," he said. "I know there've been quite a few men in this house, I mean I'm not the light of your life, I . . .''

"Stop it. I could fall in love with you and you know it.''

"Well, then listen to what I'm saying, because it is about two living people. And maybe I've already . . . well, I . . . what I mean is, if you want to go back there, if you need to go back just to see for yourself where you were born and who your parents were . . . Well, why the hell don't you come with me?'' He sighed and sat back, shoving his hands in his pants pockets. "I suppose that would be an awfully big step, wouldn't it? And all this is selfish of me. I just want you to come. Some nice guy.''

She was staring off again, frozen, then her mouth stiffened. And he realized she was again about to cry. "I'd like to go,'' she said. The tears were rising.

"God, Rowan, I'm sorry,'' he said. "I had no right to ask.''

The tears won out. She continued to look out towards the water, as if that were the only way to hold the line for the moment. But she was crying, and he could see the subtle movement of her throat as she swallowed, and the tightening in her shoulders. The thought flashed through him that this was the most alone person he'd ever known. California was full of them, but she was really isolated, and in a purely unselfish way, he was afraid for her, afraid to leave her in this house.

"Look, Rowan, I really am sorry. I can't do this to you,'' he said. "It's between you and Ellie. When you get ready to go, you'll go. And for now, I have to do it for totally different reasons. I've got to get out of here, and I hate like hell to go.''

The tears had begun to spill down her cheeks again.

"Rowan . . .''

"Michael," she whispered. "I'm the one who's sorry. I'm the one who's fallen in your arms. Now, stop worrying about me."

"No, don't say it." He started to get up, because he wanted to hug her again, but she wouldn't allow it. She reached for his hand across the table and held it.

Gently he spoke to her: "If you don't think I loved it, holding you, wiping your tears, well then you're not using your powers, Rowan. Or you just don't understand a man like me."

She shivered, arms tight across her chest, her bangs falling down in her eyes. She looked so forlorn he wanted to gather her to himself and kiss her again.

"What are you afraid of, really?" he asked.

When she answered, she spoke in a whisper, so low that he could scarcely hear. "That I'm bad, Michael, a bad person, a person who could really do harm. A person with a terrible potential for evil. That is what all my powers, such as they are, tell me about me."

"Rowan, it wasn't a sin to be a better person than Ellie or Graham. And it isn't a sin to hate them for your loneliness, for rearing you in a state of isolation from every blood tie you might have."

"I know all that, Michael." She smiled, a warm sweet smile full of gratitude and quiet acceptance, but she did not trust the things he'd said. She felt that he had failed to see something crucial about her, and he knew it. She felt that he had failed, just as he failed on the deck of the boat. She looked out at the deep blue water and then back at him.

"Rowan, no matter what happens in New Orleans, you and I are going to see each other again, and soon. I could swear to you now on a stack of Bibles that I'll be back here, but in truth, I don't think I ever will. I knew when I left Liberty Street I wasn't ever going to live there again. But we're going to meet somewhere, Rowan. If you can't set foot in New Orleans, then you pick the place, and you say the word, and I'll come."

Take that, you bastards out there, he thought looking at the water, and up at the dirty blue California sky, you creatures whoever you are that did this to me, and won't come back to guide me. I'll go to New Orleans, I'll follow where you lead. But there is something here between me and this woman, and that belongs to me.

She wanted to drive him to the airport, but he insisted on taking a cab. It was just too long a drive for her, and she was tired, he knew it. She needed her sleep.

He showered and shaved. He hadn't had a drink now in almost twelve hours. Truly amazing.

When he came down he found her sitting with her legs folded, on the hearth again, looking very pretty in white wool pants and another one of those great swallowing cable-knit sweaters that made her look all the more long-wristed and long-legged and delicate as a deer. She smelled faintly of some perfume he used to know the name of, and which he still loved.

He kissed her cheek, and then held her for a long moment. Eighteen years, maybe more than that, separated him in age from her and he felt it painfully, felt it when he let his lips again graze her firm, plump cheek.

He gave her a slip of paper on which he'd written down the name of the Pontchartrain Hotel and the number. "How can I reach you at the hospital, or is that not the right thing to do?"

"No, I want you to do that. I pick up my messages all day, at intervals." She went to the kitchen counter and wrote out the numbers on the telephone pad, tore off the page, and put it in his hand. "Just raise hell if they give you any trouble. Tell them I'm expecting your call. And I'll tell them."

"Gotcha."

She stood back a pace from him, slipping her hands in her pockets, and she lowered her head slightly as she looked at him. "Don't get drunk again, Michael," she said.

"Yes, Doctor." He laughed. "And I could stand right here and tell you I was going to take the pledge, honey, but somehow or other the minute that stewardess . . ."

"Michael, don't drink on the plane and don't drink when you get there. You're going to be bombarded with memories. You're going miles away from anybody you know."

He shook his head. "You're right, Doc," he said. "I'll be careful. I'll be all right."

He went to his suitcase, took out his Sony Walkman from the zipper pocket, and checked that he had remembered to bring a book for the plane.

"Vivaldi," he said, slipping the Walkman with its tiny earphones into his jacket pocket. "And my Dickens. I go nuts when I fly without them. It's better than Valium and vodka, I swear."

She smiled at him, the most exquisite smile, and then she laughed. "Vivaldi and Dickens," she whispered. "Imagine that."

He shrugged. "We all have our weaknesses," he said. "God, why am I leaving like this?" he asked. "Am I crazy?"

"If you don't call me this evening . . ."

"I'll call you, sooner and more often than you could possibly expect."

"The taxi's there," she said.

He had heard the horn, too.

He took her in his arms, kissing her, crushing her to him. And for one moment, he almost couldn't pull away. He thought of what she'd said again, about *them* causing the accident, causing the amnesia, and a dark chill went through him, something like real fear. What if he forgot about them, forever, what if he just stayed here with her? It seemed a possibility, a last chance of sorts, it really did.

"I think I love you, Rowan Mayfair," he whispered.

"Yes, Michael Curry," she said, "I think something like that might be happening on both sides right now."

She gave him another of her soft, radiant smiles, and he saw in her eyes all the strength he'd found so seductive in these last few hours, and all the tenderness and sadness, too.

All the way to the airport, he listened to Vivaldi with his eyes closed. But it didn't help. He thought of New Orleans, and then he thought of her; and back and forth the pendulum swung. It was a simple thing she'd said, but how it jarred him. It seemed all these weeks he'd clung to the idea of a magnificent pattern and a purpose that served some higher value, but when she'd asked a few simple and logical questions, his faith had fallen apart.

Well, he didn't believe the accident had been caused by anyone. The wave had simply knocked him off the rock. And then he'd gone somewhere, a stratum others have visited, and there he'd found these beings, and they had found him. But they couldn't do things to people to hurt them, to manipulate them as if they were puppets on strings!

Then what about the rescue, buddy? What about her coming, alone in that boat, just before dark to that very spot in the sea?

God, he was going crazy again already. All he could think about was being with her again, or getting a good slug of bourbon with ice.

Only when he was waiting for the plane to board did something occur to him, something he had not given the slightest thought to before.

He'd lain with her three times in the last few hours, and he had not taken the usual precautions against conception. He had not even thought about the prophylactics he always carried in his wallet. He had not asked her about the matter, either. And

213

to think, in all these years, this was the first time he had let such a thing slip by.

Well, she was a doctor, for the love of heaven. Surely she had the matter covered. But maybe he should call her about it now. It wouldn't hurt to hear her voice. He closed the copy of *David Copperfield* and started looking for a phone.

Then he saw that man again, that Englishman with the white hair and the tweed suit. Only a few rows away he sat, with his briefcase and his umbrella, a folded newspaper in his hand.

Oh, no, Michael thought dismally, as he took his seat again. All I need now is to run into him.

The call came for boarding. Michael watched anxiously as the Englishman rose, collected his things, and moved to the gate.

But moments later, the old gentleman didn't even glance up when Michael passed him and took a seat by the window in the rear of first class. The old fellow had had his briefcase open already, and he'd been writing, very rapidly it seemed, in a large leather-bound book.

Michael ordered his bourbon with an ice-cold beer chaser before the plane took off. By the time they reached Dallas for a forty-minute stopover, he was on his sixth beer and his seventh chapter of *David Copperfield*, and he didn't even remember anymore that the Englishman was there.

Seven

H E'D MADE THE cab driver stop on the way in for a six-pack, already jubilant to be in the warm summer air, and now as they made the turn off the freeway and came down into the familiar and unforgettable squalor of lower St. Charles Avenue, Michael felt like weeping at the sight of the black-barked oak trees with their dark foliage, and the long narrow St. Charles streetcar, exactly as he had remembered it, roaring and clattering along its track.

Even on this stretch, in the midst of the ugly hamburger joints and the seedy wooden barrooms and the new apartment buildings towering over boarded-up shopfronts and deserted gas stations, it was his old, verdant, and softly beautiful town. He loved even the weeds exploding in the cracks. The grass grew rich and green on the neutral ground. The crepe myrtle trees were covered with frothy blooms. He saw pink crepe myrtle and purple crepe myrtle, and a red as rich as the red of watermelon meat.

"Look at that, will you!" he said to the driver, who had been talking on and on about the crime, and the bad times here. "The sky's violet, it's violet just like I remembered it, and goddamnit, all these years out there I thought I imagined all this, I thought I colored it in with a crayon in my memory, you know."

He felt like crying. All the time he'd held Rowan while she'd cried, he'd never shed a tear. But now he felt like bawling, and oh, how he wished Rowan were here.

The driver was laughing at him. "Yeah, well, that's a purple sky all right, I guess you could call it that."

"Damn right it is," said Michael. "You were born between Magazine and the river, weren't you?" Michael said. "I'd have known that voice anywhere."

"What you talking about, boy, what about your own voice," the driver teased him back. "I was born on Washington and St. Thomas for your information, youngest of nine children. They don't make families like that anymore." The cab was just crawling down the avenue, the soft moist August breeze washing through the open windows. The street lamps had just gone on.

Michael closed his eyes. Even the cab driver's endless diatribe was music. But for this, this fragrant and embraceable warmth, he had longed with his whole soul. Was there anyplace else in the world where the air was such a living presence, where the breeze kissed you and stroked you, where the sky was pulsing and alive? And oh God, what it meant to be no longer cold!

"Oh, I am telling you, nobody's got a right to be as happy as I am now," Michael said. "Nobody. Look at the trees," he said opening his eyes, staring up at the black curling branches.

"Where the hell you been, son?" asked the driver. He was a short man in a bill cap, with his elbow half out the window.

"Oh, I've been in hell, buddy, and let me tell you something about hell. It's not hot. It's cold. Hey, look, there's the Pontchartrain Hotel and it's still the same, damn, it's still the same." In fact, it looked if anything more elegant and aloof than it had in the old days. It had trim blue awnings, and the old complement of doormen and bellmen standing at the glass doors.

Michael could hardly sit still. He wanted to get out, to walk, to cover the old pavements. But he'd told the driver to take him up to First Street, that they'd double back to the hotel later, and for First Street he could wait.

215

He finished the second beer just as they came to the light at Jackson Avenue, and at that point everything changed. Michael hadn't remembered the transition as so dramatic; but the oaks grew taller and infinitely denser; the apartment buildings gave way to the white houses with the Corinthian columns; and the whole drowsy twilight world seemed suddenly veiled in soft, glowing green.

"Rowan, if only you were here," he whispered. There was the James Gallier house on the corner of St. Charles and Philip, splendidly restored. And across the street the Henry Howard house, spiffed up with a new coat of paint. Iron fences guarded lawns and gardens. "Christ, I'm home!" he whispered.

When he first landed he had regretted getting so drunk—it was just too damned hard to handle his suitcase and find a taxi—but now he was past that. As the cab turned left on First Street and entered the dark leafy core of the Garden District, he was in ecstasy.

"You realize it's just the way it used to be!" he told the driver. An immense gratitude flooded him. He passed the fresh beer to him, but the driver only laughed and waved it away.

"Later, son," he said. "Now where are we going?" In the slow motion of dream time, it seemed, they glided past the massive mansions. Michael saw brick sidewalks, the tall stiff magnolia grandiflora with their shiny dark leaves.

"Just drive, real slow, let this guy here pass us, yeah, very slow, until I tell you to stop."

He had chosen the most beautiful hour of the evening for his return, he thought. He wasn't thinking now of the visions or the dark mandate. He was so brimful of happiness all he could think about was what lay before him, and about Rowan. That was the test of love, he thought dreamily, when you can't bear to be this happy without the other person with you. He was really afraid that the tears were going to come pouring down his face.

The cab driver started talking again. He had never really stopped talking. Now he was talking about the Redemptorist Parish and how it had been in the old days, and how it was all run-down now. Yeah, Michael wanted to see the old church. "I was an altar boy at St. Alphonsus," Michael said.

But that didn't matter, that could wait forever. Because, looking up, Michael saw the house.

He saw its long dark flank stretching back from the corner; he saw the unmistakable iron railings with their rose pattern; he saw the sentinel oaks stretching out their mammoth branches like mighty and protective arms.

"That's it," he said, his voice dropping senselessly and

216

breathlessly to a whisper. "Pull over to the right. Stop here." Taking the beer with him, he stepped out of the cab and walked to the corner, so that he could stand diagonally opposite the house.

It was as if a hush had fallen over the world. For the first time he heard the cicadas singing, the deep churning song rising all around him, which made the shadows themselves seem alive. And there came another sound he had forgotten completely, the shrill cry of birds.

Sounds like the woodland, he thought, as he gazed at the darkened and forlorn galleries, shrouded now in early darkness, not a single light flickering from behind the high narrow and numerous wooden blinds.

The sky was glazed and shining over the rooftop, soft and shot with violet and gold. It revealed starkly and beautifully the farthest end column of the high second gallery and, beneath the bracketed cornice, the bougainvillea vine tumbling down luxuriantly from the roof. Even in the gloom he could see the purple blossoms. And he could trace the old rose pattern in the iron railings. He could make out the capitals of the columns, the curious Italianate mixture of Doric for the side columns, Ionic for the lower ones set in ante, and Corinthian for those above.

He drew in his breath in a long mournful sigh. Again, he felt inexpressible happiness but it was mixed with sorrow, and he was not sure why. All the long years, he thought wearily, even in the midst of this joy. Memory had deceived in only one aspect, he reflected. The house was larger, far larger than he had remembered. All of these old places were larger; the very scale of everything here seemed for the moment almost unimaginable.

Yet there was a breathing, pulsing closeness to everything— the soft overgrown foliage behind the rusted iron fence blending in the darkness, and the singing of the cicadas, and the dense shadows beneath the oaks.

"Paradise," he whispered. He gazed up at the tiny green ferns that covered the oak branches, and the tears came to his eyes. The memory of the visions was perilously close to him. It brushed him like dark wings. *Yes, the house, Michael.*

He stood riveted, the beer cold against the palm of his gloved hand. Was she talking to him, the woman with the dark hair?

He only knew for certain that the twilight was singing; the heat was singing; he let his gaze drift to the other mansions around him, noting nothing perhaps but the flowing harmony of fence and column and brickwork and even tiny faltering crepe myrtles struggling for life on strips of velvet green. A warm peace flooded him, and for a second the memory of the visions and their awful mandate lost its hold. Back, back into childhood he reached, not for a memory, but for a continuity. The moment expanded, moving beyond all thought, all helpless and inadequate words.

The sky darkened. It was still the brave color of amethyst, as if fighting the night with a low and relentless fire. But the light was nevertheless going. And turning his head ever so slightly to look down the long street in the direction of the river, Michael saw that there the sky was pure gold.

Deep, deep in him were memories, naturally, memories of a boy walking out this street from the crowded little houses near the river, of a boy standing in this very place when evening fell. But the present continued to eclipse everything, and there was no straining to recollect, to impress or to improve the soft inundation of his senses by everything around him, this moment of pure quiet in his soul.

Only now as he looked lovingly and slowly again at the house itself, at its deep doorway, shaped like a giant keyhole, did the impression of the visions grow strong again. Doorway. Yes, they had told him about the doorway! But it was not a literal doorway. Yet the sight of the giant keyhole and the shadowy vestibule behind it . . . No, couldn't have been a literal doorway. He opened his eyes and closed them. He found himself gazing trancelike up at the windows of a northern room on the second story, and to his sudden worry, he saw the lurid glare of fire.

No, that could not happen. But within the same instant, he realized it was only the light of candles. The flicker remained constant, and he merely wondered at it, wondered that those within would choose this form of light.

The garden was thickening and closing up in the darkness. He would have to rouse himself if he wanted to walk down along the fence and look back into the side yard. He wanted to do it, but the high northern window held him. He saw now the shadow of a woman moving against the lace curtain. And through the lace, he was able to make out a dingy flower pattern on the high corner of the wall.

Suddenly he looked down at his feet. The beer had fallen from his hand. It was foaming into the gutter. Drunk, he thought, too drunk, you idiot, Michael. But it didn't matter. On the contrary, he felt rather powerful, and suddenly he blundered across the intersection, aware of his heavy and uneven steps, and came to the front gate of the house.

He pushed his fingers through the iron webbing, staring at the dust and debris tossed about on the peeling boards of the front porch. The camellias had grown into trees which towered over the railings. And the flagstone path was covered over with leaves. He stuck his foot into the iron webbing. Easy enough to jump this gate.

"Hey, buddy, hey!"

Astonished, he turned to see the cab driver next to him, and how short he was when he wasn't inside the cab. Just a little man with a big nose, his eyes in shadow under the bill cap, like a troll of the oaks in this heightened moment. "What are you trying to do? You lost your key?"

"I don't live here," Michael said. "I don't have a key." And suddenly he laughed at the pure absurdity of it. He felt giddy. The sweet breeze coming from the river was so luscious and the dark house was right here in front of him, almost close enough for him to touch.

"Come on, let me take you back to your hotel, you said the Pontchartrain? Right? I'll help you get upstairs to your room."

"Not so fast," Michael said, "just hang on a minute." He turned and walked down the street, distracted suddenly by the broken and uneven flagstones, pure purple, too, as he'd remembered. Was there nothing that would be faded and disappointing? He wiped at his face. Tears. Then he turned and looked into the side yard.

The crepe myrtles here had grown enormously. Their pale waxy trunks were now quite thick. And the great stretch of lawn he remembered was sad with weeds now, and the old boxwood was growing wild and unkempt. Nevertheless he loved it. Loved even the old trellis in the back, leaning under its burden of tangled vines.

And that's where the man always stood, he thought, as he made out the faraway crepe myrtle, the one that went high up the wall of the neighboring house.

"Where are you?" he whispered. The visions hung thick over him suddenly. He felt himself fall forward against the fence, and heard its iron tendons groan. A soft rustling came from the foliage on the other side, just exactly to his right. He turned; movement in the leaves. Camellia blossoms, bruised and falling on the soft earth. He knelt and reached through the fence and caught one of them, red, broken. Was the cab driver talking to him?

"It's OK, buddy," Michael said, looking at the broken camellia in his hand, trying the better to see it in the gloom. Was that the gleam of a black shoe right in front of him, on the other side? Again came the rustling. Why, he was staring at a man's pant leg. Someone was standing only an inch away. He lost his balance as he looked up. And as his knees struck the flagstones, he saw a figure looming over him, peering through the fence at him, eyes catching only a spark of light. The figure appeared frozen, wide-eyed, perilously close to him, and violently alert and focused upon him. A hand reached out, no more than a streak of white in the shadows. Michael moved away on the flags, the alarm in him instinctive and unquestioned. But now as he stared at the overgrown foliage, he realized that there was no one there.

The emptiness was as terrifying suddenly as the vanished figure. "God help me," he whispered. His heart was knocking against his ribs. And he could not get up. The cab driver tugged on his arm.

"Come on, son, before a patrol car passes here!"

He was pulled, swaying dangerously, to his feet.

"Did you see that?" he whispered. "Christ almighty, that was the same man!" He stared at the cab driver. "I tell you it was the same man."

"I'm telling you, son, I gotta take you back to the hotel now. This is the Garden District, boy, don't you remember? You can't go staggering drunk around here!"

Michael lost his footing again. He was going over. Heavily he backed off the flags into the grass, and then turned, reaching out for the tree but there was no tree. Again the driver caught him. Then another pair of hands steadied him. He spun round. If it was the man again, he was going screaming crazy.

But of all people, it was that Englishman, that white-haired fellow in the tweed suit who'd been on the plane.

"What the hell are you doing here?" Michael whispered. But even through his drunkenness he caught the man's benign face, his reserved and refined demeanor.

"I want to help you, Michael," the man said, with the utmost gentleness. It was one of those rich and limitlessly polite English voices. "I'd be so grateful if you'd allow me to take you back to the hotel."

"Yeah, that seems to be the appropriate course of action," Michael said, keenly aware that he could hardly make the words come out clear. He stared back at the garden, at the high facade of the house again, now quite lost in the darkness, though the sky in bits and pieces beyond the oak branches still carried a latent gleam. It seemed that the cab driver and the Englishman were talking together. It seemed the Englishman was paying the fare.

Michael tried to reach into his pants pocket for his money clip, but his hand kept sliding right past the cloth again and again. He moved away from the two men, falling forward and then against the fence once more. Almost all the light was gone from the lawn now, from the distant encroaching shrubs. The trellis and its weight of vines was a mere hooded shape in the night.

Yet beneath the farthest crepe myrtle, quite distinctly, Michael could make out a thin human shape. He could see the pale oval of the man's face, and to his disbelieving eye came clear the same stiff white collar of the old days, the same silk tie at the throat.

Like a man right out of a novel. And he had seen these very same details only moments before in his panic.

"Come on, Michael, let me take you back," said the Englishman.

"First you have to tell me something," Michael said. He was beginning to shake all over. "Look, tell me, do you see that man?"

But now he saw only the various shades of darkness. And out of memory, there came his mother's voice, young and crisp and painfully immediate. "Michael, now you know there is no man there."

Eight

AFTER MICHAEL LEFT, Rowan sat on the western deck for hours, letting the sun warm her, and thinking in a rather incoherent and sleepy way about all that had taken place. She was slightly shocked and bruised by what had happened, rather deliciously bruised.

Nothing could efface the shame and guilt she felt for having burdened Michael with her doubts and her grief. But this was of no real concern to her now.

One did not become a good neurosurgeon by dwelling for very long on one's mistakes. The appropriate thing, and the instinctive thing for Rowan, was to assess the error for what it was, consider how to avoid it in the future, and then to go on from there.

And so she took stock of her aloneness, her sadness, the revelation of her own need, which had caused her to fall into

221

Michael's arms, and she took stock also of the fact that Michael had enjoyed comforting her, that it had drawn the two of them together, deeply coloring their new relationship in a wholly unforeseen way.

Then she moved on to thinking about him.

Rowan had never loved a man of Michael's age; she had never imagined the degree of selflessness and simplicity which was evident in Michael's most spontaneous words or gestures. She had been unprepared for and quite enthralled by Michael's mellowness of soul. As for his lovemaking, well, it was damn near perfect. He liked it rough and tumble the way she did; rather like a rape from both sides, it seemed to her. She wished they could do it again right now.

And for Rowan, who had so long kept her spiritual hungers and her physical hungers completely separated, satisfying the first through medicine and the second through near anonymous bed partners, the sudden convergence of the two in one good-hearted, intelligent, irresistibly huggable and charmingly cheerful and handsome figure with a captivating combination of mysterious psychological and psychic problems was just about more than she could handle. She shook her head, laughing softly to herself, then sipping her coffee. "Dickens and Vivaldi," she whispered aloud. "Oh, Michael, please come back to me. Come back soon." This was a gift from the sea, this man.

But what the hell was going to happen to him, even if he did come back right away? This idée fixe about the visions and the house and the purpose was destroying him. And furthermore, she had the distinct feeling that he wasn't going to come back.

There wasn't any doubt in her mind, as she sat half dreaming in the clear afternoon sun, that Michael was drunk by now and that he would get drunker before he ever reached his mysterious house. It would have been a lot better for him if she had gone with him, to look after him and to try to steady him through the shocks of this trip.

In fact, it occurred to her now that she had abandoned Michael twice—once when she had given him up too soon and too easily to the Coast Guard; and this morning, when she had let him go on to New Orleans alone.

Of course no one would have expected her to go with him to New Orleans. But then nobody knew what she felt for Michael, or what Michael had felt for her.

As for the nature of Michael's visions, and she thought about these at length, she had no conclusive opinion except that they could not be attributed to a physiological cause. And again, their particularity—their eccentricity—startled her and frightened her

222

somewhat. And there persisted in her a sense of Michael's dangerous innocence, his naivete, which seemed to her to be connected to his attitudes about evil. He understood good better than he did evil.

Yet why, when they'd been driving over from San Francisco, did he ask her that curious question: had she been trying to throw him some sort of warning?

He had seen Graham's death when he touched her hand because she had been thinking of Graham's death. And the thought of it tortured her. But how could Michael construe this to be a deliberate warning? Had he sensed something of which she was wholly unaware?

The longer she sat in the sun, the more she realized that she could not think clearly and that she could not endure this longing for Michael, which was reaching the point of anguish.

She went upstairs to her room. She was just stepping into the shower when she thought of something. She had forgotten completely to use a contraceptive with Michael. It wasn't the first time in her life she had been so stupid, but it was the first time in many years.

But it was done now, wasn't it? She turned on the tap and stood back against the tile, letting the water flood over her. Imagine having a child by him. But that was crazy. Rowan didn't want babies. She had never wanted babies. She thought again of that fetus in the laboratory, with all the wires and the tubes connected to it. No, her destiny was to save lives, not to make them. So what did that mean? For two weeks or so she'd be anxious; then when she knew she wasn't pregnant, she'd be all right.

She was so sleepy when she came out of the shower that she was scarcely aware of what she was doing. She found Michael's discarded shirt by the bed, the one he'd taken off the night before. It was a blue work shirt, starched and pressed as well as a dress shirt, which she had liked. She folded it neatly, and then lay down with it in her arms as if it were a child's favorite blanket or stuffed toy.

And there she slept for six hours.

When she awoke, she knew she could not stay alone in the house. It seemed Michael had left his warm imprint on everything. She could hear the timbre of his voice, his laughter, see his enormous blue eyes peering at her earnestly through the horn-rimmed glasses, feel his gloved fingers touching her nipples, her cheek.

It was too early still to expect to hear from him, and now the house seemed all the more empty in the aftermath of his warmth.

At once she called the hospital. Of course they needed her. It was Saturday night in San Francisco, wasn't it? The Emergency Rooms at San Francisco General had already overflowed. Accident victims were pouring into the Trauma Center at University from a multicar crash on Highway 101, and there had been several shootings in the Mission.

As soon as she arrived, there was a patient waiting for her in surgery, already intubated and anesthetized, the victim of an attempted ax murder, who had lost a great deal of blood. The intern ran through the history as Rowan scrubbed. Dr. Simmons had already opened. She saw as soon as she entered the ice-box-cold Operating Room that Dr. Simmons was relieved that she had come.

She surveyed the scene carefully as she stretched out her arms to receive the sterile green gown and the plastic gloves. Two of the best nurses on duty; one intern getting sick, the other powerfully excited by the proceedings; the anesthetists not her favorites but adequate; Dr. Simmons having done a good and tidy job of things so far.

And there was the patient, the anonymous patient, mounted in a slump of a sitting position, head bowed, the skull opened, the face and limbs hidden completely beneath layers and layers of green cotton drapery, except for two naked, helpless feet.

She moved towards the head of the table, behind the slumped body, nodding to the few rapid words the anesthetist spoke to her, and with her right foot she pressed down on the pedal that adjusted the giant double surgical scope, bringing into focus the opened brain, its tissues held back by the shining metal retractors.

"What a god-awful mess," she whispered.

Soft, delicate laughter all around.

"She knew you were coming in, Dr. Mayfair," said the older of the two nurses, "so she just told her husband to go on and give her another whack with that ax."

Rowan smiled behind her mask, her eyes crinkling. "What do you think, Dr. Simmons?" she asked. "Can we clean up all this blood in here without sucking out too much of this lady's brain?"

For five hours, she did not think of Michael at all.

It was two o'clock when she reached home. The house was dark and cold as she expected it to be when she came in. But for the first time since Ellie's death she did not find herself brooding over Ellie. She didn't think uneasily and painfully of Graham.

No message on her machine from Michael. She was disappointed but not surprised. She had a vivid image of him staggering off the plane, drunk. It was four o'clock in New Orleans, she figured. She couldn't ring the Pontchartrain Hotel now.

Best not to think too much about it, she reasoned as she went up to bed once more.

Best not to think about the paper in the safe that said she couldn't go back to New Orleans. Best not to think about getting on a plane and going to him. Best not to think about Andrew Slattery, her colleague, who still hadn't been hired at Stanford, and who might be all too happy to fill in for her at University for a couple of weeks. Why the hell had she asked Lark tonight about Slattery, calling him just after midnight, to ask specifically whether Slattery had found a job. Something was going on in her feverish little brain.

It was three o'clock when next she opened her eyes. Someone was in the house. She did not know what noise or vibration had caused her to waken, only that someone else was there. The numerals of the digital clock were the only illumination other than the distant lights of the city. A great gust of wind hit the windows suddenly and with it a shower of glittering spray.

She realized the house was moving violently on its pilings. There was the faint rattle of glass.

She rose as quietly as she could, removed a .38- caliber pistol from the dresser drawer, cocked it, and went to the head of the stairs. She held the gun with two hands as Chase, her cop friend, had taught her to do. She had practiced with this gun and she knew how to use it. She was not afraid so much as angry, deeply angry, and quietly alert.

She heard no footsteps. She heard only the wind, howling distantly in the chimney, and making the thick glass walls ever so faintly groan.

She could see the living room directly below, in the usual glaze of bluish lunar light. Another volley of droplets struck the windows. She heard the *Sweet Christine* slam dully against the rubber tires fixed along the northern pier.

Quietly she went down, step by step, her eyes sweeping the empty rooms with each curve of the staircase, until she reached the lower floor. There was not a crevice of the house she could not see from where she stood, except the bathroom behind her. And seeing only emptiness everywhere she looked, and the *Sweet Christine* rocking awkwardly, she moved cautiously towards the bathroom door.

225

The little room was empty. Nothing disturbed there. Michael's coffee cup on the vanity counter. Scent of Michael's cologne.

Looking out once more through the front rooms, she rested back against the frame of the door. The ferocity of the wind slamming the glass walls alarmed her. She had heard it in the past, many a time, however. And only once had it been strong enough to break the glass. Such a storm had never come during the month of August. It had always been a winter phenomenon, coupled with the heavy rains that poured down on the hills of Marin County, washing mud into the streets, and sometimes washing houses off their foundations as well.

Now she watched, vaguely fascinated as the water splashed and spattered onto the long decks, staining them darkly. She could see a frost of drops on the windshield of the *Sweet Christine*. Had this sudden storm deceived her? She sent out her invisible antennae. She listened.

Beyond the groaning of glass and wood, she heard no alien sound. But something was wrong here. She wasn't alone. And the intruder was not on the second floor of the house, she was certain of that. He was near. He was watching her. But where? She could find no explanation for what she felt.

The digital clock in the kitchen made a tiny, near imperceptible clicking sound as it rolled over to reveal that the time was five minutes after three A.M.

Something moved in the corner of her eye. She did not turn to stare at it. She chose not to move at all. And gradually, shifting her gaze sharply to the left without moving her head, she took in the figure of a man standing on the western deck.

He appeared to be slight of build, white-faced, with dark hair. His posture was not furtive or threatening. He stood unaccountably straight, arms natural at his sides. Surely she wasn't seeing this figure clearly, for the clothes seemed improbable to the point of impossibility—formal, and elegantly cut.

Her rage grew stronger, and a cold calm settled over her. Her reasoning was instantaneous. He could not gain entrance to the house through the deck doors. He could not batter his way through the thick glass either. And if she fired the gun at him, which she would have loved to do, she'd put a hole in the glass. Of course he might fire a gun at her as soon as he saw her. But why would he do it? Intruders want to get in. Besides, she was almost certain that he had already seen her, that he'd been watching her, and was watching her now.

Very slowly she turned her head. However dark the living room might have appeared to him, there was no doubt that he could see her, that he was looking at her, in fact.

His boldness infuriated her. And her sense of the danger of the situation mounted. She watched coldly as he moved towards the glass.

"Come on, you bastard, I'll cheerfully kill you," she whispered, feeling the hairs rise on her neck. A delicious chill passed through her whole body. She wanted to kill him, whoever he was, trespasser, madman, thief. She wanted to blow him right off the deck with the .38-caliber bullet. Or to put it simply, with any power she had at her command.

Slowly, with both hands, she lifted the gun. She pointed it directly at him and stretched out her arms as Chase had taught her to do.

Undeterred, the intruder continued to look at her, and through her quiet, iron-cold fury, she marveled at the physical details that she could make out. The dark hair was wavy, the face wan and thin, and there seemed something sad and beseeching in the shadowy expression. The head turned gently on the neck as though the man were pleading with her, speaking to her.

Who in God's name are you? she thought. The incongruity of it struck her slowly, along with a completely alien thought. This is not what it appears to be. This is some form of illusion I'm looking at! And with a sudden interior shift, her anger passed into suspicion and finally fear.

The dark eyes of the being implored her. He raised his pale hands now and placed his fingers on the glass.

She could neither move nor speak. Then, furious at her helplessness and at her terror, she cried:

"You go back to hell where you came from!" her voice sounding loud and terrible in the empty house.

As if to answer her, to unsettle her and vanquish her totally, the intruder slowly disappeared. The figure went transparent, then dissolved utterly, and nothing was left but the faintly horrible and completely unsettling sight of the empty deck.

The immense pane of glass rattled. There came another boom from it as though the wind had pushed against it head on. Then the sea seemed to settle. The rushing of water died away. And the house grew still. Even the *Sweet Christine* settled uneasily in the channel beside the pier.

Rowan continued to look at the empty deck. Then she realized her hands were wet with perspiration, and shaking. The gun felt enormously heavy and dangerously uncontrollable. In fact, she was shaking all over. Nevertheless, she went directly to the glass wall. Furious at her defenselessness against this thing, she touched the glass where the being had touched it. The glass was faintly but distinctly warm. Not warm as it might be from a

227

human hand, for that would be too subtle a thing to warm such a cold surface, but warm as if heat had been directed at it.

Again she studied the bare boards. She stared out at the dark, faceted water and the distant cozy lights of Sausalito on the other side of the bay.

She moved swiftly to the kitchen counter, set down the gun, and picked up the phone.

"I have to reach the Pontchartrain Hotel in New Orleans. Please dial it," she said, her voice quaking. And the only thing she could do to calm herself as she waited was to listen, to reassure herself of what she already knew, that she was completely alone.

Useless to check locks and latches. Useless to go poking in drawers and nooks and crannies. Useless, useless, useless.

She was frantic by the time the hotel answered. "I have to speak to Michael Curry," she said. He was to have checked in that night, she explained. No, it didn't matter that it was five-twenty in New Orleans. Please ring his room.

It seemed forever that she stood there alone, too shaken to question the selfishness of waking Michael at this hour. Then came the operator again: "I'm sorry, but Mr. Curry is not answering."

"Try him again. Send someone up to the room, please. I have to talk to him."

Finally, when they had failed to rouse him altogether, and refused of course to enter the suite without his permission—and for that she couldn't blame them—she left an urgent message, hung up and sank down on the hearth, and tried to think.

She was certain of what she'd seen, absolutely certain of it. An apparition there on the deck, looking at her, drawing close to her, examining her! Some being that could appear and disappear entirely at will. Yet why had she seen the gleam of light on the edge of his collar; why the droplets of moisture in his hair? Why was the glass warm to the touch? She wondered if the thing had substance to it when it was visible, and if that substance dissolved when the creature "appeared to disappear."

In sum, her mind ran to science as it always had, and she knew this was her tack, but it could not stop the panic in her, the great awful feeling of helplessness that had come over her and stayed with her now, making her afraid in her own safe place, where she'd never been afraid before.

Why had the wind and the rain been part of it, she wondered. Surely she hadn't imagined that part. And why, above all else, had this creature appeared to *her*?

"Michael," she whispered. It was like a prayer dropping from her lips. Then she gave a little whispered laugh. "I'm seeing them, too."

She rose from the hearth and went about the house slowly, with steady steps, turning on every light.

"All right," she said calmly, "if you come back, it will have to be in a blaze of illumination." But this was absurd, wasn't it? Something that could move the very waters of Richardson Bay could trip a circuit breaker easily enough.

But she wanted these lights on. She was scared. She went into the bedroom, locked the door behind her, locked the door of the closet, and closed the door of the bathroom, and then lay down, plumping the pillows under her head, and placing the gun within reach.

She lit a cigarette, knowing it was dreadful to smoke in bed, checked out the tiny winking red light on the smoke alarm, and then continued to smoke.

A ghost, she thought. Imagine it, I have seen one. I never believed in them, but I've seen one. It had to be a ghost. There's nothing else it could have been. But why did this ghost appear to me? Again, she saw its imploring expression, and the vividness of the experience returned to her.

It made her miserable suddenly that she couldn't reach Michael, that Michael was the only one in the whole world who might believe what had happened, that Michael was the only one she trusted enough to tell.

The fact was, she was excited; it was curiously like her feeling after the rescue that night. *I have been through something awful and thrilling.* She wanted to tell someone. She lay there, wide-eyed in the bright shadowless yellow light of the bedroom thinking, Why did it appear to me?

So curious the way it had walked across the deck and peered through the glass at her. "You would have thought I was the strange one."

And the excitement continued. But she was very relieved when the sun finally rose. Sooner or later, Michael would wake up out of his drunken sleep. He'd see the message light on his phone; and surely, he would call.

"And here I am wanting something from him again, reaching out to him right in the midst of whatever is happening there, needing him . . ."

But now she was drifting off, in the warm sweet safety of the sunlight pouring through the glass, snuggling into the warm pillows and pulling the patchwork quilt over her, thinking about him, about the dark fleecy hair on the backs of his arms and his hands, about his large eyes again peering at her through the glasses. And only on the cusp of dream did she think, Could this ghost possibly have something to do with him?

The visions. She wanted to say, "Michael, is it something to do with the visions?" Then the dream swung into absurdity, and she wakened, resisting the irrelevance and the grotesqueness as she always did, consciousness being so much better, thinking— of course, Slattery could fill in for her, and if Ellie existed somewhere she no longer cared whether Rowan went back to New Orleans, certainly, for we had to believe that, didn't we? That what was beyond this plane was infinitely better; and then she fell back into exhausted sleep again.

Nine

MICHAEL AWOKE ABRUPTLY, thirsting, and hot in the bed covers though the air in the room was quite cool. He was wearing his shorts and his shirt, cuffs unbuttoned, collar undone. He was also wearing his gloves.

A light burned at the end of the little carpeted corridor. Over the soft engulfing roar of the air conditioner, he heard what sounded like the rustle of papers.

Good heavens, where am I? he thought. He sat up. At the end of the little hallway, there appeared to be a parlor, and a baby grand piano of pale and lustrous wood standing against a bank of flowered drapes. His suite at the Pontchartrain Hotel, it had to be.

He had no memory of coming here. And he was instantly angry with himself for having gotten so drunk. But then the euphoria of the earlier evening returned to him, the vision of the house on First Street beneath the violet sky.

I'm in New Orleans, he thought. And he felt a surge of happiness which effaced all his present confusion and guilt. "I'm home," he whispered. "Whatever else I've done, I'm home."

But how had he managed to get into this hotel? And who was in the parlor? The Englishman. His last clear memory was of speaking to the Englishman in front of the First Street house. And with that little recollection came another: he saw the brownhaired man behind the black iron fence again, staring down at him. He saw the glittering eyes only a few feet above him, and the strangely white and impassive face. A curious feeling passed over him. It wasn't fear precisely. It was more purely visceral. His body tensed as it might against a threat.

How could that man have changed so little over the years? How could he have been there one minute and gone the next?

It seemed to Michael that he knew the answers to these questions, that he'd always understood the man was no ordinary man. But his sudden familiarity with such a completely unfamiliar notion almost made him laugh.

"You're losing it, buddy," he whispered.

But he had to get his bearings now, in this strange place, and find out what the Englishman wanted, and why he was still here.

Quickly he surveyed the room. Yes, the old hotel. A feeling of comfort and security came to him as he saw the slightly faded carpet, the painted air conditioner beneath the windows, and the heavy old-fashioned telephone sitting on the small inlaid desk with its message light pulsing in the darkness.

The door of the bath stood open revealing a dim slash of white tile.

To his left, the closet, and his suitcase, opened on its stand, and wonder of wonders, on the table beside him an ice bucket, beaded over beautifully with tiny drops of moisture, and crammed into the ice three tall cans of Miller's beer.

"Well, isn't that just about perfect?"

He removed his right glove and touched one of the beer cans. Immediate flash of a uniformed waiter, same old load of distracting, irrelevant information. He put the glove back on and opened the can. He drank down half of it in deep cold swallows. Then he climbed to his feet and went into the bathroom and pissed.

Even in the soft morning light coming through the slatted blinds, he could see his shaving kit laid out on the marble dresser. He took out his toothbrush and toothpaste and brushed his teeth.

Now he felt a little less headachy, hung over, and downright miserable. He combed his hair, swallowed the rest of the can of beer, and felt almost good.

He changed into a fresh shirt, pulled on his trousers, and taking another beer from the ice bucket, he went down the hallway and stood looking into a large, elegantly furnished room.

Beyond a gathering of velvet couches and chairs, the Englishman sat at a small wooden table, bent over a mass of manila folders and typewritten pages. He was a slightly built man with a heavily lined face and rather luxuriant white hair. He wore a gray velvet smoking jacket, tied at the waist, and gray tweed trousers, and he was looking at Michael with an extremely friendly and agreeable expression.

He rose to his feet.

"Mr. Curry, are you feeling better?" he asked. It was one of those eloquent English voices which make the simplest words take on new meaning, as if they've never been properly pronounced before. He had small yet brilliant blue eyes.

"Who are you?" Michael asked.

The Englishman drew closer, extending his hand.

Michael didn't take it, though it hurt him to be this rude to somebody who looked so friendly and earnest and sort of nice. He took another sip of the beer.

"My name's Aaron Lightner," the Englishman said. "I came from London to see you." Softly spoken, unobtrusive.

"My aunt told me that part. I saw you hanging around my house on Liberty Street. Why the hell did you follow me here?"

"Because I want to talk to you, Mr. Curry," the man said politely, almost reverentially. "I want to talk to you so badly that I'm willing to risk any discomfort or inconvenience I might incur. That I've risked your displeasure is obvious. And I'm sorry for it, truly sorry. I only meant to be helpful in bringing you here, and please allow me to point out that you were entirely cooperative at the time."

"Was I?" Michael found he was bristling. Yet this guy was a real charmer, he had to give him that. But another glance at the papers spread out on the table made Michael furious. For fifty bucks, or considerably less, the cab driver would have lent him a hand. And the cab driver wouldn't be here now.

"That's quite true," said Lightner in the same soft, well-tempered voice. "And perhaps I should have retired to my own suite above, but I wasn't certain whether or not you'd be ill, and frankly I was worried on another count."

Michael said nothing. He was fully aware that the man had just read his mind, so to speak. "Well, you just caught my attention with that little trick," he said. And he thought, Can you do it again?

"Yes, if you like," said the Englishman. "A man in your frame of mind is, unfortunately, quite easy to read. Your increased sensitivity works both ways, I fear. But I can show you how to hide your thoughts, how to throw up a screen if you wish. On the other hand, it isn't really necessary. Because there aren't very many people like me walking about."

Michael smiled in spite of himself. All this was said with such genteel humility that he was a little overwhelmed and definitely reassured. The man seemed completely truthful. In fact, the only emotional impression received by Michael was one of goodness, which surprised him somewhat.

Michael walked past the piano to the flowered draperies and pulled the cord. He loathed being in an electrically lighted room in the morning, and he felt immediately happy again when he looked down on St. Charles Avenue, on the wide band of grass and the streetcar tracks, and the dusty foliage of the oaks. He had not remembered the leaves of the oaks as being so darkly green. It seemed everything he saw was remarkably vivid. And when the St. Charles car passed beneath him, moving slowly uptown, the old familiar roar—a sound like no other—brought the excitement back to him. How drowsy and wonderfully familiar it all seemed.

He had to get back outside, walk over to the First Street house again. But he was keenly aware of the Englishman watching him. And again, he could detect nothing but honesty in the man, and nothing but a sort of wholesome goodwill.

"OK, I'm curious," he said turning around. "And I'm grateful. But I don't like all this. I really don't. So out of curiosity and in gratitude, if you follow me, I'll give you twenty minutes to explain who you are, and why you are here, and what this is all about." He sat down on the velvet couch opposite the man and the messy table. He switched off the lamp. "Oh, and thanks for the beer. I really appreciate the beer."

"There's more in the refrigerator in the kitchen behind me," said the Englishman. Unflappably pleasant.

"Thoughtful," said Michael. He felt comfortable in this room. He could not remember it really from childhood, but it was pleasant with its dark papered walls and soft upholstered pieces and low brass lamps.

The man seated himself at the table, facing Michael. And for the first time Michael noticed a small bottle of brandy and a glass. He saw that the man's suit coat was on the back of the other chair. A briefcase, the briefcase Michael had seen in the airport, was standing by the chair.

"You wouldn't care for a little cognac?" the man asked.

"No. Why do you have the suite just overhead? What's going on?"

"Mr. Curry, I belong to an old organization," said the man. "It's called the Talamasca. Have you ever heard the name?"

Michael thought for a moment. "No."

"We go back to the eleventh century. More truly, we go back before that. But sometime during the eleventh century we took the name Talamasca, and from that time on we had a constitution, so to speak, and certain rules. What we are in modern parlance is a group of historians interested primarily in psychic research. Witchcraft, hauntings, vampires, people with remarkable psychic ability—all of these things interest us and we keep an immense archive of information regarding them.''

''You've been doing this since the eleventh century?''

''Yes, and before, as I said. We are in many respects a passive group of people; we do not like to interfere. As a matter of fact, let me show you our card and our motto.''

The Englishman drew the card out of his pocket, gave it to Michael, and returned to his chair.

Michael read the card:

THE TALAMASCA

We watch
And we are always here.

There were phone numbers given for Amsterdam, Rome, and London.

''You have headquarters in all those places?'' Michael asked.

''Motherhouses, we call them,'' said the Englishman. ''But to continue, we are largely passive, as I said. We collect data; we correlate, cross-reference, and preserve information. But we are very active in making our information available to those who might benefit from it. We heard about your experience through the London papers, and through a contact in San Francisco. We thought we might be able to . . . be of assistance to you.''

Michael took off his right glove, tugging slowly at each finger, and then laid the glove aside. He picked up the card again. Jarring flash of Lightner putting several such cards in his pocket in another hotel room. New York City. Smell of cigars. Noise of traffic. Flash of some woman somewhere, speaking to Lightner fast in a British accent . . .

''Why not ask it a specific question, Mr. Curry?''

The words brought Michael out of it. ''All right,'' he said. *Is this man telling me the truth?* The load continued, debilitating and discouraging, voices growing louder, more confused. Through the din, Michael heard Lightner speak to him again:

''Focus, Mr. Curry, extract what you want to know. Are we good people or are we not?''

Michael nodded, repeating the question silently, then he couldn't take all this any longer. He set the card down on the table, careful not to brush the table itself with his fingertips. He was shaking slightly. He slipped his glove back on. His vision cleared.

"Now, what do you know?" asked Lightner.

"Something about the Knights Templar, you stole their money," Michael said.

"What?" Lightner was flabbergasted.

"You stole their money. That's why you have all these Motherhouses all over kingdom come. You stole their money when the king of France arrested them. They gave it to you for safekeeping and you kept it. And you're rich. You're all filthy rich. And you're ashamed of what happened with the Knights Templar, that they were accused of witchcraft and destroyed. I know that part, of course, from the history books. I was a history major. I know all about what happened to them. The king of France wanted to crack their power. Apparently he didn't know about you." Michael paused. "Very few people really know about you."

Lightner stared in what seemed innocent amazement. Then his faced colored. His discomfort seemed to be increasing.

Michael laughed, though he tried not to. He moved the fingers of the right glove. "Is that what you mean by focus and extract information?"

"Well, I suppose that is what I meant, yes. But I never thought you would extract such an obscure—"

"You're ashamed of what happened with the Knights Templar. You always have been. Sometimes you go down into the basement archives in London and you read through all the old material. Not the computer abstracts, but the old files, written in ink on parchment. You try to convince yourself there was nothing that the order could have done to help the Knights."

"Very impressive, Mr. Curry. But, Mr. Curry, if you know your history, you'll know that no one except the Pope in Rome could have saved the Knights Templar. We certainly were not in a position to do it, being an obscure and small and completely secret organization. And frankly, when the persecutions were over, when Jacques de Molay and the others had been burnt alive, there wasn't anyone left to whom the money could be returned."

Michael laughed again. "You don't have to tell all this to me, Mr. Lightner. But you're really ashamed of something that happened six hundred years ago. What an odd bunch of guys you must be. By the way, for what it's worth, I did write a paper once on the Knights, and I agree with you. Nobody could have helped them, not even the Pope, as far as I can figure. If you guys had surfaced, they would have burnt you at the stake too."

Again, Lightner flushed. "Undoubtedly," he said. "Are you satisfied that I've been telling you the truth?"

"Satisfied? I'm impressed!" Michael studied him for a long moment. Again, the distinct impression of a wholesome human being, one who shared the values which mattered very much to Michael himself. "And this work of yours is the reason you followed me," Michael asked, "enduring, what was it, discomfort and inconvenience, and my displeasure?" Michael picked up the card, which took some doing with his gloved fingers, and slipped the card into the pocket of his shirt.

"Not entirely," said the Englishman. "Though I want to help you very much, and if that sounds patronizing or insulting, I'm sorry. Truly sorry. But it's true, and it's pointless to lie to someone like you."

"Well, I don't suppose it will come as any surprise to you that there have been times in the last few weeks when I have prayed out loud for help. I'm a little better off now than I was two days ago, however. A good deal better off. I'm on my way to doing . . . what I feel I have to do."

"You have an enormous power, and you don't really understand it," Lightner said.

"But the power is unimportant. What I'm talking about is the purpose. Did you read the articles on me in the papers?"

"Yes, everything in print that I could find."

"Well, then you know I had these visions when I was dead; and that they involved a purpose in my coming back; and that somehow or other, the entire memory has been wiped out. Well, almost the entire memory."

"Yes, I understand."

"Then you know the thing about the hands doesn't matter," said Michael. Uneasiness. He took another deep swallow of beer. "Nobody much believes about the purpose. But it's been over three months since the accident happened, and the feeling I have is the same. I came back here on account of the purpose. It has something to do with that house I went to last night. That house on First Street. I intend to keep trying to figure out what that purpose is."

The man was scanning him intently. "It does? The house is connected to the visions you saw when you were drowned?"

"Yes, but don't ask me how. For months, I've seen that house over and over again in my mind. I've seen it in my sleep. It's connected. I came two thousand miles because it's connected. But again, don't ask me how or why."

"And Rowan Mayfair, how is she connected?"

Michael set the beer down slowly. He took a hard appraising look at the man. "You know Dr. Mayfair?" he asked.

"No, but I know a great deal about her, and about her family," said the Englishman.

"You do? About her family? She might be very interested to know that. But how do you know about her family? What is her family to you? I thought you said you were waiting outside my house in San Francisco because you wanted to talk to me."

Lightner's face darkened for a moment. "I'm very confused, Mr. Curry. Perhaps you'll enlighten me. How did Dr. Mayfair happen to be there?"

"Look, I'm getting sick of your questions. She was there because she was trying to help me. She's a doctor."

"She was there in her capacity as a doctor?" Lightner asked in a half whisper. "I've been laboring under a misimpression. Dr. Mayfair didn't send you here?"

"Send me here? Good Lord, no. Why the hell would she do that? She wasn't even in favor of my coming, except that I'd get it out of my system. The truth is, I was so drunk when she picked me up it's a wonder she didn't have me committed. I wish I was that drunk right now. But why would you have an idea like that, Mr. Lightner? Why would Rowan Mayfair send me here?"

"Indulge me for a moment, won't you?"

"I don't know if I will."

"You didn't know Dr. Mayfair before you had the visions?"

"No. Not till five minutes afterwards."

"I don't follow you."

"She's the one who rescued me, Lightner. The one who pulled me out of the sea. That's the first time I ever laid eyes on her, when she brought me around on the deck of her boat."

"Good Lord, I had no idea."

"Well, neither did I until Friday night. I mean I didn't know her name or who she was or anything about her. The Coast Guard flubbed it. They didn't get her name or the registry of the boat when the call came in. But she saved my life out there. She's got some kind of powerful diagnostic sense, some sort of sixth sense about when a patient's going to live or die. She started trying to revive me immediately. I sometimes wonder if the Coast Guard had spotted me, whether or not they would even have tried."

Lightner lapsed into silence, staring at the carpet. He seemed deeply troubled.

"Yes, she is a remarkable physician," he whispered, but this did not seem to be a full expression of his thoughts. He seemed to be struggling to concentrate. "And you told her about these visions."

"I wanted to get back on her boat. I had this idea, that maybe if I knelt down on the deck and touched the boards, well, something might come through my hands. Something that might jog my memory. And the amazing thing was, she went along with it. She's not an ordinary doctor at all."

"No, I quite agree with you there," said Lightner. "And what happened?" he asked.

"Nothing, that is, nothing except that I got to know Rowan." He paused. He wondered if this man could guess how it was between him and Rowan. He was not going to say.

"Now I think you owe me some answers," Michael said. "Exactly what do you know about her and her family, and what made you think she sent me here? Me, of all people. Why the hell would she send me here?"

"Well, that's what I was trying to discover. I thought perhaps it had to do with the power in your hands, that she'd asked you to do some secretive research for her. Why, it was the only explanation I could think of. But Mr. Curry, how did you know about this house? I mean, how did you make the connection between what you saw in the visions and . . ."

"I grew up here, Lightner. I loved that house when I was a little kid. I used to walk past it all the time. I never forgot it. Even before I drowned I used to think about that house. I aim to find out who owns it and what this all means."

"Really . . ." said Lightner, again in a half whisper. "You don't *know* who owns it?"

"No, I just said I aim to find out."

"You don't have any idea . . ."

"I just told you, I aim to find out!"

"You tried to climb over the fence last night."

"I remember. Now would you mind telling me a few things, please? You know about me. You know about Rowan Mayfair. You know about the house. You know about Rowan's family—" Michael stopped, staring fixedly at Lightner. "Rowan's family!" he said. "They own that house?"

Gravely, Lightner nodded.

"That's really true?"

"They have for centuries," said Lightner quietly. "And if I'm not sadly mistaken that house will belong to Rowan Mayfair, upon her mother's death."

"I don't believe you," Michael whispered. But in truth he did. Once again the atmosphere of the visions enveloped him, only to dissolve immediately as it always did. He stared at Lightner, unable to form any of the questions teeming in his head.

"Mr. Curry. Indulge me again. Please. Explain to me in detail how the house is connected with the visions. Or more specifically, how you came to know it and remember it when you were a child."

"Not till you tell me what you know about all this," said Michael. "Do you realize that Rowan—?"

Lightner interrupted him:

"I am willing to tell you a great deal about the house and about the family," he said, "but I ask in exchange that you speak first. That you tell me anything you can recall, anything which seems significant, even if you don't know what to make of it. Possibly I shall know what to make of it. Do you follow my drift?"

"All right, my info for your info. But you *are* going to tell me what you know?"

"Absolutely."

It was worth it, obviously. It was about the most exciting thing which had happened, outside of Rowan coming to his door. And he was surprised how much he wanted to tell this man everything, absolutely every last detail.

"OK," he began, "as I said, I used to pass that house all the time when I was a kid. I used to go out of my way to pass it. I grew up on Annunciation Street by the river, about six blocks away. I used to see a man in the garden of that house, the same man I saw last night. Do you remember me asking you if you saw him? Well, I saw him last night by the fence, and back farther, in the garden, and damned if he didn't look exactly the same as he had when I was a little kid. And I mean I was four years old the first time I saw that guy. I was six when I saw him in church."

"You saw him in church?" Again the scanning, the eyes seeming to graze Michael's face as Lightner listened.

"Right, at Christmastime, at St. Alphonsus, I've never forgotten it, because he was in the sanctuary of all places, you know what I'm talking about? The crib was set up at the altar rail, and he was back on the side altar steps."

Lightner nodded. "And you are certain it was he?"

Michael laughed. "Well, given the part of town I come from, I was certain it was him," he said. "But yes, seriously, it was the same man. I saw him another time, too, I'm almost sure of it, but I haven't thought about it for years. It was at a concert downtown, a concert I'll never forget because Isaac Stern played that night. It was the first time I heard anything like that, live,

239

you know. And anyway, I saw that man in the auditorium. He was looking at me.''

Michael hesitated, the ambience of that long-ago moment returning, without a welcome, actually, because that had been such a sad and wrenching time. He shook it off. Lightner was reading his thoughts again, he knew it.

"They are not clear when you're upset," said Lightner softly. "But this is most important, Mr. Curry—"

"You're telling me! It's all got to do with what I saw when I was drowned. I know because I kept thinking about it after the accident, when I couldn't focus on anything else. I mean I kept waking up, seeing that house, thinking yes, go back there. It's what Rowan Mayfair called an idée fixe.''

"You did tell her about it . . ."

Michael nodded. He finished the beer. "Described it to her completely. She was patient, but she couldn't figure it out. She did say something that was very on the money, however. She said it was too specific to be something simply pathological. I thought that made a lot of sense.''

"Let me ask for just a little more patience," Lightner said. "Would you tell me what you do remember of the visions? You said you had not entirely forgotten . . ."

Michael's faith in the man was increasing. Maybe it was the mildly authoritative manner. But nobody had asked about the visions with this kind of seriousness, not even Rowan. He found himself completely disarmed. The man seemed so sympathetic.

"Oh, I am," said Lightner hastily. "Believe me, I'm entirely sympathetic, not only to what's happened to you, but to your belief in it. Please, do tell me.''

Michael described briefly the woman with the black hair, the jewel that was mixed up with it, the vague image or idea of a doorway . . . "Not the doorway of the house, though, it can't be. But it's got to do with the house." And something about a number now forgotten. No, not the address. It wasn't a long number, it was two digits, had some very important significance. And the purpose, of course the purpose, the purpose was the saving thing, and Michael's strong sense that he might have refused.

"I can't believe that they would have let me die if I had not accepted. They gave me a choice on everything. I chose to come back, and to fulfill the purpose. I awoke knowing I had something terribly important to do.''

He could see that what he said was having an amazing effect upon Lightner. Lightner didn't even attempt to disguise his surprise.

"Is there anything else you remember?"

"No. Sometimes it seems I'm about to remember everything. Then it just slides away. I didn't start thinking about the house till about twenty-four hours afterwards. No, maybe even a little longer. And immediately there was the sense of connection. I felt the same sense last night. I'd come to the right place to find all the answers, but I still couldn't remember! It's enough to drive a man mad."

"I can imagine," said Lightner softly, but he was still deeply involved in his own surprise or amazement at all that Michael had said. "Let me suggest something. Is it possible that when you were revived you took Rowan's hand in yours, and that this image of the house came to you then from Rowan?"

"Well, it's possible, except for one very important fact. Rowan doesn't know anything about that house. She doesn't know anything about New Orleans. She doesn't know anything about her family, except for the adoptive mother who died last year."

Lightner seemed reluctant to believe this.

"Look," Michael said. He was getting quite carried away now on the whole subject and he knew it. The fact was, he liked talking to Lightner. But things were going too far. "You have to tell me how you know about Rowan. Friday night when Rowan came to get me in San Francisco, she saw you. She said something about having seen you before. I want you to be straight with me, Lightner. What's all this about Rowan? How do you know about her?"

"I shall tell you everything," said Lightner with the same characteristic gentleness, "but let me ask you again, are you sure Rowan has never seen a picture of that house?"

"No, we discussed that very point. She was born in New Orleans—"

"Yes . . ."

"But they took her away that very day. They made her sign a paper that she'd never come back here. I asked her if she'd ever seen pictures of the houses here. She told me she hadn't. She couldn't find a scrap of information about her family after her adoptive mother's death. Don't you see? This didn't come from Rowan! It involves Rowan just as it involves me."

"How do you mean?"

Michael felt dazed trying to compass it. "I mean, I knew that they chose me because of everything that had ever happened to me . . . who I was, what I was, where I'd lived, it was all connected. And don't you see? I'm not the center of it. Rowan is probably the center. But I have to call Rowan. I have to tell her. I have to tell her that the house is her mother's house."

241

"Please don't do that, Michael."

"What?"

"Michael, sit down, please."

"What are you talking about? Don't you understand how incredible this is! That house belongs to Rowan's family. Rowan doesn't even know anything about her family. Rowan doesn't even know her own mother's full name."

"I don't want you to call her!" said Lightner with sudden urgency. "Please, I haven't fulfilled my side of the bargain. You haven't heard me out."

"God, don't you realize? Rowan was probably just taking out the *Sweet Christine* when I was washed off that rock! We were on a collision course with each other, and then these people, these people who knew everything, chose to intervene."

"Yes, I do realize . . . all I ask is that you allow for our exchange of information now, before you call Rowan."

The Englishman was saying more, but Michael couldn't hear him. He felt a sudden violent disorientation as if he were slipping into unconsciousness, and if he didn't grab hold of the table he would black out. But this wasn't a failure of his body; it was his mind that was slipping; and for one brilliant second the visions opened again, the black-haired woman was speaking directly to him, and then from some vantage point high above, some lovely and airy place where he was weightless and free he saw a small craft on the sea below, and he said, *Yes, I'll do it.*

He held his breath. Desperate not to lose the visions, he didn't reach out for them mentally. He didn't crowd them. He remained locked in stillness, feeling them leave him again in confusion, feeling the coldness and the solidity of his body around him, feeling the old familiar longing and anger and pain.

"Oh, my God," he whispered. "And Rowan doesn't even have the slightest idea . . ."

He realized he was sitting down on the couch again. Lightner had hold of him, and he was grateful. Otherwise he might have fallen. He shut his eyes again. But the visions were nowhere near. He saw only Rowan, soft and pretty and beautifully disheveled in the big white terry-cloth robe, her neck bent, her blond hair falling down to veil her face as she cried.

When he opened his eyes, he saw that Lightner was sitting next to him. There was the horrifying feeling that he had lost seconds, possibly minutes of time. He didn't mind the presence of the man, however. The man seemed genuinely kindly and respecting, in spite of all the incredible things he had to say.

"Only a second or two has passed," said Lightner. (Mind reading again!) "But you were dizzy. You almost fell."

"Right. You don't know how awful this is, not remembering. And Rowan said the strangest thing."

"What was that?"

"That maybe they didn't mean for me to remember."

"And this struck you as strange?"

"They want me to remember. They want me to do what I'm supposed to do. It has to do with the doorway, I know it does. And the number thirteen. And Rowan said another thing that really threw me. She said how did I know that these people I saw were good? Christ, she asked me if I thought they were responsible for the accident, you know, for me being washed out to sea like that. God, I tell you I'm going crazy."

"Those are very good questions," said the man with a sigh. "Did you say the number thirteen?"

"Did I? Is that what I said? I don't . . . I guess I did say that. Yes, it was the number thirteen. Christ, I've got that back now. Yes, it was the number thirteen."

"Now I want you to listen to me. I don't want you to call Rowan. I want you to get dressed and to come with me."

"Wait a second, my friend. You're a very interesting guy. You look better in a smoking jacket than anybody I've ever seen in the movies and you have a very persuasive and charming manner. But I'm right here, exactly where I want to be. And I'm going back to that house after I call Rowan . . ."

"And what exactly are you going to do there? Ring the bell?"

"Well, I'll wait till Rowan comes. Rowan wants to come, you know. She wants to see her family. That's got to be what this is all about."

"And the man, what do you suppose he has to do with it all?" asked Lightner.

Michael was stopped. He sat there staring at Lightner. "Did you see that man?" he asked.

"No. He didn't allow time for that. He wanted you to see him. And why is what I would like to know."

"But you know all about him, don't you?"

"Yes."

"OK, it's your turn to talk, and I wish you'd start right now."

"Yes, that's our bargain," said Lightner. "But I find it's more important than ever that you know everything." He stood up, and walked slowly over to the table, and began to gather up the papers that were scattered all over it, placing them neatly into a large leather folder. "And everything is in this file."

Michael followed him. He looked down at the impossibly large mass of materials which the man was cramming into the folder. Mostly typewritten sheets, yet some were in longhand as well.

"Look, Lightner, you owe me some answers," Michael said.

"This is a compendium of answers, Michael. It's from our archives. It's entirely devoted to the Mayfair family. It goes back to the year 1664. But you must hear me out. I cannot give it to you here."

"Where then?"

"We have a retreat house near here, an old plantation house, quite a lovely place."

"No!" Michael said impatiently.

Lightner gestured for quiet. "It's less than an hour and a half away. I must insist that you dress now and you come with me, and that you read the file in peace and quiet at Oak Haven, and that you save all your questions until you've done so, and all the aspects of this case are clear. Once you've read the records you'll understand why I've begged you to postpone your call to Dr. Mayfair. I think you'll be glad that you did."

"Rowan should see this record."

"Indeed, she should. And if you were willing to place it in her hands for us, we would be eternally grateful indeed."

Michael studied the man, trying to separate the charm of the man's manner from the astonishing content of what he said. He felt drawn to the man and reassured by his knowledge on the one hand; yet suspicious on the other. And through it all, he was powerfully fascinated by the pieces of the puzzle which were falling into place.

Something else had come clear to him also. The reason he so disliked this power in his hands was that once he had touched another, or the belongings of another, a certain intimacy was established. In the case of strangers, it was fairly quickly effaced. In the case of Lightner it was gradually increasing.

"I can't go with you to the country," Michael said. "There's no doubt in my mind that you're sincere. But I have to call Rowan and I want you to give this material to me here."

"Michael, there is information here which is pertinent to everything you've told me. It concerns a woman with black hair. It concerns a very significant jewel. As for the doorway, I don't know the meaning. As for the number thirteen, I might. As for the man, the woman with the black hair and jewel are connected to him. But I shall let it out of my hands only on my terms."

Michael narrowed his eyes. "You're saying this is the woman I saw in the visions?"

"Only you can determine that for yourself."

"You wouldn't play games with me."

"No. Of course not. But don't play games with yourself either, Michael. You always knew that man was not . . . what he appeared to be, didn't you? What did you feel last night when you saw him?"

"Yeesss, I knew . . ." Michael whispered. He felt the disorientation again. Yet a dark unsettling thrill ran through him. He saw the man again peering down at him through the fence. "Christ," he whispered. And before he could stop himself, the most surprising thing happened. He raised his right hand and made a quick, reflexive sign of the cross.

Embarrassed he looked at Lightner.

Then the clearest thought came to him. The sense of excitement in him was rising. "Could they have meant for me to meet you?" Michael asked. "The woman with the black hair, could she have meant for this meeting between you and me to take place?"

"Only you can be the judge of that. Only you know what these beings said to you. Only you know who they actually were."

"God, but I don't." Michael put his hands to the side of his head. He found that he was staring down at the leather folder. There was writing on it in English. Large letters, embossed in gold, but half worn away. " 'The Mayfair Witches,' " he whispered. "Is that what those words say?"

"Yes. Would you dress now and come with me? They can have breakfast waiting for us in the country. Please?"

"You don't believe in witches!" Michael said. But *they* were coming. Again the room was fading. And Lightner's voice was once again distant, his words without meaning, merely faint, innocuous sounds coming from far away. Michael shuddered all over. Sick feeling. He saw the room again in the dusty morning light. Aunt Vivian had sat over there years ago, and his mother had sat here. But this was now. Call Rowan . . .

"Not yet," said Lightner. "After you've read the file."

"You're afraid of Rowan. There's something about Rowan herself, some reason you want to protect me from Rowan . . ." He could see the dust swirling around him in motes. How could something so particular and so material give the scene an air of unreality? He thought of touching Rowan's hand in the car. *Warning.* He thought of Rowan afterwards, in his arms.

"You know what it is," Lightner said. "Rowan told you."

"Oh, that's crazy. She imagined it."

"No, she didn't. Look at me. You know I'm telling you the

245

truth. Don't ask me to search out your thoughts for it. You know. You thought of it when you saw the word 'Witches.' ''

"I didn't. You can't kill people simply by wishing them dead.''

"Michael, I'm asking for less than twenty-four hours. This is a trust I am placing in you. I ask for your respect for our methods, I ask that you give me this time.''

Michael watched in confused silence as Lightner removed his smoking jacket, put on his suit coat, and then folded the jacket neatly and put it in the briefcase along with the leather file.

He had to read what was in that leather folder. He watched Lightner zipper the briefcase and lift it and hold it in both arms.

"I don't accept it!'' said Michael. "Rowan is no witch. That's crazy. Rowan's a doctor, and Rowan saved my life.''

And to think it was her house, that beautiful house, the house he'd loved ever since he was a little boy. He felt the evening again as it had been yesterday with the sky breaking violet through the branches and the birds crying as if they were in a wild wood.

All these years he'd known that man wasn't real. All his life he'd known it. He'd known it in the church. . . .

"Michael, that man is waiting for Rowan,'' Lightner said.

"Waiting for Rowan? But, Lightner, why, then, did he show himself to me?''

"Listen, my friend.'' The Englishman put his hand on Michael's hand and clasped it warmly. "It isn't my intention to alarm you or to exploit your fascination. But that creature has been attached to the Mayfair family for generations. It can kill people. But then so can Dr. Rowan Mayfair. In fact, she may well be the first of her kind to be able to kill entirely on her own, without that creature's aid. And they are coming together, that creature and Rowan. It's only a matter of time before they meet. Now, please, dress and come with me. If you choose to be our mediator and to give the file on the Mayfair Witches to Rowan for us, then our highest aims will have been served.''

Michael was quiet, trying to absorb all this, his eyes moving anxiously over Lightner but seeing countless other things.

He could not entirely account for his feelings towards "the man'' now, the man who had always seemed vaguely beautiful to him, an embodiment of elegance, a wan and soulful figure, almost, who seemed to possess, in his deep garden hideaway, some serenity that Michael himself wanted to possess. Behind the fence last night, the man had tried to frighten him. Or was that so?

If only in that instant, he'd been rid of his gloves, and had been able to touch the man!

He did not doubt Lightner's words. There was something ghastly in all this, something ominous, something dark as the shadows that enclosed that house. *Yet it seemed familiar.* He thought of the visions, not in a struggle to remember, but merely to sink once more in the sensations evoked by them, and a conviction of goodness settled on him, as it had before.

"I'm meant to intervene," he said, "surely I am. And maybe I'm meant to use this power through touching. Rowan said . . ."

"Yes?"

"Rowan asked why I thought the power in my hands had nothing to do with it, why I kept insisting it was separate . . ." He thought again of touching the man. "Maybe it is part of it, maybe it's not just a little curse visited on me to drive me crazy and off course."

"That's what you thought?"

He nodded. "Seemed like it. Like it was the thing preventing me from coming. I holed up on Liberty Street for two months. I could have found Rowan sooner . . ." He looked at the gloves. How he hated them. They made his hands into artificial hands.

He could think no further. He couldn't grasp all the aspects of this fully. The feeling of familiarity lingered, taking the edges off the shocks of Lightner's revelations.

"All right," he said finally. "I'll go with you. I want to read that file, all of it. But I want to be back here as soon as possible. I'm leaving word for her that I'll be back in case she should call. She matters to me. She matters to me more than you know. And it's got nothing to do with the visions. It's got to do with who she is, and how much I . . . care about her. She can't be subordinated to anything else."

"Not even to the visions themselves?" Lightner asked respectfully.

"No. Twice, maybe three times in a lifetime you feel about someone the way I do about Rowan. That involves its own priorities, its own purposes."

"I understand," said Lightner. "I'll be downstairs to meet you in twenty minutes. And I wish that you would call me Aaron, from now on, if you'd like to. We have a long way to go together. I'm afraid I lapsed into calling you Michael quite some time ago. I want us to be friends."

247

"We're friends," said Michael. "What the hell else could we possibly be?" He gave a little uneasy laugh, but he had to admit, he liked this guy. In fact, he felt distinctly uneasy letting Lightner, and the briefcase, out of his sight.

Michael showered, shaved, and dressed in less than fifteen minutes. He unpacked, except for a few essentials. And only as he picked up his suitcase did he see the message light still pulsing on the bedside phone. Why in the world hadn't he responded the first time he'd seen it? It infuriated him suddenly.

At once he called the switchboard.

"Yes. A Dr. Rowan Mayfair called you, Mr. Curry, about five-fifteen A.M." The woman gave him Rowan's number. "She insisted that we ring, and that we knock."

"And you did?"

"We did, Mr. Curry. We didn't get any answer."

And my friend Aaron was there all the time, Michael thought angrily.

"We didn't want to use the passkey to go in."

"That's fine. Listen, I want to leave word with you for Dr. Mayfair if she calls again."

"Yes, Mr. Curry?"

"That I arrived safely, and that I'll call within twenty-four hours. That I have to go out now, but I'll be here later on."

He laid a five-dollar bill for the maid on the coverlet and walked out.

The small narrow lobby was bustling when he came down. The coffee shop was crowded and cheerfully noisy. Lightner, having changed from his dark tweed into an immaculate seersucker suit, stood by the doors, looking very much the southern gentleman of the old school.

"You might have answered the phone when it rang," said Michael. He did not add that Lightner looked like the old white-haired men he remembered from the old days who used to take their evening walks through the Garden District and along the avenue uptown.

"I didn't feel I had the right to do that," said Aaron politely. He opened the door for Michael and gestured to the gray car—a stretch limousine—at the curb. "Besides, I was afraid it was Dr. Mayfair."

"Well, it was," Michael said. Delicious gust of August heat. He wanted to take off on foot. How comfortable the pavement felt to him. But he knew he had to make this journey. He climbed into the backseat of the car.

"I see," Lightner was saying. "But you haven't called her back." He seated himself beside Michael.

"A deal is a deal," Michael said with a sigh. "But I don't like it. I've tried to make it clear to you how things are with me and Rowan. You know, when I was in my twenties, falling in love with a person in one evening would have been damn near impossible. Least it never happened. And when I was in my thirties? Well maybe, but again it didn't happen, though now and then I saw just the promise . . . and maybe I ran away. But I'm in my late forties now, and I'm either more stupid than ever, or I know enough finally that I can fall in love with a person in one day or one night, I can size up the situation, so to speak, and figure when something is just about perfect, you know what I mean?"

"I think so."

The car was somewhat old but plenty agreeable enough, with well-kept gray leather upholstery and a little refrigerator tucked to one side. Ample room for Michael's long legs. St. Charles Avenue flashed by all too rapidly beyond the tinted glass.

"Mr. Curry, I respect your feelings for Rowan, though I have to confess I'm both surprised and intrigued. Oh, don't get me wrong. The woman's extraordinary by any standard, an incomparable physician and a beautiful young creature of rather amazing demeanor. I know. But what I ask that you understand is this: The File on the Mayfair Witches would never normally be entrusted to anyone but a member of our order or a member of the Mayfair family itself. Now I'm breaking the rules in showing you this material. And the reasons for my decision are obvious. Nevertheless, I want to use this precious time to explain to you about the Talamasca, how we operate, and what small loyalty, in exchange for our confidence, we should like to claim from you."

"OK, don't get so fired up. Is there some coffee in this glorified taxi?"

"Yes, of course," said Aaron. He lifted a thermos from a pocket in the side door, and a mug with it, and started to fill the mug.

"Black will do just fine," Michael said. A lump rose in his throat suddenly as he saw the big proud houses of the avenue gliding past, with their deep porches and colonnettes and gaily painted shutters, and the pastel sky enmeshed in a tangle of groping branches and softly fluttering leaves. A sudden crazy thought came to him, that some day he would buy a seersucker suit like Lightner's suit, and he would walk on the avenue, like the gentlemen of years past, walk for hours, round curve after curve as the avenue followed the distant bends of the river, past all these graceful old houses that had survived for so long. He felt drugged and crazy drifting through this ragged and beautiful landscape, in this insulated car, behind dimming glass.

"Yes, it is beautiful," Lightner said. "Very beautiful indeed."

"OK, tell me about this order. So you're driving around in limousines thanks to the Knights Templar. What else?"

Lightner shook his head reprovingly, a trace of a smile on his lips. But again he colored, surprising and amusing Michael.

"Just kidding you, Aaron," said Michael. "Come on, how did you come to know about the Mayfair family in the first place? And what the hell damn is a witch, in your book, do you mind telling me that?"

"A witch is a person who can attract and manipulate unseen forces," said Aaron. "That's our definition. It will suffice for sorcerer or seer, as well. We were created to observe such things as witches. It all started in what we now call the Dark Ages, long before the witchcraft persecutions, as I'm sure you know. And it started with a single magician, an alchemist as he called himself, who began his studies in a solitary spot, gathering together in a great book all the tales of the supernatural he had ever read or heard.

"His name and his life story are not important for the moment. But what characterized his account was that it was curiously secular for the times. He was perhaps the only historian ever to write about the occult, or the unseen, or the mysterious without making assumptions and assertions as to the demonic origin of apparitions, spirits, and the like. And of his small band of followers he demanded the same open-mindedness. 'Merely study the work of the so-called spell binder,' he would say. 'Do not assume you know whence his power comes.'

"We are very much the same now," Aaron continued. "We are dogmatic only when it comes to defending our lack of dogma. And though we are large and extremely secure, we are always on the lookout for new members, for people who will respect our passivity and our slow and thorough methods, people who find the investigation of the occult as fascinating as we do, people who have been gifted with an extraordinary talent such as the power you have in your hands . . .

"Now when I first read of you, I have to confess, I knew nothing about any connection between you and Rowan Mayfair or the house on First Street. It was membership that entered my mind. Of course I hadn't planned to tell you this immediately. But everything is changed now, you'll agree.

"But whatever was to happen on that account, I came to San Francisco to make available our knowledge to you, to show you, if you wished, how to use your power, and then perhaps to broach the subject that you might find our way of life fulfilling or enjoyable, enough to consider it, at least for a while . . .

"You see, there was something about your life which intrigued me, that is, what I could learn of it, from the public records and from, well some simple investigation that we conducted on our own. And that is, that you seemed to be at a crossroads before the accident, it was as if you had achieved your goals, yet you were unsatisfied—"

"Yeah, you're right about all that," Michael said. He had forgotten completely about the scenery beyond the windows. His eyes were fixed on Lightner. He held out the mug to be refilled with coffee. "Go on, please."

"And well, there's your background in history," said Lightner, "and the absence of any close family, except for your darling aunt, whom I have come to simply adore on short acquaintance, I must confess, and of course there is still the question of this power you possess, which is considerably stronger than I ever supposed . . .

"But to continue about the order. We have observed occult phenomena throughout the world, as well you can imagine. And our work with the witch families is but a small part of it, and one of the few parts which involve real danger, for the observation of hauntings, even cases of possession, and our work with reincarnation and mind reading and the like involve almost no danger at all. With witches, it's entirely different. . . . And as a consequence, only the most experienced members are ever invited to work with this material, even to read it or try to understand it. And almost never would a novice or even a young member be brought into the field to approach a family such as the Mayfair family because the dangers are too great.

"All of that will come clear to you when you read the File. What I want from you now is some understanding that you won't make light of what we offer and what we do. That if we should part ways, either disagreeably or agreeably, you will respect the privacy of the persons mentioned in the Mayfair history . . ."

"You know you can trust me on that score. You know what kind of a person I am," Michael said. "But what do you mean about danger? You're talking about this spirit again, this man, and you're talking about Rowan . . ."

"Prematurely. What more do you want to know about us?"

"Membership, how does it actually work?"

"It begins with a novitiate, just as it does in a religious order. But again, let me emphasize one does not embrace a slate of teachings when one comes to us. One embraces an approach to life. During one's years as a novice, one comes to live in the Motherhouse, to meet and associate with the older members, to work in the libraries, and to browse in them at will . . ."

"Now that would be heaven," Michael said, dreamily. "But I didn't mean to interrupt you. Go on."

"After two years of preparation, then we talk of serious commitment, we speak of fieldwork or scholarly pursuits. Of course one may follow the other, and again, we are not comparable to a religious order in providing our members with unrefusable assignments; we do not take vows of obedience. Allegiance, confidentiality, these are far more important to us. But you see, in the final analysis, it's all about understanding; about being inducted and absorbed into a special sort of community . . ."

"I can see it," said Michael. "Tell me about the Motherhouses. Where are they?"

"The one in Amsterdam is the oldest now," Aaron said. "Then there is the house outside of London, and our largest house, and our most secret perhaps, in Rome. Of course the Catholic Church doesn't like us. It doesn't understand us. It puts us with the devil, just as it did the witches, and the sorcerers, and the Knights Templar, but we have nothing to do with the devil. If the devil exists, he is no friend to us . . ."

Michael laughed. "Do you think the devil exists?"

"I don't know, frankly. But that's what a good member of the Talamasca would say."

"Go on, about the Motherhouses . . ."

"Well, you'd like the one in London, actually . . ."

Michael was scarcely aware that they had left New Orleans, that they were speeding on through the swampland, on a barren strip of new highway, and that the sky had narrowed to a ribbon of flawless blue overhead. He was listening to every word Aaron said, quite enthralled. But a dark troublesome feeling was brewing in him, which he tried to ignore. This was all familiar, this unfolding story of the Talamasca. It was familiar as the frightening words about Rowan and "the man" had been familiar, familiar as the house itself had been familiar. And tantalizing though this was, it discouraged him suddenly, because the great design—of which he felt he was part—seemed for all its vagueness to be growing, and the bigger it grew, the more the world itself seemed to dwindle, to lose its splendor and its promise of infinite natural wonders and ever-shifting fortune, and even some of its ragged romance.

Aaron must have realized what Michael was feeling, because Aaron paused once before continuing with his story, to say tenderly but almost absently, "Michael, just listen now. Don't be afraid . . ."

"Tell me something, Aaron," he said.

"If I can, of course . . ."

"Can you touch a spirit? That man, I mean. Can you touch him with your hand?"

"Well, there are times when I think that would be entirely possible . . . At least you could touch something. But of course, whether or not the being would allow himself to be touched is quite another story, as you'll soon see."

Michael nodded. "It's all connected, then. The hands, the visions, and even you . . . and this organization of yours. It's connected."

"Wait, wait until you've read the history. At each step of the game . . . wait and see."

Ten

WHEN ROWAN AWOKE at ten she began to doubt what she had seen. In the flood of sunlight warming the house, the ghost seemed unreal. She tried to reinvoke the moment—the eerie noises of the water and the wind. It all seemed thoroughly impossible now.

She began to be thankful that she hadn't reached Michael. She didn't want to appear foolish, and above all, she didn't want to burden Michael again. On the other hand, how could she have imagined such a thing as that? A man standing at the glass with his fingers touching it, looking at her in that imploring way?

Well, there was no evidence of the being here now. She went out on the deck, walked the length of it, studied the pilings, the water. No signs of anything out of the ordinary. But then what sort of signs would there be? She stood at the railing, feeling the brisk wind for a while, and feeling thankful for the dark blue sky. Several sailboats were making their way slowly and gracefully out of the marina across the water. Soon the bay would be covered with them. She half wanted to take out the *Sweet Christine*. But she decided against it. She went inside.

No call from Michael yet. The thing to do was to take out the *Sweet Christine*, or go to work.

She was dressed and leaving for the hospital when the phone rang. "Michael," she whispered. Then she realized that it was Ellie's old line.

"Person to person, please, for Miss Ellie Mayfair."

"I'm sorry, she can't answer," said Rowan. "She's no longer here." Was that the way to say this? It was never pleasant telling these people that Ellie was dead.

Conference on the other end.

"Can you tell us where we might reach her?"

"Can you tell me who is calling, please?" Rowan asked. She set down her bag on the kitchen counter. The house was warm from the morning sun, and she was a little hot in her coat. "I'll be glad to have you reverse the charges, if the party is willing to speak to me."

Another conference, then the crisp voice of an older woman: "I'll speak to this party."

The operator rang off.

"This is Rowan Mayfair, can I help you?"

"You can tell me when and where I can reach Ellie," said the woman, impatient, perhaps even angry, and certainly cold.

"Are you a friend of hers?"

"If she cannot be reached immediately, I would like to talk to her husband, Graham Franklin. You have his office number perhaps?"

What an awful person, Rowan thought. But a suspicion was growing in her that this was a family call.

"Graham can't be reached either. If you'll only tell me who you are, I'll be glad to explain the situation."

"Thank you, I don't care to do that." Steely. "It's imperative that I reach Ellie Mayfair or Graham Franklin."

Be patient, Rowan told herself. This is obviously an old woman, and if she is part of the family, it is worth holding on.

"I'm sorry to have to tell you this," Rowan said. "Ellie Mayfair died last year. She died of cancer. Graham died two months before Ellie. I'm their daughter, Rowan. Is there anything I can do for you? Anything else perhaps that you want to know?"

Silence.

"This is your aunt, Carlotta Mayfair," said the woman. "I'm calling you from New Orleans. Why in the name of God was I not notified of Ellie's death?"

An immediate anger kindled in Rowan.

"I don't know who you are, Miss Mayfair," she said, deliberately forcing herself to speak slowly and calmly. "I don't have an address or a phone number for any of Ellie's people in New Orleans. Ellie left no such information. Her instructions to her lawyer were that no one be notified other than friends here."

Rowan suddenly realized she was trembling, and her hand on the phone was slippery. She could not quite believe that she had been so rude, but it was too soon to be sorry. She also realized that she was powerfully excited. She didn't want this woman to hang up.

"Are you still there, Miss Mayfair?" she asked. "I'm sorry. I think you caught me a bit off guard."

"Yes," said the woman, "perhaps we were both caught off guard. It seems I have no choice but to speak to you directly."

"I wish you would."

"It's my unfortunate duty to tell you that your mother died this morning. I presume you understand what I'm saying? Your mother? It was my intention to tell Ellie, and leave it entirely in her hands as to how or when this information should be conveyed to you. I'm sorry to have to handle it in this fashion. Your mother died this morning at five minutes after five."

Rowan was too stunned to respond. The woman might as well have struck her. This wasn't grief. It was too sharp, too awful for that. Her mother had sprung to life suddenly, living and breathing and existing for a split second in spoken words. And in the same instant the living entity was pronounced dead; she existed no more.

Rowan didn't try to speak. She shrank into her habitual and natural silence. She saw Ellie dead, in the funeral home, surrounded by flowers; but there was no coherence to this, no sweet bite of sadness. It was purely terrible. And the paper lay in the safe, as it had for over a year. *Ellie, she was alive and I could have known her and now's she dead.*

"There is no need whatsoever for you to come here," said the woman with no perceptible change of attitude or tone. "What is necessary is that you contact your attorney immediately, and that you put me in touch with this person as there are pressing matters regarding your property which must be discussed."

"Oh, but I want to come," Rowan said, without hesitation. Her voice was thick. "I want to come now. I want to see my mother before she's buried." Damn the paper, and this unspeakable woman, whoever she was.

"That's scarcely appropriate," said the woman wearily.

"I insist," said Rowan. "I don't wish to trouble you but I want to see my mother before she's buried. No one there need know who I am. I simply want to come."

"It would be a useless journey. Surely Ellie would not have wanted this. Ellis assured me that—"

"Ellie's dead!" Rowan whispered, her voice scraping bottom in her effort to control it. She was shaking all over. "Look, it means something to me to see my mother. Ellie and Graham are both gone, as I told you. I . . ." She could not say it. It sounded too self-pitying and too intimate to confess that she was alone.

"I must insist," said the woman in the same tired, worn-out feelingless voice, "that you remain exactly where you are."

"Why?" Rowan asked. "What does it matter to you if I come? I told you, no one needs to know who I am."

"There isn't going to be a public wake or funeral," said the woman. "It doesn't matter who knows or doesn't know. Your mother will be buried as soon as it can be arranged. I have asked that it be done tomorrow afternoon. I am trying to save you grief with my recommendations. But if you will not listen, then do what you feel you must do."

"I'm coming," Rowan said. "What time tomorrow afternoon?"

"Your mother will be buried through Lonigan and Sons on Magazine Street. The Requiem Mass will be at St. Mary's Assumption Church on Josephine Street. And the services will take place just as soon as I can arrange for them. It is pointless for you to come two thousand miles—"

"I want to see my mother. I ask you please to wait until I can get there."

"That is absolutely out of the question," said the woman with a slight touch of anger or impatience. "I advise you to leave immediately, if you are determined to come. And please don't expect to spend the night under this roof. I have no means of properly receiving you. The house is yours, of course, and I shall vacate it as soon as possible if that is your wish. But I ask that you remain in a hotel until I can conveniently do so. Again, I have no means of making you comfortable here."

Carefully, in the same tired manner, the woman gave Rowan the address.

"You said First Street?" Rowan asked. It was the street that Michael had described to her, she was sure of it. "This was my mother's house?" she asked.

"I've been awake all night," said the woman, her words slow, spiritless. "If you're coming, then everything can be explained to you when you arrive."

Rowan was about to ask another question when, to her astonishment, the woman rang off.

She was so angry that for a moment she did not feel her hurt. Then the hurt overshadowed everything. "Who in the hell are you?" she whispered, the tears rising, but not flowing. "And why in the world would you speak this way to me!" She slammed down the phone, her teeth biting into her lip, and folded her arms. "God, what an awful, awful woman," she whispered.

But this was no time for crying or wishing for Michael. Quickly, she took out her handkerchief, blew her nose and wiped her eyes, and then reached for the pad and pen on the kitchen counter, and she jotted down the information the woman had given her.

First Street, she thought, looking at it after she'd written it. Probably no more than coincidence. And Lonigan and Sons, the words Ellie had mentioned in her delirium when she had rambled on about her childhood and home. Quickly she called New Orleans information, then the funeral home.

It was a Mr. Jerry Lonigan who answered.

"My name is Dr. Rowan Mayfair, I'm calling from California about a funeral."

"Yes, Dr. Mayfair," he said in a most agreeable voice that reminded her of Michael at once. "I know who you are. I have your mother here now."

Thank God, no subterfuge, no need for false explanations. Yet she couldn't help but wonder why did the man know about her? Hadn't the whole adoption been hush-hush?

"Mr. Lonigan," she said, trying to speak clearly and ignore the thickness in her voice, "it's very important to me that I be there for the funeral. I want to see my mother before she is put into the ground."

"Of course you do, Dr. Mayfair. I understand. But Miss Carlotta called here just now and said if we don't bury your mother tomorrow . . . Well, let's just say she's insisting on it, Dr. Mayfair. I can schedule the Mass for as late as three P.M. Do you think you could make it by that time, Dr. Mayfair? I will hold everything up just as long as I can."

"Yes, absolutely, I will make it," said Rowan. "I'll leave tonight or early tomorrow morning at the latest. But Mr. Lonigan—if I get delayed—"

"Dr. Mayfair, if I know you're on your way, I won't shut that coffin before you arrive."

"Thank you, Mr. Lonigan. I only just found out. I just . . ."

"Well, Dr. Mayfair, if you don't mind my saying so, it only just happened. I picked up your mother at six A.M. this morning. I think Miss Carlotta's rushing things. But then Miss Carlotta is so old now, Dr. Mayfair. So old . . ."

"Listen, let me give you my phone number at the hospital. If anything should happen, call me please."

He took down the numbers. "Don't you worry, Dr. Mayfair. Your mother will be here at Lonigan and Sons when you come."

Again the tears threatened. He sounded so simple, so hopelessly sincere. "Mr. Lonigan, can you tell me something else?" she said, her voice quavering badly.

"Yes, Dr. Mayfair."

"How old was my mother?"

"Forty-eight, Dr. Mayfair."

"What was her name?"

Obviously this surprised him, but he recovered quickly. "Deirdre was her name, Dr. Mayfair. She was a very pretty woman. My wife was a good friend of hers. She loved Deirdre, used to go to visit. My wife is right here with me. My wife is glad that you called."

For some reason, this affected Rowan almost as deeply as all

258

the other bits and pieces of information had affected her. She pressed the handkerchief to her eyes tightly, and swallowed.

"Can you tell me what my mother died of, Mr. Lonigan? What does the death certificate say?"

"It says natural causes, Dr. Mayfair, but your mother had been sick, real sick for many years. I can give you the name of the doctor who treated her. I think he might talk to you, being that you are a doctor yourself."

"I'll get it from you when I come," Rowan said. She could not continue this much longer. She blew her nose quickly and quietly. "Mr. Lonigan. I have the name of a hotel. The Pontchartrain. Is that convenient to the funeral home and the church?"

"Why, you could walk over here from there, Dr. Mayfair, if the weather wasn't so hot."

"I'll call you as soon as I get in. But please, again, promise me that you won't let my mother be buried without . . ."

"Don't worry about it another minute, Dr. Mayfair. But Dr. Mayfair, there's one thing more. It's my wife who wants me to take it up with you."

"Go ahead, Mr. Lonigan."

"Your aunt, Carlotta Mayfair, she doesn't want any announcement of this in the morning paper, and well, frankly, I don't think there's time for an announcement now. But there are so many Mayfairs who would want to know about the funeral, Dr. Mayfair. I mean the cousins are going to be up in arms when they find out how all this happened so fast. Now, it's entirely up to you, you understand, I'll do as you say, but my wife was wondering, would you maybe mind if she started calling the cousins. 'Course once she gets one or two of them, they'll call everybody else. Now, if you don't want her to do that, Dr. Mayfair, she won't do it. But Rita Mae, my wife, that is, she felt that it was a shame to bury Deirdre this way without anybody knowing, and she felt maybe, you know, that it might do you good to see the cousins who would turn out. God knows, they came out for Miss Nancy last year. And Miss Ellie was here, your Miss Ellie from California, as I'm sure you know . . ."

No, Rowan had not known. Another dull shock struck her at the mention of Ellie's name. She found it painful to envision Ellie back there among these numberless and nameless cousins, whom she herself had never seen. The heat of her anger and bitterness surprised her. Ellie and the cousins. And Rowan here in this house alone. Once again, she struggled for composure. She wondered if this was not one of the more difficult moments she had endured since Ellie's death.

259

"Yes, I would be grateful, Mr. Lonigan, if your wife would do what she thinks best. I would like to see the cousins . . ." She stopped because she could not continue. "And Mr. Lonigan, regarding Ellie Mayfair, my adoptive mother—she is gone too now. She died last year. If you think any of these cousins would want to be told—"

"Oh, I'd be glad to do that, Dr. Mayfair. Save you telling them when you arrive. And I'm so sorry to hear it. We had no idea."

It sounded so heartfelt. She could actually believe that he was sorry. Such a nice old-fashioned sort of man. There was almost a Damon Runyon quality to him.

"Good-bye Mr. Lonigan. I'll see you tomorrow afternoon."

For one moment, as she put down the phone, it seemed that if she let the tears go they'd never stop. The stir of emotions was so thick in her it was dizzying, and the pain demanded some violent action, and the strangest, most bizarre pictures filled her mind.

Choking back her tears, she saw herself rushing into Ellie's room. She saw herself dragging clothes out of drawers and off hangers and ripping garments to shreds at random, in a near uncontrollable rage. She saw herself smashing Ellie's mirror and the long row of bottles which still stood on her dresser, all those little bottles of scent in which the perfume had dried to nothing but color over the months. "Dead, dead, dead," she whispered. "She was alive yesterday and the day before and the day before that, and I was here, and I did nothing! Dead! Dead! Dead!"

And then the bizarre scene shifted, as if the tragedy of her rage were passing into another act. She saw herself beating with her fists on all the walls of wood and glass around her, beating with her fists until the blood ran from her bruised hands. The hands that had operated on so many, healed so many, saved so many lives.

But Rowan did none of these things.

She sat down on the stool at the kitchen corner, her body crumpling, hand up to shield her face, and she began to sob aloud in the empty house, the images still passing through her mind. Finally she laid her head down on her folded arms, and she cried and cried, until she was choked and exhausted with it, and all she could do was whisper over and over: "Deirdre Mayfair, aged forty-eight, dead dead dead."

At last, she wiped her face with the back of her hand, and she went to the rug before the fire and lay down. Her head hurt and all the world seemed empty to her and hostile and without the slightest promise of warmth or light.

It would pass. It had to. She had felt this misery on the day Ellie was buried. She had felt it before, standing in the hospital corridor as Ellie cried in pain. Yet it seemed impossible now that things could get better. When she thought of the paper in the safe, the paper which had kept her from going to New Orleans after Ellie's death, she despised herself for honoring it. She despised Ellie for ever having made her sign it.

And her thoughts continued, abysmal and miserable, sapping her spirit and her belief in herself.

It must have been an hour that she lay there, the sun hot on the floorboards around her, and on the side of her face and her arms. She was ashamed of her loneliness. She was ashamed of being the victim of this anguish. Before Ellie's death, she had been such a happy person, so carefree, utterly dedicated to her work, and coming and going in this house, assured of warmth and love, and giving warmth and love in return. When she thought of how much she had depended upon Michael, how much she wanted him now, she was doubly lost.

Inexcusable really, to have called him so desperately last night about the ghost, and to be wanting him so desperately now. She began to grow calm. Then slowly it came to her—the ghost last night, and last night her mother had died.

She sat up, folding her legs Indian-style, and trying to remember the experience in cold detail. She'd glanced at the clock last night only moments before the thing had appeared. It had been five minutes after three. And hadn't that awful woman said, "Your mother died at five minutes after five"?

Same time *exactly* in New Orleans. But what a bewildering possibility, she thought, that the two were linked.

Of course, if her mother had appeared to her it would have been splendid beyond belief. It would have been the kind of sacramental moment people talk about forever. All the lovely clichés—"life-changing, miraculous, beautiful"—could have come into play. In fact, it was almost impossible to contemplate the comfort of such a moment. But it was not a woman who had appeared there, it was a man, a strange and curiously elegant man.

Just thinking about it again, thinking about the beseeching expression of the being, made her feel her alarm of the night before. She turned and glanced anxiously at the glass wall. Nothing there of course but the great empty blue sky over the dark distant hills, and the flashing, sparkling panorama of the bay.

She grew coldly and unexpectedly calm as she puzzled over it, as she reviewed in her mind all the popular myths she'd heard about such apparitions, but then this brief interlude of excitement began to fade.

Whatever it was, it seemed vague, insubstantial, even trivial beside the fact of the death of her mother. That was what had to be dealt with. And she was wasting precious time.

She climbed to her feet and went to the phone. She called Dr. Larkin at home.

"Lark, I have to go on leave," she explained. "It's unavoidable. Can we talk about Slattery filling in?"

How cool her voice sounded, how like the old Rowan. But that was a lie. As they spoke, she stared at the glass wall again, at the empty space on the deck where the tall, slender being had stood. She saw his dark eyes again, searching her face. She could scarcely follow what Lark was saying. No way I imagined that damned thing, she thought.

Eleven

THE DRIVE TO the Talamasca retreat house took less than an hour and a half. The limousine took the dull path of the interstate, cutting over the river road only when they were within a few miles of the house.

But it seemed like far less to Michael, who was for the entire time immersed in his conversation with Aaron.

By the time they reached the house, Michael had a fairly good understanding of what the Talamasca was, and he had assured Aaron that he would keep confidential forever what he was about to read in the files. Michael loved the idea of the Talamasca; he loved the genteel civilized way in which Aaron presented things; and he thought to himself more than once, that had he not been hell-bent on this "purpose" of his, he would cheerfully have embraced the Talamasca.

But those were foolish thoughts, because it was the drowning which led to the sense of purpose and to his psychic ability; and these things had led the Talamasca to him.

There also had sharpened in Michael a sense of his love for Rowan—and it was love, he felt—as something apart from his involvement with the visions, even though he knew now that the visions had involved Rowan.

He tried to explain this to Aaron as they approached the retreat house gates.

"All you've told me sounds familiar; there is a sense of recognition, just as I felt when I saw the house last night. And you know of course that the Talamasca couldn't be familiar to me, it's not possible that I would have heard of you and forgotten except if *they* told me while I was drowned. But the point I'm trying to make is that my affection for Rowan doesn't feel familiar. It doesn't feel like something meant to be. It's fresh; it's tied up in my mind somehow with rebellion. Why, I remember when I was with her out there, you know, talking over breakfast, at her house in Tiburon, I looked out over the water and I said almost defiantly to those beings, that this thing with Rowan mattered to me."

Aaron listened to all this carefully, as he had listened to Michael, intermittently, all along.

It seemed to Michael that both knew their knowledge of each other had deepened and become seemingly natural to them, that they were now completely at ease.

Michael had drunk only coffee since they'd left New Orleans. He intended to keep it that way, at least until he had read all that Aaron had to give him to read.

Michael was also weary of the limousine, weary of the smooth, brutal way it shot through the old swampy landscape. He wanted to breathe fresh air.

As soon as they entered the gates of the retreat house, turning left off the river road with the levee behind them, Michael knew the place from the picture books. The oak-lined avenue had been photographed countless times over the decades. It seemed lavishly dreamlike in its southern Gothic perfection, the gargantuan black-barked trees extending their gnarled and heavy limbs to form an unbroken ceiling of crude and broken arches leading all the way to the verandas of the house.

Great streaks of gray Spanish moss hung from the deep knotty elbows of these branches. Bulging roots crowded, on either side, the narrow rutted gravel drive.

Michael loved it. It lay its hands silently on his heart the same way that the beauty of the Garden District had done so; a quiet faith sprang up in him, that no matter what else happened to him, he was home in the south and things were somehow going to be all right.

The car tunneled deeper and deeper into the green-tinted light, ragged rays of sun here and there piercing the shadows, while beyond, the low country on both sides, full of high grass, and tall shapeless shrubbery seemed to close in upon the sky and upon the house itself.

Michael pressed the button to lower the window. "God, feel that air," he whispered.

"Yes, rather remarkable I think," Aaron said softly. But he was smiling indulgently at Michael. The heat was wilting. Michael didn't care.

It seemed a hush fell over the world as the car came to a stop, and they climbed out before the broad two-story house. Built before the Civil War, it was one of those sublimely simple structures—massive yet tropical, a square box graced with floor-length windows, and surrounded on all sides by deep galleries and thick unfluted columns rising to support its flat roof.

It seemed a thing made to capture the breezes, for sitting and gazing out over fields and river—a strong brick structure made to survive hurricanes and drenching rains.

Hard to believe, Michael thought, that beyond the distant levee was the river traffic of tugs and barges which they had glimpsed less than an hour ago as a chugging ferry brought them to the southern bank. All that was real now was this soft breeze stealing over the brick floor on which they stood, the broad double doors of the house suddenly open to receive them, the errant sun glinting in the glass of the beautifully arched fanlight window above.

Where was the rest of the world? It didn't matter. Michael heard again the wondrous sounds that had lulled him on First Street—the singing of insects, the wild, seemingly desperate cry of birds.

Aaron pressed his arm as he led Michael inside, apparently ignoring the shock of the artificially chilled air. "We'll have a quick tour," he said.

Michael scarcely followed his words. The house had caught him up, as houses always did. He loved houses made in this fashion with a wide central hallway, a simple staircase, and large square rooms in perfect balance on either side. The restoration and furnishings were sumptuous as well as meticulous. And rather characteristically British, what with dark green carpets, and books in mahogany cases and shelves rising to the ceilings in all the main rooms. Only a few ornate mirrors recalled the antebellum period, and a little harpsichord pushed into a corner. All the rest was solidly Victorian, but not unpleasing by any means.

"Like a private club," Michael whispered. It was almost comical to him, the occasional person seated deep in a tapestried chair who did not even glance up from a book or a paper as they glided soundlessly past. But the overall atmosphere was unmistakably inviting. He felt good here. He liked the quick smile of the woman who passed him on the staircase. He wanted to find a chair himself at some time or other in the library. And through all the many French doors, he caught the greenery outside, a great sprawling net swallowing up the blue sky.

"Come, we'll take you to your room," Aaron said.

"Aaron, I'm not staying. Where's the file?"

"Of course," Aaron said, "but you must have quiet to read as you like."

He led Michael along the upper corridor to the front bedroom on the eastern side of the house. Floor-length windows opened onto both the front and the side galleries. And though the carpet was as dark and thick as everywhere else, the decor had yielded to the plantation tradition with a couple of marble-top bureaus and one of those overpowering poster beds which seemed made for this kind of house. Several layers of handmade quilts covered its shapeless feather mattress. No carvings ornamented its eight-foot-high posts.

But the room had a surprising array of modern conveniences, including the small refrigerator and television fitted into a carved armoire, and a chair and desk nestled in the inside corner, so that they faced both the front windows and those to the east. The phone was covered with buttons and tiny carefully inscribed numerals for various extensions. A pair of Queen Anne wing chairs stood on tiptoe before the fireplace. A door was open to an adjoining bath.

"I'm moving in," Michael said. "Where's the file?"

"But we should have lunch."

"You should. I can get a sandwich and eat it while I'm reading. Please, you promised. The file."

Aaron insisted that they go at once to a small screened porch off the back of the second story, and there, overlooking a formal garden with gravel paths and weathered fountains, they sat down to eat. It was an enormous southern breakfast, complete with biscuits, grits, and sausage; and plenty of chicory café au lait to drink.

Michael was ravenous. Again, he had that feeling he'd had with Rowan—good to be off the booze. Good to be clear-headed, looking out on the green garden with the branches of the oaks dipping down to the very grass. Divine to be feeling the warm air again.

"This has all happened so fast," Aaron said, passing him the basket of steaming biscuits. "I feel I should say something more, yet I don't know what I can say. We wanted to approach you slowly, we wanted to get to know you and for you to know us.''

Michael couldn't stop thinking about Rowan suddenly. He resented it powerfully that he couldn't call Rowan. Yet it seemed useless to try to explain to Aaron how worried about Rowan he was.

"If I had made the contact I hoped to make," said Aaron, "I would have invited you to our Motherhouse in London, and your introduction to the order might have been slow and graceful there. Even after years of fieldwork, you would not have been asked to undertake a task as dangerous as intervention with regard to the Mayfair Witches. There is no one in the order even qualified to undertake such a task except for me. But you are involved, to use the simple modern expression.''

"In it up to the eyeballs," Michael said, eating steadily as he listened. "But I hear what you're saying. It would be like the Catholic church asking me to participate in an exorcism when they knew I wasn't an ordained priest.''

"Very nearly so," he said. "I sometimes think that on account of our lack of dogma and ritual, we are all the more stringent. Our definition of right and wrong is more subtle, and we become more angry with those who don't comply.''

"Aaron, look. I won't tell a blessed soul in Christendom about that file, except for Rowan. Agreed?''

Aaron was thoughtful for a moment. "Michael," he said, "when you've read the material we must talk further about what you should do. Wait before you say no. At least commit yourself to listening to my advice.''

"You're personally afraid of Rowan, aren't you?''

Aaron drank a swallow of coffee. He stared at the plate for a moment. He had eaten nothing but half a biscuit. "I'm not sure," he answered. "My one meeting with Rowan was very peculiar. I could have sworn . . .''

"What?''

"That she wanted desperately to talk to me. To talk to someone. And then again, there was a hostility I perceived in her, a rather generalized hostility, as if the woman were superhuman and bristled with something instinctively alien to other human beings. Oh, I know that sounds farfetched. Of course she isn't superhuman. But if we think of these psychic powers of ours as mutations, then we can begin to think of a creature like Rowan as something different, as one species of bird is different from another. I felt her differentness, so to speak.''

He paused. He seemed to notice for the first time that Michael was wearing his gloves as he ate. "Do you want to try it without those? Perhaps I can teach you how to block the images. It isn't really as difficult as you . . .''

"I want the file," said Michael. He wiped his mouth with the napkin and swallowed the rest of his coffee.

"Of course you do, and you shall have it," said Aaron with a sigh.

"Can I go to my room now? Oh, and if they could manage another pot of this lovely black syrupy coffee and hot milk . . .''

"Of course."

Aaron led Michael out of the breakfast room, stopping only to give the order for the coffee, and then he led Michael back down the broad central hallway to the front bedroom.

The dark damask drapes covering the front floor-length windows had been opened, and through every pane of glass shone the gentle summer light, filtered through the trees.

The briefcase with the bulging file in its leather folder lay on the quilt-covered four-poster bed.

"All right, my friend," Aaron said. "They'll bring in the coffee without knocking so as not to disturb you. Sit out on the front gallery if you like. And please read carefully. There's the phone if you need me. Dial the operator and ask for Aaron. I'm going to be down the hall, a couple of doors, catching a little sleep."

Michael took off his tie and his jacket, went into the bathroom and washed his face, and was just getting his cigarettes out of his suitcase when the coffee arrived.

He was surprised and a little disturbed to see Aaron reappear, with a troubled expression on his face. Scarcely five minutes had passed, or so it seemed.

Aaron told the young boy servant to set the tray down on the desk facing out from the corner, and then he waited for the boy to leave.

"Bad news, Michael."

"What do you mean?"

"I just called London for my messages. Seems they tried to reach me in San Francisco to tell me Rowan's mother was dying. But we failed to connect."

"Rowan will want to know this, Aaron."

"It's over, Michael. Deirdre Mayfair died this morning, around five A.M." His voice faltered slightly. "You and I were talking at the time, I believe."

"How awful for Rowan," said Michael. "You can't imagine how this will affect her. You just don't know."

"She's coming, Michael," said Aaron. "She contacted the funeral parlor, and asked them to postpone the services. They agreed. She inquired about the Pontchartrain Hotel when she called. We'll check, of course, to see whether or not she's made reservations. But I believe we can count on her arriving very soon."

"You're worse than the Federal Bureau of Investigation, you know it?" Michael said. But he wasn't angry. This was precisely the information he wanted. With a bit of relief he reviewed in his mind the time of his arrival, his visit to the house, and his waking afterwards. No, there was nothing he could have done to effect a meeting with Rowan and her mother.

"Yes, we are very thorough," said Aaron sadly. "We think of everything. I wonder if God is as indifferent as we are to the proceedings we watch." His face underwent a distinct change, as he appeared to draw inward. Then he moved to leave, apparently without another word.

"You actually knew Rowan's mother?" Michael asked.

"Yes, I knew her," said Aaron bitterly, "and I was never able to do a single solitary thing to help her. But that's often how it is with us, you see. Perhaps this time things will be different. And then again, perhaps not." He turned the knob to go. "It's all there," he said pointing to the folder. "There's no time anymore for talk."

Michael watched helplessly as he left in silence. The little display of emotion had surprised him completely, but it had also reassured him. He felt sad that he had been unable to say anything comforting. And if he started to think of Rowan, of seeing her and holding her, and trying to explain all this to her, he would go crazy. No time to lose.

Taking the leather folder from the bed, he set it on the desk. He collected his cigarettes, and he took his seat in the leather desk chair. Almost absently he reached for the silver coffeepot, and poured himself a cup of coffee, and then added the hot milk.

The sweet aroma filled the room.

He opened the cover, and took up the manila folder inside it, marked simply "THE MAYFAIR WITCHES: Number One." It contained a thick bound typescript, and an envelope marked "Photocopies of the Original Documents."

His heart ached for Rowan.

He began to read.

Twelve

IT WAS AN hour later that Rowan called the hotel. She had
packed the few light summery things she had. In fact, her
packing had been a bit of a surprise to her, as she watched her
own choices and actions, seemingly from a remove. Light silk
things had gone into the suitcases, blouses and dresses bought
for vacations years back and never worn since. A load of jewelry, neglected since college. Unopened perfumes. Delicate high-
heel shoes never taken out of the box. Her years in medicine
had left no time for such things. Same with the linen suits she'd
worn a couple of times in the Hawaiian Islands. Well, they would
serve her well now. She also packed a cosmetic kit which she
hadn't opened for over a year.

The flight was arranged for midnight that night. She would
drive in to the hospital, go over all the patient histories in detail
with Slattery, who would be filling in for her, and then go on to
the airport from there.

Now she must make her reservation at the hotel and leave
word for Michael that she was coming in.

An amiable southern voice answered her at the hotel. Yes,
they did have a suite vacant. And no, Mr. Curry was not in. He
had left a message for her, however, that he was out but he would
call within twenty-four hours. No, no word on where he was or
when he'd return.

"OK," Rowan said with a weary sigh. "Please take this message down for him. Tell him I'm coming in. Tell him my mother
died. That the funeral is tomorrow at Lonigan and Sons. Have
you got that?"

"Yes, ma'am. And let me tell you how sorry we all are to
hear about your mother. I got kind of used to seeing her on that
screened porch whenever I passed."

Rowan was amazed.

"Tell me something, if you will," Rowan said. "The house
where she lived is on First Street?"

"Yes, Doctor."

"Is that in a neighborhood called the Garden District?"

"Yes, Doctor, it sure is."

She murmured her thanks and hung up. Then it is the same stretch that Michael described to me, she thought. And how is it they know about it, she wondered. Why, I didn't even tell that woman my mother's name.

But it was time to go. She went out on the north deck and made sure the *Sweet Christine* was thoroughly secured, as she might be for the worst weather. Then she locked the wheelhouse and went back into the house. She set the various household alarm systems, which she had not used since Ellie died.

Time now to take one last look about.

She thought of Michael standing before that graceful old Victorian on Liberty Street, talking of foreboding, of never coming back. Well, she had no such clear feeling. But merely to look at everything here made her feel sad. The house felt cast off, used up. And when she looked at the *Sweet Christine* she felt the same way.

It was as if the *Sweet Christine* had served her well, but did not matter anymore. All the men she'd made love to in the cabin below deck no longer mattered. In fact, it was quite remarkable really that she had not taken Michael down the little ladder into the snug warmth of the cabin. She had not even thought of it. Michael seemed part of a different world.

She had the strongest urge to sink the *Sweet Christine* suddenly, along with all the memories attached to it. But that was foolish. Why, the *Sweet Christine* had led her to Michael. She must be losing her mind.

Thank God she was going to New Orleans. Thank God she was going to see her mother before the burial, and thank God she'd soon be with Michael, telling him everything, and having him there with her. She had to believe that would happen, no matter why he hadn't called. She thought bitterly of the signed document in the safe. But it didn't matter to her now, not even enough to go to the safe, look at it, or tear it up.

She shut the door without looking back.

PART TWO

THE MAYFAIR WITCHES

Thirteen

THE FILE ON THE MAYFAIR WITCHES

Translator's Foreword to Parts I through IV:

The first four parts of this file contain material written by Petyr van Abel expressly for the Talamasca—in Latin, and primarily in our Latin code, a form of Latin used by the Talamasca in the fourteenth through the eighteenth centuries to keep its epistles and diary entries secret from prying eyes. Enormous amounts of material were written in English as well, as it was Petyr van Abel's custom to write in English when he was among the French, and in French when he was among the English, to render the dialogue and certain thoughts and feelings more naturally than the old Latin code would allow.

Almost all of this material is in the form of epistles, as this was, and still is, the primary form in which reports to the archives of the Talamasca are made.

Stefan Franck was at this time the head of the order, and most of the following material is addressed to him in an easy and intimate and sometimes informal style. However, Petyr van Abel was always aware that he was writing for the record, and he took great pains to explain and to clarify for the inevitable uninformed reader as he went along. This is the reason that he might describe a canal in Amsterdam, though writing to the man who lived on the very canal.

The translator has omitted nothing. The material is adapted only where the original letters and diary entries have been damaged and are no longer legible. Or where words or phrases in the old Latin code elude the modern scholars within the order, or where obsolete words in English obscure the meaning for the modern reader. The spelling has been modernized, of course.

The modern reader should take into account that English at this time—the late seventeenth century—was already the tongue that we know. Such phrases as "pretty good" or "I guess" or

273

"I suppose" were already current. They have not been added to the text.

If Petyr's world view seems surprisingly "existential" for the period, one need only reread Shakespeare, who wrote nearly seventy-five years before, to realize how thoroughly atheistic, ironical, and existential were the thinkers of those times. The same may be said of Petyr's attitude towards sexuality. The great repression of the nineteenth century sometimes causes us to forget that the seventeenth and eighteenth centuries were far more liberal in matters of the flesh.

Speaking of Shakespeare, Petyr had a special love of him and read the plays as well as the sonnets for pleasure. He often said that Shakespeare was his "philosopher."

As for the full story of Petyr van Abel, quite a tale in its own right, it is told in the file under his name, which consists of seventeen volumes in which are included complete translations of every report he ever made, on every case which he investigated, in the order in which those reports were written.

We also possess two different portraits painted of him in Amsterdam, one by Franz Hals, done expressly for Roemer Franz, our director of the period, showing Petyr to be a tall, fair-haired youth—of almost Nordic height and blondness—with an oval face, prominent nose, a high forehead, and large inquisitive eyes; and the other, dated some twenty years later and painted by Thomas de Keyser, reveals a heavier build and a fuller face, though still distinctly narrow, with a neatly trimmed mustache and beard and long curling blond hair beneath a large-brimmed black hat. In both pictures Petyr appears relaxed and somewhat cheerful, as was so typical of the men featured in Dutch portraits of the time.

Petyr belonged to the Talamasca from boyhood until he died in the line of duty at the age of forty-three—as this, his last complete report to the Talamasca, will make clear.

By all accounts, Petyr was a talker, a listener, and a natural writer, and a passionate and impulsive man. He loved the artistic community of Amsterdam and spent many hours with painters in his leisure time. He was never detached from his investigations, and his commentary tends to be verbose, detailed, and at times excessively emotional. Some readers may find it annoying. Others may find it priceless, for not only does he give us florid pictures of what he witnessed, he provides more than a glimpse of his own character.

He was himself a limited mind reader (he confessed that he was not competent in the use of this power because he disliked and distrusted it), and he possessed the ability to move small objects, to stop clocks, and do other "tricks" at will.

As an orphan wandering the streets of Amsterdam, he first came into contact with the Talamasca at the age of eight. The story goes that, perceiving that the Motherhouse sheltered souls who were "different" just as he was different, he hung about, finally falling asleep one winter night on the doorstep, where he might have frozen had not Roemer Franz found him and brought him in. He was later discovered to be educated and able to write both Latin and Dutch, and to understand French as well.

All his life his memory of his early years with his parents was sporadic and unreliable, though he did undertake the investigation of his own background, and discovered not only the identity of his father, Jan van Abel, the famous surgeon of Leiden, but also voluminous writings by the man containing some of the most celebrated anatomical and medical illustrations of the time.

Petyr often said that the order became his father and mother. No member was ever more devoted.

Aaron Lightner
the Talamasca, London, 1954

THE MAYFAIR WITCHES

PART I / TRANSCRIPT ONE

From the Writings of Petyr van Abel
for the Talamasca
1689

September 1689, Montcleve, France

Dear Stefan,

I have at last reached Montcleve on the very edge of the Cévennes mountains—to wit in the foothills of the region—and the grim little fortified town with its tiled roofs and dreary bastions is indeed in readiness for the burning of a great witch as I had been told.

It is early autumn here, and the air from the valley is fresh, perhaps even touched with the heat of the Mediterranean, and from the gates one has the most pleasing view of vineyards where the local wine, Blanquette de Limoux, is made.

As I have drunk more than my fill of it on this first evening, I can attest it is quite as good as these poor townsfolk insist.

But you know, Stefan, I have no love of this region, for these mountains echo still with the cries of the murdered Cathars who were burned in such great numbers all through this region centuries ago. How many centuries must pass before the blood of so many has soaked deep enough into the earth to be forgotten?

The Talamasca will always remember. We who live in a world of books and crumbling parchment, of flickering candles and eyes sore and squinting in the shadows, have always our hands on history. It is *now* for us. And I can remember, aye, long before I ever heard the word Talamasca, how my father spoke of those murdered heretics, and of the lies that were promulgated against them. For he had read much of them as well.

Alas, what has this to do with the tragedy of the Comtesse de Montcleve, who is to die tomorrow on the pyre built beside the doors of the Cathedral of Saint-Michel? It is all stone, this old fortified town, but not the hearts of its inhabitants, though nothing can prevent this lady's execution as I mean to show.

My heart is aching, Stefan. I am more than helpless, for I am besieged by revelations and memories. And have the most surprising story to tell.

But I shall take things in order as best I can, attempting to confine myself as always—and failing—to those aspects of this sad adventure which are worthy of note.

Allow me to say first off that I cannot prevent this burning. For not only is the lady in question deemed to be an unrepentant and powerful witch, but she stands accused of killing her husband by poison, and the testimony against her is exceedingly grievous, as I shall go on to make plain.

It is the mother of her husband who had come forth to accuse her daughter-in-law of intercourse with Satan, and of murder; and the two small sons of the unfortunate Comtesse have joined with their grandmother in her accusations, while the only daughter of the accused witch, one Charlotte, aged twenty and exceedingly beautiful, has already fled to the West Indies with her young husband from Martinique and their infant son, seeking to avert a charge of witchcraft against herself.

But not all of this is as it seems. And I shall explain fully what I have discovered. Only bear with me as I shall begin at the very beginning and then plunge into the dim past. There is much here that is of interest to the Talamasca, but little that the Talamasca can hope to do. And I am in torment as I write, for I know this lady, and came here on the suspicion perhaps that I would know her, though I hoped and prayed that I would be wrong.

When last I wrote you, I was just leaving the German states, and weary to death of their awful persecutions, and of how little I was able to interfere. I had witnessed two mass burnings in Treves, of the most despicable suffering made all the worse by the Protestant clerics who are as fierce as the Catholics and in complete agreement with them that Satan is afoot in the land and waging his victories through the most unlikely of towns-folk—mere simpletons in some cases, though in most merely honest housewives, bakers, carpenters, beggars, and the like.

How curious it is that these religious people believe the devil to be so stupid that he should seek to corrupt only the poor and powerless—why not the king of France for once?—and the population at large to be so weak.

But we have pondered these things many times, you and I.

I was drawn here, rather than home to Amsterdam for which I long with all my soul, because the circumstances of this trial were well-known far and wide, and are most peculiar in that it is a great Comtesse who is accused, and not the village midwife, a stammering fool wont to name every other poor soul as her accomplice and so forth and so on.

But I have found many of the same elements which are found elsewhere in that there is present here the popular inquisitor, Father Louvier, who has bragged for a decade that he had burned hundreds of witches, and will find witches here if they be here to be found. And there is present also a popular book on witch-craft and demonology by this very same man, much circulated throughout France, and read with extreme fascination by half-literate persons who pore over its lengthy descriptions of demons as if they were biblical Scripture, when in fact they are stupid filth.

And oh, I must not fail to make mention of the engravings in this fine text which is passed from hand to hand with such reverence, for they are the cause of much clamor, being skillfully done pictures of devils dancing by moonlight, and old hags feasting upon babies or flying about on brooms.

This book has held this town spellbound, and it will surprise no one of our order that it was the old Comtesse who produced it, the very accuser of her daughter-in-law, who has said straight out on the church steps that were it not for this worthy book she should not have known a witch was living in her very midst.

Ah, Stefan, give me a man or woman who has read a thousand books and you give me an interesting companion. Give me a man or woman who has read perhaps three and you give me a dangerous enemy indeed.

But again, I stray from my story.

I arrived here at four o'clock this evening, coming through

the mountains and down south towards the valley, a slow and laborious journey on horseback indeed. And once in sight of the town, which hovered above me like a great fortress, for that is what it once was, I straightaway divested myself of all those documents which might prove me to be other than as I have presented myself—a Catholic priest and student of the witchcraft pestilence, making his way through the countryside to study convicted witches so that he might better weed them out of his own parish at home.

Placing all of my extraneous and incriminating possessions in the strongbox, I buried it safely in the woods. Then wearing my finest clerical garb and silver crucifix and other accoutrements to present me as a rich cleric, I rode up and towards the gates, and past the towers of the Château de Montcleve, the former home of the unfortunate Comtesse whom I knew only by the title of the Bride of Satan, or the Witch of Montcleve.

Straightaway, I began to question those I met as to why there was such a great pyre set in the very middle of the open place before the cathedral doors, and why the peddlers had set up their stands to sell their drinks and cakes when there was no fair to be seen, and what was the reason for the viewing stands having been built to the north of the church and beside it against the walls of the jail? And why are the four inn yards of the town overflowing with horses and coaches, and why are so many milling and talking and pointing to the high barred window of the jail above the viewing stand, and then to the loathsome pyre?

Was it to do with the Feast of St. Michael, which is tomorrow, the day that is called Michaelmas?

Not a person to whom I spoke hesitated to enlighten me that it had nought to do with the saint, though this is his cathedral, except that they had chosen his feast the better to please God and all his angels and saints, with the execution tomorrow of the beautiful Comtesse who is to be burnt alive, without benefit of being strangled beforehand, so as to set an example to all witches in the neighborhood of whom there were many, though the Comtesse had named absolutely none as her accomplices even under the most unspeakable torture, so great was the devil's power over her, but the inquisitors would indeed find them out.

And from these sundry persons who would have talked me into a stupor had I allowed it, I did learn further that there was scarce a family in the vicinity of this prosperous community who had not seen firsthand the great powers of the Comtesse, as she did freely heal those who were sick, and prepare for them herb potions, and lay her own hands upon their afflicted limbs and bodies, and for this she asked nothing except that she be remembered in their prayers. She had in fact great fame for countering the black magic of lesser witches; and those suffering from spells went to her often for bread and salt to drive away the devils inflicted on them by persons unknown.

Such raven hair you never saw, said one of these to me, and ah, but she was so beautiful before they broke her, said another, and yet another, my child is alive on account of her, and yet a fourth that the Comtesse could cool the hottest fever, and that to those under her she had given gold on feast days, and had nothing for anyone but kind words.

Stefan, you would have thought I was on my way to a canonization, not a burning. For no one whom I met in this first hour, during which I took my time in the narrow streets, riding hither and thither as if lost, and stopping to talk with any and all I passed, had a cruel word for the lady at all.

But without a doubt, these simple folk seemed all the more tantalized by the fact that it was a good and great lady who would be committed to the flames before them, as if her beauty and her kindnesses made her death a grand spectacle for them to enjoy. I tell you, it was with fear in my heart of their eloquent praise of her, and their quickness to describe her, and the glitter that came over them when they spoke of her death, that I finally had enough of it and went on to the pyre itself and rode back and forth before it, inspecting its great size.

Aye, it takes a great deal of wood and coal to burn a human being complete and entire. I gazed on it with dread as always, wondering why it is that I have chosen this work when I do not ever enter a town such as this, with its barren stone buildings, and its old cathedral with its three steeples, but that I do not hear in my ears the noise of the mob, the crackling of the fire, and the coughing and gasping and finally the shrieks of the dying. You know that no matter how often I witness these despicable burnings, I cannot inure myself to them. What is it in my soul that forces me to seek this same horror again and again?

Do I do penance for some crime, Stefan? And when will I have done penance enough? Do not think I ramble on. I have a point in all this, as you will soon see and understand. For I have come face to face once more with a young woman I once loved as dearly as I have loved anyone, and I remember more vividly than her charms the blankness of her face when I first beheld her, chained to a cart on a lonely road in Scotland, only hours after she had seen her own mother burnt.

Perhaps if you remember her at all you have guessed the truth already. Do not read ahead. Bear with me. For as I rode back and forth before the pyre, listening to the stammering and stupidity of a pair of local wine sellers who boasted of having seen other burnings as if this were something to be proud of, I did not know the full history of the Comtesse. I do now.

At last, at perhaps five of the clock, I went to the finest of the inns of the town, and the oldest, which stands right opposite the church, and commands from all its front windows a view of the doors of Saint-Michel and the place of execution which I have described.

As the town was obviously filling up for this event, I fully expected to be sent away. You can imagine my surprise when I discovered that the occupants of the very best rooms on the front of the house were being turned out for, in spite of their fine clothes and airs, they had been discovered to be penniless. I at once paid the small fortune required for these "fine chambers," and, asking for a quantity of candles, that I might write late into the night as I am doing now, I went up the crooked little stair and found that this was a tolerable place with a decent straw mattress, not too filthy all things considered and one of them being that this is not Amsterdam, and a small hearth of which I have no need on account of the beautiful September weather, and the windows though small do indeed look out upon the pyre.

"You can see very well from here," said the innkeeper to me proudly, and I wondered how many times he had seen such a spectacle, and what were his thoughts on the proceedings, but then he went to talking on his own of how beautiful was the Comtesse Deborah and shaking his head sadly as did everyone else when they spoke of her, and what was to come.

"Deborah you said, that is her name?"

"Aye," he answered, "Deborah de Montcleve, our beautiful Comtesse, though she is not French you know, and if only she had been a little bit of a stronger witch—" and then he broke off with a bowed head.

I tell you the knife was at my breast then, Stefan. I guessed who she was, and could scarce endure to press him further. Yet I did. "Pray continue," I said.

"She said when she saw her husband dying that she could not save him, that it was beyond her power . . ." And here with sad sighs he broke off once more.

Stefan, we have seen countless such cases. The cunning woman of the village becomes a witch only when her powers to heal do not work. Before that, she is everyone's good sorceress, and there is nary the slightest talk of devils. And so here it was again.

I set up my writing desk, at which I sit now, put away the candles, and then betook myself to the public rooms below, where a little fire was going against the damp and dark in this stony place, about which several local philosophers were warming themselves, or drying out their besotted flesh, one or the other, and seating myself at a comfortable table and ordering supper, I tried to banish from my mind the curious obsession I have with all comfortable hearth fires, that the condemned feel this cozy warmth before it turns to agony and their bodies are consumed.

"Bring me the very best of your wine," I said, "and let me share it with these good gentlemen here, in the hopes that they will tell me about this witch, as I have much to learn."

My invitation was at once accepted and I ate at the very center of a parliament who commenced to talk all at once, so that I might pick and choose at different times the one to whom I wished to listen, and shut all the others out.

"How were the charges brought?" I asked straightaway.

And the chorus began its various unharmonized descriptions, that the Comte had been riding in the forest when after a fall from his horse, he staggered into the house. After a good meal and a good sleep, he rose well restored and prepared to go hunting, when a pain came over him and he took to his bed again.

All night long the Comtesse sat at his bedside, along with his mother, and listened to his groans. "The injury is *deep* inside," declared the wife. "I can do nothing to help it. Soon the blood will come to his lips. We must give him what we can for his pain."

And then as foretold the blood did appear in his mouth, and his groans grew louder, and he cried to his wife who had cured so many to bring her finest remedies to him. Again the Comtesse confided to her mother-in-law and to her children that this was an injury beyond her magic. The tears sprang to her eyes.

"Now, can a witch cry, I ask you," said the innkeeper, who had been listening as he wiped the table.

I confessed that I did not think that a witch could.

They went on to describe how the Comte lingered, and finally screamed as his pains grew sharper, though his wife had given him wine and herbs aplenty to dull his suffering and deliver his mind.

"Save me, Deborah," he screamed, and would not see the priest when he came to him. But then in his last hour, white and feverish, and bleeding from the bowels and from his mouth, he drew the priest close to him and declared that his wife was a witch and always had been, that her mother had been burnt for witchcraft and now he was suffering for all their wrongs.

In horror the priest drew away, thinking these are the ravings of a dying man. For all his years here, he had worshiped the Comtesse and lived on her generosity, but the old Comtesse took her son by the shoulders and set him down on the pillow, and said, "Speak, my son."

"A witch, that's what she is, and what's she always been. All these things she confessed to me, bewitching me, with the wiles of a young bride, crying upon my chest. And by this means she bound me to her and her evil tricks. In the town of Donnelaith in Scotland, her mother taught her the black arts, and there her mother was burnt before her very eyes."

And to his wife, who knelt with her arms beneath her face on the side of the bed, sobbing, he cried, "Deborah, for the love of God. I am in agony. You saved the baker's wife; you saved the miller's daughter. Why will you not save me!"

So maddened was he that the priest could not give him the viaticum, and he died cursing, a horrible death indeed.

The young Comtesse went wild as his eyes closed, calling out to him, and professing her love for him, and then lay as if dead herself. Her son Chrétien and her son Philippe gathered about her, and her fair daughter Charlotte, and they sought to comfort her and hold tight to her as she lay prostrate on the very floor.

But the old Comtesse had her wits about her and had marked what her son said. To her daughter-in-law's private apartments she went, and found in the cabinets not only her countless unguents and oils and potions for the curing of the ill and for poisoning, but also a strange doll carved crudely of wood with a head made of bone, and eyes and mouth drawn upon it, and black hair fixed to it, and tiny flowers in its hair made from silk. In horror the old Comtesse dropped this effigy upon knowing that it could only be evil, and that it looked far too much like the corn dolls made by the peasants in their old Beltane rituals against which the priests are forever preaching; and throwing open the other doors, she beheld jewels and gold beyond all reckoning, in heaps and in caskets, and in little sacks of silk, which, said the old Comtesse, the woman surely meant to steal when her husband was dead.

The young Comtesse was arrested that very hour, while the grandmother took into her private chambers her grandchildren that she might instruct them in the nature of this terrible evil, so that they might stand with her against the witch, and come to no harm.

"But it was well-known," said the innkeeper's son, who talked more than anyone else present, "that the jewels were the property of the young Comtesse and had been brought with her from Amsterdam where she had been the widow of a rich man, and our Comte before he went in search of a rich wife had little more than a handsome face, and threadbare clothes, and his father's castle and land.''

Oh, how these words bruised me, Stefan, you cannot compass. Only wait and hear my tale.

Sad sighs came from the entire little company.

''And with her gold, she was so generous,'' said another, ''for you had but to go to her and beg for help and it was yours.''

''Oh, she's a powerful witch, no doubt of it,'' said another, ''for how else could she bind so many to herself as she bound the Comte?'' But even this was not said with hate and fear.

I was reeling, Stefan.

''So now the old Comtesse has taken this money into her charge,'' I remarked, seeing the bare bones of the plot. ''And what, pray tell, was the fate of the doll?''

''Disappeared,'' they said all in a chorus, as if they were answering the litany in the cathedral. ''Disappeared.'' But Chrétien swore that he had seen this hideous thing and knew it to be from Satan, and bore witness that his mother had spoken to it, as if it were an idol.

And on they went, breaking up into Babel again, and warring diatribes, that no doubt the beautiful Deborah had more than likely murdered the Amsterdam husband before the Comte had ever met her, for that was the way of a witch, wasn't it, and could anyone deny that she was a witch, once the story of her mother was known?

''But is this story of the mother's death proven to be true?'' I pressed.

''Letters were written from the Parliament of Paris, to which the lady appealed, to the Scottish Privy Council and they did send verification that indeed a Scottish witch had been burnt in Donnelaith over twenty years before, and a daughter Deborah had survived her, and been taken away from that place by a man of God.''

How my heart sank to hear this, for I knew now there was no hope at all. For what worse testimony could there be against her, than that her mother had been burnt before her? And I did not even need to ask, had the Parliament of Paris turned down her appeal?

''Yes, and with the official letter from Paris, there came also an illustrated leaflet, much circulated in Scotland still, which told of the evil witch of Donnelaith who had been a midwife and a cunning woman of great renown until her fiendish practices were made known.''

Stefan, if you do not recognize the Scottish witch's daughter now from this account you do not remember the story. But I no longer held out the slightest doubt. "My Deborah," I whispered in my heart. There was no chance that I could be wrong.

Claiming that I had witnessed many an execution in my time, and hoped to witness more, I asked the name of the Scottish witch, for perhaps I had perused the record of her trial in my own studies. "Mayfair," they said, "Suzanne of the Mayfair, who called herself Suzanne Mayfair for want of any other name."

Deborah. It could be no other than the child I had rescued from the Highlands so very long ago.

"Oh, but Father, there are such dreadful truths in that little book of the Scottish witch, that I hesitate to say."

"Such books are not Scripture," I replied in defiance. But they went on to enlighten me to the effect that the entire trial of Suzanne of the Mayfair had been sent on through the Parliament of Paris, and was in the hands of the inquisitor now.

"Was poison found in the Comtesse's chambers?" I asked, trying for what bit of truth I could obtain.

No, they said, but so heavy was the testimony against her that this did not matter, for her mother-in-law had heard her address beings that were invisible, and her son Chrétien had seen this also, and her son Philippe, and even Charlotte, though Charlotte had fled rather than answer questions against her mother, and other persons too had seen the power of the Comtesse, who could move objects without touching them, and judge the future, and know countless impossible things.

"And she confesses nothing?"

"It was the devil who would put her in a trance when she was tortured," said the innkeeper's son. "For how else could any human being slip into a stupor when a hot iron is applied to the flesh?"

At this I felt myself sicken and grow weary, and almost overcome. Yet I continued to question them. "And named no accomplices?" I asked. "For the naming of accomplices they are always much urged to do."

"Ah, but she was the most powerful witch ever heard of in these parts, Father," said the vintner. "What need had she of others? The inquisitor, when he heard the names of those whom she had cured, likened her to the great sorceresses of mythology, and to the Witch of Endor herself."

"And would there were a Solomon about," I said, "so that he might concur."

But this they did not hear.

"If there was another witch, it was Charlotte," said the old vintner. "You never saw such a sight as her Negroes, coming into the very church with her to Sunday Mass, with fine wigs and satin clothes! And the three mulatto maids for her infant boy. And her husband, tall and pale and like unto a willow tree, and suffering as he does from a great weakness which has afflicted him from childhood and which not even Charlotte's mother could cure. And oh, to see Charlotte command the Negroes to carry their master about the village, down the steps and up the steps, and to pour his wine for him and hold the cup to his lip and the napkin to his chin. At this very table they sat, the man as gaunt as a saint on the church wall, and the black shining faces around him, and the tallest and blackest of them all, Reginald, they called him, reading to his master from a book in a booming voice. And to think Charlotte has lived among such persons since the age of eighteen, having married this Antoine Fontenay of Martinique at that tender age."

"Surely it was Charlotte who stole the doll from the cabinet," said the innkeeper's son, "before the priest could lay hands on it, for who else in the terrified household would have touched such a thing?"

"But you have said that the mother could not cure the husband's illness?" I asked gently. "And plainly Charlotte herself could not cure it. Maybe these women are not witches."

"Ah, but curing and cursing are two separate things," said the vintner. "Would they had applied their talent merely to curing! But what had the evil doll to do with curing?"

"And what of Charlotte's desertion?" asked another, who had only just joined the congregation and seemed powerfully excited. "What can it mean but that they were witches together? No sooner was the mother arrested than Charlotte fled with her husband and her child, and her Negroes, back to the West Indies whence they came. But not before Charlotte had gone to be with her mother in the prison, and been locked up with her alone for more than an hour, this request granted only for those in attendance were foolish enough to believe that Charlotte would persuade her mother to confess, which of course she did not do."

"Seemed the wise thing to have done," said I. "And where has Charlotte gone?"

"To Martinique once more, it is said, with the pale skin and bone crippled husband, who has made a fortune there in the plantations, but no one knows that this is true. The inquisitor has written to Martinique to demand of the authorities that they question Charlotte, but they have not answered him, though there has been time enough, and what hope has he of justice being done in such a place as that?"

For over half an hour I listened on to this chatter, as the trial was described to me, and how Deborah protested her innocence, even before the judges and before those of the village who were admitted to witness it, and how she herself had written to His Majesty King Louis, and how they had sent to Dole for the witch pricker, and had then stripped her naked in her cell, and cut off her long raven hair, shaving her head after that, and searched her for the devil's mark.

"And did they find it?" I asked, trembling inside with disgust at these proceedings, and trying not to recall in my mind's eyes the girl I remembered from the past.

"Aye, two marks they found," said the innkeeper, who had now joined us with a third bottle of white wine paid for by me and poured it out for all to enjoy. "And these she claimed she had from birth and that they were the same as countless persons had upon their bodies, demanding that all the town be searched for such marks, if they were to prove anything, but no one believed her, and she was by then worn white and thin from starvation and torture, yet her beauty was not gone."

"How so, not gone?" asked I.

"Oh, like a lily she looks now," said the old vintner sadly, "very white and pure. Even her jailers love her, so great is her power to charm everyone. And the priest weeps when he takes her Communion, for though she is unconfessed, he will not deny it to her."

"Ah but you see, she could seduce Satan. And that is why they have called her his bride."

"But she cannot seduce the witch judge," says I. And they all nodded, not seeming to know that I spoke this in bitter jest.

"And the daughter," I asked, "what did she say on the matter of her mother's guilt before she made her escape?"

"Not a single word to any person. And in the dead of night, she slipped away."

"A witch," said the innkeeper's son, "or how could she have left her mother to die alone with her sons turned against her?"

This no one could answer, but I could well guess.

By this time, Stefan, I had little appetite for anything but to get clear of this inn and speak to the parish priest, though this, as you know, is always the most dangerous part. For what if the inquisitor were to be roused from wherever he sat feasting and drinking on the money earned from this madness, and he should know me from some other place, and horror of horrors know my work and my impostures.

Meanwhile my newfound friends drank even more of my wine, and talked on that the young Comtesse had been painted by many a renowned artist in Amsterdam, so great was her beauty; but then I might have told them that part of the story, and so fell silent, in anguish, quietly paying for another bottle for the company before I took my leave.

The night was warm and full of talk and laughter everywhere it seemed, with windows open and some still coming and going from the cathedral, and others camped along the walls and ready for the spectacle, and no light in the high barred window of the prison beside the steeple where the woman was held.

I stepped over those seated and chatting in the dark as I went to the sacristy on the other side of the great edifice and there struck the knocker until an old woman led me in and called the pastor of the place. A bent and gray-haired man came at once to greet me saying that he wished he had known of a traveling priest come to visit, and I must move from the inn at once and lodge with him.

But my apologies he accepted quick enough as well as my excuses about the pain in my hands which prevents me now from saying Mass any longer, for which I have a dispensation, and all the other lies I have to tell.

As luck would have it, the inquisitor was being put up in fine style by the old Comtesse at the château outside the town gates, and as all the great cronies of the place were gone thither to dine with him, he would not show his face again tonight.

On this account the pastor was obviously injured, as he had been by the whole proceedings, for everything had been taken out of his hands by the witch judge and the witch pricker and all the other ecclesiastic filth which rains down upon such affairs as this.

How fortunate you are, I thought as he showed me into his dingy rooms, for had she broken under the torture and named names, half your town would be in jail and everyone in a state of terror. But she has chosen to die alone, by what strength I cannot conceive of.

Though you know, Stefan, there are always persons who do resist, though we have naught but sympathy for those who find it impossible.

"Come in and sit with me for a while," said the priest, "and I'll tell you what I know of her."

To him immediately I put my most important questions, on the thin hope that the townsfolk might have been wrong. Had there been an appeal to the local bishop? Yes, and he had condemned her. And to the Parliament of Paris? Yes, and they had refused to hear her case.

"You have seen these documents yourself?"

He gave me a grave nod, and then from a drawer in his cabinet produced for me the hated pamphlet of which they had spoken, with its evil engraving of Suzanne Mayfair perishing in artful flames. I put this bit of trash away from me.

"Is the Comtesse such a terrible witch?" I said.

"It was known far and wide," he said in a whisper, with a great lift of his eyebrows, "only no one had the courage to speak the truth. And so the dying Comte spoke it, to clear his conscience as it were, and the old Comtesse, having read the *Demonologie* of the inquisitor, found in it the proper descriptions of all the strange things which she and her grandsons had long seen." He gave a great sigh. "And I shall tell you another loathsome secret." And here he dropped his voice to a whisper. "The Comte had a mistress, a very great and powerful lady whose name must not be spoken in connection with these proceedings. But we have it from her own lips that the Comte was terrified of the Comtesse, and took great pains to banish all thoughts of his mistress from his mind when he entered the presence of his wife, for she could read such things in his heart."

"Many a married man might follow that advice," I said in disgust. "So what does it prove? Nothing."

"Ah, but don't you see? This was her reason for poisoning her husband, once he had fallen from the horse, and she thought that on account of the fall, she might not be blamed."

I said nothing.

"But it is known hereabout," he said slyly, "and tomorrow when the crowd gathers, watch the eyes and upon whom they settle, and you will see the Comtesse de Chamillart, from Carcassonne, in the viewing stand before the jail. However, mark me. I do not say that it is she."

I said nothing, but sank only further into hopelessness.

"You cannot imagine the power which the devil has over the witch," he continued.

"Pray, enlighten me."

"Even after the rack on which she was cruelly tortured, and the boot being put on her foot to crush it, and the irons being applied to the soles of her feet, she confessed nothing, but did scream for her mother in torment, and cry out: 'Roelant, Roelant,' and then 'Petyr,' which were surely the names of her devils, as they belong to no one of her acquaintance here, and at once, through the agency of these daimons she fell to dreaming, and could not be made to feel the slightest pain."

I could listen no more!

"May I see her?" I asked. "It is so important for me to gaze with my own eyes upon the woman, to question her if I might."

And here I produced my big thick book of scholarly observations in Latin, which this old man could scarcely read, I should say, and I babbled on about the trials I had witnessed at Bramberg, and the witch house there, where they had tortured hundreds, and many other things which impressed this priest sufficiently enough.

"I'll take you to her," he said finally, "but I warn you, it is most dangerous. When you see her you'll understand."

"How exactly?" I inquired, as he led me down the stairs with a candle.

"Why, she is still beautiful! That is how much the devil loves her. That is why they call her the devil's bride."

He then directed me to a tunnel which ran beneath the nave of the cathedral where the Romans had buried their dead in olden times in this region, and through this we passed to the jail on the other side. Then up the winding stairs we went to the highest floor, where she was kept beyond a door so thick the jailers themselves could scarce open it, and holding his candle aloft, the priest pointed then to the far corner of a deep cell.

Only a trace of light came through the bars. The rest fell from the candle. And there on a heap of hay I beheld her, bald and thin and wretched, in a ragged gown of coarse cloth, yet pure and shining as a lily as her admirers had so described. They had shaved even the eyebrows from her, and the perfect shape of her bare head and her hairlessness gave an unearthly radiance to her eyes and to her countenance as she looked up at us, from one to the other, carefully, with a slight and indifferent nod.

It was the face one expects to see at the center of a halo, Stefan. And you, too, have seen this face, Stefan, rendered in oil on canvas, as I shall clarify for you by and by.

She did not move, but merely regarded us calmly and in silence. Her knees were drawn up in front of her, and she had wrapped her arms about her legs, as if she were cold.

Now you know, Stefan, that as I knew this woman, there was the strong chance that at this moment she would know me, that she should speak to me or implore me or even curse me in some way as to cause my authenticity to be questioned, but I tell you in truth I had not even thought of this in my haste.

But let me break off my account of this miserable night, and tell you now the whole tale before I proceed to relate what little did here take place.

Before you read another word I have written, leave your chamber, go down the stairs into the main hall of the Motherhouse, and look at the portrait of the dark-haired woman by Rembrandt van Rijn which hangs just at the foot of the stairs. That is my

Deborah Mayfair, Stefan. This is the woman, now shorn of her long dark hair, who sits shivering now as I write, in the prison across the square.

I am in my room at the inn, having only lately left her. I have candles aplenty, as I have told you, and too much wine to drink and a bit of a fire to drive out the cold. I am seated at the table facing the window, and in our common code I will now tell you all.

For it was twenty-five years ago that I first came upon this woman, as I have told you, and I was a young man of eighteen years then and she only a girl of twelve.

This was before your time in the Talamasca, Stefan, and I had come to it only some six years before as an orphaned child. It seemed the pyres of the witches were burning from one end of Europe to the other, and so I had been sent out early from my studies to accompany Junius Paulus Keppelmeister, our old witch scholar, on his travels throughout Europe, and he had only just begun to show to me his few poor methods of trying to save the witches, by defending them where he could and inclining them in private to name as accomplices their accusers as well as the wives of the most prominent citizens of the town so the entire investigation might be discredited, and the original charges be thrown out.

And I had only lately been made to understand, as I traveled with him, that we were always in search of the true magical person—the reader of minds, the mover of objects, the commander of spirits, though seldom if ever, even in the worst persecutions, was any true sorcerer to be found.

It was my eighteenth year as I have told you, and my first to venture out of the Motherhouse since I had begun my education there, and when Junius took ill and died in Edinburgh, I was at my wit's end. We had been on our way to investigate the trial of a Scottish cunning woman, very much famed for her healing power, who had cursed a milkmaid in her village and been accused of witchcraft though no evil had befallen the maid.

On his last night in this world, Junius ordered me to continue to the Highland village without him; and told me to cling fast to my disguise as a Swiss Calvinist scholar. I was far too young to be called a minister by anyone, and so could not make use of Junius's documents as such; but I had traveled as his scholarly companion in plain Protestant clothes, and so went on in this manner on my own.

You cannot imagine my fear, Stefan.

And the burnings of Scotland terrified me. The Scots are and were, as you know, as fierce and terrible as the French and

Germans, learning nothing it seems from the more merciful and reasonable English. And so afraid was I on this my first journey that even the beauty of the Highlands did not work its spell upon me.

Rather when I saw that the village was small and at a great remove from its nearest neighbor, and that its people were sheepherders, I knew even greater dread for their ignorance and the ferocity of their superstition. And to the dreary aspect of the whole was added the nearby ruins of a once great cathedral, rising like the bones of a leviathan out of the high grass, and far beyond across a deep valley, the forlorn picture of a castle of rounded towers and tiny windows, which might have been an empty ruin, for all I could see.

How shall I ever be of assistance here, I thought, without Junius to aid me? And riding into the village proper I soon discovered I had come too late, for the witch had been burnt that very day, and the wagons had just come to clear away the pyre.

Cart after cart was filled with ashes and charred bits of wood and bone and coal, and then the procession moved out of the little place, with its solemn-faced folk standing about, and into the green country again, and it was then that I laid eyes upon Deborah Mayfair, the witch's daughter.

Her hands bound, her dress ragged and dirty, she had been taken to witness the casting of her mother's ashes to the four winds.

Mute she stood there, her black hair parted in the middle and hanging down her back in rich waves, her blue eyes dry of all tears.

" 'Tis the mark of the witch," said an old woman who stood by watching, "that she cannot shed a tear."

Ahh, but I knew the child's blank face; I knew her sleeplike walk, her slow indifference to what she saw as the ashes were dumped out and the horses rode through them to scatter them. I knew because I knew myself in childhood, orphaned and roaming the streets of Amsterdam after the death of my father; and I remembered how when men and women spoke to me, it did not even cross my mind to answer, or to look away, or to change my manner for any reason. And even when I was slapped or shaken, I retained this extraordinary quietude, only wondering mildly why they would bother to do such a curious thing; better to look perhaps at the slant of the sunlight striking the wall behind them, as at the furious expressions on their faces, or take heed of the growls that came from their lips.

This tall and stately girl of twelve had been flogged as they burnt her mother. They had turned her head to make her watch, as the lash fell.

"What will they do with her?" I asked the old woman.

"They should burn her, but they are afraid to," she answered. "She is so young and a merry-begot, and no one would bring harm to a merry-begot, and who knows who her father might be." And with that the old woman turned and gave a grave look to the castle that stood, leagues away across the green valley, clinging to the high and barren rocks.

You know, Stefan, many a child has been executed in these persecutions. But each village is different. And this was Scotland. And I did not know what was a merry-begot or who lived in the castle or how much any of this might mean.

I watched in silence as they put the child on a cart and drove her back towards the town. Her dark hair blew out with the wind as the horses picked up speed. She did not turn her head to left or right, but stared straight forward, the ruffian beside her holding onto her to keep her from falling as the rough wooden wheels bounced over the ruts of the road.

"Ah, but they should burn her and be done with it," said the old woman now, as if I had argued with her, when in truth I had said nothing, and then she spat to one side, and said: "If the Duke does not move to stop them," and here she looked once more to the distant castle, "I think that burn her they will."

Then and there I made my decision. I would take her, by some ruse if I could.

Leaving the old woman to return on foot to her farm, I followed the girl in the cart back to the village, and only once did I see her wake from her seeming stupor, and this was when we passed the ancient stones outside the village, and I mean by this those huge standing stones in a circle, from the dark times before history, of which you know more than I will ever know. To a circle of these she looked with great and lingering curiosity, though why it was not possible to see.

For naught but a lone man stood far out in the field, in their midst, staring back at her, with the powerful light of the open valley beyond him—a man no older than myself perhaps, tall and slight of build with dark hair, but I could hardly see him, for so bright was the horizon that he seemed transparent, and I thought perhaps he was a spirit and not a man at all.

It did seem that their glances met as the girl's cart passed, but of none of this part am I certain, only that some person or thing was momentarily there. I marked it only for she was so lifeless, and it may have some bearing upon our story; and I think now that it does indeed have bearing; but that is for us both to determine at some later time. I shall go on.

I went to the minister at once, and to the commission which had been appointed by the Scottish Privy Council and had not yet disbanded, for it was at this very hour dining, as was the custom, with a good meal being provided by the estate of the dead witch. She had had much gold in her hut, said the innkeeper to me as I entered, and this gold had paid for her trial, her torture, the witch pricker, the witch judge who tried her, and the wood and the coal used to burn her, and indeed the carts that carried her ashes away.

"Sup with us," said the fellow to me as he explained all this, "for the witch is paying. And there's more gold still."

I declined. And was not pressed for explanation, thank heaven, and going right to the men at the board I declared myself to be a student of the Bible and a God-fearing man. Might I take the witch's child with me to Switzerland, to a good Calvinist minister there who would take her in and educate her and make a Christian of her and wipe the memory of her mother from her mind?

I said far too much to these men. Little was required. To wit, only the word Switzerland was required. For they wanted to rid themselves of her, they said it straight out, and the Duke wanted them to be rid of her, and not to burn her, and she was a merry-begot, which made the villagers most afraid.

"And what is that, pray tell?" I asked.

To which they explained that the people of Highland villages were most attached still to the old customs, and that on the eve of May 1 they built great bonfires in the open grass, these being lighted only from the needfire, or the fire they made themselves from sticks, and they danced all night about the bonfires, making merry. And in such revelry, this child's mother, Suzanne, the fairest in the village and the May Queen of that year, had conceived of Deborah, the surviving child.

A merry-begot she was, and therefore much beloved, for no one knew who was her father and it could have been any of the village men. It could have been a man with noble blood. And in the olden times, which were the times of the pagans and best forgotten, though they could never make these villagers forget them, the merry-begots were the children of the gods.

"Take her now, brother," they said, "to this good minister in Switzerland and the Duke will be glad of it, but have something to eat and drink before you go, for the witch has paid for it, and there is plenty for all."

Within the hour, I rode out of the town with the child on my horse before me. And we rode right through the ashes at the crossroads, to which she did not to my knowledge give even a glance. To the circle of stones, she never once looked that I could tell. And she gave no farewell to the castle either as we rode down to the road that runs on the banks of Loch Donnelaith.

As soon as we reached the first inn in which we had to lodge, I knew full well what I had done. The girl was in my possession, mute, defenseless, and very beautiful, and big as a woman in some respects, and there I was, little more than a boy, but plenty more to make the difference, and I had taken her with no permission from the Talamasca and might face the most terrible storm of reprimands when I returned.

We put up in two rooms as was only proper, for she looked more woman than child. But I was afraid to leave her alone lest she run away, and wrapping my cloak about me, as if it would somehow restrain me, I lay down on the hay opposite her and stared at her, and tried to think what to do.

I observed now by the light of the reeking candle that she wore a few locks of her black hair in two small knots on either side of her head, high up, so as to keep back the bulk of it, and that her eyes were very like the eyes of a cat. By this I mean they were oval and narrow and turned up ever so little on the outside ends, and they had a shine to them. And beneath them she had rounded though dainty cheeks. It was no peasant face by any measure, but far too delicate, and beneath her ragged gown hung the high full breasts of a woman, and her ankles which she crossed before her as she sat on the floor were very shapely indeed. Her mouth I could not look at without wanting to kiss it, and I was ashamed of these fancies in my head.

I had not given the slightest thought to anything but rescuing her. And now my heart beat with desire for her. And she a girl of twelve merely sat looking at me.

What were her thoughts, I wondered, and sought to read them, but it seemed she knew this, and closed her mind to me.

At last I thought of the simple things, that she must have food and decent clothes—this seemed rather like discovering that sunlight makes one warm and water satisfies thirst—and so I went out to procure food for her and wine, and to acquire a proper dress, and a bucket of warm water for washing, and a brush for her hair.

She stared at these things as if she did not know what they were. And I could see now, by the light of the candle, that she was covered with filth and marks from the lash, and that the bones showed through her skin.

Stefan, does it take a Dutchman to abhor such a condition? I swear to you that I was consumed with pity as I undressed her and bathed her, but the man in me was burning in hell. Her skin was fair and soft to the touch, and she was ready for childbearing, and she gave me not the slightest resistance as I cleaned her, and then dressed her and at last brushed her hair.

Now I had by that time learned something of women, but it was not as much as I knew of books. And this creature seemed all the more mysterious to me for her nakedness and helpless quiet; but all the while, she peered out at me from the prison of her body with fierce, silent eyes that frightened me somewhat, and made me feel that, were my hands to stray in some improper way upon her body, she might strike me dead.

She did not flinch when I washed the marks of the lash on her back.

I fed her the food with a wooden spoon, Stefan, and though she took each morsel from me, she would reach for nothing and assist in nothing, on her own.

During the night I woke dreaming that I had taken her, much relieved to discover that I had not. But she was awake and watching me, and with the eyes of a cat. For some time I stared at her, again trying to divine her thoughts. The moonlight was pouring into the uncovered window, along with a good deal of bracing cold air, and I saw by the light that she had lost her blank expression and now seemed malevolent and angry, and this was frightening to me. She seemed a wild thing, dressed in her stiff starched white collar and bonnet, and blue dress.

In a soothing voice I tried to tell her in English that she was safe with me, that I would take her to a place where no one would accuse her of witchcraft, and that those who had descended upon her mother were themselves wicked and cruel.

At this she seemed puzzled, but she said nothing. I told her that I had heard tell of her mother, that her mother was a healer and could help the afflicted, and that such persons have always existed, and no one called them witches until these terrible times. But an awful superstition was afoot in Europe; and whereas in the olden days, men were admonished not to believe that people could speak to devils, now the church itself believed such things, and went looking for witches in every hamlet and town.

Nothing came from her, but it seemed her face grew less terrible, as though my words had melted her anger. And I saw the look of bewilderment again.

I told her I was of an order of good people who did not want to hurt or burn the old healers. And that I would take her to our Motherhouse, where men scoffed at the things which the witch hunters believed. "This is not in Switzerland," I said, "as I told the bad men in your village, but in Amsterdam. Have you ever heard of this city? It is a great place indeed."

It seemed then the coldness came back to her. Surely she understood my words. She gave a faint sneer at me, and I heard her whisper under her breath in English, "You are no churchman. You are a liar!"

At once I went to her and took her hand. I was greatly pleased to see she understood English and did not speak only the hopeless dialects one finds in these places, for now I could talk to her with more courage. I explained that I had told these lies to save her, and that she must believe that I was good.

But then she faded before my eyes, drawing away from me, like a flower closing up.

All the next day she spoke nothing to me, and all the next night the same, though she ate now unaided and well, I thought, and seemed to be gaining in strength.

When we reached London, I woke in the night in the inn to hear her speaking. I climbed up off the straw and beheld her looking out the window, and I heard her say in English, and with a thick Scottish accent to it, "Go away from me, devil! I will not see you anymore."

When she turned round, there were tears shining in her eyes. More than ever she had the aspect of a woman, looming over me, with her back to the window, and the light of my candle stub rising up into her face. She saw me without surprise and with the same coldness as she had shown me before. She lay down and turned her face to the wall.

"But to whom did you speak?" I demanded. She said nothing to me. In the dark I sat and talked to her, not knowing whether or not she heard. I told her that if she had seen something, be it a ghost or a spirit, it need not be the devil. For who was to say what these invisible things were? I begged her to talk to me of her mother and tell me what her mother had done to bring the charge of witchcraft against her, for now I was certain that she herself had powers and that her mother had possessed them, but she would not answer even one word.

I took her to a bathing house, and bought her another dress. These things brought no interest from her. At the crowds and the passing coaches she stared with coldness. And wanting to hurry from the place and reach home, I divested myself of my clerical black, and put on the garments of a Dutch gentleman, as these would most likely bring respect and good service.

But this change in me provided her with some grim and secret amusement and again she sneered at me, as if to say she knew

I had some sordid purpose, but I did nothing to confirm her in this suspicion any more than I had in the past. Could she read my thoughts, I wondered, and know that every waking moment I imagined her as she had been when I bathed her? I hoped it was not so.

She looked so pretty in her new dress, I thought to myself, I had never seen any young woman who was prettier. Because she would not, I had braided a part of her hair for her, and wound this braid around the top of her head, to hold her long locks back out of her face, as I had seen women do, and ah, but she was a picture.

Stefan, it is agony for me to write of these things, but I do it I think not only for our voluminous records, but because the night is so still here in Montcleve, though it is not yet even midnight, and I am so sick at heart. I wish to look at the wounds I cannot heal. But you do not have to accept my pledges as to the woman's beauty, you have yourself seen her likeness; as I have said before.

On to Amsterdam we went, she and I, posing now as the rich Dutch brother and sister, for all anyone might know; and as I had hoped and dreamed, our city waked her from her torpor, with its pretty tree-lined canals and all the handsome boats and the fine four- and five-story houses which she did inspect with a new vigor.

And coming upon the grand Motherhouse, with the canal at its feet, and seeing that it was "my home," and was to be hers, she could not conceal her wonder. For what had this child seen of the world but a miserable sheep-farming village and the dirty inns in which we'd lodged; so you can quite understand how it was when she saw a proper bedstead, in a clean Dutch bedroom. She spoke not a single word, but the bit of a smile on her lips spoke volumes.

I went directly to my superiors, to Roemer Franz and Petrus Lancaster, both of whom you fondly remember, and confessed all that I had done.

I broke down in tears and said the child was alone and so I had taken her, and I had no other excuse for spending so much money, except that I did it; and to my astonishment, they forgave me, but they also laughed because they knew my innermost secrets.

And Roemer said: "Petyr, you have done such penance between here and Scotland that surely you deserve an increase in your allowance, and perhaps a better room within the house."

More laughter greeted these words. I had to smile to myself, for I was drenched in fantasies of Deborah's beauty even then, but soon the good spirits had left me and I was again in pain.

Deborah would answer no questions put to her. But when the wife of Roemer, who lived with us all her life, went to Deborah and put the needle and the embroidery in her hands, Deborah did, with some skill, begin to sew.

By the end of week, Roemer's wife and the other wives had taught her through example to make lace, and she was hard at work at it by the hour, acknowledging nothing said to her, but staring at those around her whenever she looked up and then returning to her work without a word.

To the female members, those who were not wives, but were scholars and had powers of their own, she seemed to possess an obvious aversion. To me she would say nothing, but she had stopped giving me hateful glances, and when I asked her to walk out with me, she accepted and was soon dazzled by the city, and allowed me to buy her a drink in the tavern, though the spectacle of respectable women drinking and eating there seemed to amaze her, as it amazes other foreigners who have traveled far more widely than she.

All the while I described our city to her, I told of its history and its tolerance, of how Jews had come here to escape persecution in Spain, and how Catholics even lived here in peace among the Protestants, and there were no more executions for such things as witchcraft here, and I took her to see the printers and the booksellers. And to the house of Rembrandt van Rijn we went for a brief visit, as he was always so very pleasant to visit, and there were always pupils about.

His beloved Hendrickje, of whom I was always fond, had been gone two years, but Titus, his son, was still living, and with him. And I for one preferred the paintings which he did at this time of his life, for their curious melancholy, to those he did earlier when he was all the fashion. We drank a glass of wine with the young painters who were always gathered there to study with the master and this is when Rembrandt first caught sight of Deborah, though it was later that he painted her.

All the while, my intention was to amuse her, and divert her out of her hellish thoughts, and show to her the wide world of which she could now be a part.

She kept her silence, but I could see that the painters delighted her, and the portraits of Rembrandt in particular drew her, and so did this kindly and genial man himself. We went on to other studios and spoke to other artists—to see Emmanuel de Witte and others who were then painting in our city, some friends of ours then as they are today. And she appeared to warm to this, and to come alive as it were, her face at moments most gentle and sweet.

But it was when we passed the shops of the jewelers that she begged me with a light touch of her white fingers on my arm to stop. White fingers. I write this because I remember it so well—her delicate hand shining like a lady's hand as she touched me, and the weak desire for her I felt at this touch.

She showed a great fascination with those who were cutting and polishing diamonds and with the comings and goings of the merchants and the rich patrons who had come from all over Europe, nay the world, to buy their fine jewels. I wished that I had the money to buy something pretty for her, and of course the merchants being much taken with her beauty, and her fine clothes—for Roemer's wife had turned her out beautifully—began to play to her, and ask would she like to see their wares.

A fine Brazilian emerald set in gold was being shown to a rich Englishman, and this caught her eye. When the Englishman forswore it on account of the expense, she sat down at the table to look at it, as if she could well purchase it or I might for her, and it seemed she fell into a spell staring at this rectangular gem, fixed in its filigree of old gold. And then in English, she asked the price of it, and did not bat an eye when told.

I assured the merchant we would take it under consideration most deeply, as obviously the lady wanted it, and with a smile, I helped her to the street. Then I fell into sadness that I could not buy it for her.

And as we walked along the quay together back to the house, she said to me, "Do not be sad. For who expects such things of you?" and for the very first time she smiled at me, and pressed my hand. My heart leapt at this, but she lapsed again into her coldness and her silence and would say nothing more.

I confessed all this to Roemer, who advised me that we had not taken vows of chastity but that I was behaving most honorably, which was as he expected, and that I should study my English books now, as my writing in English was still dreadful, and thereby occupy my mind.

On the seventh day of Deborah's time in the Motherhouse, one of our members of whom you have heard and studied much, though she is dead these many years, came home from Haarlem where she had been visiting her brother, a rather ordinary sort of man. But she was no ordinary woman, and it is of the great witch, Geertruid van Stolk, that I speak. She was at that time the most powerful of all our members, be they men or women; and at once the story of Deborah was told to her, and she was asked to speak to the child and see if she could read Deborah's thoughts.

"She will not tell us whether she can read or write," said Roemer, "in fact, she will tell us nothing, and we cannot divine what she reads from our minds or of our intentions, and we do not know how to proceed. We feel in our hearts that she has powers, but we are not sure of it; she has locked her mind to us."

At once Geertruid went to her, but Deborah, on merely hearing this woman approach, rose from her stool, overturning it, and threw down her sewing and backed up against the wall. There she stared at Geertruid with a look of pure hatred on her face, and then sought to get out of the room, clawing at the walls as if to go through them, and at last finding the door and rushing down the passage towards the street.

Roemer and I restrained her, begging her to be calm, and telling her that no one meant to hurt her, and at last Roemer said, "We must break the silence of this child." Meantime Geertruid gave to me a note, hastily scratched on paper, which said in Latin, "The child is a powerful witch," and this I passed on to Roemer without a word.

We implored Deborah to come with us into Roemer's study, a large and commodious room as you well know as you inherited it, but in his time it was filled with clocks, for he loved them, and these have since been distributed about the house.

Roemer always kept the windows over the canal open, and all the healthy noises of the city flowed, it seemed, into this room. It had about it a cheerful aspect. And as he brought Deborah now into the sunlight, and bid her sit down and calm herself, she seemed quieted and comforted, and then sat back and with a weary, pained manner looked up into his eyes.

Pained. I saw such pain in this instant as to nearly bring the tears to my own eyes. For the mask of blankness had utterly melted, and her very lips were trembling, and she said in English:

"Who are you men and women here? What in the name of God do you want with me!"

"Deborah," he said, speaking soothingly to her. "Listen to my words, child, and I shall tell you plainly. All this while we have sought to know how much you could understand."

"And what is there," she demanded hatefully, "that I should understand!" It seemed a woman's vibrant voice coming from her heaving bosom, and as her cheeks flamed, she became a woman, hard and cold inside and bitter from the horrors she had seen. Where was the child in her, I thought frantically, and then she turned and glared at me, and again at Roemer, who was intimidated if I ever saw him, but he worked fast to overcome it and he spoke again.

"We are an order of scholars, and it is our purpose to study those with singular powers, powers such as your mother had, which were said wrongly to have come from the devil, and powers which you yourself may possess as well. Was it not true that your mother could heal? Child, such a power does not come from the devil. Do you see these books around you? They are full of stories of such persons, called in one place sorcerer, and in another witch, but what has the devil to do with such things? If you have such powers, place your trust in us that we may teach you what they can and cannot do."

Roemer spoke further to her of how we had helped witches to escape their persecutors and to come here, and to be safe with us. And he spoke even to her about two of the women with us who were both powerful seers of spirits, and of Geertruid, who could make the very glass rattle in the windows with her mind, if she chose.

The child's eyes grew large but her face was hard. Her hands tightened on the arms of the chair, and she cocked her head to the left as she fixed Roemer and looked him up and down.

I saw the look of hate come back into her face, and Roemer whispered: "She is reading our thoughts, Petyr, and she can hide her own thoughts from us."

This gave her a start. But still she said nothing.

"Child," Roemer said, "what you have witnessed is terrible, but surely you did not believe the accusations made against your mother. Tell us, please, to whom did you speak the night in the inn when Petyr heard you? If you can see spirits, tell these things to us. No harm will ever come to you."

No answer.

"Child, let me show you my own power. It does not come from Satan, and no evocation of him is required for its use. Child, I do not believe in Satan. Now, behold the clocks around you—the tall case clock there, and the pendulum clock to the left of you, and the clock on the mantelshelf, and that clock there on the far desk."

She looked at all these, which greatly relieved us for at least she understood, and then she stared in consternation as Roemer, without moving a particle of his physical being, made them all come abruptly to a stop. The endless ticking was gone from the room and had left a great silence after it, which seemed strong enough in its emptiness to hush even the sounds from the canal below.

"Child, trust in us, for we share these powers," said Roemer, and then pointing to me, he told me to start the clocks again by the power of my mind. I shut my eyes and said to the clocks: "Start," and the clocks did as they were told and the room was full of ticking once more.

The face of Deborah was transformed from cold suspicion to sudden contempt, as she looked from me to Roemer. She sprang from the chair. Backwards against the books she crept, fixing me and then Roemer with her malevolent gaze.

"Ah, witches!" she cried. "Why did you not tell me? You are all witches! You are an order of Satan." And then as the tears poured down her face, she sobbed. "It is true, true, true!"

She wrapped her arms around her to cover her breasts and she spit at us in her rage. Nothing we could say would quiet her.

"We are all damned! And you hide here in this city of witches where they can't burn you!" she cried. "Oh, clever, clever witches in the devil's house!"

"No, child," cried Roemer. "We know nothing of the devil! We seek to understand what others condemn."

"Deborah," I cried out, "forget the lies they taught you. There is no one in the city of Amsterdam who would burn you! Think of your mother. What did she say of what she did, before they tortured her and made her sing their songs?"

Ah, but these were the wrong words! I could not know it, Stefan. I could not know it. Only as her face was stricken, as she put her hands over her ears, did I realize my error. Her mother had believed she was evil!

And then from Deborah's trembling mouth came more denunciations. "Wicked, are you? Witches, are you? Stoppers of clocks! Well, I shall show you what the devil can do in the hands of this witch!"

She moved into the very center of the room and looking up and out the window, it seemed, to the blue sky, she cried:

"Come now, my Lasher, show these poor witches the power of a great witch and her devil. Break the clocks one and all!"

And at once a great dark shadow appeared in the window, as if the spirit upon whom she had called had condensed himself to become small and strong within the room.

The thin glass over the faces of the clocks was shattered, the fine glued seams of their wooden cases sprung open, the very springs breaking out of them, and the clocks tumbled off the mantelshelf and the desk, and the tall case clock crashed to the floor.

Roemer was alarmed for seldom had he seen a spirit of such power, and we could all but feel the thing in our midst, brushing our garments, as it swept past us and shot out its invisible tentacles, as it were, to obey the witch's commands.

"Damn you into hell, witches. I shall not be your witch!" Deborah cried, and as the books began to fall around us, she fled once more from us, and the door slammed shut after her and we could not pry it open, try as we might.

But the spirit was gone. We had nothing more to fear from the thing. And after a long silence, the door was made to open again, and we wandered out, bewildered to discover that Deborah had long since left the house.

Now, you know, Stefan, by that time, Amsterdam was one of the very great cities of all Europe, and she held perhaps one hundred and fifty thousand persons, or more. And into this great city Deborah had vanished. And no inquiry we made of her in the brothels or the taverns bore fruit. Even to the Duchess Anna, the richest whore in Amsterdam, we went, for that is where with certainty a beautiful girl like Deborah might find refuge, and though the Duchess was as always glad to see us and talk with us, and serve us good wine, she knew nothing of the mysterious child.

I was now in such abject misery that I did nothing but lie in my bed, with my face on my arms, and weep, though all told me this was foolish, and Geertruid swore that she would find "the girl."

Roemer told me that I must write down what had happened with this young woman as part of my scholarly work, but I can tell you, Stefan, that what I wrote was most pitiful and brief and that is why I have not asked that you consult these old records. When I return to Amsterdam, God willing, I shall replace my old entries with this more vivid chronicle.

But to continue with what little more there is to say, it was a fortnight later that a young student of Rembrandt lately from Utrecht came to me and said that the girl for whom I had been searching was now living with the old portraitist Roelant, who was known by that name only, who had studied many years in Italy in his youth and still had many flocking to him for his work, though he was exceedingly ill and infirm, and could scarce pay his debts anymore.

You may not remember Roelant, Stefan, but let me tell you now he was a fine painter, whose portraits always evinced the happiness of Caravaggio, and had it not been for the malady which struck his bones and crippled him before his time, he might have been better regarded than he was.

At this time, he was a widower with three sons, and a kindly man.

At once I went to see Roelant, who was known to me and had always been genial, but now I found the door shut in my face. He had no time for visiting with us "mad scholars" as he called us, and warned me in heated terms that even in Amsterdam those as strange as we might be driven out.

Roemer said that I was to leave it alone for a while, and you know, we survive, Stefan, because we avoid notice, and so we kept our council. But in the days that followed we saw that Roelant paid all his back debts, which were many, and that he and his children by his first wife now dressed in fine clothes, which could only be called exceedingly rich.

It was said that Deborah, a Scottish girl of great beauty, taken in by him to nurse his children, had prepared an unguent for his crippled fingers, which had heated them as it were and loosened them and he could hold the brush again. Rumor had it he was being well paid for his new portraits, but he would have had to paint three and four a day, Stefan, to make the money to pay for the furnishings and clothes that now went into that house.

So the Scottish woman was rich, it was soon learned, the love child of a nobleman of that country, who though he could not acknowledge her, sent her money aplenty which she shared with the Roelants, who had been kind enough to take her in.

And who might that be, I wondered? The nobleman in that great hulking Scottish castle which glowered like a pile of natural rock over the valley from which I'd taken her, his merrybegot, barefoot and filthy and scarred to the bone from the lash, unable even to feed herself? Oh, what a pretty tale!

Roemer and I watched all of these goings-on with trepidation, for you know as well as I the reason for our own rule that we shall never use our powers for gain. And how was this wealth being got, we wondered, if not through that spirit which had come crashing into Roemer's chamber to break the clocks as Deborah commanded him to do?

But all was contentment now in the Roelant household and the old man married the young girl before the year was out. But two months before this wedding took place, Rembrandt, the master, had already painted her, and a month after the wedding the portrait was displayed in Roelant's parlor for all to see.

And around her neck in this portrait was the very Brazilian emerald which Deborah had so coveted the day I had taken her out. She had long ago bought it from the jeweler, along with every bit of plate or jewelry that struck her fancy, and the paintings of Rembrandt and Hals and Judith Leister which she so admired.

Finally I could stay away no longer. The house was open for

the viewing of the portrait by Rembrandt, of which Roelant was justly proud. And as I crossed the threshold to see this picture, old Roelant made no move to bar my entrance, but rather hobbled up to me on his cane, and offered me with his own hand a glass of wine, and pointed out to me his beloved Deborah in the library of the house, learning with a tutor to read and write Latin and French, for this was her greatest wish. She learnt so fast, said Roelant, that it amazed him, and she had of late been reading the writing of Anna Maria van Schurman who held that women were indeed as open to learning as men.

How brimming with joy he seemed.

I doubted what I knew of her age when I saw her. Arrayed in jewels and green velvet, she looked to be a young woman of perhaps seventeen. Great sleeves she wore, and voluminous skirts, and a green ribbon with satin rosettes in her black hair. Her eyes too seemed green against the magnificent fabric that surrounded her. And it struck me that Roelant himself did not know of her youth. Not a word had passed my lips to expose any of the lies that circulated around her, and I stood stung by her beauty as if she had rained blows on my head and shoulders, and then the fatal blow to my heart was struck when she looked up and smiled.

Now I shall have to go, I thought, and made to set down my wine. But she came towards me, smiling still, and she held my hands, and said "Petyr, come with me," and took me into a small chamber of cabinets where the household linen was kept.

What polish she had now, and grace. A lady at court could not have done it better. But when I considered this, I considered also my memory of her in the cart that day at the crossroads, and how like the little Princess she had seemed.

Yet she was changed from those times in every way. In the few thin shafts of light that pierced the little linen room, I could inspect her in every detail, and I found her robust, and perfumed, and red-cheeked, and there sat the great Brazilian emerald in its filigree of gold upon her high plump breast.

"Why have you not told everyone what you know of me?" she asked as if she did not know the answer.

"Deborah, we told you the truth about ourselves. We only wanted to offer you shelter, and our knowledge of the powers you possess. Come to us whenever you wish."

She laughed. "You are a fool, Petyr, but you brought me out of darkness and misery into this wondrous place." She reached into the hidden right pocket of her great skirt and pulled up out of it a handful of emeralds and rubies. "Take these, Petyr."

I drew back and shook my head.

"You say you are not of the devil," she said to me. "And your leader says that he does not even believe in Satan, were those not his words? But what of God and the Church, do you believe in, then, that you must live like monks in retreat with your books, never knowing the pleasures of the world? Why did you not take me in the inn, Petyr, when you had the chance to do it? You wanted it badly enough. Take my thanks, for that is all you can have now. And these gems which will make you rich. You need no longer depend on your monkish brethren. Stretch out your hand?"

"Deborah, how did you come by these jewels!" I whispered. "For what if you are accused of stealing them?"

"My devil is too clever for that, Petyr. They come from far away. And I have but to ask for them to have them. And with but a fraction of their endless supply I bought this emerald which I wear about my neck. The name of my devil is carved on the back of the gold fitting, Petyr. But you know his name. I admonish you, never call upon him, Petyr, for he serves me and will only destroy anyone else who seeks to command him through his given name."

"Deborah, come back to us," I begged, "only by day if you wish, for a few hours here and there, to talk to us, when your husband would certainly allow. This spirit of yours is no devil, but he is powerful, and can do evil things out of recklessness and the prankishness that characterizes spirits. Deborah, this is no plaything, surely you must know!"

But I could see such concerns were far from her thoughts.

I pressed her further. I explained that the first and foremost rule of our order was that no one of us, regardless of his powers, would ever command a spirit for gain. "For there is an old rule in the world, Deborah, among all sorcerers and those who address powers unseen. That those who strive to use the invisible for evil purposes cannot but invite their own ruin."

"But why is gain an evil thing, Petyr?" she said as if we were the same age, she and I. "Think of what you are saying! What is rich is not evil! Who has been hurt by what my devil brings to me? And all these in the household of Roelant have been helped."

"There are dangers in what you do, Deborah! This thing grows stronger the more you speak to it—"

She hushed me. She had contempt for me now. Again, she pressed me to take the jewels. She told me bluntly I was a fool, for I did not know how to use my powers, and then she thanked me for having taken her to the perfect city for witches, and with an evil smile she laughed.

306

"Deborah, we do not believe in Satan," I said, "but we believe in evil, and evil is what is destructive to mankind. I beg you beware of this spirit. Do not believe what it tells you of itself and its intentions. For no one knows what these beings really are."

"Stop, you anger me, Petyr. What makes you think this spirit tells me anything? It is I who speak to it! Look to the demonologies, Petyr, the old books by the rabid clergy who do believe in devils, for those books contain more true knowledge of how to control these invisible beings than you might think. I saw them on your shelves. I knew that one word in Latin, demonology, for I have seen such books before."

The books were full of truth *and* lies and I told her so. I drew back from her sadly. Once again she pressed me to take the jewels. I would not. She slipped them in my pocket and pressed her warm lips to my cheek. I went out of the house.

Roemer forbade me after that to see her. What he did with the gems I have never asked. The great treasure stores of the Talamasca have never been of much concern to me. I knew then only what I know now: that my debts are paid, my clothes are bought, I have the coins in my pockets I require.

Even when Roelant took ill, and this was not her doing, Stefan, I quite assure you, I was told I could not visit Deborah again.

But the strange thing was, that very often in odd places, Stefan, I beheld her, alone, or with one of Roelant's sons in hand, watching me from afar. I saw her thus in the public streets, and once passing the house of the Talamasca, beneath my window, and when I went to call upon Rembrandt van Rijn, there she sat, sewing, with Roelant beside her, staring at me out of her sideways eye.

There were times even when I imagined that she pursued me. For I would be alone, walking and thinking of her, and remembering moments of our first beginning together when I had fed her and washed her like a child. I cannot pretend I thought of her as a child, however, when I thought of this. But all of a sudden, I would break my stride, turn, and there she would be, walking behind me in her rich velvet cloak and hood, and she would fix me with her eye before she turned down another lane.

Oh, Stefan, imagine what I suffered. And Roemer said, do not go to her. I forbid it. And Geertruid warned me over and over that this fiercesome power of hers would grow too strong for her to command.

The month before Roelant died, a young female painter of exquisite talent, Judith de Wilde, came to reside under his roof with Deborah, and to remain in the house with her aging father, Anton de Wilde, when Roelant was gone.

Roelant's brothers took his sons home to the countryside, and the Widow Roelant and Judith de Wilde now together maintained the house, caring for the old man with great gentleness, but living a life of gaiety and many diversions as the rooms were thrown open all day and evening to the writers and poets and scholars and painters who chose to come there, and the students of Judith, who admired her as much as they admired any male painter, for she was just as fine, and had her membership in the Guild of St. Luke the same as a man.

Under Roemer's edict, I could not enter. But many was the time I passed, and I swear to you, if I lingered long enough, Deborah would appear at the upstairs window, a shadow behind the glass. Sometimes I would see no more of her than a flashing light from the green emerald, and at other times she would open the window and beckon, in vain, for me to come inside.

Roemer himself went to see her, but she only sent him away.

"She thinks she knows more than we do," he said sadly. "But she knows nothing or she would not play with this thing. This is always the mistake of the sorceress, you see, to imagine her power is complete over the unseen forces that do her bidding, when in fact, it is not. And what of her will, her conscience, and her ambition? How the thing does corrupt her! It is unnatural, Petyr, and dangerous, indeed."

"Could I call such a thing, Roemer, if I chose to do it?"

"No one knows the answer, Petyr. If you tried perhaps you could. And perhaps you could not get rid of it, once you had called it, and therein lies the old trap. You will never call up such a thing with my blessings, Petyr. You are listening to my words?"

"Yes, Roemer," I said, obedient as always. But he knew my heart had been corrupted and won over by Deborah, just as surely as if she had bewitched me, but it was not bewitching, it was stronger even than that.

"This woman is beyond our help now," he said. "Turn your mind to other things."

I did my best to obey the order. Yet I could not help but learn that Deborah was being courted by many a lord from England or France. Her wealth was so vast and solid that no one anymore thought to question the source of it, or to ask if there had been a time when she was not rich. Her education was proceeding with great speed, and she had a pure devotion to Judith de Wilde and her father, and so was in no hurry to marry, as she allowed the various suitors to call.

Well, one of those suitors finally took her away!

I never knew who it was that she married, or whence the marriage took place. I saw Deborah but once more, and I did not know then what I know now—that it was perhaps her last night before she left the place.

I was awakened in the dark by a sound at my window, and realizing that it was a steady tapping on the glass, such as could not be made by nature, I went to see if some knave had come over the roof. I was after all on the fifth story then, being still little more than a boy in the order, and given only a mean but very comfortable room.

The window was locked and undisturbed as it ought to be. But far below on the quay stood a lone woman in a garment of black cloth, who appeared to be gazing up at me, and when I opened the glass, she made a motion with her arm, which meant that I must come down.

I knew it was Deborah. But I was maddened, as if a succubus had come into my chamber and pulled the covers off me and gone to work with her mouth.

I crept out of the house so as to avoid all questions, and she stood waiting for me with the green emerald winking in the darkness, like a great eye about her neck. She took me with her through the back streets and into her house.

Now by this point, Stefan, I thought myself to be dreaming. But I did not wish for this dream to end. The lady had no maid or footman or anyone about her. She had come alone to me— which is not I must say so dangerous in Amsterdam as it might be someplace else—but it was enough to stir my blood to see her so unprotected and so deliberate and mysterious, and clinging to me and urging me to hurry along.

How rich were this lady's furnishings, how thick her many rugs, how fine her parquet floors. And past silver and fine china behind glimmering glass, she drew me up the stairs to her private chamber, and there to a bed draped in green velvet.

"I go to be married tomorrow, Petyr," she said.

"Then why have you brought me here, Deborah?" I asked, but I was shaking with desire, Stefan. When she let loose of her outer garment and let it drop on the floor, and I saw her full breasts plumped up by the tight lacing of her dress, I went mad to touch them, though I did not move. Even her waist so tightly cinched warmed me, and the sight of her fair neck and sloping shoulders. There was not a succulent particle of her flesh for which I did not hunger. I was a rabid beast in a cage.

"Petyr," she said looking up into my eyes, "I know that you gave the gems to your order, and that you took nothing of my thanks for yourself. So let me give you now what you wanted from me in our long journey here, and which you were too gentle to take.''

"But Deborah, why do you do this?'' I asked, determined not to take the slightest advantage of her. For in deep distress she was, I could read this in her eyes.

"Because I want it, Petyr,'' she said to me suddenly, and wrapping her arms around me, she covered me with kisses. "Leave the Talamasca, Petyr, and come with me,'' she said. "Be my husband, and I will not marry this other man.''

"But Deborah, why do you want this of me?'' I asked again.

With bitterness and sadness she laughed. "I am lonely for your understanding, Petyr. I am lonely for one from whom I need hide nothing. We are witches, Petyr, whether we belong to God or the devil, we are witches, you and I.''

Oh, how her eyes glittered as she said this, how plain was her triumph, yet how bitter. Her teeth were clenched together for an instant. Then she put her hands on me and stroked my face and neck and I was further maddened.

"You know that you desire me, Petyr, as you have always. Why do you not give in? Come with me; we will leave Amsterdam if the Talamasca will not allow you to be free; we will go away together, and there is nothing that I cannot get for you, nothing that I will not give you, only be with me, and let me be close to you and no longer afraid. I can speak to you of who I am and what befell my mother. I can speak to you of all that troubles me, Petyr, and of you I am never afraid.''

At this her face grew sad and the tears came to her eyes.

"My young husband is beautiful and all that I ever dreamed of when I sat, dirty and barefoot, at the cottage door. He is the lord who rode by on his way to the castle, and to a castle he shall take me now, though it be in another land. It is as if I have entered into the fairy tales told by my mother, and I shall be the Comtesse, and all those rhymes and songs shall be made real.

"But Petyr, I love him and do not love him. You are the first man that I loved, you who brought me here, you who saw the pyre on which my mother died, and you who bathed me and fed me and clothed me when I could not do these things for myself.''

I was past all hope of leaving this chamber without having her. I knew it. Yet so fascinated was I by the smallest fall of her lashes or the tiniest dimple of her cheek, that I let her draw me not to the bed but down upon the carpet before the little coal fire, and there in the flickering warmth she began to tell me of her woes.

"My past is like phantoms now to me,'' she cried softly, her eyes growing wide at the wonder of it. "Did I ever live in such a place, Petyr? Did I watch my mother die?"

"Do not bring it back into the light, Deborah," I said. "Let the old pictures fade away."

"But Petyr, you remember when you first spoke to me and you told me that my mother was not evil, that men had done evil to her. Why did you believe those things?"

"You tell me if she was a witch, Deborah, and what is a witch, by God!"

"Oh, Petyr, I remember going out into the fields with her, under the moonless sky where the stones were."

"And what happened, my dear?" I begged her. "Did the devil come with cloven hoofs?"

She shook her head, and gestured for me to listen to her and be still and be good. "Petyr," she said, "it was a witch judge that taught her the black magic! She showed me the very book. He had come through our village when I was but a small thing, crawling still, and he came out to our hut for the mending of a cut in his hand. By the fire he sat with her and told her of all the places he had gone in his work and the witches he had burnt. 'Be careful, my girl,' he said to her, or so she told me afterwards, and then he took from his leather pouch the evil book. *Demonologie* it was called and he read it to her, for she could not read Latin, or any language for that matter, and the pictures he held to the light of the fire all the better for her to see.

"Hour by hour he taught these things to her, what witches had done, and what witches could do. 'Be careful, my girl,' he would say, 'lest the devil tempt you, for the devil loves the midwife and the cunning woman!' and then he would turn another page.

"That night as he lay with her, he talked on of the torture houses, and of the burnings, and of the cries of the condemned. 'Be careful, my girl,' he said again when he left her.

"And all these things she later told to me. I was a child of six, maybe seven when she told the story. At the kitchen fire we sat together. 'Now, come,' she said, 'and you shall see.' Out into the field we went, feeling for the stones before us, and finding the very middle of the circle and standing stock-still in it to feel the wind.

"Nary a sound in the night, I tell you. Nary a glimmer of light. Not even the stars to show the towers of the castle, or the far-away bit of water that one could see from there of Loch Donnelaith.

"I heard her humming as she held my hand; then in a circle we danced together, making small circles round and round as we did. Louder she hummed and then the Latin words she spoke to call the demon, and then flinging out her arms she cried to him to come.

"The night was empty. Nothing answered. I drew close to her skirts and held her cold hand. Then over the grasslands I felt it coming, a breeze it seemed, and then a wind as it gathered itself about us. I felt it touching my hair and the back of my neck, I felt it wrapping us round as it were with air. I heard it speak then, only not in words, and yet I heard it and it said: 'I am here, Suzanne!'

"Oh, how she laughed with delight; how she danced. Like a child, she wrung her hands, and laughed again and threw back her hair. 'Do you see him, my baby?' she said to me. And I answered that I could feel him and hear him very near.

"And once again, he spoke, 'Call me by my name, Suzanne.'

"'Lasher,' she said, 'for the wind which you send that lashes the grasslands, for the wind that lashes the leaves from the trees. Come now, my Lasher, make a storm over Donnelaith! And I shall know that I am a powerful witch and that you do this for my love!'

"By the time we reached the hut, the wind was howling over the fields, and in the chimney as she shut our door. By the fire, we sat laughing like two children together, 'You see, you see, I did it,' she whispered. And looking into her eyes, I saw what I had always seen and always would even to her last hour of agony and pain: the eyes of a simpleton, a dim-witted girl laughing behind her fingers with the stolen sweet in the other hand. It was a game to her, Petyr. It was a game!"

"I see it, my beloved," I said.

"Now, tell me there is no Satan. Tell me that he did not come through the darkness to claim the witch of Donnelaith and lead her to the fire! It was Lasher who found for her the objects which others lost, it was Lasher who brought the gold to her, which they took from her, it was Lasher who told her the secrets of treachery which she revealed to willing ears. And it was Lasher who rained hail upon the milkmaid who quarreled with her, Lasher who sought to punish her enemies for her and thereby made her power known! She could not instruct him, Petyr. She did not know how to use him. And like a child playing with a candle, she kindled the very fire that burnt her to death."

"Do not make the same error, Deborah!" I whispered, even as I kissed her face. "No one instructs a daimon, for that is what this is."

"Oh, no, it is more than that," she whispered, "and you are most mistaken. But don't fear for me, Petyr. I am not my mother. There is no cause."

312

We sat then in quiet by the little fire, though I could not think that she would want to be near it, and as she leaned her forehead on the stones above it, I kissed her again on her soft cheek, and brushed back the long vagrant strands of her moist black hair.

"Petyr," she said, "I shall never live in hunger and filth as she lived. I shall never be at the mercy of foolish men."

"Don't marry, Deborah. Don't go! Come with me. Come into the Talamasca and we shall discover the nature of this creature together . . ."

"No, Petyr. You know I will not." And here she smiled sadly. "It is you who must come with me, and we shall go away. Speak to me now with your secret voice, the voice in you that can command clocks to stop or spirits to come, and be with me, and be my bridegroom, and this shall be the witches' wedding night."

I went to answer her with a thousand protests, but she covered my mouth with her hand, and then with her mouth, and she went to kissing me with such heat and charm that I knew nothing anymore, but that I had to tear from her the garments that bound her, and have her there in the bed with the green curtains drawn around us, this tender childlike body with its woman's breasts and woman's secrets which I had bathed and clothed.

Why do I torture myself to write this? I am confessing my old sin, Stefan. I am telling you all that I did, for I cannot write of this woman without this confession and so I go on.

Never have I celebrated the rites with such abandon. Never have I known such voluptuousness and sweetness as I knew in her.

For she believed herself to be a witch, Stefan, and therefore to be evil, and these were the devil's rites to her that she celebrated with such willfulness. Yet hers was a tender and loving heart, I swear it, and so the mixture was a rare and powerful witch's brew indeed.

I did not leave her bed till morning. I slept against her perfumed breast. I wept now and then like a boy. With a temptress's skill, she had wakened all of my flesh to her. She had discovered my most secret hungers and had toyed with them, and fed them. I was her slave. But she knew that I would not stay with her, that I had to go back to the Talamasca, and for hours finally she lay quiet and sad staring at the wooden ceiling of the bed, as the light came through the seams of the curtains and the bed began to grow warm from the sun.

I dressed wearily and without desire for anything in the whole of Christendom but her soul and her flesh. Yet I was leaving her. I was going home to tell Roemer what I had done. I was going

313

back to the Motherhouse, which was indeed my mother and my father, and I knew no other choice.

I thought now she will send me off with curses. But it was not to be. One last time, I begged her to remain in Amsterdam, to come with me.

Good-bye, my little priest, she said to me. Fare thee well, and may the Talamasca reward you for what you have given up in me. Tears she shed, and I kissed her open hands hungrily before I left her, and put my face once more into her hair. "Go now, Petyr," she said finally. "Remember me."

Perhaps a day or two passed before I was told that she had gone. I was disconsolate and lay weeping and trying to listen to Roemer and to Geertruid, but I could not hear what they had to say. They were not angry with me as I had thought they would be, that much I knew.

And it was Roemer who went to Judith de Wilde and purchased from her the portrait of Deborah by Rembrandt van Rijn which hangs in our house to this day.

It was a full year perhaps before I regained true health of body and soul. And never after that did I break the rules of the Talamasca as I had in those days, and went out again through the German states and through France and even to Scotland to do my work to save the witches, and to write of them and their tribulations as we have always done.

So now you know, Stefan, the story of Deborah, such as it is. And my shock to come upon the tragedy of the Comtesse de Montcleve, so many years later, in this fortified town in the Cévennes of the Languedoc and to discover that she was Deborah Mayfair, the daughter of the Scottish witch.

Oh, if only that bit of knowledge—that the mother had been burnt—had been kept from these townsfolk. If only the young bride had not told her secrets to the young lord when she cried on his chest. And her face lo, those many years ago, is fixed in my memory, when she said to me, "Petyr, I can speak to you and not be afraid."

Now you see with what fear and misery I entered the prison cell, and how in my haste, I gave no thought until the very last moment that the lady, crouched there in rags upon her bed of straw, might look up and recognize me and call out my name, and in her despair, cheerfully give my disguise away.

But this did not happen.

As I stepped into the cell, lifting the hem of my black cassock so as to appear as a cleric who did not wish to soil himself with this filth, I looked down upon her and saw no look of recognition in her face.

That she did look steadily at me alarmed me however, and straightaway I said to the old fool of a parish priest that I must examine her alone. He was loathe to leave me with her, but I told him that I had seen many a witch and she did not frighten me in the slightest and that I must ask her many questions, and if only he would wait for me at the rectory I should be back soon. Then I took from my pockets several gold coins, and said, "You must take these for your church, for I know I have given you much trouble." And that sealed it. The imbecile was gone.

Need I tell you how contemptible all these proceedings were, that this woman should be put into my hands thus without guards? For what might I have done to her, had I chosen to do it? And who had done such things before me?

At once the door was shut up, and though I could hear much whispering in the passage beyond, we were alone. I set down the candle upon the only furnishing in the place, which was a wooden bench, and as I struggled not to give way to tears at the sight of her, I heard her voice coming low, scarce more than a whisper as she said:

"Petyr, can it really be you?"

"Yes, Deborah," I said.

"Ah, but you have not come to save me, have you?" she asked wearily.

My heart was struck by the very tone of her voice, for it was the same voice that had spoken to me in her bedchamber in Amsterdam that last night. It had but a tiny fraction of deeper resonance, and perhaps a dark music to it which suffering imparts.

"I cannot do it, Deborah. Though I shall try, I know that I will fail."

This came as no surprise to her, yet she smiled at me.

Taking up the candle once more, I drew closer to her, and went down on my knees in the hay before her so that I might look into her eyes. I saw the very same eyes I remembered, and the same cheeks as she smiled, and it seemed this spare and waxen form was but my Deborah made already into a spirit, with all her beauty intact.

She made no move towards me but perused my face as she might a painting, and then in a rush of feeble and pitiful words I told her that I had not known of her distress, but had come upon this place alone, in my work for the Talamasca, and had discovered with great sorrow that she was the one of whom I had heard so much talk. I had ascertained that she had appealed to the bishop, and to the Parliament of Paris, but here she silenced me with a simple gesture and said:

315

"I shall die here on the morrow, and there is nothing that you can do."

"Ah, but there is one small mercy," I said, "for I have in my possession a powder, which when mixed with water and drunk, will make you stuporous and you will not suffer as you might. Nay, I can give you such a measure of it that you will die, if that is your wish, and thereby cheat the flames altogether. I know that I can put this into your hands. The old priest is a fool."

She seemed most deeply affected by my offer, though in no urgency to accept it. "Petyr, I must have my wits about when I am taken down into the square. I warn you, do not be in the town when this takes place. Or be safe behind a shuttered window, if you must remain to see it for yourself."

"Are you speaking of escape, Deborah?" I asked, for I had to admit that my imagination was at once inflamed. If only I could save her, cause a great confusion and then take her away by some means. But how could I do such a thing?

"No, no, Petyr, that is beyond my power and the power of him whom I command. It is a simple thing for a spirit to transport a small jewel or a gold coin into the hands of a witch, but to open prison doors, to overcome armed guards? This cannot be done." Then, as if distracted, her eyes glancing wildly about, she said, "Do you know my own sons have testified against me? That my beloved Chrétien has called his mother a witch?"

"I think they made him do it, Deborah. Shall I go to see him? What can I do that will help?"

"Oh, kind, dear Petyr," she said. "Why did you not listen to me when I begged you to come with me? But this is not your doing, all this. It is mine."

"How so, Deborah? That you were innocent I never doubted. If you could have cured your husband of his injury, there never would have been a cry of 'witch.' "

She shook her head at this. "There is so much more to the story. When he died I believed myself to be blameless. But I have spent many a long month in this cell thinking on it, Petyr. And hunger and pain make the mind grow sharp."

"Deborah, do not believe what your enemies say of you, no matter how often or well they say it!"

She did not answer me. She seemed indifferent to it. And then she turned to me again. "Petyr, do these things for me. If on the morrow I am brought bound into the square, which is my worst fear, demand that my arms and legs be freed that I may carry the heavy candle in penance, as has always been the custom in these parts. Do not let my crippled feet wring pity from you, Petyr. I fear the bonds worse than I fear the flames!''

''I will do it,'' I said, ''but there is no cause for concern. They will make you carry the candle, and make you walk the length of the town. You will be made to bring it to the steps of the cathedral, and only then will they bind you and take you to the pyre.'' I could scarce continue.

''Listen, I have more to ask of you,'' she said.

''Yes, please, go on.''

''When it is finished, and you leave this town, then to my daughter, Charlotte Fontenay, wife of Antoine Fontenay, in Saint-Domingue, which is in Hispaniola, in care of the merchant Jean-Jacques Toussaint, Port-au-Prince, write what I tell you to say.''

I repeated the name and full address to her.

''Tell Charlotte that I did not suffer in the flames even if this is not true.''

''I will make her believe it.''

At this she smiled bitterly. ''Perhaps not,'' she said. ''But do your best at it, for me.''

''What else?''

''Give her a further message, and this you must remember word for word. Tell her to proceed with care—that he whom I have sent to obey her sometimes does those things for us which he *believes* we want him to do. And further tell her that he whom I am sending to her draws his belief in our purpose as much from our random thoughts, as from the careful words we speak.''

''Oh, Deborah!''

''You understand what I am saying to you, and why you must convey this to her?''

''I see it. I see it all. You wished your husband dead, on account of his treachery. And the demon struck him down.''

''It is deeper than that. Do not seek to compass it. I never wished him dead. I loved him. And I did not know of his treachery! But you must make known what I have said to Charlotte, for her protection, for my invisible servant cannot tell her of his own changing nature. He cannot speak to her of what he himself does not understand.''

''Oh, but . . .''

''Do not stand on conscience with me now, Petyr. Better that you had never come here, if you do. She has the emerald in her possession. He will go to her when I am dead.''

''Do not send him, Deborah!''

She sighed, with great disappointment and desperation. ''Please, I beg you, do as I ask.''

"What took place with your husband, Deborah?"

It seemed she would not answer, and then she said, "My husband lay dying when my Lasher came to me, and made known to me that he had tricked my husband and made him fall in the woods. 'How could you do such a thing,' I demanded, 'which I never told you to do?' And then came his answer: 'But Deborah, had you seen into his heart as I did, *it is what you would have told me to do.*' "

I was chilled to my very bones then, Stefan, and I ask that when you have this letter copied out for our records, that the above words be underlined. For when have we ever heard of such conniving and willfulness from an invisible devil, such wit and such stupidity in one?

I saw this imp, as if loosed from a bottle, cavorting and wreaking havoc at will. I remembered Roemer's old warnings. I remembered Geertruid and the things which she had said. But this was worse even than they might have imagined.

"Aye, you are correct," she said to me, sadly, having read this from my mind. "You must write this to Charlotte," she beseeched me. "Be careful with your words, lest the letter fall into the wrong hands, but write it, write it so that Charlotte sees the whole of what you have to say!"

"Deborah, restrain this thing. Let me tell her, at the behest of her mother, to drop the emerald into the sea."

"It is too late for that now, Petyr, and the world being what it is, I would send my Lasher to Charlotte even if you had not come tonight to hear this last request from me. My Lasher is powerful beyond your dreams of a daimon, and he has learnt much."

"Learned," I repeated in amazement. "How learned, Deborah, for he is merely a spirit, and they are forever foolish and therein lies the danger, that in granting our wishes they do not understand the complexity of them, and thereby prove our undoing. There are a thousand tales that prove it. Has this not happened? How so do you say learned?"

"Think on it, Petyr, what I have told you. I tell you my Lasher has learnt much, and his error came not from his unchangeable simplicity but from the sharpening of purpose in him. But promise me, for all that passed between us once, write to my beloved daughter! This you must do for me."

"Very well!" I declared, wringing my hands. "I shall do it, but I shall tell her also all that I have just said to you."

"Fair enough, my good priest, my good scholar," she said bitterly, and smiling. "Now go, Petyr. I cannot bear your presence here any longer. And my Lasher is near to me, and we would talk together, and on the morrow, I beg you, get indoors and safe once you see that my hands and feet are unfettered and that I have come to the church doors.''

"God in heaven help me, Deborah, if only I could take you from this place, if it were possible by any means—'' And here I broke down, Stefan. I lost all conscience. "Deborah, if your servant, Lasher, can effect an escape with my assistance, you have only to tell me how it might be done!''

I saw myself wresting her from the mad crowds that surrounded us and of stealing her away over the walls of the town and into the woods.

How she smiled at me then, how tenderly and sadly. It was the way she had smiled when we had parted years before.

"What fancies, Petyr,'' she said. Then her smile grew even broader, and she looked half mad in the candlelight, or even more like an angel or a mad saint. Her white face was as beautiful as the candle flame itself. "My life is over, but I have traveled far and wide from this little cell,'' she said. "Now go. Go and send my message to Charlotte, but only when you are safely away from this town.''

I kissed her hands. They had burnt the palms when they tortured her. There were deep scabs on them, and these too I kissed. I did not care.

"I have always loved you,'' I said to her. And I said other things, many things, foolish and tender, which I will not write here. All this she bore with perfect resignation, and she knew what I had only just discovered: that I *regretted* that I had not gone off with her, that I despised myself and my work and all my life.

This will pass, Stefan. I know it. I knew it then, only hours ago when I left her cell. But it is true now, and I am like St. John of the Cross in his "Dark Night of the Soul.'' I tell you all consolation has left me. And on what account?

That I love her, and only that. For I know that her daimon has destroyed her, as surely as it destroyed her mother. And that all the warnings of Roemer and Geertruid and all the wizards of the ages, have been proven here to be true.

I could not leave her without embracing her and kissing her. But I could feel her agony when I held her—the agony of the burns and the bruises on her body, and her muscles torn from the rack. And this had been my beautiful Deborah, this ruin that clung to me, and wept suddenly as if I had turned a key in a lock.

"I am sorry, my beloved,'' I said, for I blamed myself for these tears.

319

"It is sweet to hold you," she whispered. And then she pushed me away from her. "Go now, and remember everything that I have said."

I went out a madman. The square was still filling with those who had come to see the execution. By torchlight there were those putting up their stalls, and others sleeping under blankets along the walls.

I told the old priest I was not at all convinced the woman was a witch, and I wanted to see the inquisitor at once. I tell you, Stefan, I was bound to move heaven and earth for her.

But you know how it went.

We came to the château and they admitted us, and this fool priest was very glad to be with someone of importance, barging in upon the banquet to which he had not been invited, but I pulled myself up now, and used my most impressive manner, questioning the inquisitor directly in Latin, and the old Comtesse, a dark-skinned woman, very Spanish in appearance, who received me with extraordinary patience considering the manner in which I began.

The inquisitor, Father Louvier, handsome and very well fed, with fine groomed beard and hair and twinkling black eyes, saw nothing suspicious in my manner, and became obsequious to me as if I were from the Vatican, which I might be for all he knew, and merely sought to comfort me when I said perhaps an innocent woman was to be burnt.

"You never saw such a witch," said the Comtesse, who laughed in an ugly deep-throated fashion and offered me some wine. She then presented me to the Comtesse de Chamillart, who sat beside her, and to every other noble of the surrounding area who had come to lodge at the château and see the witch burnt.

Every question I asked and objection I raised and suggestion I made to offer was met with the same easy conviction by this assemblage. For them the battle had been fought and won. All that remained was the celebration that would take place in the morning.

The boys were crying in their chambers, true, but they would recover. And there was nothing to fear from Deborah, for if her demon were strong enough to free her he would have done so by now. And was it not so with all witches? Once they were in chains, the devil left them to their fate.

"But this woman has not confessed," I declared, "and her husband fell from his horse in the forest, by his own admission. Surely you cannot convict on the evidence of a feverish and dying man!"

It was as if I were flinging dry leaves into their faces, for all the effect it had upon them.

"I loved my son before all things in this world," said the old Comtesse, her small black eyes hard and her mouth ugly. Then as if thinking the better of her tone, she said with complete hypocrisy, "Poor Deborah, have I ever said that I did not love Deborah, that I did not forgive Deborah a thousand things?"

"You say too much!" declared Louvier very sanctimoniously, and with an exaggerated gesture as he was drunk, the fiend.

"I don't speak of witchcraft," said the old woman, quite unperturbed by his manner, "I speak of my daughter-in-law and all her weaknesses and secrets, for who in this town does not know that Charlotte was born too soon after the wedding, yet my son was so blind to the charms of this woman, and so adoring of Charlotte, and so grateful to Deborah for her dowry and so much a fool in all respects . . ."

"Must we speak of it!" whispered the Comtesse de Chamillart, who appeared to tremble. "Charlotte is gone from our midst."

"She will be found and burnt like her mother," declared Louvier, and there were nods and assents all around.

And they went to talking amongst themselves about how very content they would all be after the executions, and as I sought to question them, they merely gestured for me to be quiet, to drink, not to concern myself.

It was horrible the manner in which they then ignored me, like beings in a dream who cannot hear our screams. Yet I persisted that they had no evidence of night flying, of Sabbats, of intercourse with demons, and all the other foolish evidence which elsewhere sends these creatures to the stake. As for the healing, what was this but the skill of the cunning woman, and why convict for that? The doll might not have been anything more than an instrument of healing.

To no avail!

How convivial and calm they were as they dined at the table, which had been her table, and on silver which had been her silver, and she in that wretched cell.

At last I pleaded that she should be allowed to die by strangulation before the burning. "How many of you have seen for yourselves a person die by fire!" But this was met with the weariest of dismissals.

"The witch is unrepentant," said the Comtesse de Chamillart, the only one of them who seemed sober and even touched with a slight fear.

"She will suffer what? A quarter of an hour at most?" the

inquisitor asked, wiping his mouth with his filthy napkin. "What is that to the eternal fires of hell!"

At last I went out and back through the crowded square where it seemed a drunken revel was being held around all the little fires burning, and I stood looking at the grim pyre, and the stake high above with its iron manacles, and then by chance I found myself looking to the left of it at the triple arches of the church doors. And there in the crude carving of ages past were the imps of hell being driven down into the flames by St. Michael the Archangel with his trident through the fiend's belly.

The words of the inquisitor rang in my ears as I looked at this ugly thing in the firelight. "She will suffer what? A quarter of an hour at most? And what is that to the eternal fires of hell?"

Oh, Deborah, who never willfully harmed anyone, and had brought her healing arts to the poorest and the richest, and been so unwise!

And where was her vengeful spirit, her Lasher, who sought to save her grief by striking down her husband, and had brought her to that miserable cell? Was he with her, as she had told me? It was not his name she had cried out when she was tortured, it was my name, and the name of her old and kindly husband Roelant.

Stefan, I have written this tonight as much to stave off madness, as to make the record. I am weary now. I have packed my valise, and I am ready to leave this town when I have seen this bitter story to the end. I will seal this letter and put it in my valise with the customary note affixed to it, that in the event of my death, a reward will be waiting for it in Amsterdam, should it be delivered there, and so forth and so on.

For I do not know what the daylight will bring. And I shall continue this tragedy by means of a new letter if I am settled tomorrow evening in another town.

The sunlight is just coming through the windows. I pray somehow Deborah can be saved; but I know it is out of the question. And Stefan, I would call her devil to me, if I thought he would listen. I would try to command him in some desperate action. But I know I have no such power, and so I wait.

Yours Faithfully in the Talamasca,

Petyr van Abel
Montcleve
Michaelmas, 1689

Michael had now finished the first typescript. He withdrew the second from its manila folder, and he sat for a long moment, his hands clasped on top of it, praying stupidly that somehow Deborah was not going to burn.

Then unable to sit still any longer, he picked up the phone, called the operator, and asked to speak to Aaron.

"That picture in Amsterdam, Aaron, the one painted by Rembrandt," he said, "do you still have it?"

"Yes, it is still there, Michael, in the Amsterdam Motherhouse. I've already sent for a photograph from the Archives. It's going to take a little time."

"Aaron, you know this is the dark-haired woman! You know it is. And the emerald—that must be the jewel I saw. Aaron, I could swear I know Deborah. She must be the one who came to me, and she had the emerald around her neck. And Lasher . . . Lasher is the word I spoke when I opened my eyes on the boat."

"But you do not actually remember it?"

"No, but I'm sure . . . And Aaron—"

"Michael, try not to interpret, or to analyze. Go on with your reading. There isn't much time."

"I need a pen and paper to take notes."

"What you need is a notebook in which you can record all your thoughts, and anything that comes back to you about the visions."

"Exactly, I wish I'd been keeping a notebook all along."

"I'll have one sent up. Let me recommend that you merely date each entry as you would in a free-form diary. But please continue. There'll be some fresh coffee for you shortly. Anything else, simply ring."

"That will do it. Aaron, there are so many things . . ."

"I know, Michael. Try to stay calm. Just read."

Michael hung up, lighted a cigarette, drank a little more of the old coffee, and stared at the cover of the second file.

At the first sound of a knock, he went to the door.

The kindly woman he'd seen earlier in the hallway was there with the fresh coffee, and several pens and a nice leather notebook with very white lined paper. She set the tray down on the desk and removed the old service, and quietly went out.

He seated himself again, poured a fresh cup of black coffee, and immediately opened the notebook, entered the date, and made his first note:

"After reading the first folder of the file, I know that Deborah is the woman I saw in the visions. I know her. I know her face, and her character. I can hear her voice if I try.

"And it is more than a safe guess that the word I spoke to

Rowan when I came around was Lasher. But Aaron is right. I don't really remember this. I simply know it.

"And of course the power in my hands is connected. But how is it meant to be used? Surely not to touch things at random, the way I've been doing, but to touch something specific . . .

"But it's too soon to draw conclusions . . ."

But if I only had something of Deborah's to touch, he thought. But he sensed there was nothing, or else Aaron would have sent for it too. He examined the photocopies of Petyr van Abel's letters. That's all they were—photocopies. No good for his anxious hands.

He thought for a moment, if such confusion in one's mind could be called thought, and then he drew a picture in the notebook of a necklace, showing a rectangular jewel in the center, and a filigree border, and a chain of gold. He drew it the way he would draw an architectural design, with very clean, straight lines and slightly shaded detail.

He studied it, the gloved fingers of his left hand working nervously in his hair, and then curling into a fist as he rested his hand on the desk. He was about to scratch out the drawing when he decided against it, and then he opened the second file and began to read.

Fourteen

THE FILE ON THE MAYFAIR WITCHES

PART II

Marseille, France
October 4, 1689

Dear Stefan,

I am here in Marseille after several days' journey from Montcleve, during which I rested at Saint-Rémy and made my way very slowly from there, on account of my wounded shoulder and wounded soul.

I have already drawn money from our agent here, and will

post this letter no later than one hour after I finish it, and so you will receive it on the heels of my last, which I posted upon my arrival last night.

I am heartsick, Stefan. The comforts of a large and decent inn here mean little or nothing to me, though I am glad to be out of the small villages and in a city of some size, where I cannot help but feel at ease and somewhat safe.

If word has reached this place of what happened at Montcleve, I have not heard of it yet. And as I put away my clerical garb on the outskirts of Saint-Rémy and have been since then the Dutch traveler of means, I do not think that anyone will trouble me about those recent events in the mountains, for what would I know about such things?

I write once more to stave off madness as much as to report to you, which I am bound to do, and to continue the business at hand.

The execution of Deborah began in a manner similar to many others, in that as the morning light fell down on the square before the doors of the Cathedral of Saint-Michel all the town collected there with the wine sellers making their profits, and the old Comtesse, somberly dressed, coming forward with the two trembling children, both dark-haired and dark-skinned with the stamp of the Spanish blood on them, but with a height and delicacy of bone that betrayed the blood of their mother, and very much frightened, as they were taken high to the very top of the viewing stand before the jail, and facing the pyre.

It seemed the little one, Chrétien, began to weep and cling to his grandmother, whereupon there ran through the crowd excited murmurs, "Chrétien, look at Chrétien." This child's lip trembled as he was seated, but his elder brother, Philippe, evinced only fear and perhaps loathing of what he beheld around him, and the old Comtesse embraced and comforted both of them, and on her other side welcomed the Comtesse de Chamillart and the inquisitor Father Louvier, with two young clerics in fine robes.

Four more priests, I know not from where, also filled the topmost places in the stand, and a small band of armed men stood at the very foot of it, these constituting the local authorities, or so I presumed.

Other important personages, or a great collection of those who think themselves very important, filled up the rest of the elevated seats very quickly, and if there had been any window anywhere that had not been opened beforehand, it was opened now and full of eager faces, and those on foot pressed so close to the

pyre that I could not help but wonder how they would save themselves from being burnt.

A small band of armed men, bearing a ladder with them,
appeared from the thick of the crowd and laid this ladder against
the pyre. The young Chrétien saw this and turned fearfully once
more to his grandmother, his shoulders shaking as he cried, but
the young Philippe remained as before.

At last the doors of Saint-Michel were thrown open, and there
appeared beneath the rounded arch, on the very threshold, the
pastor and some other despicable official, most likely the mayor
of this place, who held in his hands a rolled parchment, and a
pair of armed guards came forth to the left and to the right.

And between them there emerged to a hushed and wonder-
stricken audience my Deborah, standing straight and with her
head high, her thin body covered by a white robe which hung to
her bare feet, and in her hands the six-pound candle which she
held before her as her eyes swept the crowd.

Never have I seen such fearlessness in all my life, Stefan,
though as I looked down from the window of the inn opposite,
and my eyes met the eyes of Deborah, my own eyes were blurred
by tears.

I cannot say for certain what then followed, except that at the
very instant when heads might have turned to see this person at
whom "the witch" stared so fixedly, Deborah did look away,
and again her eyes took in the scene before her, lingering with
equal care upon the stalls of the wine sellers and the peddlers,
and the groups of random persons who backed away from her
as she looked at them, and finally up at the viewing stand which
loomed down upon her, and at the old Comtesse, who steeled
herself to this silent accusation, and then to the Comtesse de
Chamillart, who at once squirmed in her seat, her face redden-
ing, as she looked in panic to the old Comtesse, who remained
as unmoved as before.

Meantime Father Louvier, the great and triumphant inquisitor,
was shouting hoarsely to the mayor that he should read the proclamation in his hands, and that "these proceedings must commence!"

A hubbub rose from all assembled, and the mayor cleared his
throat to begin reading, and I then satisfied myself of what I had
already seen but failed to note, that Deborah's hands and feet
were unbound.

It was now my intention to come down from the window and
to push my way, by the roughest means if need be, to the very
front of the crowd so that I might stand near her, regardless of
what danger this might mean to me.

And I was in the act of turning from the window when the mayor began to read the Latin with torturous slowness, and Deborah's voice rang out, silencing him and commanding that the crowd be still.

"I never did you harm, not the poorest of you!" she declared, speaking slowly and loudly, her voice echoing off the stone walls, and as Father Louvier stood and shouted for silence, she raised her voice even louder and declared that she would speak.

"Silence her!" declared the old Comtesse, now in a fury, and again Louvier bellowed for the mayor to read the proclamation and the frightened pastor looked to his armed guards, but they had drawn away on either side and seemed fearful as they stared at Deborah and at the frightened crowd.

"I will be heard!" my Deborah called out again, as loudly as before. And as she took but one step forward, to stand more fully in the sunlight, the crowd drew back in a great swarming mass.

"I am unjustly condemned of witchcraft," cried Deborah, "for I am no heretic and I do not worship Satan, and I have done no malice against any being here!"

And before the old Comtesse could roar again, Deborah continued:

"You, my sons, you testified against me and I disown you! And you, my beloved mother-in-law, have damned yourself to hell with your lies!"

"Witch!" screamed the Comtesse de Chamillart, now in panic. "Burn her. Throw her on the pyre."

And at this it seemed a number did press forward, as much out of fear as a desire for heroism and to draw favor upon themselves perhaps, or maybe it was mere confusion. But the armed guards did not move.

"Witch, you call me!" Deborah answered at once. And with a great gesture, she threw down the candle on the stones and threw up her hands before the men who would have taken hold of her but did not. "Hearken to me!" she declared. "I shall show you witchcraft I have never shown you before!"

The crowd was now in complete fright and some were leaving the square and others pressing to reach the narrow streets leading away from it, and even those in the viewing stand had risen to their feet, and the young Chrétien buried his face against the old Comtesse and again shook with sobs.

Yet the eyes of hundreds in this narrow place remained fixed upon Deborah, who had raised her thin and bruised arms. Her lips moved, but I could hear no words from her, and shrieks now rang out from some below the window, and then a rumbling was heard over the rooftops, far fainter than thunder and therefore more terrible, and a great wind was gathering suddenly, and with it came another noise, a low creaking and ripping sound, which at first I did not know and then I remembered from many another storm—the old roofs of the place were giving up to the wind their loose and broken tiles.

At once the tiles began to fall from the parapets, raining down singly and here and there by the half dozen, and the wind was howling and gathering itself over the square. The wooden shutters of the inns had begun to flap on their hinges, and my Deborah screamed again over this noise and over the frantic cries of the crowd.

"Come now, my Lasher, be my avenger, strike down my enemies!" Bending double, she raised her hands, her face red and stricken with her rage. "I see you, Lasher, I know you! I call you!" And straightening and flinging out her arms: "Destroy my sons, destroy my accusers! Destroy those who have come to see me die!"

And the tiles came crashing down off the roofs, off the church and the jail and the sacristy, and off the roofs of the inns, striking the heads of those screaming below, and in the wind, the viewing stand, built of fragile boards and sticks and ropes with crude mortar, began to rock as those clinging to it shrieked for their lives.

Only Father Louvier stood firm. "Burn the witch!" he shouted, trying to get through the panic-stricken men and women who tumbled over one another to get away. "Burn the witch and you stop the storm."

No one moved to obey him, and though the church alone could provide shelter from this tempest, no one dared moved towards it as Deborah commanded the door, her arms outstretched. The armed men had run away from her in their panic. The parish priest had shrunk to the far side. The mayor was gone from view.

Overhead the very sky had gone dark, and people were fighting and cursing and falling in the crush, and in the fierce rain of tiles the old Comtesse was struck and slumped over, losing her balance and vaulting down over the bodies writhing in front of her, onto the very stones. The two boys clung to each other as a shower of loose stones broke upon them from the facade of the church. Chrétien was bowed under the stones as a tree in a hail storm, and then struck unconscious, falling to his knees. The stand itself now collapsed, taking down with it both boys and some twenty or more persons still struggling to get clear.

As far as I could see, all the guards had deserted the square, and the pastor had run away. And now I beheld my Deborah move backwards into the shadows, though her eyes were still on the heavens:

"I see you, Lasher!" she cried out. "My strong and beautiful Lasher!" And she vanished into the dark of the nave.

At this I ran from the window and down the stairs and into the frenzy of the square. What was in my mind I could not tell you, save somehow I could reach her, and under cover of the panic around us, get her free from this place.

But as I ran across the open space, the tiles flew every which way, and one struck my shoulder, and another my left hand. I could see nothing of her, only the doors of the church which were, in spite of their great heaviness, swinging in the wind.

Shutters had broken loose and were coming down upon the mad folk who could not get out through the little streets. Bodies lay piled at every arch and doorway. The old Comtesse lay dead, staring upwards, men and women tripping over her limbs. And in the ruin of the viewing stand lay the body of Chrétien, the little one, twisted so as it could not have had life in it.

Philippe, the elder, crawled upon his knees to seek shelter, his leg broken it appeared, when a wooden shutter came down striking his neck and breaking it as well so that he fell dead.

Then someone near me, cowering against the wall, screamed: "The Comtesse!" and pointed up.

There she stood, high on the parapets of the church, for she had gone in and upwards, and balancing perilously upon the wall, she once again raised her hands to heaven and cried out to her spirit. But in the howling of the wind, in the screaming of the afflicted, in the falling of the tiles and the stones and the broken wood, I could not hope to hear her words.

I ran for the church, and once inside searched in panic for the steps. There was Louvier, the inquisitor, running back and forth, and then finding the steps before me, leading the way.

Up and up I ran after him, seeing his black skirts high above me, and his heels clacking on the stones. Oh, Stefan, if I had had a dagger, but I had no dagger.

And as we reached the open parapets, as he ran out before me, I saw Deborah's thin body fly, as it were, from the roof. Reaching the edge, I peered down upon the carnage and saw her lying broken on the stones. Her face was turned upwards—one arm beneath her head, and the other limp across her chest—and her eyes were closed as though she slept.

Louvier cursed when he saw her. "Burn her, take her body up to the pyre," he cried, but it was useless. No one could hear him. In consternation he turned, perhaps to go back down and further command the proceedings, when he beheld me standing there.

And with a great look of amazement on his face, he regarded me helplessly and in confusion as, without hesitation, I pushed him with all my might, squarely in the chest, and backwards, so that he went flying off the edge of the roof.

No one saw this, Stefan. We were at the highest point of Montcleve. No other rooftop rose above that of the church. Even the distant château had no view of this parapet, and those below could not have seen me, as I was shielded from view by Louvier himself as I struck the blow.

But even if I am wrong as to the possibility of it, the fact of it is that no one did see me.

Retreating at once, making certain that no one had followed me to this place, I went down and to the church door. There lay my handiwork, Louvier, as dead as my Deborah, and lying very near her, his skull crushed and bleeding and his eyes open, in that dull stupid expression that the dead have which is almost never approximated by a human being in life.

How long the gale continued I cannot tell you, only that it was already falling off when I reached the church door. Perhaps a quarter of an hour, the very time the fiend had allotted for Deborah to die on the pyre.

From the shadows of the church foyer, I saw the square finally emptied, the very last climbing over the bodies that now blocked the side streets. I saw the light brighten. I heard the storm die away. I stood still regarding in silence the body of my Deborah, and saw that the blood now poured from her mouth, and that her white gown was stained with blood as well.

After a great while, numerous persons moved into the open place, examining the bodies of the dead, and the bodies of those who were still living and weeping and begging for assistance; and here and there the wounded were picked up and carried away. The innkeeper ran out, with his son beside him, and knelt down beside the body of Louvier.

It was the son who saw me and came to me and told me in great agitation that the parish priest had perished and so had the mayor. The son had a wild look to him, as if he could not believe that he was still living, and had witnessed such a thing.

"I told you she was a great witch," he whispered to me. And as he stood beside me, staring at her, we saw the armed guards gathering, very shaken and bruised and fearful as, at the command of a young cleric with a bleeding forehead, they lifted up Deborah and looking about as if they feared the storm would come again, though it did not, they took her to the pyre. The wood and coal began to tumble down as they climbed the ladder propped against it, and they laid her gently down and hurried away.

Others gathered as the young cleric in his torn robe, and with his head still bleeding, lighted the torches, and very soon the thing was set ablaze. The young cleric stood very near, watching the wood burn, and then backed away from it, and weaving, finally fell over in a faint, or perhaps dead.

I hoped dead.

Once again I climbed the steps. I went out upon the roof of the church. I looked down upon the body of my Deborah, dead and still and beyond all pain, as it was consumed by the flames. I looked out over the rooftops, now spotted all over where the tiles had been ripped out, and I thought of the spirit of Deborah and wondered if it had risen into the clouds.

Only when the rising smoke had become so thick and odoriferous from the coals and wood and pitch that I could no longer breathe the air did I retreat. And going to the inn, where men were drinking and babbling away in confusion and peering out at the fire and then backing away from the doors timidly, I gathered my valise and went down to seek my horse. It was gone in the melee.

But seeing another, in the charge of a frightened stable boy, and in readiness for a rider, I managed to buy it from him for twice what it was worth, though in all likelihood it was not his to sell, and I rode out of the town.

After many hours of riding very slowly through the forest, with much pain in my shoulder, and much more pain in my mind, I came to Saint-Rémy and there fell into a dead sleep.

No one there had heard of the trouble yet, and I rode out very early on my way south to Marseille.

For the last two nights, I have lain on my bed half sleeping, half dreaming, and thinking of the things I saw. I wept for Deborah until there were no more tears in me. I thought of my crime and knew that I felt no guilt, but only the conviction that I would do it again.

All my life in the Talamasca, I have never once raised my hand to another man. I have reasoned, sought to persuade, connived and lied, and done my best to defeat the powers of darkness as I knew them, and to serve the powers of good. But in Montcleve, my anger rose, and with it my righteousness, and my vengeance. I rejoice that I threw that fiend off the roof of the church, if this quiet satisfaction can be called rejoicing.

Nevertheless, I have done murder, Stefan. You have in your possession my confession of this. And I anticipate nothing but your censure and the censure of the order, for when have our scholars gone forth to do murder, to push witch judges off the roofs of churches as I have done?

All I can say in my defense is that the crime was committed in a moment of passion and thoughtlessness. But I have no regret of it. You will know this as soon as you set eyes on me. I have no lies to tell you to make it a simpler thing.

My thoughts are not on this murder, as I write now. They are on my Deborah, and the spirit Lasher, and what I saw with my own eyes at Montcleve. They are on Charlotte Fontenay, the daughter of Deborah, who has gone on, not to Martinique as her enemies believe, but to Port-au-Prince in Saint-Domingue, as perhaps only I know.

Stefan, I cannot but continue my inquiry into this matter. I cannot lay down my pen and fall on my knees and say I have murdered a priest and therefore I must renounce the world and my work. So I, the murderer, continue as if I had never tainted this matter with my own crime, or my confession.

What I must do now is go to this unfortunate Charlotte—no matter how long the journey—and speak to her from my heart and tell her all that I have seen and all that I know.

This can be no simple exposition; no plea to sanity; no sentimental entreaty as I made in my youth to Deborah. There must be meat to these arguments, there must be talk between me and this woman, so that she will allow me to examine with her this thing brought out of invisibility and out of chaos to do more harm than any daimon or spirit of which I have ever heard tell.

For that is the essence of it, Stefan, the thing is horrific, and each and every witch that seeks to command it shall in the end lose control of it, I have no doubt. But what is the career of the thing itself?

To wit, it struck down Deborah's husband on account of what it knew of the man. Why did it not tell the witch herself? And what was meant by Deborah's statements that this being was learning, statements which have been made to me twice—the first time years ago in Amsterdam, the second time only lately before these tragic events.

What I mean to do is consider the nature of the thing, that it meant to spare Deborah pain in striking down her husband for her, without telling her the why of it, though it had to confess when it was asked. Or that it sought to leap ahead and do for her what she would have had done, to show itself a good and clever spirit.

Whatever the answer, this is a most unusual and interesting spirit, indeed. And consider its strength, Stefan, for I have exaggerated nothing of what befell the populace at Montcleve. You will soon hear of this, for it was too horrifying and remarkable for the story not to spread far and wide.

Now, during these long hours of soreness and torment, as I have lain here, I have considered carefully in memory all I have ever read of the old lore on spirits and daimons and the like.

I have considered the writings of wizards, through their warnings, and through anecdotes and the teachings of the Church Fathers, for no matter what fools they be in some matters, the Church Fathers do know a thing or two of spirits, in which they are in agreement with the ancients, and that agreement is a significant point.

Because if the Romans, the Greeks, the Hebrew scholars, and the Christians all describe the same entities, and issue the same warnings and formulae for controlling them, then surely that is something not to be dismissed.

And no nation or tribe to my knowledge has not acknowledged that there are many invisible beings, and that they divide into good spirits and evil spirits, according to how they benefit man.

In the early days of the Christian Church, the Church Fathers believed that these daimons were, in fact, the old gods of the pagans. That is they believed in the existence of those gods and that they were creatures of lesser power, a belief which the Church surely does not hold now.

However, the witch judges do hold this belief, crudely and in ignorance, for when they accuse the witch of riding out at night, they are accusing her in foolish words of the old belief in the goddess Diana, which did infect pagan Europe before the coming of Christianity, and the goat devil whom the witch kisses is none other than the pagan god Pan.

But the witch judge does not know that this is what he is doing. Dogmatically he believes only in Satan, "the Devil," and the devil's demons. And the historian must point out to him, for all the good it will do, that the fabrications of his demonologies come from the pagan peasant lore.

But to return to the main consideration, all peoples have believed in spirits. And all peoples have told us something of spirits, and it is what they have told us that I must examine here. And if memory serves me now, I must aver that what we see through the legends, the books of magic, and the demonologies is a legion of entities which can be called up by name, and commanded by witches or sorcerers. Indeed, the Book of Solomon lists them as numerous, giving not merely names and properties of the beings, but in what manner they choose to appear.

And though we in the Talamasca have long held that most of this is pure fancy, we know that there are such entities, and we know that the books contain some worthwhile warnings as to the danger inherent in evoking these beings, for they may grant our wishes in ways that cause us to cry to heaven in desperation as the old tale of King Midas and the peasant story of the three wishes make plain.

Indeed, the wisdom of the wizard in any language is defined as knowing how to restrain and carefully use the power of these invisible creatures, so that it is not turned upon the wizard in some unforeseen way.

But no matter how much one reads of learning about the spirits, where does one hear of teaching the spirits to learn? Where does one hear of them changing? Growing strong with evocation, yes, but changing?

And twice Deborah spoke to me of that very thing, the education of her spirit, Lasher, which says that the thing can change.

Stefan, what I perceive is that this thing, called forth from invisibility and chaos, by the simpleton Suzanne, is a complete mystery at this stage of its existence as the servant of these witches, and that it has advanced itself, through the guidance of Deborah, from a lowly spirit of the air, a storm maker that is, to a horrid daimon capable of killing the witch's enemies upon command. And I hold that there is even more to it than that, which Deborah had not time or strength to make known to me, but which I must make known to Charlotte, though not for the purpose of guiding her in her devotion to this thing, but in the hope of coming between her and the daimon and effecting the dissolution of it by some means.

For Stefan, when I consider the words of the being which Deborah quoted to me, I believe that the spirit has not only characteristics to be learned by the witch, but a *character* through which he learns; in sum, not only a nature to be understood, but a soul perhaps through which he understands.

Further, I am also willing to wager that this Charlotte Fontenay knows next to nothing of this daimon, that she never learnt the black arts from Deborah; that only in the eleventh hour did Deborah make known to Charlotte her secrets, and command Charlotte's loyalty, and send her away with her blessing that Charlotte might survive her, and not see her suffer in the fire. My beloved daughter, she called her, which I remember well.

Stefan, I *must* be allowed to go to Charlotte. I must not shrink from it as I did years before from Deborah on Roemer Franz's command. For had I argued with Deborah and studied with Deborah, perhaps I would have won ground with her, and this thing could have been sent away.

And finally, Stefan, consider my request for this mission on two further counts. One, I loved Deborah and I met defeat with her; and therefore I must go to her daughter, for this much is required of me on account of what passed between me and the woman before.

And two, that I have in my possession money enough to go to Saint-Domingue and can get more from our agent here, who will advance me plenty, and I may go even if you do not allow.

But please, do not make me break the rule of the order. Give me permission. Send me to Saint-Domingue.

For it so happens that I am going.

Yours Faithfully in the Talamasca,

Petyr van Abel
Marseille

The Talamasca
Amsterdam

Petyr van Abel
Marseille

Dear Petyr,

Your letters never fail to surprise us, but you have surpassed even all your past triumphs with these two lately from Marseille.

All here have read them, word for word, and the council has come together and these are our recommendations:

That you come home at once to Amsterdam.

We understand full well your reasons for wishing to journey to Saint-Domingue but we cannot allow such a thing. And we beg you to understand, that by your own admission, you have become part of the evil of Deborah Mayfair's daimon. In striking down Father Louvier from the roof, you carried out the wishes of the woman and of her spirit.

That you violated the rules of the Talamasca by this rash action concerns us heavily because we fear for you and we are of one mind that you must come home to take the advice of those here, and to restore your conscience and your judgment.

Petyr, you are being ordered under threat of excommunication: Return to us at once.

To the story of Deborah Mayfair we have devoted much study, taking into account your letters to us, as well as the very few observations which Roemer Franz saw fit to commit to paper (Translator's note: to date these have not been found); and we do agree with you that this woman and what she has done with her daimon is of considerable interest to the Talamasca; and please understand that we do intend to learn what we can of Charlotte Fontenay, and her life in Saint-Domingue.

It is not beyond possibility that we should in future send to the West Indies a nuncio to speak with this woman, and to learn what can be learned. But such cannot be contemplated now.

Wisdom dictates that after your return here, you write to this woman and make known to her the circumstances of her mother's death, with the omission of your crime against Father Louvier, as there would be no good reason to broadcast your guilt, and that you make known to Charlotte Fontenay also all that her mother has said. That you invite her to enter into correspondence with you would be more than advisable; and it is possible that you might exert upon her an influence that is beneficial with no risk to yourself.

This is all that you may do with regard to Charlotte Fontenay, and once more we order you to return at once; please come to us over land or sea, as quickly as possible.

But please be assured of our love and high regard for you, of our concern. We are of the opinion that if you disobey only misery awaits you in the West Indies if not worse. We judge this as much from your own words, and confessions, as from our premonitions regarding the matter. We have laid hands on the letters. We see darkness and disaster ahead.

Alexander, who as you know has the greatest power to see through touch of any among us, is most adamant that if you go on to Port-au-Prince, we will never see you again. He has taken to his bed over this, and lies there, refusing food and speaking only in strange sentences when he does choose to speak.

I should tell you further that Alexander went into the hall at the foot of the stair and laid hands upon the portrait by Rembrandt of Deborah, and withdrew near to fainting, and refusing to speak, and was helped by the servants to his room.

"To what purpose is this silence?" I demanded of him. To which he responded, that what he saw made plain that it was futile to speak. I went into a rage at this and demanded that he tell me. "I saw only death and ruin," he said. "There were no figures or numbers or words in it. What do you want of me?" And then he went on to say that if I would know how it was, look again to the portrait, to the darkness from which Rembrandt's subjects are forever emerging, and see how the light strikes the face of Deborah only partially, for that was the only light he could divine in the history of these women, a partial and fragile light, forever swallowed by darkness. Rembrandt van Rijn caught but a moment, no more.

"One can say that of any life and any history," I persisted.

"No, it is prophetic," he announced. "And if Petyr goes on to the West Indies he will vanish into the darkness from which Deborah Mayfair emerged only for a little while."

Make of that lovely exchange what you will! I cannot withhold from you that Alexander said further that you *would* go to the West Indies, that you would ignore our orders and you would ignore the pronouncement of excommunication, and that the darkness would descend.

You may defy this prediction, and if you do indeed defy it, you will work wonders for the health of Alexander, who is wasting away. Come home, Petyr!!!!

Surely you are aware, as a sensible man, that in the West Indies you need not meet with daimons or witches to endanger your life. Fever, pestilence, rebellious slaves, and the beasts of the jungle await you there, after all the perils of the sea voyage.

But let us leave the matter of common injunctions against such travel, and the matter of our private powers, and look at the documents which you have laid before us.

An interesting tale indeed. We have long known that "witch-craft" is a great concoction of judges, priests, philosophers, and so-called learned men. That by means of the printing press they have disseminated this fantasy throughout Europe, and into the Highlands of Scotland, and perhaps into the New World.

We have long known as well that the peasant populations of the rural districts now see their cunning women and midwives as witches, and the bits and pieces of custom and superstition once held in high regard by them have now been woven into fantasies of goat-footed devils, sacrilege, and preposterous Sabbats.

But where have we ever perceived a more exquisite example of how the fantasies of these men have created a witch than in the simpleton Suzanne Mayfair, who taking guidance directly from the demonologies has done what one in a million women could do—conjured up for herself a true spirit, and one of redoubtable power, a fiend which was passed on to her clever and embittered daughter, Deborah, who has gone further into the practice of Black Magic to perfect her hold over this being and now has passed him on, along with her superstitions no doubt, to her daughter in the New World.

Who among us does not wish that he or she had stood with you at Montcleve to see the great power of this spirit, and the

337

ruin of the lady's enemies, and surely had there been one of us at your side, that one would have stayed your hand and let the good Father Louvier meet his fate without your help.

I should say further that no one among us fails to understand your desire to pursue this fiend and its witch to Saint-Domingue. What would I not give to speak to such a person as this Charlotte, and to ask what she has learnt from her mother, and what she means to do.

But Petyr, you yourself have described the power of this demon. You have related faithfully the strange statements made in regard to it by the late Comtesse Deborah Mayfair de Montcleve. You must know that this thing will seek to prevent your coming between it and Charlotte, and that it is capable of bringing you to a bad end as it did with the late Comte de Montcleve.

You cannot be other than right in your conclusion that the thing is more clever than most daimons, if only in what it has said to the witch, if not in what it does.

Aye, it is quite irresistible to us, this tragic story. But you must come home to write your letters to the daughter of Deborah, from the safety of Amsterdam allowing our Dutch ships to take them over the sea.

It may interest you to know as you prepare for your return journey, that we have only lately heard that word of Father Louvier's death has reached the French court.

That a storm struck the town of Montcleve on the day of the execution of Deborah de Montcleve you will not be surprised to know. That it was sent by God to show his displeasure over the extent of witchcraft in France, and his condemnation in particular of this unrepentant woman who would not confess even under torture, you may be very interested to learn.

And that the good Father Louvier died attempting to shelter others from falling brickbats will no doubt touch your heart. The dead numbered some fifteen, we are told, and the brave people of Montcleve burnt the witch, thereby ending the tempest, God willing, and the lesson in all this is that the Lord Jesus Christ would see more witches discovered and burnt. Amen.

How soon I wonder will we see this in a pamphlet replete with the usual drawings, and a litany of untruths? No doubt the printing presses, which forever feed the flames that burn witches, are already hard at work.

And where, pray tell, is the witch judge who spent a warm night by the fire of the cunning woman of Donnelaith, and showed her the dark drawings in his demonology? Is he dead and burning in hell? We shall never know.

Petyr, do not take time to write to us. Only come home. Know that we love you, and that we do not condemn you for what you have done, or for anything that you may do. We say what we believe we must say!

Yours Faithfully in the Talamasca,

Stefan Franck
Amsterdam

Dear Stefan,

I write in haste as I am already on board the French ship *Sainte-Hélène,* bound for the New World, and a boy is waiting here to take this to be posted to you at once.

Before your letter reached me I had drawn from our agents all that I required for the journey, and have purchased what clothing and medicines I fear I shall need.

I go to Charlotte as I can do nothing else, and this will not surprise you, and please tell Alexander for me that I know he would do nothing else were he in my place.

But Stefan, you judge me wrongly when you say that I have been caught up in the evil of this daimon. True, I have broken the rules of the order only on account of Deborah Mayfair, both in the past and in the present; but the daimon was never any part of my love of Deborah, and when I struck down the witch judge I did what I wanted to do.

I struck him down for Deborah, and for all the poor and ignorant women I have seen screaming in the flames, for the women who have expired on the rack or in cold prison cells, for the families destroyed and for the villages laid waste by these awful lies.

But I waste time with this defense of myself. You are good not to condemn me, for it was murder, nevertheless.

Let me also say in great haste that the tale of the storm of Montcleve reached here some time ago, and is much garbled. It is ascribed to the power of the witch in one breath, and put down to simple nature on the other, and the death of Louvier is judged an accident in the melee, and there is much tiresome and endless argument over what actually took place.

Now I can speak of what most concerns me and that is what I have lately learnt of Charlotte Fontenay. She is much remembered here as it was at Marseille that she arrived and from Marseille that she sailed. And what has been told me by various persons is that she is very rich, very beautiful, and very fair, with flowing flaxen locks and bewitching blue eyes, and that her husband is indeed deeply crippled by a childhood illness which has caused a progressive weakness in his limbs. He is a wraith of a man. It was on this account that Charlotte brought him to Montcleve, with a great retinue of Negroes to attend him, to appeal to her mother that she might cure him, and also detect any sign of the illness in Charlotte's infant son. Indeed Deborah pronounced that the son was healthy. And mother and daughter devised for the husband a salve for his limbs which gave him much relief, but could not restore the feeling altogether, and it is thought that he shall soon be as helpless as his father, who is afflicted with the same malady, and though his mind is sharp and he can direct the affairs of his plantation, he is rumored to lie helpless in a splendid bed with Negroes to feed him and clean him as if he were a child. It was hoped the illness would progress with less speed in young Antoine, who was quite the figure at court when Charlotte first beheld him and accepted his proposal of marriage, though she was very young at that time.

It is commonly known here as well that Charlotte and young Antoine were enjoying their visit with Deborah, and had been with her many weeks when tragedy befell the family with the death of the Comte, and the rest you know. Except perhaps that those in Marseille do not believe so much in witchcraft and ascribe the madness of the persecution to the superstition of the mountain people, though what is that superstition without the famous witch judge to goad it on?

It is most easy for me to inquire about these two for no one here knows that I have been in the mountains, and it seems that those whom I invite to join me in a cup of wine do love to speak of Charlotte and Antoine Fontenay as the townspeople of Montcleve loved to speak of the entire family.

A great stir was caused here by Charlotte and young Fontenay, for apparently they live with much extravagance and generosity to everyone, handing out coins as if they were nothing, and they appeared at the church here for Mass with a retinue of Negroes as they did in Montcleve, which drew all eyes. It is said also that they paid very well every doctor here whom they did consult with regard to Antoine's affliction and there is much talk about the cause of this illness, as to whether it springs from the intense heat of the West Indies, or is an old malady of which many Europeans have suffered in ages past.

There is no doubt among these people as to the wealth of the Fontenays, and they did have agents in this city for trade until very recently, but taking their departure here in great haste, before the arrest of Deborah had become common knowledge, they broke their ties with the local agents, and no one knows where they have gone.

Now, I have more to tell you. Maintaining myself at great expense as the rich Dutch merchant, I managed to discover the name of a very gracious and beautiful young woman, of fine family, who was a friend to Charlotte Fontenay, a name mentioned in connection with that of Charlotte whenever the name Charlotte is mentioned in a conversation of any length. Saying only that I had known and loved Deborah de Montcleve in her youth in Amsterdam, I managed to secure this lady's trust, and learned more from her lips.

Her name being Jeanne Angélique de Roulet, she was at court during which time Charlotte was at court, and they were presented to His Majesty together.

Jeanne de Roulet, fearing nothing of the superstition in the mountains, avers that Charlotte is of a beguiling and sweet disposition and could never be a witch. She too lays it down to the ignorance of the mountainfolk that anyone could believe such a thing. She has offered a Mass for the repose of the soul of the unfortunate Comtesse.

As for Antoine, the lady's impression of him is that he bears his illness with great fortitude, and indeed loves his wife and is not, all things taken into account, a poor companion to his wife. However, the cause of their long journey home to Deborah was that the young man may not now father any more children, so great is his weakness, and the one boy child now living, though very strong and healthy, may inherit the malady. No one knows.

It was further stated that the father of Antoine, the master of the plantation, was in favor of the journey, so eager is he for male children through Antoine and so disapproving of his other sons, who are most dissolute and cohabit with their Negro mistresses, rarely bothering to enter their father's house.

This young woman by the way maintains a great devotion to Charlotte and laments that Charlotte did not take leave of her before sailing from Marseille. However, on account of the horrors in the Cévennes, all is forgiven.

When asked why no one came to the defense of Deborah in these recent proceedings, the woman had to confess that the Comte de Montcleve had himself never been to court, and neither had his mother, and that they had been Huguenots at one time in their history, and that no one in Paris knew the Comtesse, that Charlotte herself had been there only briefly, and that when the tale went round that Deborah de Montcleve was in fact the fatherless daughter of a Scottish witch, a mere peasant by all accounts, outrage over her predicament turned to pity and finally to nothing at all.

"Ah," says the young woman, "those mountains and those

towns." She herself is eager to return to Paris, for what is there outside Paris? And who can hope to obtain favor or advancement if he or she is not in attendance upon the king?

That is all that I have time to write. We sail within the hour.

Stefan, must I make it more plain to you? I must see the girl; I must warn her against the spirit; and where, for the love of heaven, do you imagine, that this child, born eight months after Deborah took leave of me in Amsterdam, got her fair skin and her flaxen hair?

I shall see you again. My love to all of you, my brothers and sisters in the Talamasca. I go to the New World with great anticipation. I shall see Charlotte. I shall conquer this being, Lasher, and perhaps I myself shall commune with this thing that has a voice and such power, and learn from it wherefore it learns from us.

Yours Faithfully as Ever in the Talamasca,

Petyr van Abel
Marseille

Fifteen

THE FILE ON THE MAYFAIR WITCHES

PART III

Port-au-Prince
Saint-Domingue

Stefan,

Having sent you two brief missives from the ports at which we dropped anchor before our arrival, I now begin the bound journal of my travels, in which all of my entries shall be addressed to you.

If time allows, I shall copy my entries into letters and send them to you. If time does not allow, you shall receive from me the entire journal.

As I write this I am in most comfortable if not luxurious lodgings here in Port-au-Prince, and have spent two hours in walking about the colonial city, much dazzled with its fine houses, splendid public buildings, including a theater for the performance of Italian opera, and with its richly dressed planters and their wives, and the great plenitude of slaves.

No place equals Port-au-Prince in my travels for its exotic qualities, and I do not think that any city in Africa could offer so much to the eye.

For not only are there Negroes everywhere performing all tasks here, there is a multitude of foreigners engaged in all manner of trade. I have also discovered a large and prosperous "colored" population, composed entirely of the offspring of the planters and their African concubines, most of which have been freed by their white fathers, and have gone on to make a good living as musicians or craftsmen, shopkeepers and undoubtedly women of ill fame. The women of color I have seen are surpassingly beautiful. I cannot fault the men for choosing them as mistresses or evening companions. Many have golden skin and great liquid black eyes, and they are quite obviously aware of their charms. They dress with great ostentation, possessing many black slaves of their own.

This class is increasing daily I am told. And one cannot help but wonder what will be its fate as the years pass.

As for the slaves, they are imported by the thousands. I watched two ships unload their miserable cargo. The stench was past describing. It was horrible to see the conditions in which these poor human beings have been maintained. It is said that they are worked to death on the plantations for it is cheaper to import them than to keep them alive.

Harsh punishments are visited upon them for the smallest crimes. And the entire island lives in terror of uprisings, and the masters and mistresses of the great houses live in fear of being poisoned, for that is the slave's weapon, or so I am told.

As for Charlotte and her husband, all know of them here, but nothing of Charlotte's family in Europe. They have purchased one of the very largest and most prosperous plantations very close to Port-au-Prince, yet near to the sea. It is perhaps an hour's carriage ride from the outskirts of the city, and borders great cliffs over the beaches; and is famed for its large house and other fine buildings, containing as it does an entire city with blacksmith and leatherworks and seamstresses and weavers and furniture makers all within its many arpents, which are planted with coffee and indigo, and yield a great fortune with each harvest.

This plantation has made rich men of three different owners in the short time that the French have been here, engaged in endless battles with the Spanish who inhabit the southeast portion of the island, and two of those owners quit it for Paris with their earnings, whilst the third died of a fever, and now it is in possession of the Fontenays, Antoine Pére and Antoine Fils, but all know that it is Charlotte who runs this plantation, and she is known far and wide as Madame Charlotte, and every merchant in this city pays court to her, and the local officials beg for her favor and for her money, of which she has a seemingly endless amount.

It is said that she has taken the management of the plantation into her own hands down to the smallest detail, that she rides the fields with her overseer—Stefan, no one is held in more contempt than these overseers—and that she knows the names of all her slaves. She spares nothing to provide them with food and with drink and so binds them to her with extraordinary loyalty, and she inspects their houses, and dotes upon their children, and looks into the souls of the accused before meting punishment. But her judgment upon those who are treacherous is already legendary, for there is no limit here to the power of these planters. They can flog their slaves to death if they wish.

As for the household retinue, they are sleek, overly dressed, privileged, and audacious to hear the local merchants tell it; five maids alone attend Charlotte. Some sixteen slaves keep the kitchen; and no one knows how many maintain the parlors, music rooms, and ballrooms of the house. The famous Reginald accompanies the master everywhere that he goes, if he goes anywhere at all. And having much free time, these slaves appear often in Port-au-Prince, with gold in their pockets, at which time all shop doors are open to them.

It is Charlotte who is almost never seen away from this great preserve, which is named Maye Faire by the way, and this is always written in English as I have spelled it above, and never in French.

The lady has given two splendid balls since her arrival, during which her husband took a chair to view the dancing, and even the old man was in attendance, weak as he was. The local gentry, who think of nothing but pleasure in this place for there is not much else to think of, adore her for these two entertainments and long for others, with the certainty that Charlotte will not disappoint them.

Her own Negro musicians provided the music; the wine flowed without cease; exotic native dishes were offered, as well as splendid plain-cooked fowl and beef. Charlotte herself danced with every gentleman present except of course her husband, who looked on approvingly. She herself put the wineglass to his lips.

As far as I am able to learn, this lady is called a witch only by her slaves and in awe and respect on account of her healing powers which have already gained a reputation but allow me to repeat—*no one here knows anything of the occurrence in France*. The name of Montcleve is never spoken by anyone. The history of this family is that it has come from Martinique.

It is said that Charlotte is most eager for all the planters to join together to create a sugar refinery here, so that they may reap higher profits from their crops. There is also much talk of driving our Dutch ships out of the Caribbean, as it seems we are still most prosperous, and the French and Spanish envy us. But no doubt you know more of that than I do, Stefan. I did see many Dutch ships in the port, and have no doubt that my return to Amsterdam will be a simple matter, as soon as my work here is done. As "a Dutch merchant" I am certainly treated with every courtesy.

This afternoon, when I grew tired of my meanderings, I came back here to my lodgings, where there are two slaves to undress me and bathe me if I should allow it, and I wrote to the lady and said that I should like to visit her, that I have a message for her which is of the utmost importance and comes from someone very dear to her, dearer perhaps than any other, who entrusted me with the proper address on the night before her death. I have come in person, I said, because my message was too important to be enclosed in a letter. I signed my full name.

Just before I began this entry, the reply arrived. I should come to Maye Faire this very evening. Indeed a carriage will be waiting for me at the entrance of the inn just before dark. I am to bring what provisions I need to stay the night, and the night after, as suits me. This I intend to do.

Stefan, I am most excited and not at all fearful. I know now, after having given it the greatest thought, that I go to see my own daughter. But how to make this known to her—whether to make it known—deeply troubles me.

I am strongly convinced that the tragedy of the Mayfair women will come to an end in this strange and fertile place, this rich and exotic land. It will come to an end here with this strong and clever young woman who has the world in her grasp, and surely has seen enough to know what her mother and her grandmother have suffered in their brief and tragic lives.

I go now to bathe and properly dress and prepare for this adventure. I do not mind at all that I shall see a great colonial plantation. Stefan, how shall I say what is in my heart? It is as if my life before this were a thing painted in pale colors; but now it takes on the vibrancy of Rembrandt van Rijn.

I feel the darkness near me; I feel the light shining. And more keenly I feel the contrast between the two.

Until I pick up this pen again,

Your servant,
Petyr

Post Script: copied out and sent by letter to Stefan Franck this same evening. PVA

Port-au-Prince
Saint-Domingue

Dear Stefan,

It has been a full fortnight since I last wrote to you. How can I describe all that has taken place? I fear there is not time, my beloved friend—that my reprieve is short—yet I must write all of it. I must tell you what I have seen, what I have suffered, and what I have done.

It is late morning as I write this. I did sleep two hours upon my return to this inn. I have also eaten, but only that I may have a little strength. I hope and pray that the thing which has followed me here and tormented me on the long road from Maye Faire has at last returned to the witch who sent it after me, to drive me mad and destroy me, which I have not allowed it to do.

Stefan, if the fiend has not been defeated, if the assault upon me is renewed with mortal vigor, I shall break off my narrative and give you the most important elements in simple sentences and close and seal this letter away in my iron box. I have already this very morning spoken to the innkeeper, that in the event of my demise he is to see that this box reaches Amsterdam. I have also spoken with a local agent here, cousin and friend to our agent in Marseille, and he is instructed to ask for the box.

Allow me to say, however, that on account of my appearance these two men believe me to be a madman. Only my gold commanded their attention, and they have been promised a rich reward upon delivery of the box and this letter into your hands.

Stefan, you were right in all your warnings and presentiments. I am sunk now deeper and deeper into this evil; I am beyond redemption. I should have come home to you. For the second time in my life I know the bitterness of regret.

I am now scarcely alive. My clothes are in tatters, my shoes broken and useless, my hands scratched by thorns. My head aches from my long night of running through darkness. But there is no time to rest further. I dare not leave by ship this very hour, for if the thing means to come after me, it will do it here or at sea. And it is better that it make its assault on land so that my iron box will not be lost.

I must use what time I have left to recount all that has taken place . . .

. . . It was early evening on the day I last wrote to you when I left this place. I had dressed in my finest clothes and went down to meet the coach at the appointed time. All that I had seen in the streets of Port-au-Prince had prepared me for a splendid equipage, yet this surpassed my imaginings, being an exquisite glass carriage with footman, coachmen, and two armed guards on horseback, all of them black Africans, in full livery with powdered wigs and satin clothes.

The journey into the hills was most pleasant, the sky overhead stacked with high white clouds and the hills themselves covered with beautiful woodland and fine colonial dwellings, many surrounded by flowers, and the banana trees which grow here in abundance.

I do not think you can imagine the lushness of this landscape, for the tenderest hot house blooms grow here in wild profusion all year round. Great clumps of banana trees rise up everywhere. And so do giant red flowers upon slender stems which grow as high as trees.

No less enchanting were the sudden glimpses of the distant blue sea. If there is any sea as blue as the Caribbean I have never beheld it, and when it is seen at twilight, it is most spectacular, but then you will hear more of this later, for I have had much time to contemplate the color of this sea.

On the road I also passed two smaller plantation houses, very pleasing structures, set back from the road behind great gardens. And also just beside a small river, a graveyard laid out with fine marble monuments inscribed with French names. As we went very slowly over the little bridge I had time to contemplate it, and think about those who had come to live and die in this savage land.

I speak of these things for two reasons, the important one to state now being that my senses were lulled by the beauties I saw on this journey, and by the heavy moist twilight, and by the long stretch of tended fields and the sudden spectacle of Charlotte's plantation house before me, grander than any I had beheld, at the end of a paved road.

It is a giant colonial-style mansion, and by that I mean it has a great pitched roof with many dormers, and beneath there are porches stretching the length of it, supported by mud-brick columns which have been plastered over to look not unlike marble.

All of its many windows extend to the floor and are decorated with very green wooden shutters which can be bolted both against enemy attack and against storms.

A heady profusion of light came from the place as we approached. Never have I seen so many candles, not even at the French court. Lanterns were hung in the branches of the trees. As we drew nearer, I saw that every window was open to the porches both above and below, and I could see the chandeliers and the fine furnishings, and other bits of color gleaming in the dark.

So distracted was I by all this, that with a start I beheld the lady of the house, come out to the garden gate to see me, and standing among the many flowers, waiting, her lemon-colored satin dress very like the soft blooms that surrounded her, her eyes fixing me harshly and perhaps coldly in her young and tender face so that she appeared, if you can see it, a tall and angry child.

As I climbed down with the aid of the footman onto the purple flags, she drew closer, and only then did I judge her full height to be great for a woman, though she was much smaller than I.

Fair-haired and beautiful I found her, and so would anyone else looking at her, but the descriptions of her could not prepare me for the picture she presented. Ah, if Rembrandt had ever seen her, he would have painted her. So young yet so like hard metal. Very richly dressed she was, her gown ornamented with lace and pearls and displaying a high full bosom, half naked one might say, and her arms were beautifully shaped in their tight lace-trimmed sleeves.

Ah, I linger on every detail for I seek to understand my own weakness, and that you may forgive it. I am mad, Stefan, mad over what I have done. But please, when you and the others judge me, consider all that I have written here.

It seemed as we faced each other that something silent and frightening passed between us. This woman, her face sweet and youthful almost to an absurdity of tender cheeks and lips and large innocent blue eyes, studied me as if a very different soul lurked within her, old and wise. Her beauty worked like a spell upon me. I stared foolishly at her long neck, and at the tender slope of her shoulders and again at her shapely arms.

It struck me stupidly that it would be sweet to press my thumbs into the softness of her arms. And it did seem to me that she regarded me very much as her mother had regarded me many years ago, when in the Scottish inn I had fought the devil of her beauty not to ravage her there.

"Ah, so, Petyr van Abel," she said to me in English and with a touch of the Scottish to it, "you have come." I swear to you, Stefan, it was Deborah's youthful voice. How much they must have spoken together in English, why, it might have been a secret language for them.

"My child," I answered, in the same language, "thank you for receiving me. I have made a long journey to see you, but nothing could have kept me away."

But all the while she was coldly taking my measure, as surely as if I were a slave on the auction block, not disguising her appraisal as I had taken pains to disguise mine. And I was shocked by what I saw in her face, a thin nose and deep-set eyes, for all their size very like my own. Cheeks a little low and full, very like my own. And her hair, though it was a glorious mane of pale gold, brushed straight back from her forehead and held in place by a great jeweled comb, in color and texture very like my own.

A great sadness consumed me. She was my daughter. I knew that she was. And there came to me again that terrible regret I had known in Montcleve. I saw my Deborah, a broken puppet of white wax on the stones before the church of Saint-Michel.

Perhaps my sadness was felt by Charlotte, for a shadow fell over her countenance, and she seemed determined to defy this feeling as she spoke:

"You are as handsome as my mother told me," she said, half musing, and half under her breath and with a slight raise of one eyebrow. "You are tall and straight and strong, and in the fullness of health, are you not?"

"Mon Dieu, madam. What strange words," I said. I laughed uneasily. "I do not know whether you flatter me or not."

"I like the look of you," she said. And the strangest smile spread over her face, very clever and disdaining, yet at the same time childishly sweet. She gave a little bitter stretch to her lips as a child might do it, almost to a pout, it seemed, and I found this unspeakably charming. Then she seemed lost in contemplating me, and said finally: "Come with me, Petyr van Abel. Tell me what you know of my mother. Tell me what you know of her death. And whatever your purpose do not lie to me."

And there seemed in her then a great vulnerability as if I might hurt her suddenly and she knew it, and was afraid.

I felt such tenderness for her. "No, I haven't come to tell lies," I said. "Have you heard nothing at all?"

She was silent, and then coldly she said: "Nothing," as if she

349

were lying. I saw that she was scanning me in the very way that I have scanned others when trying to pry loose their secret thoughts.

She led me towards the house, bowing her head ever so slightly as she took my arm. Even the grace of her movements distracted me, and the brush of her skirts against my leg. She did not even look at the slaves who flanked the path, a very regiment of them, all holding lanterns to light our way. Beyond lay the flowers glimmering in the darkness, and the massive trees before the house.

We had all but reached the front steps when we turned and followed the flags into the trees, and there sought out a wooden bench.

I was seated at her behest. Darkness came fast around us, and the lanterns strung here and there burned bright and yellow, and the house itself gave forth an even greater dazzle of light.

"Tell me how I shall begin, madam," I said. "I am your servant. How would you hear it?"

"Straight out," she answered, her eyes fixing on me again. She sat composed, turned slightly towards me, her hands in her lap.

"She did not die in the flames. She threw herself from the church tower, and died when she struck the stones."

"Ah, thank God!" she whispered. "To hear it from human lips."

I pondered these words for a moment. Did she mean the spirit Lasher had already told her this, and she had not believed it? She was most dejected and I was not sure I should say more.

Yet I continued. "A great storm hit Montcleve," I said, "called down by your mother. Your brothers died. So did the old Comtesse."

She said nothing, but looked straight forward, heavy with sadness, and perhaps despair. Girlish she looked, not a woman at all.

I continued, only now I took several steps backwards in my account and told her how I had come to the town, how I had met with her mother, and all the things which her mother had said to me about the spirit Lasher, that he had caused the death of the Comte, unbeknownst to Deborah, and how she had upbraided him for this, and what the spirit had said to her in his defense. And how Deborah would have her know and be warned.

Her face grew dark as she listened; still she looked away from me. I explained what I thought was the meaning of her mother's warnings, and then what were my thoughts on this spirit and how no magician had ever written of a spirit that could learn.

Still she did not move or speak. Her face was so dark now she seemed in a pure rage. Finally, when I sought to resume on this subject, saying that I knew something of spirits, she interrupted me: "Don't speak of this anymore," she said. "And never speak of it to anyone here."

"No, I would not," I hastened to answer. I proceeded to explain what followed my meeting with Deborah, and then to describe the day of her death in great detail, leaving out only that I had thrown Louvier from the roof. I said merely that he had died.

But here she turned to me, and with a dark smile she asked:

"How died, Petyr van Abel? Did you not push him off the roof?"

Her smile was cold and full of anger, though I did not know whether it was against me or all that had taken place. It did seem that she was defending her daimon, that she felt I had insulted him, and this was her loyalty, for surely he had told her what I had done. But I do not know if I am right in this conjecture. I know only that to think she knew of my crime frightened me a little, and perhaps more than I cared to say.

I didn't answer her question. She fell silent for a long time. It seemed she would cry but then she did not. Finally:

"They believed I deserted my mother," she whispered. "You know I did not!"

"I know this, madam," I said to her. "Your mother sent you here."

"Ordered me to leave!" she said, imploring me. "Ordered me." She stopped only to catch her breath. " 'Go, Charlotte,' she said, 'for if I must see you die before me or with me, my life is nothing. I will not have you here, Charlotte. If I am burnt I cannot bear it that you should see it, or suffer the same.' And so I did what she told me to do." Her mouth gave that little twist again, that pout, and it seemed again she would cry. But she ground her teeth, and widened her eyes, considering all of it, and then fell into her anger again.

"I loved your mother," I said to her.

"Aye, I know that you did," she said. "They turned against her, her husband and my brothers."

I noticed that she did not speak of this man as her father, but I said nothing. I did not know whether I should ever say anything on this account or not.

"What can I say to soothe your heart?" I asked her. "They are punished. They do not enjoy the life which they took from Deborah."

"Ah, you put it well." And here she smiled bitterly at me,

351

and she bit her lip, and her little face looked so tender and so soft to me, so like something which could be hurt, that I leant over and kissed her and this she allowed, with her eyes downcast.

She seemed puzzled. And so was I, for I had found it so indescribably sweet to kiss her, to catch the scent of her skin and to be so near her breasts, that I was in a state of pure consternation actually. At once I said that I wished to talk of this spirit again, for it seemed my only salvation was the business at hand. "I must make known to you my thoughts on this spirit, on the dangers of this thing. Surely you know how I came to know your mother. Did she not tell you the whole tale?"

"You try my patience," she said suddenly.

I looked at her and saw her anger again.

"How so?"

"You know things that I would not have you know."

"What did your mother tell you?" I asked. "It was I who rescued her from Donnelaith."

She considered my words, but her anger did not cool. "Answer me this," she said. "Do you know how her mother came to summon her daimon, as you call him!"

"From the book the witch judge showed her, she took her idea. She learnt it all from the witch judge, for before that she was the cunning woman and the midwife, as are so many, and nothing more."

"Oh, she might have been more, much more. We are all more than we seem. We only learn what we must. To think what I have become here, since I left my mother's house. And listen to what I say, it was my mother's house. It was her gold which furnished it and put the carpets on the stone floors, and the wood in the fireplaces."

"The townsfolk talked of that," I said. "That the Comte had nothing but his title before he met her."

"Aye, and debts. But that is all past now. He is dead. And I know that you have told me all that my mother said. You have told me the truth. I only wonder that I want to tell you what you do not know, and cannot guess. And I think on what my mother told me of you, of how she could confess anything to you."

"I'm glad she said this of me. I never betrayed her to anyone."

"Except to your order. Your Talamasca."

"Ah, but that was never betrayal."

She turned away from me.

"My dearest Charlotte," I said to her. "I loved your mother, as I told you. I begged her to beware of the spirit and the spirit's power. I do not say I predicted what happened to her. I did not. But I was afraid for her. I was afraid of her ambition to use the spirit for her ends—''

"I don't want to hear any more." She was in a rage again.

"What would you have me do?" I asked.

She thought, but not apparently on my question, and then she said: "I will never suffer what my mother suffered, or her mother before her."

"I pray not. I have come across the sea to . . ."

"No, but your warnings and your presence have nothing to do with it. I will not suffer those things. There was something sad in my mother, sad and broken inside, which had never healed from girlhood."

"I understand."

"I have no such wound. I was a woman here before these horrors befell her. I have seen other horrors and you will see them tonight when you look upon my husband. There isn't a physician in all the world who can cure him. And no cunning woman either. And I have but one healthy son by him, and that is not enough."

I sighed.

"But come, we'll talk more," she said.

"Yes, please, we must."

"They are waiting for us now." She stood up, and I with her. "Say nothing about my mother in front of the others. Say nothing. You have come to see me . . ."

"Because I am a merchant and would set up in Port-au-Prince, and want your advice on it."

She gave a weary nod to that. "The less you say," she said, "the better." She turned away and started towards the steps.

"Charlotte, please don't close your heart to me," I said to her, and tried to take her hand.

She stiffened against me, and then assuming a false smile, very sweet and very calm, she led me up the short steps to the main floor of the house.

I was miserable as you can imagine. What was I to make of her strange words? And she herself baffled me for she seemed at one moment child and at another old woman. I could not say that she had even considered my warnings, or rather the very warnings that Deborah had implored me to give. Had I added too much of my own advice to it?

"Madame Fontenay," I said as we reached the top of the short stairs and the door to the main floor. "We must talk some more. I have your promise?"

"When my husband is put to bed," she said, "we will be

alone." She allowed her gaze to linger on me as she pronounced this last phrase, and I fear a blush rose to my face as I looked at her, and I saw the high color in her rounded cheeks also, and then the little stretch of her lower lip and her playful smile.

We entered a central hallway, very spacious, though nothing on the order of a French château, mind you, but with much fancy plasterwork, and a fine chandelier all ablaze with pure wax candles, and a door open at the far end to the rear porch, beyond which I could just make out the edge of a cliff where the lanterns hung from the tree branches as they did from those in the front garden, and very slowly I realized that the roar I heard was not wind but the gentle sound of the sea.

The supper room, which we entered to our right, gave an even greater view of the cliffs and the black water beyond them which I saw as I followed Charlotte, for this room was the entire width of the house. A bit of light still played upon the water or I would not have been able to make it out. The roar filled this room most delightfully and the breeze was moist and warm.

As for the room itself it was splendid, every European accoutrement having been brought to bear upon the colonial simplicity. The table was draped in the finest linen, and laid with the heaviest and most elegantly carved plate.

Not anywhere in Europe have I seen finer silver; the candelabra were heavy and well embossed with designs. Each place had its lace-trimmed napkin, and the chairs themselves were well upholstered with the finest velvet, replete with fringes, and above the table, a great square wooden fan hung from a hinge, moved back and forth by means of a rope, threaded through hooks across the ceiling and down the wall, at the end of which, in the far corner, sat a small African child.

What with the fan and all the many doors open to the porch, the room had a coolness and a sweet fragrance to it, and was most inviting, though the candle flames did fight for their lives. No sooner had I been seated at the chair to the left of the head of the table, than numerous slaves entered, all finely dressed in European silks and lace, and began to set the table with platters. And at the same time, the young husband of whom I had heard so much appeared.

He was upright, and did slide his feet along the floor, but his entire weight was supported by the large, heavily muscled black man who had an arm about his waist. As for his arms, they seemed as weak as his legs, with the wrists bent, and the fingers hanging limp. Yet he was a handsome young man.

Before the advance of this illness, he must have cut a likely figure at Versailles where he won his bride. And in well-fitted princely clothes, and with his fingers covered with jeweled rings, and with his head adorned with an enormous and beautiful Parisian wig, he did look very fine indeed. His eyes were of a piercing gray, and his mouth very broad and narrow, and his chin very strong.

Once settled in the chair, he struggled as it were to move himself backwards for more comfort, and when he failed to accomplish his aim, the powerful slave moved him and then placed the chair as the master wanted it, and then took his place at the master's back.

Charlotte had now taken her place not at the end of the table, but at her husband's right, just opposite my place, so that she might feed and assist her husband. And two other persons came, the brothers, I was soon to discover, Pierre and André, both of them besotted and full of dull slurred drunken humor, and four ladies, fancily dressed, two young and two old, cousins, it seemed, and permanent residents of this house, the old ones being silent except for occasional confused questions as they were both hard of hearing and a little decrepit, the young ones past their prime but lively of mind and well-bred.

Just before we were served, a doctor appeared, having just ridden over from a neighboring plantation—a rather old and befuddled fellow dressed in somber black as was I, and he was at once invited to join the company and sat down and began to drink the wine in great gulps.

That composed the company, each of us with a slave behind his chair, to reach forward and to serve our plates from the platters before us, and to fill our wineglasses if we drank so much as a sip.

The young husband spoke most pleasantly to me, and it was at once perfectly clear that his mind was wholly unaffected by his illness, and that he still had an appetite for good food, which was fed to him both by Charlotte and by Reginald, Charlotte taking the spoon in hand, and Reginald breaking the bread. Indeed the man had a desire for living, that was plain enough. He remarked that the wine was excellent and that he approved of it, and talking in a polite way with all the company, consumed two bowls of soup.

The food was highly spiced and very delicious, the soup being a seafood stew filled with much pepper, and the meats being garnished with fried yams and fried bananas and much rice and beans and other delicious things.

All the while everyone conversed with vigor except for the old women, who seemed nevertheless to be amused and content.

Charlotte spoke of the weather and the business of the plantation, and how her husband must ride out with her to see the crops tomorrow, and how the young slave girl bought last winter was now coming along well with her sewing, and so forth and so on. This chatter was in French for the most part, and the young husband was spirited in his response, breaking off to ask me many polite questions as to the conditions of my voyage, and my liking of Port-au-Prince, and how long I would be staying with them, and other polite remarks as to the friendliness of the country, and how they had prospered at Maye Faire and meant to buy the adjacent plantation as soon as the owner, a drunken gambler, could be persuaded to sell.

The drunken brothers were the only ones prone to argument and several times made sneering remarks, for it seemed to the youngest, Pierre, who had none of the good looks of his ailing brother, that they had enough land and did not need the neighboring plantation, and Charlotte knew more about the business of the planter's life than a woman should.

This was met with cheers by the loud and nasty André, who spilt his food all down his lace shirtfront, and ate with his mouth stuffed, and put a greasy stain from his mouth upon his glass when he drank. He was for selling all this land when their father died and going back to France.

"Do not speak of his death," declared the eldest, the crippled Antoine. To which the others sneered.

"And how is he today?" asked the doctor, belching as he did so. "I fear to inquire if he is any better or worse."

"What can be expected?" asked one of the female cousins, who had once been beautiful and was still pleasing to look at, handsome one might say. "If he speaks a word today, I shall be surprised."

"And why shouldn't he speak?" asked Antoine. "His mind is as it always was."

"Aye," said Charlotte, "he rules with a steady hand."

There ensued a great verbal brawl, with everyone talking at once, and one of the feeble old ladies demanding to be told what was going on.

Finally the other old woman, a crone if ever there was one, who had nibbled at her plate all the while with the fixed attention of a busy insect, suddenly raised her head and cried to the drunken brothers, "You are neither of you fit to run this plantation," to which the drunken brothers replied with boisterous laughter, though the two younger females regarded this with much seriousness, their eyes passing over Charlotte fearfully and then sweeping gently the near paralyzed and useless husband, whose hands lay like dead birds beside his plate.

Then the old woman, apparently approving of the response to her words, issued another pronouncement. "It is Charlotte who rules here!" and this produced even more fearful looks from the women, and more laughter and sneering from the drunken brothers, and a winsome smile from the crippled Antoine.

Then the poor fellow became most agitated, so that he in fact began to tremble, but Charlotte hastily spoke of pleasant things. Once again I was questioned about my journey, about life in Amsterdam, and the present state of things in Europe, which related to the importation of coffee and indigo, and told that I should become very weary of life in the plantations, for nobody did anything but eat and drink and seek pleasure, and so forth and so on, until suddenly Charlotte broke off gently and gave the order to the black slave, Reginald, that he should go and fetch the old man and bring him down.

"He has been talking to me all day," she said quietly to the others, with a vague look of triumph.

"Indeed, a miracle!" declared the drunken André, who now ate in slovenly fashion without the aid of a knife or fork.

The old doctor narrowed his eyes as he regarded Charlotte, quite indifferent to the food he had slopped down his lace ruff, or the wine spilling from the glass which he held in his uncertain hand. That he should drop it was a distinct possibility. The young slave boy behind him looked on anxiously.

"What do you mean spoken to you all day?" asked the doctor. "He was stuporous when last I saw him."

"He changes hourly," said one of the cousins.

"He'll never die!" roared the old woman, who was again nibbling.

Then into the room came Reginald, holding a tall gray-haired and much emaciated man, with one thin arm flung about the slave's shoulder, and head hanging, though his bright eyes fixed all of us one by one.

Into the chair at the foot of the table he was put, a mere skeleton, and as he could not sit upright, bound to it with sashes of silk. Then the slave Reginald, who seemed a very artist at all this, lifted the man's chin as he could not hold up his head on his own.

At once the female cousins began to chatter at him, that it was good to see him so well. But they were amazed at him, and so was the doctor, and then as the old man began to speak so was I.

One hand lifted off the table with a floppy, jerky movement and then came crashing down. At the same moment his mouth opened, though his face remained so smooth that only the lower jaw dropped, and out came his hollow and toneless words.

"I am nowhere near death and will not hear of it!" And again, the limp hand rose in a spasm and came down with a bang.

Charlotte was studying this all the while with narrow and glittering eyes. Indeed for the first time I perceived her concentration, and how every particle of her attention was directed to the man's face and his one flopping hand.

"Mon Dieu, Antoine," cried the doctor, "you cannot blame us for worrying."

"My mind is as it ever was!" declared the old creature in the same toneless voice, and then turning his head very slowly as though it were made of wood and grinding away in a socket, he looked from right to left and then at Charlotte and gave a crooked smile.

Only now as I bent forward, escaping the dazzle of the nearest candles and marveling at this strange performance, did I perceive that his eyes were bloodshot, and that indeed his face appeared frozen, and the expressions that broke out upon it were like cracks in ice.

"I trust in you, my beloved daughter-in-law," he said to Charlotte, and this time his total lack of modulation resulted in a great noise.

"Yes, mon père," said Charlotte with sweetness, "and I shall take care of you, be assured of it."

And drawing closer to her husband, she gave a squeeze to his useless hand. As for the husband, he was staring at his father with suspicion and fear.

"But Father, are you in pain?" he asked now softly.

"No, my son," said the father, "no pain, never any pain." And this seemed as much a reassurance as an answer, for this picture was surely what the son saw as a prophecy. Or was it?

For as I beheld this creature, as I saw him turn his head again in that odd way, very like a doll made of wooden parts, I knew that this was not the man at all speaking to us, but something inside of him which had gained possession of him, and at the moment of recognition, I perceived the true Antoine Fontenay trapped within this body, unable to command his vocal chords any longer, and peering out at me with terrified eyes.

It was but a flash, yet I saw it. And in the same instant, I turned to Charlotte, who stared at me coldly, defiantly, as if daring me to acknowledge what I had realized, and the old man himself stared at me, and with a suddenness that startled everyone gave forth a loud cackling laugh.

"Oh, for the love of God, Antoine!" cried the handsome female cousin.

"Father, take a little wine," said the feeble eldest son.

The black man Reginald reached for the glass, but the old man suddenly lifted both hands, bringing them down upon the table with a crash, and then lifting them again, his eyes glittering, took the wineglass as if between two paws and, bringing it to his mouth, slopped the contents onto his face so that it washed into his mouth and down his chin.

The company was appalled. The black Reginald was appalled. Only Charlotte gave a small steely smile as she beheld this trick, and then said, "Good, Father, go to bed," as she rose from the table.

Reginald tried to catch the glass as it was suddenly released and the old man's hand thumped down beside it. But it fell to one side, the wine splattering all over the tablecloth.

Once more the frozen mouth cracked open and the hollow voice spoke. "I weary of this conversation. I would go now."

"Yes, to bed," said Charlotte, approaching his chair, "and we will come to see you by and by."

Did no one else perceive this horror? That the useless limbs of the old man were being worked by the demonic agency? The female cousins stared at the man in silence and revulsion as he was drawn up out of the chair, his chin flopping down on his chest, and taken away. Reginald was now quite completely responsible for the old man's movements and took him towards the door. The drunken brothers appeared angry and petulant, and the old doctor, who had just downed another entire glass of red wine, was merely shaking his head. Charlotte quietly observed all this and then returned to her place at the table.

Our eyes met. I would swear it was hatred I saw staring back at me. Hatred for what I knew. In awkwardness I took another drink of the wine, which was most delicious, though I had begun to notice already that it was uncommonly strong or I was uncommonly weak.

Very loudly again spoke the old deaf woman, the insectile one, saying to everyone and no one, "I have not seen him move his hands like that in years."

"Well, he sounds to me like the very devil!" said the handsome female.

"Damn him, he'll never die," whispered André and then fell to sleep, face down in his plate, his overturned glass rolling off the table.

Charlotte, watching all of this and more, with equal calm, gave a soft laugh, and said, "Oh, he is very far from dead."

Then a horrid sound startled the entire company, for at the top of the stairs, or somewhere very close to the head of it, the old man gave forth another loud terrible laugh.

Charlotte's face grew hard. Patting her husband's hand gently, she took her leave with great speed, but not so much speed that she did not look at me as she left the room.

Finally the old doctor, who was at this point almost too besotted to rise from the table, which he started to do once and then thought the better of, declared with a sigh that he must go home. At which moment two other visitors arrived, well-dressed Frenchmen, to whom the handsome older female cousin went immediately, as the three other women rose and made their way out, the crone glaring back in condemnation at the drunken brother, who had fallen into the plate, and muttering at him. The other son meantime had risen to assist the drunken doctor, and these two staggered out on the gallery.

Alone with Antoine and a host of slaves cleaning the table, I asked the man if he would enjoy with me a cigar, as I had bought two very good ones in Port-au-Prince.

"Ah, but you must have my own, from the tobacco I grow here," he declared. A young slave boy brought the cigars to us and lighted them, and this young man stood there to take the thing from the master's mouth and replace it as he should.

"You must excuse my father," said Antoine to me softly, as if he did not like the slave to hear it. "He is most keen of mind. This illness is a very horror."

"I can well imagine," I said. Much laughter and conversation came from the parlor across the hall where the females had settled, it seemed, with the visitors, and possibly with the drunken brother and the doctor.

Two black slave boys meantime attempted to pick up the other brother, who suddenly shot to his feet, indignant and belligerent, and struck one of the boys so that he began to cry.

"Don't be a fool, André," said Antoine wearily. "Come here, my poor little one."

The slave obeyed, as the drunken brother rampaged out.

"Take the coin from my pocket," said the master. The slave, familiar with the ritual, obeyed, his eyes shining as he held up his reward.

At last, Reginald and the lady of the house appeared and this time with the rosy-cheeked infant son, a blessed lambkin, two mulatto maids hovering behind the child as though the child were made of porcelain and might any moment be hurled to the floor.

The lambkin laughed and kicked its little limbs with joy at the sight of his father. And what a sad spectacle it was that its father could not even lift his miserable hands.

But he did smile at the lambkin, and the lambkin was placed upon his lap for an instant, and he did bend and kiss its blond head.

The child gave no sign of infirmity, but neither had Antoine at such a tender age, I wager. And surely the child had beauty both from its mother and father, for it had more than any such child I have ever beheld.

At last, the mulatto maids, both very pretty, were allowed to descend upon it, and rescue it from the world at large, and carry it away.

The husband then took his leave of me, bidding me remain at Maye Faire for as long as I should please. I took another drink of the wine, though I was resolved it should be my last, for I was dizzy.

Immediately, I found myself led out onto the darkened gallery by the fair Charlotte, so as to look out over the front garden with its melancholy lanterns, the two of us quite alone as we took our places on a wooden bench.

My head was most surely swimming from the wine, though I could not quite determine how I had managed to drink so much of it, and when I pleaded to have no more, Charlotte would not hear of it, and insisted that I take another glass. "It is my finest, brought from home."

To be polite I drank it, feeling then a wave of intoxication; and remembering in a blur the image of the drunken brothers and wishing to get clearheaded, I rose and gripped the wooden railing and looked down into the yard. It seemed the night was full of dark persons, slaves perhaps moving in the foliage, and I did see one very shapely light-skinned creature smiling up at me as she passed. In a dream, it seemed, I heard Charlotte speaking to me:

"All right, handsome Petyr, what more would you say to me?"

Strange words I thought, between father and daughter, for surely she knows it, she cannot but know it. Yet again, perhaps she does not. I turned to her and began my warnings. Did she not understand that this spirit was no ordinary spirit? That this thing which could possess the body of the old man and make it do her bidding could turn upon her, that it was, in fact, obtaining its very strength from her, that she must seek to understand what spirits were, but she bid me hush.

And then it did seem to me that I was seeing the most bizarre things through the window of the lighted dining room, for the slave boys in their shining blue satin appeared to me to be dancing as they dusted and swept the room, dancing like imps.

"What a curious illusion," I said. Only to realize that the young boys, dusting the seats of the chairs and gathering the fallen napkins, were only cavorting, and playing, and did not know that I watched.

Then staring back at Charlotte, I beheld that she had let her hair down free over her shoulders and that she was staring up at me with cold, beautiful eyes. It seemed also that she had pushed down the sleeves of her dress, as a tavern wench might do it, the better to reveal her magnificent white shoulders and the tops of her breasts. That a father should stare at a daughter as I stared at her was plainly wicked.

"Ah, you think you know so much," she said, obviously referring to the conversation which in my general confusion I had all but forgot. "But you are like a priest, as my mother told me. You know only rules and ideas. Who told you that spirits are evil?"

"You misunderstand. I do not say evil, I say dangerous. I say hostile to man perhaps, and impossible to control. I do not say hellish, I say unknown."

I could feel my tongue thick in my mouth. Yet still I continued. I explained to her that it was the teaching of the Catholic church that anything "unknown" was demonic, and that was the greatest difference between the Church and the Talamasca. It was upon that great difference that we had been founded long ago.

Again, I saw the boys were dancing. They whirled about the room, leaping, turning, appearing and reappearing at the windows. I blinked to clear my head.

"And what makes you think that I do not know this spirit intimately," said she, "and that I cannot control it? Do you really think that my mother did not control it? Can you not see that there is a progression here from Suzanne to Deborah to me?"

"I see it, yes, I see it. I saw the old man, did I not?" I said, but I was losing the thought. I could not form my words properly. And the remembrance of the old man upset my logic. I wanted the wine, but did not want it, and did not drink any more.

"Yes," she said, quickening it seemed, and taking the wineglass from me, thank God. "My mother did not know that Lasher could be sent into a person, though any priest might have told her demons possess humans all the time, though of course they do it to no avail."

362

"How so, no avail?"

"They must leave eventually; they cannot become that person, no matter how truly they want to become that person. Ah, if Lasher could become the old man . . ."

This horrified me, and I could see that she smiled at my horror, and she bid me sit down beside her. "What is it however that you truly mean to convey to me?" she pressed.

"My warning, that you give up this being, that you move away from it, that you not found your life upon its power, for it is a mysterious thing, and that you teach it no more. For it did not know it could go into a human until you taught it so, am I right?"

This gave her pause. She refused to answer.

"Ah, so you are teaching it to be a better demon for your sake!" I said. "Well, if Suzanne could have read the demonology shown her by the witch judge, she would have known you can send a demon into people. Deborah would have known had she read enough too. But ah, it must be left to you to teach it this thing so that the witch judge is upheld in the third generation! How much more will you teach it, this thing which can go into humans, create storms, and make a handsome phantom of itself in an open field?"

"How so? What do you mean phantom?" she asked.

I told her what I had seen at Donnelaith—the gauzy figure of the being among the ancient stones, and that I had known it was not real. At once I saw that nothing I had said so far caught her interest as this caught it.

"You saw it?" she asked me incredulously.

"Yes, indeed I did see it, and I saw her see it, your mother."

She whispered, "Ah, but he has never appeared thus to me." And then, "But do you see the error, for Suzanne, the simpleton, thought he was the dark man, the Devil as they call him, and so he was for her."

"But there was nothing monstrous in his appearance, rather he made himself a handsome man."

At this she gave a mischievous laugh, and her eyes flashed with sudden vitality. "So she imagined the Devil to be handsome and for her Lasher made himself handsome. For you see, all that he is proceeds from us."

"Perhaps, lady, perhaps." I looked at the empty glass. I was thirsty. But I would not be drunk again. "But perhaps not."

"Aye, and that is what makes it so interesting to me," she said. "That on its own it cannot think, do you not see? It cannot gather its thoughts together; it was the call of Suzanne which gathered it; it was the call of Deborah which concentrated it further, and gave it the purpose to raise the storm; and I have called it into the old man, and it delights in these tricks, and peers through his eyes at us as if it were human, and is much amused. Do you not see, I love this being for its changing, for its development, as it were.''

"Dangerous!" I whispered. "The thing is a liar."

"No, that is impossible. I thank you for your warnings, but they are so useless as to be laughable." Here she reached for the bottle and filled my glass again.

But I did not take it.

"Charlotte, I implore you . . ."

"Petyr," she said, "let me be plainspoken with you, for you deserve as much. We strive for many things in life; we struggle against many obstacles. The obstacle of Suzanne was her simple mind and her ignorance; of Deborah that she had been brought up a peasant girl in rags. Even in her castle, she was that frightened country lass always, counting Lasher as the sole cause of her fortune, and nothing else.

"Well, I am no village cunning woman, no frightened merry-begot, but a woman born to riches, and educated from the time I can remember, and given all that I could possibly desire. And now in my twenty-second year, already a mother and soon perhaps to be a widow, I rule in this place. I ruled before my mother gave to me all her secrets, and her great familiar, Lasher, and I mean to study this thing, and make use of it, and allow it to enhance my considerable strength.

"Now surely you understand this, Petyr van Abel, for we are alike, you and I, and with reason. You are strong as I am strong. Understand as well that I have come to love this spirit, love, do you hear me? For this spirit has become my will!"

"It killed your mother, beautiful daughter," I said. Whereupon I reminded her of all that was known of the trickery of the supernatural in tales and fables, and what the moral was: this thing cannot be fully understood by reason, and cannot by reason be ruled.

"My mother knew you for what you were," she said sadly, shaking her head, and offering me the wine which I did not take. "You of the Talamasca are as bad as the Catholics and the Calvinists, when all is said and done."

"No," I said to her. "Of a different ilk entirely. We draw our knowledge from observation and experience! We are of this age, and like unto its surgeons and physicians and philosophers, not the men of the cloth!"

"Which means what?" she sneered.

"The men of the cloth look to revelation, to Scripture as it were. When I tell you of the old tales of demons, it is to draw attention to a distilled knowledge! I do not say take the *Demonologie* on its face, for it is poison. I say read what is worthwhile and discard the rest.''

She gave no reply.

"You say you are educated, my daughter, well then consider my father, a surgeon at the University of Leiden, a man who went to Padua to study, and then to England to hear the lectures of William Harvey, who learned French that he might read the writings of Paré. Great doctors cast aside the 'scripture' of Aristotle and Galen. They learn from the dissection of dead bodies, and from the dissection of live animals! They learn from what they observe! That is our method. I am saying look at this thing, look at what it has done! I say that it brought down Deborah with its tricks. It brought down Suzanne.''

Silence.

"Ah, but you give me the means to study it better. You tell me to approach it as a doctor might approach it. And be done with incantations and the like.''

"Ah, for this I came here," I sighed.

"You have come here for better things than this," she said, and gave me a most devilish and charming smile. "Come now, let us be friends. Drink with me.''

"I would go to bed now.''

She gave a sweet laugh. "So would I," she said. "By and by.''

Again she pushed the glass at me, and so to be polite I took it and drank, and there came the drunkenness again as if it had been hovering like an imp in the bottle. "No more," I said.

"Oh, yes, my finest claret, you must drink it." And once again she pushed it at me.

"All right, all right," I said to her and drank.

Did I know, then, Stefan, what was to happen? Was I even then peering over the edge of the glass at her succulent little mouth and juicy little arms?

"Oh, sweet beautiful Charlotte," I said to her. "Do you know how I love you? We have spoken of love, but I have not told you . . .''

"I know," she whispered lovingly to me. "Don't upset yourself, Petyr. I know." She rose and took me by the arm.

"Look," I said to her, for it seemed the lights below were dancing in the trees, dancing as if they were fireflies, and the trees themselves seemed quite alive and to be watching us, and the night sky to rise higher and higher, its moonlit clouds rising beyond the stars.

"Come, dearest," she said, now pulling me down the stairs, for I tell you, Stefan, my limbs were weakened by the wine. I was stumbling.

A low music had meantime commenced, if one could call it that, for it was made up entirely of African drums, and some eerie and mournful horn playing which I found I liked and then did not like at all.

"Let me go, Charlotte," I said to her, for she was pulling me towards the cliffs. "I would go to bed now."

"Yes, and you shall."

"Then why do we go to the cliffs, my dear? You mean to throw me over the edge?"

She laughed. "You are so handsome in spite of all your propriety and your Dutch manners!" She danced in front of me, with her hair blowing in the breeze, a lithesome figure against the dark glittering sea.

Ah, such beauty. More beautiful even than my Deborah. I looked down and saw the glass was in my left hand, most strange, and she was filling it once more, and I was so thirsty for it that I drank it down as if it were ale.

Taking my arm once more, she pointed the way down a steep path, which led perilously close to the edge, but I could see a roof beyond and light and what seemed a whitewashed wall.

"Do you think I am ungrateful for what you've told me?" she said in my ear. "I am grateful. We must talk more of your father, the physician, and of the ways of those men."

"I can tell you many things, but not so that you use them to do evil." I looked about me, stumbling still, and trying to see the slaves who played the drums and the horn, for surely they were very near. The music seemed to echo off the rocks and off the trunks of the trees.

"Ah, and so you do believe in evil!" She laughed. "You are a man of angels and devils, and you would be an angel, like the angel Michael who drove the devils into hell." She placed her arm about me so that I did not fall, her breasts crushed up against me, and her soft cheek touching my shoulder.

"I do not like that music," I said. "Why must they play it?"

"Oh, it makes them happy. The planters hereabouts do not think sufficiently about what makes them happy. If they did they would get more from them, but now we are back to observations, are we not? But come now, such pleasures await you," she told me.

"Pleasures? Oh, but I do not care for pleasures," I said, and my tongue was thick again and my head swimming and I could not get accustomed to the music.

"What on earth are you saying, you do not care for pleasures!" she scoffed. "How can one not care for pleasures?"

We had come to the small building, and I saw in the bright light of the moon that it was a house of sorts with the usual pitched roof, but that it was built to the very edge of the cliff. Indeed the light I had seen came from the front of it, which perhaps was open, but we could gain entrance only through a heavy door, which she did unbar from the outside.

She was still laughing at me, for what I had said, when I stopped her.

"What is this, a prison!"

"You are in prison, within your body," she said, and pushed me through the door.

I drew myself up and meant to go back out, but the door was shut and being bolted by others. I heard the bolt slide into place. I looked about me, in anger and confusion.

A spacious apartment I saw, with a great four-poster bed, fit for the king of England, though it was fitted out in muslin rather than velvet, and in the netting they use here to fend off the mosquitoes, and on either side of it burned candles. Rugs covered the tiled floor, and indeed the front of the little house was entirely open, its shutters back, but I soon saw why, for to walk even ten steps out was to come to a balustrade, and beyond that, I soon saw upon clumsy investigation, as she held my arm to steady me, was nothing but a great plunge to the beach below and the lapping sea.

"I do not care to spend the night here," I said to her, "and if you will not provide me with a coach, I shall walk to Port-au-Prince."

"Explain this to me, that you do not like pleasure," she said gently, tugging at my coat. "Surely you are hot in these miserable garments. Do all Dutchmen wear such clothes?"

"Stop those drums, will you?" I said. "I cannot bear the sound." For the music seemed to come through the walls. There was a melody to it now, however, and that was a slight bit reassuring, though the melody kept putting its hooks into me and dragging me with it mentally so that I was dancing in my head against my will.

And somehow or other I was now on the side of the bed, with Charlotte removing my shirt. On the table but a few feet away sat a silver tray with bottles of wine and fine glasses, and to this she went now, and poured a glass full of claret and brought this to me and put it in my hand. I went to dash it to the floor, but she held it, and looked into my eyes, and said:

"Petyr, drink a little only that you may sleep. When you wish to leave you may leave."

"You are lying to me," I said. Whereupon I felt other hands upon me, and other skirts brushing my legs. Two stately mulatto women had somehow managed to enter this chamber, both of them exquisitely pretty, and voluptuous in their freshly pressed skirts and ruffled blouses, moving with ease no doubt through the general fog which now shrouded all my perceptions, to pound the pillows, and straighten the netting of the bed, and take my boots from me and my trousers.

Hindu princesses they might have been with their dark eyes and dark eyelashes and dusky arms and innocent smiles.

"Charlotte, I will not have this," I said, yet I was drinking the wine, as she held it to my mouth, and again there came the swoon. "Oh, Charlotte, why, what is this?"

"Surely you want to observe pleasure," she whispered, stroking my hair in such a way that I was very disturbed by it. "I am quite serious. Listen to me. You must experiment with pleasure to be certain that you do not care for it, if you know what I mean."

"I don't. I wish to go."

"No, Petyr. Don't now," she said as if talking to a child.

She knelt before me, looking up at me, her dress binding her naked breasts so tightly that I wanted to free them. "Drink some more, Petyr," she said.

I shut my eyes, and at once lost my balance. The music of the drums and the horn was now slower and even more melodic, and put me in mind of madrigals though it was far more savage. Lips brushed my cheeks and my mouth, and when I opened my eyes in alarm, I saw the mulatto women were naked and offering themselves to me, for how else could their gestures be described?

At some remove Charlotte stood, with her hand upon the table, a picture in the stillness, though everything was now quite beyond my grasp. She seemed a statue against the dim blue light of the sky; the candles sputtered in the breeze; the music was as strong as ever, and I found myself lost in contemplating the two naked women, their huge breasts and their dark fleecy private hair.

It then came to me that in this warmth I did not mind at all being naked, which had seldom been the case in my life. It seemed quite fine to be naked, and that the women should be, and I fell into contemplating their various secrets, and how they differed from other women, and how all women were alike.

One of them kissed me again, her hair and skin very silky against me, and this time I opened my mouth.

368

But by then, you know, Stefan, I was a lost man.

I was now covered with kisses by these two and laid back on the pillows, and there was no part of my anatomy which did not receive their skilled attentions, and each gesture was prolonged and rendered all the more exquisite in my drunkenness. And so loving and cheerful they seemed, the two women, so innocent, and the silkiness of their skin was maddening me.

I knew that Charlotte watched these proceedings but that did not seem of importance any longer, so much as kissing these women and touching them all over as they touched me, for the potion I had drunk was working no doubt to remove all restraint and yet to slow down the natural rhythm of a man under such circumstances, as there seemed all the time in the world.

The room grew darker; the music more soothing. I grew more impassioned, slowly, deliciously, and completely consumed by sensations of the most extraordinary sort. One of the women, very ripe and yielding in my arms, showed me now a band of black silk, and as I puzzled what this could be, this broad ribbon, she put it over my eyes, and the other tied it tight behind my head.

How can I explain how this sudden bondage fanned the flame in me, how, blindfolded like Cupid, I lost whatever decency remained to me, as we tumbled together in the bed?

In this intoxicating darkness, I finally mounted my victim, feeling my hands fall gently upon a great mass of hair.

A mouth sucked at me, and strong arms drew me down into a veritable field of soft breasts and belly and sweet perfumed female flesh, and as I cried out in my passion, a lost soul, unquestioning, the blindfold was ripped from me, and I looked down in the dim light to see the face of Charlotte beneath me, her eyes closed demurely, her lips parted, and her face flushed with an ecstasy equal to my own.

There was no one but the two of us in this bed! No one, I saw, but the two of us in this little house.

Like a madman I was up and away from her. But it had been done. I had reached the very edge of the cliff, when she came after me.

"What would you do!" she cried miserably. "Jump into the sea!"

I could not answer her but clung to her lest I fall. If she had not pulled me back, I would have fallen. And all I could think was, this is my daughter, my daughter! What have I done?

Yet when I knew it, my daughter, and repeated it, my daughter, and looked full in the face of it, I found myself turning to her, and catching hold of her, and bringing her to me. Would I punish her with kisses? How could rage and passion be so melded? I have never been a soldier in a siege but are they so inflamed when they tear the garments from their screaming female captives?

I only knew I would crush her in my lust. And as she threw back her head and sighed, I whispered "My daughter." I buried my face in her naked breasts.

It was as if I had never spent my passion, so great was it then. Into the room she dragged me, for I would have taken her in the sand. My roughness held no fear for her. She pulled me down onto the bed, and never since that night in Amsterdam with Deborah have I known such release. Nay, I was not even checked by the tenderness I knew then.

"You foul little witch," I cried out to her. And she took it like kissing. She writhed on the bed beneath me, rising to meet me, as I came down upon her.

At last I fell back into the pillow. I wished to die, and to have her again at once.

Twice more before dawn, I took her surely unless I had gone completely mad. But I was so drunk then I scarce knew what I did, except that all I had ever wanted in a woman was there for the taking.

Close to morning, I remember that I did lie with her, and study her, as if to know her and her beauty, for she was sleeping, and nothing came between me and my observations—ah, yes, I thought bitterly on her mockery of me, but that is what they were, Stefan, observations—and I learnt more of a woman I suppose in that hour than ever in my entire life.

How lovely in its youth was her body, how firm and sweet to the touch her young limbs and her fresh skin. I did not want her to wake and look at me with the wise and cunning eyes of Charlotte. I wanted to weep that all this had taken place.

It seemed she did wake and that we talked for a while, but I remember more truly the things I saw than the words we spoke.

She was again plying me with her drink, her poison, and had added to the mix an even greater inducement, for now she seemed deep and saddened and more eager than ever to know my thoughts. As she sat there with her golden hair falling all about her, the Lady Godiva of the English, she puzzled again that I had seen Lasher in the stone circle in Donnelaith.

And it seemed the trick of the potion now, Stefan, that I was there! For I heard the creaking of the cart once more, and saw my precious little Deborah, and in the distance the thin image of the dark man.

"Ah, but you see, it was to Deborah that he meant to appear," I heard myself explain, "and that I saw him proves only that anyone could see him, that he had gathered by some mysterious means a physical shape."

"Aye, and how did he do it?"

And once more I pulled out of the archive of my head the teachings of the ancients. "If this thing can gather jewels for you . . ."

"—that he does."

"—then he can gather tiny particles to create a human shape."

Then in a twinkling, I found myself in Amsterdam in bed with my Deborah, and all her words to me of that night were spoken again, as if I stood with her in the very room. And all this I then told to my daughter, the witch in my arms, who poured the wine for me, whom I meant to take a thousand times before I should be released.

"But if you know then that I am your father, why did you do this?" I asked, while at the same time seeking to kiss her again.

She held me off as she might hold off her child. "I need your height and your strength, Father. I need a child by you—a son that will not inherit Antoine's illness, or a daughter that will see Lasher, for Lasher will not show himself to a man." She considered for a moment and then said to me: "And you see, you are not merely a man to me, but a man bound to me by blood."

So it was all planned.

"But there is more to it," she said. "Do you know what it is to me to feel a true man with his arms about me?" she asked. "To feel a true man on top of me? And why should it not be my father, if my father is the most pleasing of all the men I have ever seen?"

I thought of you, Stefan. I thought of your warnings to me. I thought of Alexander. Was he at this moment mourning for me still in the Motherhouse?

Surely I shed tears, for I remember her comforting me, and how touching was her distress. Then she did cling to me, like a child herself curled beside me, and said that we two knew things that no one else had ever known save Deborah and Deborah was dead. She cried then. She cried for Deborah.

"When she came to me and told me that she was dead, I wept and wept. I could not stop weeping. And they beat on the doors and said, 'Charlotte, come out.' I had not seen him or known him until that moment. My mother had said: 'Put on the emerald necklace, and by its light he will find you.' But he did not need that thing. I know it now. I was lying in the darkness alone when he came to me. I will tell you a terrible secret. Until that mo-

371

ment I did not believe in him! I did not. I had held the little doll she gave me, the doll of her mother . . ."

"It was described to me in Montcleve."

"Now that is made of the bone and the hair of Suzanne, or so my mother claimed it was, for Lasher, she said, had brought the hair to her after they cut it from Suzanne in prison, and the bone after she was burnt. And from this she had made the doll as Suzanne had told her to do, and she would hold it and call upon Suzanne.

"Now, I had this, and I had done as she had instructed me. But Suzanne didn't come to me! I heard nothing and felt nothing, and I wondered about all the things which my mother had believed.

"Then he came, as I told you. I felt him come in the darkness, I felt his caress."

"How so, caress?"

"Touching me as you have touched me. I lay in the darkness, and there were lips upon my breasts. Lips upon my lips. Between my legs he stroked me. I rose up, thinking, Ah well, this is a dream, a dream of when Antoine was still a man. But *he was there*! 'You have no need of Antoine,' he said to me. 'My beautiful Charlotte.' And then, you see, I put on the emerald. I put it on as she had told me to do."

"He told you that she was dead?"

"Aye, that she had fallen from the cathedral battlements, and that you had thrown the evil priest to his death. Ah, but he speaks most strangely. You cannot imagine how strange his words are. As if he had picked them up from all over the world the way he picks up bits and pieces of jewels and gold."

"Tell me," I said to her.

She thought. "I cannot," she said with a sigh. Then she tried it, and now I shall do my best to recount it. " 'I am here, Charlotte, I am Lasher, and I am here. The spirit of Deborah went up out of her body; it did not see me; it left the earth. Her enemies ran to the left and to the right and to the left in fear. See me, Charlotte, and hear me, for I exist to serve you, and only in serving you, do I exist.' " She gave another sigh. "But it is even stranger than that when he tells me a long tale. For I questioned him as to what happened to my mother and he said, 'I came and I drew together, and I lifted the tiles of the roofs and made them fly through the air. And I lifted the dirt from the ground and made it fly through the air.' "

"And what else does this spirit say as to his own nature?"

"Only that he always was. Before there were men and women, he was."

"Ah, and you believe this?"

"Why should I not believe it?"

I did not answer her, but in my soul I did not believe it, and I did not know why.

"How did he come to be near the stones of Donnelaith?" I asked her. "For that was where Suzanne first called him, was it not?"

"He was nowhere when she called him; he came into being at her call. That is to say, he has no knowledge of himself before that time. His knowledge of himself begins with her knowledge of him, and strengthens with mine."

"Ah, but you see this could be flattery," I said to her.

"You speak of him as if he were without feeling. That isn't so. I tell you I have heard him weep."

"Over what, pray tell?"

"The death of my mother. If she had allowed it, he could have destroyed all the citizenry of Montcleve. The innocent and the guilty would have been punished. But my mother could not imagine such a thing. My mother sought only her release when she threw herself from the battlements. Had she been stronger . . ."

"And you are stronger."

"Using his powers for destruction is nothing."

"Aye, in that I think you are wise, I have to confess."

I puzzled over all of it, trying to memorize what was said which I believe I have done. And perhaps she understood, for next she said sadly to me:

"Ah, how can I allow you to leave this place when you know these things of him and of me?"

"So you would kill me?" I asked her.

She wept. She turned her head into the pillow. "Stay with me," she said. "My mother asked this of you, and you refused her. Stay with me. By you I could have strong children."

"I am your father. You are mad to ask this of me."

"What does it matter!" she declared. "All around us there is nothing but darkness and mystery. What does it matter?" And her voice filled me with sadness.

It seemed I too was weeping, but more quietly. I kissed her cheeks and soothed her. I told her what we had come to believe in the Talamasca, that, with or without God, we must be honest men and women, that we must be saints, for only as saints can we prevail. But she merely cried all the more sadly.

"All your life has been in vain," she said. "You have wasted it. You have forsworn pleasure and for nothing."

"Ah, but you miss the depths," I said. "For my reading and

my study have been my pleasures, as surgery and study were the pleasures for my father, and these pleasures are lasting. I do not need the pleasure of the flesh. I never did. I do not need riches, and therefore I am free.''

"Are you lying to me or to yourself? You are afraid of the flesh. The Talamasca offered safety to you as convents offer it to nuns. You have always done what is safe . . .''

"Was it safe for me to go into Donnelaith, or safe for me to go to Montcleve?''

"No, you were brave in that, true. And brave I suppose to come here. But I speak not of that part of you but the private, secret part of you which might have known love and known passion and shrank from it for fear of it, disliking the very heat. You must realize that sin such as we have committed tonight can only strengthen us and cause us to grow more solitary and willful and cold towards others as if our secrets were shields.''

"But my dearest,'' I said, "I do not want to be solitary and willful and cold towards others. I am that enough already when I go into the towns where witches are to be burnt. I want my soul to be in harmony with other souls. And this sin has made of me a monster in my eyes.''

"And so what, then, Petyr?''

"I don't know,'' I said. "I don't know. But you are my daughter all right. You think about what you do, that much I give you. You ponder and you consider. But you do not suffer enough!''

"And why should I?'' She gave the most innocent laugh. "Why should I!'' she cried out, staring right into my face.

And unable to answer that question, sick to death of my guilt, and of this drunkenness, I fell into a deep sleep.

Before dawn I awakened.

The morning sky filled with great pink-tinged clouds, and the roar of the sea was a wondrous sound. Charlotte was nowhere about. I could see that the door to the outside world was shut, and I knew without testing it that it was bolted from the outside. As for the small windows in the walls on either side of me, they were not large enough to allow a child to escape. Slatted shutters covered them now, through which the breeze ran, singing; and the little room was filled with the fresh air of the sea.

Dazed I stared out at the brightening light. I wanted to be back in Amsterdam, though I felt tainted beyond reprieve. And as I tried to rouse myself, to ignore the sickness in my head and belly, I perceived a ghostly shape standing to the left of the open doors, in the shady corner of the room.

For a long time, I considered it, whether it was not some product of the drug I had imbibed, or indeed of the light and the shadow playing together; but it was not. A man it appeared to be, tall, and dark of hair, and gazing down upon me as I lay there, and wanting to speak or so it seemed.

"Lasher," I whispered aloud.

"Fool of a man that you should come here," said the being. But its lips did not move and I did not hear this voice through the ears. "Fool that you should seek to come between me and the witch whom I love, once again."

"And what did you do with my precious Deborah?"

"You know but you do not know."

I laughed. "Should I be honored that you pass judgment on me?" I sat up in my bed. "Show yourself more plainly," I said.

And before my eyes, the shape grew denser and more vivid, and I saw the aspects of a particular man. Thin of nose, dark of eye, and dressed in the very same garments I had spied for but an instant years ago in Scotland, a leather jerkin and coarse-cut breeches, and a homespun shirt of bag sleeves.

Yet even as I surmised these things, it seemed that the nose became plainer, and the dark eyes more vivid, and the leather of the jerkin more plainly leather.

"Who are you, spirit?" I asked. "Tell me your true name, not the name my Deborah gave you."

A terrible bitter expression came over its face; or no, it was only that the illusion had begun to crumple, and the air was filled with lamentation, a terrible soundless crying. And the thing faded away.

"Come back, spirit!" I declared. "Or more truly, if you love Charlotte, go away! Go back into the chaos from which you came and leave my Charlotte alone."

And I could have sworn that in a whisper the being spoke again to say, "I am patient, Petyr von Abel. I see very far. I shall drink the wine and eat the meat and know the warmth of the woman when you are no longer even bones."

"Come back!" I cried. "Tell me the meaning of this! I saw you, Lasher, as clearly as the witch saw you, and I can make you strong."

But there was only silence. And I fell back upon the pillow, knowing that this was the strongest spirit I have ever beheld. No ghost has ever been stronger, more truly visible. And the words spoken to me by the demon had nothing to do with the will of the witch.

Oh, if only I had my books with me. If only I had had them then.

Once more in my mind's eye I see the circle of stones at Donnelaith. I tell you there is some reason that the spirit came from that spot! This is no mean daimon, no familiar, no Ariel ready to bow to Prospero's wand! So feverish was I finally that I drank the wine again so that it would dull my pain.

And so there, Stefan, you have but the first day of my captivity and wretchedness.

How well I came to know the little house. How well I was to know the cliff beyond from which no path led down to the beach. Even if I had had a seaman's rope, wrapped about the balustrade, I could not have made that awful descent.

But let me go on with my tale.

It was noon perhaps before Charlotte came to me, and when I saw the mulatto maids enter with her I knew that I had not created them out of my imagination, and only watched them in cold silence as they put fresh flowers about the room. They had my shirt clean and ironed for me and more clothing, of the lighter fabrics worn in these places. And a large tub they brought, sliding it across the sandy earth like a boat, with two heavily muscled male slaves to guard them lest I rush out the door.

This they filled with hot water, and said that I might have a bath whenever I chose.

I took it, hoping to wash away my sins, I guess, and then when I was clean and dressed and my beard and mustache properly trimmed, I sat down and ate the food given me without looking at Charlotte who alone remained.

Finally, putting the plate aside, I asked: "How long do you mean to keep me in this place?"

"Until I have conceived a child by you," she said. "And I may have a sign of that very soon."

"Well, you have had your chance," I said, but even as the words came out, I felt last night's lust again, and saw myself, as if in a dream, ripping her pretty silk frock from her and tearing loose her breasts again so that I might suckle them savagely as a babe. There came again the delicious idea that she was wicked and therefore I might do anything to her and with her, and I should avail myself of that opportunity as soon as I could.

She knew. Undoubtedly she knew. She came and sat on my lap, and looked into my eyes. A very tender little weight indeed. "Rip the silk if you like," she said. "You cannot get out of here. So do what you can in your prison."

I reached for her throat. At once I was thrown back upon the floor. The chair was turned over. Only she had not done it, she had merely moved aside so as not to be hurt.

"Ah, so he is here," I said with a sigh. I could not see him, but then again I could, a gathering as it were just over me, and then the dispersal as the billowy presence grew broader and thinner and then disappeared. "Make yourself a man as you did this morning," I said. "Speak to me as you did this morning, little coward, little spirit!"

All the silver in the place began to rattle. A great ripple ran through the mosquito netting. I laughed. "Stupid little devil," I said, climbing to my feet and brushing off my clothes. The thing struck me again, but I caught the back of the chair. "Mean little devil," I said. "And such a coward, too."

Amazed, she watched all this. I could not tell what it was in her face, suspicion or fear. Then she whispered something under her breath, and I saw the netting hung from the windows move as though the thing had flown out. We were alone.

She turned her face away from me, but I could see her cheeks burning, and see the tears in her eyes. She looked so tender then. I hated myself for wanting her.

"Surely you do not blame me for trying to hurt you," I said politely to her. "You hold me here against my will."

"Don't challenge him again," she said fearfully, her lip trembling. "I would not have him hurt you."

"Oh, and cannot the powerful witch restrain him?"

Lost she seemed, clinging to the bedpost, her head bowed. And so beguiling! So seductive! She did not need to be a witch to be a witch.

"You want me," she said softly. "Take me. And I shall tell you something that will warm your blood better than any drug I can give you." Here she looked up, her lip trembling as if she would cry.

"What is that?" I said to her.

"That I want you," she said. "I find you beautiful. I find I ache for you as I lie beside Antoine."

"Your misfortune, daughter," I said coldly, but what a lie. "Is it?"

"Steel yourself. Remember that a man does not have to find a woman beautiful to ravage her. Be as cold as a man. It suits you better, for you hold me here against my will."

She said nothing for a moment, and then she came towards me and began her seduction again, with soft daughterly kissing, and then her hand seeking me out, and her kisses growing more ardent. And I was just as much a fool as before.

Only my anger would not permit it, so I fought her. "Does your spirit like it?" I asked, looking up and around in the emptiness. "That you let me touch you when he would touch you?"

"Don't play with him!" she said fearfully.

"Ah, for all his touching of you, caressing of you, kissing of you, he cannot get you with child, can he? He is not the incubus

377

of the demonologies who can steal the seed from sleeping men. And so he suffers me to live until I get you with child!''

"He will not hurt you, Petyr, for I will not allow it. I have forbidden it!''

Her cheeks grew red again as she looked at me, and now she searched the emptiness around her.

"Keep that thought in your mind, daughter, for he can read what you think, remember. And he may tell you that he does what you wish, but he does what he wishes. He came to me this morning; he taunted me.''

"Don't lie to me, Petyr.''

"I never lie, Charlotte. He came.'' And I described to her the full apparition, and I confessed his strange words. "Now, what can that mean, my pretty? You think he has no will of his own? You are a fool, Charlotte. Lie with him instead of me!'' I laughed at her, and seeing the pain in her eyes, I laughed more. "I should like to see it, you and your daimon. Lie there and call him to come now.''

She struck me. I laughed all the more, the sting feeling sweet to me, suddenly, and again she slapped me, and again, and then I had what I wanted, which was the rage to take hold of her by her wrists and hurl her onto the bed. And there I tore loose her dress and the ribbons binding her hair. With the fine clothes her maids had put on me, she was just as rough, and we were together in it as hot as before.

Finally it was over three times, and as I lay in half sleep, she left me in silence, with only the roar of the sea to keep me company.

By late afternoon, I knew that I could not get out of the house, for I had tried. I had tried to batter down the door, using the one chair in the place to help me. I had tried to climb around the edges of the walls. I had tried to fit through the small windows. All in vain. This place had been carefully made as a prison. I tried even to get up on the roof, but that too had been studied and provided for. The slope was impossibly steep, and the tiles slippery, and the climb far too long and too great. And as twilight came, a supper was brought to me, being put, plate by plate, through one of the small windows, which after a long hesitation, I did take, more out of boredom and near madness than hunger.

And as the sun sank in the sea, I sat by the balustrade, drinking wine and looking at it, and looking at the dark blue of the waves, as they broke with their white foam upon the clean beach below.

No one ever came or went there on the beach in all my captivity. I suspect that it is a spot which could be reached only by sea. And anyone reaching it would have died there, for there was no way up the cliff, as I have said.

But it was most beautiful to look at. And getting drunker and drunker I fell into watching the colors of the sea and the light change, as if in a spell.

When the sun had vanished, a great fiery layer lay upon the horizon from end to end of the world. That lasted perhaps an hour and then the sky was but a pale pink and at last a deep blue, blue as the sea.

I resolved, naturally, that I should not touch Charlotte again, no matter what the provocation, and that finding me useless to her she would soon allow me to go. But I suspected that she would indeed kill me, or that the spirit would kill me. And that she could not stop him, I did not doubt.

I do not know when I fell to sleep. Or how late it was when I awoke and saw that Charlotte had come, and was seated inside by the candle. I roused myself to pour another glass of wine, for I was now completely taken up with drinking, and conceived an insupportable thirst within minutes of the last drink.

I said nothing to her, but I was frightened by the beauty she held for me, and that at the very first sight of her, my body had quickened and wanted her, and expected the old games to begin. I gave myself stern lectures in silence; but my body is no schoolboy.

It laughed in my face, so to speak. And I shall never forget the expression on her face as she looked at me, and looked into my heart.

I went to her, as she came to me. And this affection humiliated us both.

Finally when we were finished with it again, and sitting quietly, she began to talk to me.

"There are no laws for me," she said. "Men and women are not merely cursed with weaknesses. Some of us are cursed with virtues as well. And my virtue is strength. I can rule those around me. I knew it when I was a child. I ruled my brothers, and when my mother was accused, I begged to remain in Montcleve, for I felt certain I could turn their testimony to her side.

"But she would not allow it, and she I never could rule. I rule my husband and have from our first meeting. I rule the house so skillfully that the other planters remark upon it, and come to me for advice. One might say that I rule the parish, as I am the richest planter in it, and I could rule the colony perhaps if I chose.

"I have always had this strength, and I see that you too have it. It is the strength which enables you to defy all civil and church authority, to go into villages and towns with a pack of lies, and believe in what you do. You have submitted to but one authority on earth, and that is the Talamasca, and you are not entirely in submission even to them.''

I had never thought of this, but it was true. You know, Stefan, we have members who cannot do the work in the field for they haven't the skepticism regarding pomp and ceremony. And so she was right.

I did not tell her so, however. I drank the wine, and looked out over the sea. The moon had risen and made a path across it. I wondered that I had spent so little time in my life regarding the sea.

It seemed I had been a long time on the edge of this cliff in my little prison, and there was nothing remarkable about it now.

She continued to talk to me. ''I have come to the very place in which my strength can be best used,'' she said. ''And I mean to have many children before Antoine dies. I mean to have many! If you remain with me as my lover, there is nothing that you cannot have.''

''Don't say such things. You know that cannot be.''

''Consider it. Envision it. You learn by observation. Well, what have you learned by observing things here? I could make a house for you on my land, a library as large as you like. You could receive your friends from Europe. You could have whatever you wish.''

I thought for a long time before I answered, as this was her request.

''I need more than what you offer me,'' I said. ''Even if I could accept that you are my daughter and that we are outside the laws of nature, so to speak.''

''What laws,'' she sneered.

''Allow me to finish and then I shall tell you,'' I explained. ''I need more than the pleasures of the flesh, and even more than the beauty of the sea, and more than my every wish granted. I need more than money.''

''Why?''

''Because I am afraid of death,'' I said. ''I believe nothing, and therefore like many who believe nothing, I must make something, and that something is the meaning which I give to my life. The saving of witches, the study of the supernatural, these are my lasting pleasures; they make me forget that I do not know why we are born, or why we die, or why the world is here.

''Had my father not died, I would have been a surgeon, and studied the workings of the body, and made beautiful drawings of my studies as he did. And had not the Talamasca found me after my father's death, I might have been a painter, for they make worlds of meaning on the canvas. But I cannot be those things now, as I have no training in them, and it is too late for that, and so I must return to Europe and do what I have always done. I must. It is not a matter of choice. I should go mad in this savage place. I should come to hate you more than I already do."

This greatly intrigued her, though it hurt her and disappointed her. Her face took on the look of soft tragedy as she studied me, and never did my heart go out to her so much as it did at that moment, when she heard my answer and sat there pondering it before me, without a word.

"Talk to me," she said. "Tell me all your life."

"I will not!"

"Why?"

"Because you want it, and you hold me against my will."

She thought again in silence, her eyes very beautiful in their sadness as before.

"You came here to sway me and to teach me, did you not?"

I smiled at her, for it was true. "All right, then, daughter. I'll tell you everything I know. Will it do the trick?"

And at that moment, on my second day in this prison, it was changed, changed until the very hour many days later when I went free. I did not yet realize it, but it was changed.

For after that, I fought her no more. And I fought no more my love for her, and my lust for her, which were not always mingled, but always very much alive.

Whatever happened in the days that followed, we talked together by the hour, I in my drunkenness and she in her pointed sobriety, and all the story of my life came out for her to examine and discuss and a great deal which I knew of the world.

It seemed then that my life was nothing but drunkenness, making love to her, and talking to her; and then those long periods of dreaminess in which I continued my studies of the changing sea.

Some time and I do not know how long it was after—perhaps five days, perhaps more—she brought pen and paper to me and asked that I write for her what I knew of my lineage—of my father's people, and how he had come to be a physician as was his father, and how they had both studied at Padua, and what they had learnt and written. And the names of my father's books.

This I did with pleasure, though I was drunk so much that it took me hours, and after I lay, trying to remember my former self as she took my writing away.

Meantime, she had had fine clothes made for me, and she had her maids dress me each day, though I lay now indifferent to such things, and in a similar indifference I allowed them to pare my fingernails and trim my hair.

I suspected nothing in this, only that it was their regular meticulous attention to which I had become accustomed, but she then revealed to me a cloth mannequin made from the shirt I had worn when I first came to her, and explained to me that within its various knots were my fingernails, and that the hair affixed to its head was my hair.

I was stuporous then, as she had planned, no doubt. And in silence I watched as she slit my finger with her knife, and let my blood fall into the body of this doll. Nay, all of it she stained with my blood until it was a red thing with blond hair.

"What do you mean to do with this hideous thing?" I asked her.

"You know what I mean to do," she said.

"Ah, then my death is assured."

"Petyr," she said most imploringly, the tears springing to her eyes, "it may be years before you die, but this doll gives me power."

I said nothing. When she had gone I took up the rum which had always been there for me, and which was naturally much stronger than the wine, and I drank myself into horrid dreams with that.

But late in the night, this little incident of the doll produced in me a great horror, and so I went once more to the table, and took up my pen, and wrote for her all I knew of daimons, and this time it was with no hope of warning her, so much as guiding her.

I felt she must know that:

—the ancients had believed in spirits as we do, but they believed that they might grow old and die away; and there was in Plutarch the story of the Great Pan dying finally and all the daimons of the world weeping for they realized they would one day die as well.

—when a people of ancient times were conquered, it was believed that their fallen gods became daimons and hovered about the ruins of their cities and temples. And she must remember that Suzanne had called up the daimon Lasher at the ancient stones in Scotland, though what people had assembled those stones no one knows.

—the early Christians believed that the pagan gods were daimons, and that they could be called up for curses and spells.

And that in summary, all of these beliefs have to them a consistency, for we know that daimons are strengthened by our belief in them. So naturally, they might become as gods to those who invoke them, and when their worshipers are conquered and scattered, the daimons would once more lapse back into chaos, or be but minor entities answering the occasional magician's call.

I wrote further about the power of daimons. That they can create illusions for us; that they can enter bodies as in possession; that they can move objects; that they can appear to us, though whence they gather their bodies we do not know.

As for Lasher, it was my belief that his body was made of matter and held together by his power, but this could only be done by him for a short spell.

I did further describe how the daimon had appeared to me, and the strange words he said to me, and how I had puzzled over them, and how she must be aware that this thing might be the ghost of some long dead person—earthbound and vengeful, for all the ancients believed that the spirits of those who died in youth, or by violence, might become vengeful daimons, whereas the spirits of the good go out of this world.

Whatever else I wrote—and there was much—I no longer now remember, for I was utterly given over to drunkenness, and perhaps what I placed into her tender hands the next day was no more than a sorry scrawl. But many things I did attempt to explain to her, over her protests, though she claimed I had said them all before.

As for Lasher's words to me that morning, his strange prediction, she only smiled at this, and told me whenever I did mention it, that Lasher took his speech from us in fragments and much that he said did not make sense.

"That is only partly true," I warned her. "He is unaccustomed to language, but not to thinking. That is your mistake."

More and more as the days passed, I gave myself over to the rum and to sleeping. I would open my eyes only to see if she was there.

And just when I was maddened by her absence, nay, ready to beat her in a rage, she would appear without fail. Beautiful, yielding, soft in my arms, the embodiment of all poetry, the very face I would endlessly paint were I Rembrandt, the very body the Succubus would take to win me to the Devil complete and entire.

I was satiated in all ways, yet always craving for more. I did crawl from bed now and then to watch the sea. And I woke often to see and study the falling of the rain.

For the rain in this place was most warm and gentle, and I

loved the song of it on the rooftop, and the sheet of it, catching the light as the breeze carried it at an angle past the doors.

Many thoughts came to me, Stefan, thoughts nourished by loneliness and warmth and the singing of the birds in the distance and the sweet fresh air from the waves roaring gently on the beach below.

In my little prison, I knew what I had wasted in life, but it is so simple and sad to put it into words. At times I fancied myself mad Lear on the moors, putting the flowers in his hair, having become king of nothing but the wilderness.

For I, in this savage place, had become so simplified, the grateful scholar of the rain and of the sea.

At last one afternoon late when the light was just dying, I was wakened by the savory aroma of a hot supper, and I knew that I had been drunk for a full day round the clock, and that she had not come.

I devoured the supper, as liquor never stops my hunger, and then I dressed in fresh clothes, and sat to thinking of what had become of me, and trying to calculate how long I had been in this place.

I thought it was twelve days.

I resolved then that no matter how despondent I became, I would drink nothing further. That I must be released or go mad.

And feeling disgust for all my weakness, I put on my boots, which I had not touched in all this time, and the new coat brought to me long ago by Charlotte, and went to the balustrade to look out over the sea. I thought, surely she will kill me rather than let me go. But it must be known one way or the other. This I can no longer endure.

Many hours passed; I drank nothing. Then Charlotte came. She was weary from her long day of riding and tending to the plantation, and when she saw that I was dressed, when she saw that I wore my boots and my coat, she sank down into the chair and wept.

I said nothing, for surely it was her decision whether or not I should leave this place, not mine.

Then she said: "I have conceived; I am with child."

Again, I made no answer. But I knew it. I knew that it was the reason she had been away for so long.

Finally when she would do nothing but sit there, dejected, and sad, with her head down, crying, I said:

"Charlotte, let me go."

At last she said that I must swear to her to leave the island at once. And that I must not tell anyone what I knew of her or her mother or of anything that had passed between us.

"Charlotte," I said, "I will go home to Amsterdam on the first Dutch ship I can find in the harbor, and you will see me no more."

"But you must swear to tell no one—not even your brethren in the Talamasca."

"They know," I said. "And I shall tell them all that has taken place. They are my father and my mother."

"Petyr," she said. "Haven't you the good sense even to lie to me?"

"Charlotte," I said. "Either let me go or kill me now."

Again, she wept, but I felt cold towards her, cold towards myself. I would not look at her, lest my passion be aroused again.

At last she dried her eyes. "I have made him swear that he will never harm you. He knows that I shall withdraw all love and trust from him if he disobeys my command."

"You have made a pact with the wind," I said.

"But he protests that you will tell our secrets."

"That I shall."

"Petyr, give me your pledge! Give it to me so that he can hear."

I considered this, for I wanted so to be free of this place, and to live, and to believe that both were still possible, and finally I said:

"Charlotte, I will never do you harm. My brothers and sisters in the Talamasca are not priests or judges. Nor are they witches. What they know of you is secret in the true sense."

She looked at me with sad tear-filled eyes, and then she came to me, and kissed me, and though I tried to make of myself a wooden statue, I could not do it.

"Once more, Petyr, once more, from your heart," she said, her voice full of sorrow, and longing. "And then you may leave me forever, and I will never look into your eyes again until I look some day into the eyes of our child."

I fell to kissing her again, for I believed her that she would let me go. I believed her that she did love me; and I believed for that last hour as we lay together, that perhaps there were no laws for us, as she had said, and that there was a love between us which perhaps no one else would ever understand.

"I love you, Charlotte," I whispered to her as she lay beside me, and I kissed her forehead. But she would not answer. She would not look at me.

And as I dressed once more, she turned her face into the pillow and cried.

Going to the door, I discovered that it had never been bolted behind her, and I wondered how many times that had been the case.

But it did not matter now. What mattered was that I go, if that damnable spirit would not stop me, and that I not look back, or speak to her again, or catch the scent of her sweetness, or think about the soft touch of her lips or her hand.

And on this account I asked her for no horse or coach to take me into Port-au-Prince, but resolved that I should simply leave without a word.

It had been an hour's ride out and so I fancied that it not being yet midnight I should easily make the city by dawn. Oh, Stefan, thanks be to God, I did not know what that journey would be! Would I have ever had the courage to set out!

But let me break my story here, to say that for twelve hours I have been scribbling. And now it is midnight once more, and the thing is near.

For that reason I shall shut up in my iron box this and all the other pages I have written, so that at least this much of my tale will reach you, if what I write from here on is lost.

I love you, my dear friend, and I do not expect your forgiveness. Only keep my record. Keep it, for this story is not finished and may not be for many a generation. I have that from the spirit's own voice.

Yours in the Talamasca,

Petyr van Abel
Port-au-Prince

Sixteen

THE FILE ON THE MAYFAIR WITCHES

PART IV

Stefan,
After a bit of refreshment, I begin again. The thing is here. Only a moment ago, it made itself visible, in its manly guise,

an inch from me, as is its wont, and then caused my candle to go out, though it had no breath of its own with which to do it.

I had to go downstairs to procure another light. Coming back I found my windows open and flapping in the breeze, and had to bolt them again. My ink was spilt. But I have more ink. The covers had been snatched from the bed, and my books had been scattered about.

Thank God the iron box is on its way to you. Enough said, for perhaps the thing can read.

It makes the sound of wings flapping in this close space, and then laughter.

I wonder if far away in her bedroom at Maye Faire Charlotte sleeps, and that is why I am the victim of these tricks.

Only the bawdy houses and taverns are open; all the rest of the little colonial city is quiet.

But let me relate the events of last night as fast as I can . . .

. . . I started out upon the road on foot. The moon was high; the path was clear before me with all its twists and turns, rising and falling gently here and there over what we would scarce call hills.

I walked fast, with great vigor, all but giddy with my freedom, and the realization that the spirit had not stopped me, and that I was smelling the sweet air around me, and thinking that I might make Port-au-Prince well before dawn.

I am alive, I thought; I am out of my prison; and perhaps I shall live to reach the Motherhouse again!

With each step I believed it all the more, and wondered at it, for during my captivity I had given up all hope of such a thing.

Again and again, however, my mind was overtaken by thoughts of Charlotte, as though a spell had fallen over me, and I remembered her in the bed where I had left her, and I weakened, thinking even that I was a fool to leave such beauty and such excitement, for indeed I loved her; I loved her madly! And what would it mean, I wondered, were I to remain and become her lover, and see the birth of one child after another, and live in luxury as she had suggested to me? That I should within a matter of hours be separated from her forever was more than I could endure.

So I would not think on it. I drove the thoughts from my mind whenever I became aware that they had once more stolen in.

On and on I walked. Now and then I spied a light over the darkened fields on either side of me. And once a rider passed, thundering along the road, as if driven on an important mission. He did not even see me. And I continued alone, with only the moon and the stars for witnesses, and plotted out my letter to you and how I would describe what had taken place.

I had been on my way perhaps three-quarters of an hour when I saw a man at some distance ahead of me, merely standing and watching me approach, so it seemed. And what was so remarkable was that he was a Dutchman, which I saw by his enormous black hat.

Now, my hat I had left behind me. I had worn it as always when I had come to Maye Faire, but had not seen it from the time I gave it up to the slaves before supper on my first night.

And now as I saw this tall man ahead of me I thought of it, and lamented it, and wondered also who was this Dutchman standing by the side of the road, facing me and staring at me, it seemed, a shadowy thing with blond hair and a blond beard.

I slowed my pace, for as I approached, the figure did not move, and the closer I came to it, the more I perceived the strangeness of it, that a man should stand alone in this darkness, so idly, and then it came to me that I was being foolish, for it was only another man there, and so why should it make me feel all the more undefended in the dark of night?

But no sooner had that thought occurred to me, when I drew close enough to see the man's face. And in the same instant as I beheld that this was my own double standing there, the creature leapt out at me, drawing up not one inch from me as my own voice issued from his lips.

"Ah, Petyr, but you have forgot your hat!" he cried, and gave forth a terrible laugh.

I fell backwards onto the road, my heart roaring in my chest.

Over me, he bent like a vulture. "Oh, come on, Petyr, pick up your hat for you have let it drop in the dust!"

"Get away from me!" I screamed in my terror, and turning away, I covered my head. Like a miserable crab, I scrambled to escape the thing. Then rising, I rushed at him, as a bull might have done it, only to find myself charging the empty air.

Nothing on this road but my miserable self and my black hat lying crushed in the dirt.

Shaking like a child, I took it up and brushed it off.

"Damn you, spirit!" I cried. "I know your tricks."

"Do you?" a voice spoke to me, and this time it was a woman speaking. I spun around to see the creature! And there beheld my Deborah, as she had been in girlhood, but for a flash.

"It isn't she," I declared. "You liar from hell!"

But Stefan, that one glimpse of her was a sword passing through me. For I had caught her girlish smile and her flashing eye. A sob rose in my throat. "Damn you, spirit," I whispered.

I searched the blackness for her. I would have seen her, real or illusion. And I felt the fool.

The night was quiet. But I did not trust it. Only slowly did I stop my shaking, and put on my hat.

I walked on, but nothing as fast as before. Everywhere I looked, I thought I beheld a face and figure, only to discover that it was a trick of the darkness—the banana trees shifting in the breeze, or those giant red flowers drowsing on their weak stems as they hung over the fences bordering the road.

I resolved to look straight ahead. But then I heard a footfall behind me; I heard the breathing of another man. Steady came the feet, out of step with my own walking; and as I resolved to ignore it, I felt the hot breath of the creature on my very neck.

"Damn you!" I cried again, spinning round, only to see a perfect horror looming over me, the monstrous image of myself once more but with nothing but a naked and blazing skull for my face.

Flames leapt from the empty eye sockets beneath the blond hair and the great Dutch hat.

"Go to hell!" I screamed and shoved it with all my might as it fell forward on me, the fire scorching me. And where I had been certain there would be nothing, was a solid chest.

Growling like a monster myself, I fought it, forcing it to stagger backwards, and only then did it vanish, with a great blast of warmth.

I found I had fallen without even realizing it. I was on my knees and had torn my breeches. I could think of nothing but the flaming skull I had just beheld. Once more my body shook stupidly and uncontrollably. And the night was darker as the moon was no longer high, and God only knew how long I must walk on this road until I reached Port-au-Prince.

"All right, evil one," I said, "I shall not believe my eyes no matter what they reveal to me."

And without further hesitation, I turned back to the right direction, and began to run. I ran, with my eyes down, until I was out of breath. And slowing to a walk, went on doggedly in the same manner, looking only at the dust beneath my feet.

It was only a little while before I saw feet next to mine, naked, bleeding, but I paid no mind to them for I knew they could not be real. I smelled flesh burning but I took no note of it, for I knew it could not be real.

"I know your game," I said. "You have pledged not to hurt me, and so you go by the letter of the pledge. You would drive me mad, would you?" And then remembering the rules of the ancients, that I was but strengthening it by talking to it, I stopped talking and fell to saying the old prayers.

"May all the forces of goodness protect me, may the higher spirits protect me, may no harm come to me; may the white light shine upon me, and keep me from this thing."

The feet that had walked along with me were gone now, and so was the stench of burning flesh. But far ahead I heard an eerie noise. It was the sound of wood splintering, aye, of many pieces of wood splintering, and perhaps of things being ripped up from the earth.

This is no illusion, I thought. The thing has uprooted the very trees and will now hurl them down in my path.

On I walked, confident that I should dodge such dangers, and remembering that it was playing games with me, and I must not fall into its trap. But then I saw the bridge ahead of me, and I realized that I had come to the little river, and the sounds I heard were coming from the graveyard! The thing was breaking open the graves!

A terror seized me which was far worse than any I had felt before. We all have our private fears, Stefan. A man can fight tigers, yet shrink from the sight of a beetle; another can cut his way through an enemy regiment, yet not remain with a dead body in a closed-up room.

For me, the places of the dead have always held terror; and now to know what the spirit meant to do, and that I must cross the bridge and pass through the graveyard held me petrified and dripping with sweat. And to hear ever more loudly the ripping and the tearing; to see the trees above the graves swaying, I did not know how I should ever move again.

But to remain here was folly. I forced myself to move, drawing closer, step by step to the bridge. Then I beheld the ravaged graveyard, I saw the coffins torn up from the soft wet earth. I saw the things climbing out of them, or rather pulled from them, for they were lifeless, surely they were lifeless, and he moved them as he would move puppets!

"Petyr, run!" I cried, and tried to obey my own command.

I crossed the bridge in an instant, but I could see them coming up the banks on both sides. I heard them! I heard the rotted coffins breaking under their feet. Illusion, trickery, I told myself once more, but as the first of these horrid cadavers came into my path, I screamed like a frightened woman, "Get away from me!" and then found myself unable to touch the putrid arms that flailed at me, merely stumbling away from this assault, only to fall against another such rotted corpse, and at last to collapse upon my knees.

I prayed, Stefan. I cried out loud to the spirit of my father and to Roemer Franz, please help me! These things had now surrounded me and were pushing against me, and the stench was unbearable, for some of them were newly buried, and others but half decomposed, and others reeked purely of the earth itself.

My arms and hair were drenched from their disgusting wetness, and shivering I covered my head with both arms.

Then I heard a voice speaking to me, clearly, and I knew it was the voice of Roemer, and he said: "Petyr, they are lifeless! They are as fruit fallen on the floor of the orchard. Rise and push them aside; you cannot offend them!"

And emboldened, I did.

On I'ran once more, crashing into them, tripping over them and then dancing back and forth to catch my balance and go on ahead. At last I ripped off my coat to flail at them, and discovering them weak and unable to sustain an assault upon me, I beat them back with the coat, and got clear of the graveyard. And I knelt down once more to rest.

I could still hear them back there; hear the trudge of their aimless dead feet.

Then glancing over my shoulder, I saw that they struggled to follow, a legion of horrid corpses, pulled as if by strings.

Again I rose; again I went on; my coat I carried now, for it was filthy from the battle, and my hat, ah, my priceless hat, I had lost. Within minutes I outdistanced the dead ones. I suppose that he let them drop finally.

And as I continued, my feet aching now, and my chest burning from my exertions, I saw that my sleeves were covered with stains from the battle. Dead flesh clung to my hair. My boots were smeared with it. And the smell would follow me all the way to Port-au-Prince. But it was still and quiet around me. The thing was resting! The thing had exhausted itself. So this was no time to worry about stenches and garments. I must rush on.

I began in my madness to talk to Roemer. "What shall I do, Roemer? For you know this thing will follow me to the ends of the earth."

But there came no answer, and I thought that I had imagined his voice when I heard it before. And all the while I knew the spirit might take on his voice, if I thought too long and too hard on Roemer, and that would drive me mad, madder than I already was.

The peace continued. The sky was growing light. I heard carts upon the road behind me, and saw that the fields were coming alive to the right and the left. Indeed, coming to the top of a rise I saw the colonial city below me, and I breathed a great sigh.

Now one of these carts approached, a small rickety wooden cart, laden with fruit and vegetables for market, and driven by two pale-skinned mulattoes, and they did stop and stare at me, at which point I said in my best French that I needed their help and God would bless them if they gave it to me. And then remembering that I had money, or had had, I went into my pockets for it, and gave them several livres which they took with gratitude, and I climbed upon the tail of the cart.

I lay back against a great heap of vegetables and fruits, and went to sleeping, and the cart rocked me and knocked me about, but it was as if I were in the most luxurious coach.

Then as a dream overcame me, as I imagined I was back in Amsterdam, I felt a hand touch mine. A gentle hand. It patted my left hand and I lifted my right to touch it in the same gentle manner, and opening my eyes, and rolling my head to my left, I beheld the burnt and blackened body of Deborah peering at me, bald and shriveled with only her blue eyes alive, and the teeth grinning at me from behind her burnt lips.

I screamed so loud I frightened the drivers of the cart and the horse. But no matter; I had fallen off onto the road. Their horse ran away, and they could not stop it, and they were soon gone way ahead, and over the rise.

I sat cross-legged, crying, "You damnable spirit! What is it you want of me! Tell me! Why do you not kill me! Surely you have it in your power if you can do such things!"

No voice answered me. But I knew that he was there. Looking up, I saw him, and in no horrible guise now. Merely the dark-haired one again, in the leather jerkin, the handsome man I had seen twice before.

Very solid he appeared, so that even the sunlight fell on him, as he sat idly on the fence at the edge of the road. He peered down at me, thoughtfully, it would seem, for his face was all blank.

And I found myself staring at him, studying him as if he were nothing to fear. And I perceived something now which was most important for me to understand.

The burnt body of Deborah, it had been illusion! From within my mind, he had taken this image and made it bloom. My double, that too had been illusion! It was as perfect as my reflection in a mirror. And the other demon follower whom I fought—his weight had been an illusion.

And of course the corpses had been real, and they were corpses and nothing more.

But this was no illusion, the man sitting on the fence. It was a body which this thing had made.

"Aye," he said to me, and again his lips did not move. And I understand why. For he could not yet make them move. "But I shall," he said. "I shall."

I continued to peer at him. Perhaps in my exhaustion, I had lost my wits. But I knew no fear. And as the morning sun grew brighter, I saw it shine through him! I saw the particles of which he was made swirling in it, like so much dust.

"Dust thou art," I whispered, thinking of the biblical phrase. But he had at that very instant begun to dissolve. He went pale and then was nothing, and the sun rose over the field, more beautiful than any morning sun that I have ever seen.

Had Charlotte waked? Did Charlotte stay his hand?

I cannot answer. I may never know. I reached my lodgings here less than an hour later, after meeting with the agent and speaking again to the innkeeper, as I related to you before.

And now it is long past midnight by my good watch, which I set by the clock in the inn at noon today. And the fiend has not left the room for some time.

For over an hour, he has come and gone in his manly shape, watching me. He sits in one corner and then in another; once I spied him in the looking glass peering out at me—Stefan, how does the spirit do such things? Does he trick my eyes? For surely he cannot be in the glass!—but I refused to raise my eyes to it, and finally the image faded away.

He has now begun to move the furniture about, and once again to make the sound of wings flapping, and I must flee this room. I go to send this letter with the rest.

Yours in the Talamasca,
Petyr

Stefan,

It is dawn, and all my letters are on their way to you, the ship having sailed an hour ago with them, and much as I would have gone with it, I knew that I must not. For if this thing means to destroy me, better he play with me here, whilst my letters be carried safely on.

I fear, too, that the thing may have the strength to sink a ship, for no sooner had I set foot on it, to speak with the captain and make certain that my letters would be safely conveyed, than a wind came up and rain struck the windows, and the boat itself began to move.

My reason told me the fiend does not have such strength as

would be required to drown the vessel; but horror of horrors, what if I am wrong. I cannot be the cause of such harm to others.

So I remain, here in a crowded tavern in Port-au-Prince—the second to which I have gone this morning—and I fear to be alone.

A short while ago, as I returned from the docks, the thing so affrighted me with the image of a woman falling before a coach that I ran out into the path of the horses to save her, only to discover that there was no woman, and I myself was all but trampled. How the coachman did curse me, calling me a madman.

And that is surely how I seem. In the first tavern, I fell asleep for perhaps a quarter of an hour, and was waked by flames around me, only to discover that the candle had been overturned into the spilt brandy. I was blamed for it, and told to take my money elsewhere. And there the thing stood, in the shadows behind the chimneypiece. It would have smiled if it could make its waxy face move.

Mark what I say now about its power. When it would be itself, it is a made-up body over which it has scant control.

Nevertheless my understanding of its art is imperfect. And I am so weary, Stefan. I went again to my room and tried to sleep, but it flung me from my bed.

Even here in this public room full of late night drinkers and early morning travelers, it plays its tricks with me, and no one is the wiser, for they do not know that the image of Roemer seated by the fire is not truly there. Or that the woman who appears for an instant on the stairs, scarcely noticed by them, is Geertruid—dead now twenty years. The thing snatches these images from my mind, surely, and then expands them, though how I cannot guess.

I have tried to talk with it. In the street, I pleaded with it to tell me its purpose. Is there any chance that I shall live? What could I do for it that it would cease its evil tricks? And what had Charlotte commanded it to do?

Then when I had seated myself here and ordered my wine, for I am thirsty for it again, and drinking too much of it, I beheld that it did move my pen and make scrawl marks on my paper which say: "Petyr will die."

This I enclose with the letter, for it is the writing of a spirit. I myself had no hand in it. Perhaps Alexander might lay his hands on the paper and learn from it. For I can learn nothing from the fool thing except that he and I together can make images the like of which would have driven Jesus from the desert, mad.

I know now there is only one means of salvation for me. As soon as I finish this communication and leave it with the agent I shall go to Charlotte and beg her to make the fiend stop. Nothing else will do for it, Stefan. Only Charlotte can save me. And I pray I can reach Maye Faire unharmed.

I shall rent a mount for the trip, and count upon the road at midmorning being well traveled and that Charlotte is awake and in control of the fiend.

But I have one terrible fear, my friend, and that is, that Charlotte knows what this devil does to me, and has commanded it to do so. That Charlotte is the author of the entire diabolical plan.

If you hear nothing more from me—and allow me to remind you that Dutch ships leave here daily for our fair city—follow these instructions.

Write to the witch and tell her of my disappearance. But see to it that your letter does not originate from the Motherhouse; and that no address provided for my reply is given which should enable the fiend to penetrate our walls.

Do not, and I beg you, do not send anyone after me! For he will only meet with a worse fate than mine.

Learn what you can of the progress of this woman from other sources, and remember the child she bears within nine months will surely be mine.

What else can I tell you?

After my death, I shall try to reach you or to reach Alexander if such be possible. But my beloved friend, I fear there is no "after." That only darkness waits for me, and my time in the light is at an end.

I have no regrets in these final hours. The Talamasca has been my life, and I have spent many years in the defense of the innocent and in the pure seeking of knowledge. I love you, my brothers and sisters. Remember me not for my weakness, for my sins, or for my poor judgment. But that I loved you.

Ah, allow me to tell you what just happened for it was very interesting indeed.

I saw Roemer again, my beloved Roemer, the first director of our order I knew and loved. And Roemer looked so young and fine to me, and I was so glad to see him that I wept, and did not want the image to disappear.

Let me play with this, I thought, for it comes from my mind, does it not? And the fiend does not know what he does. And so I spoke to Roemer. I said, "My dearest Roemer, you do not know how I have missed you, and where have you been, and what have you learned?"

And the stout handsome figure of Roemer comes towards me, and I know now that no one else sees it for they are glancing at me, the muttering madman, but I do not care. Again I say, "Sit down, Roemer, drink with me." And this, my beloved teacher, sits and leans against the table, and speaks the most foul obscenities to me, ah, you have never heard such language, as he tells me that he would strip off my clothes in this very tavern, and what pleasure he would give me, and how he had always wanted to do it when I was a boy, and even that he did do it, in the night, coming into my room, and laughing afterwards about it, and letting others watch.

Like a statue, I must have appeared, staring into the face of this monster, who with Roemer's smile whispered like an old bawd to me, such filth, and then finally this creature's mouth ceases to move, but merely grows bigger and bigger, and the tongue inside it becomes a black thing, big and shining like the humpback of a whale.

Like a puppet, I reach for my pen and dip it and begin to write the above description, and now the thing is gone.

But you know what it has done, Stefan? It has turned my mind inside out. Let me tell you a secret. Of course, my beloved Roemer never took such liberties with me! But I used to pray that he would! And the fiend drew that out of me, that as a boy I lay in my bed in the Motherhouse dreaming that Roemer would come and pull down the covers and lie with me. I dreamed those things!

Had you asked me last year, did I ever have such a dream, I would have said never, but I had it, and the fiend remembered me of it. Should I thank him?

Maybe he can bring my mother back and she and I will sit by the kitchen fire once more and sing.

I go now. The sun is fully risen. The thing is not near. I will entrust this to our agent before I go on towards Maye Faire—that is, if I am not stopped by the local constables, and thrown into jail. I do look like a vagabond and a madman. Charlotte will help me. Charlotte will restrain this demon.

What else is there to say?

Petyr

NOTE TO THE ARCHIVES:
   This was the last letter ever received from Petyr van Abel.

On the Death of Petyr van Abel

SUMMARY OF TWENTY-THREE LETTERS, AND NUMEROUS REPORTS
TO THE FILES
(SEE INVENTORY):

Two weeks after Petyr's last letter reached the Motherhouse, a communication was received from a Jan van Clausen, Dutch merchant in Port-au-Prince, that Petyr was dead. This letter was dated only twenty-four hours after Petyr's last letter. Petyr's body had been discovered some twelve hours after he was known to have rented a horse at the livery stables and to have ridden out of Port-au-Prince.

It was the assumption of the local authorities that Petyr had met with foul play on the road, perhaps coming upon a band of runaway slaves in the early morning, who might have been in the process of again desecrating a cemetery in which they had wreaked considerable havoc only a day or two before. The original desecration had caused a great disturbance among the local slaves, who, much to the dismay of their masters, were reluctant to participate in the restoration of the site, and it was still in a state of considerable disarray and deserted when the assault upon Petyr occurred.

Petyr was apparently beaten and driven into a large brick crypt where he was trapped by a fallen tree and much heavy debris. When he was found, the fingers of his right hand were entangled in the debris as if he had been trying to dig his way out. Two fingers from his left hand had been severed and were never found.

The perpetrators of the desecration and the murder were never discovered. That Petyr's money, his gold watch, and his papers were not stolen added to the mystery of his death.

Ongoing repairs to the site led to the early discovery of Petyr's remains. In spite of extensive head wounds, Petyr was easily and undeniably identified by van Clausen, as well as by Charlotte Fontenay, who rode into Port-au-Prince when she heard tell of it, and was violently disturbed by Petyr's death, and "took to her bed" in grief.

Van Clausen returned Petyr's possessions to the Motherhouse, and at the behest of the order undertook a further investigation of Petyr's death.

The files contain letters not only to and from van Clausen, but also to and from several priests in the colony, and other persons as well.

Essentially, nothing of any real importance was discovered,

except that Petyr was thought to be mad during his last day and night in Port-au-Prince, what with his repeated requests for letters to be mailed to Amsterdam, and repeated instructions that the Motherhouse be notified in the event of his death.

Several mentions are made of his having been in the company of a strange dark-haired young man, with whom he conversed at length.

It is difficult to know how to interpret these statements. But more analysis of Lasher and Lasher's powers is contained in the later chapters of these files. It is sufficient to say that others saw Lasher with Petyr, and believed Lasher to be a human being.

Via Jan van Clausen, Stefan Franck wrote to Charlôtte Fontenay a letter which could not have been understood by anyone else, explaining what Petyr had written in his last hours, and imploring her to take heed of whatever Petyr had told her.

No response to this was ever received.

The desecration of the cemetery, along with Petyr's murder, led to its abandonment. No further burials were made there, and some bodies were moved elsewhere. Even one hundred years later it was still regarded as a "haunted place."

Before Petyr's last letters reached Amsterdam, Alexander announced to the other members in the Motherhouse that Petyr was dead. He asked that the portrait of Deborah Mayfair by Rembrandt be taken down from the wall.

Stefan Franck complied, and the painting was stored in the vaults.

Alexander laid hands upon the piece of paper on which Lasher had written the words "Petyr will die," and said only that the words were true, but the spirit was "a liar."

He could ascertain nothing more. He warned Stefan Franck to abide by Petyr's wishes that no one be sent to Port-au-Prince to speak further with Charlotte as such a person would be going to his most certain death.

Stefan Franck frequently attempted to make contact with the spirit of Petyr van Abel. With relief he reported again and again in notes to the file that his attempts had been a failure and he was confident that Petyr's spirit had "moved on to a higher plane."

Ghost stories regarding the stretch of road where Petyr died were copied into the files as late as 1956. However none of them pertain to any recognizable figures in this tale.

This brings to a conclusion the story of Petyr's investigation of the Mayfair Witches, who can reliably be considered Petyr's descendants on the basis of his reports.

The story continues . . . Please go to Part V.

Seventeen

THE FILE ON THE MAYFAIR WITCHES

PART V

The Mayfair Family from 1689 to 1900
Narrative Abstract by Aaron Lightner

After Petyr's death, it was the decision of Stefan Franck that no further direct contact with the Mayfair Witches would be attempted in his lifetime. This judgment was upheld by his successors, Martin Geller and Richard Kramer, respectively.

Though numerous members petitioned the order to allow them to attempt contact, the decision of the governing board was always unanimously against it, and the cautionary ban remained in effect into the twentieth century.

However, the order continued its investigation of the Mayfair Witches from afar. Information was frequently sought from people in the colony who never knew the reason for the inquiry, or the meaning of the information which they sent on.

RESEARCH METHODS

The Talamasca, during these centuries, was developing an entire network of "observers" worldwide who forwarded newspaper clippings and gossip back to the Motherhouse. And in Saint-Domingue several people were relied upon for such information, including Dutch merchants who thought the inquiries of a strictly financial nature, and various persons in the colony who were told only that people in Europe would pay dearly for information regarding the Mayfair family. No professional investigators, comparable to the twentieth century "private eye," existed at this time. Yet an amazing amount of information was gathered.

Notes to the archives were brief and often hurried, sometimes no more than a small introduction to the material being transcribed.

Information about the Mayfair legacy was obtained surreptitiously and probably illegally through people in the banks involved who were bribed into revealing it. The Talamasca has always used such means to acquire information and was only a little less unscrupulous than it is now in years past. The standard excuse was then, and is today, that the records obtained in this manner are usually seen by scores of people in various capacities. Never were private letters purloined, or persons' homes or businesses violated in criminal fashion.

Paintings of the plantation house and of various members of the family were obtained through various means. One portrait of Jeanne Louise Mayfair was obtained from a disgruntled painter after the lady had rejected the work. A daguerreotype of Katherine and her husband, Darcy Monahan, was obtained in similar fashion, as the family bought only five of the ten different pictures attempted at that sitting.

There was evidence from time to time that the Mayfairs knew of our existence and of our observations. At least one observer— a Frenchman who worked for a time as an overseer on the Mayfair plantation in Saint-Domingue—met with a suspicious and violent death. This led to greater secrecy and greater care, and less information in the years that followed.

The bulk of the original material is very fragile. Numerous photocopies and photographs of the materials have been made, however, and this work continues with painstaking care.

THE NARRATIVE YOU ARE NOW READING

The history which follows is a narrative abstract based upon all of the collected materials and notes, including several earlier fragmentary narratives in French and in Latin, and in Talamasca Latin. A full inventory of these materials is attached to the documents boxes in the Archives in London.

I began familiarizing myself with this history in 1945 when I first became a member of the Talamasca, and before I was ever directly involved with the Mayfair Witches. I finished the first "complete version" of this material in 1956. I have updated, revised and added to the material continuously ever since. The full revision was done by me in 1979 when the entire history, including Petyr van Abel's reports, was entered into the computer system of the Talamasca. It has been extremely easy to fully update the material ever since.

I did not become directly involved with the Mayfair Witches until the year 1958. I shall introduce myself at the appropriate time.

Aaron Lightner, January 1989

THE HISTORY CONTINUES

Charlotte Mayfair Fontenay lived to be almost seventy-six years old, dying in 1743, at which time she had five children and seventeen grandchildren. Maye Faire remained throughout her lifetime the most prosperous plantation in Saint-Domingue. Several of her grandchildren returned to France, and their descendants perished in the Revolution at the end of the century.

Charlotte's firstborn, by her husband Antoine, did not inherit his father's disability, but grew up to be healthy, to marry, and to have seven children. However, the plantation called Maye Faire passed to him only in name. It was in fact inherited by Charlotte's daughter Jeanne Louise, who was born nine months after Petyr's death.

All his life Antoine Fontenay III deferred to Jeanne Louise and to her twin brother, Peter, who was never called by the French version of that name, Pierre. There is little doubt that these were the children of Petyr van Abel. Both Jeanne Louise and Peter were fair of complexion, with light brown hair and pale eyes.

Charlotte gave birth to two more boys before the death of her crippled husband. The gossip in the colonies named two different individuals as the fathers. Both these boys grew to manhood and emigrated to France. They used the name Fontenay.

Jeanne Louise went only by the name of Mayfair on all official documents, and though she married young to a dissolute and drunken husband, her lifelong companion was her brother, Peter, who never married. He died only hours before Jeanne Louise, in 1771. No one questioned the legality of her using the name Mayfair, but accepted her word that it was a family custom. Later, her only daughter, Angélique, was to do the same thing.

Charlotte wore the emerald necklace given her by her mother until she died. Thereafter Jeanne Louise wore it, and passed it on to her fifth child, Angélique, who was born in 1725. By the time this daughter was born, Jeanne Louise's husband was mad and confined to "a small house" on the property, which from

401

all descriptions seems to be the house in which Petyr was imprisoned years before.

It is doubtful that this man was the father of Angélique. And it seems reasonable, though by no means certain, that Angélique was the child of Jeanne Louise and her brother Peter.

Angélique called Peter her "Papa" in front of everyone, and it was said among the servants that she believed Peter was her father as she had never known the madman in the outbuilding, who was chained in his last years rather like a wild beast. It should be noted that the treatment of this madman was not considered cruel or unusual by those who knew the family.

It was also rumored that Jeanne Louise and Peter shared a suite of connecting bedrooms and parlors added to the old plantation house shortly after Jeanne Louise's marriage.

Whatever gossip circulated about the secret habits of the family, Jeanne Louise wielded the same power over everyone that Charlotte had wielded, maintaining a hold upon her slaves through immense generosity and personal attention in an era that was famed for quite the opposite.

Jeanne Louise is described as an exceptionally beautiful woman, much admired and much sought after. She was never described as evil, sinister, or a witch. Those whom the Talamasca contacted during Jeanne Louise's lifetime knew nothing of the family's European origins.

Runaway slaves frequently came to Jeanne Louise to implore her intervention with a cruel master or mistress. She often bought such unfortunates, binding them to her with a fierce loyalty. She was a law unto herself at Maye Faire, and did execute more than one slave for treachery. However, the goodwill of her slaves towards her was well known.

Angélique was Jeanne Louise's favorite child, and Angélique was devoted to her grandmother, Charlotte, and was with the old woman when she died.

A fierce storm surrounded Maye Faire on the night of Charlotte's death, which did not abate till early morning, at which time one of Angélique's brothers was found dead.

Angélique married a very handsome and rich planter by the name of Vincent St. Christophe in the year 1755, giving birth five years later to Marie Claudette Mayfair, who later married Henri Marie Landry and was the first of the Mayfair witches to come to Louisiana. Angélique also had two sons, one of whom died in childhood, and the second of whom, Lestan, lived into old age.

Every evidence indicates that Angélique loved Vincent St. Christophe and was faithful to him all their lives. Marie Claudette was also devoted to him and there seems no question that he was her father.

The pictures which we possess of Angélique show her to be not as beautiful as either her mother or her daughter, her features being smaller and her eyes being smaller. But she was nevertheless extremely attractive, with very curly dark brown hair, and was thought of as a beauty in her prime.

Marie Claudette was exceptionally beautiful, strongly resembling her handsome father Vincent St. Christophe as much as her mother. She had very dark hair and blue eyes, and was extremely small and delicate. Her husband, Henri Marie Landry, was also a good-looking man. In fact, it was said of the family by that time that they always married for beauty, and never for money or for love.

Vincent St. Christophe was a sweet, gentle soul who liked to paint pictures and play the guitar. He spent much time on a small lake built for him on the plantation, making up songs which he would later sing to Angélique. After his death Angélique had several lovers, but refused to remarry. This too was a pattern with the Mayfair women; they usually married once only, or only once with any success.

What characterizes the family through the lifetimes of Charlotte, Jeanne Louise, Angélique, and Marie Claudette is respectability, wealth, and power. Mayfair wealth was legendary within the Caribbean world, and those who entered into disputes with the Mayfairs met with violence often enough for there to be talk of it. It was said to be "unlucky" to fight with the Mayfair family.

The slaves regarded Charlotte, Jeanne Louise, Angélique, and Marie Claudette as powerful sorceresses. They came to them for the curing of illnesses; and they believed that their mistresses "knew" everything.

But there is scant evidence that anyone other than the slaves took these stories seriously. Or that the Mayfair Witches aroused either suspicion or "irrational" fear among their peers. The preeminence of the family remained completely unchallenged. People vied for invitations to Maye Faire. The family entertained often and lavishly. Both the men and the women were much sought after in the marriage market.

How much other members of the family understood about the power of the witches is uncertain. Angélique had both a brother and a sister who emigrated to France, and another brother, Maurice, who remained at home, having two sons—Louis-Pierre and Martin—who also married and remained part of the Saint-Domingue family. They later went to Louisiana with Marie

Claudette. Maurice and his sons went by the name of Mayfair, as do their descendants in Louisiana to the present day.

Of Angélique's six children, two girls died early, and two boys emigrated to France, the other, Lestan, going to Louisiana with his sister Marie Claudette.

The men of the family never attempted to claim the plantation or to control the money, though under French law they were entitled to do both. On the contrary, they tended to accept the dominance of the chosen women; and financial records as well as gossip indicate that they were enormously wealthy men.

Perhaps some compensation was paid to them for their submissiveness. Or perhaps they were accepting by nature. No tales of rebellion or quarrels have been passed on. The brother of Angélique who died during the storm on the night of Charlotte's death was a young boy said to be kindly and acquiescent by nature. Her brother Maurice was known to be an agreeable, likable man, who participated in the management of the plantation.

Several descendants of those who emigrated to France during the 1700s were executed in the French Revolution. None of those emigrating before 1770 used the name Mayfair. And the Talamasca has lost track of these various lines.

During this entire period the family was Catholic. It supported the Catholic church in Saint-Domingue, and one son of Pierre Fontenay, Charlotte's brother-in-law, became a priest. Two women in the family became Carmelite nuns. One was executed in the French Revolution, along with all the members of her community.

The money of the colonial family, during all these years as their coffee and sugar and tobacco poured into Europe and into North America, was frequently deposited in foreign banks. The degree of wealth was enormous even for the multimillionaires of Hispaniola, and the family seems always to have possessed quite fantastic amounts of gold and jewels. This is not at all typical of a planter family, whose fortunes are generally connected with the land and easily subject to ruin.

As a consequence the Mayfair family survived the Haitian revolution with enormous wealth, though all of its land holdings on the island were irretrievably lost.

It was Marie Claudette, who established the Mayfair legacy in 1789, right before the revolution that forced the family to leave Saint-Domingue. Her parents were by that time dead. The legacy was later enhanced and refined by Marie Claudette after she was settled in Louisiana, at which time she shifted a great portion of her money from banks in Holland and Rome to banks in London and in New York.

THE LEGACY

The legacy is an immensely complicated and quasi-legal series of arrangements, made largely through the banks holding the money, which establishes a fortune that cannot be manipulated by any one country's inheritance laws. Essentially it conserves the bulk of the Mayfair money and property in the hands of one person in each generation, this heir to the fortune being designated by the living beneficiary, except that should the beneficiary die without making the designation, the money goes to her eldest daughter. Only if there is no living female descendant will the legacy go to a man. However, the beneficiary may designate a male, if she chooses.

To the knowledge of the Talamasca, the beneficiary of the legacy has never died without designating an heir, and the legacy has never passed to a male child. Rowan Mayfair, the youngest living Mayfair Witch, was designated at birth by her mother Deirdre, who was designated at birth by Antha, who was designated by Stella, and so forth and so on.

However, there have been times in the history of the family when the designee has been changed. For example, Marie Claudette designated her first daughter, Claire Marie, and then later changed this designation to Marguerite, her third child, and there is no evidence that Claire Marie ever knew that she was designated, though Marguerite knew she was the heiress long before Marie Claudette's death.

The legacy also provides enormous benefits for the beneficiary's other children (the siblings of the heir) in each generation, the amount for women usually being twice that given to the men. However, no member of the family could inherit from the legacy unless he or she used the name Mayfair publicly and privately. Where laws prohibited the heir from using the name legally, it was nevertheless used customarily, and never legally challenged.

This served to keep alive the name of Mayfair well into the present century. And in numerous instances, members of the family passed the rule on to their descendants along with their fortunes, though nothing legally required them to do so, once they were one step removed from the original legacy.

The original legacy also contains complex provisions for destitute Mayfairs claiming assistance, as long as they have always used the name Mayfair and are descended from those who used it. The beneficiary may also leave up to ten percent of the legacy to other "Mayfairs" who are not her children, but once more, the name Mayfair must be in active use by such a person or the provisions of the will are null and void.

In the twentieth century, numerous "cousins" have received money from the legacy, primarily through Mary Beth Mayfair, and her daughter Stella, but some also through Deirdre, the money being administered for her by Cortland Mayfair. Many of these people are now "rich," as the bequest was frequently made in connection with investments or business ventures of which the beneficiary or her administrator approved.

The Talamasca knows today of some five hundred and fifty descendants all using the name Mayfair; easily one half of these people know the core family in New Orleans, and know something about the legacy, though they are many generations removed from their original inheritance.

Stella gathered together some four hundred Mayfairs and related families in 1927 at the house on First Street, and there is considerable evidence that she was interested in the other psychic members of the family, but the story of Stella will be related further on.

DESCENDANTS

The Talamasca has investigated numerous descendants, and found that among them mild psychic powers are common. Some exhibit exceptional psychic powers. It is also common to speak of the ancestors of Saint-Domingue as "witches" and to say that they were "lovers of the devil" and sold their souls to him, and that the devil made the family rich.

These tales are now told lightly and often with humor or with wonder and curiosity, and the majority of the descendants with whom the Talamasca has made limited contact do not really know anything concrete about their history. They do not even know the names of the "witches." They know nothing of Suzanne or Deborah, though they do banter about statements such as "Our ancestors were burnt at the stake in Europe," and "We have a long history of witchcraft." They have rather vague notions about the legacy, knowing that one person is the main beneficiary of the legacy and they know the name of that one person, but not much else.

However, descendants in the New Orleans area know a great deal about the core family. They attend wakes and funerals, and were gathered together on countless occasions by Mary Beth and by Stella, as we shall see. The Talamasca possesses numerous pictures of these people, in family gatherings and singly.

Stories among all these people of seeing ghosts, of precognition, of "phone calls from the dead," and of mild telekinesis are by no means uncommon. Mayfairs who know almost nothing of the New Orleans family have been involved in no less than ten different ghost stories contained in various published books. Three different distantly related Mayfairs have exhibited enormous powers. But there is no evidence that they understood or used these powers to any purpose. To the best of our knowledge, they have no connection to the witches, to the legacy, to the emerald necklace, or to Lasher.

There is a saying that all the Mayfairs "feel it" when the beneficiary of the legacy dies.

Descendants of the Mayfair family fear Carlotta Mayfair, the guardian of Deirdre Mayfair, the present beneficiary, and regard her as a "witch," but the word in this case is more closely related to the vernacular term for an unpleasant woman than to anything pertaining to the supernatural.

SUMMARY OF MATERIALS
RELATING TO THE SAINT-DOMINGUE YEARS

To return to an appraisal of the family in the seventeen hundreds, it is undeniably characterized by strength, success, and wealth, by longevity and enduring relationships. And the witches of the period must be perceived as extremely successful. It can safely be assumed that they controlled Lasher completely to their satisfaction. *However, we honestly do not know whether or not this is true.* We simply have no evidence to the contrary. There are no specific sightings of Lasher. There is no evidence of tragedy within the family.

Accidents befalling enemies of the family, the family's continued accumulation of jewels and gold, and the countless stories told by the slaves as to the omnipotence or infallibility of their mistresses constitute the only evidence of supernatural intervention, and none of this is reliable evidence.

Closer observation through trained investigators might have told a very different tale.

Several days before the Haitian revolution (the only successful slave uprising in history), Marie Claudette was warned by her slaves that she and her family might be massacred. She and her children, her brother Lestan and his wife and children, and her uncle Maurice and his two sons and their wives and children escaped with apparent ease and an amazing amount of personal possessions, a veritable caravan of wagons leaving Maye Faire for the nearby port. Some fifty of Marie Claudette's personal slaves, half of whom were of mixed blood, and some of whom were undoubtedly the progeny of Mayfair men, went with the family to Louisiana. We can assume that numerous books and written records also went with them, and some of these materials have been glimpsed since, as these reports will show.

Almost from the moment of their arrival in Louisiana, the Talamasca was able to acquire more information about the Mayfair Witches. Several of our contacts in Louisiana were already established on account of two dramatic hauntings that had taken place in that city; and at least two of our members had visited the city, one to investigate a haunting and the other on his way to other places in the South.

Another reason for the increased information was that the Mayfair family itself seems to have become more "visible" to people. Torn from its position of near feudal power and isolation in Saint-Domingue, it was thrown into contact with countless new persons, including merchants, churchmen, slave traders, brokers, colonial officials, and the like. And the wealth of the Mayfairs, as well as their sudden appearance on the scene so to speak, aroused immense curiosity.

All sorts of tales were collected about them from the very hour of their arrival. And the flow of information became even richer as time went on.

Changes in the nineteenth century also contributed, inevitably, to the increased flow of information. The growth of newspapers and periodicals, the increase in the keeping of detailed records, the invention of photography, all made it easier to compile a more detailed anecdotal history of the Mayfair family.

Indeed, the growth of New Orleans into a teeming and prosperous port city created an environment in which dozens of people could be questioned about the Mayfairs without anyone's ever noticing us or our investigators.

So what must be borne in mind as we study the continued history of the Mayfairs is that, *though the family appears to change dramatically in the nineteenth century, it could be that the family did not change at all.* The only change may have been in our investigative methods. We learned more about what went on behind closed doors.

In other words, if we knew more about the Saint-Domingue years, we might have seen greater continuity. But then again, perhaps not.

Whatever the case, the witches of the 1800s—with the exception of Mary Beth Mayfair, who was not born until 1872—*appear* to have been much weaker than those who ruled the family during the Saint-Domingue years. And the decline of the Mayfair Witches, which became so marked in the twentieth century, can be seen—on the basis of our fragmentary evidence—to have begun before the Civil War. But the picture is more complicated than that, as we shall see.

Changing attitudes and changing times in general may have played a significant role in the decline of the witches. That is, as the family became less aristocratic and feudal, and more "civilized" or "bourgeois," its members might have become more confused regarding their heritage and their powers, and more generally inhibited. For though the planter class of Louisiana referred to itself as "the aristocracy," it was definitely not aristocratic in the European sense of that word, and was characterized by what we now define as "middle-class values."

"Modern psychiatry" also seems to have played a role in inhibiting and confusing the Mayfair Witches, and we will go into that in greater detail when we deal with the Mayfair family in the twentieth century.

But for the most part we can only speculate about these things. Even when direct contact between the order and the Mayfair Witches was established in the twentieth century, we were unable to learn as much as we had hoped.

Bearing all this in mind . . .

THE HISTORY CONTINUES . . .

Upon arrival in New Orleans, Marie Claudette moved her family into a large house in the Rue Dumaine, and immediately acquired an enormous plantation at Riverbend, south of the city, building a plantation house that was larger and more luxurious than its counterpart in Saint-Domingue. This plantation was called La Victoire at Riverbend, and was known later simply as Riverbend. It was carried away by the river in 1896; however, much of the land there is still owned by the Mayfairs, and is presently the site of an oil refinery.

Maurice Mayfair, Marie Claudette's uncle, lived out his life at this plantation, but his two sons purchased adjacent plantations of their own, where they lived in close contact with Marie Claudette's family. A few descendants of these men stayed on that land up until 1890, and many other descendants moved to New Orleans. They made up the ever increasing number of "cousins" who were a constant factor in Mayfair life for the next one hundred years.

There are numerous published drawings of Marie Claudette's plantation house and even several photographs in old books, now out of print. It was large even for the period and, predating the ostentatious Greek Revival style, it was a simple colonial structure with plain rounded columns, a pitched roof, and galleries, much like the house in Saint-Domingue. It was two rooms thick, with hallways bisecting it from north to south and east to west, and had a full lower floor, as well as a very high and spacious attic floor.

The plantation included two enormous *garçonnières* where the male members of the family lived, including Lestan in his later widowhood, and his four sons, all of whom went by the name of Mayfair. (Maurice always lived in the main house.)

Marie Claudette was every bit as successful in Louisiana as she and her ancestors had been in Saint-Domingue. Once again, she cultivated sugar, but gave up the cultivation of coffee and tobacco. She bought smaller plantations for each of Lestan's sons, and gave lavish gifts to their children and their children's children.

From the first weeks of their arrival, the family was regarded with awe and suspicion. Marie Claudette frightened people, and entered into a number of disputes in setting up business in Louisiana, and was not above threatening anyone who stood in her path. She bought up enormous numbers of slaves for her fields, and in the tradition of her ancestors, treated these slaves very well. But she did not treat merchants very well, and drove more than one merchant off her property with a whip, insisting that he had tried to cheat her.

She was described by the local witnesses as "formidable" and "unpleasant," though still a handsome woman. And her personal slaves and free mixed-blood servants were greatly feared by the slaves she purchased in Louisiana.

Within a short time, she was heralded as a sorceress by the slaves on her land; it was said that she could not be deceived, and that she could give "the evil eye," and that she had a demon whom she could send after anyone who crossed her. Her brother

Lestan was more generally liked, and apparently fell in at once with the drinking and gambling planter class of the area.

Henri Marie Landry, her husband, seems to have been a likable but passive individual who left absolutely everything to his wife. He read botanical journals from Europe and collected rare flowers from all over the South and designed and cultivated an enormous garden at Riverbend.

He died in bed, in 1824, after receiving the sacraments.

In 1799 Marie Claudette gave birth to the last of her children, Marguerite, who later became the designee of the legacy, and who lived in Marie Claudette's shadow until Marie Claudette's death in 1831.

There was much gossip about Marie Claudette's family life. It was said that her oldest daughter, Claire Marie, was feeble-minded, and there are numerous stories about this young woman wandering about in her nightgown, and saying strange though often delightful things to people. She saw ghosts and talked to them all the time, sometimes right in the middle of supper before amazed guests.

She also "knew" things about people and would blurt out these secrets at odd moments. She was kept at home, and though more than one man fell in love with her, Marie Claudette never allowed Claire Marie to marry. In her old age, after the death of her husband, Henri Marie Landry, Marie Claudette slept with Claire Marie, to watch her and keep her from roaming about and getting lost.

She was often seen on the galleries in her nightgown.

Marie Claudette's only son, Pierre, was never allowed to marry either. He "fell in love" twice, but both times gave in to his mother when she refused to grant permission for the wedding. His second "secret fiancée" tried to take her own life when she was rejected by Pierre. After that he seldom went out, but was often seen in the company of his mother.

Pierre was a doctor of sorts to the slaves, curing them with various potions and remedies. He even studied medicine for a while with an old drunken doctor in New Orleans. But nothing much came of this. He also enjoyed botany and spent much time working in the garden, and drawing pictures of flowers. Botanical sketches done by Pierre are in existence today in the famous Mayfair house on First Street.

It was no secret that about the year 1820 Pierre took a quadroon mistress in New Orleans, an exquisite young woman who might have passed for white, according to the gossip. By her Pierre had two children, a daughter who went north and passed into the white race, and a son, François, born in 1825, who remained in Louisiana and later handled substantial amounts of paperwork for the family in New Orleans. A genteel clerk, he seems to have been thought of affectionately by the white Mayfairs, especially the men who came into town to conduct business.

Everyone in the family apparently adored Marguerite. When she was ten years old, her portrait was painted, showing her wearing the famous emerald necklace. This is an odd picture, because the child is small and the necklace is large. As of 1927, the picture was hanging on a wall in the First Street house in New Orleans.

Marguerite was delicate of build, with dark hair and large slightly upturned black eyes. She was considered a beauty, and called La Petite Gypsy by her nurses, who loved to brush her long black wavy hair. Unlike her feeble-minded sister and her compliant brother, she had a fierce temper and a violent and unpredictable sense of humor.

At age twenty, against Marie Claudette's wishes, she married Tyrone Clifford McNamara, an opera singer, and another "very handsome" man, of an extremely impractical nature, who toured widely in the United States, starring in operas in New York, Boston, St. Louis, and other cities. It was only after he had left on one such tour that Marguerite returned from New Orleans to Riverbend and was received once more by her mother. In 1827 and 1828, she gave birth to boys, Rémy and Julien. McNamara came home frequently during this period, but only for brief visits. In New York, Boston, Baltimore, and other places where he appeared he was famous for womanizing and drinking, and for getting into brawls. But he was a very popular "Irish tenor" of the period, and he packed houses wherever he went.

In 1829, Tyrone Clifford McNamara and an Irishwoman, presumably his mistress, were found dead after a fire in a little house in the French Quarter which had been bought for the woman by McNamara. Police reports and newspaper stories of the time indicate the pair was overcome with smoke when trying vainly to escape. The lock on the front door had been broken. There was a child from this union, apparently, who was not in the house at the time of the fire. He later went north.

This fire engendered considerable gossip in New Orleans, and it was at this time that the Talamasca gained more personal information about the family than it had been able to acquire in years.

A French Quarter merchant told one of our "witnesses" that Marguerite had sent her devil to take care of "those two" and that Marguerite knew more about voodoo than any black person in Louisiana. Marguerite was reputed to have a voodoo altar in her home, to work with unguents and potions as cures and for love, and to go everywhere in the company of two beautiful quadroon servants, Marie and Virginie, and a mulatto coachman named Octavius. Octavius was said to be a bastard son of one of Maurice Mayfair's sons, Louis-Pierre, but this was not a well-circulated tale.

Marie Claudette was still living then, but seldom went out anymore, and it was said that she had taught her daughter the black arts learned in Haiti. It was Marguerite who drew attention everywhere that she went, especially in view of the fact that her brother Pierre lived a fairly respectable life, was very discreet about his quadroon mistress, and Uncle Lestan's children were also entirely respectable and well liked.

Even by her late twenties, Marguerite had become a gaunt and somewhat frightening figure, with often unkempt hair and glowing dark eyes, and a sudden disconcerting laugh. She always wore the Mayfair emerald.

She received merchants and brokers and guests in an immense book-lined study at Riverbend which was full of "horrible and disgusting" things such as human skulls, stuffed and mounted swamp animals, trophy heads from African safaris, and animal-skin rugs. She had numerous mysterious bottles and jars, and people claimed to have seen human body parts in these jars. She was reputed to be an avid collector of trinkets and amulets made by slaves, especially those who had recently been imported from Africa.

There were several cases of "possession" among her slaves at the time, which involved frightened slave witnesses running away and priests coming to the plantation. In every case, the victim was chained up and exorcism was tried without success, and the "possessed" creature died either from hunger because he could not be made to eat, or from some injury sustained in his wild convulsions.

There were rumors that such a possessed slave was chained in the attic, but the local authorities never acted upon this investigation.

At least four different witnesses mention Marguerite's "mysterious dark-haired lover," a man seen in her private apartments by her slaves, and also seen in her suite at the St. Louis Hotel when she came into New Orleans, and in her box at the French Opera. Much gossip surrounded the question of this lover or companion. The mysterious manner in which he came and went puzzled everyone.

"Now you see him, now you don't," was the saying.

These constitute the first mentions of Lasher in over one hundred years.

Marguerite married almost immediately after Tyrone Clifford McNamara's death, a tall penniless riverboat gambler named Arlington Kerr who vanished completely six months after the marriage. Nothing is known about him except that he was "as beautiful as a woman," and a drunkard, and played cards all night long in the *garçonnière* with various drunken guests and with the mulatto coachman. It is worth noting that more was heard about this man than was ever seen of him. That is, most of our stories about him are thirdhand or even fourthhand. It is interesting to speculate that perhaps such a person never existed.

He was however legally the father of Katherine Mayfair, born 1830, who became the next beneficiary of the legacy and the first of the Mayfair Witches in many generations who did not know her grandmother, as Marie Claudette died the following year.

Slaves up and down the river coast circulated the tale that Marguerite had murdered Arlington Kerr and put his body in pieces in various jars, but no one ever investigated this tale, and the story let out by the family was that Arlington Kerr could not adapt to the planter's life, and so left Louisiana, penniless as he had come, and Marguerite said "good riddance."

In her twenties, Marguerite was famous for attending the dances of the slaves, and even for dancing with them. Without doubt she had the Mayfair power to heal, and presided at births regularly. But as time passed she was accused of stealing the babies of her slaves, and this is the first Mayfair Witch whom the slaves not only feared but came to personally abhor.

After the age of thirty-five, she did not actively manage the plantation but put everything in the hands of her cousin Augustin, a son of her uncle Lestan, who proved a more than capable manager. Pierre, Marguerite's brother, helped somewhat in the decisions that were made; but it was principally Augustin, answering only to Marguerite, who ran things.

Augustin was feared by the slaves, but they apparently regarded him as predictable and sane.

Whatever, the plantation during these years made a fortune. And the Mayfairs continued to make enormous deposits in foreign banks and northern American banks, and to throw money around wherever they went.

By forty, Marguerite was "a hag," according to observers, though she could have been a handsome woman had she bothered to pin up her hair and give even the smallest attention to her clothing.

When her eldest son, Julien, was fifteen, he began to manage the plantation along with his cousin Augustin, and gradually Julien took over the management completely. At his eighteenth birthday supper, an unfortunate "accident" took place with a new pistol, at which time "poor Uncle Augustin" was shot in the head and killed by Julien.

This may have been a legitimate accident, as every report of it indicates that Julien was "prostrate with grief" afterwards. More than one story maintains that the two were wrestling with the gun when the accident happened. One story says that Julien had challenged Augustin's honesty, and Augustin had threatened to blow his own brains out on account of this, and Julien was trying to stop him. Another story says that Augustin accused Julien of a "crime against nature" with another boy and on that account they began to quarrel, and Augustin brought out the gun, which Julien tried to take from him.

Whatever the case, no one was ever charged with any crime, and Julien became the undisputed manager of the plantation. And even at the tender age of fifteen, Julien had proved well suited to it, and restored order among the slaves, and doubled the output of the plantation in the next decade. Throughout his life he remained the true manager of the property, though Katherine, his younger sister, inherited the legacy.

Marguerite spent the last decades of her very long life reading all the time in the library full of "horrible and disgusting" things. She talked to herself out loud almost all the time. And would stand in front of mirrors and have very long conversations in English with her reflection. She would also talk at length to her plants, many of which had come from the original garden created by her father, Henri Marie Landry.

She was very fond of her many cousins, children and grandchildren of Maurice Mayfair and Lestan Mayfair, and they were fiercely loyal to her, though she engendered talk continuously.

The slaves grew to hate Marguerite and would not go near her, except for her quadroons Virginie and Marie, and it was said that Virginie bullied her a bit in her old age.

A runaway in 1859 told the parish priest that Marguerite had stolen her baby and cut it up for the devil. The priest told the local authorities and there were inquiries, but apparently Julien and Katherine, who were very well liked and admired by everyone and quite capably running Riverbend, explained that the slave woman had miscarried and there was no baby to speak of, but that it had been baptized and buried properly.

Whatever else was going on, Rémy, Julien, and Katherine grew up apparently happy and inundated with luxury, enjoying all that antebellum New Orleans had to offer at its height, including the theater, the opera, and endless private entertainments.

They frequently came to town as a trio, with only a quadroon governess to watch over them, staying in a lavish suite at the St. Louis Hotel and buying out the fashionable stores before their return to the country. There was a shocking story at the time that Katherine wanted to see the famous quadroon balls where the young women of mixed blood danced with their white suitors; and so she went with her quadroon maid to the balls, and had herself presented there as being of mixed blood, and fooled everyone. She had very dark hair and dark eyes and pale skin, and did not look in the least African, but then many of the quadroons did not. Julien had a hand in the affair, introducing his sister to several white men who had not met her before and believed her to be a quadroon.

The tale stunned the old guard when they heard it. The young white men who had danced with Katherine, believing her to be "colored," were humiliated and outraged. Katherine and Julien and Rémy thought the story was amusing. Julien fought at least one duel over the affair, badly wounding his opponent.

In 1857, when Katherine was seventeen, she and her brothers bought a piece of property on First Street in the Garden District of New Orleans and hired Darcy Monahan, the Irish architect, to build a house there, which is the present Mayfair home. It is likely that the purchase was the idea of Julien, who wanted a permanent city residence.

Whatever the case, Katherine and Darcy Monahan fell deeply in love, and Julien proved to be insanely jealous of his sister and would not permit her to marry so young. An enormous family squabble ensued. Julien moved out of the family home at Riverbend and spent some time in a flat in the French Quarter with a male companion of whom we know little except that he was from New York and rumored to be very handsome and devoted to Julien in a way that caused people to whisper that the pair were lovers.

The gossip further relates that Katherine stole away to New Orleans to be alone with Darcy Monahan in the unfinished house at First Street, and there the two lovers pledged their fealty in roofless rooms, or in the wild unfinished garden. Julien became increasingly miserable in his anger and disapproval, and implored his mother, Marguerite, to interfere, but Marguerite would take no interest in the matter.

At last Katherine threatened to run away if her wishes were not granted; and Marguerite gave her official consent to a small church wedding. In a daguerreotype taken after the ceremony, Katherine is wearing the Mayfair emerald.

Katherine and Darcy moved into the house on First Street in 1858, and Monahan became the most fashionable architect and builder in uptown New Orleans. Many witnesses of the period mention Katherine's beauty and Darcy's charm, and what fun it was to attend the balls given by the two in their new home. The Mayfair emerald is mentioned any number of times.

It was no secret that Julien Mayfair was so bitter about the marriage, however, that he would not even visit his sister. He did go back to Riverbend, but spent much time in his French Quarter flat. At Riverbend, in 1863, Julien and Darcy and Katherine had a violent quarrel. Before the servants and some guests, Darcy begged Julien to accept him, to be affectionate to Katherine, and to be "reasonable."

Julien threatened to kill Darcy. And Katherine and Darcy left, never returning as a couple to Riverbend.

Katherine gave birth to a boy named Clay in 1859 and thereafter to three children who all died in babyhood. Then in 1865, she gave birth to another boy named Vincent, and to two more children who died in babyhood.

It was said that these lost children broke her heart, that she took their deaths as a judgment from God, and that she changed somewhat from the gay, high-spirited girl she had been to a diffident and confused woman. Nevertheless her life with Darcy seems to have been rich and full. She loved him very much, and did everything to support him in his various building enterprises.

We should mention here that the Civil War had brought no harm whatever to the Mayfair family or fortune. New Orleans was captured and occupied very early on, with the result that it was never shelled or burned. And the Mayfairs had much too much money invested in Europe to be affected by the occupation or subsequent boom-and-bust cycles in Louisiana.

Union troops were never quartered on their property, and they were in business with "the Yanquees" almost as soon as the occupation of New Orleans began. Indeed Katherine and Darcy Monahan entertained Yanquees at First Street much to the bitter disgust of Julien and Rémy, and other members of the family.

This happy life came to an end when Darcy himself died in 1871 of yellow fever. Katherine, broken-hearted and half mad, pleaded with her brother Julien to come to her. He was in his French Quarter flat at the time, and came to her immediately, setting foot in the First Street house for the first time since its completion.

Julien then remained with Katherine night and day while the

servants took care of the forgotten children. He slept with her in the master bedroom over the library on the north side of the house, and even people passing in the street below could hear Katherine's continued crying and miserable exclamations of grief over Darcy and her dead babies.

Twice, Katherine tried to take her life through poison. The servants told stories of doctors rushing to the house, of Katherine being given antidotes and made to walk about though she was only semiconscious and ready to drop, and of a distraught Julien who could not keep back his tears as he attended to her.

Finally Julien brought Katherine and the two boys home to Riverbend, and there in 1872 Katherine gave birth to Mary Beth Mayfair, who was baptized and registered as Darcy Monahan's child, though it seems highly unlikely that Mary Beth was Darcy's child, since she was born ten and one-half months after the death of her father. Julien is almost certainly Mary Beth's father.

As far as the Talamasca could determine the servants spread the tale that Julien was, and so did various nurses who took care of the children. It was common knowledge that Julien and Katherine slept in the same bed, behind closed doors, and that Katherine could not have had a lover after Darcy's death as she never went out of the house except to make the journey home to the plantation.

But this tale, though circulated widely among the servant class, never seems to have been accepted or acknowledged by the peers of the Mayfairs.

Katherine was not only completely respectable in every other regard, she was enormously rich and generous and well liked for it, often giving money freely to family and friends whom the war had devastated. Her attempts at suicide had aroused only pity. And the old tales of her having gone to the quadroon balls had been completely erased from the public memory. Also the financial influence of the family was so far-reaching at the time as to be almost immeasurable. Julien was very popular in New Orleans society. The talk soon died away and it is doubtful that it ever had any impact whatsoever on the private or public life of the Mayfairs.

Katherine is described in 1872 as still pretty, in spite of being prematurely gray, and was said to have a wholesome and engaging manner that easily won people over. A lovely and very well-preserved tintype of the period shows her seated in a chair with the baby in her lap, asleep, and the two little boys beside her. She appears healthy and serene, an attractive woman with a hint of sadness in her eyes. She is not wearing the Mayfair emerald.

While Mary Beth and her older brothers, Clay and Vincent, were growing up in the country, Julien's brother, Rémy Mayfair, and his wife—a Mayfair cousin and grandchild of Lestan Mayfair—took possession of the Mayfair house, and lived there for years, having three children, all of whom went by the name of Mayfair and two of whom have descendants in Louisiana.

It was during this time that Julien began to visit the house, and to make an office for himself in the library there. (This library, and master bedroom above it, were part of a wing added to the original structure by Darcy in 1867.) Julien had bookcases built into two walls of the room, and stocked them with many of the Mayfair family records that had always been kept at the plantation. We know that many of these books were very very old and some were written in Latin. Julien also moved many old paintings to the house, including "portraits from the 1600s."

Julien loved books and filled the library as well with the classics and with popular novels. He adored Nathaniel Hawthorne and Edgar Allan Poe, and also Charles Dickens.

There is some evidence that quarrels with Katherine drove Julien into town, away from Riverbend, though he never neglected his duties there. But if Katherine drove him away, certainly his little niece (or daughter) Mary Beth brought him back, for he was always swooping down upon her with cartloads of gifts and stealing her away for weeks on end in New Orleans. This devotion did not prevent him from getting married, in 1875, to a Mayfair cousin, a descendant of Maurice and a celebrated beauty.

Her name was Suzette Mayfair, and Julien so loved her that he commissioned no less than ten portraits of her during the first years of their marriage. They lived together in the First Street house apparently in complete harmony with Rémy and his family, perhaps because in every respect Rémy deferred to Julien.

Suzette seems to have loved little Mary Beth, though she had four children of her own in the next five years, including three boys and a girl, named Jeannette.

Katherine never voluntarily returned to the First Street house. It reminded her too much of Darcy. When in old age she was forced to return, it unsettled her mind; and at the turn of the century she became a tragic figure, eternally dressed in black, and roaming the gardens in search of Darcy.

Of all the Mayfair Witches studied to date, Katherine was perhaps the weakest and the least significant. Her children Clay and Vincent were both entirely respectable and unremarkable. Clay and Vincent married early and had large families, and their descendants now live in New Orleans.

What we know seems to indicate that Katherine was "broken" by Darcy's death. And is thereafter never described as anything but "sweet" and "gentle" and "patient." She never took part in the management of Riverbend, but left it all to Julien, who eventually put it in the hands of Clay and Vincent Mayfair and of paid overseers.

Katherine spent more and more of her time with her mother, Marguerite, who had become with each decade ever more peculiar. A visitor in the 1880s describes Marguerite as "quite impossible," a crone who went about night and day in stained white lace, and spent hours reading aloud in a horrid unmodulated voice in her library. She is said to have insulted people carelessly and at random. She was fond of her niece Angeline (Rémy's daughter) and of Katherine. She constantly mistook Katherine's children Clay and Vincent for their uncles, Julien or Rémy. Katherine was described as gray-haired and worn, and always at work on her embroidery.

Katherine seems to have been a strict Catholic in later life. She went to daily Mass at the parish church and lavish christening parties were held for all of Clay's children and Vincent's children.

Marguerite did not die until she was ninety-two, at which time Katherine was sixty-one years old.

But other than the tales of incest, which characterize the Mayfair history since the time of Jeanne Louise and Pierre, there are no occult stories about Katherine.

The black servants, slave or free, were never afraid of Katherine. There are no sightings of any mysterious dark-haired lover. And there is no evidence to indicate that Darcy Monahan died of anything but plain old yellow fever.

It has even been speculated by the members of the Talamasca that Julien was actually "the witch" of this entire period—that perhaps no other natural medium was presented in this generation of the family, and as Marguerite grew old, Julien began to exhibit the power. It has also been speculated that Katherine was a natural medium but that she rejected her role when she fell in love with Darcy, and that is why Julien was so against her marriage, for Julien knew the secrets of the family.

Indeed, we have an abundance of information to suggest that Julien was a witch, if not the witch of the Mayfair family.

It is therefore imperative that we study Julien in some detail. As late as the 1950s, fascinating information about Julien was recounted to us. At some point, the history of Julien must be enlarged through further investigation and further collation and examination of the existing documents. Our reports on the Mayfairs throughout these decades are voluminous and repetitive. And there are numerous public and recorded mentions of Julien, and there are three oil portraits of him in American museums, and one in London.

Julien's black hair turned completely white while he was still quite young, and his numerous photographs as well as these oil paintings show him to be a man of considerable presence and charm, as well as physical beauty. Some have said that he resembled his opera singer father, Tyrone Clifford McNamara.

But it has struck some members of the Talamasca that Julien strongly resembled his ancestors Deborah Mayfair and Petyr van Abel, who of course in no way resembled each other. Julien seems a remarkable combination of these two forebears. He has Petyr's height, profile, and blue eyes, and Deborah's delicate cheekbones and mouth. His expression in several of his portraits is amazingly like that of Deborah.

It is as if the nineteenth-century portraitist had seen the Rembrandt of Deborah—which was of course impossible as it has always been in our vault—and consciously sought to imitate the "personality" captured by Rembrandt. We can only assume that Julien evinced that personality. It is also worth noting that in most of his photographs, in spite of the somber pose and other formal aspects of the work, Julien is smiling.

It is a "Mona Lisa" smile, but it is nevertheless a smile, and strikes a bizarre note since it is wholly out of keeping with nineteenth-century photographic conventions. Five tintypes of Julien in our possession show the same subtle little smile. And smiles in tintypes of this era are completely unknown. It is as if Julien found "picture taking" amusing. Photographs taken near the end of Julien's life, in the twentieth century, also show a smile, but it is broader and more generous. It is worth noting that in these later pictures he appears extremely good-natured, and quite simply happy.

Julien was certainly the magnate of the family all of his life, more or less governing nieces and nephews as well as his sister, Katherine, and his brother, Rémy.

That he incited fear and confusion in his enemies was well-known. It was reported by one furious cotton factor that Julien had, in a dispute, caused another man's clothing to burst into flame. The fire was hastily put out, and the man recovered from his rather serious burns, and no action was ever taken against Julien. Indeed, many who heard the story—including the local police—did not believe it. Julien laughed whenever he was asked about it. But there is also a story, told by only one witness, that

Julien could set anything on fire by his will, and that his mother teased him about it.

In another famous incident, Julien caused all the objects of a room to fly about when he went into a rage, and then could not bring a halt to the confusion. He went out, shut the door on the little storm, and sank into helpless laughter. There is also an isolated story, dependent upon one witness, that Julien murdered one of his boyhood tutors.

None of the Mayfairs up to this period attended any regular school. But all were well educated privately. Julien was no exception, having several tutors during his youth. One of these, a handsome Yankee from Boston, was found drowned in a bayou near Riverbend, and it was said that Julien strangled him and threw him in the water. Again, this was never investigated, and the entire Mayfair family was indignant at this gossip. Servants who spread the story at once retracted it.

This Boston schoolteacher had been a great source of information about the family. He gossiped continuously about Marguerite's strange habits, and about how the slaves feared her. It is from him that we gained our descriptions of her bottles and jars full of strange body parts and objects. He claimed to have fought off advances from Marguerite. Indeed, so vicious and unwise was his gossip that more than one person warned the family about it.

Whether Julien did kill the man cannot be known, but if he did, he had—given the attitudes of the day—at least some reason.

Julien was said to give out foreign gold coins as if they were copper pennies. Waiters at the fashionable restaurants vied with one another to serve his table. He was a fabled horseman and maintained several horses of his own, as well as two carriages and teams in his stables near to First Street.

Even into old age, he often rode his chestnut mare all the way up St. Charles Avenue to Carrolton and back in the morning. He would toss coins to the black children whom he passed.

After his death, four different witnesses claimed to have seen his ghost riding through the mist on St. Charles Avenue, and these stories were printed in the newspapers of the period.

Julien was also a great supporter of the Mardi Gras, which began as we know it today around 1872. He entertained lavishly at the First Street house during the Mardi Gras season.

It was also said countless times that Julien had the gift of "bilocation," that is, he could be in two places at the same time. This story was widely circulated among the servants. Julien would appear to be in the library, for instance, but then would be sighted almost immediately in the back garden. Or a maidservant would see Julien go out the front door, and then turn around to see him coming down the stairway.

More than one servant quit working in the First Street house rather than cope with the "strange Monsieur Julien."

It has been speculated that appearances of Lasher might have been responsible for this confusion. Whatever the case, later descriptions of Lasher's clothes bear a remarkable resemblance to those worn by Julien in two different portraits. Lasher as cited throughout the twentieth century is invariably dressed as Julien might have been dressed in the 1870s and 1880s.

Julien stuffed handfuls of bills into the pockets of the priests who came to call or the visiting Little Sisters of the Poor or other such persons. He gave lavishly to the parish church, and to every charitable fund whose officials approached him. He often said that money didn't matter to him. Yet he was a tireless accumulator of wealth.

We know that he loved his mother, Marguerite, and though he did not spend much time in her company, he purchased books for her all the time in New Orleans, and ordered them for her from New York and Europe. Only once did a quarrel between them attract attention and that was over Katherine's marriage to Darcy Monahan, at which time Marguerite struck Julien several times in front of the servants. By all accounts he was deeply emotionally hurt and simply withdrew, in tears, from his mother's company.

After the death of Julien's wife, Suzette, Julien spent less time than ever at Riverbend. His children were brought up entirely at First Street. Julien, who had always been a debonair figure, took a more active role in society. Long before that, however, he appeared at the opera and the theater with his little niece (or daughter) Mary Beth. He gave many charity balls and actively supported young amateur musicians, presenting them in small private concerts in the double parlor at First Street.

Julien not only made huge profits at Riverbend, he also went into merchandising with two New York affiliates and made a considerable fortune in that endeavor. He bought up property all over New Orleans, which he left to his niece Mary Beth, even though she was the designee of the Mayfair legacy and thereby stood to inherit a fortune larger than Julien's.

There seems little doubt that Julien's wife, Suzette, was a disappointment to him. Servants and friends spoke of many unfortunate arguments. It was said that Suzette for all her beauty was deeply religious and Julien's high-spirited nature disturbed her. She eschewed the jewels and fine clothes which he wanted her to wear. She did not like to go out at night. She disliked loud music. A lovely creature, with pale skin and shining eyes, Suzette was always sickly and died young after the birth in rapid succession of her four children, and there is no doubt that the one girl, Jeannette, had some sort of "second sight" or psychic power.

More than once Jeannette was heard by the servants to scream in uncontrollable panic at the sight of some ghost or apparition. Her sudden frights and mad dashes from the house into the street became well-known in the Garden District, and were even written up in the papers. In fact, it was Jeannette who gave rise to the first "ghost stories" surrounding First Street.

There are several stories of Julien's being extremely impatient with Jeannette and locking her up. But by all accounts he loved his children. All three of his sons went to Harvard, returning to New Orleans to practice civil law, and to amass great fortunes of their own. Their descendants are Mayfairs to this day, regardless of sex or marital connection. And it is the law firm founded by Julien's sons which has, for decades, administered the Mayfair legacy.

We have at least seven different photographs of Julien with his children, including some with Jeannette (who died young). In every one, the family seems extremely cheerful, and Barclay and Cortland strongly resemble their father. Though Barclay and Garland both died in their late sixties, Cortland lived to be eighty years old, dying in late October of 1959. This member of the Talamasca made direct contact with Cortland the preceding year, but we shall come to that at the proper time.

(Ellie Mayfair, adoptive mother of Rowan Mayfair, *the present designee of the legacy*, is a descendant of Julien Mayfair, being a granddaughter of Julien's son Cortland, the only child of Cortland's son Sheffield Mayfair and his wife, a French-speaking cousin named Eugenie Mayfair, who died when Ellie was seven years old. Sheffield died before Cortland, of a severe heart attack in the family law offices on Camp Street in 1952, at which time he was forty-five. His daughter Ellie was a student at Stanford in Palo Alto, California at the time, where she was already engaged to Graham Franklin, whom she later married. She never lived in New Orleans after that, though she returned for frequent visits and came back to adopt Rowan Mayfair in 1959.)

Some of our most interesting evidence regarding Julien himself has to do with Mary Beth, and with the birth of Belle, her first daughter. Upon Mary Beth Julien bestowed everything she could possibly desire, holding balls for her at First Street that rivaled any private entertainment in New Orleans. The garden walks, balustrades, and fountains at First Street were all designed and laid out for Mary Beth's fifteenth birthday party.

Mary Beth was already tall by the age of fifteen, and in her photographs from this period she appears stately, serious, and darkly beautiful, with large black eyes and very clearly defined and beautifully shaped eyebrows. Her air is decidedly indifferent however. And this apparent absence of narcissism or vanity was to characterize her photographs all her life. Sometimes her mannish posture is almost defiantly casual in these pictures; but it highly doubtful that she was ever defiant so much as simply distracted. It was frequently said that she looked like her grandmother Marguerite and not like her mother, Katherine.

In 1887, Julien took his fifteen-year-old niece to New York with him. There Julien and Mary Beth visited one of Lestan's grandsons, Corrington Mayfair, who was an attorney and in the merchandising business with Julien. Julien and Mary Beth went on to Europe in 1888, remaining an entire year and a half, during which time New Orleans was informed by numerous letters to friends and relatives that sixteen-year-old Mary Beth had "married" a Scottish Mayfair—an Old World cousin—and given birth to a little girl named Belle. This marriage, taking place in a Scottish Catholic church, was described in rich detail in a letter which Julien wrote to a friend in the French Quarter, a notorious gossip of a woman, who passed the letter around to everyone. Other letters from both Julien and Mary Beth described the marriage in more abbreviated form for other talkative friends and relatives.

It is worth noting that when Katherine heard of her daughter's marriage, she took to her bed and would not eat or speak for five days. Only when threatened with a private asylum did she sit up and agree to drink some soup. "Julien is the devil," she whispered, at which point Marguerite drove everyone out of the room.

Unfortunately the mysterious Lord Mayfair died in a fall from his ancestral tower in Scotland two months before the birth of his little daughter. Again, Julien wrote home full accounts of everything which took place. Mary Beth wrote tearful letters to her friends.

This Lord Mayfair is almost certainly a fictitious character. Mary Beth and Julien did visit Scotland; indeed they spent some time in Edinburgh and even visited Donnelaith, where they purchased the very castle on the hill above the town described in detail by Petyr van Abel. But the castle, once the family home of the Donnelaith clan, had been an abandoned ruin since the

425

late 1600s. There is no record anywhere in Scotland of any lord or lords Mayfair.

However, inquiries made by the Talamasca in this century have unearthed some rather startling evidence about the Donnelaith ruin. A fire gutted it in the year 1689, in the fall, apparently very near the time of Deborah's execution in Montcleve, France. It might have been the very day, but that we have been unable to discover. In the fire, the last of the Donnelaith clan—the old lord, his eldest son, and his young grandson—perished.

It is tantalizing to suppose that the old lord was the father of Deborah Mayfair. It is also tantalizing to suppose that he was a wretched coward, who did not dare to interfere with the burning of the poor simpleminded peasant girl Suzanne, even when their "merry-begot" daughter Deborah was in danger of the same awful fate.

But we cannot know. And we cannot know whether or not Lasher played any role in starting the fire that wiped out the Donnelaith family. History tells us only that the old man's body was burnt, while the infant grandson smothered in the smoke, and several women in the family leapt to their death from the battlements. The eldest son apparently died when a wooden stairway collapsed under him.

History also tells us that Julien and Mary Beth purchased Donnelaith castle after only one afternoon spent in the ruins. It remains the property of the Mayfair family to this day, and other Mayfairs have visited it.

It has never been occupied or restored, but it is kept cleared of all debris and rather safely maintained, and during Stella's life in the twentieth century, it was open to the public.

Why Julien bought the castle, what he knew about it and what he meant to do with it has never been known. Surely he had some knowledge of Deborah and Suzanne, either through the family history, or through Lasher.

The Talamasca has devoted an enormous amount of thought to this whole question—who knew what and when—because there is strong evidence to indicate that the Mayfairs of the nineteenth century did not know their full history. Katherine confessed on more than one occasion that she really didn't know much about the family's beginnings, only that they had come from Martinique to Saint-Domingue sometime in the sixteen hundreds. Many other Mayfairs made similar remarks.

And even Mary Beth as late as 1920 told the parish priests at St. Alphonsus Church that it was "all lost in the dust." She seemed even a little confused when talking to local architecture students about who built Riverbend and when. Books of the period list Marguerite as the builder when, in fact, Marguerite was born there. When asked by the servants to identify certain persons in the old oil portraits at First Street, Mary Beth said that she could not. She wished somebody back then had had the presence of mind to write the names on the backs of the pictures.

As far as we have been able to ascertain, the names are on the backs of at least some of the pictures.

Perhaps Julien, and Julien alone, read the old records, for certainly there were old records. And Julien had started to move them from Riverbend to First Street as early as 1872.

Whatever the case, Julien went to Donnelaith in 1888 and bought the ruined castle. And Mary Beth Mayfair told the story to the end of her days that Lord Mayfair was the father of her poor sweet little daughter Belle, who turned out to be the very opposite of her powerful mother.

In 1892, an artist was hired to paint a picture of the ruin, and this oil painting hangs in the house on First Street.

To return to the chronology, the supposed uncle and niece returned home with baby Belle in late 1889, at which time Marguerite, aged ninety and extremely decrepit, took a special interest in the baby.

In fact, Katherine and Mary Beth had to keep watch on the child all the time it was at Riverbend, lest Marguerite go walking with it in her arms and then forget about it, and drop it or lay it on a stairstep or a table. Julien laughed at these cautions and said before the servants numerous times that the baby had a special guardian angel who would take care of it.

By this time there seems to have been no talk at all about Julien having been Mary Beth's father, and none whatsoever about his being the father, by his daughter, of Belle.

But for the purposes of this record, we are certain that he was Mary Beth's father and the father of her daughter Belle.

Mary Beth, Julien, and Belle all lived together happily at First Street, and Mary Beth, though she loved to dance and to go to the theater and to parties, showed no immediate interest in finding "another" husband.

Eventually, she did remarry, as we shall see, a man named Daniel McIntyre, giving birth to three more children—Carlotta, Lionel, and Stella.

The night before Marguerite's death in 1891, Mary Beth woke up in her bedroom on First Street, screaming. She insisted she had to leave for Riverbend at once, that her grandmother was dying. Why had no one sent for her? The servants found Julien sitting motionless in the library of the first floor, apparently weeping. He seemed not to hear or see Mary Beth as she pleaded with him to take her to Riverbend.

A young Irish maid then heard the old quadroon housekeeper remark that maybe that wasn't Julien at all sitting at the desk, and they ought to go look for him. This terrified the maid, especially since the housekeeper began to call out to "Michie Julien" about the house while this motionless weeping individual remained at the desk, staring forward as if he could not hear her.

At last Mary Beth set out on foot, at which point Julien leapt up from the desk, ran his fingers through his white hair, and ordered the servants to bring round the brougham. He caught up with Mary Beth before she had reached Magazine Street.

It is worth noting that Julien was sixty-three at this time, and described as being a very handsome man with the flamboyant appearance and demeanor of a stage actor. Mary Beth was nineteen and exceedingly beautiful. Belle was only two years old and there is no mention of her in this story.

Julien and Mary Beth arrived at Riverbend just as messengers were being sent to fetch them. Marguerite was almost comatose, a wraith of a ninety-two-year-old woman, clutching a curious little doll with her bony fingers, which she called her *maman* much to the confusion of the attending doctor and nurse, who told all of New Orleans about it afterwards. A priest was also in attendance and his detailed account of the whole matter has also worked its way into our records.

The doll was reputedly a ghastly thing with real human bones for limbs, strung together by means of black wire, and a mane of horrid white hair affixed to its head of rags with its crudely drawn features.

Katherine, then aged sixty-one, and her two sons were both sitting by the bed, as they had been for hours. Rémy was also there, having been at the plantation for a month before his mother took ill.

The priest, Father Martin, had just given Marguerite the last sacraments, and the blessed candles were burning on the altar.

When Marguerite breathed her last, the priest watched with curiosity as Katherine rose from her chair, went to the jewel box on the dresser which she had always shared with her mother, took out the emerald necklace, and gave it to Mary Beth. Mary Beth received it gratefully, put it around her neck, and then continued to weep.

The priest then observed that it had begun to rain, and the wind about the house was extremely strong, banging the shutters and causing the leaves to fall. Julien seemed to be delighted by this and even laughed.

Katherine appeared weary and frightened. And Mary Beth cried inconsolably. Clay, a personable young man, seemed fascinated by what was going on. His brother Vincent merely looked indifferent.

Julien then opened the windows to let in the wind and rain, which frightened the priest somewhat and certainly made him uncomfortable, as it was winter. He nevertheless stayed at the bedside as he thought proper, though rain was actually falling on the bed. The trees were crashing against the house. The priest was afraid one of the limbs might come right through the window nearest him.

Julien, quite unperturbed and with his eyes full of tears, kissed the dead Marguerite and closed her eyes, and took the doll from her, which he put inside his coat. He then laid her hands on her chest and made a speech to the priest explaining that his mother had been born at the end of the "old century" and had lived almost a hundred years, that she had seen and understood things which she could never tell anyone.

"In most families," Julien declared in French, "when a person dies, all that the person knows dies with that person. Not so with the Mayfairs. Her blood is in us, and all she knew is passed into us and we are stronger."

Katherine merely nodded sadly to this speech. Mary Beth continued to weep. Clay stood in the corner with his arms folded, watching.

When the priest asked timidly if the window might be closed, Julien told him that the heavens were weeping for Marguerite, and that it would be disrespectful to close the window. Julien then knocked the blessed candles off the Catholic altar by the bed, which offended the priest. It also startled Katherine.

"Now, Julien, don't go crazy!" Katherine whispered. At which Vincent laughed in spite of himself, and Clay smiled unwillingly also. All glanced awkwardly at the priest, who was horrified. Julien then gave the company a playful smile and a shrug, and then looking at his mother again, he became miserable, and knelt down beside the bed, and buried his face in the covers beside the dead woman.

Clay quietly left the room.

As the priest was taking his leave, he asked Katherine about the emerald. Rather offhandedly she said that it was a jewel she had inherited from her mother, but never much liked, as it was so big and so heavy. Mary Beth could have it.

The priest then left the house and discovered that within a few hundred yards, the rain was not falling and there was no wind. The sky was quite clear. He came upon Clay sitting in a white straight-backed chair by the picket fence at the very end of the frontage of the plantation; Clay was smoking and watching the distant storm which was quite visible in the darkness. The priest greeted Clay but Clay did not appear to hear him.

This is the first detailed account of the death of a Mayfair witch that we possess since Petyr van Abel's description of the death of Deborah.

There are many other stories about Julien which could be included here, and indeed perhaps they should be in future. We will hear more of him as the story of Mary Beth unfolds.

But we should not move on to Mary Beth without treating one more aspect of Julien, that is, his bisexuality. And it is worthwhile to recount in detail the significant stories told of Julien by one of his lovers, Richard Llewellyn.

As indicated above, Julien was mentioned in connection with a "crime against nature" very early in his life, at which point he killed—either accidentally or deliberately—one of his uncles. We have also made mention of his male companion in the French Quarter in the late 1850s.

Julien was to have such companions throughout his life, but of most of them we know nothing.

Two of whom we have some record are a quadroon named Victor Gregoire and an Englishman named Richard Llewellyn.

Victor Gregoire worked for Julien in the 1880s, as a private secretary of sorts, and even a sort of valet. He lived in the servants' quarters on First Street. He was a remarkably handsome man as were all Julien's companions, male or female. And he was rumored to be a Mayfair descendant.

Investigation has confirmed in fact that he was the great-grandson of a quadroon maid who emigrated from Saint-Domingue with the family, a possible descendant of Peter Fontenay Mayfair, brother of Jeanne Louise, and son of Charlotte and Petyr van Abel.

Whatever, Victor was much beloved by Julien, but the two had a quarrel in about 1885, around the time of Suzette's death. The one rather thin story we have about the quarrel indicates that Victor accused Julien of not treating Suzette in her final illness with sufficient compassion. And Julien, outraged, beat Victor rather badly. Cousins repeated this tale within the family enough for outsiders to hear of it.

The consensus seemed to be that Victor was probably right, and as Victor was a most devoted servant to Julien he had a servant's right to tell his master the truth. It was common knowledge at this time that no one was closer to Julien than Victor, and that Victor did everything for Julien.

It should also be added, however, that there is strong evidence that Julien loved Suzette, no matter how disappointed he was in her, and that he took good care of her. His sons certainly thought that he loved their mother; and at Suzette's funeral, Julien was distraught. He comforted Suzette's father and mother for hours after; and took time off from all business pursuits to remain with his daughter Jeannette, who "never recovered" from her mother's death.

We should also note that Julien was near hysteria at Jeannette's funeral, which occurred several years later. Indeed, at one point he held tight to the coffin and refused to allow it to be placed in the crypt. Garland, Barclay, and Cortland had to physically support their father as the entombment took place.

Descendants of Suzette's sisters and brothers say in the present time that "Great-aunt Suzette" who once lived at First Street was, in fact, driven mad by her husband Julien—that he was perverse, cruel, and mischievous in a way that indicated congenital insanity. But these tales are vague and contain no real knowledge of the period.

To proceed with the story of Victor, the young man died tragically while Julien and Mary Beth were in Europe.

Walking home one night through the Garden District, Victor stepped in the path of a speeding carriage at the corner of Philip and Prytania streets, and suffered a dreadful fall and a blow to the head. Two days later he succumbed from massive cerebral injuries. Julien received word on his return to New York. He had a beautiful monument built for Victor in the St. Louis No. 3 Cemetery.

What argues for this having been a homosexual relationship is circumstantial except for a later statement by Richard Llewellyn, the last of Julien's male companions. Julien bought enormous amounts of clothes for Victor. He also bought Victor beautiful riding horses, and gave him exorbitant amounts of money. The two spent days and nights together, traveled together to and from Riverbend, and to New York, and Victor often slept on the couch in the library at First Street, rather than retire to his room at the very back of the house.

As for the statement of Richard Llewellyn, he never knew Victor, but he told this member of the order personally that Julien had once had a colored lover named Victor.

* * *

Richard Llewellyn is the only observer of Julien ever personally interviewed by a member of the order, and he was more than a casual observer.

What he had to say—concerning other members of the family as well as Julien—makes his testimony of very special interest even though his statements are for the most part uncorroborated. He has given some of the most intimate glimpses of the Mayfair family which we possess.

Therefore, we feel that it is worthwhile to quote our reconstruction of his words in its entirety.

Richard Llewellyn came to New Orleans in 1900 at the age of twenty and he became an employee of Julien, just as Victor had once been, for Julien, though he was then seventy-two years old, still maintained enormous interests in merchandizing, cotton factoring, real estate, and banking. Until the week of his death some fourteen years later, Julien kept regular business hours in the library at First Street.

Llewellyn worked for Julien until his death, and Llewellyn admitted candidly to me in 1958, when I first began my field investigation of the Mayfair Witches, that he had been Julien's lover.

Llewellyn was in 1958 just past seventy-seven years of age. He was a man of medium height, healthy build, and had curly black hair, heavily streaked with gray, and very large and slightly protruding blue eyes. He had acquired by that time what I would call a New Orleans accent, and no longer sounded like a Yankee or a Bostonian, though there are definite similarities between the ways that New Orleanians and Bostonians speak. Whatever the case, he was unmistakably a New Orleanian and he looked the part as well.

He owned an antiquarian bookstore in the French Quarter, on Chartres Street, specializing in books on music, especially opera. There were always phonograph records of Caruso playing in the store, and Llewellyn, who invariably sat at a desk to the rear of the shop, was always dressed in a suit and tie.

It was a bequest from Julien which had enabled him to own the building, where he also lived in the second floor flat, and he worked in his shop until one month before his death in 1959.

I visited him several times in the summer of 1958 but I was only able to persuade him to talk at length on one occasion, and I must confess that the wine he drank, at my invitation, had a great deal to do with it. I have of course shamelessly employed this method—lunch, wine, and then more wine—with many a witness of the Mayfair family. It seems to work particularly well in New Orleans and during the summer. I think I was a little too brash and insistent with Llewellyn, but his information has proved invaluable.

An entirely ''causal'' meeting with Llewellyn was effected when I happened into his bookstore one July afternoon, and we commenced to talk about the great castrati opera singers, especially Farinelli. It was not difficult to persuade Llewellyn to lock up the shop for a Caribbean siesta at two-thirty and come with me for a late lunch at Galatoire's.

I did not broach the subject of the Mayfair family for some time, and then only timidly and in connection with the old house on First Street. I said frankly that I was interested in the place and the people who lived there. By then Llewellyn was pleasantly ''high'' and plunged into reminiscences of his first days in New Orleans.

At first he would say nothing about Julien but then began to speak of Julien as if I knew all about the man. I supplied various well-known dates and facts and that moved the conversation along briskly. We left Galatoire's finally for a small, quiet Bourbon Street café and continued our conversation until well after eight-thirty that evening.

At some point during this conversation Llewellyn realized that I had no prejudice whatsoever against him on account of his sexual preferences, indeed that nothing he was saying came as a shock to me, and this added to his relaxed attitude towards the story he told.

This was long before our use of tape recorders, and I reconstructed the conversation as best I could as soon as I returned to my hotel, trying to capture Llewellyn's particular expressions. But it is a reconstruction. And throughout I have omitted my own persistent questions. I believe the substance to be accurate.

Essentially, Llewellyn was deeply in love with Julien Mayfair, and one of the early shocks of Llewellyn's life was to discover that Julien was at least ten to fifteen years older than Llewellyn ever imagined, and Llewellyn only discovered this when Julien suffered his first stroke in early 1914. Until that time Julien had been a fairly romantic and vigorous lover of Llewellyn, and Llewellyn remained with Julien until he died, some four months later. Julien was partially paralyzed at that time, but still managed to spend an hour or two each day in his office.

Llewellyn supplied a vivid description of Julien in the early 1900s, as a thin man who had lost some of his height, but was generally spry and energetic, and full of good humor and imagination.

433

Llewellyn said frankly that Julien had initiated him in the erotic secrets of life, and not only had Julien taught Llewellyn how to be an attentive lover, he also took the young man with him to Storyville—the notorious red-light district of New Orleans—and introduced him to the better houses operating there.

But let us move on directly to his account:

"Oh, the tricks he taught me," Llewellyn said, referring to their amorous relationship, "and what a sense of humor he had. It was as if the whole world were a joke to him, and there was never the slightest bitterness in it. I'll tell you a very private thing about him. He made love to me just as if I were a woman. If you don't know what I mean, there's no use explaining it. And that voice he had, that French accent. I tell you when he started talking in my ear . . .

"And he would tell me the funniest stories about his antics with his other lovers, about how they fooled everyone, and indeed, one of his boys, Aleister by name, used to dress up as a woman and go to the opera with Julien and no one ever had the slightest suspicion about it. Julien tried to persuade me to do that, but I told him I could never carry it off, never! He understood. He was extremely good-natured. In fact, it was impossible to involve him in a quarrel. He said he was done with all that, and besides he had a horrible temper, and couldn't bear to lose it. It exhausted him.

"The one time I was unfaithful and came back after two days, fully expecting a terrible argument, he treated me with what would you call it? Bemused cordiality. It turned out he knew everything that I had done and with whom, and in the most pleasant and sincere way he asked me why I had been such a fool. It was positively eerie. At last I burst into tears and confessed that I had meant to show my independence. After all he was such an overwhelming man. But I was then ready to do anything to get back into his good graces. I don't know what I would have done if he'd thrown me out!

"He accepted this with a smile. He patted my shoulder and said not to worry. I'll tell you it cured me of wandering out forever! It was no fun at all to feel so dreadful and have him so calm and so accepting. Taught me a few things, it really did.

"And then he went into all that about being a reader of minds, and of being able to see what was going on in other places. He talked a lot about that. I could never tell whether or not he meant it, or if it was just another one of his jokes. He had the prettiest eyes. He was a very handsome old man, really. And there was a flare to the way he dressed. I suppose you might say he was something of a dandy. When he was dressed up in a fine white linen suit with a yellow silk waistcoat and a white Panama hat, he looked splendid.

"I think I imitate him to this day. Isn't that sad? I go about trying to look like Julien Mayfair.

"Oh, but that reminds me, I'll tell you, he did the strangest thing to frighten me once! And to this day I don't really know what happened. We had been talking the night before about what Julien looked like when he was young, how handsome he appeared in all the photographs, and you know it was like going through a veritable history of photography to study all that. The first pictures of him were daguerreotypes, and then came the tintypes and the later genuine photographs in sepia on cardboard, and finally the sort of black-and-white pictures we have today. Anyway, he had shown me a batch of them and I had said, 'Oh, I wish I'd known you when you were young, I imagine you were truly beautiful.' Then I'd stopped. I was so ashamed. I thought perhaps I'd hurt him. But there he was, merely smiling at me. I shall never forget it. He was seated at the far end of his leather couch, legs crossed, just looking at me through the smoke from his pipe, and he said, 'Well, Richard, if you'd like to know how I was then, maybe I'll show you. I'll surprise you.'

"That night, I was downtown. I don't remember why I went out. I had to get out perhaps. You know sometimes that house could be so oppressive! It was full of children and old people, and Mary Beth Mayfair was always about, and she was such a presence, to put it politely. Don't get me wrong, I liked Mary Beth, everybody liked Mary Beth. And I liked her a great deal, until Julien died, at least. She was easy to talk to, actually. She would really listen to you when you talked to her, that is one thing I always found rather unusual about her. But she had a way of filling up a room when she came in. She outshined everyone else, you might say, and then there was her husband, Judge McIntyre.

"Judge McIntyre was a terrible sot. He was always drunk. And what a quarrelsome drunk. I tell you I had to go looking for him more than once and bring him home from the Irish bars on Magazine Street. You know, the Mayfairs weren't his kind of people, really. He was an educated man, lace curtain Irish, to be sure. Yet I think Mary Beth made him feel inferior. She was always saying little things to him, such as that he ought to put his napkin in his lap, or not smoke his cigars in the dining room, or that he was biting the edge of his silver when he ate, and the noise annoyed her. He was eternally offended by her. But I think he really loved her. That's why she could hurt him so easily. He really loved her. You would have had to have known her to un-

435

derstand. She wasn't beautiful. That wasn't it. But she was . . . she was absolutely captivating! I could tell you about her and the young men, but then I don't want to talk about all that. But what I was trying to say was that they would sit there at the table till all hours after dinner, Mary Beth and Judge McIntyre and Julien, of course, and Clay Mayfair, too, while he was there. I never saw people who liked to talk so much after dinner.

"Julien could put away half a fifth of brandy. And little Stella would fall asleep in his lap. Ah, Stella with the ringlets, dear pretty Stella. And beautiful little Belle. She'd come wandering in with her doll. And Millie Dear. They called her Millie Dear then but they stopped later on. She was younger than Belle, but she, you know, sort of watched out for Belle. It took a long time to catch on about Belle. You just thought she was sweet at first, an angel of a girl, if you know what I mean. There were some other cousins who used to come. Seems Julien's boy, Garland, was around plenty after he came home from school. And Cortland, I really liked Cortland. And for a while there was talk he might marry Millie, but she was only a first cousin, being Rémy's girl, and people didn't do that sort of thing anymore. Millie has never married. What a sad thing . . .

"But you know, Judge McIntyre was the kind of Irishman who really can't stand to be around his wife, if you follow my meaning. He had to be with men, drinking and arguing all the time, and not men like Julien, but men like himself, hard-drinking, hard-talking Irishmen. He spent a great deal of time downtown at his club, but many an evening he went to those rougher drinking places on Magazine Street.

"When he was home, he was always very noisy. He was a good judge however. He wouldn't drink till he came home from court, and since he always came home early he had plenty of time to be completely drunk by ten o'clock. Then he would go wandering, and round midnight Julien would say, 'Richard, I think you had better go look for him.'

"Julien just took it all in stride. He thought Judge McIntyre was funny. He would laugh at anything Judge McIntyre said. Judge McIntyre would go on and on about Ireland and the political situation over there, and Julien would wait until he was finished and say cheerfully and with a twinkle in his eye, 'I don't care if they all kill each other.' Judge McIntyre would go crazy. Mary Beth would laugh and shake her head and kick Julien under the table. But Judge McIntyre was so far gone in those last years. How he ever managed to live so long I cannot imagine. Didn't die till 1925, three months after Mary Beth died. They said it was pneumonia. The hell it was pneumonia! They found him in the gutter, you know. And it was Christmas Eve and so cold the pipes were freezing. Pneumonia. I heard when Mary Beth was dying, she was in such pain they gave her almost enough morphia to kill her. She would be lying there out of her mind, and in he'd come, drunk, and wake her up, saying, 'Mary Beth, I need you.' What a poor drunken fool he was. And she would say to him, 'Come, Daniel, lie beside me, Daniel.' And to think she was in such pain. It was Stella who told me that . . . the last time I ever saw her. Alive that is. I went up there one last time after that—for Stella's funeral. And there she was in the coffin, it was a miracle the way Lonigan closed up that wound. Just beautiful she was, lying there, and all the Mayfairs in that room. But that was the last time I saw her alive, as I was saying . . . And the things she said about Carlotta, of how Carlotta was cold to Mary Beth in those last months, why, it would make your hair stand on end.

"Imagine a daughter being cold to a mother who was dying like that. But Mary Beth took no notice of it. She just lay there, in pain, half dreaming, Stella said, not knowing where she was, sometimes talking out loud to Julien as if she could see him in the room, and of course Stella was by her night and day, you can be sure of that; how Mary Beth loved Stella.

"Why, Mary Beth told me once that she could put all her other children in a sack and throw them in the Mississippi River, for all she cared. Stella was the only one that mattered. 'Course she was joking. She was never mean to those children. I remember how she used to read by the hour to Lionel when he was little, and help him with his schooling. She got him the best teachers when he didn't want to go to school. None of the children did well in school, except for Carlotta, naturally. Stella was expelled from three different schools, I believe. Carlotta was the only one who really did well, and a lot of good it did her.

"But what was I saying? Oh, yes. Sometimes I felt I had no place in the house. Whatever the case, I went out. I went to the Quarter. It was the days of Storyville, you know, when prostitution was legal here, and Julien had taken me down to Lulu White's Mahogany Hall himself one night and to the other fashionable places, and he didn't much care if I went on my own.

"Well, I said I was going that night. And Julien didn't mind. He was up there snug in the third-floor bedroom with his books and his hot chocolate, and his Victrola. Besides, he knew I was only looking. And so I went down there, strolling past all those little houses—you know, the cribs they used to call them—with the girls in the front doors beckoning for me to come in, and of course I had not the slightest intention of doing it.

"Then my eyes fell on this beautiful young man, I mean a simply beautiful young man. And he stood in one of the alleyways down there, with his arms folded, leaning against the side of the house, simply looking at me. 'Bon soir, Richard,' he said to me and I recognized the voice at once, the French accent. It was Julien's. And I saw that the man was Julien! Only he couldn't have been past twenty! I tell you I never had such a start. I almost cried out. It was worse than seeing a ghost. And the fellow was gone, like that, vanished.

"I couldn't get to a cab fast enough and I went right straight home to First Street. Julien opened the front door for me. He was wearing his robe, and puffing on his obnoxious pipe and laughing. 'I told you I would show you what I looked like when I was twenty!' he said. He laughed and laughed.

"I remember I followed him into the parlor. And it was such a lovely room, then, nothing like it is now, you should have seen it. Absolutely lovely French pieces, mostly Louis Cinque, which Julien had bought himself in Europe when he went with Mary Beth. So light and elegant and simply lovely. That art deco furniture was all Stella's doing. She thought it was quite the thing, what with potted palms everywhere! The only good piece of furniture was that Bözendorfer piano. The place looked perfectly mad when I went up there for the funeral, and you know of course that Stella was buried from the house. No funeral parlor for Stella. Why, Stella was laid out in the very front room in which she'd been shot, do you know that? I kept looking around, wondering where exactly it had happened. And don't you know everybody else was doing that, and they had already locked up Lionel, of course. Oh, I couldn't believe it. Lionel had been such a sweet boy, and so good-looking. And he and Stella used to go everywhere together. But what was I saying?

"Oh, yes, that incredible night. I'd just seen young Julien downtown, beautiful young Julien, speaking French to me, and then I was home again and following old Julien into the parlor and he sat down on the couch there, and stretched out his legs and said, 'Ah, Richard, there are so many things I could tell you, so many things I could show you. But I'm old now. And what's the point? One very fine consolation of old age is you don't need to be understood anymore. A sort of resignation sets in with the inevitable hardening of the arteries.'

"Of course I was still upset. 'Julien,' I said. 'I demand to know how you did it.' He wouldn't answer me. It was as if I wasn't there. He was staring at the fire. He always had both fires going in that room in winter. It has two fireplaces, you know, and one is slightly smaller than the other.

"A little later he waked from his dream and he reminded me that he was writing his life story. I might read that after his death, perhaps. He wasn't sure.

" 'I have enjoyed my life,' he said. 'Perhaps a person shouldn't enjoy his life as much as I have enjoyed mine. Ah, there is so much misery in the world and I have always had such a splendid time! Seems unfair, doesn't it? I should have done more for others, much more. I should have been more inventive! But all of that is in my book. You can read it later.'

"He said more than once that he was writing his life story. He really had quite an interesting life, you know, being born so long before the Civil War, and seeing so very much. I used to ride with him uptown, and we would ride through Audubon Park and he would talk about the days when all that land had been a plantation. He talked about taking the steamboat from River-bend. He talked about the old opera house and the quadroon balls. On and on, he talked. I should have written it down. He used to tell little Lionel and Stella those stories too, and how they both listened. He'd take them downtown in the carriage with us, and he would point out places in the French Quarter to them, and tell them wonderful little tales.

"I tell you I wanted to read that life story. I remember several occasions on which I came into the library and he was writing away, and remarked that it was the autobiography. He wrote by hand, though he did have a typewriter. And he didn't mind at all that the children were underfoot. Lionel would be in there reading by the fire, or Stella would be playing with her doll on the couch, didn't matter one bit, he would just be writing away on his autobiography.

"And what do you think? When he died, there was no life story. That's what Mary Beth told me. I begged her to let me see whatever he'd written. She said offhandedly there was nothing. She would not let me touch anything on his desk. She locked me out of the library. Oh, I hated her for it, positively hated her. And she did it in such an offhanded way. She would have convinced anybody else she was telling the truth, that's how sure of herself she was. But I had seen the manuscript. She did give me something which belonged to him, and I've always been grateful."

At that point Llewellyn produced a beautiful carbuncle ring and showed it to me. I complimented him on it, and told him I was curious about the days of Storyville. What had it been like to go there with Julien? His answer was quite lengthy:

"Oh, Julien loved Storyville, he really did. And the women at Lulu White's Hall of Mirrors adored him, I can tell you.

They waited on him as if he were a king. Same thing everywhere he went. Lots of things happened down there, however, that I don't much like to talk about. It wasn't that I was jealous of Julien. It was very simply shocking to a clean-living Yankee boy such as I had been." Llewellyn laughed. "But you'll understand better what I mean if I tell you.

"The first time Julien took me it was winter, and he had his coachman drive us up to the front doors of one of the best houses. There was a pianist playing there then—I'm not sure who it was now, maybe Manuel Perez, maybe Jelly Roll Morton—I was never the fan of jazz and ragtime that Julien was. He just loved that pianist—they always called those pianists the professor, you know—and we sat in the parlor listening, and drinking champagne, and it was quite good champagne, and of course the girls came in with all their tawdry finery and foolish airs—there was the Duchess this and the Countess that—and they tried to seduce Julien, and he was just perfectly charming to all of them. Then finally he made his choice and it was this older woman, rather plain, and that puzzled me, and he said we were both going upstairs. Of course I didn't want to be with her; nothing could have persuaded me to be with her, but Julien only smiled at that, and said that I should watch and that way I'd learn something of the world. Very typical Julien.

"And what do you think happened when we went into the bedroom? Well, it wasn't the woman Julien was interested in, it was her two daughters, nine and eleven years old. They sort of helped with preparations—the examination of Julien, to put it delicately, to make certain that he didn't have you know . . . and then the washing. I tell you I was stunned to watch those children perform these intimate duties, and do you know that when Julien went to it with the mother, the two little girls were there on the bed? They were both very pretty, one with dark hair, the other with blond curls. They wore little chemises, and dark stockings, if you can imagine, and they were enticing, I think even to me. Why, you could see their little nipples through the chemises. Didn't have hardly any breasts at all. I don't know why that was so enticing. They sat against the high carved back of the bed—you know, it was one of those machine-made atrocities that went clear to the ceiling with the half tester and the crown—and they even kissed him like attending angels when he . . . he . . . mounted the mother, so to speak.

"I'll never forget those children, the way it all seemed so natural to them! And natural to Julien.

"Of course he behaved throughout all this as gracefully in such a situation as a human being could possibly behave. You would have thought that he was Darius, King of Persia, and that these ladies were his harem, and there was not the slightest bit of self-consciousness in him or crudery. Afterwards, he drank some more champagne with them, and even the little girls drank it. The mother tried to work her charms on me, but I would have none of it. Julien would have stayed there all night if I hadn't asked him to leave. He was teaching both the girls 'a new poem.' Seems he taught them a poem every time he came down; and they recited three or four of the past lessons for him, one a Shakespeare sonnet. The new one was Elizabeth Barrett Browning.

"I couldn't wait to leave that place. And on the way home, I really lit into him. 'Julien, whatever we are, we are grown people. Those were just children,' I said. He was his usual genial self. 'Come on, now, Richard,' he said, 'don't be foolish. Those were what are called trick babies. They were born in a house of prostitution; and they'll live out their lives that way. I didn't do anything to them that would hurt them. And if I hadn't been with their mother this evening, somebody else would have been with her and with them. But I'll tell you what strikes me, Richard, about the whole matter. It's the way that life asserts itself, no matter what the circumstances. Of course it must be a miserable existence. How could it not be? Yet those little girls manage to live; to breathe; to enjoy themselves. They laugh and they are full of curiosity and tenderness. They adjust, I believe that's the word. They adjust and they reach for the stars in their own way. I tell you it's wondrous to me. They make me think of the wildflowers that grow in the cracks of the pavements, just pushing up into the sun, no matter how many feet crush them down.'

"I didn't argue with him any further. But I remember that he talked on and on. He said there were children in every city in the country who were more miserable than those children. Of course that didn't make it all right.

"I know he went to Storyville often, and he didn't take me along. But I'll tell you something else rather strange . . ." (Here he hesitated. He required some prodding.) "He used to take Mary Beth with him. He took her to Lulu White's and to the Arlington, and the way they managed it was that Mary Beth dressed as a man.

"I saw them go out together on more than one occasion, and of course if you ever saw Mary Beth you would understand. She was not an ugly woman in any sense, but she wasn't delicate. She was tall and strongly built, and she had rather large features. In one of her husband's three-piece suits, she made a damned good-looking man. She'd wrap her long hair up under a hat, and

441

wear a scarf around her neck, and sometimes she wore glasses, though I'm not sure why, and off she went with Julien.

"I remember that happening at least five times. And I heard them talking about it after, how she fooled everyone. And Judge McIntyre sometimes went with them, but I think in truth that Julien and Mary Beth didn't want him along.

"And then once Julien told me that that was how Judge McIntyre had met Mary Beth Mayfair—that it was in Storyville about two years before I came. He wasn't Judge McIntyre yet, then, just Daniel McIntyre. And he'd met Mary Beth down there and spent the evening gambling with her and with Julien, and didn't know till the next morning that Mary Beth was a woman, and when he discovered that he wouldn't leave her alone.

"Julien told me all about it. They had gone down just to roam around and to catch what they could of the Razzy Dazzy Spasm Band. Now you've heard of them, I imagine, and they were good, they really were. And somehow Julien and Mary Beth, who went by the name of Jules on these excursions, went into Willie Piazza's and there they ran into Daniel McIntyre, and after that they wandered from place to place, looking for a good pool game, because Mary Beth was very good at pocket billiards, always was.

"Anyway, it must have been daylight when they decided to go home, and Judge McIntyre had talked a lot of business with Julien, since he wasn't the Judge yet of course and he was a lawyer, and it was determined they would meet uptown for lunch and that maybe Julien would do something to help McIntyre get into a firm. And at that point, when the Judge was giving 'Jules' a big hug of farewell, she pulled off her fedora, and down came all her black hair, and she told him she was a woman, and he almost died on the spot.

"I think he was in love with her from that day on. I came the year after they were married, and they already had Miss Carlotta, a baby in the crib, and Lionel came along within ten months, and then a year and half later, Stella, the prettiest of them all.

"To tell you the truth, Judge McIntyre never fell out of love with Mary Beth. That was his trouble. Nineteen hundred thirteen was the last full year I spent in that house, and of course he had been a judge for over eight years by then, thanks to Julien's influence, and I tell you he was just as much in love with Mary Beth as he had ever been. And in her own way she was in love with him, too. Don't guess she could have put up with him if she hadn't been.

"Of course there were the young men. People talked about

those young men. You know, her stable boys and her messenger boys, and they were good-looking, they really were. You'd see them coming down the back steps, you know, looking scared sort of, as they went out the back door. But she loved Judge McIntyre, she really did, and I'll tell you another thing. I don't think he ever guessed. He was so damned drunk all the time. And Mary Beth was just as cool about all that as she was about anything else. Mary Beth was the calmest person I ever knew, in a way. Nothing ruffled her, not for very long, at any rate. She didn't have much patience with anyone who opposed her, but she wasn't interested in being enemies with a person, you know. She wasn't one to fight or pit her will against anyone else.

"It always amazed me the way she put up with Carlotta. Carlotta was thirteen years old when I left. She was a witch, that child! She wanted to go to school away from home, and Mary Beth tried to persuade her not to do it, but that girl was determined, and so Mary Beth finally just let her go.

"Mary Beth dismissed people like that, that's the way it was, really, and you might say she dismissed Carlotta. Part of her coldness, I suppose, and it could be maddening. When Julien died, the way she locked me out of the library, and out of the third-floor bedroom, that I'll never forget. She never did get the least bit excited. 'Go on, now Richard, you go downstairs, and have some coffee, and then you best get packed,' she said, as if she was talking to a little child. She bought a building for me down here, lickety split. I mean Julien wasn't in the ground when she had bought that building and moved me downtown. Of course, it was Julien's money.

"But no, she never got excited. Except when I told her Julien was dead. Then she got excited. Yes, to tell the truth, she went mad. But just for a little while. Then when she saw he really was gone, she just snapped to and started straightening him up and straightening up the bedcovers. And I never saw her shed another tear.

"I'll tell you a strange thing about Julien's funeral, though. Mary Beth did a strange thing. It was in that front room, of course, and the coffin was open and Julien was a handsome corpse and every Mayfair in Louisiana was there. Why, there were carriages and automobiles lined up for blocks on First and Chestnut streets. And it rained, oh, did it rain! I thought it would never stop. It was so thick it was like a veil around the house. But the main thing was this. They were waking Julien, you know, and it wasn't really what you'd call an Irish wake, of course, because they were far too high-toned for that sort of thing, but there was wine and food, and the Judge was blind drunk naturally. And at one point, with all those people in the room and all the goings-on, and people all over the hallway and back in the dining room and in the library and up the steps, well, with all that just going on, Mary Beth just moved a straight-backed chair up, right beside the coffin, and she put her hand in the coffin and clasped Julien's dead hand, and she just went to dozing right there, in that chair, with her head to one side, holding on to Julien as the cousins came and went to see him, and kneel on the prie-dieu and so forth and so on.

"It was a tender thing that. But jealous as I had always been of her, I loved her for it. I wish I could have done it. Julien certainly did look fine in the coffin. And you should have seen the umbrellas in the Lafayette Cemetery the next day! I tell you when they slipped that coffin inside the vault, I died myself inside. And Mary Beth came up to me at that very moment, and she put her arm around my shoulder, and so that I could hear it, she whispered, 'Au revoir, mon cher Julien!' She did it for me, I know she did. She did it for me, but that was about the warmest thing she ever did. And to her dying day, she denied that he had ever written any autobiography."

I prodded him at this point, asking him if Carlotta had cried at the funeral.

"Indeed not. I don't even remember seeing her there. She was such an awful child. So humorless and antagonistic to everyone. Mary Beth could take it in stride. But Julien used to get so upset with her. It was Mary Beth who calmed him down. Julien told me once that Carlotta would waste her life the same way his sister, Katherine, had wasted hers.

" 'Some people don't like living,' he said to me. Wasn't that strange? 'They just can't stand life. They treat it like it's a terrible disease.' I laughed at that. I've thought about it since many a time. Julien loved being alive. He really did. He was the first one in the family to ever buy a motor car. A Stutz Bearcat it was, quite incredible! And we went riding in that thing, all over New Orleans. He thought it was wonderful!

"He would sit on the front seat next to me—I had to do the driving, of course—all wrapped up in a lap rug, and with his goggles on, just laughing and enjoying the whole affair, what with me climbing out to crank the thing! It was fun, though, it really was. Stella loved that car too. I wish I had that car now. You know, Mary Beth tried to give it to me. And I refused it. Didn't want the responsibility of the thing, I suppose. I should have taken it.

"Mary Beth later gave that car to one of her men, some young Irish fella she'd hired as a coachman. Didn't know a thing about horses as I recall. Didn't have to. I believe he went back to being a policeman later on. But she gave him that car. I know because I saw him in it once and we talked and he told me about it. Of course he didn't say a word against her to me. He knew better than that. But imagine, your lady employer giving you a car like that. I tell you, some of the things she did just drove the cousins up the wall. But they didn't dare talk about it. And it was her manner that carried things through. She just acted as if the strangest things she did were perfectly normal.

"But for all her coolness, you know, you might say that she loved being alive as much as Julien. She really did. Yes, Julien loved being alive. He was never old, not really.

"Julien told me all about how it had been with his sister Katherine in the years before the war. He had done the same tricks with her he did with Mary Beth later on. Only there was no Storyville in those days. They'd gone to Gallatin Street, to the roughest riverfront bars in town. Katherine had dressed up as a young sailor, and she put a bandage on her head to cover up her hair.

" 'She was adorable,' Julien said, 'you should have seen her. Then that Darcy Monahan destroyed her. She sold her soul to him. I tell you, Richard, if you ever get ready to sell your soul, don't bother to sell it to another human being. It's bad business to even consider such a thing.'

"Julien said so many strange things. Of course by the time I came along, Katherine was a burnt-out, crazy old woman. Just crazy, I tell you, the stubborn repetitious kind of crazy that gets on people's nerves.

"She would sit on a bench in the back garden talking to her dead husband, Darcy. It disgusted Julien. So did her religion. And I think she had some influence on Carlotta, little as she was. Though I was never sure of it. Carlotta used to go to Mass at the Cathedral with Katherine.

"I recall once later on Carlotta had a terrible fight with Julien, but I never knew what it was about. Julien was such an ingratiating man; he was so easy to like. But that child couldn't stand him. She couldn't stand to be near him. And then they were shouting at each other behind closed doors in the library. They were shouting in French, and I couldn't understand a word. Finally Julien came out and went upstairs. There were tears in his eyes. And there was a cut on his face, and he was holding his handkerchief to it. I think that little beast actually struck him. That's the only time I ever saw him cry.

"And that awful Carlotta, she was such a cold mean little person. She just stood there watching him go upstairs, and then she said she was going out on the front steps to wait for her daddy to come home.

"Mary Beth was there, and she said, 'Well you are going to be waiting a very long time, because your father is drunk right now at the club, and they won't load him into a carriage till about ten o'clock. So you had better wear a coat when you go outside.'

"This wasn't said in a mean way, really, just matter-of-fact, the way she said everything, but you should have seen the way that girl looked at her mother. I think she blamed her mother for her father's drinking, and if she did what a little fool of a child she was. A man like Daniel McIntyre would have been a drunk if he had married the Virgin Mary or the Whore of Babylon. Didn't matter a particle at all. He told me himself how his father had died of drink, and his father before him. And both of them at the age of forty-eight, no less. And he was afraid he'd die at forty-eight. I don't know whether he made it past forty-eight or not. And you know his family had money. Plenty of money. You ask me, Mary Beth kept Judge McIntyre up and running a bit longer than anyone else might have been able to do.

"But Carlotta never understood. Never for a moment. I think Lionel understood, and Stella too. They loved both their parents, at least it always seemed that way to me. Maybe Lionel was a little embarrassed by the Judge from time to time, but he was a good boy, a devoted boy. And Stella, why, Stella adored her mother and father.

"Ah, that Julien. I can remember that last year, he did the damnedest thing. He took Lionel and Stella both with him down to the French Quarter to see the unseemly sights, so to speak, when they were no more than ten and eleven years old, I kid you not! And you know, I don't think it was the first time either. I think it was just the first time that he couldn't keep it from me, the mischief he was up to. And you know he had Stella dressed as a little sailor boy and did she ever look cute. And they had driven around all evening down there, with him pointing out the fancy clubs to them, though of course he didn't take them in, not even Julien could have pulled that off, I suppose, but they'd been drinking, I can tell you.

"I was awake when they came home. Lionel was quiet, he was always quiet. But Stella was all fired up with everything she'd seen down there in those cribs, you know, with the women right on the street. And we sat on the steps together, Stella and I, talking about it in whispers long after Lionel had helped Julien up to the third floor and put him to bed.

"Stella and I went out and opened up a bottle of champagne in the kitchen. She said she was old enough to have a few drinks, and of course she didn't listen to me, and who was I to stop her. And she and Lionel and I ended up dancing out on the back patio as the sun came up. Stella was doing some ragtime dance she'd seen down there. She said Julien was going to take them to Europe, and to see the whole world, but of course that never happened. I don't think they really knew how old Julien was, any more than I did. When I saw the year 1828 written on that stone, I was shocked, I tell you. But then so much about Julien made sense to me. No wonder he had such a peculiar perspective. He had seen an entire century pass, he really had.

"Stella should have lived so long, really she should have. I remember she said something to me I never forgot. It was long after Julien died. We had lunch down here together at the Court of Two Sisters. She had already had Antha by then, and of course she hadn't bothered to marry or even identify the father. Now, that's a story, let me tell you. She just about turned society on its ear with that one. But what am I trying to say? We had lunch, and she told me she was going to live to be as old as Julien. She said Julien had looked into her palm and told her so. A long life, she would have.

"And think of it, shot dead like that by Lionel when she wasn't even thirty years old. Good God! But you know it was Carlotta all along, don't you?"

Llewellyn was by this time almost incoherent. I pressed on the matter of Carlotta and the shooting, but he would say no more about it. The whole subject began to frighten him. He returned to the subject of Julien's "autobiography" and how much he wanted it. And what he wouldn't give to get into that house some day and lay hands on those pages if they were still in that upstairs room. But then so long as Carlotta was there, he didn't have a chance of it.

"You know there were storage rooms up there, right along the front of the house under the roof. You can't see the roof slope from the street, but they're there. Julien had trunks in there. I'll bet that's where she put the autobiography. She didn't bother to burn it. Not Mary Beth. She just didn't want it to fall into my hands. But then that beast Carlotta, who knows what she's done with all those things?"

Not wanting to miss an opportunity, I pressed as to whether there was ever anything strange in the house, anything supernatural. (That is, other than Julien's power to cause apparitions.) This was of course the kind of leading question that I try not to ask, but I had been with him for hours and he had volunteered nothing on this score other than his strange experiences with Julien. I was searching for something more.

His reaction to my question about a ghost was very strong. "Oh, that," he said. "That was awful, just awful. I can't tell anyone about that. Besides, it must have been my imagination." He all but passed out.

I helped him back to his flat above the bookstore on Chartres Street. Over and over, he mentioned that Julien had left him the money for the building, and for the opening of a shop. Julien knew Llewellyn loved poetry and music and really despised his work as a clerk. Julien sought to set him free, and he had done it. But the one book he wished he had was Julien's life story.

I was never able to obtain another interview of similar depth and length.

When I tried to talk to Llewellyn again a few days later, he was very polite but cautious. He apologized for having gotten so drunk and talked so much, though he said he had enjoyed it. And I could never persuade him to lunch with me again or to speak again at any length about Julien Mayfair.

Several times after that, I stopped in his shop. I asked him many questions about the family and its various members. But I could never regain his trust. Once I asked again if that house on First Street was haunted as people said. There were so many stories.

The very same expression came over him that I had seen the first night I spoke with him. He looked away, his eyes wide, and he shuddered. "I don't know," he said. "It might have been what you call a ghost. I don't like to think about those things. I always thought it was my . . . guilt, you know, that I was imagining it."

When I found myself pressing, perhaps a little too much, he said to me that the Mayfair family was a hard and strange family. "You don't want to run afoul of those people. That Carlotta Mayfair, she's a monster. A real monster." He looked very uncomfortable.

I asked if she had ever given him trouble, to which he replied dismissively that she gave everyone trouble. He seemed distracted, troubled. Then he said a most curious thing, which I wrote down as soon as I returned to my hotel room. He said that he had never believed in life after death, but when he thought of Julien, he was convinced that Julien was still in existence somewhere.

"I know you think I'm out of mind to say something like that," he said, "but I could swear it's true. The night after we first met, I could swear I dreamed of Julien and Julien told me a lot of things. When I woke up, I couldn't remember the dream clearly, but I felt that Julien didn't want us to talk again. I don't even like talking about it now except that . . . well, I feel I have to tell you.''

I said I believed him. He went on to say that Julien in the dream wasn't the Julien he remembered. Something was definitely changed. "He seemed wiser, kinder, just the way you hope someone would be who has crossed over. And he didn't look old. Yet he wasn't exactly young either. I shall never forget that dream. It was . . . absolutely real. I could swear he was standing at the foot of my bed. And I do remember one thing he said. *He said that certain things were destined but that they could be averted.*''

"What sort of things?" I asked.

He shook his head. He would say nothing more after that, no matter how I pressed. He did admit that he could recall no censure from Julien on account of our conversation. But the sense of Julien's being there again had made him feel disloyal. I could not even get him to repeat the story when next I asked him about it.

The last time I saw him was in late August 1959. He had obviously been ill. He had a bad tremor affecting both his mouth and his left hand, and his speech was no longer entirely distinct. I could understand him, but it was difficult. I told him frankly that what he had told me of Julien meant a great deal to me, that I was still interested in the Mayfair history.

At first I thought he did not remember me or the incident in question, so vague did he seem. Then he appeared to recognize me. He became excited.

"Come in the back with me," he said, and as he struggled to rise from the desk I lent him a hand. He was unsteady on his feet. We passed through a dusty curtained doorway into a small storage room, and there he stopped just as if he were staring at something, but I could see nothing.

He gave a strange little laugh and made a dismissive gesture with his hand. Then he took out a box, and with trembling hands, he removed a packet of photographs. These were all of Julien. He gave them to me. It seemed he wanted to say something but he couldn't find the words.

"I cannot tell you what this means to me," I said.

"I know," he answered. "That is why I want you to have them. You are the only person who has ever understood about Julien.''

I felt sad then, dreadfully sad. Had I understood? I suppose I had. He had caused the figure of Julien Mayfair to come to life for me, and I had found it a seductive figure.

"My life might have been different," he said, "had I not met Julien. No one ever after seemed to measure up, you see. And then the store, well, I fell back on the store, and didn't really accomplish very much in the long run."

Then he appeared to shrug it all off, and he smiled.

I put several questions to him but he only shrugged them off too. Finally one caught his attention.

"Did Julien suffer when he died?" I asked.

He became absorbed, then he shook his head. "No, not really. He didn't much care for being paralyzed, of course. Who would? But he loved books. I read to him all the time. He died in the early morning. I know because I was with him till two o'clock, and then I blew out the lamp and went downstairs.

"Well, around six o'clock a storm waked me. It was raining so hard it was coming in at the windowsills. And the limbs of the maple tree outside were making quite a racket. I ran up at once to see to Julien. His bed was right by the window.

"And what do you think? He had somehow managed to sit up, and open the window; and there he was, dead, across the windowsill, his eyes closed, looking quite peaceful, as if he'd wanted a breath of fresh air, and when he had had it he gave up, just like that, falling dead as if he were falling asleep, with his head to one side. Would have been a very peaceful scene if it hadn't been for the storm, for the rain pouring in on him and even the leaves blowing into the room.

"They said later it was a massive stroke. They couldn't figure how he had ever managed to open the window. I never said anything, but you know it occurred to me . . ."

"Yes?" I prodded him.

He gave a little shrug and then went on, his speech extremely slurred. "Mary Beth went mad when I called her. She pulled him off the windowsill and back onto the pillow. She even slapped him. 'Wake up, Julien,' she said. 'Julien, don't leave me yet!' I had a hell of a time closing that window. Then one of the panes blew out. It was dreadful.

"And that horrible Carlotta came up. All the others were coming to kiss him, you know, and to pay their respects, and Millie Dear, Rémy's daughter, you know, was helping us with the bedcovers. But that dreadful Carlotta wouldn't go near him, wouldn't even help us. She stood there on the landing, with her hands clasped, like a little nun, just staring at the door.

"And Belle, precious Belle. Belle, the angel. She came in

with her doll, and she started crying. Then Stella climbed in the bed and lay beside him, with her hand over his chest.

"Belle said, 'Wake up, Oncle Julien.' I guess she had heard her mama say it. And Julien, poor sweet Julien. He was such a peaceful picture, finally, with his head on the pillow, and his eyes closed."

Llewellyn smiled and shook his head, then he began to laugh softly under his breath as though remembering something that aroused tenderness in him. He said something but it wasn't clear. Then he cleared his throat with difficulty. "That Stella," he said. "Everybody loved Stella. Except Carlotta. Carlotta never did . . ." His voice trailed off.

I pressed him further, once more asking the sort of leading questions I made it a rule to avoid. I broached the subject of a ghost. So many people said the house was haunted.

"I should think if it was, you would have known," I said.

I could not tell if he understood me. He made his way back to his desk and sat down, and just when I was quite certain he'd forgotten me altogether, he said that there was something in the house, but he didn't know how to explain it.

"There were things," he said, and that look of revulsion came over him again. "And I could have sworn they all knew about it. Sometimes it was just a sense . . . a sense of somebody always watching."

"Was there more to it than that?" I pressed, being young and ruthless and full of curiosity, and not knowing yet what it means to be old.

"I told Julien about it," he said, "I said it was there in the room with us, you know, that we weren't alone, and that it was . . . watching us. But he would just laugh it off, the way he laughed at everything. He would tell me not to be so self-conscious. But I could swear it was there! It came when, you know, Julien and I were . . . together."

"Was it something you saw?"

"Only at the end," he said. He said something else but I couldn't understand it. When I pressed, he shook his head, and pressed his lips together for emphasis as he did it. Then he dropped his voice to a whisper. "Must have imagined it. But I could swear in those last days when Julien was so sick, that the thing was there, definitely there. It was in Julien's room, it was in the bed with him."

He looked up at me to gauge my reaction. His mouth turned down at the ends and he was scowling, his eyes glaring up at me from beneath his bushy eyebrows.

451

"Awful, awful thing," he whispered, shaking his head. He shivered.

"Did you see it?"

He looked away. I asked him several more questions, but I knew I had lost him. When he answered again, I caught something about the others knowing about that thing, knowing and pretending they didn't.

Then he looked up at me again and he said, "They didn't want me to know that they knew. They all knew. I told Julien, 'There's somebody else in this house, and you know it, and you know what it likes, and what it wants, and you won't tell me you know,' and he said, 'Come now, Richard,' and he'd use all his . . . persuasion, so to speak, to you know, make me forget about it. And then that last week, that awful last week, it was there, in that bed. I know it was. I woke up in the chair and I saw it. I did. I saw it. It was the ghost of a man, and it was making love to Julien. Oh, God, what a sight. Because you see, I knew it wasn't real. Wasn't real at all. Couldn't be. And yet I could see it."

He looked away, the tremor in his mouth worsening. He tried to take out his pocket handkerchief but was merely fumbling with it. I did not know whether or not I should help him.

I asked more questions as gently as I could. He either didn't hear me or didn't care to answer. He sat slumped in the chair, looking as if he might die of old age at any moment.

Then he shook his head and said he couldn't talk anymore. He did seem quite exhausted. He said he didn't stay in the shop all day anymore and he would soon be going upstairs. I thanked him profusely for the pictures, and he murmured that yes, he was glad I'd come, he'd been waiting for me to give me those pictures.

I never saw Richard Llewellyn again. He died about five months after our last interview, in early 1959. He was buried in the Lafayette Cemetery not far from Julien.

There are many other stories which could be included here about Julien. There is much more that might be discovered.

It is sufficient for the purposes of this narrative to add nothing more at this point except that Julien had one other male companion of whom we know, a man to whom he was very strongly attached, and this was the man already described in this narrative as Judge Daniel McIntyre, who later married Mary Beth Mayfair.

But we can discuss Daniel McIntyre in connection with Mary Beth. Therefore it is appropriate to move on now to Mary Beth herself, the last great nineteenth-century Mayfair Witch, and the only female Mayfair Witch of the nineteenth century to rival her eighteenth-century forebears in power.

It was ten minutes past two. Michael stopped only because he had to stop. His eyes were closing, and there was nothing to do but give in and sleep for a while.

He sat still for a long moment, staring at the folder, which he had just closed. He was startled by the knock on the door.

"Come in," he said.

Aaron entered quietly. He was dressed in his pajamas and a quilted silk robe, sashed at the waist. "You look tired," he said. "You should go to bed now."

"I have to," Michael said. "When I was young, I could just keep swilling the coffee. But it's not like that anymore. My eyes are shutting down on me." He sat back in the leather chair, fished in his pocket for a cigarette, and lighted it. The need to sleep was suddenly so heavy, he closed his eyes and almost let the cigarette slip from his fingers. Mary Beth, he thought, have to get on to Mary Beth. So many questions . . .

Aaron settled into the wing chair in the corner. "Rowan canceled her midnight flight," he said. "She'll have a layover tomorrow, and won't reach New Orleans before afternoon."

"How do you find out things like that?" Michael asked sleepily. But that was the least of the questions on his mind. He took another lazy drag off the cigarette and stared at the plate of uneaten sandwiches before him. A sculpture now. He had not wanted any supper. "That's good," he said. "If I wake up at six, and read right on through, I'll make it by evening."

"And then we should talk," Aaron said. "We should talk a great deal before you go to see her."

"I know. Believe me, I know. Aaron, why the hell am I involved in this? Why? Why have I been seeing that man since I was a kid?" He took another drag off the cigarette. "Are you afraid of that spirit thing?" he asked.

"Yes, of course," Aaron answered without the slightest hesitation.

Michael was surprised. "You believe all this then? And you yourself have seen him?"

Aaron nodded. "I have," he said.

"Thank God. Every word of this story has a different meaning for us than it would for someone else who hasn't seen! Someone who doesn't know what it's like to see an apparition like that."

"I believed before I saw," Aaron said. "My colleagues have

seen him. They have reported what they've seen. And as a seasoned member of the Talamasca, I accepted the testimony.''

"Then you accept that this thing can kill people.''

Aaron reflected for a moment. ''Look, I might as well tell you this now. And try to remember it. This thing can do harm, but it has a devil of a time doing it.'' He smiled. ''No pun intended there,'' he said. ''What I'm trying to say is, Lasher kills largely through trickery. He can certainly cause physical effects—move objects, cause tree limbs to fall, rocks to fly—that sort of thing. But he wields this power awkwardly and often sluggishly. Trickery and illusion are his strongest weapons.''

"He forced Petyr van Abel into a tomb,'' Michael said.

"No, Petyr was found trapped in a tomb. What likely happened was that he went into it himself in a state of madness in which he could no longer distinguish illusion from reality.''

"But why would Petyr do that when he was terrified of . . .''

"Oh, come now, Michael, men are often irresistibly drawn to the very thing they fear.''

Michael didn't say anything. He drew on the cigarette again, seeing in his mind's eye the surf crashing on the rocks off Ocean Beach. And remembering the moment of standing there, his scarf blowing in the wind, his fingers frozen.

"To put it bluntly,'' Aaron said, ''never overestimate this spirit. It's weak. If it wasn't it wouldn't need the Mayfair family.''

Michael looked up. ''Say that again.''

"If it wasn't weak, it wouldn't need the Mayfair family,'' Aaron said. ''It needs their energy. And when it attacks, it uses the victim's energy.''

"You just reminded me of something I said to Rowan. When she asked whether or not these spirits I saw had caused me to fall from the rock into the ocean. I told her they couldn't do something like that. They weren't that strong. If they were strong enough to knock a man into the sea and cause him to drown, they wouldn't need to come to people in visions. They wouldn't need to give me a crucial mission.''

Aaron didn't reply.

"You see my point?'' Michael asked.

"Yes, I do. But I see the point of her question also.''

"She asked me why I assumed that they were good, these spirits. I was shocked by that. But she thought it was a logical question.''

"Maybe it is.''

"Oh, but I know they are good.'' Michael stubbed out the cigarette. ''I know. I know that it was Deborah I saw. And that she wants me to oppose that spirit, Lasher. I know that as surely as I know . . . who I am. Remember what Llewellyn told you? I just finished reading it. Llewellyn told you that when Julien came to him in a dream Julien was different. Julien was wiser than he had been when he was alive. Well, that's how it was with Deborah in my vision. Deborah wants to stop this thing that she and Suzanne brought into the world and into this family!"

"Then comes the question. Why has Lasher shown himself to you?"

"Yes. We're going in a circle."

Aaron switched off the light in the corner, and then the lamp on the desk. This left only the lamp on the bedside table. "I'll have them call you at eight. I think you can finish the entire file by late afternoon, perhaps a little sooner. Then we can talk, and you can come to some sort of . . . well . . . decision."

"Have them call me at seven. That's one good thing about being this age. I get sleepy but I sleep less. I'll be fine if they ring me at seven. And Aaron . . ."

"Yes?"

"You never really answered me about last night. Did you see that thing when he was standing right in front of me on the other side of the fence! Did you or didn't you?"

Aaron opened the door. He seemed reluctant to speak. Then he said, "Yes, Michael. I saw him. I saw him very clearly and distinctly. More clearly and distinctly than ever before. And he was smiling at you. It even seemed he was . . . reaching out for you. I would say from what I saw that he was welcoming you. Now, I must go, and you must go to sleep. I'll talk to you in the morning."

"Wait a minute."

"Lights out, Michael."

The phone woke him up. The sunlight was pouring through the windows on either side of the head of the bed. For one moment he was completely disoriented. Rowan had just been talking to him, saying something about how she wanted him to be there before they closed the lid. What lid. He saw a dead white hand lying against black silk.

Then he sat up, and he saw the desk, and the briefcase, and the folders heaped there, and he whispered: "The lid of her mother's coffin."

Drowsily he stared at the ringing phone. Then he picked up the receiver. It was Aaron.

"Come down for breakfast, Michael."

"Is she on the plane yet, Aaron?"

"She's just left the hospital. As I believe I told you last night, she'll have a layover. I doubt she'll reach the hotel before two o'clock. The funeral begins at three. Look, if you won't come down we'll send something up, but you must eat."

"Yes, send it up," he said. "And Aaron. Where is this funeral?"

"Michael, don't bolt on me after you've finished. That wouldn't be fair to anyone."

"No, I'm not going to do that, Aaron. Believe me. But I just want to know. Where is the funeral?"

"Lonigan and Sons. Magazine Street."

"Oh, yeah, do I ever know that place." Grandmother, grandfather, and his father, too, all buried from Lonigan and Sons. "Don't worry, Aaron, I'll be right here. Come up and keep me company if you want. But I've got to get started."

He took a quick shower, put on fresh clothes, and came out of the bathroom to find his breakfast waiting for him under a series of high polished silver domes on a lace-covered tray. The old sandwiches were gone. And the bed was made. There were fresh flowers by the window. He smiled and shook his head. He had a flash of Petyr van Abel in some fine little chamber in the seventeenth-century Motherhouse in Amsterdam. Was Michael a member now? Would they enfold him with all these trappings of security and legitimacy and safety? And what would Rowan think of that? There was so much he had to explain to Aaron about Rowan . . .

Drinking his first cup of coffee absently, he opened the next folder, and began to read.

Eighteen

I T WAS FIVE thirty in the morning as Rowan finally headed to the airport, Slattery driving the Jaguar for her, her eyes glassy and red as she instinctively and anxiously watched the traffic, uncomfortable to have given over the control of the car to anyone else. But Slattery had agreed to keep the Jag in her absence, and he ought to get used to it, she figured. And besides, all she wanted now was to be in New Orleans. The hell with the rest.

Her last evening at the hospital had gone almost as planned. She had spent hours making the rounds with Slattery, introducing him to patients, nurses, interns, and residents, doing what she could to make the transition less painful for everyone involved. It had not been easy. Slattery was an insecure and envious man. He made random deprecating remarks under his breath continuously, ridiculing patients, nurses, and other doctors in a manner that suggested Rowan was in complete sympathy with him when she was not. There was a deep unkindness in him towards those he believed to be inferior. But he was far too ambitious to be a bad doctor. He was careful, and smart.

And much as Rowan disliked turning it all over to him, she was glad he was there. The feeling was growing ever stronger in her that she wasn't coming back here. She tried to remind herself that there was no reason for such a feeling. Yet she couldn't shake it. The special sense told her to prepare Slattery to take over for her indefinitely, and that was what she had done.

Then at eleven P.M., when she was scheduled to leave for the airport, one of her patients—an aneurysm case—began to complain of violent headaches and sudden blindness. This could only mean the man was hemorrhaging again. The operation which had been scheduled for the following Tuesday—to be performed by Lark—had to be performed by Rowan and Slattery right then.

Rowan had never gone into surgery more distracted; even as they were tying on her sterile gown, she had been worried about her delayed flight to New Orleans, worried about the funeral, worried that somehow she'd be trapped for hours during the layover in Dallas, until after her mother had been lowered into the ground.

Then looking around the OR, she had thought, This is the last time. I'm not going to be in this room again, though why I don't know.

At last the usual curtain had fallen, cutting her off from past and future. For five hours, she operated with Slattery beside her, refusing to allow him to take over though she knew he wanted to do it.

She stayed in recovery with her patient for an additional forty-five minutes. She didn't like leaving this one. Several times she placed her hands on his shoulders and did her little mental trick of envisioning what was going on inside the brain. Was she helping him or merely calming herself? She had no idea. Yet she worked on him mentally, as hard as she had ever worked on anyone, even whispering aloud to him that he must heal now, that the weakness in the wall of the artery was repaired.

"Long life to you, Mr. Benjamin," she whispered under her breath. Against her closed eyes, she saw the brain circuitry. A vague tremor passed through her. Then, slipping her hand over his, she knew he would be all right.

Slattery was in the doorway, showered and shaved, and ready to take her to the airport.

"Come on, Rowan, get out of here, before anything else happens!"

She went to her office, showered in the small private bathroom, put on her fresh linen suit, decided it was much too early to call Lonigan and Sons in New Orleans, even with the time difference, and then walked out of University Hospital, with a lump in her throat. So many years of her life, she thought, and the tears hovered. But she didn't let them come.

"You all right?" Slattery had asked as he pulled out of the parking lot.

"Oh, yeah," she said. "Just tired." She was damned sick of crying. She'd done more of it in the last few days than in all her life.

Now, as he made the left turn off the highway at the airport, she found herself thinking that Slattery was about as ambitious as any doctor she'd ever met. She knew quite emphatically that he despised her, and that it was for all the simple, boring reasons—that she was an extraordinary surgeon, that she had the job he coveted, that she might soon be back.

A debilitating chill passed over her. She knew she was picking up his thoughts. If her plane crashed, he could take her place forever. She glanced at him, and their eyes met for a second, and she saw the flush of embarrassment pass over him. Yes, his thoughts.

How many times in the past had it happened that way, and so frequently when she was tired? Maybe her guard was down when she was sleepy, and this evil little telepathic power could assert itself wantonly, and serve up to her this bitter knowledge whether she wanted it or not. It hurt her. She didn't want to be near him.

But it was a good thing that he wanted her job, a good thing that he was there to take it so that she could go.

It struck her very clearly now that, much as she had loved University, it wasn't important where she practiced medicine. It could be any well-equipped medical center in which the nurses and technicians could give her the backup she required.

So why not tell Slattery she wasn't coming back? Why not end the conflict inside him for his sake? The reason was simple.

She didn't know why she felt so strongly that this was a final farewell. It had to do with Michael; it had to do with her mother; but it was as purely irrational as anything she'd ever felt.

Before Slattery even stopped at the curb, she had the door open. She climbed out of the car and gathered up her shoulder bag.

Then she found herself staring at Slattery as he handed her the suitcase from the trunk. The chill passed over her again, slowly, uncomfortably. She saw malice in his eyes. What an ordeal the night had been for him. He was so eager. And he disliked her so much. Nothing in her manner, either personally or professionally, evoked a finer response in him. He simply disliked her. She could taste it as she took the suitcase from his hand.

"Good luck, Rowan," he said, with a metallic cheerfulness. *I hope you don't come back.*

"Slat," she said, "thank you for everything. And there's something else I should tell you. I don't think . . . Well, there's a good possibility I may not come back."

He could scarcely conceal his delight. She felt almost sorry for him, watching the tense movement of his lips as he tried to keep his expression neutral. But then she felt a great warm, wondrous delight herself.

"It's just a feeling," she said. (And it's great!) "Of course I'll have to tell Lark in my own time, and officially—"

"—Of course."

"But go ahead and hang your pictures on the office walls," she continued. "And enjoy the car. I guess I'll send for it sooner or later, but probably later. If you want to buy it, I'll give you the bargain of your life."

"What would you say to ten grand for it, cash, I know it's—"

"That will do it. Write me a check when I send you my new address." With an indifferent wave, she walked off towards the glass doors.

The sweet excitement washed over her like sunlight. Even sore-eyed and sluggishly weary, she felt a great sense of momentum. At the ticket desk, she specified first class, one way.

She drifted into the gift shop long enough to buy a pair of big dark glasses, which struck her as very glamorous, and a book to read—an absurd male fantasy of impossible espionage and relentless jeopardy, which seemed slightly glamorous too.

The *New York Times* said it was hot in New Orleans. Good that she had worn the white linen, and she felt pretty in it. For a few moments, she lingered in the lounge, brushing her hair, and taking care with the pale lipstick and cream rouge she hadn't touched in years. Then she slipped on the dark glasses.

Sitting in the plastic chair at the gate, she felt absolutely anchorless. No job, no one in the house in Tiburon. And Slat double-clutching Graham's car all the way back to San Francisco. You can have it, Doctor. No regret, no worry. Free.

Then she thought of her mother, dead and cold on a table at Lonigan and Sons, beyond the intervention of scalpels, and the old darkness crept over her, right amid the eerie monotonous fluorescent lights and the shining early morning air commuters with their briefcases and their blue all-weather suits. She thought of what Michael had said about death. That it was the only supernatural event most of us ever experience. And she thought that was true.

The tears came again, silently. She was glad she had the dark glasses. Mayfairs at the funeral, lots and lots of Mayfairs . . .

She fell asleep as soon as she was settled on the plane.

Nineteen

THE FILE ON THE MAYFAIR WITCHES

PART VI

The Mayfair Family from 1900 through 1929

RESEARCH METHODS IN THE TWENTIETH CENTURY

As mentioned earlier, in our introduction to the family in the nineteenth century, our sources of information about the Mayfair family became ever more numerous and illuminating with each passing decade.

As the family moved towards the twentieth century, the Talamasca maintained all of its traditional kinds of investigators. But it also acquired professional detectives for the first time. A number of such men worked for us in New Orleans and still do. They have proved excellent not only at gathering gossip of all sorts but at investigating specific questions through reams of records, and at interviewing scores of persons about the Mayfair family, much as an investigative "true crime" writer might do today.

These men seldom if ever know who we are. They report to an agency in London. And though we still send our own specially trained investigators to New Orleans on virtual "gossip-gathering sprees" and carry on correspondence with numerous other watchers, as we have all through the nineteenth century, these private detectives have greatly improved the quality of our information.

Yet another source of information became available to us in the late nineteenth and twentieth century, which we—for want of a better phrase—will call family legend. To wit, though Mayfairs are often absolutely secretive about their contemporaries, and very leery of saying anything whatsoever about the family legacy to outsiders, they had begun by the 1890s to repeat little stories and anecdotes and fanciful tales about figures in the dim past.

Specifically, a descendant of Lestan who would say absolutely nothing about his dear cousin Mary Beth when invited by a stranger at a party to gossip about her, nevertheless repeated several quaint stories about Great-aunt Marguerite, who used to dance with her slaves. And later the grandson of that very cousin repeated quaint stories about old Miss Mary Beth, whom he never knew.

Of course much of this family legend is too vague to be of interest to us, and much concerns "the grand plantation life" which has become mythic in many Louisiana families and does not shed light upon our obsessions. However, sometimes these family legends tie in quite shockingly with bits of information we have been able to gather from other sources.

And when and where they have seemed especially illuminating, I have included them. But the reader must understand "family legend" always refers to something being told to us recently about someone or something in the "dim past."

Yet another form of gossip which came to the fore in the twentieth century is what we call legal gossip—and that is, the gossip of legal secretaries, legal clerks, lawyers, and judges who knew the Mayfairs or worked with them, and the friends and families of all these various non-Mayfair persons.

Because Julien's sons, Barclay, Garland, and Cortland, all became distinguished lawyers, and because Carlotta Mayfair was a lawyer, and because numerous grandchildren of Julien also went into law, this network of legal contacts has tended to grow larger than one might suppose. But even if this had not been the case, the financial dealings of the Mayfairs have been so extensive that many, many lawyers have been involved.

When the family began to squabble in the twentieth century, when Carlotta began to fight over the custody of Stella's daughter; when there were arguments about the disposition of the legacy, this legal gossip became a rich source of interesting details.

Let me add in closing that the twentieth century saw even greater and more detailed record keeping in general than the nineteenth. And our paid investigators of the twentieth century availed themselves of these numerous public records concerning the family. Also as time went on, the family was mentioned more and more in the press.

THE ETHNIC CHARACTER OF THE CHANGING FAMILY

As we carry this narrative towards the year 1900, we should note that the ethnic character of the Mayfair family was changing.

Though the family had begun as a Scottish-French mix, incorporating in the next generation the blood of the Dutchman Petyr van Abel, it had become after that almost exclusively French.

In 1826, however, with the marriage of Marguerite Mayfair to the opera singer Tyrone Clifford McNamara, the legacy family began to intermarry fairly regularly with Anglo-Saxons.

Other branches—notably the descendants of Lestan and Maurice—remained staunchly French, and if and when they moved to New Orleans they preferred to live "downtown" with other French-speaking Creoles, in or around the French Quarter or on Esplanade Avenue.

The legacy family, with Katherine's marriage to Darcy Monahan, became firmly ensconced in the uptown "American" Garden District. And though Julien Mayfair (half Irish himself) spoke French all his life, and married a French-speaking cousin, Suzette, he gave his three boys distinctly American or Anglo names, and saw to it that they received American educations. His son Garland married a girl of German-Irish descent with Julien's blessing. Cortland also married an Anglo-Saxon girl, and eventually Barclay did also.

As we have already noted Mary Beth was to marry an Irishman, Daniel McIntyre, in 1899.

Though Katherine's sons Clay and Vincent spoke French all their lives, both married Irish-American girls—Clay the daughter of a well-to-do hotel owner, and Vincent the daughter of an Irish-German brewer. One of Clay's daughters became a member of the Irish Catholic Order of the Sisters of Mercy (following in the footsteps of her father's sister), to which the family contributes to this day. And a great-granddaughter of Vincent entered the same order.

Though the French Mayfairs worshiped at the St. Louis Cathedral in the French Quarter, the legacy family began to attend services at their parish church, Notre Dame, on Jackson Avenue, one of a three-church complex maintained by the Redemptorist Fathers which sought to meet the needs of the waterfront Irish and German immigrants as well as the old French families. When this church was closed in the 1920s a parish chapel was established on Prytania Street in the Garden District, quite obviously for the rich who did not want to attend either the Irish church of St. Alphonsus or the German church of St. Mary's.

The Mayfairs attended Mass at this chapel, and indeed residents of First Street attend Mass there to this day. But as far back as 1899, the Mayfairs began to use the Irish church of St. Alphonsus—a very large, beautiful, and impressive structure—for important occasions.

Mary Beth was married to Daniel McIntyre in St. Alphonsus Church in 1899, and every First Street Mayfair baptism since has been held there. Mayfair children—after their expulsion from better private schools—went to St. Alphonsus parochial school for brief periods.

Some of our testimony about the family comes from Irish Catholic nuns and priests stationed in this parish.

After Julien died in 1914, Mary Beth was rarely heard to speak French, even to the French cousins, and it may be that the language died out in the legacy family. Carlotta Mayfair has never been known to speak French; and it is doubtful that Stella or Antha or Deirdre knew more than a few words of any foreign language.

Our investigators observed on numerous occasions that the speech of the twentieth-century Mayfairs—Carlotta; her sister, Stella; Stella's daughter, Antha; and Antha's daughter, Deirdre—showed distinct Irish traits. Like many New Orleanians, they had no discernible French or southern American accent. But they tended to call people they knew by both their names, as in "Well, how are you now, Ellie Mayfair?" and to speak with a certain lilt and certain deliberate repetitions which struck the listeners as Irish. A typical example would be this fragment picked up at a Mayfair funeral in 1945: "Now don't you tell me that story, now, Gloria Mayfair, you know I won't believe such a thing and shame on you for telling it! And poor Nancy with all she has on

463

her mind, why, she's a living saint and you know she is, if ever there was one!''

With regard to appearance, the Mayfairs are such a salad of genes that any combination of coloring, build, or facial characteristics can appear at any time in any generation. There is no characteristic look. Yet some members of the Talamasca aver that a study of all the existing photographs, sketches, and reproductions of paintings in our files does reveal a series of recurring types.

For example, there is a group of tall blond Mayfairs (including Lionel Mayfair) who resemble Petyr van Abel, all of whom have green eyes and strong jaw lines.

Then there is a group of very pale, delicately built Mayfairs who are invariably blue-eyed and short, and this group includes not only the original Deborah but also Deirdre Mayfair, the present beneficiary and ''witch'' and the mother of Rowan.

A third group of dark-eyed, dark-haired Mayfairs with very large bones includes Mary Beth Mayfair, and her uncles Clay and Vincent, and also Angélique Mayfair of Saint-Domingue.

Another group of smaller black-eyed, black-haired Mayfairs looks distinctly French, and every one of this group has a small round head and rather prominent eyes and overly curly hair.

Lastly, there is a group of very pale, cold-looking Mayfairs, all blond, with grayish eyes and fairly delicate of build, though always tall, and this group includes Charlotte of Saint-Domingue (the daughter of Petyr van Abel); Marie Claudette, who brought the family to Louisiana; Stella's daughter, Antha Mayfair; and her granddaughter—Dr. Rowan Mayfair.

Members of the order have also noted some very specific resemblances. For instance, Dr. Rowan Mayfair of Tiburon, California, strongly resembles her ancestor Julien Mayfair, much more than she does any blond members of the family.

And Carlotta Mayfair in her youth strongly resembled her ancestor Charlotte.

(This investigator feels obligated to note with regard to this entire subject of looks that he does not see all this in these pictures! There are similarities, but the differences far outweigh them! The family does not look distinctly Irish, French, Scottish, or anything else.)

In any discussion of Irish influence and Irish traits we should remind ourselves that the history of this family is such that one can never be certain who is the father of any child. And as the later ''legends'' repeated in the twentieth century by descendants will show, the incestuous entanglements of each generation

464

were not really secret. Nevertheless an Irish cultural influence is definitely discernible.

We should also note—for what it's worth—that the family in the late 1800s began to employ more and more Irish domestic servants, and these servants became for the Talamasca priceless sources of information. How much they contributed to our vision of the family as Irish is not easy to determine.

The hiring of these Irish workers had nothing to do with the family's Irish identity, per se. It was the trend in the neighborhood of the period, and many of these Irish-Americans lived in the so-called Irish Channel or riverfront neighborhood lying between the Mississippi wharves and Magazine Street, the southernmost boundary of the Garden District. Some of them were live-in maids and stable boys; others came to work by the day, or only on certain occasions. And as a whole, they were not as loyal to the Mayfair family as the colored and black servants were; and they talked much more freely about what went on at First Street than servants of past decades.

But though the information they made available to the Talamasca is extremely valuable, it is information of a certain kind and must be evaluated carefully.

The Irish servants working in and around the house tended on the whole to believe in ghosts, in the supernatural, and in the power of the Mayfair women to make things happen. They were what we must call highly superstitious. Hence their stories of what they saw or heard sometimes border on the fantastic, and often contain vivid and lurid passages of description.

Nevertheless, this material is—for obvious reasons—extremely significant. And much of what was recounted by the Irish servants has—for us—a familiar ring to it.

All things considered, it is not unfair to say in summary that by the first decade of this century the First Street Mayfairs thought of themselves as Irish, often making remarks to that effect; and that they emerged in the consciousness of many who knew them—servants and peers alike—as almost stereotypically Irish in their madness and eccentricity and penchant for the morbid. Several critics of the family have called them "raving Irish loonies." And a German priest of St. Alphonsus Church once described them as existing in "a perpetual state of Celtic gloom." Several neighbors and friends referred to Mary Beth's son, Lionel, as a "raving Irish drunk," and his father, Daniel McIntyre, was certainly considered to be one, by just about every bartender on Magazine Street.

Perhaps it is safe to say that with the death of "Monsieur Julien" (who was in fact half Irish) the house on First Street lost the very last of its French or Creole character. Julien's sister, Katherine, and his brother, Rémy, had already preceded him to the grave, and so had his daughter, Jeannette. Thereafter—in spite of the huge family gatherings which included French-speaking cousins by the hundreds—the core family was an Irish-American Catholic family.

As the years passed, the French-speaking branches lost their Creole identity as well, as have so many other Louisiana Creole families. The French language has all but died out in every known branch. And as we move towards the last decade of the twentieth century, it is difficult to find a true French-speaking Mayfair descendant anywhere.

This brings us to one other crucial observation—which is all too easily overlooked when proceeding with this narrative.

With the death of Julien, the Mayfair family may have lost the last member who really knew its history. We cannot know. But it seems more than likely. And as we converse more with descendants and gather more of their preposterous legends about the plantation days, it seems a certainty.

As a consequence, from 1914 on, any member of the Talamasca investigating the Mayfair family could not help but be aware that he or she knew more about the family than the family appeared to know about itself. And this has led to considerable confusion and stress on the part of our investigators.

Even before Julien's death, the question of whether or not to attempt contact with the family had become a pressing one for the order.

After the death of Mary Beth, it became agonizing.

But we must now continue our story, backtracking to the year 1891, so that we may focus sharply upon Mary Beth Mayfair, who will carry us into the twentieth century, and who was perhaps the last of the truly powerful Mayfair Witches.

We know more about Mary Beth Mayfair than we know about any other Mayfair Witch since Charlotte. Yet when all the information is examined, Mary Beth remains a mystery, revealing herself to us in only occasional blinding flashes through the anecdotes of servants and family friends. Only Richard Llewellyn gave us a truly intimate portrait, and as we have already seen, Richard knew very little about Mary Beth's business interests or her occult powers. She seems to have fooled him, as she fooled everyone around her, into believing that she was very simply a strong woman, when the truth was far more complex than that.

* * *

The week after Marguerite's death in 1891, Julien removed Marguerite's personal possessions from Riverbend to the First Street house. Hiring two wagons to transport the goods, he moved numerous jars and bottles, all properly crated, several trunks of letters and other papers, and some twenty-five cartons of books, as well as several trunks of miscellaneous contents.

We know that the jars and bottles disappeared into the third floor of the First Street house, and we never heard of these bottles and jars again from any contemporary witness.

Julien made his bedroom on the third floor at this time, and this is the room in which he died as described by Richard Llewellyn.

Many of Marguerite's books, including obscure texts in German and French having to do with black magic, were put on the shelves in the ground-floor library.

Mary Beth was given the old master bedroom in the north wing, above the library, which has always since been occupied by the beneficiary of the legacy. Little Belle, too young perhaps to be displaying signs of feeblemindedness, was given the first bedroom across the hall, but Belle often slept with her mother in the early years.

Mary Beth began to wear the Mayfair emerald regularly. And it may be said that she came into her own at this time as an adult and as mistress of the house. New Orleans society certainly became more aware of her, and the first business transactions bearing her signature appear in the public records at this time.

She appears in numerous photographic portraits wearing the emerald, and many people talked about it and spoke of it with admiration. And in many of these photographs she is wearing men's clothing. In fact, scores of witnesses verify Richard Llewellyn's statement that Mary Beth cross-dressed, and that it was common for her to go out, dressed as a man, with Julien. Before Mary Beth's marriage to Daniel McIntyre, these wanderings included not only the bordellos of the French Quarter, but an entire spectrum of social activity, Mary Beth even appearing at balls in the handsome "white tie and tails" of a man.

Though society in general was shocked by this behavior, the Mayfairs continued to pave the way for it with money and charm. They lent money freely to those who needed it during the various postwar depressions. They gave to charities almost ostentatiously, and under the management of Clay Mayfair, Riverbend continued to make a fortune with one bountiful sugar crop after another.

In these early years, Mary Beth herself seems to have aroused little enmity in others. She is never spoken of, even by her detractors, as vicious or cruel, though she is often much criticized as cold, businesslike, indifferent to people's feelings, and mannish in manner.

For all her strength and height, however, she was not a mannish woman. Numerous people describe her as voluptuous, and occasionally she is described as beautiful. Numerous photographs bear this out. She presented an alluring figure in male attire, particularly in these early years. And more than one member of the Talamasca has observed that whereas Stella, Antha, and Deirdre Mayfair—her daughter, granddaughter, and great-granddaughter respectively—were delicate "southern belle" women, Mary Beth greatly resembled the striking and "larger than life" American film stars who came after her death, particularly Ava Gardner and Joan Crawford. Mary Beth also bore a strong resemblance in photographs to Jenny Churchill, the celebrated American mother of Winston Churchill.

Mary Beth's hair remained jet black until her death at the age of fifty-four. We do not know her exact height but we can guess that it was close to five feet eleven inches. She was never a heavy woman, but she was big-boned, and very strong. She walked with large steps. The cancer that killed her was not discovered until six months before her death, and she remained an "attractive" woman up until the final weeks, when she finally disappeared into the sickroom never to leave it.

There can be no doubt, however, that Mary Beth had scant interest in her physical beauty. Though always well groomed, and sometimes stunning in a ball gown and fur wrap, she is never spoken of by anyone as seductive. In fact, those who called her "unfeminine" dwelt at length upon her straightforward and brusque manner, and her seeming indifference to her own considerable endowments.

It is worth noting that almost all of these traits—straightforward manner, businesslike attitude, honesty, and coldness—are later associated with her daughter Carlotta Mayfair, who is not and never was a designee of the legacy.

Those who liked Mary Beth and did business successfully with her praised her as a "straight shooter," and a generous person, quite incapable of pettiness. Those who did not do well with her called her feelingless and inhuman. This is also the case with Carlotta Mayfair.

Mary Beth's business interests and her appetite for pleasure will be dealt with extensively below. It is sufficient to say here that, in the early years, she set the tone for what went on at First

Street as much as Julien. Many family dinner parties were planned by her completely, and she persuaded Julien to make his last trip to Europe in 1896, at which time she and he toured the capitals from Madrid to London.

Mary Beth shared Julien's love of horses from girlhood on, and frequently went riding with Julien. They also loved the theater and attended almost any sort of play, from the very grand Shakespearean productions to very small and insignificant local theatricals. And both were passionate lovers of opera. In later years, Mary Beth had a Victrola of some sort in almost every room of the house, and she played opera records continuously.

Mary Beth also seems to have enjoyed living with a large number of people under one roof. Her interest in the family was not limited to reunions and get-togethers. On the contrary, she opened her doors all her life to visiting cousins.

Some casual accounts of her hospitality suggest that she enjoyed having power over people; she enjoyed being the center of attention. But even in those stories in which such opinions are quite literally expressed, Mary Beth emerges as a person more interested in others than in herself. In fact, the total absence of narcissism or vanity in this woman continues to be astonishing to those who peruse the record. Generosity, rather than a lust for power, seems a more appropriate explanation for her family relationships.

(Allow us to note here that Nancy Mayfair, an illegitimate child of a descendant of Maurice Mayfair, was adopted by Mary Beth and brought up along with Antha Mayfair as Stella's daughter. Nancy lived in the First Street house until 1988. It was commonly believed even by scores of Mayfairs that she was really Stella's daughter.)

In 1891, the First Street household consisted of Rémy Mayfair, who seemed years older than his brother Julien, though he was not, and was rumored to be dying of consumption, which he finally did in 1897; Julien's sons, Barclay, Garland, and Cortland, who were the first Mayfairs to be sent off to boarding schools on the upper East Coast where they did well; Millie Mayfair, the only one of Rémy's children never to marry; and finally, in addition to Julien and Mary Beth, their daughter, little Belle, who as already mentioned was slightly feebleminded.

By the end of the century the house included Clay Mayfair, Mary Beth's brother, and also the unwilling and heartbroken Katherine Mayfair after the destruction of Riverbend, and from time to time other cousins.

During all this time, Mary Beth was the undisputed lady of the house, and it was Mary Beth who inspired and carried out a great refurbishing of the structure before 1900, at which time three bathrooms were added and the gaslight was expanded to the third floor, and to the entire servants' quarters, and to two large outbuildings as well, one of which was a stable with living accommodations above it.

Though Mary Beth lived until 1925, dying of cancer in September of that year, we can safely say that she changed little over time—that her passions and priorities in the late nineteenth century were pretty much the same as in the last year of her life.

If she ever had a close friend or confidant outside the family, we know nothing of it. And her true character is rather hard to describe. She was certainly never the playful, cheerful person that Julien was; she seemed to have no desire for great drama; and even at the countless family reunions where she danced and supervised the taking of photographs and the serving of food and drink, she is never described as "the life of the party." Rather she seems to have been a quiet, strong woman, with very definite goals. And it is possible that no one was ever really close to her except her daughter Stella. But we shall get to that part of the story by and by.

To what extent Mary Beth's occult powers furthered her goals is a very significant question. And there is a variety of evidence to help one make a series of educated guesses as to what went on behind the scenes.

To the Irish servants who came and went at First Street, she was always a "witch" or a person with voodoo powers. But their stories of her differ from other accounts which we possess, quite markedly, and must be taken with the proverbial grain of salt.

Nevertheless . . .

The servants spoke often of Mary Beth going down to the French Quarter to consult with the voodooiennes and of having an altar in her room at which she worshiped the devil. They said that Mary Beth knew when you told a lie, and knew where you had been, and knew where every member of the Mayfair family was, even those who had gone up north, and knew at any moment what these people were doing. They said Mary Beth made no effort to keep such things a secret.

They also said that Mary Beth was the person to whom the black servants turned when they were in trouble with the local voodooiennes and Mary Beth knew what powder to use or candle to burn in order to counteract a spell, and that she could command spirits; and Mary Beth declared more than once that this was all that voodoo was about. Command the spirits. All the rest is for show.

One Irish cook who worked in the house off and on from 1895 to 1902 told one of our investigators casually that Mary Beth told her there were all kinds of spirits in the world, but the lowly spirits were the easiest to command, and anybody could call them up if such a person had a mind to. Mary Beth had spirits guarding all the rooms of the house and all the things in them. But Mary Beth warned the cook not to try to call spirits on her own. It had its dangers and was best left to people who could see spirits and feel them the way that Mary Beth could.

"You could feel the spirits in that house, all right," said the cook, "and if you closed your eyes halfway, you could see them. But Miss Mary Beth didn't have to do that. She could just see them plain as day all the time, and she talked to them and called them by name."

The cook also said Mary Beth drank brandy straight from the bottle, but that was all right, because Mary Beth was a real lady and a lady could do what she pleased, and Mary Beth was a kind and generous person. Same held true for old Monsieur Julien, but he would not have thought of drinking brandy straight from a bottle, or anything else straight from a bottle, and always liked his sherry in a crystal glass.

A laundress reported that Mary Beth could make doors close behind her without bothering to touch them, as she made her way through the house. The laundress was asked once to take a basket of folded linen to the second floor, but she refused, she was so frightened. Then Mary Beth scolded her in a rather good-natured way for being so foolish, and the laundress wasn't afraid anymore.

There are at least fifteen different accounts of Mary Beth's voodoo altar, on which she burned incense and candles of various colors, and to which she added plaster saints from time to time. But no account tells us precisely where this altar was. (It is interesting to note that no black servant ever questioned about this altar would utter one word about it.)

Some of the other stories we have are very fanciful. It was told to us several times, for instance, that Mary Beth didn't just dress like a man, she turned into a man when she went out in her suit, with her cane and hat. And she was strong enough at such times to beat off any other man who assaulted her.

One morning early when she was riding her horse on St. Charles Avenue alone (Julien was ill at the time, and would very soon die), a man tried to pull her from the horse, at which time she herself turned into a man and beat him half to death with her fist, and then dragged him at the end of a rope behind her horse to the local police station. "Lots of people saw that," we are told. That story was repeated in the Irish Channel as late as 1935. Indeed police records of the time indicate the assault, and the "citizen's arrest" did take place in 1914. The man died in his cell several hours later.

There is another story of a foolish maidservant who stole one of Mary Beth's rings, and awoke that night in her smothering little room on Chippewa Street to discover Mary Beth bending over her, in manly form, and demanding that she give back the ring immediately, which the woman did, only to die by three o'clock the following afternoon from the shock of the experience.

That story was told to us once in 1898, and again in 1910. It has proved impossible to investigate.

By far the most valuable story we have from the earlier period was told to us by a taxi driver in 1910, who said that he once picked up Mary Beth downtown in the Rue Royale one day in 1908, and though he was certain she had gotten into his taxi alone (this was a horse-drawn hansom), he heard her talking to someone all the way uptown. When he opened the door for her before the carriage block at First Street, he saw a handsome man with her in the cab. She seemed deep in conversation with him, but broke off when she saw the driver, and uttered a short laugh. She gave the driver two beautiful gold coins and told him they were worth far more than the fare, and to spend them quickly. When the taxi driver looked for the man to follow her out of the cab he saw there was no one there.

There are numerous other servant stories in our files concerning Mary Beth's powers, but all have a common theme—that Mary Beth was a witch and that she showed her powers whenever she or her possessions or her family was threatened. But once more, let us emphasize that the stories of these servants differ markedly from the other material we have.

However, if we consider the entire scope of Mary Beth's life, we will see that there is convincing evidence of witchcraft from other sources.

As far as we can deduce, Mary Beth had three overriding passions.

First but not foremost was Mary Beth's desire to make money, and to involve members of her own family in the building of an immense fortune. It is an understatement to say that she was successful.

Almost from the beginning of her life, we hear stories of treasure troves of jewels, of purses full of gold coins which can never be emptied, and of Mary Beth tossing gold coins to the poor at random.

She was said to have warned many persons to "spend the coins fast," saying that whatever she gave away from her magic purse always returned to her.

Regarding the jewels and the coins—it could be that a thorough study of all the Mayfair finances, made entirely from public records and analyzed by those versed in such matters, might indicate that mysterious and unaccountable infusions of wealth have played a role in their entire financial history. But on the basis of what we know, we cannot make this assumption.

More pertinent is the question of Mary Beth's use of precognition or occult knowledge in her investments.

Even a casual examination of Mary Beth's financial achievements indicates that she was a financial genius. She was far more interested in making money than Julien had ever been, and she possessed an obvious knack for knowing what was going to happen before it did, and she often warned all her peers about impending crises and bank failures, though they often did not listen to her.

In fact, Mary Beth's diversified investments defy conventional explanation. She was, as they say, "into" everything. She engaged directly in cotton brokering, real estate, shipping, railroads, banking, merchandising, and later bootlegging. She continuously invested in highly unlikely ventures that proved astonishingly successful. She was "in on the ground floor" of several chemicals and inventions which made her incalculable amounts of money.

One can go so far as to say that her story—on paper—doesn't make sense. She knew too much too often and made too much out of it.

Whereas Julien's successes, great as they were, could be attributed to one man's knowledge and skill, it is almost impossible to explain Mary Beth's success in this simple a fashion. Julien had no interest for example in modern inventions, as far as investment was concerned. Mary Beth had a positive passion for gadgets and technology, and never ever made a mistake in this area. The same held true for shipping, about which Julien knew little, and Mary Beth knew a great deal. Whereas Julien loved to purchase buildings, including factories and hotels, he never bought undeveloped land, but Mary Beth bought enormous tracts of it all over the United States and sold it at unbelievable profits. In fact, her knowledge of when and where towns and cities would develop is totally unaccountable.

Mary Beth was also very canny about presenting her wealth in a favorable light to other people. She made enough of a show to suit her purposes. Consequently she never inspired the wonder

473

or disbelief that would have inevitably followed full disclosures of her success. And she was careful all her life to avoid publicity. Her life-style at First Street was never particularly ostentatious, except that she came to love motor cars and had so many at one time that she had to rent garages all over the neighborhood for them. In sum, the picture she presented to Richard Llewellyn, quoted at length in the last chapter, is pretty much the picture she presented to everyone. Very few people knew how much money or power she had.

In fact, there is some evidence that Mary Beth possessed an entire business life of which other people weren't aware, in the sense that she had a troop of financial employees whom she met in downtown offices, who never came near her office on First Street. There is talk even today in New Orleans of the men who worked "downtown" for Mary Beth, and how generously they were rewarded. It was a "plush job," according to one old gentleman, who recalls that his friend often went on long trips for Mary Beth, to London and Paris and Brussels and Zurich, sometimes carrying enormous sums of money with him. Shipboard and hotel accommodations were always first class, said this old man. And Mary Beth handed out bonuses regularly. Another source insists that Mary Beth herself frequently went on such trips without the knowledge of her family, but we can make no verification of this.

We also have five different stories of Mary Beth's taking revenge on those who tried to cheat her. One story recounts how her secretary, Landing Smith, ran off with three hundred thousand dollars of Mary Beth's cash, taking a liner to Europe under an assumed name, quite convinced that he'd gotten away with it. Three days out of New York, he woke up in the middle of the night to discover Mary Beth sitting on the side of his bed. Not only did she take the money from him, she beat him soundly with her riding crop, and left him bloody and half mad on the cabin floor where the ship's steward later found him. His full confession followed at once. But Mary Beth was not found on board the ship, and neither was the money. This story was recounted in the local papers, though Mary Beth herself refused to confirm or deny that anything was ever stolen.

Another story, told by two different elderly men in the year 1955, recounts how a meeting was held by one of Mary Beth's companies which sought to dissociate itself from her and cheat her by a series of entirely legal maneuvers. The meeting was half over perhaps when all at the table realized Mary Beth was sitting there with them. Mary Beth told them simply what she thought of them, severed her tie with the company, and it soon met with financial ruin. Descendants of those involved despise the Mayfairs to this day for this tragedy.

One branch of the Mayfair family—descendants of Clay Mayfair who now live in New York—will have nothing to do with the New Orleans Mayfairs on account of such an entanglement with Mary Beth which took place in 1919.

It seems Mary Beth was investing heavily in New York banking at this time. But an altercation had occurred between her and a cousin. In sum, he did not believe Mary Beth's plan of action would work. She thought it would. He sought to undercut her plan without her knowledge. She appeared in New York, in his office, and tore the pertinent papers from his hands and threw them into the air, where they caught fire and burnt without ever touching the ground. She then warned him if he ever tried to cheat his own blood again, she'd kill him. He then told this story over and over again compulsively to anyone and everyone who would listen, effectively ruining his reputation and destroying his professional life. People thought he was crazy. He committed suicide by jumping out of the office window three months after Mary Beth's appearance. To this day the family blames Mary Beth for the death, and speaks of her and her descendants with hatred.

It should be noted that these New York Mayfairs are very well off. And Stella made friendly overtures to them on numerous occasions. They insist that Mary Beth used Black Magic in all her dealings, but the more they talk to our representatives, the more we come to understand that they really know very little of the New Orleans family from which they came, and they have a very small concept of Mary Beth's dealings.

Of course it is common to have a very small idea of Mary Beth's dealings. As mentioned before, she was very good at keeping her immense power and influence a secret.

But to the Talamasca, stories of Mary Beth putting a curse on a farmer who wouldn't sell her a horse sound perfectly absurd when we know that Mary Beth was buying up railroads in South America and investing in Indian tea and purchasing enormous amounts of land surrounding the city of Los Angeles, California.

Some day perhaps someone will write a book about Mary Beth Mayfair. It is all there in the records. But as it stands now, it seems that the Talamasca alone is the only group of persons outside the family who knows that Mary Beth Mayfair expanded her financial influence and power globally—that she built a financial empire so immense, so strong, and so diversified that its gradual dismantling is still going on to this day.

But the entire subject of Mayfair finances deserves more attention than we can give it. If those with the knowledge of such matters were to make a thorough study of the entire Mayfair history—and we refer here to public documents available to anyone diligent enough to search for them—it is possible that we would perceive a very strong case for occult power being used throughout the centuries for the acquisition and expansion of wealth. The jewels and the gold coins might represent the smallest part of it.

Alas, we have no such expertise for that kind of study. And given what we do know, Mary Beth rises head and shoulders above Julien as an entrepreneur, and it is almost certain that no one human being could have accomplished, without supernatural aid, what she accomplished.

To conclude, Mary Beth left her family far richer than most of them ever knew, apparently, or ever appreciated. And the wealth exists to this day.

Mary Beth's second passion was the family. And from the beginning of her active business life, she involved her cousins (or brothers) Barclay, Garland, Cortland and other Mayfairs in her dealings; she brought them into the companies she formed and used Mayfair attorneys and Mayfair bankers for her transactions. In fact, she always used Mayfairs for business, if she possibly could, instead of strangers. And she put great pressure on other Mayfairs to do the same. When her daughter Carlotta Mayfair went to work for a non-Mayfair law firm, she was disappointed and disapproving, but she took no restrictive or punitive action regarding Carlotta's decision. She let it be known that Carlotta was guilty of lack of vision.

With regard to Stella and Lionel, Mary Beth was notoriously indulgent and allowed them to have their friends over for days or weeks on end. She sent them to Europe with tutors and governesses when she herself was too busy to go; and she gave them birthday parties of legendary size and extravagance, to which countless Mayfair cousins were invited. She was equally generous to her daughter Belle, her adopted daughter Nancy, and to Millie Dear, her niece, all of whom continued to live at First Street after Mary Beth's death, though they were the recipients of large trust funds which granted them indisputable financial independence.

Mary Beth stayed in contact with Mayfairs all over the country, and fostered numerous get-togethers of the Mayfair cousins in Louisiana. Even after Julien's death and right on until the twilight of Mary Beth's life, delicious food and drink were served at these affairs, with Mary Beth supervising the menu and the wine tasting herself, and often musicians were hired to provide entertainment.

Enormous family dinners were very common at First Street. And Mary Beth paid out fabulous salaries to hire the best cooks for her kitchen. Many reports indicate that the Mayfair cousins loved going to First Street, that they loved the long after-dinner discussions (described by Richard Llewellyn), and that they were personally devoted to Mary Beth, who had an uncanny ability to remember birthdays, wedding anniversaries, and graduation dates, and to send appropriate and very welcome cash presents.

As already indicated, when she was young, Mary Beth loved to dance with Julien at these family parties, and encouraged dancing among young and old, and sometimes hired instructors to teach the cousins the latest dances. She and Julien would amuse the children with their spry antics. And sometimes the dance bands they hired from the Quarter shocked the more staid Mayfairs. After Julien's death, Mary Beth did not dance so much but she loved to see other people dance, and she almost always provided some music. In her last years, these affairs were managed by her daughter Stella, and her son, Lionel, and they were as spirited as ever.

Mayfairs were not only invited to these get-togethers, they were expected to attend, and Mary Beth was sometimes unpleasant to those who refused to accept her invitations. And there are two stories of her becoming extremely angry with members of the family who discarded the name Mayfair in favor of the name of their father.

Several stories we have gathered from friends of the family indicate that Mary Beth was both loved and feared by the cousins; whereas Julien, especially in his old age, was considered sweet and charming, Mary Beth was considered slightly formidable.

There are several stories which indicate that Mary Beth could see the future but disliked using the power. When asked to predict or to help make a decision, she frequently warned the family members involved that "second sight" wasn't a simple thing. And that predicting the future could be "tricky." However, she did now and then make outright predictions. For example, she told Maitland Mayfair—Clay's son—that he would die if he took up airplane flying, and he did. Maitland's wife, Therese, blamed Mary Beth for his death. Mary Beth shrugged it off with the simple words, "I warned him, didn't I? If he hadn't gone up in the damned plane, he couldn't have crashed in it."

Maitland's brothers were distraught over Maitland's death, and begged Mary Beth to try to stop such events if she could, to which she replied that she could give it a try, and would the next time something of that kind came to her attention. Again, she warned them that such things were tricky. In 1921, Maitland's son, Maitland Junior, wanted to go on an expedition in the African jungles, of which his mother Therese strongly disapproved, and she appealed to Mary Beth either to stop the boy or to make some sort of prediction.

Mary Beth considered the matter for a long time, and then explained in her simple straightforward manner that the future wasn't predetermined, it was merely predictable. And her prediction was that this boy would die if he went to Africa. But if he stayed here worse things might happen. Maitland Junior changed his own mind about the expedition, stayed home, and was killed in a fire six months later. (The young man was drunk and was smoking in bed.) At the funeral Therese accosted Mary Beth and demanded to know why she didn't prevent such horrors. Mary Beth said almost casually that she foresaw the whole thing, yes, but there wasn't much she could do to change it. To change it, she would have had to change Maitland Junior and that was not her job in life, and besides, she'd tried, to no avail, to talk to Maitland countless times; but she certainly felt dreadful about it, and she wished the cousins would stop asking her to look into the future.

"When I look into the future," she reportedly said, "all I see is how weak most people are, and how little they do to fight fate or fortune. You can fight, you know. You really can. But Maitland wasn't going to change anything." Then she shrugged, or so the story goes, and walked with her characteristic big steps out of the Lafayette Cemetery.

Therese was horrified by these statements. She never forgave Mary Beth for her "involvement" (?) in the death of her husband or her son. And to her dying day, she maintained that an aura of evil surrounded the First Street house, and that whatever power the Mayfairs possessed worked only for the chosen ones.

(This story was told to us by a friend of Therese's sister, Emilie Blanchard, who died in 1935. An abbreviated version was passed on to us by a nonrelative who overheard the conversation at the cemetery and made inquiries about it. Yet a third version was repeated to us by a nun who was present at the cemetery. And the agreement among the three as to Mary Beth's statements makes this one of our most powerful pictures of her, albeit small. The two deaths involved were reported in the papers.)

There are countless other stories about Mary Beth's predictions, advice, and the like. They are all very similar. Mary Beth advised against certain marriages, and her advice always turned out to be correct. Or Mary Beth advised people to enter into certain ventures and it worked out wonderfully. But everything points to the fact that Mary Beth was very cautious about the power, and disliked direct prediction. We have one other quote from her on the matter, and this was made to the parish priest who later told it to his brother, a police officer, who apparently remembered it because he thought it was interesting.

Mary Beth is rumored to have told the priest that any one strong individual could change the future for countless others, that it happened all the time. Given the number of human beings alive in this world, such persons were so rare that predicting the future was deceptively simple.

"Then we are possessed of free will, you grant that much," the priest had said, to which Mary Beth replied, "Indeed we are, in fact, it is absolutely crucial that we exercise our free will. Nothing is predetermined. And thank God there aren't many strong people who upset the predictable scheme, for there are as many bad ones who bring on war and disaster as there are visionaries who do good for others."

(It is worth noting that these statements are interesting in light of Richard Llewellyn's description of Julien coming to him in a dream and telling him that nothing is predetermined. And it is also worth noting that two hundred years before, Lasher, according to Petyr van Abel, made a mysterious prediction which deeply disturbed Petyr. If only we had more direct quotations regarding this and other subjects from the powerful psychic members of the Mayfair family! But alas we do not, and this immediate connection between two quotes makes us painfully aware of it.)

Regarding family attitudes towards Mary Beth, many family members—according to their talkative friends—were aware that there was something strange about Mary Beth and Monsieur Julien, and whether or not to go to them in times of trouble was an ever present question in each generation. Going to them was perceived as having advantages and definite liabilities.

For example, one descendant of Lestan Mayfair who was pregnant out of wedlock went to Mary Beth for help and, though she received a great deal of money to assist with her child, became convinced afterwards that Mary Beth had caused the death of the child's irresponsible father.

Another Mayfair, a favorite of Mary Beth's, who was convicted of assault and battery after a drunken brawl in a French Quarter nightclub, was said to be more afraid of Mary Beth's disapproval and retribution than of any criminal court. He was fatally shot trying to escape from jail. And Mary Beth refused to allow him to be buried in the Lafayette Cemetery.

Another unfortunate girl—Louise Mayfair—who was pregnant out of wedlock and gave birth at First Street to Nancy Mayfair (whom Mary Beth adopted and accepted as one of Stella's children), died two days after the birth, and numerous stories were circulated that Mary Beth, displeased by the girl's behavior, had let her die alone and unattended.

But the stories of Mary Beth's occult powers, or evil doings, regarding the family are relatively few. Even when one considers the secretiveness of the family, the reluctance of most Mayfairs to gossip in any way about the legacy family to anyone, there simply isn't very much evidence that Mary Beth was a witch to her own kindred, so much as a magnate. When she did use her powers, it was almost always with reluctance. And we have numerous indications that many Mayfairs did not believe the "superstitious foolishness" repeated about Mary Beth by servants, neighbors, and occasionally by family members. They considered the story of the purse of golden coins to be laughable. They blamed superstitious servants for these tales, they considered them to be a holdover from the romantic plantation days, and they complained against the gossips of the neighborhood and the church parish.

We cannot emphasize enough that the vast majority of tales about Mary Beth's powers do come from the servants.

All things taken into account, the family lore indicates that Mary Beth was loved and respected by her family, and that she did not dominate people's lives or decisions, except to pressure them towards some show of family loyalty, and that, in spite of a few noteworthy mistakes, she picked excellent candidates for business ventures from among her kindred, and that they trusted her and admired her and liked to do business with her. She kept her outlandish accomplishments secret from those with whom she did business, and possibly she kept her occult powers secret from others, too, and she enjoyed being with the family in a simple and ordinary fashion.

It is also worth noting that the little children of the family loved Mary Beth. She was photographed scores of times with Stella, Lionel, Belle, Millie Dear, Nancy, and dozens of other little children all around her. And every Sunday for years the south lawn of the First Street property was covered with children tumbling and playing ball and tag while the grown-ups napped inside after dinner.

The third great passion or obsession of Mary Beth's life, as far as we can determine, was her desire for pleasure. As we have seen, she and Julien enjoyed dancing, parties, the theater, etc. She also had many lovers.

Though family members are absolutely mute on the subject, servant gossip, often coming to us second- or thirdhand through friends of the servant's family, is the largest source of such information. Neighbors also gossiped about "good-looking boys" who were always hanging about, supposedly to do jobs for which they were often utterly unqualified.

And Richard Llewellyn's story of the gift of the Stutz Bearcat to a young Irish coachman has been verified through simple registration records. The giving of other large gifts—sometimes bank drafts for enormous amounts—also indicate that these good-looking boys were Mary Beth's lovers. For there are no other explanations as to why she should give five thousand dollars as a Christmas present to a young coachman who could not in fact manage a team; or to a handyman who could never so much as hammer in a nail without assistance.

It is interesting to note that when all the information on Mary Beth is studied as a whole, we have more stories about her sensual appetites than any other aspect of her. In other words, stories about her lovers, her wine drinking, her love of food, and her dancing far outnumber (seventeen to one) stories about her occult powers or her abilities in making money.

But when all the many descriptions of Mary Beth's love of wine, food, music, dancing, and bed partners are considered, one can see that she behaved more like a man of the period than a woman in this regard, merely pleasing herself as a man might, with little thought for convention or respectability. In sum, there is nothing too unusual about her behavior if one sees it in this light. But of course people at the time did not see it in that light, and they thought her love of pleasure to be rather mysterious and even sinister. She deepened this sense of the mysterious by her casual attitude towards what she did, and her refusal to attach importance to the shallow reactions of others. More than one Mayfair close cousin begged her to "behave" (or so the servants said), and more than once Mary Beth shrugged off this suggestion.

As for her cross-dressing, she did it so long and so well that just about everyone became accustomed to it. In the last years of her life she would often go out in her tweed suit, and with her walking stick, and stroll around the Garden District for hours. She did not bother to pin up her hair any more or hide it beneath a hat. She wore it in a simple twist or bun; and people took her appearance entirely for granted. She was Miss Mary Beth to servants and neighbors for blocks around, walking with her head slightly bowed, and with very big steps, and waving in a lackadaisical fashion to those who greeted her.

As for her lovers, the Talamasca has been able to find out almost nothing about them. Of a young cousin, Alain Mayfair, we know the most, and it is not even certain that he was Mary Beth's lover. He worked for Mary Beth as a secretary or chauffeur or both from 1911 until 1913, but was frequently in Europe for long periods. He was in his twenties at the time, and very handsome and spoke French very well, but not to Mary Beth, who preferred English. There was some disagreement between him and Mary Beth in 1914, but no one seems to know what it was. He then went to England, joined the forces fighting in World War I, and was killed in combat. His body was never recovered. Mary Beth held an immense memorial service for him at First Street.

Kelly Mayfair, another cousin, also worked for Mary Beth in 1912 and 1913, and continued in her employ until 1918. He was a strikingly handsome red-haired, green-eyed young man (his mother was Irish-born); he took care of Mary Beth's horses and, unlike other boys whom Mary Beth kept, did know what he was doing in that capacity. The case for his having been Mary Beth's lover rests entirely on the fact that they did dance together at many family gatherings, and later had many noisy quarrels which were overheard by maids, laundresses, and even chimney sweeps.

Also Mary Beth settled an immense sum of money on Kelly so that he could try his luck as a writer. He went to Greenwich Village in New York with this money, worked for a while as a reporter for the *New York Times*, and froze to death in a cold-water flat there, while drunk, apparently quite by accident. It was his first winter in New York and he may not have understood the dangers. Whatever the case, Mary Beth was distraught over his death, and had the body brought home and buried properly, though Kelly's parents were so disgusted with what had happened that they would not attend the funeral. She had three words inscribed on his tombstone: "Fear no more." And this may be a reference to the famous lines of Shakespeare in *Cymbeline*, "Fear no more the heat of the sun, nor the furious winter's rages." But we do not know. She refused to explain it even to the undertaker or the tombstone workers.

The other "good-looking boys" who caused so much talk are unknown to us. We have only gossip descriptions which indicate they were all very handsome and what one might call "rough trade." Full-time maids and cooks were highly suspicious of them and resentful towards them. And most accounts of these young men say nothing per se about their being Mary Beth's lovers. They run something like this, "And then there was one of those boys of hers about, you know, one of those good-looking ones she always had around, and don't ask me for what, and he was sitting on the kitchen steps doing nothing but whittling you know and I asked him to carry the laundry basket down but he was too good for that, you can well imagine, but of course he did it, because she came into the kitchen then, and he wouldn't dare do nothing to run against her, you can be sure, and she give him one of her smiles, you know and said, 'Hello there, Benjy.'"

Who knows? Maybe Mary Beth only liked to look at them.

What we do know for certain is that from the day she met him she loved and cared for Daniel McIntyre, though he certainly began his role in the Mayfair history as Julien's lover.

Richard Llewellyn's story notwithstanding, we know that Julien met Daniel McIntyre sometime around 1896, and that he began to place a great deal of important business with Daniel McIntyre, who was an up-and-coming attorney in a Camp Street firm founded by Daniel's uncle some ten years before.

When Garland Mayfair finished law school at Harvard he went to work in this same firm, and later Cortland joined him, and both worked with Daniel McIntyre until the latter was appointed a judge in 1905.

Daniel's photographs of the period show him to be pale, slender, with reddish-blond hair. He was almost pretty—not unlike Julien's later lover, Richard Llewellyn, and not unlike the darker Victor who died from the fall beneath the carriage wheels. The facial bone structure of all three men was exceptionally beautiful and dramatic, and Daniel had the added advantage of remarkably brilliant green eyes.

Even in the last years of his life, when he was quite heavy and continually red-faced from drink, Daniel McIntyre elicited compliments on his green eyes.

What we know of Daniel McIntyre's early life is fairly cut and dry. He was descended from "old Irish," that is, the immigrants who came to America long before the great potato famines of the 1840s, and it is doubtful that any of his ancestors were ever poor.

His grandfather, a self-made millionaire commission agent, built a magnificent house on Julia Street in the 1830s, where Daniel's father, Sean McIntyre, the youngest of four sons, grew up. Sean McIntyre was a distinguished medical doctor until he died abruptly of a heart attack at the age of forty-eight.

By then Daniel was already a practicing lawyer, and had moved with his mother and unmarried sister to an uptown St. Charles Avenue mansion where Daniel lived until his mother died. Neither McIntyre home is still standing.

Daniel was by all accounts a brilliant business lawyer, and numerous records attest to his having advised Julien well in a variety of business ventures. He also represented Julien successfully in several crucial civil suits. And we have one very interesting little anecdote told to us years later by a clerk in the firm to the effect that, about one of these civil suits, Julien and Daniel had a terrible argument in which Daniel repeatedly said, "Now Julien, let me handle this legally!" to which Julien repeatedly replied, "All right, if you are so damned set on doing it, then do it. But I tell you I could very easily make this man wish he had never been born."

Public records also indicate that Daniel was highly imaginative in finding ways for Julien to do things he wanted to do, and for helping him discover information about people who opposed him in business.

On February 11, 1897, when Daniel's mother died, he moved out of their uptown St. Charles Avenue home, leaving his sister in the care of nurses and maids, and took up residence in an ostentatious and lavish four-room suite at the old St. Louis Hotel. There he began to live "like a king," according to bellhops and waiters and taxi drivers who received enormous tips from Daniel and served him expensive meals in his parlor which fronted on the street.

Julien Mayfair was Daniel's most frequent visitor, and he often stayed the night in Daniel's suite.

If this arrangement aroused any enmity or disapproval in Garland or Cortland, we know nothing of it. They became partners in the firm of McIntyre, Murphy, Murphy, and Mayfair, and after the retirement of the two Murphy brothers, and the appointment of Daniel to the bench, Garland and Cortland became the firm of Mayfair and Mayfair. In later decades, they devoted their entire energies to the management of Mayfair money, and they were almost partners with Mary Beth in numerous ventures; though there were other ventures in which Mary Beth was involved of which Garland and Cortland apparently knew nothing.

Daniel was already by this time a heavy drinker, and there are numerous accounts of hotel staff members having to help him to his suite. Cortland also kept an eye on him continuously, and in later years when Daniel bought a motor car, it was Cortland who was always offering to drive Daniel home so that he wouldn't kill himself or someone else. Cortland seems to have liked Daniel very much. He was the defender of Daniel to the rest of the family, which became—over the years—an ever more demanding role.

We have no evidence that Mary Beth ever met Daniel during this early period. She had already become very active in business, but the family had numerous lawyers and connections, and we have no testimony to indicate that Daniel ever came to the First Street house. It may have been that he was embarrassed by his relationship with Julien, and a bit more puritanical about such things in general than Julien's other lovers had been.

He was certainly the only one of Julien's lovers of whom we know who had a professional career of his own.

Whatever the explanation, he met Mary Beth Mayfair in late 1897, and Richard Llewellyn's version of the meeting—in Storyville—is the only one we have. We do not know whether or not they fell in love as Llewellyn insisted, but we do know that Mary Beth and Daniel began to appear together at numerous social affairs.

Mary Beth was by that time about twenty-five years old and extremely independent. And it was no secret that little Belle—the child of the mysterious Scottish Lord Mayfair—was not right in the head. Though very sweet and amiable, Belle was obviously unable to learn even simple things, and reacted emotionally to life forever as though she were about four years old, or so the cousins later described it. People hesitated to use the word feebleminded.

Everyone knew of course that Belle was not an appropriate designee for the legacy as she might never marry. And the cousins discussed this fairly openly at the time.

Another Mayfair tragedy was also a topic of conversation and that was the destruction, by the river, of the plantation of Riverbend.

The house, built by Marie Claudette before the beginning of the century, was built on a thumb of land jutting into the river, and sometime around 1896 it became clear that the river was determined to take this thumb of land. Everything was tried, but nothing could be done. The levee had to be built behind the house and finally the house had to be abandoned; the ground around the house was slowly flooded; then one night the house itself collapsed into the marsh, and within a week it was gone altogether, as if it had never been there.

That Mary Beth and Julien regarded this as a tragedy was obvious. There was much talk in New Orleans of the engineers they consulted, in attempting to avert the tragedy. And no small part of it was Katherine, Mary Beth's aging mother, who did not want to move to New Orleans to the house Darcy Monahan had built for her decades ago.

At last, Katherine had to be sedated for the move to the city, and as stated earlier, she never recovered from the shock, and soon went insane, wandering around the First Street gardens, talking all the time to Darcy, and searching also for her mother, Marguerite, and endlessly turning out the contents of drawers to find things which she claimed to have lost.

Mary Beth tolerated her, and was heard to say once, much to the shock of the doctor in attendance, that she was happy to do what she could for her mother, but she did not find the woman or her plight "particularly interesting," and she wished there was some drug they could give the woman to quiet her down.

Julien was present at the time, and naturally found this very funny and went into one of his disconcerting riffs of laughter. He was understanding of the doctor's shock, however, and explained to him that the great virtue of Mary Beth was that she always told the truth, no matter what the consequences.

If they did give Katherine "some drug," we know nothing of it. She began to wander the streets around 1898, and a young mulatto servant was hired simply to follow her around. She died in bed at First Street, in a rear bedroom, in 1905, on the night of January 2, to be exact, and to the best of our knowledge there was no storm to mark her death, and no unusual event of any kind. She had been in a coma for days, according to the servants, and Mary Beth and Julien were at her side when she died.

On January 15, 1899, in an enormous wedding held at St. Alphonsus Church, Mary Beth married Daniel McIntyre. It is interesting to note that up until this time the family had worshiped at the Notre Dame church (the French church of the tri-church parish), but for the wedding it chose the Irish church, and thereafter went to all services at St. Alphonsus.

Daniel seems to have been on very friendly terms with the Irish-American priests of the parish, and to have been lavish in his support of the parish. He also had a cousin in the Irish-American Sisters of Mercy who taught at the local school.

It seems safe therefore to assume that the change to the Irish church was Daniel's idea. And it is also safe to assume that Mary Beth was almost indifferent to the matter, though she did go to church often with her children and great-nieces and nephews, though what she believed about it one cannot say. Julien never went to church, except for the customary weddings, funerals, and christenings. He also seems to have preferred St. Alphonsus to the humbler French church of Notre Dame.

The wedding of Daniel and Mary Beth was, as already mentioned, an enormous affair. A reception of dazzling proportions was held at the First Street house, with cousins coming from as far away as New York. Daniel's family, though much much smaller than the Mayfair family, was also in attendance, and by all reports the couple were deeply in love and deeply happy, and the dancing and singing went on late into the night.

The couple went to New York for a honeymoon trip, and from there to Europe, where they remained for four months, cutting short their journey in May because Mary Beth was already expecting a child.

Indeed, Carlotta Mayfair was born seven and one-half months after her parents' marriage, on September 1, 1899.

On November 2 of the following year, 1900, Mary Beth gave birth to Lionel, her only son. And finally, on October 10 of the year 1901, she gave birth to her last child, Stella.

These children were of course all the legal offspring of Daniel McIntyre, but one can legitimately ask for the purposes of this history, who was their real father?

There is overwhelming evidence, both from medical records and from pictures, to indicate that Daniel McIntyre was Carlotta Mayfair's father. Not only did Carlotta inherit Daniel's green eyes, she also inherited his beautiful reddish-blond curly hair.

As for Lionel, he was also of the same blood type as Daniel McIntyre, and also tended to resemble him though he bore a strong resemblance to his mother as well, having her dark eyes and her "expression," especially as he grew older.

As for Stella, her blood type, as recorded in her superficial postmortem examination in 1929, indicates that she could not have been Daniel McIntyre's daughter. We know that this information came to the notice of her sister Carlotta at the time. In fact, talk about Carlotta's request for blood typing is what brought it to the attention of the Talamasca.

It is perhaps superfluous to add that Stella bore no resemblance to Daniel. On the contrary, she resembled Julien with her delicate bones, black curling hair, and very brilliant, if not twinkling dark eyes.

As we have no blood type for Julien, and do not know that any was ever recorded, we cannot add that scrap of evidence to the case.

Stella might have been fathered by any of Mary Beth's lovers, though we do not know that she had a lover in the year before Stella was born. Indeed, the gossip concerning Mary Beth's lovers came after, but that may only mean that she grew careless about her lovers as the years passed.

One other definite possibility is Cortland Mayfair, Julien's second son, who was, at the time of Stella's birth, twenty-two years old and an extremely appealing young man. (His blood type was finally obtained in 1959 and is compatible.) He was in residence off and on at First Street, as he was studying law at Harvard and did not finish until 1903. That he was very fond of Mary Beth was well-known to everyone, and that he took an interest all his life in the family legacy is also well-known.

Unfortunately for the Talamasca, Cortland was throughout most of his life a very secretive and guarded man. He was known even to his brothers and his children as a reclusive individual who disliked any sort of gossip outside the family. He loved reading, and was something of a genius at investment. To our knowledge, he confided in no one. Even those closest to him give contradictory versions of what Cortland did, and when, and why.

The one aspect of the man of which everyone is certain is that he was devoted to the management of the legacy and to making money for himself, his brothers and their children, and Mary Beth. His descendants are among the richest among the Mayfair clan to this day.

When Mary Beth died, it was Cortland who prevented Carlotta Mayfair from virtually dismantling her mother's financial empire by taking over its complete management on behalf of Stella, who was in fact the designee, and did not care what happened to it as long as she could do as she pleased.

Stella never "cared a thing about money" by her own admission. And over Carlotta's wishes, she placed her interests entirely in Cortland's hands. Cortland and his son Sheffield continued to manage the bulk of the fortune on behalf of Antha after Stella's death.

We should stress here, however, that after Mary Beth died her empire began to fall apart. No one individual could take her place. And though Cortland did a marvelous job of consolidating and investing and preserving, the dizzying expansion which had gone on under Mary Beth essentially came to an end.

But to return to our principal concern here, there are other indications that Cortland was Stella's father. Cortland's wife, Amanda Grady Mayfair, had a deep aversion to Mary Beth and to the entire Mayfair family, and she would never accompany Cortland to the First Street house. This did not stop Cortland from visiting there all the time, and he took all of his five children there, so that they grew up knowing his family quite well.

Amanda eventually left Cortland when their youngest son, Pierce Mayfair, finished Harvard in 1935, leaving New Orleans forever and going to live with her younger sister, Mary Margaret Grady Harris, in New York.

In 1936 Amanda told one of our investigators at a cocktail party (a casual chance meeting had been arranged) that her husband's family was evil, that if she were to tell the truth about it people would think she was crazy, and that she would never go south again to be among those people, no matter how much her sons begged her to do so. A little later during the evening, when she was quite intoxicated, she asked our investigator, whose name she did not know, whether or not he believed people could sell their souls to the devil. She said that her husband had done it, and he was "richer than Rockefeller" and so was she and so were her sons. "They will all burn in hell some day," she told him. "Of that you can be sure."

When our investigator asked if the lady really believed this sort of thing, she replied that there were witches alive in the modern world who could throw spells.

"They can make you believe you are some place you aren't, that you're seeing things when there's nothing there. They did that to my husband. And you know why? Because my husband is a witch, a powerful witch. Don't quibble over words like warlock. It doesn't matter. The man is a witch. I myself saw what he could do."

Asked point-blank if her husband had ever done any evil to her, Cortland's wife said (to this apparent stranger) that no, she had to confess he hadn't. It was what he condoned in others, what he went along with, and what he believed. She then began to cry and to say that she missed her husband, and she didn't want to talk about it anymore.

"I'll tell you this much," she said when she had recovered herself slightly. "If I wanted my husband to come to me tonight, he'd do it. How he'd do it I couldn't tell you, but he could make himself materialize in this very room. All his family can do things like that. They could drive you out of your mind with it. But he'd be here in this very room. Sometimes he's in the room with me when I don't want him to be. And I can't make him go away."

At this point the lady was rescued by a Grady niece, and no further contact was ever accomplished until some years later.

One further circumstance argues for a close bond between Cortland and Stella, and that is that after Julien's death, Cortland took Stella and her brother Lionel to England and to Asia, for well over a year. Cortland already had five children at this time, all of which he left behind with his wife. Yet he seems to have been the instigator of this trip, and was completely in charge of the arrangements and greatly prolonged the venture so that the party did not actually return to New Orleans for some eighteen months.

After the Great War, Cortland left his wife and children again to travel for a year with Stella. And he seems always to have been on Stella's side in family disputes.

In sum, this evidence is certainly not conclusive, but it does indicate Cortland might have been Stella's father. But then again, Julien, in spite of his great age, may have been her father. We don't know.

Whatever the case, Stella was pretty much "the favorite child" from the time of her birth. Daniel McIntyre certainly seems to have loved her as if she were his own daughter, and it is entirely possible that he never knew she was not.

Of the early childhood of all three children, we know little that is specific, and Richard Llewellyn's portrait is the most intimate we possess.

As the children grew older, there was more and more talk about dissension, however; and when Carlotta went to board at the Sacred Heart at the age of fourteen, everyone knew it was against Mary Beth's wishes, and that Daniel, too, was heartbroken, and wanted his daughter to come home more often than she did. Carlotta is never described as a happy child by anyone. But it is difficult to this day to gather information about her, because she is still living, and even people who knew her fifty years ago are extremely afraid of her, and of her influence, and very reluctant to say anything about her at all.

The people who are willing to talk are those who most dislike her. Possibly if the others were not so afraid, we might hear something to balance the picture.

Whatever the case, Carlotta was admired for her brilliance from the time she was a little girl. She was even called a genius by the nuns who taught her. She boarded at Sacred Heart through high school, and went on to Loyola law school when she was very young.

Meantime, Lionel began attending day school when he was eight years old. He seems to have been a quiet, well-behaved boy who never gave anyone very much trouble, and to have been liked. He had a full-time tutor to assist him with his homework, and as time passed, he became something of an exceptional student. But he never made friends outside the family. His cousins were his only companions when he wasn't at school.

The history of Stella was markedly different from the start. By all accounts Stella was a particularly beguiling and seductive child. She had soft black rippling hair and enormous black eyes.

When one considers the numerous photographs of her from 1901 to her death in 1929, it seems impossible to imagine her living in any other era, so suited to the times was she with her slender boyish hips, pouty little red mouth, and bobbed hair.

In her earliest pictures she is the image of the luscious child in the Pears Soap advertisements, a white-skinned little temptress, gazing soulfully yet playfully at the spectator. By the time she was eighteen, she was Clara Bow.

On the night of her death, she was, according to numerous eyewitnesses, a femme fatale of unforgettable power, dancing the Charleston wildly in her short fringed skirt and glittering stockings, flashing her enormous jewellike eyes on everyone and no one as she commanded the attention of every man in the room.

When Lionel was sent off to school, Stella begged to be allowed to go to school also, or so she told the nuns at Sacred Heart herself. But within three months of her admission as a day student she was privately and unofficially expelled. The talk was that she frightened the other students. She could read their minds, and she enjoyed demonstrating the power, and also she could fling people about without touching them, and she had an unpredictable sense of humor and would laugh at things the nuns said which she considered to be blatant lies. Her conduct was mortifying to Carlotta, who was powerless to control her, though by all accounts Carlotta also loved Stella, and did make every effort to persuade Stella to fit the mold.

It may be surprising to learn in light of all this that the nuns and the children at Sacred Heart actually liked Stella. Numerous classmates remember her fondly, and even with delight.

When she wasn't up to her tricks she was "charming," "sweet," absolutely "lovable," "a darling little girl." But nobody could stand being around her very long.

Stella next attended the Ursuline Academy long enough to make her First Communion with the class, but was expelled immediately after in the same private and unofficial manner and more or less for the same complaints. This time, apparently, she was crushed at being sent home, because she regarded school as great fun, and she did not like to be about the house all day with her mother and Uncle Julien telling her they were busy. She wanted to play with other children. Her governesses annoyed her. She wanted to go out.

Stella then attended four different private schools, spending no more than three or four months in each before ending up at the St. Alphonsus parochial school, where she was the only one, among an Irish-American proletarian student body, to be driven to school each day in a chauffeured Packard limousine.

Sister Bridget Marie—an Irish-born nun who lived at Mercy Hospital in New Orleans until she was ninety—remembered Stella vividly, even fifty years afterwards, and told this investigator in 1969 that Stella Mayfair was undoubtedly some sort of witch.

Once again, Stella was accused of reading minds, of laughing when people lied to her, of flinging things about by the power of the mind, and talking to an invisible friend, "a familiar" according to Sister Bridget Marie, who did Stella's bidding, which included finding lost objects and making things fly through the air.

But Stella's manifestation of these powers was by no means continuous. She often tried to behave herself for long periods; she enjoyed reading and history and English; she liked to play with the other girls in the school yard on St. Andrew Street, and she liked the nuns very much.

The nuns found themselves seduced by Stella. They let her into the convent garden to cut flowers with them; or took her into the parlor after school to teach her embroidery, for which she had a knack.

"You know what she was up to? I'll tell you. Every sister in that convent felt that Stella was her special little friend. She led you to believe that. She told you little secrets about herself, just as if she'd never told them to another soul. And she knew all about you, she did. She knew things you'd never told anyone, and she'd talk to you about your secrets and your fears and the things you always wanted to tell someone, and she'd make you feel better about it. And later, hours later, or maybe even days later, you'd think about it, think about what it had been like to be sitting there in the garden whispering with her, and you'd know she was a witch! She was from the devil. And she was up to no good.

"But she wasn't mean, I'll say this much for her. She wasn't mean. If she had been, she'd have been a monster, that one. God knows the evil she might have done. I don't think she really wanted to make trouble. But she took a secret pleasure in her powers, if you know what I mean. She liked knowing your secrets. She liked seeing the look of amazement when she told you what you dreamed the night before.

"And oh, how she pitched herself into things. She would draw pictures all day long for weeks on end, then throw out the pencils and never draw another thing. Then it was embroidery with her, she had to learn it, and she'd make the most beautiful thing,

492

fussing at herself for the least little mistake, then throw down the needles and be done with that forevermore. I never saw a child so changeable. It was as though she was looking for something, something to which she could give herself, and she never found it. Least ways not while she was a little girl.

"I'll tell you one thing she loved to do, and she never tired of it, and that was to tell stories to the other girls. They'd gather around her at big recess, and she'd keep them hanging on her every word until the bell rang. And such stories they were that she told them—ghost stories of old plantation houses full of horrible secrets, and people foully murdered, and of voodoo in the islands long years ago. She knew stories of pirates, oh, they were the worst, the things she would tell about the pirates. It was positively shocking. And all this had the ring of truth to it, to hear her tell it. But you knew she had to be making it up. What did she know of the thoughts and feelings of some group of poor souls on a captured galleon in the hours before a brute of a pirate made them walk the plank?

"But I'll tell you, some of the things she said were most interesting, and I always wanted to ask someone else about them, you know, someone who read the history books and really knew.

"But the girls had nightmares from the things she told them and wouldn't you know it, the parents were coming and asking us, 'Now, Sister, where did my little girl ever hear such a thing!'

"We were always calling Miss Mary Beth. 'Keep her home for a few days,' we'd ask. For that was the thing about Stella. You couldn't take it day in and day out. Nobody could take it.

"And thank the Lord she'd get tired of school and disappear on her own for months at a time.

"Sometimes it went on so long we thought she was never coming back. We heard she was running wild over there on First and Chestnut, playing with the servants' children and making a voodoo altar with the cook's son, him black as coal, you can be sure of it, and we'd think, well, somebody ought to go round and talk to Miss Mary Beth about it.

"Then lo and behold, one morning, perhaps ten o'clock it would be—the child never did care what time she came to school—the limousine would appear on the corner of Constance and Saint Andrew and out would step Stella in her little uniform, a perfect doll, if you can imagine, but with a great big ribbon in her hair. And what would she have with her, but a sack of gaily wrapped presents for each of the sisters she knew by name, and hugs for all of us, too, you can be sure of it. 'Sister Bridget Marie,' she'd whisper in my ear, 'I missed you.' And sure enough, I'd open the box, and I can tell you this happened more than once, and there'd be some little thing I so wanted with all my heart. Why, one time it was a tiny Infant Jesus of Prague she gave me, all dressed in silk and satin, and another time, the most beautiful rosary of crystal and silver. Ah, what a child. What a strange child.

"But it was God's will, she stopped coming as the years went on. She had a governess all the time teaching her, and I think she was bored with St. Alphonsus, and they said she could get the chauffeur to drive her anywhere that she pleased. Lionel didn't go to high school either as I recollect. He started just running around with Stella, and seems it was about that time or maybe a little after that old Mr. Julien died.

"Oh, how that child cried at his funeral. We didn't go to the cemetery of course, none of the sisters did in those days, but we went to the Mass, and there was Stella, slumped over in the pew, just sobbing, and Carlotta holding her. You know, after Stella died, they said Carlotta never liked her. But Carlotta was never mean to that child. Never. And I remember at Julien's Mass, the way Carlotta held her sister, and Stella just cried and cried and cried.

"Miss Mary Beth, she was in a trance of sorts. It was deep grief I saw in her eyes as she came down the aisle after the coffin. She had the children with her, but it was a faraway look I saw in her eye. 'Course her husband wasn't with her, no, not him. Judge McIntyre never was with her when she needed him, or at least that's how I heard it. He was dead drunk when old Mr. Julien passed, they couldn't even wake him up, though they shook him and threw cold water on him and stood him up out of the bed. And on the day of the funeral, the man was nowhere to be seen at all. Heard later they'd carried him home from a tavern on Magazine Street. It's a wonder that man lived as long as he did."

Sister Bridget Marie's view of Carlotta's affection for her sister has been corroborated by many witnesses, though of course Richard Llewellyn would not have agreed. There are several accounts of Julien's funeral, and in all of them, Carlotta is mentioned as holding on to her sister, and even wiping her tears.

In the months following Julien's death, Lionel left school altogether and he and Stella went to Europe, with Cortland and Barclay, making the Atlantic crossing on a great luxury liner only months before the outbreak of the Great War.

As travel in continental Europe was all but impossible, the party spent several weeks in Scotland, visiting Donnelaith Castle, and then set out for more exotic climes. At considerable risk, they made their way to Africa, spent some time in Cairo and Alexandria, and then went on to India, sending home countless crates of carpets, statuary, and other relics as they went along.

In 1915, Barclay, sorely missing his family, and very weary of traveling, left the party and made the dangerous crossing back to New York. The *Lusitania* had only just been sunk by a German U-boat, and the family held its breath for Barclay's safety, but he soon turned up at the house on First Street with fabulous stories to tell.

Conditions were no better six months later when Cortland, Stella, and Lionel decided to come home. However, luxury liners were making the crossing in spite of all dangers, and the trio managed to make the journey without mishap, arriving in New Orleans just before Christmas of 1916.

Stella was then fifteen years old.

In a photograph taken that year, Stella is wearing the Mayfair emerald. It was common knowledge that she was the designee of the legacy. Mary Beth seems to have been exceptionally proud of her, called her "the intrepid" on account of her wanderings, and though she was disappointed that Lionel did not want to go back to school with a view to going on to Harvard, she seemed to have been accepting of all her children. Carlotta had her own apartment in one of the outbuildings, and went to Loyola University every day in a chauffeur-driven car.

Anyone passing on Chestnut Street in the evening could see the family, through the windows, seated at dinner, an enormous gathering, waited on by numerous servants, and always lasting until quite late.

Family loyalty always has made it very difficult for us to determine what the cousins actually thought of Stella, or what they actually knew of her troubles at school.

But by this time, there are numerous mentions on record of Mary Beth telling the servants almost casually that Stella was the heiress, or that "Stella was the one who would inherit everything," and even the remarkable comment—one of the most remarkable in our entire record—quoted twice and without context: *"Stella has seen the man."*

We have no record of Mary Beth's ever explaining this strange statement. We are told only that she made it to a laundress named Mildred Collins, and to an Irish maid named Patricia Devlin, and we received the stories thirdhand. We were further given to understand that there was no agreement among the descendants of these two women as to what the famous Miss Mary Beth meant by this comment. One person believed "the man" to be the devil, and another that he was "a ghost" who had haunted the family for hundreds of years.

Whatever the case, it seems clear that Mary Beth made remarks like this offhandedly at intimate moments with her servants, and we get the impression that she was confiding something to them, in a moment perhaps of understanding with them, which she could not or would not confide in people of her own rank.

And it is very possible that Mary Beth made similar remarks to other people, for by the 1920s old people in the Irish Channel knew about "the man." They talked about "the man." Two sources are simply not enough to explain the extent of this supposed "superstition" about the Mayfair women—that they had a mysterious "male spirit or ally" who helped them work their voodoo or witchcraft or tricks.

Certainly, we see this as an unmistakable reference to Lasher, and its implications are troubling, and it reminds us of how little we really understand about the Mayfair Witches and what went on among them, so to speak.

Is it possible, for instance, that the heiress in each generation has to manifest her power by independently seeing "the man"? That is, did she have to see "the man" when she was alone, and away from the older witch who could act as a channel, and was it required of her that of her own free will she mention what she had seen?

Once more, we must confess that we cannot know.

What we do know is that people who knew of "the man" and spoke of him did not apparently connect him with any dark-haired anthropomorphic figure which they had personally seen. They did not even connect "the man" with the mysterious being once seen with Mary Beth in her taxi, for the stories come from entirely different sources and were never put together by anyone, so far as we know, except us.

And so it is with so much of the Mayfair material. The references which come later to the mysterious dark-haired man at First Street are not connected with this earlier talk of "the man." Indeed even people who knew of "the man" and who later saw an anonymous dark-haired man about the place did not make the connection, believing that the man they'd seen was simply some stranger or relative they did not know.

Witness Sister Bridget Marie's statement in 1969 when I asked her specifically about "the man."

"Ah, that. That was the invisible companion who hovered near that child night and day. The selfsame demon, I might add, who later hovered about her daughter Antha, ever ready to do the child's bidding. And later around poor little Deirdre, the sweetest and most innocent of them all. Don't ask me if I ever actually saw the creature. For as God is my witness, I don't know if I ever saw him, but I tell you, and I've told the priest myself many a time, I knew when he was there!''

But it is very likely that at this time Lasher was not eager to be seen by people outside the family. And certainly we have not a single account of his ever showing himself deliberately to anyone, and as I have already mentioned, we get quite a few later on.

To return to the chronology. After Julien's death, Mary Beth was at the very height of her financial influence and accomplishments. It was as if the loss of Julien left her a driven woman, and for a time gossip and rumor speak of her as ''unhappy.'' But this did not last. Her characteristic calm seems to have returned to her well before the children came home from abroad.

We know that she had a brief and bitter fight with Carlotta before Carlotta entered the law firm of Byrnes, Brown and Blake, in which she works to this very day. But Mary Beth finally accepted Carlotta's decision to work ''outside the family,'' and Carlotta's small apartment over the stables was completely renovated for her, and she lived there for many years, coming and going without having to enter the house.

We also know that Carlotta took her meals every day with her mother—breakfast in the morning on the back terrace when the weather allowed it, and supper in the dining room at seven o'clock.

When asked why she did not go into the firm of Mayfair and Mayfair with Julien's sons, her reply was usually stiff and brief and to the effect that she wanted to be on her own.

From the beginning of her career, she was known as a brilliant lawyer, but she had no desire ever to enter a courtroom, and to this day, she works in the shadow of the men of the firm.

Her detractors have described her as no more than a glorified legal clerk. But kinder evidence seems to indicate she became ''the backbone'' of Byrnes, Brown and Blake; she is the one who knows everything; and that with her demise, the firm will be hard put to find anyone to take her place.

Many lawyers in New Orleans have credited Carlotta with teaching them more than they ever learned in law school. In sum one might say that she started out and has continued to be an efficient and brilliant civil lawyer, with a tremendous and completely reliable knowledge of business law.

Other than the skirmish with Carlotta, Mary Beth's life continued upon a predictable course almost to the very end. Even

Daniel McIntyre's drinking does not seem to have weighed heavily on her.

Family legend avers that Mary Beth was extremely kind to Daniel in the last years of their lives.

From this point on the story of the Mayfair Witches is really Stella's story, and we will deal with Mary Beth's final illness and death at the proper time.

THE CONTINUING STORY OF STELLA AND MARY BETH

Mary Beth continued to enjoy her three main pursuits in life, and also to derive a great deal of pleasure from the antics of her daughter Stella, who at sixteen became something of a scandal in New Orleans society, driving her automobiles at breakneck speed, drinking in speakeasies, and dancing till dawn.

For eight years Stella lived the life of a flapper, or a young reckless southern belle, utterly unperturbed by business concerns or thoughts of marriage or any future. And whereas Mary Beth was the most quiet and mysterious witch ever produced by the family, Stella seems the most carefree, the most flamboyant, the most daring, and the only Mayfair Witch ever bent entirely upon "having fun."

Family legend holds that Stella was arrested all the time for speeding, or for disturbing the peace with her singing and dancing in the streets, and that "Miss Carlotta always took care of it," going to get Stella and bring her home. There is some gossip to the effect that Cortland sometimes became impatient with his "niece," demanding that she straighten up and pay more attention to her "responsibilities," but Stella had not the slightest interest in money or business.

A secretary for Mayfair and Mayfair describes in vivid detail one of Stella's visits to the office, when she appeared in a dashing fur coat and very high heels, with a bottle of bootleg whiskey in a brown paper bag from which she drank all during the meeting, erupting into wild laughter at all the funny legal phrases read out to her regarding the transaction involved.

Cortland seemed to have been charmed, but also a little weary. Finally, in a good-natured way, he told Stella to go on to her luncheon, and he would take care of the whole thing.

If there was ever anyone who did not find Stella "bewitching" and "attractive" during this period, other than Carlotta Mayfair, we have not heard of such a person.

In 1921 Stella apparently "got pregnant," but by whom no one was ever to know. It might have been Lionel, and certainly family legend indicates that everyone suspected it at the time.

Whatever the case, Stella announced that she didn't need a husband, wasn't interested in marriage in general, and would have her baby with all appropriate pomp and ceremony, as she was utterly delighted at the prospect of being a mother, and would name the baby Julien if it was a boy or Antha if it was a girl.

Antha was born in November of 1921, a healthy, eight-pound baby girl. Blood tests indicate that Lionel could have been the father. But Antha in no way resembled Lionel, for what that is worth, and there is simply something wrong with the picture of Lionel being the father. But more on that as we go on.

In 1922 the Great War was over, and Stella declared that she would make the Grand Tour of Europe which she had been denied before. With a nurse for the baby, and Lionel in tow quite reluctantly (he had been reading law with Cortland and he did not want to go), and Cortland happy to take off from the firm though his wife disliked his doing it, the party went to Europe first class, and spent a full year wandering about.

Stella was now an exceptionally beautiful young girl with a reputation for doing anything that she pleased. Cortland, as he grew older, more and more resembled his father Julien, except that his hair remained black until the end of his long life. In his photographs Cortland is lean and handsome at this period. The resemblance between him and Stella was frequently remarked upon.

According to the gossip of Cortland's descendants, the Grand Tour was a drunken bash from start to finish, with Stella and Lionel gambling at Monte Carlo for weeks on end. In and out of luxury hotels all over Europe they went, and in and out of museums and ancient ruins, often carrying their bottles of bourbon with them in paper sacks. To this day the grandchildren of Cortland talk about his letters home, full of humorous descriptions of their antics. And countless presents arrived for Cortland's wife, Amanda, and his sons.

Family legend also maintains that the party suffered one tragedy while abroad. The nurse who went along to take care of baby Antha experienced some sort of "breakdown" while they were in Italy, and took a severe fall on the Spanish Steps in Rome. She died in the hospital within hours of the fall.

Only recently have our investigators been able to shed some light on this incident, uncovering a simple written record (in Italian) of the incident in the Holy Family Hospital in Rome.

The woman's name was Bertha Marie Becker. And we have verified that she was half Irish and half German, born in New Orleans in the Irish Channel in 1905. She was admitted with severe head wounds and went into a coma about two hours afterwards from which she never revived.

But before that time she did a considerable amount of talking to the English-speaking doctor who was called to assist her and to the English-speaking priest who arrived later on.

She told the doctors that Stella, Lionel, and Cortland were "witches" and "evil" and that they had cast a spell on her and that "a ghost" traveled with the party, a dark evil man who appeared by baby Antha's cradle at all hours of the night and day. She said the baby could make the man appear, and would laugh with delight when he stood over her; and that the man did not want Bertha to see him, and he had driven Bertha to her death, stalking her through the crowds at the Spanish Steps.

The doctor and the priest concurred that Bertha, an illiterate servant girl, was insane. Indeed the record ends with the doctor noting that the girl's employers, very gracious, well-to-do people who spared no expense to make her comfortable, were heartbroken at her deterioration, and arranged for her body to be shipped home.

To our knowledge no one in New Orleans ever heard this story. Only Bertha's mother was living at the time of the girl's death, and she apparently suspected nothing when she heard that her daughter had died from a fall. She was given an enormous sum of money by Stella in compensation for her lost daughter, and descendants of the Becker family were talking about that as late as 1955.

What interests us about the story is that the dark man is obviously Lasher. And except for the one mention of a mysterious man in a taxi with Mary Beth, we have no other mention of him in the twentieth century before this time.

The truly remarkable thing about this story is that the nurse said the baby could make the man appear. One wonders if Stella had any control over the situation. And what would have been Mary Beth's thoughts on the subject? Again, we shall never know. Poor Bertha Marie Becker faced it entirely alone, or so the record appears to show.

In spite of the tragedy the party did not return home. Cortland wrote a "sad letter" about the whole affair to his wife and sons, and explained that they had hired a "lovely Italian woman" who took better care of Antha than Bertha, poor child, had ever managed to do.

This Italian woman, who was in her thirties at the time, was named Maria Magdalene Gabrielli, and she returned with the family and was Antha's nurse until the girl was nine years old.

If she ever saw Lasher we don't know anything about it. She

lived at First Street until she died, and never spoke to anyone outside the family as far as we know. Family legend holds she was highly educated, could read and write both English and French as well as Italian, and had "a scandal in her past."

Cortland finally left the party in 1923, when the trio had arrived in New York, and there Stella and Lionel, along with Antha and her nurse, remained in Greenwich Village, where Stella took up with numerous intellectuals and artists, and even did some painting of her own, which she always called "quite atrocious" and some writing, "hideous," and some sculpture, "absolute trash." At last she settled down to simply enjoying the company of truly creative individuals.

Every source of gossip in New York avers that Stella was extremely generous. She gave huge "handouts" to various painters and poets. She bought one penniless friend a typewriter and another an easel, and for one old gentleman poet she even bought a car.

During this time Lionel resumed his studies, reading constitutional law with one of the New York Mayfairs (a descendant of Clay Mayfair, who had joined descendants of Lestan Mayfair in a New York firm). Lionel also spent considerable time in the museums of New York City, and he frequently dragged Stella to the opera, which had begun to bore her, and to the symphony, which she liked only a little better, and to the ballet, which she did genuinely enjoy.

Family legend among the New York Mayfairs (available to us only now, as no one would talk at the time) depicts Lionel and Stella as absolutely devil-may-care and charming, people of tireless energy who entertained continuously, and often woke up other members of the family with early morning knocks on the door.

Two photographs taken in New York show Stella and Lionel as a happy, smiling duo. Lionel was all his life a slender man, and as indicated he inherited Judge McIntyre's remarkable green eyes and strawberry blond hair. He did not in any way resemble Stella and it was remarked more than once by those who knew them that sometimes newcomers into the crowd were shocked to discover that Lionel and Stella were brother and sister; they had presumed them to be something else.

If Stella had any particular lover, we know nothing of it. In fact, Stella's name was never coupled with that of anyone else (up till this point) except Lionel, though Stella was believed to be absolutely careless with her favors where young men were concerned. We have accounts of two different young artists falling passionately in love with her, but Stella "refused to be tied down."

What we know of Lionel reinforces over and over again that he was quiet and somewhat withdrawn. He seems to have delighted in watching Stella dance, and laugh, and carry on with her friends. He enjoyed dancing with her himself, which he did all the time and rather well; but he was definitely in Stella's shadow. He seemed to get his vitality from Stella. And when Stella wasn't around, he was "like an empty mirror." You hardly knew he was there.

There are several rumors that he was writing a novel while they were in New York, and that he was quite vulnerable with regard to the matter, and that an older novelist destroyed his confidence by telling him his pages were "pure rot."

But from most sources, we hear only that Lionel enjoyed the arts, that he was a contented human being, and that as long as no one came between him and Stella he was "just fine."

Finally, in 1924, Stella, Lionel, little Antha and her nurse, Maria, came home. Mary Beth threw a huge family party at First Street, and descendants still mention sadly that it was the last affair before Mary Beth took sick.

At this time a very strange incident occurred.

As mentioned, the Talamasca had a team of trained investigators working in New Orleans, private eyes who never asked why they were being asked to gather information on a certain family or a certain house. One of these investigators, a man who specialized in divorce cases, had let it out among the fashionable photographers of New Orleans that he would pay well for any discarded pictures of the Mayfair family, particularly those who lived in the First Street house.

One of these photographers, Nathan Brand, who had a fashionable studio on St. Charles Avenue, was called to the First Street house for this big homecoming party, and there took a whole series of pictures of Mary Beth, Stella, and Antha, as well as pictures of other Mayfairs throughout the afternoon as a wedding photographer might do.

A week later when he brought the pictures to the house for Mary Beth and Stella to choose what it was they wanted, the women picked out a fair number and laid the discards aside.

But then Stella retrieved one of the discards—a group shot of her with her mother and her daughter in which Mary Beth was holding a big emerald necklace around little Antha's neck. On the back of it, Stella wrote:

"To the Talamasca, with love, Stella! P.S. There are others who watch, too," and then, giving it back to the photographer, she went into peels of laughter, explaining that his investigator friend would know what the writing meant.

The photographer was embarrassed; he claimed innocence, then made excuses for his arrangement with the investigator, but no matter what he said, Stella only laughed. Then Stella said to him in a very charming and reassuring manner, "Mr. Brand, you're working yourself into a fit. Just give the picture to the investigator." And that is what Mr. Brand did.

It reached us about a month later. And was to have a decisive effect upon our approach to the Mayfair family.

At this time the Talamasca had no specific member assigned to the Mayfair investigation, and information was being added to the file by several archivists as it came in. Arthur Langtry—an outstanding scholar and a brilliant student of witchcraft—was familiar with the entire record, but he had been busy all of his adult life with three other cases, which were to obsess him till the day he died.

Nevertheless, the whole family history had been discussed numerous times by the grand council, but the judgment not to make contact had never been lifted. And indeed, it is doubtful that anyone among us at that time knew the full story.

This photograph, with its obvious message, caused quite a stir. A young member of the order, an American from Texas named Stuart Townsend (who had been Anglicized by years of living in London), asked to make a study of the Mayfair Witches with a view to direct investigation, and after careful consideration the entire file was placed in his hands.

Arthur Langtry agreed to reread all the material, but pressing matters kept him from ever doing it, though he was responsible for increasing the number of investigators in New Orleans from three professional private eyes to four and of discovering another excellent contact—a man named Irwin Dandrich, the penniless son of a fabulously rich family, who moved in the highest circles while selling information secretly to anyone who wanted it, including detectives, divorce lawyers, insurance investigators, and even scandal sheets.

Allow me to remind the reader that the file did not then include this narrative, as no such collation of materials had yet been done. It contained Petyr van Abel's letters and diary and a giant compendium of witness testimony, as well as photographs, articles from newspapers, and the like. There was a running chronology, updated periodically by the archivists, but it was very sketchy, to say the least.

Stuart was at that time engaged in several other significant investigations, and it took him some three years to complete his examination of the Mayfair material. We shall return to him and to Arthur Langtry at the appropriate time.

After Stella's return, she began to live very much as she had before she ever went to Europe, that is, she frequented speakeasies, once again gave parties for her friends, was invited to numerous Mardi Gras balls where she created something of a sensation, and in general behaved as the ne'er-do-well femme fatale she had been before.

Our investigators had no trouble at all gathering information about her, because she was highly visible and the subject of gossip all over town. Indeed, Irwin Dandrich wrote to our detective agency connection in London (he never knew to whom his information was going or for what purpose) that all he had to do was step into a ballroom and he heard all about what Stella was up to. A few phone calls made on Saturday morning also provided reams of information.

(It is worth noting here that Dandrich, by all accounts, was not a malicious man. His information has proved to be ninety-nine percent accurate. He was our most voluminous and intimate witness regarding Stella, and though he never said so, one can easily infer from his reports that he went to bed with her numerous times. But he didn't really know her; and she remains at a distance even at the most dramatic and tragic moments described in his reports.)

Thanks to Dandrich and others, the picture of Stella after her return from Europe took on greater and greater detail.

Family legend says that Carlotta severely disapproved of Stella during this period, and argued with Mary Beth about it, and demanded repeatedly and in vain that Stella settle down. Servant gossip (and Dandrich's gossip) corroborated this, but said that Mary Beth paid very little attention to the matter, and thought Stella was a refreshingly carefree individual and should not be tied down.

Mary Beth is even quoted as saying to one society friend (who promptly passed it on to Dandrich), "Stella is what I would be if I had my life to live over again. I've worked too hard for too little. Let her have her fun."

We must note that Mary Beth was already gravely ill and possibly very tired when she said this. Also she was far too clever a woman not to appreciate the various cultural revolutions of the 1920s, which may be hard for readers of this narrative to appreciate as the twentieth century draws to a close.

The true sexual revolution of the twentieth century began in its tumultuous third decade, with one of the most dramatic changes in female costume the world has ever witnessed. But not only did women abandon their corsets and long skirts; they threw out old-fashioned mores with them, drinking and dancing in speakeasies in a manner which would have been unthinkable only ten years before. The universal adoption of the closed automobile gave everyone unprecedented privacy, as well as freedom of movement. Radio reached into private homes throughout rural as well as urban America. Motion pictures made images of "glamour and wickedness" available to people worldwide. Magazines, literature, drama were all radically transformed by a new frankness, freedom, tolerance, and self-expression.

Surely Mary Beth perceived all this on some level. We have absolutely no reports of her disapproval of the "changing times." Though she never cut her long hair or gave up long skirts (when she wasn't cross-dressing), she begrudged Stella nothing. And Stella was, more than any other member of the family, the absolute embodiment of her times.

In 1925 Mary Beth was diagnosed as having incurable cancer, after which she lived only five months, and most of them in such severe pain that she no longer went out of the house.

Retiring to the north bedroom over the library, she spent her last comfortable days reading the novels she had never got around to reading when she was a girl. Indeed, numerous Mayfair cousins called upon her, bringing her various copies of the classics. And Mary Beth expressed a special interest in the Brontë sisters, in Dickens, which Julien used to read to her when she was little, and in random other English classics, which she seemed determined to read before she died.

Daniel McIntyre was terrified at the prospect of his wife's leaving him. When he was made to understand that Mary Beth wasn't going to recover, he commenced his final binge, and according to the gossips and the later legends was never seen to be sober again.

Others have told the same story that Llewellyn told, of Daniel waking Mary Beth constantly in her final days, frantic to know whether or not she was still alive. Family legend confirms that Mary Beth was endlessly patient with him, inviting him to lie down beside her, and comforting him for hours on end.

During this time, Carlotta moved back into the house so that she could be close to her mother and, indeed, sat with her through many a long night. When Mary Beth was in too much pain to read, she asked Carlotta to read to her, and family legend says that Carlotta read all of *Wuthering Heights* to her, and some of *Jane Eyre*.

Stella was also in constant attendance. She stopped her carousing altogether, and spent her time preparing meals for her mother—who was frequently too sick to eat anything—and consulting doctors all over the world, by letter and phone, about cures.

A perusal of the scant medical records that exist on Mary Beth indicate her cancer had metastasized before it was ever discovered. She did not suffer until the last three months and then she suffered a great deal.

Finally on the afternoon of September 11, 1925, Mary Beth lost consciousness. The attending priest noted that there was an enormous clap of thunder. "Rain began to pour." Stella left the room, went down to the library, and began to call the Mayfairs all over Louisiana, and even the relatives in New York.

According to the priest, the servant witnesses, and numerous neighbors, the Mayfairs started to arrive at four o'clock and continued to arrive for the next twelve hours. Cars lined First Street all the way to St. Charles Avenue, and Chestnut Street from Jackson to Washington.

The "cloudburst" continued, slacking off for a few hours to a drizzle and then resuming as a regular rain. Indeed it was raining all over the Garden District, though it was not raining in any other part of the city; however, no one took particular notice of that fact.

On the other hand, the majority of the New Orleans Mayfairs came equipped with umbrellas and raincoats, as though they fully expected some sort of storm.

Servants scurried about serving coffee and contraband European wine to the cousins, who filled the parlors, the library, the hallway, the dining room, and even sat on the stairs.

At midnight the wind began to howl. The enormous sentinel oaks before the house began to thrash so wildly some feared the branches would break loose. Leaves came down as thick as rain.

Mary Beth's bedroom was apparently crowded to overflowing with her children and her nieces and nephews, yet a respectful silence was maintained. Carlotta and Stella sat on the far side of her bed, away from the door, as the cousins came and went on tiptoe.

Daniel McIntyre was nowhere to be seen, and family legend holds that he had "passed out" earlier, and was in bed in Carlotta's apartment over the stables outside.

By one o'clock, there were solemn-faced Mayfairs standing on the front galleries, and even in the wind and rain, under their unsteady umbrellas, on the front walk. Many friends of the family had come merely to hover under the oak trees, with newspapers over their heads and their collars turned up against the wind. Others remained in their cars double-parked along Chestnut and First.

At one thirty-five, the attending physician, Dr. Lyndon Hart, experienced some sort of disorientation. He confessed later to several of his colleagues that ''something strange'' happened in the room.

To Irwin Dandrich, he confided in 1929 the following account:

''I knew she was almost gone. I had stopped taking her pulse. It seemed so undignified, to get up over and over, only to nod to the others that she was still alive. And each time I made a move towards the bed, naturally the cousins noticed it, and you would hear the anxious whispers in the hall.

''So for the last hour or so I did nothing. I merely waited and watched. Only the immediate family was at the bedside, except for Cortland and his son Pierce. She lay there with her eyes half open, her head turned towards Stella and Carlotta. Carlotta was holding her hand. She was breathing very irregularly. I had given her as much morphine as I dared.

''And then it happened. Perhaps I'd fallen asleep and was dreaming, but it seemed so real at the time—that a whole group of entirely different persons were there, an old woman, for example, whom I knew but didn't know was bending over Mary Beth, and there was a very tall old gentleman in the room, who looked distinctly familiar. There were all sorts of persons, really. And then a young man, a pale young man who was very primly dressed in beautiful old-fashioned clothes, was bending over her. He kissed her lips, and then he closed her eyes.

''I was on my feet with a start. The cousins were crying in the hallway. Someone was sobbing. Cortland Mayfair was crying. And the rain had started to really pour again. Indeed the thunder was deafening. And in a sudden flash of lightning I saw Stella staring at me with the most listless and miserable expression. And Carlotta was crying. And I knew my patient was dead, without doubt, and indeed her eyes were closed.

''I have never explained it really. I examined Mary Beth at once, and confirmed that it was over. But they already knew. All of them knew. I looked about, trying desperately to conceal my momentary confusion, and I saw little Antha in the corner, a few feet behind her mother, and that tall young gentleman was with her, and then, quite suddenly, he was gone. In fact, he was gone so suddenly that I'm not sure I saw him at all.

''But I'll tell you why I think he was really there. Someone else also saw him. It was Pierce Mayfair, Cortland's son. I turned around right after the young man vanished, and I realized Pierce was staring at that very spot. He was staring at little Antha, and

507

then he looked at me. At once he tried to appear natural, as if nothing was the matter, but I know he saw that man.

"As to the rest of what I saw, there certainly wasn't any old lady about, and the tall old gentleman was nowhere to be seen. But do you know who he was? I believe he was Julien Mayfair. I never knew Julien, but I saw a portrait of him later that very morning on the wall of the hallway, opposite the library door.

"To tell you the truth, I don't think any of those in the sick-room paid me the slightest notice. The maids started to wipe Mary Beth's face, and to get her ready for the cousins to come in and see her for the last time. Someone was lighting fresh candles. And the rain, the rain was dreadful. It was just flooding down the windows.

"The next thing I remember, I was pushing through a long line of the cousins, to get to the bottom of the stairs. Then I was in the library with Father McKenzie, and I was filling out the death certificate, and Father McKenzie was sitting on the leather couch with Belle and trying to comfort her, telling her all the usual things, that her mother had gone to heaven and she would see her mother again. Poor Belle. She kept saying, 'I don't want her to go away to heaven. I want to see her again right now.' How do people like that ever come to understand?

"It was only when I was leaving that I saw the portrait of Julien Mayfair and realized with a shock that I had seen that man. In fact a rather curious thing happened. I was so startled when I saw the portrait that I blurted it aloud: 'That's the man.'

"And there was someone standing in the hallway, having a cigarette, I believe, and that person looked up, saw me, and saw the portrait to his left, on the wall, and then said with a little laugh, 'Oh, no, that's not the man. That's Julien.'

"Of course I didn't bother to argue. I can't imagine what the person thought I meant. And I certainly don't know what he meant by what he said, and I just left it at that. I don't even know who the person was. A Mayfair, you can be sure of it, but other than that, I wouldn't make a guess.

"I told Cortland about it all afterwards, when I thought an appropriate amount of time had passed. He wasn't at all distressed. He listened to everything I said, and told me he was glad I'd told him. But he said he hadn't seen anything particular in that room.

"Now, you mustn't go telling everyone this story. Ghosts are fairly common in New Orleans, but doctors who see them are not! And I don't think Cortland would appreciate me telling that story. And of course, I've never mentioned it to Pierce. As for

Stella, well, frankly I doubt Stella cares about such things at all. If Stella cares about anything, I'd like to know what it is."

These apparitions undoubtedly included another appearance of Lasher, but we cannot leave this vivid and noteworthy story without discussing the strange exchange of words at the library door. What did the Mayfair cousin mean when he said, "Oh, no, that's not the man"? Did he mistakenly think that the doctor was referring to Lasher? And did the little comment slip out before he realized that the doctor was a stranger? And if so, does this mean that members of the Mayfair family knew all about "the man" and were used to talking about him? Perhaps so.

Mary Beth's funeral was enormous, just as her wedding had been some twenty-six years before. For a full account of it we are indebted to the undertaker, David O'Brien, who retired a year later, leaving his business to his nephew Red Lonigan, whose family has given us much testimony since.

We also have some family legends regarding the event, and considerable gossip from parish ladies who attended the funeral and had no compunction about discussing the Mayfairs critically at all.

All agree that Daniel McIntyre did not make it through the ceremony. He was taken home from the Requiem Mass by Carlotta, who then rejoined the party before it left the church.

Before the interment in Lafayette Cemetery several short speeches were made. Pierce Mayfair spoke of Mary Beth as a great mentor; Cortland praised her for her love of her family and her generosity to everyone. And Barclay Mayfair said that Mary Beth was irreplaceable; and she would never be forgotten by those who knew her and loved her. Lionel had his hands full consoling the stricken Belle and the crying Millie Dear.

Little Antha was not there, and neither was little Nancy (an adopted Mayfair mentioned earlier whom Mary Beth introduced to everyone as Stella's child).

Stella was despondent, yet not so much that she failed to shock scores of the cousins, and the undertaker, and numerous friends of the family, by sitting on a nearby grave during the final speeches, with her legs dangling and swilling liquor from her famous bottle in the brown bag. When Barclay was concluding his speech, she said to him quite loudly, "Barclay, get on with it! She hated this sort of thing. She's going to rise from the dead and tell you to shut up if you don't stop."

The undertaker noted that many of the cousins laughed at these remarks, and others tried to stop themselves from laughing. Barclay also laughed, and Cortland and Pierce merely smiled. Indeed, the family may have been divided with regard to this response entirely on ethnic lines. One account holds that the French cousins were mortified by Stella's conduct but that all the Irish Mayfairs laughed.

But then Barclay wiped his nose, and said, "Good-bye my beloved," and kissed the coffin, and then backed up, into the arms of Cortland and Garland, and began to sob.

Stella then hopped down off the grave, went to the coffin and kissed it, and said to the priest, "Well, Father, carry on."

During the final Latin words, Stella pulled a rose off one of the funeral arrangements, broke the stem to a manageable length, and stuck the rose in her hair.

Then the closest of the kin retired to the First Street house, and before midnight the piano music and singing was coming so loud from the parlor that the neighbors were shocked.

When Judge McIntyre died, the funeral was a lot smaller but extremely sad. He had been much loved by many Mayfairs, and tears were shed.

Before continuing, let us note once more that, to our knowledge, Mary Beth was the last really strong witch the family produced. One can only speculate as to what she might have done with her powers if she had not been so family oriented, so thoroughly practical, and so utterly indifferent to vanity or notoriety of any kind. As it was, everything that she did eventually served her family. Even her pursuit of pleasure expressed itself in the reunions which helped the family to identify itself and to maintain a strong image of itself in changing times.

Stella did not have this love of family, nor was she practical; she did not mind notoriety, and she loved pleasure. But the keynote to understanding Stella is that she wasn't ambitious either. She seemed to have few real goals at all.

"Live" might have been the motto of Stella.

The history from this point until 1929 belongs to her and little Antha, her pale-faced, sweet-voiced little girl.

STELLA'S STORY CONTINUES

Family legend, neighborhood gossip, and parish gossip all seem to agree that Stella went wild after her parents' death.

While Cortland and Carlotta battled over the legacy fortune and how it should be managed, Stella began to throw scandalous parties for her friends at First Street; and the few she held for the family in 1926 were equally shocking, what with the bootleg beer and bourbon, and Dixieland bands and people dancing the

Charleston until dawn. Many of the older cousins left these last parties early, and some never returned to the First Street house.

Many of them were never invited again. Between 1926 and 1929, Stella slowly dismantled the extended family created by her mother. Or rather, she refused to guide it further, and it slowly fell apart. Large numbers of cousins lost contact altogether with the house on First Street, rearing children who knew little or nothing about it, and these descendants have been for us the richest source of legend and other lore.

Other cousins were alienated but remained involved. All of Julien's descendants, for example, remained close to the legacy family, if for no other reason than because they were legally and financially connected, and because Carlotta could never effectively drive them away.

"It was the beginning of the end," according to one cousin. "Stella just didn't want to be bothered," said another. And yet another, "We knew too much about her, and she knew it. She didn't want to see us around."

The image of Stella we have during this period is of a very active, very happy person who cared less about the family than her mother had, but who nevertheless cared passionately about many things. Young writers and artists in particular interested Stella, and scores of "interesting" people came to First Street, including writers and painters whom Stella had known in New York. Several friends mentioned that she encouraged Lionel to take up his writing again, and even had an office refurbished for him in one of the outbuildings, but it is not known if Lionel ever wrote anything more.

A great many intellectuals attended Stella's parties. Indeed, she became fashionable with those who were not afraid to take social risks. Old guard society of the sort in which Julien moved was essentially closed to her, or so Irwin Dandrich maintained. But it is doubtful Stella ever knew or cared.

The French Quarter of New Orleans had been undergoing something of a revival since the early 1920s. Indeed, William Faulkner, Sherwood Anderson, Edmund Wilson, and other famous writers lived there at various times.

We have no evidence to connect any individual person with Stella; but she was very familiar with the Bohemian life of the Quarter, she frequented the coffee houses and the art galleries, and she brought the musicians home to First Street to play for her and threw open her doors to penniless poets and painters very much as she had done in New York.

To the servants this meant chaos. To the neighbors it meant scandal and noise. But Stella was no dissolute drunk, as her legal father had been. On the contrary, for all her drinking, she is never described as being intoxicated; and there seems to have been considerable taste and thought at work in her during these years.

At the same time, she undertook a refurbishing of the house, spending a fortune on new paint, plaster, draperies, and delicate expensive furniture in the art deco style. The double parlor was crowded with potted palms as Richard Llewellyn has described. A Bözendorfer grand piano was purchased, an elevator was eventually installed (1927), and before that an immense swimming pool was built to the rear of the lawn, and a cabana was built to the south side of the pool so that guests could shower and dress without bothering to go into the house.

All of this—the new friends, the partying, and the refurbishing—shocked the more staid cousins, but what really turned them against Stella, thereby creating numerous legends for us to gather later, was that, within a year after Mary Beth's death, Stella abandoned the large family gatherings altogether.

Try as he might, Cortland could not persuade Stella to give any family parties after 1926. And though Cortland frequently attended her soirées or balls or whatever they were called, and his son Pierce was often there with him, other cousins who were invited refused to go.

In the Mardi Gras season of 1927, Stella gave a masked ball which caused talk in New Orleans for six months. People from all ranks of society attended; the First Street house was splendidly lighted; contraband champagne was served by the case. A jazz band played on the side porch. (This porch was not screened in until later for Deirdre Mayfair when she became an invalid.) Dozens of guests went swimming in the nude, and by morning a full-scale orgy was in progress, or so the bedazzled neighbors were heard to say. Cousins who had been excluded were furious. Indeed, Irwin Dandrich says they appealed to Carlotta Mayfair for explanations, but everyone knew the explanation: Stella didn't want a bunch of dreary cousins hanging about.

Servants reported Carlotta Mayfair was outraged by the noise and duration of this party, not to mention the expense. Some time before midnight she left the house, taking little Antha and little Nancy (the adopted one) with her, and she did not return until the afternoon of the following day.

This was the very first public quarrel between Stella and Carlotta, but cousins and friends soon learned that they had made it up. Lionel had made peace between the sisters, and Stella had agreed to stay home more with Antha, and not to spend so much money, or make so much noise. The money seems to have been a matter of particular concern to Carlotta, who thought filling an entire swimming pool with champagne was "a sin."

(It is interesting to note that Stella was worth hundreds of millions of dollars at this time. Carlotta had four different fabulous trust funds in her own right. It is possible that Carlotta was offended by excess. In fact, numerous people have indicated that that was the case.)

Late that year, the first of a series of mysterious social events occurred. What the family legends have told us is that Stella sought out certain Mayfair cousins and brought them together for "an interesting evening" in which they were to discuss family history, and the family's unique "psychic gifts." Some said a séance was held at First Street, others that voodoo was involved.

(Servant gossip was rife with stories of Stella's involvement with voodoo. Stella told several of her friends that she knew all about voodoo. She had colored relations in the Quarter who told her all about it.)

That many cousins did not understand the reason for this get-together, that they did not take the talk of voodoo seriously and resented being snubbed, was plainly obvious.

Indeed, the meeting sent veritable shock waves through the family. Why was Stella bothering to dig into genealogies and to call this and that cousin whom nobody had seen of late, when she did not even have the courtesy to call those who had known and loved Mary Beth so much? The doors at First Street had always been open to everyone; now Stella was picking and choosing, Stella who didn't bother to attend school graduations, or to send presents to christenings and weddings, Stella who behaved like "a perfect you know what."

It was argued that Lionel agreed with the cousins, that he thought Stella was going too far. Holding family get-togethers was extremely important, and one descendant told us later that Lionel had complained bitterly to his Uncle Barclay that things were never going to be the same, now that his mother was gone.

But for all the gossip, we have been unable to find out who attended this strange evening affair, except that we know Lionel was in attendance, and that Cortland and his son Pierce were also there. (Pierce was only seventeen at the time and a student at the Jesuits. He had already been accepted to Harvard.)

We know also from family gossip that the gathering lasted all night, and that some time before it was over Lionel "left in disgust." Cousins who attended and would say nothing of what happened were much criticized by the others. Society gossip, filtered through Dandrich, thought it was Stella playing on her "black magic past" and that it was all a big game.

Several gatherings like it followed, but these were deliberately shrouded in secrecy with all parties being sworn to divulge nothing of what went on.

Legal gossip spoke of Carlotta Mayfair arguing with Cortland about these affairs, and about wanting to get little Antha and little Nancy out of the house. Stella wouldn't agree to a boarding school for Antha and "everybody knew it."

Lionel meantime was having fights with Stella. An anonymous person called one of our private eyes who had let it be known that he was interested in gossip pertaining to the family, and told him that Stella and Lionel had had a row in a downtown restaurant and that Lionel had walked out.

Dandrich quickly reported similar stories. Lionel and Stella were fighting. Was there at last another man?

When the investigator began to ask about the matter, he discovered it was well-known about town that the family was in the midst of a battle over little Antha. Stella was threatening to go away to Europe again with her daughter, and was begging Lionel to go with her, while Carlotta was ordering Lionel not to go.

Meantime Lionel began to appear at Mass at the St. Louis Cathedral with one of the downtown cousins, a great-niece of Suzette Mayfair named Claire Mayfair, whose family lived in a beautiful old house on Esplanade Avenue owned by descendants to this day. Dandrich insists this caused considerable talk.

Servant gossip told of countless family quarrels. Doors were being slammed. People were screaming.

Carlotta forbid further "voodoo gatherings." Stella told Carlotta to get out of the house.

"Nothing's the same without Mother," said Lionel. "It started to fall apart when Julien died, but without Mother it's impossible. Carlotta and Stella are oil and water in that house."

It does seem to have been entirely Carlotta's doing that Antha and Nancy ever went to any school. Indeed, the few school records we have been able to examine with regard to Antha indicate that Carlotta enrolled her and attended the subsequent meetings at which she was asked to take Antha out of the school.

Antha was by all accounts completely unsuited for school.

By 1928, Antha had already been sent home from St. Alphonsus.

Sister Bridget Marie, who remembers Antha perhaps as well as she remembers Stella, tells very much the same stories about her as she told about her mother. But her testimony regarding

514

this entire period and its various developments is worth quoting in full. This is what she told me in 1969.

"The invisible friend was always with Antha. She would turn and talk to him in a whisper as if no one else were there. Of course he told her the answers when she didn't know them. All the sisters knew it was going on.

"And if you want to hear the worst part of it, some of the children saw him with their very eyes. I wouldn't have believed it if it hadn't been so many; but when four children all tell you the same story, and each of them is afraid, and worried, and the parents are worried, well, then what can you do but believe?

"It was in the school yard that they would see him. Now, I told you the girl was shy. Well, she'd go over to the far brick wall at the back, and there she'd sit and read her book in a little patch of sun coming through the trees. And soon he would be there with her. A man, they said he was, can you imagine? And you ask me do I know the meaning of the words, 'the man'?

"Ah, you see, it was a shock to everyone when it came out that he was a full-grown man. For they thought he was a little child before that, or some sort of child spirit, if you follow me now. But then it was a man, a tall dark-haired man. And that really set everyone to talking. That it was a man.

"No, I never did see him. None of the sisters saw him. But the children saw him. And the children told Father Lafferty. I told Father Lafferty. And he was the one that called Carlotta Mayfair and said, 'You have to take her out of school.'

"Now I don't criticize the priests, no, never. But I will say this. Father Lafferty wasn't a man you could buy with a big donation to the church, and he said, 'Miss Carlotta, you've got to take her out of school.'

"No use calling up Stella by that time. Everyone knew Stella was practicing witchcraft. She went down to the French Quarter and bought the black candles for her voodoo, and do you know, she was bringing the other Mayfairs into it? Yes, she was doing it. I heard it a long time after, that she had gone to look for the other cousins who were witches and she had told them all to come up to the house.

"It was a séance they had in that house. They lighted black candles and they burned incense and they sang songs to the devil, and they asked that their ancestors appear. That's what I heard happened. I can't tell you where I heard it. But I heard it. And I believe it, too."

In the summer of 1928, Pierce Mayfair, Cortland's son, canceled his plans to go to Harvard, and decided to go to Tulane University, though his father and his uncles were dead against it. Pierce had been to all of Stella's secret parties, reported Dandrich, and the two were beginning to be linked by the gossips, and Pierce was not yet eighteen.

By the end of 1928, legal gossip indicated that Carlotta had declared that Stella was an unfit mother, and somebody ought to take her child away from her "in court." Cortland denied such rumors to his friends. But everybody knew it was "coming to that," said Dandrich. Legal gossip told of family meetings at which Carlotta demanded that the Mayfair brothers stand by her.

Meantime, Stella and Pierce were running around day and night together, with little Antha often in tow. Stella bought dolls for little Antha incessantly. She took her to breakfast every morning at a different hotel in the French Quarter. Pierce went with Stella to purchase a building on Decatur Street which Stella meant to turn into a studio where she could be alone.

"Let Millie Dear and Belle have that house and Carlotta," Stella told the real estate agent. Pierce laughed at everything Stella said. Antha, a thin seven-year-old with porcelain skin and soft blue eyes, stood about clutching a giant teddy bear. They all went to lunch together, including the real estate agent, who told Dandrich later, "She is charming, absolutely charming. I think those people up on First Street are merely too gloomy for her."

As for Nancy Mayfair, the dumpy little girl adopted at birth by Mary Beth and introduced to everyone as Antha's sister, Stella paid no attention to her at all. One Mayfair descendant says bitterly that Nancy was no more than "a pet" to Stella. But there is no evidence of Stella's ever being mean to Nancy. Indeed, she charged truckloads of clothes and toys for Nancy. But Nancy seems to have been a generally unresponsive and sullen little girl.

Meantime Carlotta alone took Antha and Nancy to Mass on Sundays, and it was Carlotta who saw that Nancy went to the Academy of the Sacred Heart.

In 1928, gossip had it that Carlotta Mayfair had taken the shocking legal step of trying to gain custody of Antha, with a view, apparently, to sending her away to school. Certain papers had been signed and filed.

Cortland was horrified that Carlotta would take things so far. At last Cortland, who had been on friendly terms with Carlotta until this juncture, threatened to oppose her legally if she did not drop the matter out of hand. Barclay, Garland, and young Sheffield and other members of the family agreed to go along with Cortland. Nobody was going to take Stella to court and take her child away from her while Cortland was alive.

Lionel too agreed to stand behind Cortland. He is described as being tortured by the whole incident. He even suggested that he and Stella go away to Europe together for a while and leave Antha in Carlotta's hands.

Finally Carlotta withdrew her petition for custody.

But between her and Julien's descendants, things were never the same. They began to fight over money, and they have continued that fight to this day.

Sometime in 1927, Carlotta had persuaded Stella to sign a power of attorney so that Carlotta could handle certain matters for her about which Stella didn't want to be concerned.

Carlotta attempted now to use this power of attorney to make sweeping decisions regarding the enormous Mayfair legacy which had since Mary Beth's death been entirely in Cortland's hands.

Family legend and contemporary legal gossip, as well as society gossip, all concur that the Mayfair brothers—Cortland, Garland, and Barclay, and later Pierce, Sheffield, and others—refused to honor this piece of paper. They refused to follow Carlotta's orders to liquidate the hugely profitable and daring investments which they had been making with tremendous success on behalf of the legacy for years. They rushed Stella to their offices so that she might revoke the power of attorney and reaffirm that everything was to be handled by them.

Nevertheless endless squabbles resulted between the brothers and Carlotta, which have gone on into the present time. Carlotta seems never to have trusted Julien's sons after the custody battle, and not even to have liked them. She made endless demands upon them for information, full disclosures, detailed accounts and explanations of what they were doing, constantly implying that if they did not give a good account of themselves she would take them to court on behalf of Stella (and later on behalf of Antha, and later on behalf of Deirdre unto the present time).

They were hurt and baffled by her distrust. By 1928 they had made near incalculable amounts of money on behalf of Stella, whose affairs of course were completely entangled with their own. They could not understand Carlotta's attitude, and they seemed to have persisted in taking it literally over the years.

That is, they patiently answered all her questions, and again and again attempted to explain what they were doing, when of course Carlotta only asked them more questions and demanded more answers and brought up new topics for examination, and called for more meetings, and made more phone calls, and made more veiled threats.

It is interesting to note that almost every legal secretary or clerk who ever worked for Mayfair and Mayfair seemed to understand this "game." But Julien's sons continued to be hurt and bitter about it always, as if they did not see through it to the core.

Only reluctantly did they allow themselves to be forced away from the house on First Street where all of them had been born.

By 1928, they were already being forced away but they didn't know it. Twenty-five years later, when Pierce and Cortland Mayfair asked to examine some of Julien's belonging in the attic, they were not allowed past the front door. But in 1928 such a thing would have been unimaginable.

Cortland Mayfair probably never guessed that the battle over Antha was the last personal battle with Carlotta that he would ever win.

Meantime, Pierce practically lived at First Street in the fall of 1928. Indeed by the spring of 1929, he was going everywhere with Stella, and had styled himself her "personal secretary, chauffeur, punching bag and crying pillow." Cortland put up with it, but he didn't like it. He told friends and family that Pierce was a fine boy, and he would tire of the whole thing and go east to school just as all the other boys had done.

As it turned out, Pierce never really had a chance to tire of Stella. But we have now come to the year 1929, and we should interrupt this story to include the strange case of Stuart Townsend, our brother in the Talamasca, who wanted so badly to make contact with Stella in the summer of that year.

Twenty

THE FILE ON THE MAYFAIR WITCHES

PART VII

The Disappearance of Stuart Townsend

In 1929, Stuart Townsend, who had been studying the Mayfair materials for years, petitioned the council in London to allow him to attempt contact with the Mayfair family.

He felt strongly that Stella's cryptic message to us on the back of the photograph meant that she wanted such contact.

And Stuart was also convinced that the last three Mayfair Witches—Julien, Mary Beth, and Stella—were not murderers or evildoers in any sense; that it would be entirely safe to contact them, and that, indeed, "wonderful things" might result.

This forced the council to take a hard look at the entire question, and also to reexamine, as it does constantly, the aims and standards of the Talamasca.

Though an immense body of written material exists in our archives as to our aims and standards, as to what we find acceptable and unacceptable, and though this is a constant topic of conversation at our council meetings worldwide, let me summarize *for the purposes of this narrative* the issues which are relevant here, all of which were raised by Stuart Townsend in 1929.

First and foremost: We had created in the File on the Mayfair Witches an impressive and valuable history of a psychic family. We had proved to ourselves beyond a doubt that the Mayfairs had contact with the realm of the invisible, and that they could manipulate unseen forces to their advantage. But there were still many things about what they did that we did not know.

What if they could be persuaded to talk to us, to share our secrets? What might we then learn?

Stella was not the secretive or guarded person that Mary Beth had been. Maybe, if she could be convinced of our discretion and our scholarly purpose, she would reveal things to us. Possibly Cortland Mayfair would talk to us too.

Second and perhaps less important: Certainly we had over the years violated the privacy of the Mayfair family with our vigilance. We had, according to Stuart, "snooped" into every aspect of their lives. Indeed we had studied these people as specimens, and again and again, we justify the lengths to which we go by arguing that we will, and do, make our records available to those we study.

Well, we had not done that with the Mayfairs ever. And perhaps there was no excuse for not trying now.

Third: We existed in an absolutely unique relationship to the Mayfairs because the blood of Petyr van Abel, our brother, ran in their veins. They were "related" to us, one might say. Should we not seek to make contact merely to tell them about this ancestor? And who knows what would follow from there?

Fourth: Could we do some real good by making contact? And here of course we come to one of our highest purposes. Could the reckless Stella benefit from knowing about other people like herself? Would she not enjoy knowing there were people who studied such persons, with a view to understanding the realm of the invisible? In other words, would Stella not like to talk to us, and not like to know what we knew about the psychic world at large?

Stuart argued vociferously that we were obligated to make contact. He also raised the pertinent question: what did Stella already know? He also insisted that Stella needed us, that the entire Mayfair clan needed us, that little Antha in particular needed us, and it was time that we introduced ourselves and offered what we knew.

The council considered everything that Stuart had to say; it considered what it knew of the Mayfair Witches, and it concluded that the good reasons for making contact far outweighed any bad reasons. *It dismissed out of hand the idea of danger.* And it told Stuart that he might go to America and he might make contact with Stella.

In a welter of excitement, Stuart sailed for New York the very next day. The Talamasca received two letters from him postmarked New York. He wrote again when he reached New Orleans, on stationery from the St. Charles Hotel, saying that he had contacted Stella and indeed had found her extremely receptive, and that he was going to meet her for lunch the next day.

Stuart Townsend was never seen or heard from again. We do not know where or when or even if his life ended. We simply know that sometime in June of 1929 he vanished without a trace.

When one looks back upon these council meetings, when one reads over the transcript, it is very easy to see that the Talamasca made a tragic mistake. Stuart was not really prepared for this mission. A narrative should have been written embracing all the materials, so that the Mayfair history could be seen as a whole. Also the question of danger should have been more carefully evaluated. Throughout the anecdotal history of the Mayfairs there are references to violence being done to the enemies of the Mayfair Witches.

But in all fairness, it must be admitted that there were no such stories associated with Stella or her generation. And certainly no such stories in relationship to other contemporary residents of the First Street house. (The exceptions, of course, are the playground stories concerning Stella and Antha. They were accused of using their invisible friend to hurt other little children. But there is nothing comparable about Stella as an adult.)

Also the full story of Antha's nurse who died of a fall in Rome was not then known to the Talamasca. And it is possible that Stuart knew nothing about this incident at all.

Nevertheless Stuart was not fully prepared for such a mission. And when one reviews his comments to the council and to other members it becomes obvious that Stuart had fallen in love with Stella Mayfair. He had fallen in love with her under the very worst circumstances—that is, he had fallen in love with her image in her photographs, and with the Stella who emerged from people's descriptions of her. She had become a myth to him. And so, full of zeal and romance, he went to meet her, dazzled not only by her powers but by her proverbial charms.

It is also obvious to anyone who considers this case dispassionately that Stuart was not the best person for this mission, for a number of reasons.

And before we go with Stuart to New Orleans, allow us to explain briefly who Stuart was. A full file on Stuart exists in the archives, and it is certainly worth reading in its own right. For some twenty-five years, he was a devoted and conscientious member of the order and his investigations of cases of possession cover some one hundred and fourteen different files.

THE LIFE OF STUART TOWNSEND

How much of Stuart's life is relevant to what happened to him, or to the story of the Mayfair Witches, I cannot say. I know that I am including more of it here than I need to include. And especially in view of what little I say of Arthur Langtry, I must explain.

I think I have included this material here as some sort of memorial to Stuart, and as some sort of warning. Be that as it may. . . .

Stuart came to the attention of the order when he was twenty-two years old. Our offices in London received from one of its many investigators in America a small newspaper article about Stuart Townsend, or "The Boy Who Had Been Somebody Else for Ten Years."

Stuart had been born in a small town in Texas in the year 1895. His father was the local doctor, a deeply intellectual and widely respected man. Stuart's mother was from a well-to-do

521

family, and engaged in charity work of the fashionable sort for a lady of her position, having two nurses for her seven children, of which Stuart was the firstborn. They lived in a large white Victorian house with a widow's walk, on the town's one and only fashionable street.

Stuart went to boarding school in New England when he was six years old. He was from the beginning an exceptional student, and during his summer vacations home, he was something of a recluse, reading in his attic bedroom until late in the night. He did have a number of friends, however, among the town's small but vigorous aristocracy—sons and daughters of city officials, lawyers, and well-to-do ranchers; and he seems to have been well liked.

When he was ten years old Stuart came down with a serious fever which could not be diagnosed. His father concluded finally that it was of infectious origin, but no real explanation was ever found. Stuart went into a crisis during which he was delirious for two days.

When he recovered, he wasn't Stuart. He was somebody else. This somebody else claimed to be a young woman named Antoinette Fielding who spoke with a French accent and played the piano beautifully, and seemed generally confused about how old she was, where she lived, or what she was doing in Stuart's house.

Stuart himself did know some French; but he did not know how to play the piano. And when he sat down at the dusty grand in the parlor and began to play Chopin the family thought they were losing their minds.

As for his believing he was a girl, and crying miserably when he saw his reflection in a mirror, his mother could not endure this and actually ran from the room. After about a week of hysterical and melancholic behavior, Stuart-Antoinette was persuaded to stop asking for dresses, to accept the fact that she had a boy's body now, and to believe that she was Stuart Townsend, and get back to doing what Stuart was expected to do.

However, any return to school was out of the question. And Stuart-Antoinette, who became known to the family as Tony for the sake of simplicity, spent his or her days playing the piano endlessly and scribbling out memories in a huge diary as she-he tried to solve the mystery of who she was.

As Dr. Townsend perused these scribbled recollections he perceived that the French in which they were written was far beyond the level of expertise which ten-year-old Stuart had attained. He also began to realize that the child's memories were all of Paris, and of Paris in the 1840s, as direct references to operas and plays and modes of transportation clearly showed.

It emerged from these written documents that Antoinette Fielding had been of English-French parentage, that her Frenchman father had not married her English mother—Louisa Fielding—and that she had lived a strange and reclusive life in Paris, the pampered daughter of a high-class prostitute who sought to protect her only child from the filth of the streets. Her great gift and consolation was her music.

Dr. Townsend, enthralled, and reassuring his wife that they would get to the bottom of this mystery, began an investigation by mail with a view to discovering whether or not this person Antoinette Fielding had ever existed in Paris.

This occupied him for some five years.

During that time, "Antoinette" remained in Stuart's body, playing the piano obsessively, venturing out only to get lost or into some dreadful scrape with the local toughs. At last Antoinette never left the house, and became something of a hysterical invalid, demanding that meals be left at her door, and going down to play the piano only at night.

Finally, through a private detective in Paris, Dr. Townsend ascertained that a certain Louisa Fielding had been murdered in Paris in 1865. She was indeed a prostitute, but there was no record whatsoever of her having a child. And at last Dr. Townsend came to a dead end. He was by this time weary of trying to solve the mystery. And he came to terms with the situation as best he could.

His handsome young son Stuart was gone forever, and in his place was a wasted, warped invalid, a white-faced boy with burning eyes and a strange sexless voice, who lived now entirely behind closed blinds. The doctor and his wife grew used to hearing the nocturnal concerts. Every now and then the doctor went up to speak to the pale-faced "feminine" creature who lived in the attic. He could not help but note a mental deterioration. The creature could no longer remember much of "her past." Nevertheless they conversed pleasantly in French or in English for a little while; then the emaciated and distracted young person would turn to his books as if the father weren't there, and the father would go away.

It is interesting to note that no one ever discussed the possibility that Stuart was "possessed." The doctor was an atheist; the children were taken to the Methodist church. The family knew nothing of Catholics or Catholic rites of exorcism, or the Catholic belief in demons or possession. And as far as we know the local minister, whom the family did not like, was never personally consulted as to the case.

This situation continued until Stuart was twenty years old. Then one night he fell down the steps, suffering a severe concussion. The doctor, half awake and waiting for the inevitable music to rise from the parlor, discovered his son unconscious in the hallway and rushed him to the local hospital, where Stuart lay in a coma for two weeks.

When he woke up, he was Stuart. He had absolutely no recollection of ever having been anyone else. Indeed, he believed he was ten years old, and when he heard a manly voice issuing from his own throat, he was horrified. When he discovered he had a grown man's body, he was speechless with shock.

Dumbfounded he sat in his hospital bed listening to stories of what had been happening to him for the last ten years. Of course he did not understand French. He'd had a terrible time with it in school. And of course he couldn't play the piano. Why, everybody knew he had no musical ability. He could not even carry a tune.

In the next few weeks, he sat staring at the dinner table at his "enormous" brothers and sisters, at his now gray-haired father, and at his mother, who could not look at him without bursting into tears. Telephones and automobiles—which had hardly existed in 1905 when he had ceased to be Stuart—startled him endlessly. Electric lights filled him with insecurity. But the keenest source of agony was his own adult body. And the ever deepening realization that his childhood and adolescence were now gone without a trace.

Then he began to confront the inevitable problems. He was twenty with the emotions and education of a ten-year-old boy. He began to gain weight; his color improved; he went riding on the nearby ranches with his old friends. Tutors were hired to educate him; he read the newspapers and the national magazines by the hour. He took long walks during which he practiced moving and thinking like an adult.

But he lived in a perpetual state of anxiety. He was passionately attracted to women, but did not know how to deal with this attraction. His feelings were easily hurt. As a man he felt hopelessly inadequate. At last he began to quarrel with everyone, and discovering that he could drink with impunity, he began to "hit the bottle" in the local saloons.

Soon the whole town knew the story. Some people remembered the first "go round" when Antoinette had been born. Others only heard the whole tale in retrospect. Whatever the case, there was ceaseless talk. And though the local paper never, out of deference to the doctor, made mention of this bizarre story, a reporter from Dallas, Texas, got wind of it from several sources, and without the family's cooperation, wrote a long article on it which appeared in the Sunday edition of a Dallas paper in 1915. Other papers picked up this story. It was eventually forwarded to us in London about two months after it appeared.

Meantime curiosity seekers descended upon Stuart. A local author wanted to write a novel about him. Representatives from national magazines rang the front door bell. The family was up in arms. Stuart was once again driven indoors, and sat brooding in the attic room, staring at the treasured possessions of this strange person Antoinette, and feeling that ten years of his life had been stolen from him, and he was now a hopeless misfit, driven to antagonizing everyone he knew.

No doubt the family received a great deal of unwelcome mail. On the other hand, communication in that day and age was not what it is now. Whatever the case, a package from the Talamasca reached Stuart in late 1916, containing two well-known books about such cases of "possession," along with a letter from us informing him that we had a good deal of knowledge about such things and would be very glad to talk to him about it, and about others who had experienced the same thing.

Stuart at once fired off a reply. He met with our representative Louis Daly in Dallas in the summer of 1917, and gratefully agreed to go with us to London. Dr. Townsend, at first deeply concerned, was finally won over by Louis, who assured him that our approach to such things was entirely scholarly, and at last Stuart came to us on September 1, 1917.

He was received into the order as a novice the following year, and he remained with us from then on.

His first project of course was a thorough study of his own case, and a study of every other known case of possession on record. His conclusion finally, and that of the other Talamasca scholars assigned to this area of research, was that he indeed had been possessed by the spirit of a dead woman.

He believed then and ever after that the spirit of Antoinette Fielding could have been driven out of him, if anyone knowledgeable had been consulted, even a Catholic priest. For though the Catholic Church holds that such cases are purely demonic—which we do not—there is no doubt that their techniques for exorcising such alien presences do work.

For the next five years Stuart did nothing but investigate past

525

cases of possession the world over. He interviewed victims by the dozens, taking voluminous notes.

He came to the conclusion long held by the Talamasca that there are a great variety of entities who engage in possession. Some may be ghosts; some may be entities who were never human; some may be "other personalities" within the host. But he remained convinced that Antoinette Fielding had been a real human being, and that like many such ghosts, she had not known or understood that she was dead.

In 1920 he went to Paris to find evidence of Antoinette Fielding. He was unable to discover anything at all. But the few bits of information about the dead Louisa Fielding did fit with what Antoinette had written about her mother. Time, however, had long ago erased any real trace of these persons. And Stuart remained forever dissatisfied on this account.

In late 1920 he resigned himself to the fact that he might never know who Antoinette was, and then he turned to active fieldwork on behalf of the Talamasca. He went out with Louis Daly to intervene in cases of possession, carrying out with Daly a form of exorcism which Daly used very effectively to drive such alien presences out of the victim-host.

Daly was very impressed with Stuart Townsend. He became Stuart's mentor, and Stuart was throughout these years noted for his compassion, patience, and effectiveness in this field. Not even Daly could comfort the victims afterwards the way Stuart could do it. After all, Stuart had been there. Stuart knew.

Stuart worked in this field tirelessly until 1929, reading the File on the Mayfair Witches only when a busy schedule allowed. Then he made his plea to the council and won.

At that point in time, Stuart was thirty-five. He stood six feet tall, had ash-blond hair and dark gray eyes. He was lean of build and had a light complexion. He tended to dress elegantly, and was one of those Americans who deeply admires English manners and ways of doing things, and aspires to imitate them. He was an attractive young man. But his greatest appeal to friends and acquaintances was a sort of boyish spontaneity and innocence. Stuart was really missing ten years of his life, and he never got them back.

He was capable at times of impetuousness, and of flying off the handle, of getting furious when he encountered even small obstacles to his plans. But he controlled this very well when he was in the field; and when he threw a tantrum in the Motherhouse he could always be brought round.

He was also capable of falling deeply and passionately in

love, which he did with Helen Kreis, a member of the Talamasca who died in an auto accident in 1924. He grieved excessively and even dangerously for Helen for two years after her death.

What happened between him and Stella Mayfair we may never know. But it is possible to conjecture that she was the only other love of his life.

I should like to add my personal opinion here that Stuart Townsend never should have been sent to New Orleans. It was not only that he was too emotionally involved with Stella; it was that he lacked experience in this particular field.

In his novitiate, he had dealt with various kinds of psychic phenomena; and undoubtedly he read widely in the occult all his life. He discussed a great variety of cases with other members of the order. And he did spend some time with Arthur Langtry.

But he did not really know anything about witches, per se. And like so many of our members who have dealt only with hauntings, possessions, or reincarnation, he simply did not know what witches can do.

He did not understand that the strongest manifestations of discarnate entities come through mortal witches. There are even some suggestions that he thought the Talamasca was being archaic and silly in calling these women witches. And it is very likely that though he accepted the seventeenth-century descriptions of Deborah Mayfair and her daughter Charlotte, he could not "relate" this material to a clever, fashionable twentieth-century "jazz baby" like Stella, who seemed to be beckoning to him across the Atlantic with a smile and a wink.

Of course the Talamasca encounters a certain amount of incredulity in all new workers in the witchcraft field. The same holds true for the investigation of vampires. More than one member of the order has had to see these creatures in action before he or she could believe in them. But the solution to that problem is to introduce our members to fieldwork under the guidance of experienced persons, and in cases which do not involve direct contact.

To send an inexperienced man like Townsend to make contact with the Mayfair Witches is like sending a little child directly to hell to interview the devil.

In sum Stuart Townsend went off to New Orleans unprepared and unwarned. And with all due respect to those who governed the order in 1929, I do not believe that such a thing would happen today.

Lastly, let me add that Stuart Townsend, to the best of our knowledge, possessed no extraordinary powers. He wasn't "psychic," as they say. So he had no extrasensory weapons at his command when he confronted the foe, whom he did not even perceive to be a foe.

Stuart's disappearance was reported to the New Orleans police on July 25, 1929. This was a full month after his arrival in New Orleans. The Talamasca had tried to reach him by telegram and by phone. Irwin Dandrich had tried to find him but in vain. The St. Charles Hotel, from which Stuart claimed to have written his only letter from New Orleans, denied ever having such a person registered. No one remembered such a person ever having been there.

Our private investigators could discover nothing to prove Townsend had ever reached New Orleans. And the police soon came to doubt that he had.

On July 28, the authorities told our local investigators that there was nothing further that they could do. But under severe pressure both from Dandrich and from the Talamasca the police finally agreed to go to the Mayfair house and ask Stella if she had ever seen or spoken to the young man. The Talamasca held out no hope at this point, but Stella surprised everyone by recalling Stuart at once.

Yes indeed, she had met Stuart, she said, the tall Texan from England, how could she ever forget such an interesting person? They had had lunch together and later dinner, and spent an entire night in talk.

No, she couldn't imagine what had happened to him. In fact, she became quite instantly and visibly distressed at the possibility that he had met with foul play.

Yes, he was staying at the St. Charles Hotel, he mentioned that to her, and why on earth would he lie about such a thing? She began to cry. Oh, she hoped nothing had happened to him. In fact, she became so upset that the police almost terminated the interview. But she held them there asking questions. Had they talked to the people at the Court of Two Sisters? She'd taken Stuart there, and he'd liked it. Maybe he had been back. And there was a speakeasy on Bourbon Street where they had talked early the following morning, after some more respectable place—dreadful hole!—had kicked them out.

The police covered these establishments. Everyone knew Stella. Yes, Stella could have been there with a man. Stella was always there with a man. But nobody had any particular recollection of Stuart Townsend.

Other hotels in town were canvassed. No belongings of Stuart Townsend were found. Cabbies were questioned but with the same dismal lack of result.

At last the Talamasca decided to take the investigation into its own hands. Arthur Langtry sailed from London to discover what had happened to Stuart. He was conscience-stricken that he had ever agreed to let Stuart undertake this assignment alone.

THE STORY OF STELLA CONTINUES

Arthur Langtry's Report

Arthur Langtry was certainly one of the most able investigators whom the Talamasca ever produced. The study of several great "witch families" was his lifelong work. The story of his fifty-year career with the Talamasca is one of the most interesting and amazing histories contained in our archives, and his detailed studies of the witch families with whom he became involved are some of the most valuable documents we possess.

It is a great sadness to those of us who have been obsessed all our lives with the Mayfair Witches that Langtry was never able to devote his time to their history. And in the years before Stuart Townsend became involved, Langtry expressed his own regrets regarding the whole affair.

But Langtry owed no one an apology for not having time or life enough for every witch family in our files.

Nevertheless, when Stuart Townsend disappeared, Langtry felt responsible, and nothing could have kept him from sailing to Louisiana in August of 1929. As already mentioned, he blamed himself for Stuart's disappearance, because he had not opposed Stuart's assignment; and he had known in his heart that Stuart should not go.

"I was so eager for someone to go there," he confessed before he left London. "I was so eager for something to happen. And of course I felt I couldn't go. And so I thought, well, maybe that strange young Texan will crack through that wall."

Langtry was nearing seventy-four years of age at this time, a tall, gaunt man with iron gray hair, a rectangular face, and sunken eyes. He had an extremely pleasant speaking voice and meticulous manners. He had the usual minor infirmities of old age, but, all things considered, he was in good health.

He had seen "everything" during his years of service. He was a powerful psychic or medium; and he was absolutely fearless when it came to any manifestation of the supernatural. But he was never rash or careless. He never underestimated any sort of phenomena. He was, as his own investigations show, extremely confident and extremely strong.

As soon as he heard of Stuart's disappearance, he became convinced that Stuart was dead. Quickly rereading the Mayfair material, he saw the error which the order had made.

He arrived in New Orleans on August 28, 1929, at once registering at the St. Charles Hotel and dispatching a letter home as Stuart had done. He gave his name, address, and London phone number to several people at the hotel desk so that there could be no question later that he had been there. He made a long distance call to the Motherhouse from his room, reporting the room number and several other particulars about his arrival.

Then he met with one of our investigators—the most competent of the private detectives—in the hotel bar, charging all of the drinks to the room.

He confirmed for himself everything that the order had already been told. He was also informed that Stella was no longer cooperating with the investigation, such as it was. Insisting that she didn't know anything and couldn't help anyone, she had at last become impatient and refused to talk to the investigators anymore.

"As I said good-bye to this gentleman," he wrote in his report, "I knew for certain that I was being watched. It was no more than a feeling, yet it was a profound one. And I sensed that it was connected to Stuart's disappearance, though I myself had made no inquiry regarding Stuart of any person at the hotel.

"At this point I was sorely tempted to roam the premises, seeking to detect some latent indication of Stuart's having been in this or that room. But I was also deeply convinced that Stuart had not met with foul play in this hotel. On the contrary, the people who were watching me, indeed, taking note of my movements and what I did, were doing so only because someone had paid them to do it. I decided to contact Stella Mayfair at once."

Langtry rang Stella from his room. Though it was past four o'clock, she had obviously only just awakened when she answered her private phone. Only reluctantly did she allow the subject to be reopened. And it soon became obvious that she was genuinely upset.

"Look, I don't know what happened to him!" she said, and again began to cry. "I liked him. I really did. He was such a strange man. We went to bed, you know."

Langtry couldn't think of a thing to say to such a frank admission. Even her disembodied voice proved somewhat charming. And he was convinced that her tears were real.

"Well, we did," she continued, undaunted. "I took him to some awful little place in the Quarter. I told the police about it. Anyway, I liked him, very very much! I told him not to come around this family. I told him! He had the most peculiar ideas about things. He didn't know anything. I told him to go away. Maybe he did go away. That is what I thought happened, you know, that he simply took my advice and went away."

Langtry implored her to help him discover what had happened. He explained that he was a colleague of Townsend's, that they had known each other very well.

"Colleague? You mean you're part of that group."

"Yes, if you mean the Talamasca . . ."

"Shhh, listen to me. Whoever you are, you can come on up here if you like. But do it tomorrow night. I'm giving a party, you see. You can just well, sort of blend in. If anyone asks you who you are, which they probably won't, just say Stella invited you. Ask to speak to me. But for God's sakes don't say anything about Townsend and don't say the name of your . . . whatever you call it . . ."

"Talamasca . . ."

"Yes! Now please listen to what I'm saying. There'll be hundreds of people there, white tie to rags, you know, and do be discreet. Just come up to me, and when you kiss me, whisper your name in my ear. What is it again?"

"Langtry. Arthur."

"Hmmmm. Unhuh. Right. That's simple enough to remember, isn't it? Now, do be careful. I can't stay on any longer. You will come, won't you? Look, you must come!"

Langtry averred that nothing could keep him away. He asked her if she remembered the photograph on which she'd written "To the Talamasca, with love, Stella! P.S. There are others who watch, too."

"Of course I remember it. Look, I can't talk to you about this right now. It was years and years ago, when I wrote that note. My mother was alive then. Look, you can't imagine how bad things are for me now. I've never been in a worse jam. And I don't know what happened to Stuart, really I don't. Look, will you please come tomorrow night?"

"Yes, I shall," said Langtry, struggling silently to determine whether or not he was being lured into some sort of trap. "But why must we be so circumspect about the whole arrangement, I don't . . ."

"Darling, look," she said, dropping her voice, "it's all very nice about your organization, and your library and all your marvelous psychic investigations. But don't be a perfect fool. Ours is not a world of séances and mediums and dead relatives telling you to look between the pages of the Bible for the deed to the property on Eighth Street or whatever. As for the voodoo nonsense, that was a perfect scream. And by the way, we do not have any Scottish ancestors. We were all French. My Uncle Julien made up something about a Scottish castle he bought when he went to Europe. So do forget about all that, if you please. But there are things I can tell you! That's just the point. Look, come early. Come around eight o'clock, will you? But whatever you do, don't be the first one to arrive. Now, I've got to get off, you really cannot imagine how dreadful everything is just now. I'll tell you frankly. I never asked to be born into this mad family! Really! There are three hundred people invited tomorrow night, and I haven't a single friend in the world.''

She rang off.

Langtry, who had taken down the entire conversation in shorthand, immediately copied it out in longhand, with a carbon, and posted one copy to London, going directly to the post office to do it, for he no longer trusted the situation at the hotel.

Then he went to rent a tailcoat and boiled shirt for the party the following night.

''I am thoroughly confused,'' he had written in his letter. ''I had been certain she had a hand in getting rid of poor Stuart. Now I don't know what to think. She wasn't lying to me, I am sure of it. But why is she frightened? Of course I cannot make an intelligent appraisal of her until I see her.''

Late that afternoon, he called Irwin Dandrich, the socialite spy for hire, and asked him to have dinner at a fashionable French Quarter restaurant blocks from the hotel.

Though Dandrich had nothing to say about Townsend's disappearance, he appeared to enjoy the meal thoroughly, gossiping nonstop about Stella. People said Stella was burning out.

''You can't drink a fifth of French brandy every day of your life and live forever,'' said Dandrich with weary, mocking gestures, as if to suggest the subject bored him, when in fact, he loved it. ''And the affair with Pierce is outrageous. Why, the boy is scarcely eighteen. It really is so perfectly stupid of Stella to do this. Why, Cortland was her chief ally against Carlotta, and now she's gone and seduced Cortland's favorite son! I don't think Barclay or Garland much approves of the situation either. And God only knows how Lionel stands it.

Lionel is a monomaniac and the name of his monomania is Stella, of course.''

Was Dandrich going to the party?

"Wouldn't miss it for anything in this world. Bound to be some interesting pyrotechnics. Stella's forbidden Carlotta to take Antha out of the house during these affairs. Carlotta is simmering. Threatening to call the police if the rowdies get out of hand.''

"What is Carlotta like?" asked Langtry.

"She's Mary Beth with vinegar in her veins instead of vintage wine. She's brilliant but she has no imagination. She's rich but there's nothing she wants. She's endlessly practical and meticulous and hardworking, and an absolutely insufferable bore. Of course she does take care of absolutely everything. Millie Dear, Belle, little Nancy, and Antha. And they have a couple of old servants up there who don't know who they are or what they're doing anymore, and she takes care of them, right along with everyone else. Stella has herself to blame for all this, really. She always did let Carlotta do the hiring and the firing, the check writing, and the shouting. And what with Lionel and Cortland turning against her, well, what can she do? No, I wouldn't miss this party, if I were you. It may be the last one for quite some time.''

Langtry spent the following day exploring the speakeasies and the small French Quarter hotel (a dump) where Stella had taken Stuart. He was plagued continuously with the strong feeling that Stuart had been in these places, that Stella's account of their wanderings had been the complete truth.

At seven o'clock, dressed and ready for the evening, he wrote another very short letter to the Motherhouse, which he mailed on the way to the party from the post office at Lafayette Square:

"The more I think about our phone conversation, the more I'm troubled. Of what is this lady so afraid? I find it hard to believe that her sister Carlotta can really inflict harm upon her. Why can't someone hire a nurse for the troubled child? I tell you, I find myself being drawn into this head over heels. Surely that is how Stuart felt.''

Langtry had the cab drop him at Jackson and Chestnut so that he might walk the remaining two blocks to the house, approaching it from the rear.

"The streets were completely blocked with automobiles. People were piling in through the back garden gate, and every window in the place was lighted. I could hear the shrill screams of the saxophone long before I reached the front steps.

"There was no one on the front door, as far as I ever saw,

and I simply went in, pushing through a regular jam of young persons in the hallway, who were all smoking and laughing and greeting each other, and took no notice of me at all.''

The party did include every manner of dress, exactly as Stella had promised. There were even quite a few elderly people there. And Langtry found himself comfortably anonymous as he made his way to the bar in the living room where he was served a glass of extremely good champagne.

''There were more and more people streaming in every minute. A crowd was dancing in the front portion of the room. In fact, there were so many persons everywhere I looked, all chattering and laughing and drinking amid a thick bluish cloud of cigarette smoke, that I could hardly gain a fair impression of the furnishings of the room. Rather lavish, I suppose, and rather like the salon of a great liner, actually, with the potted palms, and the tortured art deco lamps, and the delicate, vaguely Grecian chairs.

''The band, stationed on the side porch just behind a pair of floor-length windows, was deafening. How people managed to talk over it, I cannot imagine. I could not sustain a coherent train of thought.

''I was about to make my way out of all this when my eyes fastened on the dancers before the front windows, and I soon realized I was gazing directly at Stella—far more dramatic than any picture of her could possibly be. She was clad in gold silk— a skimpy little dress, no more than a remnant of a chemise layered with fringe, it seemed, and barely covering her shapely knees. Tiny gold sequins covered her gossamer stockings, and indeed the dress itself, and there was a gold satin band of yellow flowers in her short wavy black hair. Around her wrists were delicate glittering gold bracelets, and at her throat the Mayfair emerald, looking quite absurdly old-fashioned, yet stunning in its old filigree, as it rested against her naked flesh.

''A child-woman, she appeared, slim, breastless, yet entirely feminine, her lips brazenly rouged, and her enormous black eyes literally flashing like gems as she took in the crowd gazing at her in adoration, without ever missing a beat of dance. Her little feet in their flimsy high-heel shoes came down mercilessly on the polished floor, and throwing back her head, she laughed delightedly as she made a little circle, swishing her tiny hips, her arms flung out.

'' 'That's it, Stella!' someone roared, and yet another, 'Yeeeah, Stella!' and all of this with the rhythm, if you can imagine, and Stella managing somehow to be lovingly responsive to her worshipers, while at the same time giving herself over, limply and exquisitely, to the dance.

"If I have ever seen a person enjoy music and attention with such innocent abandon, I did not recall it then and I do not recall now. There was nothing cynical or vain in her exhibition. On the contrary, she seemed to have soared past all such self-conscious nonsense, and to belong both to those who admired her, and to her self.

"As for her partner, I only came to see him by and by, though in any other setting I'm sure I would have noticed him immediately, given that he was very young and indeed resembled her remarkably, having the same fair skin, black eyes, and black hair. But he was scarcely more than a boy. And his face still had a porcelain purity to it, and his height seemed to have gotten the better of his weight.

"He was bursting with the same careless vitality as Stella. And as the dance came to a finish, she threw up her hands, and let herself fall, with perfect trust, straight backwards into his waiting arms. He embraced her with shameless intimacy, letting his hands run over her boyish little torso and then kissing her tenderly on the mouth. But this was done without a particle of theatricality. Indeed, I don't think he saw anyone in the room save for her.

"The crowd closed about them. Someone was pouring champagne into Stella's mouth, and she was draping herself over the boy, as it were, and the music was starting up again. Other couples—all quite modern and very gay—began to dance.

"This was no time to approach her, I reasoned. It was only ten past eight, and I wanted to take a few moments to look about. Also I was for the moment entirely disarmed by her appearance. A great blank had been filled in. I felt certain she had not harmed Stuart. And so, hearing her laughter ringing over the fresh onslaught of the band, I resumed my journey towards the hall doors.

"Now, let me say here that this house is possessed of an exceptionally long hallway and a particularly long and straight stairs. I would say, offhand, there were some thirty steps to it. (There are in fact twenty-seven.) The second floor appeared to be completely dark and the staircase was deserted, but dozens of people were squeezing past this stairway towards a brightly lighted room at the end of the first-floor hall.

"I meant to follow suit, and thereby make a little exploration of the place, but as I placed my hand on the newel post I saw someone at the top of the stairs. Quite suddenly I realized it was

Stuart. My shock was so great I almost called out to him. But then I realized that something was very wrong.

"He appeared absolutely real, you must understand. Indeed the way that the light struck him from below was altogether realistic. But his expression alerted me at once to the fact that I was seeing something that couldn't be real. For though he was looking straight at me and obviously knew me, there was no urgency in his face, only a profound sadness, a great and weary distress.

"It seemed he took his time even acknowledging that I had seen him, and then he gave a very weary and forbidding shake of his head. I continued to stare at him, pushed and shoved by God knows how many individuals, the noise a perfect din around me, and once again, he shook his head in this forbidding way. Then he lifted his right hand and made a definite gesture for me to go away.

"I didn't dare move. I remained absolutely calm as I always do at such moments, resisting the inevitable delirium, concentrating upon the noise, the press of the crowd, even the thin scream of the music. And very carefully I memorized what I saw. His clothes were dirty and disheveled. The right side of his face was bruised or at least discolored.

"Finally I came round to the foot of the steps and started up. Only then did the phantom wake from its seeming languor. Once again, he shook his head and gestured for me to go away.

" 'Stuart!' I whispered. 'Talk to me, man, if you can!'

"I continued upwards, my eyes fixed upon him, as his expression grew ever more fearful; and I saw that he was covered with dust; that his body, even as he stared back at me, showed the first signs of decay. Nay, I could smell it! Then the inevitable happened; the image begin to fade. 'Stuart!' I appealed to him desperately. But the figure darkened, and through it, quite unconscious of it, stepped a flesh and blood woman of extraordinary beauty, who hurried down the stairs towards me and then past me, in a flurry of peach-colored silk and clattering jewelry, carrying with her a cloud of sweet perfume.

"Stuart was gone. The smell of human decay was gone. The woman murmured an apology as she brushed by me. Seems she was shouting to any number of people in the lower hall.

"Then she turned, and as I stood staring upwards still, quite oblivious to her, and gazing at nothing but empty shadows, I felt her hand grip my arm.

" 'Oh, but the party's down here,' she said. And gave me a little tug.

536

" 'I'm looking for the lavatory,' I said, for at that moment, I could think of nothing else.

" 'Down here, ducky,' she said. 'It's off the library. I'll show you, right around in back of the stairs.'

"Clumsily, I followed her down around the staircase and into a very large but dimly lighted northside room. The library, yes, most certainly, with bookshelves to the ceiling and dark leather furnishings, and only one lamp lighted, in a far corner, beside a blood red drape. A great dark mirror hung over the marble fireplace, reflecting the one lamp as if it were a sanctuary light.

" 'There you go,' she said, pointing to a closed door, and quickly made her exit. I was suddenly conscious of a man and woman huddled together on the leather couch who rose and hurried away. It seemed the party with its continued merriment bypassed this room. Everything here was dust and silence. One could smell moldering leather and paper. And I was immensely relieved to be alone.

"I sank down into the wing chair facing the fireplace, with my back to the crowd passing in the hallway, glancing up at the reflection of it in the mirror, and feeling quite safe from it for the moment, and praying that no other loving couple would seek this shadowy retreat.

"I took out my handkerchief and wiped my face. I was sweating miserably, and I struggled to remember every detail of what I'd seen.

"Now, you know we all have our theories regarding apparitions—as to why they appear in this or that guise, or why they do what they do. And my theories probably don't agree with those of anyone else. But I was certain of one thing as I sat there. Stuart had chosen to show himself to me in decayed and disheveled form for one very good reason—his remains were in this house! Yet he was imploring me to leave here! He was warning me to get out.

"Was this warning intended for the entire Talamasca? Or merely for Arthur Langtry? I sat brooding, feeling my pulse return to normal, and feeling as I always do in the aftermath of such experiences, a rush of adrenaline, a zeal to discover all that lies behind the faint shimmer of the supernatural which I had only just glimpsed.

"I was also enraged, deeply and bitterly, at whoever or whatever had brought Stuart's life to a close.

"How to proceed, that was the vital question. Of course I should speak to Stella. But how much of the house might I explore before I made myself known to her? And what of Stuart's

537

warning? Precisely what was the danger for which I must be prepared?

"I was considering all this, aware of no perceptible change in the racket from the hallway behind me, when there suddenly came over me the realization that something in my immediate environment had undergone a radical and significant change. Slowly I looked up. There was someone reflected in the mirror—a lone figure, it seemed. With a start I looked over my shoulder. No one there. And then back again to the dim and shadowy glass.

"A man was gazing out from the immaterial realm beyond it, and as I studied him, the adrenaline pumping and my senses sharpening, his image grew brighter and clearer, until he was vividly and undeniably a young man of pale complexion and dark brown eyes, staring angrily and malevolently and unmistakably down at me.

"At last the image reached its fullest potency. And so vital was it, that it seemed a mortal man had secreted himself in a chamber behind the mirror, and having removed the glass was peering at me from the empty frame.

"Never in all my years with the Talamasca had I seen an apparition so exquisitely realized. The man appeared to be perhaps thirty years of age; his skin was deliberately flawless, yet carefully colored, with a blush to the cheeks and a faint paling beneath the eyes. His clothing was extremely old-fashioned, with an upturned white collar and a rich silk tie. As for the hair, it was wavy and ever so slightly unkempt, as if he had only just run his fingers through it. The mouth appeared soft, youthful, and slightly ruddy. I could see the fine lines in the lips. Indeed I could see the barest shadow of a shaven beard on his chin.

"But the effect was horrible, for it was not a human being, or a painting, or a reflection. But something infinitely more brilliant than any of these; and yet silently alive.

"The brown eyes were full of hatred, and as I looked at the creature, his mouth quivered ever so slightly with anger, and finally rage.

"Quite slowly and deliberately, I raised my handkerchief to my lips. 'Did you kill my friend, spirit?' I whispered. Seldom have I felt so enlivened, so heated for adversity. 'Well, spirit?' I whispered again.

"I saw it weakening. I saw it lose its solidity, indeed, its very animation. The face, so beautifully modeled and expressive of negative emotion, was slowly going blank.

" 'I'm not so easily dispatched, spirit,' I said under my breath.

'Now we have two accounts to settle, do we not! Petyr van Abel and Stuart Townsend, are we agreed on that much?'

"The illusion seemed powerless to answer me. And quite suddenly the entire mirror shivered, becoming merely a dark glass again as the door to the hallway was slammed shut.

"Footsteps sounded on the bare floor beyond the edge of the Chinese carpet. The mirror was definitely empty, reflecting no more than woodwork and books.

"I turned and saw a young woman advancing across the carpet, her eyes fixed on the mirror, her whole demeanor one of anger, confusion, distress. It was Stella. She stood before the mirror, with her back to me, gazing into it, and then turned round.

" 'Well, you can describe that to your friends in London, can't you?' she said. She seemed on the edge of hysteria. 'You can tell them you saw that!'

"I realized she was shaking all over. The flimsy gold dress with its layers of fringe was shivering. And anxiously she clutched the monstrous emerald at her throat.

"I struggled to rise, but she told me to sit down, and immediately took a place on the couch to my left, her hand laid firmly on my knee. She leant over very close to me, so close that I could see the mascara on her long lashes, and the powder on her cheeks. She was like a great kewpie doll looking at me, a cinema goddess, naked in her gossamer silk.

" 'Listen, can you take me with you?' she said. 'Back to England, to these people, this Talamasca? Stuart said you could!'

" 'You tell me what happened to Stuart and I'll take you anywhere you like.'

" 'I don't know!' she said, and at once her eyes watered. 'Listen, I have to get out of here. I didn't hurt him. I don't do things like that to people. I never have! God, don't you believe me? Can't you tell that I'm speaking the truth?'

" 'All right. What do you want me to do?'

" 'Just help me! Take me with you, back to England. Look, I've got my passport, I've got plenty of money—' At this point she broke off, and pulled open a drawer in the couchside table and took out of it a veritable sheaf of twenty-dollar bills. 'Here, you can buy the tickets. I can meet you. Tonight.'

"Before I could answer, she looked up with a start. The door had opened, and in came the young boy with whom she'd been dancing earlier, quite flushed, and full of concern.

" 'Stella, I've been looking for you . . .'

" 'Oh, sweetheart, I'm coming,' she said, rising at once, and glancing at me meaningfully over her shoulder. 'Now, go back out and get me a drink, will you, sweetheart?' She straightened his tie as she spoke to him, and then turned him around with quick little gestures and actually shoved him towards the door.

"He was highly suspicious, but very obviously well bred. He did as he was told. As soon as she had shut the door, she came back to me. She was flushed, and almost feverish, and absolutely convincing. In fact, my impression of her was that she was a somewhat innocent person, that she believed all the optimism and rebellion of the 'jazz babies.' She seemed authentic, if you know what I mean.

" 'Go to the station,' she implored me. 'Get the tickets. I'll meet you at the train.'

" 'But which train, what time?'

" 'I don't know what train!' She wrung her hands. 'I don't know what time! I have to get out of here. Look, I'll come with you.'

" 'That certainly seems to be a better plan. You could wait for me in the taxi while I get my things from the hotel.'

" 'Yes, that's a fine idea!' she whispered. 'And we'll get out of here on any train that's leaving, we can always change our destination further on.'

" 'And what about him?'

" 'Who! Him!' she demanded crossly. 'You mean Pierce? Pierce isn't going to be any trouble! Pierce is a perfect darling. I can handle Pierce.'

" 'You know I don't mean Pierce,' I said. 'I mean the man I saw a moment ago in that mirror, the man you forced to disappear.'

"She looked absolutely desperate. She was the cornered animal, but I don't believe I was the one cornering her. I couldn't figure it out.

" 'Look, I didn't make him disappear,' she said under her breath. 'You did!' She made a conscious effort to calm herself, her hand resting for a moment on her heaving breast. 'He won't stop us,' she said. 'Please trust me that he won't.'

"At this moment, Pierce returned, pushing open the door once more and letting in the great cacophony from outside. She took the glass of champagne from him gratefully and drank down half of it.

" 'I'll talk to you in a few minutes,' she said to me with deliberate sweetness. 'In just a few minutes. You'll be right here, won't you? No, as a matter of fact, why don't you get some air? Go out on the front porch, ducky, and I'll come talk to you there.'

"Pierce knew she was up to something. He looked from her

540

to me, but obviously he felt quite helpless. She took him by the arm and led him out with her ahead of me. I glanced down at the carpet. The twenty-dollar bills had fallen and were scattered everywhere. Hastily, I gathered them up, put them back into the drawer, and went into the hall.

"Just opposite the library door, I caught a glimpse of a portrait of Julien Mayfair, a very well-done canvas in heavy dark Rembrandt-style oils. I wished I had time to examine it.

"But I hurried around the back of the staircase and started pushing and shoving as gently as I could towards the front door.

"Three minutes must have passed, and I had made it only so far as the newel post, when I saw *him* again, or thought I did for one terrible instant—the brown-haired man I had seen in the mirror. This time he was gazing at me over someone's shoulder, as he stood in the front corner of the hall.

"I tried to pick him out again. But I couldn't. People crushed against me as if they were deliberately trying to block me, but of course they weren't.

"Then I realized someone ahead of me was pointing to the stairs. I was now past it, and within only a few feet of the door. I turned round, and saw a child on the stairway, a very pretty little blond-haired girl. No doubt it was Antha, though she looked rather small for eight years. She was dressed in a flannel nightgown and barefoot, and she was crying, and looking over the railing into the doors of the front room.

"I too turned and looked into the front room, at which point someone gasped aloud, and the crowd parted, people falling to the left and the right of the door, in apparent fear. A red-haired man stood in the doorway, slightly to my left, facing into the room. And as I watched with sickening horror, he lifted a pistol with his right hand and fired it. The deafening report shook the house. Panic ensued. The air was filled with screams. Someone had fallen by the front door, and the others simply ran over the poor devil. People were struggling to escape back through the hall.

"I saw Stella lying on the floor in the middle of the front room. She was on her back, with her head turned to the side, staring towards the hall. I raced forward, but not in time to stop the red-haired man from standing over her and firing the pistol again. Her body convulsed as blood exploded from the side of her head.

"I grabbed for the bastard's arm, and he fired again as my hand tightened on his wrist. But this bullet missed her and went through the floor. It seemed the screams were redoubled. Glass was breaking. Indeed, the windows were shattering. Someone attempted to grab the man from behind, and I managed somehow to get the gun away from him, though I was accidentally stepping on Stella, indeed, tripping over her feet.

"I fell to my knees with the gun, and then pushed it quite deliberately away across the floor. The murderer was struggling vainly against a half-dozen men now. Glass from the windows blew inward all over us; I saw it rain down upon Stella. Blood was running down her neck, and over the Mayfair emerald which lay askew on her breast.

"Next thing I knew a monstrous clap of thunder obliterated the deafening screams and shrieks still coming from all quarters. And I felt the rain gusting in; then I heard it coming down on the porches all around, and then the lights went out.

"In repeated flashes of lightning I saw the men dragging the murderer from the room. A woman knelt at Stella's side, and lifted her lifeless wrist, and then let out an agonizing scream.

"As for the child, she had come into the room, and stood barefoot staring at her mother. And then she too began to scream. Her voice rose high and piercing over the others. 'Mama, Mama, Mama,' as though with each new burst her realization of what had happened deepened helplessly.

" 'Someone take her out!' I cried. And indeed, others had gathered around her, and were attempting to draw her away. I moved out of their path, only climbing to my feet when I reached the side porch window. In another crackle of white light, I saw someone pick up the gun. It was then handed to another person, and then to another, who held it as if it were alive. Fingerprints were no longer of consequence, if ever they were, and there had been countless witnesses. There was no reason for me not to get out while I could. And turning, I made my way out onto the side porch and into the downpour, as I stepped onto the lawn.

"Dozens of people were huddled there, the women crying, the men doing what they could to cover the women's heads with their jackets, everyone soaked and shivering and quite at a loss. The lights flickered on for a second, but another violent slash of lightning signaled their final failure. When an upstairs window suddenly burst in a shower of glittering shards, panic broke out once more.

"I hurried towards the back of the property, thinking to leave unobserved through a back way. This meant a short rush along a flagstone path, a climb of two steps to the patio around the swimming pool, and then I spied the side alley to the gate.

"Even through the dense rain I could see that it was open, and see beyond it the wet gleaming cobblestones of the street. The thunder rolled over the rooftops, and the lightning laid bare the whole garden hideously in an instant, with its balustrades and towering camellias, and beach towels draped over so many skeletal black iron chairs. Everything was helplessly thrashing in the wind.

"I heard sirens suddenly. And as I rushed towards the waiting sidewalk, I glimpsed a man standing motionless and stiff, as it were, in a great clump of banana trees to the right of the gate.

"As I drew closer, I glanced to the right, and into the man's face. It was the spirit, visible to me once more, though for what reason under God I had no idea. My heart raced dangerously, and I felt a momentary dizziness and tightening in my temples as if the circulation of my blood were being choked off.

"He presented the same figure he had before; I saw the unmistakable glint of brown hair and brown eyes, and dim unremarkable clothing save for its primness and a certain vagueness about the whole. Yet the raindrops glistened as they struck his shoulders and his lapels. They glistened in his hair.

"But it was the face of the being which held me enthralled. It was monstrously transfigured by anguish, and his cheeks were wet with soundless crying as he looked into my eyes.

" 'God in heaven, speak if you can,' I said, almost the same words I'd spoken to the poor desperate spirit of Stuart. And so crazed was I by all I had seen that I lunged at him, seeking to grab hold of him by the shoulders and make him answer if I could.

"He vanished. Only this time I felt him vanish. I felt the warmth and the sudden movement in the air. It was as if something had been sucked away, and the bananas swayed violently. But then the wind and the rain were knocking them about. And suddenly I did not know what I had seen, or what I had felt. My heart was skipping dangerously. I felt another wave of dizziness. Time to get out.

"I hurried up Chestnut Street past scores of wandering, weeping, dazed individuals and then down Jackson Avenue out of the wind and the rain, into a fairly clear and mild stretch where the traffic swept by without the slightest knowledge, apparently, of what had happened only blocks away. Within a matter of seconds, I caught a taxi for the hotel.

"As soon as I reached it, I gathered up my belongings, lugging them downstairs myself without the aid of a bellboy, and immediately checked out. I had the cab take me to the train station, where I caught the midnight train for New York, and I am in my sleeping car now.

"I shall post this as soon as I possibly can. And until such time, I shall carry the letter with me, on my person, hoping for

543

what it's worth that if anything happens to me the letter will be found.

"But as I write this I do not think anything will happen to me! It is over, this chapter! It has come to a ghastly and bloody end. Stuart was part of it. And God only knows what role the spirit played in it. But I shall not tempt the demon further by turning back. Every impulse in my being tells me to get away from here. And if I forget this for a moment, I have the haunting memory of Stuart to guide me, Stuart gesturing to me from the top of the stairs to go away.

"If we never talk in London, please pay heed to the advice I give you now. Send no one else to this place. At least not now. Watch, wait, as is our motto. Consider the evidence. Try to draw some lesson from what has taken place. And above all, study the Mayfair record. Study it deeply and put its various materials in order.

"My belief, for what it is worth at such a moment, is that neither Lasher nor Stella had a hand in the death of Stuart. Yet his remains are under that roof.

"But the council may consider the evidence at its leisure. Send no one here again.

"We cannot hope for public justice with regard to Stuart. We cannot hope for legal resolutions. Even in the investigation that will inevitably follow tonight's horrors, there will be no search of the Mayfair house and its grounds. And how could we ever demand such a step be taken?

"But Stuart will never be forgotten. And I am man enough, even in my twilight years, to believe that there must be a reckoning—both for Stuart, and for Petyr—though with whom or with what that reckoning will be I do not know.

"I do not speak of retribution. I do not speak of revenge. I speak of illumination, understanding, and above all, resolution. I speak of the final light of truth.

"These people, the Mayfairs, do not know who they are anymore. I tell you the young woman was an innocent. I'm convinced of it. But we know. We know; and Lasher knows. And who is Lasher? Who is this spirit who chose to reveal his pain to me; who chose to show to me his very tears?"

Arthur posted this letter from St. Louis, Missouri. A bad carbon was sent two days later from New York, with a brief postscript, explaining that Arthur had booked passage home, and would be sailing at the end of the week.

After two days at sea, Arthur rang the ship's doctor, complaining of chest pains and asking for a standard remedy for indigestion. A half hour later, the doctor discovered Arthur dead of an apparent heart attack. The time was half past six on the evening of September 7, 1929.

Arthur had written one more brief letter on shipboard the day before his death. It was in his robe pocket when he was found.

In it, he said that he was not well, and suffering from violent seasickness, which he hadn't experienced in years. There were times when he feared he was really ill, and might not see the Motherhouse again.

"There are so many things I want to discuss with you about the Mayfairs, so many ideas going through my head. What if we were to draw off that spirit? That is, what if we were to invite it to come to us?

"Whatever you do, do not send another investigator to New Orleans—not now, not while that woman, Carlotta Mayfair, lives."

Twenty-one

H E WAS KISSING her as his fingers stroked her breasts. The pleasure was so keen. Paralyzing. She tried to lift her head. But she couldn't move. The constant roar of the jet engines lulled her. Yes, this is a dream. Yet it seemed so real, and she was slipping back into it. Only forty-five minutes until they landed at New Orleans International. She ought to try to wake up. But then he kissed her again, forcing his tongue very gently between her lips, so gently yet forcefully, and his fingers touched her nipples, pinching them as if she were naked under the small woolen blanket. Oh, he knew how to do it, pinch them slowly but hard. She turned more fully towards the window, sighing, drawing up her knees against the side of the cabin. No one noticing her. First class half empty. Almost there.

Again, he pinched her nipples, just a little more cruelly, ah, so delicious. You cannot be too rough, really. Press your lips harder against mine. Fill me with your tongue. She opened her mouth against his, and then his fingers touched her hair, sending another, unexpected sensation through her, a light tingling. That was the miracle of it, that it was such a blending of sensations, like soft and bright colors mingling, the chills moving down her naked back and arms, and yet the heat pounding between her legs. *Come inside me! I want to be filled up, yes, with your tongue, and with you, come in harder.* It was enormous, yet smooth, bathed as it was in her fluids.

She came silently, shuddering beneath the blanket, her hair fallen down over her face, only dimly aware that she wasn't naked, that no one could be touching her, no one could be creating this pleasure. Yet it went on and on, her heart stopping, the blood pounding in her face, the shocks moving down through her thighs and her calves.

You are going to die if it doesn't stop, Rowan. His hand brushed her cheek. He kissed her eyelids. *Love you* . . .

Suddenly, she opened her eyes. For a moment nothing registered. Then she saw the cabin. The little blind was drawn, and everything about her seemed a pale luminous gray, drenched in the sound of the engines. The shocks were still passing through her. She lay back in the large soft airline seat and yielded to them, rather like dim, beautifully modulated jolts of electricity, her eyes drifting sluggishly over the ceiling as she struggled to keep them open, to wake up.

God, how did she look after this little orgy? Her face must be flushed.

Very slowly, she sat up, smoothing back her hair with both hands. She tried to reinvoke the dream, not for the sensuality but for information, tried to travel back to the center of it, to know who he had been. Not Michael. No. That was the bad part.

Christ, she thought. I've been unfaithful to him with nobody. How strange. She pressed her hands to her cheeks. Very warm. She was still feeling the low, vibrant, debilitating pleasure even now.

"How long before we land in New Orleans?" she asked the stewardess who was passing.

"Thirty minutes. Seat belt buckled?"

She sat back, feeling for the buckled seat belt, and then letting herself go deliciously limp. But how could a dream do that, she thought. How could a dream carry it so far?

When she was thirteen, she used to have those dreams, before she knew they were natural or what to do about them. But she'd always wake before the finish. She couldn't help it. This time, it had just taken its own course. And the odd thing was, she felt violated, as if the dream lover had assaulted her. Now, that was really absurd. But it wasn't a good feeling, and it was extremely strong.

Violated. . . .

She raised her hands to her breasts under the blanket, covering them protectively. But that was nonsense, wasn't it? Besides, it wasn't rape at all.

"You want a drink before we land?"

"No. Coffee." She closed her eyes. Who had he been, her dream lover? No face, no name. Only the sense of someone more delicate than Michael, someone almost ethereal, or at least that was the word that came to her mind. The man had spoken to her, however, she was sure of it, but everything except the memory of the pleasure was gone.

Only as she sat up to drink the coffee did she realize there was a faint soreness between her legs. Possibly an aftereffect of the powerful muscular contractions. Thank God there was no one else near at hand, no one beside her or across the aisle from her. But then she never would have let it go so far if she hadn't been concealed, under the blanket. That is, if she could have forced herself awake. If she had had a choice.

She felt so sleepy!

Slowly she took a sip of the coffee and raised the white plastic shade.

Green swampland down there in the deepening afternoon sun. And the dark brown serpentine river curving around the distant city. She felt a sudden elation. Almost there. The sound of the engines grew harsher, louder with the plane's descent.

She didn't want to think about the dream anymore. She honestly wished it hadn't happened. In fact, it was dreadfully distasteful to her suddenly, and she felt soiled and tired and angry. Even a little revolted. She wanted to think about her mother, and about seeing Michael.

She had called Jerry Lonigan from Dallas. The parlor was open. And the cousins were already arriving. They had been calling all morning. The Mass was set for three P.M. and she wasn't to worry. She should just come on over from the Pontchartrain as soon as she arrived.

"Where are you, Michael?" she whispered, as she sat back again, and closed her eyes.

Twenty-two

THE FILE ON THE MAYFAIR WITCHES

PART VIII

The Family from 1929 to 1956

THE IMMEDIATE AFTERMATH OF STELLA'S DEATH

In October and November of 1929, the stock market crashed and the world entered the Great Depression. The Roaring Twenties came to an end. Wealthy people everywhere lost their fortunes. Multimillionaires jumped out of windows. And in a time of new and unwelcome austerity, there came an inevitable cultural reaction to the excesses of the twenties. Short skirts, booze-swilling socialites, and sexually sophisticated motion pictures and books went out of style.

At the Mayfair house on First and Chestnut Streets in New Orleans, the lights went dim with Stella's death and were never turned up again. Candles lighted Stella's open-casket funeral in the double parlor. And when Lionel, her brother, who had shot her dead with two bullets in front of scores of witnesses, was buried a short time after, it was not from the house but from a sterile funeral parlor on Magazine Street blocks away.

Within six months of Lionel's death, Stella's art deco furniture, her numerous contemporary paintings, her countless records of jazz and ragtime and blues singers, all disappeared from the rooms of First Street. What did not go into the immense attics of the house went out on the street.

Countless staid Victorian pieces, stored since the loss of Riverbend, came out of storage to fill the rooms. Shutters were bolted on the Chestnut Street windows never to be opened again.

But these changes had little to do with the death of the Roaring Twenties, or the crash of the stock market, or the Great Depression.

The family firm of Mayfair and Mayfair had long ago shifted

its enormous resources out of the railroads, and out of the dangerously inflated stock market. As early as 1924, it had liquidated its immense land holdings in Florida for boom profits. It continued to hold its California property for the western land boom yet to come. With millions invested in gold, Swiss francs, South African diamond mines, and countless other profitable ventures, the family was once again in a position to lend money to friends and distant cousins who had lost all they had.

And lend money right and left the family did, pumping new blood into its incalculably large body of political and social contacts, and further protecting itself from interference of any sort as it had always done.

Lionel Mayfair was never questioned by a single police officer as to why he shot Stella. Two hours after her death, he was a patient in a private sanitarium, where in the days that followed weary doctors nodded off listening to Lionel rave about the devil walking the hallways of the house at First Street, about little Antha taking the devil into her bed.

"And there he was with Antha and I knew it. It was happening all over again. And Mother wasn't there, you see, no one was there. Just Carlotta fighting endlessly with Stella. Oh, you can't imagine the door slamming and the screaming. We were a household of children without Mother. There was my big sister Belle clinging to her doll, and crying. And Millie Dear, poor Millie Dear, saying her rosary on the side porch in the dark, shaking her head. And Carlotta struggling to take Mother's place, and unable to do it. She's a tin soldier compared to Mother! Stella threw things at her. 'You think you're going to lock me up!' Stella was hysterical.

"Children, I tell you, that's what we were. I'd knock on her door and Pierce was in there with her! I knew it and all this in broad daylight. She was lying to me, and *him* with Antha, I saw him. All the time I saw him! I saw him! I saw them together in the garden. But she knew, she knew all along that he was with Antha. She let it happen.

" 'Are you going to let him have her?' That's what Carlotta said. How the hell was I supposed to stop it? She couldn't stop it. Antha was under the trees out there singing with him, tossing the flowers in the air, and he was making them float there. I saw that! I saw that so many times! I could hear her laughing. That's how Stella used to laugh! And what did Mother ever do, for Christ's sake! Oh, God, you don't understand. A household of children. And why were we children? Because we didn't know how to be evil. Did Mother know how? Did Julien know how?

"Do you know why Belle's an idiot? It was inbreeding! And

Millie Dear's no better! Good God, do you know that Millie Dear is Julien's daughter! Oh, yes, she is! As God is my witness, yes, she is. And she sees *him* and she lies about it! I know she sees him.

" 'Leave her alone,' Stella says to me, 'It doesn't matter.' I know Millie can see him. I know she can. They were carrying cases of champagne for the party. Cases and cases, and there was Stella up there dancing to her phonograph records. 'Just try to be decent for the party, will you, Lionel?' For the love of heaven. Didn't anybody know what was going on?

"And Carl talking about sending Stella to Europe! How could anyone get Stella to do anything! And what did it matter if Stella was in Europe? I tried to tell Pierce. I grabbed that young man by the throat and I said, 'I'm going to make you listen.' I would have shot him too if I could have done it. I would have, oh God, in heaven, why did they stop me! 'Don't you see, it's Antha he's got now! Are you blind?' That's what I said. You tell me! Are they all blind!''

On and on it went, we are told, for days on end. Yet the above is the only fragment noted verbatim in the doctor's file, after which we are informed that "the patient continues on about she and her and him and he, and one of these persons is supposed to be the devil." Or, "Raving again, incoherent, implying someone put him up to it, but it is not clear who this person is."

On the eve of Stella's funeral, three days after the murder, Lionel tried to escape. Thereafter he was kept permanently in restraints.

"How they managed to patch up Stella, I'll never know," one of the cousins said long after. "But she looked lovely.

"That was Stella's last party, really. She'd left detailed instructions as to how it was to be handled, and do you know what I heard later? That she'd written all that out when she was thirteen! Imagine, the romantic notions of a girl of thirteen!''

Legal gossip indicated otherwise. Stella's funeral instructions (which were in no way legally binding) had been included with the will she made in 1925 after Mary Beth's death. And for all their romantic effect they were extremely simple. Stella was to be buried from home. Florists were to be informed that the "preferred flower" was the calla or some other white lily, and only candles would be used to light the main floor. Wine should be served. The wake should continue from the time of laying out until the body was removed to the church for the Requiem Mass.

But romantic it was, by anyone's standards, with Stella dressed in white in an open coffin at the front end of the long parlor, and dozens of wax candles giving off a rather spectacular light.

"I'll tell you what it was like," said one of the cousins long after. "The May processions! Exactly, with all those lilies, all that fragrance, and Stella like the May Queen in white."

Cortland, Barclay, and Garland greeted the cousins who came by the hundreds. Pierce was allowed to pay his respects, though he was immediately thereafter packed off to his mother's family in New York. Mirrors were draped in the old Irish fashion, though by whose order no one seemed to know.

The Requiem Mass was even more crowded, for cousins whom Stella had not invited to First Street while she was alive went directly to the church. The crowd in the cemetery was as big as it had been for Miss Mary Beth.

"Oh, but you must realize that it was a scandal!" said Irwin Dandrich. "It was the murder of 1929! And Stella was Stella, you see. It couldn't have been more interesting to certain types of people. Did you know that the very night of her murder, two different young men of my acquaintance fell in love with her! Can you imagine? Neither of them had ever met her before and there they were quarreling over her, one demanding that the other let him have his chance with her, and the other saying that he had spoken to her first. My dear man, the party only started at seven. And by eight-thirty, she was dead!"

The night after Stella's funeral, Lionel woke up screaming in the asylum, "He's there, he won't leave me alone."

He was in a straitjacket by the end of the week, and finally on the fourth of November, he was placed in a padded cell. As the doctors debated whether to try electric shock, or merely to keep him sedated, Lionel sat crouched in the corner, unable to free his arms from the straitjacket, whimpering and trying to turn his head away from his invisible tormentor.

The nurses told Irwin Dandrich that he screamed for Stella to help him. "He's driving me mad. Oh, why in the name of God doesn't he kill me? Stella, help me. Stella, tell him to kill me."

The corridors rang with his screams. "I didn't want to give him any more injections," one of the nurses told Dandrich. "He never really went to sleep. He'd wrestle with his demons, mumbling and cursing. It was worse for him that way, I think."

"He is judged to be completely and incurably insane," wrote one of our private detectives. "Of course, if he were cured he might have to stand trial for the murder. God knows what Carlotta has told the authorities. Possibly she hasn't told them anything. Possibly no one has asked."

On the morning of the sixth of November, alone and unattended, Lionel apparently went into a convulsion and died of suffocation, having swallowed his tongue. No wake was held in the funeral parlor on Magazine Street. Cousins were turned away the morning of the funeral, and told to go directly to the Mass at St. Alphonsus Church. There they were told by hired funeral directors not to continue on to the cemetery, that Miss Carlotta wanted things quiet.

Nevertheless they gathered at the Prytania Street gates of Lafayette No. 1, watching from a distance as Lionel's coffin was placed beside Stella's.

Family legend:

"It was all over, everyone knew it. Poor Pierce eventually managed to get over it. He studied at Columbia for a while, then entered Harvard the following year. But to the day he died no one ever mentioned Stella in his presence. And how he hated Carlotta. The only time I ever heard him speak of it, he said she was responsible. She ought to have pulled the trigger herself."

Not only did Pierce recover, he became a highly capable lawyer, and played a major role in guiding and expanding the Mayfair fortune over the decades. He died in 1986. His son, Ryan Mayfair, born in 1936, is the backbone of Mayfair and Mayfair today. Young Pierce, Ryan's son, is at present the most promising young man in the firm.

But those cousins who said "It was all over" were right.

With the death of Stella, the power of the Mayfair Witches was effectively broken. Stella was the first of Deborah's gifted descendants to die young. She was the first one to die by violence. And never after would a Mayfair Witch "rule" at First Street, or assume direct management of the legacy. Indeed, the present designee is a mute catatonic and her daughter—Rowan Mayfair—is a young neurosurgeon living over two thousand miles from First Street who knows nothing of her mother, her heritage, her inheritance, or her home.

How did it all come to this? And can any one person be blamed? These are questions over which one could agonize eternally. But before we consider them in greater detail, let us draw back and consider the position of the Talamasca after Arthur Langtry's death.

THE STATUS OF THE INVESTIGATION
IN 1929

No autopsy was ever performed on Arthur Langtry. His remains were buried in England in the Talamasca cemetery, as he had long ago arranged for them to be. There is no evidence that he died by violence; indeed, his last letter, describing Stella's murder, indicates that he was already suffering from heart trouble. But one can say with some justification that the stress of what he saw in New Orleans took its toll. Arthur might have lived longer had he never gone there. On the other hand, he was not retired, and he might have met his death in the field on some other case.

To the ruling council of the Talamasca, however, Arthur Langtry was another casualty of the Mayfair Witches. And Arthur's glimpse of Stuart's spirit was fully accepted by these experienced investigators as proof that Stuart had died within the Mayfair house.

But how exactly did Stuart die, the Talamasca wanted to know. Had Carlotta done it? And if so, why?

The outstanding argument against Carlotta as the murderer is perhaps obvious already and will become even more obvious as this narrative continues. Carlotta has been throughout her life a practicing Catholic, a scrupulously honest lawyer, and a law-abiding citizen. Her strenuous criticisms of Stella were apparently founded upon her own moral convictions, or so family, friends, and even casual observers have assumed.

On the other hand, Carlotta is credited by scores of persons with driving Lionel to shoot Stella, for doing everything but putting the gun in his hand.

Even if Carlotta did put the gun in Lionel's hands, such an emotional and public act as Stella's murder is a very different thing from the secret and cold-blooded killing of a stranger one hardly knows.

Was Lionel perhaps the murderer of Stuart Townsend? What about Stella herself? And how can we rule out Lasher? If one considers this being to have a personality, a history, indeed a profile as we say in the modern world, does not the killing of Townsend more logically fit the modus operandi of the spirit than anyone else in the house?

Unfortunately none of these theories can provide for the cover-up, and certainly there was a cover-up with employees of the St. Charles Hotel being paid to say that Stuart Townsend was never there.

Perhaps an acceptable scenario is one which accommodates all of the suspects involved. For instance, what if Stella did invite Townsend to First Street, where he met his death through some violent intervention of Lasher. And what if a panic-stricken Stella then turned to Carlotta or Lionel or even Pierce to help her conceal the body and make sure no one at the hotel said a word?

Unfortunately this scenario, and others like it, leaves too many unanswered questions. Why, for instance, would Carlotta have participated in such treachery? Mightn't she have used the death of Townsend to get rid of her baby sister once and for all? As for Pierce, it is highly unlikely that such an innocent young man could have become involved in such a thing. (Pierce went on to live a very respectable life.) And when we consider Lionel we must ask: if he did have knowledge of Stuart's death or disappearance, what prevented him from saying something about it when he went "stark raving mad"? He certainly said enough about everything else that happened at First Street, or so the records show.

And lastly, we should ask—if one of these unlikely people did help Stella bury the body in the backyard, why bother to remove Townsend's belongings from the hotel and bribe the employees to say he was never there?

Perhaps the Talamasca was wrong, in retrospect, for not pursuing the matter of Stuart further, for not demanding a full-scale investigation, for not badgering the police into doing something more. The fact is, we did push. And so did Stuart's family when they were informed of his disappearance. But as one distinguished law firm in New Orleans informed Dr. Townsend: "We have absolutely nothing to go on. You cannot prove the young man was ever here!"

In the days that followed Stella's murder, no one was willing to "disturb" the Mayfairs with further questions about a mysterious Texan from England. And our investigators, including some of the best in the business, could never crack the silence of the hotel employees, nor get so much as a clue as to who might have paid them off. It is foolish to think the police could have done any better.

But there is one very interesting bit of contemporary "opinion" to consider before we leave this crime unsolved; and that is the final word on the subject by Irwin Dandrich, gossiping with one of our private detectives in a French Quarter bar during the Christmas season of 1929.

"I'll tell you the secret to understanding that family," said Dandrich, "and I've watched them for years. Not just for your queer birds in London, mind you. I've watched them the way everybody watches them—forever wondering what goes on behind those drawn blinds. The secret is realizing that Carlotta Mayfair isn't the clean-living, righteous Catholic woman she has always pretended to be. There's something mysterious and evil about that woman. She's destructive, and vengeful too. She'd rather see little Antha go mad than grow up to be like Stella.

She'd rather see the place dark and deserted than see other people having fun."

On the surface, these remarks seem simplistic, but there may be more truth to them than anyone realized at the time. To the world Carlotta Mayfair certainly did represent clean living, sanity, righteousness, and the like. From 1929, she attended Mass daily at Our Mother of Perpetual Help Chapel on Prytania, gave generously to the church and all its organizations, and though she carried on a private war with Mayfair and Mayfair over the administration of Antha's money, she was always extremely generous with her own. She lent money freely to any and all Mayfairs who had need of it, sent modest gifts for birthdays, weddings, christenings, and graduations, attended funerals, and now and then met with cousins outside the house for lunch or tea.

To those who had been so grievously offended by Stella, Carlotta was a good woman, the backbone of the house on First Street, the able and endlessly self-sacrificing caretaker of Stella's insane daughter, Antha, and the other dependents, Millie Dear, Nancy, and Belle.

She was never criticized for her failure to open the house to the family, or her refusal to reinstate reunions and get-togethers of any kind. On the contrary, it was understood that "she had her hands full." No one wanted to make any demands on her. Indeed, she became a sort of sour saint to the family as the years passed.

My opinion—for what it's worth—after forty years of studying the family, is that there is a great deal of truth to Irwin Dandrich's estimation of her. It is my personal conviction that she presents a mystery as great as that of Mary Beth or Julian. And we have only scratched the surface of what goes on in that house.

THE POSITION OF THE ORDER
FURTHER CLARIFIED

With regard to the future, it was decided by the Talamasca in 1929 that no further attempt at personal contact would be made.

Our director, Evan Neville, believed that first and foremost we should abide by Arthur Langtry's advice, and that second, the warning from the specter of Stuart Townsend should be taken seriously. We should stay away from the Mayfairs for the time being.

Several younger members of the council believed, however, that we must attempt to make contact with Carlotta Mayfair by mail. What harm could result from doing this, they argued, and *what right had we to withhold our information from her?* To what purpose had we acquired this information? We must prepare some sort of discreet digest for her of the information we had acquired. Certainly our very earliest records—Petyr van Abel's letters—should be made available to her, along with the genealogical tables we had made.

This precipitated a furious and acrimonious debate. Older members of the order reminded the younger ones that Carlotta Mayfair was in all probability responsible for the death of Stuart Townsend, and more than likely responsible for the death of her sister, Stella. What obligation could we possibly have to such a person? Antha was the person to whom we should make our disclosure, and such a thing could not even be considered until Antha reached the age of twenty-one.

Besides, in the absence of any guiding personal contact, how was information to be given to Carlotta Mayfair and what information could we possibly give?

The history of the Mayfair family as it existed in 1929 was in no way ready for "outside eyes." A discreet digest would have to be prepared, with the names of witnesses and investigators thoroughly expunged from the record, and once again, what would be the purpose of giving this to Carlotta? What would she do with it? How might she use it in regard to Antha? What would be her overall reaction? And if we were going to give this history to Carlotta, why not give it also to Cortland and his brothers? Indeed, why not give it to every member of the Mayfair family? And if we did do such a thing, what would be the effects of such information upon these people? What right had we to contemplate such a spectacular intervention in their lives?

Indeed, the nature of our history was so special, it included such bizarre and seemingly mysterious material, that no disclosure of it could be arbitrarily contemplated.

. . . And so on and on the debate raged.

As always at such times, the rules, the goals, and the ethics of the Talamasca were completely reevaluated. We were forced to reaffirm for ourselves that the history of the Mayfair family— due to its length and its detail—was invaluable to us as scholars of the occult, and that we were going to continue to gather information on the Mayfairs, no matter what the younger members of the council said about ethics and the like. But our attempt at "contact" had been an abysmal failure. We would wait until Antha Mayfair was twenty-one, and then a careful approach would be considered, depending upon who was available within the order for such an assignment at that time.

It also became clear as the council continued its wrangling

that almost no one there—Evan Neville included—really knew the full story of the Mayfair Witches. In fact there was considerable arguing not only about what to do and how it should be done, but about what had happened and when in the Mayfair family. For the file had simply become too big and too complicated for anyone to examine effectively within a reasonable period of time.

Obviously the Talamasca must find a member willing to take on the Mayfair Witches as a full-time assignment—someone able to study the file in detail and then make intelligent and responsible decisions about what to do in the field. And considering the tragic death of Stuart Townsend, it was determined that such a person must have first-rate scholarly credentials, as well as great field experience; indeed, he must prove his knowledge of the file by putting all of its materials into one long coherent and readable narrative. Then, and only then, would such a person be allowed to broaden his study of the Mayfair Witches by more direct investigation with a view to a contact eventually being made.

In sum, the enormous task of translating the file into a narrative was seen as a necessary preparation for field involvement. And there was great wisdom to this approach.

The one sad flaw in the whole plan was that such a person was not found by the order until 1953. And by that time Antha Mayfair's tragic life had come to a close. The designee of the legacy was a wan-faced twelve-year-old girl who had already been expelled from school for "talking with her invisible friend," and making flowers fly through the air, or finding lost objects, and reading minds.

"Her name is Deirdre," said Evan Neville, his face creased with worry and sadness, "and she is growing up in that gloomy old house just the way her mother did, alone with those old women, and God only knows what they know or believe about their history, and about her powers, and about this spirit who has already been seen at the child's side."

The young member, greatly inflamed by this and by earlier conversations, and much random reading of the Mayfair papers, decided he had better act fast.

As I myself, obviously, am that member, I shall now pause before relating the brief and sad story of Antha Mayfair, to introduce myself.

A complete biography of me is available under the heading Aaron Lightner. For the purposes of this narrative the following is more than sufficient.

I was born in London in 1921. I became a full member of the order in 1943, after I had finished my studies at Oxford. But I had been working with the Talamasca since the age of seven, and living in the Motherhouse since the age of fifteen.

Indeed, I had been brought to the attention of the order in 1928 by my English father (a Latin scholar and translator) and my American mother (a piano teacher) when I was six years old. It was a frightening telekinetic ability that precipitated their search for outside help. I could move objects just by concentrating upon them or telling them to move. And though this power was never very strong, it proved very disturbing to those who saw examples of it.

My concerned parents suspected that this power went along with other psychic traits, of which they had indeed seen an occasional glimpse. I was taken to several psychiatrists, on account of my strange abilities, and finally one of these said, "Take him to the Talamasca. His powers are genuine, and they are the only ones who can work with someone like this."

The Talamasca was more than willing to discuss the question with my parents, who were greatly relieved. "If you try to crush this power in your son," Evan Neville said, "you will get nowhere with him. Indeed you place his well-being at risk. Let us work with him. Let us teach him how to control and use his psychic abilities." Reluctantly my parents agreed.

I began to spend every Saturday at the Motherhouse outside of London, and by the age of ten I was spending weekends and summers there as well. My father and mother were frequent visitors. Indeed my father began doing translations for the Talamasca from its old crumbling Latin records in 1935, and worked with the order until his death in 1972, at which time he was a widower living in the Motherhouse. Both my parents loved the General Reference Library at the Motherhouse, and though they never sought official membership in the order, they were in a very real sense a part of it all their lives. They did not object when they saw me drawn into it, only insisting that I complete my education, and not allow my "special powers" to draw me prematurely away from "the normal world."

My telekinetic power never became very strong, but with the aid of my friends in the order, I became keenly aware that—

under certain circumstances—I could read people's thoughts. I also learned to veil my thoughts and feelings from others. I learned also how to introduce my powers to people when and where it was appropriate, and how to reserve them primarily for constructive use.

I have never been what anyone would call a powerful psychic. Indeed my limited mind-reading ability serves me best in my capacity as a field investigator for the Talamasca, particularly in situations which involve jeopardy. And my telekinetic ability is seldom called upon for anything of a practical nature.

By the time I was eighteen, I was devoted to the order's way of life and its goals. I could not easily conceive of a world without the Talamasca. My interests were the interests of the order, and I was completely compatible with its spirit. No matter where I went to school, no matter how much I traveled with my parents or with school friends, the order had become my true home.

When I completed my studies at Oxford, I was received into full membership, but I was really a member long before then. The great witch families had always been my chosen field. I had read extensively in the history of the witchcraft persecutions. And those persons fitting our particular definition of witch were of great fascination to me.

My first fieldwork was done in connection with a witch family in Italy, under the guidance of Elaine Barrett, who was at that time, and for many years later, the most able witch investigator in the order.

It was she who first introduced me to the Mayfair Witches, in a casual conversation over dinner, telling me firsthand of what had happened to Petyr van Abel, Stuart Townsend, and Arthur Langtry, and inviting me to begin my reading of the Mayfair materials in my spare time. Many a night during the summer and winter of 1945 I fell asleep with the Mayfair papers all over the floor of my bedroom. I was already jotting down notes for a narrative in 1946.

The year 1947, however, took me completely away from the Motherhouse and the File on the Mayfair Witches for work in the field with Elaine. I did not realize until later that these years provided me with precisely the field record I would need for the romance with the Mayfair Witches which would become my life's work.

I was given the assignment formally in 1953: begin the narrative; and when it is complete in acceptable form, we will discuss sending you to New Orleans to see the inhabitants of the First Street house for yourself.

Again and again, I was reminded that whatever my aspirations I would only be allowed to proceed with caution. Antha Mayfair had died violently. So had the father of her daughter, Deirdre. So had a Mayfair cousin from New York—Dr. Cornell Mayfair—who had come to New Orleans in 1945 expressly to see little eight-year-old Deirdre and investigate Carlotta's claim that Antha had been congenitally insane.

I accepted the terms of the assignment. I set to work translating the diary of Petyr van Abel. In the meantime, I was given an unlimited budget to amplify the research in any and all directions. So I also commenced a "long distance" investigation into the present state of things with twelve-year-old Deirdre Mayfair, Antha's only child.

I should like to add in conclusion that two factors apparently play a large role in any investigation which I undertake. The first of these seems to be that my personal manner and appearance put people at ease, almost unaccountably. They talk to me more freely perhaps than they might talk to someone else. How much I control this by any sort of "telepathic persuasion" is quite difficult or impossible to determine. In retrospect, I would say it has more to do with the fact that I appear to be "an Old World gentleman," and that people assume that I am basically good. I also empathize strongly with those I interview. I am in no way an antagonistic listener.

I hope and pray that in spite of the deceptions I have maintained in connection with my work that I have never really betrayed anyone's trust. To do good with what I know is my life's imperative.

The second factor which influences my interviews and fieldwork is my mild mind-reading ability. I frequently pick up names and details from people's thoughts. In general I do not include this information in my reports. It's too unreliable. But my telepathic discoveries have certainly provided me with significant "leads" over the years. And this trait is definitely connected with my keen ability to sense danger, as the following narrative will eventually reveal . . .

It is time now to return to the narrative, and to reconstruct the tragic tale of Antha's life and Deirdre's birth.

Antha Mayfair

With the death of Stella, an era ended for the Mayfairs. And the tragic history of Stella's daughter Antha, and her only child, Deirdre, remains shrouded in mystery to this day.

As the years passed, the household staff at First Street dwindled to a couple of silent, unreachable, and completely loyal servants; the outbuildings, no longer needed for housemaids and coachmen and stable boys, fell slowly into disrepair.

The women of First Street maintained a reclusive existence, Belle and Millie Dear becoming "sweet old ladies" of the Garden District as they walked to daily Mass at the Prytania Street chapel, or stopped in their ceaseless and ineffectual gardening to chat with neighbors passing the iron fence.

Only six months after her mother's death, Antha was expelled from a Canadian boarding school, which was the last public institution she was ever to attend. It was a surprisingly simple matter for a private investigator to learn from teacher gossip that Antha had frightened people with her mind reading, her talking to an invisible friend, and threats against those who ridiculed her or talked behind her back. She was described as a nervous girl, always crying, complaining of the cold in all kinds of weather, and subject to long unexplained fevers and chills.

Carlotta Mayfair took Antha home by train from Canada, and to the best of our knowledge, Antha never spent another night out of the First Street house until she was seventeen.

Nancy, a sullen, dumpy young woman, only two years older than Antha, continued to go to school every day until she was eighteen. At that point she went to work as a file clerk in Carlotta's law offices, where she worked for four years. Every morning, without fail, she and Carlotta walked from First and Chestnut to St. Charles Avenue, where they caught the St. Charles car for downtown.

By this time the First Street house had taken on an air of perpetual gloom. Its shutters were never opened. Its violet-gray paint began to peel, and its garden grew wild along the iron fences, with cherry laurels and rain trees sprouting among the old camellias and gardenias, which had been so carefully tended years before. When the old unoccupied stable burned to the ground in 1938, weeds soon filled up the open space at the back of the property. Another dilapidated building was razed shortly after, and nothing remained but the old *garçonnières*, and one great and beautiful oak, its branches poignantly outstretched above the wild grass towards the distant main house.

In 1934, we started to receive the first reports from workmen who found it impossible to complete repairs or other jobs on the house. The Molloy brothers told everyone in Corona's Bar on Magazine Street that they couldn't paint that place because every time they turned around their ladders were on the ground, or their paint was spilled, or their brushes somehow got knocked in the dirt. "It must have happened six times," said Davey Molloy, "that my paint just went right over, off the ladder, and poured out on the ground. Now, I know I never knocked over a full paint can! And that's what she said to me, Miss Carlotta, she said, 'You knocked it over yourself.' Well, when that ladder went over with me on it, I tell you, that was it. I quit."

Davey's brother, Thompson Molloy, had a theory as to who was responsible. "It's that brown-haired fella, the one who was always watching us. I told Miss Carlotta, 'Don't you think he could be doing it? That fella that's always over there under the tree?' She acted like she didn't know what I was talking about. But he was always watching us. We were trying to patch the wall on Chestnut Street and I seen him looking at us through the library shutters. Gave me the creeps, it did. Who is he? Is he one of them cousins? I'm not working there. I don't care how bad times are. I'm not working on that house again."

Another workman, hired only to paint the black cast-iron railings, reported the same "goings-on." He gave up after half a day during which time debris fell on him from the roof and leaves constantly fell into his paint.

By 1935, it was common knowledge in the Irish Channel that nothing could be done "on that old house." When a couple of young men were hired to clean out the pool that same year, one of them was knocked into the stagnant water and almost drowned. The other had a hell of a time getting him out. "It was like I couldn't see anything. I had a hold of him, and I was hollering for somebody to help me, and we were going down in all that muck, and then thank God he had a hold of the side and he was saving me. That old colored woman, Aunt Easter, come out there with a towel for us and she hollered, 'Just get away from that swimming pool. Never mind cleaning it. Just get away.'"

Even Irwin Dandrich heard the gossip. "They're saying it's haunted, that Stella's spirit won't let anyone touch anything. It's as if the whole place is in mourning for Stella." Had Dandrich heard of a mysterious brown-haired man? "I hear all kinds of things. Some say it's Julien's ghost. That he's keeping an eye on Antha. Well, if he is, he isn't doing a very good job.''

Shortly thereafter a vague story appeared in the *Times-Picayune* describing a ''mysterious uptown mansion'' where no work could be done. Dandrich clipped it and sent it to London with the note ''My Big Mouth'' in the margin.

One of our investigators took the reporter to lunch. She was happy to talk about it, and yes indeed it was the Mayfair house. Everyone knew it. A plumber said he was trapped under that house for hours when he tried to fix a pipe. He actually lost consciousness. When he finally came to himself and got out of there, he had to be taken to the hospital. Then there was the telephone man who was called to fix a phone in the library. He said he would never set foot in that house again. One of the portraits on the wall had actually looked at him. And he thought sure he saw a ghost in that very room.

''I could have written a great deal more,'' said the young woman, ''but the people at the paper don't want any trouble with Carlotta Mayfair. Did I tell you about the gardener? He goes in there regularly to cut the grass, you know, and he said the weirdest thing when I called him. He said, 'Oh, *he* never bothers me. He and I get along just fine. He and I are just real regular friends.' Now, who do you suppose this man was referring to? When I asked him he said, 'You just go up there. You'll see him. He's been there forever. My grandfather used to see him. He's all right. He can't move or talk to you. He just stands there looking at you from the shadows. One minute you see him. Then he's gone. He don't bother me. He's all right by me. I get paid plenty to work there. I've always worked there. He don't frighten me.''

Family gossip of the period dismissed the ''ghost stories.'' So did uptown society, according to Dandrich, though he implied he thought that people were naive.

''I think Carlotta herself started all those silly ghost stories,'' said one of the cousins years after. ''She wanted to keep people away. We just laughed when we heard it.''

''Ghosts at First Street? Carlotta was responsible for that house becoming a ruin. She always was penny-wise and pound-foolish. That's the difference between her and her mother.''

But whatever the attitudes of the cousins and the local society, the priests at the Redemptorist rectory heard countless stories of ghosts and mysterious mischief at First Street. Father Lafferty called regularly at First Street, and rumor had it that he would not allow himself to be turned away.

His sister told one of our investigators, ''My brother knew

plenty about what was going on, but he never gossiped about it. I asked him how Antha was doing, and he wouldn't answer me. But I know he saw Antha. He got into that house. After Antha died, he came over here one Sunday, and he just put his head on his arms on the dining table and he cried. That's the only time I ever saw my brother, Father Thomas Lafferty, break down and cry.''

The family remained concerned about Antha throughout this period. The official story was that Antha was ''insane,'' and that Carlotta was always taking her to psychiatrists, but that ''it didn't do any good.'' The child had been irreparably shocked by the shooting of her mother. She lived in a fantasy world of ghosts and invisible companions. She could not be left unattended; she could not visit outside the house.

Legal gossip indicates that the cousins frequently called Cortland Mayfair to beg him to look in on Antha, but that Cortland was no longer welcome at First Street. Neighbors report seeing him turned away several times.

''He used to go up there every Christmas Eve,'' said one of the neighbors much later. ''His car would pull up at the front gate, and his driver would hop out and open the door, and then take all the presents out of the trunk. Lots and lots of presents. Then Carlotta would come out and shake hands with him on the steps. He never got inside that house.''

The Talamasca has never found any record of doctors who saw Antha. It is doubtful Antha was ever taken outside the house except to go to Sunday Mass. Neighbors reported seeing her frequently in the garden at First Street.

She read her books under the big oak at the rear of the property; she sat for hours on the side gallery, her elbows on her knees.

A maid who worked across the street reported seeing her talking to ''that man all the time, you know that browned-haired man, he is always up there to see her, must be one of the cousins, and he sure do dress nice.''

By the time Antha reached the age of fifteen, she sometimes went out the gate by herself. A mail carrier mentioned seeing her often, a thin girl with a dreamy expression walking alone and sometimes with a ''good-looking young fella'' through the streets. ''The good-looking fella'' had brown hair and brown eyes, and was always dressed in a suitcoat and tie.

''They liked to scare the hell out of me,'' said a local milkman. ''One time I was just whistling to myself, coming out of the gate of Dr. Milton's house on Second Street, and there they were just right in front of me, under the magnolia tree, in the shadows, and she was real still, and he was standing beside her. I nearly ran into them. I think they were just sort of whispering together, and maybe I scared her as bad as she scared me.''

There are no photographs in our files from this period. But all these witnesses and others describe Antha as pretty.

''She had a remote look to her,'' said a woman who used to see her at the chapel. ''She wasn't vibrant like Stella; she always seemed wrapped in her dreams, and to tell you the truth, I felt sorry for her all alone in that house with those women. Don't quote me on this but that Carlotta is a mean person. She really is. My maid and my cook knew all about her. They said she would grab that girl by the wrist and dig her nails into her flesh.''

Irwin Dandrich reported that old friends of Stella's tried to call on the girl from time to time, only to be turned away. ''No one gets past Nancy or the colored maid, Aunt Easter,'' Dandrich wrote to the London investigators. ''And the talk is that Antha is a veritable prisoner in that house.''

Other than these few glimpses, we know virtually nothing of Antha during the years 1930 to 1938, and it seems nobody in the family knew much of her either. But we can safely conclude that all the references to the ''brown-haired man'' apply to Lasher; and if this is the case, *we have more sightings of Lasher during this period than for all the decades before.*

Indeed, the sightings of Lasher are so numerous that our investigators got in the habit of merely jotting down notes such as ''Maid working on Third Street says she saw Antha and the man walking together.'' Or ''Woman on First and Prytania saw Antha standing under the oak tree talking to the man.''

The First Street house had now taken on an air of sinister mystery even for the descendants of Rémy Mayfair and of Suzette's brothers and sisters, who had once been quite close.

Then, in April of 1938, neighbors witnessed a violent family quarrel at First Street. Windows were broken, people heard screaming, and finally a distraught young woman, clutching only a shoulder bag of a purse, was seen running out the front gate and towards St. Charles Avenue. Without question it was Antha. Even the neighbors knew that much, and they watched from behind lace curtains as a police car pulled up only moments after and Carlotta went to the curb to confer with the two officers who drove off at once, siren screaming, apparently to catch the errant girl.

That night Mayfairs in New York received phone calls from Carlotta, informing them that Antha had run away from home and was headed for Manhattan. Would they help with the search? It was these New York cousins who told the family in New Orleans. Cousins called cousins. Within days Irwin Dandrich wrote to London that "poor little Antha" had made her bid for freedom. She had run off to New York City. But how far would she ever get?

As it turned out, Antha got quite far.

For months no one knew the whereabouts of Antha Mayfair. Police, private investigators, and family members failed to find a clue to Antha's whereabouts. Carlotta made three separate train trips to New York during this period, and offered substantial rewards to anyone in the New York police department who could offer help in the search. She called on Amanda Grady Mayfair, who had only recently left her husband, Cortland, and actually threatened Amanda.

As Amanda told our "undercover" society investigator later, "It was simply dreadful. She asked me to meet her for lunch at the Waldorf. Well, of course I didn't want to do it. Rather like going into a cage at the zoo to have lunch with a lion. But I knew she was all upset about Antha, and I suppose I wanted to give her a piece of my mind. I wanted to tell her that she had driven Antha away, that she never should have isolated that poor little girl from her uncles and aunts and cousins who loved her.

"But, as soon as I sat down at the table, she started to threaten me. 'Let me tell you, Amanda, if you are harboring Antha I can make trouble for you that you won't believe.' I wanted to throw my drink in her face. I was furious. I said, 'Carlotta Mayfair, don't you ever talk to me again, don't you ever call me, or write to me, or come to my home. I had enough of you in New Orleans. I had enough of what your family did to Pierce and to Cortland. Don't you ever ever come near me again.' I tell you the smoke was coming out of my ears when I left the Waldorf. But you know, it is a regular technique with Carlotta. She makes an accusation as soon as she sees you. She's been doing it for years, really. That way, you don't have a chance to make an accusation against her."

In the winter of 1939, our investigators located Antha in a very simple way. Elaine Barrett, our witchcraft scholar, in a routine meeting with Evan Neville suggested that Antha must have financed her escape with the famous Mayfair jewels and gold coins. Why not try the shops in New York where such items could be sold for quick money? Antha was located within the month.

Indeed, she had been selling rare and exquisite gold coins steadily to support herself since her arrival in 1939. Every coin dealer in New York knew her—the beautiful young woman with the fine manners and the cheerful smile who always brought in the rarest of merchandise, taken from a family collection in Virginia, she said.

"At first I thought her stuff was stolen," said one coin dealer. "I mean these were three of the finest French coins I'd ever seen. I gave her a fraction of what they were worth and just waited. But absolutely nothing happened. When I made the sale, I saved her a percentage. And when she brought me some marvelous Roman coins, I paid her what they were worth. Now she's a regular. I'd rather deal with her than some of the other people who come in here, I'll tell you that much."

It was a simple thing to follow Antha from one of these shops to a large apartment on Christopher Street in Greenwich Village where she had been living with Sean Lacy, a handsome young Irish-American painter who showed considerable promise and had already exhibited with some critical approval several pieces of his work. Antha herself had become a writer. Everyone in the building and on the block knew the young couple. Our investigators collected reams of information almost overnight.

Antha was the sole support of Sean Lacy, friends said openly. She bought him anything he wanted, and he treated her like a queen. "He calls her his Southern Belle, actually, does everything for her. But then why shouldn't he?" The apartment was "a wonderful place," full of bookshelves to the ceiling, and big old comfortable overstuffed chairs.

"Sean has never painted so well. He's done three portraits of her, all of them very interesting. And you can hear Antha's typewriter going constantly. She sold one story, I heard, to some little literary magazine in Ohio. They threw a party over that one. She was so happy. She really is a little on the naive side. But she's a swell kid."

"She'd be a good writer if she'd write about what she knows," said one young woman in a bar who claimed to have once been Sean's lover. "But she writes these morbid fantasies about an old violet-colored house in New Orleans and a ghost who lives there—all very high-pitched, and hardly what will sell. She really ought to get away from all that rot and write about her experiences here in New York."

Neighbors were fond of the young couple. "She can't cook or do anything practical," reported a female painter who lived above them, "but then why should she? She pays all the bills as it is. I asked Sean one time wherever does she get her money? He said she had a bottomless purse. All she ever had to do was reach in it. Then he laughed."

Finally in the winter of 1940, Elaine Barrett, writing from London, urged our most responsible private investigator in New

York to attempt to interview Antha. Elaine wanted desperately to go to New York herself, but it was out of the question. So she talked directly by phone to Allan Carver, a suave and sophisticated man who had worked for us for many years. Carver was a well-dressed and well-mannered gentleman of fifty. He found it a simple matter to make contact. A pleasure, in fact.

"I followed her to the Metropolitan Museum of Art, then happened upon her as she was sitting in front of one of the Rembrandts, just staring at it, rather lost in her thoughts. She is pretty, quite pretty, but very Bohemian. She was all wrapped up in wool that day, with her hair loose. I sat down beside her, flashed a copy of Hemingway's short stories, and engaged her in conversation about him. Yes, she'd read Hemingway and she loved him. Did she love Rembrandt? Yes, she did. How about New York in general? Oh, she loved living here. She never wanted to be anyplace else. The city of New York was a person to her. She had never been so happy as she was now.

"There wasn't a chance of getting her out of there with me. She was too guarded, too proper. So I made the most of it as quickly as I could.

"I got her talking about herself, her life, her husband, and her writing. Yes, she wanted to be a writer. And Sean wanted her to be. Sean wouldn't be happy unless she was successful too. 'You know, the only thing I can be is a writer,' she said. 'I'm absolutely unprepared for anything else. When you've lived the kind of life I have, you are good for nothing. Only writing can save you.' It was all very touching actually, the way she spoke about it. She seemed altogether defenseless and absolutely genuine. I think, had I been thirty years younger, I would have fallen in love with her.

" 'But what kind of life did you have?' I pressed her. 'I can't place your accent. But I know you're not from New York.'

" 'Down south,' she said. 'It's another world.' She grew sad instantly, even agitated. 'I want to forget all that,' she said, 'I don't mean to be rude, but I've made this rule for myself. I'll write about my past but I won't talk about it. I'll turn it into art if I can, but I won't talk about it. I won't give it life here, outside of art, if you follow what I mean.'

"I found this rather clever and interesting. I liked her. I cannot tell you how much I liked her. And you know, in my line of work, one gets so accustomed to just using people!

" 'Well, then tell me about what you write,' I begged. 'Just tell me about one of your stories for instance, assuming you write stories, or tell me about your poems.'

" 'If they're any good, you'll read them some day,' she said, and then she gave me a parting smile and left. I think she'd become suspicious. I don't know really. She was glancing around in a rather defensive way the whole time we talked. I even asked her at one point if she was expecting someone. She said not really, but 'You never know.' She acted as if she thought someone was watching her. And of course my people were watching her all the time. I felt pretty uncomfortable about it at that moment, I can tell you.''

Reports continued to pour in for months that Antha and Sean were happy. Sean, a big burly individual with an endearing sense of humor, had a one-man show in the Village which was quite a success. Antha had a short poem (seven lines) in *The New Yorker*. The couple were ecstatic. Only in April of 1941 did the gossip change.

''Well, she's pregnant,'' said the upstairs painter, ''and he doesn't want the baby, you know, and of course she wants it and God knows what's going to happen. He knows a doctor who can take care of it, you see, but she won't hear of it. I hate to see her going through this, really. She's much too fragile. I hear her crying down there in the night.''

On July 1, Sean Lacy died in a single car accident (mechanical failure) coming back from a visit to his ailing mother in upstate New York. A hysterical Antha had to be hospitalized at Bellevue. ''We just didn't know what to do with her,'' said the upstairs painter. ''For eight hours straight she screamed. Finally we called Bellevue. I'll never know if we did the right thing.''

Records at Bellevue indicate Antha stopped screaming or indeed making any sound or movement as soon as she was admitted. She remained catatonic for over a week. Then she wrote the name ''Cortland Mayfair'' on a slip of paper, along with the words ''Attorney, New Orleans.'' Cortland's firm was contacted at ten-thirty the following morning. At once Cortland called his estranged wife, Amanda Grady Mayfair, in New York and begged her to go to Bellevue and see to Antha until he could get there himself.

A horrid battle then began between Cortland and Carlotta, Cortland insisting that he should take care of Antha because Antha had sent for him. Contemporary gossip tells us Carlotta and Cortland took the train together to New York to get Antha and bring her home.

At an emotional drunken lunch, Amanda Grady Mayfair poured out the whole story to her friend (and our informant) Allan Carver, who made it a point to inquire about her old southern family and its gothic goings-on. Amanda told him all about the poor little niece in Bellevue:

". . . It was simply awful. Antha couldn't talk. She couldn't. She'd tried to say something and she'd simply stammer. She was so fragile. The death of Sean had destroyed her utterly. It was twenty-four hours before she wrote down the address of the apartment in Greenwich Village. I went there immediately with Ollie Mayfair, you know, one of Rémy's grandchildren, and we got Antha's things. Oh, it was so sad. Of course all Sean's paintings belonged to Antha, as she was his wife, I supposed; but then the neighbors came in and they told us Antha had never married Sean. Sean's mother and brother had already been there. They were coming back with a truck to take everything away. Seems that Sean's mother despised Antha because she believed Antha had led her son into this Greenwich Village artist life.

"I told Ollie, well, they can have everything else but they aren't taking the portraits of Antha. I took those and all her clothes and things, and this old velvet purse filled with gold coins. Now, I'd heard of that purse, and don't tell me you haven't if you know the Mayfairs. And her writings, oh, yes, her writings. I packed up all of that—her stories, and chapters of a novel, and some poems she'd written. And do you know later on I found out she'd published a poem in *The New Yorker*. *The New Yorker*. But I didn't find out about that until my son, Pierce, told me. And he went to the library and looked it up. It was very brief, something about snow falling and the museum in the park. Not what I would call a poem, actually. Rather a little bit of life, so to speak. But she was published in *The New Yorker*. That is the point. It was so sad taking everything out of that apartment. You know, dismantling a life.

"When I got back to the hospital, Carlotta and Cortland were already there. They were fighting with each other in the hallway. But you had to see and hear a fight between Carl and Cort to believe it, it was all whispers, and little gestures, and tight lips. It was really something. But there they stood, talking to each other like that and I knew they were ready to kill each other.

" 'That girl's pregnant you know,' I said. 'Did the doctors tell you?'

" 'She ought to get rid of it,' Carl said. I thought Cortland was going to die. I was so shocked myself I didn't know what to say.

"I absolutely hate Carlotta. I don't care who knows it. I hate her. I have hated her all my life. It gives me nightmares to think of her being alone with Antha. I told Cortland right there in front of her, 'That girl needs care.'

"But Cortland had tried to get custody of Antha, he had tried it in the very beginning, and Carlotta had threatened to fight him, to expose all kinds of things about us, she said. Oh, she is dreadful. And Cortland had given up. And I think he knew he wasn't going to get control of Antha now. 'Look, Antha's a woman now,' I said. 'Ask her where she wants to go. If she wants to stay in New York she can stay with me. She can stay with Ollie.' Not a chance!

"Carlotta went in to talk to those doctors. She did her routine. She managed some sort of official transfer of Antha to a mental hospital in New Orleans. She ignored Cortland as if he wasn't even there. I got on the phone to all the cousins in New Orleans. I called everyone. I even called young Beatrice Mayfair on Esplanade Avenue—Rémy's granddaughter. I told them that child was sick, and she was pregnant and she needed loving care.

"Then the most sad thing happened. They were taking Antha to the train station, and she gestured for me to come over to her, and she whispered in my ear. 'Save my things for me, please, Aunt Mandy. She'll throw them all away if you don't,' and to think I had already shipped all her things back home. I called my son Sheffield and told him about it. I said, 'Sheff, do what you can for her when she gets back.' "

Antha traveled back to Louisiana by train with her uncle and her aunt, and was immediately committed to St. Ann's Asylum, where she remained for six weeks. Numerous Mayfair cousins came to see her. Family gossip indicated she was pale and at times incoherent but that she was coming along just fine.

In New York, our investigator Allan Carver arranged another chance meeting with Amanda Grady Mayfair. "How is the little niece coming along?"

"Oh, I could tell you the worst story!" said Amanda Grady Mayfair. "You cannot imagine. Do you know that girl's aunt told the doctors in the asylum she wanted them to abort the girl's baby? That she was congenitally insane and must never be allowed to have a child? Have you ever heard anything worse? When my husband told me that I told him if you don't do something now, I'll never forgive you. Of course he said no one was going to hurt that baby. The doctors weren't going to do such a thing, not for Carlotta, not for anyone. Then when I called Beatrice Mayfair on Esplanade Avenue and told her all about it, Cortland was furious. 'Don't get everybody up in arms,' he said. But that is exactly what I meant to do. I told Bea, 'Go see her. Don't let anyone keep you out.' "

The Talamasca has never been able to corroborate the story about the proposed abortion. But nurses at St. Ann's later told our investigators that scores of Mayfair cousins came to see Antha at the asylum.

"They are not taking no for an answer," Irwin Dandrich wrote. "They insist upon seeing her, and by all reports she is doing well. She is excited about her baby, and of course they have deluged her with presents. Her young cousin, Beatrice, brought her some antique lace baby clothes that had once belonged to somebody's Great-aunt Suzette. Of course, it is common knowledge here that Antha never married the New York artist; but then what does it matter when your name is Mayfair, and Mayfair it will always be."

The cousins proved just as aggressive after Antha was released from St. Ann's and came home to First Street to convalesce in Stella's old bedroom on the north side of the house. She had nurses with her round the clock, and obtaining information from them proved very simple for our investigators.

The place was described as "insufferably dreary." But Millie Dear and Belle took excellent care of Antha. In fact, they didn't leave the nurses much to do at all. Millie Dear sat with Antha all the time on the little upstairs porch outside her bedroom. And Belle knitted beautiful clothes for the baby.

Cortland stopped by every evening after work. "The lady of the house didn't want him there, I don't believe," said one of the nurses. "But he came. Without fail he came. He and another young gentleman, I believe his name was Sheffield. They sat with the patient every night for a little while and talked."

Family gossip said that Sheffield had read some of Antha's writings from the New York days, and that Antha was "very good." The nurses talked about the boxes from New York—crates of books and papers, which Antha examined but was too weak in general to truly unpack.

"I don't really see anything mentally wrong with her," said one of the nurses. "The aunt takes us out in the hallway and asks us the strangest questions. She implies the girl is congenitally insane, and may harm someone. But the doctors didn't say anything to us about it. She's a quiet, melancholy girl. She looks and sounds much younger than she is. But she's not what I would call insane."

Deirdre Mayfair was born on October 4, 1941, at the old Mercy Hospital on the river, which was later torn down. Apparently the birth presented no particular difficulty, and Antha was heavily anesthetized as was the custom in those days. Mayfairs packed the corridors of the hospital during visiting hours for the entire five days that Antha was there. Her room was full of flowers. The baby was a beautiful healthy little girl.

But the flow of information, so dramatically increased with the involvement of Amanda Grady Mayfair, came to an abrupt halt two weeks after Antha returned home. The cousins found themselves turned away by the black maid, Aunt Easter, or by Nancy when they came for their second and third visits. Indeed, Nancy had quit her job as a file clerk to take care of the baby ("Or to lock us out!" said Beatrice to Amanda long distance) and she was adamant that the mother and the baby not be disturbed.

When Beatrice called to inquire about the christening, she was told the baby had already been baptized at St. Alphonsus. Outraged, she called Amanda in New York. Some twenty of the cousins "crashed" the house on a Sunday afternoon.

"Antha was overjoyed to see them!" said Amanda to Allan Carver. "She was simply thrilled. She had no idea they'd been calling and dropping by. No one had even told her. She didn't know people gave parties for a christening. Carlotta had arranged everything. She was hurt when she realized what had happened, and everyone changed the subject at once. But Beatrice was furious with Nancy. But Nancy is just doing what Carlotta told her to do."

On October 30 of that year, Antha was officially declared the recipient and full manager of the Mayfair legacy. She signed a power of attorney naming Cortland and Sheffield Mayfair as her legal representatives in all matters concerning the money; and she requested that they immediately establish a large trust for the management of the "restoration" of the First Street house. She expressed concern about the condition of the entire property.

Legal gossip says that Antha was stunned to discover that she owned the place. She had never had the slightest idea. She wanted to redecorate, paint, restore everything.

Carlotta was not at Antha's meeting with her uncles. Carlotta had demanded of the law firm of Mayfair and Mayfair that they provide her with a complete audit on behalf of Antha of everything that had been done since Stella's death, saying that the present records were inadequate, and she refused to participate in any sort of legal discussion until she received this audit "for review."

Sheffield told his mother, Amanda, later, that Antha had been deliberately misled with regard to the legacy. She seemed hurt and even a little shocked as things were explained to her. And it was Carlotta who had hurt her. But all she would say was that Carlotta had probably had her good in mind all along.

The party went for a late lunch at Galatoire's to celebrate. Antha was nervous about leaving the baby, but she seemed to have a good time. As they were leaving, Sheffield heard her ask his father the following question: "Then you mean she couldn't have thrown me out of the house if she had wanted to? She couldn't have put me on the street?"

"It's your house, *ma chérie*," Cortland told her. "She has permission to live there, but that is subject entirely to your approval."

Antha looked so sad. "She used to threaten me," she said under her breath. "She used to say she'd put me in the street if I didn't do what she said."

Cortland then took Antha away from the party and drove her home alone.

Antha and the baby went to lunch a few days later with Beatrice Mayfair at another fashionable French Quarter restaurant. A nurse was on hand to take the baby walking in its beautiful white wicker buggy while the two women enjoyed their wine and fish. When Beatrice described it all to Amanda later she told her Antha had really become a young woman. Antha was writing again. She was working on a novel, and she was going to have the First Street house completely fixed up.

She wanted to repair the swimming pool. She talked about her mother a little, how her mother had loved to give big parties. She seemed full of life.

Indeed, several contractors were approached to give estimates for "a complete restoration, including painting, carpentry repairs and some masonry work." Neighbors were delighted to hear this from the servants. Dandrich wrote that a distinguished architectural firm had been consulted about rebuilding the carriage house.

Antha wrote a brief letter to Amanda Grady Mayfair in mid-November, thanking her for her help in New York. She thanked her for forwarding the mail from Greenwich Village. She said that she was writing short stories, and working on her novel again.

When Mr. Bordreaux, the mailman, passed on his regular rounds at nine A.M. on December 10, Antha was waiting for him at the gate. She had several large manila envelopes ready to go to New York. Could she buy the postage from him? They made a guess at the weight—she said she couldn't leave the baby to go to the post office—and he took the packages with him. Antha also gave him a bundle of regular mail for various New York addresses.

"She was all excited," he said. "She was going to be a writer. Such a sweet girl. And I'll never forget. I made some remark about the bombing of Pearl Harbor, that my son had enlisted the day before, and now we were in the war at last. And do you know? She'd never heard a thing about it. She didn't even know about the bombing, or the war. Just like she was living in a dream."

The "sweet girl" died that very afternoon. When the same postman came around with the afternoon mail at three-thirty, there was a cloudburst over that area of the Garden District. It was raining "cats and dogs." Yet a crowd was assembled in the Mayfair garden, and the undertaker's wagon was in the middle of the street. The wind was blowing "something fierce." Mr. Bordreaux hung around in spite of the weather.

"Miss Belle was on the porch sobbing. And Miss Millie tried to tell me what was happening but she couldn't say a word. Then Miss Nancy came to the edge of the porch and shouted at me. 'You go on, Mr. Bordreaux. We've had a death here. You go on and get out of the rain.' "

Mr. Bordreaux crossed the street and sought shelter on the porch of a neighboring house. The housekeeper told him through the screen door that it was Antha Mayfair who was dead. She'd apparently fallen from the third-floor porch roof.

The storm was terrible, said the mailman, a regular hurricane. Yet he remained to watch as a body was put into the undertaker's wagon. Red Lonigan was there, with his cousin Leroy Lonigan. Then the wagon drove away. Finally Mr. Bordreaux went back to delivering the mail, and very soon, about the time he reached Prytania Street, the weather had cleared up. When he passed the next day the sidewalk was littered with leaves.

Over the years, the Talamasca has collected numerous stories connected with Antha's death, but what actually happened on the afternoon of December 10, 1941, may never be known. Mr. Bordreaux was the last "outsider" ever to see or speak with Antha. The baby's nurse, an elderly woman named Alice Flanagan, had called in sick that day.

What is known from the police records and from guarded talk emanating from the Lonigan family and the priests of the parish is that Antha jumped or fell from the porch roof outside the attic window of Julien's old room some time before three P.M.

Carlotta's story, gleaned from these same sources, was as follows:

She had been arguing with the girl about the baby, because Antha had deteriorated to such a point that she was not even feeding the child.

"She was in no way prepared to be a mother," said Miss Carlotta to the police officer. Antha spent hours typing letters and stories and poetry, and Nancy and the others had to beat on the door of the room to make her realize that Deirdre was crying in the cradle and needed to be given a bottle or nursed.

Antha became "hysterical" during this last argument. She ran up the two flights of steps to the attic, screaming to be left alone. Carlotta, fearing that Antha would hurt herself—which she often did, according to Carlotta—pursued her into Julien's old room. There Carlotta discovered that Antha had tried to scratch her own eyes out, and indeed had succeeded in drawing considerable blood.

When Carlotta tried to control her, Antha broke away, falling backwards through the window, and onto the roof of the cast-iron porch. She apparently crawled to the edge of it, and then lost her balance or deliberately jumped. She died instantly when her head struck the flagstones three stories below.

Cortland was beside himself when he learned of his niece's death. He went immediately to First Street. What he told his wife in New York later was that Carlotta was absolutely distraught. The priest was with her, a Father Kevin, from the Redemptorist Parish. Carlotta said over and over that nobody understood how fragile Antha had been. "I tried to stop her!" Carlotta said. "What in the name of God was I expected to do!" Millie Dear and Belle were too upset to talk about it. Belle seemed to be confusing it all with the death of Stella. Only Nancy had frankly disagreeable things to say, complaining that Antha had been spoiled and sheltered all her life, that her head was full of silly dreams.

When Alice Flanagan, the nurse, was contacted by Cortland, she seemed afraid. She was elderly, and partially blind. She said she didn't know anything about Antha's ever hurting herself or becoming hysterical or anything like that. She took her orders from Miss Carlotta. Miss Carlotta had been good to her family. Miss Flanagan didn't want to lose her job. "I just want to take care of that darling baby," she told the police. "That darling baby needs me now."

Indeed she took care of Deirdre Mayfair until the girl was five years old.

Finally, Cortland told Beatrice and Amanda to leave Carlotta in peace. Carlotta was the only witness to what had happened. And whatever had gone on that afternoon, surely Antha's death had been a terrible accident. What could anyone do?

No true investigation followed the death of Antha. There had been no autopsy. When the undertaker became suspicious after examining the corpse and concluding that Antha's facial scratches were not self-inflicted, he contacted the family doctor and was advised or told to let the matter drop. Antha was insane, that was the unofficial verdict. All her life she had been unstable.

She had been committed to Bellevue and St. Ann's Asylum. She had depended upon others to care for her and her child.

After Stella's death, the Mayfair emerald was never mentioned in connection with Antha. No relative or friend ever reported seeing it. Sean Lacy never painted Antha with it. No one in New York had ever heard of it.

But when Antha died she had the emerald around her neck.

The question is obvious. Why was Antha wearing the emerald on that day of all days? Was it the wearing of the emerald that precipitated the fatal argument? And if the scratch marks on Antha's face were not self-inflicted, did Carlotta try to scratch out Antha's eyes, and if so why?

Whatever the case, the house on First Street was once again shrouded in secrecy. Antha's plans for a restoration were never carried out. After furious arguments in the offices of Mayfair and Mayfair—Carlotta stormed out once, actually breaking the glass on the door—Cortland went so far as to petition the court for custody of baby Deirdre. Clay Mayfair's grandson Alexander also came forward. He and his wife, Eileen, had a lovely mansion in Metairie. They could officially adopt the child or just take her informally, whatever Carlotta would allow.

Amanda Grady Mayfair told our undercover society man, Allan Carver, ''Cortland wants me to go home to take care of the baby. I tell you I feel so sorry for that baby. But I can't go back to New Orleans after all these years.''

Carlotta all but laughed in the face of these ''do-gooders,'' as she called them. She told the judge and indeed anyone in the family who asked her that Antha had been gravely ill. It was a congenital insanity, without question, and might well surface in Antha's little girl. She had no intention of allowing anyone to take Deirdre out of her mother's house, or away from darling Miss Flanagan, or from dear sweet Belle, or darling Millie, all of whom adored the child, and had time on their hands to care for her day in and day out as no one else could.

When Cortland refused to back down, Carlotta threatened him directly. His wife had left him, hadn't she? Wouldn't the family like to know after all these years just what sort of a man Cortland was? Cousins pondered her slurs and innuendoes. The judge in the case became ''impatient.'' To his mind, Carlotta Mayfair was a woman of impeccable virtue and excellent judgment. Why couldn't this family accept the situation? Good Lord, if every orphan baby had aunts as sweet as Millie and Belle and Carlotta, this would be a better world.

The legacy was left in the hands of Mayfair and Mayfair, and the child was left in the hands of Carlotta. And the matter was abruptly closed.

Only one other assault on Carlotta's authority was ever attempted. It was in 1945.

Cornell Mayfair, one of the New York cousins and a descendant of Lestan, had just finished his residency at Massachusetts General. He was training to be a psychiatrist. He had heard "incredible stories" about the First Street house from his cousin (by marriage) Amanda Grady Mayfair. And also from Louisa Ann Mayfair, Garland's eldest granddaughter who went to Radcliffe and had an affair with Cornell while she was there. What was all this talk of congenital insanity? Cornell was fascinated. Also he was still in love with Louisa Ann, who had gone back to New Orleans rather than marry him and live in Massachusetts, and he could not understand the girl's devotion to her home. He wanted to visit New Orleans and the family at First Street, and the New York cousins thought it was a good idea.

"Who knows?" he told Amanda over lunch at the Waldorf. "Maybe I'll like the city, and maybe Louisa Ann and I can somehow work things out."

On February 11, Cornell came to New Orleans, checking into a downtown hotel. He begged Carlotta to talk to him and she agreed to let him come uptown.

As he later told Amanda by long distance, he remained at the house for perhaps two hours, visiting with little four-year-old Deirdre alone for some of that time. "I can't tell you what I've found out," he said. "But that child has to be removed from this environment. And frankly I don't want Louisa Ann involved. I'll tell you the whole thing when I get back to New York."

Amanda insisted that he call Cortland, that he tell Cortland all about his concerns. Cornell confessed that Louisa Ann had suggested the same thing.

"I don't want to do that just now," said Cornell. "I've just had a bellyful of Carlotta. I don't want to meet any more of these people this afternoon."

Trusting that Cortland could be of help, Amanda called him and told him what was going on. Cortland appreciated Dr. Mayfair's interest. He called Amanda later that afternoon to tell her he had made an appointment with Cornell for dinner at Kolb's downtown. He'd call her after they had talked together, but as things stood now, he liked the young doctor. He was eager to hear what he had to say.

Cornell never kept the appointment for dinner. Cortland waited for an hour at Kolb's Restaurant and then rang Cornell's room.

No answer. The following morning, the hotel maid found Cornell's dead body. He lay fully dressed on a rumpled bed, eyes half open, a half full glass of bourbon on the table at his side. No immediate cause of death could be found.

When an autopsy was performed, at the behest of Cornell's mother as well as the New Orleans coroner, Cornell was found to have a small amount of a strong narcotic, mixed with alcohol, in his veins. It was ruled an accidental overdose and never investigated further. Amanda Grady Mayfair never forgave herself for sending young Dr. Cornell Mayfair to New Orleans. Louisa Ann "never recovered" and is to this day unmarried. A distraught Cortland accompanied the coffin back to New York.

Was Cornell a casualty of the Mayfair Witches? Once more we are forced to say that we do not know. One detail, however, gives us some indication that Cornell did not die from the small amount of narcotic and alcohol in his blood. The coroner who examined Cornell's body before it was removed from the hotel room noted that Cornell's eyes were full of hemorrhaged blood vessels. We now know that this is a symptom of asphyxiation. It is possible that someone severely disabled Cornell by slipping a drug into his drink (bourbon was found in the glass on the table), and then smothered him with a pillow when he could not defend himself.

By the time the Talamasca attempted to investigate this case (through a reputable private detective), the trail was cold. No one at the hotel could remember if Cornell Mayfair had had any callers that afternoon. Had he ordered his bourbon from room service? No one had ever asked these questions before. Fingerprints? None had been taken. After all, this wasn't a murder . . .

But it is now time to turn to Deirdre Mayfair, the present heiress of the Mayfair legacy, orphaned at the age of two months and left in the hands of her aging aunts.

Deirdre Mayfair

The First Street house continued to deteriorate after Antha's death. The swimming pool had by this time become a rank swamp pond of duckweed and wild irises, its rusted fountain jets spewing green water into the muck. Shutters were once again bolted on the windows of the northside master bedroom. The paint continued to peel from the violet-gray masonry walls.

Elderly Miss Flanagan, almost completely blind in her last year, cared for little Deirdre until just before the child's fifth birthday. Now and then she took the baby walking around the block in a wicker buggy, but she never crossed the street.

Cortland came on Christmas. He drank sherry in the long front parlor with Millie Dear and Belle and Nancy.

"I told them I wasn't going to be turned away this time," he explained to his son Pierce, who later told his mother. "No, sir. I was going to see that child with my own eyes on her birthday and on Christmas. I was going to hold her in my arms." He made similar statements to his secretaries at Mayfair and Mayfair, who often bought the presents which Cortland took uptown.

Years later, Cortland's grandson Ryan Mayfair talked about it to a sympathetic "acquaintance" at a wedding reception:

"My grandfather hated to go up there. Our place in Metairie was always so cheerful. My father said that Grandfather would come home crying. When Deirdre was three years old, Grandfather made them get their first Christmas tree in all those years. He took a package of ornaments up there for it. He bought the lights at Katz and Bestoff and put them on himself. It's so hard to imagine people living in that sort of gloom. I wish I had really known my grandfather. He was born in that house. Think of it. And his father, Julien, had been born before the Civil War."

Cortland, by this point in time, had become the image of his father, Julien. Pictures of him even as late as the mid-1950s show him as a tall, slender man with black hair, and gray only at the temples. His heavily lined face was remarkably like that of his father, except for the fact that his eyes were much larger, reminiscent of Stella's eyes, though he had Julien's agreeable expression, and frequently Julien's cheerful smile.

By all accounts Cortland's family loved him; his employees veritably worshiped him; and though Amanda Grady Mayfair had left him years before, even she seems to have always loved him, or so she told Allan Carver in New York the year she died. Amanda cried on Allan's shoulder about the fact that her sons never understood why she had left their father, and she had no intention of telling them, either.

Ryan Mayfair, who knew his grandfather Cortland only briefly, was absolutely devoted to him. To him and his father, Cortland was a hero. He could never understand how his grandmother could "defect" to New York.

What was Deirdre like during this early period? We are unable to discover a single account of her in the first five years, except the legend in Cortland's family that she was a very pretty little girl.

Her black hair was fine and wavy, like that of Stella. Her blue eyes were large and dark.

But the First Street house was once more closed to the outside world. A generation of passersby had become accustomed to its hopelessly forbidding and neglected facade. Once again, workmen couldn't complete repairs on the premises. A roofer fell off his ladder twice and then refused to come back. Only the old gardener and his son came willingly to now and then cut the weed-infested grass.

As people in the parish died, certain legends concerning the Mayfairs died with them. Other stories became so miserably transformed by time as to be unrecognizable. New investigators replaced old investigators. Soon no one questioned about the Mayfairs mentioned the names of Julien or Katherine or Rémy or Suzette.

Julien's son Barclay died in 1949, his brother Garland in 1951. Cortland's son Grady died the same year as Garland, after a fall from a horse in Audubon Park. His mother, Amanda Grady Mayfair, died only shortly after, as if the death of her beloved Grady was more than she could take. Of Pierce's two sons, only Ryan Mayfair "knows the family history" and regales the younger cousins—many of whom know nothing—with strange tales.

Irwin Dandrich died in 1952. However, his role had been already filled by another "society investigator," a woman named Juliette Milton, who collected numerous stories over the years from Beatrice Mayfair and the other downtown cousins, many of whom lunched with Juliette regularly and did not seem to mind that she was a gossip who told them everything about everybody and told everybody everything about them. Like Dandrich, Juliette was not a particularly vicious person. Indeed, she doesn't even seem to have been unkind. She loved melodrama, however, and wrote incredibly long letters to our lawyers in London, who paid her an annual amount equal to the annuity which had once been her sole support.

As was the case with Dandrich, Juliette never knew to whom she was supplying all this information about the Mayfairs. And though she broached the subject at least once a year, she never pressed.

In 1953, as I began my full-time translation of Petyr van Abel's letters, I read the contemporary reports regarding twelve-year-old Deirdre as they poured in. I sent the investigators after every scrap of information. "Dig," I said. "Tell me all about her from the very beginning. There is nothing I do not want to know." I called Juliette Milton personally. I told her I would pay well for anything extra she could turn up.

* * *

During the early years at least Deirdre had followed in the footsteps of her mother, being expelled from one school after another for her "antics" and "strange behavior," her disruption of the classes, and strange crying fits for which nothing could be done.

Once more Sister Bridget Marie, then in her sixties, saw the "invisible friend" in action in the St. Alphonsus school yard, finding things for little Deirdre and making flowers fly through the air. Sacred Heart, Ursulines, St. Joseph's, Our Lady of the Angels—they all expelled little Deirdre within a couple of weeks. For months at a time, the child stayed home. Neighbors saw her "running wild" in the garden, or climbing the big oak tree on the back of the lot.

There was no real staff anymore at First Street. Aunt Easter's daughter Irene did all the cooking and the cleaning thoroughly but steadily. Every morning she swept the pavements or the banquettes as they were called. Three o'clock saw her ringing out her mop at the tap by the rear garden gate.

Nancy Mayfair was the actual housekeeper, managing things in a brusque and offensive manner, or so said deliverymen and priests who now and then came to call.

Millie Dear and Belle, both picturesque if not beautiful old women, tended the few roses growing by the side porch which had been saved from the wilderness that now covered the property from the front fence to the back wall.

All the family appeared for nine o'clock Mass on Sundays at the chapel, little Deirdre a picture in her navy blue sailor dress and straw hat with its ribbons, Carlotta in her dark business suit and high-necked blouse, and the old ladies, Millie Dear and Belle, exquisitely attired in their black high string shoes, gabardine dresses with lace, and dark gloves.

Miss Millie and Miss Belle often went shopping together on Mondays, taking a taxi from First Street to Gus Mayer or Godchaux's, the finest stores in New Orleans, where they bought their pearl gray dresses and flowered hats with veils, and other genteel accoutrements. The ladies at the cosmetic counters knew them by name. They sold them face powder and cream rouge and Christmas Night perfume. The two old women had lunch at the D.H. Holmes lunch counter before taking the taxi home. And they, and they alone, represented the First Street family at funerals, and even now and then at christenings, and even once in a while at a wedding, though they seldom went to the reception after the Nuptial Mass.

Millie and Belle even attended funerals of other persons in the parish, and would go to the wake if it was held at Lonigan and Sons, nearby. They went to the Tuesday night Novena service at the chapel, and sometimes on summer nights they brought little Deirdre with them, clucking over her proudly and feeding her little bits of chocolate during the service so that she would be quiet.

No one remembered anymore that anything had ever been "wrong" with sweet Miss Belle.

Indeed, the two old ladies easily won the goodwill and respect of the Garden District, especially among families who knew nothing of the Mayfair tragedies or secrets. The First Street house was not the only moldering mansion behind a rusted fence.

Nancy Mayfair, on the other hand, seemed to have been born and reared in an entirely different class. Her clothes were always dowdy, her brown hair unwashed and only superficially combed. It would have been easy to mistake her for a hired servant. But nobody ever questioned the story that she was Stella's sister, which of course she was not. She began to wear black string shoes when she was only thirty. Grumpily she paid the delivery boys from a worn pocketbook, or called down from the upstairs gallery to tell the peddler at the gate to go away.

It was with these women that little Deirdre spent her days when she was not struggling to pay attention in a crowded classroom, which always ended in failure and disgrace.

Over and over the parish gossips compared her to her mother. The cousins said maybe it was "congenital insanity," though honestly no one knew. But to those who observed the family more closely—even from a distance of many miles—certain differences between mother and daughter were apparent very early on.

Whereas Antha was always slender and shrinking by nature, there was something rebellious and unmistakably sensuous in Deirdre from the start. Neighbors frequently saw her running "like a tomboy" through the garden. At the age of five she could climb the great oak tree to the top. Sometimes she concealed herself in the shrubbery along the fence so that she could deliberately startle those who passed by.

At nine years old she ran away for the first time. Carlotta rang Cortland in panic; then the police were called in. Finally a cold and shivering Deirdre showed up on the front porch of St. Elizabeth's Orphanage on Napoleon Avenue, telling the sisters that she was "cursed" and "possessed of the devil." They had to call a priest for her. Cortland came with Carlotta to take her home.

"Overactive imagination," said Carlotta. It was to become a stock phrase.

A year later, police found Deirdre wandering in a rainstorm along the Bayou St. John, shivering and crying, and saying she was afraid to go home. For two hours she told the police lies about her name and background. She was a gypsy who had come to town with a circus. Her mother had been murdered by the animal trainer. She had tried to "commit suicide with rare poison" but had been taken to a hospital in Europe where they drew all the blood out of her veins.

"There was something so sad about that child and so crazy," said the officer afterwards to our investigator. "She was absolutely in earnest and the wildest look would come into her blue eyes. She didn't even look up when her uncle and her aunt came to get her. She pretended she didn't know them. Then she said they kept her chained in an upstairs room."

At ten years of age, Deirdre was packed off to Ireland, to a boarding school recommended by an Irish-born priest at St. Patrick's Cathedral, Father Jason Power. Family gossip said it was Cortland's idea.

"Grandfather wanted to get her away from there," Ryan Mayfair gossiped later.

But the sisters in County Cork sent Deirdre home within the month.

For two years Deirdre studied with a governess named Miss Lampton, an old friend of Carlotta's from the Sacred Heart. Miss Lampton told Beatrice Mayfair (on Esplanade Avenue downtown) that Deirdre was a charming girl, and very bright indeed. "She has too much imagination, that is all that's wrong with her, and she spends much too much time alone." When Miss Lampton moved north to marry a widower she'd met during his summer vacation, Deirdre cried for days.

Even during these years there were quarrels at First Street, however. People heard shouting. Deirdre frequently ran out of the house crying. She would climb the oak tree until she was well out of the reach of Irene or Miss Lampton. Sometimes she stayed up there until after dark.

But with adolescence a change came over Deirdre. She became withdrawn, secretive, no longer the tomboy. At thirteen she was far more voluptuous than Antha had been as a grown woman. She wore her black wavy hair long and parted in the middle, and held back by a bit of lavender ribbon. Her large blue eyes looked perpetually distrustful and faintly bitter. Indeed, the child had a bruised look to her, said the parish gossips who saw her at Sunday Mass.

"She was already a beautiful woman," said one of the ma-

584

trons who went to the chapel regularly. "And those old ladies didn't know it. They dressed her as if she were still a child."

Legal gossip revealed other problems. One afternoon Deirdre rushed into the waiting room outside Cortland's office.

"She was hysterical," said the secretary later. "For an hour she screamed and cried in there with her uncle. And I'll tell you something else, something I didn't even notice till she was leaving. She wasn't wearing matching shoes! She had on one brown loafer and one black flat shoe. I don't think she ever realized it. Cortland took her home. I don't know that he noticed it either. I never saw her after that."

In the summer before Deirdre's fourteenth birthday, she was rushed to the new Mercy Hospital. She had tried to slash her wrists. Beatrice went to see her.

"That girl has a spirit that Antha simply didn't have," she told Juliette Milton. "But she needs womanly advice on things. She wanted me to buy her cosmetics. She said she's only been in a drugstore once in her entire life."

Beatrice brought the cosmetics to the hospital, only to be told that Carlotta had put a stop to all visits. When Beatrice called Cortland, he confessed he didn't know why Deirdre had slit her wrists. "Maybe she just wanted to get out of that house."

That very week, Cortland arranged for Deirdre to go to California. She flew to Los Angeles to stay with Garland's daughter, Andrea Mayfair, who had married a doctor on the staff of Cedars of Lebanon Hospital. But Deirdre was home again at the end of two weeks.

The Los Angeles Mayfairs said nothing to anyone about what happened, but years afterwards their only son, Elton, told investigators that his poor cousin from New Orleans was crazy. That she had believed herself to be cursed by some sort of legacy, that she had talked of suicide to him, horrifying his parents. That they had taken her to see doctors who said she would never be normal.

"My parents wanted to help her, especially my mother. But the entire family was disrupted. I think what really finished it however was that they saw her out in the backyard one night with a man, and she wouldn't admit to it. She kept denying it. And they were afraid something would happen. She was thirteen, I believe, and very pretty. They sent her home."

Beatrice recounted pretty much the same story to Juliette Milton. "I think Deirdre looks too mature," she said. But she wouldn't believe Deirdre had lied about male companions. "She's confused." And Beatrice was adamant that there was no congenital insanity. That was just a family legend that Carlotta had started, and one which really ought to be stopped.

Beatrice went up to First Street to see Deirdre and take her some presents. Nancy wouldn't let her in.

The same mysterious male companion was responsible for Deirdre's most traumatic expulsion from St. Rose de Lima boarding school when she was sixteen. Deirdre had attended the school for a full semester without mishap, and was in the middle of the spring term when the incident occurred. Family gossip said Deirdre had been blissfully happy at St. Ro's, that she had told Cortland she never wanted to go home. Even over Christmas, Deirdre had remained at the boarding school, only going out with Cortland for an early supper on Christmas Eve.

Yet she loved the swings in the back play yard, which were big enough for the older children, and at twilight she would sing songs there with another girl, Rita Mae Dwyer (later Lonigan), who remembered Deirdre as a rare and special person, elegant and innocent; romantic and sweet.

As recently as 1988, more data was obtained about this expulsion directly from Rita Mae Dwyer Lonigan in a conversation with this investigator.

Deirdre's "mysterious friend" met her in the nuns' garden in the moonlight, and spoke softly but audibly enough for Rita Mae to hear. "He called her 'my beloved,' " Rita Mae told me. She had never heard such romantic words spoken except in a movie.

Defenseless and sobbing bitterly, Deirdre did not utter a word when the nuns accused her of "bringing a man onto the school grounds." They had spied upon Deirdre and her male companion, peering through the slats of the convent kitchen into the garden where the two met in the dark. "This was no boy," said one of the nuns in a rage afterwards to the assembled boarders. "This was a man! A grown man!"

The record from the period is almost vicious in its condemnations. "The girl is deceitful. She allowed the man to touch her indecently. Her innocence is a complete facade."

There can be no doubt that this mysterious companion was Lasher. He is described by the nuns, and later by Mrs. Lonigan, as having brown hair and brown eyes, and beautiful old-fashioned clothes.

But the remarkable point is that Rita Mae Lonigan, unless she is exaggerating, actually heard Lasher speak.

Other startling information given us by Mrs. Lonigan is that Deirdre had the Mayfair emerald in her possession at the boarding school, that she showed it to Rita Mae, and showed her a word engraved on the back of it: "Lasher." If Rita Mae's story is true, Deirdre knew little about her mother or her grandmother. She understood that the emerald had come to her from these women, but she did not even know how Stella or Antha had died.

It was common knowledge in the family in 1956 that Deirdre was crushed by her expulsion from St. Rose de Lima's. She was admitted to St. Ann's Asylum for six weeks. Though the records have proved unobtainable, nurses gossiped that Deirdre begged for shock treatment, and was given it twice. She was at this point almost seventeen.

From what we know of medical practice at this period, we can safely conclude that these treatments involved a higher voltage than is common now; they were probably very dangerous, resulting in a loss of memory for hours if not days.

Why a whole course was not pursued as was the custom we do not know. Cortland was dead set against the shock treatment, or so he told Beatrice Mayfair. He couldn't believe in something so drastic for one so young.

"What is wrong with that girl?" Juliette asked Beatrice finally, to which Beatrice answered, "Nobody knows, darling. Nobody knows."

Carlotta brought Deirdre home from the asylum, and there she languished for another month.

Relentless canvassing by our investigators indicated that a dark shadowy figure was often seen with Deirdre in the garden. A deliveryman from Solari's grocery was "scared out of his wits" as he was leaving the property when he saw "that wild-eyed girl and that man" in the tall bamboo thicket by the old pool.

A spinster who lived on Prytania Street saw the pair in the chapel after dark. "I told Miss Belle. I stopped by the gate the following morning. I didn't think it was quite proper. It had happened in the evening, just after dark. I went into the chapel to light a candle and say my rosary as I always do, and there she was in a back pew with this man. I could scarcely see them at first. I was a little frightened. Then when she got up and hurried out I saw her clearly under the street lamp. It was Deirdre Mayfair. I don't know what happened to the young man."

Several other persons reported similar sightings. The images were always the same—Deirdre and the mysterious young man in the shadows. Deirdre and the mysterious young man flushed from their place, or peering out at the stranger in an unsettling manner. We have fifteen different variations on these two themes.

Some of these stories reached Beatrice on Esplanade Avenue. "I don't know if anyone is watching out for her. And she is so

". . . so well developed physically," she told Juliette. Juliette went with Beatrice to First Street.

"The girl was wandering in the garden. Beatrice went up to the fence and called to her. For a few minutes she didn't seem to know who Bea was. Then she went to get the key to the gate. Of course Bea did all the talking after that. But the girl is shockingly beautiful. It has to do with the strangeness of her personality as much as anything else. She seems wild and deeply suspicious of people, and at the same time keenly interested in things about her. She fell in love with a cameo I was wearing. I gave it to her, and she was absolutely childlike in her delight. I hesitate to add that she was barefoot and wearing a filthy cotton dress."

As fall came on, there were more reports of fights and screaming. Neighbors went so far as to call the police on two different occasions. Of the first occasion in September I was personally able, two years later, to obtain a full account.

"I didn't like going there," the officer told me. "You know, bothering these Garden District families just isn't my line. And that lady really put us through it at the front door. It was Carlotta Mayfair, the one they call Miss Carl; the one who works for the judge.

" 'Who called you here? What do you want? Who are you? Let me see your identification. I'll have to talk to Judge Byrnes about this if you come here again.' Finally my partner said that people had heard the young lady in the house screaming, and we would like to talk to her and make certain for ourselves she was all right. I thought Miss Carl was going to kill him on the spot. But she went and got the young girl, Deirdre Mayfair, the one they talk about. She was crying and shaking all over. She said to my partner, C. J., 'You make her give me my mother's things. She took my mother's things.'

"Miss Carl said she had had enough of this 'intrusion,' that this was a family argument and the police weren't needed here. If we didn't leave, she'd call Judge Byrnes. Then this girl, Deirdre, ran out of the house and towards the squad car. 'Take me away!' she screamed.

"Then something happened to Miss Carl. She was looking at the girl standing at the curb by our squad car, and she started crying. She tried to hide it. She took out her handkerchief and covered her face. But we could see, the lady was crying. The girl really had the lady at her wit's end.

"C. J. said, 'Miss Carl, what do you want us to do?' She went past him down to the sidewalk, and she laid her hand on the girl and she said, 'Deirdre, do you want to go back to the asylum? Please, Deirdre. Please.' And then she just broke down. She couldn't talk. The girl stared at her, all wild-eyed and crazy, and then she broke into sobs. And Miss Carl put her arm around the girl and took her back up the steps and inside."

"Are you sure it was Carl?" I asked the officer.

"Oh, yeah, everybody knows her. Boy, I'll never forget her. She called the captain the next day and tried to have C. J. and me fired."

A different squad car answered the neighbor's call a week later. All we know of this occasion is that Deirdre was trying to leave the house when the police arrived; they persuaded her to sit down on the porch steps and wait until her Uncle Cortland arrived.

Deirdre ran away the following day. Legal gossip reports of numerous phone calls back and forth, of Cortland rushing up to First Street, and Mayfair and Mayfair calling the New York cousins in search for Deirdre as they had when Antha disappeared years before.

Amanda Grady Mayfair was dead. Dr. Cornell Mayfair's mother, Rosalind Mayfair, wanted nothing to do with "the First Street crowd" as she called them. Nevertheless she called the other New York cousins. Then the police contacted Cortland in New Orleans. Deirdre had been found wandering around barefoot and incoherent in Greenwich Village. There was some evidence that she had been raped. Cortland flew to New York that night. The following morning he brought Deirdre back with him.

The repeat of history came full circle with Deirdre's second commitment to St. Ann's Asylum. A week later she was released, and went to live with Cortland in his old family home in Metairie.

Family gossip described Carlotta as beaten down and discouraged. She told Judge Byrnes and his wife that she had failed with her niece. She feared the girl would "never be normal."

When Beatrice Mayfair went to call on Carlotta one Saturday, she found her sitting alone in the parlor at First Street with all the curtains drawn. Carlotta wouldn't talk.

"I realized later she had been staring at the very spot where they put the coffin in the old days when the funerals were still at home. All she said to me was yes or no, or hmmmm when I asked her questions. Finally that horrible Nancy came in and offered me some iced tea. She acted put upon when I accepted. I told her I would get it myself and she said, oh, no Aunt Carl wouldn't have that."

When Beatrice had had her fill of sadness and rudeness she

left. She went out to Metairie to visit Deirdre at Cortland's house on Country Club Lane.

This house had been in the Mayfair family since Cortland built it when he was a young man. A brick mansion with white columns and French windows and every "modern convenience," it later passed to Ryan Mayfair, Pierce's son, who lives there now. For years Sheffield and Eugenie Mayfair shared it with Cortland. Their only child, Ellie Mayfair, the woman who later adopted Deirdre's daughter, Rowan, was born in this house.

At this period, Sheffield Mayfair had already died of a heart attack; Eugenie had been gone for years. Ellie lived in California, where she had just gotten married to a lawyer named Graham Franklin. And Cortland lived in the Metairie mansion on his own.

By all reports, the house was extremely cheerful, filled with bright colors, gay wallpaper, traditional furnishings, and books. Numerous French doors opened to the garden, the pool, and the front lawn.

The entire family seems to have thought it was the best place for Deirdre. Metairie had none of the gloom of the Garden District. Cortland assured Beatrice that Deirdre was resting, that the girl's problems had been compounded by a lot of secrecy and bad judgment on the part of Carlotta.

"But he won't really tell me what's happening," Beatrice complained to Juliette. "He never does. What does he mean, secrecy?"

Beatrice queried the maid by phone whenever she could. Deirdre was just fine, said the maid. The girl's color was excellent. She had even had a guest, a very nice-looking young man. The maid had only seen him for a second or two—he and Deirdre had been out in the garden—but he was a handsome, gentlemanly sort of young man.

"Now, who could that be?" Beatrice wondered over lunch with Juliette Milton. "Not that same scoundrel who sneaked into the nuns' garden to bother her at St. Ro's!"

"Seems to me," wrote Juliette to her London contact, "that this family does not realize this girl has a lover. I mean one lover—one very distinguished and easily recognized lover, who is seen in her company over and over. All the descriptions of this young man are the same!"

The significant thing about this story is that Juliette Milton had never heard any rumors about ghosts, witches, curses, or the like associated with the Mayfair family. She and Beatrice truly believed this mysterious person was a human being.

Yet at the very same time, in the Irish Channel old people

gossiped over kitchen tables about "Deirdre and the man." And by "the man," they did not mean a human being. The elderly sister of Father Lafferty knew about "the man." She tried to talk to her brother about it; but he would not confide in her. She gossiped with an elderly friend named Dave Collins about it; she gossiped with our investigator, who walked along with her on Constance Street as she made her way home from Sunday Mass.

Miss Rosie, who worked in the sacristy, changing the altar cloths and seeing to the sacramental wine, also knew the shocking facts about those Mayfairs and "the man." "First it was Stella, then Antha, now Deirdre," she told her nephew, a college boy at Loyola who thought she was a superstitious fool.

An old black maid who lived in the same block knew all about "that man." He was the family ghost, that's who he was, and the only ghost she ever saw in broad daylight, sitting with that girl in the back garden. That girl was going to hell when she died.

It was at this point, in the summer of 1958, that I prepared to go to New Orleans.

I had finished putting the entire Mayfair history into an early version of the foregoing narrative, which was substantially the same as what the reader has only just read. And I was deeply and passionately concerned about Deirdre Mayfair.

I felt that her psychic powers, and especially her ability to see and communicate with spirits, were driving her out of her mind.

After numerous discussions with Scott Reynolds, our new director, and several meetings with the entire council, it was decided that I should make the trip, and that I should use my own judgment as to whether Deirdre Mayfair was old enough or stable enough to be approached.

Elaine Barrett, one of the oldest and most experienced members of the Talamasca, had died the preceding year, and I was now considered (undeservedly) the leading expert in the Talamasca on witch families. My credentials were never questioned. And indeed, those who had been most frightened by the deaths of Stuart Townsend and Arthur Langtry—and most likely to forbid my going to New Orleans—were no longer alive.

Twenty-three

THE FILE ON THE MAYFAIR WITCHES

PART IX

The Story of Deirdre Mayfair
Revised Completely 1989

I arrived in New Orleans in July of 1958, and immediately checked into a small, informal French Quarter hotel. I then proceeded to meet with our ablest professional investigators, and to consult some public records, and to satisfy myself upon other points.

Over the years we had acquired the names of several people close to the Mayfair family. I attempted contact. With Richard Llewellyn I was quite successful, as has already been described, and this report alone occupied me for days.

I also managed "to run into" a young lay teacher from St. Rose de Lima's who had known Deirdre during her months there, and more or less clarified the reasons for the expulsion. Tragically this young woman believed Deirdre to have had an affair with "an older man" and to have been a vile and deceitful girl. Other girls had known of the Mayfair emerald. It was concluded that Deirdre had stolen it from her aunt. For why else would the child have had such a valuable jewel at school?

The more I talked with the woman the more I realized that Deirdre's aura of sensuality had made an impression on those around her. "She was so . . . mature, you know. A young girl has no business really having enormous breasts like that at the age of sixteen."

Poor Deirdre. I found myself on the verge of asking whether or not the teacher thought mutilation was appropriate in these circumstances, then terminated the interview. I went back to the hotel, drank a stiff brandy, and lectured myself on the dangers of becoming emotionally involved.

Unfortunately I was no less emotional when I visited the Garden District the following day, and the day after that, during which time I spent hours walking through the quiet streets and observing the First Street house from all angles. After years of reading of this place and its inhabitants, I found this extremely exciting. But if ever a house exuded an atmosphere of evil, it was this house.

Why? I asked myself.

By this time it was extremely neglected. The violet paint had faded from the masonry. Weeds and tiny ferns grew in crevices on the parapets. Flowering vines covered the side galleries so that the ornamental ironwork was scarcely visible, and the wild cherry laurels screened the garden from view.

Nevertheless it ought to have been romantic. Yet in the heavy summer heat, with the burnished sun shining drowsily and dustily through the trees, the place looked damp and dark and decidedly unpleasant. During the idle hours that I stood contemplating it, I noted that passersby invariably crossed the street when they approached it. And though its flagstone walk was slick with moss and cracked from the roots of the oak trees, so were other sidewalks in the area which people did not seek to avoid.

Something evil lived in this house, lived and breathed as it were, and waited, and perhaps mourned.

Accusing myself again, and with reason, of being overemotional, I defined my terms. This something was evil because it was destructive. It "lived and breathed" in the sense that it influenced the environment and its presence could be felt. As for my belief that this "something" was in mourning, I needed only to remind myself that no workman had made any repairs on the place since Stella's death. Since Stella's death the decline had been steady and unbroken. Did not the thing want the house to rot even as Stella's body decayed in the grave?

Ah, so many unanswered questions. I went to the Lafayette Cemetery and visited the Mayfair tomb. A kindly caretaker volunteered the information that there were always fresh flowers in the stone vases before the face of the crypt, though no one ever saw the person who put them there.

"Do you think it is some old lover of Stella Mayfair's?" I asked.

"Oh, no," said the elderly man, with a cracking laugh. "Good heavens, no. It's him, that's who it is, the Mayfair ghost. He's the one that puts those flowers there. And you want to know something? Sometimes he takes them off the altar at the chapel. You know, the chapel, down there on Prytania and Third? Father Morgan came here one afternoon just steaming. Seems he had just put out the gladiolus, and there they were in the vases before the Mayfair grave. He went by and rang the bell over there on First Street. I heard Miss Carl told him to go to hell.'' The man laughed and laughed at such an idea . . . somebody telling a priest to go to hell.

Renting a car, I drove down the river road to Riverbend and explored what was left of the plantation, and then I called our undercover society investigator, Juliette Milton, and invited her to lunch.

She was more than happy to provide me with an introduction to Beatrice Mayfair. Beatrice agreed to meet me for lunch, accepting without the slightest question my superficial explanation that I was interested in southern history and the history of the Mayfair family.

Beatrice Mayfair was thirty-five years old, an attractively dressed dark-haired woman with a charming blend of southern and New Orleans (Brooklyn, Boston) accent, and something of a ''rebel'' as far as the family was concerned.

For three hours she talked to me nonstop at Galatoire's, pouring out all sorts of little stories about the Mayfair family, and verifying what I had already suspected, that little or nothing was known in the present time about the family's remote past. It was the most vague sort of legend, in which names were confused, and scandal had become near preposterous.

Beatrice didn't know who built Riverbend, or when. Or even who had built First Street. She thought Julien had built it. As for stories of ghosts and legends of purses full of coins, she had believed all that when she was young, but not now. Her mother had been born at First Street (this woman, Alice Mayfair, was the second to the last daughter of Rémy Mayfair; Millie Dear, or Miss Millie as she was known, was Rémy's youngest child, and Beatrice's aunt) and she had said some awfully strange things about that house. But she'd left it when she was only seventeen to marry Aldrich Mayfair, a great-grandson of Maurice Mayfair, and Aldrich didn't like Beatrice's mother to talk about that house.

''Both my parents are so secretive,'' said Beatrice. ''I don't think my dad really remembers anything anymore. He's past eighty, and my mother just won't tell me things. I myself didn't marry a Mayfair, you know. My husband knows nothing about the family, really.'' (Note: Beatrice's husband died of throat cancer in the seventies.) ''I don't remember Mary Beth. I was only two years old when she died. I have some pictures of myself at her feet at one of the reunions, you know, with all the other little Mayfair babies. But I remember Stella. Oh, I loved Stella. I loved her so.

"It kills me not to be able to go up there. Years ago I stopped visiting Aunt Millie Dear. She's sweet, but she doesn't really know who I am. Every time I have to say, I'm Alice's daughter, Rémy's granddaughter. She remembers for a little while and then blanks out. And Carlotta doesn't really want me there. She doesn't want anyone there. She's simply awful. She killed that house! She drove all the life out of it. I don't care what anyone else says, she's to blame."

"Do you believe the house is haunted, that there's something evil perhaps . . ."

"Oh! Carlotta. She's evil! But you know, if it's that sort of thing you're after, well, it's too bad you couldn't have talked to Amanda Grady Mayfair. She was Cortland's wife. She's been dead for years. She believed some fantastic things! But it was interesting actually . . . Well, in a way. They said that was why she left Cortland. She said Cortland knew the house was haunted. That he could see and talk to spirits. I was always shocked that a grown woman would believe things like that! But she became completely convinced of some sort of Satanic plot. I think Stella caused all that, inadvertently. I was too young then to really know. But Stella was no evil person! No voodoo queen. Stella went to bed with anybody and everybody, and if that's witchcraft, well, half the city of New Orleans ought to be burnt at the stake."

. . . And so on it went, the gossip becoming slightly more intimate and reckless as Beatrice continued to pick at her food and smoke Pall Mall cigarettes.

"Deirdre's oversexed," she said, "that's all that's wrong with her. She's been ridiculously sheltered. No wonder she takes up with strange men. I'm relying upon Cortland to take care of Deirdre. Cortland has become the venerable elder of the family. And he is certainly the only one who can stand up to Carlotta. Now, that's a witch in my book. Carlotta. She gives me the shivers. They ought to get Deirdre away from her."

Indeed, there was already some talk about a school in Texas, a little university where Deirdre might go in the fall. It seemed that Rhonda Mayfair, a great-granddaughter of Suzette's sister Marianne (this was an aunt of Cortland's), had married a young man in Texas who taught at this school. It was in fact a small state school for women, heavily endowed, and with many of the traditions and accoutrements of an expensive private school. The whole question was, would that awful Carlotta let Deirdre go. "Now, Carlotta. That is a witch!"

Once more, Beatrice became quite worked up on the subject of Carlotta, her criticisms including Carlotta's style of dressing (business suits) and style of talking (businesslike), when abruptly she leaned across the table and said:

"And you know that witch killed Irwin Dandrich, don't you?"

Not only did I not know this, I had never heard the faintest whisper of such a thing. It had been reported to us in 1952 that Dandrich died of a heart attack in his apartment some time after four in the afternoon. It had been well-known that he had a heart condition.

"I talked to him," Beatrice said, her manner one of great self-importance and thinly concealed drama. "I talked to him the day he died. He said Carlotta had called. Carlotta had accused him of spying on the family, and had said, 'Well, if you want to know about us, come up here to First Street. I'll tell you more than you'll ever want to hear.' I told him not to go. I said: 'She'll sue you. She'll do something terrible to you. She's out of her mind.' But he wouldn't listen to me. 'I'm going to see that house for myself,' he said. 'Nobody I know has been in it since Stella died.' I made him promise to call me as soon as he got home. Well, he never did call me. He died that very afternoon. She poisoned him. I know she did. She poisoned him. And they said it was a heart attack when they found him. She poisoned him but she gave it to him so he could go home on his own steam and die in his own bed."

"What makes you so certain?" I asked.

"Because it isn't the first time something like that has happened. Deirdre told Cortland there was a dead body in the attic of the house at First Street. Yes, a dead body."

"Cortland told you this?"

She nodded gravely. "Poor Deirdre. She tells these doctors things like that and they give her shock treatment! Cortland thinks she's seeing things!" She shook her head. "That's Cortland. He believes the house is haunted, that there are ghosts up there you can talk to! But a body in the attic? Oh, no, he won't believe in that!" She laughed softly, then became extremely serious. "But I'll bet it's true. I remember something about a young man who disappeared right before Stella died. I heard about it years later. Aunt Millie Dear said something about it to my cousin, Angela. Later on, Dandrich told me about it. The police were looking for him. Private detectives were looking. A Texan from England, Irwin said, who had actually spent the night with Stella, and then just disappeared.

"I'll tell you who else knew about it. Amanda knew about it. Last time I saw her in New York we were rehashing the whole thing, and she said, 'And what about that man who strangely disappeared!' Of course she connected it with Cornell, you know the one who died in the hotel downtown after he called on Carlotta. I tell you, she poisons them and they go home and die afterwards. It's one of those chemicals with a delayed effect. This Texan was some sort of historian from England. Knew about our family's past—"

Suddenly she made a connection. I was a historian from England. She laughed. "Mr. Lightner, you better watch your step!" she said. She sat back laughing softly to herself.

"I suppose you're right. But you don't really believe all this, do you, Miss Mayfair?"

She thought for a moment. "Well, I do and I don't." Again, she laughed. "I wouldn't put anything past Carlotta. But if the truth be known, the woman's too dull to actually poison somebody. But I thought about it! I thought about it when Irwin Dandrich died. I loved Irwin. And he did die right after he went to see Carlotta. I hope Deirdre goes to college in Texas. And if Carlotta invites you up for tea, don't go!"

"About the ghost particularly . . ." I said. (Throughout this interview, it was rarely necessary for me to complete a sentence.)

"Oh, which one! There's the ghost of Julien—everybody's seen that ghost. I thought I saw it once. And then there's the spook that throws over people's ladders. That's a regular invisible man."

"But isn't there one whom they call 'the man'?"

She had never heard that expression. But I ought to talk to Cortland. That is, if Cortland would talk to me. Cortland didn't like outsiders asking him questions. Cortland lived in a family world.

We parted ways at the corner as I helped her into her taxi. "If you do talk to Cortland," she said, "don't tell him you talked to me. He thinks I'm an awful gossip. But do ask him about that Texan. You never know what he might say."

As soon as the cab drove away, I called Juliette Milton, our society spy.

"Don't ever go near the house," I said. "Don't ever have anything to do personally with Carlotta Mayfair. Don't ever go to lunch again with Beatrice. We'll give you a handsome check. Simply bow out."

"But what did I do? What did I say? Beatrice is an impossible gossip. She tells everyone those stories. I haven't repeated anything that wasn't common knowledge."

"You've done a fine job. But there are dangers. Definite dangers. Just do as I say."

"Oh, she told you that about Carlotta killing people. That's nonsense. Carlotta's an old stick. To hear her tell it, Carlotta went to New York and killed Deirdre's father, Sean Lacy. Now, that is sheer nonsense!''

I repeated my warnings, or orders, for what they were worth.

The following day I drove out to Metairie, parked my car, and took a walk in the quiet streets around Cortland's house. Except for the large oak trees and the soft velvet green of the grass, the neighborhood had nothing of the atmosphere of New Orleans. It might as well have been a rich suburb near Houston, Texas, or Oklahoma City. Very beautiful, very restful, very seemingly safe. I saw nothing of Deirdre. I hoped she was happy in this wholesome place.

I was convinced that I must see her from afar before I attempted to speak to her. In the meantime, I tried to make direct contact with Cortland, but he did not return my calls. Finally his secretary told me he did not want to talk to me, that he had heard I'd been talking to his cousins and he wished that I would leave the family alone.

I was undecided as to whether I should press the matter with Cortland. Same old questions that always plague us at such junctures—what were my obligations, my goals? I left the message finally that I had a great deal of information about the Mayfair family, going back to the 1600s, and would welcome an interview. I never received a response.

The following week, I learned from Juliette Milton that Deirdre had just left for Texas Woman's University in Denton, Texas, where Rhonda Mayfair's husband, Ellis Clement, taught English to small classes of well-bred girls. Carlotta was absolutely against it; it had been done without her permission, and Carlotta was not speaking to Cortland.

Cortland had driven Deirdre to Texas, and remained long enough to see that she was comfortable in the home of Rhonda Mayfair and Ellis Clement, and then came home.

It was not difficult for us to ascertain that Deirdre had been admitted as a "special student," educated at home. She had been assigned a private room in the freshman dormitory, and was registered for a full schedule of routine course work.

I arrived in Denton two days later. Texas Woman's University was a lovely little school situated on low rolling green hills with vine-covered brick buildings, and neatly tended lawns. It was quite impossible to believe that it was a state institution.

At the age of thirty-six, with prematurely gray hair and addicted to well-tailored linen suits, I found it effortlessly easy to roam about the campus, probably passing for a faculty member to anyone who took notice. I stopped on benches for long periods to write in my notebook. I browsed in the small open library. I wandered the halls of the old buildings, exchanging pleasantries with a few elderly women teachers and with fresh-faced young women in blouses and pleated skirts.

I caught my first glimpse of Deirdre unexpectedly on the second day after my arrival. She came out of the freshman dormitory, a modest Georgian-style building, and walked for about an hour around the campus—a lovely young woman with long loose black hair, strolling idly up and down small winding paths beneath old trees. She wore the usual cotton blouse and skirt.

Seeing her at last overwhelmed me with confusion. I was glimpsing a great celebrity. And as I followed her, at a remove, I suffered unanticipated agonies over what I was doing. Should I leave this woman alone? Should I tell her what I knew of her early history? What right had I to be here?

In silence, I watched her return to her dormitory. The following morning, I followed her to the first of her classes, and then afterwards into a large basement canteen area where she drank coffee alone at a small table and put nickels into the jukebox over and over to play one selection repeatedly—a mournful Gershwin tune sung by Nina Simone.

It seemed to me she was enjoying her freedom. She read for a while, then sat looking around her. I found myself utterly unable to move from the chair and go towards her. I dreaded frightening her. How terrible to discover that one is being followed. I left before she did and went back to my little downtown hotel.

That afternoon, I again wandered the campus, and as soon as I approached her dormitory, she appeared. This time she wore a white cotton dress with short sleeves and a beautifully fitted bodice, and a rather loose billowy skirt.

Once again, she appeared to be walking aimlessly; however this time she took an unexpected turn towards the back of the campus, so to speak, away from the groomed lawns and the traffic, and I soon found myself following her into a large, deeply neglected botanical garden—a place so shadowy and wild and overgrown that I became fearful for her as she proceeded, way ahead of me, along the uneven path.

At last the large stands of bamboo blotted out all signs of the distant dormitories, and all noise from the even more distant streets. The air felt heavy as it feels in New Orleans, yet slightly more dry.

I came down a small walkway over a little bridge, and looked up to see Deirdre facing me as she stood quite still beneath a large flowering tree. She lifted her right hand and beckoned for me to come closer. Were my eyes deceiving me? No. She was staring straight at me.

"Mr. Lightner," she said, "what is it you want?" Her voice was low, and faintly tremulous. She seemed neither angry nor afraid. I was unable to answer her. I realized suddenly she was wearing the Mayfair emerald around her neck. It must have been under her dress when she came out of the dormitory. Now it was plainly in view.

A tiny alarm sounded inside me. I struggled to say something simple and honest and thoughtful. Instead, I said, "I've been following you, Deirdre."

"Yes," she said, "I know."

She turned her back to me, beckoning for me to follow, and went down a narrow overgrown set of steps to a near secret place where cement benches formed a circle, all but hidden from the main path. The bamboo was crackling faintly in the breeze. The smell of the nearby pond was rank. But the spot had an undeniable beauty to it.

She settled on the bench, her dress a shining whiteness in the shadows, the emerald flashing against her breast.

Danger, Lightner, I said to myself. You are in danger.

"Mr. Lightner," she said, looking up as I sat opposite, "just tell me what you want!"

"Deirdre, I know many things," I said. "Things about you and your mother, and your mother's mother, and about her mother before her. History, secrets, gossip, genealogies . . . all sorts of things really. In a house in Amsterdam there is a portrait of a woman, your ancestor. Her name was Deborah. She was the one who bought that emerald from a jeweler in Holland hundreds of years ago."

None of this seemed to surprise her. She was studying me, obviously scanning for lies and ill intentions. I myself was unaccountably shaken. I was talking to Deirdre Mayfair. I was sitting with Deirdre Mayfair at last.

"Deirdre," I said, "tell me if you want to know what I know. Do you want to see the letters of a man who loved your ancestor, Deborah? Do you want to hear how she died in France, and how her daughter came across the sea to Saint-Domingue? On the day she died, Lasher brought a storm to the village . . ."

I stopped. It was as if the words had dried up in my mouth. Her face had undergone a shocking change. For a moment I thought it was rage that had overwhelmed her. Then I realized it was some consuming inner struggle.

"Mr. Lightner," she whispered, "I don't want to know. I want to forget what I do know. I came here to get away."

"Ah." I said nothing for a moment.

I could feel her growing more calm. I was the one at a loss, quite completely. Then she said:

"Mr. Lightner"—her voice very steady yet infused with emotion—"my aunt says that you study us because you believe we are special people. That you would help the evil in us, out of curiosity, if you could. No, don't misunderstand me. She means that by talking about the evil, you would feed it. By studying it, you would give it more life." Her soft blue eyes pleaded for my understanding. How remarkably poised she seemed; how surprisingly calm.

"I understand your aunt's point of view," I said. In fact, I was amazed. Amazed that Carlotta Mayfair knew who we were, or understood even that much of our purpose. And then I thought of Stuart. Stuart must have spoken to her. There was the proof of it. This, and a thousand other thoughts were crowding my brain.

"It's like the spiritualists, Mr. Lightner," Deirdre said in the same polite sympathetic manner. "They want to speak with the spirits of dead ancestors; and in spite of all their good intentions, they merely strengthen demons about whom they understand nothing . . ."

"Yes, I know what you're saying, believe me I know. I wanted only to give you the information, to let you know that if you . . ."

"But you see, I don't want it. I want to put the past behind me." Her voice faltered slightly. "I want never to go home again."

"Very well then," I said. "I understand perfectly. But will you do this for me? Memorize my name. Take this card from me. Memorize the phone numbers on it. Call me if ever you need me."

She took the card from me. She studied it for a length of time and then slipped it into her pocket.

I found myself looking at her in silence, looking into her large innocent blue eyes, and trying not to dwell upon the beauty of her young body, her exquisitely molded breasts in the cotton dress. Her face seemed full of sadness to me in the shadows.

"He's the devil, Mr. Lightner," she whispered. "He really is."

"Then why are you wearing the emerald, my dear?" I asked her impulsively.

A smile came over her face. She reached for it, closing her right hand around it, and then pulled hard on it so the chain broke. "For one very definite reason, Mr. Lightner. It was the

601

simplest way to bring it here, and I mean to give it to you.'' She reached out and dropped it in my hand.

I looked down at it, scarce believing that I was holding the thing. Off the top of my head, I said, "He'll kill me, you know. He'll kill me and he'll take it back.''

"No, he can't do that!'' she said. She stared at me blankly, in shock.

"Of course he can,'' I said. But I was ashamed that I'd made such a statement. "Deirdre, let me tell you what I know about this spirit. Let me tell you what I know about others who see such things. You are not alone in this. You needn't fight it alone.''

"Oh God,'' she whispered. She closed her eyes for an instant. "He can't do that,'' she said again, but there was no conviction. "I don't believe he can do something like that.''

"I'll take my chances with him,'' I said. "I'll take the emerald. Some people have weapons of their own, so to speak. I can help you understand your weapons. Does your aunt do this? Tell me what you want of me.''

"That you go away,'' she said miserably. "That you . . . that you . . . never speak to me about these things again.''

"Deirdre, can he make you see him when you don't want him to come?''

"I want you to stop it, Mr. Lightner. If I don't think of him, if I don't speak of him''—she raised her hands to her temples— "if I refuse to look at him, maybe. . . .''

"What do you want? For yourself.''

"Life, Mr. Lightner. Normal life. You can't imagine what the words mean to me! Normal life. Life like they have, the girls over there in the dormitory, life with teddy bears and boyfriends and kissing in the back of cars. Just life!''

She was now so upset that I was fast becoming upset. And all this was so unforgivably dangerous. And yet she'd put this thing in my hand! I felt of it, rubbing my thumb across it. It was so cold, so hard.

"I'm sorry, Deirdre, I'm so sorry I disturbed you. I'm so sorry . . .''

"Mr. Lightner, can't you make him go away! Can't you people do that? My aunt says no, only the priest can do it, but the priest doesn't believe in him, Mr. Lightner. And you can't exorcise a demon when you have no faith.''

"He doesn't show himself to the priest, does he, Deirdre?''

"No,'' she said bitterly with a trace of a smile. "What good would it do if he did? He's no lowly spirit who can be driven off with holy water and Hail Marys. He makes fools of them.''

She had begun to cry. She reached for the emerald and pulled it by its chain from my fingers, and then flung it as far as she could through the underbrush. I heard it strike water, with a dull short sound. She was shaking violently. "It'll come back," she said. "It will come back! It always comes back."

"Maybe you can exorcise him!" I said. "You and only you."

"Oh, yes, that's what she says, that's what she always said. 'Don't look at him, don't speak to him, don't let him touch you!' But he always comes back. He doesn't ask my permission! And . . ."

"Yes."

"When I'm lonely, when I'm miserable . . ."

"He's there."

"Yes, he's there."

This girl was in agony. Something had to be done!

"And what if he does come, Deirdre? What I am saying is, what if you do not fight him, and you let him come, let him be visible. What then?"

Stunned and hurt she looked at me. "You don't know what you're saying."

"I know it's driving you mad to fight him. What happens if you don't fight him?"

"I die," she answered. "And the world dies around me, and there's only him." She wiped her mouth with the back of her hand.

How long she has lived with this misery, I thought. And how strong she is, and so helpless and so afraid.

"Yes, Mr. Lightner, that's true," she said. "I am afraid. But I am not going to die. I'm going to fight him. And I'm going to win. You're going to leave me. You're never going to come near me again. And I'm never going to say his name again, or look at him, or invite him to come. And he'll leave me. He'll go away. He'll find someone else to see him. Someone . . . to love."

"Does he love you, Deirdre?"

"Yes," she whispered. It was growing dark. I could no longer see her features clearly.

"What does he want, Deirdre?" I asked.

"You know what he wants!" she answered. "He wants me, Mr. Lightner. The same thing you want! Because I make him come through."

She took a little knot of handkerchief out of her pocket and wiped at her nose. "He told me you were coming," she said. "He said something strange, something I can't remember. It was like a curse, what he said. It was 'I shall eat the meat and drink the wine and have the woman when he is moldering in the grave.' ''

"I've heard those words before," I answered.

"I want you to go away," she said. "You're a nice man. I like you. I don't want him to hurt you. I'll tell him that he mustn't—'' She stopped, confused.

"Deirdre, I believe I can help you . . .''

"No!''

"I can help you fight him if that's your decision. I know people in England who . . .''

"No!''

I waited, then said softly, "If you ever need my help, call me.'' She didn't answer. I could feel her utter exhaustion. Her near despair. I told her where I was staying in Denton, that I would be there until tomorrow, and that if I didn't hear from her I would go. I felt an utter failure, but I could not hurt her any more! I gazed off into the whispering bamboo. It was getting darker and darker. And there were no lights in this rank garden.

"But your aunt is wrong about us,'' I said, unsure of her attention. I stared up at the little bit of sky above which was now quite white. "We want to tell you what we know. We want to give you what we have. It's true we care about you because you are a special person, but we care far more about you than we care about him. You could come to our house in London. Stay there as long as you like. We'll introduce you to others who've seen such things, battled them. We'll help you. And who knows, perhaps we can somehow make him go away. And any time you want to go, we'll help you to go.'' (She didn't answer.) "You know I'm speaking the truth,'' I said. "And I know that you know.''

I looked at her, quite afraid to see the pain in her face. She was staring at me exactly the way she had been before, her eyes sad and glazed with tears, and her hands limp in her lap. And directly behind her, *he stood*, not even an inch from her, brilliantly realized, staring with his brown eyes at me.

I cried out before I could stop myself. Like a fool, I leapt to my feet.

"What is it!'' she cried. She was terrified. She sprang up off the bench and threw herself in my arms. "Tell me! What is it?''

He was gone. A gust of heated breeze moved the towering shoots of bamboo. Nothing but shadows there. Nothing but the rank closeness of the garden. And a gradual drop in temperature. As if the door to a furnace room had been swung shut.

I closed my eyes, holding her as firmly as I could, trying not to shake right out of my shoes, and to comfort her, while I memorized what I had seen. A malicious young man, smiling coldly as he stood behind her, clothes prim and dark and without detail as if the entire energy of the being were absorbed in the lustrous eyes and the white teeth and the gleaming skin. Otherwise he had been the man whom so many others had described.

She was now quite hysterical. Her hand was clamped over her mouth, and she was swallowing her sobs. She pushed away from me roughly. And ran up the small overgrown stairs to the path.

"Deirdre!" I called out. But she was already out of sight in the darkness. I glimpsed a smear of white through the distant trees, and then I did not even hear her footfall any longer.

I was alone in the old botanical garden, and it was dark, and I was mortally afraid for the first time in my life. I was so afraid that I became angry. I started to follow her, or rather the path she had taken, and I forced myself not to run, but to take one firm step after another until at last I saw the distant lights of the dormitories, and the service road behind them, and heard the traffic, and felt once again that I was safe.

Entering the freshman dormitory, I inquired of the gray-haired woman at the desk as to whether Deirdre Mayfair had just come in. She had. Safe and sound, I thought.

"It's supper now, sir. You can leave a message if you like."

"Yes, of course, I'll call her later." I took out a small plain envelope, wrote Deirdre's name on it, then wrote a note explaining once more that I was at the hotel if she wished to contact me, and placing my card in the envelope with the note, I sealed the envelope and gave it to the woman for delivery, and went out.

Without mishap I reached the hotel, went to my room, and rang London. It was an hour before my call could be put through, during which time I lay there on the bed, with the phone beside me, and all I could think was, I've seen him. I've seen "the man." I've seen "the man" for myself. I've seen what Petyr saw and what Arthur saw. I've seen Lasher with my own eyes.

Scott Reynolds, our director, was calm but adamant when I finally made the connection.

"Get the hell out of there. Come home."

"Take a deep breath, Scott. I haven't come this far to be frightened off by a spirit we have studied from afar for three hundred years."

"This is how you use your own judgment, Aaron? You who know the history of the Mayfair Witches from beginning to end? The thing isn't trying to frighten you. It's trying to entice you. It wants you to torment the girl with your inquiries. It's losing her, and you're its hope of getting her back. The aunt, whatever else she may be, is on to the truth. You make that girl talk to you about what she's been through and you'll give that spirit the energy it wants.''

''I'm not trying to make her do anything, Scott. But I don't think she is winning her battle. I'm going back to New Orleans. I want to be near at hand.''

Scott was on the verge of ordering me to leave when I pulled rank. I was older than he was. I had declined the appointment as director. Hence he'd received it. I was not going to be ordered off this case.

''Well, this is like offering a bromide to a person who's burning to death, but don't drive back to New Orleans. Take the train.''

That was a surprisingly welcome suggestion. No dark dismal shoulderless roads through the Louisiana swampland. But a nice cheerful, crowded train.

The following day, I left a note for Deirdre that I would be at the Royal Court in New Orleans. I drove the rental car to Dallas and took the train back to New Orleans from there. It was only an eight-hour trip, and I was able to write in my diary the entire way.

At length I considered what had happened. The girl had renounced her history and her psychic powers. Her aunt had reared her to reject the spirit, Lasher. But for years she'd been losing the battle, quite obviously. But what if we gave her our assistance? Might the hereditary chain be broken? Might the spirit depart the family like a spirit fleeing a burning house which it has haunted for years?

Even as I wrote out these thoughts, I was dogged by my remembrance of the apparition. The thing was so powerful! It was more seemingly incarnate and powerful than any such phantom I had ever beheld. Yet it had been a fragmentary image.

In my experience only the ghosts of people who have very recently died appear with such seeming substance. For example, the ghost of a pilot killed in action may appear on the very day of his death in his sister's parlor, and she will say after, ''Why, he was so real. I could see the mud on his shoes!''

Ghosts of the long departed almost never had such density or vividness.

And discarnate entities? They could possess bodies of the living and of the dead, yes, but appear on their own with such solidity and such intensity?

This thing liked to appear, didn't it? Of course it did. That was why so many people saw it. It liked to have a body if only for a split second. So it didn't just speak with a soundless voice to the witch, or make an image which existed entirely in her mind. No, it made itself somehow material so that others saw it and even heard it. And with great effort—perhaps very great effort, it could make itself appear to cry or smile.

So what was the agenda of this being? To gain strength so that it might make appearances of greater and greater duration and perfection? And above all what was the meaning of the curse, which in Petyr's letter had read: "I shall drink the wine and eat the meat and know the warmth of the woman when you are no longer even bones"?

Lastly, why was it not tormenting me or enticing me now? Had it used the energy of Deirdre to make this appearance, or my energy? (I had seen very few spirits in my life. I was not a strong medium. In fact, at that point, I had never seen an apparition which could not have been explained as some sort of illusion created by light and shadow, or an overactive mind.)

Perhaps foolishly I had the feeling that as long as I was away from Deirdre it couldn't do me harm. What had happened with Petyr van Abel had to do with his powers of mediumship and how the thing manipulated them. I had very little of that sort of power.

But it would be a very bad mistake to underestimate the being. I needed to be on guard from here on out.

I arrived in New Orleans at eight in the evening, and strange unpleasant little things began to happen at once. I was nearly run down by a taxi outside Union Station. Then the taxi which took me to my hotel nearly collided with another car as we pulled up to the curb.

In the small lobby of the Royal Court, a drunken tourist bumped into me and then tried to start a brawl. Fortunately, his wife diverted him, apologizing repeatedly, as the bellhops assisted her in getting the man upstairs. But my shoulder was bruised from this small incident. I was shaken from the close calls in the cab.

Imagination, I thought. Yet as I climbed the stairs to my first-floor room, a weak portion of the old wooden railing came loose in my hands. I almost lost my balance. The bellhop was immediately apologetic. An hour later, as I was noting all these things in my diary, a fire broke out on the third floor of the hotel.

I stood in the cramped French Quarter street with other uncomfortable guests for the better part of an hour before it was determined that the small blaze had been put out without smoke or water damage to any other rooms. "What was the cause?" I asked. An embarrassed employee murmured something about rubbish in a storage closet, and assured me that everything was all right.

For a long time, I considered the situation. Really, all this might have been coincidence. I was unharmed, and so was everyone else involved in these little incidents, and what was required of me now was a stalwart frame of mind. I resolved to move just a little bit more slowly through the world, to look around myself with greater care, and to try to remain conscious of all that was going on around me at all times.

The night passed without any further mishap, though I slept very uneasily and woke often. And the following morning after breakfast, I called our investigative detectives in London, asked them to hire a Texas investigator and to find out as discreetly as possible what he could about Deirdre Mayfair.

I then sat down and wrote a long letter to Cortland. I explained who I was, what the Talamasca was, and how we had followed the history of the Mayfair family since the seventeenth century during which one of our representatives had rescued Deborah Mayfair from serious jeopardy in her native Donnelaith. I explained about the Rembrandt of Deborah in Amsterdam. I went on to explain that we were interested in Deborah's descendants because they seemed to possess genuine psychic powers, manifesting in every generation, and we were desirous of making contact with the family, with a view to sharing our records with those who were interested, and in offering information to Deirdre Mayfair, who seemed to be a person deeply burdened by her ability to see a spirit who in former times was called Lasher and might still be called Lasher to this day.

"Our representative, Petyr van Abel, first glimpsed this spirit in Donnelaith in the 1600s. It has been seen countless times since in the vicinity of your home on First Street. I have only just seen it in another location, with my own eyes."

I then copied out the identical letter to Carlotta Mayfair, and after much consideration, put down the address and phone number of my hotel. After all, what was the point of hiding behind a post office box?

I drove up to First Street, placed Carlotta's letter in the mailbox, and then drove out to Metairie, where I put Cortland's letter through the slot in his door. After that, I found I was overcome by foreboding, and though I went back to my hotel, I did not go up to my room. Rather I told the desk I would be in the first-floor bar, and there I remained all evening, slowly savoring a good sample of Kentucky sipping whiskey and writing in my diary about the whole affair.

The bar was small and quiet, and opened onto a charming

courtyard, and though I sat with my back to this view, facing the lobby doors for reasons I cannot quite explain, I enjoyed the little place. The feeling of foreboding was slowly melting away.

At about eight o'clock, I looked up from my diary to realize that someone was standing very near my table. It was Cortland.

I had only just completed my narrative of the Mayfair file, as indicated. I had studied countless photographs of Cortland. But it was not a photograph of Cortland which came to mind as our eyes met.

The tall, black-haired man smiling down at me was the image of Julien Mayfair, who had died in 1914. The differences seemed unimportant. It was Julien with larger eyes, darker hair, and perhaps a more generous mouth. But Julien nevertheless. And quite suddenly the smile appeared grotesque. A mask.

I made a mental note of these odd thoughts, even as I invited the man to sit down.

He was wearing a linen suit, much like my own, with a pale lemon-colored shirt and pale tie.

Thank God it's not Carlotta, I thought, at which point he said: "I don't think you will hear from my cousin Carlotta. But I think it's time you and I had a talk." Very pleasant and completely insincere voice. Deeply southern but in a unique New Orleans way. The gleam in the dark eyes was charming and faintly awful.

This man either hated me or regarded me as a damnable nuisance. He turned and signaled the bartender. "Another drink for Mr. Lightner, please, and a sherry for me."

He sat opposite me across the little marble table, his long legs crossed and turned to one side. "You don't mind if I smoke, do you, Mr. Lightner? Thank you." He withdrew a beautiful gold cigarette case from his pocket, laid it down, offered me a cigarette, and when I refused, lit one for himself. Again his cheerful demeanor struck me as entirely contrived. I wondered how it might appear to a normal person.

"I'm so glad you've come, Mr. Mayfair," I said.

"Oh, do call me Cortland," he said. "There are so many Mr. Mayfairs, after all."

I felt danger emanating from him, and made a conscious effort to veil my thoughts.

"If you will call me Aaron," I said, "I shall call you Cortland with pleasure."

He gave a little nod. Then he threw an offhanded smile at the young woman who set down our drinks, and at once he took a sip of his sherry.

He was a compellingly attractive person. His black hair was lustrous, and there was a touch of thin mustache, dappled with gray, above his lip. It seemed the lines in his face were an embellishment. I thought of Llewellyn and his descriptions of Julien, which I had heard only a few days before. But I had to put all this out of my mind completely. I was in danger. That was the overriding intuition and the man's subdued charm was part of it. He thought himself very attractive and very clever. And both of these things he was.

I stared at the fresh bourbon and water. And was suddenly struck by the position of his hand on his gold cigarette case only an inch from the glass. I knew, absolutely knew, this man meant to do me harm. How unexpected. I had thought it was Carlotta all along.

"Oh, excuse me," he said with a sudden look of surprise as though he had just remembered something. "A medicine I have to take, that is, if I can find it." He felt of his pockets, then drew something out of his coat. A small bottle of tablets. "What a nuisance," he said, shaking his head. "Have you enjoyed your stay in New Orleans?" He turned and asked for a glass of water. "Of course you've been to Texas to see my niece, I know that. But you've been touring the city as well, no doubt. What do you think of this garden here?" He pointed to the courtyard behind him. "Quite a story about that garden. Did they tell you?"

I turned in my chair and glanced over my shoulder at the garden. I saw the uneven flagstones, a weathered fountain, and beyond, in the shadows, a man standing before the fanlight door. Tall thin man, with the light behind him. Faceless. Motionless. The chill which ran down my back was almost delicious. I continued to look at the man, and slowly the figure melted completely away.

I waited for a draft of warm air, but I felt nothing. Perhaps I was too far from the being. Or perhaps I was altogether wrong about who or what it had been.

It seemed an age passed. Then, as I turned around, Cortland said, "A woman committed suicide in that little garden. They say that the fountain turns red with her blood once a year."

"Charming," I said under my breath. I watched him lift his glass of water and drink half the contents. Was he swallowing his tablets? The little bottle had disappeared. I glanced at my bourbon and water. I would not have touched it for anything in this world. I looked absently at my pen, lying there beside my diary, and then placed it in my pocket. I was so utterly absorbed in everything that I saw and heard that I felt not the slightest urge to speak a word.

"Well, then, Mr. Lightner, let's get to the point." Again that smile, that radiant smile.

"Of course," I said. What was I feeling? I was curiously excited. I was sitting here with Julien's son, Cortland, and he had just slipped a drug, no doubt lethal, into my drink. He thought he was going to get away with this. The whole dark history glittered suddenly in my mind. I was in it. I wasn't reading about it in England. I was here.

Perhaps I smiled at him. I knew that a crushing misery would follow this curious peak of emotion. The damned son of a bitch was trying to kill me.

"I've looked into this matter, the Talamasca, etcetera," he said in a bright, artificial voice. "There's nothing we can do about you people. We can't force you to disclose your information about our family because apparently it's entirely private, and not intended for publication or for any malicious use. We can't force you to stop collecting it either as long as you break no laws."

"Yes, I suppose that's all true."

"However we can make you and your representatives uncomfortable, very uncomfortable; and we can make it legally impossible for you to come within so many feet of us and our property. But that would be costly to us, and wouldn't really stop you, at least not if you are what you say you are."

He paused, took a draw off his thin dark cigarette, and glanced at the bourbon and water. "Did I order the wrong drink for you, Mr. Lightner?"

"You didn't order any drink," I said. "The waiter brought another of what I had been drinking all afternoon. I should have stopped you. I've had quite enough."

His eyes hardened for a moment as he looked at me. In fact, his mask of a smile vanished completely. And in a moment of blankness and lack of contrivance he looked almost young.

"You shouldn't have made that trip to Texas, Mr. Lightner," he said coldly. "You should never have upset my niece."

"I agree with you. I shouldn't have upset her. I was concerned about her. I wanted to offer my help."

"That's very presumptuous of you, you and your London friends." Touch of anger. Or was it simply annoyance that I wasn't going to drink the bourbon. I looked at him for a long moment, my mind emptying itself until there was no sound intruding, no movement, no color—only his face there, and a small voice in my head telling me what I wanted to know.

"Yes, it is presumptuous, isn't it?" I said. "But you see, it was our representative Petyr van Abel who was the father of Charlotte Mayfair, born in France in 1664. When he later journeyed to Saint-Domingue to see his daughter, he was imprisoned

611

by her. And before your spirit, Lasher, drove him to his death on a lonely road outside of Port-au-Prince, he coupled with his own daughter Charlotte, and thereby became the father of her daughter, Jeanne Louise. That means he was grandfather of Angélique and the great-grandfather of Marie Claudette, who built Riverbend, and created the legacy which you administer for Deirdre now. Do you follow my tale?''

Clearly he was utterly incapable of a response. He sat still looking at me, the cigarette smoking in his hand. I caught no emanation of malice or anger. Watching him keenly, I went on:

"Your ancestors are the descendants of our representative, Petyr van Abel. We are linked, the Mayfair Witches and the Talamasca. And then there are other matters which bring us together after all these years. Stuart Townsend, our representative who disappeared here in New Orleans after he visited Stella in 1929. Do you remember Stuart Townsend? The case of his disappearance was never solved.''

"You are mad, Mr. Lightner,'' he said with no perceptible change of expression. He drew on his cigarette and crushed it out though it was not half spent.

"That spirit of yours, Lasher—he killed Petyr van Abel,'' I said calmly. "Was it Lasher whom I saw only a moment ago? Over there?'' I gestured to the distant garden. "He is driving your niece out of her mind, isn't he?'' I asked.

A remarkable change had now come over Cortland. His face, beautifully framed by his dark hair, looked totally innocent in its bewilderment.

"You're perfectly serious, aren't you?'' he asked. These were the first honest words he'd spoken since he came into the bar.

"Of course I am,'' I said. "Why would I try to deceive people who can read other people's thoughts? That would be stupid, wouldn't it?'' I looked at the glass. "Rather like you expecting me to drink this bourbon and succumb to the drug you put into it, the way Stuart Townsend did, or Cornell Mayfair after that.''

He tried to shroud his shock behind a blank, dull look. "You are making a very serious accusation,'' he said under his breath.

"All this time, I thought it was Carlotta. It was never Carlotta, was it? It was you.''

"Who cares what you think!'' he whispered. "How dare you say such things to me.'' Then he checked his anger. He shifted slightly in his chair, his eyes holding me as he opened the cigarette case and withdrew another cigarette. His whole demeanor changed suddenly to one of honest inquiry. "What the hell do you want, Mr. Lightner!'' he asked, dropping his voice earnestly. "Seriously now, sir, what do you want?''

I reflected for a moment. I had been asking myself this very question for weeks on end. What did I mean to accomplish when I went to New Orleans? What did we, and what did I, really want?

"We want to know you!" I said, rather surprised myself to hear it come out. "To know you because we know so much about you and yet we don't know anything at all. We want to tell you what we know about you—all the bits and pieces of information we've collected, what we know about the deep past! We want to tell you all we know about the whole mystery of who you are and what *he* is. And we wish you would talk to us. We wish you would trust us and let us in! And lastly, we want to reach out to Deirdre Mayfair and say, 'There are others like you, others who see spirits. We know you're suffering, and we can help you. You aren't alone.' "

He studied me, eyes seemingly open, his face quite beyond dissembling. Then pulling back and glancing away, he tapped off the ash of his cigarette and motioned for another drink.

"Why don't you drink the bourbon?" I asked. "I haven't touched it." Again, I had surprised myself. But I let the question stand.

He looked at me. "I don't like bourbon," he said. "Thank you."

"What did you put in it?" I asked.

He shrank back into his thoughts. He appeared just a little miserable. He watched as the boy set down his drink. Sherry as before, in a crystal glass.

"This is true," he asked, looking up at me, "what you wrote in your letter, about the portrait of Deborah Mayfair in Amsterdam?"

I nodded. "We have portraits of Charlotte, Jeanne Louise, Angélique, Marie Claudette, Marguerite, Katherine, Mary Beth, Julien, Stella, Antha, and Deirdre . . ."

He made a sudden impatient motion for me to stop.

"Look, I came here because of Deirdre," I said. "I came because she's going mad. The girl I spoke to in Texas is on the edge of breakdown."

"Do you think you helped her?"

"No, and I deeply regret that I didn't. If you don't want contact with us, I understand. Why the hell should you? But we can help Deirdre. We really can."

No answer. He drank the sherry. I tried to see this from his point of view. I couldn't. I'd never tried to poison someone. I didn't have the faintest idea of who he really was. The man I'd known in the history wasn't this man.

"Would your father, Julien, have spoken to me?" I asked.

"Not a chance of it," he said, looking up as though awakening from his thoughts. For a moment he looked deeply distressed. "But don't you know from all your observations," he asked, "that he was *one of them*?" Again, he seemed completely earnest, his eyes searching my face as if to assure himself that I was earnest too.

"And you're not one of them?" I asked.

"No," he said with great quiet emphasis, slowly shaking his head. "Not really. Not ever!" He looked sad suddenly, and when he did he looked old. "Look, spy on us if you wish. Treat us as if we were a royal family . . ."

"Exactly."

"You're historians, that's what my contacts in London tell me. Historians, scholars, utterly harmless, completely respectable . . ."

"I'm honored."

"But leave my niece alone. My niece has a chance for happiness now. And this thing must come to an end, you see. It must. And perhaps she can see to it that it does."

"Is she *one of them*?" I asked, echoing his early intonation.

"Of course she isn't!" he said. "That's just the point! There is no *one of them* now! Don't you see that? What's been the theme of your study of us? Haven't you seen the disintegration of the power? Stella wasn't one of them either! The last one was Mary Beth. Julien—my father, that is—and then Mary Beth."

"I've seen it. But what about your spectral friend? Will he allow it to come to a finish?"

"You believe in him?" He cocked his head with a faint smile, his dark eyes creasing at the edges with silent laughter. "Really, now, Mr. Lightner? Do you believe in Lasher yourself?"

"I saw him," I said simply.

"Imagination, sir. My niece told me it was a very dark garden."

"Oh, please. Have we come this far to say such things to each other? I saw him, Cortland. He smiled when I saw him. He made himself very substantial and vivid indeed."

Cortland's smile became smaller, more ironic. He raised his eyebrows and gave a little sigh. "Oh, he would like your choice of words, Mr. Lightner."

"Can Deirdre make him go away and leave her alone?"

"Of course she can't. But she can ignore him. She can live her life as if he weren't there. Antha couldn't. Stella didn't want to. But Deirdre's stronger than Antha, and stronger than Stella too. Deirdre has a lot of Mary Beth in her. That's what the others

614

often don't realize—'' He appeared to catch himself suddenly in the act of saying more than he had ever intended to say.

He stared at me for a long moment, and then he gathered up his cigarette case and his lighter and slowly rose to his feet.

"Don't go yet," I said, imploringly.

"Send me your history. Send it to me and I'll read it. And then maybe we can talk again. But don't ever approach my niece again, Mr. Lightner. Understand that I would do anything to protect her from those who mean to exploit her or hurt her. Anything at all!"

He turned to go.

"What about the drink?" I asked, rising. I gestured to the bourbon. "Suppose I call the police and I offer the contaminated drink in evidence?"

"Mr. Lightner. This is New Orleans!" He smiled and winked at me in the most charming fashion. "Now please, go home to your watchtower and your telescope and gaze at us from afar!"

I watched him leave. He walked gracefully with very long, easy steps. He glanced back when he reached the doorway and gave me a quick, agreeable wave of his hand.

I sat down, ignoring the drugged bourbon, and wrote an account of the whole affair in my diary. I then took a small bottle of aspirin out of my pocket, emptied out the tablets, and poured some of the drugged bourbon into it, and capped it and put it away.

I was about to collect my diary and pen and make for the stairs when I looked up and saw the bellhop standing in the lobby just beyond the door. He came forward. "Your bags are ready, Mr. Lightner. Your car is here." Bright, agreeable face. Nobody had told him he was personally throwing me out of town.

"Is that so?" I said. "Well, and you packed everything?" I surveyed the two bags. My diary I had with me, of course. I went into the lobby. I could see a large old black limousine stopping up the narrow French Quarter street like a giant cork. "That's my car?"

"Yes sir, Mr. Cortland said to see you made the ten o'clock flight to New York. Said he'd have someone meet you at the airport with the ticket. You ought to have plenty of time."

"Isn't that thoughtful?" I fished into my pocket for a couple of bills, but the boy refused them.

"Mr. Cortland's taken care of everything, sir. You'd better hurry. You don't want to miss your plane."

"That's true. But I have a superstition about big black cars. Get me a taxi, and do take this for it, please."

615

The taxi took me not to the airport but to the train. I managed to get a sleeper for St. Louis, and went on to New York from there. When I spoke to Scott he was adamant. This data required a reevaluation. Don't do any more research in New York. Come home.

Halfway across the Atlantic, I became ill. By the time I reached London I was running a high fever. An ambulance was waiting to take me to hospital, and Scott was there to ride with me. I was going in and out of consciousness. "Look for poison," I said.

Those were my last words for eight hours. When I finally came around, I was still feverish and uncomfortable, but much reassured to be alive and to discover Scott and two other good friends in the room.

"You've been poisoned all right, but the worst is over. Can you remember your last drink before you boarded the plane?"

"That woman," I said.

"Tell me."

"I was in the bar at the New York airport, had a Scotch and soda. She was stumbling alone with an impossible bag, then asked me if I'd fetch the skycap for her. She was coughing as if she were tubercular. Very unhealthy-looking creature. She sat at my table while I went for the skycap. Probably a hireling, off the streets."

"She slipped you a poison called ricin; its from the castor bean. Very powerful, and extremely common. Same thing Cortland put in your bourbon. You're out of the woods, but you're going to be sick for two more days."

"Good Lord." My stomach was cramping again.

"They aren't ever going to talk to us, Aaron," Scott said. "How could they? They kill people. It's over. At least for now."

"They always killed people, Scott," I said weakly. "But Deirdre Mayfair doesn't kill people. I want my diary." The cramps became unbearable. The doctor came in and started to prepare me for an injection. I refused.

"Aaron, he's the head of toxicology here, impeccable reputation. We've checked out the nurses. Our people are here in the room."

It was the end of the week before I could return to the Motherhouse. I could scarcely bring myself to take any nourishment. I was convinced the entire Motherhouse might soon be poisoned. What was to stop them from hiring people to put commonplace toxins in our food? The food might be poisoned before it even reached our kitchen.

And though no such thing happened, it was a year before such thoughts left me, so shaken was I by what had occurred.

A great deal of shocking news came to us from New Orleans during that year . . .

During my convalescence I reviewed the entire Mayfair history. I revised some of it, including the testimony of Richard Llewellyn, and a few other persons I'd seen before I went to Texas to see Deirdre.

I concluded that Cortland had done away with Stuart, and probably with Cornell. It all made sense. Yet so many mysteries remained. What was Cortland protecting when he committed these crimes? And why was he engaged in constant battle with Carlotta?

We had in the meantime heard from Carlotta Mayfair—a barrage of threatening legal letters from her law firm to ours in London, demanding that we "cease and desist" with our "invasion" of her privacy, that we make "full disclosure" of any personal information we had obtained about her and her family, "that we restrict ourselves to a safe distance of one hundred yards from any person in her family, and any piece of family property, and that we make no effort whatsoever to contact in any way shape or form, Deirdre Mayfair," et cetera, and so forth and so on ad nauseam, none of these legal threats or demands having the slightest validity.

Our legal representatives were instructed to make no response.

We discussed the matter with the full council.

Once again, we had tried to make contact and we had been pushed back. We would continue to investigate, and for this purpose I might have a carte blanche, but no one was going near the family in the foreseeable future. "If ever again," Reynolds added with great emphasis.

I did not argue. I could not drink a glass of milk at the time without wondering if I was going to die from it. And I could not get the memory of Cortland's artificial smile out of my mind.

I doubled the number of investigators in New Orleans and in Texas. But I also warned these people, personally by phone, that the objects of their surveillance were hostile and potentially very dangerous. I gave each and every one of our investigators full opportunity to refuse the job.

As it turned out, I lost no investigators whatsoever. But several raised their price.

As for Juliette Milton, our socialite undercover gossip, we retired her with an unofficial pension, over her protests. We did everything we could to make her sensible that certain members of this family were capable of violence. Reluctantly, she stopped writing to us, pleading in her letter of December 10, 1958 to understand what she had done wrong. We were to hear from her again several times over the years, however. She is still living *as of 1989*, in an expensive boarding house for elderly people in Mobile, Alabama.

DEIRDRE'S STORY CONTINUES

My investigators in Texas were three highly professional detectives, two of whom had once worked for the United States government; and all three were cautioned that Deirdre was never to be disturbed or frightened by what we were doing in any way.

"I am very concerned for this girl's happiness, and for her peace of mind. But understand, she is telepathic. If you come within fifty feet of her, she is likely to know you are watching her. Please take care."

Whether they believed me or not, they followed my instructions. They kept a safe distance, gathering information about her through the school offices and from gossiping students, from old women who worked the desk in her dormitory, and from teachers who talked freely about her over coffee. If Deirdre ever knew she was being watched, we never found out.

Deirdre did well in the fall semester at Texas Woman's University. She made excellent grades. The girls liked her. Her teachers liked her. About every six weeks or so she signed out of the dormitory for dinner with her cousin Rhonda Mayfair and Rhonda's husband, Professor Ellis Clement, who was Deirdre's English teacher at this time. There is also a record of one date on December 10 with a boy named Joey Dawson, but it lasted one hour if the register is to be believed.

The same register indicates that Cortland visited Deirdre often, frequently signing her out for a Friday or Saturday night in Dallas from which she returned before the "Late Check In" time of one A.M.

We know that Deirdre went home to Metairie to Cortland's house for Christmas, and family gossip declared that she would not even see Carlotta when Carlotta came to call.

Legal gossip supports the idea that Carlotta and Cortland were still not speaking. Carlotta would not return Cortland's routine business calls. Acrimonious letters went back and forth between the two over the smallest financial matters concerning Deirdre.

"He's trying to get complete control of her for her own sake," said one secretary to a friend, "but that old woman won't have it. She's threatening to take him to court."

Whatever the particulars of that struggle, we know that Deirdre began to deteriorate during the spring term. She began to miss classes. Dorm mates said she cried all night sometimes, but would not answer their knocks on her door. One evening she was picked up by the campus police in a small downtown park, apparently confused as to where she was.

Finally she was called to the dean's office for disciplinary action. She had missed too many classes. She was put on Compulsory Attendance, and though she did manage to appear in the classroom, teachers reported her as inattentive, and possibly ill.

Finally in April, Deirdre began to suffer nausea every morning. Girls up and down the hallway could hear her struggling with her sickness in the communal washroom. The girls went to the dorm mother.

"Nobody wanted to squeal on her. We were afraid. What if she tried to hurt herself?"

When the dorm mother finally suggested she might be pregnant, Deirdre broke down sobbing, and had to be hospitalized until Cortland could come and get her, which he did on May 1.

What happened afterwards has remained a mystery to this day. The records at the new Mercy Hospital in New Orleans indicate that Deirdre was probably taken there directly upon arrival from Texas, and that she was given a private room. Gossip among the old nuns, many of whom were retired teachers from St. Alphonsus School who remembered Deirdre, quickly verified that it was Carlotta's attending physician, Dr. Gallagher, who visited Deirdre and ascertained that yes, she was going to have a child.

"Now, this girl is going to be married," he told the sisters. "And I don't want anything mean being said. The father is a college professor from Denton, Texas, and he is on his way to New Orleans now."

By the time Deirdre was taken by ambulance to First Street three weeks later, heavily sedated and with a registered nurse in attendance, the gossip was all over the Redemptorist Parish that she was pregnant and soon to be married, and that her husband, the college professor, was "a married man."

Quite the scandal it was to those who had watched the family for generations. Old ladies whispered about it on the church steps. Deirdre Mayfair and a married man! People glanced furtively at Miss Millie and Miss Belle as they passed. Some said that Carlotta would have no part of it. But then Miss Belle and Miss Millie took Deirdre with them to Gus Mayer and there they bought her a lovely blue dress and blue satin shoes for the wedding, and a new white purse and hat.

"She was so drugged, I don't think she knew where she was,"

said one of the salesgirls. "Miss Millie made all the choices for her. She just sat there, white as a sheet, and saying 'Yes, Aunt Millie,' in a slurred voice."

Juliette Milton could not resist writing to us. We received a long letter from her detailing how Beatrice Mayfair had been to First Street to see Deirdre and brought her a whole shopping bag of gifts. "Why ever did she go home to that house, instead of Cortland's!" wrote Juliette.

There is some indication that Deirdre had little choice in the matter. Medical science in those days believed the placenta of the baby protected it from drugs injected into the mother. And nurses said that Deirdre was so heavily drugged when she left the hospital that she did not even know what was happening to her. Carlotta had come in the early afternoon on a weekday and obtained her release.

"Now, Cortland Mayfair came looking for her that very evening," Sister Bridget Marie told me later in strictest confidence. "And was he ever fit to be tied when he discovered that child was gone!"

Legal gossip deepened the mystery. Cortland and Carlotta were screaming at each other over the phone behind the office doors. Cortland told his secretary in a rage that Carlotta thought she could keep him out of the house where he was born. Well, she was out of her mind, if she thought so!

Years later, Ryan Mayfair talked about it. "They said my grandfather was simply locked out. He went up to First Street and Carlotta met him at the gate and threatened him. She said, 'You come in here and I'll call the police.' "

On the first of July, another volley of information rocked the parish gossips. Deirdre's future husband, the "college professor" who was leaving his wife to marry her, had been killed driving to New Orleans on the river road. His car had suffered a broken tie rod and veered to the right at great speed, striking an oak tree, whereupon it exploded into flames. Deirdre Mayfair, unmarried and not yet eighteen, was going to be giving up her baby. It was to be a family adoption, and Miss Carlotta was arranging the whole thing.

"My grandfather was outraged when he heard about the adoption," said Ryan Mayfair many years later. "He wanted to talk to Deirdre, hear it from her own lips that she wanted to give up this child. But he still couldn't get in the house on First Street. Finally he went to Father Lafferty, the parish priest, but Carlotta had him in her pocket. The priest was squarely on Carlotta's side."

All this sounds extremely tragic. It sounds as if Deirdre almost escaped the curse of First Street, if only the father of her baby, driving from Texas to marry her, had not died. For years this sad scandalous story has been repeated throughout the Redemptorist Parish. It was repeated to me as late as *1988* by Rita Mae Lonigan. There is every indication that Father Lafferty believed the story of the Texas father of the baby. And countless reports indicate that the Mayfair cousins believed it. Beatrice Mayfair believed it. Pierce Mayfair believed it. Even Rhonda Mayfair and her husband, Ellis Clement, in Denton, Texas seemed to have believed it, or at least the vague version which they were eventually told.

But the story wasn't true.

Almost from the beginning, our investigators shook their heads in puzzlement. College professor with Deirdre Mayfair? Who? Constant surveillance ruled out completely the possibility of Rhonda Mayfair's husband, Ellis Clement. He scarcely knew Deirdre.

Indeed, there never was any such man in Denton, Texas, who dated Deirdre Mayfair, or was ever observed by anyone in her company. And there was no college professor employed at that university or any other school in the vicinity who died in a car crash on the Louisiana river road. Indeed, no one died in such a crash on the river road in 1959, as far as we know.

Did an even more scandalous and tragic story lie behind this fabrication? We were slow in putting the pieces together. Indeed, by the time we learned of the River Road car accident, the adoption of Deirdre's baby was already being legally arranged. By the time we learned that there had been no river road accident, the adoption was a fait accompli.

Later court records indicate that some time during August, Ellie Mayfair flew to New Orleans to sign adoption papers in the office of Carlotta Mayfair, though no one in the family seems to have known at the time that Ellie was there.

Graham Franklin, Ellie's husband, told one of his business associates years later that the adoption had been a real kettle of fish. "My wife stopped speaking to her grandfather altogether. He didn't want us to adopt Rowan. Fortunately the old bastard died before the baby was even born."

Father Lafferty told his aging sister in the Irish Channel that the whole thing was a nightmare, but that Ellie Mayfair was a good woman and she would take the child to California where it would have a chance at a new life. All of Cortland's grandchildren approved of the decision. It was only Cortland who was carrying on. "That girl can't keep that baby. She's crazy," said the old priest. He sat at his sister's kitchen table, eating his red beans and rice and drinking his small glass of beer. "I mean it, she's crazy. It's just got to be done."

"It won't work," the old woman later told our representative. "You can't escape a family curse by moving away."

Miss Millie and Miss Belle bought beautiful bed jackets and nightgowns for Deirdre at Gus Mayer. The salesgirls asked about "poor Deirdre."

"Oh, she is doing the best she can," said Miss Millie. "It was a terrible, terrible thing." Miss Belle told a woman at the chapel that Deirdre was having those "bad spells again."

"She doesn't even know where she is half the time!" said a grumpy Nancy, who was sweeping the walk when one of the Garden District matrons passed the gate.

What did happen behind the scenes all those months at First Street? We pressed our investigators to find out everything that they could. Only one person of whom we know saw Deirdre during the last months of her "confinement"—to use the old-fashioned term for it, which in this instance may be the correct one—but we did not interview that person until 1988.

At the time, the attending physician came and went in silence. So did the nurse who assisted Deirdre for eight hours each day.

Father Lafferty said the girl was resigned to the adoption. Beatrice Mayfair was told she couldn't see Deirdre when she came to call, but she had a glass of wine with Millie Dear, who said the whole thing was heartbreaking indeed.

But by October 1, Cortland was desperate with worry over the situation. His secretaries report that he made continuous calls to Carlotta, that he took a taxi to First Street and was turned away over and over again. Finally on the afternoon of October 20, he told his secretary he would get into that house and see his niece even if he had to break down the door.

At five o'clock that afternoon a neighbor spotted Cortland sitting on the curbstone at First and Chestnut Streets, his clothes disheveled and blood flowing from a cut on his head.

"Get me an ambulance," he said. "He pushed me down the stairs!"

Though the neighbor woman sat with him until the ambulance arrived, he would say nothing more. He was rushed from First Street to nearby Touro Infirmary. The intern on duty quickly ascertained that Cortland was covered with severe bruises, that his wrist was broken, and that he was bleeding from the mouth. "This man has internal injuries," he said. He called for immediate assistance.

Cortland then grabbed the intern's hand and told him to listen, that it was very important that he help Deirdre Mayfair, who was being held prisoner in her own home. "They're taking her baby away from her against her will. Help her!" Then Cortland died.

A superficial postmortem indicated massive internal bleeding and severe blows to the head. When the young intern pressed for some sort of police investigation, Cortland's sons immediately quieted him. They had talked to their cousin Carlotta Mayfair. Their father fell down the steps and then refused medical assistance, leaving the house on his own. Carlotta had never dreamed he was so badly hurt. She had not known he was sitting on the curb. She was beside herself with grief. The neighbor should have rung the bell.

At Cortland's funeral—a huge affair out in Metairie—the family was told the same story. While Miss Belle and Miss Millie sat quietly in the background, Cortland's son, Pierce, told everyone that Cortland had been confused when he made some vague statement to the neighbor about a man pushing him down the steps. In fact there had been no man in the First Street house who could have done such a thing. Carlotta herself saw him fall. So did Nancy, who rushed to try to catch him, but failed.

As for the adoption, Pierce was firmly behind it. His niece Ellie would give the baby exactly the environment it needed to have every chance. It was tragic that Cortland had been against the adoption, but Cortland had been eighty years old. His judgment had been impaired for some time.

The funeral proceeded, grandly and without incident, though the undertaker remembered years later that several of the cousins, older men, standing in the very rear of the room during Pierce's "little speech" had joked bitterly and sarcastically amongst themselves. "Sure, there's no man in that house," one of them said. "Nooooo, no man at all. Just those nice ladies." "I've never seen a man there, have you?" And so on it went. "Nope, no man at First Street. No sir!"

When cousins came to call on Deirdre, they were told pretty much the same story that Pierce had told at the funeral. Deirdre was too sick to see them. She hadn't even wanted to see Cortland, she was so sick. And she didn't know and mustn't know that Cortland was dead.

"And look at that dark stairs," said Millie Dear to Beatrice. "Cortland should have used the elevator. But he never would use the elevator. If he had just used the elevator, he would never have taken such a fall."

Family legend today indicates that everyone agreed the adoption was for the best. Cortland should have stayed out of it. As Ryan Mayfair, Cortland's grandson, said, "Poor Deirdre was no more fit to be a mother than the Madwoman of Chaillot. But I think my grandfather felt responsible. He had taken Deirdre to Texas. I think he blamed himself. He wanted to be sure she wanted to give up the baby. But maybe what Deirdre wanted wasn't the important thing.''

At the time, I dreaded each new piece of news from Louisiana. I lay in bed at night in the Motherhouse thinking ceaselessly of Deirdre, wondering if there were not some way that we could discover what she truly wanted or felt. Scott Reynolds was more adamant than ever that we could not intervene further. Deirdre knew how to reach us. So did Cortland. So did Carlotta Mayfair, for what that was worth. There was nothing further that we could do.

Only in January of 1988, nearly thirty years later, did I learn in an interview with Deirdre's old school friend Rita Mae Dwyer Lonigan that Deirdre had tried desperately to reach me, and failed.

In 1959, Rita Mae had only just married Jerry Lonigan of Lonigan and Sons funeral home, and when she heard that Deirdre was at home, pregnant, and had already lost the father of her baby, Rita Mae screwed up her courage and went to call. As so many others have been, she was turned away at the door, but not before she saw Deirdre at the top of the stairs. Deirdre called out to Rita Mae desperately:

"Rita Mae, they're going to take my baby! Rita Mae, help me." As Miss Nancy sought to force Deirdre back up to the second floor, Deirdre threw a small white card down to Rita Mae. "Contact this man. Get him to help me. Tell him they're going to take my baby away."

Carlotta Mayfair physically attacked Rita Mae and tried to get the card away from her, but Rita, even though her hair was being pulled and her face scratched, held it tight as she ran through a hail of leaves out the gate.

When she got home she discovered the card was almost unreadable. Carlotta had torn part of it; and Rita had inadvertently clenched the little card in the moist palm of her hand. Only the word Talamasca, and my name, handwritten on the back, could be made out.

Only in 1988, when I encountered Rita Mae at the funeral of Nancy Mayfair—and gave her a card identical to the one destroyed in 1959—did she recognize the names and call me at my hotel to report what she remembered from that long ago day.

It was heartbreaking to this investigator to learn of Deirdre's vain plea for help. It was heartbreaking to remember those nights thirty years before when I lay in bed in London thinking, "I cannot help her, but I have to try to help her. But how do I dare to do it? And how could I possibly succeed?''

The fact is I probably could not have done anything to help Deirdre, no matter how hard I might have tried. If Cortland couldn't stop the adoption, it is sensible to assume that I couldn't have stopped it either. Yet in my dreams I see myself taking Deirdre out of the First Street house to London. I see her a healthy normal woman today.

The reality is utterly different.

On November 7, 1959, Deirdre gave birth at five o'clock in the morning to Rowan Mayfair, nine pounds, eight ounces, a healthy, fair-haired baby girl. Hours afterwards, emerging from the general anesthesia, Deirdre found her bed surrounded by Ellie Mayfair, Father Lafferty, and Carlotta Mayfair, and two of the Sisters of Mercy who later described the scene in detail to Sister Bridget Marie.

Father Lafferty held the baby in his arms. He explained that he had just baptized it in the Mercy Hospital chapel, naming it Rowan Mayfair. He showed her the signed baptismal certificate.

''Now kiss your baby, Deirdre,'' said Father Lafferty, ''and give her to Ellie. Ellie is ready to go.''

Parish gossip says that Deirdre did as she was told. She had insisted that the child have the name Mayfair and once that condition was met, she let her baby go. Crying so as she could scarce see, she kissed the baby and let Ellie Mayfair take it from her arms. Then she turned her head, sobbing, into the pillow. Father Lafferty said, ''Best leave her alone.''

Over a decade later, Sister Bridget Marie explained the meaning of Rowan's name.

''Carlotta stood godmother to the child. I believe they got some doctor off the ward to be its godfather, so determined were they to have the baptism done. And Carlotta said to Father Lafferty, the child's to be named Rowan, and he said to her, 'Now, you know, Carlotta Mayfair, that that is not a saint's name. It sounds like a pagan name to me.'

''And she to him in her manner, you know the way she was, she says, 'Father, don't you know what the rowan tree was and that it was used to ward off witches and all manner of evil? There's not a hut in Ireland where the woman of the house did not put up the rowan branch over the door to protect her family from witches and witchcraft, and that has been true throughout Christian times. Rowan is to be the name of this child!' And Ellie Mayfair, the little mealymouth that she always was, just nodded her head.''

"Was it true?" I asked. "Did they put the rowan over the door in Ireland?"

Gravely Sister Bridget Marie nodded. "Lot of good that it did!"

Who is the father of Rowan Mayfair?

Routine blood typing done at the hospital indicates that the baby's blood type matched that of Cortland Mayfair, who had died less than a month before. Allow us to repeat here that Cortland may also have been the father of Stella Mayfair, and that recent information obtained from Bellevue Hospital has at last confirmed that Antha Mayfair may have been his daughter as well.

Deirdre "went mad" before she ever left Mercy Hospital after Rowan's birth. The nuns said she cried by the hour, then screamed in an empty room, "You killed him!" Then wandering into the hospital chapel during Mass, she shouted once more, "You killed him. You left me alone among my enemies. You betrayed me!" She had to be taken out by force, and was quickly committed to St. Ann's Asylum, where she became catatonic by the end of the month.

"It was the invisible lover," Sister Bridget Marie believes to this day. "She was shouting and cursing at him, don't you know it, for he'd killed her college professor. He'd done it, because the devil wanted her for himself. The demon lover, that's what he was, right here in the city of New Orleans. Walking the streets of the Garden District by night."

That is a very lovely and eloquent statement, but since it is more than highly likely that the college professor never existed, what other meaning can we attach to Deirdre's words? Was it Lasher who pushed Cortland down the staircase, or startled him so badly that he fell? And if so, why?

This is the end of the life of Deirdre Mayfair really. For seventeen years she was incarcerated in various mental institutions, given massive doses of drugs and ruthless courses of electric shock treatment, with only brief respites when she returned home, a ghost of the girl she had once been.

At last in 1976, she was brought back to First Street forever, a wide-eyed and mute invalid, in a perpetual state of alertness, yet with no connective memory at all.

The side porch downstairs was screened in for her. For years she has been led out every day, rain or shine, to sit motionless in a rocking chair, her face turned ever so slightly towards the distant street.

"She cannot even remember from moment to moment," said

one physician. "She lives entirely in the present, in a way we simply cannot imagine. You might say there is no mind there at all." It is a condition described in some very old people who reach the same state in advanced senility, and sit staring in geriatric hospitals throughout the world. Regardless, she is drugged heavily, to prevent bouts of "agitation," or so her various doctors and nurses have been told.

How did Deirdre Mayfair become this "mindless idiot," as the Irish Channel gossips call her, "this nice bunch of carrots" sitting in her chair? Shock treatments certainly contributed to it, course after course of them, given by every hospital in which she had ever stayed since 1959. Then there were the drugs—massive doses of near paralytic tranquilizers—given to her in astonishing combinations, or so the records, as we continue to gain access to them, reveal.

How does one justify such treatment? Deirdre Mayfair ceased to speak coherently as early as 1962. When not tranquilized, she screamed or cried incessantly. Now and then she broke things. Sometimes she simply lay back, with her eyes rolling up in her head, and howled.

As the years have passed, we have continued to collect information about Deirdre Mayfair. Every month or so we manage to "interview" some doctor or nurse, or other person who has been in the First Street house. But our record of what really happened remains fragmentary. Hospital files are, naturally, confidential and extremely difficult to obtain. But in at least two of the sanitariums where Deirdre was treated, we now know that no record of her treatment exists.

One of her doctors has clearly and by his own admission to an inquiring stranger destroyed his records of Deirdre's case. Another physician retired shortly after he had treated Deirdre, leaving only a few cryptic notes in his brief file. "Incurable. Tragic. Aunt demands continued medication, yet Aunt's descriptions of behavior not credible."

We continue, for obvious reasons, to rely upon anecdotal evidence, for our assessment of Deirdre's history.

Though Deirdre has slumbered in a twilight induced by drugs all of her adult life, there have been countless sightings by those around her of "a mysterious brown-haired man." Nurses in St. Ann's Asylum claimed to have seen him—"some man going into her room! Now I know I saw that." At a Texas hospital where she was incarcerated briefly, a doctor claimed to have seen "a mysterious visitor" who always "seemed somehow to just disappear when I wanted to question him or ask him who he was."

At least one nurse in a northern Louisiana sanitarium insisted to her superiors that she had seen a ghost. Black orderlies in the various hospitals saw "that man all the time." One woman told us, "He not human. I know him when I see him. I see spirits. I call them up. I know him and he know me and he don't come near me at all."

Most workmen cannot work on the First Street house any more today than they could in the days when Deirdre was a girl. There are the same old stories. There is even some talk of "a man around there" who doesn't want things done.

Nevertheless some repairs are completed; air-conditioning units have been installed in some rooms, and some upgrading of the electricity has been carried out—these tasks almost invariably being done under Carlotta Mayfair's on-site supervision.

The old gardener still comes, and he occasionally paints the rusted fence.

Otherwise First Street slumbers beneath the oak branches. The frogs sing in the night around Stella's pool with its lily pads and wild irises. Deirdre's wooden swing has long ago fallen from the oak at the far end of the property. The wooden seat—a mere slat of wood—lies bleached and warping in the high grass.

Many a person stopping to look at Deirdre in her rocking chair on the side porch has glimpsed "a handsome cousin" visiting her. Nurses have sometimes quit because of "that man who comes and goes like some kinda spook," or because they kept seeing things out of the corner of their eye, or thought they were being watched.

"There's some kind of ghost hovering near her," said one young practical nurse who told the agency she would never, never go back to that house. "I saw him once, in the bright sunlight. Scariest thing I've ever seen."

When I asked this nurse about it over lunch, she had few details to add to the story. "Just a man. A man with brown hair and brown eyes in a nice-looking coat and white shirt. But dear God, if I have ever seen anything more terrifying than that! He was just standing there in the sunlight beside her looking at me. I dropped the tray and just screamed and screamed."

Numerous other medical persons left the service of the family abruptly. One doctor was fired off the case in 1976. We continue to track down these people, to take their testimony and record it. We try to tell them as little as we can of why we want to know what they saw and when.

What emerges from this data is a frightening possibility—that Deirdre's mind has been destroyed to the point where she cannot control her evocation of Lasher. That is, she subconsciously gives him the power to appear near her in very convincing form. Yet she is not conscious enough to control him further, or indeed to drive him away, if on some level she does not want him there.

In sum, she is a mindless medium; a witch rendered inoperative, and at the mercy perhaps of her familiar, who is ever at hand.

There is another very distinct possibility. That Lasher is there to comfort her, to look out for her, and to keep her happy in ways perhaps that we do not understand.

In 1980, over eight years ago, I managed to obtain an article of Deirdre's clothing, a cotton duster, or loose-fitting garment, which had been put in the dustbin in back of the house. I took this garment back with me to England, and placed it in the hands of Lauren Grant, the most powerful psychometric in the order today.

Lauren knew nothing per se about the Mayfair Witches, but one cannot rule out telepathy in such situations. I tried to keep out of it with my own thoughts as much as I could.

"I see happiness," she said. "This is the garment of someone who is blissfully happy. She lives in dreams. Dreams of green gardens and twilight skies, and exquisite sunsets. There are low-hanging branches there. There is a swing hanging from a beautiful tree. Is this a child? No, this is a woman. There is a warm breeze." Lauren massaged the garment ever more tightly, pressing its fabric to her cheek. "Oh, and she has the most beautiful lover. Oh, such a lover. He looks like a picture. Steerforth out of *David Copperfield*, that sort of man. He's so gentle, and when he touches her, she yields to him utterly. Who is this woman? All the world would like to be this woman. At least for a little while."

Is that the subconscious life of Deirdre Mayfair? Deirdre herself will never tell.

In closing allow me to add a few details. Since 1976, Deirdre Mayfair, whether clothed in a white flannel nightgown or a cotton duster, has always worn the Mayfair emerald around her neck.

I have seen Deirdre myself several times from a distance since 1976. By that time, I had made three visits to New Orleans to gather information. I have returned numerous times since.

I invariably spend some time walking in the Garden District on these return visits; I have attended the funerals over the years of Miss Belle, Miss Millie, and Miss Nancy, as well as Pierce, the last of Cortland's sons, who died of a heart attack in 1984.

At each funeral, I have seen Carlotta Mayfair. Our eyes have met. I have three times during this decade placed my card in her hand as I passed her. She has never contacted me. She has never made any more legal threats.

She is very old now, white-haired, painfully thin. Yet she still goes to work every day. She can no longer climb up on the step of the St. Charles car, so she is taken by a regular taxi. Only one black servant works in the house regularly, with the exception of Deirdre's devoted nurse.

With each visit, I encounter some new "witness" who can tell me more about "the brown-haired man" and the mysteries surrounding First Street. The stories are all much the same. But we have indeed come to the end of Deirdre's history, though she herself is not yet dead.

It is time to examine in detail her only child and heir, Rowan Mayfair, who has never set foot in her native city since the day she was taken away from it, six hours after her birth, on a cross-continental jet flight.

And though it is much too soon to attempt to put the information on Rowan into a coherent narrative, we have made some critically important notes from our random material, and there is considerable indication that Rowan Mayfair—who knows nothing of her family, her history, or her inheritance—may be the strongest witch the Mayfair family has ever produced.

Twenty-four

THE AIR-CONDITIONING FELT good after the hot streets. But as she stood quietly for a moment in the foyer of Lonigan and Sons, unobserved and therefore anonymous, she realized the heat had already made her faintly sick. The icy stream of air was now shocking her. She felt the kind of chill you have when you have fever. The enormous crowd milling only a few feet away took on a curious dreamlike quality.

When she'd first left the hotel, the humid summer afternoon had seemed manageable. But by the time she'd reached the dark house on Chestnut and First, she was feeling weak and already feeling the chill, though the air itself had been moist and warm and close, full of the raw smell of earth and green things.

Yes, dreamlike all of this—this room now with its white damask walls and small new crystal chandeliers, and the noisy well-dressed people in ever shifting clusters. Dreamlike as the shaded world of old houses and iron fences through which she had just walked.

From where she stood, she could not see into the coffin. It was mounted against the far wall of the second room. As the noisy gathering shifted here and there, she caught glimpses of the deeply polished wood and the silver handles, and of the tufted satin inside the open lid.

She felt an involuntary tightening of her facial muscles. In that coffin, she thought. You have to go through this room, and through the next room, and look. Her face felt so curiously rigid. Her body felt rigid too. Just go up to the coffin. Isn't that what people do?

She could see them doing it. She could see one person after another stepping up close to the coffin, and looking down at the woman inside.

And sooner or later someone would notice her anyway. Someone would ask, perhaps, who she was. "You tell me. Who are all these people? Do they know? Who is Rowan Mayfair?"

But for this moment, she was invisible, watching the rest of them, the men in their pale suits, the women in pretty dresses, and so many of the women wearing hats, and even gloves. It had been years since she had seen women in gaily colored dresses with belted waists and soft full skirts. There must have been two hundred people roaming about, and they were people of all ages.

She saw bald, pink-scalped old men in white linen with canes, and young boys slightly uncomfortable in their tight collars and ties. The backs of the necks of old men and young boys looked equally naked and vulnerable. There were even little children playing around the adults, babies in white lace being bounced on laps, toddlers crawling on the dark red carpet.

And there a girl, perhaps twelve years old, staring at her, with a ribbon in her red hair. Never in all her years in California had she seen a girl of that age—or any child, for that matter—with a real ribbon in her hair, and this was a big bow of peach-colored satin.

Everyone in their Sunday best, she thought. Was that the expression? And the conversation was almost festive. Like a wedding, it seemed suddenly, though she had never been to such a wedding, she had to admit. Windowless this room, though there were white damask draperies hung here and there utterly concealing what might have been windows.

The crowd shifted, broke again, so that she could see the coffin almost completely. A fragile little old man in a gray seersucker suit was standing alone looking down at the dead woman. With great effort, he lowered himself onto the velvet kneeler. What had Ellie called such things? *I want there to be a prie-dieu by my coffin.* Rowan had never seen a seersucker suit before in her life. But she knew that's what it was, because she'd seen it in the movies—in the old black-and-white films in which the fans churned and the parrot clucked on its perch and Sidney Green-street said something sinister to Humphrey Bogart.

And that is what this was like. Not the sinister quality, merely the time frame. She had slipped into the past, a world now buried beneath the earth in California. And maybe that was why it was so unexpectedly comforting, rather like that "Twilight Zone" television episode where the harried businessman gets off the commuter train at a town happily fixed in the leisurely nineteenth century.

Our funerals in New Orleans were the way they ought to be. Tell my friends to come. But Ellie's stark uncomfortable service had been nothing like this, with her bone-thin, suntanned friends, embarrassed by death, sitting resentfully on the edge of their folding chairs. *She didn't really want us to send flowers, did she?* And Rowan had said, "I think it would be terrible if there were no flowers . . ." Stainless steel cross, meaningless words, the man speaking them a total stranger.

Oh, and look at these flowers! Everywhere she looked she saw them, great dazzling sprays of roses, lilies, gladiolus. She did not know the names of some of these flowers. Nestled among the small curly-legged chairs, they stood, great wreaths on wire legs, and behind the chairs, and thrust five and six deep into the corners. Sprinkled with glistening droplets of water, they shivered in the chilly air, replete with white ribbons and bows, and some of the ribbons even had the name Deirdre printed on them in silver. Deirdre.

Suddenly, it was everywhere she looked. Deirdre, Deirdre, Deirdre, the ribbons soundlessly crying her mother's name, while the ladies in the pretty dresses drank white wine from stemmed glasses, and the little girl with the hair ribbon stared at her, and a nun, even a nun in a dark blue dress and white veil and black stockings, sat bent over her cane, on the edge of a chair, with a man speaking into her ear, her head cocked, her small beak of a nose gleaming in the light, and little girls gathered around her.

They were bringing in more flowers now, little wire trees sprouting red and pink roses amid spikes of shivering fern. How beautiful. A big blond beefy man with soft jowls set down a gorgeous little bouquet very near the distant coffin.

And such an aroma rose from all these many bouquets. Ellie

used to say the flowers in California had no scent. A lovely sweet perfume hung in this room. Now Rowan understood. It was sweet the way the warm air outside had been warm, and the moist breeze moist. It seemed that all the colors around her were becoming increasingly vivid.

But she felt sick again, and the strong perfume was making it worse. The coffin was far away. The crowd completely obscured it now. She thought about the house again, the high dark house on the "riverside downtown corner," as the clerk at the hotel had described it. It had to be the house that Michael kept seeing. Unless there were a thousand like it, a thousand with a rose pattern in the cast iron, and a great dark cascade of bougainvillea pouring down the faded gray wall. Oh, such a beautiful house.

My mother's house. My house? Where was Michael? There was a sudden opening in the crowd, and once again she saw the long flank of the coffin. Was she seeing a woman's profile against the satin pillow from where she stood? Ellie's coffin had been closed. Graham had had no funeral. His friends had gathered at a downtown bar.

You are going to have go up to that coffin. You are going to have to look into it and see her. This is why you came, why you broke with Ellie and the paper in the safe, to see with your own eyes your mother's face. But are these things actually taking place, or am I dreaming? Look at the young girl with her arm around the old woman's shoulder. The young girl's white dress has a sash! She is wearing white stockings.

If only Michael were here. This was Michael's world. If only Michael could take off his glove and lay his hand on the dead woman's hand. But what would he see? An undertaker shooting embalming fluid into her veins? Or the blood being drained into the gutter of the white embalming table? Deirdre. Deirdre was written in silver letters on the white ribbon that hung from the nearby wreath of chrysanthemums. Deirdre on the ribbon across the great bouquet of pink roses . . .

Well, what are you waiting for? Why don't you move? She moved back, against the door frame, watching an old woman with pale yellow hair open her arms to three small children. One after another they kissed the old woman's wobbling cheeks. She nodded her head. Are all these people my mother's family?

She envisioned the house again, stripped of detail, dark and fantastically large. She understood why Michael loved that house, loved this place. And Michael didn't know that that was her mother's house. Michael didn't know any of this was happening. Michael was gone. And maybe that was all there would ever be, just that one weekend, and forever this unfinished feeling . . .

I gotta go home, it isn't just the visions, it's that I don't belong out here anymore. I knew it that day I went down to the ocean . . .

The door opened behind her. Silently she stepped to the side. An older couple passed her as if she were not there, a stately woman with beautiful iron gray hair swept back in a twist, in a perfect silk shirtwaist dress, and a man in a rumpled white suit, thick-necked and soft-voiced as he talked to the woman.

"Beatrice!" Someone spoke a greeting. A handsome young man came to kiss the pretty woman with the iron gray hair. "Darling, come in," said a female voice. "No, no one's seen her, she's due to arrive anytime." Voices like Michael's voice, yet different. A pair of men talking in whispers over their wine-glasses came between her and the couple as they moved on into the second room. Once again, the front door was opening. Gust of heat, traffic.

She moved over into the far corner, and now she could see the coffin clearly, see that half the lid was closed over the lower portion of the woman's body, and why that struck her as grotesque she didn't know. A crucifix was set into the tufted silk above the woman's head, not that she could see that head, but she knew it was there, she could just see a dash of flesh color against the gleaming white. Go on, Rowan, go up there.

Go up to the coffin. Is this more difficult than going into an Operating Room? Of course they will all see you, but they won't know who you are. The constriction came again, the tightening in the muscles of her face and her throat. She couldn't move.

And then someone was speaking to her, and she knew she ought to turn her head and answer, but she did not. The little girl with the ribbon watched her. Why wasn't she answering, thought the little girl.

". . . Jerry Lonigan, can I help you? You're not Dr. Mayfair, are you?"

She looked at him stupidly. The beefy man with the heavy jowls and the prettiest china blue eyes. No, like blue marbles, his eyes, just perfectly round and blue.

"Dr. Mayfair?"

She looked down at his hand. Large, heavy, a paw. Take it. Answer that way if you can't talk. The tightening in her face grew worse. It was affecting her eyes. What was this all about?— her body frozen in alarm though her mind was in this trance, this awful trance. She made a little gesture with her head at the distant coffin. I want to . . . but no words would come out. Come on, Rowan, you flew two thousand miles for this.

The man slipped his arm around her. Pressure against her back. "You want to see her, Dr. Mayfair?"

See her, talk to her, know her, love her, be loved by her. . . . Her face felt as if it were carved of ice. And her eyes were unnaturally wide, she knew it.

She glanced up into his small blue eyes, and nodded. It seemed a hush had fallen over everyone. Had she spoken that loud? But she hadn't said anything at all. Surely they didn't know what she looked like, yet it seemed they were all turning to look at her as she and this man walked into the first room, and the message traveled by whispers. She looked closely at the red-haired girl with the ribbon as she passed. In fact, she stopped without meaning to, stranded, on the threshold of the second room, with this nice man, Jerry Lonigan, beside her.

Even the children had stopped playing. The room seemed to darken as everyone moved soundlessly and slowly, but only a few steps. Mr. Lonigan said:

"You wanna sit down, Dr. Mayfair?"

She was staring at the carpet. The coffin was twenty feet away. Don't look up, she thought, don't look up until you actually reach the coffin. Don't see something horrible from a distance. But what was so horrible about all this, how could this be worse than the autopsy table, except that this was . . . this was her mother.

A woman stepped up behind the little girl, placing her hand on the girl's shoulder. "Rowan? Rowan, I'm Alicia Mayfair, I was Deirdre's fourth cousin once removed. This is Mona, my little girl."

"Rowan, I'm Pierce Mayfair," said the handsome young man on her right, extending his hand suddenly. "I'm Cortland's great-grandson."

"Darling, I'm Beatrice, your cousin." Whiff of perfume. The woman with the iron gray hair. Soft skin touching Rowan's cheek. Enormous gray eyes.

"—Cecilia Mayfair, Barclay's granddaughter, my grandfather was Julien's second son born at the First Street house, and here, Sister, come, this is Sister Marie Claire. Sister, this is Rowan, this is Deirdre's girl!"

Weren't you supposed to say something respectable to nuns, but this sister couldn't have heard. They were shouting in her ear. "Deirdre's girl, Rowan!"

"—Timothy Mayfair, your fourth cousin, we're glad to see you, Rowan—"

"—glad to see you on this sad . . . ."

"Peter Mayfair, we'll talk later on. Garland was my father. Did Ellie ever talk about Garland?"

Dear God, they were all Mayfairs. Polly Mayfair, and Agnes Mayfair, and Philip Mayfair's girls, and Eugenie Mayfair, and on and on it went. How many of them could there possibly be? Not a family but a legion. She was clasping one hand after another, and at the same time cleaving to the beefy Mr. Lonigan, who held her so firmly. Was she trembling? No, this is what they call shaking, not trembling.

Lips brushed her cheek. " . . . Clancy Mayfair, Clay's great-granddaughter. Clay was born at First Street before the Civil War. My mother is Trudy Mayfair, here, Mother, come, let Mother through . . ."

" . . . so glad to see you, darling. Have you seen Carlotta?"

"Miss Carlotta's feeling pretty bad," said Mr. Lonigan. "She'll meet us at the church—"

"—ninety years old now, you know."

"—do you want a glass of water? She's white as a sheet, Pierce, get her a glass of water."

"Magdalene Mayfair, Rémy's great-granddaughter. Rémy lived at First Street for years. This is my son, Garvey, and my daughter, Lindsey. Here, Dan, Dan say hello to Dr. Mayfair. Dan is Vincent's great-grandson. Did Ellie tell you about Clay and Vincent and . . ."

No, never, about anyone. *Promise me you will never go back, that you'll never try to find out.* But why, why in the name of God? All these people—why the paper, the secrecy?

"—Gerald's with her. Pierce stopped by. He saw her. She's fine, she'll be at the church."

"Do you want to sit down, honey?"

"Are you all right?"

"Lily, darling, Lily Mayfair, you'll never remember all our names, don't try."

"Robert, honey. We'll talk to you later."

"—here if you need us, Rowan. Are you feeling all right?"

I am. I'm fine. I just can't talk. I can't move. I . . .

There was tightening again of the facial muscles. Rigid, rigid all over. She held tighter to Mr. Lonigan's hand. He said something to them about her paying her respects now. Was he telling them to go away? A man touched her left hand.

"I'm Guy Mayfair, Andrea's son, and this is my wife, Stephanie, she's Grady's daughter. She was Ellie's first cousin."

She wanted to respond, was clasping each hand enough, was nodding enough? Was kissing back the old woman who kissed her enough? Another man was talking to her but his voice was too soft. He was old, he was saying something about Sheffield. The coffin was twenty feet away at most. She didn't dare look up, or look away from them, for fear she'd see it accidentally.

But this is what you came for, and you have to do it. And they are here, hundreds of them . . .

"Rowan," said someone to her left, "this is Fielding Mayfair, Clay's son." Such a very old man, so old she could see all the bones of his skull through his pale skin, see the lower and upper teeth and the ridges around his sunken eyes. They were holding him up; he couldn't stand by himself, and all this struggle, so that he might see her? She put out her hand. "He wants to kiss you, honey." She brushed his cheek with her lips.

His speech was low, his eyes yellowed as he looked up at her. She tried to hear what he was saying, something about Lestan Mayfair and Riverbend. What was Riverbend? She nodded. He was too old to be treated badly. She had to say something! He was too old to be struggling like this just to pay his respects to her. When she squeezed his hand, it felt so smooth and silky and knotted and strong.

"I think she's going to faint," someone whispered. Surely they weren't talking about *her*.

"Do you want me to take you up to the coffin?" The young man again, the handsome one, with the clean preppie face, and the brilliant eyes. "I'm Pierce, I met you just a second ago." Flash of perfect teeth. "Ellie's first cousin."

Yes, to the coffin. It's time, isn't it? She looked towards it, and it seemed that someone stepped back so that she might see, and then her eyes shifted instantly upwards, beyond the face on the propped-up pillow. She saw the flowers clustered about the raised lid, a whole jungle of flowers, and far to the right at the foot of the coffin a white-haired man she knew. The dark-haired woman beside him was crying, and saying her rosary, and they were both looking at her, but how in the world could she possibly know that man, or anyone here? But she knew him! She knew he was English, whoever he was, she knew just how his voice would sound when he spoke to her.

Jerry Lonigan helped her step forward. The handsome one, Pierce, was standing beside her. "She's sick, Monty," said the pretty old woman. "Get her some water."

"Honey, maybe you should sit down . . ."

She shook her head, mouthing the word no. She looked at that white-haired Englishman again, the one with the woman who was praying. Ellie had wanted her rosary in the last week. Rowan had had to go to a store in San Francisco to buy one. The woman was shaking her head and crying, and wiping her nose, and the white-haired man was whispering to her, but his eyes were fixed on Rowan. *I know you.* He looked at her as if she'd spoken to him, and then it came to her—the cemetery in Sonoma County where Graham and Ellie were buried, this was the man she had seen that day by the grave. *I know your family in New Orleans.* And quite unexpectedly another piece of the same puzzle fell into place. This was the man who'd been standing outside Michael's house two nights ago on Liberty Street.

"Honey, do you want a glass of water?" said Jerry Lonigan.

But how could that be? How could that man have been there, and here, and what had all this to do with Michael, who had described to her the house with the iron roses in the railing?

Pierce said he would go get a chair. "Let her just sit right here."

She had to move. She couldn't just remain here staring at the white-haired Englishman, demanding of him that he explain himself, explain what he'd been doing on Liberty Street. And out of the corner of her eye, something she couldn't bear to see, something in the coffin waiting.

"Here, Rowan, this is nice and cold." Smell of wine. "Take a drink, darling."

I would like to, I really would, but I can't move my mouth. She shook her head, tried to smile. I don't think I can move my hand. And you are all expecting me to move, I really should move. She used to think the doctors who fainted at an autopsy were fools, really. How could such a thing affect one so physically? If you hit me with a baseball bat, I might pass out. Oh, God, what you don't know about life is really just beginning to reveal itself in this room. And your mother is in that coffin.

What did you think, that she would wait here, alive, until you came? Until you finally realized . . . Down here, in this strange land! Why, this is like another country, this.

The white-haired Englishman came towards her. Yes, who are you? Why are you here? Why are you so dramatically and grotesquely out of place? But then again, he wasn't. He was just like all of them, the inhabitants of this strange land, so decorous and so gentle, and not a touch of irony or self-consciousness or false sentiment in his kindly face. He drew close to her, gently making the handsome young man give way.

Remember those tortured faces at Ellie's funeral. Not a one under sixty yet not a gray hair, not a sagging muscle. Nothing like this. Why, this is what they mean when they talk about "the people."

She lowered her eyes. Banks of flowers on either side of the velvet prie-dieu. She moved forward, her nails digging into Mr.

Lonigan before she could stop herself. She struggled to relax her hand and to her utter amazement, she felt she was going to fall. The Englishman took hold of her left arm, as Mr. Lonigan held her by the right one.

"Rowan, listen to me," said the Englishman softly in her ear, in that clipped yet melodious accent. "Michael would be here if he could. I'm here in Michael's place. Michael will come tonight. Just as soon as he can."

She looked at him, shocked, the relief almost making her shudder. Michael was coming. Michael was somewhere close. But how could this be?

"Yes, very close, and unavoidably detained," he said, as sincerely as if he'd invented the words, "and truly put out that he cannot be here . . ."

She saw the dim dark featureless First Street house again, the house Michael had been talking about all that time. And when she'd first seen him in the water, he had looked like a tiny speck of clothes floating on the surface, that can't be a drowned man, not out here, miles and miles from the land . . .

"What can I do for you now?" said the Englishman, his voice low and secretive and utterly solicitous. "Do you want to step up to the coffin?"

Yes, please, take me up. Please help me! Make my legs move. But they were moving. He had slipped his arm around her and he was guiding her, so easily, and the conversation had started up again, thank God, though it was a low respectful hum, from which she could extract various threads at will. ". . . she just didn't want to come to the funeral parlor, that's the truth of it. She's furious that we're all here." "Keep quiet, she's ninety if she's a day and it's a hundred degrees outside." "I know, I know. Well, everyone can come to my place afterwards, I told you . . ."

She kept her eyes down, on the silver handles, on the flowers, on the velvet kneeler right in front of her now. Sick again. Sick from the heat and this motionless cool air with the scent of the flowers hanging around her like an invisible mist. But you have to do this. You have to do it calmly and quietly. You cannot lose it. *Promise me you'll never go back there, you'll never try to find out.*

The Englishman was holding her, *Michael will come*, his right hand comfortingly against her arm, his left hand steadying her left wrist as she touched the velvet-covered side of the casket.

Slowly, she forced herself to look up from the floor, to raise her eyes until she saw the face of the dead woman lying right there on the satin pillow. And slowly her mouth began to open, to pull open, the rigidity shifting into a spasm. She struggled with all her strength to keep from opening her mouth. She clenched her teeth. And the shudder that passed through her was so violent that the Englishman tightened his grip. He too was looking down. He had known her!

Look at her. Nothing else matters now. It is not important to hurry, or to think of anything else, or to worry. Just look at her, look at her face with all its secrets locked away now forever.

And Stella's face was so beautiful in the coffin. She had such beautiful black hair . . .

"She is going to faint, help her! Pierce, help her."

"No, we have her, she's all right," said Jerry Lonigan.

So perfectly, hideously dead she looked, and so lovely. Groomed she was for eternity—with the pink lipstick gleaming on her shapely mouth and the rouge on the flawless girlish cheeks, and her black hair brushed out on the satin, like girl's hair, free and beautiful, and the rosary beads, yes, rosary beads, threaded through her fingers, which are like dough as they lie on her breast, not human hands at all, but something made crudely by a sculptor.

In all these years, Rowan had never seen such a thing. She had seen them drowned, and stabbed, and after they had died on the wards in their sleep. She had seen them colorless and pumped with chemicals, slit open after weeks and months and even years, for the anatomy lesson. She had seen them at the autopsy with the bloodred organs being lifted out in the doctor's gloved hands.

But never this. Never this dead and pretty thing in blue silk and lace, smelling of face powder, with her hands clasped over the rosary beads. Ageless she looked, almost like a giant little girl with her innocent hair, her face devoid of lines, even the shiny lipstick the color of rose petals.

Oh, if it were only possible to open her eyes! I wish I could see my mother's eyes! And in this room filled with the very old, she is so young still . . .

She bent down. She withdrew her hands ever so gently from the Englishman. She laid them on her pale hands, her softly melting hands. Hard! Hard as the rosary beads. Cold and hard. She closed her eyes, and pressed her fingers into this unyielding white flesh. So absolutely dead, so beyond any breath of life, so firmly finished.

If Michael were here, could he know from her hands if she had died without pain or fear? Could he know why the secrecy? Could he touch this horrid, lifeless flesh and hear the song of life still from it? Oh, please God, whoever she was, why ever she gave me away, I hope it was without fear and pain that she died. In peace, in a sweetness like her face. Look at her closed eyes, her smooth forehead.

Slowly, she raised her hand and wiped the tears off her own cheek, and realized that her face was relaxed now. That she could speak if she wanted to, and that others around her were crying too, that the woman with the iron gray hair was crying, and that the poor black-haired woman who had been crying all along was sobbing silently against the chest of the man beside her, and that the faces of those who didn't cry—everywhere she looked in the glow beyond the coffin—had become thoughtful and quiet, and rather like those faces in great Florentine paintings where the passive, faintly sad souls regard the world beyond the frame as if from a dream, gazing out from the corners of their eyes, languidly.

She backed away, but her eyes remained fixed on the woman in the coffin. She let the Englishman guide her again, away, to a small room that waited. Mr. Lonigan was saying it was time for them all to come up one by one, that the priest was here, and he was ready.

In astonishment, Rowan saw a tall old man bend gracefully and kiss the dead woman's forehead. Beatrice, the pretty one with the gray hair, came next and whispered something as she kissed the dead woman in the same manner. A child was lifted next to do the same; and the old bald man came, heavy with his big belly making it hard, but he bent to give the kiss, whispering hoarsely for everyone to hear, "Good-bye, darlin'."

Mr. Lonigan pushed her gently down in the chair. As he turned, the crying woman with the black hair suddenly bent near and looked into her eyes. "She didn't want to give you up," she said, her voice so thin and quick it was like a thought.

"Rita Mae!" Mr. Lonigan hissed, turning on her, taking her by the arm, and drawing her back.

"Is that true?" Rowan whispered. Rowan reached out to capture her retreating hand. Mr. Lonigan's face flushed, his jowls shivering slightly. He pushed the black-haired woman away, out of the door, down a small hallway.

The Englishman looked down at her from the door to the big room. He gave her a little nod, his eyebrows rising as if it filled him with sadness and wondering.

Slowly Rowan withdrew her gaze from him. She stared at the procession, still coming one by one, each bending as if to drink from the cool splash of a low water fountain. "Good-bye, Deirdre, dear." Did they all know? Did they all remember, the older ones, the ones who had come up to her at first? Had all the children heard, in one form or another, at some time or another? The handsome one was watching her from far away.

"Good-bye, sweetheart . . ." On and on they came, seemingly without end, the rooms behind them dark and crowded as the line pressed in tighter.

Didn't want to give you up.

What must it feel like to kiss her smooth hard skin? And they did it as if it were the most natural thing in the world, the simplest thing in the world, the baby held aloft, the mother bending, the man coming so quick and then another very old one with spotted hands and thinning hair, "Help me up, Cecil," her foot on the velvet prie-dieu. The twelve-year-old with the hair ribbon stood on tiptoe.

"Rowan, do you want to be alone with her again?" Lonigan's voice. "That's your time at the end, when they've all passed. The priest will wait. But you don't have to."

She looked into the Englishman's mild, gray eyes. But he wasn't the one who'd spoken. It was Lonigan with his flushed and shining face, and china blue eyes. Far down the little hallway stood his wife, Rita Mae, not daring now to come closer.

"Yes, alone, one more time," Rowan whispered. Her eyes searched out the eyes of Rita Mae, in the shadows at the end of the little hall. "True," Rita Mae mouthed the word, as she nodded gravely.

Yes. To kiss her good-bye, yes, the way they are kissing her . . .

Twenty-five

THE FILE ON THE MAYFAIR WITCHES

PART X

Rowan Mayfair

STRICTLY CONFIDENTIAL THIS SUMMARY AND UPDATED 1989
SEE CONFIDENTIAL FILE: ROWAN MAYFAIR, LONDON FOR ALL
RELATED MATERIALS.
COMPUTER PASSWORD REQUIRED.

Rowan Mayfair was adopted legally by Ellen Louise Mayfair and her husband Graham Franklin, on the date of Rowan's birth, November 7, 1959.

At this point Rowan was taken by plane to Los Angeles, where she lived with her adopted parents until she was three years old. The family then moved to San Francisco, California, where they lived in Pacific Heights for two years.

When Rowan was five, the family made its final move to a house on the shore of Tiburon, California—across the bay from San Francisco—which had been designed by architects Trammel, Porter and Davis expressly for Graham and Ellie and their daughter. The house is a marvel of glass walls, exposed redwood beams, and modern plumbing fixtures and appliances. It includes enormous decks, its own twenty-five-foot pier, and a boat channel, which is dredged twice yearly. It commands a view of Sausalito across Richardson Bay and San Francisco to the south. Rowan lives alone in this house now.

At the time of this writing, Rowan is almost thirty years old. She is five feet ten inches tall. She has short, softly bobbed blond hair and large pale gray eyes. She is undeniably attractive, with remarkably beautiful skin, and dark straight eyebrows and dark eyelashes and an extremely beautiful mouth. Yet for the sake of comparison, it can be said that she has none of the glamour of Stella, or the sweet prettiness of Antha, or the dark sensuality of Deirdre. Rowan is delicate yet boyish; in some of her pictures, her expression—on account of her straight dark eyebrows—is reminiscent of Mary Beth.

It is my belief that she resembles Petyr van Abel, but there are definite differences. She does not have his deep-set eyes, and her blond hair is ashen rather than gold. But her face is narrow like that of Petyr van Abel; and there is a Nordic look to Rowan, just as there is to Petyr in his portraits.

Rowan appears cold to people. Yet her voice is warm, and deep and slightly husky—what is called a whiskey voice in America. People say you have to know her, really, to like her. This is strange because our investigation indicates that very few people know her. But she is almost universally liked.

Ellen Louise Mayfair was the only daughter of Sheffield, son of Cortland Mayfair. She was born in 1923, and six years old when Stella died. Ellie lived in California almost exclusively from the time that she entered Stanford University at eighteen years of age. She married Graham Franklin, a Stanford law graduate, when she was thirty-one. Graham was eight years younger than Ellie. Ellie seems to have had very little contact with her family even before she went to California, as she went away to a boarding school in Canada when she was only eight, six months after her mother's death.

Her father, Sheffield Mayfair, seems never to have recovered from the loss of his wife, and though he visited Ellie often, taking her on shopping sprees in New York, he kept her away from home. He was the most quiet and reclusive of Cortland's sons, and possibly the most disappointing, in that he worked doggedly in the family firm but seldom excelled or participated in important decisions. Everyone depended upon him, Cortland said after his death.

What is relevant here is that after the age of eight, Ellie saw very little of the Mayfairs, and her lifelong friends in California were people she had met there, along with a few girls from the Canadian boarding school with whom she kept in touch. We don't know what she knew of Antha's life and death, or even of Deirdre's life.

Her husband, Graham Franklin, knew nothing about Ellie's family apparently, and some of the remarks he made over the years are entirely fanciful. "She came from a great plantation down there." "They are the sort of people who keep gold under the floorboards." "I think they were probably descended from the buccaneers." "Oh, my wife's people? They were slave traders, weren't they, honey? They all have colored blood."

Family gossip at the time of the adoption said that Ellie had signed papers for Carlotta Mayfair saying she would never let Rowan discover anything about her true background, and never permit her to return to Louisiana.

Indeed, these papers are part of the official adoption records, being formalized personal agreements between the parties, and involving staggering transfers of money.

During the first year of Rowan's life, over five million dollars was transferred in successive installments from the account of Carlotta Mayfair in New Orleans to the accounts of Ellie Mayfair in California, in the Bank of America and the Wells Fargo Bank.

Ellie, rich in her own right, through the trust funds left to her from her father Sheffield, and later from her grandfather Cortland (maybe Cortland would have changed this arrangement had there been time, but the paperwork had been done decades before), set up an immense trust fund for her adoptive daughter, Rowan, to which half of this five million was added over the next two years.

The remaining half was transferred, as it came in, directly to Graham Franklin, who invested the money prudently and successfully, largely in real estate (a gold mine in California), and who continued to invest Ellie's money—regular payments from her trust—in community property and investments over the years. Though he made a very high salary as a successful lawyer, Graham had no family money, and his enormous estate—owned in common with his wife—at the time of his death was the result of his skillful use of her inherited money.

There is considerable evidence that Graham resented his wife, and resented his emotional as well as financial dependence upon her. He could not have possibly supported his life-style—yachts, sports cars, extravagant vacations, a palatial modern house in Tiburon—on his salary. And he funneled enormous sums of Ellie's money directly out of their joint account into the hands of various mistresses over the years.

Several of these women have told our investigators that Graham was a vain and slightly sadistic man. Yet they found him irresistible, giving up on him only when they realized that he really loved Ellie. It wasn't just her money. He couldn't live without her. "He has to get back at her from time to time, and that's the only reason he cheats."

Graham once explained to a young airline stewardess whom he subsequently put through college that his wife swallowed him, and that he had to have "something on the side" (meaning a woman) or he was nothing and nobody at all.

When he discovered that Ellie had fatal cancer, he went into a panic. Legal partners and friends have described in detail his "total inability" to deal with Ellie's sickness. He would not discuss the illness with her; he would not listen to her doctors; he refused to enter her hospital room. He moved his mistress into a Jackson Street apartment right across from his office in San Francisco, and went over to see her as often as three times a day.

He immediately instigated an elaborate scheme to strip Ellie of all the family property—which now amounted to an immense fortune—and was in the process of trying to declare Ellie incompetent so that he could sell the Tiburon house to his mistress when he himself died suddenly—two months before Ellie—from a stroke. Ellie inherited his entire estate.

Graham's last mistress, Karen Garfield, an exquisite young fashion model from New York, poured out her woes to one of our investigators over cocktails. She had been left with half a million and that was just fine, but she and Graham had planned a whole life together—"the Virgin Islands, the Riviera, the works."

Karen herself died of a series of massive heart attacks, the first of which occurred an hour after Karen visited Graham's house in Tiburon to try to "explain things" to his daughter Rowan. "That bitch! She wouldn't even let me have his things! All I wanted were a few keepsakes. She said, 'Get out of my mother's house.' "

Karen lived for two weeks after the visit, long enough to say many unkind things about Rowan, but apparently Karen never connected her sudden and inexplicable cardiac deterioration to her visit. Why should she?

We did make this connection as the following summary will show.

When Ellie died, Rowan told Ellie's closest friends that she had lost her best and only friend in this world. This was probably true. Ellie Mayfair was all her life a very sweet and somewhat fragile human being, beloved by her daughter and her numerous friends. According to these friends, she always evinced something of a southern belle charm, though she was an athletic, modern California woman in every way, easily passing for twenty years younger than she was, which was not uncommon with her contemporaries. Indeed, her youthful looks may have constituted her only obsession, other than the welfare of her daughter, Rowan.

She had cosmetic surgery twice in her fifties (facial tightening), frequented expensive beauty salons, and dyed her hair continuously. In pictures with her husband, taken a year before her death, she appears to be the younger person. Devoted to Graham and completely dependent upon him, she ignored his affairs, and with reason. As she told one friend, "He's always home at six o'clock for dinner. And he's always there when I turn out the lights."

Indeed, the source of Graham's charm for Ellie and for others, other than his looks, was apparently his great enthusiasm for living, and the easy affection he lavished on those around him, including his wife.

One of his lifelong friends, an older lawyer, explained it this way to our investigator. "He got away with those affairs because he was never inattentive to Ellie. Some of the other guys around here should take a lesson from that. What women hate is when you turn cold to them. If you treat them like queens, they'll let you have a concubine or two outside the palace."

At this point, we simply do not know how important it is to gather more information about Graham Franklin and Ellie Mayfair. What seems relevant here is that they were normal upper-middle-class Californians, and extremely happy in spite of Graham's deceptions, until the very last year of their lives. They went to the San Francisco Opera on Tuesday nights, the symphony on Saturday, the ballet now and then. They owned a dazzling succession of Bentleys, Rolls-Royces, Jaguars, and other fine cars. They spent as much as ten thousand dollars a month on clothes. On the open decks of their beautiful Tiburon home, they entertained friends lavishly and fashionably. They flew to Europe or Asia for brief, luxurious vacations. And they were extremely proud of "our daughter, the doctor," as they called Rowan, lightheartedly, to their many friends.

Though Ellie was supposed to be telepathic, it was a parlor-game type of thing. She knew who it was when the phone rang. She could tell you what playing card you were holding in your hand. Otherwise there was nothing unusual about this woman, except perhaps that she was very pretty, resembling many other descendants of Julien Mayfair, and had her great-grandfather's ingratiating manner and seductive smile.

The last time I myself saw Ellie was at the funeral of Nancy Mayfair in New Orleans in January of 1988; she was at that time sixty-three or -four, a beautiful woman, about five feet six inches in height, with darkly tanned skin and jet black hair. Her blue eyes were concealed behind white-rimmed sunglasses; her fashionable cotton dress flattered her slender figure, and indeed, she had something of the glamour of a film actress, to wit a California patina. Within half a year, she was dead.

When Ellie died, Rowan inherited everything, including Ellie's family trust fund, and an additional trust fund which had been set up—Rowan knew nothing about it—when Rowan was born.

As Rowan was then, and is now, an extremely hardworking physician, her inheritance has made almost no appreciable difference in her day-to-day life. But more on that in the proper time.

Nonobtrusive surveillance of Rowan indicated that this child was extremely precocious from the beginning, and may have had a variety of psychic powers of which her adoptive parents appeared unaware. There is also some evidence that Ellie Mayfair refused to acknowledge anything "strange" about her daughter. Whatever the case, Rowan seems to have been "the pride and joy" of both Ellie and Graham.

As already indicated, the bond between mother and child was extremely close until the time of Ellie's death. However, Rowan never shared her mother's love of parties, lunches, shopping sprees, and other such pursuits, and was never, even in later adolescence or young adulthood, drawn into Ellie's wide circle of female friends.

Rowan did share her parents' passion for boating. She accompanied the family on boat trips from her earliest years, learning to manage Graham's small sailboat, *The Wind Singer*, on her own when she was only fourteen. When Graham bought an ocean-going cruiser named the *Great Angela*, the whole family took long trips together several times a year.

By the time Rowan was sixteen, Graham had bought her her own seaworthy twin-engine full displacement hull yacht, which Rowan named the *Sweet Christine*. The *Great Angela* was at that time retired, and the whole family used the *Sweet Christine*, but Rowan was the undisputed skipper. And over everyone's advice and objections, Rowan frequently took the enormous boat out of the harbor by herself.

For years it was Rowan's habit to come directly home from school and to go out of San Francisco Bay into the ocean for at least two hours. Only occasionally did she invite a close friend to go along.

"We never see her till eight o'clock," Ellie would say. "And I worry! Oh, how I worry. But to take that boat away from Rowan would be to kill her. I just don't know what to do."

Though an expert swimmer, Rowan is not a daredevil sailor, so to speak. The *Sweet Christine* is a heavy, slow, forty-foot Dutch-built cruiser, designed for stability in rough seas, but not for speed.

What seems to delight Rowan is being alone in it, out of sight of land, in all kinds of weather. Like many people who respond to the northern California climate, she seems to enjoy fog, wind, and cold.

All who have observed Rowan seem to agree that she is a

loner, and an extremely quiet person who would rather work than play. In school she was a compulsive student, and in college a compulsive researcher. Though her wardrobe was the envy of her classmates, it was, she always said, Ellie's doing. She herself had almost no interest in clothes. Her characteristic off-duty attire has been for years rather nautical—jeans, yachting shoes, oversized sweaters and watch caps, and a sailor's peacoat of navy blue wool.

In the world of medicine, particularly that of neurosurgery, Rowan's compulsive habits are less remarkable, given the nature of the profession. Yet even in this field, Rowan has been seen as "obsessive." In fact, Rowan seems born to have been a doctor, though her choice of surgery over research surprised many people who knew her. "When she was in the lab," said one of her colleagues, "her mother had to call her and remind her to take time out to sleep or eat."

One of Rowan's early elementary-school teachers noted in the record, when Rowan was eight, that "this child thinks she is an adult. She identifies with adults. She becomes impatient with other children. But she is too well behaved to show it. She seems terribly, terribly alone."

TELEPATHIC POWERS

Rowan's psychic powers began to surface in school from the time she was six years old. Indeed, they may have surfaced long before that, but we have not been able to find any evidence before that time. Teachers queried informally (or deviously) about Rowan tell truly amazing stories about the child's ability to read minds.

However, nothing we have discovered indicates that Rowan was ever considered an outcast or a failure or maladjusted. She was throughout her school years an overachiever and an unqualified success. Her school pictures reveal her to have been an extremely pretty child, always, with tanned skin and sun-bleached blond hair. She appears secretive in these pictures, as if she does not quite like the intrusion of the camera, but never affected, or ill at ease.

Rowan's telepathic abilities became known to teachers rather than to other students, and they follow a remarkable pattern:

"My mother had died," said a first-grade teacher. "I couldn't go back to Vermont for the funeral, and I felt terrible. Nobody knew about this, you understand. But Rowan came up to me at recess. She sat beside me and she took my hand. I almost burst into tears at this tenderness. 'I'm sorry about your mother,' she said. She sat there with me in silence. Later when I asked her how she knew, she said, 'It just popped into my head.' I think that child knew all kinds of things that way. She knew when the other kids were envious of her. How lonely she always was!''

Another time, when a little girl was absent from school for three days without explanation and school authorities could not reach her, Rowan quietly told the principal there was no reason to be alarmed. The girl's grandmother had died, said Rowan, and the family had gone off to the funeral in another state, completely forgetting to call the school. This turned out to be true. Again Rowan could not explain how she had known except to say "It just came into my head."

We have some two dozen stories similar to this one, and what characterizes almost all of them is that they involve not only telepathy, but empathy and sympathy on the part of Rowan—*a clear desire to comfort or minister to a suffering or confused person*. That person was invariably an adult. The telepathic power is never connected with tricks, frightening people, or quarrels of any kind.

In 1966, when Rowan was eight, she used this telepathic ability of hers for the last time *as far as we know*. During her fourth-grade term at a private school in Pacific Heights, she told the principal that another little girl was very sick and ought to see a doctor, but Rowan didn't know how to tell anyone. The little girl was going to die.

The principal was horrified. She called Rowan's mother and insisted that Rowan be taken to a psychiatrist. Only a deeply disturbed little girl would say "something like that." Ellie promised to talk with Rowan. Rowan said nothing further.

However, the little girl in question was diagnosed within a week as having a rare form of bone cancer. She died before the end of the term.

The principal has told the story over dinner countless times. She deeply regretted her censure of Rowan. She wished in particular that she had not called Mrs. Mayfair, because Mrs. Mayfair became so terribly upset.

It may have been concern on Ellie's part which put an end to this sort of incident in Rowan's life. Ellie's friends all knew about it. "Ellie was damned near hysterical. She wanted Rowan to be normal. She said she didn't want a daughter with strange gifts."

Graham thought the whole thing was a coincidence, according to the principal. He bawled out the woman for calling and telling Ellie when the poor little girl died.

Coincidence or not, this entire affair seems to have put an end to Rowan's demonstrations of her power. It is safe to assume that she shrewdly decided to "go underground" as a mind reader. Or even that she deliberately suppressed her power to the point where it became nonexistent or extremely weak. Try as we might, we find nothing about her telepathic abilities from then on. People's memories of her all have to do with her quiet brilliance, her indefatigable energy, and her love of science and medicine.

"She was that girl in high school who collected the bugs and the rocks, calling everything by a long Latin name."

"Frightening, absolutely frightening," said her high school chemistry teacher. "I wouldn't have been surprised if she had reinvented the hydrogen bomb one weekend in her spare time."

It has been speculated within the Talamasca that Rowan's suppression of her telepathic power may have something to do with the growth of her telekinetic power, that she rechanneled her energy, so to speak, and that the two powers represent both sides of the same coin. To put it differently, Rowan turned away from mind and toward matter. Science and medicine became her obsessions from her junior high school years on.

Rowan's only real boyfriend during her teen-age years was also brilliant and reclusive. He seems to have been unable to take the competition. When Rowan was admitted to U.C. Berkeley and he was not, they broke up bitterly. Friends blamed the boyfriend. He later went east and became a research scientist in New York.

One of our investigators "bumped into him" at a museum opening, and brought the conversation around to psychics and mind readers. The man opened up about his old high school sweetheart who had been psychic. He was still bitter about it. "I loved that girl. Really loved her. Her name was Rowan Mayfair and she was very unusual-looking. Not pretty in an ordinary way. But she was impossible. She knew what I was thinking even before I knew it. She knew when I'd been out with someone else. She was so damned quiet about it, it was eerie. I heard she became a neurosurgeon. That's scary. What will happen if the patient thinks something negative about her before he goes under the anesthesia? Will she slice the thought right out of his head?"

The fact is, no one reporting on Rowan mentions pettiness in connection with her. She is described as "formidable," just as Mary Beth Mayfair was once described, but never small-minded or vindictive, or unduly aggressive in any personal way.

By the time Rowan entered U.C. Berkeley in 1976, she knew that she wanted to be a doctor. She was a straight A student in the premedicine program, took courses every summer (though she still went on vacation often with Graham and Ellie), skipped an entire year, and graduated at the top of her class in 1979. She entered medical school when she was twenty, apparently believing that neurological research would be her life's work.

Her academic progress during this period was thought to be phenomenal. Numerous teachers speak of her as "the most brilliant student I have ever had."

"She isn't just smart. She's intuitive! She makes astonishing connections. She doesn't just read a book. She swallows it, and comes up with six different implications of the author's basic theory of which the author never dreamed."

"The students have nicknamed her Dr. Frankenstein because of her talk about brain transplants and creating whole new brains out of parts. But the thing about Rowan is, she's a real human being. No need to worry about brilliance without a heart."

"Oh, Rowan. Do I remember Rowan? You have to be kidding! Rowan could have been teaching the class instead of me. You want to know something funny—and don't you ever tell anyone this! I had to go out of town at the end of the term, and I gave Rowan all the class papers to grade. She graded her own class! Now if that ever gets out I'm ruined, but we struck a bargain, you see. She wanted a key to the laboratory over the Christmas break, and I said, 'Well, how about grading these papers?' And the worst part of it was it was the first time I didn't get a single student complaint about a grade. Rowan, I wish I could forget her. People like Rowan make the rest of us feel like jerks."

"She isn't brilliant. That's what people think, but there's more to it. She's some sort of mutant. No, seriously. She can study the research animals and tell you what's going to happen. She would lay her hands on them and say, 'This drug isn't going to do it.' I'll tell you something else she did too. She could cure those little creatures. She could. One of the older doctors told me once that if she didn't watch it, she could upset the experiments by using her powers to cure. I believe it. I went out with her one time, and she didn't cure me of anything, but boy, was she ever hot. I mean literally hot. It was like making love to somebody with a fever. And that's what they say about faith healers, you know, the ones who've been studied. You can feel a heat coming from their hands. I believe it. I don't think she should have gone into surgery. She should have gone into oncology. She could have really cured people. Surgery? Anybody can cut them up."

(Let us add that this doctor himself is an oncologist, and non-surgeons frequently make extremely pejorative statements about surgeons, calling them plumbers and the like; and surgeons make similar pejorative remarks about nonsurgeons, saying things such as "All they do is get the patients ready for us.")

As soon as Rowan entered the hospital as an intern (her third year of medical school), stories of her healing powers and diagnostic powers became so common that our investigators could pick and choose what they wanted to write down.

In sum, Rowan is the first Mayfair witch to be described as a healer since Marguerite Mayfair at Riverbend before 1835.

Just about every nurse ever questioned about Rowan has some "fantastic" story to tell. Rowan could diagnose anything; Rowan knew just what to do. Rowan patched up people who looked like they were ready for the morgue.

"She can stop bleeding. I've seen her do it. She grabbed a hold of this boy's head and looked at his nose. 'Stop,' she whispered. I heard her. And he just didn't bleed any more after that."

Her more skeptical colleagues—including some male and female doctors—attribute her achievements to the "power of suggestion." "Why, she practically uses voodoo, you know, saying to a patient, Now we're going to make this pain stop! Of course it stops, she's got them hypnotized."

Older black nurses in the hospital know Rowan has "the power," and sometimes ask her outright to "lay those hands" on them when they are suffering severe arthritis or other such aches and pains. They swear by Rowan.

"She looks into your eyes. 'Tell me about it, where it hurts,' she says. And she rubs with those hands, and it *don't* hurt! That's a fact."

By all accounts, Rowan seems to have loved working in the hospital, and to have experienced an immediate conflict between her devotion to the laboratory and her newfound exhilaration on the wards.

"You could see the research scientist being seduced!" said one of her teachers sadly. "I knew we were losing her. And once she stepped into the Operating Room it was all over. Whatever they say about women being too emotional to be brain surgeons, no one would ever say such a thing about Rowan. She's got the coolest hands in the field."

(Note the coincidental use of cool and hot in reference to the hands.)

There are indications that Rowan's decision to abandon research for surgery was a difficult, if not traumatic one. During the fall of 1983, she apparently spent considerable time with a Dr. Karl Lemle, of the Keplinger Institute in San Francisco, who was working on cures for Parkinson's disease.

Rumors at the hospital indicated that Lemle was trying to lure Rowan away from University, with an extremely high salary and ideal working conditions, but that Rowan did not feel she was ready to leave the Emergency Room or the Operating Room or the wards.

During Christmas of 1983, Rowan seems to have had a violent falling out with Lemle, and thereafter would not take his calls. Or so he told everyone at University over the next few months.

We have never been able to learn what happened between Rowan and Lemle. Apparently Rowan did agree to see him for lunch in the spring of 1984. Witnesses saw them in the hospital cafeteria where they had quite an argument. A week later Lemle entered the Keplinger private hospital having suffered a small stroke. Another stroke followed and then another, and he was dead within the month.

Some of Rowan's colleagues criticized her severely for her failure to visit Lemle. Lemle's assistant, who later took his place at the Institute, said to one of our investigators that Rowan was highly competitive and jealous of his boss. This seems unlikely.

No one to our knowledge has ever connected the death of Lemle with Rowan. However, we have made the connection.

Whatever happened between Rowan and her mentor—she frequently described him as such before their falling out—Rowan committed herself to neurosurgery shortly after 1983, and began operating exclusively on the brain after she completed her regular residency in 1985. She is at the time of this writing completing her residency in neurosurgery, and will undoubtedly be Board-certified, and probably hired as the Staff Attending at University within the year.

Rowan's record as a neurosurgeon so far—though she is still a resident and technically operating under the eye of the Attending—is as exemplary as one might expect.

Stories abound of her saving lives on the operating table, of her uncanny ability to know in the Emergency Room whether surgery will save a patient, of her patching up ax wounds, bullet wounds, and skull fractures resulting from falls and car collisions, of her operating for ten hours straight without fainting, of her quiet and expert handling of frightened interns and cranky nurses, and of disapproving colleagues and administrators who have advised her from time to time that she takes too many risks.

Rowan, the miracle worker, has become a common epithet.

In spite of her success as a surgical resident, Rowan remains extremely well liked at the hospital. She is a doctor upon whom others can rely. Also she elicits exceptional devotion from the nurses with whom she works. In fact, her relationship with these women (there are a few male nurses but the profession is still predominately female) is so exceptional as to beg for an explanation.

And the explanation seems to be that Rowan goes out of her way to establish personal contact with nurses, and that indeed, she displays the same extraordinary empathy regarding their personal problems that she displayed with her teachers years ago. Though none of these nurses report telepathic incidents, they say repeatedly that Rowan seems to know when they are feeling bad, to be sympathetic with their family difficulties, and that Rowan finds some way to express her gratitude to them for special services, and this from an uncompromising doctor who expects the highest standards of those on the staff.

Rowan's conquest of the Operating Room nurses, including those famous for being uncooperative with women surgeons, is something of a legend in the hospital. Whereas other female surgeons are criticized as "having a chip on their shoulder," or being "too superior" or "just plain bitchy"—remarks which seem to reflect considerable prejudice, all things considered—the same nurses speak of Rowan as if she were a saint.

"She never screams or throws a tantrum like the men do, she's too good for that."

"She's as straight as a man."

"I'd rather be in there with her than some of these men doctors, I tell you."

"She's beautiful to work with. She's the best. I love just to watch her work. She's like an artist."

"She's the only doctor who's ever going to open my head, I can tell you that."

To put this more clearly into perspective, we are still living in a world in which Operating Room nurses sometimes refuse to hand instruments to women surgeons, and patients in Emergency Rooms refuse to be treated by women doctors and insist that young male interns treat them while older, wiser, and more competent women doctors are forced to stand back and watch.

Rowan appears to have transcended this sort of prejudice entirely. If there is any complaint against her among members of her profession it is that she is too quiet. She doesn't talk enough about what she's doing to the young doctors who must learn from her. It's hard for her. But she does the best she can.

As of 1984, she seemed to have escaped completely the curse

of the Mayfairs, the ghastly experiences that plagued her mother and her grandmother, and to be on the way to a brilliant career.

An exhaustive investigation of her life had turned up no evidence of Lasher's presence, or indeed any connection between Rowan and ghosts or spirits or apparitions.

And her strong telepathic powers and healing powers seemed to have been put to extraordinarily productive use in her career as a surgeon.

Though everyone around her admired her for her exceptional accomplishments, no one thought of her as "weird" or "strange" or in any way connected with the supernatural.

As one doctor put it when asked to explain Rowan's reputation, "She's a genius. What else can I say?"

LATER DISCOVERIES

However, there is more to the story of Rowan which has surfaced only in the last few years. One part of that story is entirely personal and no concern of the Talamasca. The other part of it has us alarmed beyond our wildest expectations as to what may happen to Rowan in the years that lie ahead.

Allow us to deal with the insignificant part first.

In 1985, the complete lack of any social life on the part of Rowan aroused our curiosity. We asked our investigators to engage in closer surveillance.

Within weeks, they discovered that Rowan, far from having no social life, has a very special kind of social life including very virile working-class men whom she picks up from time to time in any one of four different San Francisco bars.

These men are predominately fire fighters or uniformed policemen. They are invariably single; they are always extremely good-looking and extremely well built. Rowan sees them only on the *Sweet Christine*, in which they sometimes go out to sea and other times remain in the harbor, and she rarely sees any one of them more than three times.

Though Rowan is very discreet and unobtrusive, she has become the subject of some gossip in the bars she frequents. At least two men have been embittered by their inevitable rejection by her and they talked freely to our investigators, but it became apparent that they knew almost nothing about Rowan. They thought she was "a rich girl from Tiburon" who had snubbed them, or used them. They had no idea she was a doctor. One of them repeatedly described the *Sweet Christine* as "Daddy's fancy boat."

Other men who have known Rowan are more objective. "She's

a loner, that's all. I liked it, actually. She didn't want any string attached and neither did I. I would have liked it once or twice more maybe, but it's got to be mutual. I understand her. She's an educated girl who likes old-fashioned men.''

A superficial investigation of twelve different men seen leaving Rowan's house between 1986 and 1987 indicated that all were highly regarded fire fighters or policemen, some with sterling records and decorations, and all considered by their peers and later girlfriends to be "nice guys."

Further digging also confirmed that Rowan's parents knew about her preference for this sort of man as early as her undergraduate years. Graham told his secretary that Rowan wouldn't even speak to a guy with a college degree. That she only went out with "hairy-chested galoots," and one of these days she was going to discover that these non-compos-mentis apes were dangerous.

Ellie also expressed her concern to her friends. "She says they're all cops and firemen and that those kind of men only save lives. I don't think she knows what she's doing. But as long as she doesn't marry one of those men I suppose it's all right. You should see the one she brought home last night. I got a glimpse of him on the side deck. Beautiful red hair and freckles. Just the cutest Irish cop you ever saw.''

As things stand now, I have put a halt to this investigation. I feel we had no grounds to pursue this aspect of Rowan's life further. And indeed, the bars in which Rowan picks up her cops and firemen are so few that asking questions about Rowan truly violates her privacy by drawing attention to her; and in some instances our questions have encouraged rather degrading talk on the part of crude men, who actually knew nothing about Rowan, but claimed to have heard this or that vulgar detail from someone else.

I do not think that this aspect of Rowan's life is any concern of ours, except to note that her taste seemed similar to that of Mary Beth Mayfair, and that such a pattern of random and limited contacts reinforces the idea that Rowan is a loner, and a mystery to everyone who knows her. That she does not talk about herself to these bed partners is obvious. Perhaps she cannot talk about herself to anyone, and this may be one key to understanding her compulsions and her ambitions.

The other aspect of Rowan's life, only lately discovered, is far more significant, and represents one of the most disturbing chapters in the entire history of the Mayfair family. We have only begun to document this second secret aspect of Rowan, and we feel compelled to continue our investigations, and to consider the possibility of contact with Rowan in the very near future, though we are deeply troubled about disturbing her ignorance regarding her family background, and we cannot in conscience make contact without disturbing her ignorance. The responsibilities involved are immense.

In 1988, when Graham Franklin died of a cerebral hemorrhage, our investigator in the area wrote us a brief description of the event, adding only a few details, namely that the man had died in Rowan's arms.

As we knew of the deep division between Graham Franklin and his dying wife, Ellie, we read this report with some care. Could Rowan have somehow caused Graham's death? We were curious to know.

As our investigators sought more information about Graham's plan to divorce his wife, they came in contact with Graham's mistress, Karen Garfield, and reported in due time that Karen had suffered several severe heart attacks. Then they reported her death, two months following that of Graham.

Attaching no significance to it whatsoever, they had also reported a meeting between Rowan and Karen the day that Karen was rushed to the hospital with her first major attack. Karen had spoken to our investigator—"You're a cute guy, I like you"—only hours after seeing Rowan. She was, in fact, talking to the man when she broke off because she wasn't feeling well.

The investigations did not make the connection, but we did. Karen Garfield was only twenty-seven. Her autopsy records, which we obtained fairly easily, indicated that she had had an apparent congenital weakness of the heart muscle, and a congenital weakness of the artery wall. She sustained a hemorrhage in the artery and then major heart failure, and after the initial damage to the heart muscle, she simply could not recover. The subsequent bouts of heart failure weakened her progressively until she finally died.

Only a heart transplant could have saved her, and as she had a very rare blood type, that was out of the question. And besides, there wasn't time.

The case struck us as very unusual, especially since Karen's condition had never given her any trouble before. When we studied Graham's autopsy we discovered that he too had died of an aneurysm, or weakness of the artery wall. A massive hemorrhage had killed him almost instantly.

We ordered our investigators to go back through Rowan's life as best they could, and look for any sudden deaths through heart failure, cerebrovascular accident, or any such internal traumatic cause. In sum, this meant making casual and unobtrusive inquiries of teachers who might remember Rowan and her classmates, and inquiries of students who might remember such things at U.C. Berkeley, or University Hospital. Not such an easy thing to accomplish, but easier than one unfamiliar with our methods might suppose.

In truth, I expected the investigation to turn up nothing.

People with this kind of telekinetic power—the power to inflict severe internal damage—are almost unheard of, even in the annals of the Talamasca. And certainly we had never seen anyone in the Mayfair family who could bring death with that kind of force.

Many Mayfairs moved objects, slammed doors, caused windows to rattle. But in almost every incidence it could have been pure witchcraft—to wit, the manipulation of Lasher or other lowly spirits, rather than telekinesis. And if it was telekinesis it was the garden variety and nothing more.

Indeed, the history of the Mayfairs was the history of witchcraft, with only mild touches of telepathy or healing power or other psychic abilities mixed in.

In the meantime, I studied all the information we had on Rowan. I could not help but believe that Deirdre Mayfair would be happy if she could read such a history, if she could know that her daughter was so deeply admired and so uniformly successful, and I vowed to myself that I would never do anything to disturb the happiness or the peace of mind of Rowan Mayfair—that if the Mayfair history, as we knew it and understood it, was coming to an end in the liberated figure of Rowan, then we could only be glad for Rowan, and could do nothing to affect that history in any way.

After all, only a tiny bit of information about the past might change the course of Rowan's life. We could not risk such intervention. In fact, I felt we had to be prepared to close the file on Rowan, and on the Mayfair Witches, as soon as Deirdre was released in death. On the other hand we had to be prepared to do something if, when Ellie died, Rowan went back to New Orleans to find out about her past.

Within two weeks of Ellie's funeral, we knew that Rowan was not going back. She had just commenced her final year as senior resident in neurosurgery and could not possibly take the time. Also our investigators had discovered that Rowan had been asked by Ellie to sign a paper swearing officially that she would never go to New Orleans or seek to know who her real parents were. Rowan had signed this paper. There was no indication that she did not mean to honor it.

Perhaps she would never set eyes on the First Street house. Perhaps somehow "the curse" would be broken. And Carlotta Mayfair would be victorious in the end.

On the other hand, it was too soon to know. And what was to stop Lasher from revealing himself to this highly psychic young woman who could read people's minds more strongly perhaps than her mother or grandmother, and whose enormous ambition and strength echoed that of ancestors like Marie Claudette, or Julien, or Mary Beth, about whom she knew nothing, but about whom she might soon find out a lot.

As I pondered all these things, I also found myself thinking often of Petyr van Abel—Petyr whose father had been a great surgeon and anatomist in Leiden, a name in the history books to this day. I longed to tell Rowan Mayfair: "See that name, that Dutch doctor who was famous for his study of anatomy. That is your ancestor. His blood and his skill perhaps have come down to you through all the generations and the years."

These were my thoughts when in the fall of 1988 our investigators began to report some amazing findings regarding traumatic deaths in Rowan's past. It seems that a little girl fighting with Rowan on the playground in San Francisco had suffered a violent cerebral hemorrhage and died within a few feet of the hysterical Rowan before an ambulance could even be called.

Then in 1974, when Rowan was a teenager, she was saved from assault at the hands of a convicted rapist when the man suffered a fatal heart attack as Rowan struggled to fight him off.

In 1984, on the afternoon that he first complained of a severe headache, Dr. Karl Lemle of the Keplinger Institute told his secretary, Berenice, that he had just seen Rowan unexpectedly and that he could not understand the animosity she felt for him. She had become so angry when he tried to speak to her that she had cut him off in front of the other doctors at University. In fact, she'd given him a bad headache. He needed some aspirin. He was hospitalized for the first of his successive hemorrhages that night, and died within a matter of weeks.

That made five deaths from cerebrovascular or cardiovascular accident among Rowan's close associates. Three of these people had died while Rowan was present. Two had seen her within hours of taking ill.

I told my investigators to run an exhaustive check on every single one of Rowan's classmates or colleagues, and to check each and every name with the death records in San Francisco and in the city of the person's birth. Of course this would take months.

But within weeks, they had found yet another death. It was Owen Gander who called me, a man who has worked directly for the Talamasca for twenty years. He is not a member of the order, but he has visited the Motherhouse and he is one of our most trusted confidants, and one of the best investigators we have.

This was his report. At U.C. Berkeley in 1978, Rowan had had a terrible argument with another student over some laboratory work. Rowan felt that the girl had deliberately meddled with her equipment. Rowan had lost her temper—an extremely rare occurrence—and thrown a piece of equipment to the ground, breaking it, and then turned her back on the girl. The girl then ridiculed Rowan until other students came between them insisting that the girl stop.

The girl went home that night to Palo Alto, California, as the spring break began the following day. By the end of spring break she had died of a cerebrovascular hemorrhage. There was no indication from the record that *Rowan ever knew*.

When I read this, I called Gander immediately from London. "What makes you think Rowan didn't know?" I asked.

"None of her friends knew. After I found the girl's death in the Palo Alto records, I researched her with Rowan's friends. They all remembered the fight, but they didn't know what happened to the girl afterwards. Not a single one knew. I asked them pointedly. 'Never saw her again.' 'Guess she dropped out of school.' 'Never knew her very well. Don't know what happened to her. Maybe she went back to Stanford.' That's it. U.C. Berkeley is an enormous university. It could have happened like that."

I then advised the investigator to proceed with the utmost discretion to discover whether Rowan knew what had happened to Graham's mistress, Karen Garfield. "Call her some time in the evening. Ask for Graham Franklin. When she tells you Graham is dead, explain that you are trying to find Karen Garfield. But try to upset her as little as possible, and don't stay on the line very long."

The investigator called back the following evening.

"You're right."

"About what?" I asked.

"She doesn't know she's doing it! She doesn't have any idea

that Karen Garfield is dead. She told me Karen lived somewhere on Jackson Street in San Francisco. She suggested I try Graham's old secretary. Aaron, she doesn't know."

"How did she sound?"

"Weary, faintly annoyed, but polite. She has a beautiful voice, really. Rather exceptional voice. I asked her if she'd seen Karen. I was really pushing it. She said that she didn't actually know Karen, that Karen had been a friend of her father's. I believe she was perfectly sincere!"

"Well, she had to know about her stepfather, and about the little girl on the playground. And she had to know about the rapist."

"Yes, but Aaron, probably none of them was deliberate. Don't you see? She was hysterical when that little girl died; she was hysterical after the rape attempt. As for the stepfather, she was doing everything she could to resuscitate him when the ambulance arrived. She doesn't know. Or if she does know, she can't control it. It might be scaring her half to death."

I told Gander to reconsider the matter of the young lovers in greater detail. Look for any relevant deaths among policemen or fire fighters in San Francisco or Marin County. Go back to the bars Rowan frequented; start a conversation with one of her former lovers; say you're looking for Rowan Mayfair. Has anybody seen her? Does anybody know her? Be as discreet and nondisruptive as possible. But dig.

Gander called four days later. There had been no such suspicious deaths among any young men in the departments who could conceivably be connected to Rowan. But one thing had emerged from the investigator's talks in the bar. One young fireman, who admitted to knowing Rowan and liking her, said she was no mystery to him, rather she was an open book. "She's a doctor; she likes saving people's lives and she hangs around with us because we do the same thing."

"Did Rowan actually say that to the young man?"

"Yes, she told him that. He made a joke about it. 'Imagine, I went to bed with a brain surgeon. She fell in love with my medals. It was great while it lasted. You think if I pull somebody out of a burning building, she'll give me another chance?' " Gander laughed. "She doesn't know, Aaron. She's hooked on saving people, and maybe she doesn't even know why."

"She has to know. She's too good a doctor not to know," I said. "Remember, this girl is a diagnostic genius. She must have known about the stepfather. Unless of course we're wrong about the whole thing."

"We're not wrong," said Gander. "What you've got here,

Aaron, is a brilliant neurosurgeon descended from a family of witches, who can kill people just by looking at them; and on some level she knows it, she has to, and she spends every day of her life making up for it in the Operating Room, and when she goes out on the town it's with some hero who's just saved a kid from a burning attic, or a cop who's stopped a drunk from stabbing his wife. She's sort of mad, this lady. Maybe as mad as all the rest.''

In December of 1988, I went to California. I had been to the States in January to attend the funeral of Nancy Mayfair, and I deeply regretted not having gone on to the coast at that time to try to get a glimpse of Rowan. But no one had an inkling, then, that both Ellie and Graham would be dead within six months.

Rowan was now all alone in the house in Tiburon. I wanted to have a look at her, even if it was from a distance. I wanted to make some appraisal which depended upon my seeing her in the flesh.

By that time, we had not—thank God—turned up any more deaths in Rowan's past. As the senior resident in neurosurgery, she was working a hectic if not inhuman schedule at the hospital, and I found it far more difficult to get a glimpse of her than I ever imagined. She left the hospital from a covered parking lot and drove into a covered garage at home. The *Sweet Christine*, moored at her very doorstep, was concealed entirely by a high redwood fence.

At last I entered University Hospital, sought out the doctors' cafeteria, and hovered near it in a small visitors' area for seven hours. To my knowledge Rowan never passed.

I resolved to follow her from the hospital only to discover that there was no way to discover when she might be leaving. When she arrived was also a mystery. There was no discreet way to press anyone for details. I could not risk hanging about in the area adjacent to the Operating Rooms. It wasn't open to the public. The waiting room for the family members of those having surgery was strictly monitored. And the rest of the hospital was like a labyrinth. I didn't know finally what to do.

I was thrown into consternation. I wanted to see Rowan, but I dreaded disturbing her. I could not bear the thought of bringing darkness into her life, of clouding the isolation from the past which seemed, on the surface, to have served her so well. On the other hand, if she was actually responsible for the deaths of six human beings! Well, I had to see her before I could make a decision. I had to see her.

Unable to come to any decision, I invited Gander for a drink at the hotel. Gander felt Rowan was deeply troubled. He had watched her off and on for over fifteen years. She had had the wind knocked out of her by the death of her parents, he said. And we could now pretty fairly well confirm that her random contact with the "boys in blue," as he called her lovers, had dropped off in the last few months.

I told Gander I would not leave California without a glimpse of her, if I had to hover in the underground parking lot near her car—the absolutely worst way possible to achieve a sighting—until she appeared.

"I wouldn't try that, old man," said Gander. "Underground parking lots are the spookiest places. Her little psychic antennae will pick you up instantly. Then she'll misinterpret the intensity of your interest in her, and you'll get a sudden stabbing pain in the side of your head. Next you'll suddenly . . ."

"I follow the drift, Owen," I said dismally. "But I must get a good look at her in some public place where she isn't aware of me."

"Well, make it happen," said Gander. "Do a little witchcraft yourself. Synchronicity? Isn't that what they call it?"

The following day I decided to do some routine work. I went to the cemetery where Graham and Ellie were buried, to photograph the inscriptions on the stones. I had twice asked Gander to do this, but somehow he had never gotten around to it. I think he enjoyed the other aspects of the investigation much more.

While I was there, the most remarkable thing happened. Rowan Mayfair appeared.

I was down on my knees in the sun, making a few notes on the inscriptions, having already taken the photographs, when I became aware of this tall young woman in a sailor's coat and faded dungarees coming up the hill. She seemed all legs and blowing hair for a moment, a very fresh-faced and lovely young creature. Quite impossible to believe she was thirty years old.

On the contrary, her face had almost no lines in it at all. She looked exactly like the photographs taken of her years ago, yet she looked very much like someone else, and for one moment the resemblance so distracted me that I could not think who it was. Then it came to me. It was Petyr van Abel. She had the same blond, pale-eyed look. It was very nearly Scandinavian, and she appeared extremely independent and extremely strong.

She approached the grave, and stopped only a few feet away where I knelt, clearly taking notes from her stepmother's headstone.

At once I began to talk to her. I cannot remember precisely what I said. I was so flustered that I didn't know what I should say to explain my appearance there, and very slowly I sensed danger just as surely as I had sensed it with Cortland years ago. I sensed enormous danger. In fact, her smooth pale face with its large gray eyes seemed suddenly filled with pure malice. Then a wall went up behind her expression. She closed down, rather like a giant receiver which is suddenly and soundlessly turned off.

I realized with horror that I had been talking about her family. I had told her that I knew the Mayfairs of New Orleans. It was my feeble excuse for what I was doing there. Did she want to have a drink, talk about old family matters. Dear God! What if she said yes!

But she said nothing. Absolutely nothing, at least not in words. I could have sworn, however, that the closed receiver suddenly became a highly focused speaker and she communicated to me quite deliberately that she couldn't avail herself of my offer, something dark and terrible and painful prevented her from doing it, and then she seemed lost in confusion; lost in misery. In fact, I have seldom if ever in my life felt such pure pain.

It came to me in a silent flash that she knew she had killed people. She knew she was different in a horrible and mortal way. She knew it and the knowledge sealed her up as if she were buried alive inside herself.

Perhaps it had not been malice which I felt only moments before. But whatever had taken place was now concluded. I was losing her. She was turning away. Why she had come, what she meant to do, I would never know.

At once I offered her my card. I put it in her hand. She gave it back to me. She wasn't rude when she did it. She simply did it. She put it right back in my hand. The malice leapt out of her like a flash of light from a keyhole. Then she went dim. Her body tensed and she turned and walked off.

I was so badly shaken that for a long moment I could not move. I stood in the cemetery watching her walk down the hill. I saw her get into a green Jaguar sedan. Off she drove without glancing back.

Was I ill? Had I suffered a severe pain somewhere? Was I about to die? Of course not. Nothing like that had happened. Yet I knew what she could do. I knew and she knew and she had told me! But why?

By the time I reached the Campton Place Hotel in San Francisco, I was thoroughly confused. I decided I would do nothing further for the present.

When I met with Gander, I said: "Keep up the surveillance. Get as close as you dare. Watch for anything that indicates she is using the power. Report to me at once."

"Then you're not going to make contact."

"Not now. I can't justify it. Not until something else happens and that could be either of two things: she kills someone else, deliberately or accidentally. Or her mother dies in New Orleans and she decides to go home."

"Aaron, that's madness! You have to make contact. You can't wait until she goes back to New Orleans. Look, old man, you have pretty much told me the whole story over the years. And I don't claim to know what you people know about it. But from everything you've told me, this is the most powerful psychic the family has ever produced. Who's to say she's not a powerful witch as well? When her mother finally goes, why would this spook Lasher miss an opportunity like this?"

I couldn't answer, except to say what Owen already knew. There were absolutely no sightings of Lasher in Rowan's history.

"So he's biding his time. The other woman's still alive. She has the necklace. But when she dies, they have to give it to Rowan. From what you've told me, it's the law."

I called Scott Reynolds in London. Scott is no longer our director, but he is the most knowledgeable person in the order on the subject of the Mayfair Witches, next to me.

"I agree with Owen. You have to make contact. You have to. What you said to her in the cemetery was exactly what you should have said, and on some level you know it. That's why you told her you knew her family. That's why you offered her the card. Talk to her. You have to."

"No, I disagree with you. It isn't justified."

"Aaron, this woman is a conscientious physician, yet she's killing people! Do you think she wants to do that sort of thing? On the other hand . . ."

". . . what?"

"If she does know, this contact could be dangerous. I have to confess, I don't know how I would feel about all this if I were there, if I were you."

I thought it over. I decided that I would not do it. Everything that Owen and Scott had said was true. But it was all conjecture. We did not know whether Rowan had ever deliberately killed anyone. Possibly she was not responsible for the six deaths.

We could not know whether she would ever lay her hands on the emerald necklace. We did not know if she would ever go to New Orleans. We did not know whether or not Rowan's power included the ability to see a spirit, or to help Lasher to materialize . . . ah, but of course we could pretty well conjecture that Rowan could do all that . . . But that was just it, it was conjecture. Conjecture and nothing more.

And here was this hardworking doctor saving lives daily in a big city Operating Room. A woman untouched by the darkness that shrouded the First Street house. True, she had a ghastly power, and she might again use it, either deliberately or inadvertently. And if that happened, then I would make contact.

"Ah, I see, you want another body on the slab," said Owen.

"I don't believe there is going to be another," I said angrily. "Besides, if she doesn't know she's doing it, why should she believe us?"

"Conjecture," said Owen. "Like everything else."

SUMMATION

As of January 1989, Rowan has not been connected with any other suspicious deaths. On the contrary, she has worked tirelessly at University Hospital at "working miracles," and will very likely be appointed Attending Physician in neurosurgery before the end of the year.

In New Orleans, Deirdre Mayfair continues to sit in her rocking chair, staring out over the ruined garden. The last sighting of Lasher—"a nice young man standing beside her"—was reported two weeks ago.

Carlotta Mayfair is nearing ninety years of age. Her hair is entirely white, though the style of it has not changed in fifty years. Her skin is milky and her ankles are perpetually swollen over the tops of her plain black leather shoes. But her voice remains quite steady. And she still goes to the office every morning for four hours. Sometimes she has lunch with the younger lawyers before she takes her regular taxi home.

On Sundays she walks to Mother of Perpetual Help Chapel to go to Mass. People in the parish have offered to drive her to Mass, and indeed, anyplace else that she would like to go. But she says that she likes walking. She needs the fresh air. It keeps her in good health.

When Sister Bridget Marie died in the fall of 1987, Carlotta attended the funeral with her nephew (cousin, actually) Gerald Mayfair, a great-grandson of Clay Mayfair. She is said to like Gerald. She is said to be afraid she may not live long enough to see Deirdre at peace. Maybe Gerald will have to take care of Deirdre after Carlotta is gone.

To the best of our knowledge Rowan Mayfair knows none of these people. She knows no more today of her family history than she did when she was a little girl.

"Ellie was so afraid Rowan would try to find out about her real parents," said a friend recently to Gander. "I got the feeling it was an awful story. But Ellie would never talk about it, except to say that Rowan must be protected, at all costs, from the past.''

I am content to watch and to wait.

I feel, irrationally perhaps, that I owe this much to Deirdre. That she did not want to give up Rowan is quite obvious to me. That she would have wanted Rowan to have a normal life is beyond doubt. There are times when I am tempted to destroy our file on the Mayfair Witches. Has any other history involved us in so much violence and so much pain? Of course such a thing is unthinkable. The Talamasca would never allow it. And never forgive it, if I did it on my own.

Last night after I completed my final draft of the above summary, I dreamed of Stuart Townsend, whom I had met only once when I was a small boy. In the dream, he was in my room and had been talking to me for hours. Yet when I awoke, I could recall only his last words. ''You see what I am saying? It's all planned!''

He was dreadfully upset with me.

''I don't see!'' I said out loud when I woke up. In fact, it was my own voice which awakened me. I was amazed to discover that the room was empty, that I had been dreaming, that Stuart wasn't really there.

I don't see. That is the truth. I don't know why Cortland tried to kill me. I don't know why such a man would go to such a ghastly extreme. I don't know what really happened to Stuart. I don't even really know why Stella was so desperate that Arthur Langtry take her away. I don't know what Carlotta did to Antha, or whether or not Cortland fathered Stella, Antha, and Deirdre's baby. I don't see!

But there is one thing of which I am certain. Some day, regardless of whatever she promised Ellie Mayfair, Rowan Mayfair may go back to New Orleans and if she does, she will want answers. Dozens upon dozens of answers. And I fear I am the only one now—we in the Talamasca are the only ones—who can possibly hope to reconstruct for her this sad tale.

Aaron Lightner,
The Talamasca
LONDON
January 15, 1989

Twenty-six

O N AND ON it went, exotic and dreamlike still in its strangeness, a ritual from another country, quaint and darkly beautiful, as the whole party spilled out into the warm air and then into a fleet of limousines which drove them silently through narrow, crowded, treeless little streets.

Before a high brick church—St. Mary's Assumption—the long lumbering shiny cars stopped, one after another, oblivious to the derelict school buildings with their broken windows, and the weeds rising triumphant from every fissure and crack.

Carlotta stood on the church steps, tall, stiff, her thin spotted hand locked on the curve of her gleaming wooden cane. Beside her an attractive man, white-haired and blue-eyed, and not much older than Michael perhaps, whom the old woman dismissed with a brittle gesture beckoning for Rowan to follow her.

The older man stepped back with young Pierce, after quickly clasping Rowan's hand. There was something furtive in the way he whispered his name, "Ryan Mayfair," glancing anxiously at the old woman. Rowan understood he was young Pierce's father.

And into the immense nave they all moved, the entire assemblage following the coffin on its rolling bier. Footfalls echoed softly and loudly under the graceful Gothic arches, light striking brilliantly the magnificent stained-glass windows and the exquisitely painted statues of the saints.

Seldom even in Europe had she seen such elegance and grandeur. Faintly Michael's words came back to her about the old parish of his childhood, about the jam-packed churches which had been as big as cathedrals. Could this have been the very place?

There must have been a thousand people gathered here now, children crying shrilly before their mothers shushed them, and the words of the priest ringing out in the vast emptiness as if they were a song.

The straight-backed old woman beside her said nothing to her. In her wasted, fragile-looking hands, she held with marvelous capability a heavy book, full of bright and lurid pictures of the

669

saints. Her white hair, drawn back into a bun, lay thick and heavy against her small head, beneath her brimless black felt hat. Aaron Lighter remained back in the shadows, by the front doors, though Rowan would have had him stay beside her. Beatrice Mayfair wept softly in the second pew. Pierce sat on the other side of Rowan, arms folded, staring dreamily at the statues of the altar, at the painted angels high above. His father seemed to have lapsed into the same trance, though once he turned and his sharp blue eyes fixed deliberately and unself-consciously on Rowan.

By the hundreds they rose to take Holy Communion, the old, the young, the little children. Carlotta refused assistance as she made her way to the front and then back again, her rubber-tipped cane thumping dully, then sank down into the pew, with her head bowed, as she said her prayers. So thin was she that her dark gabardine suit seemed empty, like a garment on a hanger, with no contour of a body at all within it, her legs like sticks plunging to her thick string shoes.

The smell of incense rose from the silver censer as the priest circled the coffin. At last the procession moved out to the waiting fleet in the treeless street. Dozens of small black children—some barefoot, some shirtless—watched from the cracked pavements before a shabby, neglected gymnasium. Black women stood with bare arms folded, scowling in the sun.

Can this really be America?

And then through the dense shade of the Garden District the caravan plunged, bumper to bumper, with scores of people walking on either side of it, children skipping ahead, all advancing through the deep green light.

The walled cemetery was a veritable city of peaked-roof graves, some with their own tiny gardens, paths running hither and thither past this tumbling down crypt or this great monument to fire fighters of another era, or the orphans of this or that asylum, or to the rich who had had the time and money to etch these stones with poetry, words now filled with dust and wearing slowly away.

The Mayfair crypt itself was enormous, and surrounded by flowers. A small iron fence encircled the little building, marble urns at the four corners of its gently sloping peristyle roof. Its three bays contained twelve coffin-sized vaults, and from one of these the smooth marble stone had been removed, so that it gaped, dark and empty, for the coffin of Deirdre Mayfair to be placed inside like a long pan of bread.

Urged politely to the front ranks, Rowan stood beside the old woman. The sun flashed in the old woman's small round silver-rimmed glasses, as grimly she stared at the word "Mayfair" carved in giant letters within the low triangle of the peristyle.

And Rowan too looked at it, her eyes once again dazzled by the flowers and the faces surrounding her, as in a hushed and respectful voice young Pierce explained to her that though there were only twelve slots, numerous Mayfairs had been buried in these graves, as the stones on the front revealed. The old coffins were broken up in time to make way for new burials, and the pieces, along with the bones, were slipped into a vault beneath the grave.

Rowan gasped faintly. "So they're all down there," she whispered, half in wonder. "Higgledy-piggledy, underneath."

"No, they are in hell or heaven," said Carlotta Mayfair, her voice crisp and ageless as her eyes. She had not even turned her head.

Pierce backed away, as if he were frightened of Carlotta, a quick flash of an uncomfortable smile illuminating his face. Ryan was staring at the old woman.

But the coffin was now being brought forward, the pallbearers actually supporting it on their shoulders, their faces red from the exertion, sweat dripping from their foreheads as they set down the heavy weight upon its wheeled stand.

It was time for the last prayers. The priest was here again with his acolyte. The heat seemed motionless and impossible suddenly. Beatrice was blotting her flushed cheeks with a folded handkerchief. The elderly, save for Carlotta, were sitting down where they could on the ledges surrounding the smaller graves.

Rowan let her eyes drift to the top of the tomb, to the ornamented peristyle with the words "Mayfair" in it, and above the name, in bas-relief, a long open door. Or was it a large open keyhole? She wasn't sure.

When a faint, damp breeze came, stirring the stiff leaves of the trees along the pathway, it seemed a miracle. Far away, by the front gates, the traffic moving in sudden vivid flashes behind him, Aaron Lightner stood with Rita Mae Lonigan, who had cried herself out and looked merely bereft like those who have waited on hospital wards with the dying all through a long night.

Even the final note struck Rowan as a bit of picturesque madness. For as they drifted back out the main entrance, it became clear that a small party of them would now move into the elegant restaurant directly across the street!

Mr. Lightner whispered his farewell to her, promising that Michael would come. She wanted to press him, but the old woman was staring at him coldly, angrily, and he had seen this, obviously, and was eager to withdraw. Bewildered Rowan waved good-bye, the heat once again making her sick. Rita Mae Lonigan murmured a sad farewell to her. Hundreds said their good-byes as they passed quickly; hundreds came to embrace the old woman; it seemed to go on forever, the heat bearing down and then lifting, the giant trees giving a dappled shade. "We'll talk to you again, Rowan." "Are you staying, Rowan?" "Good-bye, Aunt Carl. You took care of her." "We'll see you soon, Aunt Carl. You have to come out to Metairie." "Aunt Carl, I'll telephone you next week." "Aunt Carl, are you all right?"

At last the street stood empty except for the steady stream of bright noisy indifferent traffic and a few well-dressed people wandering out of the obviously fancy restaurant and squinting in the sudden bright light.

"I don't want to go in," said the old woman. She gazed coldly at the blue and white awnings.

"Oh, come on, Aunt Carl, please, just for a little while," said Beatrice Mayfair. Another slender young man, Gerald was his name, held the old woman's arm. "Why don't we go for a few minutes?" he said to Carlotta. "Then I'll take you home."

"I want to be alone now," said the old woman. "I want to walk home alone." Her eyes fixed on Rowan. Unearthly their ageless intelligence flashing out of the worn and sunken face. "Stay with them as long as you wish," she said as if it were an order, "and then come to me. I'll be waiting. At the First Street house."

"When would you like for me to come?" Rowan asked carefully.

A cold, ironic smile touched the lips of the old woman, ageless like the eyes and the voice. "When you want to come. That will be soon enough. I have things to say to you. I'll be there."

"Go with her, Gerald."

"I'm taking her, Aunt Bea."

"You may drive along beside me, if you wish," Carlotta said as she bowed her head and placed her cane before her, "but I am walking alone."

Once the glass doors of the restaurant called Commander's Palace had shut behind them, and Rowan had realized they were now in a faintly familiar world of uniformed waiters and white tablecloths, she glanced back through the glass at the white-washed wall of the graveyard, and at the little peaked roofs of the tombs visible over the top of the wall.

The dead are so close they can hear us, she thought.

"Ah, but you see," said the tall white-haired Ryan, as if he'd read her mind, "in New Orleans, we never really leave them out."

Twenty-seven

A<small>N ASHEN TWILIGHT</small> was deepening over Oak Haven. The sky was scarcely visible anymore. The oaks had become black and dense, the shadows beneath them broadening to eat the last of the warm summer light that clung to the dim gravel road.

Michael sat on the deep front gallery, chair tipped back, foot on the wooden railing, cigarette on his lip. He had finished the Mayfair history, and he felt raw and exhilarated and filled with quiet excitement. He knew that he and Rowan were now the new chapter yet unwritten, he and Rowan who had been characters in this narrative for some time.

For a long moment, he clung almost desperately to the enjoyment of the cigarette, and watched the changes in the dusky sky. The darkness gathered itself everywhere now on the far-flung landscape, the distant levee vanishing so that he could no longer make out the cars as they passed on the road, but only see the yellow twinkle of their lights. Each sound, scent, and shift of color aroused in him a deluge of sweet memories, some without place or mark of any kind. It was simply the certainty of familiarity, that this was home, that this was where the cicadas sang like no place else.

But it was an agony, this silence, this waiting, this many thoughts crowding his brain.

The lighted lamps in the room behind him grew brighter as the day died around him. Now it was their soft illumination falling on the manila folders in his lap.

Why hadn't Aaron called him? Surely the funeral of Deirdre Mayfair was over. Aaron had to be on his way back, and maybe Rowan was with him, maybe Rowan had instantly forgiven Michael for not being there—he hadn't forgiven himself yet—and was coming here to be with him, and they would talk together tonight, talk over everything in this safe and wholesome place.

But there was one more folder to read, one more sheaf of notes, obviously intended for his eyes. Better get to it now quickly. He crushed out the cigarette in the ashtray on the little camp table beside him, and lifting the folder into the yellow light, he opened it now.

Loose papers, some handwritten, some typed, some printed. He began to read.

COPY MAIL GRAM sent to TALAMASCA MOTHERHOUSE LONDON from Aaron Lightner

August 1989:
Parker Meridien Hotel
New York.

Just completed ''casual meeting'' interview with Deirdre Mayfair's doctor (from 1983) here in New York, as assigned. Several surprises.

Will send full handwritten transcript of interview (tape was lost; doctor requested it from me and I gave it to him) which I will complete on the plane to California.

But want to communicate an extremely interesting development, and ask for a file search and study.

This doctor claims to have seen Lasher not only near Deirdre but some distance away from the First Street house, on two occasions, and on at least one of these occasions—in a Magazine Street bar—Lasher clearly materialized. (Note the heat, the movement of the air, all fully described by the man.)

Also the doctor became convinced that Lasher was trying to stop him from giving Deirdre her tranquilizing medication. And that when Lasher later appeared to him, he was trying to get this doctor to come back to First Street and intervene in some way with Deirdre.

The doctor only came to this interpretation at a later time. When the appearances were happening he was frightened. He heard no words from Lasher; he received no clear telepathic message. On the contrary, he felt the spirit was trying desperately to communicate and could only do it through his mute appearances.

This doctor shows no evidence at all of being any sort of natural medium.

Appropriate Action: Pull every sighting of Lasher since 1958 and study each carefully. Look for any such sighting when Deirdre was not in the vicinity. Make a list of all sightings and give approximate distance from Deirdre.

As it stands now, preliminary to such an investigation, I can only conclude that Lasher may have gained considerable strength in the last twenty years, or has always had more strength than we realize; and can in fact materialize where he chooses.

I don't want to be hasty in drawing such a conclusion. But this seems more than likely. And Lasher's failure to implant any clear words or suggestions in the doctor's mind only reinforces my opinion that the doctor himself was not a natural medium and could not have been assisting these materializations.

As we well know, with Petyr van Abel, Lasher was working with the energy and imagination of a powerful psyche with profound moral guilts and conflicts. With Arthur Langtry, Lasher was dealing with a trained medium, and those appearances and/or materializations happened only on the First Street property, in proximity to Antha and Stella.

Can Lasher materialize when and where he wants to? Or does he merely have the strength to do it at greater distances from the witch?

This is what we have to discover.

Yours in the Talamasca,
Aaron

P.S. Will not attempt sighting of Rowan Mayfair while in San Francisco. Attempted contact with Michael Curry takes precedence this trip. Phone call earlier today from Gander before I left New York indicated Curry is now a semi-invalid in his house. However please notify me at the Saint Francis Hotel if there are any new developments in the Mayfair case. Will remain in San Francisco as long as required to make contact and offer assistance to Curry.

Notes to File, August 1989
(Handwritten, neatly, black ink on lined paper)

I'm aboard a 747 heading for the Coast. Have just reread the transcript. It's my firm opinion that there is something very unusual in this doctor's story. As I review the Mayfair file hastily, what hits me is this:

Rita Mae Dwyer Lonigan heard Lasher's voice in 1955–56.

This doctor claims to have seen Lasher a great distance from the First Street house.

Maybe a casual meeting between Gander and Rowan should be attempted so that Gander can try to determine whether or not Rowan has seen Lasher. But it seems so unlikely . . .

Can't attempt this myself. Absolutely cannot do it now. Curry situation too important.

Feelings about Curry . . . I continue to believe that there is something very special about this man, apart from his harrowing experience.

He needs us, there's no question of that, Gander is right about that. But my feeling has to do with him and us. I think he might want to become one of us.

How can I justify such a feeling?

1) I have read over all the articles pertaining to his experience several times, and there is something unsaid here, something to do with his life being at a point of stasis when he was drowned. I have a strong impression of a man who was waiting for something.

2) The man's background is remarkable, especially his formal education. Gander confirms background in history, especially European history. We need that kind of person, desperately.

He is weak in languages, but everyone today is weak in languages.

3) But the main question regarding Curry is this: How do I get to see him? I wish the entire Mayfair family would go away for a while. I don't want to think of Rowan while I am on Curry . . .

Michael quickly leafed through the rest of the last folder. All articles on him, and articles he had read before. Two large glossy United Press International photographs of him. A typewritten biography of him, compiled mostly from the attached materials.

Well, he knew the file on Michael Curry. He put all this aside, lighted a fresh cigarette, and returned to the handwritten account of Aaron's meeting in the Parker Meridien with the doctor.

It was very easy to read Aaron's fine script. The descriptions of Lasher's appearances were neatly underlined. He finished the account, agreeing with Aaron's remarks.

Then he got up from the porch chair, taking the folder with him, and went inside, to the desk. His leather-covered notebook lay there where he'd left it. He sat down, staring blindly at the room for a moment, not really seeing that the river breeze was blowing the curtains, or that the night was utter blackness outside. Or that the supper tray lay on the ottoman before the wing chair, just as it had since it arrived, with the food beneath its several silver-domed covers untouched.

He lifted his pen and began to write:

"I was six years old when I saw Lasher in the church at Christmas behind the crib. That would have been 1947. Deirdre would have been the same age, and she might have been in the church. But I have the strongest feeling that she wasn't there.

"When Lasher showed himself to me in the Municipal Auditorium, she might have been there too. But again—we can't know, to quote Aaron's favorite clause.

"Nevertheless the appearances per se have nothing to do with Deirdre. I have never seen Deirdre in the garden of First Street, nor anywhere, to my knowledge.

"Undoubtedly Aaron has already written up what I've told him. And the same suggestion is relevant: Lasher appeared to me when he was not in the vicinity of the witch. He can probably materialize where he wants to.

"The question is still why. Why me? And other connections are even more tantalizing and nerve-racking.

"For example—this may not matter much—but I know Rita Mae Dwyer Lonigan. I was with her and Marie Louise on the riverboat the night she got drunk with her boyfriend, Terry O'Neill. For that she was sent to St. Ro's, where she met Deirdre Mayfair. I remember Rita Mae going to St. Ro's.

"Does this mean nothing?

"And something else too. What if my ancestors worked in the Garden District? I don't know that they did or didn't. I know my father's mother was an orphan, reared at St. Margaret's. I don't think she had a legal father. What if her mother had been a maid in the First Street house . . . but my mind is just going crazy.

"After all, look what these people have done in terms of breeding. When you do this with horses and dogs, it's called inbreeding or line breeding.

"Over and over again, the finest male specimens have inbred with the witches, so that the genetic mix is strengthened in terms of certain traits, undoubtedly including psychic traits, but what about others? If I read this damn thing properly, Cortland wasn't just the father of Stella and Rowan. He could have been the father of Antha too, though everybody thought it was Lionel.

"Now if Julien was Mary Beth's father, ah, but they ought to do some kind of computer thing just on that aspect of it, the inbreeding. Make a chart. And if they have the photographs, they can get into more genetic science. But I have to tell all this to Rowan. Rowan will understand all this. When we were talking Rowan said something about genetic research being so unpopular. People don't want to admit what they can determine about human beings genetically. Which brings me to free will, and my belief in free will is part of why I'm going crazy.

"Anyway, Rowan is the genetic beneficiary of all this—tall, slim, sexy, extremely healthy, brilliant, strong, and successful. A medical genius with a telekinetic power to take life who chooses instead to save life. And there it is, free will, again. Free will.

"But how the hell do I fit in with my free will intact, that is?

I mean what is 'all planned' to use Townsend's words in the dream. Christ!

"Am I perhaps related somehow to these people through the Irish servants that worked for them? Or is it simply that they outcross when they need stamina? But any of Rowan's police/fire fighter heroes would have done the job. Why me? Why did I have to drown, if indeed, they accomplished the drowning, which I still don't believe they did—but then Lasher was revealing himself alone to me all the way back to my earliest years.

"God, there is no one way to interpret any of this. Maybe I was destined for Rowan all along, and my drowning wasn't meant, and that's why the rescue happened. If the drowning was meant, I can't accept it! Because if that was meant, then too much else could be meant. It's too awful.

"I cannot read this history and conclude that the terrible tragedies here were inevitable—Deirdre to die like that.

"I could write on like this for the next three days, rambling, discussing this point or that. But I'm going crazy. I still haven't a clue to the meaning of the doorway. Not a single thing in what I've read illuminates this single image. Don't see any specific number involved in this either. Unless the number thirteen is on a doorway, and that has some meaning.

"Now the doorway may simply be the doorway to First Street; or the house itself could be some sort of portal. But I'm reaching. There is no feeling of rightness to what I say.

"As for the psychometric power in my hands, I still don't know how that is to be used, unless I am to touch Lasher when he materializes, and thereby know what this spirit really is, whence he comes and what he wants of the witches. But how can I touch Lasher unless Lasher chooses to be touched?

"Of course I will remove the gloves and lay my hands on objects related to this history, to First Street, if Rowan, who is now the mistress of First Street, will allow. But somehow the prospect fills me with terror. I can't see it as the consummation of my purpose. I see it as intimacy with countless objects, surfaces, and images . . . and also . . . for the first time I'm afraid of touching objects which belonged to the dead. But I must attempt it. I must attempt everything!

"Almost nine o'clock. Still Aaron isn't here. And it's dark and creepy and quiet out here. I don't want to sound like Marlon Brando in *On the Waterfront*, but the crickets make me nervous in the country too. And I'm jumpy in this room, even with its nice brass lamps. I don't want to look at the pictures on the wall, or in the mirrors for fear something's going to scare me.

"I hate being scared.

"And I can't stand waiting here. Perhaps it's unfair to expect Aaron to arrive the minute I finish reading. But Deirdre's funeral is over, and here I sit waiting for Aaron, with Mayfairs on the brain and pressing on my heart, but I wait! I wait because I promised I would, and Aaron hasn't called, and I have to see Rowan.

"Aaron is going to have to trust me on this, he really is. We'll talk tonight, tomorrow, and the next day, but tonight I am going to be with Rowan!

"One final note: if I sit here and close my eyes, and I think back on the visions. If I evoke the feeling, that is, for all the facts are gone, I still find myself believing that the people I saw were good. I was sent back for a higher purpose. And it was my choice—free will—to accept that mission.

"Now I cannot attach any negative or positive feeling to the idea of the doorway or the number thirteen. And that is distressing, deeply distressing. But I continue to feel that my people up there were good.

"I don't believe Lasher is good. Not at all. The evidence seems incontrovertible that he has destroyed some of these women. Maybe he has destroyed everyone who ever resisted him. And Aaron's question, *What is the agenda of this being*? is the pertinent one. This creature does things on his own. But why am I calling him a creature? Who created him? The same person who created me? And who is that, I wonder. Go for entity.

"This entity is evil.

"So why did he smile at me in the church when I was six? Surely he can't want me to touch him and discover his agenda? Or can he?

"Again the words 'meant' and 'planned' are driving me mad. Everything in me revolts against such an idea. I can believe in a mission, in a destiny, in a great purpose. All those words have to do with courage and heroism, with free will. But 'meant' and 'planned' fill me with this despair.

"Whatever the case, I don't feel despair right now. I feel crazed, unable to stay in this room much longer, desperate to reach Rowan. And desperate to put all these pieces together, to fulfill the mission I was given out there, because I believe that the best part of me accepted that mission.

"Why do I hear that guy in San Francisco, Gander or whatever his name was, saying, 'Conjecture!'

"I wish Aaron were here. For the record, I like him. I like them. I understand what they did here. I understand. None of us likes to believe that we are being watched, written about,

679

spied upon, that sort of thing. But I understand. Rowan will understand. She has to.

"The resulting document is just too nearly unique, too important. And when I think about how deeply implicated in all this I am, how involved I've been from the moment that entity looked out at me through the iron fence—well, thank God, they're here, that they 'watch,' as they say. That they know what they know.

"Because otherwise . . . And Rowan will understand that. Rowan will understand perhaps better than I understand, because she will see things I don't see. And maybe that's what's planned, but there I go again.

"Aaron! Come back!"

Twenty-eight

S HE STOOD BEFORE the iron gate as the cab crawled away, the rustling silence closing in around her. Impossible to imagine a house that was any more desolate or forbidding. The merciless light of the street lamp poured down like the full moon through the branches of the trees—on the cracked flags and the marble steps banked with dead leaves, and on the high thick fluted columns with their peeling white paint and black patches of rot, on the crumbling boards of the porch which ran back unevenly to the open door and the dull pale light from within wobbling ever so faintly.

Slowly she let her eyes roam the shuttered windows, the dense overgrown garden. A thin rain had begun to fall even as she left the hotel, and it was so very faint now that it was little more than a mist, giving its shine to the asphalt street, and hovering in the gleaming leaves above the fence, and just touching her face and shoulders.

Here my mother lived out her life, she thought. And here her mother was born, and her mother before her. Here in this house where Ellie sat near Stella's coffin.

For surely it had been here, though all the late afternoon long, over the cocktails and the salad and the highly spiced food, they had spoken only superficially of such things. "Carlotta will want to tell you . . ." ". . . after you talk to Carlotta."

Was the door open for her now? Had the gate been pushed back to welcome her? The great wooden frame of the door looked like a giant keyhole, tapering as it did from a flared base to a narrower top. Where had she seen that very same doorway shaped like a keyhole? Carved on the tomb in the Lafayette Cemetery. How ironic, for this house had been her mother's tomb.

Even the sweet silent rain had not alleviated the heat. But a breeze came now, the river breeze they had called it when they had said their farewells only blocks away at the hotel. And the breeze, smelling of the rain, flowed over her as deliciously as water. What was the scent of flowers in the air, so savage and deep, so unlike the florist scents that had surrounded her earlier?

She didn't resist it. She stood dreaming, feeling light and almost naked in the fragile silk garments she had just put on, trying to see the dark house, trying to take a deep breath, trying to slow the stream of all that had happened, all she'd witnessed and only half understood.

My life is broken in half, she thought; and all the past is the discarded part, drifting away, like a boat cut loose, as if the water were time, and the horizon was the demarcation of what would remain meaningful.

Ellie, why? Why were we cut off? Why, when they all knew? Knew my name, knew yours, knew I was her daughter! What was it all about, with them there by the hundreds and speaking that name, Mayfair, over and over?

"Come to the office downtown after you've talked," the young Pierce had said, Pierce with his rosy cheeks who was already a partner in the firm founded so long ago by his great-grandfather. "Ellie's grandfather, too, you know," said Ryan of the white hair and the carefully chiseled features who had been Ellie's first cousin. She did not know. She did not know who was who or whence they came, or what it meant, and above all why no one had ever told her. Flash of bitterness! Cortland this, and Cortland that . . . and Julien and Clay and Vincent and Mary Beth and Stella and Antha and Katherine.

Oh, what sweet southern music, words rich and deep like the fragrance she breathed now, like the heat clinging to her, and making even the soft silk shirt she wore feel suddenly heavy.

Did all the answers lie beyond the open door? Is the future beyond the open door? For after all, why could this not become, in spite of everything, a mere chapter of her life, marked off and seldom reread, once she had returned to the outside world where she had been kept all these years, quite beyond the spells and enchantments which were now claiming her? Oh, but it wasn't going to be. Because when you fell prey to a spell this strong, you were never the same. And each moment in this alien world of family, South, history, kinship, proffered love, drove her a thousand years away from who she'd been, or who she had wanted to be.

Did they know, did they guess for a second, how seductive it was? How raw she'd felt as they offered their invitations, their promises of visits and conversations yet to come, of family knowledge and family loyalty and family intimacy.

Kinship. Could they guess how indescribably exotic that was after the barren, selfish world in which she'd spent her life, like a potted plant that had never seen the real sun, nor the real earth, nor heard the rain except against double-paned glass?

"Sometimes I'd look around," Michael had said of California, "and it all seemed so sterile here." She had known. She had understood before she had ever dreamed of a city such as this, where every texture, every color, leapt out at you, where every fragrance was a drug, and the air itself was something alive and breathing.

I went into medicine to find the visceral world, she thought, and only in the waiting rooms and corridors outside the Emergency Room have I ever glimpsed the gatherings of clans, the generations weeping and laughing and whispering together as the angel of death passes over them.

"You mean Ellie never even told you her father's name? She never spoke to you about Sheffield or Ryan or Grady or . . . ?" Again and again, she had said no.

Yet Ellie had come back, to stand in that very cemetery at Aunt Nancy's funeral, whoever the hell Aunt Nancy had been, and afterwards in that very restaurant had shown them Rowan's photograph from her wallet! *Our daughter the doctor!* And dying, in a morphine dream, she had said to Rowan, "I wish they would send me back down home, but they can't. They can't do that."

There had been a moment after they'd left her off at the hotel, and after she had gone upstairs to shower and change on account of the muggy heat, when she had felt such bitterness that she could not reason or rationalize or even cry. And of course, she knew, knew as surely as she knew anything else, that there were countless ones among them who would have loved nothing more than to escape it all, this immense web of blood ties and memories. Yet she couldn't really imagine it.

All right, that had been the sweet side, overwhelming as the perfume of this flower in the dark, all of them there opening their arms.

But what truths lay ahead behind this door, about the child woman in the casket? For a long time, as they talked, voices splashing together like champagne, she had thought, *Do any of you by any miracle know the name of my father?*

"Carlotta will want to . . . well, have her say."

". . . so young when you were born."

"Father never actually told us . . ."

From here, in the electric moonlight on the broken flags, she could not see the side gallery which Ryan and Bea had described to her, the gallery on which her mother had sat in a rocking chair for thirteen years. "I don't think she suffered."

But all she had to do now was open this iron gate, go up the marble steps, walk across the rotted boards, push back the door that had been left open. Why not? She wanted to taste the darkness inside so badly that she did not even miss Michael now. He couldn't do this with her.

Suddenly, as if she'd dreamed it, she saw the light brighten behind the door. She saw the door itself moved back, and the figure of the old woman there, small and thin. Her voice sounded crisp and clear in the dark, with almost an Irish lilt to it, somber and low as it was:

"Are you coming in or not, Rowan Mayfair?"

She pushed at the gate, but it didn't give, and so she moved past it. The steps were slippery, and she came up slowly and felt the soft boards of the wooden porch give ever so slightly under her.

Carlotta had disappeared, but as Rowan entered the hallway now she saw her small dim figure far, far away at the entrance to a large room where the lone light was shining that illuminated all of the dim high-ceilinged distance before her.

She walked slowly after the old woman.

She walked past a stairway, rising straight and impossibly high to a dark second floor of which she could see nothing, and on past doors to the right opening onto a vast living room. The lights of the street shone through the windows of this room beyond, making them smoky and lunar white, and revealing a long stretch of gleaming floor, and a few indefinable pieces of scattered furniture.

At last passing a closed door to the left, she moved on into the light and saw that she had come into a large dining room.

Two candles stood on the oval table, and it was their faintly dancing flames which gave the only interior illumination to everything. Amazingly even it seemed, rising thinly to reveal the murals on the walls, great rural scenes of moss-hung oaks, and furrowed farmland. The doors and the windows soared to some twelve feet above her head; indeed as she looked back down the long hallway, the front door seemed immense, its surrounding frame covering the entire wall to the shadowy ceiling.

She turned back, staring at the woman who sat at the end of the table. Her thick wavy hair looked very white in the dark, massed more softly around her face than before, and the candlelight made two distinct and frightening flames in her round glasses.

"Sit down, Rowan Mayfair," she said. "I have many things to say to you."

Was it stubbornness that caused her to take one last slow look around her, or merely her fascination which wouldn't be interrupted? She saw that the velvet curtains were almost ragged in some places, and the floor was covered with threadbare carpet. A smell of dust or mold rose from the upholstered seats of the carved chairs. Or was it from the carpet, perhaps, or the sad draperies?

Did not matter. It was everywhere. But there was another smell, another delicious smell that made her think of wood and sunlight, and strangely, of Michael. It smelled good to her. And Michael, the carpenter, would understand that smell. The smell of the wood in the old house, and the heat which had built up in it all day long. Faintly blended with the whole was the smell of the wax candles.

The darkened chandelier above caught the candlelight, reflecting it in hundreds of crystal teardrops.

"It takes candles," said the old woman. "I'm too old now to climb up to change them. And Eugenia is also too old. She can't do it." With a tiny gesture of her head, she pointed to the far corner.

With a start Rowan realized that a black woman was standing there, a wraith of a creature with scant hair and yellowed eyes and folded arms, seemingly very thin, though it was hard to tell in the dark. Nothing was visible of her clothes but a soiled apron.

"You can go now, dear," said Carlotta to the black woman. "Unless my niece would like something to drink. But you don't, do you, Rowan?"

"No. No thank you, Miss Mayfair."

"Call me Carlotta, or Carl if you will. It doesn't matter. There are a thousand Misses Mayfair."

The old black woman moved away, past the fireplace, and around the table and out the door into the long hall. Carlotta watched her go, as if she wanted to be completely alone before she said another word.

Suddenly there was a clanging noise, oddly familiar yet completely undefinable to Rowan. And then the click of a door being shut, and a dull deep throb as of a great motor churning and straining within the depths of the house.

"It's an elevator," Rowan whispered.

The old woman appeared to be monitoring the sound. Her face looked shrunken and small beneath the thick cap of her hair. The dull clank of the elevator coming to a halt seemed to satisfy her. She looked up at Rowan, and then gestured to a lone chair on the long flank of the table.

Rowan moved towards it, and sat down, her back to the windows that opened on the yard. She turned the chair so that she might face Carlotta.

More of the murals became visible to her as she raised her eyes. A plantation house with white columns, and rolling hills beyond it.

She looked past the candles at the old woman and was relieved to see no reflection any more of the tiny flames in her glasses. Only the sunken face, and the glasses gleaming cleanly in the light, and the dark flowered fabric of the woman's long-sleeved dress, and her thin hands emerging from the lace at the sleeves, holding with knotted fingers what seemed a velvet jewel box.

This she pushed forward sharply towards Rowan.

"It's yours," she said. "It's an emerald necklace. It's yours and this house is yours and the land upon which it stands, and everything of any significance contained in it. Beyond that, there is a fortune some fifty times beyond what you have now, perhaps a hundred times, though that is now beyond my reckoning. But listen to what I say before you lay claim to what is yours. Listen to all I have to tell you."

She paused, studying Rowan's face, and Rowan's sense of the agelessness of the woman's voice, indeed of her manner altogether, deepened. It was almost eerie, as if the spirit of some young person inhabited the old frame, and gave it a fierce contradictory animation.

"No," said the woman. "I'm old, very old. What's kept me alive is waiting for her death, and for the moment I feared above all, the moment of your coming here. I prayed that Ellie would live a long life, that Ellie would hold you close in those long years, until Deirdre had rotted in the grave, and until the chain was broken. But fate has dealt me another little surprise. Ellie's death. Ellie's death and not a word to tell me of it."

"It was the way she wanted it," Rowan said.

"I know." The old woman sighed. "I know what you say is true. But it's not the telling of it, it's the death itself that was the blow. And it's done, and couldn't be prevented."

"She did what she could to keep me away," Rowan said simply. "She insisted I sign a promise that I'd never come. I chose to break it."

The old woman was silent for a moment.

"I wanted to come," Rowan said. And then as gently, as imploringly as she could, she asked: "Why did you want me kept away? Was it such a terrible story?"

The woman sat silent regarding her. "You're a strong woman," she said. "You're strong the way my mother was strong."

Rowan didn't answer.

"You have her eyes, did they tell you that? Were there any of them old enough to remember her?"

"I don't know," Rowan answered.

"What have you seen with your eyes?" asked the old woman. "What have you seen that you knew should not be there?"

Rowan gave a start. At first she had thought she misunderstood the words; then in a split second she realized she had not, and she thought instantly of the phantom who had appeared at three o'clock, and confused with it suddenly and inexplicably was her dream on the plane of someone invisible touching her and violating her.

In confusion she saw the smile spread over the old woman's face. But it wasn't bitter or triumphant. It was merely resigned. And then the face went smooth again and sad and wondering. In the dim light, the old woman's head looked like a skull for a moment.

"So he did come to you," she said with a soft sigh, "and he laid his hands on you."

"I don't know," Rowan said. "Explain this to me."

But the woman merely looked at her and waited.

"It was a man, a thin elegant man. He came at three o'clock. At the hour of my mother's death. I saw him as plainly as I see you, but it was only for a moment."

The woman looked down. Rowan thought she had closed her eyes. Then she saw the little gleam of light beneath her lids. The woman folded her hands before her on the table.

"It was 'the man'," she said. "It was 'the man' who drove your mother mad, and drove her mother mad before her. 'The man' who served my mother who ruled all those around her. Did they speak of him to you, the others? Did they warn you?"

"They didn't tell me anything," she said.

"That's because they don't know, and at last they realize they don't know, and now they leave the secrets to us, as they should have always done."

"But what did I see? Why did he come to me?" Once again, she thought of the dream on the plane, and she could find no answer for connecting the two.

"Because he believes that you are his now," said the woman. "His to love and his to touch and his to rule with promises of servitude."

Rowan felt the confusion again, and a dull heat in her face. His to touch. The haunting ambience of the dream came back.

"He will tell you it's the other way around," said the old woman. "When he speaks into your ear so that no one can hear, he will say he is your slave, that he's passed to you from Deirdre. But it's a lie, my dear, a vicious lie. He'll make you his and drive you mad if you refuse to do his will. That is what he's done to them all." She stopped, her wrinkled brows tightening, her eyes drifting off across the dusty surface of the table. "Except for those who were strong enough to rein him in and make him the slave he claimed to be, and use him for their own ends . . ." Her voice trailed off. "Their own endless wickedness."

"Explain it to me."

"He touched you, did he not?"

"I don't know."

"Oh yes you do. The color flies into your cheeks, Rowan Mayfair. Well, let me ask you, my girl, my independent young girl who has had so many men of her own choice, was it as good as a mortal man? Think before you speak. He'll tell you that no mortal man could give you the pleasure he gives. But was it true? It carries a terrible price, that pleasure."

"I thought it was a dream."

"But you saw him."

"That was the night before. The touching was in a dream. It was different."

"He touched her until the very end," said the woman. "No matter how much drugs they gave her. No matter how stupid her stare, how listless her walk. When she lay in bed at night he came, he touched her. Like a common whore she writhed on the bed, under his touch . . ." She bit down on her words, then the smile came again playing on her lips, like the light. "Does that make you angry? Angry with me that I tell you this? Do you think it was a pretty sight?"

"I think she was sick and out of her mind, and it was human."

"No, my dear, their intercourse was never human."

687

"You want me to believe that this is a ghost I saw, that he touched my mother, that I have somehow inherited him."

"Yes, and swallow back your anger. Your dangerous anger."

Rowan was stunned. A wave of fear and confusion passed over her. "You're reading my mind, you've been doing it all along."

"Oh yes, as best as I can, I do. I wish I could read it better. Your mother was not the only woman in this house with the power. Three generations before I was the one meant for the necklace. I saw him when I was three years old, so clear and strong that he could slip his warm hand in mine, he could lift me in the air, yes, lift my body, but I refused him. I turned my back on him. I told him, You go back to the hell from which you came. And I used my power to fight him."

"And this necklace now, it comes to me because I can see him?"

"It comes to you because you are the only girl child and choice is not possible. It would come to you no matter how weak your powers were. But that doesn't matter. Because your powers are strong, very strong, and always have been." She paused, considering Rowan again, her face unreadable for a moment, perhaps devoid of any specific judgment. "Imprecise, yes, and inconsistent, of course, and uncontrolled perhaps—but strong."

"Don't overestimate them," said Rowan softly. "I never do."

"Long ago, Ellie told me all about it," said the old woman. "Ellie told me you could make the flowers wither. Ellie told me you could make the water boil. 'She's a stronger witch than ever Antha was, or Deirdre was,' that's what she told me, crying and begging me for advice as to what she could do! 'Keep her away!' I said. 'See that she never comes home, see that she never knows! See that she never learns to use it.' "

Rowan sighed. She ignored the dull pain at the mention of Ellie, of Ellie speaking to these people about her. Cut off alone. And all of them here. Even this wretched old woman here.

"Yes, and I can feel your anger again, anger against me, anger for what you think you know that I did to your mother!"

"I don't want to be angry with you," said Rowan in a small voice. "I only want to understand what you're saying, I want to know why I was taken away . . ."

Again, the old woman lapsed into a thoughtful silence. Her fingers hovered over the jewel case and then folded down upon it and lay still, all too much like the flaccid hands of Deirdre in the casket.

Rowan looked away. She looked at the far wall, at the panorama of painted sky above the fireplace.

"Oh, but don't these words bring you even the slightest consolation? Haven't you wondered all these years, were you the only one in the world who could read others' thoughts, the only one who knew when someone near you was going to die? The only one who could drive a person back away from you with your anger? Look at the candles. You can make them go out and you can light them again. Do it.''

Rowan did nothing. She stared at the little flames. She could feel herself trembling. *If only you really knew, if only you knew what I could do to you now . . .*

"But I do, you see, I can feel your strength, because I too am strong, stronger than Antha or Deirdre. And that is how I have kept him at bay in this house, that is how I have prevented him from hurting me. That is how I have put some thirty years between him and Deirdre's child. Make the candles go out. Light them again. I want to see you do it.''

"I will not. And I want you to stop playing with me. Tell me what you have to tell. But stop your games. Stop torturing me. I have never done anything to you. Tell me who he is, and why you took me from my mother.''

"But I have. I took you from her in order to get you away from him, and from this necklace, from this legacy of curses and wealth founded upon his intervention and power.'' She studied Rowan, and then went on, her voice deepening yet losing nothing of its preciseness. "I took you away from her to break her will, and separate her from a crutch upon which she would lean, and an ear into which she would pour her tortured soul, a companion she would warp and twist in her weakness and her misery.''

Frozen in anger, Rowan gave no answer. Miserably, she saw in her mind's eyes the black-haired woman in her coffin. She saw the Lafayette Cemetery in her mind, only shrouded with the night, and still and deserted.

"Thirty years you've had to grow strong and straight, away from this house, away from this history of evil. And what have you become, a doctor the like of which your colleagues have never seen, and when you've done evil with your power, you've drawn away in righteous condemnation of yourself, in shame that drove you on to greater self-sacrifice.''

"How do you know these things?''

"I see. What I see is imprecise, but I see. I see the evil, though I cannot see the acts themselves, for they're covered up in the very guilt and shame that advertises them.''

"Then what do you want of me? A confession? You said yourself I turned my back on what I've done that was wrong. I sought for something else, something infinitely more demanding, something finer.''

" 'Thou shalt not kill,' '' whispered the woman.

A shock of raw pain passed through Rowan, and then in consternation she watched the woman's eyes grow wide, mocking her. In confusion, Rowan understood the trick, and felt defenseless. For in a split second the woman had, with her utterance, provoked the very image in Rowan's mind for which the old woman had been searching.

You have killed. In anger and rage, you have taken life. You have done it willfully. That is how strong you are.

Rowan sank deeper into herself, peering at the flat round glasses as they caught the light and then let it go, and the dark eyes scarcely visible behind them.

"Have I taught you something?'' the woman asked.

"You try my patience,'' Rowan said. "Let me remind you that I have done nothing to you. I have not come to demand answers of you. I have made no condemnation. I haven't come to claim this jewel or this house or anything in it. I came to see my mother laid to rest, and I came through that front door because you invited me to do so. And I am here to listen. But I won't be played with much longer. Not for all the secrets this side of hell. And I don't fear your ghost, even if he sports the cock of an archangel.''

The old woman stared at her for a moment. Then she raised her eyebrows and laughed, a short, sudden little laugh, that had a surprisingly feminine ring to it. She continued to smile. "Well put, my dear,'' she said. "Seventy-five years ago, my mother told me he could have made the Greek gods weep with envy, so beautiful was he, when he came into her bedroom.'' She relaxed slowly in her chair, pursing her lips, then smiling again. "But he never kept her from her handsome mortal men. She liked the same kind of men you do.''

"Ellie told you that too?''

"She told me many things. But she never told me she was sick. She never told me she was dying.''

"When people are dying, they become afraid,'' said Rowan. "They are all alone. Nobody can die for them.''

The old woman lowered her eyes. She remained still for a long moment, and then her hands moved over the soft dome of the jewel box again, and grasping it, she snapped it open. She turned it ever so slightly so that the light of the candles blazed in the emerald that lay inside, caught on a bed of tangled golden chain. It was the largest jewel Rowan had ever seen.

"I used to dream of death,'' Carlotta said, gazing at the stone.

"I've prayed for it." She looked up slowly, measuring Rowan, and once again her eyes grew wide, the soft thin flesh of her forehead wrinkling heavily above her gray brows. Her soul seemed closed and sunk in sadness, and it was as if for a moment, she had forgotten to conceal herself somehow, behind meanness and cleverness, from Rowan. She was merely staring at Rowan.

"Come," she said. She drew herself up. "Let me show what I have to show you. I don't think there's much time now."

"Why do you say that!" Rowan whispered urgently. Something in the old woman's change of demeanor terrified her. "Why do you look at me like that?"

The woman only smiled. "Come," she said. "Bring the candle if you will. Some of the lights still burn. Others are burnt out or the wires have long ago frayed and come loose. Follow me."

She rose from the chair, and carefully unhooked her wooden cane from the back of it, and walked with surprising certainty across the floor, past Rowan who stood watching her, guarding the tender flame of the candle in the curve of her left hand.

The tiny light leapt up the wall as they proceeded down the hallway. It shone for a moment on the gleaming surface of an old portrait of a man who seemed suddenly to be alive and to be staring at Rowan. She stopped, turning her head sharply to look up, to see that this had only been an illusion.

"What is it?" said Carlotta.

"Only that I thought . . . ." She looked at the portrait, which was very skillfully done and showed a smiling black-eyed man, most certainly not alive, and buried beneath layers of brittle, crazed lacquer.

"What?"

"Doesn't matter," Rowan said, and came on, guarding the flame as before. "The light made him look as though he'd moved."

The woman looked back fixedly at the portrait as Rowan stood beside her. "You'll see many strange things in this house," she said. "You'll pass empty rooms only to double back because you think you've seen a figure moving, or a person staring at you."

Rowan studied her face. She seemed neither playful nor vicious now, only solitary, wondering and thoughtful.

"You aren't afraid of the dark?" Carlotta asked.

"No."

"You can see well in the dark."

"Yes, better than most people."

The woman turned around, and went on to the tall door at the foot of the stairs and pressed the button. With a muffled clank the elevator descended to the lower floor and stopped heavily and jerkily; the woman turned the knob, opening the door and revealing a gate of brass which she folded back with effort.

Inside they stepped, onto a worn patch of carpet, enclosed by dark fabric-covered walls, a dim bulb in the metal ceiling shining down on them.

"Close the doors," said the woman, and Rowan obeyed, reaching out for the knob and then pushing shut the gate.

"You might as well learn how to use what is yours," she added. A subtle fragrance of perfume rose from her clothes, something sweet like Chanel, mingled with the unmistakable scent of powder. She pressed a small black rubber button to her right. And up they went, fast, with a surge of power that surprised Rowan.

The hallway of the second floor lay in even thicker darkness than the lower corridor. The air was warmer. No open doorway or window gave even a seam of light from the street, and the candle light burst weakly on the many white-paneled doors and yet another rising stairway.

"Come into this room," the old woman said, opening the door to the left and leading the way, her cane thumping softly on the thick flowered carpet.

Draperies, dark and rotting like those of the dining room below, and a narrow wooden bed with a high half roof, carved it seemed, with the figure of an eagle. A similar deeply etched symmetrical design was carved into the headboard.

"In this bed your mother died," said Carlotta.

Rowan looked down at the bare mattress. She saw a great dark stain on the striped cloth that gave off a gleam that was almost a sparkling in the shadows. Insects! Tiny black insects fed busily on the stain. As she stepped forward, they fled the light, scurrying to the four corners of the mattress. She gasped and almost dropped the candle.

The old woman appeared wrapped in her thoughts, protected somehow from the ugliness of it.

"This is revolting," said Rowan under her breath. "Someone should clean this room!"

"You may have it cleaned if you like," said the old woman, "it's your room now."

The heat and the sight of the roaches sickened Rowan. She moved back and rested her head against the frame of the door. Other smells rose, threatening to nauseate her.

"What else do you want to show me?" she asked calmly.

Swallow your anger, she whispered within herself, her eyes drifting over the faded walls, the little nightstand crowded with plaster statues and candles. Lurid, ugly, filthy. Died in filth. Died here. Neglected.

"No," said the old woman. "Not neglected. And what did she know of her surroundings in the end? Read the medical records for yourself."

The old woman turned past her once more, returning to the hallway. "And now we must climb these stairs," she said. "Because the elevator goes no higher."

Pray you don't need my help, Rowan thought. She shrank from the mere thought of touching the woman. She tried to catch her breath, to still the tumult inside her. The air, heavy and stale and full of the faintest reminders of worse smells, seemed to cling to her, cling to her clothes, her face.

She watched the woman go up, managing each step slowly but capably.

"Come with me, Rowan Mayfair," she said over her shoulder. "Bring the light. The old gas jets above have long ago been disconnected."

Rowan followed, the air growing warmer and warmer. Turning on the small landing, she saw yet another shorter length of steps and then the final landing of the third floor. And as she moved up, it seemed that all the heat of the house must be collected here.

Through a barren window to her right came the colorless light of the street lamp far below. There were two doors, one to the left and one directly before them.

It was the left door which the old woman opened. "See there, the oil lamp on the table inside the door," she said. "Light it."

Rowan set down the candle and lifted the glass shade of the lamp. The smell of the oil was faintly unpleasant. She touched the burning candle to the burnt wick. The large bright flame grew even stronger as she lowered the shade. She held up the light to let it fill a spacious low-ceilinged room, full of dust and damp, and cobwebs. Once more tiny insects fled the light. A dry rustling sound startled her, but the good smell of heat and wood was strong here, stronger even than the smell of rotted cloth and mold.

She saw that trunks lay against the walls; packing crates crowded an old brass bed in the far corner beneath one of two square windows. A thick mesh of vines half covered the glass, the light caught in the wetness from the rain which still clung to the leaves, making them ever more visible. The curtains had long ago fallen down and lay in heaps on the windowsills.

Books lined the wall to the left, flanking the fireplace and its small wooden mantel, shelves rising to the ceiling. Books lay helter-skelter upon the old upholstered chairs which appeared soft now, spongy with dampness and age. The light of the lamp glinted on the dull brass of the old bed. It caught the dull gleaming leather of a pair of shoes, tossed it seemed against a long thick rug, tied in a lumpy roll and shoved against the unused fireplace.

Something odd about the shoes, odd about the lumpy roll of rug. Was it that the rug was bound with rusted chain, and not the rope that seemed more probable?

She realized the old woman was watching her.

"This was my uncle Julien's room," said the old woman. "It was through that window there that your grandmother Antha went out on the porch roof, and fell to her death below, on the flagstones."

Rowan steadied the lamp, grasping it more firmly by the pinched waist of its glass base. She said nothing.

"Open the first trunk there to your right," said the old woman.

Hesitating just a moment, though why she didn't know, Rowan knelt down on the dusty bare floor, and set the lamp beside the trunk, and examined the lid and the broken lock. The trunk was made of canvas and bound with leather and brass tacks. She lifted the lid easily and threw it back gently so as not to scar the plaster wall.

"Can you see what's inside?"

"Dolls," Rowan answered. "Dolls made of . . . of hair and bone."

"Yes, bone, and human hair, and human skin, and the parings of nails. Dolls of your female ancestors so far back there are no names for the oldest dolls, and they'll fall to dust when you lift them."

Rowan studied them, row after row set out carefully on a bed of old cheesecloth, each doll with its carefully drawn face and long hank of hair, some with sticks for arms and legs, others soft-bodied, and almost shapeless. The newest and finest of all the dolls was made of silk with a bit of pearl stitched to its little dress, its face of shining bone with nose and eyes and mouth drawn in dark brown ink, perhaps, even in blood.

"Yes, blood," said the old woman. "And that is your great-grandmother, Stella."

The tiny doll appeared to grin at Rowan. Someone had stuck the black hair to the bone skull with glue. Bones protruded from the hem of the little tube of a silk dress.

"Where did the bones come from?"

"From Stella."

Rowan reached down, then drew back, her fingers curling. She couldn't bring herself to touch it. She lifted the edge of the cheesecloth tentatively, seeing beneath yet another layer, and here the dolls were fast becoming dust. They had sunk deep into the cloth, and probably could not be lifted intact from it.

"All the way back to Europe they go. Reach in. Take the oldest doll. Can you see which one it is?"

"It's hopeless. It will fall to pieces if I touch it. Besides, I don't know which one it is." She laid the cloth back, smoothing the top layer gingerly. And when her fingers touched the bones, she felt a sudden jarring vibration. It was as if a bright light had flashed before her eye. Her mind registered the medical possibilities . . . temporal lobe disturbance, seizure. Yet the diagnosis seemed foolish, belonging to another realm.

She stared down at the tiny faces.

"What's the purpose? Why?"

"To speak to them when you would, and invoke their help, so they can reach out of hell to do your bidding." The woman pressed her withered lips into a faint sneer, the light rising and distorting her face unkindly. "As if they would come from the fires of hell to do anyone's bidding."

Rowan let out a long low derisive sigh, looking down again at the dolls, at the horrid and vivid face of Stella.

"Who made these things?"

"They all did, all along. Cortland crept down in the night and cut the foot off my mother, Mary Beth, as she lay in the coffin. It was Cortland who took the bones from Stella. Stella wanted to be buried at home. Stella knew what he would do, because your grandmother Antha was too little to do it."

Rowan shuddered. She lowered the lid of the trunk, and lifting the lamp carefully, rose to her feet, brushing the dust from her knees. "This Cortland, this man who did this, who was he? Not the grandfather of Ryan at the funeral?"

"Yes, my dear, the very same," said the old woman. "Cortland the beautiful, Cortland the vicious, Cortland the instrument of him who has guided this family for centuries. Cortland who raped your mother when she clung to him for help. I mean the man who coupled with Stella, to father Antha who then gave birth to Deirdre, who by him conceived you, his daughter and great-granddaughter."

Rowan stood quiet, envisioning the scheme of births and entanglements.

"And who has made a doll of my mother?" she asked, as she

stared into the old woman's face which now appeared ghastly in the light of the lamp playing on it.

"No one. Unless you yourself care to go to the cemetery and unscrew the stone and take her hands out of the coffin. Do you think you could do that? He will help you do it, you know, the man you have already seen. He'll come if you put on the necklace and call him."

"You have no cause to want to hurt me," Rowan said. "I am no part of this."

"I tell you what I know. Black Magic was their game. Always. I tell you what you must know to make your choice. Would you bow to this filth? Would you continue it? Would you lift those wretched pieces of filth and call upon the spirits of the dead so that all the devils in hell could play dolls with you?"

"I don't believe in it," Rowan said. "I don't believe that you do."

"I believe what I have seen. I believe what I feel when I touch them. They are endowed with evil, as relics are endowed with sanctity. But the voices who speak through them are all his voice, the voice of the devil. Don't you believe what you saw when he came to you?"

"I saw a man with dark hair. He wasn't a human being. He was some sort of hallucination."

"He was Satan. He will tell you that is not so. He will give you a beautiful name. He will talk poetry to you. But he is the devil in hell for one simple reason. He lies and he destroys, and he will destroy you and your progeny if he can, for his ends, for his ends are what matter."

"And what are they?"

"To be alive, as we are alive. To come through and to see and feel what we see and feel." The woman turned her back, and moving her cane before her, walked to the left wall, by the fireplace, stopping at the lumpy roll of rug, and then looking up at the books that lined the shelves on either side of the paneled chimney above the mantel.

"Histories," she said, "histories of all those who came before, written by Julien. This was Julien't room, Julien's retreat. In here he wrote his confessions. How with his sister Katherine he lay to make my mother, Mary Beth, and then with her he lay to make my sister Stella. And when he would have lain with me, I spit into his face. I clawed at his eyes. I threatened to kill him." She turned to look fixedly at Rowan.

"Black magic, evil spells, records of his petty triumphs as he punished his enemies and seduced his lovers. Not all the seraphim in heaven could have satisfied his lust, not Julien's."

"This is all recorded there?"

"All this and more. But I have never read his books, and I never shall. It was enough to read his mind as he sat day by day in the library below, dipping his pen and laughing to himself, and giving vent to his fantasies. That was decades and decades ago. I have waited so long for this moment."

"And why are the books still here? Why didn't you burn them?"

"Because I knew that if you ever came, you would have to see for yourself. No book has the power of a burned book! No. . . . You must read for yourself what he was, for what he says in his own words can't do anything else but convict and condemn him." She paused. "Read and choose," she whispered. "Antha couldn't make the choice. Deirdre couldn't make the choice. But you can make it. You are strong and clever and wise already in your years, wise. I can see this in you."

She rested both hands on the crook of her cane and looked away, out of the corner of her eyes, pondering. Once again, her cap of white hair seemed heavy around her small face.

"I chose," she said softly, almost sadly. "I went to church after Julien touched me, after he sang me his songs and told me his lies. I honestly think he believed his charms would win me over. I went to the shrine of Our Lady of Perpetual Help and I knelt and prayed, and the strongest truth came through to me. Didn't matter if God in his heaven was a Catholic or a Protestant God, or the God of the Hindus. What mattered was something deeper and older and more powerful than any such image—it was a concept of goodness based upon the affirmation of life, the turning away from destruction, from the perverse, from man using and abusing man. It was the affirmation of the human and the natural." She looked up at Rowan. "I said, 'God, stand by me. Holy Mother, stand by me. Let me use my power to fight them, to beat them, to win against them.' "

Again her eyes moved off, gazing back into the past perhaps. For a long moment they lingered on the rug at her feet, bulging in its circles of rusted chain. "I knew what lay ahead, even then. Years after I learned what I needed. I learned the same spells and secrets they used. I learned to call up the very lowly spirits whom they commanded. I learned to fight *him* in all his glory, with spirits bound to me, whom I could then dismiss with the snap of my fingers. In sum, I used their very weapons against them."

She looked sullen, remote, studying Rowan's reactions yet seemingly indifferent to them.

"I told Julien I would bear no incestuous child by him. To

show me no fantasies of the future. To play no tricks on me, changing himself to a young man in my arms, when I could feel his withered flesh, and knew it was there all along. 'Do you think I care if you are the most beautiful man in the world? You or your evil familiar? Do you think I measure my choices by such vanity and self-indulgence?' That's what I said to him. If he touched me again, I promised I would use the power I had in me to drive him back. I would need no human hands to help me. And I saw fear in his eyes, fear even though I myself hadn't learned yet how to keep my threats, fear of a power in me which he knew was there even when I was uncertain of it. But maybe it was only fear of one he couldn't seduce, couldn't confuse, couldn't win over.'' She smiled, her thin lips revealing a shining row of even false teeth. ''That is a terrible thing, you know, to one who lives solely by seduction.''

She lapsed into silence, caught perhaps in remembering.

Rowan took a deep long breath, ignoring the sweat that clung to her face and the warmth of the lamp. Misery was what she felt, misery and waste and long lonely years, as she looked at the woman. Empty years, years of dreary routine, and bitterness and fierce belief, belief that can kill . . .

''Yes, kill,'' sighed the woman. ''I have done that. To protect the living from him who was never living, and would possess them if he could.''

''Why us?'' Rowan demanded. ''Why are we the playthings of this spirit you are talking about, why us in all the world? We aren't the only ones who can see spirits.''

The old woman gave a long sigh.

''Did you ever speak to him?'' Rowan asked. ''You said he came to you when you were a child, he spoke in your ears words that no one could hear. Did you ever ask who he was and what he really wanted?''

''Do you think he would have told me the truth? He won't tell you the truth, mark my words. You feed him when you question him. You give him oil as if he were the flame in that lamp.''

The old woman drew closer to her suddenly.

''He'll take from your mind the answer best suited to lead you on, to enthrall you. He'll weave a web of deceits so thick you won't see the world through it. He wants your strength and he'll say what he must say to get it. Break the chain, child! You're the strongest of them all! Break the chain and he'll go back to hell for he has no other place to go in all the wide world to find strength like yours. Don't you see? He's created it. Bred sister to brother, and uncle to niece, and son to mother, yes, that too, when he had to do it, to make an ever more powerful witch, only faltering now and then, and gaining what he lost in one generation by even greater strength in the next. What was the cost of Antha and Deirdre if he could have a Rowan!''

"Witch? You spoke the word *witch*?" Rowan asked.

"They were witches, every one, don't you see?" The old woman's eyes searched Rowan's face. "Your mother, her mother, and her mother before her, and Julien, that evil despicable Julien, the father of Cortland who was your father. I was marked for it myself until I rebelled."

Rowan clenched her left hand, cutting her palm with her nails, staring into the old woman's eyes, repelled by her yet unable to draw away from her.

"Incest, my dear, was the least of their sins, but the greatest of their schemes, incest to strengthen the line, to double up the powers, to purify the blood, to birth a cunning and terrible witch in each generation, going so far back it's lost in European history. Let the Englishman tell you about that, the Englishman who came with you to the church, the Englishman who held your arm. Let him tell you the names of the women whose dolls lie in that trunk. He knows. He'll sell you his brand of the black arts, his genealogy."

"I want to get out of this room," Rowan whispered. She turned around, throwing the beam of the light on the landing.

"You know that it's true," said the old woman behind her. "You've always known deep inside that an evil lived in you."

"You choose your words badly. You speak of the potential for evil."

"Well, know that you can put it to a finish! That can be the significance of your greater strength, that you can do as I have done and turn it against him. Turn it against all of them!"

She pushed past Rowan, the hem of her dress scraping Rowan's ankle, her cane thudding lightly as before, as she walked out onto the landing, gesturing for Rowan to follow.

Into the only remaining door on the third floor they went, a noxious overpowering smell flooding out over them. Rowan drew back, scarcely able to breathe. Then she did what she knew she had to do. She breathed in the stench, and swallowed it, because there was no other way to tolerate it.

Lifting the lamp high, she saw this was a narrow storage chamber. It was filled with jars and bottles on makeshift shelves and the jars and bottles were filled with blackish, murky fluid. Specimens in these containers. Rotting, putrid things. Stench of alcohol and other chemicals, and most of all of putrefying flesh. Unbearable to think of these glass containers broken open and the horrid smell of their exposed contents.

"They were Marguerite's," said the old woman, "and Marguerite was Julien's mother and the mother of Katherine, who was my grandmother. I don't expect you to remember these names. You can find them in the ledger books in the other room. You can find them in the old records in the downstairs library. But mark what I say. Marguerite filled these jars with horrors. You'll see when you pour out the contents. And mind me, do it yourself if you don't want trouble. Horrible things in those jars. . . . and she, the healer!" She almost spat the word with contempt. "With the same powerful gift that you have now, to lay hands on the ill, and bring together the cells to patch the rupture, or the cancer. And that's what she did with her gift. Bring your lamp closer."

"I don't want to see this now."

"Oh? You're a doctor, are you not? Haven't you dissected the dead of all ages? You cut them open now, do you not?"

"I'm a surgeon. I operate to preserve and lengthen life. I don't want to see these things now . . ."

Yet even as she spoke she was peering at the jars, looking at the largest of them in which the liquid was still clear enough to see the soft, vaguely round thing floating there, half shrouded in shadow. But that was impossible what she saw there. That looked just like a human head. She drew back as if she'd been burnt.

"Tell me what you saw."

"Why do you do this to me?" she said in a low voice, staring at the jar, at the dark rotted eyes swimming in the fluid and the seaweed hair. She turned her back on it and looked at the old woman. "I saw my mother buried today. What do you want of me?"

"I told you."

"No, you punish me for coming back, you punish me for merely wanting to know, you punish me because I violated your schemes."

Was that a grin on the old woman's face?

"Don't you understand that I am alone out there now? I want to know my people. You can't make me bend to your will."

Silence. It was sweltering here. She did not know how long she could stand it. "Is that what you did to my mother?" she said, her voice burning out in her anger. "You made her do your will?"

She stepped backwards, as if her anger was forcing her away from the old woman, her hand tightening uncomfortably on the glass lamp which was now hot from the burning wick, so hot she could scarcely hold it any longer.

"I'm getting sick in this room."

"Poor dear," said the woman. "What you saw in that jar was a man's head. Well, look closely at him when the time comes. And at the others you find there."

"They're rotted, deteriorated; they're so old they're no good for any purpose if they ever were. I want to get out of here."

Yet she looked back at the jar, overcome with horror. Her left hand went to her mouth as if it could somehow protect her, and gazing at the clouded fluid she saw again the dark hole of a mouth where the lips were slowly deteriorating and the white teeth shone bright. She saw the gleaming jelly of the eyes. No, don't look at it. But what was in the jar beside it? There were things moving in the fluid, worms moving. The seal had been broken.

She turned and left the room, leaning against the wall, her eyes shut, the lamp burning her hand. Her heart thudded in her ears, and it seemed for a moment the sickness would get the better of her. She'd vomit on the very floor at the head of these filthy stairs, with this wretched vicious woman beside her. Dully, she heard the old woman passing her again. She heard her progress as she went down the stairs, steps slower than before, gaining only a little speed as the woman reached the landing.

"Come down, Rowan Mayfair," she said. "Put out the lamp, but light the candle before you do, and bring it with you."

Slowly Rowan righted herself. She pushed her left hand back through her hair. Fighting off another wave of nausea, she moved slowly back into the bedroom. She set down the lamp, on the little table by the door from which she'd taken it, just when she thought her fingers couldn't take the heat anymore, and for a moment she held her right hand to her lips, trying to soothe the burn. Then slowly she lifted the candle and plunged it down the glass chimney of the lamp, because she knew the glass of the chimney was too hot to touch now. The wick caught, wax dripping on the wick, and then she blew out the lamp, and stood still for a moment, her eyes falling on that rolled rug and the pair of leather shoes tossed against it.

No, not tossed, she thought. No. Slowly she moved towards the shoes. Slowly, she extended her own left foot until the toe of her shoe touched one of those shoes, and then she kicked the shoe and realized that it was caught on something even as it fell loose and she saw the gleaming white bone of the leg extending from the trouser within the rolled carpet.

Paralyzed, she stared at the bone. At the rolled rug itself. And then walking along it, she saw at the other end what she could not see before, the dark gleam of brown hair. Someone wrapped in the rug. Someone dead, dead a long time, and look, the stain on the floor, the blackish stain on the side of the rug, near the bottom where the fluids long ago flowed out and dried up, and see, even the mashed and tiny insects fatally caught in the sticky fluid so long ago.

Rowan, promise me, you will never go back, promise me.

From somewhere far below, she heard the old woman's voice, so faint it was no more than a thought. "Come down, Rowan Mayfair."

Rowan Mayfair, Rowan Mayfair, Rowan Mayfair . . .

Refusing to hurry, she made her way out, glancing back once more at the dead man concealed in the rug, at the slender spoke of white bone protruding from it. And then she shut the door and walked sluggishly down the stairs.

The old woman stood at the open elevator door, merely watching, the ugly gold light from the elevator bulb shining full on her.

"You know what I found," Rowan said. She steadied herself as she reached the newel post. The little candle danced for a moment, throwing pale translucent shadows on the ceiling.

"You found the dead man, wrapped in the rug."

"What in God's name has gone on in this house!" Rowan gasped. "Are you all mad?"

How cold and controlled the old woman seemed, how utterly detached. She pointed to the open elevator. "Come with me," she said. "There is nothing more to see and only a little more to say . . ."

"Oh, but there's a lot more to say," Rowan said. "Tell me— did you tell my mother these things? Did you show her those horrible jars and dolls?"

"I didn't drive her mad if that's your meaning."

"I think anyone who grew up in this house might go mad."

"So do I. That's why I sent you away from it. Now come."

"Tell me what happened with my mother."

She stepped after the woman into the small dusty chamber again, closing the door and the gate angrily. As they moved down, she turned and stared at the woman's profile. Old, old, yes, she was. Her skin as yellow all over as parchment, and her neck so thin and frail, the veins standing out under her fragile skin. Yes, so fragile.

"Tell me what happened to her," Rowan said, staring at the floor, not daring to look closely at the woman again. "Don't tell me how he touched her in her sleep, but tell me what happened, really happened!"

The elevator stopped with a jerk. The woman opened the gate, and pushed back the door, and walked out into the hallway.

As Rowan closed the door, the light died out as if the elevator and its bare bulb had never existed. The darkness swept in close and faintly cool, and smelling of the rain from beyond the open front door. The night gleamed outside, noisy with comforting sounds.

"Tell me what happened," Rowan said again, softly, bitterly.

Through the long front parlor they walked, the old woman leading the way, listing slightly to the left as she followed her cane, Rowan coming patiently behind her.

The pale light of the candle slowly crept throughout the whole room, lighting it thinly to the ceiling. Even in decay, it was a beautiful room, its marble fireplaces and high mantel mirrors shining in the dreary shadows. All its windows were floor-length windows. Mirrors at the far ends gazed across the length of the room into each other. Dimly Rowan saw the chandeliers reflected again and again and into infinity. Her own small figure was there, repeated over and over and vanishing finally in darkness.

"Yes," said the old woman. "It is an interesting illusion. Darcy Monahan bought these mirrors for Katherine. Darcy Monahan tried to take Katherine away from all the evil around her. But he died in this house of yellow fever. Katherine wept for the rest of her life. But the mirrors stand today, there and there, and over the fireplaces, just as Darcy fixed them."

She sighed, once more resting her two hands on the crook of her cane.

"We have all . . . from time to time . . . been reflected in these mirrors. And you see yourself in them now, caught in the same frame."

Rowan didn't respond. Sadly, distantly, she longed to see the room in the light, to see the carvings in the marble fireplaces, to see the long silk draperies for what they really were, to see the plaster medallions fixed to the high ceilings.

The old woman proceeded to the nearest of the two side floor-length windows. "Raise it for me," she said. "It slides up. You are strong enough." She took the candle from Rowan and set it on a small lamp table by the fireplace.

Rowan reached up to unsnap the simple lock, and then she raised the heavy nine-paned window, easily pushing it until it was almost above her head.

Here was the screened porch, and the night outside, and the air fresh as it was warm, and full of the breath of the rain again. She felt a rush of gratitude, and stood silently letting the air kiss her face and her hands. She moved to the side as the old woman passed her.

The candle, left behind, struggled in an errant draft. Then went out. Rowan stepped out into the darkness. Again that strong perfume came on the breeze, drenchingly sweet.

"The night jasmine," said the old woman.

All around the railings of this porch vines grew, tendrils dancing in the breeze, fine tiny leaves moving like so many little insect wings beating against the screen. Flowers glimmered in the dark, white and delicate and beautiful.

"This is where your mother sat day after day," said the old woman. "And there, out there on the flagstones is where her mother died. Where she died when she fell from that room above which had been Julien's. I myself drove her out of that window. I think I would have pushed her with my own hands if she hadn't jumped. With my own hands I'd scratched at her eyes, the way I'd scratched at Julien's."

She paused. She was looking out through the rusted screen into the night, perhaps at the high faint shapes of the trees against the paler sky. The cold light of the street lamp reached long and bright over the front of the garden. It fell upon the high unkempt grass. It even shone on the high back of the white wooden rocking chair.

Friendless and terrible the night seemed to Rowan. Awful and dismal this house, a terrible engulfing place. Oh, to live and die here, to have spent one's life in these awful sad rooms, to have died in that filth upstairs. It was unspeakable. And the horror rose like something black and thick inside her, threatening to stop her breath. She had no words for what she felt. She had no words for the loathing inside her for the old woman.

"I killed Antha," the old woman said. Her back was turned to Rowan, her words low and indistinct. "I killed her as surely as if I did push her. I wanted her to die. She was rocking Deirdre in the cradle and he was there, by her side, he was staring down at the baby and making the baby laugh! And she was letting him do it, she was talking to him in her simpering, weak little voice, telling him he was her only friend, now that her husband was dead, her only friend in this whole world. She said, 'This is my house. I can put you out if I want to.' She said that to me.

"I said, 'I'll scratch your eyes out of your head if you don't give him up. You can't see him if you don't have eyes. You won't let the baby see him.' "

The old woman paused. Sickened and miserable, Rowan waited in the muffled silence of the night sounds, of things moving and singing in the dark.

"Have you ever seen a human eye plucked out of its socket, hanging on a woman's cheek by the bloody threads? I did that to her. She screamed and sobbed like a child, but I did that. I did it and chased her up the stairs as she ran from me, trying to hold her precious eye in her hands. And do you think he tried to stop me?"

"I would have tried," Rowan said thickly, bitterly. "Why are you telling me this?"

"Because you wanted to know! And to know what happened to one, you must know what happened to the one before her. And you must know, above all, that this is what I did to break the chain."

The woman turned and stared at Rowan, the cold white light shining in her glasses and making them blind mirrors suddenly. "This I did for you, and for me, and for God, if there is a God. I drove her through that window. 'Let's see if you can see him if you're blind,' I cried. 'Then can you make him come!' And your mother, your mother screaming in the cradle in that very room there. I should have taken her life. I should have snuffed it out then and there while Antha lay dead outside on the flagstones. Would to God I had had the courage."

Again the old woman paused, raising her chin slightly, the thin lips once again spreading in a smile. "I feel your anger. I feel your judgment."

"Can I help it?" Rowan whispered.

The old woman bowed her head. The light of the street lamp settled on her white hair, her face in shadow. "I couldn't kill such a small thing," she said wearily. "I couldn't bring myself to take the pillow and put it over Deirdre's face. I thought of the stories from the old days of the witches who had sacrificed babies, who'd stirred the baby fat in the cauldron at the Sabbats. We are witches, we Mayfairs. And was I to sacrifice this tiny thing as they had done? There I stood ready to take the life of a small baby, a crying baby, and I could not bring myself to do what they had done."

Silence once again.

"And of course he knew I couldn't do it! He would have ripped the house apart to stop me had I tried."

Rowan waited, until she could wait no longer, until the hate and anger in her were silently choking her. In a thick voice, she asked:

"And what did you do to her later on—my mother—to break the chain, as you've said?"

Silence.

"Tell me."

The old woman sighed. She turned her head slightly, gazing through the rusted screen.

"From the time she was a small child," she said, "playing in that garden there, I begged her to fight him. I told her not to look at him. I schooled her in turning him away! And I had won my fight, won over her fits of melancholy and madness and crying, and sickening confessions that she had lost the battle and let him come into her bed, I had won, until Cortland raped her! And then I did what I had to do to see that she gave you up and she never went after you.

"I did what I had to do to see that she never gained the strength to run away, to search for you, to claim you again and bring you back into her madness, and her guilt and her hysteria. When they wouldn't give her electric shock at one hospital, I took her to another. And if they wanted to take her off the drugs at that hospital, I took her to another. And I told them what I had to tell them to make them tie her to her bed, and give her the drugs, and give her the shock. I told her what I had to tell her to make her scream so they would do it!"

"Don't tell me any more."

"Why? You wanted to know, didn't you? And yes, when she writhed in her bedcovers like a cat in heat, I told them to give her the shots, give them to her—"

"Stop!"

"—twice a day or three times a day. I don't care if you kill her, but give it to her, I won't have her lie there, his plaything writhing in the dark, I won't—"

"Stop it. Stop."

"Why? Till the day she died, she was his. Her last and only word was his name. What good was it all, except that it was for you, for you, Rowan!"

"Stop it!" Rowan hissed at her, her own hands rising helplessly in the air, fingers splayed. "Stop it. I could kill you for what you are telling me! How dare you speak of God and life when you did that to a girl, a young girl that you had brought up in this filthy house, you did that to her, you did that to her when she was helpless and sick and you . . . God help you, you are the witch, you sick and cruel old woman, that you could do that to her, God help you, God help you, God damn you!"

A look of sullen shock swept the old woman's face. For one second in the weak light, she seemed to go blank, with her round blank glass eyes shining like two buttons, and her mouth slack and empty.

Rowan groaned, her own hands moved to the sides of her head, slipping into her hair, her lips pressed shut to stop her words, to stop her rage, to stop the hurt and pain. "To hell with you for what you did!" she cried, half swallowing the words, her body bent with the rage she couldn't swallow.

The old woman frowned. She reached out, and the cane fell from her hand. She took a single shuffling step forward. And then her right hand faltered, and plunged towards the left knob of the rocking chair in front of her. Her frail body twisted slowly and sank down into the chair. As her head fell back against the high slats, she ceased to move. Then her hand slipped off the arm of the chair and dangled beside it.

There was no single noise in the night. Only a dim continuous purring as if the insects sang and the frogs sang and the faraway engines and cars, wherever they were, sang with them. It seemed a train passed somewhere close, clicking rhythmically and fast beneath the song. And there came the dull faraway sound of a whistle, like a guttural sob in the darkness.

Rowan stood motionless, her hands dropped at her sides, limp and useless, as she stared dumbly through the rusted mesh of the screen, at the soft lacy movement of the trees and the sky. The deep singing of the frogs slowly broke itself away from the other night songs, and then faded. A car came down the empty street beyond the front fence, headlights piercing the thick wet foliage.

Rowan felt the light on her skin. She saw it flash over the wooden cane lying on the floor of the porch, over Carlotta's black high-top shoe, bent painfully in as if the thin ankle had snapped.

Did anyone see through the thick shrubs the dead woman in the chair? And the tall blond woman figure behind her?

Rowan shuddered all over. She arched her back, her left hand rising and gripping a hank of her hair and pulling it until the pain in her scalp was sharp, so sharp she couldn't quite bear it.

The rage was gone. Even the faintest most bitter flash of anger had died away; and she stood alone and cold in the dark, clinging to the pain as she held her own hair tight in her trembling fingers, cold as if the warm night were not there, alone as if the darkness were the darkness of the abyss from which all promise of light was gone, and all promise of hope or happiness. The world gone. The world with all its history, and all its vain logic, and all its dreams, and accomplishments.

Slowly, she wiped her mouth with the back of her hand, sloppily like a child, and she stood looking down at the limp hand of the dead woman, her own teeth chattering as the cold ate deep into her, truly chilling her. Then she went down on her knee and lifted the hand and felt for the pulse, which she knew wasn't there, and then laid it down in the woman's lap, and looked at the blood trickling down from the woman's ear, running down her neck and into her white collar.

"I didn't mean to . . ." she whispered, barely forming the words.

Behind her the dark house yawned, waited. She couldn't bear to turn around. Some distant unidentifiable sound shocked her. It filled her with fear; it filled her with the worst and only real fear she'd ever known of a place in all her life, and when she thought of the dark rooms, she couldn't turn around. She couldn't go back into it. And the enclosed porch held her like a trap.

She rose slowly and looked out over the deep grass, over a tangle of vine that clawed at the screen, and shivered now against it with its tiny pointed leaves. She looked up at the clouds moving beyond the trees, and she heard an awful little sound issuing from her own lips, a kind of awful desperate moaning.

"I didn't mean to . . ." she said again.

This is when you pray, she thought miserably and quietly. This is when you pray to nothing and no one to take away the terror of what you've done, to make it right, to make it that you never never came here.

She saw Ellie's face in the hospital bed. *Promise me, you'll never never* . . .

"I didn't mean to do it!" It came so low, the whisper, that nobody but God could have heard. "God, I didn't mean to. I swear it. I didn't mean to do this again."

Far away somewhere in another realm other people existed. Michael and the Englishman and Rita Mae Lonigan, and the Mayfairs gathered at the restaurant table. Even Eugenia, lost somewhere within the house, asleep and dreaming perhaps. All those others.

And she stood here alone. She, who had killed this mean and cruel old woman, killed her as cruelly as she herself had ever killed, God damn her for it. God damn her into hell for all she said and all she'd done. God damn her. But I didn't mean it, I swear . . .

Once again, she wiped her mouth. She folded her arms across her breasts and hunched her shoulders and shivered. She had to turn around, walk through the dark house. Walk back to the door, and leave her.

Oh, but she couldn't do that, she had to call someone, she had to tell, she had to cry out for that woman Eugenia, and do what had to be done, what was right to be done.

Yet the agony of speaking to strangers now, of telling official lies, was more than she could endure.

She let her head fall lazily to one side. She stared down at the helpless body, broken and collapsed within its sack of a dress. The white hair so clean and soft-looking. All her paltry and miserable life in this house, all her sour and unhappy life. And this is how it ends for her.

She closed her eyes, bringing her hands up wearily to her face, and then the prayers did come, Help me, because I don't know what to do, I don't know what I've done, and I can't undo it. And everything the old woman said was true, and I've always known, known it was evil inside me and inside them and that's why Ellie took me away. Evil.

She saw the thin pale ghost outside the glass in Tiburon. She felt the invisible hands touching her, as she had on the plane. Evil.

"And where are you?" she whispered in the darkness. "Why should I be afraid to walk back into this house?"

She raised her head. In the long parlor, there came another faint, cracking noise behind her. Like an old board creaking under a step. Or was it just a rafter breathing? So faint it might have been a rat in the dark, creeping along the boards with its tiny repulsive feet. But she knew it wasn't. With every instinct in her, she felt a presence there, someone near, someone in the dark, someone in the parlor. Not the old black woman. Not the scratching of her slippers.

"Show yourself to me," she whispered, the last of her fear turning to anger. "Do it now."

Once again she heard it. And slowly she turned around. Silence. She looked down one last time at the old woman. And then she walked into the long front room. The high narrow mirrors stared at one another in the shadowy stillness. The dusty chandeliers gathered the light to themselves sullenly in the gloom.

I'm not afraid of you. I'm not afraid of anything here. Show yourself as you did before.

The very furniture seemed alive for one perilous instant, as if the small curved chairs were watching her, as if the bookcases with their glass doors had heard her vague challenge, and would bear witness to whatever took place.

"Why don't you come?" she whispered aloud again. "Are you afraid of me?" Emptiness. A dull creak from somewhere overhead.

With quiet even steps she made her way into the hallway, painfully aware of the sound of her own labored breathing. She gazed dumbly at the open front door. Milky the light from the street, and dark and shining the leaves of the dripping oaks. A long sigh came out of her, almost involuntarily, and then she turned and moved away from this comforting light, back through the hallway, against the thick shadows and towards the empty dining room, where the emerald lay, waiting, in its velvet box.

He was here. He had to be.

"Why don't you come?" she whispered, surprised at the frailty of her own voice. It seemed the shadows stirred, but no shape materialized. Maybe a tiny bit of breeze had caught the dusty draperies. A thin dull snap sounded in the boards under her feet.

There on the table lay the jewel box. Smell of wax lingering in the air. Her fingers were trembling as she raised the lid, and touched the stone itself.

"Come on, you devil," she said. She lifted the emerald, vaguely thrilled by its weight, in spite of her misery, and she lifted it higher, until the light caught it, and she put it on, easily manipulating the small strong clasp at the back of her neck.

Then, in one very strange moment, she saw herself doing this. She saw herself, Rowan Mayfair, ripped out of her past, which had been so far removed from all of this that it now lacked detail, standing like a lost wanderer in this dark and strangely familiar house.

And it was familiar, wasn't it? These high tapering doors were familiar. It seemed her eyes had drifted over these murals a thousand times. Ellie had walked here. Her mother had lived and died here. And how otherworldly and irretrievable seemed the glass and redwood house in faraway California. Why had she waited so long to come?

She had taken a detour in the dark gleaming path of her destiny. And what were all her past triumphs to the confrontation of this mystery, and to think, this mystery in all its dark splendor belonged by right to her. It had waited here all these years for her to claim it and now, at last she was here.

The emerald lay against the soft silk of her blouse heavily. Her fingers seemed unable to resist it, hovering about it as if it were a magnet.

"Is this what you want?" she whispered.

Behind her, in the hallway, an unmistakable sound answered her. The whole house felt it, echoed it, like the case of a great piano echoes the tiniest touch to a single string. Then again, it came. Soft but certain. Someone there.

Her heart thudded almost painfully. She stood stranded, her head bowed, and as if in dreamy sleep, she turned and raised her eyes. Only a few feet away, she made out a dim and indistinct figure, what seemed a tall man.

All the smallest sounds of the night seemed to die away and leave her in a void as she struggled to pick this thing out from the murky dark that enmeshed it. Was she deceiving herself or was that the scheme of a face? It seemed that a pair of dark eyes was watching her, that she could just make out the contour of a head. Perhaps she saw the white curve of a stiff collar.

"Don't play games with me," she whispered. Once again, the whole house echoed the sound with its uncertain creaks and sighs. And then wondrously, the figure brightened, confirmed itself magically, and yet even as she gasped aloud, it began to fade.

"No, don't go!" she pleaded, doubting suddenly that she had ever seen anything at all.

And as she stared into the confusion of light and shadow, searching desperately, a darker form suddenly loomed against the dull faint light from the distant door. Closer it came, through the swirling dust, with heavy distinct footfalls. Without any chance of mistake she saw the massive shoulders, the black curly hair.

"Rowan? Is that you, Rowan?"

Solid, familiar, human.

"Oh Michael," she cried, her voice soft and ragged. She moved into his waiting arms. "Michael, thank God!"

Twenty-nine

WELL, SHE THOUGHT to herself, silent, hunched over, sitting alone at the dining table, the supposed victim of the horrors in this dark house—I am becoming one of those women now who just falls into a man's arms and lets him take care of everything.

But it was beautiful to watch Michael in action. He made the calls to Ryan Mayfair, and to the police, to Lonigan and Sons. He spoke the language of the plainclothesmen who came up the steps. If anyone noticed the black gloves he wore, they did not say so, maybe because he was talking too fast, explaining things, and moving things along to hasten the inevitable conclusions.

"Now she just got here, she does not have the faintest idea

who in the hell this guy is up in the attic. The old woman didn't tell her. And she's in shock now. The old woman just died out there. Now this body in the attic has been there a long time, and what I'm asking you is not to disturb anything else in the room, if you can just take the remains, and she wants to know who this man was as much as you want to know.

"And look, this is Ryan Mayfair coming. Ryan, Rowan is in there. She's in awful shape. Before Carlotta died, she showed her a body upstairs."

"A body. Are you serious?"

"They need to take it out. Could you or Pierce go up there, see that they don't touch all those old records and things? Rowan's in there. She's exhausted. She can talk in the morning."

At once Pierce accepted the mission. Thunder of people going up the old staircase.

In hushed voices Ryan and Michael talked. Smell of cigarette smoke in the hall. Ryan came into the dining room and spoke to Rowan in a whisper.

"Tomorrow, I'll call you at the hotel. Are you sure you don't want to come with me and with Pierce out to Metairie?"

"Have to be close," she said. "Want to walk over in the morning."

"Your friend from California is a nice man, a local man."

"Yes. Thank you."

Even to old Eugenia, Michael had been the protector, putting his arm around her shoulder as he escorted her in to see "old Miss Carl" before Lonigan lifted the body from the rocker. Poor Eugenia who cried without making a sound. "Honey, do you want me to call someone for you? You don't want to stay tonight in the house alone, do you? You tell me what you want to do. I can get someone to come here and stay with you."

With Lonigan, his old friend, he fell right into stride. He lost all the California from his voice, and was talking just like Jerry, and just like Rita, who had come out with him in "the wagon." Old friends, Jerry drinking beer with Michael's father on the front steps thirty-five years ago, and Rita double-dating with Michael in the Elvis Presley days. Rita threw her arms around him. "Michael Curry."

Roaming to the front, Rowan had watched them in the glare of the flashing lights. Pierce was talking on the phone in the library. She had not even seen the library. Now a dull electric light flooded the room, illuminating old leather and Chinese carpet.

". . . well, now, Mike," said Lonigan, "you have to tell Dr. Mayfair this woman was ninety years old, the only thing keeping

712

her going was Deirdre. I mean we knew it was just a matter of time once Deirdre went, and so she can't blame herself for whatever happened here tonight, I mean, she's a doctor, Mike, but she ain't no miracle worker.''

No, not much, Rowan had thought.

"Mike Curry? You're not Tim Curry's son!'' said the uniformed policeman. "They told me it was you. Well, hell, my dad and your dad were third cousins, did you know that? Oh, yeah, my dad knew your dad real well, used to drink beer with him at Corona's.''

At last the body in the attic, bagged and tagged, was taken away, and the small dried body of the old woman had been laid on the white padded stretcher as if it were alive, though it was only being moved into the undertaker's wagon—perhaps to lie on the same embalming table where Deirdre had lain a day earlier.

No funeral, no interment ceremony, no nothing, said Ryan. She had told him that herself yesterday. Told Lonigan too, the man said. "There will be a Requiem Mass in a week,'' said Ryan. "You'll still be here?''

Where would I go? Why? I found where I belong. In this house. I'm a witch. I'm a killer. And this time I did it deliberately.

". . . And I know how terrible this has been for you.''

Wandering back into the dining room, she heard young Pierce in the library door.

"Now, she isn't considering staying in this house, tonight, is she?''

"No, we're going back to the hotel,'' Michael said.

"It's just that she shouldn't be here alone. This can be a very unsettling house. A truly unsettling house. Would you think me crazy if I told you that just now when I went into the library there was a portrait of someone over the fireplace and that now there's a mirror?''

"Pierce!'' said Ryan wrathfully.

"I'm sorry, Dad, but . . .''

"Not now, son, please.''

"I believe you,'' said Michael with a little laugh. "I'll be with her.''

"Rowan?'' Ryan approached her again carefully—she the bereaved, the victim, when in fact she was the murderer. Agatha Christie would have known. But then I would have had to do it with a candle stick.

"Yes, Ryan.''

He settled down at the table, careful not to touch the dusty

713

surface with the sleeve of his perfectly tailored suit. The funeral suit. The light struck his thoroughbred face, his cold blue eyes, much lighter blue than Michael's. "You know this house is yours."

"She told me that."

Young Pierce stood respectfully in the doorway.

"Well, there's a lot more to it," said Ryan.

"Liens, mortgages?"

He shook his head. "No, I don't think you'll ever have to worry about anything of that sort as long as you live. But the point is, that whenever you want you can come downtown and we'll go over it."

"Good God," said Pierce, "is that the emerald?" He had spied the jewel case in the shadows at the other end. "And with all these people just trooping through there."

His father gave him a subdued, patient look. "Nobody's going to steal that emerald, son," he said with a sigh. He glanced anxiously at Rowan. He gathered up the jewel case and looked at it as if he didn't quite know what to do with it.

"What's wrong?" Rowan asked. "What's the matter?"

"Did she tell you about this?"

"Did anyone ever tell *you*?" she asked quietly, unchallengingly.

"Quite a story," he said, with a subtle, forced smile. He laid the jewel box down in front of her and patted it with his hand. He stood up.

"Who was the man in the attic, do they know?" she asked.

"They will soon. There was a passport, and other papers with the corpse, or what was left of it."

"Where's Michael?" she asked.

"Here, honey, over here. Look, you want me to leave you alone?" In the dark, his gloved hands were almost invisible.

"I'm tired, can we go back? Ryan, can I call you tomorrow?"

"When you want, Rowan."

Ryan hesitated at the door. Glanced at Michael. Michael made a move to leave. Rowan reached out and caught his hand, startled by the leather.

"Rowan, listen to me," said Ryan, "I don't know what the hell Aunt Carl told you, I don't know how that body got upstairs, or what that's about, or what she's told you about the legacy. But you have to clean out this old place, you've got to burn the trash up there, get people to come here, maybe Michael will help you, and throw things out, all those old books, those jars. You have to let the air in and take stock. You don't have to go through this place, examining every speck of dust and dirt and ugliness. It's an inheritance but it isn't a curse. At least it doesn't have to be.''

"I know," she said.

Noise at the front door.

The two young black men who had come to collect Grandma Eugenia were now standing in the hallway. Michael went upstairs to help her. Ryan and then Pierce swept down to kiss Rowan on the cheek. Rather like kissing the corpse, it seemed to her suddenly. Then she realized it was the other way around. They kissed the dead people here the way they kissed the living.

Warm hands, and the parting flash of Pierce's smile in the dark. Tomorrow, phone, lunch, talk, et cetera.

Sound of the elevator making its hellish descent. People did go to hell in elevators in the movies.

"And you have your key, Eugenia, you just come on over tomorrow, you come in as you always did, if you need or want anything. Now, honey, do you need any money?"

"I got my pay, Mr. Mike. Thank you, Mr. Mike."

"Thank you, Mr. Curry," said the younger black man. Smooth, educated voice.

The older policeman came back. He must have been in the very front hall because she could barely hear him. "Yeah, Townsend."

". . . passport, wallet, everything right there in the shirt."

Doors closed. Darkness. Quiet.

Michael coming back the hallway.

And now we are two, and the house is empty. He stood in the dining room doorway looking at her.

Silence. He drew a cigarette out of his pocket, mashing the pack back into it. Couldn't be easy with the gloves, but they did not seem to slow him down.

"What do you say?" he asked. "Let's get the hell out of here for tonight." He packed his cigarette on the face of his watch. Explosion of a match, and the flash of light in his blue eyes as he looked up, taking in the dining room again, taking in the murals.

There are blue eyes and blue eyes. Could his black hair have grown so much in such a short time? Or was it just the moisture in the warm air that made it so thick and curly?

The silence rang in her ears. They were actually all gone.

And the whole place lay empty and vulnerable to Rowan's touch, with its many drawers and cabinets and closets and jars and boxes. Yet the idea of touching anything was repugnant. It wasn't hers, it was the old woman's, all of it. Dank and stale, and awful, like the old woman. And Rowan had no spirit to move, no spirit to climb the stairs again, or to see anything at all.

"His name was Townsend?" she asked.

"Yeah. Stuart Townsend."

"Who the hell was he, do they have any idea?"

Michael thought for a moment, flicked a tiny bit of tobacco off his lip, shifted his weight from one hip to another. Pure beefcake, she thought. Downright pornographic.

"I know who he was," he said with a sigh. "Aaron Lightner, you remember him? He knows all about him."

"What are you talking about?"

"You want to talk here?" His eyes moved over the ceiling again, like antennae. "I've got Aaron's car outside. We could go back to the hotel, or downtown somewhere."

His eyes lingered lovingly on the plaster medallion, on the chandelier. There was something furtive and guilty about the way he was admiring it in the middle of this crisis. But he didn't have to hide it from her.

"This is the house, isn't it?" she asked. "The one you told me about in California."

His eyes homed to her, locked.

"Yeah, it's the one." He gave a little sad smile and a shake of his head. "It's the one all right." He tapped the ash into his cupped hand, and then moved slowly away from the table towards the fireplace. The heavy shift of his hips, the movement of his thick leather belt, all distractingly erotic. She watched him tip the ashes into the empty grate, the invisible little ashes that probably would have made no difference at all, had they been allowed to drift to the dusty floor.

"What do you mean, Mr. Lightner knows who that man was?"

He looked uncomfortable. Extremely sexy and very uncomfortable. He took another drag off the cigarette, and looked around, figuring.

"Lightner belongs to an organization," he said. He fished in his shirt pocket, and drew out a little card. He placed it on the table. "They call it an order. Like a religious order, but it isn't religious. The name of it is the Talamasca."

"Dabblers in the black arts?"

"No."

"That's what the old woman said."

"Well, that's a lie. Believers in the black arts, but not dabblers or practitioners."

"She told a lot of lies. There was truth in what she said, too, but every damned time it was entangled with hate, and venom and meanness, and awful awful lies." She shuddered. "I'm hot

716

and I'm cold," she said. "I saw one of those cards before. He gave one to me in California. Did he tell you that? I met him in California."

Michael nodded uneasily. "At Ellie's grave."

"Well, how is that possible? That you're his friend, and that he knows all about this man in the attic? I'm tired, Michael. I feel like I might start screaming and never be able to stop. I feel like if you don't start telling me . . ." She broke off, staring listlessly at the table. "I don't know what I'm saying," she said.

"That man, Townsend," said Michael apprehensively, "he was a member of the order. He came here in 1929 trying to make contact with the Mayfair family."

"Why?"

"They've been watching this family for three hundred years, compiling a history," Michael said. "It's going to be hard for you to understand all this . . ."

"And just by coincidence, this man's your friend?"

"No. Slow down. None of it was coincidence. I met him outside this house the first night I got here. And I saw him in San Francisco, too, you saw him, remember, the night you picked me up at my place, but we both thought he was a reporter. I had never spoken to him, and before that night I'd never seen him before."

"I remember."

"And then outside this house, he was there. I was drunk, I'd gotten drunk on the plane. Remember I promised you I wouldn't, well, I did. And I came here, and I saw this . . . this other man in the garden. Only it wasn't a real man. I thought it was, and then I realized it wasn't. I'd seen that guy when I was a kid. I'd seen him every time I ever passed this house. I told you about him, do you remember? Well, what I have to somehow explain is . . . he's not a real man."

"I know," she said. "I've seen him." The most electrical feeling passed through her. "Keep talking. I'll tell you about it when you finish, please."

But he didn't keep talking. He looked at her anxiously. He was frustrated, worried. He was leaning on the mantel, looking down at her, the light from the hallway half illuminating his face, his eyes darting over the table, and finally returning to her. It aroused a complete tenderness in her to see the protectiveness in him, to hear in his voice the gentleness and the fear of hurting her.

"Tell me the rest," she said. "Look, don't you understand, I have some terrible things I have to tell you because you're the only one I can tell. So you tell me your story because you're

717

actually making it easier for me. Because I didn't know how I was going to tell you about seeing that man. I saw him after you left, on the deck in Tiburon. I saw him at the very moment my mother died in New Orleans, and I didn't know she was dying then. I didn't know anything about her."

He nodded. But he was still confused, stymied.

"If I can't trust you, for what it's worth, I don't want to talk to anybody. What are you holding back? Just tell me. Tell me why that man Aaron Lightner was kind to me this afternoon at the funeral when you weren't there? I want to know who he is, and how you know him. Am I entitled to ask that question?"

"Look, honey, you can trust me. Don't get mad at me, please."

"Oh, don't worry, it takes more than a lover's quarrel for me to blow somebody's carotid artery."

"Rowan, I didn't mean . . ."

"I know, I know!" she whispered. "But you know I killed that old woman."

He made a small, forbidding gesture. He shook his head.

"You know I did." She looked up at him. "You are the only one who knows." Then a terrible suspicion came into her mind. "Did you tell Lightner the things I told you? About what I could do?"

"No," he said, shaking his head earnestly, pleading with her quietly and eloquently to believe him. "No, but he knows, Rowan."

"Knows what?"

He didn't answer. He gave a little shrug, and drew out another cigarette, and stood there, staring off, considering, apparently, as he pulled out his matchbook, and without even noticing it, did that wonderful one-handed match trick of bending out one book match, and closing the book and then bending that match and striking it and putting the flame to the cigarette.

"I don't know where to begin," he said. "Maybe at the beginning." He let out the smoke, resting his elbow on the mantel again. "I love you. I really do. I don't know how all this came about. I have a lot of suspicions and I'm scared. But I love you. If that was meant, I mean destined, well, then I'm a lost man. Really lost, because I can't accept the destined part. But I won't give up the love. I don't care what happens. Did you hear what I said?"

She nodded. "You have to tell me everything about these other people," she said. But she also said without words, *Do you know how much I love you and desire you?*

She turned sideways in the chair, the better to face him. She rubbed the back of her arms, again, and hung the heel of her shoe on the chair rung. Looking up at him, she saw his hips again, the slant of his belt, the shirt tight across his chest. She couldn't stop wanting him physically. Best to get it over with, wasn't it? Oh, all right, let's eat all this delicious ice cream just to get rid of it. And so you can tell me what you're talking about with all this, and I can tell you. About the man on the plane. And the old woman's question. Was it better than a mortal man?

His face darkened as he looked at her. Loved her. Yes. This man, just the best man she had ever known or touched or wanted ever. What would all this have been like without him?

"Michael, talk straight to me, please," she said.

"Oh, yeah. But Rowan, don't freak out on me. Just listen to what I have to say."

He picked up one of the dining room chairs from along the wall, swung it around so that the back faced her, and straddled it cowboy style, folding his arms on the back of it, as he looked at her. That was pornographic too.

"For the last two days," he said, "I've been holed up about sixty miles from here, reading the history of the Mayfair family compiled by these people."

"The Talamasca."

He nodded. "Now, let me explain to you. Three hundred years ago, there was this man named Petyr van Abel. His father had been a famous surgeon at the University of Leiden in Holland. There are books still in existence that were written by this doctor, Jan van Abel."

"I know who he is," she said. "He was an anatomist."

He smiled and shook his head. "Well, he's your ancestor, babe. You look like his son. At least that's what Aaron says. Now when Jan van Abel died, Petyr was orphaned and he became a member of the Talamasca. He could read minds, he could see ghosts. He was what other people might have called a witch, but the Talamasca gave him shelter. Eventually, he went to work for them, and part of his work was saving people accused in other countries of witchcraft. And if they had real gifts, you know, the gifts that I have and you have and Petyr van Abel had, well, he would help those people to reach the Motherhouse of the Talamasca in Amsterdam.

"Now, this Petyr van Abel went to Scotland to try to intervene in the trial of a witch named Suzanne Mayfair. But he came too late, and all he was able to do, which was plenty as it turned out, was take her daughter Deborah away from the town where she might eventually have been burnt too, and bring her to Holland. But before he did, he saw this man, this spirit. He saw too that the child Deborah saw it, and Petyr conjectured that Deborah had made it appear, which proved to be accurate.

"Deborah didn't stay with the order. Eventually she seduced Petyr, and by him had a child named Charlotte. Charlotte went to the New World and it was she who founded the Mayfair family. But when Deborah died in France, a convicted witch, that brown-haired man, that spirit, went to Charlotte. So did this emerald necklace that is lying right here in this box. It passed along with the spirit, to Charlotte.

"All the Mayfairs since are Charlotte's descendants. And in each generation of those descendants down to the present time at least one woman has inherited the powers of Suzanne and Deborah, which included, among other things, the ability to see this brown-haired man, this spirit. And they are what the Talamasca calls the Mayfair Witches."

She made a little sound, half amazement, half nervous amusement. She drew herself up in the chair, and watched the little changes in his face, as he silently sorted all the things he wanted to tell. Then she decided to say nothing.

"The Talamasca," he said, choosing his words with care. "They're scholars, historians. They've documented a thousand sightings of that brown-haired man in and around this house. Three hundred years ago in Saint-Domingue, when Petyr van Abel went there to talk to his daughter Charlotte, this spirit drove him mad. It eventually killed him."

He took another drag off the cigarette, eyes moving around the room again, but not seeing it this time, rather seeing something else, and then returning to her.

"Now as I explained before," he said, "I've seen that man since I was six years old. I saw him every time I ever passed this house. And unlike the countless people interviewed by the Talamasca over the years, I've seen him other places. But the point is . . . the other night when I came back here, after all these years, I saw that man again. And when I told Aaron what I saw, when I told him that I'd been seeing that man since I was yea high, and when I told him that it was you who rescued me, well, then he showed me the Talamasca's file on the Mayfair Witches."

"He hadn't known I was the one who pulled you out of the ocean?"

Michael shook his head. "He'd come to San Francisco to see me because of my hands. That's their territory, so to speak, people who have special powers. It was routine. He was reaching out to me, as routinely perhaps as Petyr van Abel went to try to intervene in the execution of Suzanne Mayfair. And then he saw you outside my house. He saw you come to pick me up, and do you know he thought you'd hired me to come back here? He thought you'd hired a psychic to come back here and investigate your background.''

He took a final drag off the cigarette and pitched it into the grate. ''Well, for a while anyway, he thought that. Until I told him why you'd really come to see me, and how you'd never seen this house, or even seen a picture of it. But there you have it, you see.

''And what you have to do now is read the File on the Mayfair Witches. But there's more to it . . . as far as I'm concerned, I mean more to it that has to do with me.''

''The visions.''

''Exactly.'' He smiled, his face warm and beautiful. ''Exactly! Because you remember I told you I saw a woman and there was a jewel . . .''

''And you're saying it's the emerald.''

''I don't know, Rowan. I don't know. And then I do know. I know as surely as I know I'm sitting here that it was Deborah Mayfair I saw out there, Deborah, and she was wearing the emerald around her neck, and I was sent here to do something.''

''To fight that spirit?''

He shook his head. ''It's more complicated. That's why you have to read the File. And Rowan, you have to read it. You have to not be offended that such a file exists. You have to read it.''

''What does the Talamasca get from all this?'' she asked.

''Nothing,'' he answered. ''To know. Yes, they'd like to know. They'd like to understand. It's like, you know, they're psychic detectives.''

''And filthy rich, I suppose.''

''Yeah,'' he said, nodding. ''Filthy rich. Loaded.''

''You're kidding.''

''No, they've got money like you've got. They've got money like the Catholic Church has got. Like the Vatican. Look, it's got nothing to do with their wanting anything from you . . .''

''OK, I believe it. It's just you're naive, Michael. You really are. You really are naive.''

''What in the hell makes you say that, Rowan! Christ, where do you get the idea that I am naive! You said this before and this is really crazy!''

''Michael, you are. You really are. OK, tell me the truth, do you still believe that these visions were good? That these people who appeared to you were higher beings?''

''Yes, I do,'' he said.

''This black-haired woman, this convicted witch, as you called her, with the jewel was good . . . the one who knocked you off the rock right into the Pacific Ocean where . . .''

"Rowan, no one can prove a chain of controlled events like that! All I know . . .''

"You saw this spirit man when you were six? Let me tell you something, Michael, this man is not good. And you saw him here two nights ago? And this black-haired woman is not good either.''

"Rowan, it's too early for you to make these interpretations.''

"OK. All right. I don't want to make you mad. I don't want to make you angry even for one second. I'm so glad you're here, you can't know how glad I am that you're here, that you're here with me in this house, and you understand all this, that you're . . . oh, it's a terrible thing to say, but I'm glad I'm not in it alone. And I want you here, that's the whole truth.''

"I know, I understand, and the important thing is, I am here, and you aren't alone.''

"But don't you make too many interpretations either. There is something terribly evil here, something I can feel like the evil in me. No, don't say anything. Just listen to me. There's something so bad that it could spill out and hurt lots of people. More than it's ever hurt in the past. And you're like some starry-eyed knight who just rode over the drawbridge out of the castle!''

"Rowan, that is not true.''

"All right. OK. They didn't drown you out there. They didn't do that. And your knowing all these people, Rita Mae and Jerry Lonigan, it's all not connected.''

"It's connected, but the question is, how is it connected? It's crucial not to jump to conclusions.''

She turned back towards the table, resting her elbows on it and holding her head in her hands. She had no idea now what time it was. The night seemed quieter than before; now and then something in the house would snap or creak. But they were alone. Completely alone.

"You know,'' she said, "I think about that old woman, and it's like a cloud of evil descending on me. It was like walking with evil to be with her. And she thought she was the good one. She thought she was fighting the devil. It's tangled, but it's tangled even more obscurely than that.''

"She killed Townsend,'' he said.

She turned and looked at him again. "You know that for sure?''

"I laid my hands on him. I felt the bone. She did it. She tied him up in that rug. He was maybe drugged at the time, I don't

722

know. But he died in the rug, I know that much. He chewed a hole in it.''

"Oh, God!'' She closed her eyes, her imagination filling in the implications too vividly.

"And there were people in this house all the time and they couldn't hear him. They didn't know he was dying up there, or if they did they didn't do anything about it.''

"Why would she do it!''

"'Cause she hated us. I mean she hated the Talamasca.''

"You said 'us.' ''

"That was a slip, but a very informative one. I feel like I'm part of them. They've come to me and they've asked me to be, more or less. They've taken me into their confidence. But maybe what I really meant, is that she hated anyone from outside who knew anything. There are dangers still to anybody from outside. There's danger to Aaron. You asked me what the Talamasca stands to get out of this. It stands to lose another member.''

"Explain.''

"On the way home from the funeral, coming back out to the country to get me, he saw a man on the road and swerved, rolled over twice, and just got out of the damned car before it exploded. It was that spirit thing. I know it was. So does he. I guess whatever this big plan is, this entanglement, Aaron has served his purpose.''

"Is he hurt?''

Michael shook his head. "He knew what was going down, even as it was happening. But he couldn't take a chance. Suppose it hadn't been an apparition and he'd run down a real man. Just couldn't chance it. He was belted in, too. I think he got slammed on the head pretty bad.''

"Did they take him to a hospital?''

"Yes, Doctor. He's OK. That is why I took so long to get here. He didn't want me to come. He wanted you to come to them, out there in the country, read the file out there. But I came on anyway. I knew that thing wasn't going to kill me. I haven't served my purpose yet.''

"The purpose of the visions.''

"No. He has his purpose, and they have theirs. And they don't work together. They work against each other.''

"What happens if you try to run away to Tibet?'' she asked.

"You want to go?''

"If I go with you, you're not running away. But really, what if you do run away?

"I don't know. I don't intend to, so it doesn't compute. They

723

want me to fight him, to fight him and the little scheme he's been laying down all along. I'm convinced of it.''

"They want you to break the chain,'' she said. "That's what the old woman said. She said, 'Break the chain,' meaning this legacy that comes all the way down from Charlotte, I guess, though she didn't talk about anyone that far back. She said she herself had tried. And that I could do it.''

"That's the obvious answer, yes. But there has to be more to it than that, having to do with him, and why he's shown himself to me.''

"OK,'' she said. "You listen to me now. I'm going to read the File, every page of it. But I've seen this thing too. And it doesn't simply appear. It affects matter.''

"When did you see it?''

"The night my mother died, at the very hour. I tried to call you. I rang the hotel, but you weren't there. It scared the hell out of me. But the apparition isn't the significant part. It's what else happened. It affected the water around the house. It made the water so turbulent that the house was swaying on its pilings. There was absolutely no storm that night on Richardson Bay or San Francisco Bay or any earthquake or any natural reason for that to happen. And there's something else too. The next time, I felt this thing touch me.''

"When did that happen?''

"On the plane. I thought it was a dream. But it wasn't. I was sore afterwards, just as if I'd been with a large man.''

"You mean it . . . ?''

"I thought I was asleep, but the distinction I'm trying to make is, this thing isn't limited to apparitions. It's involved with the physical in some very specific way. And what I have to understand is its parameters.''

"Well, that's a commendable scientific attitude. Could I ask whether or not its touching you evoked any other, less scientific response?''

"Of course it did. It was pleasurable, because I was half asleep. But when I woke up, I felt like I'd been raped. I loathed it.''

"Oh, lovely,'' he said anxiously. "Just lovely. Well, look, you've got the power to stop this thing from that sort of violation.''

"I know, and now that I know that's what it is, I will. But if anybody had tried to tell me day before yesterday that some invisible being was going to slip under my clothes on a flight to New Orleans, I wouldn't have been any more prepared than I was because I wouldn't have believed it. But we know it doesn't want to hurt me. And we are fairly certain that it doesn't want to hurt you. What we have to keep in mind is that it does want to hurt anyone who interferes with its plans, apparently, and now this includes your friend Aaron."

"Right," Michael said.

"Now you look tired, like you're the one who needs to be taken back to the hotel and put to bed," she said. "Why don't we go there?"

He didn't answer. He sat up, and rubbed the back of his neck with his hands. "There's something you're not saying."

"What?"

"And I'm not saying it either."

"Well then say it," she said softly, patiently.

"Don't you want to talk to him? Don't you want to ask him yourself who he is and what he is? Don't you think you can communicate with him better and more truly maybe than any of the rest of them? Maybe you don't. But I do. I want to talk to him. I want to know why he showed himself to me when I was a kid. I want to know why he came so close to me the other night that I almost touched him, touched his shoe. I want to know what he is. And I know, that no matter what Aaron's told me, or what Aaron will tell me, I think I'm smart enough to get through to that thing, and to reason with it, and maybe that's exactly the kind of pride it expects to find in everyone who ever sees it. Maybe it counts on that.

"Now, if you haven't felt that, well, then, you're smarter and stronger than I am, by a long, long way. I never really talked to a ghost or a spirit, or whatever he is. And boy, I wouldn't pass up the opportunity, not even knowing what I know, and knowing what he did to Aaron."

She nodded. "Yeah, you've covered it all right. And maybe it does play on that, the vanity in some of us that we won't run the way the others did. But there's something else between me and this thing. It touched me. And it left me feeling raped. I didn't like it."

They sat there in silence for a moment. He was looking at her, and she could all but hear the wheels turning in his head.

He stood up and reached for the jewel case, sliding it across the smooth surface of the table. He opened it and looked at the emerald.

"Go ahead," she said. "Touch it."

"It doesn't look like the drawing I made of it," he whispered. "I was imagining it when I made the drawing, not remembering it." He shook his head. He seemed about to close the lid of the box again; then he removed his glove, and laid his fingers on the stone.

In silence she waited. But she could tell by his face that he was disappointed and anxious. When he sighed and closed the box, she didn't press him.

"I got an image of you," he said, "of your putting it around your neck. I saw myself standing in front of you." He put the glove back on, carefully.

"That's when you came in."

"Yeah," he said, nodding. "I didn't even notice that you were wearing it."

"It was dark."

"I saw only you."

"What does that matter?" she shrugged. "I took it off and put it back in the case."

"I don't know."

"Just now, when you touched it. Did you see anything else?"

He shook his head. "Only that you love me," he said in a small voice. "You really do."

"You only have to touch me to discover that," she said.

He smiled, but the smile was sad, and confused. He shoved his hands in his pockets, as if he were trying to get rid of them, and he bowed his head. She waited for a long moment, hating to see him miserable.

"Come on, let's go," she said. "This place is getting to you worse than me. Let's go back to the hotel."

He nodded. "I need a glass of water," he said. "Do you think there's some cold water in this house? I'm dry and I'm hot."

"I don't know," she said. "I don't even know if there's a kitchen. Maybe there's a well with a moss-covered bucket. Maybe there's a magic spring."

He laughed softly. "Come on, let's find some water."

She got up and followed him out of the rear door of the dining room. Some sort of butler's pantry, it was, with a little sink in it, and high glassed cabinets filled with china. He took his time passing through. He seemed to be measuring the thickness of the walls with his hands.

"Back here," he said, passing through the next door. He pushed in an old black wall button. A dingy overhead bulb flashed on, weak and dismal, revealing a long split-level room, the upper portion a sterile workplace, and the lower, two steps down, a small breakfast room with a fireplace.

A long series of glass doors revealed the overgrown yard outside. It seemed the song of the frogs was louder here, clearer.

The dark outline of an immense tree obscured the northern corner of the view completely.

The rooms themselves were very clean and very streamlined in an old-fashioned way. Very efficient.

The built-in refrigerator covered half the inside wall, with a great heavy door like the doors of walk-in vaults in restaurants.

"Don't tell me if there's a body in there, I don't want to know," she said wearily.

"No, just food," he said smiling, "and ice water." He took out the clear glass bottle. "Let me tell you about the South. There's always a bottle of ice water." He rummaged in one of the cabinets over the corner sink, and caught up two jelly glasses with his right hand and set them down on the immaculate counter.

The cold water tasted wonderful. Then she remembered the old woman. Her house, really, her glass, perhaps. A glass from which she'd drunk. She was overcome with revulsion, and she set the glass in the small steel sink before her.

Yes, like a restaurant, she thought, detaching herself slowly, rebelliously. The place was that well equipped long long ago when someone had ripped out the Victorian fixtures they so love these days in San Francisco. And put in all this shining steel.

"What are we going to do, Michael?" she said.

He stared down at the glass in his hand. Then he looked at her, and at once the tenderness and the protectiveness in his eyes went to her heart.

"Love each other, Rowan. Love each other. You know, as sure as I am about the visions, I'm sure that it isn't part of anyone's plan that we really love each other."

She stepped up to him and slipped her arms around his chest. She felt his hands come up her back and close warmly and tenderly on her neck and her hair. He held her deliciously tight, and buried his face in her neck, and then kissed her again on the lips gently.

"Love me, Rowan. Trust me and love me," he said, his voice heartbreakingly sincere. He drew back, and seemed to retreat into himself a little, and then he took her hand, and led her slowly towards the French door. He stood looking out into the darkness.

Then he opened the door. No lock on it. Maybe there was no lock on any of them. "Can we go outside?" he asked.

"Of course, we can. Why do you ask me?"

He looked at her as if he wanted to kiss her but he didn't do it. And then she kissed him. But at the mere delicious taste of

727

him, all the rest of it returned. She snuggled against him for a long moment. And then she led the way out.

They found that they had come onto a screened porch, much smaller than the one on which the old woman had died, and they went out another door, like many an old-fashioned screened door, even to the spring that caused it to shut behind them. They went down the wooden steps to the flagstones.

"All this is OK," he said, "it's not in bad repair really."

"But what about the house itself? Can it be saved, or is it too far gone?"

"This house?" He smiled, shaking his head, his blue eyes shining beautifully as he glanced at her and then up at the narrow open porch high overhead. "Honey, this house is fine, just fine. This house will be here when you and I are gone. I've never been in such a house. Not in all my years in San Francisco. Tomorrow, we'll come back and I'll show you this house in the sunlight. I'll show you how thick these walls are. I'll show you the rafters underneath if you want." He stopped, ashamed it seemed of relishing it so much, and caught again in the unhappiness and the mourning for the old woman, just as she had been.

And then there was Deirdre, and so many questions yet unanswered about Deirdre. So many things in this history he described, and yet it seemed the darkest journey . . . Much rather look at him and see the excitement in him as he looks up at the walls, as he studies the door frames and the sills and the steps.

"You love it, don't you?"

"I've loved it ever since I was a kid," he said. "I loved it when I saw it two nights ago. I love it now even though I know all kinds of things that happened in it, even what happened to that guy in the attic. I love it because it's your house. And because . . . because it's beautiful no matter what anybody has done in it, or to it. It was beautiful when it was built. It will be beautiful a hundred years from now."

He put his arm around her again, and she clung to him, nestling against him, and feeling him kiss her hair again. His gloved fingers touched her cheek. She wanted to rip off the gloves. But she didn't say so.

"You know, it's a funny thing," he said. "In all my years in California, I worked on many a house. And I loved them all. But none of them ever made me feel my mortality. They never made me feel small. This house makes me feel that. It makes me feel it because it *is* going to be here when I'm gone."

They turned and walked deeper into the garden, finding the flagstones in spite of the weeds that pressed against them, and the bananas that grew so thick and low that the great bladelike leaves brushed their faces.

The shrubs closed out the kitchen light behind them as they climbed the low flagstone steps. Dark it was here, dark as the rural dark.

A rank green smell rose, like the smell of a swamp, and Rowan realized that she was looking out at a long pool of water. They stood on the flagstone lip of this great black pool. It was so heavily overgrown that the surface of the water showed only in dim flashes. The water lilies gleamed boldly in the faintest light from the far-off sky. Insects hummed thickly and invisibly. The frogs sang, and things stirred the water so that the light skittered on the surface suddenly, even deep among the high weeds. There came a busy trickling sound as though the pond were fed by fountains, and when she narrowed her eyes, she saw the spouts, pouring forth their thin sparkling streams.

"Stella built this," he said. "She built it over fifty years ago. It wasn't meant to be like this at all. It was a swimming pool. And now the garden's got it. The earth has taken it back."

How sad he sounded. It was as if he had seen something confirmed that he did not quite believe. And to think how that name had struck her when Ellie said it in the final weeks of fever and delirium. "Stella in the coffin."

He was looking off towards the front of the house, and when she followed his gaze, she saw the high gable of the third floor with its twin chimneys floating against the sky, and the glint of the moon or the stars, she didn't know which, in the square windows high up there, in the room where the man had died, and where Antha had fled Carlotta. All the way down past those iron porches she had fallen—all the way down to the flagstones, before her cranium cracked on the flagstones, and the soft tissue of the brain was crushed, the blood oozing out of it.

She pressed herself more closely against Michael. She locked her hands behind his back, resting her weight against him.

She looked straight up at the pale sky and its few scattered yet vivid stars, and then the memory of the old woman came back again, and it was like the evil cloud wouldn't let go of her. She thought of the look on the old woman's face as she'd died. She thought of the words. And the face of her mother in the casket, slumbering forever on white satin.

"What is it, darlin'?" he asked. A low rumble from his chest.

She pressed her face against his shirt. She started to shiver as she had been doing on and off all night, and when she felt his arms come down tighter and almost hard, she loved it.

The frogs were singing here, that loud grinding woodland

song, and far away a bird cried in the night. Impossible to believe that streets lay near at hand, and that people lived beyond the trees, that the distant tiny yellow lights twinkling here and there through the glossy leaves were the lights of other people's houses.

"I love you, Michael," she whispered. "I do. I love you."

But she couldn't shake the evil spell. It seemed to be part of the sky and the giant tree looming over her head, and the glittering water down deep in the rank and wild grass. But it was not part of any one place. It was in her, part of her. And she realized, her head lying still against his chest, that this wasn't only the remembrance of the old woman and her brittle and personal malice, but a foreboding. Ellie's efforts had been in vain, for Rowan had known this foreboding long ago. Maybe even all her life, she'd known that a dread and dark secret lay ahead, and that it was a great and immense and greedy and multilayered secret, which once opened would continue to unfold forever. It was a secret that would become the world, its revelations crowding out the very light of ordinary life.

This long day in the balmy tropical city of old-fashioned courtesies and rituals had merely been the first unfolding. Even the secrets of the old woman were the mere beginning.

And it draws its strength, this big secret, from the same root from which I draw my strength, both the good and the bad, because in the end, they cannot be separated.

"Rowan, let me get you away from here," he said. "We should have left before. This is my fault."

"No, it doesn't matter, leaving here," she whispered. "I like it here. It doesn't matter where I go, so why not stay here where it's dark and quiet and beautiful?"

The soft heavy smell of that flower came again, the one the old woman had called the night jasmine.

"Ah, do you smell it, Michael?" She looked at the white water lilies glowing in the dark.

"That's the smell of summer nights in New Orleans," he answered. "Of walking alone, and whistling, and beating the iron pickets with a twig." She loved the deep vibration of his voice coming from his chest. "That's the smell of walking all through these streets."

He looked down at her, struggling to make out her face, it seemed. "Rowan, whatever happens, don't let this house go. Even if you have to go away from it and never see it again, even if you come to hate it. Don't let it go. Don't let it ever fall into the hands of anyone who wouldn't love it. It's too beautiful. It has to survive all this, just as we do."

She didn't answer. She didn't confess this dark fear that they weren't going to survive, that somehow everything that had ever given her consolation would be lost. And then she remembered the old woman's face, upstairs in the death room where the man had died years and years ago, and the old woman saying to her, "You can choose. You can break the chain!" The old woman, trying to break through her own crust of malice and viciousness and coldness. Trying to offer Rowan something which she herself perceived to be shining and pure. And in the same room with that man who had died, bound helplessly in that rug, while life went on in the rooms below.

"Let's go, darling dear," he said. "Let's go back to the hotel. I insist. And let's just get into one of those big soft hotel beds and snuggle together."

"Can we walk, Michael? Can we walk slowly through the dark?"

"Yes, honey, if you want to."

They had no keys to lock up. They left the lights shining behind soiled or draped windows. They went down the path and out the rusted gate.

Michael unlocked the car and took out a briefcase and showed it to her. It was the whole story, he said, but she couldn't read it before he explained a few things. There were things in there that were going to shock her, maybe even upset her. Tomorrow, they'd talk about it over breakfast. He had promised Aaron that he wouldn't put it into her hands without explanations, and it was for her that he was doing this. Aaron wanted her to understand.

She nodded. She had no distrust of Aaron Lightner. It wasn't possible for people to fool her, and Lightner had no need to fool anyone. And when she thought of him now, remembering his hand on her arm at the funeral, she had the uneasy feeling that he too was an innocent, an innocent like Michael. And what made them innocent was that they really didn't understand the malice in people.

She was so tired now. No matter what you see or feel or come to know, you get tired. You cannot grieve on and on hour after hour day after day. Yet glancing back at the house she thought of the old woman, cold and small, and dead in the rocker, her death never to be understood or avenged.

If I had not killed her, I could have hated her with such freedom! But now I have this guilt on account of her, as well as all the other doubts and misery she brought to the fore.

Michael stood stranded, staring at the front door. She gave a little tug to his sleeve as she drew close to him.

"Looks like a great keyhole, doesn't it?" she asked.

He nodded, but he seemed far away, lost in his thoughts. "That's what they called that style—the keyhole doorway," he murmured. "Part of the Egyptian Greek Italianate mishmash they loved so much when they built this house."

"Well, they did a good job of it," she said wearily. She wanted to tell him about the door being carved on the tomb in the cemetery but she was so tired.

They walked on slowly together, winding over to Philip Street and then up to Prytania and over to Jackson Avenue. They passed lovely houses in the dark; they passed garden walls. Then down to St. Charles they walked, past the shut-up stores and bars, and past the big apartment houses, and towards the hotel, only an occasional car slipping by, and the streetcar appearing once with a great iron clatter as it rounded the bend, and then roared out of sight, its empty windows full of butter yellow light.

In the shower, they made love, kissing and touching each other hastily and clumsily, the feel of the leather gloves exciting Rowan almost madly when they touched her naked breasts and went down between her legs. The house was gone now; so was the old woman; and the poor sad beautiful Deirdre. Just Michael, just this hard chest of which she'd been dreaming, and his thick cock in her hands, rising out of its nest of dark glossy curling hair.

Years ago some idiot friend had told her over coffee on the campus that women didn't find men's bodies beautiful, that it was what men did that mattered. Well, she had always loved men for both what they did, and their bodies. She loved this body, loved its hardness and its tiny silky soft nipples, and the hard belly, and this cock, which she took into her mouth. She loved the feel of these strong thighs under her fingers, the soft hair in the curve of this backside. Silky and hard, that's what men were.

She ran her hands down Michael's legs, scratching the backs of his knees, and squeezing the muscles of his calves. So strong. She shoved him back against the tile, sucking in longer more delicious strokes, her hands up to cup his balls, and lift them and bind them against the base of the cock.

Gently, he tried to lift her. But she wanted him to spill in her mouth. She brought his hips more tightly against her. She wouldn't let him go, and then he spilled over, and the moan was as good as everything else.

Later when they climbed into the bed, warm and dry, with the air-conditioning blowing softly, Michael stripped off the gloves and they began again. "I can't stop touching you," he said. "I can't stand it, and I want to ask you what it was like when that thing happened, but I know I shouldn't ask you that, and you know, it's like I've seen the face of the man who touched you . . ."

She lay back on the pillow, looking at him in the dark, loving the delicious crush of his weight against her, and his hands almost pulling her hair. She made a fist of her right hand and rubbed her knuckles along the dark shadowy stubble on his chin.

"It was like doing it yourself," she said softly, reaching up and catching his left hand and bringing it down so that she could kiss the palm of it. He stiffened, his cock poking against her thigh. "It wasn't the thunder and crackle of another person. It wasn't living cells against living cells."

"Hmmmm, I love these living cells," he purred in her ear, kissing her roughly. He mauled her with his kisses, her mouth coming back at him as disrespectful and hungry and demanding as his own.

When she awoke it was four o'clock. *Time to go to the hospital. No.* Michael was deep asleep. He didn't feel the very gentle kiss she laid on his cheek. She put on the heavy white terry-cloth robe she found hanging in the closet and went silently out into the living room of the suite. The only light came from the avenue.

Deserted down there. Quiet as a stage set. She loved early morning streets when they were like that, when you felt you could go down and dance on them if you wanted as if they were stages, because their white lines and signal lights meant nothing.

She felt clearheaded and all right, and safe here. The house was waiting, but the house had waited for a long time.

The switchboard told her there was no coffee yet. But there was a message for her and for Mr. Curry, from a Mr. Lightner, that he would return to the hotel later that day and could be reached this morning at the retreat house. She jotted down the number.

She went into the small kitchen, found a pot, and coffee, and made it herself, and then went back and carefully shut the bedroom door, and the door to the little hallway between the bedroom and the living room.

Where was the File on the Mayfair Witches? What had Michael done with the briefcase he'd taken from the car?

She searched the little living room with its skirted chairs and couch. She searched the small den and the closets and even the kitchen. Then she slipped back into the hallway and watched him sleeping there in the light from the window. Curly hair on the back of his neck.

In the closet, nothing. In the bathroom nothing.

Clever, Michael. But I'm going to find it. And then she saw the very edge of the briefcase. He had slipped it behind the chair.

Not very trusting, but then I'm doing just what I more or less promised I wouldn't, she thought. She drew it out, stopping to listen to the pace of his deep breathing, and then she shut the door, and tiptoed down the hall and shut the second door, and laid the briefcase on the coffee table in the light of the lamp.

Then she got her coffee, and her cigarettes, and sat down on the couch and looked at her watch. It was four fifteen. She loved this time, absolutely loved it. It was a good time to read. It had been her favorite time, too, for driving to the hospital, running one red light after another in the great quiet vacuum, her mind filled with orderly and detailed thoughts of the operations waiting for her. But it was an even better time to read.

She opened the briefcase and removed the great stack of folders, each of which carried the curious title: The File on the Mayfair Witches. It made her smile.

It was so literal. "Innocent," she whispered. "They are all innocent. The man in the attic probably innocent. And that old woman, a witch to the core." She paused, taking her first drag off the cigarette and wondering how she understood it so completely, and why she was so certain that they—Aaron and Michael—did not.

The conviction remained with her.

Flipping quickly through the folders, she sized up the manuscript, the way she always did the scientific texts she wanted to devour in one sitting, and then she scanned one page at random for the proportion of abstractions to concrete words, and found it very comfortable, the latter outnumbering the former to an extremely high degree.

A snap to cover this in four hours. With luck, Michael would sleep that long. The world would sleep. She snuggled back on the couch, put her bare feet against the rim of the coffee table, and began to read.

At nine o'clock, she walked slowly back First Street until she reached the corner of Chestnut. The morning sun was already high in the sky, and the birds were singing almost furiously in the leafy canopy of branches overhead. The sharp caw of a crow cut through the softer chorus. Squirrels scurried along the thick heavy branches that reached out low and far over the fences and the brick walls. The clean swept brick sidewalks were deserted; and the whole place seemed to belong to its flowers, its trees, and its houses. Even the noise of the occasional traffic was swallowed by the engulfing stillness and greenness. The clean blue sky shone through the web of overhead foliage, and the light even in the shade seemed somehow bright and pure.

Aaron Lightner was already waiting for her at the gate, a small-boned man in light, tropical clothing, with a prim British look to him, even to the walking stick in his hand.

She had called him at eight and asked for this appointment, and she could see even from a distance that he was deeply worried about her reaction to what she'd read.

She took her time crossing the intersection. She approached him slowly, her eyes lowered, her mind still swimming with the long story and all the detail which she'd so quickly absorbed.

When she found herself standing in front of him, she took his hand. She had not rehearsed what she meant to say. It would be an ordeal for her. But it felt good to be here, to be holding his hand, pressing it warmly, as she studied the expression on his open and agreeable face.

"Thank you," she said, her voice sounding weak and inadequate to her. "You've answered all the worst and most tormenting questions of my life. In fact, you can't know what you've done for me. You and your watchers—they found the darkest part of me; and you knew what it was, and you turned a light on it—and you connected it to something greater and older, and just as real." She shook her head, still holding his hand, struggling to continue. "I don't know how to say what I want to say," she confessed. "I'm not alone anymore! I mean me, all of me, not merely the name and the part that the family wants. I mean who I am." She sighed. The words were so clumsy, and the feelings behind them so enormous, as enormous as her relief. "I thank you," she said, "that you didn't keep your secrets. I thank you from the bottom of my heart."

She could see his amazement, and his faint confusion. Slowly he nodded. And she felt his goodness, and above all his willingness to trust.

"What can I do for you now?" he asked, with total and disarming candor.

"Come inside," she said. "Let's talk."

Thirty

ELEVEN O'CLOCK. He sat up in the dark, staring at the digital clock on the table. How ever did he sleep that long? He'd left the drapes open so the light would wake him. But somebody had closed them. And his gloves? Where were his gloves? He found them and slipped them on, and then climbed out of bed.

The briefcase was gone. He knew it before he looked behind the chair. Foiled.

At once he put on his robe and walked down the little hallway to the living room. No one here. Just the scorched smell of old coffee coming from the kitchen, and the lingering perfume of a cigarette. Made him want one immediately.

And there on the coffee table, the empty sack of a briefcase, and the file—manila folders in two neat stacks.

"Ah Rowan," he groaned. And Aaron was never going to forgive him. And Rowan had read the part about Karen Garfield and Dr. Lemle dying after they had seen her. She'd read all the delicious gossip gleaned over the years from Ryan Mayfair and from Bea and from others whom she had most surely met at the funeral. That, and a thousand other things he couldn't even think of at the moment.

If he went into the bedroom and discovered that all her clothes were gone . . . But her clothes weren't here anyway, they were in her room.

He stood there scratching his head, uncertain what to do first—ring her room, call Aaron, or go screaming crazy. And then he saw the note.

It was right beside the two stacks of manila folders—a single sheet of hotel stationery covered in a very clear, straight hand.

Eight thirty A.M.
Michael,
Read the file. I love you. Don't worry. Going to nine o'clock appointment with Aaron. Can you meet me at the house at three o'clock? I need some time alone there. I'll

be looking for you around three. If not, leave word for me here.

The Witch of Endor

"The Witch of Endor." Who was the Witch of Endor? Ah, the woman to whom King Saul had gone to conjure the faces of his ancestors? Don't overinterpret. It means she has survived the file. The whiz kid. The brain surgeon. Read the file! It had taken him two days. Read the file!

He peeled off his right glove and laid his hand on the note. Flash of Rowan, dressed, bending over the desk in the little room off this parlor. Then a flash of someone who'd put the stationery here days ago, a uniformed maid, and other foolish things, cascading in, none of which mattered. He lifted his fingers, waited until the tingling stopped. "Give me Rowan," he said, and touched the paper again. Rowan and Rowan not angry, but deeply secretive and . . . what? In the midst of an adventure?

Yes, what he was sensing was a strange, defiant excitement. And this he understood perfectly. He saw her again, with shocking clarity, only it was someplace else, and at once the image was confused, and then he lost it, and he put back on the glove.

He sat there for a moment, drawing back into himself, instinctively hating this power, yet thinking about the question of excitement. He remembered what Aaron had told him last night. "I can teach you how to use it; but it will never be precise; it will always be confusing." God, how he hated it. Hated even the sharp sense of Rowan that had invaded him and wouldn't leave him; he would have much preferred the visceral memories of the bedroom and her lovely deep grosgrain voice speaking to him so softly and honestly and simply. Much preferred to hear it from her own lips. Excitement!

He called Room Service.

"Send me a big breakfast, Eggs Benedict, grits, yeah, a big bowl of grits, extra side of ham, toast, and a full pot of coffee. And tell the waiter to use his key. I'll be getting dressed, and add a twenty percent tip for the waiter, please, and bring me some cold cold water."

He read the note again. Aaron and Rowan were together now. This filled him with apprehension. And now he understood how fearful Aaron had been when he himself had begun to read the materials. And he hadn't wanted to listen to Aaron. He had wanted to read. Well, he couldn't blame Rowan.

He couldn't shake this uneasiness either. She didn't understand Aaron. And he certainly didn't understand her. And she

737

thought he was naive. He shook his head. And then there was Lasher. What did Lasher think?

Last night, before he'd left Oak Haven, Aaron had said, "It was the man. I saw him in the headlights. I knew it was a trick, but I couldn't chance it."

"So what are you going to do?" Michael had asked.

"Be careful," said Aaron. "What else can I do?"

And now she wanted him to meet her at the house at three o'clock, because she needed some time alone there. With Lasher? How was he going to put a lid on his emotions until three o'clock?

Well, you're in New Orleans, aren't you, old buddy? You haven't been back to the old neighborhood. Maybe it's time to go.

He left the hotel at eleven forty-five, the engulfing warm air surprising and delighting him as he stepped outside. After thirty years in San Francisco, he had been braced for the chill and the wind reflexively.

And as he walked in the direction of uptown, he found he had been braced for a hill climb or hill descent in the same subconscious fashion. The flat wide pavements felt wonderful to him. It was as if everything was easier—every breath he took of the warm breeze, every step, the crossing of the street, the gentle looking around at the mature black-barked oaks that changed the cityscape as soon as he had crossed Jackson Avenue. No wind cutting his face, no glare of the Pacific coast sky blinding him.

He chose Philip Street for the walk out to the Irish Channel, and moved slowly as he would have in the old days, knowing the heat would get worse, that his clothes would get heavy, and that even the insides of his shoes would become moist after a little while, and he'd take off this khaki safari jacket sooner or later and sling it over his shoulder.

But he soon forgot about all that; this was the landscape of too many happy memories. It drew him away from worrying about Rowan; it drew him away from worrying about the man; and he was just sliding back into the past, drifting by the old ivy-covered walls, and the young crepe myrtles growing thin and weedy and full of big floppy blossoms. He had to slap them back as he went on. And it came to him again, as strongly as it had before, that longing had embellished nothing. Thank God so much was still here! The tall Queen Anne Victorians, so much larger than those of San Francisco, were still standing right beside the earlier antebellum houses with their masonry walls and columns, as sturdy and magnificent as the house on First Street.

At last, he crossed Magazine, wary of the speeding traffic,

and moved on into the Irish Channel. The houses seemed to shrink; columns gave way to posts; the oaks were no more; even the giant hackberry trees didn't go beyond the corner of Constance Street. But that was all right, that was just fine. This was his part of town. Or at least it had been.

Annunciation Street broke his heart. The fine renovations and fresh paint jobs he had glimpsed on Constance and Laurel were few and far between on this neglected street. Garbage and old tires littered the empty lots. The double cottage in which he'd grown up was abandoned, with big slabs of weathered plywood covering all its doors and windows; and the yard in which he'd played was now a jungle of weeds, enclosed by an ugly chain-link fence. He saw nothing of the old four o'clocks which had bloomed pink and fragrant summer and winter; and gone were the banana trees by the old shed at the end of the side alley. The little corner grocery was padlocked and deserted. And the old corner bar showed not the slightest sign of life.

Gradually he realized he was the only white man to be seen.

He walked on deeper it seemed into the sadness and the shabbiness. Here and there was a nicely painted house; a pretty black child with braided hair and round quiet eyes clung to the gate, staring up at him. But all the people he might have known were long gone.

And the dreary decay of Jackson Avenue at this point hurt him to see it. Yet on he walked, towards the brick tenements of the St. Thomas Project. No white people lived in there anymore. No one had to tell him that.

This was the black man's town back here now, and he felt cold appraising eyes on him as he turned down Josephine Street towards the old churches and the old school. More boarded-up wooden cottages; the lower floor of a tenement completely gutted. Ripped and swollen furniture piled at a curb.

In spite of what he had seen before, the decay of the abandoned school buildings shocked him. There was glass broken out from the windows of the rooms in which he'd studied in those long-ago years. And there, the gymnasium he had helped to build appeared so worn, so past its time, so utterly forgotten.

Only the churches of St. Mary's and St. Alphonsus stood proud and seemingly indestructible. But their doors were locked. And in the sacristy yard of St. Alphonsus, the weeds grew up to his knees. He could see the old electrical boxes open and rusted, the fuses torn out.

"Ya wanna see the church?"

He turned. A small balding man with a rounded belly and a

sweating pink face was talking to him. "Ya can go in the rectory and they'll take ya in," the man said.

Michael nodded.

Even the rectory was locked. You had to ring a bell and wait for the buzzer; and the little woman with the thick glasses and the short brown hair spoke through a glass.

He drew out a handful of twenty-dollar bills. "Let me make a donation," he said. "I'd love to see both churches if I could."

"You can't see St. Alphonsus," she said. "It isn't used now. It isn't safe. The plaster's falling."

The plaster! He remembered the glorious murals on the ceiling, the saints peering down at him from a blue sky. Under that roof, he had been baptized, made his First Communion, and later Confirmation. And that last night here, he had walked down the aisle of St. Alphonsus in his white cap and gown, with the other high school graduates, not even thinking to take a last slow look around because he was excited to be going with his mother out west.

"Where did they all go?" he asked.

"Moved away," she said, as she beckoned for him to follow her. She was taking him through the priest house itself into St. Mary's. "And the colored don't come."

"But why is it all locked?"

"We've had one robbery after another."

He couldn't conceive of it, not being able to wander into a quiet, shadowy church at any hour. Not being able to escape the noisy sun-cooked street, and sit in the dim light, talking to the angels and the saints, while old women in flowered dresses and straw hats knelt whispering with dried lips their rosaries.

She led him through the sanctuary. He had been an altar boy here. He had prepared the sacramental wine. He felt a little throb of happiness when he saw the rows and rows of wooden saints, when he saw the long high nave with its successive Gothic arches. All splendid, all intact.

Thank God this was still standing. He was getting choked up. He shoved his hands in his pockets and lowered his head, only looking up slowly under his brows. His memories of Masses here and Masses across the street at St. Alphonsus mingled completely. There had been no German-Irish quarrel by his time, just all the German and Irish names jumbled together. And the grammar school had used the other church for morning Mass. The high school had filled up St. Mary's.

It took no imagination to see again the uniformed students filing out of the rows to go to Communion. Girls in white blouses and blue wool skirts, boys in their khaki shirts and trousers. But memory scanned all the years; when he was eight years old he'd swung the smoking incense here, on these steps, for Benediction.

"Take your time," the little woman said. "Just come back through the rectory when you're finished."

For a half hour he sat in the first pew. He did not know precisely what he was doing. Memorizing, perhaps, the details he could not have called forth from his recollections. Never to forget again the names carved in the marble floor of those buried under the altar. Never to forget perhaps the painted angels high above. Or the window far to his right in which the angels and the saints wore wooden shoes! How curious. Could anyone now have explained such a thing? And to think he'd never noticed it before, and when he thought of all those hours spent in this church . . .

Think of Marie Louise with her big breasts beneath the starched white uniform blouse, reading her missal at Mass. And Rita Mae Dwyer, who had looked like a grown woman at fourteen. She wore very high heels and huge gold earrings with her red dress on Sunday. Michael's father had been one of the men who moved down the aisles with the collection basket on its long stick, thrusting it into row after row, face appropriately solemn. You did not even whisper in a Catholic church in those days unless you had to.

What did he think, that they would have all been here, waiting for him? A dozen Rita Maes in flowered dresses, making a noon visit?

Last night, Rita Mae had said, "Don't go back there, Mike. Remember it the way it used to be."

Finally he climbed to his feet. He wandered up the aisle towards the old wooden confessionals. He found the plaque on the wall listing those who had in the recent past paid for restoration. He closed his eyes, and just for a moment imagined he heard children playing in the school yards—the noontime roar of mingled voices.

There was no such sound. No heavy swish of the swinging doors as the parishioners came and went. Only the solemn empty place. And the Virgin under her crown on the high altar.

Small, far away, the image seemed. And it occurred to him intellectually that he ought to pray to it. He ought to ask the Virgin or God why he had been brought back here, what it meant that he'd been snatched from the cold grip of death. But he had no belief in the images on the altar. No memory of childlike belief came back to him.

Instead the memory that came was specific and uncomfortable, and shabby and mean. He and Marie Louise had met to exchange secrets right inside one of these tall front doors. In the pouring rain it had been. And Marie Louise had confessed, reluctantly, that no, she wasn't pregnant, angry for being made to confess it, angry that he was so relieved. "Don't you want to get married? Why are we playing these stupid games!"

What would have happened to him if he had married Marie Louise? He saw her big, sullen brown eyes again. He felt her sourness, her disappointment. He could not imagine such a thing.

Marie Louise's voice came back again. "You know you're going to marry me sooner or later. We're meant for each other."

Meant. Had he been meant to leave here, meant to do the things he'd done in his life, meant to travel so far? Meant to fall from the rock into the sea and drift slowly out, away from all the lights of land?

He thought of Rowan—not merely of the visual image, but of everything Rowan was to him now. He thought of her sweetness and sensuality, and mystery, of her lean taut body snuggled against his under the covers, of her velvety voice and her cold eyes. He thought of the way she looked at him before they made love, so unself-conscious, forgetting her own body completely, absorbed in his body. In sum, looking at him the way a man looked at a woman. Just as hungry and just as aggressive and yet yielding so magically in his arms.

He was still staring at the altar—staring at the whole vast and gorgeously ornamented church.

He wished he could believe in something. And then he realized that he did. He still believed in his visions, in the goodness of the visions. He believed in them and their goodness as surely as people believed in God or saints, or the God-given rightness of a certain path, as truly as they believed in a vocation.

And this seemed as foolish as the other beliefs. "But I saw, but I felt, but I remember, but I know . . ." So much stammering. After all he still couldn't remember. Nothing in the entire Mayfair history had really brought him back to those precious moments, except the image of Deborah, and for all his certainty that she had been the one who had come to him, he had no real details, no truly remembered moments or words.

On impulse, his eyes still fixed on the altar, he made the sign of the cross.

How many years had it been since he'd done that every day, three times a day? Curiously, thoughtfully, he did it again. "In the Name of the Father, and of the Son, and of the Holy Ghost," his eyes still fixed on the Virgin.

"What do they want of me?" he whispered. And trying to reinvoke what little he could of the visions, he realized in despair that the image of the dark-haired woman he had seen was now replaced by the descriptive image of Deborah in the history. One had blotted out the other! He had lost through his reading, not gained.

After a little while more, of standing there in silence, his gloved hands shoved in his pockets, he went slowly back down the aisle, until he had come to the altar rail, and then he walked up the marble steps, crossed the sanctuary, and found his way out through the priest house.

The sun was beating down on Constance Street the way it always had. Merciless and ugly. No trees here. And the garden of the priest house hidden behind its high brick wall, and the lawn beside St. Mary's burned and tired and dusty.

The holy store on the far corner, with all its pretty little statues and holy pictures, was no more. Boards on the windows. A real estate sign on the painted wooden wall.

The little bald man with the sweaty red face sat on the rectory steps, his arms folded on his knees, eyes following a gust of gray-winged pigeons as they flew up the dreary peeling façade of St. Alphonsus.

"They oughtta poison them birds," he said. "They dirty up everything."

Michael lighted a cigarette, offered one to the man. The man took it with a nod. Michael gave him the near empty matchbook.

"Son, why don't you take off that gold watch and slip it inside your pocket?" the man said. "Don't walk around here with that thing on your wrist, ya hear?"

"They want my watch," Michael said, "they're gonna take my wrist with it, and the fist that's attached to it."

The old man just shrugged and shook his head.

Up on the corner of Magazine and Jackson Michael went in a dark, evil-looking bar, in the sorriest old sagging wooden clapboard building. In all his years in San Francisco, he had never seen such a run-down place. A white man hung like a shadow at the far end, staring at him with glittering eyes out of a cracked and caved-in face. The bartender too was white.

"Give me a beer," Michael said.

"What kind?"

"I don't give a damn."

He timed it perfectly. At three minutes before three he was crossing Camp Street, walking slowly, so the heat would not kill him, and soothed once more by the sweet shade and random

743

beauty of the Garden District. Yes, all this was as it had always been. And at once he felt good; at once he felt he was where he wanted to be, and maybe even where he ought to be, if one could chart a course of one's own.

At three P.M. exactly he stood at the open gate. This was the first time he had seen the house in the sunlight, and his pulse quickened. *Here, yes.* Even in its neglect it was dignified, grand, merely slumbering beneath the overhanging vines, its long shutters caked with flaking green paint yet still hanging straight on their iron hinges. Waiting . . .

A giddiness overtook him as he looked at it, a swift delight that for whatever reasons, he had come back. *Doing what I am supposed to be doing . . .*

He went up the marble steps, and pushed at the door, and when it opened he walked into the long broad hallway. Never in San Francisco had he been in such a structure, had he stood under such a high ceiling, or looked at doorways so graceful and tall.

A deep luster clung to the heart pine boards in spite of the margin of sticky dust that ran along the walls. Paint flaked from the high crown moldings but they themselves were sound. He felt love for everything he saw—love for the workmanship of the tapering keyhole doorways, and the fine newel post and balusters of the long stairway. He liked the feel of the floor beneath his feet, so solid. And the warm good wood smell of the house filled him with a sudden welcome contentment. A house smelled like this in only one place in the whole world.

"Michael? Come in, Michael."

He walked to the first of the two living room doors. Dark and shadowy still, though she had opened all the drapes. The light was slatted coming through the shutters, and dim and soft pouring through the dirty screens of the porch beyond the side windows. Whiff of honeysuckle. So sweet and good. And was that the Queen's Wreath bursting in little bright pink sprigs along the screens? He had not seen that lovely wild vine in all this time.

She was sitting, small and very pretty, on the long brown velvet couch with its back to the front of the house. Her hair was falling down beautifully against her cheek. She had on one of those loose wrinkled cotton overshirts that is as light as silk, and her face and throat looked darkly tanned against the white T-shirt under it. Legs long in the white pants, her toes naked and surprisingly sexy, with a thin flash of red polish, in her white sandals.

"The Witch of Endor," he said, swooping down to kiss her cheek and hold her face in his left hand, warm, tender.

She took hold of both his wrists, clinging to him, kissing him roughly and sweetly on the mouth. He could feel the tremor in her limbs, the fever in her.

"You've been here all alone?"

She sat back as he took his place beside her.

"And why the hell not?" she asked in her slow deep voice. "I quit the hospital officially this afternoon. I'm going to apply for a job here. I'm going to stay here, in this house."

He let out a long whistling sigh and smiled. "You mean it?"

"Well, what do you think?"

"I don't know. All the way over here . . . coming back from the Irish Channel, I kept thinking maybe you'd be here with your bag packed to go back."

"No. Not a chance. I've already discussed three or four different hospitals here with my old boss in San Francisco. He's making calls for me. But what about you?"

"What do you mean what about me?" he asked. "You know why I'm here. Where am I going to go? They brought me here. They're not telling me to go anyplace else. They're not telling me anything. I still can't remember. I read four hundred pages of the history and I can't remember. It was Deborah I saw, I know that much, but I don't really know what she said."

"You're tired and hot," she said, touching her hand to his forehead. "You're talking crazy."

He gave a little surprised laugh. "Listen to you," he said, "the Witch of Endor. Didn't you read the history? What's going on, Rowan? Didn't you read all that? We're in a big spiderweb, and we don't know who's done the weaving." He held out his gloved hands, looking down at his fingers. "We just don't know."

She gave him a quiet, remote look, which made her face seem very cold, even though it was flushed, and her gray eyes were picking up the light wonderfully.

"Well, you read it, didn't you? What did you think when you read it? What did you think?"

"Michael, calm down," she said. "You're not asking me what I think. You're asking me what I feel. I've been telling you what I think. We're not stuck in any web, and nobody's doing the weaving. And you want my advice? Forget about them. Forget about what they want, these people you saw in your visions. Forget them from now on."

"What do you mean 'forget'?"

"OK, listen to me. I've been sitting here thinking for hours, thinking about it all. This is my decision. I'm staying here, and I'm staying here because this is my house and I like it. And I like the family I met yesterday. I like them. I want to know them. I want to hear their voices and know their faces, and learn what they have to teach. And also, I know I wouldn't be able to forget that old woman and what I did to her no matter where I went.'' She stopped, a flash of sudden emotion transfiguring her face for a second, then gone again, leaving it taut and cool. She folded her arms lightly, one foot up on the edge of the small coffee table. "Are you listening?"

"Yeah, of course."

"OK, I want you to stay here, too. I hope and pray you will stay here. But not because of this pattern or this web or whatever it is. Not because of these visions or because of the man. Because there is absolutely no way to figure out what these things mean, Michael, or what's meant, to use the word you wrote in your notes, or why you and I were thrown together. There is no way to know."

She paused, her eyes scanning him intently. Then she went on:

"So I've made my decision," she said, her words coming more slowly, "based on what I can know, and what I can see, and what I can define and understand, and that is, that this place is where I belong, because I want to belong."

He nodded. "I hear you," he said.

"What I'm saying is that I'm staying here in spite of this man and this seeming pattern, this coincidence of me pulling you up out of the ocean and you being what you are."

He nodded again, a little hesitantly, and then sat back taking a deep breath, his eyes not letting go of hers. "But you can't tell me," he said, "that you don't want to communicate with this thing, that you don't want to understand the meaning of all this . . ."

"I do want to understand," she said. "I do. But that wouldn't keep me here by itself. Besides, it doesn't matter to this being whether or not we're in Montcleve, France, or Tiburon, California, or Donnelaith, Scotland. And as for what matters to those beings you saw, they're going to have to come back and tell you what matters! You don't know."

She paused, deliberately and obviously trying to soften her words as if she feared she'd become too sharp.

"Michael," she said, "if you want to stay, make up your mind based on something else. Like maybe wanting to be here for me or because it's where you were born, or because you think you'd be happy here. Because it was the first place you loved, this neighborhood, and maybe you could love it again."

"I never stopped loving it."

746

"But don't do anything else to give in to them! Do things in spite of them."

"Rowan, I'm here now in this room because of them. Don't lose sight of that fact. We did not meet at the yacht club, Rowan."

She let out a long breath.

"I insist on losing sight of it," she said.

"Did Aaron talk to you about all this? Was this his advice to you?"

"I didn't ask him for his advice," she said patiently. "I met with him for two reasons. Firstly, I wanted to talk with him again, and confirm for myself that he was an honest man."

"And?"

"He's everything you said he was. But I had to see him again, really talk to him." She paused. "He's a bit of a spellbinder, that man."

"I know."

"I felt this when I saw him at the funeral; and there was the other time, when I met him at Ellie's grave."

"And you feel all right about him now?"

She nodded. "I know him now," she said. "He's not so different from you and me."

"How do you mean?"

"He's dedicated," she said. She gave a little shrug. "Just the way I'm a dedicated surgeon, and you're dedicated when you're bringing a house like this back to life." She thought for a minute. "He has illusions, the way you and I have illusions."

"I understand."

"The second thing was—I wanted to tell him that I was grateful for what he'd given me in the history. That he didn't have to worry about resentment or a breach of confidence from me."

He was so relieved that he didn't interrupt her, but he was puzzled.

"He filled in the largest and the most crucial blank in my life," she said. "I don't think even he understands what it meant to me. He's too wary. And he doesn't really know about loneliness. He's been with the Talamasca ever since he was a boy."

"I know what you mean. But I think he does understand."

"But still he's wary. This thing—this charming brown-haired apparition, or whatever he is—really tried to hurt him, you know."

"I know."

"But I tried to make him understand how grateful I was. That wasn't challenging him in any way. Two days ago I was a person without a past or a family. And now I have both of those things. The most agonizing questions of my life have been answered. I don't think the full meaning of it has really sunk in. I keep thinking of my house in Tiburon and each time I realize 'You don't have to go back there, you don't have to be alone there anymore.' And it's a wonderful shock all over again.''

"I never dreamed you'd respond that way. I have to confess. I thought you'd be angry, maybe even offended.''

"Michael, I don't care what Aaron did to get the information. I don't care what his colleagues did, or what they've done all along. The point is, the information wouldn't be there in any form whatsoever if he hadn't collected it. I'd be left with that old woman, and the vicious things she said. And all the shiny-faced cousins, smiling and offering sympathy, and incapable of telling the whole story because they don't know it. They only know little glittering parts.'' She took a deep breath. ''You know, Michael, some people can't receive gifts. They don't know how to claim them and make use of them. I have to learn how to receive gifts. This house is a gift. The history was a gift. And the history makes it possible for me to accept the family! And God, they are the greatest gift of all.''

Again he was relieved, profoundly relieved. Her words held a charm for him. Nevertheless he could not get over his surprise.

"What about the part of the file on Karen Garfield?'' he asked. "And Dr. Lemle? I was so afraid for you, reading that.''

The flash of pain in her face this time was stronger, brighter. Instantly he regretted his bluntness. It seemed suddenly unforgivable to have blurted out these words.

"You don't understand me,'' she said, her voice as even as before. ''You don't understand the kind of person I am. I wanted to know whether or not I had that power! I went to you because I thought if you touched me with your hands you could tell me if this power was really there. Well, you couldn't. But Aaron has told me. Aaron has confirmed it. And nothing, nothing could be worse than suspecting it and being unsure.''

"I see.''

"Do you?'' She swallowed, her face working hard suddenly to preserve its expression of tranquillity. And then her eyes went dull for a moment, and only brightened again with an obvious act of will. In a dry whisper, she said, ''I hate what happened to Karen Garfield. I hate it. Lemle? Lemle was sick already. He'd had a stroke the year before. I don't know about Lemle, but Karen Garfield . . . that was my doing, all right, and Michael, it was because I didn't know!''

"I understand,'' he said softly.

For a long moment, she struggled silently to regain her composure. When she spoke again, her voice was weary and a little frayed.

"There was still another reason I had to see Aaron."

"What?"

She thought for a moment, then:

"I'm not in communication with this spirit, and that means I can't control it. It hasn't revealed itself to me, not really. And it may not."

"Rowan, you've already seen it, and besides—it's waiting for you."

She was pondering, her hand playing idly with a little thread on the edge of her shirt.

"I'm hostile to it, Michael," she said. "I don't like it. And I think it knows. I've been sitting here for hours alone, inviting it to come, yet hating it, fearing it."

Michael puzzled over this for a moment.

"It may have overplayed its hand," she said.

"You mean, the way it touched you . . ."

"No. I mean in *me*, it may have overplayed its hand. It may have helped to create the very medium who can't be seduced by it, or driven crazy by it. Michael, if I could kill a flesh and blood human being with this invisible power of mine, what do you think my hostility feels like to Lasher?"

He narrowed his eyes, studying her. "I don't know," he confessed.

Her hand shook just a little as she swept her hair back out of her face, the sunlight catching it for one moment and making it truly blond.

"My dislikes run very deep. They always have. They don't change with time. I feel an inveterate dislike for this thing. Oh, I remember what you said last night, about wanting to talk to it, reason with it, learn what it wants. But the dislike is what's strongest right now."

Michael watched her for a long silent moment. He felt a curious, near inexplicable, quickening of his love for her.

"You know, you're right in what you said before," he said. "I don't really understand you, or what kind of person you are. I love you, but I don't understand you."

"You think with your heart," she said, touching his chest gently with her left fist. "That's what makes you so good. And so naive. But I don't do that. There's an evil in me equal to the evil in people around me. They seldom surprise me. Even when they make me angry."

He didn't want to argue with her. But he was not naive!

"I've been thinking for hours about all this," she said. "About this power to rupture blood vessels and aortas and bring about death as if with a whispered curse. If this power I have is good for anything, maybe it's good for destroying this entity. Maybe it can act on the energy controlled by him as surely as it acts upon flesh and blood cells."

"That never even crossed my mind before."

"That's why we have to think for ourselves," she said. "I'm a doctor, first and foremost. Only a woman and a person, second. And as a doctor, it's perfectly easy for me to see that this entity is existing in some continuous relationship with our physical world. It's knowable, what this being is. Knowable the way the secret of electricity was knowable in the year 700 though no one knew it."

He nodded. "Its parameters. You used that word last night. I keep wondering about its parameters. If it's solid enough when it materializes for me to touch it."

"Right. Exactly. What is it when it materializes? I have to learn its parameters. And my power also works according to the rules of our physical world. And I have to learn the parameters of my power, too."

The pain came back into her face, again like a flash of light, somehow distorting her expression, and then broadening until her smooth face threatened to rumple like that of a doll in a flame. Only gradually did she go blank again, calm and pretty and silent. Her voice was a whisper when she resumed.

"That's my cross, the power. Just as your cross is the power in your hands. We'll learn to control these things, so that we decide when and where to use them."

"Yeah, that's exactly what we have to do."

"I want to tell you something about that old woman, Carlotta, and about the power . . ."

"You don't have to, if you don't want to."

"She knew I was going to do it to her. She foresaw it, and then she calculatedly provoked me. I could swear she did."

"Why?"

"Part of her scheme. I go back and forth thinking about it. Maybe she meant to break me, break my confidence. She always used guilt to hurt Deirdre, and she used it probably with Antha. But I'm not going to get drawn into the lengthy pondering of her scheme. This is the wrong thing for us to do now, talk about them and what they want—Lasher, the visions, that old woman—they've drawn a bunch of circles for us and I don't want to walk in circles."

"Yeah, do I ever know what you mean."

He let go of her eyes slowly, and rummaged in his pocket for his cigarettes. Three left. He offered her one, but she shook her head. She was watching him.

"Some day, we can sit at the table," she said, "drink white wine together, beer, whatever, and talk about them. Talk about Petyr van Abel, and about Charlotte, and about Julien and all that. But not now. Now I want to separate the worthy from the unworthy, the substantial from the mystical. And I wish you would do the same thing."

"I follow you," he said. He searched for his matches. Ah, no matches. Gave them to that old man.

She slipped her hand in her pants pocket, drew out a slender gold lighter, and lighted his cigarette.

"Thanks," he said.

"Whenever we do focus on them," she said, "the effect is always the same. We become passive and confused."

"You're right," he said. He was thinking about all the time he'd spent in the darkened bedroom on Liberty Street, trying to remember, trying to understand. But here he was in this house at last and except for two instances last night—when he'd touched Townsend's remains and when he'd touched the emerald—he hadn't removed the gloves. The mere thought of it scared him. Touching the door frames and the tables and the chairs that had belonged to the Mayfairs, touching the older things, the trunk of dolls in the attic, which Rowan had described to him, and the jars, those stinking jars . . .

"We become passive and confused," she said again, commanding his attention, "and we don't think for ourselves, which is exactly what we must do."

"I agree with you," he said. "I only wish I had your calmness. I wish I could know all these half truths and not go spinning off into the darkness trying to figure things out."

"Don't be a pawn in somebody's game," she said. "Find the attitude which gives you the maximum strength and the maximum dignity, no matter what else is going on."

"You mean strive to be perfect," he said.

"What?"

"You said in California that you thought we should all aim to be perfect."

"Yes, I did, didn't I? Well, I believe that. I'm trying to figure the perfect thing to do. So don't act like I'm a freak if I don't burst into tears, Michael. Don't think I don't know what I did to Karen Garfield or Dr. Lemle, or that little girl. I know. I really do."

"I didn't mean—"

"Oh, yeah, you did too," she said with slight sharpness. "Don't like me better when I cry than when I don't."

"Rowan, I didn't—"

"I cried for a year before I met you. I started crying when Ellie died. And then I cried in your arms. I cried when the call came from New Orleans that Deirdre was dead, and I'd never even known her or spoken to her or laid eyes on her. I cried and I cried. I cried when I saw her in the coffin yesterday. I cried for her last night. And I cried for that old woman, too. Well, I don't want to go on crying. What I have here is the house, the family, and the history Aaron has given me. I have you. A real chance with you. And what is there to cry about, I'd like to know."

She was glaring at him, obviously sizzling with anger and with the conflict in herself, gray eyes flashing at him in the half light.

"You're gonna make me cry, Rowan, if you don't stop," he said.

She laughed in spite of herself. Her face softened beautifully, her mouth twisting unwillingly into a smile.

"All right," she said. "And there is one thing more that could make me cry. I should tell you that, in order to be perfectly truthful. And that is . . . I'd cry if I lost you."

"Good," he whispered. He kissed her quickly before she could stop him.

She made a little gesture for him to sit back, to stay serious, and to listen. He nodded and shrugged.

"Tell me—what do *you* want to do? I mean what do you *want* to do? I'm not talking about what these beings want you to do. What's inside you now?"

"I want to stay here," he said. "I wish to hell I hadn't stayed away so long. I don't know why I did."

"OK, now you're talking," she said. "You're talking about something real."

"No doubt about it," he said. "I've been walking—back there, in the old streets, where I grew up. It's not the old neighborhood now. It was never beautiful, but it's squalid and ruined and . . . all gone."

He saw the concern in her eyes immediately.

"Yeah, well it's changed," he said with a little weary and accepting gesture. "But New Orleans never was just that neighborhood to me. It was never Annunciation Street. It was here, the Garden District, and it was uptown, it was down in the French Quarter, it was all the other beautiful parts. And I love it. And I'm glad I'm back here. I don't want to leave again."

"OK," she said. She smiled, the light glinting on the curve of her cheek and the edge of her mouth.

"You know, I kept thinking, I'm home. I'm home. And no matter what does happen with all the rest—I don't want to leave home."

"The hell with them, Michael," she said. "The hell with them, whoever they are, until they give us some reason to feel otherwise."

"Well put," he said. He smiled.

How mysterious she was, such a baffling mixture of sharpness and softness. Maybe his mistake was that he had always confused strength and coldness in women. Maybe most men did.

"They'll come to us again," she said. "They have to. And when they do, then we'll think and we'll decide what to do."

"Yeah, right," he said. And what if I took off the gloves? Would they come to me now?

"But we're not holding our breath until then."

"No." He gave a little laugh.

He grew quiet, filled with excitement, and yet filled with worry though every word she spoke gladdened him and made him feel that this anxiety would lift any second.

He found himself looking off to the mirror at the far end of the room, and seeing their tiny reflection there, and the repeated chandeliers, caught in the two mirrors, marching on, countless, in a blur of silver light, to eternity.

"Do you like loving me?" she asked.

"What?"

"Do you like it?" Her voice had a decided tremor in it for the first time.

"Yeah, I love loving you. But it's scary, because you aren't like anyone else I've ever known. You're so strong."

"Yes, I am," she said thickly. "Because I could kill you right now if I wanted to. All your manly strength wouldn't do you any good."

"No, that isn't what I meant," he said. He turned and looked at her, and for one moment in the shadows her face looked unspeakably cold and cunning, with her eyelids at half mast, and her eyes gleaming. She looked malicious the way she had for one instant in the house in Tiburon in the cold light coming through the glass into a darkened room.

She sat up slowly, with a soft rustle of cloth, and he found himself shrinking from her, instinctively, every hair standing on end. It was the hard wariness you feel when you see a snake in the grass two inches from your shoe, or you realize the man on the next bar stool has just turned towards you and opened a switchblade knife.

"What the hell's the matter with you?" he whispered.

But then he saw. He saw she was shaking and her cheeks were blotched with pink yet deathly white, and her hands reached out for him and then shrank back and she looked at them and then clasped them together, as if trying to contain something unspeakable. "God, I didn't even hate Karen Garfield," she whispered. "I didn't! So help me God, I . . ."

"No, it was all a mistake," he said, "a terrible mistake, and you won't ever make that mistake again."

"No, never," she said. "Even with that old woman, I swear, I didn't really believe it."

Desperately he wanted to help her but he didn't know what to do. She was quivering like a flame in the shadows, her teeth stabbing her lower lip, her right hand clenching her own left hand cruelly.

"Stop, honey, stop—you're hurting yourself," he said. But she felt like something made of steel, unbending, when he touched her.

"I swear, I didn't believe it. It's like an impulse, you know and you don't really believe you can possibly . . . I was so angry with Karen Garfield. It was outrageous, her coming there, her walking into Ellie's house, so stupidly outrageous!"

"I know, I understand."

"What do I do to neutralize it? Does it come back inside me and burn me from within?"

"No."

She turned away from him, drawing up her knees and peering out into the room dully, a little calmer now, though her eyes were unnaturally wide, and her fingers were still working anxiously.

"I'm surprised you haven't hit upon the obvious answer," she said, "the one that is so clear and so neat."

"What do you mean?"

"Maybe your purpose is simple. It's to kill me."

"God, how could you think of such a thing?" He drew closer to her, brushing her hair back out of her face, and gathering her near to him.

She looked at him as if from a long long distance away.

"Honey, listen to me," he said. "Anybody can take a human life. It's easy. Very easy. There are a million ways. You know ways I don't know because you're a doctor. That woman, Carlotta, small as she was, she killed a man strong enough to strangle her with one hand. When I sleep next to any woman, she

754

can kill me if she wants to. You know that. A scalpel, a hat pin, a bit of lethal poison. It's easy. And we don't do those things, nothing on earth can make most of us ever even think of them, and that's how it's been all your life with you. And now you find you've got a mutant power, something that exceeds the laws of choice and impulse and self-control, something that calls for a more subtle understanding, and you have that understanding. You have the strength to know your own strength.''

She nodded; but she was still shaking all over. And he could tell that she didn't believe him. And in a way, he wasn't sure he believed himself. What was the use of denying it? If she didn't control this power, she would inevitably use it again.

But there was something else he had to say, and it had to do with the visions and the power in his hands.

''Rowan,'' he said, ''you asked me to take off the gloves the first night we met. To hold your hands. I've made love to you without the gloves. Just your body and my body, and our hands touching and my hands touching you all over, and what is it I see, Rowan? What do I feel? I feel goodness and I feel love.''

He kissed her cheek. He kissed her hair and brought it back off her forehead with his hand.

''You're right in many things you've said, Rowan, but not in that. I'm not meant to hurt you. I owe my life to you.'' He turned her head towards him and kissed her, but she was still cold and trembling, and far far beyond his reach.

She took his hands and moved them down and away from her, gently, nodding, and then she kissed him gently, but she didn't want to be touched now. It didn't do any good.

He sat there for a while, thinking, looking at the long ornate room. Looking at the high mirrors in their dark carved frames, and the dusty old Bözendorfer piano at the far end, and the draperies like long streaks of faded color in the gloom.

Then he climbed to his feet. He couldn't sit still any longer. He paced the floor in front of the couch, and found himself at the side window, looking out over the dusty screen porch.

''What did you say a moment ago?'' he asked, turning around. ''You said something about passivity and confusion. Well, this is it, Rowan, the confusion.''

She didn't answer him. She was sitting crouched there, staring at the floor.

He went back to her and gathered her up, off the couch and into his arms. Her cheeks were still splotched with pink, and very pale. Her lashes were dark and long as she looked down.

He pressed his lips against her mouth softly, feeling no resistance, almost no awareness, as if it were the mouth of someone unconscious or deep asleep. Then slowly she came back to life. She slipped her hands up around his neck, and kissed him back.

"Rowan, there is a pattern," he whispered in her ear. "There is a great web and we're in it, but I believe now as I believed then, they were good, the people who brought us together. And what they want of me is good. I gotta figure it out, Rowan. I have to. But I know it's good. Just as I know that you are good, too."

He heard her sigh against him, felt the lift of her warm breasts against his chest. When at last she slipped away, it was with great tenderness, kissing his fingers as she let them go.

She walked out towards the center of the long room. She stood under the high broad archway that divided the space into two parlors, and she looked up at the beautiful carving in the plaster, and at the way the arch curved down to meet the cornices at either end. She seemed to be studying this, to be lost in contemplating the house.

He felt bruised and quiet. The whole exchange had hurt him. He couldn't shake a feeling of misery and suspicion, though it was not suspicion of her.

"Who gives a damn!" she whispered as if she were talking to herself, but she seemed fragile and uncertain.

The dusty sunlight crept in from the screened porch and showed the amber wax on the old boards. The motes of dust swirled around her.

"Talk, talk, talk," she said. "The next move is theirs. You've done everything you could. And so have I. And here we are. And let them come to us."

"Yes, let them come."

She turned to him, inviting him silently to draw closer, her face imploring and almost sad. A split second of dread shocked him, and left him empty. The love he felt for her was so precious to him, and yet he was afraid, actually afraid.

"What are we going to do, Michael?" she said. And suddenly she smiled, a very beautiful and warm smile.

He laughed softly. "I don't know, honey." He shrugged and shook his head. "I don't know."

"You know what I want from you right now?"

"No. But whatever it is, you can have it."

She reached out for his hand. "Tell me about this house," she said, looking up into his eyes. "Tell me everything you know about a house like this, and tell me if it really can be saved."

"Honey, it's just waiting for that, just waiting. It's solid as any castle in Montcleve or Donnelaith."

"Could you do it? I don't mean with your own hands . . ."

"—I'd love to do it with my own hands." He looked at them suddenly, these wretched gloved hands. How long since he'd held a hammer and nails, or the handle of a saw, or laid a plane to wood. And then he looked up at the painted arch above them, at the long sweep of the ceiling with its fractured and peeling paint. "Oh, how I'd love to," he said.

"What if you had carte blanche, what if you could hire anybody and everybody you wanted—plasterers, painters, roofers, people to bring it all back, to restore every nook and cranny . . ."

Her words went on, slow yet exuberant. But he knew everything she was saying, he understood. And he wondered if she could possibly understand all that it really meant to him. To work on a house like this had always been his greatest dream, but it wasn't merely a house like this, it was this house. And back and back he traveled in memory, until he was a boy again, outside at the gate, a boy who went off to the library to pull down off the shelves the old picture books which had this house inside them, this very room and that hallway, because he never dreamed he would see these rooms except in books.

And in the vision the woman had said, *converging upon this very moment in time, in this house, in this crucial moment when . . .*

"Michael? You want to do it?"

Through a veil, he saw her face had lighted up like the face of a child. But she seemed so far away, so brilliant and happy and far away.

Is that you, Deborah?

"Michael, take off the gloves," Rowan said, her sudden sharpness startling him. "Go back to work! Go back to being you. For fifty years nobody's been happy in this house, nobody's loved in this house, nobody's won! It's time for us to love here and to win here, it's time for us to win the house back itself. I knew that when I finished the File on the Mayfair Witches. Michael, this is our house."

But you can alter . . . Never think for a moment that you do not have the power, for the power derives from . . .

"Michael, answer me."

Alter what? Don't leave me like this. Tell me!

But they were gone, just as if they'd never come near, and here he stood, with Rowan, in the sunshine and on the warm amber-colored floor, and she was waiting for him to answer.

And the house waited, the beautiful house, beneath its layers of rust and soil, beneath its shadows and its tangled ragged vines, and in its heat and its dampness, it waited.

"Oh, yes, honey, yes," he said as if waking from a dream, his senses flooded suddenly with the fragrance of the honeysuckle on the screens, and the singing of the birds outside, and the warmth of the sun itself coming in on them.

He turned around in the middle of the long room. "The light, Rowan, we have to let in the light. Come on," he said, taking her hand. "Let's see if these old shutters still open."

Thirty-one

QUIETLY, REVERENTLY, THEY began to explore the house. At first it was as if they had crept away from the guards in a museum, and dared not abuse their accidental freedom.

They were too respectful to touch the personal belongings of those who had once lived here. A coffee cup lying on a glass table in the sun room. A magazine folded on a chair.

Rather they traveled the rooms and the hallways, opening the drapes and shutters, merely peeking now and then into closets and cabinets and drawers, with the greatest care.

But slowly, as the shadowy warmth became more and more familiar, they grew bolder.

In the library alone, they browsed for an hour, examining the spines of the leather-bound classics and the old plantation ledgers from Riverbend, saddened when they saw the pages were spongy and ruined. Almost nothing of the old accounts could be read.

They did not touch the papers on the desk which Ryan Mayfair would collect and examine. They studied the framed portraits on the walls.

"That's Julien, it has to be." Darkly handsome, smiling at them as they stood in the hallway. "What is that in the background?" It had darkened so badly Michael couldn't make it out. Then he realized, Julien was standing on the front porch of this house.

"Yes, and there, that old photograph, that's apparently Julien with his sons. The one closest to Julien is Cortland. That's my father.'' Once again, they were grouped on the porch, smiling through the faded sepia, and how cheerful, even vivacious, they seemed.

And what would you see if you touched them, Michael? And how do you know it isn't what Deborah wants you to do?

He turned away quickly. He wanted to follow Rowan. He loved the way Rowan walked, her long loose strides, the way her hair swayed with the rhythm. She turned in the dining room doorway and smiled back at him. Coming?

In the small high-ceilinged pantry, they discovered shelves on top of shelves of gorgeous china: Minton, Lenox, Wedgwood, Royal Doulton—flowered patterns, Oriental patterns, patterns bordered in silver and gold. Old white ware and Oriental porcelain, antique Blue Willow, and old Spode.

There were chests upon chests of sterling, heavy ornate pieces by the hundreds, nestled in felt, including very old sets with the English marks and the initial M in the European style engraved on the back.

Michael was the one who knew such things; his long love affair with Victoriana in all forms stood him well. He could identify the fish knives and the oyster forks and the jelly spoons, and dozens of other tiny special items, of which there were a countless number in a dozen different ornate patterns.

Sterling candlesticks they found, elaborate punch bowls and serving platters, bread plates and butter dishes and old water pitchers, and coffee urns and teapots and carafes. Exquisite chasing. Magically the darkest tarnish gave way to a hard rub of the finger, revealing the old luster of pure silver beneath.

Cut-glass bowls of all sizes were pushed to the back of the cabinets, leaded crystal dishes and plates.

Only the tablecloths and the piles of old napkins were too far gone, the fine linen and lace having rotted in the inevitable damp, the letter M showing proudly still here and there beneath the dark stain of mildew.

Yet even a few of these had been carefully preserved in a dry cedar-lined drawer, wrapped in blue paper. Heavy old lace that had yellowed beautifully. And tumbled among them were napkin rings of bone and silver and gold.

Touch them? Did the MBM stand for Mary Beth Mayfair? And here, here is a ring with the letters JM and you know to whom that must have belonged. He put it back, gloved fingers now as agile as bare fingers, though his hands were hot and uncomfortable, and the cross as she called it was biting into him with its weight.

The late afternoon sun came in long slanting rays through the

759

dining room windows. Look at her again in this setting. Rowan Mayfair. The murals sprang to life, revealing a whole population of little figures lost in the dreamy plantation fields. The great oblong table stood sturdy and fine as it had perhaps for a century. The Chippendale chairs, with their intricately carved backs, lined the walls.

Shall we dine here together soon with high flickering candles? "Yes," she whispered. "Yes!"

Then in the butler's pantry they found the delicate glassware, enough for a royal banquet. They found thin fine-spun goblets and thick-bottomed tumblers etched with flowers—sherry glasses, glasses for brandy, for champagne, for white wine and red wine, and shot glasses, and dessert glasses, and decanters to go with them, with glass stoppers, and crystal cut-glass pitchers, and pretty dishes again, stacks of them, glimmering in the light.

So many treasures, Michael thought, and all of them waiting it seemed for the touch of a wand to bring them back into service.

"I'm dreaming of parties," Rowan said, "of parties like in the old days, of bringing them all together, and piling the table with food. Of Mayfairs and Mayfairs."

Michael gazed in silence at her profile. She held a delicate stem glass in her right hand, letting it catch the fragile sun.

"It's all so graceful, so seductive," she said. "I didn't know life could be the way that it seems here. I didn't know there were houses like this anywhere in America. How strange it all is. I've traveled the whole world, and never been to a place like this. It's as if time forgot this place completely."

Michael couldn't help but smile. "Things change very slowly here," he said. "Thank God for that."

"Yet it's as if I dreamed of these rooms, and of a way of life that can be lived here, and never remembered on waking. But something in me, something in me must have remembered. Something in me felt alien and lost in the world we made out there."

They wandered out into the sunshine together, roaming around the old pool and through the ruined cabana. "This is all solid," Michael explained as he examined the sliding doors, and the washbasin and shower. "It can be repaired. Look, this is built of cypress. And the pipes are copper. Nothing destroys cypress. I could fix that plumbing in a couple of days."

Back into the high grass they walked, where the old outbuildings had once stood. Nothing remained but one lone sad tumbledown wooden structure on the very inside edge of the rear lot.

"Not so bad, not so bad at all," Michael said, peering through the dusty screens. "Probably the menservants lived out here, it's a sort of *garçonniére.*"

Here was the oak tree in which Deirdre had sought refuge, soaring to perhaps eighty feet over their heads. The foliage was dark and dusty and tight with the heat of the summer. It would break into a glorious mint green in the spring. Great clumps of banana trees sprang like monstrous grass in patches of sunlight. And a long beautifully built brick wall stretched across the back of the property, overgrown with ivy and tangled wisteria right to the hinges of the Chestnut Street gates.

"The wisteria is still blooming," Michael said. "I love these purple blossoms—how I used to love to touch them when I went walking, to see the petals shiver."

Why the hell can't you take off the gloves for a moment, just to feel those tender little petals in your hand?

Rowan stood with her eyes closed. Was she listening to the birds? He found himself staring at the long back wing of the main house, at the servants' porches with their white wooden railings and white privacy lattice, and just the sight of this lattice subdued him and made him feel happy. These were all the random colors and textures of home.

Home. As if he had ever lived in such a place. Well, had any wandering observer ever loved it more? And in a way he had always lived in it, it was the place he had longed for when he went away, the place he had dreamed of . . .

You cannot imagine the strength of the assault . . .

"Michael?"

"What is it, honey?" He kissed her, catching the delicious smell of the sun in her hair. The warmth gave a glisten to her skin. But the frisson of the visions lingered. He opened his eyes wide, letting the burnt afternoon light fill them, letting the soft hum of the insects lull him.

tangle of lies . . .

Rowan went before him in the high grass.

"There are flagstones here, Michael." Her voice so thin in the great openness. "All of this is flagstone. It's covered over."

He wandered after her, back into the front garden. They found little Greek statues, cement satyrs beautifully weathered, peeping with blind eyes from beneath the overgrown boxwood; a marble nymph lost in the dark waxen leaf camellias, and the tiny yellow lantana blooming beautifully wherever the sun broke in.

"Bacon and eggs, we called this little flower," he said, picking a sprig of it for her. "See the tiny brown and yellow petals, mingled with the orange. And there, there's the blue kind. And see that flower, that's impatiens, and look, that's hollyhock—the big blue flowers growing by the porch, but we always called it althaea."

"Althaea, that's so lovely."

"That vine there is the Queen's Wreath, or the Coral Wreath, but we called it Rose of Montana."

They could just see the white streak of Deirdre's old rocking chair above the lace of the vines. "They must have trimmed them for her to see out," he said. "See how they've grown up the other side, fighting the bougainvillea? Ah, but it's the queen of the wall, isn't it?"

Almost violent the fluorescent purple bracts that everyone thought were flowers.

"Lord God, how many times did I try to make all this in some little backyard in California, before I turned over the key to the new owner. After I'd hung the Quaker Lace curtains on the windows, and done the floors with Minwax Golden Oak, and found the claw-footed tub from the salvage yard. And here the place looms, the genuine article . . ."

"And it's yours, too," she said. "Yours and mine." How innocent she seemed now, how full of eager sincerity her soft smile.

She wound her arm around him again, squeezed his gloved hand with her naked fingers. "But what if it's all decayed inside, Michael? What would it take to cure everything that's wrong?"

"Come here, stand back here, and look," he said. "See the way the servants' porches run completely straight up there? There's no weakness in the foundation of this house at all. There are no leaks visible on the first floor, no dampness seeping through. Nothing! And in the old days those porches were the hallways by which the servants came and went. That's why there are so many floor-length windows and doors, and by the way every window and door I've tried is level. And the house is all open on this side to catch the river breeze. All over the city, you'll see that, houses open on the river side, to catch the river breeze."

She gazed up at the windows of Julien's old room. Was she thinking again of Antha?

"I can feel the curse lifting from this place," she whispered. "That's what was meant, that you and I should come, and love each other here."

Yes, I believe that, he thought, but somehow or other he didn't say it. Maybe the stillness around him seemed too alive; maybe he was afraid to challenge something unseen that watched and listened.

"All these walls are solid brick, Rowan," he went on, "and some of them as much as twenty inches thick. I measured them with my hands when I walked through the various doorways. Twenty inches thick. They'd been plastered over outside to make the house look like stone because that was the fashion. See the scoring in the paint? To make it look like a villa built of great blocks of stone?

"It's a polyglot," he confessed, "with its cast-iron lace and Corinthian columns and Doric and Ionic columns, and the key-hole doorways—"

"Yeah, keyholes," she said. "And I'll tell you about another place where I saw a doorway like that. It's on the tomb. At the very top of the Mayfair tomb."

"How do you mean at the top?"

"Just the carving of a doorway, like the doorways in this house. I'm sure that's what it was, unless it's really meant to be a keyhole. I'll show you. We can walk over there today or to-morrow. It's right off the main path."

Why did that fill him with uneasiness? A doorway carved on the tomb? He hated graveyards, he hated tombs. But sooner or later he had to see it, didn't he? He went on talking, stifling the feeling, wanting to have the moment and the sight of the house before him, bathed in the lovely sun.

"Then there are those curved Italianate windows on the north side," he said, "and that's another architectural influence. But it's all of a piece, finally. It works because it works. It's built for this climate with its fifteen-foot ceilings. It's a great trap for light and cool breezes, a citadel against the heat."

Slipping her arm around him, she followed him back inside and up the long shadowy stairs.

"See, this plaster is firm," he explained. "It's almost surely the original, but it was done by master craftsmen. They probably ran those crown moldings by hand. There aren't even the minimum cracks you'd expect from settlement. When I get under the house I'm going to find these are chain walls that go clear down to the ground, and that the sills that support this house are enormous. They have to be. Everything is level, firm."

"And I thought it was hopeless when I first saw it."

"Take this old wallpaper down with your imagination," he said. "Paint the walls in your mind's eyes with bright warm colors. See all this woodwork shining white and clean."

"It's ours now," she whispered. "Yours and mine. We're writing the file from now on."

"The File on Rowan and Michael," he said with a faint smile. He paused at the top of the stairs. "Things up here on the second floor are simpler. The ceilings are about a foot lower, and you don't have the ornate crown moldings. It's all a smaller scale."

She laughed and shook her head. "And how high are these smaller rooms, thirteen feet, perhaps?"

They turned and went down the hall to the first bedroom on the very front of the house. Its windows opened both to the front and the side porches. Belle's prayer book lay on the chest of drawers, with her name engraved in the cover in gold letters. There were photographs in gilt frames behind dim glass hanging on dulled and rusted chains.

"Julien again. Has to be," said Michael. "And Mary Beth, look, that woman looks like you, Rowan."

"So they told me," she said softly.

Belle's rosary, with her named engraved on the back of the crucifix, lay still on the pillow of the four-poster bed. Dust rose from the feather comforter when Michael touched it. A wreath of roses peered down at him from the satin tester above.

Gloomy it all seemed with its fading flowered paper, and the heavy armoires tilting ever so slightly forward, and the carpet threadbare and the color of dust itself. The branches of the oaks looked like ghosts beyond the pongee curtains. The bathroom was clean and very plain—tile from Stella's time, Michael figured. A great old tub such as one still finds now and then in old hotels, and a high pedestal lavatory, and stacks of towels, layered with dust, on a wicker stand.

"Oh, but Michael, this is the best room," Rowan said behind him. "This is the one that opens to the south and the west. Help me with this window."

They forced the stubborn sash. "It's like being in a tree house," she said as she stepped outside on the deep front gallery. She laid her hand on the fluted Corinthian column and looked into the twisted branches of the oaks. "Look, Michael, there are ferns growing in the branches, hundreds of little green ferns. And there, a squirrel. No, there are two of them. We've frightened them. This is so strange. It's like we're in the woods, and we can jump out there and start climbing. We could just wander heavenward through this tree."

Michael tested the rafters underneath. "Solid, just like everything else. And the iron lace isn't rusted, not really. All it needs is paint." No leaks in the roof above either.

Just waiting, waiting all this time to be restored. He stopped, and slipped off his khaki jacket. The heat was getting to him finally, even here where the river breezes did flood by.

He slung the jacket over his shoulder and held it with one hooked finger.

Rowan stood, with arms folded, leaning on the cast-iron railing. She looked out over the quiet still corner.

He was looking down through the tangle of the little sweet olive trees, at the front gate. He was seeing himself as a boy standing there, just seeing himself so clearly. She clasped his hand suddenly and drew him after her back inside.

"Look, that door connects to the next bedroom. That could be a sitting room, Michael. And both lead on to that side porch."

He was staring at one of the oval photographs. Stella? Had to be Stella.

"Wouldn't it be wonderful?" she was saying. "It has to be the sitting room."

He glanced down again at the white leather cover of the prayer book with the words Belle Mayfair inscribed in gold. Just for a second, he thought, Touch it. And to think, Belle was so sweet, so good.

How could Belle hurt you? You're in this house and not using the power.

"Michael?"

But he couldn't do it. If he began, how could he stop? And it would kill him, those electrical shocks passing through him, and the blindness, the inevitable blindness when the images swam around him like murky water, and the cacophony of all the voices. No. You don't have to. Nobody has told you that you have to.

The thought suddenly that someone might make him do it, might tear off the glove and force his hand on these objects, made him cringe. He felt cowardly. And Rowan was calling him. He looked down at the prayer book as he moved away.

"Michael, this must have been Millie's room. It has a fireplace, too." She stood before a high dresser, holding a small monogrammed handkerchief. "These rooms are like shrines," she said.

Beyond the long window, the bougainvillea grew so thick over the side porch that the lower railings could no longer be seen. This was the porch above Deirdre's porch. Open, because only that lower part had been screened in.

"Yes, all these rooms have fireplaces," he said absently, his eyes on the fluorescent purple blossoms of the bougainvillea. "I'm going to have a look at the firebricks in the chimneys. These little shallow grates were never used for wood, they were used for coal."

Now they housed gas heaters, and he rather liked that, for in all this time, he'd never seen a little gas heater blazing away in the cozy winter dark, with all those tiny blue and gold flames.

Rowan stood at the closet door. "What is that smell, Michael?"

"Lord, Rowan Mayfair, you never smelled camphor in an old closet?"

She laughed softly. "I've never even seen an old closet, Michael Curry. I've never lived in an old house, nor visited an old hotel. State of the art was my adoptive father's motto. Rooftop restaurants and brass and glass. You can't imagine the lengths to which he went to maintain those standards. And Ellie couldn't stand the sight of anything old or used. Ellie threw out all her clothes after a year's wear."

"You must think you slipped off the planet."

"No, not really. Just slipped into another interpretation," she said, her voice trailing off. Thoughtfully she touched the old clothes hanging there. All he saw were shadows.

"And to think," she whispered, "the century is almost over, and she lived all her life right here in this room." She stepped back. "God, I hate this wallpaper. Look, there's a leak up there."

"Nothing major, honey. Just a little leak. There's bound to be one or more in a house this size. That's nothing. But I think the plaster's dead up there."

"Dead? The plaster is dead?"

"Too old to take a patch. See the way it's crumbled. So we'll put in a new ceiling," he said, shrugging. "Two days' work."

"You're a genius."

He laughed and shook his head.

"Look, there's an old bathroom there," she said. "Each room has its own bathroom. I'm trying to see everything cleaned and finished . . ."

"I see it," he said. "I see it all with every step I take."

Carlotta's room was the last major room at the end of the hallway—a great gloomy cavern it seemed, with its black four-poster bed and its faded taffeta ruffles, and a few dreary slip-covered chairs. A stale smell rose around them. A bookshelf held law texts and reference books. And there, the rosary and the prayer book as if she'd only just laid them down. Her white gloves in a tangle, and a pair of cameo earrings, and a string of jet beads.

"We used to call those Grandma beads," he said with vague surprise. "I forgot all about those." He moved to touch them and then drew back his gloved hand as if he'd drawn near to something hot.

"I don't like it in here, either," Rowan whispered. She was hugging the backs of her arms again in that chilled, miserable gesture. Scared maybe. "I don't want to touch what belonged to her," she said, looking vaguely repelled by the items strewn on the dresser, repelled by the old furniture, beautiful as it was.

"Ryan will take care of it," she murmured, becoming ever more uneasy. "He said that Gerald Mayfair will come and take away her things. She left her personal things to Gerald's grandmother." At last she turned as if something had startled her, then stared almost angrily at the mirror between the side windows. "There's that smell again, that camphor. And something else."

"Verbena, and rose water," he said. "See the bottle? They plant little things like that now in quaint northern California bed-and-breakfast hotels. I've planted them on many a marble-top table. And there they sit. The real thing."

"It's too real," she whispered, "it's dreary and unhappy."

They moved on to the rear door of the room which opened onto a little corridor and a short stairs, and then two small rooms, following one upon the other.

"The maids slept here in the old days," Michael explained. "Eugenia has that room back there now. Technically we are looking into the servants' wing, and they would never have used this connecting door, because it wasn't here until recent years. They cut through the brick wall to put it in. In the old days the servants would have come into the main house by means of the porch."

At the far end of the wing, they could see a dull light burning. "That's the stairway that leads down to the kitchen. And that old bathroom back there was Eugenia's. In the old days southern people had the black servants use a different bathroom. You've heard enough about all *that*, I imagine."

They turned back into the larger room. Rowan moved carefully across the faded rug, and Michael followed her to the window and gently pushed back the soft frail curtain, so that they could look down on the brick sidewalks of Chestnut Street, and the artful façade of the grand house across the way.

"See, open to the river side," said Michael, looking at the other building. "And look at the oak trees on that property and the old carriage house is still standing. See the stucco peeling from the bricks. It, too, was made to look like stone."

"From every window you see the oaks," Rowan said, speaking low as if not to disturb the dust. "And the sky, such a deep blue. Even the light is different here. It's like the soft light of Florence or Venice."

"That it is," Michael said.

Again, he found himself staring apprehensively at the belongings of this woman. Maybe Rowan's uneasiness had communicated itself to him. He imagined, compulsively and painfully, having to take off his glove and lay his naked hand upon things that had been hers.

"What is it, Michael?"

"Let's go," he said under his breath, clasping her hand again and moving back into the main hall.

Only reluctantly did she follow Michael into Deirdre's old room. Here her confusion and revulsion seemed to deepen. Yet he knew she was compelled to make this journey. He saw the way her eyes moved hungrily over the framed photographs, and the little Victorian cane-seated chairs. Michael hugged her close as she stared down at the vicious stain on the mattress.

"That's awful. I've got to call someone," he said, "to clean that up."

"I'll do it," she said.

"No, I will. You asked downstairs if I could take over, hire the people I needed to restore the whole place. Well, I can take care of that too."

He looked at the stain, a great oval of brown, the center of it sticky. Had the woman hemorrhaged when she was dying? Or had she lain there with her waste seeping out in the heat of this awful old room?

"I don't know," Rowan whispered, though he hadn't voiced the question. She gave a ragged sigh. "I've already asked for the records. Ryan's requesting everything through legal channels. I talked to him today. I called the doctor. I talked to the nurse, too, Viola. Sweet old woman. She told it like Dickens. All the doctor said was that there was no reason to take her to the hospital. The whole thing was crazy. He didn't like my asking him questions. He suggested that I was wrong to ask him. He said it was the humane thing to let her die."

He held her more tightly, grazing her cheek with his lips.

"What are those candles?" she asked, staring at the little bedside altar. "And that awful statue. What's that?"

"The Blessed Mother," he said. "When there's a naked heart on it like that I guess you call it the Immaculate Heart of Mary. I don't really remember. The candles are blessed candles. I saw them flickering up here, when I was outside that first night. I never dreamed she was dying. If I'd known I . . . I don't know. I didn't even know who lived here when I first came."

"But why did they burn these blessed candles?"

"It's to comfort the dying. The priest comes. He gives her

768

what they call the Last Sacraments. I went with the priest a couple of times when I was an altar boy.''

"They did that for her, but they didn't take her to the hospital."

"Rowan, if you had known, if you had come, do you think she could have been brought around? I don't think so, honey. I don't think it matters now."

"Ryan says no. She was hopeless. He says that once about ten years ago, Carlotta took her off the drugs. There was no response to any stimulus except reflex. Ryan says they did everything they could, but then Ryan is covering Ryan, isn't he? But I'll know when I see the records, and then I'll feel better . . . or worse."

She moved away from the bed, her eyes drifting more sluggishly over the room. She seemed to be forcing herself to evaluate it the way they had evaluated everything else.

Tentatively he pointed out to her that only in this room was there the ornamentation that was common to the lower floor. He drew her attention to the scrollwork crowning the windows. A crystal chandelier, covered with dust, hanging from an ornate plaster medallion. The bed itself was huge and vaguely ugly.

"It's not like the others, the four-posters," she said.

"It's newer, machine made," he explained, "It's American. That was the kind they bought by the millions near the end of the last century. Probably Mary Beth bought it and it was very much the thing."

"She stopped time, didn't she?"

"Mary Beth?"

"No, that hateful Carlotta. She stopped time here. She made everything grind to a halt. Think of young girls growing up in a house like this. There isn't a scrap of evidence that they ever had anything beautiful or special or contemporary of their own."

"Teddy bears," Michael whispered. Hadn't Deirdre said something about teddy bears in the garden in Texas?

Rowan had not heard him. "Well, her reign is over," she said, but it was without triumph or resolution.

She suddenly moved forward and picked up the plaster Virgin with the exposed red heart, and pitched it across the room. It landed on the marble floor of the open bathroom, the body breaking into three uneven pieces. She stared at it as if shocked by what she'd done.

He was astonished. Something purely irrational and completely superstitious shook him. The Virgin Mary broken on the bathroom floor. He wanted to say something, some magic words or prayers to undo it; like tossing salt over your shoulder or knocking on wood. Then his eye caught something glittering in the shadows. A heap of tiny glittering things on the table at the far side of the bed.

"Look, Rowan," he said softly, slipping his fingers around the back of her neck. "Look, on the other table, over there."

It was the jewel box, and it stood open. It was the velvet purse. Gold coins heaped everywhere, and ropes of pearls, and gems, hundreds of small glittering gems.

"Good God," she whispered. She moved around the bed, and stared down at it as if it were alive.

"Didn't you believe it?" he asked her. But he wasn't sure now whether he had believed it himself. "They look fake, don't they? Like a motion-picture treasure. Couldn't possibly be real."

She looked at him across the barren empty bed. "Michael," she said softly, "would you touch them? Would you . . . lay your hands on them?"

He shook his head. "I don't want to, Rowan," he said.

She stood silent, drawing into herself, it seemed, her eyes becoming vague and unfocused. She hugged her arms again, the way she always did it seemed when she was upset, as if her interior misery made her cold.

"Michael," she said again softly, "would you touch something of Deirdre's? Her nightgown. Maybe the bed."

"I don't want to, Rowan. We said we wouldn't . . ."

She looked down, her hair tumbling over her eyes so that he couldn't see them.

"Rowan, I can't interpret it. It will just be confusion. I'll see the nurse that helped her dress, or maybe the doctor, or maybe a car that passed when she was sitting out there, watching. I don't know how to use it. Aaron's taught me a little. But I'm still not very good. I'll see something ugly and I'll hate it. And it scares me, Rowan, because she's dead. I touched all kinds of things for people in the beginning. But I can't now. Believe me, I . . . I mean when Aaron teaches me . . ."

"What if you saw happiness? What if you saw something beautiful like that woman in London saw, who touched her robe for Aaron?"

"Did you believe in that, Rowan? They aren't infallible, these people in the Talamasca. They're just people."

"No, they aren't just people," she said. "They're people like you and me. They have preternatural powers like you and I have preternatural powers."

Her voice was mild, unchallenging. But he understood what she felt. He stared again at the blessed candles, and then at the broken statue, which he could just see in the shadows behind

770

her on the bathroom floor. Flash of the May procession and the giant statue of the Virgin tilting as it was carried through the streets. Thousands of flowers. And he thought again of Deirdre, Deirdre in the botanical garden, talking in the dark to Aaron. "I want normal life."

He moved around the bed and went to the old-fashioned dresser. He opened the top drawer. Nightgowns of soft white flannel, whiff of sachet, very sweet. And lighter summer garments of real silk.

He lifted one of these nightgowns—a thin sleeveless thing sewn with pale pastel flowers. He laid it down in a wrinkled heap on the dresser, and he took off his gloves. For a second he clasped his hands together tightly and then he picked up the garment in both hands. He closed his eyes. "Deirdre," he said, "only Deirdre."

An enormous place gaped before him. Through the lurid flickering glare he saw hundreds of faces, he heard voices wailing and screaming. An unbearable sound. A man came towards him stepping over the bodies of the others! "No. Stop!" He had dropped the nightgown. He stood there with his closed eyes trying to remember what he'd just glimpsed, though he couldn't bear to be surrounded by it again. Hundreds of people shifting and turning, and someone speaking to him in a rapid ugly mocking voice. "Christ, what was it?" He stared down at his hands. He had heard a drum behind all of it, a marching cadence, a sound he knew.

Mardi Gras, years ago. Rushing through the winter street with his mother. "Going to see the Mystic Krewe of Comus." Yes, that had been the very drum song. And the glare had been the glare of the flickering reeking flambeaux.

"I don't understand," he said.

"What are you saying?"

"I didn't see anything that made any sense." He looked down angrily at the nightgown. Slowly he reached out for it. "Deirdre, in the last days," he said. "Only Deirdre in the last days." He touched the soft wrinkled cloth very gently. "I'm seeing the view from the porch, the garden," he whispered. Yes, the Queen's Wreath vine, and that is a butterfly climbing the screen, and his hand right there beside her. "Lasher's there, she's glad he's there, and he's right beside her." And if he turned his head and looked up from the rocker he'd see Lasher. He set the nightgown down again. "And it was all sunlight and flowers, and she was . . . was all right."

"Thank you, Michael."

"I don't want to do it again, Rowan, I'm sorry I can't do it. I don't want to."

"I understand," she said. She came towards him. "I'm sorry." Her voice was low and sincere and soothing, but her eyes were full of bewilderment. What had he seen that first time around, she wanted to know.

So did he. But what chance had he of knowing?

Yet he was here, inside the house, and he had the power, which had been given to him, presumably by them! And he was being a coward with the power, he, Michael Curry, a coward, and he kept saying he meant to do what they wanted him to do.

Hadn't they wanted him to come here? Didn't they want him to touch things? And she wanted him to. How could she not?

He reached out and touched the foot of Deirdre's bed. Flash of midday, nurses, a cleaning woman pushing a tired vacuum, someone complaining, ceaselessly, a whine. It came so fast finally it was blurred; he ran his fingers along the mattress: her white leg like a thing made out of dough, and Jerry Lonigan there, lifting her, saying under his breath to his assistant, Look at this place, will you look at it, and when he touched the walls, her face suddenly, Deirdre, idiot smile, drool on her chin. He touched the door to the bathroom, a white nurse bullying her, telling her to come now, and move her feet, she knew that she could, pain inside Deirdre, pain eating her insides, a man's voice speaking, the cleaning woman coming, going, the flush of the toilet, the hum of the mosquitoes, the sight of a sore on her back, good God, look at it, where she has rubbed against the rocker over the years, a festering sore, caked with baby powder, are you people crazy, and the nurse just holds her on the toilet. I can't . . .

He turned and pushed past Rowan, brushing her hand away as she tried to stop him. He touched the post of the stairs. Flash of a cotton dress passing him, beat of footsteps on the old carpet. Someone screaming, crying.

"Michael!"

He ran up the steps after them. The baby was roaring in the cradle. It echoed all the way up the three flights from the parlor.

Stench of chemicals, rotted filth in those jars. He'd glimpsed it last night, she'd told him about it, but now he had to see it, didn't he? And touch it. Touch Marguerite's filthy jars. He'd smelled it last night when he'd come up to find Townsend's body, only it wasn't the body. His hand on the railing, caught a flash of Rowan with the lamp in her hand. Rowan angry and miserable and trying to escape the old woman, who was beating her with words, viciousness, and then the black woman with her dust

772

mop, and a carpenter putting a pane of glass in this window that looked out over the roof. God, that is an awful smell up here, lady. Just do your job. Deirdre's bedroom, shrill clang of other voices, rising to a peak, then washing away, and another wave coming. And the door, the door straight ahead, someone laughing, a man speaking French, what he's saying, let me hear one distinct word, the stench is behind it.

But no, first Julien's room, Julien's bed. The laughing grew louder, but a baby's crying was mixed up with it, someone rushing up the stairs just behind him. The door gave him Eugenia again, dusting, complaining about the stench, Carlotta's voice droning on, the words indistinguishable, and then that awful stain there in the darkness where Townsend died, drawing his last breath through the hole in the carpet, and the mantel, wavering flash of Julien! The same man, yes, the same man he'd seen when he held Deirdre's nightgown, yes, you, Julien, staring at him, *I see you*, and then footsteps running, no, I don't want to see this, but he reached out for the windowsill, grabbed the little cord of the shade, and up it ran, rattling at the top, revealing the dirty windowpanes.

She flew past him, Antha, through the glass, scuttling out on the roof, terrified, tangle of hair over her wet face, her eye, look at her eye, it's on her cheek, dear God. Sobbing, "Don't hurt me, don't hurt me! Lasher, help me!"

"Rowan!"

And Julien, why didn't he do something, why did he stand there crying silently, doing nothing. "You can call on the devil in hell and the saints in heaven, they won't help you," said Carlotta, her voice a snarl as she climbed through the window.

And Julien helpless. "Kill you, bitch, kill you, you will not . . ."

She's gone, she's fallen, her scream unfurling like a great billowing red flag against the blue sky. Julien with his face in his hands. Helpless. Shimmering gone, a ghost witness. The chaos again, Carlotta fading. He clamped his hands on the iron bed, Julien sitting there, wavering yet distinct for an instant, I know you, dark eyes, smiling mouth, white hair, yes, you, don't touch me! "*Eh bien*, Michel, at last!"

His hand struck the packing crates lying on the bed, but he couldn't see them. He could see nothing but the light wavering and forming the image of the man sitting there under the covers, and then it was gone, and then it was there. Julien was trying to get out of the bed . . . No, get away from me.

"Michael!"

He had shoved the boxes off the bed. He was stumbling over

the books. The dolls, where were the dolls? In the trunk. Julien said that, didn't he? He said it in French. Laughter, a chorus of laughter. Rustle of skirts around him. Something broke. His knee struck something sharp, but he crawled on towards the trunk. Latches rusted, no problem, throw back the lid.

Wavering, vanishing, Julien stood there, nodding, pointing down into the trunk.

The rusted hinges broke completely as the lid slammed back into the old plaster and fell loose. What was that rustling, like taffeta all around him, feet scraping the floor around him, figures looming over him, like flashes of light through shutters, here and then gone, let me breathe, let me see. It was like the rustle of the nuns' skirts when he was in school and they came thundering down the hallway to hit the boys, to make the boys get back in line, rustling of beads and cloth and petticoats . . .

But there are the dolls.

Look, the dolls! Don't hurt them, they are so old and so fragile, with their dumb scribble scratch faces looking at you, and look, that one, with the button eyes, and the braids of gray, in her tiny little perfect man clothes of tweed to the very trousers. God, bones inside!

He held it. Mary Beth! The flapping gores of her skirts came against him; if he looked up he'd see her looking down; he did see her, there was no limit to what he could see, he could see the backs of their heads as they closed in on him, but nothing would hold steady even for an instant. It was all gossamer, and solid for one second and then nothing, the room full of dusty nothing and crowded to overflowing. Rowan came through as if through the tear in a fabric, grabbing him by the arm, and in a glimmering flash he saw Charlotte, knew it was Charlotte. Had he touched the doll? He looked down, they were all higgledy piggledy and so fragile on the layer of cheesecloth.

But where is Deborah? Deborah, you have got to tell me . . . He folded back the cloth, tumbling the newer dolls on each other, were they crying, somebody was crying, no, that was the baby screaming in the cradle, or Antha on the roof. Or both of them. Flash of Julien again, talking rapidly in French, down on one knee beside him, *I can't understand you.* One millimeter of a second, and gone. You're driving me crazy, what good am I to you or to anyone if I am crazy?

Get these skirts away from me! It was so much like the nuns. "Michael!"

He groped under the cloth—where?—easy to tell for there lay the oldest, a mere stick thing of bones and one over from it, the blond hair of Charlotte, and that meant that the frail little thing

774

between them was his Deborah. Tiny beetles raced from beneath it as he touched it. Its hair was disintegrating, oh, God, it's falling apart, even the bones are turning to dust. And in horror, he drew back. He had left the print of his finger in its bone face. The blast of a fire caught him, he could smell it; her body all crumpled up like a wax thing on top of the pyre, and that voice in French ordering him to do something, but what?

"Deborah," he said, touching it again, touching its little ragged dress of velvet. "Deborah!" It was so old his breath was going to blow it away. Stella laughed. Stella was holding it. "Talk to me," she said with her eyes squeezed shut, the young man beside her laughing. "You don't really think this is going to work!"

What do you want of me?

The skirts pushed closer around him, mingling voices in French and English. He tried to catch Julien this time. It was like trying to catch a thought, a memory, something flitting through your mind when you listened to music. His hand lay on the little Deborah doll, crushing it down into the trunk, the blond hair doll tumbling against him. I'm destroying them.

"Deborah!"

Nothing, nothing.

What have I done that you won't tell me!

Rowan was calling him. Shaking him; he almost hit her.

"Stop it!" he shouted. "They're all here, in this house! Don't you see? They're waiting, they're . . . they're . . . there's a name for it, they're hovering . . . earthbound!"

How strong she was. She wouldn't stop. She pulled him to his feet. "Let me go." He saw them everywhere he looked, as if they were woven into a veil that was moving in the wind.

"Michael, stop it, it's enough, stop . . ."

Have to get out of here. He grabbed for the door frame. When he looked back at the bed he saw only the packing crates. He stared at the books. He had not touched the books. The sweat was pouring down his face, his clothes, look at his clothes, he ran his naked hands over his shirt, trembling, flash of Rowan, shimmer of them all around him again, only he couldn't see their faces and he was tired of looking for their faces, tired of the draining zapping feelings running through him, "I can't do this, goddamn it!" he shouted. This was like being underwater, even the voices he heard as he clamped his hands to his ears were like wavering hollow voices under water. And the stench, not possible to avoid it. The stench from the jars that were waiting, the jars . . .

775

Is this what you wanted of me, to come back here and to touch things and to know and to find out? Deborah, where are you?

Were they laughing at him? Flash of Eugenia with her dust mop. Not you! Go away. I want to see the dead not the living. And that was Julien's laughter, wasn't it? Someone was definitely crying, a baby crying in a cradle, and a dull low voice cursing in English, kill you, kill you, kill you.

"It's enough, stop, don't . . ."

"No, it isn't. The jars are there. It is not enough. Let me do it, once and for all, with all of it."

He pushed her aside, amazed again at the strength with which she tried to stop him, and shoved open the door to the room of the jars. If only they would shut up, if only that baby would stop crying, and the old woman cursing, and that voice in French . . . "I can't . . ."

The jars.

A gust of air came up the stairway and moved the sluggish stench for an instant. He was standing with his hands over his ears looking at the jars. He took a deep breath, but the stench went into his lungs. Rowan was watching him. *Is this what you want me to touch?* And they wanted to come back, like a great sloppy veil again closing around him, but he wouldn't let them. He sharpened his focus. The jars only. He took another breath.

The smell was enough to kill you, but it can't. It can't really hurt you. Look. And now in the swimming ugly light, he put his hand on the dingy glass, and through his splayed fingers saw an eye looking at him. "Christ," it's a human head, but what was he getting from the jar itself, through his tortured fingers, nothing, nothing but images so faint they were like the thing inside, a cloud surrounding him, in which the visual and the audial were blended and ever dissolving, and trying to be solid and breaking apart again. The jar was there, shining.

These were his fingers scratching at the wax seal.

And the beautiful flesh and blood woman in the door was Rowan.

He broke the seal open, and plunged his hand into the liquid, while the fumes from it went up his nose like poison gas. He gagged, but that didn't stop him. He grabbed the head inside by the hair though it fell away in his fingers, slipped like seaweed.

The head was slimy and falling to pieces. Chunks of it rose against the glass, pushing against his wrist. But he had a hold of it, his thumb sinking into the putrid cheek. He drew it up out of the jar, knocking the jar on the floor so that the stinking liquid splattered on him. He held the head—dim flash of the head speaking, the head laughing, the features mobile though the head

776

was dead, and the hair was brown hair, the eyes bloodshot but brown, and blood seeping from the dead mouth that talked.

Aye, Michael, flesh and blood when you are nothing but bones.

The whole man sat on the bed, naked, and dead, yet alive with Lasher in him, the arms thrashing and the mouth opening. And beside him Marguerite, with her hag hair and her hands on his shoulders, her big wide taffeta skirts out like a circle of red light around her, holding the dead thing, just as Rowan was trying to hold him now.

The head slipped out of his hands. It slid in the muck on the floor. He went down on his knees. God! He was sick. He was going to vomit. He felt the convulsion, and the pain in a circle around his ribs. Vomit. I can't help it. He turned towards the corner, tried to crawl away . . . It poured out of him.

Rowan held him by the shoulder. When you're this sick you don't give a damn who's touching you, but again, he saw the dead thing on the bed. He tried to tell her. His mouth was sour and full of vomit. God. Look at his hands. The mess was all over the floor, on his clothes.

But he got to his feet, his fingers slipping off the doorknob. Pushing Julien out of the way, and Mary Beth, and then Rowan, and groping for the fallen head, squashed fruit on the floor, breaking apart like a melon.

"Lasher," he said to her, wiping at his mouth. "Lasher, in that head, in the body of that head."

And the others? Look at them, filled with heads. Look at them! He snatched at another, smashed it against the wood of the shelf, so that the greenish remains slid down soft and rotten, like a giant greenish egg yoke onto the floor, oozing off the skull that emerged dark and shrunken as he caught it and held it, the face just dripping away.

Aye, Michael, when you are nothing but bones, like the bones you hold in your hands.

"Is this flesh?" he cried. "Is this flesh!" He kicked the rotten head on the floor. He threw down the skull and kicked the skull. Like rubber. "You aren't going to get her, not for this, not for anything."

"Michael!"

He was sick again, but he wasn't going to let it come. His hand caught the edges of the shelf. Flash of Eugenia.

"Sure hate the smell of this attic, Miss Carl." "You leave it, Eugenia."

He turned around and wiping both his hands on his coat, wiping them furiously, he said to Rowan, "He came into the dead bodies. He possessed them. He looked through their eyes

777

and he spoke through their vocal cords, and used them, but he couldn't make them come alive again, he couldn't make the cells begin to multiply again. And she saved the heads. He came into the heads, long after the bodies were gone, and he looked through the eyes.''

Turning, he snatched up one jar after another. She stood beside him. They were peering through the glass, the shimmer of the images almost blinding him to what he meant to see, but he was determined to see. Heads with brown hair, and look, a blond head with streaks of brown in it, and look, the face of a black man, with blotches of white skin on it, and streaks of lighter hair, and here another, with the white hair streaked with brown.

''Dear God, don't you see? He not only went into them, he changed the tissues, he caused the cells to react, he changed them but he couldn't keep them alive.''

Heads, heads, heads. He wanted to smash all the jars.

''You see that? He caused a mutation, a new cell growth! But it was nothing, nothing compared to being alive! They rotted. He couldn't stop them! And they won't tell me what they want me to do!''

His slippery fingers closed in a fist. He smashed at one of the jars and saw it fall. She didn't try to stop him. But she had her arms around him. And she was begging him to come out of the room with her, dragging him. If she didn't watch it, they were both going to go down in this muck, for sure, this filthy muck.

''But look! You see that!'' Far back on the shelf, behind the jar he'd just broken. The finest of them, the liquid clear, the thick seal tarlike and intact. Through the flicker of meaningless indistinguishable images and sounds he heard her:

''Open it, break it,'' she said.

He did. The glass fell away soundlessly into the ashy layer of whispering voices, and he held this head, no longer even caring about the stench, or the spongy, moldering texture of the thing he held.

Again the bedroom, Marguerite at the dressing table, tiny-waisted, big skirts, turning to smile at him, toothless, eyes dark and quick, hair like a great ugly cascade of Spanish moss, and Julien reed thin and white-haired and young with his arms folded, you devil. *Let me see you, Lasher.* And then the body on the bed, beckoning for her to come, and then her lying down beside him and the dead rotting fingers tearing open her bodice, and touching her living breast. The dead cock erect between his legs. ''Look at me, change me, look at me, change me.''

Had Julien turned his back? No such luck. He stood at the

778

foot of the bed, his hands on the pillars of the bed, his face beating with the faint light of the candle blowing in the wind from the open windows. Fascinated, fearless.

Yes, and look at this thing in your hands, now, this was his face, wasn't it? His face! The face you saw in the garden, in the church, in the auditorium, the face that you saw all those many times. And the brown hair, oh yes, the brown hair.

He let it slide to the floor with the others. He backed away from it, but the eye pits were staring up at him, and the lips were moving. Did Rowan see it?

"Do you hear it talking?"

Voices all around him, but there was only one voice, one clear searing soundless voice:

You cannot stop me. You cannot stop her. You do my bidding. My patience is like the patience of the Almighty. I see to the finish. I see the thirteen. I shall be flesh when you are dead.

"He's speaking to me, the devil's speaking to me! You hear it?"

He was out of the door and down the stairs before he realized what he was doing, or that his heart was thundering in his ears, and that he couldn't breathe. He couldn't endure it any longer, he had always known it would be like this, the plunging into the nightmare, and that was enough, wasn't it, what did they want of him, what did she want? That bastard had spoken to him! That thing he had seen standing in the garden had spoken to him, and through that rotted head! He was no coward, he was a human man! But he couldn't take any more of it.

He'd torn off his coat and thrown it away in the corner of the hallway. Ah, the muck on his fingers, he couldn't wipe it off.

Belle's room. Clean and quiet. I'm sorry about the filth, please let me lie down on the clean bed. She was helping him, thank God for that, not trying to stop him.

The bedspread was clean and white and full of dust but the dust was clean, and the sun coming through the opened windows was beautiful and full of dust. Belle. Belle is what he touched now, the soft sweet spirit of Belle.

He was lying on his back. She had the gloves for him. She was wiping his hands with the warm washcloth, so lovingly, and her face was full of concern. She pressed her fingers to his wrist.

"Lie quiet, Michael. I have the gloves here. Lie quiet."

What was that cold hard thing near his cheek? He reached up. Belle's rosary, and it was tangling painfully in his hair when he pulled it loose, but that was OK. He wanted it.

And there was Belle. Oh, how lovely.

He tried to tell Rowan Belle was standing there. Rowan was

listening to his pulse. But Belle was gone. He had a rosary in his hands; he'd felt its cold beads next to his face, and Belle had been right there, talking to him.

There she was.

"Rest, Michael," Belle said. Sweet tremulous voice like Aunt Viv. She was fading but he could still see her. "Don't be afraid of me, Michael, I'm not one of them, that's not why I'm here."

"Make them talk to me, make them tell me what they want. Not them, but the ones who came to me. Was it Deborah?"

"Lie quiet, Michael, please."

What did you say, Rowan? His mouth hadn't moved.

"We aren't meant to have these powers," he said. "They destroy the human in us. You're human when you're at the hospital. I was human when I had the hammer and nails in my hands."

Everything was sliding. How could he explain to her, it had been like scaling a mountain, it had been like all the physical work he'd ever put his hands to, and his back to, done in a single hour. But she wasn't there. She'd kissed him and laid a quilt over him and gone out because he was asleep. Belle was sitting at the dresser, such a lovely picture. Sleep, Michael.

"Are you going to be here when I wake up?"

"No, darling, I'm not really here now. It's their house, Michael. I'm not one of them."

Sleep.

He clutched at the rosary beads. Millie Dear said, Time to go to church. The rooms are so clean and quiet. They love each other. Pearl gray gabardine. It has to become our house. That's why I loved it so when I was small and I'd walk here. Loved it. Our house. Never any quarrel between Belle and Millie Dear. So nice . . . Something almost adorable about Belle with her face so pretty in old age, like a flower pressed in a book, tinted still and fragrant.

Deborah said to him, . . . *incalculable power, power to transmute* . . .

He shuddered.

. . . *not easy, so difficult you can scarce imagine it, the hardest thing perhaps that you* . . .

I can do this!

Sleep.

And through his sleep, he heard the comforting sound of breaking glass.

When he awoke, Aaron was there. Rowan had brought him a change of clothes from the hotel, and Aaron helped him into the bathroom, so that he could wash and change. It was spacious and actually comfortable.

Every muscle in him ached. His back ached. His hands burned. He had the antsy awful feeling that he'd had all those weeks on Liberty Street, until he pulled the gloves back on and took a swallow of the beer Aaron gave him at his request. The pain in his muscles was awful, and even his eyes were tired, as if he'd been reading for hours by a poor light.

"I'm not going to get drunk," he told both of them.

Rowan explained that his heart had been racing, that whatever had happened it had been an extreme physical exertion, that a pulse reading like that was something you expected after a man had run a four-minute mile. It was important that he rest, and that he not remove the gloves again.

OK by him. He would have loved nothing better than to encase his hands in concrete!

They went back to the hotel together, ordered supper, and sat quietly in the living room of the suite. For two hours, he told them everything he had seen:

He told them about the little snatches of the visions that were coming back to him even before he'd taken off the gloves. He told them about the first vision when he held Deirdre's nightgown, and how it was Julien he'd seen in the hellish place, and how he'd seen him upstairs.

He told and he told. He described and described. He wished Aaron would speak, but he understood why Aaron did not.

He told them about Lasher's ugly prophecy, and the weird feeling of intimacy he had with the thing now though he had not really touched it but merely that rotted stinking head.

He told them finally about Belle, and then exhausted from the telling, he sat there, wanting another beer, but afraid they'd think he was a drunk if he drank another, then giving in and getting up and getting it out of the refrigerator no matter what they thought.

"I don't know why I'm involved, any more than I did before," he said. "But I know they're there, in that house. You remember Cortland said he wasn't one of them. And Belle said to me she wasn't one of them . . . if I didn't imagine it . . . well, the others who are part of it are there! And that thing altered matter, just a little but it did it, it possessed the dead bodies and worked on the cells.

"It wants Rowan, I know it does. It wants Rowan to use her power to alter matter! Rowan has more of that power than any of the others before her. Hell, she knows what the cells are, how they operate, how they're structured!''

Rowan seemed struck by those words. Aaron explained that after Michael had gone to sleep, and Rowan was sure his pulse was normal, that she had called Aaron and asked him to come to the house. He'd brought crates of ice in which to pack the specimens in the attic, and together they had opened each jar, photographed the contents, and then packed it away.

The specimens were at Oak Haven now. They were frozen. They'd be shipped to Amsterdam in the morning, which was what Rowan wanted. Aaron had also removed Julien's books, and the trunk of dolls, and they too would go to the Mother-house. But Aaron wanted to photograph the dolls first and he wanted to examine the books, and of course Rowan had agreed to all this, or it wouldn't have happened.

So far, the books appeared to be no more than ledgers, with various cryptic entries in French. If there was an autobiography such as Richard Llewellyn had indicated, it had not been in that attic room.

It gave Michael an irrational relief to know those things were no longer in the house. He was on his fourth beer now, as they sat together on the velvet couches. He didn't care what they thought about it. Just one night's peace, for Chrissakes, he thought. And he had to slow down his brain so he could think it through. Besides, he wasn't getting drunk. He didn't want to be drunk.

But what was one more beer now, and besides they were here where they were safe.

At last, they fell quiet. Rowan was staring at Michael, and suddenly for the whole disaster Michael felt mortally ashamed.

''And how are you, my dear?'' asked Michael. ''After all this madness. I'm not being very much help to you, am I? I must have scared you to death. Do you wish you'd followed your adoptive mother's advice and stayed in California?''

''You didn't scare me,'' she said affectionately, ''and I liked taking care of you. I told you that once before. But I'm thinking. All the wheels in my head are turning. It's the strangest mixture of elements, this whole thing.''

''Explain.''

''I want my family,'' she said. ''I want my cousins, all nine hundred of them or however many there are. I want my house. I want my history—and I mean the one Aaron gave to us. But I don't want this damned thing, this secret mysterious evil thing. I don't want it, and yet it's so . . . so seductive!''

Michael shook his head. "It's like I told you last night. It's irresistible."

"No, not irresistible," she said, "but seductive."

"And dangerous?" Aaron suggested. "I think we are more certain of that now than ever. I think we *know* we are talking of a creature which can change matter."

"I'm not so sure," said Rowan. "I examined those stinking things as best I could. The changes were insignificant; they were changes in the surface tissue. But of course the samples were hopelessly old and corroded . . ."

"But what about the one with the face like Lasher?" Michael asked. "The duplicate?"

She shook her head. "No evidence to indicate it wasn't a look-alike person," she said. "Julien looked like Lasher. Remarkably so. Again the changes may have been skin deep. Impossible to tell."

"OK, skin deep, but what about that?" Michael pressed. "You ever heard of a thing that could do that? We aren't talking about a blush, we're talking about something permanent! Something there after a century."

"You know what the mind can do," said Rowan. "I don't have to tell you that people can control their bodies to an amazing extent by thought. They can make themselves die if they want to. They've been known to make themselves levitate, if you believe the anecdotal evidence. Stilling heart rates, raising temperatures, that's all well documented. The saints in their trances could make the wounds of the stigmata open in their hands. They can also make these same wounds close. Matter is subject to mind, and we are only beginning to understand the extent of it. And besides, we know that when this thing materializes it has a solid body. At least it seems solid. So the thing changed the subcutaneous tissue of a corpse. What of it? It wasn't even a live body, from what you've told me. It's all rather crude and imprecise."

"You amaze me," said Michael almost coldly.

"Why?"

"I don't know. I'm sorry. But I have a horrible feeling it's all planned that you're who you are, that you're a brilliant doctor! It's all planned."

"Calm down, Michael. There are too many flaws in this whole story for everything to be planned. Nothing's planned in this family. Consider the history."

"It wants to be human, Rowan," said Michael, "that's the meaning of what it said to Petyr van Abel and to me. It wants

783

to be human, and it wants you to help it. What did the ghost of Stuart Townsend say to you, Aaron. It said, 'It's all planned.' "

"Yes," said Aaron thoughtfully, "but it's a mistake to over-interpret that dream. And I think Rowan is right. You cannot assume that you know what is planned. And by the way, for what it's worth, I don't think this thing can become human. It wants to have a body, perhaps, but I don't think that it would ever be human."

"Oh, that's beautiful," said Michael, "just beautiful. And I do think it planned everything. It planned for Rowan to be taken away from Deirdre. That's why it killed Cortland. It planned for Rowan to be kept away until she'd become not only a witch, but a witch doctor. It planned the very moment of her return."

"But again," said Rowan, "why did it show itself to you? If you're to intervene, why did it show itself to you?"

He sighed. With a sinking heart he thought about his pleas to Deborah, about touching the old doll of Deborah, and not seeing her or hearing her voice. The delirium came back to him, the stench of the room, and the ugliness of the rotted specimens. He thought of the mystery of the doorway. Of the spirit's strange words, *I see the thirteen.*

"I'm going on with *my* own plan," said Rowan calmly. "I'm going to claim the legacy and the house, just as I told you. I still want to restore the house. I want to live in it. I won't be deterred from it." She looked at him, expecting him to say something. "And this being, no matter how mysterious he is, is not going to get in the way of that, if I have something to say about it. I told you it's overplayed its hand."

She looked at Michael, almost angrily. "Are you with me?" she demanded.

"Yes, I'm with you, Rowan. I love you! And I think you're right to go ahead. We can start on the house any damn time you want. I want that too."

She was pleased, immensely pleased, but still her calm distressed him. He looked at Aaron.

"What do you think, Aaron?" he asked. "About what the creature said, about my role in this? You have to have an interpretation."

"Michael, what's important is that *you* interpret. That you regain an understanding of what happened to you. I have no certain interpretation of anything.

"This may sound frightfully strange to you, but as a member of the Talamasca, as the brother of Petyr, and Arthur and Stuart, I've already accomplished my most important goals here. I've made successful contact with both of you. The Mayfair history has been given to Rowan. And you have some knowledge now, fragmentary and biased as it may be, to assist you."

"You guys are a bunch of monks," said Michael grumpily. He lifted his beer in a careless toast. " 'We watch, and we are always here.' Aaron, why did all this happen?"

Aaron laughed good-naturedly, but he shook his head. "Michael, Catholics always want us to offer the consolations of the church. We can't do it. I don't know why it's happened. I do know that I can teach you to control the power in your hands, to shut it off at will so it stops tormenting you."

"Maybe," said Michael wearily. "Right now I wouldn't take off these gloves to shake hands with the president of the United States."

"When you want to work with it," said Aaron, "I'm at your service. I'm here for both of you." He looked at Rowan for a long moment and then back to Michael. "I don't have to warn you to be careful, do I?"

"No," said Rowan. "But what about you? Has anything else happened since the traffic accident?"

"Little things," said Aaron. "They're not important in themselves. And it might very well be my imagination. I'm as human as the next man, as far as that goes. I feel I'm being watched however, and menaced in a rather subtle way."

Rowan started to interrupt, but he gestured for silence.

"I have my guard up. I've been in these situations before. And one very odd aspect of the whole thing is this: when I'm with you—either of you—I don't feel this . . . this presence near me. I feel completely safe."

"If it harms you," said Rowan, "it makes its final tragic error. Because I shall never address it or recognize it in any way. I'll try to kill it when I see it. All its schemes will be in vain."

Aaron reflected for a moment.

"Do you think it knows that?" asked Rowan.

"Possibly," said Aaron. "But it's like everything else. A puzzle. A pattern can be a puzzle. It can involve great and intricate order; or it can be a labyrinth. I honestly don't know what it knows. I do believe that Michael is entirely right. It wants a human body. There seems no doubt of it. But what it knows and what it doesn't know . . . I can't say. I don't know what it really is. I don't guess anyone knows."

He took a sip of his coffee and then moved the cup away. Then he looked at Rowan.

"There's no doubt it will approach you, of course. You realize this. This antipathy you feel won't keep it at bay forever. I doubt

785

it's keeping it at bay now. It's simply waiting for a proper opportunity.''

"God," Michael whispered. It was like hearing that an assailant would soon attack the person he loved most in all the world. He felt a crippling jealousy and anger.

Rowan was looking at Aaron. "What would you do if you were me?" asked Rowan.

"I'm not sure," Aaron answered. "But I cannot emphasize enough that it is dangerous."

"The history told me that."

"And that it's treacherous."

"The history told me that too. Do you think I should try to make contact with it?"

"No. I don't. I think letting it come to you is the wisest thing you can do. And for the love of God, try to remain in complete control always."

"There's no getting away from it, is there?"

"I don't think so. And I can make a guess as to what it will do when it approaches you."

"What?"

"It will demand your secrecy and your cooperation. Or it will refuse to reveal itself or its purposes fully."

"It will divide you from us," said Michael.

"Exactly," Aaron went on.

"Why do you think it will do that?"

Aaron shrugged. "Because that is what I would do if I were it."

"What's the chance of driving it out? Of a straight-out exorcism?"

"I don't know," said Aaron. "Those rituals certainly do work, but I myself don't know how to make them work, and I don't know what the effect would be upon an entity this powerful. You see, that is the remarkable thing. This being is a monarch among its kind. A sort of genius."

She laughed softly.

"It's so cunning and unpredictable," Aaron said. "I'd be dead right now if it wanted me to be dead. Yet it doesn't kill me."

"For God's sake, Aaron," Michael said, "don't challenge it."

"It knows I would hate it," said Rowan, "if it hurt you."

"Yes, that may explain why it hasn't gone farther. But there we are again, at the beginning. Whatever you do, Rowan, never lose sight of the history. Consider the fate of Suzanne, and Deborah, and Stella, and Antha and Deirdre. Maybe if we knew the full story of Marguerite or Katherine, or Marie Claudette or the others from Saint-Domingue their stories would be just as tragic. And if any one character in the drama can be held responsible for so much suffering and death, it is Lasher.''

Rowan seemed lost in her thoughts for a moment. "God, I wish it would go away," she murmured.

"That would be too much to ask for, I think," said Aaron. He sighed and took out his pocket watch, and then rose from the couch. "I'm going to leave you now. I'll be upstairs in my suite if you need me.''

"Thank God you're staying," said Rowan. "I was afraid you'd go back to Oak Haven."

"No. I have Julien's books upstairs, and I think I should like to be in town just now. As long as I don't crowd you."

"You don't crowd us at all," said Rowan.

"Let me ask you one more thing," Michael said. "When you were in the house, what did it feel like?"

Aaron gave a little laugh and shook his head. He considered for a minute. "I think you can imagine," he said gently. "But one thing did surprise me—that it was so beautiful; so grand and yet so inviting, with all the windows opened and the sun coming in. I suppose I thought it would be forbidding. But nothing could have been farther from the truth."

This was the answer Michael had hoped to hear, but the mood was still on him from the long ordeal of the afternoon, and it failed to cheer him.

"It's a wonderful house," said Rowan, "and it's already changing. We're already making it ours. How long will it take, Michael, to bring it back to what it was meant to be?"

"Not long, Rowan, two, three months, maybe less. By Christmas it could be finished. I'm itching to do it. If I could just lose this feeling . . ."

"What feeling?"

"That it's all planned."

"Forget about that," said Rowan crossly.

"Let me make a suggestion," Aaron said. "Get a good night's sleep, then proceed with what you really want to do—with the legal questions at hand, with the settling of the estate, with the house perhaps—all the good things you want to do. And be on guard. Be on guard always. When our mysterious friend approaches, insist upon your own terms."

Michael sat sullenly staring at the beer as Rowan walked Aaron to the door. She came back, settled down beside him, and slipped her arm around him.

"I'm scared, Rowan," he said, "and I hate it. Positively hate it."

"I know, Michael," she said, "but we're going to win."

That night, after Rowan had been asleep for hours, Michael got up, went into the living room, and took the notebook out of his valise which Aaron had given him at the retreat house. He felt normal now. And the abnormalities of the day seemed strangely distant. Though he was still sore all over, he felt rested. And it was comforting to know Rowan was only a few feet away, and that Aaron slept in the suite above.

Now Michael wrote down everything he had told them. He went through it in writing as he had gone through it in words, only more slowly, and perhaps more thoughtfully, and he talked about it with himself in the notebook as he would in a diary because that is what the notebook had become.

He wrote down all he could remember of the little fragments that had come back before he had taken off the gloves. And it was not surprising that he could remember almost nothing at all. And then the beginning of the catastrophe when he'd held Deirdre's nightgown in his hand:

"Same drums as the Comus Parade. Or any such parade. The point is, an awful frightening sound, a sound to do with some sort of dark and potentially destructive energy."

He stopped. Then went on. "I remember something else too, now. At Rowan's house in Tiburon. After we made love. I woke up thinking the place was on fire and there were all kinds of people downstairs. I remember now. It was the same ambience, the same lurid sort of light, the same sinister quality.

"And the fact of the matter was, that Rowan was just down there by the fire she'd lighted in the fireplace.

"But it was the same feeling. Fire and people there, many many people, crowded together, a commotion in the flickering light.

"And I had no sense of recognition when I saw Julien upstairs, or when I saw Charlotte, or Mary Beth, or Antha, poor, tragic Antha scrambling over that roof. To see something like that is to feel it; it swallows you. There's nothing left of you inside while you're seeing it. But they weren't in my visions. None of them. And Deborah was just a body crumpled on the pyre. She wasn't standing there with them. Now surely that means something in itself."

He reread what he had written. He wanted to add more but he was leery of embellishment. He was leery of logic. Deborah's not one of them? That's why she wasn't there?

He went on to describe the rest. "Antha was wearing a cotton dress. I saw the patent leather belt she wore. When she crawled

788

across the roof, she tore her stockings. Her knees were bleeding. But her face, that was the unforgettable part, her eye torn out of the socket. And the sound of her voice. I'll carry that sound to the grave with me. And Julien. Julien looked as solid as she did while he was watching. Julien wore black. And Julien was young. Not a boy, by any means. But a vigorous man, not an old man. Even in the bed he wasn't old.''

Again he paused. ''And what else did Lasher say that was new. Something about patience, about waiting . . . and then that mention of the thirteen.

''But the thirteen what? If it's a number on a doorway, I haven't seen it. The jars, there weren't thirteen jars. There were more like twenty, but I'll verify this with Rowan.''

Again, he stopped, thought about embellishments, but didn't add them.

''The cheerful fiend didn't say a damn thing about a doorway,'' he wrote. ''No, just his threat that I'd be dead while he'd be flesh and blood.''

Dead. Tombs. Something Rowan had said before the day was shattered, like a piece of glass. Or like a glass jar. Something about a keyhole doorway carved on the Mayfair tomb.

''I'll go there tomorrow, and see for myself. If the number thirteen is carved somewhere on that doorway, I hope to God it brings me more enlightenment than what happened today.

''Whatever happens, no matter what I see, or what I think it means, I begin some serious work tomorrow. And so does Rowan. She goes downtown early with Ryan and Pierce to talk about the legacy. I start to talk to the other contractors in town. I start real, true, honest work on the house.

''And that feels better than any other course of action. It feels like a form of salvation.

''Let's see how Lasher likes it. Let's see what he chooses to do.''

He left the notebook on the table and went back to bed.

In sleep, Rowan was so smooth and expressionless that she was like a perfect wax mannequin beneath the sheets. The warmth of her skin surprised him when he kissed her. Stirring slowly, she turned and wound her arms around him, and nuzzled against his neck. ''Michael . . .'' she whispered in a dreamy voice. ''St. Michael, the archangel . . .'' Her fingers touched his lips, as if groping in the dark to know that he was really there. ''Love you . . .''

''I love you, too, darlin','' he whispered. ''You're mine, Rowan.'' And he felt the heat of her breasts against his arm, as he drew her close to him. She turned over and her soft fleecy sex was a little flame against his thigh, as she settled back into sleep.

Thirty-two

THE LEGACY.

It had come into her mind sometime during the night: a half dream of hospitals and clinics, and magnificent laboratories, peopled by brilliant researchers . . .

And all of this you can do.

They wouldn't understand. Aaron would and Michael would. But the rest of them wouldn't because they didn't know the secrets of the file. They didn't know what had been in the jars.

They knew things but they didn't know all the way back over the centuries to Suzanne of the Mayfair, midwife and healer in her filthy Scottish village, or Jan van Abel at his desk in Leiden, drawing his clean ink illustration of a flayed torso to reveal the layers of muscle and vein. They didn't know about Marguerite and the dead body flopping on the bed, and roaring with the voice of a spirit, or Julien watching, Julien who had put the jars in the attic instead of destroying them almost a century ago.

Aaron knew and Michael knew. They would understand the dream of hospitals and clinics and laboratories, of healing hands laid upon sore and aching bodies by the thousands.

What a joke on you, Lasher!

Money was no mystery to her; she was not frightened by the legacy. She could already imagine to the limits that it might allow. She'd never been charmed by money as she had been by anatomy and microsurgery, by biophysics or neurochemistry. But it was no mystery. She'd studied it before, and she'd study it now. And the legacy was something that could be mastered like any other subject . . . and converted into hospitals, clinics, laboratories . . . lives saved.

If only she could get the memory of the dead woman out of the house. For that was the real ghost to her, not the ghosts whom Michael had seen, and when she thought of his suffering she could scarcely bear it. It was like seeing everything she loved in him dying inside. She would have driven all the demons in

790

the world back away from him if only she'd known how to do it.

But the old woman. The old woman lay in the rocker still as if she would never leave it. And her stench was worse than the stench of the jars, because it was Rowan's murder. And the perfect crime.

The stench corrupted the house; it corrupted the history. It corrupted the dream of the hospitals. And Rowan waited at the door.

We want in, old woman. I want my house and my family. The jars have been smashed and the contents are gone now. I have the history in my hand, brilliant as a jewel. I shall atone for it all. Let me in so that I can fight the battle.

Why were they not friends, she and the old woman? Rowan had only contempt for the evil, spiteful voice which had taunted Michael from the contents of the broken jars.

And the spirit knew she loathed it. That when she remembered its secretive touch, she loathed it.

Alone yesterday, hours before Michael had come, she had sat there, waiting for Lasher, listening to every creak and whisper in the old walls.

If you think you can frighten me, you are tragically mistaken. I have no fear of you, and no love either. You are mysterious. Yes. And I am curious. But that is a very cold thing for a scientific mind such as mine. Very cold. You stand between me and the things I could love warmly.

She should have destroyed the jars then. She should have never urged Michael to take off the gloves, and she never would again, of that she was certain. Michael couldn't endure this power in his hands. He couldn't really endure his memory of the visions. It made him suffer, and it filled her with dread to see him afraid.

It was the fact of the drowning that had brought them together, not these mysterious dark forces that lurked in the house. Voices speaking from rotted heads in jars. Ghosts in taffeta. His strength and her strength, that had been the origin of their love, and the future was the house, the family, the legacy which could bring the miracles of medicine to thousands, even millions.

What were all the dark ghosts and legends on earth compared to those hard and glittering realities? In her sleep, she saw the buildings rise. She saw the immensity. And the words of the history ran through her dreams. No, never meant to kill the old woman, the one awful flaw. To have killed. To have done something so wrong. . . .

* * *

791

At six o'clock, when her breakfast arrived, the newspaper came with it.

SKELETON FOUND IN FAMOUS GARDEN DISTRICT HOUSE

Well, that was inevitable, wasn't it? Seems Ryan had warned her that they couldn't quash it. Numbly, she scanned the several paragraphs, amused in spite of herself, at the gothic tale unfolding in a quaint old-fashioned journalistic style.

Who could argue with the statement that the Mayfair mansion had always been associated with tragedy? Or that the one person who might have shed light upon the demise of Texan Stuart Townsend was Carlotta Mayfair, who had died the very night that the remains were discovered, after a long and distinguished legal career?

The rest was an elegy to Carlotta, which filled Rowan with coldness and guilt.

Surely someone from the Talamasca was clipping this story. Perhaps Aaron was reading it in his rooms above. What would he write in the file about it? It comforted her to think of the file.

In fact, she was a lot more comfortable now than a sane person ought to be. For no matter what was happening, she was a Mayfair, among all the other Mayfairs; and her secret sorrows were tangled with older, more intricate sorrows.

Even yesterday when Michael had been smashing the jars and wrestling with the power, it had not been the worst for her, not by any means. She had him, she had Aaron, she had all the cousins. She wasn't alone. Even with the murder of the old woman, she wasn't alone.

She sat still for a long time after reading the story, her hands clasped on top of the folded newspaper, as rain came down hard outside, and the food on the breakfast table grew cold.

No matter what else she felt, she ought to grieve in silence for the old woman. She ought to let the misery coagulate in her soul. And the woman was going to be dead forever now. Wasn't she?

The truth was, so much was happening to her, and so rapidly, that she could no longer catalog her responses; or even manifest any response at all. She passed in and out of emotion. Yesterday when Michael was lying on the bed, his pulse racing and his face flushed, she had been frantic. She had thought, If I lose this man, I'll die with him. I swear it. And an hour after, she had broken one jar after another, spilling the contents into the white dishpan, and poking at it with an ice pick as she examined it, before handing it over to Aaron to be packed in the ice. Clinical as any doctor. No difference at all.

In between these moments of crisis, she was drifting, watching, remembering, because it was all too different, too purely unusual, and finally too much.

This morning, waking at four A.M., she had not known where she was. Then it all came back to her, the mingled flood of curses and blessings, her dream of the hospitals, and Michael beside her, and the desire for him like a drug.

Not his fault really that his every gesture, word, movement, or facial expression was electrically erotic to her, no matter what else might be going on. He was a sex object and delightfully oblivious to it, because in his innocence he didn't really understand the greed of her desire.

Sitting up in bed with her arms wrapped around her knees, she had wondered if this wasn't somehow worse for a woman than a man, because a woman could find the smallest things about a man violently erotic, such as the way his curly hair was mashed down now on his forehead, or the way it curled on the back of his neck.

Weren't men a little more direct about things? Did they go mad over a woman's ankle? Seems Dostoyevski said they did. But she had doubted it. It was excruciating for her to look at the dark fleece on the back of Michael's wrist, to see his gold watchband cutting into it, to imagine his arm later, with the white cuff rolled up, which for some reason made it even more sexy than when the arm was naked, and the flash of his fingers as he lighted his cigarettes. All directly genitally erotic. Everything done with a sharp edge, a punch. Or his low growly voice, full of tenderness, when he talked on the phone to his Aunt Viv.

When he'd been on his knees in that foul, ugly room, he'd been battling, striking out. And on the dusty bed after, he had been irresistible to her in his exhaustion, his large, strong hands curled and lying empty on the counterpane. Loosening his thick leather belt and the zipper of his jeans, all erotic, that this powerful thing was suddenly dependent upon her. But then the terror had gripped her when she felt his pulse.

She'd sat with him for a long tense time, until the pulse returned to normal; until his skin had cooled. Until he was breathing in regular sleep. So coarsely and perfectly beautiful he'd been, the white undershirt stretched tight over his chest, just a real man and so exquisitely mysterious to her, with that dark hair on his chest and on the backs of his arms, and the hands so much bigger than hers.

Only his fear cooled her passion, and his fear never lasted very long.

This morning, she had wanted to wake him up by clamping her mouth on his cock. But he needed his sleep now after all that had happened. He needed it badly. She only prayed he had peace in his dreams. And besides she was going to marry him as soon as it seemed polite to ask him. And they had all their lives in the First Street house, didn't they, to do things like that?

And it seemed wrong to do what she'd done several mornings with Chase, her old palomino cop from Marin County, which was roll over next to him, press her hips against his flank and her face against his suntanned upper arm, and squeeze her legs tightly together, until the orgasm ran through her like a wash of blinding light.

It wasn't much fun to do that, either—nothing, in fact, compared to being tacked to the mattress by an adorable brute, with a little gold crucifix dangling from a chain around his neck.

He hadn't even stirred when the thunder rolled overhead, when the crack came so loud and sudden that it was like guns tearing loose the roof.

And now, two hours later, as the rain fell, and the breakfast grew cold, she sat dreaming, her mind running over all the past and all the possibilities, and this crucial meeting, soon to begin.

The phone startled her. Ryan and Pierce were in the lobby, ready to take her downtown.

Quickly she wrote a note for Michael, saying she was off on Mayfair legal business, and would be back for dinner, no later than six. "Please keep Aaron with you and don't go over to the house alone." She signed it with love.

"I want to marry you," she said aloud as she placed the note on the bedside table. Softly he snored into the pillow. "The archangel and the witch," she said, even more loudly. He slept on. She chanced one kiss on his naked shoulder, felt gently of the muscle in his upper arm, enough to drag her right into the bed if she lingered on it, and went out and shut the door.

Skipping the fancy paneled elevator, she walked down the carpeted stairs, staring for a moment at smooth-faced Ryan and his handsome son as if they were aliens from another universe in their tropical wool suits, with their mellow southern voices, there to guide her to a spaceship disguised as a limousine.

The small quaint brick buildings of Carondelet Street glided past in a curious silence, the sky like polished stone beyond the delicate downpour, the lightning opening a vein in the stone, the thunder crackling menacingly and then dying away.

At last they came into a region of burnished skyscrapers, a shining America for two blocks, followed by an underground garage that might have been anywhere in the world.

No surprises in the spacious thirtieth-floor offices of Mayfair and Mayfair, with its traditional furnishings and thick carpet, not even that two of the assembled Mayfair lawyers were women, and one was a very old man, or that the view through the high glass windows was of the river, gray as the sky, dotted with interesting tugs and barges, beneath the rain's silver veil.

Then coffee and conversation of the most vague and frustrating sort with the white-haired Ryan, his light blue eyes as opaque as marbles, speaking interminably it seemed of "considerable investments," and "long term holdings," and "tracts of land which have been held for over a century," and hard-core conservative investments "larger than you might expect."

She waited; they had to give her more than this; they had to. And then like a computer she analyzed the precious names and details when he at last began to let them slip.

Here it was, finally, and she could see the hospitals and the clinics shimmering against the dream horizon, though she sat there motionless, expressionless, letting Ryan talk on.

Blocks of real estate in downtown Manhattan and Los Angeles? The major financing for the Markham Harris Resorts worldwide hotel chain? Shopping malls in Beverly Hills, Coconut Grove, Boca Raton, and Palm Beach? Condominiums in Miami and Honolulu? And then once more references to the "very large" hard-core investments in treasury bills, Swiss francs, and gold.

Her mind drifted but never very far. So Aaron's descriptions in the file had been completely accurate. He had given her the backdrop and the proscenium arch for this little drama to be fully appreciated. Indeed he had given her knowledge of which these clean-faced lawyers in their shining pastel office garments could not possibly dream.

And once again, it struck her as positively strange that Aaron and Michael had ever feared her displeasure for placing a tool of that power in her hands. They didn't understand power, that was their problem. They'd never sliced into a cerebellum.

And this legacy was a cerebellum, wasn't it?

She drank her coffee in silence. Her eyes ran over the other Mayfairs, who also sat there in silence, as Ryan continued drawing his vague pictures of municipal bonds, oil leases, some cautious financing in the entertainment industry and of late in computer technology. Now and then she nodded, and made a small note with her silver pen.

Yes, of course, she understood that the firm had managed things for over a century. That deserved a nod and a heartfelt murmur. Julien had founded the firm for such management. And of course she could well envision how the legacy was entangled with the finances of the family at large—''all to the benefit of the legacy, of course. For the legacy is first and foremost, but there has never been a conflict, in fact, to speak of a conflict is to misunderstand the scope . . .''

''I understand.''

''Ours has always been a conservative approach, but to appreciate fully what I'm saying, one must understand what such an approach means when one is speaking of a fortune of this size. You might, realistically, think in terms of a small oil-producing nation and I do not exaggerate—and of policies aimed at conserving and protecting rather than expanding and developing, because when capital in this amount is properly conserved against inflation or any other erosion or encroachment, the expansion is virtually unstoppable, and the development in countless directions is inevitable, and you are faced with the day-to-day issue of investing revenues so large that . . .''

''You're talking billions,'' she said in a quiet voice.

Silent ripples passed through the assemblage. A Yankee blunder? She caught no vibration of dishonesty, only confusion, and fear of her and what she might eventually do. After all, they were Mayfairs, weren't they? They were scrutinizing her as she was scrutinizing them.

Pierce glanced at his father, Pierce who was of all of them the most purely idealistic and the least tarnished. Ryan glanced at the others, Ryan who understood the scope of what was at stake in a way perhaps that the others could not.

But no answer was forthcoming.

''Billions.'' She spoke again. ''In real estate alone.''

''Well, actually, yes, I have to say that is correct, yes, billions in real estate alone.''

How embarrassed and uncomfortable they all seemed, as if a strategic secret had been revealed.

She could smell the fear suddenly, the revulsion of Lauren Mayfair, the older blond-haired woman lawyer, in her seventies perhaps, with the soft powdery wrinkled skin, who eyed her from the end of the table and imagined her shallow, spoilt, and programmed to be totally ungrateful for what the firm had done. And then there was Anne Marie Mayfair to the right, dark-haired, pretty, forty years or more, skillfully rouged, and smoothly dressed in her gray suit and blouse of saffron silk, and more frankly curious, peering at Rowan steadily through horn-rimmed glasses, but convinced that disaster of one sort or another must lie ahead.

And Randall Mayfair, grandson of Garland, slender, with a hoary thatch of gray hair, and a soft wattle of a neck spilling over his collar, who merely sat there, eyes sleepy under his heavy brows and faintly purpled lids, not fearful, but watchful and by nature, resigned.

And when their eyes met, Randall answered her silently. *Of course you don't understand. How could you? How many people can understand? And so you'll want control, and for that you are a fool.*

She cleared her throat, ignoring the revealing manner in which Ryan made his hands into a church steeple just beneath his chin and stared at her hard with his marble blue eyes.

"You're underestimating me," she said in a monotone, her eyes sweeping the group. "I'm not underestimating you. I only want to know what's involved here. I cannot remain passive. It would be irresponsible to remain passive."

Moments of silence. Pierce lifted his coffee cup and drank without a sound.

"But what we're really talking about," said Ryan calmly and courteously, the steeple having fallen, "to be completely practical here, you understand, is that one can live in queenly luxury on a fraction of the interest earned by the reinvestment of a fraction of the interest earned by the reinvestment of . . . et cetera, if you follow me, without the capital ever being touched in any incidence or for any reason . . ."

"Again, I cannot be passive, nor complacent, nor negligently ignorant. I do not believe that I should be any of those things."

Silence, and once again Ryan to break it. Conciliatory and gentlemanly. "What specifically would you like to know?"

"Everything, the nuts and bolts of it. Or perhaps I should say the anatomy. I want to see the entire body as if it were stretched on a table. I want to study the organism as a whole."

A quick exchange of glances between Randall and Ryan. And then Ryan again. "Well, that's perfectly reasonable but it may not be as simple as you imagine . . ."

"Yet there must be a beginning to it somewhere, and at some point, an end."

"Well, undoubtedly, but I think you're envisioning this, if I may say so, in the wrong way."

"One thing specifically," she said. "How much of this money goes into medicine? Are there any medical institutions involved?"

How startled they were. A declaration of war, it seemed, or

so said the face of Anne Marie Mayfair, glancing at Lauren and then at Randall, in the first undisguised bit of hostility which Rowan had witnessed since she'd come to this town. The older Lauren, a finger hooked beneath her lower lip, eyes narrow, was too polished for such a display and merely looked fixedly at Rowan, her gaze now and then shifting very slowly to Ryan, who again began to speak.

"Our philanthropic endeavors have not in the past involved medicine, per se. Rather the Mayfair Foundation is more heavily involved with the arts and with education, with educational television in particular, and with scholarship funds at several universities, and of course we donate enormous sums through several established charities, quite independent of the Foundation, but all of this, you see, is carefully structured, and does not involve the release of the control of the money involved, so much as the release of the earnings . . ."

"I know how that works," Rowan said quietly. "But we are talking about billions, and hospitals, clinics, and laboratories are profit-making institutions. I wasn't thinking of the philanthropic question, really. I was thinking of an entire area of involvement, which could have considerable beneficial impact upon human lives."

How curiously cold and exciting this moment was. How private too. Rather like the first time she had ever approached the operating table and held the microinstruments in her own hands.

"We have not tended to go in the direction of medicine," said Ryan with an air of finality. "The field would require intense study, it would require an entire restructuring . . . and Rowan, you do realize that this network of investments, if I may call it that, has evolved over a century's time. This isn't a fortune which can be lost if the silver market crashes, or if Saudi Arabia floods the world with free oil. We are talking about a diversification here which is very nearly unique in financial annals, and carefully planned maneuvers which have proven profitable through two world wars and numberless smaller upheavals."

"I understand," she said. "I really do. But I want information. I want to know everything. I can start with the paper you filed with the IRS, and move on from there. Perhaps what I want is an apprenticeship, a series of meetings in which we discuss various areas of involvement. Above all I want statistics, because statistics are the reality finally . . ."

Again, the silence, the inner confusion, the glances ricocheting off each other. How small and crowded the room had become.

"You want my advice?" asked Randall, his voice deeper and

rougher than that of Ryan, but equally patient in its mellow southern cadences. "You're paying for it, actually, so you might as well have it."

She opened her hands. "Please."

"Go back to being a neurosurgeon; draw an income for anything and everything you will ever need; and forget about understanding where the money comes from. Unless you want to cease being a doctor and become what we are—people who spend their lives at board meetings, and talking to investment counselors and stockbrokers and other lawyers and accountants with little ten-key adding machines, which is what you pay us to do."

She studied him, his dark unkempt gray hair, his droopy eyes, the large wrinkled hands now clasped on the table. Nice man. Yes, nice man. Man who isn't a liar. None of them are liars. None of them are thieves either. Intelligently managing this money requires all their skill and earns them profits beyond the dreams of those with a taste for thievery.

But they are all lawyers, even pretty young Pierce with the porcelain skin is a lawyer, and lawyers have a definition of truth which can be remarkably flexible and at odds with anyone else's definition.

Yet they have ethics. This man has his ethics; but he is profoundly conservative, and those who are profoundly conservative are not interventionists; they are not surgeons.

They do not even think in terms of great goodness, or saving thousands, even millions of lives. They cannot guess what it would mean if this legacy, this egregious and monumental fortune, could be returned to the hands of the Scottish midwife and the Dutch doctor as they approached the sickbed, hands out to heal.

She looked away, out towards the river. For a moment her excitement had blinded her. She wanted the warmth to die away from her face. Salvation, she whispered inside her soul. And it was not important that they understand it. What was important was that she understood it, and that they withheld nothing, and that as things were removed from their control, they were not hurt or diminished, but that they too should be saved.

"What does it all amount to?" she asked, her eyes fixed on the river, on the long dark barge being pushed upstream by the shabby snub-nosed tug.

Silence.

"You're thinking of it in the wrong way," said Randall. "It's all of a piece, a great web . . ."

"I can imagine. But I want to know, and you mustn't blame me for it. How much am I worth?"

No answer.

"Surely you can make a guess."

"Well, I wouldn't like to, because it might be entirely unrealistic if viewed from a . . ."

"Seven and one half billion," she said. "That's my guess."

Protracted silence. Vague shock. She had hit very close to it, hadn't she? Close perhaps to an IRS figure, which had surfaced in one of these hostile and partially closed minds.

It was Lauren who answered, Lauren whose expression had changed ever so slightly, as she drew herself up to the table and held her pencil in both hands.

"You're entitled to this information," she said in a delicate, almost stereotypically feminine voice, a voice that suited her carefully groomed blond hair and pearl earrings. "You have every legal right to know what is yours. And I do not speak only for myself when I say that we will cooperate with you completely, for that we are ethically bound to do. But I must say, personally, that I find your attitude rather morally interesting. I welcome the chance to talk with you about every aspect of the legacy, down to the smallest detail. My only fear is that you're going to tire of this game, long before all the cards are on the table. But I am more than willing to take the initiative and begin."

Did she realize how very patronizing this was? Rowan doubted it. But after all, the legacy had belonged to these people for over fifty years, hadn't it? They deserved patience. Yet she could not quite give them what they deserved.

"There really isn't any other way for either of us to go about it," Rowan said. "It isn't merely morally interesting that I want to know what's involved, it's morally imperative that I find out."

The woman chose not to respond. Her delicate features remained tranquil, her small pale eyes widening slightly, her thin hands trembling only a little as they held the pencil at both ends. The others at the table were watching her, though each in his or her own fashion tried to disguise it.

And Rowan realized; this is the brains behind the firm, this woman, Lauren. And all the time, Rowan had thought it was Ryan. Silently she acknowledged her mistake, wondering if the woman could possibly perceive what she was thinking. *We have been wrong about each other* . . .

But one could not read anything into such an impassive face and such a graceful slow manner.

"May I ask you a question," the woman asked, still looking directly at Rowan. "It's a purely business question, you understand."

"Of course."

"Can you take being rich? I mean really, really rich? Can you handle it?"

Rowan was tempted to smile. It was such a refreshing question, and again, so patronizing and so insulting. Any number of replies came to her lips. But she settled for the simplest.

"Yes," she said. "And I want to build hospitals."

Silence.

Lauren nodded. She folded her arms on the table, her eyes taking in the entire assembly. "Well, I don't see any problem with that," she said calmly. "Seems like an interesting idea. And we're here to do what you want, of course."

Yes, she was the brains behind the firm. And she had allowed Ryan and Randall to do the talking. But she was the one who would be the teacher and eventually the obstacle.

No matter.

Rowan had what she wanted. The legacy was as real as the house was real, as real as the family was real. And the dream was going to be realized. In fact, she knew: it could be done.

"I think we can talk about the immediate problems now, don't you?" Rowan asked. "You'll need to make an inventory of the possessions at the house? I believe someone mentioned this. Also, Carlotta's things. Is there anyone who wants to remove them?"

"Yes, and regarding the house," said Ryan. "Have you come to any decision?"

"I want to restore it. I want to live in it. I'll be marrying Michael Curry soon. Probably before the end of the year. We'll make our home there."

It was as if a bright light had snapped on, bathing each one of them in its warmth and illumination.

"Oh, that's splendid," said Ryan.

"So glad to hear it," said Anne Marie.

"You don't know what the house means to us," said Pierce.

"I wonder if you know," said Lauren, "how very happy everyone will be to hear of this."

Only Randall was quiet, Randall with his droopy lids, and his fleshy hands, and then even he said almost sadly, "Yes, that would be very simply wonderful."

"But can someone come and take the old woman's things away?" Rowan asked. "I don't want to go in until that's done."

"Absolutely," said Ryan. "We'll begin the inventory tomorrow. And Gerald Mayfair will call at once for Carlotta's things."

"And a cleaning team, I need a professional team to scrub

down a room on the third floor and to remove all the mattresses."

"Those jars," said Ryan, with a look of distaste. "Those disgusting jars."

"I emptied all of them."

"Whatever was in them?" asked Pierce.

Randall was studying her with his heavy sagging eyes half mast.

"It was all rotted. If they can get the stench out, and take away the mattresses, we can begin the restoration. All the mattresses, I think . . ."

"Start fresh, yes. I'll take care of it. Pierce can go up there now."

"No, I'll go myself," she said.

"Nonsense, Rowan, let me handle it," said Pierce. He was already on his feet. "Do you want replacements for the mattresses? They're doubles, aren't they, those antique beds? Let me see, there are four. I can have them delivered and installed this afternoon."

"That's splendid," said Rowan. "The maid's room needn't be touched, and Julien's old bed can be dismantled and stored."

"Got it. What else can I do for you?"

"That's more than enough. Michael will take care of the rest. Michael will handle the renovation himself."

"Yes, he is quite successful at that, isn't he?" said Lauren quietly. Instantly she realized the slip she had made. She lowered her eyes, then looked up at Rowan, attempting to mask her slight confusion.

They had already investigated him, hadn't they? Had they found out about his hands?

"We'd love to keep you awhile longer," said Ryan quickly. "Just a few papers we have to show you, in connection with the estate, and perhaps some basic documents pertaining to the legacy . . ."

"Yes, of course, let's get to work. I'd like nothing better."

"Then it's settled. And we'll take you to lunch afterwards. We wanted to take you to Galatoire's, if you have no other plans."

"Sounds wonderful."

And so it was begun.

It was three o'clock when she reached the house. In the full heat of the day, though the sky was still overcast. The warmth seemed collected and stagnant beneath the oaks. As she stepped out of the cab, she could see the tiny insects swarming in the pockets of shadow. But the house caught her up instantly. Here alone again. And the jars are gone, thank God, and the dolls, and very soon all that belonged to Carlotta. Gone.

She had the keys in her hand. They had shown her the papers pertaining to the house, which had been entailed with the legacy in the year 1888 by Katherine. It was hers and hers alone. And so were all the other billions which they wouldn't speak of aloud. *All mine.*

Gerald Mayfair, a personable young man with a bland face and nondescript features, came out the front door. Quickly he explained that he was just leaving, he had only just placed the last carton of Carlotta's personal possessions in the trunk of his car.

The cleaning team had finished about a half hour before.

He eyed Rowan a little nervously as she offered her hand. He couldn't have been more than twenty-five, and did not resemble Ryan's family. His features were smaller and he lacked the poise she'd observed in the others. But he seemed nice—what one would call a nice young guy.

His speaking voice was certainly agreeable.

Carlotta had wanted his grandmother to have her things, he explained. Of course the furniture would remain. It belonged to Rowan. It was all quite old, dating from the time that Carlotta's grandmother, Katherine, had furnished the house.

Rowan thanked him for taking care of things so quickly. She assured him she would be at the Requiem Mass for Carlotta.

"Do you know if she's been . . . buried?" Was that the proper word for being slipped into one of those stone drawers?

Yes, he said, she had been interred this morning. He'd been there with his mother. They'd gotten her message to come for the things when they returned home.

She told him how much she appreciated it, how much she wanted to meet all the family. He nodded.

"It was nice of your two friends to come," he said.

"My friends? Come to what?"

"This morning at the cemetery, Mr. Lightner and Mr. Curry."

"Oh, of course. I . . . I should have been there myself."

"Doesn't matter. She didn't want any fuss, and frankly . . ."

He stood quiet for a moment on the flagstone walk, looking up at the house, and wanting to say something, but seemingly unable to speak.

"What is it?" Rowan asked.

Perhaps he'd wandered up there and seen all that broken glass before the cleaning team had arrived. Surely he would have wanted to see where the "skeleton" had lain, that is, if he'd read the papers, or if the other Mayfairs had told him, which maybe they had.

"You plan to live in it?" he asked suddenly.

"To restore it, to bring it back to the old splendor. My husband . . . the man I'm going to marry. He's an expert on old houses; he says it's absolutely solid. He's eager to begin."

Still he stood quiet in the simmering air, his face glistening slightly, and his expression full of expectation and hesitancy. Finally he said:

"You know it has seen so many tragedies. That's what Aunt Carlotta always said."

"And so did the morning paper," she said, smiling. "But it's seen much happiness, hasn't it? In the old days, for decades at a stretch. I want it to see happiness again."

She waited patiently, and then finally, she asked:

"What is it you really want to say to me?"

His eyes moved over her face, and then with a little shift to his shoulders, and a sigh, he looked back up at the house.

"I think I should tell you that Carlotta . . . Carlotta wanted me to burn the house after her death."

"You're serious?"

"I never had any intention of doing it. I told Ryan and Lauren. I told my parents. But I thought I should tell you. She was adamant. She told me how to do it. That I was to start the fire in the attic with an oil lamp that was up there, and then move down to the second floor and start the drapes burning and finally come down to the first. She made me promise. She gave me a key."

He handed this key to Rowan.

"You don't really need it," he said. "The front door hasn't been locked in fifty years, but she was afraid someone might lock it. She knew she wouldn't die till Deirdre died, and those were her instructions."

"When did she tell you this?"

"Many times. The last time was a week ago, maybe less. Right before Deirdre died . . . when they first knew she was dying. She called me late at night and reminded me. 'Burn it all,' she said."

"She would have hurt everyone if she had done that!" Rowan whispered.

"I know. My parents were horrified. They were afraid she'd burn it herself. But what could they do? Ryan said she wouldn't.

She wouldn't have asked me to do it if she'd been able to do it. He told me to humor her. Tell her I'd do it so that she'd be sure of that, and not go to some other extreme."

"That was wise."

He gave a little nod, then his eyes drifted away from hers and back to the house.

"I just wanted you to know," he said. "I thought you should know."

"And what else can you tell me?"

"What else?" He gave a little shrug. Then he looked at her, and though he meant to turn away, he didn't. He locked in. "Be careful," he said. "Be very careful. It's old and it's gloomy and it's . . . it's not perhaps what it seems."

"How so?"

"It's not a grand house at all. It's some sort of domicile for something. It's a trap, you might say. It's made up of all sorts of patterns. And the patterns form a sort of trap." He shook his head. "I don't know what I'm saying. I'm speaking off the top of my head. It's just . . . well, all of us have a little talent for feeling things . . ."

"I know."

"And well, I guess I wanted to warn you. You don't know anything about us."

"Did Carlotta say that about the patterns, about its being a trap?"

"No, it's only my opinion. I came here more than the others. I was the only one Carlotta would see in the last few years. She liked me. I'm not sure why. Sometimes I was only there out of curiosity, though I wanted to be loyal to her, I really did. It's been like a cloud over my life."

"You're glad it's finished."

"Yes. I am. It's dreadful to say it, but then she didn't want to live on any longer. She said so. She was tired. She wanted to die. But one afternoon, when I was alone here, waiting for her, it came to me that it was a trap. A great big trap. I don't really know what I mean. I'm only saying perhaps that if you feel something, don't discount it. . . ."

"Did you ever *see* anything when you were here?"

He thought for a moment, obviously picking up her meaning with no difficulty.

"Maybe once," he said. "In the hallway. But then again, I could have imagined it."

He fell silent. So did she. That was the end of it, and he wanted to be going.

"It was very nice to talk to you, Rowan," he said with a feeble smile. "Call me if you need me."

She went inside the gate, and watched almost furtively as his silver Mercedes, a large sedan, drove slowly away.

Empty now. Quiet.

She could smell pine oil. She climbed the stairs, and moved quickly from room to room. New mattresses, still wrapped in shining plastic, on all the beds. Sheets and counterpanes neatly folded and stacked to one side. Floors dusted.

Smell of disinfectant from the third floor.

She went upstairs, moving into the breeze from the landing window. The floor of the little chamber of the jars was scrubbed immaculate except for a dark deep staining which probably would never scrub away. Not a shard of glass to be seen in the light from the window.

And Julien's room, dusted, straightened, boxes stacked, the brass bed dismantled and laid against the wall beneath the windows, which had also been cleaned. Books nice and straight. The old dark sticky substance scraped away from the spot where Townsend had died.

All else was undisturbed.

Going back down to Carlotta's room, she found the drawers empty, the dresser bare, the armoire with nothing left but a few wooden hangers. Camphor.

All very still. She saw herself in the mirrored door of the armoire, and was startled. Her heart beat loudly for a moment. No one else here.

She walked downstairs to the first floor, and back down the hallway to the kitchen. They had mopped these floors and cleaned the glass doors of the cabinets. Good smell of wax again, and pine oil, and the smell of wood. That lovely smell.

An old black phone stood on the wooden counter in the pantry.

She dialed the hotel.

"What are you doing?" she asked.

"Lying here in bed feeling lonely and sorry for myself. I went over to the cemetery this morning with Aaron. I'm exhausted. I still ache all over, like I've been in a fight. Where are you? You aren't over there, are you?"

"Yes, and it's warm and empty and all the old woman's things are gone, and the mattresses are gone, and the attic room is scrubbed clean."

"Are you the only one there?"

"Yes," she said. "And it's beautiful. The sun's coming out."

She stood looking about herself, at the light pouring through the French windows into the kitchen, at the light in the dining room, falling on the hardwood floor. "I'm definitely the only one here."

"I want to come over there," he said.

"No, I'm leaving now to walk back to the hotel. I want you to rest. I want you to go for a checkup."

"Be serious."

"Have you ever had an electrocardiogram?"

"You're going to scare me into a heart attack. I had all that after I drowned. My heart's perfect. What I need is erotic exercise in large doses sustained over an endless period of time."

"Depends on your pulse when I get there."

"Come on, Rowan. I'm not going for any checkup. If you're not here in ten minutes, I'm coming to get you."

"I'll be there sooner than that."

She hung up.

For a moment she thought about something she'd read in the file, something Arthur Langtry had written about his experience of seeing Lasher, something about his heart skipping dangerously, and about being dizzy. But then Arthur had been a very old man.

Peace here. Only the cries of the birds from the garden.

She walked slowly through the dining room and through the high keyhole doorway into the hall, glancing back at it to enjoy its soaring height and her own seeming smallness. The light poured in through the sun room, shining on the polished floor.

A great lovely sense of well-being came over her. *All mine.*

She stood still for a few seconds, listening, feeling. Trying to take full possession of the moment, trying to remember the anguish of yesterday and the day before, and to feel this in comparison, this wonderful lighthearted feeling. And once again the whole lurid tragic history comforted her, because she with all her own dark secrets had a place in it. And she would redeem it. That was the most important thing of all.

She turned to walk to the front of the house, and for the first time noticed a tall vase of roses on the hall table. Had Gerald put them there? Perhaps he had forgotten to mention it.

She stopped, studying the beautiful drowsy blooms, all of them bloodred, and rather like the florist-perfect flowers for the dead, she thought, as if they'd been picked from those fancy sprays left in the cemetery.

Then with a chill, she thought of Lasher. Flowers tossed at Deirdre's feet. Flowers put on the grave. In fact, she was so violently startled that for a moment she could hear her heart again, beating in the stillness. But what an absurd idea. Probably Gerald had put the flowers here, or Pierce when he had seen to the mattresses. After all, this was a commonplace vase, half filled with fresh water, and these were simply florist roses.

Nevertheless the thing looked ghastly to her. In fact, as her heartbeat grew steady again, she realized there was something distinctly odd about the bouquet. She was not an expert on roses, but weren't they generally smaller than this? How large and floppy these flowers looked. And such a dark blood color. And look at the stems, and the leaves; the leaves of roses were invariably almond-shaped, were they not, and these leaves had many points on them. As a matter of fact, there wasn't any leaf in this entire bouquet which had the same pattern or number of points as another. Strange. Like something grown wild, genetically wild, full of random and overwhelming mutation.

They were moving, weren't they? Swelling. No, just unfolding, as roses often do, opening little by little until they fall apart in a cascade of bruised petals. She shook her head. She felt a little dizzy.

Probably left there by Pierce. And what did it matter? She'd call him from the hotel just to make sure, and tell him she appreciated it.

She moved on to the front of the house, trying to capture the feeling of well-being again, breathing in the luxurious warmth around her. Very like a temple, this house. She looked back at the stairs. All the way up there, Arthur had seen Stuart Townsend.

Well, there was no one there now.

No one. No one in the long parlor. No one out there on the porch where the vines crawled on the screens.

No one.

"Are you afraid of me?" she asked out loud. It gave her a curious tingling excitement to speak the words. "Or is it that you expected me to be afraid of you and you're angry that I'm not? That's it, isn't it?"

Only the stillness answered her. And the soft rustling sound of the rose petals falling on the marble table.

With a faint smile, she went back to the roses, picked one

from the vase, and gently holding it to her lips to feel its silky petals, she went out the front door.

It really was just an enormous rose, and look how many petals, and how strangely confused they seemed. And the thing was already withering.

In fact, the petals were already brown at the edges and curling. She savored the sweet perfume for another slow second, and then dropped the rose into the garden as she went out the gate.

PART THREE

COME INTO MY
PARLOR

Thirty-three

THE MADNESS OF restoration began on Thursday morning, though the night before over dinner at Oak Haven with Aaron and Rowan, he had begun to outline what steps he would take.

As far as the grave was concerned, and all his thoughts about it and the doorway and the number thirteen, they had gone into the notebook, and he did not wish to dwell on them anymore.

The whole trip to the cemetery had been grim. The morning itself had been overcast yet beautiful, of course, and he had liked walking there with Aaron, and Aaron had shown him how to block some of the sensations that came through his hands. He'd been practicing, going without the gloves, and here and there touching gateposts, or picking sprigs of wild lantana, and turning off the images, pretty much the way one blocks a bad or obsessive thought, and to his surprise it more or less worked.

But the cemetery. He had hated it, hated its crumbling romantic beauty, and hated the great heap of withering flowers from Deirdre's funeral which still surrounded the crypt. And the gaping hole where Carlotta Mayfair was soon to be laid to rest, so to speak.

Then as he was standing there, realizing in a sort of stunned miserable state that there were twelve crypts in the tomb and the doorway carved on the top made thirteen portals, up came his old friend Jerry Lonigan with some very pale-faced Mayfairs, and a coffin on wheels which could only belong to Carlotta, which was slipped, with only the briefest ceremony by the officiating priest, into the vacant slot.

Twelve crypts, the keyhole door, and then that coffin sliding in, blam! And his eyes moving up to that keyhole door again, which did look exactly like the doors in the house, but why? And then they were all going, with a quick exchange of pleasantries, for the Mayfairs assumed he and Aaron were there for the ceremony and expressed their appreciation before they went away.

813

"Come have a beer with me sometime," said Jerry.

"Best to Rita."

The cemetery had dropped into a buzzing, dizzying silence. Not a single thing he had seen since the beginning of this odyssey, not even the images from the jars, had filled him with as much dread as the sight of this tomb. "There's the thirteen," he had said to Aaron.

"But they have buried so many in those crypts," Aaron had explained. "You know how it's done."

"It's a pattern," he'd murmured halfheartedly, feeling the blood drain from his face. "Look at it, twelve crypts and a doorway. It's a pattern, I tell you. I knew the number and the door were connected. I just don't know what they mean."

Later that afternoon waiting for Rowan, while Aaron typed away on his computer in the front room, presumably on the Mayfair history, Michael had drawn the doorway in his notebook. He hated it. He hated the empty middle of it, for that's what it had been in the bas-relief, not a door, but a doorway.

"And I've seen that doorway somewhere else, in some other representation," he wrote. "But I don't know where."

He had hated even thinking about it. Even the thing trying to be human had not filled him with such apprehension.

But over supper, on the patio at Oak Haven, with the ashen twilight surrounding them and the candles flickering in their glass shades, they had resolved again to spend no more time poring over interpretations. They would move forward as they said. He and Rowan had spent the night in the front bedroom of the plantation, a lovely change from the hotel, and in the morning when he woke up at six, with the sun beating on his face, Rowan was already on the gallery, enjoying her second pot of coffee, and raring to go.

As soon as he arrived back in New Orleans, at nine o'clock, the work began.

He had never had so much fun.

He rented a car and roamed the city, taking down the names of the construction crews who were working on the finest of the uptown houses and the classy restorations going on in the Quarter downtown. He got out and talked to the bosses and the men; sometimes he went inside with the more talkative people who were willing to show him their work in progress, discussing the local wage scales and expectations, and asking for the names of carpenters and painters who needed work.

He called the local architectural firms who were famous for handling the grand homes, and requested various recommendations. The sheer friendliness of people astonished him. And the mere mention of the Mayfair house kindled excitement. People were only too eager to give advice.

For all the work that was going on, the city was full of unemployed craftsmen. The oil boom of the 1970s and early 1980s had generated tremendous interest and activity in restoration. And now the city lay under the cloud of the oil depression, with an economy bruised by numerous foreclosures. Money was tight. There were mansions on the market for half of what they were worth.

By one o'clock he had hired three crews of excellent painters, and a team of the finest plasterers in the city—quadroons descended from the colored families who had been free long before the Civil War, and who had been plastering the ceilings and walls of New Orleans houses for over seven and eight generations.

He had also signed up two teams of plumbers, one excellent roofing company, and a well-known uptown landscaping expert to begin the clearing and the restoration of the garden. At two P.M. the man walked the property with Michael for half an hour, pointing out the giant camellias and azaleas, the bridal wreath and the antique roses, all of which could be saved.

Two cleaning women had also been hired—upon recommendation of Beatrice Mayfair—who began the detailed dusting of furniture, the polishing of the silver, and the washing of the china which had lain under its layer of dust for many a year.

A special crew was scheduled to come in Friday morning to commence draining the pool, and seeing what had to be done to restore it and revamp its antiquated equipment. A kitchen specialist was also scheduled for Friday. Engineers were scheduled to examine the foundation and the porches. And an excellent carpenter and jack-of-all-trades named Dart Henley was eager to become Michael's second in command.

At five o'clock, while there was still plenty of light, Michael went under the house with a flashlight and a dust mask and confirmed, after forty-five minutes of serious crawling, that indeed the interior walls were chain walls, descending directly to the ground, that the underneath was dry and clean, and that there was ample space for a central air and heat duct system.

Meantime, Ryan Mayfair came through the house to take the official and legal inventory for the estates of Deirdre and Carlotta Mayfair. A team of young lawyers, including Pierce, Franklin, Isaac, and Wheatfield Mayfair—all descendants of the original brothers of the firm—accompanied a group of appraisers and antique dealers who identified, appraised, and tagged every chandelier, picture, mirror, and fauteuil.

Priceless French antiques were brought down from the attic, including some fine chairs which needed only reupholstering and tables which required no repair at all. Stella's art deco treasures, equally delicate and equally preserved, were also brought into the light.

Old oil paintings by the dozens were discovered, as well as rugs rolled in camphor balls, old tapestries, and all the chandeliers from Riverbend, each crated and marked.

It was after dark when Ryan finished.

"Well, my dear, I'm happy to report: no more bodies."

Indeed, a call from him later in the evening confirmed that the enormous inventory was almost the same as the one taken at the death of Antha. Things had not even been moved. "All we did most of the time was check them off the list," he said. Even the count of the gold and jewels was the same. He'd have the inventory for her right away.

By that time, Michael was back at the hotel, had feasted on delicious room service from the Caribbean Room downstairs, and was perusing all the architecture books he'd gleaned from the local stores, pointing out to Rowan the pictures of the various houses that surrounded hers, and the other mansions scattered throughout the Garden District.

He had bought a "house" notebook in the K&B drugstore on Louisiana Avenue, and was making lists of what he meant to do. He would have to call tile men early in the morning, and take a more careful look at the old bathrooms, because the fixtures were absolutely marvelous, and he did not want to change what did not need to be changed.

Rowan was reading over some of the papers she would sign. She had opened a joint account at the Whitney Bank that afternoon just for the renovations, depositing three hundred thousand dollars in it, and she had the signature cards for Michael and a book of checks.

"You can't spend too much money on this house," she said. "It deserves the best."

Michael gave a little delighted laugh. This had always been a dream—to do it without a budget, as if it were a great work of art, every decision being made with the purest aims.

At eight o'clock, Rowan went down to meet Beatrice and Sandra Mayfair for drinks in the bar. She was back within the hour. Tomorrow she would have breakfast with another couple of cousins. It was all rather pleasant and easy. They did the talking. And she liked the sound of their voices. She'd always liked to listen to people, especially when they talked so much that she didn't have to say anything much herself.

"But I'll tell you," she said to Michael, "they do know things and they aren't telling me what they know. And they know the older ones know things. They're the ones I have to talk to. I have to win their trust."

On Friday, as the plumbers and the roofers swarmed over the property, and the plasterers went in with their buckets and ladders and drop cloths, and a loud chugging machine began to pump the swimming pool dry, Rowan went downtown to sign papers.

Michael went to work with the tile men in the front bathroom. It had been decided to fix up the front bath and bedroom first so that he and Rowan could move in as soon as possible. And Rowan wanted a shower without disturbing the old tub. That meant ripping out some tile, and building in more, and fitting the tub with a glass enclosure.

"Three days we'll have it for you," the workman promised.

The plasterers were already removing the wallpaper from the bedroom ceiling. The electrician would have to be called in, as the wires to the old brass chandelier had never been properly insulated. And Rowan and Michael would want a ceiling fan in place of the old fixture. More notes.

Some time around eleven, Michael wandered out on the screened porch off the parlor. Two cleaning women were working noisily and cheerfully in the big room behind him. The decorator recommended by Bea was measuring the windows for new draperies.

Forgot about these old screens, Michael thought. He made a note in his book. He looked at the old rocker. It had been scrubbed clean, and the porch itself had been swept. The bees hummed in the vines. Through the thick stand of banana trees to the left, he could just see the bright occasional flashes of the workmen surrounding the pool. They were shoveling two feet of earth from off the flagstone patio. Indeed, the area of paving was far larger than anyone had supposed.

He took a deep breath, staring out at the crepe myrtle across the lawn.

"No ladders thrown down yet, am I right, Lasher?" His whisper seemed to die on the empty air.

Nothing but the hum of the bees, and the mingled sounds of the workmen—the low grind of a lawn mower just starting up, and the sound of the diesel leaf blowers navigating the paths. He glanced at his watch. The air-conditioning men were due any minute. He had sketched out a system of eight different heat pumps which would provide both cooling and heating, and the worst problem would be the placement of the equipment, what with the attics filled with boxes and furniture and other items. Maybe they could go directly to the roof.

Then there were the floors. Yes, he had to get an estimate on the floors right away. The floor of the parlor was still very beautifully finished, apparently from the time Stella had used it as a dance floor. But the other floors were deeply soiled and dull. Of course nobody would do any interior painting or floor finishing until the plasterers were out. They made too much dust. And the painters, he had to go see how they were coming along on the outside. They had to wait until the roofers had sealed the parapet walls at the top. But the painters had plenty of work to do sanding and preparing the window frames and the shutters. And what else? Oh, the phone system, yes, Rowan wanted something state of the art. I mean the house was so big. And then there was the cabana, and that old servants' quarters building way at the back. He was thinking of turning a small contractor loose on that little building now, for an entire renovation.

Ah, this was fun. But why was he getting away with it? That was the question. Who was biding whose time?

He didn't want to confess to Rowan that he couldn't shake an underlying apprehensiveness, an underlying certainty that they were being watched. That the house itself was something alive. Maybe it was only the lingering impression of the images in the attic—of all the skirts gathered around him, of all of *them* earth-bound and here. He didn't really believe in ghosts in that sense. But the place had absorbed the personalities of all the Mayfairs, hadn't it, as old houses are supposed to do. And it seemed every time he turned that he was about to see someone or something that really wasn't there.

What a surprise to step into the parlor and see only the sunlight and the solemn neglected furniture. The enormous mirrors, towering over the room like guardians. The old pictures lifeless and dim in their frames. For a long moment he looked at the soft portrait of Stella—a painted photograph. So sweet her smile, and her black shining marcelled hair. Out of the corners of her eyes, she looked at him, through the filth that clung to the dim glass.

"Did you want something, Mr. Mike?" the young cleaning woman asked him. He shook his head.

He turned back and looked at the empty rocker. Had it moved? This was foolish. He was inviting something to happen. He closed his notebook and went back to work.

Joseph, the decorator, was waiting for him in the dining room. And Eugenia was here. Eugenia wanted to work. Surely there was something she could do. Nobody knew this house the way she did, she'd worked in this house for five years, she had. Eugenia had told her son this very morning that she was not too old to work, that she would work until she dropped dead.

Did Dr. Mayfair want silk for these draperies? asked the decorator. Was she sure about that? He had a score of damasks and velvets to show her that wouldn't cost half as much.

When Michael met Rowan for lunch at Mayfair and Mayfair she was still signing. He was surprised at the ease and trust with which Ryan greeted him and began to explain things.

"It was always the custom before Antha and Deirdre to make bequests at a time such as this," he said, "and Rowan wants to revive the custom. We're making a list now of the Mayfairs who might accept a bequest, and Beatrice is already on the phone to anybody and everybody in the family. Please understand this isn't as insane as it sounds. Most Mayfairs have money in the bank, and always have had. Nevertheless, there are cousins in college, and a couple in medical school, and others who are saving to buy a first home. You know—that sort of thing. I think it's commendable of Rowan to want to revive the custom. And of course considering the size of the estate . . ."

Nevertheless there was something cunning in Ryan, something calculating and watchful. And wasn't that natural? He seemed to be testing Michael with these riffs of information. Michael only nodded, and shrugged. "Sounds great."

By late afternoon, Michael and Rowan were back at the house conferring with the men around the pool. The stench of the muck that had been dredged from the bottom was unbearable. Shirtless and barefooted, the men carried it away in wheelbarrows. There were no real leaks in the old cement. You could tell because there was no sogginess in the ground anywhere. The foreman told Michael they could have the whole thing patched and replastered by the middle of next week.

"Sooner if you can," said Rowan. "I don't mind paying you overtime to work this weekend. Bring it back fast. I can't stand the sight of it the way it is now."

They were glad for the extra paychecks. In fact, just about every workman on the place was happy to work the weekend.

All new heating and filtering equipment was being installed for the pool. The gas connections were satisfactory. The new electric service was already going in.

And Michael got on the phone to another painting crew to take care of the cabana. Sure, they'd work Saturday, for time and a half. Wouldn't take much to paint its wooden doors, and refit its shower, lavatory, and small changing rooms.

"So what color do you want the house to be?" Michael asked. "They'll get to the outside painting faster than you think. And you want the cabana and the *garçonnière* painted the same color, don't you?"

"Tell me what you want," she said.

"I'd leave it the violet color it's always been. The dark green shutters go with it just fine. I'd keep the whole scheme, actually—blue for the roofs of the porches, and gray for the porch floors, and black for the cast iron. By the way, I found a little man who can replace the pieces of the iron that are missing. He's already making the molds. He has his own shop back by the river. Did anyone tell you about the iron fence that runs around this property?"

"Tell me."

"It's even older than the house. It was the early nineteenth century version of chain link. That is, it was prefab. And it goes all the way down First Street and turns on Camp because that's how big the property once was. Now, we should paint it, just a nice coat of black paint is all it needs, just like the railings . . ."

"Bring in all the crews you need," she said. "The violet color is perfect. And if you have to make a decision without me, make it. Make it look like you think it should look. Spend what you think ought to be spent."

"You're a contractor's dream, darling," he said. "We're off to a roaring start. Gotta go. See that man who just came out the back door? He's coming to tell me he ran into a problem with the upstairs bathroom walls. I knew he would."

"Don't work too hard," she said in his ear, her deep velvety voice bringing the chills up on him. A nice little throb of excitement caught him between the legs as she crushed her breasts against his arm. No time for it.

"Work too hard? I'm just warming up. And let me tell you something else, Rowan. There are a couple of damn near irresistible houses I'd like to tackle in this town when we're through here. I see the future, Rowan. I see Great Expectations with offices on Magazine Street. I could bring those houses back slowly and carefully and ride out the bad market. This house is only the first."

"How much do you need to pick them up?"

"Honey, I have the money to do that," he said, kissing her quickly. "I've got plenty of money. Ask your cousin Ryan if you don't believe me. If he hasn't already run a complete credit check on me, I'd be very surprised."

"Michael, if he says one wrong word to you . . ."

"Rowan, I'm in paradise. Relax!"

Saturday and Sunday rolled by at the same grand pace. The gardeners worked until after dark mowing down the weeds and digging the old cast-iron furniture out of the brush.

Rowan and Michael and Aaron set up the old table and chairs in the center of the lawn, and there they had their lunch each day.

Aaron was making some progress with Julien's books, but they were mostly lists of names, with brief enigmatic statements. No real autobiography at all. "So far, my most unkind guess is that these are lists of successful vendettas." He read a sampling.

" 'April 4, 1889 Hendrickson paid out as he deserved.'

" 'May 9, 1889, Carlos paid in kind.'

" 'June 7, 1889, furious with Wendell for his display of temper last night. Showed him a thing or two. No more worries there.'

"It goes on like that," said Aaron, "page after page, book after book. Occasionally there are little maps and drawings, and financial notes. But for the most part that's all it is. I'd say there are approximately twenty-two entries per year. I've yet to come upon a coherent full paragraph. No, if the autobiography exists, it's not here."

"What about the attic, are you game to go up there?" asked Rowan.

"Not now. I had a fall last night."

"What are you talking about?"

"On the staircase at the hotel. I was impatient with the elevator. I fell to the first landing. It might have been worse."

"Aaron, why didn't you tell me?"

"Well, this is soon enough. There's nothing out of the ordinary about it, except that I don't recall losing my footing. But I've a sore ankle, and I'd like to put off going up into the attic."

Rowan was crestfallen, angry. She gazed up at the façade of the house. There were workmen everywhere. On the parapets, on the porches, in the open bedroom windows.

"Don't become unduly alarmed," said Aaron. "I want you to know, but I don't want you to fret."

It was clear to Michael that Rowan was speechless. He could feel her fury. He could see the disfigurement of the anger in her face.

"We've seen nothing here," said Michael to Aaron. "Absolutely nothing. And no one else has seen anything, at least not anything worth mentioning to either of us."

"You were pushed, weren't you?" asked Rowan in a low voice.

"Perhaps," said Aaron.

"He's deviling you."

"I think so," said Aaron with a little nod. "He likes to knock Julien's books about too, when he has the opportunity, which seems to be whenever I leave the room. Again, I thought it important you know about it, but I don't want you to fret."

"Why's he doing it?"

"Maybe he wants your attention," said Aaron. "But I hesitate to say. Whatever the case, trust that I can protect myself. The work here does seem to be coming along splendidly."

"No problems," said Michael, but he was pitched into gloom.

After lunch, he walked Aaron to the gate.

"I'm having too much fun, aren't I?" he asked.

"Of course you aren't," said Aaron. "What a strange thing to say."

"I wish it would come to a boil," said Michael. "I think I'll win when it does. But the waiting is driving me nuts. After all, what is he waiting for?"

"What about your hands? I do wish you'd try to go without the gloves."

"I have. I take off the gloves for a couple of hours each day. I can't get used to the heat, the zinging feeling, even when I can blot everything else out. Look, do you want me to walk with you back to the hotel?"

"Of course not. I'll see you there tonight if you have time for a drink."

"Yeah, it's like a dream coming true, isn't it?" he asked wistfully. "I mean for me."

"No, for both of us," said Aaron.

"You trust me?"

"Why on earth would you ask?"

"Do you think I'm going to win? Do you think I'm going to do what they want of me?"

"What do you think?"

"I think she loves me and that it's going to be wonderful what happens."

"So do I."

He felt good, and each successive hour brought some new realization of it; and in his time at the house, there had been no other fragmentary memories of the visions. No sense of the ghosts.

It was comfortable each night being with Rowan, comfortable

being in the spacious old suite, and making love, and then getting up again, to go back to work on the books and on the notes. It was comfortable being tired from a day of physical exertion, and feeling his body springing back from those two months of torpor and too much beer.

He was drinking little or no beer now; and in the absence of the dulling alcohol, his senses were exquisitely sharpened; he could not get enough of Rowan's sleek, girlish body and her inexhaustible energy. Her total lack of narcissism or self-consciousness awakened in him a roughness that she seemed to love. There were times when their lovemaking was like horse-play, and even more violent than that. But it always ended in tenderness and a feverish embrace, so that he wondered how he had ever slept all these years, without her arms around him.

Thirty-four

HER PRIVATE TIME was still the early morning. No matter how late she read, she opened her eyes at four o'clock. And no matter how early he went to bed, Michael slept like the dead till nine unless someone shook him or screamed at him.

It was all right. It gave her the margin of quiet that her soul demanded. Never had she known a man who accepted her so completely as she was; nevertheless there were moments when she had to get away from everyone.

Loving him these last few days, she had understood for the first time why she had always taken her men in small doses. This was slavery, this persistent passion—the inability to even look at his smooth naked back or the little gold chain around his powerful neck without wanting him, without gritting her teeth silently at the thought of reaching under the covers and stroking the dark hair around his balls and making his cock grow hard in her hand.

That his age gave him some leverage against her—the ability to say after the second time, tenderly but firmly, No, I can't do it again—made him all the more tantalizing, worse perhaps than a teasing young boy, though she didn't really know, because she'd never been teased by a young boy. But when she considered the kindness, the mellowness, the total lack of young-man self-centeredness and hatefulness in him, the trade-off of age against boundless energy was a perfect bargain indeed.

"I want to spend the rest of my life with you," she had whispered this morning, running her finger down the coarsened black stubble which covered not only his chin but his throat, knowing that he wouldn't stir. "Yes, my conscience and my body need you. Everything I'll ever be needs you."

She had even kissed him without a chance of waking him.

But now was her time alone, with him safely out of sight and out of mind.

And it was such an extraordinary time to walk through the deserted streets just as the sun was rising, to see the squirrels racing through the oaks, and to hear the violent birds crying mournfully and even desperately.

A mist sometimes crawled along the brick pavements. And the iron fences shimmered with the dew. The sky was shot through and through with red, bloody as a sunset, fading slowly into blue daylight.

The house was cool at this hour.

And this morning, she was glad of it because the heat in general had begun to wear on her. And she had an errand to perform which gave her no pleasure.

She should have attended to it before now, but it was one of those little things she wanted to ignore, to weed out from all the rest that was being offered her.

But as she went up the stairs now, she found herself almost eager. A little twinge of excitement caught her by surprise. She went into the old master bedroom, which had belonged to her mother, and moved to the far side of the bed, where the velvet purse of gold coins still lay, ignored, on the marble top bedside table. The jewel box was there, too. In all the hubbub no one had dared touch them.

On the contrary, at least six different workmen had come to report that these items were there, and somebody ought to do something about them.

Yes, something about them.

She stared down at the gold coins, which spilled out of the old velvet bag in a grimy heap. God only knew where they had actually come from.

Then she gathered up the sack, put the loose coins inside, picked up the jewel box, and took them down to her favorite room, which was the dining room.

The soft morning light was just breaking through the soiled windows. A plasterer's drop cloth covered half the floor, and a tall spidery ladder reached to the unfinished patchwork on the ceiling.

She pushed back the canvas that covered the table, and removed the draping from the chair, and then she sat down with her load of treasures and put them in front of her.

"You're here," she whispered. "I know you are. You're watching me." She felt cold as she said it. She laid out a handful of coins, and pushed them apart the better to see them in the gathering light. Roman coins. It didn't take an expert to see it. And here, this was a Spanish coin, with amazingly clear numerals and letters. She reached into the sack and pulled out another little trove. Greek coins? About these she wasn't certain. A stickiness clung to them, part damp and part dust. She longed to polish them.

It struck her suddenly that that would be a good task for Eugenia, polishing all these coins.

And no sooner had the thought made her smile, than she thought she heard a sound in the house. A vague rustling. Just the singing of the boards, Michael would say if he were here. She paid no attention.

She gathered up all the coins and shoved them back in the purse, pushed it aside, and took up the jewel box. It was very old, rectangular, with tarnished hinges. The velvet had worn through in some places to show the wood beneath, and it was deep inside, with six large compartments.

The various jewels were in no order, however. Earrings, necklaces, rings, pins, they were all tangled together. And in the bottom of the box, like so many pebbles, were what appeared to be raw stones, gleaming dully. Were these real rubies? Emeralds? She could not imagine it. She did not know a real pearl from a fake. Nor gold from an imitation. But these necklaces were fine artifacts, skillfully fashioned, and a sense of reverence and sadness came over her as she touched them.

She thought of Antha hurrying through the streets of New York with a handful of coins to sell. And a stab of pain went through her. She thought of her mother, lying in the rocker on the porch, the drool slipping down her chin, and all this wealth so near at hand, and the Mayfair emerald around her neck, like some sort of child's bauble.

The Mayfair emerald. She hadn't even thought of it since the first night when she'd tucked it away in the china pantry. She rose and went to the pantry now—unlocked all this time like everything else—and there was the small velvet case on the wooden shelf behind the glass door, among the Wedgwood cups and saucers, just where she'd left it.

She took it to the table, set it down, and carefully opened it. The jewel of jewels—large, rectangular, glinting exquisitely in its dark gold setting. And now that she knew the history, how she had changed towards it.

On the first night it had seemed unreal, and faintly repulsive. Now it seemed a living thing, with a tale to tell of its own, and she found herself hesitant to remove it from the soiled velvet. Of course it did not belong to her! It belonged to those who had believed in it, and who had worn it with pride, those who had wanted *him* to come to them.

Just for a moment, she felt a longing to be one of them. She tried to deny it, but she felt it—a longing to accept with a whole heart the entire inheritance.

Was she blushing? She felt the warmth in her face. Maybe it was simply the humid air and the sun rising slowly outside, and the garden filling up with a bright light that made the trees come alive beyond the glass, and made the sky suddenly blue in the topmost panes of the windows.

But it was more likely shame that she felt. Shame that Aaron or Michael might know what she'd been thinking.

Lusting after the devil like a witch. She laughed softly.

And it seemed unfair suddenly, very unfair that *he* should be her sworn enemy before they'd even met.

"What are you waiting for?" she asked aloud. "Are you like the shy vampire of myth who must be invited in? I think not. This is your home. You're here now. You're listening to me and watching me."

She sat back in the chair, her eyes running over the murals as they slowly came to life in the pale sunlight. For the first time she spied a tiny woman naked in the window of the dim plantation house in the painting. And another faded nude seated upon the dark green bank of the small lagoon. It made her smile. Rather like discovering a secret. She wondered if Michael had seen these two tawny beauties. Oh, the house was full of undiscovered things, and so was its sad and melancholy garden.

Beyond the windows, the cherry laurel suddenly swayed in the breeze. In fact, it began to dance as if a wind had caught its stiff dark limbs. She heard it stroke the banister of the porch. It scraped against the roof above, and then settled back to itself, as the wind moved on, it seemed, to the distant crepe myrtle.

Entrancing the way the high thin branches, full of pink blossoms, succumbed to the dance, and the entire tree thrashed against the gray wall of the neighboring house, and sent down a shower of dappled, fluttering leaves. Like so much light falling in tiny pieces.

Her eyes misted slightly; she was conscious of the relaxation of her limbs, of giving in to a vague dreaminess. Yes, look at the tree dance. Look at the cherry laurel again, and the shower of green coming down on the boards of the porch. Look at the thin limbs reaching all the way in to scrape the windowpanes.

With a dull shock, she focused her eyes, staring at the branches, staring at their concerted, deliberate movement as they stroked the glass.

"You," she whispered.

Lasher in the trees, Lasher the way Deirdre would make him come outside the boarding school. And Rita Mae never knew what she'd actually described to Aaron Lightner.

She was rigid now in the chair. The tree was bending close, and then swaying back ever so gracefully, and this time the branches veritably blotted out the sun, and the leaves tumbled down the glass, broken and spinning. Yet the room was warm and airless.

She did not remember rising to her feet. But she was standing. Yes, he was there. He was making the trees move, for nothing else on earth could make them move like that. And the tiny hairs were standing up on the backs of her arms. And she felt a vague chill over her scalp, as if something were touching her.

It seemed the air around her changed. Not a breeze, no. More like a curtain brushing her. She turned around, and stared out through the empty window at Chestnut Street. Had there been something there, a great dense shadow for a moment, a thing contracting and then expanding, like a dark sea being with tentacles? No. Nothing but the oak across the street. And the sky growing ever more radiant.

"Why don't you speak?" she said. "I'm here alone."

How strange her voice sounded.

But there were other sounds intruding now. She heard voices outside. A truck had stopped; and she could hear the scrape of the gate as the workmen pushed it back on the flagstones. Even as she waited, her head bowed, there came the turning of the knob.

"Hey, there, Dr. Mayfair . . ."

"Morning, Dart. Morning, Rob. Morning, Billy."

Heavy feet mounted the stairs. With a soft deep vibration, the little elevator was being brought down, and soon its brass door opened with the familiar dull clang.

Yes, their house now.

She turned sluggishly, almost stubbornly, and gathered together the entire trove of treasures. She took them into the china pantry and put them in the large drawer, where the old tablecloths had once been, moldering, before they were discarded. The old key was still in the lock. She turned it and put the key in her pocket.

Then she went back out, steps slow, uneasy, relinquishing the house to the others.

At the gate, she turned and looked back. No breeze at all in the garden. Just to make certain of what she'd seen, she turned and followed the path, around and past her mother's old porch, and back to the servants' gallery that ran along the dining room.

Yes, littered with curling green leaves. Something brushed her again, and she turned around, her arm up as if to defend herself from a dangling spiderweb.

A stillness seemed to drop down around her. No sounds had followed her here. The foliage grew high and dense over the balustrade.

"What keeps you from speaking to me?" she whispered. "Are you really afraid?"

Nothing moved. The heat seemed to rise from the flagstones beneath her. Tiny gnats congregated in the shadows. The big drowsy white ginger lilies leaned over close to her face, and a dull crackling sound slowly drew her eye to the depths of the garden patch, to a dark tangle from which a vagrant purple iris sprang, savage and shivering, a hideous mouth of a flower, its stem snapping back now as though a cat darting through the brush had bent it down carelessly.

She watched it sway and then right itself and grow still, its ragged petals trembling. Lurid, it looked. She had the urge to put her finger into it, as if it were an organ. But what was happening to it? She stared, the heat heavy on her eyelids, the gnats rising so that she lifted her right hand to drive them away. Was the flower actually growing?

No. Something had injured it, and it was breaking from its stem, that was all, and how monstrous it looked, how enormous; but it was all in her perspective. The heat, the stillness, the sudden coming of the men like intruders into her domain right at the moment of her greatest peace. She could be sure of nothing.

She took her handkerchief out of her pocket and blotted her cheeks, and then walked down the path towards the gate. She felt confused, unsure—guilty that she'd come alone, and uncertain that anything unusual had happened.

All her many plans for the day came back to her. So much to do, so many real things to do. And Michael would be getting up just about now. If she hurried, they might have breakfast together.

Thirty-five

MONDAY MORNING MICHAEL and Rowan went downtown together to obtain their Louisiana driver's licenses. You couldn't buy a car here until you had the state driver's license.

And when they turned in their California licenses, which they had to do in order to receive the Louisiana license, it was sort of ceremonial and final and oddly exciting. Like giving up a passport or citizenry, perhaps. Michael found himself glancing at Rowan, and he saw her secretive and delighted smile.

They had a light dinner Monday night at the Desire Oyster Bar. A searing hot gumbo, full of shrimp and andouille sausage; and ice-cold beer. The doors of the place were open along Bourbon Street, the overhead fans stirring the cool air around them, the sweet, lighthearted jazz pouring out of the Mahogany Hall bar across the street.

"That's the New Orleans sound," Michael said, "that jazz with a real song in it, a joie de vivre. Nothing ever dark in it. Nothing ever really mournful. Not even when they play for the funerals."

"Let's take a walk," she said. "I want to see all these seedy joints for myself."

They spent the evening in the Quarter, roaming away from the garish lights of Bourbon Street finally, and past the elegant shop windows of Royal and Chartres, and then back to the river lookout opposite Jackson Square.

The size of the Quarter obviously amazed Rowan, as well as the feeling of authenticity which had somehow survived the renovations and the various improvements. Michael found himself overwhelmed again by the inevitable memories—Sundays down here with his mother. He could not argue against the improvements of curbs and street lamps, and new cobblestones laid around Jackson Square. The place seemed if anything more vital now than it had been in its shabbier and more volatile past.

It felt so good after the long walk to sit on the bench at the riverfront, merely watching the dark glitter of the water, watching the dancing boats, strung with lights like big wedding cakes, as they swept past the distant indistinct shapes of the far bank.

A gaiety prevailed among the tourists who came and went from the lookout. Soft conversation and random bursts of laughter. Couples embraced in the shadows. A lone saxophonist played a ragged, soulful song for the quarters people tossed into the hat at his feet.

Finally, they walked back into the thick of the pedestrian traffic, making their way to the soiled old Café du Monde for the famous café au lait and sugared doughnuts. They sat for a while in the warm air, as the others came and went from the sticky little tables around them; then meandered out among the glitzy shops which now filled the old French Market, across from the sad and graceful buildings of Decatur Street with their iron-lace balconies and slender iron colonettes.

Because she asked him to, he drove her up through the Irish Channel, skirting the dark brooding ruin of the St. Thomas Project, and following the river with its deserted warehouses for as long as he could. Annunciation Street looked a little better in the night maybe, with cheerful lights in the windows of the little houses. They drove on, uptown, on a narrow tree-lined street, into the Victorian section where the rambling houses were full of gingerbread and fretwork, and he pointed out to her his old-time favorites, and those he would love to restore.

How extraordinary it felt to have money in his pockets in his old home town. To know he could buy those houses, just the way he'd dreamed of it in the long-ago hopelessness and desperation of childhood.

Rowan seemed eager, happy, curious about things around her. No regrets apparently. But then it was so soon . . .

She talked now and then in easy bursts, her deep grosgrain voice always charming him and distracting him slightly from the content of what she said. She agreed the people here were incredibly friendly. They took their time about everything they did; but they were so completely without meanness it was almost hard to figure out. The accents of the family members baffled her. Beatrice and Ryan spoke with a touch of New York in their voices. Louisa had a completely different accent, and young Pierce didn't sound like his father; and all of them sounded just a little bit like Michael sooner or later on some words.

"Don't tell them that, honey," he cautioned her. "I'm from the other side of Magazine Street and they know it. Don't think they don't."

"They think you're wonderful," she said dismissing his comment. "Pierce says you're an old-fashioned man."

He laughed. "Well, hell," Michael said, "maybe I am."

They stayed up late, drinking beer and talking. The old suite was as large as an apartment with its den and its kitchen, as well as the living room and the bedroom. He wasn't getting drunk at all these days, and he knew she was aware of it, but she didn't say anything, which was just as well. They talked about the house and all the little things they meant to do.

Did she miss the hospital? Yes, she did. But that wasn't important right now. She had a plan, a great plan for the future, which she would disclose soon enough.

"But you can't give up medicine. You don't mean that?"

"Of course I don't," she said patiently, dropping her voice a little for emphasis. "On the contrary. I've been thinking about medicine in an entirely different light."

"How do you mean?"

"It's too soon to explain. I'm not sure myself. But the question of the legacy changes things, and the more I learn about the legacy the more things are going to change. I'm in a new internship with Mayfair and Mayfair. The subject is money." She gestured to the papers on the table. "And it's moving along pretty well."

"You really want to do this?"

"Michael, everything we do in life, we do with certain expectations. I grew up with money. That meant I could go to medical school and proceed right through a long residency in neurosurgery. I didn't have a husband or kids to worry about. I didn't have anything to worry about. But now the sums of money have changed radically. With money like the Mayfair money, one could fund research projects, build whole laboratories. Conceivably one could set up a clinic, adjacent to a medical center, for work in one specialty of neurosurgery." She shrugged. "You see what I mean."

"Yeah, but if you become involved in that way, it will take you out of the Operating Room, won't it? You'll have to be an administrator."

"Possibly," she said. "The point is, the legacy presents a challenge. I have to use my imagination, as the cliché goes."

He nodded. "I see what you're saying," he responded. "But are they going to give you trouble?"

"Ultimately, yes. But it's not important. When I'm ready to make my moves, that won't matter. And I'll make the changes as smoothly and tactfully as I can."

"What changes?"

"Again, it's too early. I'm not ready yet to draw up a grand plan. But I'm thinking of a neurological center here in New

Orleans, with the finest equipment obtainable and laboratories for independent research.''

"Good Lord, I never thought of anything like that.''

"Before now, I never had the remotest chance of inaugurating a research program and completely controlling it—you know, determining the goals, the standards, the budget.'' She had a faraway look in her eye. "The important thing is to think in terms of the *size* of the legacy. And to think for myself.''

A vague uneasiness seized him. He didn't know why. He felt a chill rise on the back of his neck as he heard her say:

"Wouldn't that be the redemption, Michael? If the Mayfair legacy went into healing? Surely you see it. All the way from Suzanne and Jan van Abel, the surgeon, to a great and innovative medical center, devoted of course to the saving of lives.''

He sat there pondering and unable to answer,

She gave a little shrug and put her hands to her temples. "Oh, there's so much to study,'' she said, "so much to learn. But can't you see the continuity?''

"Yeah, continuity,'' he said under his breath.

Like the continuity he was so certain of when he woke in the hospital after he drowned—everything connected. They chose me because of who I was, and it's all connected . . .

"It's all possible,'' she said, scanning him for reaction. A little flame danced in her cheeks, in her eyes.

"Very near to perfect,'' he said.

"So why do you look like that? What's the matter?''

"I don't know.''

"Michael, stop thinking about those visions. Stop thinking about invisible people in the sky giving our lives meaning. There are no ghosts in the attic! Think for yourself.''

"I am, Rowan. I am. Don't get angry. It's a stunning idea. It's perfect. I don't know why it makes me uneasy. Have a little patience with me, honey. Like you said, our dreams have to be in proportion to our resources. And so it's a little over my head.''

"All you have to do is love me and listen to me, and let me think out loud.''

"I'm with you, Rowan. Always. I think it's great.''

"You're having trouble imagining it,'' she said. "I understand. I've only begun myself. But goddamn it, the money's there, Michael. There is something absolutely obscene about the amount of that money. For two generations, these corporation lawyers have tended this fortune, allowing it to feed upon itself and multiply like a monster.''

"Yeah, I know,'' he said.

"Long ago, they lost sight of the fact that it was the property of one person. It belongs to itself in some horrible way, it's greater than any human being should have or control.''

''A lot of people would agree with you,'' he said.

But he couldn't shake that memory of lying in the hospital bed in San Francisco and believing that his whole life had meaning, that everything he'd ever done and been was about to be re-deemed.

''Yes, it would redeem everything,'' he said. ''Wouldn't it?''

So why did he see the grave in his mind, with its twelve slots, and the doorway above, and the name Mayfair inscribed in big letters, and the flowers withering in the suffocating heat?

He forced himself out of this, and went for the best distraction he knew. Just looking at her, just looking and thinking about touching her, and resisting the urge, though she was only inches from him, and willing, yes, almost surely, willing to be touched.

It was working. A little switch was suddenly thrown in the ruthless mechanism called his brain. He was thinking of how her naked legs looked in the lamplight, and how delicate and full her breasts looked beneath her short silk gown.

Breasts always struck him as miracles; when you touched them and suckled them, they seemed entirely too luscious to be more than momentary—like sherbet or whipped cream, you expected them to melt in your mouth. That they stayed there, day after day, just waiting for you, was part of the whole impossibility of the female sex for him. That was all the science he knew. He bent forward, pressed his lips against her neck, and gave a little determined growl.

''Now you've done it,'' she whispered.

''Yeah, well, it's about time,'' he said in the same deep voice. ''How would you like to be carried to bed?''

''I'd love it,'' she purred. ''You haven't done that since the first time.''

''Christ! How could I have been so thoughtless!'' he whis-pered. ''What kind of an old-fashioned man am I?'' He shoved his left arm under her hot silky thighs and cradled her shoulders with his right, kissing her as he picked her up, secretly exultant that he didn't lose his balance and go sprawling. But he had her—light and clinging, and suddenly feverishly compliant. Making it to the bed was a cinch.

On Tuesday, the air-conditioning men began their work. There were enough gallery roofs for every piece of equipment. Joseph, the decorator, had taken away all the French furniture that needed restoration. The beautiful old bedroom sets, all dating from the plantation era, needed no more than polishing, and the cleaning women could take care of that.

The plasterers had finished in the front bedroom. And the painters sealed off the area with plastic drapery so that they could get a clean job in spite of the dust from the work going on in the rest of the house. Rowan had chosen a light champagne beige for the bedroom walls, and white for the ceiling and the woodwork. The carpet men had come to measure upstairs. The floor men were sanding the dining room where for some reason a fancy oak floor had been laid over the old heart pine, which needed only a fresh coat of polyurethane.

Michael had checked out the chimneys himself from the roof. The wood-burning fireplaces of the library and the double parlor were all in good condition with an excellent draft. The rest of the hearths had long ago been fitted for gas, and some of them were sealed. It was decided to change the heaters to the more attractive kind which looked like real coal fires.

Meantime the appliances in the kitchen had all been replaced. The old wooden butcher-block countertops were being sanded. They would be varnished by the end of next week.

Rowan sat cross-legged on the parlor floor with the decorator, surrounded by swatches of brilliant-colored cloth. It was a beige silk she chose for the front room draperies. She wanted something in darker damask for the dining room, something that would blend with the faded plantation murals. Upstairs, everything was to be cheerful and light.

Michael went through books of paint chips, choosing soft peach tones for the lower floor, a dark beige for the dining room which would pick up a major color in the murals, and white for the kitchen and pantries. He was soliciting bids from the window cleaners, and from the companies which cleaned chandeliers. The grandfather clock in the parlor was being repaired.

By late Friday morning, Beatrice's housekeeper, Trina, had purchased all new bedding for the various upstairs rooms, including new down pillows and comforters, and the linens had been packed with sachets into the armoires and the dresser drawers. The duct work had been completed in the attics. The old wallpaper was down in Millie's room and the old sickroom and Carlotta's room, and the plasterers had almost completed the proper preparation of the walls for fresh paint.

The burglar alarm system had also been finished, including smoke detectors, glass protectors, and buttons to summon emergency medical help.

Meantime, another crew of painters was at work in the parlor. The only flaw in the day perhaps was Rowan's noontime argument by phone with Dr. Larkin in San Francisco. She had told him she was taking an extended vacation. He felt she had sold out. An inheritance and a fancy house in New Orleans had lured her away from her true vocation. Clearly her vague statements as to her purpose and her future only further inflamed him. Finally she became exasperated. She wasn't turning her back on her life's work. She was thinking in terms of new horizons, and when she wanted to talk about it with him, she'd let him know.

When she got off the phone, she was exhausted. She wasn't even going back to California to close up the Tiburon house.

"It chills me even to think of it," she said. "I don't know why I feel so strongly. I just don't ever want to see the place again. I can't believe I've escaped. I could pinch myself to know for sure that I'm not dreaming."

Michael understood; nevertheless he advised her not to sell the house until a certain amount of time had passed.

She shrugged. She'd put it on the market tomorrow if she hadn't already rented the place to Dr. Slattery, her San Francisco replacement. In exchange for an extremely low rent and a waiver of deposits, Slattery had cheerfully agreed to box up everything personal in the house and ship it south. Ryan had arranged for warehouse storage.

"Those boxes will probably stay there unopened," she said, "for twenty years."

At about two on Friday, Michael went with Rowan to the Mercedes-Benz dealer on St. Charles Avenue. Now this was a fun errand. It was in the same block as the hotel. When he was a kid walking home from the old library at Lee Circle, he used to go into this big showroom and open the doors of the stunningly beautiful German cars and swoon over them for as long as he could get away with it before a salesman took notice. He didn't bother mentioning it. The fact was, he had a memory for every block they passed, everything they did.

He merely watched with quiet amusement as Rowan wrote out a check for two cars—the jaunty little 500 SL two-seater convertible, and the big classy four-door sedan. Both in cream with caramel leather upholstery, because that is what they had there on the floor.

The day before, he himself had picked up a neat, shiny, and luxurious American van, in which he could stow anything he wanted, yet still speed around in comfort and ease with the air-conditioning and the radio roaring. It amused him that Rowan did not seem to find the experience of buying these two cars to be anything remarkable. She did not even seem to find it interesting.

She asked the salesman to deliver the sedan to First Street, drive it in the back carriage gates, and drop the keys at the Pontchartrain. The convertible they would take with them.

She drove it out of the showroom and up St. Charles Avenue, to a crawl in front of the hotel.

"Let's get out of here this weekend," she said. "Let's forget about the house and the family."

"Already?" he asked. He had been dreaming of taking one of the riverboats for the supper cruise tonight.

"I'll tell you why. I made the interesting discovery that the best white beaches in Florida are less than four hours from here. Did you know that?"

"That's right, they are."

"There are a couple of houses for sale in a Florida town called Destin, and one of them has its own boat slip nearby. I picked up all this from Wheatfield and Beatrice. Wheatfield and Pierce used to go to Destin at spring break. Beatrice goes all the time. Ryan made the calls for me to the real estate agent. What do you say?"

"Well, sure, why not?"

Another memory, thought Michael. That summer when he was fifteen and the family drove to those very white beaches on the panhandle of Florida. Green water under the red sunset. And he'd been thinking about it the day he drowned off Ocean Beach, almost an hour exactly before he met Rowan Mayfair.

"I didn't know we were so close to the Gulf," she said. "Now, the Gulf is serious water. I mean like the Pacific Ocean is serious water."

"I know." He laughed. "I know serious water when I see it." He really broke up.

"Well, look, I'm dying to see the Gulf."

"Of course."

"I haven't been in the Gulf since I was in high school and we went to the Caribbean. If it's as warm as I remember it—"

"Yes, that is definitely worth a trip."

"You know, I can probably get somebody to bring the *Sweet Christine* down here, or better yet, buy a new boat. Ever cruise the Gulf or the Caribbean?"

"No." He shook his head. "I should have known after I saw that house in Tiburon."

"Just four hours, Michael," she said, "Come on, it won't take us fifteen minutes to pack a bag."

They made one last stop at the house.

Eugenia was at the kitchen table, polishing up all the silver plate from the kitchen drawers.

"It's a joy to see this place come back," she said.

"Yes, it is, isn't it?" said Michael. He put his arm lightly around her thin shoulder. "How about moving back into your old room, Eugenia? You want to?"

Oh, yes, she said she'd love to. She'd stay this weekend, certainly. She was too old for all those children at her son's house. She was screaming too much at those children. She'd be happy to come back. And yes, she still had her keys. "But you don't never need no keys around here."

The painters were working late upstairs. The yard crew would be there until dark. Dart Henley, Michael's second in command, gladly agreed to oversee everything for the weekend. No worry at all.

"Look, the pool's almost finished," Rowan said. Indeed, all the patchwork inside had been done, and they were applying the final paint.

All the wild growth had been cleared from the flagstone decking, the diving boards had been restored, and the graceful limestone balustrade had been uncovered throughout the garden. The thick boxwood had been taken out; more old cast-iron chairs and tables had been discovered in the disappearing brush. And the lower flagstone steps of the side screen porch had been uncovered, proving that before Deirdre's time it had been open. One could once again walk out from the side windows of the parlor, across the flags, and down and onto the lawn.

"We ought to leave it that way, Rowan. It needs to be open," Michael said. "And besides, we have that nice little screened porch off the kitchen in back. They've already put up the new screen back there. Come, take a look."

"You think you can tear yourself away?" Rowan asked. She tossed him the car keys. "Why don't you drive?" she asked. "I think I make you nervous."

"Only when you run lights and stop signs at such high speeds," he said. "I mean, it's breaking two laws simultaneously that makes me nervous."

"OK, handsome, as long as you get us there in four hours."

He took one last look at the house. The light here was like the light of Florence, on that score she had been right. Washing down the high south façade, it made him think of the old palazzi of Italy. And everything was going so well, so wonderfully well.

He felt an odd pain inside him, a twinge of sadness and pure happiness.

I am here, really here, he thought silently. Not dreaming about it any longer far away, but here. And the visions seemed distant, fading, unreal to him. He had not had another flash of them in so long.

But Rowan was waiting, and the clean white southern beaches were waiting. More of his wonderful old world to be reclaimed. It crossed his mind suddenly that it would be luscious to make love to her in yet another new bed.

Thirty-six

THEY RODE INTO the town of Fort Walton, Florida, at eight o'clock after a long slow crawl out of Pensacola. The whole world had come down to the beach tonight, bumper to bumper. To press on to Destin was to risk finding no accommodations.

As it was, the older wing of a Holiday Inn was the only thing left. All the money in the world couldn't buy a suite at the fancier hotels. And the little helter-skelter town with all its neon signs was a mite depressing in its highway shabbiness.

The room itself seemed damned near unbearable, smelly and dimly lighted, with dilapidated furniture and lumpy beds. But then they changed into their bathing suits and walked out the glass door at the end of the corridor and found themselves on the beach.

The world opened up, warm and wondrous under a heaven of brilliant stars. Even the glassy green of the water was visible in the pouring moonlight. The breeze had not the faintest touch of a chill in it. It was even silkier than the river breeze of New Orleans. And the sand was a pure surreal white, and fine as sugar under their feet.

They walked out together into the surf. For a moment, Michael could not quite believe the delicious temperature of the water, nor its glassy, shining softness as it swirled around his ankles. In a strange moment of circular time, he saw himself at Ocean Beach on the other side of the continent, his fingers frozen, the bitter Pacific wind lashing his face, thinking of this very place, this seemingly mythical and impossible place, beneath the southern stars.

If only they could receive all this, and hold it to their breasts, and keep it, and cast off the dark things that waited and brooded and were sure to reveal themselves . . .

Rowan threw herself forward into the water. She gave a slow, sweet laugh. She nudged at his leg with her foot, and he let himself tumble down into the shallow warm waves beside her. Going back on his elbows, he let the water bathe his face.

They swam out together, with long lazy strokes, through gentle waves, where their feet still scraped the bottom, until it was so deep finally that they could stand with the water up to their shoulders.

The white dunes down the beach gleamed like snow in the moonlight, and the distant lights of the larger hotels twinkled softly and silently beneath the black star-filled sky. He hugged Rowan, feeling her wet limbs sealed against him. The world seemed altogether impossible—something imagined in its utter easiness, its absence of all barriers or harshness or assaults upon the senses or the flesh.

"This is paradise," she said. "It really is. God, Michael, how could you ever leave?" She broke from him, not waiting for an answer, and swam with swift strong strokes towards the horizon.

He remained where he was, his eyes scanning the heavens, picking out the great constellation of Orion with its belt of jewels. If he had ever been this happy before in his life, he couldn't remember it. He absolutely couldn't. No one had ever created in him the happiness that she did. Nothing ever created in him the happiness of this moment—this freshness and beauty and motherly warmth.

Yes, back where I belong, and I have her with me, and I don't care about all the rest. Not now . . . , he thought.

Saturday they spent looking at the available property. Much of the beachfront from Ft. Walton to Seaside was taken up by the large resorts and high-rise condominiums. The individual houses were few and at a great price.

At about three o'clock, they walked into "the house"—a Spartan modern affair with low ceilings and severe white walls. The rectangular windows made the Gulf view into a series of paintings in simple frames. The horizon cut the paintings exactly in half. Down below the high front decks were the dunes, which must be preserved, it was explained to them, as they were the protection against the high waves when the hurricanes came.

By means of a long pier they walked out over the dunes and then went down weathered wooden steps to the beach itself. In the dazzle of the sun the whiteness was again unbelievable. The water was a perfect foaming green.

Far, far down the beach to either side the high rises broke the vista with their white towers, seemingly as clean and geometric as this little house itself. The cliffs and crags and trees of California were utterly absent. It was a wholly different environment—suggestive of the Greek islands, in spite of its flatness, a cubist landscape of blinding light and sharp lines.

He liked it. He told her that immediately, yes, he really did like it, and this house would be just fine.

Above all he liked the contrast to the lushness of New Orleans. The house was well built, with its coral-colored tile floors and thick carpets, and its gleaming stainless steel kitchen. Yes, cubist, and stark. And inexplicably beautiful in its own way.

The one disappointment for Rowan was that a boat couldn't be docked here, that she would have to drive a couple of miles to the marina on the bay side of the highway, and take the boat out through Destin harbor into the Gulf. But that was not so terribly inconvenient when one measured it against the luxury of this long stretch of unspoiled beach.

As Rowan and the agent wrote up the offer to purchase, Michael walked out on the weathered deck. He shaded his eyes as he studied the water. He tried to analyze the sense of serenity it produced in him, which surely had to do with the warmth and the deep brilliance of the colors. In retrospect it seemed that the hues and tints of San Francisco had always been mixed with ashes, and that the sky had always been half invisible beyond a fog, or a deep mist, or a fleece of unremarkable clouds.

He could not connect this brilliant seascape to the cold gray Pacific, or to his scant awful memories of the rescue helicopter, of lying there chilled and aching on the stretcher, his clothes drenched. This was his beach and his water, and it wouldn't hurt him. What the hell, maybe he could even get to like being on the *Sweet Christine* down here. But he had to confess, the thought of that made him slightly sick.

Late in the afternoon, they dined in a little fish restaurant near the marina in Destin, very rough and noisy with the beer in plastic cups. The fresh fish was better than very good. At sunset they were on the motel beach again, sprawled in the weathered wooden chairs. Michael was making notes on things back at First Street. Rowan slept, her tanned skin quite noticeably darkened from the last week of time outdoors, and this one hour perhaps on the burning beach. Her hair was streaked with yellow. It made a pain in him to look at her, to realize how very young she was still.

He woke her gently as the sun began to sink. Enormous and

blood red, it made its spectacular path across the glittering emerald sea.

He shut his eyes finally because it was too much. He had to veer away from it, and come back again, slowly, as the hot breeze ruffled his hair.

At nine o'clock that evening, after they had enjoyed a tolerable meal at a bayside restaurant, the call came from the real estate agent. Rowan's offer on the house had been accepted. No complications. The wicker and painted wood furniture was included. Fireplace fittings, dishes, everything would remain. They would move to clear title and close escrow as soon as possible. She could probably claim the keys in two weeks.

On Sunday afternoon, they visited the Destin Marina. The choice of boats was fabulous. But Rowan was still toying with the idea of sending for the *Sweet Christine*. She wanted something seaworthy. And there was really nothing here that surpassed the luxury and solidity of the old *Sweet Christine*.

It was late afternoon when they started back. With the radio playing Vivaldi, they saw the sunset as they sped along Mobile Bay. The sky seemed limitless, gleaming with magical light beyond an endless terrain of darkening clouds. The scent of rain mingled with the heat.

Home. Where I belong. Where the sky looks as I remember it. Where the low country spreads out forever. And the air is my friend.

Fast and silent the traffic flowed on the interstate highway; the low cushy Mercedes-Benz cruised easily at eighty-five. The music ripped the air with its high pure violin glissandos. Finally the sun died to a wash of blinding gold. The dark swampy woodlands closed around them as they sped into Mississippi, the eighteen-wheelers rumbling by, the lights of the little towns flickering for an instant, then vanishing, as the last of the tarnished light died away.

Did she miss the drama of California? he asked her. Miss the cliffs and the yellow hills?

She was looking at the sky just as he was. You never saw such a sky out there. No, she said softly. She missed nothing. She was going to be sailing different waters, warm waters.

After a long while, when it was truly dark, and the only view now was the view of the glowing red tail lamps before them, she said:

"This is our honeymoon, isn't it?"

"I guess it is."

"I mean, it's the easy part. Before you realize what kind of a person I really am."

"And what kind is that?"

"You want to ruin our honeymoon?"

"It won't ruin it." He glanced at her. "Rowan, what are you talking about?" No answer. "You know you're the only person in this world I really know right now. You're the only one I don't handle literally with kid gloves. I know more about you than you realize, Rowan."

"What would I do without you?" she whispered, snuggling back against the seat, stretching out her long legs.

"Meaning?"

"I don't know. But I've figured something out."

"I'm afraid to ask."

"He's not going to show himself till he gets ready."

"I know."

"He wants you here right now. He's standing back out of the way for you. He showed himself to you that first night just to entice you."

"This is giving me the creeps. Why is he so willing to share you?"

"I don't know. But I've given him opportunities, and he's not really showing himself. Strange things happen, crazy things, but I'm never sure . . ."

"Like what things?"

"Oh, not worth dwelling on. Look, you're tired. You want me to drive for a while?"

"Good Lord, no. And I'm not tired. I just don't want him here with us right now, in this conversation. I have a feeling he'll come soon enough."

Late that night, he woke up in the big hotel bed alone. He found her sitting in the living room. He realized she'd been crying.

"Rowan, what is it?"

"Nothing, Michael. Nothing that doesn't happen to a woman once a month," she said. She gave a little forced smile, faintly bitter. "It's just . . . well, you'll probably think I'm insane, but I was hoping I was pregnant."

He took her hand, not knowing whether it was the right thing to kiss her. He too felt the disappointment, but more significant, he felt happy that she had actually wanted to have a child. All this time, he'd been afraid to ask her what her feelings were about such a thing. And his own carelessness had been worrying him. "That would have been great, darling," he said. "Just great."

"You think so? You would have been happy?"

"Absolutely."

"Michael, let's do it then. Let's go on and get married."

"Rowan, nothing would make me happier," he said simply. "But are you sure this is what *you* want?"

She gave him a slow patient smile. "Michael, you're not getting away," she said, with a small playful frown. "What's the point of waiting?"

He couldn't help but laugh.

"And what about Mayfair Unlimited, Rowan? The cousins and company. You know what they're going to say, honey."

She shook her head, with the same knowing smile as before. "Do you want to hear what I have to say? We're fools if we don't do it."

Her gray eyes were still rimmed in red, but her face was very tranquil now, and so pretty to look at, so soft to touch. So unlike the face of anyone he'd ever known, or loved, or even dreamed of.

"Oh, I want to do it," he whispered. "But I'm forty-eight years old, Rowan. I was born in the same year your mother was born. Yes, I want it. I want it with all my heart. But I have to think of you."

"Let's have the wedding at First Street, Michael," she said in her soft husky voice, her eyes puckering slightly. "What do you think? Wouldn't it be perfect? On that beautiful side lawn."

Perfect. Like the plan for the hospitals built upon the Mayfair legacy. Perfect.

He wasn't sure why he was hesitating. He couldn't resist. Yet it was all too good to be true, too sweet actually, her openness and her love, and the pride it engendered in him—that this woman of all women should need and love him just the way he needed and loved her.

"Those cousins of yours will draw up all the papers to protect you . . . you know, the house, the legacy. All that."

"It's automatic. It's all entailed or something. But they'll probably manufacture a storehouse of papers of one kind or another."

"I'll sign on the dotted line."

"Michael, the papers really don't mean anything. What I have is yours."

"What I want is you, Rowan."

Her face brightened; she drew her knees up, turning sideways on the couch to face him, and she leaned over and kissed him.

Suddenly it hit him, grandly and deliciously. Getting married. Marrying Rowan. And the promise, the absolutely dazzling promise of a child. This kind of happiness was so completely unfamiliar to him that he was almost afraid. Almost. But not quite.

It seemed the very thing that they must do at all costs. Preserve what they had and what they wanted, against the dark current that had brought them together. And when he thought of the years ahead—of all the simple and heartbreakingly important possibilities—his happiness was too great to be expressed.

He knew better than to even try. After a few moments of silence, bits of poetry came to him, little phrases that barely caught the light of his contentment the way a bit of glass catches light. They left him. He was contented and empty, and full of nothing but a quiet inarticulate love.

In perfect understanding, it seemed, they looked at each other. Questions of failure, of haste, all the what if's of life, did not matter. The quiet in her was talking to the quiet in him.

When they went into the bedroom, she said she wanted to spend their wedding night at the house, and then go on to Florida for the honeymoon. Wouldn't that be the best way to handle it? A wedding night under that roof, and slipping away afterwards.

Surely the workmen could get the front bedroom ready in a couple of weeks.

"I guarantee it," he said.

In that big antique bed in the front room. He could almost hear the ghost of Belle say, "How lovely for both of you."

Thirty-seven

UNEASY SLEEP. SHE shifted, turned and put her arm over his back, drawing her knees under his, warm and snug again. The air-conditioning was almost as good as the Florida Gulf breeze.

But what was it tugging at her neck, tangling in her hair, and hurting her? She moved to brush it away, to free her hair. Something cold pressed against her breast. She didn't like it.

She turned over on her back, half dreaming once again that she was in the Operating Room, and this was a most difficult procedure. She had to envision carefully what she meant to do— to guide her hands every step with her mind—commanding the blood not to flow, commanding the tissues to come together. And the man lay split open all the way from his crotch to the top of his head, all his tiny organs exposed, quivering, red, impossible for his size, waiting for her somehow to make them grow.

"Too much, I can't do this," she said. "I'm a neurosurgeon, not a witch!"

She could see every vessel now in his legs and arms as if he were one of those clear plastic dummies threaded through and through with red, to teach children about circulation. His feet quivered. They too were small, and he was wriggling his toes trying to make them grow. How blank was the expression on his face, but he was looking at her.

And that tugging in her hair again, something pulling at her hair. Again, she pushed it away, and this time her finger caught it—what was it, a chain?

She didn't want to lose the dream. She knew it was a dream now, but she wanted to know what was going to happen to this man, how this operation was to end.

"Dr. Mayfair, put down your scalpel," said Lemle. "You don't need that anymore."

"No, Dr. Mayfair," said Lark. "You can't use it here."

They were right. It was past the point for something so crude as the tiny flickering steel blade. This was not a matter of cutting, but of construction. She was staring at the long open wound, at the tender organs shivering like plants, like the monstrous iris in the garden. Her mind raced with the proper specifications as she guided the cells, explaining as she went along so that the young doctors would understand. "There are sufficient cells there, you see, in fact, they exist in profusion. The important thing is to provide for them a superior DNA, so to speak, a new and unforeseen incentive to form organs of the proper size." And behold, the wound was closing over organs of the proper size and the man was turning his head, and his eyes snapped open and shut like the eyes of a doll.

Applause rose all around her, and looking up she was amazed to see that they were all Dutchmen here, gathered at Leiden; even she wore the big black hat and the gorgeous thick sleeves, and this was a painting by Rembrandt, of course, *The Anatomy Lesson*, and that is why the body looked so perfectly neat, though it hardly explained why she could see through it.

"Ah, but you have the gift, my child, you are a witch," said Lemle.

"That's right," said Rembrandt. Such a sweet old man. He

sat in the corner, his head to one side, his russet hair wispy now in old age.

"Don't let Petyr hear you," she said.

"Rowan, take the emerald off," Petyr said. He stood at the foot of the table. "Take it off, Rowan, it's around your neck. Remove it!"

The emerald?

She opened her eyes. The dream lost its vibrancy like a taut veil of silk suddenly torn free and furling. The darkness was alive around her.

Very slowly the familiar objects came to light. The closet doors, the table by the bed, Michael, her beloved Michael, sleeping beside her.

She felt the coldness against her naked breast, she felt the thing caught in her hair, and she knew what it was.

"Oh God!" She covered her mouth with her left hand but not before that little scream had escaped, her right hand snatching the thing off her neck as if it had been a loathsome insect.

She sat up, hunched over, staring at it in the palm of her hand. Like a clot of green blood. Her breath caught in her throat, and she saw that she had broken the old chain, and her hand was shaking uncontrollably.

Had Michael heard her cry out? He didn't move even as she leaned against him.

"Lasher!" she whispered, her eyes moving up as if she could find him in the shadows. "Do you want to make me hate you!" Her words were a hiss. For one second the fabric of the dream was clear again, as if the veil had once more been lowered. All the doctors were leaving the table.

"Done, Rowan. Magnificent, Rowan."

"A new era, Rowan."

"Very simply miraculous, my dear," said Lemle.

"Cast it away, Rowan," said Petyr.

She flung the emerald over the foot of the bed. Somewhere in the small hallway it struck the carpet, with a dull impotent little sound.

She put her hands to her face, and then feverishly, she felt of her neck, felt of her breasts as if the damnable thing had left some layer of dust or grime on her.

"Hate you for this," she whispered again in the dark. "Is that what you want?"

Far off it seemed she heard a sigh, a rustling. Through the far hallway door, she could just barely make out the curtains in the living room against the light of the street, and they moved as if ruffled by a low draft, and that was the sound she heard, wasn't it?

That and the slow measured song of Michael's breathing. She felt foolish for having flung the stone away. She sat with her hands over her mouth, knees up, staring into the shadows.

Well, didn't you believe the old tales? Why are you shaking like this? Just one of his tricks, and no more difficult for him than making the dance of the wind in the trees. Or making that iris move in the garden. Move. It did more than move, though, didn't it? It actually . . . And then she remembered those roses, those strange large roses on the hall table. She had never asked Pierce where they had come from. Never asked Gerald.

Why are you so frightened?

She got up, put on her robe, and walked barefoot into the hall, Michael sleeping on, undisturbed, in the bed behind her.

She picked up the jewel and wound the two strands of broken chain around it carefully. Seemed dreadful to have broken those fragile antique links.

"But you were stupid to do this," she whispered. "I'll never put it on now, not of my own free will."

With a low creak of the springs, Michael turned over in the bed. Had he whispered something? Her name maybe?

She crept silently back into the bedroom, and dropping to her knees, found her purse in the corner of the closet and put the necklace into the side zipper pocket.

She wasn't shaking now. But her fear had alchemized perfectly to rage. And she knew she couldn't sleep any more.

Sitting alone in the living room as the sun rose, she thought of all the old portraits at the house, the ones she'd been going through, and wiping clean, and preparing to hang, the very old ones she could identify which no one else in the family could. Charlotte with her blond hair, so deeply faded beneath the lacquer that she seemed a ghost. And Jeanne Louise, with her twin brother standing behind her. And gray-haired Marie Claudette with the little painting of Riverbend on the wall above her.

All of them wore the emerald. So many paintings of that one jewel. She closed her eyes and dozed on the velvet couch, wishing for coffee, yet too sleepy to make it. She'd been dreaming before this happened, but what was it all about—something to do with the hospital and an operation, and now she couldn't remember. Lemle there. Lemle whom she hated so much. . . .

And that dark-mouthed iris that Lasher had made. . . .

Yes, I know your tricks. You made it swell and break from its stem, didn't you? Oh, nobody really understands how much power you have. To make whole leaves sprout from the stem of a dead rose. Where do you get your handsome form when you appear, and why won't you do it for me? Are you afraid I'll scatter you to the four winds, and you'll never have the strength to gather yourself together?

She was dreaming again, wasn't she? Imagine, a flower changing like that iris, altering before her eyes, the cells actually multiplying and mutating . . .

Unless it was just a trick. A trick like putting the necklace on her in her sleep. But wasn't everything a trick?

"Well, boys and girls," said Lark once as they stood over the bed of a comatose and dying man, "we've done all our tricks, haven't we?"

What would have happened if she had tried a couple of her own? Like telling the cells of that dying man to multiply, to mutate, to restructure, and seal off the bruised tissue. But she hadn't known. She still didn't know how far she could go.

Yes, dreaming. Everyone walking through the halls at Leiden. You know what they did to Michael Servetus in Calvinist Geneva, when he accurately described the circulation of the blood in 1553, they burnt him at the stake, and all his heretical books with him. Be careful, Dr. van Abel.

I am not a witch.

Of course, none of us are. It's a matter of constantly reevaluating our concept of *natural* principles.

Nothing natural about those roses.

And now the air in here, moving the way it was, catching the curtains and making them dance, stirring the papers on the coffee table in front of her, even lifting the tendrils of her hair, and cooling her. Your tricks. She didn't want this dream anymore. Do the patients at Leiden always get up and walk away after the anatomy lesson?

But you won't dare show yourself, will you?

She met Ryan at ten o'clock and told him all about the plans for the marriage, trying to make it matter-of-fact and definite, so as to invite as few questions as possible.

"And one thing I wish you could do for me," she said. She took the emerald necklace out of her purse. "Could you put this in some sort of vault? Just lock it away, where no one can possibly get at it."

"Of course, I can keep it here at the office," he said, "but Rowan, there are several things I ought to explain to you. This legacy is very old—you have to have a little patience now. The rules and rubrics, so to speak, are quaint and bizarre, but nevertheless explicit. I'm afraid you're required to wear the emerald at the wedding.''

''You don't mean this.''

''You understand, of course, these small requirements are probably quite vulnerable to contest or revision in a court of law, but the point of following them to the letter is—and has always been—to avoid even the remotest possibility of anyone ever challenging the inheritance at any point in its history, and with a personal fortune of this size and this . . .''

And on and on he went in familiar lawyerly fashion, but she understood. Lasher had won this round. Lasher knew the terms of the legacy, didn't he? He had simply given her the appropriate wedding present.

Her anger was cold and dark and isolating just as it had always been at its worst. She gazed off, out the office window, not even seeing the soft cloud-filled sky, or the deep winding gash of the river below it.

''I'll have this gold chain repaired,'' Ryan said. ''Seems to be broken.''

It was one o'clock when she reached First Street with lunch in a little brown sack—two sandwiches and a couple of bottles of Dutch beer. Michael was all excited. They'd found a treasure trove of old New Orleans red bricks under the earth on the back lot. Beautiful bricks, the kind they couldn't make anymore. They could now build the new gateposts with the perfect material. And they'd also found a stash of old blueprints in the attic.

''They look like the original plans,'' he said. ''They may have been drawn by Darcy himself. Come on. I left them up there. They're so fragile.''

She went with him up the stairs. How fresh it all looked with the new paint; even Deirdre's room was lovely now, the way it should have always been.

''Nothing's the matter, is it?'' he asked.

Wouldn't he know? she thought. Wouldn't he have to sense it? And to think she had to wear the damned thing at the wedding. Her great dream of the Mayfair Medical Center, and everything else would go right out the window if she didn't. He'd go crazy when she told him. And she couldn't bear to see the scared look in his eyes again. She couldn't bear to see him agitated and weak, that was the truth of it.

''No, nothing's wrong,'' she said. ''I was just downtown all morning with the lawyers again, and I missed you.'' She threw her arms around him, nuzzling her head under his chin. ''I really really missed you.''

Thirty-eight

N O ONE SEEMED the least surprised at the news. Aaron drank a toast with them over breakfast, and then went back to work in the library at First Street, where at Rowan's invitation he was cataloging the rare books.

Smooth-talking Ryan of the cold blue eyes came by Tuesday afternoon, to shake Michael's hand. In a few words of pleasant conversation, he made it clear that he was impressed with Michael's accomplishments, which could only mean of course that Michael had been investigated, through the regular financial channels, just as if he were bidding on a job.

"It's all sort of annoying, I'm sure," Ryan admitted finally, "investigating the fiancée of the designee of the Mayfair legacy, but you see, I don't have much choice in the matter . . ."

"I don't mind," Michael said with a little laugh. "Anything you couldn't find out and you wanna know, just ask."

"Well, for starters, how did you ever do so well without committing a crime?"

Michael laughed off the flattery. "When you see this house in a couple of months," he said, "you'll understand." But he wasn't fool enough to think his modest fortune had impressed this man. What were a couple of million in blue chip securities compared to the Mayfair legacy? No, this was a little talk about the geography of New Orleans—that he had come from the other side of Magazine Street, and that he still had the Irish Channel in his voice. But Michael had been too long out west to worry about something like that.

They walked together over the newly clipped grass. The new boxwood—small and trim—was now in place throughout the garden. It was possible to see the flower beds as they had been laid out a century before—to see the little Greek statues placed at the four corners of the yard.

Indeed, the entire classical plan was reemerging. The long octagonal shape of the lawn was the same as the long octagonal shape of the pool. The perfectly square flagstones were set in a diamond pattern against the limestone balustrades which broke the patio into distinct rectangles and marked off paths which met at right angles, framing both garden and house. Old trellises had been righted so that they once again defined the gateways. And as the black paint went up on the cast-iron lace railings, it brought to life their ornate and repetitive design of curlicues and rosettes.

Yes, patterns—everywhere he looked he discerned patterns—struggling against the sprawling crepe myrtle and the glossy-leafed camellias, and the antique rose as it fought its way up the trellis, and against the sweet little four o'clocks which fought for light in the brightest patches of unhindered sun.

Beatrice, very dramatic in a great pink hat and large square silver-rimmed glasses, met with Rowan at two o'clock to discuss the wedding. Rowan had set the date for Saturday a week. "Less than a fortnight!" Beatrice declared with alarm. No, everything had to be done right. Didn't Rowan understand what the marriage would mean to the family? People would want to come from Atlanta and New York.

It couldn't be done before the last of October. And surely Rowan would want the renovations of the house to be complete. It meant so much to everyone to see the house.

All right, said Rowan, she guessed she and Michael could wait that long, especially if it meant they could spend their wedding night in the house, and the reception could be held here.

Definitely, said Michael; that would give him almost eight solid weeks to get things in shape. Certainly the main floor could be finished and the front bedroom upstairs.

"It would be a double celebration, then, wouldn't it?" said Bea. "Your wedding, and the reopening of the house. Darlings, you will make everyone so very happy."

And yes, every Mayfair in creation must be invited. Now Beatrice went to her list of caterers. The house could hold a thousand if tents were arranged over the pool and over the lawn. No, not to worry. And the children could swim, couldn't they?

Yes, it would be like old times, it would be like the days of Mary Beth. Would Rowan like to have some old photographs of the last parties given before Stella died?

"We'll gather all the photographs for the reception," said Rowan. "It can be a reunion. We'll put out the photographs for everyone to enjoy."

"It's going to be marvelous."

Suddenly Beatrice reached out and took Michael's hand.

"May I ask you a question, darling? Now that you're one of the family? Why in the world do you wear these horrible gloves?"

851

"I see things when I touch people," he said before he could stop himself.

Her large gray eyes brightened. "Oh, that's most intriguing. Did you know Julien had that power? That's what they always told me. And Mary Beth too. Oh, darling, please let me." She began to roll the leather back, her long pink almond-shaped fingernails lightly scraping his skin as she did it. "Please? May I? You don't mind?" She ripped the glove off and held it up with a triumphant yet innocent smile.

He did nothing. He remained passive, his hand open, fingers slightly curled. He watched as she laid her hand on his, and then squeezed his hand firmly. In a flash the random images crowded into his head. The miscellany came and went so fast he caught none of it—merely the atmosphere, the wholesomeness, the equivalent of sunshine and fresh air, and the very distinct register of *Innocent. Not one of them.*

"What did you see?" she asked.

He saw her lips stop moving before the words came clear.

"Nothing," he said as he drew back. "It's considered to be the absolute confirmation of goodness, and good fortune. Nothing. No misery, no sadness, no illness, nothing at all." And in a way, that had been perfectly true.

"Oh, you are a darling," she said, blank-faced and sincere, and then swooped in to kiss him. "Where did you ever find such a person?" she asked Rowan. And without waiting for an answer, she said, "I like you both! And that's better than loving you, for that's expected, you know. But liking you, what a curious surprise. You really are the most adorable couple, you with your blue eyes, Michael, and Rowan with that scrumptious butterscotch voice! I could kiss you on your eyes every time you smile at me—and don't do it now, how dare you?—and I could kiss her on her throat every time she utters a word! A single solitary word!"

"May I kiss you on the cheek, Beatrice?" he asked tenderly.

"Cousin Beatrice to you, you gorgeous hunk of man," she said with a little theatrical pat of her heaving bosom. "Do it!" She shut her eyes tight, and then opened them with another dramatic and radiant smile.

Rowan was merely smiling at them both in a vague, bemused fashion. And now it was time for Beatrice to take her downtown to Ryan's office. Interminable legal matters. How horrible. Off they went.

He realized the black leather glove had fallen to the grass. He picked it up, and put it on.

Not one of them . . .

But who had been speaking? Who had been digesting and relaying that information? Maybe he was simply getting better at it, learning to ask the questions, as Aaron had tried to teach him to do.

Truth was, he hadn't paid much attention to that aspect of the lessons. He mainly wanted to shut the power off. Whatever the case, there had, for the first time since the debacle of the jars, been a clear and distinct message. In fact, it was infinitely more concise and authoritative than the majority of the awful signals he'd received that day. It had been as clear as Lasher's prophecy in its own way.

He looked up slowly. Surely there was someone on the side porch, in the deep shade, watching him. But he saw nothing. Only the painters at work on the cast iron. The porch looked splendid now that the old screen had been stripped away and the makeshift wooden railings removed. It was a bridge between the long double parlor and the beautiful lawn.

And here we will be married, he thought dreamily. And as if to answer the great crepe myrtles caught the breeze, dancing, their light pink blossoms moving gracefully against the blue sky.

When he got back to the hotel that afternoon, there was an envelope waiting for him from Aaron. He tore it open even before he reached the suite. Once the door was soundly shut on the world, he pulled out the thick glossy color photograph and held it to the light.

A lovely dark-haired woman gazed out at him from the divine gloom spun by Rembrandt—alive, smiling the very same smile he had only just seen on Rowan's lips. The Mayfair emerald gleamed in this masterly twilight. So painfully real the illusion, that he had the feeling the cardboard on which it was printed might melt and leave the face floating, gossamer as a ghost, in the air.

But was this his Deborah, the woman he had seen in the visions? *He didn't know.* No shock of recognition came to him no matter how long he studied it.

Taking off the gloves and handling it yielded nothing, only the maddeningly meaningless images of intermediaries and incidental persons he had come by now to expect. And as he sat on the couch holding the photograph, he knew it would have been the same had he touched the old oil painting itself.

"What do you want of me?" he whispered.

Out of innocence and out of time, the dark-haired girl smiled back at him. A stranger. Caught forever in her brief and desperate girlhood. Fledgling witch and nothing more.

But somebody had told him something this afternoon when Beatrice's hand had touched his! Somebody had used the power for some purpose. Or was it simply his own inner voice?

He put aside his gloves, as he was accustomed to do now when alone here, and picked up his pen and his notebook, and began to write.

"Yes, it was a small constructive use of the power, I think. Because the images were subordinate to the message. I'm not sure that ever happened before, not even the day I touched the jars. The messages were mingled with the images, and Lasher was speaking to me directly, but it was mixed together. This was quite something else."

And what if he were to touch Ryan's hand tonight at dinner, when they all gathered around the candlelighted table in the Caribbean Room downstairs? What would the inner voice tell him? For the first time, he found himself eager to use the power. Perhaps because this little experiment with Beatrice had turned out so well.

He had liked Beatrice. He had seen perhaps what he wanted to see. An ordinary human being, a part of the great wave of the real which meant so much to him and to Rowan.

"Married by November 1. God, I have to call Aunt Viv. She'll be so disappointed if I don't call."

He put the photograph on Rowan's bedside table for her to see.

There was a lovely flower there, a white flower that looked like a familiar lily, yet somehow different. He picked it up, examining it, trying to figure why it looked so strange, and then he realized it was much longer than any lily he'd ever seen, and its petals seemed unusually fragile.

Pretty. Rowan must have picked it when she was walking back from the house. He went into the bathroom, filled a glass with water, and put the lily in it, and brought it back to the table.

He didn't remember about touching Ryan's hand until the dinner was long over and he was alone upstairs again, with his books. He was glad he hadn't done it. The dinner had been too much fun, what with young Pierce regaling them with old legends of New Orleans—all the lore he remembered but which Rowan had never heard—and entertaining little anecdotes about the various cousins, all of it loosely strung together in a natural and beguiling way. But Pierce's mother, Gifford, a trim, beautifully groomed brunette, and also a Mayfair by birth, had stared at him and Rowan fearfully and silently throughout the meal, and talked almost not at all.

And of course the whole dinner was, for him, another one of those secretly satisfying moments—comparing this night to the event of his boyhood when Aunt Viv had come from San Francisco to visit his mother, and he had dined in a real restaurant—the Caribbean Room—for the very first time.

And to think, Aunt Viv would be here before the end of next week. She was confused, but she was coming. What a load off his mind.

He'd sock her away in some nice comfortable condominium on St. Charles Avenue—one of the new brick town houses with the pretty mansard roofs and the French windows. Something right on the Mardi Gras parade route so she could watch from her balcony. In fact, he ought to be scanning the want ads now. She could take cabs anywhere she had to go. And then he'd break it to her very gently that he wanted her to stay down here, that he didn't want to go back to California, that the house on Liberty Street wasn't home to him anymore.

About midnight, he left his architecture books and went into the bedroom. Rowan was just switching off the light.

"Rowan," he said, "if you saw that thing you'd tell me, wouldn't you?"

"What are you talking about, Michael?"

"If you saw Lasher, you'd tell me. Right away."

"Of course I would," she said. "Why would you even ask me that? Why don't you put away the picture books and come to bed?"

He saw that the picture of Deborah had been propped up behind the lamp. And the pretty white lily in the water glass was standing in front of the picture.

"Lovely, wasn't she?" Rowan said. "I don't suppose there is a way in the world to get the Talamasca to part with the original painting."

"I don't know," he said. "Probably not likely. But you know that flower is really remarkable. This afternoon, when I put it in the glass, I could swear it had only a single bloom, and now there are three large blooms, look at it. I must not have noticed the buds."

She looked puzzled. She reached out, took the flower carefully from the water and studied it. "What kind of lily is it?" she asked.

"Well, it's kind of like what we used to call an Easter lily, but they don't bloom at this time of year. I don't know what it is. Where did you get it?"

"Me? I've never seen it before."

"I assumed you'd picked it somewhere."

"No, I didn't."

Their eyes met. She was the first to look away, raising her eyebrows slowly, and then giving a little tilt to her head. She put the lily back in the glass. "Maybe a little gift from someone."

"Why don't I throw it away?" he said.

"Don't get upset, Michael. It's just a flower. He's full of little tricks, remember?"

"I'm not upset, Rowan. It's just that it's already withering. Look at it, it's turning brown, and it looks weird. I don't like it."

"All right," she said, very calmly. "Throw it away." She smiled. "But don't worry about anything!"

"Of course not. What is there to worry about? Just a three-hundred-year-old demon with a mind of his own, who can make flowers fly through the air. Why shouldn't I be overjoyed about a strange lily popping up out of nowhere? Hell, maybe he did it for Deborah. What a nice thing to do."

He turned and stared at the photograph again. Like a hundred Rembrandt subjects, his dark-haired Deborah appeared to be looking right back at him.

He was startled by Rowan's soft little laugh. "You know, you are cute when you're angry," she said. "But there's probably a perfectly good explanation for how the flower got here."

"Yeah, that's what they always say in the movies," he said. "And the audience knows they're crazy."

He took the lily into the bathroom and dropped it into the trash. It really was withering. No waste, wherever the hell it came from, he figured.

She was waiting for him when he came out, her arms folded, looking very serene and inviting. He forgot all about his books in the living room.

The next evening he walked over alone to First Street. Rowan was out with Cecilia and Clancy Mayfair, making the rounds of the city's fashionable malls.

The house was hushed and empty when he got there. Even Eugenia was out tonight, with her two boys and their children. He had it all to himself.

Though all the work was progressing wonderfully, there were still ladders and drop cloths virtually everywhere. The windows were still bare, and it was too soon to clean them. The long shutters, removed for sanding and painting, lay side by side like great long planks on the grass.

He went into the parlor, stared for a long time at his own

shadowy reflection in the mirror over the first fireplace, the tiny red light of his cigarette like a firefly in the dark.

A house like this is never quiet, he thought. Even now he could hear a low singing of creaks and snaps in the rafters and the old floors. You could have sworn someone was walking upstairs, if you didn't know better. Or that far back in the kitchen, someone had just closed a door. And that funny noise, it was like a baby crying, far far away.

But nobody else was here. This wasn't the first night he'd slipped away to test the house and test himself. And he knew it wouldn't be the last.

Slowly he walked back through the dining room, through the shadowy kitchen and out the French doors. A flood of soft light bathed the night around him, pouring from the lanterns on the freshly restored cabana, and from the underwater lights of the pool. It shone on the neatly trimmed hedges and trees, and on the cast-iron furniture, all sanded and newly painted, and arranged in little groups on the clean-swept flagstones.

The pool itself was completely restored, and filled to the brim. Very glamorous it seemed, the long rectangle of deep blue water, rippling and shining in the dusk.

He knelt down and put his hand in the water. A little too hot really for this early September weather, which was no cooler than August when you got right down to it. But good for swimming now in the dark.

A thought occurred to him. Why not go into the pool now? It seemed wrong somehow without Rowan—that the first splash was one of those moments that ought to be shared. But what the hell? Rowan was having a good time, no doubt, with Cecilia and Clancy. And the water was so tempting. He hadn't swum in a pool in years.

He glanced back up at the few lighted windows scattered throughout the dark violet wall of the house. Nobody to see him. Quickly he peeled off his coat, shirt and trousers, his shoes and his socks. He stripped off his shorts. And walking to the deep end, he dove in without another thought.

God! This was living! He plunged down until his hands touched the deep blue bottom, then turned over so that he could see the light glittering on the surface above.

Then he shot upwards, letting his natural buoyancy carry him right through that surface, shaking his head and treading water, as he looked up at the stars. There was noise all around him! Laughter, chatter, people talking in loud, animated voices to one another, and underneath it all, the fast-paced wail of a Dixieland band.

He turned, astonished, and saw the lawn strung with lanterns and filled with people; everywhere young couples were dancing on the flagstones or even right on the grass. Every window in the house was lighted. A young man in a black dinner jacket suddenly dove into the pool right in front of him, blinding him with a violent splash of water.

The water suddenly filled his mouth. The noise was now deafening. At the far end of the pool stood an old man in a tailcoat and white tie, beckoning to him.

"Michael!" he shouted. "Come away at once, man, before it's too late!"

A British accent; it was Arthur Langtry. He broke into a rapid swim for the far end. But before he'd taken three strokes, he lost his wind. A sharp pain caught him in the ribs, and he veered for the side.

As he caught hold of the lip of the pool and pulled himself up again, the night around him was empty and quiet.

For a second he did nothing. He remained there, panting, trying to control the beating of his heart, and waiting for the pain in his lungs to go away. His eyes moved all the while over the empty patio, over the barren windows, over the emptiness of the lawn.

Then he tried to climb up and out of the pool. His body felt impossibly heavy, and even in the heat he was cold. He stood there shivering for a moment, then he went into the cabana and picked up one of the soiled towels he used in the day, when he came in here to wash his hands. He toweled dry with it, and went back out and looked again at the empty garden and the darkened house. The freshly painted violet walls were now exactly the color of the twilight sky.

His own noisy breathing was the only sound in the quiet. But the pain was gone from his chest, and slowly he forced himself to breathe deeply several times.

Was he frightened? Was he angry? He honestly didn't know. He was in a state of shock maybe. He wasn't sure on that score either. He felt he'd run the four-minute mile again, that was certain, and his head was beginning to hurt. He picked up his clothes and dressed, refusing to hurry, refusing to be driven away.

Then for a long moment he sat on the curved iron bench, smoking a cigarette and studying things around him, trying to remember exactly what he'd seen. Stella's last party. Arthur Langtry.

Another one of Lasher's tricks?

Far away, over the lawn, all the way at the front fence, among the camellias, he thought he saw someone moving. He heard steps echoing. But it was only an evening stroller, someone peeping perhaps through the leaves.

He listened until he could no longer hear the distant footsteps, and he realized he was hearing the click of the riverfront train passing, just the way he'd heard it on Annunciation Street when he was a boy. And that sound again, the sound of a baby crying, that was just a train whistle.

He rose to his feet, stubbed out the cigarette, and went back into the house.

"You don't scare me," he said, offhandedly. "And I don't believe it was Arthur Langtry."

Had someone sighed in the darkness? He turned around. Nothing but the empty dining room around him. Nothing but the high keyhole door to the hallway. He walked on, not bothering to soften his footfalls, letting them echo loudly and obtrusively.

There was a faint clicking. A door closing? And the sound a window makes when it is raised—a vibration of wood and panes of glass.

He turned and went up the stairway. He went to the front and then through every empty room. He didn't bother with the lights. He knew his way around the old furniture, ghostly under its plastic drapery. The pale light from the street lamp floating through the doorways was plenty enough for him.

Finally he had covered every foot of it. He went back down to the first floor and out the door.

When he got back to the hotel, he called Aaron from the lobby and asked him to come down to the bar for a drink. It was a pleasant little place, right in the front, small, with a few cozy tables in a dim light, and seldom crowded.

They took a table in the corner. Swallowing half a beer in record time, he told Aaron what had happened. He described the gray-haired man.

"You know, I don't even want to tell Rowan," he said.

"Why not?" Aaron asked.

"Because she doesn't want to know. She doesn't want to see me upset again. It drives her nuts. She tries to be understanding, but things just don't affect her the same way. I go crazy. She gets angry."

"I think you must tell her."

"She'll tell me to ignore it, and to go on doing what makes me happy. And sometimes I wonder if we shouldn't get the hell out of here, Aaron, if somebody shouldn't . . ." He stopped.

"What, Michael?"

"Ah, it's crazy. I'd kill anybody who tried to hurt that house."

"Tell her. Just tell her simply and quietly what happened. Don't give her the reaction which will upset her, unless of course she asks for it. But don't keep any secrets, Michael, especially not a secret like that."

He was quiet for a long time. Aaron had almost finished his drink.

"Aaron, the power she has. Is there any way to test it, or work with it, or learn what it can do?"

Aaron nodded. "Yes, but she feels she's worked with it all her life in her healing. And she's right. As for the negative potential, she doesn't want to develop it; she wants to rein it in completely."

"Yes, but you'd think she'd want to play with it once in a while, in a laboratory situation."

"In time, perhaps. Right now I think she's focused completely upon the idea of the medical center. As you said, she wants to be with the family and realize these plans. And I have to admit this Mayfair Medical is a magnificent conception. I think Mayfair and Mayfair are impressed, though they're reluctant to say so." Aaron finished his wine. "What about you?" Aaron gestured to Michael's hands.

"Oh, it's getting better. I take the gloves off more and more often. I don't know . . ."

"And when you were swimming?"

"Well, I took them off, I guess. God, I didn't even think about it. I . . . You don't think it had to do with that, do you?"

"No, I don't think so. But I think you're very right to assume it might not have been Langtry. It's no more than a feeling perhaps, but I don't think Langtry would try to come through in that way. But do tell Rowan. You want Rowan to be perfectly honest with you in return, don't you? Tell her the whole thing."

He knew Aaron was right. He was dressed for dinner and waiting in the living room of the suite when Rowan came in. He fixed her a club soda with ice, and explained the whole incident as briefly and concisely as he could.

At once, he saw the anxiety in her face. It was almost a disappointment, that something ugly and dark and awful had once again blighted her stubborn sense that everything was going well. She seemed incapable of saying anything. She merely sat on the couch, beside the heap of packages she'd brought home with her. She did not touch the drink.

"I think it was one of his tricks," said Michael. "That was

my feeling. The lily, that was some kind of trick. I think we should just go right on.''

That's what she wanted to hear, wasn't it?

"Yes, that's exactly what we should do," she said, with slight irritation. "Did it . . . shake you up?" she asked. "I think I might have gone crazy seeing something like that."

"No," he said. "It was shocking. But it was sort of fascinating. I guess it made me angry. I kind of . . . well, had one of those attacks, sort of . . ."

"Oh, Christ, Michael."

"No, no! Sit back down, Dr. Mayfair. I'm fine. It's just that when these things happen, there's an exertion, an overall systemic reaction or something. I don't know. Maybe I'm scared and I don't know it. That's probably what it is. One time when I was a kid, I was riding the roller coaster at Pontchartrain Beach. We got right to the top and I figured, well, I won't brace myself for once. I'll just go down the big dip completely relaxed. Well, the strangest thing happened. I felt these cramps in my stomach and my chest. Painful! It was like my body tensed for me, without permission. It was sort of like that. In fact, it was exactly like that."

She was really losing it. She sat there with her arms folded, and her lips pressed together, and she was losing it. Finally in a low voice she said, "People die of heart attacks on roller coasters. Just the way they die from other forms of stress."

"I'm not going to die."

"What makes you so sure?"

"Because I've done it before," he said. "And I know it's not time."

She gave a little bitter laugh. "Very funny," she said.

"I'm completely serious."

"Don't go over there anymore alone. Don't give it any opportunity to do this to you."

"Bullshit, Rowan! I'm not scared of that damned thing. Besides, I like going over there. And . . ."

"And what?"

"The thing is going to show itself sooner or later."

"And what makes you so sure it was Lasher?" she asked in a quiet voice. Her face had gone suddenly smooth. "What if it *was* Langtry, and Langtry wants you to leave me?"

"That doesn't compute."

"Of course it computes."

"Look. Let's drop it. I only want to be straight with you, to tell you everything that happens, not to hold back on something like that. And I don't want you to hold back either."

"Don't go over there again," she said, her face clouding. "Not alone, not at night, not asking for trouble."

He made some little derisive noise.

But she had risen and stalked out of the room. He'd never seen her behave in quite that manner. In a moment she reappeared, with her black leather bag in hand.

"Open your shirt, would you please?" she asked. She was removing her stethoscope.

"What! What is this? You gotta be kidding."

She stood in front of him, holding the stethoscope and staring at the ceiling. Then she looked down at him, and smiled. "We're going to play doctor, OK? Now open your shirt?"

"Only if you open your shirt too."

"I will immediately afterwards. In fact, you can listen to my heart too if you want."

"Well, if you put it that way. Christ, Rowan, this thing is cold."

"I only warm it in my hands for children, Michael."

"Well, hell, don't you think big brave guys like me feel hot and cold?"

"Stop trying to make me laugh. Take a slow deep breath."

He did what she asked. "So what do you hear in there?"

She stood up, gathered the stethoscope in one hand, and put it back in the bag. She sat beside him and pressed her fingers to his wrist.

"Well?"

"You seem fine. I don't hear any murmur. I don't pick up any congenital problems, or any dysfunction or weakness of any kind."

"That's good old Michael Curry!" he said. "What does your sixth sense tell you?"

She reached over and placed her hands on his neck, slipping her fingers down inside his open collar and gently caressing the flesh. It was so gentle and so unlike her regular touch that it brought chills up all over his back, and it stirred the passion in him to a quick, surprising little bonfire.

He was one step from being a pure animal now as he sat there, and surely she must have felt it. But her face was like a mask; her eyes were glassy and she was so still, staring at him, her hands still holding him, that he almost became alarmed.

"Rowan?" he whispered.

Slowly she withdrew her hands. She seemed to be herself again, and she let her fingers drop playfully and with maddening gentleness into his lap. She scratched at the bulge in his jeans.

862

"So what does the sixth sense tell you?" he asked again, resisting the urge to rip her clothing to pieces on the spot.

"That you're the most handsome, seductive man I've ever been in bed with," she said languidly. "That falling in love with you was an amazingly intelligent idea. That our first child will be incredibly handsome and beautiful and strong."

"Are you teasing me? You didn't really see that?"

"No, but it's going to happen," she said. She laid her head on his shoulder. "Wonderful things are going to happen," she said as he folded her against him. "Because we're going to make them happen. Let's go in there now and make something wonderful happen between the sheets."

By the end of the week, Mayfair and Mayfair held its first serious conference devoted entirely to the creation of the medical center. In consultation with Rowan, it was decided to authorize several coordinated studies as to the feasibility, the optimum size of the center, and the best possible New Orleans location.

Ryan scheduled fact-gathering trips for Anne Marie and Pierce to several major hospitals in Houston, New York, and Cambridge. Meetings were being arranged at the local level to discuss the possibility of affiliation with universities or existing institutions in town.

Rowan was hard at work reading technical histories of the American hospital. For hours she talked long distance to Larkin, her old boss, and other doctors around the country, asking for suggestions and ideas.

It was becoming obvious to her that her most grandiose dream could be realized with only a fraction of her capital, if capital was even involved at all. At least that is how Lauren and Ryan Mayfair interpreted her dreams; and it was best to allow things to proceed on that basis.

"But what if some day every penny of that money could be flowing into medicine," said Rowan privately to Michael, "going into the creation of vaccines and antibiotics, operating rooms and hospital beds?"

The renovations were going so smoothly that Michael had time to look at a couple of other properties. By mid-September, he'd acquired a big deep dusty shop on Magazine Street for the new Great Expectations, just a few blocks from First Street and from where he'd been born. It was in a vintage building with a flat above and an iron gallery that covered the sidewalk. Another one of those perfect moments.

Yes, it was all going beautifully and it was so much fun. The parlor was almost finished. Several of Julien's Chinese rugs and fine French armchairs had been returned to it. And the grandfather clock was working once again.

Of course the family besieged them to leave their digs at the Pontchartrain and come to this or that house until the wedding. But they were too comfortable there in the big suite over St. Charles Avenue. They loved the Caribbean Room, and the staff of the small elegant hotel; they even loved the paneled elevator with the flowers painted on the ceiling, and the little coffee shop where they sometimes had breakfast.

Also Aaron was still occupying the suite upstairs, and they had both become extremely fond of him. A day wasn't a day without coffee or a drink or at least a chat with Aaron. And if he was suffering any more of those accidents now, he didn't say so.

The last weeks of September were cooler. And many an evening they remained at First Street, after the workers had gone, having their wine at the iron table, and watching the sun set beyond the trees.

The very last light caught in the high attic windows which faced south, turning the panes to gold.

So quietly grand. The bougainvillea gave forth its purple blooms in dazzling profusion, and each newly finished room or bit of painted ironwork excited them, and filled them with dreams of what was to come.

Meantime Beatrice and Lily Mayfair had talked Rowan into a white dress wedding at St. Mary's Assumption Church. Apparently the legacy stipulated a Catholic ceremony. And the trappings were considered to be absolutely indispensable for the happiness and satisfaction of the whole clan. Rowan seemed pleased when she finally gave in.

And Michael was secretly elated.

It thrilled him more than he dared to admit. He had never hoped for anything so graceful or traditional in his life. And of course it was the woman's decision, and he hadn't wanted to pressure Rowan in any way. But ah, to think of it, a formal white dress wedding in the old church where he'd served Mass.

As the days grew even cooler, as they moved into a beautiful and balmy October, Michael suddenly realized how close they were to their first Christmas together, and that they would spend it in the new house. Think of the tree they could have in that enormous parlor. It would be marvelous, and Aunt Viv was finally settling in at the new condominium. She was still fussing for her personal things, and he was promising to fly to San Francisco any day now to get them, but he knew she liked it here. And she liked the Mayfairs.

Yes, Christmas, the way he had always imagined it ought to be. In a magnificent house, with a splendid tree, and a fire going in the marble fireplace.

Christmas.

Inevitably, the memory of Lasher in the church came back to him. Lasher's unmistakable presence, mingled with the smell of the pine needles and the candles, and the vision of the plaster Baby Jesus, smiling in the manger.

Why had Lasher looked so lovingly at Michael on that long-ago day when he'd appeared in the sanctuary by the crib?

Why all of it? That was the question finally.

And maybe Michael would never know. Maybe, just maybe, he had somehow completed the purpose for which his life had been given back to him. Maybe it had never been anything more than to return here, to love Rowan, and that they should be happy together in the house.

But he knew it couldn't be that simple. Just didn't make sense that way. It would be a miracle if this lasted forever. Just a miracle, the way the creation of Mayfair Medical was a miracle, and that Rowan wanted a baby was a miracle, and that the house would soon be theirs was a miracle . . . and like seeing a ghost was a miracle—a ghost beaming at you from the sanctuary of a church, or from under a bare crepe myrtle tree on a cold night.

Thirty-nine

ALL RIGHT, HERE we go again, thought Rowan. It was what? The fifth gathering in honor of the engaged couple? There had been Lily's tea, and Beatrice's lunch, and Cecilia's little dinner at Antoine's. And Lauren's little party downtown in that lovely old house on Esplanade Avenue.

And this time it was Metairie—Cortland's house, as they still called it though it had been the home of Gifford and Ryan, and their youngest son, Pierce, for years. And the clear October day was perfect for a garden party of some two hundred.

Never mind that the wedding was only ten days away, on November 1, the Feast of All Saints. The Mayfairs would hold two more teas before then, and another lunch somewhere, the place and time to be confirmed later.

"Any excuse for a party!" Claire Mayfair had said. "Darling, you don't know how long we've been waiting for something like this."

They were milling on the open lawn now beneath the small, neatly clipped magnolia trees, and through the spacious low-ceilinged rooms of the trim brick Williamsburg house. And the dark-haired Anne Marie, a painfully honest individual who seemed now utterly enchanted by Rowan's hospital schemes, introduced her to dozens of the same people she had seen at the funeral, and dozens more whom she'd never seen before.

Aaron had been so right in his descriptions of Metairie, an American suburb. They might have been in Beverly Hills or Sherman Oaks in Houston. Except perhaps that the sky had that glazed look she had never seen anywhere else except in the Caribbean. And the old trees that lined the curbs were as venerable as those of the Garden District.

But the house itself was pure elite suburbia with its eighteenth-century Philadelphia antiques and wall-to-wall carpet, and each family portrait carefully framed and lighted, and the soft propitiatory saxophone of Kenny G pouring from hidden speakers in the white Sheetrock walls.

A very black waiter with an extremely round head and a musical Haitian accent poured the bourbon or the white wine into the crystal glasses. Two dark-skinned female cooks in starched uniforms turned the fat pink peppered shrimp on the smoking grill. And the Mayfair women in their soft pastel dresses looked like flowers among the white-suited men, a few small toddlers romping on the grass, or sticking their tiny pink hands into the spray of the little fountain in the center of the lawn.

Rowan had found a comfortable place in a white lawn chair beneath the largest of the magnolias. She sipped her bourbon, as she shook hands with one cousin after another. She was beginning to like the taste of this poison. She was even a little high.

Earlier today, when she'd tried on the white wedding dress and veil for the final fitting, she'd found herself unexpectedly excited by the fanfare, and grateful that it had been more or less forced upon her.

"Princess for a Day," that's what it would be like, stepping in and out of a pageant. Even the wearing of the emerald would not really be an ordeal, especially since it had remained safely in its case since that awful night, and she'd never gotten around to telling Michael about its mysterious and unwelcome appearance. She knew that she ought to have told, and several times she'd been on the verge, but she just couldn't do it.

Michael had been overjoyed about the church wedding, everyone could see it. His parents had been married in the parish, and so had his grandparents before that. Yes, he loved the idea, probably more than she did. And unless something else happened with that awful necklace, why spoil it all for him? Why spoil it for both of them? She could always explain afterwards, when the thing was safely locked in a vault. Yes, not a deception, just a little postponement.

Also, nothing else had happened since. No more deformed flowers on her bedside table. Indeed the time had flown, with the renovations in full swing, and the house in Florida furnished and ready for their official honeymoon.

Another good stroke of luck was that Aaron had been completely accepted by the family, and was now routinely included in every gathering. Beatrice had fallen in love with him, to hear her tell it, and teased him mercilessly about his British bachelor ways and all the eligible widows among the Mayfairs. She had even gone so far as to take him to the symphony with Agnes Mayfair, a very beautiful older cousin whose husband had died the year before.

How is he going to handle that one, Rowan wondered. But she knew by now that Aaron could ingratiate himself with God in heaven or the Devil in hell. Even Lauren, the iceberg lawyer, seemed fond of Aaron. At lunch the other day, Lauren had talked to him steadily about New Orleans history. Ryan liked him. Isaac and Wheatfield liked him. And Pierce questioned him relentlessly about his travels in Europe and the East.

Aaron was also an unfailingly faithful companion to Michael's Aunt Vivian. Everybody ought to have an Aunt Vivian, the way Rowan figured it, a fragile little doll-like person brimming with love and sweetness who doted on Michael's every word. She reminded Rowan of Aaron's descriptions in the history of Millie Dear and Aunt Belle.

But the move had not been easy for Aunt Vivian. And though the Mayfairs had wined and dined her with great affection, she could not keep up with their frenetic pace and their energetic chatter. This afternoon she had begged to remain at home, sorting through the few items she'd brought with her. She was beseeching Michael to go out and pack up everything in the Liberty Street house and he was putting it off, though he and Rowan both knew such a trip was inevitable.

But to see Michael with Aunt Viv was to love him for a whole set of new reasons; for nobody could have been kinder or more patient. "She's my only family, Rowan," he'd remarked once. "Everybody else is gone. You know, if things hadn't worked out with you and me, I'd be in the Talamasca now. They would have become my family."

How well she understood; with a shock, she had been carried back by those words into her own bitter loneliness of months before.

God, how she wanted things to work here! And the ghost of First Street was keeping his counsel, as if he too wanted them to work out. Or had her anger driven him back? For days after the appearance of the necklace she had cursed him under her breath for it.

The family had even accepted the idea of the Talamasca, though Aaron was persistently vague with them about what it really was. They understood no more perhaps than that Aaron was a scholar and a world traveler, that he had always been interested in the Mayfair history because they were an old and distinguished southern family.

And any scholar who could unearth a breathtakingly beautiful ancestor named Deborah, immortalized by none other than the great Rembrandt, and authenticated beyond doubt by the appearance of the unmistakable Mayfair emerald on her breast, was their kind of historian. They were dazzled by the bits and pieces of her story as Aaron revealed them. Good Lord, they'd thought Julien made up all that foolishness about ancestors coming from Scotland.

Meantime Bea was having the photograph of the Rembrandt Deborah reproduced in oil so that it would be hanging on the wall at First Street on the day of the reception. She was furious with Ryan for not recommending the purchase of the original. But then the Talamasca wouldn't part with the original. Thank God that after Ryan's guess as to the inevitable price, the subject had been dropped altogether.

Yes, they loved Aaron and they loved Michael and they loved Rowan.

And they loved Deborah.

If they knew anything of what had happened between Aaron and Cortland or Carlotta years ago, they said not one word. They did not know that Stuart Townsend had been a member of the Talamasca; indeed, they were utterly confused about the discovery of that mysterious body. And it was becoming increasingly obvious that they thought Stella had been responsible for its presence. .

"Probably died up there from opium or drink at one of those

wild parties and she simply wrapped him up in the carpet and forgot about him.''

"Or maybe she strangled him. Remember those parties she used to give?''

It amused Rowan to listen to them talk, to hear their easy bursts of laughter. Never the slightest telepathic vibration of malice reached her. She could feel their good intentions now, their celebratory gaiety.

But they had their secrets, some of them, especially the old ones. With each new gathering, she detected stronger indications. In fact, as the date of the wedding grew closer, she felt certain that something was building.

The old ones hadn't been stopping at First Street merely to extend their best wishes, or to marvel at the renovations. They were curious. They were fearful. There were secrets they wanted to confide, or warnings perhaps which they wanted to offer. Or questions they wanted to ask. And maybe they were testing her powers, because they indeed had powers of their own. Never had she been around people so loving and so skilled at concealing their negative emotions. It was a curious thing.

But maybe this would be the day when something unusual would happen.

So many of the old ones were here, and the liquor was flowing, and after a series of cool October days the weather was pleasantly warm again. The sky was a perfect china blue, and the great curling clouds were moving swiftly by, like graceful galleons in the thrust of a trade wind.

She took another deep drink of the bourbon, loving the burning sensation in her chest, and looked around for Michael.

There he was, still trapped as he'd been for an hour by the overwhelming Beatrice, and the strikingly handsome Gifford, whose mother had been descended from Lestan Mayfair, and whose father had been descended from Clay Mayfair, and who had married, of course, Cortland's grandson, Ryan. Seems there were some other Mayfair lines tangled up in it, too, but Rowan had been drawn away from them at that point in the conversation, her blood simmering at the sight of Gifford's pale fingers wound—for no good reason—around Michael's arm.

So what did they find so fascinating about her heartthrob that they wouldn't let him out of their clutches? And why was Gifford such a nervous woman, to begin with? Poor Michael. He didn't know what was going on. He sat there with his gloved hands shoved in his pockets, nodding and smiling at their little jokes. He didn't detect the flirtatious edge to their gestures, the flaming light in their eyes, the high seductive ring to their laughter.

Get used to it. The son of a bitch is irresistible to refined women. They're all on to him now, that he's the bodyguard who reads Dickens.

Yesterday, he'd climbed the long thin ladder up the side of the house like a pirate climbing the rope ladder of a ship. And then, the sight of him, bare-chested, with his foot on the parapet, his hair blowing, one hand raised to wave as if he had no idea in the world that this series of unself-conscious gestures was driving her slowly out of her mind. Cecilia had looked up and said, "My, but he is a good-looking man, you know."

"Yes, I do," Rowan had mumbled.

Her desire for him at such moments was excruciating. And he was all the more enticing in his new three-piece white linen suit ("You mean dress like an ice-cream man?"), which Beatrice had dragged him to Perlis to buy. "Darling, you're a southern gentleman now!"

Porn, that's what he was. Walking porn. Take the times when he rolled up his sleeves and tucked his Camel cigarettes in the right-arm fold, and put a pencil behind his ear, and stood arguing with one of the carpenters or painters, and then put one foot forward and raised his hand sharply like he was going to push the guy's chin through the top of his head.

And then there were the skinny dips in the pool after everybody was off the property (no ghosts since the first time), and the one weekend they'd gotten away to Florida to claim the new house, and the sight of him sleeping naked on the deck, with nothing on but the gold wristwatch, and that little chain around his neck. Pure nakedness couldn't have been more enticing.

And he was so supremely happy! He was the only one in this world perhaps who loved that house more than the Mayfairs did. He was obsessed with it. He took every opportunity to pitch in on the job with his men. And he was stuffing the gloves away more and more often. Seems he could drain an object of the images if he really tried, and after that he'd keep it out of other hands, and it would be safe, so to speak, and now he had a whole chest of such tools which he used, barehanded, with regularity.

Thank God, the ghosts and the spooks were leaving them both alone. And she had to stop worrying about him over there with his harem.

Better to concentrate on the group gathering around her— stately old Felice had just pulled up a chair, and the pretty garrulous Margaret Ann was settling on the grass, and the dour Magdalene, the one who looked young but wasn't, had been there for some time, watching the others in an unusual silence.

Now and then a head would turn, one of them would look at her, and she would receive some vague shimmer of clandestine knowledge, and a question perhaps, and then it would fade. But it was always one of the older ones—Felice, who was Barclay's youngest daughter and seventy-five years old, or Lily, seventy-eight, they said, and the granddaughter of Vincent, or the elderly bald-headed Peter Mayfair, with the wet shining eyes and the thick neck though his body was very straight and strong—Garland's youngest son, surely a wary and knowing elder.

And then there was Randall, older perhaps than his uncle Peter, saggy-eyed and seemingly wise, slouched on an iron bench in the far corner, gazing at her steadily, no matter how many blocked his view from time to time, as if he wanted to tell her something of great importance but did not know how to begin it.

I want to know. I want to know everything.

Pierce now looked at her with undisguised awe, utterly won over to the dream of Mayfair Medical, and almost as eager as he was to make it a reality. Too bad he'd lost some of the easy warmth he'd shown before, and was almost apologetic as he brought a succession of young men to be introduced, briefly explaining the lineage and present occupation of each one. "We're a family of lawyers, or What does a gentleman do when he doesn't have to do anything?") There was something utterly lovable about Pierce as far as she was concerned. She wanted to put him at ease again. His was a friendliness behind which there was not a single shadow of self-centeredness.

She noted with pleasure as well that after each introduction, he presented the very same person to Michael with a simple, unexplained cordiality. In fact, all of them were being gracious to Michael. Gifford kept pouring the bourbon in his glass. And Anne Marie had now settled beside him and was talking intently to him, her shoulder brushing his shoulder.

Turn it off, Rowan. You can't lock up the beautiful beast in the attic.

In clusters they surrounded her, then broke away so that a new cluster might form. And all the while they talked about the house on First Street, above all about the house.

For the ongoing restoration of First Street brought them undisguised joy.

First Street was their landmark, all right, and how they had hated to see it falling down, how they had hated Carlotta. Rowan caught it behind their congratulatory words. She tasted it when she looked into their eyes. The house was free at last from despicable bondage. And it was amazing how much they knew about the very latest changes and discoveries. They even knew the colors Rowan had chosen for rooms they hadn't yet seen.

So splendid that Rowan had kept all the old bedroom furniture. Did she know that Stella had once slept in Carlotta's bed? And the bed in Millie's room had belonged to Grandmère Katherine, and Great Oncle Julien had been born in the bed in the front room, which was to be Rowan and Michael's bed.

What did they think about her plan for the great hospital? In her few brief conversations outside the firm, she'd found them amazingly receptive. The name, Mayfair Medical, delighted them.

It was crucial to her that the center break new ground, she'd explained last week to Bea and Cecilia, that it fulfill needs which others had not addressed. The ideal environment for research, yes, that was mandatory, but this was to be no ivory tower institute. It was to be a true hospital with a large proportion of its beds committed to nonpaying patients. If it could draw together the top neurologists and neurosurgeons in the nation and become the most innovative, effective, and complete center for the treatment of neurological problems, in unparalleled comfort and with the very latest equipment, it would be her dream come true.

"Sounds quite terrific if you ask me," Cecilia had said.

"It's about time, I think," said Carmen Mayfair over lunch. "You know, Mayfair and Mayfair has always given away millions, but this is the first time anyone has shown this sort of initiative."

And of course that was only the beginning. No need to explain yet that she foresaw experiments in the structure and arrangement of intensive care units, and critical care wards, that she wanted to devise revolutionary housing for the families of patients, with special educational programs for spouses and children who must participate in the ongoing rehabilitation of those with incurable diseases or disabilities.

But each day her vision gained new momentum. She dreamed of a humanizing teaching program designed to correct all the horrors and abuses which had become the clichés of modern medicine; she planned a nursing school in which a new type of supernurse, capable of a whole range of new responsibilities, could be created.

The words "Mayfair Medical" could become synonymous with the finest and most humane and sensitive practitioners in the profession.

Yes, they would all be proud. How could they not be?

"Another drink?"

"Yes, thank you. Bourbon will be fine. Too fine."

Laughter.

She took another sip as she nodded now to young Timmy Mayfair, who had come to shake hands. Yes, and hello again to Bernardette Mayfair, whom she'd met briefly at the funeral, and to the beautiful little red-haired girl with the hair ribbon, who was named Mona Mayfair, daughter of CeeCee, yes, and the tomboyish Jennifer Mayfair, Mona's best friend and fourth cousin, yes, met you before, of course. Jenn had a voice like her own, she thought, deep and husky.

Bourbon was better when it was very cold. But it was also sneaky when it was cold. And she knew she was drinking just a little too much of it. She took another sip, acknowledging a little toast from across the garden. One toast after another was being made to the house, and to the marriage. Was anybody here talking about anything else?

"Rowan, I have photographs that go all the way back—"

". . . and my mother saved all the articles from the papers . . ."

"You know, it's in the books on New Orleans, oh, yes, I have some of the very old books, I can drop them off for you at the hotel . . ."

". . . you understand, we are not going to be knocking on the door day and night, but just to know! . . ."

"Rowan, our great-grandfathers were born in that house . . . all the people you see here were . . ."

"Oh, poor Millie Dear never lived to see the day . . ."

". . . a package of daguerreotypes . . . Katherine and Darcy, and Julien. You know Julien was always photographed at the front door. I have seven different pictures of him at the front door."

The front door?

More and more Mayfairs streamed in. And there at last was the elderly Fielding—Clay's son—utterly bald, and with his fine, translucent skin and red-rimmed eyes—and they were bringing him here, to sit beside her.

No sooner had he eased down in the chair than the young ones began to appear to pay court to him as they had to her.

Hercules, the Haitian servant, put the tumbler of bourbon in the old man's hand.

"You got that now, Mr. Fielding?"

"Yes, Hercules, no food! I'm sick of food. I've eaten enough food for a lifetime."

His voice was deep, and ageless the way the old woman's voice had been.

"And so no more Carlotta," he said grimly to Beatrice, who had come to kiss him. "And I'm the only old one left."

"Don't talk about it, you're going to be with us forever," said Bea, her perfume swirling about them, sweet and floral, and expensive like her brilliant red silk dress.

"I don't know that you're all that much older than I am," declared Lily Mayfair, sitting beside him, and indeed for a moment she did seem as old as he was, with her wispy luminous white hair and sunken cheeks, and the bony hand she laid on his arm.

Fielding turned to Rowan. "So you're restoring First Street. You and that man of yours are going to live there. And so far things have gone well?"

"Why shouldn't they?" Rowan asked with a gentle smile.

But she was warmed suddenly by the blessing Fielding gave her as he rested his hand on her own.

"Splendid news, Rowan," he said, his low voice gaining resonance now that he had caught his breath after the long odyssey from the front door. "Splendid news." The whites of his eyes were yellowed, though his false teeth were shining white. "All those years, she wouldn't let anyone touch it," he said with a touch of anger. "Old witch, that's what she was."

Little gasps rose from the women gathered to the left. Ah, but this was what Rowan wanted. Let the polished surface be broken.

"Granddaddy, for heaven's sakes." It was Gifford at his elbow. She picked up his fallen cane from the grass and hooked it over the back of the chair. He ignored her.

"Well, it's the truth," he said. "She let it fall to ruin! It's a wonder it can be restored at all."

"Granddaddy," said Gifford, almost desperately.

"Oh, let him talk, darling," said Lily, with a little palsy to her small head, eyes flickering over Rowan, her thin hand knotted around her drink.

"You think anyone could shut me up," said the old man. "She said *he* was the one who wouldn't let her, she blamed it all on *him*. She believed in *him* and used *him* when she had her reasons."

A hush was falling over those around them. It seemed the light died a little as the others pressed in. Rowan was vaguely aware that the dark gray figure of Randall was moving in the corner of her eye.

"Granddaddy, I wish you wouldn't . . ." said Gifford.

Oh, but I wish you would!

"She was the one," Fielding said. "She wanted it to fall

874

lown around her. I wonder sometimes why she didn't burn it, like that wicked housekeeper in *Rebecca*. I used to worry that he'd do it. That she'd burn all the old pictures. You see the pictures? You see Julien and his sons standing in front of the doorway?''

''The doorway. You mean the keyhole door at the front of the house?''

Had Michael heard him? Yes, he was coming towards them, obviously trying to silence Cecilia who whispered nonstop in his ear, oblivious to the dazed expression on his face, and Aaron stood not very far away, under the magnolia, unnoticed, eyes fixed on the group. If only she could put a spell on them so that they didn't see Aaron.

But they weren't noticing anything except each other, Fielding nodding, and Felice speaking up, her silver bracelets jangling as she pointed at Fielding.

''Tell her about it,'' said Felice, ''I say you should. You want my opinion? Carlotta wanted that house. She wanted to rule in that house. She was mistress of it till the day she died, wasn't she?''

''She didn't want anything,'' grumbled Fielding, with a flopping dismissive gesture of his left hand. ''That was her curse. She only wanted to destroy.''

''What about the doorway?'' asked Rowan.

''Granddaddy, I'm going to take you . . .''

''You're not going to take me anywhere, Gifford,'' he said, his voice almost youthful in its determination. ''Rowan's moving back into that house. I have things to say to Rowan.''

''In private!'' Gifford declared.

''Let him talk, darling, what's the harm?'' said Lily. ''And this is private. We're all Mayfairs here.''

''It's a beautiful house, she'll love it!'' said Magdalene sharply. ''What are you all trying to do, scare her?''

Randall stood behind Magdalene, eyebrows raised, lips slightly pursed, all the wrinkles of his saggy old face drawn long and deep, as he looked down at Fielding.

''But what were you going to say?'' asked Rowan.

''It's just a package of old legends,'' said Ryan, with a faint touch of irritation, though he spoke more slowly, obviously trying to hold it in. ''Stupid old legends about a doorway and they don't mean anything.''

Michael drew up behind Fielding, and Aaron came a little closer. Still they took no notice.

''I want to know, actually,'' said Pierce. He was standing to the left behind Felice and beside Randall. Felice stared intently at Fielding, her head wagging ever so slightly because she was drunk. "My great-grandfather was painted in front of the doorway," said Pierce. "That portrait's inside. They were always in front of that doorway."

"And why shouldn't they stand on the front porch of the house in these pictures?" asked Ryan. "They lived there. We have to remember, before Carlotta it was our great-great-grandfather's house."

"That's it," Michael murmured. "That's where I saw the door. In the pictures. God, I should have taken a closer look at those pictures . . ."

Ryan glanced at him. Rowan reached out for him, gestured for him to come to her, and Ryan's eyes followed as Michael came around to the back of Rowan's chair. Pierce was talking again as Michael slipped down on the grass beside Rowan, so that she could rest her hand on his shoulder. Aaron now stood quite close by.

"But even in the old photos," Pierce was saying, "they're in front of the door. Always a keyhole door. Either the front door or one of the doors . . ."

"Yes, the door," said Lily. "And the door's on the grave. The same keyhole doorway carved right above the crypts. And nobody even knows who had it done."

"Well, it was Julien, of course," said Randall in a low stentorian voice. They all paid a quick heed to him. "And Julien knew what he was doing, because the doorway had a special meaning for him, and for all of them back then."

"If you tell her all this craziness," said Anne Marie, "she isn't going to . . ."

"Oh, but I want to know," said Rowan. "And besides, nothing could prevent us from moving into the house."

"Don't be so sure of that," said Randall solemnly.

Lauren threw him a cold disapproving glance. "This is no time for scary tales," she whispered.

"Do we have to drag up all this dirt!" cried Gifford. The woman was clearly upset. Rowan could see Pierce's concern. But he was on the very opposite side of the little gathering from his mother. Ryan was close to her. Ryan took her arm, and whispered something in her ear.

She's going to try to break this up, Rowan thought. "What does the doorway mean?" Rowan asked. "Why did they always stand in front of it?"

"I don't like to talk about it," Gifford cried. "I don't see why we have to dig up the past every time we get together. We ought to be thinking about the future."

"We are talking about the future," said Randall. "The young woman ought to know certain things."

"I'd like to know about the door," said Rowan.

"Well, go on, all of you, old mossbacks," said Felice. "If you mean to tell something finally after all these years of acting like the kitten who got the cream . . ."

"The doorway had to do with the pact and the promise," said Fielding. "And it was a secret handed down in each generation all the way from the very earliest times."

Rowan glanced down at Michael, who sat with knees up and his arms resting on them, merely looking up at Fielding. But even from above, she could see the expression of dread and confusion in his face, the same damned expression that came over him every time he talked of the visions. The expression was so uncharacteristic that he looked like someone else.

"I never heard them speak of any promise," said Cecilia. "Or pact, or any doorway, for that matter."

Peter Mayfair now joined them, bald as Fielding, and with the same sharp eyes. In fact, all of them were gathering in a circle, three and four deep. Isaac and Wheatfield crowded in behind Pierce.

"That's because they didn't speak of it," said Peter in a quavering and slightly theatrical voice. "It was their secret, and they didn't want anyone to know."

"But who do you mean, they?" asked Ryan. "Are you talking about my grandfather?" His voice was slightly slurred from his drinking. He took a hasty swallow. "You are talking about Cortland, aren't you?"

"I don't want to . . ." whispered Gifford, but Ryan gestured for her to be silent.

Fielding also motioned for Gifford to be quiet. In fact, the glance he threw her was vicious.

"Cortland was one of them, of course," said Fielding, looking up at bald-headed Peter, "and everybody knew he was."

"Oh, that's a dreadful thing to say," said Magdalene angrily. "I loved Cortland."

"Many of us loved Cortland," said Peter angrily. "I would have done anything for Cortland, but Cortland was one of them. He was. And so was your father, Ryan. Big Pierce was one of them as long as Stella was living, and so was Randall's father. Isn't that so?"

Randall gave a weary nod, taking a slow sip of his bourbon, the dark-faced servant going unnoticed as he refilled Randall's glass and quietly poured splashes of golden bourbon in others.

"What do you mean, one of them?" Pierce demanded. "I've

been hearing this all my life, one of them, not one of them, what does it mean?''

"Nothing," said Ryan. "They had a club, a social club."

"The hell they did," said Randall.

"That all died with Stella," said Magdalene. "My mother was close to Stella, she went to those parties, there were no thirteen witches! That was all bunk."

"Thirteen witches?" asked Rowan. She could feel the tenseness in Michael. Through a small break in the circle she could see Aaron, who had turned his back to the tree and was looking up at the sky as if he couldn't hear them, but she knew that he could.

"Part of the legend," said Fielding, coldly, firmly, as if to distinguish himself from those around him, "part of the story of the doorway and the pact."

"What was the story?" asked Rowan.

"That they would all be saved by the doorway and the thirteen witches," said Fielding, looking up once more at Peter. "That was the story, and that was the promise."

Randall shook his head. "It was a riddle. Stella never knew for sure what it meant."

"Saved?" asked young Wheatfield. "You mean like a Christian being saved?"

"Saved! Hallelujah!" said Margaret Ann, and downed her drink, spilling a few drops of it on her dress. "The Mayfairs are going to heaven. I knew with all this money, somebody would work something out!"

"You're drunk, Margaret Ann," whispered Cecilia. "And so am I!"

They touched their glasses in a toast.

"Stella was trying to get together the thirteen witches at those parties?" asked Rowan.

"Yes," said Fielding. "That was exactly what she was trying to do. She called herself a witch, and so did Mary Beth, her mother, she never made any bones about it, she said she had the power, and she could see 'the man.' "

"I'm not going to allow this . . ." said Gifford, her voice rising hysterically.

"Why? Why is it so scary?" asked Rowan softly. "Why isn't it just old legends? And who *is* 'the man' !"

Silence. They were all studying her, each waiting perhaps for the other to speak. Lauren looked almost angry as she stared at Rowan. Lily looked faintly suspicious. They knew she was deceiving them.

"You know it's not old legends," said Fielding under his breath.

"Because they believed it!" said Gifford, her chin raised, her lip trembling. "Because people have done bad things in the name of believing this old foolishness."

"But what bad things?" asked Rowan. "You mean what Carlotta did to my mother?"

"I mean the things that Cortland did," said Gifford. She was shaking now, clearly on the edge of hysterics. "That's what I mean." She glared at Ryan, and then at her son, Pierce, and then back at Rowan. "And yes, Carlotta too. They all betrayed your mother. Oh, there are so many things you don't know."

"Shhhh, Gifford, too much to drink," whispered Lily.

"Go inside, Gifford," said Randall.

Ryan took his wife by the arm, bending to whisper in her ear. Pierce left his place and came around to assist. Together they drew Gifford away from the group.

Felice was whispering anxiously to Magdalene, and someone on the edge of the circle was trying to gather up all the children and get them to come away. A little girl in a pinafore was saying, "I want to know . . ."

"I want to know," said Rowan. "What did they do?"

"Yes, tell us about Stella," said Beatrice, glancing uneasily at Gifford, who was now crying against Ryan's shoulder as he tried to lead her farther away.

"They believed in Black Magic, that's what they did," said Fielding, "and they believed in the thirteen witches and the doorway, but they never figured out how to make it all work."

"Well, what did they think it meant?" asked Beatrice. "I think all this is fascinating. Do tell."

"And you'll tell it to the whole country club," said Randall, "just the way you always have."

"And why shouldn't I?" said Beatrice. "Is somebody going to come burn one of us at the stake!"

Gifford was being forced into the house by Ryan. Pierce closed the French doors behind them.

"No, I want to know," said Beatrice, stepping forward and folding her arms. "Stella didn't know the meaning? Well, who did?"

"Julien," said Peter. "My grandfather. He knew. He knew and he told Mary Beth. He left it in writing, but Mary Beth destroyed the written record, and she told it to Stella but Stella never really understood."

"Stella never paid attention to anything," said Fielding.

"No, never to anything at all," said Lily sadly. "Poor Stella.

She thought it was all parties, and bootleg liquor and her crazy friends.''

"She didn't believe it all really," said Fielding. "That was the problem right there. She wanted to play with it. And when something went wrong, she became afraid, and drowned her fears in her bootleg champagne. She saw things that would have convinced anyone, but still she didn't believe in the doorway or the promise or the thirteen witches until it was too late and Julien and Mary Beth were both gone.''

"So she broke the chain of information?" Rowan asked. "That's what you're saying. They'd given her secrets along with the necklace and everything else?''

"The necklace was never all that important," said Lily. "Carlotta made a big fuss about the necklace. It's just that you can't take the necklace away . . . well, you're not supposed to take the necklace from the one who inherits it. It's your necklace and Carlotta had the idea that if she locked up the necklace, she'd put an end to all the strange goings-on, and she made that another one of her useless little battles.''

"And Carlotta knew," said Peter, glancing a little contemptuously at Fielding. "She knew what the doorway and the thirteen witches meant.''

"How do you know that?" It was Lauren speaking from a slight distance. "Carlotta certainly never talked of anything like that.''

"Of course not, why would she?" said Peter. "I know because Stella told my mother. Carlotta knew and Carlotta wouldn't help her. Stella was trying to fulfill the old prophecy. And it had nothing to do, by the way, with salvation or hallelujahs. That wasn't the point at all.''

"Says who?" demanded Fielding.

"Says I, that's who.''

"Well, what do you know about it?" asked Randall softly with a little touch of sarcasm in his voice. "Cortland himself told me that when they brought the thirteen witches together, the doorway would open between the worlds.''

"Between the worlds!" Peter scoffed. "And what has that got to do with salvation I'd like to know? Cortland didn't know anything. Any more than Stella. With Cortland it was all after the fact. If Cortland had known he would have helped Stella. Cortland was there. So was I.''

"There when?" asked Fielding scornfully.

"You don't mean Stella's parties," asked Lily.

"Stella was trying to discover the meaning when she held the parties," said Peter. "And I was there.''

"I never knew that," said Magdalene. "I never knew you went."

"How could you have been there?" asked Margaret Ann. "That was a hundred years ago."

"Oh, no it wasn't. It was 1928, and I was there," said Peter. "I was twelve years old when I went, and my father was furious with my mother for allowing it, but I was there. And so was Lauren. Lauren was four years old."

Lauren gave a little subdued nod of her head. Her eyes seemed dreamy, as if she remembered, but she did not share the drama of the moment.

"Stella picked thirteen of us," said Peter, "and it was based on our powers—you know, the old psychic gifts—to read minds, to see spirits, and to move matter."

"And I suppose you can do all that," scoffed Fielding. "And that's why I always beat you at poker."

Peter shook his head. "There wasn't anyone who could do it like Stella. Except Cortland, perhaps, but even he was weaker than Stella. And then there was Big Pierce, he had the touch, he really did, but he was young and entirely under Stella's domination. The rest of us were merely the best she could muster. That's why she had to have Lauren. Lauren had a strong touch of it, and Stella didn't want to waste even that much of a chance. And we were all gathered together in that house, and the purpose was to open the doorway. And when we formed our circle and we began to envision the purpose, *he* was to appear, and he was to come through and be there with us. And he wouldn't be a ghost anymore. He'd be entering into this very world."

A little hush fell over them. Beatrice stared at Peter as if he himself were a ghost. Fielding too studied Peter with seeming incredulity and maybe even a sneer.

Randall's face was impassive, behind its massive wrinkles.

"Rowan doesn't know what you're talking about," said Lily.

"No, and I think we should stop all this," said Anne Marie.

"She knows," said Randall, looking directly at Rowan.

Rowan looked at Peter. "What do you mean that he would come into this very world?" she asked.

"He wouldn't be a spirit any longer, that's what I mean. Not just to appear but to remain, to be . . . physical."

Randall was studying Rowan, as if there was something he couldn't quite determine.

Fielding gave a dry little laugh, a superior laugh. "Stella must have made up that part. That wasn't what my father told me. Saved, that's what he said. All those who were part of the pact would be saved. I remember hearing him tell my mother."

"What else did your father tell you?" Rowan asked.

"Oh, you don't believe all this!" asked Beatrice. "Good Lord, Rowan."

"Don't take it seriously, Rowan!" said Anne Marie.

"Stella was a sad case, my dear," said Lily.

Fielding shook his head. "Saved, that's what my father said. They'd all be saved when the doorway was opened. And it was a riddle, and Mary Beth didn't know the real meaning any more than anyone else. Carlotta swore she'd figured it out, but that wasn't true. She only wanted to torment Stella. I don't even think Julien knew."

"Do you know the words of the riddle?" Michael asked.

Fielding turned to the left and glanced down at him. And suddenly they all appeared to notice Michael, and to focus upon him. Rowan slipped her hand closer to his neck, clasping it affectionately and drawing her legs closer to him, as if embracing him and declaring him part of her.

"Yes, what were the words of the riddle?" Rowan asked.

Randall looked at Peter, and they both looked at Fielding.

Again Fielding shook his head. "I never knew. I never heard there were any special words. It was just that when there were thirteen witches, the doorway would be opened at last. And the night that Julien died, my father said, 'They'll never get the thirteen now, not without Julien.' "

"And who told them the riddle?" asked Rowan. "Was it 'the man' ?"

They were all staring at her again. Even Anne Marie appeared apprehensive and Beatrice at a loss, as if someone had made a fearful breach of etiquette. Lauren was gazing at her in the strangest way.

"She doesn't even know what this is all about," declared Beatrice.

"I think we should forget it," said Felice.

"Why? Why should we forget it?" asked Fielding. "You don't think 'the man' will come to her as he came to all the others? What's changed?"

"You're scaring her!" declared Cecilia. "And frankly you're scaring me."

"Was it 'the man' who gave them the riddle?" Rowan asked again.

No one spoke.

What could she say to make them start talking again, to make them yield up what they possessed. "Carlotta told me about 'the man' ," Rowan said. "I'm not afraid of him."

How still the garden seemed. Every single one of them was

gathered into the circle except for Ryan, who had taken Gifford away. Even Pierce had returned and stood just behind Peter. It was almost twilight. And the servants had vanished, as if they knew they were not wanted.

Anne Marie picked up a bottle from the nearby table, and with a loud gurgling noise filled her glass. Someone else reached for a bottle. And then another. But the eyes of all remained fixed upon Rowan.

"Do you all want me to be afraid?" Rowan asked.

"No, of course not," said Lauren.

"Indeed not!" said Cecilia. "I think this sort of talk could ruin everything."

". . . in a big shadowy old house like that."

". . . nonsense if you ask me."

Randall shook his head; Peter murmured no, but Fielding merely looked at her.

Again the silence came, blanketing the group, as if it were snow. A rustling darkness seemed to be gathering under the small trees. A light had gone on across the lawn, behind the small panes of the French windows.

"Have any of you ever seen 'the man' ?" Rowan asked.

Peter's face was solemn and unreadable. He did not seem to notice when Lauren poured the bourbon in his glass.

"God, I wish I could see him," said Pierce, "just once!"

"So do I!" said Beatrice. "I wouldn't think of trying to get rid of him. I'd talk to him. . . ."

"Oh shut up, Bea!" said Peter suddenly. "You don't know what you're saying. You never do!"

"And you do, I suppose," said Lily sharply, obviously protective of Bea. "Come here, Bea, sit down with the women. If it's going to be war, be on the right side."

Beatrice sat down on the grass beside Lily's chair. "You old idiot, I hate you," she said to Peter. "I'd like to see what you'd do if you ever saw 'the man'. "

He dismissed her with a raised eyebrow, and took another sip of his drink.

Fielding sneered, muttering something under his breath.

"I've gone up there to First Street," said Pierce, "and hung around that iron fence for hours on end trying to see him. If only I'd ever caught one glimpse."

"Oh, for the love of heaven!" declared Anne Marie. "As if you didn't have anything better to do."

"Don't let your mother hear that," Isaac murmured.

"You all believe in him," Rowan said. "Surely some of you have seen him."

"What would make you think that!" Felice laughed.

"My father says it's a fantasy, an old tale," said Pierce.

"Pierce, the best thing you could do," said Lily, "is stop taking every word that falls from your father's lips as if it were gospel because it is not."

"Have you seen him, Aunt Lily?" Pierce asked.

"Indeed, I have, Pierce," Lily said in a low voice. "Indeed I have."

The others registered undisguised surprise, except for the three elder men, who exchanged glances. Fielding's left hand fluttered, as if he wanted to gesture, speak, but he didn't.

"He's real," said Peter gravely. "He's as real as lightning; as real as wind is real." He turned and glared at young Pierce and then back at Rowan, as if demanding their undivided attention and belief in him. Then his eyes settled on Michael. "I've seen him. I saw him that night when Stella brought us together. I've seen him since. Lily's seen him. So has Lauren. You, too, Felice, I know you have. And ask Carmen. Why don't you speak up, Felice? And you, Fielding. You saw him the night Mary Beth died at First Street. You know you did. Who here hasn't seen him? Only the younger ones." He looked at Rowan. "Ask, they'll all tell you."

A loud murmuring ran through the outer edges of the gathering because many of the younger ones—Polly and Clancy and Tim and others Rowan did not know—hadn't seen the ghost, and didn't know whether to believe what they were hearing. Little Mona with the ribbon in her hair suddenly pushed to the front of the circle, with the taller Jennifer right behind her.

"Tell me what you saw," said Rowan, looking directly at Peter. "You're not saying that he came through the door the night that Stella gathered you together."

Peter took his time. He looked around him, eyes lingering on Margaret Ann, and then for a moment on Michael, and then on Rowan. He lifted his drink. He drained the glass, and then spoke:

"He was there—a blazing shimmering presence, and for those few moments, I could have sworn he was as solid as any man of flesh and blood I've ever seen. I saw him materialize. I felt the heat when he did it. And I heard his steps. Yes, I heard his feet strike the floor of that front hallway as he walked towards us. He stood there, just as real as you or me, and he looked at each and every one of us." Again, he lifted his glass, took a swallow and lowered it, his eyes running over the little assembly. He sighed. "And then he vanished, just as he always had. The heat again. The smell of smoke, and the breeze rushing through the house, tearing the very curtains off the windows. But he was gone. He couldn't hold it. And we weren't strong enough to help him hold it. Thirteen of us, yes, the thirteen witches, as Stella called us. And Lauren four years old! Little Lauren. But we weren't of the ilk of Julien or Mary Beth, or old Grandmère Marguerite at Riverbend. And we couldn't do it. And Carlotta, Carlotta who was stronger than Stella—and you mark my words, it was true—Carlotta wouldn't help. She lay on her bed upstairs, staring at the ceiling, and she was saying her rosary aloud, and after every Hail Mary, she said, Send him back to hell, send him back to hell!—and then went on to the next Hail Mary."

He pursed his lips and scowled down into the empty glass, shaking it soundlessly so that the ice cubes revolved. Then again, his eyes ran over the circle, taking in everyone, even little red-haired Mona.

"For the record, Peter Mayfair saw him," Peter declared, pulling himself up, eyebrow raised again. "Lauren and Lily can speak for themselves. So can Randall. But for the record, I saw him, and *that* you may tell to your grandchildren."

A pause again. The darkness was growing dense; and from far away came the grinding cry of the cicadas. No breeze touched the yard. The house was now full of yellow light, in all its many small neat windows.

"Yes," said Lily with a sigh. "You might as well know it, my dear." Her eyes fixed on Rowan as she smiled. "He is there. And we've all seen him many a time since, though not perhaps the way we saw him that night, or for so long, or so clearly."

"You were there, too?" Rowan asked.

"I was," said Lily. "But it wasn't only then, Rowan. We've seen him on that old screen porch with Deirdre." She looked up at Lauren. "We've seen him when we've passed the house. We've seen him sometimes when we didn't want to."

"Don't be frightened of him, Rowan," said Lauren contemptuously.

"Oh, now you tell her that," declared Beatrice. "You superstitious monsters!"

"Don't let them drive you out of the house," said Magdalene quickly.

"No, don't let us do that," said Felice. "And you want my advice, forget the legends. Forget the old foolishness about the thirteen witches and the doorway. And forget about him! He's just a ghost, and nothing more, and you may think that sounds strange, but truly it isn't."

"He can't do anything to you," said Lauren, with a sneer.

"No, he can't," said Felice. "He's like the breeze."

"He's a ghost," said Lily. "That's all he is and all he'll ever be."

"And who knows?" asked Cecilia. "Maybe he's no longer even there."

They all stared at her.

"Well, nobody's seen him since Deirdre died."

A door slammed. There was a tinkling sound, of glass falling, and a commotion on the edge of the circle. People shifted, stepped aside. Gifford pushed her way to the center, her face wet and stained, her hands shaking.

"Can't do anything! Can't hurt anyone! Is that what you're telling her! Can't do anything! He killed Cortland, that's what he did! After Cortland raped your mother! Did you know that, Rowan!"

"Hush, Gifford!" Fielding roared.

"Cortland was your father," Gifford screamed. "The hell he can't do anything! Drive him out, Rowan! Turn your strength on him and drive him out! Exorcise the house! Burn it down if you have to . . . Burn it down!"

A roar of protest came from all directions, and vague expressions of scorn or outrage. Ryan had appeared and was trying once more to restrain Gifford. She turned and slapped his face. Gasps came from all around. Pierce was obviously mortified and helpless.

Lily rose and left the group, and so did Felice, who almost fell in her haste. Anne Marie struggled to her feet, and helped Felice to get away. But the others stood firm, including Ryan, who simply wiped his face with his handkerchief, as if to regain his composure while Gifford stood with her fists clenched, lips trembling. Beatrice was clearly desperate to help but didn't know what to do.

Rowan rose and went towards Gifford.

"Gifford, listen to me," said Rowan. "Don't be afraid. It's the future we care about, not the past." She took Gifford by both arms, and reluctantly Gifford looked up into her face. "I will do what's good," said Rowan, "and what's right, and what's good and right for the family. Do you understand what I'm saying?"

Gifford broke into sobs, her head bent again as if her neck were too weak to hold it. Her hair fell down into her eyes. "Only evil people can be happy in that house," she said. "And they were evil—Cortland was evil!" Both Pierce and Ryan had their arms around her. Ryan was becoming angry. But Rowan hadn't let her go.

"Too much to drink," said Cecilia. Someone had thrown on the yard lights.

Gifford appeared to collapse suddenly, but still Rowan held her.

"No, listen to me, please, Gifford," Rowan said, but she was really speaking to the others. She saw Lily standing only a short distance away, and Felice beside her. She saw Beatrice's eyes fixed on her. And Michael was standing, watching her, as he stood behind Fielding's chair.

"I've been listening to you all," said Rowan, "and learning from you. But I have something to say. The way to survive this strange spirit and his machinations is to see him in a large perspective. Now, the family, and life itself, are part of that perspective. And he must never be allowed to shrink the family or shrink the possibilities of life. If he exists as you say he does, then he belongs in the shadows."

Randall and Peter were watching her intently. So was Lauren. Aaron stood very near to Michael, and he too was listening. Only Fielding seemed cold, and sneering, and did not look at Rowan. Gifford was staring at her in a daze.

"I think Mary Beth and Julien knew that," said Rowan. "I mean to follow their example. If something appears to me out of the shadows at First Street, no matter how mysterious it might be, it won't eclipse the greater scheme, the greater light. Surely you follow my meaning."

Gifford seemed almost spellbound. And very slowly Rowan realized how peculiar this moment had become. She realized how strange her words seemed; and how strange she must have appeared to all of them, making this unusual speech while she held this frail, hysterical woman by both arms.

Indeed they were all staring at her as if they too had been spellbound.

Gently she let Gifford go. Gifford stepped backwards, and into Ryan's embrace, but her eyes remained large, empty, and fixed on Rowan.

"I'm frightening you, aren't I?" asked Rowan.

"No, no everything is all right now," said Ryan.

"Yes, everything's fine," said Pierce.

But Gifford was silent. They were all confused. When Rowan looked at Michael she saw the same dazed expression, and behind it the old dark turbulent distress.

Beatrice murmured some little apology for all that had happened; she stepped up and led Gifford away. Ryan went with them. And Pierce remained, motionless, struck dumb.

Lily looked around, apparently confused for a moment, and then called to Hercules to please find her coat.

Randall, Fielding, and Peter remained in the stillness. Others lingered in the shadows. The little girl with the ribbon stared from a distance, her round sweet young face like a flame in the dark. The taller child, Jenn, appeared to be crying.

Suddenly Peter clasped Rowan's hand.

"You're wise in what you said. You'd waste your life if you got caught up in it."

"That's correct," said Randall. "That's what happened to Stella. Same thing with Carlotta. She wasted her life! Same thing." But he was anxious, and only too ready to withdraw. He turned and slipped off without a farewell.

"Come on, young man, help me up," said Fielding to Michael. "The party's over, and by the way, my congratulations on the marriage. Maybe I'll live long enough to see the wedding. And please, don't invite the ghost."

Michael looked disoriented. He glanced at Rowan, and then down at the old man, and then very gently he helped the old man to his feet. Then he looked at Rowan again. The confusion and dread were there as before.

Several of the young ones approached, to tell Rowan not to be discouraged by all this Mayfair madness. Anne Marie begged her to go on with her plans. A light breeze came at last with just a touch of coolness to it.

"Everybody will be heartbroken if you don't move into the house," said Margaret Ann.

"You're not giving it up?" demanded Clancy.

"Of course not," said Rowan with a smile. "What an absurd idea."

Aaron stood watching Rowan impassively. And Beatrice came back now with a flood of apologies on behalf of Gifford, begging Rowan not to be upset.

The others were coming back; they had their raincoats, purses, whatever they had gone to gather. It was full dark now; and the air was cool, deliciously cool. And the party was over.

For thirty minutes, the cousins said their good-byes, all issuing the same warnings. Stay, don't go. Restore the house. Forget all the old talk.

And Ryan apologized for Gifford and for the awful things she'd said. Surely Rowan must not take Gifford's words as truth. Rowan waved it away.

"Thank you, thank you very much for everything," said

Rowan. "And don't worry. I wanted to know the old stories. I wanted to know what the family was saying. And now I do."

"There's no ghost up there," said Ryan, looking her directly in the eye.

Rowan didn't bother to answer.

"You're going to be happy at First Street," said Ryan. "You'll change the image." As Michael appeared at her side, he shook Michael's hand.

Turning to take her leave, Rowan saw that Aaron was at the front gate, talking with Gifford of all people, and Beatrice. Gifford seemed entirely comforted.

Ryan waited, patiently, a silhouette in the front door.

"Not to worry about anything at all," Aaron was saying to Gifford, in his seductive British accent.

Gifford flung her arms around him suddenly. Graciously he returned her embrace and kissed her hand as he withdrew. Beatrice was only slightly less effusive. Then they both stood back, Gifford white-faced and weary-looking, as Aaron's black limousine lumbered to the curb.

"Don't worry about anything, Rowan," said Beatrice cheerily. "Lunch tomorrow, don't forget. And this shall be the most beautiful wedding!"

Rowan smiled. "Don't worry, Bea."

Rowan and Michael slipped into the long backseat, while Aaron took his favorite place, with his back to the driver. And the car slowly pulled away.

The flood of ice-cold air was a blessing to Rowan. The lingering humidity and the atmosphere of the twilight garden were clinging to her. She closed her eyes for a moment, and took a deep breath.

When she looked up again, she saw that they were on Metairie Road, speeding past the newer cemeteries of the city which looked grim and without romance through the dark tinted glass. The world always looked so ghastly through the tinted windows of a limousine, she thought. The worst shade of darkness imaginable. Suddenly it pierced her nerves.

She turned to Michael, and seeing that awful expression on his face again, she felt impatient. She had only been excited by what she had found out. Her resolves were the same. In fact, she had found the whole experience fascinating.

"Things haven't changed," she said. "Sooner or later he'll come, he'll wrestle with me for what he wants, and he'll lose. All we did was get more information about the number and the door, and that's what we wanted." Michael didn't answer her. "But nothing's changed," she insisted. "Nothing at all."

Still Michael didn't respond.

"Don't brood on it," Rowan said sharply. "You can be certain I'll never bring together any coven of thirteen witches. I have much more important things to do than that. And I didn't mean to frighten anybody back there. I think I said the wrong thing. I think I used the wrong words."

"They misunderstand," said Michael in a half murmur. He was staring at Aaron, who sat impassively watching them both. And she could tell by Michael's voice that he was extremely upset.

"What do you mean?"

"Nobody has to gather thirteen witches," said Michael, his blue eyes catching the light of the passing cars as he looked at her. "That wasn't the point of the riddle. They misunderstood because they don't know their own history."

"What are you talking about?"

She had never seen him so anxious since the day he'd smashed the jars. She knew if she took hold of his wrist, she'd feel his pulse racing again. She hated this. She could see the blood pumping in his face.

"Michael, for Christ's sake!"

"Rowan, count your ancestors! The thing has waited for thirteen witches, from the time of Suzanne to the present, and you are the thirteenth. Count them. Suzanne, Deborah, and Charlotte; Jeanne Louise, Angélique, and Marie Claudette; followed in Louisiana by Marguerite, Katherine, and Mary Beth. Then come Stella, Antha, Deirdre. And finally you, Rowan! The thirteenth is simply the strongest, Rowan, the one who can *be* the doorway for this thing to come through. You are the doorway, Rowan. That is why there were twelve crypts, and not thirteen, in the tomb. The thirteenth is the doorway."

"All right," she said, straining for patience. She put up her hands in a gentle plea. "And we knew this before, didn't we? And so the devil predicted it. The devil sees far, as he said to you, he sees the thirteen. But the devil doesn't see everything. He doesn't see who I am."

"No, those weren't his words," said Michael. "He said that he sees to the finish! And he also said that I couldn't stop you, and I couldn't stop him. His said his patience was like the patience of the Almighty."

"Michael," Aaron interrupted. "This being has no obligation to speak the truth to you! Don't fall into this trap. It plays with words. It's a liar."

"I know, Aaron. The devil lies. I know! I heard it from the time I was that high. But God, what is he waiting for? Why are we being allowed to go along day after day, while he bides his time? It's driving me crazy."

Rowan reached for his wrist, but as soon as he realized she was feeling his pulse he pulled away. "When I need a doctor, I'll tell you, OK?"

She was stung, and drew back, turning away from him. She was angry with herself that she couldn't be patient. She hated it that he was this upset. And she hated herself for being anguished and afraid.

It crossed her mind that every time he responded in this way, he played into the hands of the unseen forces that were striving to control them, that maybe they had picked him for their games because he was so easily controlled. But it would be awful to say such a thing to him. It would insult him and hurt him and she couldn't stand to see him hurt. She couldn't stand to see him weakened.

She sat defeated, looking down at her hands resting limp in her lap. And the spirit had said, "I shall be flesh when you are dead." She could all but hear Michael's heart pounding. Even though his head was turned away from her, she knew he was feeling dizzy, even sick. *When you are dead.* Her sixth sense had told her he was sound, strong, as vigorous as a man half his age, but there it was again, the unmistakable symptoms of enormous stress, playing havoc with him.

God, how awful it had turned out, the whole experience. How terribly the secrets of the past had poisoned the whole affair. Not what she wanted, no, the very opposite. Maybe it would have been better if they had said nothing at all. If Gifford had had her way and they had gone on in their airy sunlighted dream, talking of the house and the wedding.

"Michael," said Aaron in his characteristically calm voice. "He taunts and he lies. What right has he to prophesy? And what purpose could he have other than to try through his lies to make his prophecies come true?"

"Where the hell is he?" demanded Michael. "Aaron, maybe I'm grasping at straws. But that first night when I went to the house, would he have spoken to me if you hadn't been there? Why did he show himself only to vanish like so much smoke?"

"Michael, I could give you several explanations for every single appearance he has made. But I don't know that I'm right. The important thing is to maintain a sane course, to realize he's a trickster."

"Exactly," said Rowan.

"God, what kind of a game is it?" whispered Michael. "They give me everything I ever wanted—the woman I love, my home again, the house I dreamed of when I was a little boy. We want to have a child, me and Rowan! What kind of a game is it? He speaks and the others who came to me are silent. God, if only I could lose the feeling that it's all planned, like Townsend said in your dream, all planned. But who's planning it?''

"Michael, you've got to get a grip on yourself," Rowan said. "Everything is going beautifully, and we are the ones who made it that way. It has gone beautifully since the day after the old woman died. You know, there are times when I think I'm doing what my mother would have wanted. Does that sound crazy? I think I'm doing what Deirdre dreamed of all those years."

No answer.

"Michael, didn't you hear what I said to the others?" she asked. "Don't you believe in me?"

"Just promise me this, Rowan," he said. He grabbed her hand and slipped his fingers between hers. "Promise me if you see that thing, you won't keep it secret. You'll tell me. You won't keep it back.''

"God, Michael, you're acting like a jealous husband."

"Do you know what that old man said?" Michael asked. "When I helped him to the car?"

"You're talking about Fielding?"

"Yeah. This is what he said. 'Be careful, young man.' What the hell did he mean by that?"

"The hell with him for saying that," she whispered. She was suddenly in a rage. She pulled her hand free from Michael. "Who the hell does he think he is, the old bastard! How dare he say that to you. He doesn't come to our wedding. He doesn't come through the front gate—" She stopped, choking on the words. The anger was too bitter. Her trust in the family had been so total, she'd been just lapping it all up, the love, and now she felt as if Fielding had stabbed her, and she was crying again, goddamn it, and she didn't have a handkerchief. She felt like . . . like slapping Michael. But it was that old man she'd like to belt. How dare he?

Michael tried to take her hand again. She pushed him away. For a moment, she was so angry, she couldn't think at all. And she was furious that she was crying.

"Here, Rowan, please," Aaron said. He put his handkerchief into her hand.

She was barely able to whisper thank you. She used the handkerchief to cover her eyes.

"I'm sorry, Rowan," Michael whispered.

"The hell with you too, Michael!" she said. "You'd better stand up to them. You'd better stop spinning like a goddamned top every time another piece of the puzzle falls into place! It wasn't the Blessed Virgin Mary you saw out there in your visions! It was just them and all their tricks.''

"No, that's not true."

He sounded sad and contrite, and really raw. It broke her heart to hear it, but she wouldn't give in. She was afraid to say what she really thought— Listen, I love you, but did it ever occur to you that your role in this was only to see that I returned, that I remained, and that I have a child to inherit the legacy? This spirit could have staged your drowning, your rescue, the visions, the whole thing. And that was why Arthur Langtry came to you, that was why he warned you to get away before it was too late.

She sat there holding it in, poisoned by it, and hoping it wasn't true, and afraid.

"Please, don't go on with this," Aaron said gently. "The old man was a little bit of a fool, Rowan." His voice was like soothing music, drawing the tension out of her. "Fielding wanted to feel important. It was a boasting match among the three of them—Randall, Peter, and Fielding. Don't be harsh with him. He's simply . . . too old. Believe me, I know. I'm almost there myself."

She wiped her nose and looked up at Aaron. He was smiling and she smiled too.

"Are they good people, Aaron? What do you think?" She was deliberately ignoring Michael for the moment.

"Fine people, Rowan. Far better than most, my dear. And they love you. They love you. The old man loves you. You're the most exciting thing that's happened to him in the last ten years. They don't invite him out much, the others. He was basking in the attention. And of course, for all their secrets, they don't know what you know."

"You're right," she whispered. She felt drained now, and miserable. Emotional outbursts for her were never cathartic. They always left her shaky and unhappy.

"All right," she said, "I'd ask him to give me away at the wedding, damn it, except I have another very dear friend in mind." She wiped her eyes again with the folded handkerchief, and blotted her lips. "I'm talking about you, Aaron. I know it's late notice. But will you walk up the aisle with me?"

"Darling, I'd be honored," he said. "Nothing would give me greater happiness." He clasped her hand tightly. "Now, please, please don't think about that old fool anymore."

"Thank you, Aaron," she said. She sat back, and took a deep breath before she turned to Michael. In fact she had been deliberately leaving him out. And suddenly she felt terribly sorry. He looked so dejected and so gentle. She said: "Well, have you calmed down or have you had a heart attack? You're awfully quiet."

He laughed under his breath, warming at once. His eyes were so brilliantly blue when he smiled. "You know, when I was a kid," he said, taking her hand again, "I used to think that having a family ghost would be wonderful! I used to wish I could see a ghost! I used to think, ah, to live in a haunted house, wouldn't that be great!"

He was his old self again, cheerful and strong, even if he was a little ragged at the edges. She leaned over and pressed her lips against his roughened cheek. "I'm sorry I got angry."

"I'm sorry, too, honey. I'm really sorry. That old man didn't mean any harm. He's just crazy. They all have a little craziness. I guess it's their Irish blood. I haven't been around lace curtain Irish very much. I guess they're as crazy as all the others."

There was a little smile on Aaron's lips as he watched them, but they were all shaken now, and tired. And this conversation had sapped their last bit of vigor.

It seemed to Rowan that the gloom was descending again. If only this glass were not so dark.

She slumped back, letting her head rest against the leather, and watched the glum shabby city roll by, the outlying streets of wooden double shotgun cottages with their fretwork and long wooden shutters, and the low sagging stucco buildings that seemed somehow not to belong among the ragged oaks and high weeds. Beautiful, all beautiful. The veneer of her perfect California world had cracked, and she'd been thrown into the real true texture of life at last.

How could she let them both know that it was all going to work, that she knew in the end she would triumph, that no temptation conceivable could lure her away from her love, and her dreams, and her plans?

The thing would come, and the thing would work its charm— like the devil and the old women of the village—and she would be expected to succumb, but she would not, and the power within her, nurtured through twelve witches, would be sufficient to destroy him. Thirteen is bad luck, you devil. And the door is the door to hell.

Ah, yes, that was it exactly, the door was the door to hell.

But only when it was over would Michael believe.

She said no more.

She remembered those roses again in the vase on the hall table. Awful things, and that iris with the dark black shivering mouth. Horrid. And worse than all the rest, the emerald around her neck in the dark, cold and heavy against her naked skin. No, don't ever tell him about that. Don't talk anymore about any of it.

He was as brave and good as anyone she'd ever known. But she had to protect him now, because he couldn't protect her, that was plain. And she realized for the first time—that when things really did start to happen, she'd probably be completely alone in it. But hadn't that always been inevitable?

he back to his office and they heavy-set and for raised them.
No, sorry, we all turned to stop. Don't talk too much about any

he would I. Dave and Jack it turned the Nelson the wall
time ... lookm a gun now because his confident crackers
was time. And she reacted for the first time next week
nine-thirty said man A impulse sized probably be complete.
It is but much I am answer was inevitable.

PART FOUR

THE DEVIL'S BRIDE

Forty

WOULD SHE REMEMBER this afterwards, she wondered, as one of the happiest days of her life? Weddings must work their magic on everyone. But she was more susceptible than most, she figured, because it was so very exotic, because it was Old World, and old-fashioned, and old-fangled, and coming as she did from the world of the cold and the alone, she wanted it so much!

The night before, she'd come here to church to pray alone. Michael had been surprised. Was she really praying to someone? "I don't know," she said. She wanted to sit in the dark church, which was readied for the wedding with the white ribbons and bows and the red carpet down the aisle, and talk to Ellie, to try to explain to Ellie why she had broken her vow, why she was doing this, and how it was all going to work out.

She explained about the white wedding dress and how the family had wanted it, and so she had given in happily to the yards and yards of white silk lace and the full shimmering veil. And she explained about the bridesmaids—Mayfairs all, of course—and Beatrice, the matron of honor, and how Aaron was going to give her away.

She explained and she explained. She even explained about the emerald. "Be with me, Ellie," she said. "Extend to me your forgiveness. I want this so much."

Then she had talked to her mother. She had talked simply and without words, feeling close to her mother. And she had tried to blot all memory of the old woman out of her mind.

She had thought of her old friends from California, whom she had called in the last few weeks, and with whom she had had wonderful conversations. They were so happy for her, though they did not fully grasp how rich and vital this old-fashioned world here really was. Barbara wanted to come but the term had already begun at Princeton, and Janie was leaving for Europe, and Mattie was going to have a baby any day. They had sent

899

such exquisite presents though of course she had forbidden it. And she had the feeling they would see each other in the future, at least before her real work on the dream of the Mayfair Medical Center began.

Finally, she had ended her prayers in a strange way. She had lighted candles for her two mothers. And a candle for Antha. And even one for Stella. It was such a soothing ritual, to see the little wicks ignite, to see the fire dance before the statue of the Virgin. No wonder they did such things, these wise old Catholics. You could almost believe that the graceful flame was a living prayer.

Then she'd gone out to find Michael, who was having a wonderful time in the sacristy reminiscing about the parish with the kindly old priest.

Now at one o'clock, the wedding was at last beginning.

Stiff and still in her white raiment, she stood waiting, dreaming. The emerald lay against the lace that covered her breast, its burning glint of green the only color touching her. Even her ashen hair and gray eyes had looked pale in the mirror. And the jewel had reminded her, strangely, of the Catholic statues of Jesus and Mary with the exposed hearts, like the one she'd smashed so angrily in her mother's bedroom.

But all those ugly thoughts were very far away from her now. The huge nave of St. Mary's Assumption was packed. Mayfairs from New York and Los Angeles and Atlanta and Dallas had come. There were over two thousand of them. And one by one to the heavy strains of the organ, the bridesmaids—Clancy, Cecilia, Marianne, Polly, and Regina Mayfair—were moving up the aisle. Beatrice looked more splendid even than the younger ones. And the ushers, all Mayfairs too of course, and what a comely crew they were, stood ready to take the arms of the maids, one by one. But now had come the moment—

It seemed to her that she would forget how to put one foot before the other. But she didn't. Quickly she adjusted the long full white veil. She smiled at Mona, her little flower girl, lovely as always with the usual ribbon in her red hair. She took Aaron's arm, and together they followed Mona, in time with the stately music, Rowan's eyes moving dimly over the hundreds of faces on either side of her, and dazzled, through the haze of whiteness, by the tiers of lights and candles at the altar ahead.

Would she remember this always? The bouquet of white flowers in her hand, Aaron's soft radiant smile as he looked at her, and her own feeling of being beautiful the way brides must always be beautiful?

When at last she saw Michael, so perfectly adorable in his

gray cutaway and ascot, she felt the tears rise to her eyes. How truly splendid he was, her lover, her angel, beaming at her from his place beside the altar, his hands—without the awful gloves—clasped before him, his head bowed slightly as if he had to shelter his soul from the bright light that shone on him, though his own blue eyes were the most brilliant light of all to her.

He stepped up beside her. A lovely calm descended on her as she turned towards Aaron, and he lifted her veil and gracefully threw it back over her shoulders, bringing it softly down behind her arms. A shiver ran through her. Her life had never included any such time-honored gesture. And it was not the veil of her virginity or her modesty, but the veil of her loneliness that had been lifted away. He took her hand; he placed it in Michael's.

"Be good to her always, Michael," he whispered. She closed her eyes, wanting this pure sensation to endure forever, and then slowly looked up at the resplendent altar with its row after row of exquisite wooden saints.

As the priest began the traditional words, she saw that Michael's eyes were glazed with tears also. She could feel him trembling, as his grip tightened on her hand.

She feared that her voice might fail her. She had been faintly sick that morning, perhaps with worry, and she experienced a touch of dizziness again.

But what struck her in a moment of quiet and detachment was that this ceremony itself conveyed immense power, that it wrapped about them some invisible protective force. How her old friends had scoffed at such things, how she herself had once found them unimaginable. And now, in the very center of it, she savored it and opened her heart to receive all the grace that it could give.

Finally the language of the old Mayfair legacy, imposed upon the ceremony and reshaping it, was now being recited:

". . . now and forever, in public and in private, before your family and all others, without exception, and in all capacities, to be known only by the name of Rowan Mayfair, daughter of Deirdre Mayfair, daughter of Antha Mayfair, though your lawful husband shall be called by his own name . . ."

"I do."

"Nevertheless, and with a pure heart, do you take this man, Michael James Timothy Curry . . ."

"I do . . . ."

At last it was done. The final utterances had echoed under the high arched ceiling. Michael turned and took her in his arms as he'd done a thousand times in the secret darkness of their hotel bedroom; yet how exquisite now was this public and ceremonial kiss. She yielded to it completely, her eyes lowered, the church dissolved into silence. And then she heard him whisper:

"I love you, Rowan Mayfair."

She answered, "I love you, Michael Curry, my archangel." And pressing close to him, in all his stiff finery, she kissed him again.

The first notes of the wedding march sounded, loud and sharp and full of triumph. A great rustling noise swept through the church. She turned, facing the enormous assembly and the sun pouring through the stained-glass windows, and taking Michael's arm she commenced the long quick walk down the aisle.

On either side she saw their smiles, their nods, the irresistible expressions of the same excitement, as if the entire church were infused with the simple and overwhelming happiness she felt.

Only as they climbed into the waiting limousine, the Mayfairs showering them with rice in an exuberant chorus of cheers, did she think of the funeral in this church, did she remember that other cavalcade of shining black cars.

And now through these same streets, she thought, nestled with the white silk all around her and Michael kissing her again, kissing her eyes and her cheeks. He was murmuring all those silly wonderful things to her that husbands ought to murmur to brides, that she was beautiful, that he adored her, that he'd never been happier, that if this wasn't the most perfect day of his life, he couldn't imagine what it possibly was. And the greatest part was not what he said, but how happy he was himself.

She sank back and against his shoulder, smiling, her eyes closed, thinking quietly and deliberately of all the landmark moments, her graduation from Berkeley, the first day she'd entered the wards as an intern, the first day she'd walked into an Operating Room, the first time she'd heard the words at the end of the operation, Well done, Dr. Mayfair, you can close.

"Yes, the happiest day," she whispered. "And it's only just begun."

Hundreds milled over the grass, under the great white tents which had been erected to cover the garden, the pool, and the back lawn before the *garçonnière*. The outdoor buffet tables, draped in white linen, sagged beneath their weight of sumptuous southern dishes—crawfish étouffée, shrimp Creole, pasta jambalaya, baked oysters, blackened fish, and even the humble and beloved red beans and rice. Liveried waiters poured the champagne into the tulip glasses; bartenders fixed cocktails to order at the well-stocked bars in the parlor, the dining room, and beside the pool. Fancily dressed children of all sizes played tag among the adults, hiding behind the potted palms which had been stationed through the ground floor, or rushed in gangs up and down the stairway shrieking—to the utter mortification of various parents—that they had just seen "the ghost!"

The Dixieland band played furiously and joyously under its white canopy before the front fence, the music swallowed from time to time by the noisy animated conversation.

For hours Michael and Rowan, their backs to the long mirror at the First Street end of the parlor, received one visiting Mayfair after another, shaking hands, extending thanks, listening patiently to lineages and the tracing of connections and interconnections.

Many of Michael's old high-school chums had come, thanks to the diligent efforts of Rita Mae Lonigan, and they formed their own noisy and cheerful constituency, telling old football stories, very nearby. Rita had even located a couple of long-lost cousins, a nice old woman named Amanda Curry whom Michael remembered fondly, and a Franklin Curry who had gone to school with Michael's father.

If there was anyone here enjoying all this more than Rowan, it was Michael, and he was far less reserved than she. Beatrice came to hug him exuberantly at least twice in every half hour, always wringing a few embarrassed tears from him, and he was clearly touched by the affection with which Lily and Gifford took Aunt Vivian under their wing.

But it was a time of high emotions for all. Mayfairs from various other cities embraced cousins they hadn't seen in years, vowing to return to New Orleans more often. Some made arrangements to stay over a week or two with this or that branch of the family. Flashbulbs went off continuously; big black hulking video cameras slowly poked their way through the glittering press.

At last the receiving was over; and Rowan was free to roam from one little group to another, and to feel the success of the gathering, and approve the performance of the caterers and the band, as she felt bound to do.

The day's heat had lifted completely, thanks to a gentle breeze. Some guests were taking an early leave; the pool was full of half-naked little creatures, screaming and splashing each other, some swimming in underpants only, and a few drunken adults who had jumped in fully clothed.

More food was being heaped into the heated carafes. More cases of champagne were opened. The hard-core five hundred or so Mayfairs, whom Rowan had already come to know personally, were milling about quite at home, sitting on the staircase to talk, or wandering around in the bedrooms admiring the marvelous changes, or hovering about the huge and gaudy display of expensive gifts.

Everywhere people admired the restoration: the soft peach color of the parlor walls, and the beige silk draperies; the dark somber green of the library, and the glowing white woodwork throughout. They gazed at the old portraits, cleaned and reframed and carefully hung throughout the hallway and the lower rooms. They gathered to worship at the picture of Deborah, hanging now above the library fireplace. It was Lily and Beatrice who assisted Fielding on the entire tour, taking him upstairs in the old elevator, so that he might see each and every room.

Peter and Randall settled in the library with their pipes, arguing about the various portraits and their approximate dates, and which had been done by whom. And what would the cost be, if Ryan were to try to acquire this "alleged" Rembrandt?

With the first gust of rain, the band moved indoors to the back end of the parlor, and the Chinese carpets were rolled back as the young couples, some kicking off their shoes in the mayhem, began to dance.

It was the Charleston. And the very mirrors rattled with the stormy din of the trumpets and the constant thunder of stomping feet.

Surrounded again and again by groups of eager and enthusiastic faces, Rowan lost track of Michael. There was a moment when she fled to the small powder room off the library with a passing wave to Peter, who now remained alone, and seeming half asleep.

She stood there silent, the door locked, her heart pounding, merely staring at herself in the glass.

She seemed faded now, crushed, rather like the bouquet which she would have to toss later from the railing of the stairs. Her lipstick was gone, her cheeks looked pallid, but her eyes were shining like the emerald. Tentatively she touched it, adjusted it against the lace. She closed her eyes and thought of the picture of Deborah. Yes, it was right to have worn it. Right to have done everything the way they wanted. She stared at herself again, clinging to the moment, trying forever to save it, like a precious snapshot tucked in the pages of a diary. *This day, among them, everyone here.*

It did not mar her happiness to come on Rita Mae Lonigan crying softly next to Peter when she opened the library door. She was more than content to press Rita's hand and say, "Yes, I have thought of Deirdre often today, myself." Because that was true. And she had liked thinking of Deirdre and Ellie, and even Antha, and extracting them from the tragedies that en-snared them, and holding them to her heart.

Perhaps in some cold reasoning part of her mind, she under-stood why people had fled family and tradition to seek the brittle, chic world of California in which she had grown up. But she felt sorry for them, sorry for anyone who had never known this strange intimacy with so many of the same name and clan. Surely Ellie would understand.

Drifting back into the parlor, and back into the din of the band and the dancers, she searched for Michael, and suddenly saw him quite alone against the second fireplace staring all the way down the length of the crowded room. She knew that look on his face, the flush, and the agitation—she understood the way that his eyes had locked on some distant seemingly unimportant point.

He barely noticed her as she came up beside him. He didn't hear her as she whispered his name. She followed the line of his gaze. All she saw were the dancing couples, and the glittering sprinkle of rain on the front windows.

"Michael, what is it?"

He didn't move. She tugged on his arm, then lifting her right hand, she very gently turned his face towards her and stared at him, repeating his name clearly again. Roughly he turned away from her, looking again to the front of the room. Nothing this time. It was gone, whatever it was. Thank God.

She could see the droplets of sweat on his forehead and his upper lip. His hair was moist as though he'd been outside, when of course he hadn't. She drew close to him, leaning her head against his chest.

"What was it?" she said.

"Nothing, really . . . ." he murmured. He couldn't quite catch his breath. "I thought I saw . . . it doesn't matter. It's gone."

"But what was it?"

"Nothing." He took her by the shoulders, kissing her a little roughly. "Nothing's going to spoil this day for us, Rowan." His voice caught in his throat as he went on. "Nothing crazy and strange on this day."

"Stay with me," she said, "don't leave me again." She drew him after her out of the parlor and back into the library and into the powder room, where they could be alone. His heart was still speeding as she held him quietly, her arms locked around him, the noise and the music muffled and far away.

"It's OK, darlin'," he said finally, his breathing easier now, "honestly it is. The things I'm seeing, they don't mean anything. Don't worry, Rowan. Please. It's like the images; I'm catching impressions of things that happened long ago, that's all. Come on, honey, look at me. Kiss me. I love you and this is our day."

The party moved on vigorously and madly into the evening. The couple finally cut the wedding cake in a tempest of flashing cameras and drunken laughter. Trays of sweets were passed. Urns of coffee were brewing. Mayfairs in long heartfelt conversations with one another had settled in various corners, and onto couches, and gathered in clusters around tables. The rain came down hard outside. The thunder came and went with occasional booming violence. And the bars stayed open, for most of the gathering continued to drink.

Finally, because Rowan and Michael weren't going to Florida for their honeymoon until the following day, it was decided that Rowan should throw her bouquet from the stairway "now." Climbing halfway, and staring down at a sea of upturned faces, ranging in both directions and back into the parlor, Rowan closed her eyes and threw the bouquet up in the air. There was a great deal of cordial screaming and even pushing and scuffling. And suddenly beautiful young Clancy Mayfair held up the bouquet, amid shouts of approbation. And Pierce threw his arms around her, obviously declaring to the whole world his particular and selfish delight in her good luck.

Ah, so it's Pierce and Clancy, is it? thought Rowan quietly, coming back down. And she had not seen it before. She had not even guessed. But there seemed little doubt of it as she watched them slip away. Far off against the second fireplace, Peter stood smiling on, while Randall argued heatedly, it seemed, with Fielding, who had been planted there some time ago in a tapestried chair.

The new band of the evening had just arrived. It began to play a waltz; everyone cheered at the sound of the sweet, old-fashioned music, and someone dimmed the chandeliers until they gave off a soft, rosy light. Older couples rose to dance. Michael at once took Rowan and led her to the middle of the parlor. It was another flawless moment, as rich and tender as the music that carried them along. Soon the room around them was crowded with dancing couples. Beatrice was dancing with Randall. And Aunt Vivian with Aaron. All of the old ones were dancing, and then even the young ones were drawn into it, little Mona with the elderly Peter, and Clancy with Pierce.

If Michael had seen any other awful unwelcome thing, he gave no sign of it. Indeed, his eyes were fixed steadily and devotedly on Rowan.

As nine o'clock sounded, certain Mayfairs were crying, having reached some point of crucial confession or understanding in a conversation with a long-lost cousin; or simply because everybody had drunk too much and danced too long and some people felt they ought to cry. Rowan didn't exactly know. It just seemed a natural thing for Beatrice as she sat bawling on the couch with Aaron hugging her, and for Gifford, who for hours had been explaining something of seeming importance to a patient and wide-eyed Aunt Viv. Lily had gotten into a loud quarrel with Peter and Randall, deriding them as the "I remember Stella" crowd.

Rita Mae Lonigan was still crying when she left with her husband, Jerry. Amanda Curry, along with Franklin Curry, also made a tearful farewell.

By ten o'clock the crowd had dwindled to perhaps two hundred. Rowan had taken off her white satin high heels. She sat in a wing chair by the first fireplace of the parlor, her long sleeves pushed up, smoking a cigarette, with her feet curled under her, listening to Pierce talk about his last trip to Europe. She could not even recall when or where she had taken off her veil. Maybe Bea had taken it when she and Lily had gone to "prepare the wedding chamber," whatever that meant. Her feet hurt worse than they did after an eight-hour operation. She was hungry, and only the desserts were left. And the cigarette was making her sick. She stubbed it out.

Michael and the old gray-haired priest from the parish were in fast conversation before the mantel at the other end of the room. The band had moved from Strauss to more recent sentimental favorites. Here and there voices broke out in time with the strains of "Blue Moon" or "The Tennessee Waltz." The wedding cake, except for a piece to be saved for sentimental reasons, had been devoured down to the last crumb.

A group of Gradys, connections of Cortland, delayed on their journey from New York, flooded through the front door, full of apologies and exclamations. Others rushed to greet them. Rowan apologized for being shoeless and disheveled as she received their kisses. And in the back dining room, a large party which had come together for a series of photographs began to sing "My Wild Irish Rose."

At eleven, Aaron kissed Rowan good-bye, as he left to take Aunt Vivian home. He would be at the hotel if needed, and he wished them a safe trip to Destin in the morning.

Michael walked with Aaron and his aunt to the front door. Michael's old friends went off at last to continue their drinking at Parasol's bar in the Irish Channel, after extracting the promise from Michael that he would meet with them for dinner in a couple of weeks. But the stairway was still blocked with couples in fast conversation. And the caterers were "rustling up something" in the kitchen for the New York Gradys.

At last, Ryan rose to his feet, demanded silence, and declared that this party was over! Everyone was to find his or her shoes, coat, purse, or what have you, and get out and leave the wedding couple alone. Taking a fresh glass of champagne from a passing tray, he turned to Rowan.

"To the wedding couple," he announced, his voice easily carrying over the hubbub. "To their first night in this house."

Cheers once more. Everyone reaching for a last drink, and there were a hundred repeats of the toast as glasses clinked together. "God bless all in this house!" declared the priest, who just happened to be going out the door. And a dozen different voices repeated the prayer.

"To Darcy Monahan and Katherine," someone cried.

"To Julien and Mary Beth . . . to Stella . . ."

The leavetaking, as was the fashion in this family, took over a half hour, what with the kissing, and the promises to get together, and the renewed conversations halfway out of the powder room and halfway off the porch and halfway out the gate.

Meantime the caterers swept through the rooms, silently retrieving every last glass and napkin, righting pillows, and snuffing candles, and scattering the arrangements of flowers which had been grouped on the banquet tables, and wiping up the last spills.

At last it was over. Ryan was the last one to go, having paid the caterers and seen to it that everything was perfect. The house was almost empty!

"Good night, my dears," he said, and the high front door slowly closed.

For a long moment Rowan and Michael looked at each other, then they broke into laughter, and Michael picked her up and swung her around in a circle, before he set her gently back on her feet. She fell against him, hugging him the way she'd come to love, with her head against his chest. She was weak from laughing.

"We did it, Rowan!" he said. "The way everybody wanted it, we did it! It's over, it's done."

She was still laughing silently, deliciously exhausted and pleasantly excited at the same time. But the clock was striking. "Listen," she whispered. "Michael, it's midnight."

He took her by the hand, hit the wall button to shut off the light, and together they hurried up the darkened stairs.

Only one room on the second floor gave a light into the hallway, and it was their bedroom. They moved silently to the threshold.

"Rowàn, look what they've done," Michael said.

The room had been exquisitely prepared by Bea and Lily. A huge fragrant bouquet of pink roses stood on the mantel between the two silver candelabra.

On the dressing table, the champagne waited in its bucket of ice with two glasses beside it, on a silver tray.

The bed itself was ready, the lace coverlet turned down, the pillows fluffed, and the soft white bed curtains brought back and tied to the massive posts at the head.

A pretty nightgown and peignoir of white silk lay folded on one side of the bed and a pair of white cotton pajamas on the other. A single rose lay against the pillows, with a bit of ribbon tied to it, and another single candle stood on the small table to the right of the bed.

"How sweet of them to think of it," Rowan said.

"And so it's our wedding night, Rowan," Michael said. "And the clock's just stopped chiming. It's the witching hour, darlin', and we have it all to ourselves."

Again, they looked at each other, and both began to laugh softly, feeding each other's laughter, and quite unable to stop. They were too tired to do more than fall into bed beneath the covers, and they both knew it.

"Well, we ought to drink the champagne at least," Rowan said, "before we collapse."

He nodded, throwing aside the cutaway coat and tugging at the ascot. "I'll tell you, Rowan, you have to love somebody to dress up in a suit like this!"

"Come on, Michael, everybody here does this sort of thing. Here, the zipper, please." She turned her back to him, and then felt the hard shell of the bodice released at last, the gown falling loosely down around her feet. Carelessly, she unfastened the emerald and laid it on the end of the mantel.

At last everything was gathered away, and hung up, and they sat in bed together drinking the champagne, which was very cold and dry and delicious, and had foamed all over the glasses, as it ought to do. Michael was naked, but he loved caressing her through the silk nightgown, so she kept it on. Finally, no matter how tired they were, they were caught up in the deliciousness of the new bed, and the soft candlelight, and their usual heat was rising to a boil.

It was swift and violent, the way she loved it, the giant mahogany bed sturdy as if it were carved out of stone.

She lay against him afterwards, dozing and contented, and

listening to the steady rhythm of his heart. Finally she sat up, straightened out the wrinkled nightgown, and drank a long cool sip of the champagne.

Michael sat up beside her, naked, one knee crooked, and lighted a cigarette, his head rolling against the high headboard of the bed.

"Ah Rowan, nothing went wrong, you know, absolutely nothing. It was the perfect day. God, that a day could be so perfect."

Except that you saw something that scared you. But she didn't say it. Because it had been perfect, even with that strange little moment. Perfect! Nothing to spoil it at all.

She took another little drink of the champagne, savoring the taste and her own tiredness, realizing that she was still too wound up to close her eyes.

A wave of dizziness came over her suddenly, with just a touch of the nausea she'd felt in the morning. She waved the cigarette smoke away.

"What's the matter?"

"Nothing, just nerves I think. Walking up that aisle was sort of like lifting a scalpel or something for the first time."

"I know what you mean. Let me put this out."

"No, it's not that, cigarettes don't bother me. I smoke now and then myself." But it was the cigarette smoke, wasn't it? Same thing earlier. She got up, the light silk nightgown feeling like nothing as it fell down around her, and went barefoot into the bath.

No Alka-Seltzer, the one thing that always worked at such moments. But she had brought some over, she remembered. She had put it in the kitchen cabinet along with aspirin and Band-Aids and all the other household supplies. She came back and put on her bedroom slippers and peignoir.

"Where are you going?" he asked.

"Downstairs, for Alka-Seltzer. I don't know what's the matter with me. I'll be right back."

"Wait a minute, Rowan, I'll go."

"Stay where you are. You're not dressed. I'll be back in two seconds. Maybe I'll take the elevator, what the hell."

The house was not really dark. A pale light from the garden came in through the many windows, illuminating the polished floor of the hallway, and the dining room, and even the butler's pantry. It was easy to make her way without switching on a light.

She found the Alka-Seltzer in the cabinet, and one of the new crystal glasses she had bought on a shopping spree with Lily and Bea. She filled the glass at the little sink on the island in the middle of the kitchen, and stood there drinking the Alka-Seltzer and then closed her eyes.

Yes, better. Probably purely psychological, but better.

"Good. I'm glad you feel better."

"Thank you," she said, thinking what a lovely voice, so soft and with a touch of a Scottish accent, wasn't it? A beautiful melodious voice.

She opened her eyes, and with a violent start, stumbled backwards against the door of the refrigerator.

He was standing on the other side of the counter. About three feet away. His whisper had been raw, heartfelt. But the expression on his face was a little colder, and entirely human. Slightly hurt perhaps, but not imploring as it had been that night in Tiburon. No, not that at all.

This had to be a real man. It was a joke of some kind. This was a real man. A man standing here in the kitchen, staring at her, a tall, brown-haired man with large dark eyes, and a beautifully shaped sensuous mouth.

The light through the French doors clearly revealed his shirt, and the rawhide vest he wore. Old, old clothing, clothing made with hand stitches and uneven seams, and big full sleeves.

"Well? Where is your will to destroy me, beautiful one?" he whispered, in the same low, vibrant, and heartbroken voice. "Where is your power to drive me back into hell?"

She was shaking uncontrollably. The glass slipped out of her wet fingers and struck the floor with a dull noise and rolled to one side. She gave a deep, ragged sigh, and kept her eyes focused upon him. The reasoning part of her observed that he was tall, perhaps over six feet, that he had heavily muscled arms and powerful hands. That his face was perfect in its proportions, and that his hair was softly mussed, as if by a wind. Not that delicate androgynous gentleman she'd seen on the deck, no.

"The better to love you, Rowan!" he whispered. "What shape would you have me take? He is not perfect, Rowan, he is human but not perfect. No."

For a moment her fear was so great that she felt a tight squeezing inside of her as if she were going to die. Moving against it, defiant and enraged, she came forward, legs trembling, and reached out across the counter, and touched his cheek.

Roughened, like Michael's. And the lips silky. God! Once again, she stumbled backwards, paralyzed, and unable to move or speak. Tremors moved through her limbs.

"You fear me, Rowan?" he said, lips barely moving as she focused on them. "Why? Leave your friend, Aaron, alone, you commanded me, and I did as you commanded, did I not?"

"What do you want?"

"Ah, that would be a very long time in the telling," he answered, the Scottish accent thickened. "And he waits for you, your lover, and your husband, on this your wedding night. And he grows anxious that you do not come."

The face softened, torn suddenly with pain. How could an illusion be this vital?

"Go, Rowan, go back to him," he said sadly, "and if you tell him I am here, you will make him more miserable than even you know. And I shall hide from you again, and the fear and the suspicion will eat at him, and I will come only when I want to come."

"All right. I won't tell him," she whispered. "But don't you harm him. Don't you bring the slightest fear or worry to him. And the other tricks, stop them! Don't plague him with tricks! Or I swear to you, I will never never speak to you. And I will drive you away."

The beautiful face looked tragic, and the brown eyes grew soft and infinitely sad.

"And Aaron, you're never to harm Aaron. Never. Never to harm anyone, do you hear me?"

"As you say, Rowan," he said, the words flowing like music, full of sorrow and quiet strength. "What is there in all the world for me, but pleasing Rowan? Come to me when he sleeps. Tonight, tomorrow, come when you will. There is no time for me. I am here when you say my name. But keep faith with me, Rowan. Come alone to me, and in secret. Or I will not answer. I love you, my beautiful Rowan. But I have a will. I do."

The figure suddenly shimmered as if a sourceless light had struck it; it brightened and a thousand tiny details of it were suddenly visible. Then it became transparent, and a gust of warm air struck her, frightening her, and then leaving her alone in the darkness, with nothing there.

She put her hand to her mouth. The nausea came again. She stood waiting it out, shivering, and on the verge of screaming, when she heard Michael's soft but unmistakable tread coming through the pantry and into the kitchen. She forced herself to open her eyes.

He had slipped into his jeans, and his chest and his feet were bare.

"What's wrong, honey?" he whispered. He saw the glass gleaming in the dark, against the bottom of the refrigerator. He bent down, past her, and picked it up and put it in the sink. "Rowan, what's wrong?"

"Nothing, Michael," she said thickly, trying to control the

trembling, the tears springing to her eyes. "I'm sick, just a little sick. It happened this morning, and this afternoon and yesterday too actually. I don't know what it is. It was the cigarette just now. I'll be OK, Michael, honestly. I'll be fine."

"You don't know what it is?" he asked her.

"No, I just . . . I guess it's . . . cigarettes never did that to me before. . . ."

"Dr. Mayfair," he said. "You sure you don't know?"

She felt his hands on her shoulders. She felt his hair brush her cheek gently as he bent to kiss the tops of her breasts. She started to cry, her hands clasping his head, feeling the silkiness of his hair.

"Dr. Mayfair," he said. "Even I know what it is."

"What are you talking about?" she whispered. "I just need to sleep, to go upstairs."

"You're pregnant, honey. Go look at yourself in the mirror." And very gently he touched her breasts again, and she herself felt the plumpness, the slight soreness, and she knew, knew absolutely from all the other little unnoticed signs, that he was right. Absolutely right.

She dissolved into tears. She let him pick her up and tumble her against him, and carry her slowly through the house. Her body ached from the tension of the awful moments in the kitchen, and her sobs were coming dry and painfully from her throat. She didn't think it was possible for him to carry her up that long stairway, but he did it, and she let him do it, crying against his chest, her fingers tight around his neck.

He set her down on the bed, and kissed her. In a daze she watched him blow out the candles, and come back to her.

"I love you so much, Rowan," he said. He was crying too. "I love you so much. I've never been so happy . . . it comes in waves, and each time I think it's the pinnacle, and then it comes again. And this of all nights to know . . . God, what a wedding gift, Rowan. What did I ever do to deserve this happiness, I wish I knew."

"I love you, too, my darling. Yes . . . so happy." As he climbed under the covers, she turned away, tucking herself against him, and feeling his knees draw up under hers. She cried against the pillow, taking his hand and folding it over her breasts.

"Everything is so perfect," he whispered.

"Nothing to spoil it," she whispered, "not a single thing."

Forty-one

SHE WOKE BEFORE he did. After the first round of nausea, she packed the suitcases quickly, with all the prefolded bundles of clothes. Then she went downstairs into the kitchen.

Everything clean and quiet in the sunlight. No sign of what had taken place last night. And the pool sparkling out there beyond the screened porch. And the sun filtering down softly through the screens onto the white wicker furniture.

She examined the counter. She examined the floor. She could detect nothing. Then, filled with revulsion and anger, she made the coffee as quickly as she could, so as to get out of the room, and she brought it up to Michael.

He was just opening his eyes.

"Let's take off now," she said.

"I thought we wouldn't leave till this afternoon," he said sleepily. "But sure, we can go now, if you want to." Ever her agreeable hero. He gave her a soft kiss on the cheek, his unshaven beard deliciously scratchy. "How do you feel?" he whispered.

"I'm fine now," she said. She reached out and touched the little gold crucifix tangled in the dark hair of his chest. "It was bad for about half an hour. Probably it will come again. I'll sleep when it does. I'd love to get to Destin in time to walk on the beach in the sunshine."

"But what about seeing a doctor before we leave?"

"I am a doctor," she said with a smile. "And remember the special sense? It's doing just fine in there."

"Does the special sense tell you if he's a boy or a girl?" he asked.

"If *he* is a boy or a girl?" She laughed. "I wish it did. But then maybe I want to be surprised. What about you?"

"Wouldn't it be wonderful if it were twins?"

"Yes, that would be great," she said.

"Rowan, you're not . . . unhappy about the baby, are you?"

"No, God no! Michael, I want the baby. I'm just a little sick still. It comes and goes. Look, I don't want to tell the others just yet. Not until we come back from Florida. The honeymoon will be ruined if we do.''

"Agreed." Tentatively, he placed his warm hand on her belly. "It's awhile yet before you feel it in there, isn't it?"

"It's a quarter of an inch long," she said, smiling again. "It doesn't weigh an ounce. But *I* can feel it. It's swimming in a state of bliss, with all its tiny cells multiplying."

"What does it look like now?"

"Well, it's like a tiny sea being. It could stretch out on your thumbnail. It has eyes, and even clubby little hands, but no real fingers or even arms yet. Its brain is already there, at least the rudiments of the brain, already divided into two halves. And for some reason which nobody on earth can divine, all its tiny cells know what to do—they know exactly where to go to continue forming the organs which are already there, and only have to perfect themselves. Its tiny heart has been beating inside me for over a month now."

He gave a deep, satisfied sigh. "What are we going to name it?"

She shrugged. "What about Little Chris? Would that be . . . too hard for you?"

"No, that would be great. Little Chris. And it will be Christopher if it's a boy, and Christine if it's a girl. How old will it be at Christmas?" He started to calculate.

"Well, it's probably six to seven weeks now. Maybe eight. As a matter of fact, it could very well be eight. So that means . . . four months. It will have all its parts, but its eyes will still be closed. Why? You're wondering whether it would prefer a red fire engine to a baseball bat?"

He chuckled. "No, it's just that it's the greatest Christmas gift I could ever have dreamed of. Christmas has always been special to me, special in almost a pagan way. And this is going to be the grandest Christmas I ever had, that is, until next year when she's walking around and banging her little fire engine with her baseball bat."

He looked so vulnerable, so innocent, so completely trusting in her. When she looked at him, she could almost forget what had happened last night. She could almost forget everything. She gave him a quick kiss, slipped into the bathroom, and stood against the locked door with her eyes closed.

You devil, she whispered, you've really timed it well, haven't you? Do you like my hate? Is it what you've been dreaming of?

Then she remembered the face in the darkened kitchen, and the soft heartbroken voice, like fingers touching her. *What is there in all the world for me, but pleasing Rowan?*

They got away at about ten o'clock. Michael drove. And she felt better by that time, and managed to go to sleep for a couple of hours. When she opened her eyes, they were already in Florida, driving down through the dark pine forest from the interstate to the road that ran along the beach. She was clearheaded and refreshed, and when she caught the first glimpse of the Gulf, she felt safe, as if the dark kitchen in New Orleans and its apparition no longer existed.

The weather was cool, but no more so than any bracing summer day in northern California. They put on their heavy sweaters and strolled on the deserted beach. At sunset, they ate their supper by the fire, with the windows open to the Gulf breeze.

Some time around eight o'clock, she went to work on the plans for Mayfair Medical, continuing her study of the great "for profit" chains of hospitals, in comparison to the "not for profit" models which interested her more keenly.

But her mind was wandering. She couldn't really concentrate on the dense articles about profit and loss, and abuses within the various systems.

At last she made a few notes and went to bed, lying for hours in the darkened bedroom while Michael worked on his restoration plans in the other room, listening to the great roar of the Gulf through the open doors, and feeling the breeze wash over her.

What was she going to do? Tell Michael and Aaron, as she had sworn to do? And then he would retreat, and play his little tricks perhaps, and the tension would increase with every passing day.

She thought of her little baby again, her fingers lying on her stomach. Probably conceived right after she'd asked Michael to marry her. She'd always been highly irregular in her seasons, and she felt that she knew the very night it had happened. She'd dreamed of a baby that night. But she couldn't really remember.

Was it dreaming inside her? She pictured the tiny circuitry of its developing brain. No longer embryo by now, but an entire fetus. She closed her eyes, listening, feeling. *All right.* And then her own strong telepathic sense began to frighten her.

Had she the power within her to hurt this child? The thought was so terrifying that she couldn't bear it. And when she thought of Lasher again, he too seemed a menace to this frail and busy little being, because he was a threat to her, and she was her baby's entire world.

How could she protect it from her own dark powers, and from

the dark history that sought to ensnare it? Little Chris. You will not grow up with curses and spirits, and things that go bump in the night. She cleared her mind of dark and turbulent thoughts; she envisioned the sea outside, crashing endlessly on the beach, no one wave like another, yet all part of the same great monotonous force, full of sweet and lulling noise and incalculable variation.

Destroy Lasher. Seduce him, yes, as he is trying to seduce you. Discover what he is and destroy him! And you're the only one who can do it. Tell Michael or Aaron and he will retreat. You've got to deceive with a purpose and *do it*.

Four A.M. She must have slept. The irresistible hunk was lying there against her, his big heavy arm cradling her, his hand hugging her breasts. And a dream was just winking out, all full of misery and those Dutchmen in their big black hats, and a mob outside screaming for the blood of Jan van Abel.

"I describe what I see!" he had said. "I am no heretic! How are we to learn if we do not throw out the dogmas of Aristotle and Galen?"

Right you are. But it was gone now, along with that body on the table with all the tiny organs inside like flowers.

Ah, she hated that dream!

She rose and walked across the thick carpet, and out on the wooden deck. Oh, was ever a sky more vast and clear, and full of tiny twinkling stars. Pure white the foam of the black waves. As white as the sand which glowed in the moonlight.

But far down on the beach stood a lone figure, a lean tall man, looking towards her. *Damn you.* She saw the figure slowly thin and then vanish.

Bowing her head, she stood trembling with her hands on the wooden rail.

You'll come when I call you.

I love you, Rowan.

With horror she realized the voice came from no direction. It was a whisper inside of her, all around her, intimate and audible only to her.

I wait only for you, Rowan.

Leave me, then. Don't speak another word or show yourself again, or I'll never call for you.

Angry, bitter, she turned and went back into the darkened bedroom, the warm carpet soft under her feet, and climbed into the low bed beside Michael. She clung to him in the darkness, her fingers tight around his arm. Desperately she wanted to wake him, to tell him what had happened.

But this she had to do alone. She knew it. She'd always known. And an awful fatality gripped her.

Just give me these last days before the battle, she prayed. Ellie, Deirdre, help me.

She was sick every morning for a week. Then the nausea left her, and the days after were glorious, as if mornings had been rediscovered, and being clearheaded was a gift from the gods.

He didn't speak to her again. He didn't show himself. When she thought of him, she imagined her anger like a withering heat, striking the mysterious and unclassifiable cells of his form, and drying them up like so many minuscule husks. But most of all when she thought of him she was fearful.

Meantime life went on because she kept the secret locked inside her.

By phone she made an appointment with an obstetrician back in New Orleans, who arranged to have the early blood work done right here in Destin, with the results to be sent on. Everything was normal as she expected.

But who could expect them to understand that with her diagnostic sense she would have known if the little tucker was in trouble?

The warm days were few and far between, but she and Michael had the dreamlike beach almost to themselves. And the pure silence of the isolated house above the dunes was magical. When the air was warm, she sat for hours on the beach beneath a big glamorous white umbrella, reading her medical journals and the various materials which Ryan sent out to her by messenger.

She read the baby books, too, that she could find in the local bookstores. Sentimental and vague, but fun nevertheless. Especially the pictures of babies, with their tiny expressive faces, fat wrinkly necks, and adorable little feet and hands. She was dying to tell the family. She and Beatrice spoke almost every other day. But it was best to keep the secret. Think of the hurt to her and Michael if something were to go wrong, and if the others knew, that would only make the loss worse for everyone.

They walked on the beach for hours, on those days when it was too cold to swim. They shopped and bought little things for the house. They loved its bare white walls and sparse furnishings. It was like a place to play after the seriousness of First Street, said Michael. He liked doing the cooking with Rowan— chopping, shredding, stir frying, barbecuing steaks. It was all easy and fun.

They dined at all the fine restaurants and took drives into the pine woods, and explored the big resorts with their tennis courts and golf courses. But mostly they were happy in the house, with the endless sea so very near them.

Michael was pretty anxious about his business—he had a team working on the shotgun cottage on Annunciation Street, and he had opened up his new Great Expectations on Magazine, and he was having to handle all the little emergencies by phone. And of course there was the painting still going on at home, up in Julien's old room, and the roof repairs in the back. The brick parking area behind the house wasn't finished yet, and the old *garçonnière* was still being renovated—an excellent caretaker's cottage, they figured—and he was antsy not being there himself.

He didn't need a long honeymoon right now, that was perfectly obvious—especially not a honeymoon that was being extended day after day by Rowan.

But he was so agreeable. Not only did he do what she wanted, he seemed to have an endless capacity to make the most of the moment, whether they were strolling on the beach hand in hand, or enjoying a hasty seafood meal in a little tavern, or visiting the boats for sale in the marina, or reading in their various favorite corners of the spacious house, on their own.

Michael was a contented person by nature. She'd known that when she first met him; she'd understood why the anxiety was so terrible for him. And now it endeared him to her so much to see him lost in his own projects, drawing designs for the renovation of the little Annunciation Street cottage, clipping out pictures from magazines of little things he meant to do.

Aunt Viv was doing fine back in New Orleans. Lily and Bea gave her no peace, according to their own admission, and Michael felt it was the best thing in the world for her.

"She sounds so much younger when I talk to her," he said. "She's joined some garden club, and some committee to protect the oak trees. She's actually having fun."

So loving, so understanding. Even when Rowan didn't want to go back to town for Thanksgiving, he gave in. Aunt Viv went to dinner at Bea's, of course. And everybody forgave the wedding couple for staying in Florida, for it was their honeymoon after all, and they could take as long as they wished.

They had their own quiet Thanksgiving dinner on the deck over the beach. Then that night a cold, blustering lightning storm hit Destin. The wind shook the glass doors and windows. Up and down the coast, the power went out. It was an utterly divine and natural darkness.

They sat for hours by the fire, talking of Little Chris and which room would be the nursery, and how Rowan would not let the Medical Center interfere in the first couple of years; she'd spend every morning with the baby, not going to work until twelve o'clock, and of course they'd get all the help they needed to make things run smoothly.

Thank God he did not ask directly whether or not she'd "seen that damn thing." She did not know what she would do if forced to tell a deliberate lie. The secret was locked inside a little compartment in her mind, like Bluebeard's secret chamber, and the key had been thrown down the well.

The weather was getting colder. Soon there wouldn't be an excuse for remaining here. She knew they ought to go back.

What was she doing not telling Michael, and not telling Aaron? Running away like this, to hide?

But the longer she remained here, the more she began to understand her conflicts and her reasons.

She *wanted* to talk to the being. The memory of him in the kitchen flooded her with a powerful sense of him, all the more particular because she had heard the tender quality of his voice. Yes, she wanted to know him! It was exactly as Michael had predicted it that first awful night when the old woman had just died. What was Lasher? Where had he come from? What secrets lay beyond that flawless and tragic face? What would Lasher say about the doorway and the thirteen witches?

And all she had to do was call him, like Prospero calling to Ariel. Keep the secret, and say his name.

Oh, but you are a witch, she said to herself as her guilt deepened. And they all knew it. They knew it that afternoon you spoke to Gifford; they knew by the stark silvery power that came from you, what everybody thinks is coldness and cunning, but was never anything but unwelcome strength. The old man, Fielding, was right in his warnings. And Aaron knows, doesn't he? Of course he knows.

Everybody but Michael, and Michael is so easy to deceive.

But what if she decided that she wouldn't deceive anyone, that she wouldn't play along? Maybe she was searching for the courage to make that decision. Or maybe she was simply resisting. Maybe she was making the demon thing wait the way he had made her wait.

Whatever the case, she no longer felt that aversion for him, that awful dislike which had followed the incident on the plane. She felt the anger still, but the curiosity and the ever increasing attraction were greater . . .

It was the first really cold day, when Michael came out on the beach and sat down beside her and told her he had to go back.

She was enjoying the brisk air, actually, sunbathing in a heavy cotton sweater and long pants, the way she might have done in California on her windy deck.

"Look, this is what's going down," he said. "Aunt Viv wants her things from San Francisco and you know how old people can be. And, Rowan, there's nobody to close up Liberty Street except me. I have to make some decisions about my old store out there, too. My accountant just called me again about somebody wanting to rent it, and I have to get back there and go through the inventory myself."

He went on, about selling a couple of pieces of California property, shipping certain things, renting out his house, that sort of thing. And the truth was, he was needed in New Orleans. His new business on Magazine Street needed him. If this thing was going to work. . . .

"Truth is, I'd rather fly out there now than later. It's almost December, Rowan. Christmas is coming. You realize it?"

"Sure, I understand. We'll drive back tonight."

"But you don't have to, babe. You can stay here in Florida till I come back, or as long as you want."

"No, I'll come with you," she said. "I'll come up and pack in a little while. Besides, it's time to be leaving. It's warm now but it was really chilly this morning when I first came out."

He nodded. "Didn't you hate it?"

She laughed. "Still not as cold as any summer day back in California," she said.

He nodded. "I have to tell you something. It's going to get even colder. A lot colder. Winter in the South is going to surprise you. They're saying this may be a bad winter all over the southern states. In a way I just love it. First the dizzying heat and then the frost on the windows."

"I know what you mean." *And I love you. I love you more than anyone I've ever loved.*

She sat back in the wooden beach chair as he walked away, and she let her head roll to the side. The Gulf was now a dull silver blaze before her, as often happened when the sun was at its height. She let her left hand fall down into the soft, sugary sand. She pushed her fingers into it, and picked up a handful of , letting it run through her fingers. "Real," she whispered. "So real."

But wasn't it just too neat that he had to leave now, and she'd be alone at First Street? Wasn't it just like somebody had arranged things that way? And all this time she thought that she'd been calling the shots.

"Don't overreach, my friend," she whispered into the cool

Gulf breeze. ''Don't hurt my love, or I'll never forgive you. See that he comes back to me, safe and sound.''

They didn't leave till the following morning.

As they drove away, she felt the tiniest stab of excitement. In a flash, she pictured his face again as it had been in the darkened kitchen; she heard the soft resonant flow of his words. A caress. But she couldn't bear to think of that part of it. Only after Michael had arrived safely in California, only when she was alone in the house . . .

Forty-two

TWELVE O'CLOCK. WHY did that seem the right time? Maybe because Pierce and Clancy had stayed so late, and she had needed this hour of quiet? It was only ten o'clock in California, but Michael had already called, and, worn out after the long flight, he had probably already fallen asleep.

He'd sounded so excited about the fact that everything looked so unappetizing and he was so eager to come home. Excruciating to miss him so much already, to be lying alone in this large and empty bed.

But the other waited.

As the soft chimes of the clock died away, she got up, put on the silk peignoir over her nightgown, and the satin bedroom slippers, and went out and down the long stairs.

And where do we meet, my demon lover?

In the parlor amid the giant mirrors, with the draperies drawn over the light from the street? Seemed a better place than most.

She walked softly over the polished pine floor, her feet sinking into the Chinese carpet as she moved towards the first fireplace. Michael's cigarettes on the table. A half-drunk glass of beer. Ashes from the fire she had made earlier, on this her first bitter cold night in the South.

Yes, the first of December, and the baby has its little eyelids now inside her, and its ears have started to form.

No problems at all, said the doctor. Strong healthy parents, disease-free, and her body in excellent condition. Eat sensibly and by the way what do you do for a living?

Tell lies.

Today she'd overheard Michael talking to Aaron on the phone. "Just fine. I mean surprisingly well, I guess. Completely peaceful. Except of course for seeing that awful vision of Stella the day of the wedding. But I could have imagined that. I was drunk on all that champagne. [Pause] No. Nothing at all."

Aaron could see through the lie, couldn't he? Aaron knew. But the trouble with these dark inhuman powers was that you never knew when they were working. They failed you when you most counted upon them. After all the random flashing and decidedly unwelcome insights into the thoughts of others, suddenly the world was filled with wooden faces and flat voices. And you were alone.

Maybe Aaron was alone. He had found nothing helpful in the old notebooks of Julien's. Nothing in the ledgers in the library, except the predictable economic records of a plantation. He had found nothing in the grimoires and demonologies collected over the years, except the published information on witchcraft which anyone could obtain.

And now the house was beautifully finished, without dark or unexplored corners. Even the attics were shining clean. She and Michael had gone up to approve the last work, before he left for the airport. Everything in order. Julien's room just a pretty workroom now for Michael, with a drawing table and files for blueprints and the shelves full of his many books.

She stood in the center of the Chinese carpet. She was facing the fireplace. She had bowed her head and made a little steeple with her hands, and pressed her fingers to her lips. What was she waiting for? Why didn't she say it: *Lasher.* Slowly she looked up and into the mirror over the mantel.

Behind her, in the keyhole doorway, watching her, the light from the street all she needed to see him as it shone through the glass on either side of the front door.

Her heart was pounding, but she didn't move to turn around. She gazed at him through the mirror—calculating, measuring, defining—trying to grasp with all her powers, human and inhuman, what this creature was made of, what this body was.

"Face me, Rowan." Voice like a kiss in the darkness. Not a command, or a plea. Something intimate like the request from a lover whose heart will be broken if he is refused.

She turned around. He was standing against the door frame, his arms folded. He wore an old-fashioned dark suit, much like the ones Julien wore in the portraits of the 1890s, with the high white collar and silk tie. A beautiful picture. And in such lovely contrast were his strong hands, like Michael's, and the large, strong features of his face. The hair was streaked with blond, and the skin slightly darker. She thought of Chase, her old policeman lover, when she looked at him.

"Change what you will," he said gently.

And before she could respond, she saw the figure altering itself, saw it like a soundless boiling in the shadows, as the hair grew even lighter, more completely blond, and the skin took on the bronzed quality of Chase's skin. She saw the eyes brighten; Chase for one instant, perfectly realized; then another strain of human characteristics infused it, altering it again, until it was the same man who had appeared to her in the kitchen—possibly the same man who had appeared to all of them over the centuries—except that he was taller, and still had Chase's high dramatic coloring.

She realized she had moved closer. She was standing only a few feet away. She was not afraid so much as powerfully excited. Her heart was still pounding, but she wasn't trembling. She reached out as she had that night in the kitchen and felt his face.

Stubble of beard, skin, but it wasn't skin. The keen diagnostic sense told her it was not, and there were no bones inside this body; no internal organs. This was a shell for an energy field.

"But in time there will be bones, Rowan, in time, all miracles can be performed."

The lips had barely moved with the words; and the creature was already losing its shape. It had exhausted itself.

She stared hard at it, striving to hold it, and she saw it grow solid again.

"Help me smile, beautiful one," said the voice, with no movement of the lips this time. "I would smile on you and your power if I could."

Now she *was* trembling. With every fiber of her body she concentrated upon it, upon infusing the facial features with life. She could almost feel the energy flowing from her, feel it gathering the strange material substance and shaping it; it was purer and finer than her conception of electricity. And a great warmth enveloped her as she saw the lips begin to smile.

Serene, subtle, like the smile of Julien in the photographs. The large green eyes were filled with light. The hands rose and they reached out for her now, and she felt a delicious warmth as they came closer, almost touching the sides of her face.

Then the image shimmered, and suddenly disintegrated, and the blast of heat was so great she stepped ·backwards, her arm up to shield her eyes as she turned away.

The room was seemingly empty. The draperies had moved and they were still dancing soundlessly. And only very gradually did the room grow cold again.

She felt cold all over suddenly. She felt exhausted. And when she looked at her hand, she realized it was still shaking. She went over to the fireplace, and sank down on her knees.

Her mind was swimming. For a moment she was almost dizzy and unable to locate herself in relation to what had just happened. Then gradually her head cleared.

She laid some kindling into the small grate, and put a few sticks and a small log on top of it, then struck a long match and lighted the fire. In a second, the kindling was popping and snapping. She stared down into the flames.

"You're here, aren't you?" she whispered, staring into the fire as it grew stronger and brighter, tongues of flame licking at the dried bark of the log.

"Yes, I'm here."

"Where?"

"Near you, around you."

"Where is your voice coming from? Anyone could hear you now. You're actually speaking."

"You will understand how this is done better than I."

"Is that what you want of me?"

He gave a long sigh. She listened. No sound of breathing, merely the sound of a presence. Think of all the times you've known someone else was near you, and it's not because you heard a heartbeat or a footfall or a breath. You heard something softer, more subtle. This is the sound.

"I love you," he said.

"Why?"

"Because you are beautiful to me. Because you can see me. Because you are all the things in a human being which I myself desire. Because you are human and warm and soft. And I know you, and have known the others before you."

She said nothing. He went on:

"Because you are Deborah's child, and the child of Suzanne, and Charlotte, and all the others whose names you know. Even if you will not take the emerald which I gave to my Deborah, I love you. I love you without it. I have loved you since the first time I knew of your coming. I see far. I saw you coming from afar. I loved you in probability."

The fire was blazing strongly now, the delicious aroma comforting her, as the big thick log was engulfed in bright orange flames. But she was in a form of delirium. Even her own breathing seemed slow to her and strange. And she wasn't sure now that the voice was audible, or would be to others if they were here.

It was clear to her, however, and richly seductive.

Slowly she sat down on the warm floor beside the hearth and leaned against the marble, which was also warming, and she peered into the shadows beneath the arch in the very center of the room.

"Your voice is soothing to me, it's beautiful." She sighed.

"I want it to be beautiful for you. I want to give you pleasure. That you hated me made me sad."

"When?"

"When I touched you."

"Explain it all to me, everything."

"But there are many possible explanations. You shape the explanation by the question you ask. I can talk to you of my own volition, but what I tell you will have been shaped by what I have been taught through the questions of others over the centuries. It is a construct. If you want a new construct, ask."

"When did you begin?"

"I don't know.

"Who first called you Lasher?"

"Suzanne."

"Did you love her?"

"I love Suzanne."

"She still exists."

"She is gone."

"I'm beginning to see," she said. "There is no physical necessity in your world, and consequently no time. A mind without a body."

"Precisely. Clever. Smart."

"One of those words will do."

"Yes," he said agreeably, "but which one?"

"You're playing with me."

"No. I don't play."

"I want to get to the bottom of this, to understand you, your motives, what you want."

"I know. I knew before you spoke," he said in the same kind, seductive manner. "But you are clever enough to know that in the realm in which I exist there is no bottom." He paused and then went on slowly as before. "If you prod me to speak to you in complete and sophisticated sentences, and to allow for your persistent misconceptions, mistakes, or crude distinctions, I can do it. But what I say may not be as near to truth as you might like."

"But how will you do it?"

"Through what I've learned of human thinking from other humans, of course. What I am saying is, choose—begin at the beginning with me if you want pure truth. You will receive enigmatic and cryptic answers. And they may be useless. But they will be true. Or begin in the middle and you will receive educated and sophisticated answers. Either way, you will know of me what I learn of myself from you."

"You're a spirit?"

"What you call a spirit, I am."

"What would you call yourself?"

"I do not."

"I see. In your realm you have no need of a name."

"No understanding even of a name. But in truth just no name."

"But you have wants. You want to be human."

"I do." Something like a sigh followed, eloquent of sadness.

"Why?"

"Wouldn't you want to be human if you were me, Rowan?"

"I don't know, Lasher. I might want to be free."

"I crave it in pain," said the voice, speaking slowly and sorrowfully. "To feel heat and cold; to know pleasure. To laugh—ah, what would it be to laugh? To dance and sing, and to see clearly through human eyes. To feel things. To exist in necessity and in emotions and in time. To have the satisfaction of ambition, to have distinct dreams and ideas."

"Ah, yes, I'm understanding it all right."

"Don't be too sure."

"You don't see clearly?"

"Not the same."

"When you looked through the eyes of the dead man, did you see clearly?"

"Better, but not clear, and death was on me, hanging on me, around me, and moving fast. Finally I went blind inside."

"I can imagine. You went into Charlotte's father-in-law while he lived."

"Yes. He knew I was there. He was weak, but happy to walk, and to lift things with his hands again."

"Interesting. What we call possession."

"Correct. I saw distinct things through his eyes. I saw brilliant colors and smelled flowers and saw birds. I heard birds. I touched Charlotte with a hand. I knew Charlotte."

"You can't hear things now? You can't see the light of this fire?"

"I know all about it. But I do not see or hear or feel it the

927

way you do, Rowan. Though when I draw near to you, I can see what you see, I know you and your thoughts.''

She felt a sharp throb of fear. ''I'm getting the hang of it.''

''You think you are. But it's bigger and longer.''

''I know. I really do.''

''We know. We are. But from you we have learned to think in a line, and we have learned time. We have also learned ambition. For ambition one must know concepts of past and present and future. One must plan. And I speak only of those of us who want. Those of us who do not want, do not learn, for why should they? But to say 'us' is to approximate. There is no 'us' for me because I am alone and turned away from the others of me and see only you and your kind.''

''I understand. When you were in the dead bodies . . . the heads in the attic . . .''

''Yes.''

''Did you change the tissues of those heads?''

''I did. I changed the eyes to brown. I changed the hair in streaks. This took great heat from me and concentration. Concentration is the key to all I do. I draw together.''

''And in your natural state?''

''Large, infinite.''

''How did you change the pigment?''

''Went into the particles of flesh, altered the particles. But your understanding of this is greater than mine. You would use the word mutation. I know no better words, you know scientific words. Concepts.''

''What stopped you from taking over the entire organism?''

''It was dead. It gradually finished and was heavy and I was blind and dumb. I could not bring the spark of life back to it.''

''I see. In Charlotte's father-in-law, did you change his body?''

''That I could not do. I did not know to try to do it. And I cannot do it now if I were there then. You see?''

''Yes, I do. You're constant, yet we're in time. I see. But you are saying that you cannot change living tissue?''

''Not of that man. Not of Aaron when I am in him.''

''When are you in Aaron?''

''When he sleeps. That is the only time I can get in.''

''Why do you do it?''

''To be human. To be alive. But Aaron is too strong for me; Aaron organizes and commands the tissues of Aaron. Same with Michael. Same with almost all. Even the flowers.''

''Ah, yes, the flowers. You mutated the roses.''

''I did. For you, Rowan. To show you my love and my power.''

"And to show me your ambition?"

"Yes . . ."

"I don't want you ever to go into Aaron. I don't want you ever to hurt him or Michael."

"I will obey you, but I would like to kill Aaron."

"Why?"

"Because Aaron is finished, and Aaron has much knowledge and Aaron lies to you."

"How so, finished?"

"He has done what I saw that he would do and wanted for him to do. So I say finished. Now he may do what I can see and do not want him to do, which goes against my ambition. I would kill him, if it would not make you bitter and full of hate for me."

"You can feel my anger, can't you?"

"It hurts me deeply, Rowan."

"I would be in a rage of pain and anger if you hurt Aaron. But let's talk further about Aaron. I want you to spell this out for me. What did you want Aaron to do that he's done?"

"Give you his knowledge. His words written in a straight line of time."

"You're speaking of the Mayfair chronology."

"Yes. The history. You said spell it out so I didn't use the word 'chronology.'"

She laughed softly. "You don't have to spell it out that much," she said. "Go on."

"I wanted you to read this history from him. Petyr *saw* my Deborah burn, my beloved Deborah. Aaron *saw* my Deirdre weep in the garden, my beautiful Deirdre. Your responses and decisions are inestimably assisted by such history. But this task of Aaron has been completed."

"Yes, I see."

"Beware."

"Of thinking I understand?"

"Precisely. Keep asking. Words like 'responses' and 'inestimably' are vague. I would keep nothing from you, Rowan."

She heard him sighing again, but it was long, and soft, and became slowly a different sound. It was like the wind sighs. She continued to rest against the fireplace, basking in the heat of the fire, her eyes wide as she stared into the shadows. It seemed she had been here forever speaking to him, this disembodied yet softly resonant voice. The sound of the sigh had almost touched her all over like the wind.

She gave a little soft laugh of delight. She could see him in the room if she tried, see a rippling in the air, something swelling and filling the room.

"Yes . . ." he said. "I love your laughter. I cannot laugh."

"I can help you learn to do it."

"I know."

"Am I the doorway?"

"You are."

"Am I the thirteenth witch?"

"You are."

"Then Michael was correct in his interpretation."

"Michael is seldom ever wrong. Michael sees clearly."

"Do you want to kill Michael?"

"No. I love Michael. I would walk and talk with Michael."

"Why, why Michael of all people?"

"I do not know."

"Oh, you must know."

"To love is to love. Why do you love Michael? Is the answer the truth? To love is to love. Michael is bright and beautiful. Michael laughs. Michael has much of the invisible spirit in him, infusing his limbs and his eyes and voice. Do you see?"

"I think I do. It's what we call vitality."

"Exactly," he said.

But had the word ever been said with such meaning?

He went on.

"I saw Michael from the beginning. Michael was a surprise. Michael sees me. Michael came to the fence. Also Michael has ambition and is strong. Michael loved me. Now Michael fears me. You came between me and Michael, and Michael fears that I will come between him and you."

"But you won't hurt him."

No answer.

"You won't hurt him."

"Tell me not to hurt him and I will not hurt him."

"But you said you didn't want to! Why do you make it go like this in a circle?"

"This is no circle. I told you I didn't want to kill Michael. Michael may be hurt. What am I to do? Lie? I do not lie. Aaron lies. I do not lie. I do not know how."

"That I don't believe. But maybe you believe it."

"You hurt me."

"Tell me how this will end."

"What?"

"My life with you, how will it end?"

Silence.

"You won't tell me."

"You are the doorway."

She sat very still. She could feel her mind working. The fire gave off its low crackling, and the flames danced against the bricks, and the motion seemed entirely too slow to be real. Again the air shimmered. She thought she saw the long crystal teardrops of the chandelier moving, turning, gathering tiny fragments of light.

"What does it mean to be the doorway?"

"You know what it means."

"No, I don't."

"You can mutate matter, Dr. Mayfair."

"I'm not sure that I can. I'm a surgeon. I work with precise instruments."

"Ah, but your mind is ever more precise."

She frowned; it was bringing back that strange dream, the dream of Leiden . . .

"In your time you have stanched bleeding," he said, taking his time with his soft, slow words. "You have closed wounds. You have made matter obey you."

The chandelier gave off a low tinkling music in the silence. It caught the glint of the dancing flames.

"You have slowed the racing hearts of your patients; you have opened the clogged vessels of their brains."

"I wasn't always aware . . ."

"You have done it. You fear your power but you possess it. Go out into the garden in the night. You could make the flowers open. You can make them grow longer as I did."

"Ah, but you did it with dead flowers only."

"No. I have done it with the living. With the iris you saw, though this exhausted me and hurt me."

"And then the iris died and fell from its stem."

"Yes. I did not mean to kill it."

"You took it to its limits, you know. That's why it died."

"Yes. I did not know its limits."

She turned to the side; she felt she was in a trance, yet how perfectly clear was his voice, how precise his pronunciation.

"You did not merely force the molecules in one direction or another," she said.

"No. I pierced the chemical structure of the cells, just as you can do it. You are the doorway. You see into the kernel of life itself."

"No, you overestimate my knowledge. No one can do it."

The atmosphere of the dream came back, everyone gathered at the windows of the University of Leiden. What was that mob in the street? They thought Jan van Abel was a heretic.

"You don't know what you're saying," she said.

"I know. I see far. You have given me the metaphors and the terms. Through your books, I too have absorbed the concepts. I see to the finish. I know. Rowan can mutate matter. Rowan can take the thousands upon thousands of tiny cells and reorganize them."

"And what is the finish? Will I do what you want?"

Again, he sighed.

Something rustling in the corners of the room. The draperies swayed violently. And the chandelier sang softly again, glass striking glass. Was there a layer of vapor rising to the ceiling, stretching out to the pale peach-colored walls? Or just the fire-light dancing in the corner of her eye?

"The future is a fabric of interlacing possibilities," he said. "Some of which gradually become probabilities, and a few of which become inevitabilities, but there are surprises sewn into the warp and the woof, which can tear it apart."

"Thank God for that," she said. "So you can't see to the finish."

"I do and do not. Many humans are entirely predictable. You are not predictable. You are too strong. You can be the doorway if you choose."

"How?"

Silence.

"Did you drown Michael in the sea?"

"No."

"Did anyone do it?"

"Michael fell off a rock into the sea because he was careless. His soul ached and his life was nothing. All this was written in his face, and in his gestures. It would not take a spirit to see it."

"But you did see it."

"I saw it long before it happened, but I did not make it happen. I smiled. Because I saw you and Michael come together. I saw it when Michael was small and saw me and looked at me through the garden fence. I saw the death and rescue of Michael by Rowan."

"And what did Michael see when he drowned?"

"I don't know. Michael was not alive."

"What do you mean?"

"He was dead, Dr. Mayfair. You know what dead is. Cells cease to divide. The body is no longer under one organizing force or one intricate set of commands. It dies. Had I gone into his body, I could have lifted his limbs and heard through his

932

ears, because his body was fresh, but it was dead. Michael had vacated the body."

"You know this?"

"I see it now. I saw it before it happened. I saw it when it occurred."

"Where were you when it occurred?"

"Beside Deirdre, to make Deirdre happy, to make her dream."

"Ah, so you do see far."

"Rowan, that is nothing. I mean I see far in time. Space is not a straight line for me, either."

She laughed softly again. "Your voice is beautiful enough to embrace."

"I am beautiful, Rowan. My voice is my soul. Surely I have a soul. The world would be too cruel if I did not."

She felt so sad hearing this that she could have cried. She was staring at the chandelier again, at the hundreds of tiny reflected flames in the crystal. The room seemed to swim in warmth.

"Love me, Rowan," he said simply. "I am the most powerful being imaginable in your realm and there is but one of me for you, my beloved."

It was like a song without melody; it was like a voice made up of quiet and song, if such a thing can be imagined.

"When I am flesh I shall be more than human; I shall be something new under the sun. And far greater to you than Michael. I am infinite mystery. Michael has given you all that he can. There will be no great mystery any longer with your Michael."

"No, that can't be true," she whispered. She realized that she'd closed her eyes; she was so drowsy. She forced herself to look at the chandelier again. "There is the infinite mystery of love."

"Love must be fed, Rowan."

"You are saying I have to choose between you and Michael?"

Silence.

"Did you make the others choose?" She thought of Mary Beth in particular, and Mary Beth's men.

"I see far as I told you. When Michael stood at the gate years ago in your time, I saw that you would make a choice."

"Don't tell me any more of what you saw."

"Very well," he said. "Talk of the future always brings unhappiness to humans. Their momentum is based upon the fact that they cannot see far. Let us talk about the past. Humans like to understand the past."

"Do you have another tone of voice other than this beautiful soft tone? Could you have spoken those last few words sarcastically? Is that how they were meant to sound?''

"I can sound any way that I like, Rowan. You hear what I feel. I do feel in my thoughts, in what I am, pain and love. Emotions.''

"You're speeding up your words a little.''

"I am in pain.''

"Why?''

"To end your misunderstandings.''

"You want me to make you human?''

"I want to have flesh.''

"And I can give you flesh?''

"You have the power. And once such a thing is achieved, other such things may be achieved. You are the thirteenth, you are the door.''

"What do you mean, 'other such things'?''

"Rowan, we are talking of fusion; of chemical change; the structural reinvention of cells, of matter and energy in a new relationship.''

"I know what you mean.''

"Then you know, as with fission, if it is achieved once, it can be achieved again.''

"Why couldn't anyone else do it before me? Julien was powerful.''

"Knowledge, Rowan. Julien was born too soon. Allow me once more to use the word fusion and in a slightly different fashion. We have spoken so far of fusion within cells. Let me now talk of a fusion between your knowledge of life, Rowan, and your innate power. That is the key; that is what enables you to be the doorway.

"The knowledge of your era was unimaginable even to Julien, who saw in his time inventions that seemed purely magical. Could Julien have foreseen a heart opened on an operating table? A child conceived in a test tube? No. And there will come after you those whose knowledge is great enough even to define what I am.''

"Can you define yourself to me?''

"No, but I am certainly definable, and when I am defined by mortals, then I shall be able to define myself. I learn all things from you which have to do with such understanding.''

"Ah, but you know something of yourself which you can tell me now in precise language.''

"—that I am immense; that I must concentrate to feel my strength; that I can exert force; that I can feel pain in the thinking part of me.''

"Ah, yes, and what is that thinking part? And whence comes the force you exert? Those are the pertinent questions."

"I do not know. When Suzanne called to me I came together. I drew myself up small as if to pass through a tunnel. I felt my shape, and spread out like the five-pointed star of the pentagram which she drew, and each one of these points I elongated. I made the trees shiver and the leaves fall, and Suzanne called me her Lasher."

"And you liked what you did."

"Yes, that Suzanne saw it. And that Suzanne liked it. Or else I would never have done it again and not even remembered it."

"What is there in you that is physical, apart from energy?"

"I do not know!" The voice was soft yet full of despair. "Tell me, Rowan. Know me. End my loneliness."

The fire was dying in the grate, but the warmth had spread all through the room, and it surrounded her and held her like a blanket. She felt drowsy but sharply alert.

"Let's return to Julien. Julien had as much power as I have."

"Almost, my beloved. But not quite. And there was in Julien a playful and blasphemous soul that danced back and forth in the world, and liked to destroy as much as to build. You are more logical, Rowan."

"That is a virtue?"

"You have an indomitable will, Rowan."

"I see. Not broken with humor as Julien's will could be broken."

"Pree—cisely, Rowan!"

She laughed again under her breath. Then she fell quiet, staring at the shimmering air.

"Is there a God, Lasher?"

"I do not know, Rowan. In time I have formed an opinion and it is yes, but it fills me with rage."

"Why?"

"Because I am in pain and if there is a God, he made this pain."

"Yes, that I understand perfectly, Lasher. But he made love, too, if he exists."

"Yes. Love. Love is the source of my pain," he said. "It is the source of all my moving into time and ambition and plans. All my desires spring from love. You might say that what I was—when I was only what I am—that I was poisoned by love, that at the call of Suzanne I was awakened to love, and to the nightmare of want. But I saw. And I loved. And I came."

"You make me sad," she said suddenly.

"Love mutated me, Rowan. It created my first dissatisfaction."

"Yes."

"And now I seek to mutate into flesh, and that shall be the consummation of my love. I have waited so long for you. I have seen such suffering before you, and if I had had tears to shed, they would have been shed. God knows, for Langtry I made an illusion of myself weeping. It was a true image of my pain. I wept not merely for Stella, but for all of them—my witches. When Julien died, I was in agony. So great was my pain then, that I might have moved away, back to the realm of the moon and the stars and the silence. But it was too late for me. I could not bear my loneliness. When Mary Beth called, I came back to her. Quickening. I looked into the future. And I saw the thirteenth again. I saw the ever increasing strength of my witches."

She had closed her eyes again. The fire was gone out. The room was full of the spirit of Lasher. She could feel him against her skin though he did not move, and the fabric of him lay as lightly as the air itself.

"When I am truly flesh," he said, "the tears and the laughter will come from me by reflex, as they come in you, or in Michael. I shall be a complete organism."

"But not human."

"Better than human."

"But not human."

"Stronger, more enduring, for I shall be the organizing intelligence, and I have great power, greater than the power inside any existing human. I shall be a new thing, as I told you. I shall be a species which as of now does not exist."

"Did you kill Arthur Langtry?"

"Not necessary. He was dying. What he saw hastened his death."

"But why did you show yourself to him?"

"Because he was strong and he could see me, and I wanted to draw him in so that he might save Stella, for I knew Stella was in danger. Carlotta was the enemy of Stella. Carlotta was as strong as you are, Rowan."

"Why didn't Arthur help Stella?"

"You know the history. It was too late. I am as a child at such moments in time. I was defeated by simultaneity because I was acting in time."

"I don't follow."

"While I appeared to Langtry, the shots were fired into th

936

rain of Stella, and brought about instant death. I see far, but I cannot see all the surprises.''

''You didn't know.''

''And Carlotta tricked me. Carlotta misled me. I am not infallible. In fact, I am confused with amazing ease.''

''How so?''

''Why should I tell you? So you may all the better control me? You know how. You are as powerful a witch as Carlotta. It was through emotions. Carlotta conceived of the killing as an act of love. She schooled Lionel in what he was to think as he took the gun and fired at Stella. I was not alerted by hatred, or malice. I paid no attention to the love thoughts of Lionel. Then Stella lay dying, calling to me silently, with her eyes open, wounded beyond hope of repair. And Lionel fired the second shot which drove the spirit of Stella up and out of the body forever.''

''But you killed Lionel. You drove him to his death.''

''I did.''

''And Cortland? You killed Cortland.''

''No. I fought with Cortland. I struggled with him, and he sought to use his strength against me, and he failed, and fell in his struggle. I did not kill your father.''

''Why did you fight?''

''I warned him. He believed he could command me. He was not my witch. Deirdre was my witch. You are my witch. Not Cortland.''

''But Deirdre didn't want to give me up. And Cortland was defending her wishes.''

''For his own aims.''

''Which were what?''

''That is old now, unimportant. You went to freedom, so that you could be strong when you returned. You were freed from Carlotta.''

''But you saw to it, and this was against the wishes of both Deirdre and Cortland.''

''For your sake, Rowan. I love you.''

''Ah, but you see, there's a pattern here, isn't there? And you don't want me to understand it. Once the child is born, you are for the child and not the mother. That's what happened with Deborah and Charlotte, isn't it?''

''You misjudge me. When I act in time, sometimes I do what wrong.''

''You went against the wishes of Deirdre. You saw to it I was taken away. You advanced the plan of the thirteen witches, and

937

that was for your own aims. You have always worked for you
own aims, haven't you?''

"You are the thirteenth and the strongest. You have been my
aim, and I will serve you. Your aims and my aims are identical.'

"I think not.''

She could feel his pain now, feel the turbulence in the air, fee
the emotion as if it were the low strum of a harp string, playing
upon her unconscious ear. Song of pain. The draperies swayed
again in a warm draft and both of the chandeliers of the double
parlors danced in the shadows, full of splinters of white light
now that the fire had died and taken with it the colors.

"Were you ever a living human being?''

"I don't know.''

"Do you remember the first time you ever saw human be
ings?''

"Yes.''

"What did you think?''

"That it was not possible for spirit to come from matter, tha
it was a joke. What you would call preposterous or a blunder.'

"It came from matter.''

"It did indeed. It came out of the matter when the organiza
tion reached the appropriate point for it to emerge, and we were
surprised by this mutation.''

"You and the others who were already there.''

"In timelessness already there.''

"Did it draw your attention?''

"Yes. Because it was a mutation and entirely new. And also
because we were called to observe.''

"How?''

"The newly emerging intelligences of man, locked in matter
nevertheless perceived us, and thereby caused us to perceive
ourselves. Again, this is a sophisticated sentence and therefore
partially inaccurate. For millennia, these human spiritual intel
ligences developed; they grew stronger and stronger; they de
veloped telepathic powers; they sensed our existence; they named
us and talked to us and seduced us; if we took notice we were
changed; we thought of ourselves.''

"So you learned self-consciousness from us.''

"All things from you. Self-consciousness, desire, ambition
You are dangerous teachers. And we are discontent.''

"Then there are others of you with ambition.''

"Julien said, 'Matter created man and man created the gods.
That is partially correct.''

"Did you ever speak to a human being before Suzanne?''

"No.''

938

"Why?"

"I don't know. I saw and heard Suzanne. I loved Suzanne."

"I want to go back to Aaron. Why do you say Aaron tells lies?"

"Aaron does not reveal the whole purpose of the Talamasca."

"Are you certain of this?"

"Of course. How can Aaron lie to me? I knew of Aaron's coming before there was Aaron. Arthur Langtry's warnings were for Aaron, when he did not even know about Aaron."

"But how does Aaron lie? When, and in regard to what, did he lie?"

"Aaron has a mission. So do all the brothers of the Talamasca. They keep it secret. They keep much knowledge secret. They are an occult order, to use words you would understand."

"What is this secret knowledge? This mission?"

"To protect man from us. To make sure there are no more doorways."

"You mean there have been doorways before now?"

"There have. There have been mutations. But you are the greatest of all doorways. What you can achieve with me shall be unparalleled."

"Wait a minute. You mean other discarnate entities have come into the realm of the material?"

"Yes."

"But who? What are they?"

"Laughter. They conceal themselves very well."

"Laughter. Why did you say that?"

"Because I am laughing at your question, but I don't know how to make the sound of laughter. So I say it. I laugh at you that you don't think this would have happened before. You, a mortal, with all the stories of ghosts and monsters of the night, and other such horrors. Did you think there was not even a kernel of truth to these old tales? But it is not important. Our fusion shall be more nearly perfect than any in the past."

"Aaron knows this, that's what you're saying, that others have come through."

"Yes."

"And why does he want to stop me from being the doorway?"

"Why do you think?"

"Because he believes you're evil."

"Unnatural, that is what he would say, which is foolish, for I am as natural as electricity, as natural as the stars, as natural as fire."

"Unnatural. He fears your power."

"Yes. But he is a fool."

"Why?"

"Rowan, as I have told you before, if this fusion can be achieved once, it can be achieved again. Do you not understand me?"

"Yes, I understand you. There are twelve crypts in the graveyard and one door."

"Aye, Rowan. Now you are thinking. When you first read your books of neurology, when you first stepped into the laboratory, what was your sense? That man had only begun to realize the possibilities of the present science, that new beings might be created by means of transplants, grafts, in vitro experimentation with genes and cells. You saw the scope of the possibilities. Your mind was young, your imagination enormous; you were what men fear—the doctor with the vision of a poet. And you turned your back on your visions, Rowan. In the laboratory of Lemle, you could have created new beings from the parts of existent beings. You reached for brutal tools because you feared what you could do. You hid behind the surgical microscope and substituted for your power the crude micro tools of steel with which you severed tissues, rather than creating them. Even now you act from fear. You will build hospitals where people are to be cured, when you could create new beings, Rowan."

She sat still and quiet. No one had ever spoken to her about her innermost thoughts with greater accuracy. She felt the heat and size of her own ambition. She felt the amoral child in her who had dreamed of brain grafts and synthetic beings, before the adult put out the light.

"Haven't you a heart to understand why, Lasher?"

"I see far, Rowan. I see great suffering in the world. I see the way of accident and blundering, and what it has created. I am not blinded by illusions. I hear the cries everywhere of pain. And I know my own loneliness. I know my own desire."

"But what will you give up when you become flesh and blood? What's the price for you?"

"I do not shrink from the price. A fleshly pain could be no worse than what I have suffered these three centuries. Would you be what I am, Rowan? Drifting, timeless and alone, listening to the carnal voices of the world, apart, and thirsting for love and understanding?"

She couldn't answer.

"I have waited for all eternity to be incarnate. I have waited beyond the scope of memory. I have waited until the fragile spirit of man has finally attained the knowledge so that the barrier can come down. And I shall be made flesh, and it shall be perfect."

940

Silence.

"I see why Aaron is afraid of you," she said.

"Aaron is small. The Talamasca is small. They are nothing!" The voice grew thin with anger. The air in the room was warm and moving like the water in a pot moves before it boils. The chandeliers moved yet they made no sound, as if the sound were carried away by the currents in the air.

"The Talamasca has knowledge," he said, "they have power to open doorways, but they refuse to do so for us. They are the enemy of us. They would keep the world's destiny in the hands of the suffering and the blind. And they lie. All of them lie. They have maintained the history of the Mayfair Witches because it is the history of Lasher, and they fight Lasher. That is their avowed purpose. And they trick you with their attention to the witches. It is Lasher whose name should be emblazoned on the covers of their precious leather-bound files. The file is in a code. It is the history of the growing power of Lasher. Can you not see through the code?"

"Don't harm Aaron."

"You love unwisely, Rowan."

"You don't like my goodness, do you? You like the evil."

"What is evil, Rowan? Is your curiosity evil? That you would study me as you have studied the brains of human beings? That you would learn from my cells all that you could to advance the great cause of medicine? I am not the enemy of the world, Rowan. I merely wish to enter into it!"

"You're angry now."

"I am in pain. I love you, Rowan."

"To want is not to love, Lasher. To use is not to love."

"No, don't speak these words to me. You hurt me. You wound me."

"If you kill Aaron, I will never be your doorway."

"Such a small thing to affect so much."

"Lasher, kill him and I will not be the doorway."

"Rowan, I am at your command. I would have killed him already were I not."

"Same with Michael."

"Very well, Rowan."

"Why did you tell Michael that he couldn't stop me?"

"Because I hoped that he could not and I wanted to frighten him. He is under the spell of Aaron."

"Lasher, how am I to help you come through?"

"I will know when you know, Rowan. And you know. Aaron knows."

"Lasher, we don't know what life is. Not with all our science

941

and all our definitions do we know what life is, or how it began. The moment when it sprang into existence from inert materials is a complete mystery."

"I am already alive, Rowan."

"And how can I make you flesh? You've gone into the bodies of the living and the dead. You can't anchor there."

"It can be done, Rowan." His voice had become as soft as a whisper. "With my power and your power, and with my faith, for I must yield to achieve the bond, and only in your hands is the full merging possible."

She narrowed her eyes, trying to see shapes, patterns in the airy dark.

"I love you, Rowan," he said. "You are weary now. Let me soothe you, Rowan. Let me touch you." The resonance of the voice deepened.

"I want—I want a happy life with Michael and our child."

Turbulence in the air, something collecting, intensifying. She felt the air grow warmer.

"I have infinite patience. I see far. I can wait. But you will lose your taste for others now that you have seen and spoken to me."

"Don't be so certain, Lasher. I'm stronger than the others. I know much more."

"Yes, Rowan." The shadowy turbulence was growing denser, like a great wreath of smoke, only there was no smoke, circling the chandelier, moving out. Like cobwebs caught in a draft.

"Can I destroy you?"

"No."

"Why?"

"Rowan, you torture me."

"Why can't I destroy you?"

"Rowan, your gift is to transmute matter. I have no matter in me for you to attack. You may destroy the matter I bring into organization to make my image, but then I do this myself when I disintegrate. You have seen it. You could hurt my transitory image at such a moment of materialization, and you have already done so. When I first appeared to you. When I came to you near the water. But you cannot destroy *me*. I have always been here. I am eternal, Rowan."

"And suppose I told you it was finished now, Lasher, that I would never recognize you again. That I would not be the doorway. That I am the doorway for the Mayfairs into the future centuries, the doorway for my unborn child, and for things of which I dream with my ambition."

"Small things, Rowan. Nothing compared to the mysteries

and possibilities which I offer you. Imagine, Rowan, when the mutation is complete and I have a body, infused with my timeless spirit, what you can learn from this."

"And if it's done, Lasher, if the doorway is opened, and the fusion is effected, and you stand before me, flesh and blood, how will you treat me then?"

"I would love you beyond all human reason, Rowan, for you would be my mother and my creator, and my teacher. How could I not love you? And how tragic my need of you will be. I will cleave to you to learn how to move with my new limbs, how to see, how to speak and laugh. I will be as a helpless infant in your hands. Can't you see? I would worship you, my beloved Rowan. I would be your instrument in anything that you wished, and twenty times as strong as I am now. Why do you cry? Why are there tears in your eyes?"

"It's a trick, it's a trick of sound and light, the spell you induce."

"No. I am what I am, Rowan. It's your reason which weakens you. You see far. You always have. Twelve crypts and one doorway, Rowan."

"I don't understand. You play with me. You confuse me. I can't follow anymore."

Silence and that sound again, as if the whole air were sighing. Sadness, sadness enveloping her like a cloud, and the undulating layers of smoky shadow moving the length of the room, weaving through and around the chandeliers, filling the mirrors with darkness.

"You're all around me, aren't you?"

"I love you," he said, and his voice was low again as a whisper and close to her. She thought she felt lips touch her cheek. She stiffened, but she had become so drowsy.

"Move away from me," she said. "I want to be left alone now. I have no obligation to love you."

"Rowan, what can I give you, what gift can I bring?"

Again, something brushed her face, something touched her, bringing the chills up over her body. Her nipples were hard beneath the silk of the nightgown, and a low throbbing had started inside her, a hunger she could feel all through her throat and her chest.

She tried to clear her vision. It was dark in here now. The fire had burnt down. But only moments ago it had been a blaze.

"You're playing tricks on me." The air seemed to be touching her all over. "You've played tricks on Michael."

"No." It was a soft kiss against her ear.

"When he was drowned, the visions. You made them!"

943

"No, Rowan. He was not here. I could not follow him to where he went. I am of the living only."

"Did you make the ghosts he saw when he was alone here that night, when he went alone into the pool?"

"No."

She shivered all over, her hands up to brush away the sensations as if she'd been caught in cobwebs.

"Did you see the ghosts Michael saw?"

"Yes, but through Michael's eyes, I saw them."

"What were they?"

"I don't know."

"Why don't you know?"

"They were images of the dead, Rowan. I am of this earth. I do not know the dead. Do not talk to me of the dead. I do not know of God or of anything which is not of the earth."

"God! But what is this earth?" Something touching the back of her neck, gently lifting the tendrils of her hair.

"Here, Rowan, the realm in which you exist and the realm in which I exist, parallel and intermingled yet separate, in the physical world. I am physical, Rowan—natural as anything else which is of the earth. I burn for you, Rowan, in a purity in which fire has no end, in this our world."

"The ghosts Michael saw on our wedding night," she said, "in this very room. You made him see them."

"No."

"Did you see them?" Like a feather stroking her cheek.

"Through Michael's eyes. I do not have all the answers you demand of me."

Something touching her breasts, something stroking her breasts and her thighs. She curled her legs back under her. The hearth was cold now.

"Get away from me!" she whispered. "You *are* evil."

"No."

"Do you come from hell?"

"You play with me. I am in hell, desiring to give you pleasure."

"Stop. I want to get up now. I'm sleepy. I don't want to stay here."

She turned and looked at the blackened fireplace. There were no embers anymore. Her eyes were heavy and so were her limbs. She struggled to her feet, clinging to the mantel. But she knew she could not possibly reach the steps. She turned, and sank down again on her knees and stretched out on the soft Chinese rug. Like silk beneath her, and the hardness and the cool air felt so good to her. She felt she was dreaming when she looked up

944

into the chandelier. The white plaster medallion appeared to be moving, its acanthus leaves curling and writhing.

All the words she'd heard were suddenly swimming in her brain. Something touching her face. Her nipples throbbed and her sex throbbed. She thought of Michael miles and miles away from her, and she felt anguish. She had been so wrong to underestimate this being.

"I love you, Rowan."

"You're above me, aren't you?" She stared up into the shadows, thankful for the coolness, because she was burning as if she'd absorbed all the heat of the fire. She could feel the moisture pumping between her legs, and her body was opening like a flower. Stroking the inside of her thighs where the skin was always softest and had no down, and her legs were turning outward like petals opening.

"I'm telling you to stop, that I'll hate it."

"Love you, my darling." Kissing her ears, and her lips, and then her breasts. The sucking came hard, rhythmic, teeth grazing her nipples.

"I can't stand it," she whispered, but she meant the very opposite, that she would cry out in agony if it stopped.

Her arms were flung out, and the nightgown was being lifted off her. She heard the silk tearing and then the cloth was loose and she was sweetly, deliciously naked lying there, the hands stroking her sex, only they weren't hands. It was Lasher, Lasher sucking her and stroking her, lips on her ears, on her eyelids, all of his immense presence wrapped around her, even under her, stroking the small of her back, and parting her backside and stroking the nether mouth.

Yes, opening, like the dark purple iris in the garden. Like the roses exploding on the ends of their coarsened and darkened stems and the leaves with so many points and tiny veins to them. She tossed and twisted on the carpet.

And when she writhed like a cat in heat . . . Go away, old woman, you are not here! This is my time now.

"Yes, your time, our time."

Tongues licked her nipples, lips closing on them, pulling them, teeth scratching her nipples.

"Harder, rougher. Rape me, do it! Use your power."

He lifted her so that her head fell backwards, her hair tumbling down beneath her, her eyes closed, hands parting her sex, parting her thighs.

"Come in to me, hard, make yourself a man for me, a hard man!"

The mouths drew harder on her nipples, the tongues lapping

945

at her breasts, her belly, the fingers pulling at her backside and scratching at her thighs. "The cock," she whispered, and then she felt it, enormous and hard, driving into her. "Yes, do it, tear me, do it! Override me, do it!" Her senses were flooded with the smell of clean, hard flesh and clean hair, as the weight bore down on her and the cock slammed into her, yes, harder, make it rape. Glimpse of a face, dark green eyes, lips. And then a blur as the lips opened her lips.

Her body was pinned to the carpet, and the cock burned her as it drove inside her, scraping her clitoris, plunging deeper into her vagina. I can't stand it, I can't bear it. Split me apart, yes. Laid waste. The orgasm flooded through her, her mind blank except for the raging flow of colors like waves as the rollicking sensation washed up through her belly, and her breast and her face, and down through her thighs, stiffening her calves, and through the muscles of her feet. She heard her own cries, but they were far away, unimportant, flowing out of her mouth in a divine release, her body pumping and helpless and stripped of will and mind.

Again and again, it exploded in her, scalding her. Over and over, until all time, all guilt, all thought was burnt away.

Morning. Was there a baby crying? No. Only the phone ringing. Unimportant.

She lay in the bed, beneath the covers, naked. The sun was streaming in the windows on the front of the house. The memory of it came back to her, and a hurtful throbbing started in her. The phone, or was it a baby crying? A baby somewhere far off in the house. Half in dream she saw its little limbs working, bent knees, chubby little feet.

"My darling," he whispered.

"Lasher," she answered.

The sound of the crying had died away. Her eyes closed on the vision of the shining windowpanes and the tangle of the oak limbs over the sky.

When she opened them again, she stared up into his green eyes, into his dark face, exquisitely formed. She touched the silk of his lip with her finger, all his hard weight pressed down on her, his cock between her legs.

"God, yes, God, you are so strong."

"With you, my beauty." The lips revealed the barest glint of white teeth as the words were formed. "With you, my divine one."

Then came the blast of heat, the hot wind blowing her hair back, and the whirlwind scorching her.

And in the clean silence of the morning, in the light of the sun pouring through the glass, it was happening all over again.

At noon, she sat outside by the pool. Steam was rising from the water into the cold sunlight. Time to turn off the heater. Winter was truly here.

But she was warm in her wool dress. She was brushing her hair.

She felt him near her; and she narrowed her eyes. Yes, she could see the disturbance in the air again, very clearly actually, as he surrounded her like a veil being slowly wound around her shoulders and arms.

"Get away from me," she whispered. The invisible substance clung to her. She sat upright, and hissed the words at it this time. "Away, I told you!"

It was the shimmer from a fire in sunlight, what she saw. And then the chill afterwards as the air regained its normal density, as the subtle fragrances of the garden returned.

"I'll tell you when you may come," she said. "I will not be at the mercy of your whims or your will."

"As you wish, Rowan." It was that interior voice she'd heard once before in Destin, the voice that sounded like it was inside her head.

"You see and hear everything, don't you?" she asked.

"Even your thoughts."

She smiled, but it was a brittle, fierce smile. She pulled the long loose hairs out of her hairbrush. "And what am I thinking?" she asked.

"That you want me to touch you again, that you want me to surround you with illusions. That you would like to know what it is to be a man, and for me to take you as I would a man."

The blood rose to her cheeks. She matted up the little bit of blond hair from the brush and dropped it into the ferny garden beside her, where it vanished among the fronds and the dark leaves.

"Can you do that?" she asked.

"We can do it together, Rowan. You can see and feel many things."

"Talk to me first," she said.

"As you wish. But you hunger for me, Rowan."

"Can you see Michael? Do you know where he is?"

"Yes, Rowan, I see him. He is in his house, sorting through his many possessions. He is swimming in memories and in anticipation. He is consumed with the desire to return to you. He thinks only of you. And you think of betraying me, Rowan. You

947

think of telling your friend Aaron that you have seen me. You dream of treachery.''

"And what's to stop me if I want to speak to Aaron? What can you do?"

"I love you, Rowan."

"You couldn't stay away from me now, and you know it. You'll come if I call you.''

"I want to be your slave, Rowan, not your enemy."

She stood up, staring up into the soft foliage of the sweet olive tree, at the bits and pieces of pale sky. The pool was a great rectangle of steaming blue light. The oak beyond swayed in the breeze, and once again she felt the air changing.

"Stay back," she said.

There came the inevitable sigh, so eloquent of pain. She closed her eyes. Somewhere very far away a baby *was* crying. She could hear it. Had to be coming from one of these big silent houses, which always seemed so deserted in the middle of the day.

She went inside, letting her heels sound loudly on the floor. She took her raincoat from the front hall closet, all the protection she needed against the cold, and she went out the front door.

For an hour she walked through the quiet empty streets. Now and then a passerby nodded to her. Or a dog behind a fence would approach to be petted. Or a car would roar past.

She tried merely to see things—to focus upon the moss that grew on the walls, or the color of the jasmine twined still around a fence. She tried not to think or to panic. She tried not to want to go back into the house. But at last her steps took her back that way, and she was standing at her own gate.

Her hand was trembling as she put the key in the lock. At the far end of the hall, in the door to the dining room, he stood watching her.

"No! Not until I say!" she said, and the force of her hate went before her like a beam of light. The image vanished; and a sudden acrid smell rose to her nostrils. She put her hand over her mouth. All through the air she saw the faint wave-like movement. And then nothing, and the house was still.

That sound came again, the baby crying.

"You're doing it," she whispered. But the sound was gone. She went up the stairs to her room. The bed was neatly made now, her night things put away. The draperies drawn.

She locked the door. She kicked off her shoes, and lay down on the counterpane beneath the white canopy, and closed her eyes. She couldn't fight it any longer. The thought of last night's pleasure brought a deep charring heat to her, an ache, and she pressed her face into the pillow, trying to remember and not to remember, her muscles flexing and then letting go.

"Come then," she whispered. At once, the soft eerie substance enclosed her. She tried to see what she was feeling, tried to understand. Something gossamer and immense, loosely constructed or organized to use its own word, and now it was gathering itself, making itself dense, the way steam gathers itself when it turns to water, and the way water gathers itself when it turns to ice.

"Shall I take a shape for you? Shall I make illusions?"

"No, not yet," she whispered. "Be as you are, and as you were before with all your power." She could already feel the stroking on her insteps, and on the undersides of her knees. Delicate fingers sliding down into the tender spaces between her toes, and then the nylon of her hose snapping, and torn loose, pulled off her and the skin breathing and tingling all over on her naked legs.

She felt her dress opening, she felt the buttons slipped out of the holes.

"Yes, make it rape again," she said. "Make it rough and hard, and slow."

Suddenly she was flung over on her back, her head was forced to one side against the pillow; the dress was ripping, and the invisible hands were moving down her belly. Something like teeth grazed her naked sex, fingernails scraping her calves.

"Yes," she cried, her teeth clenched. "Make it cruel."

Forty-three

HOW MANY DAYS and nights had passed? She honestly did not know. Unopened mail stacked on the hall table. The phone, now and then ringing—to no avail.

"Yes, but who are you? Underneath it all. Who is there?"

"I told you, such questions mean nothing to me. I can be what you want me to be."

"Not good enough."

"What was I? A phantom. Infinitely satisfied. I don't know whence came the capacity to love Suzanne. She taught me what death was when she was burnt. She was sobbing when they dragged her to the stake; she couldn't believe they could do it to her. This was a child, my Suzanne, a woman with no understanding of human evil. And my Deborah was forced to watch it. And had I made the storm, they would have burnt them both.

"Even in her agony, Suzanne stayed my hand, for Deborah's sake. She went mad, her head banging against the stake. Even the villagers were terrified. Crude, stupid mortals come there to drink wine and laugh as she was burned. Even they could not bear the sound of her screaming. And then I saw the beautiful flesh and blood form which nature had given her ravaged by fire, like a corn husk in a burning field. I saw her blood pouring down on the roaring logs. My Suzanne. In the perfection of her youth, and in her strength, burnt like a wax candle for a stupid pack of villagers who gathered in the heat of the afternoon.

"Who am I? I am the one who wept for Suzanne when no one wept. I am the one who felt an agony without end, when even Deborah stood numb, staring at the body of her mother twisting in the fire.

"I am the one who saw the spirit of Suzanne leave the pain-racked body. I saw it rise upwards, freed, and without care. Do I have a soul that it could know such joy—that Suzanne would suffer no more? I reached out for her spirit, shaped still in the form of her body, for she did not know yet that such a form was not required of her, and I tried to penetrate and to gather, to take unto myself what was now like unto me.

"But the spirit of Suzanne went past me. It took no more notice of me than of the burning husk in the fire. Upwards it went away from me and beyond me, and there was no more Suzanne.

"Who am I? I am Lasher, who stretched himself out over the whole world, threaded through and through with the pain of the loss of Suzanne. I am Lasher, who drew himself together, made tentacles of his power, and lashed at the village till the terrified villagers ran for cover, once my beloved Deborah was taken away. I laid waste the village of Donnelaith. I chased the witch judge through the fields, pounding him with stones. There was no one left to tell the tale when I finished. And my Deborah gone with Petyr van Abel, to silks and satins, and emeralds, and men who would paint her picture.

"I am Lasher, who mourned for the simpleton, and carried her ashes to the four winds.

"This was my awakening to existence, to self-consciousness, to life and death, *to paying attention.*

"I learned more in that interval of twenty days than in all the gracious aeons of watching mortals grow upon the face of the earth, like a breed of insect, mind springing from matter but snared in it, meaningless as a moth with its wing nailed to a wall.

"Who am I? I am Lasher, who came down to sit at the feet of Deborah and learn how to have purpose, to obtain ends, to do the will of Deborah in perfection so that Deborah would never suffer; Lasher, who tried and failed.

"Turn your back on me. Do it. Time is nothing. I shall wait for another to come who is as strong as you are. Humans are changing. Their dreams are filled with the forecast of these changes. Listen to the words of Michael. Michael knows. Mortals dream ceaselessly of immortality, as their lives grow longer. They dream of unimpeded flight. There will come another who will break down the barriers between the carnate and discarnate. I shall pass through. I want this too much, you see, for it to fail, and I am too patient, too cunning in my learning, and too strong.

"The knowledge is here now. The full explanation for the origin of material life *is* at hand. Replication *is* possible. Look back with me if you will to Marguerite's bedroom on the night that I took her in the body of a dead man, and willed my hair to grow the color that I would have for myself. Look back on that experiment. It is closer in time to the painted savages who lived in caves and hunted with spears than it is to you in your hospital, and in your laboratory.

"It is your knowledge which sharpens your power. You understand the nucleus, and the protoplasm. You know what are chromosomes, what are genes, what is DNA.

"Julien was strong. Charlotte was strong. Petyr van Abel was a giant among men. And there is another kind of strength in you. A daring, and a hunger, and aloneness. And that hunger and aloneness I know, and I kiss with the lips I do not have; I hold with the arms I do not have; I press to the heart in me that isn't there to beat with warmth.

"Stand off from me. Fear me. I wait. I will not hurt your precious Michael. But he cannot love you as I can, because he cannot know you as I know you.

"I know the insides of your body and your brain, Rowan. I would be made flesh, Rowan, fused with the flesh and superhuman in the flesh. And once this is done, what metamorphosis may be yours, Rowan? Think on what I say.

"I see this, Rowan. As I have always seen it—that the thirteenth would be the strength to open the door. What I cannot see is how to exist without your love.

"For I have loved you always, I have loved the part of you

951

that existed in those before you. I have loved you in Petyr van Abel, who of all was most like you. I have loved you even in my sweet crippled Deirdre, powerless, dreaming of you.''

Silence.

For an hour there had been no sound, no vibrations in the air. Only the house again, with the winter cold outside it, crisp and windless and clean.

Eugenia was gone. The phone rang again in the emptiness.

She sat in the dining room, arms resting on the polished table, watching the bony crepe myrtle, scraping, leafless and shining, at the blue sky.

At last she stood up. She put on her red wool coat, and locked the door behind her, and went out the open gate and up the street.

The cold air felt good and cleansing. The leaves of the oaks had darkened with the deepening of winter, and shrunken, but they were still green.

She turned on St. Charles and walked to the Pontchartrain Hotel.

In the little bar, Aaron was already waiting at the table, a glass of wine before him, his leather notebook open, his pen in his hand.

She stood in front of him, conscious of the surprise in his face when he looked at her. Was her hair mussed? Did she look tired?

"He knows everything I think, what I feel, what I have to say."

"No, that's not possible," said Aaron. "Sit down. Tell me."

"I cannot control him. I can't drive him away. I think . . . I think I love him," she whispered. "He's threatened to go if I speak to you or to Michael. But he won't go. He needs me. He needs me to see him and be near him; he's clever, but not that clever. He needs me to give him purpose and bring him closer to life."

She was staring at the long bar, and the one small bald-headed man at the end of it, fleshly being with a slit of a mouth, and at the pale anemic bartender polishing something as bartenders always do. Rows of bottles full of poison. Quiet in here. Dim lights.

She sat down and turned and looked at Aaron.

"Why did you lie to me?" she asked. "Why didn't you tell me that you were sent here to stop him?"

"I have not been sent here to stop him. I've never lied."

"You know that he can come through. You know it's his purpose, and you are committed to stopping it. You have always been."

"I know what I read in the history, the same as you know it. I gave you everything."

"Ah, but you know it's happened before. You know there are things in the world like him that have found a doorway."

No answer.

"Don't help him," Aaron said.

"Why didn't you tell me?"

"Would you have believed me if I had? I didn't come to tell you fables. I didn't come to induct you into the Talamasca. I gave you the information I had about your life, your family, what was real to you."

She didn't answer. He was telling a form of truth as he knew it, but he was concealing things. Everyone concealed things. The flowers on the table concealed things. That all life was ruthless process. Lasher was process.

"This thing is a giant colony of microscopic cells. They feed off the air the way a sponge feeds from the sea, devouring such minuscule particles that the process is continuous and goes utterly unnoticed by the organism or organelle itself or anything in its environment. But all the basic ingredients of life are there—cellular structure most certainly, amino acids and DNA, and an organizing force that binds the whole regardless of its size and which responds now perfectly to the consciousness of the being which can reshape the entire entity at will."

She stopped, searching his face to divine whether or not he understood her. But did it matter? She understood now, that was the point.

"It is not invisible; it is simply impossible to see. It isn't supernatural. It is merely capable of passing through denser matter because its cells are far smaller. But they are eukaryote cells. The same cells that make up your body or mine. How did it acquire intelligence? How does it think? I can't tell you any more than I can tell you how the cells of an embryo know to form eyes and fingers and liver and heart and brain. There isn't a scientist on earth who knows why a fertilized egg makes a chicken, or why a sponge, crushed to powder, reassembles itself perfectly—each cell doing exactly what it should—over a period of mere days.

"When we know that, we will know why Lasher has intellect, because his is a similar organizing force without a discernible brain. It is sufficient to say now that he is Precambrian and self-sufficient, and if not immortal, his life span could be billions of years. It is conceivable that he absorbed consciousness from

953

mankind, that if consciousness gives off a palpable energy, he has fed upon this energy and a mutation has created his mind. He continues to feed upon the consciousness of the Mayfair Witches and their associates, and from this springs his learning, and his personality, and his will.

"It is conceivable as well that he has begun a rudimentary process of symbiosis with higher forms of matter, able to attract more complex molecular structures to him when he materializes, which he then effectively dissolves before his own cells are hopelessly bonded with these heavier particles. And this dissolution is accomplished in a state bordering on panic. For he fears an imperfect union, from which he can't be freed.

"But his love of the flesh is so strong he is willing now to risk anything to be warm-blooded and anthropomorphic."

Again, she stopped. "Maybe all of life has a mind," she said, her eyes roving over the small room, over the empty tables. "Maybe the flowers watch us. Maybe the trees think and hate us that we can walk. Or maybe, just maybe they don't care. The horror of Lasher is that he began to care!"

"Stop him," said Aaron. "You know what he is now. Stop him. Don't let him assume human form."

She said nothing. She looked down at the red wool of her coat, startled suddenly by the color. She did not even remember taking it out of the closet. She had the key in her hand but no purse. Only their conversation was real to her and she was aware of her own exhaustion, of the thin layer of sweat on her hands and on her face.

"What you've said is brilliant," said Aaron. "You've touched it and understood it. Now use the same knowledge to keep it out."

"He's going to kill you," she said, not looking at him. "I know he is. He wants to. I can hold him off, but what do I bargain with? He knows I'm here." She gave a little laugh, eyes moving over the ceiling. "He's with us. He knows every trick at my command. He's everywhere. Like God. Only he's not God!"

"No. He doesn't know everything. Don't let him fool you. Look at the history. He makes too many mistakes. And you have your love to bargain with. Bargain with your will. Besides, why should he kill you? What can I do to him? Persuade you not to help him? Your moral sense is stronger and finer even than mine."

"What in the world would make you think that?" she said. "What moral sense?" It struck her that she was near to collapse, that she had to get out of here, and go home where she could sleep. But he was there, waiting for her. He would be anywhere she went. And she'd come here for a reason—to warn Aaron. To give Aaron a last chance.

But it would be so nice to go home, to sleep again, if only she didn't hear that baby crying. She could feel Lasher wrapping his countless arms around her, snuggling her up in airy warmth.

"Rowan, listen to me."

She waked as if from a dream.

"All over the world there are human beings with exceptional powers," Aaron was saying, "but you are one of the rarest because you have found a way to use your power for good. You don't gaze into a crystal ball for dollar bills, Rowan. You heal. Can you bring him into that with you? Or will he take you away from it forever? Will he draw your power off into the creation of some mutant monster that the world does not want and cannot abide? Destroy him, Rowan. For your own sake. Not for mine. Destroy him for what you know is right."

"This is why he'll kill you, Aaron. I can't stop him if you provoke him. But why is it so wrong? Why are you against it? Why did you lie to me?"

"I never lied. And you know why it mustn't happen. He would be a thing without a human soul."

"That's religion, Aaron."

"Rowan, he would be unnatural. We need no more monsters. We ourselves are monstrous enough."

"He is as natural as we are," she said. "This is what I've been trying to tell you."

"He is as alien from us as a giant insect, Rowan. Would you make such a thing as that? It isn't meant to happen."

"Meant. Is mutation meant? Every second of every minute of every day, cells are mutating."

"Within limits. Upon a predictable path. A cat cannot fly. A man cannot grow horns. There is a scheme to things, and we can spend our lives studying it and marveling at it, that it is such a magnificent scheme. He is not part of the scheme."

"So you say, but what if there is no scheme? What if there is just process, just cells multiplying, and his metamorphosis is as natural as a river changing course and devouring farmland and houses and cattle and people? As a comet crashing into the earth?"

"Would you not try to save human beings from drowning? Would you not try to save them from the comet's fire? All right. Say he is natural. Let us postulate that we are better than natural. We aim for more than mere process. Our morals, our compassion, our capacity to love and to create an orderly society, make us better than nature. He has no reverence for that, Rowan. Look what he has done to the Mayfair family."

"He created it, Aaron!"

"No, I can't accept that. I can't."

"You're still talking religion, Aaron. You're talking an obdurate morality. There is no secure logical ground for condemning him."

"But there is. There has to be. Pestilence is natural, but you wouldn't let the bacillus out of the tube to destroy millions. Rowan, for the love of God, our consciousness was educated by the flesh from which it evolved. What would we be without the capacity to feel physical pain? And this creature, Lasher, has never bled from the smallest wound. He's never been chastened by hunger or sharpened by the need to survive. He is an immoral intelligence, Rowan, and you know this. You know it. And that is what I call unnatural, for want of a better word."

"Pretty moral poetry," she said. "You disappoint me. I was hoping you would give me arguments in exchange for my warning. I was hoping you would fortify my soul."

"You don't need my arguments. Look into your own soul. You know what I'm trying to tell you. He's a laser beam with ambition. He's a bomb that can think for itself. Let him in and the world will pay for it. You will be the mother of a disaster."

"Disaster," she whispered. "What a lovely word."

How frail he looked. She was seeing his age for the first time in the heavy lines of his face, in the soft pockets of flesh around his pale, imploring eyes. He seemed so weak to her suddenly, so without his usual eloquence and grace. Just an old man with white hair, peering at her, full of childlike wonder. No lure at all.

"You know what it could really mean, don't you?" she asked wearily. "When you strip away the fear?"

"He's lying to you; he's taking over your conscience."

"Don't say that to me!" she hissed. "That isn't courage on your part, it's stupidity." She settled back trying to calm herself. There had been a time when she loved this man. Even now she didn't want him harmed. "Can't you see the inevitable end of it?" she asked, reasonably. "If the mutation is successful, he can propagate. If the cells can be grafted and replicate themselves in other human bodies, the entire future of the human race can be changed. We are talking about an end to death."

"The age-old lure," Aaron said bitterly. "The age-old lie."

She smiled to see his composure stripped away.

"Your sanctimoniousness tires me," she said. "Science has always been the key. Witches were nothing but scientists, always. Black magic was striving to be science. Mary Shelley saw the future. Poets always see the future. And the kids in the third row of the theater know it when they watch Dr. Frankenstein piece the monster together, and raise the body into the electrical storm.''

''It is a horror story, Rowan. He's mutated your conscience.''

''Don't insult me like that again,'' she said, leaning once more across the table. ''You're old, you don't have many years left. I love you for what you've given me, and I don't want to hurt you. But don't tempt me and don't tempt him. What I'm telling you is the truth.''

He didn't answer her. He had dropped into a baffling state of calm. She found his small hazel eyes suddenly quite unreadable, and she marveled at his strength. It made her smile.

''Don't you believe what I'm telling you? Don't you want to write it in the file? I saw it in Lemle's laboratory when I saw that fetus connected to all those little tubes. You never knew why I killed Lemle, did you? You knew I did it, but you didn't know the cause. Lemle was in control of a project at the Institute. He was harvesting cells from live fetuses and using them in transplants. It's going on in other places. You can see the possibilities, but imagine experiments involving Lasher's cells, cells that have endured and transported consciousness for billions of years.''

''I want you to call Michael, to ask Michael to come home.''

''Michael can't stop him. Only I can stop him. Let Michael be where he's out of danger. Do you want Michael to die too?''

''Listen to me. You can close your mind to this being. You can veil your thoughts from it by a simple act of will. There are techniques as old as the oldest religions on earth for protecting ourselves from demons. It reads in your mind only what you project towards it. It's not different from telepathy. Try and you'll see.''

''And why should I do that?''

''To give yourself time. To give yourself a safe place for a moral decision.''

''No, you don't understand how powerful he is. You never did. And you don't know how well he knows me. That's the key, what he knows of me.'' She shook her head. ''I don't want to do what he wants,'' she said. ''I really don't. But it's irresistible, don't you see?''

''What about Michael? What about your dreams of Mayfair Medical?''

''Ellie was right,'' she said. She sat back against the wall and gazed off again, the lights of the bar blurring slightly. ''Ellie knew. She had Cortland's blood in her and she could see the future. Maybe it was only dim shapes and feelings, but she knew. I should never have come back. He used Michael to see to it that I came back. I knew Michael was in New Orleans, and like a randy bitch, I came back for that reason!''

"You're not talking the truth. I want you to come upstairs and stay with me.''

"You're such a fool. I could kill you here and now and no one would ever know it. No one but your brotherhood and your friend Michael Curry. And what could they do? It's over, Aaron. I may fight, and I may dance back a few steps, and I may gain an occasional advantage. But it's over. Michael was meant to bring me back and keep me here and he did.''

She started to rise, but he caught her hand. She looked down at his fingers. So old. You can always tell age by a person's hands. Were people staring at them? Didn't matter. Nothing mattered in this little room. She started to pull away.

"What about your child, Rowan?''

"Michael told you?''

"He didn't have to tell me. Michael was sent to love you so that you would drive that thing away, once and forever. So that you wouldn't fight this battle alone.''

"You knew that without being told also?''

"Yes. And so do you.''

She pulled her hand free.

"Go away, Aaron. Go far away. Go hide in the Motherhouse in Amsterdam or London. Hide. You're going to die if you don't. And if you call Michael, if you call him back here, I swear, I'll kill you myself.''

Forty-four

ABSOLUTELY EVERYTHING HAD gone wrong. The roof at Liberty Street had been leaking when he arrived and somebody had broken into the Castro Street store for a pitiful handful of cash in the drawer. His Diamond Street property had also been vandalized, and it had taken four days to clean it out before he could put it up for sale. Add to that a week to crate Aunt Viv's antiques, and to pack all her little knickknacks so that nothing would be broken. And he was afraid to trust the movers with these things. Then he'd had to sit down with his accountant for three days to put his tax records in order. December 14 already and there was still so much work to be done.

About the only good thing was that Aunt Viv had received the first two boxes safely and called to say how delighted she was to have her cherished objects with her at last. Did Michael know she'd joined a sewing circle with Lily, in which they did petit point and listened to Bach? She thought it was the most elegant thing. And now that her furniture was on the way, she could invite all the lovely Mayfair ladies over to her place at last. Michael was a darling. Just a darling.

"And I saw Rowan on Sunday, Michael, she was taking a walk, in this freezing weather, but do you know she has finally started to put on a little weight. I never wanted to say it before, but she was so thin and so pale. It was wonderful to see her with a real bloom in her cheeks."

He had to laugh at that, but he missed Rowan unbearably. He had never planned to be gone so long. Every phone call only made it worse, the famous butterscotch voice driving him out of his mind.

She was understanding about all the unforeseen catastrophes but he could hear the worry behind her questions. And he couldn't sleep after the calls, smoking one cigarette after another, and drinking too much beer, and listening to the endless winter rain.

San Francisco was in the wet season now, and the rain hadn't stopped since his arrival. No blue skies, not even over the Lib-

erty Street hill, and the wind ripped right through his clothe
when he stepped outside. He was wearing his gloves all the tim
just to keep warm.

But now at last the old house was almost empty. Nothing b
the last two boxes in the attic, and in a strange way, these littl
treasures were what he had come to retrieve and take with hi
to New Orleans. And he was eager to finish the job.

How alien it all looked to him, the rooms smaller than h
remembered, and the sidewalks in front so dirty. The tiny pe
per tree he'd planted seemed about to give up the ghost. Impo
sible that he could have spent so many years here telling himse
he was happy.

And impossible that he might have to spend another bacl
breaking week, taping and labeling boxes at the store, and goin
through tax receipts, and filling out various forms. Of course h
could have the movers do it, but some of the items weren't wor
that kind of trouble. And then the sorting was the nightmar
with all the little decisions.

"It's better now than later," Rowan had said this afternoo
when he called. "But I can hardly stand it. Tell me, have yo
had any second thoughts? I mean about the whole big change
Are there moments when you'd just like to pick up where yo
left off, as if New Orleans never happened?"

"Are you crazy? All I think about is coming back to you. I'
getting out of here before Christmas. I don't care what's goin
on."

"I love you, Michael." She could say it a thousand times an
it always sounded spontaneous. It was an agony not to be abl
to hold her. But was there a darker note to her voice, somethin
he hadn't heard before?

"Michael, burn anything that's left. Just make a bonfire in th
backyard, for heaven's sakes. Hurry."

He'd promised her he'd finish in the house by tonight if
killed him.

"Nothing's happened, has it? I mean you're not scared ther
are you, Rowan?"

"No. I'm not scared. It's the same beautiful house you lef
Ryan had a Christmas tree delivered. You ought to see it,
reaches the ceiling. It's just waiting there in the parlor for yo
and me to decorate it. The smell of the pine needles is all throug
the house."

"Ah, that's wonderful. I've got a surprise for you . . . for th
tree."

"All I want is you, Michael. Come home."

Four o'clock. The house was really truly empty now and hol

low and full of echoes. He stood in his old bedroom looking out over the dark shiny rooftops, spilling downhill to the Castro district, and beyond, the clustered steel gray skyscrapers of downtown.

A great city, yes, and how could he not be grateful for all the wonderful things it had given him? A city like no other perhaps. But it wasn't his city anymore. And in a way it never had been.

Going home.

But he'd forgotten again. The boxes in the attic, the surprise, the things he wanted most of all.

Taking the plastic wrapping material and an empty carton with him, he went up the ladder, stooping under the sloped roof, and snapped on the light. Everything clean and dry now that the leak had been patched. And the sky the color of slate beyond the front window. And the four remaining boxes, marked "Christmas" in red ink.

The tree lights he'd leave for the guys who were renting the place. Surely they could use them.

But the ornaments he would now carefully repack. He couldn't bear the thought of losing a single one. And to think, the tree was already there.

Dragging the box over under the naked overhead bulb, he opened it and discarded the old tissue paper. Over the years he'd collected hundreds of these little porcelain beauties from the specialty shops around town. Now and then he'd sold them himself at Great Expectations. Angels, wise men, tiny houses, carousel horses, and other delicate trinkets of exquisitely painted bisque. Real true Victorian ornaments could not have been more finely fashioned or fragile. There were tiny birds made of real feathers, wooden balls skillfully painted with lavish old roses, china candy canes, and silver-plated stars.

Memories came back to him of Christmases with Judith and with Elizabeth, and even back to the time when his mother had been alive.

But mostly he remembered the last few Christmases of his life, alone. He had forced himself to go through with the old rituals. And long after Aunt Viv had gone to bed, he'd sat by the tree, a glass of wine in his hand, wondering where his life was going and why.

Well, this Christmas would be utterly and completely different. All these exquisite ornaments would now have a purpose, and for the first time there would be a tree large enough to hold the entire collection, and a grand and wonderful setting in which they truly belonged.

Slowly he began work, removing each ornament from the tis-

sue, rewrapping it in plastic, and putting it in a tiny plastic sack
Imagine First Street on Christmas Eve with the tree in the parlor
Imagine it next year when the baby was there.

It seemed impossible suddenly that his life could have expe
rienced such a great and wondrous change. Should have died ou
there in the ocean, he thought.

And he saw, not the sea in his mind suddenly, but the church
at Christmas when he was a child. He saw the crib behind the
altar, and Lasher standing there, Lasher looking at him when
Lasher was just the man from First Street, tall and dark-haired
and aristocratically pale.

A chill gripped him. *What am I doing here? She's there alone.
Impossible that he hasn't shown himself to her.*

The feeling was so dark, so full of conviction, that it poisoned
him. He hurried with the packing. And when at last he was
finished, he cleaned up, threw the trash down the steps, took the
box of ornaments with him, and closed up the attic for the last
time.

The rain had slacked by the time he reached the Eighteenth
Street post office. He'd forgotten what it meant to crawl through
this dense traffic, to move perpetually among crowds on grim,
narrow, treeless streets. Even the Castro, which he had always
loved, seemed dismal to him in the late afternoon rush.

He stood in line too long to mail the box, bristled at the
routine indifference of the clerk—an abruptness he had not once
encountered in the South since his return—and then hurried off
in the icy wind, towards his shop up on Castro.

She wouldn't lie to him. She wouldn't. The thing was playing
its old game. Yet why that visitation on that long-ago Christmas?
Why that face, beaming at him over the crib? Hell, maybe it
meant nothing.

After all, he had seen the man that unforgettable night when
he first heard the music of Isaac Stern. He had seen the man a
hundred times when he walked on First Street.

But he couldn't stand this panic. As soon as he reached the
shop and had locked the door behind him, he picked up the
phone and dialed Rowan.

No answer. It was midafternoon in New Orleans, and it was
cold there, too. Maybe she'd taken a nap. He let it ring fifteen
times before he gave up.

He looked around. So much work still to be done. The entire
collection of brass bath fixtures had to be disposed of, and what
about the various stained-glass windows stacked against the back
wall? Why the hell didn't the thief who broke in steal this stuff?

At last he decided to box up the papers in the desk, trash and all. No time to sort things. He unbuttoned his cuffs, rolled up his sleeves, and began to shove the manila folders into the cardboard cartons. But no matter how quickly he worked, he knew he wouldn't get out of San Francisco for another week at best.

It was eight o'clock when he finally quit, and the streets were wet still from the rain, and crowded with the inevitable Friday night foot traffic. The lighted shopfronts looked cheerful to him, and he even liked the music thundering out of the gay bars. Yeah, he did now and then miss this bustle of the big city, that he had to admit. He missed the gay community of Castro Street and the tolerance of which its presence was proof.

But he was too tired to think much about it, and with his head bowed against the wind, he pushed his way uphill to where he'd left his car. For a moment he couldn't believe what he saw—both front tires were gone off the old sedan, and the trunk was popped, and that was his goddamned jack under the front bumper.

"Rotten bastards," he whispered, stepping out of the flow of pedestrians on the sidewalk. "This couldn't be worse if somebody had planned it."

Planned it.

Someone brushed his shoulder. "*Eh bien,* Monsieur, another little disaster."

"Yeah, you're telling me," he muttered under his breath, not even bothering to look up, and barely noticing the French accent.

"Very bad luck, Monsieur, you're right. Maybe somebody did plan it."

"Yeah, that's just what I was thinking myself," he said with a little start.

"Go home, Monsieur. That's where you're needed."

"Hey!"

He turned, but the figure was already traveling on. Glimpse of white hair. In fact, the crowd had almost swallowed him. All Michael saw was the back of his head moving swiftly away and what looked like a dark suit coat.

He rushed after the man.

"Hey!" he shouted again. But as he reached the corner of Eighteenth and Castro, he couldn't see the guy anywhere. People streamed across the intersection. And the rain had started up again. The bus, just pulling away from the curb, gave a belch of black diesel smoke.

Despairing, Michael's eyes passed indifferently over the bus, as he turned to retrace his steps, and only by chance did he see

in a flash through the back window a familiar face staring back
at him. Black eyes, white hair.

*. . . with the simplest and the oldest tools at your command
for through these you can win, even when it seems the odds are
impossible . . .*

"Julien!"

*. . . unable to believe your senses, but trust what you know
to be the truth and what you know to be right, and that you have
the power, the simple human power . . .*

"Yes, I will, I understand . . ."

With a sudden violent motion he was jerked off his feet; he
felt an arm around his waist, and a person of great strength
dragging him backwards. Before he could reason or begin to
resist, the bright red fender of a car bumped over the curb,
smashing with a deafening crunch into the light pole. Someone
screamed. The windshield of the car appeared to explode, silver
nuggets of glass flying in all directions.

"Goddamn!" He couldn't regain his balance. He tumbled back
on top of the very guy who'd pulled him out of the way. People
were running toward the car. Somebody was moving inside. The
glass was still falling out all over the pavement.

"You OK?"

"Yeah, yeah, I'm OK. There's somebody trapped in there."

The flashing light of a police car dazzled him suddenly. Some
one shouted to the policeman to call an ambulance.

"Boy, she nearly got you," said the one who'd pulled him
away—big powerfully built black man in a leather coat, shaking
his grizzled head. "Didn't you see that car coming straight at
you?"

"No. You saved my life, you know it?"

"Hell, I just pulled you out of the way. It was nothing. Didn't
even think about it." Dismissive wave of his hand as he went
on, eyes lingering for a moment on the red car, and on the two
men trying to free the woman inside, who was screaming. The
crowd was growing, and a policewoman was shouting for every
one to get back.

A bus was now blocking the intersection, and another police
car had pulled up. Newspapers were lying all over the sidewalk
from the overturned box, and the glass was sparkling in the rain
like so many scattered diamonds.

"Look, I don't know how to thank you," Michael called out.

But the black man was already far away, loping up Castro
with just a glance over his shoulder and a last casual wave of his
hand.

Michael stood shivering against the wall of the bar. People

964

pushed past those who had stopped to stare. There was that squeezing in his chest, not quite a pain but a tightening, and the pounding pulse, and a numbness creeping through the fingers of his left hand.

Christ, what actually happened? He couldn't get sick here, had to get back to the hotel.

He moved clumsily out into the street, and past the policewoman who asked him suddenly if he'd seen the car hit the light pole. No, he had to confess, he sure hadn't. Cab over there. Get the cab.

The driver could get him out of here if he backed up on Eighteenth and made a sharp right onto Castro.

"Gotta get to the St. Francis, Union Square," he said.

"You OK?"

"Yeah. Just barely."

It had been Julien who had spoken to him, no doubt about it, Julien whom he'd seen through the bus window! But what about that damned car?

Ryan could not have been more obliging. "Of course, we could have helped you with all this before, Michael. That's what we're here for. I'll have someone there tomorrow morning to inventory and crate the entire stock. I'll find a qualified real estate agent and we can discuss the listing price when you get here."

"I hate to bother you, but I can't reach Rowan and I have this feeling that I have to get back."

"Nonsense, we're here to take care of things for you, large and small. Now, do you have your plane reservation? Why don't you let me handle that? Stay right where you are and wait for my call."

He lay on the bed afterwards, smoking his last Camel cigarette, staring at the ceiling. The numbness in his left hand was gone, and he felt all right now. No nausea or dizziness or anything major, as far as he was concerned. And he didn't care. That part wasn't real.

What was real was the face of Julien in the bus window. And then that fragment of the visions catching hold of him, as powerfully as ever.

But had it all been planned, just to get him to that dangerous corner? Just to dazzle him and plant him motionless in the path of that careening car? The way he'd been planted in the path of Rowan's boat?

Oh, so engulfing that fragment of memory. He closed his eyes, saw their faces again, Deborah and Julien, heard their voices.

. . . that you have the power, the simple human power . . .

I do, I have it. I believe in you! It's a war between you and him, and once again, you reached down and you touched me at the very moment of his contrivance, as his carefully orchestrated calamity was taking place.

I have to believe that. Because if I don't I'll go out of my mind. *Go home, Monsieur. That's where you're needed.*

He was lying there, his eyes closed, dozing, when the phone rang.

"Michael?" It was Ryan.

"Yeah."

"Listen, I've arranged for you to come back by private plane. It's much simpler that way. It's the Markham Harris Hotels plane and they're more than delighted to assist us. I have someone coming to pick you up. If you need help with your bags . . ."

"No, just tell me the time, I'll be ready." What was that smell? Had he put his cigarette out?

"How about an hour from now? They'll call you from the lobby. And Michael, please, from now on, don't hesitate to ask us for anything, anything at all."

"Yeah, thanks, Ryan, yeah, I really appreciate it." He was staring at the smoldering hole in the bedspread where he'd dropped the cigarette when he fell asleep. God, the first time in his life he'd ever done anything like this! And the room was already full of smoke. "Thanks, Ryan, thanks for everything!"

He hung up, went into the bathroom, and filled the empty ice bucket with water, splashing it quickly onto the bed. Then he pulled the burnt spread away, and the sheet, and poured more water into the dark, smelly hole in the mattress. His heart was tripping again. He went to the window, struggled with it, realized it wasn't going to open, and then sat down heavily in a chair and watched the smoke gradually drift away.

When he was all packed, he tried Rowan again. Still no answer. Fifteen rings, no answer. He was just about to give up when he heard her groggy voice.

"Michael? Oh, I was asleep, I'm sorry, Michael."

"Listen to me, honey. I'm Irish, and I'm a very superstitious guy, as we both know."

"What are you talking about?"

"I'm having a string of bad luck, very bad luck. Do a little Mayfair witchcraft for me, will you, Rowan? Throw a white light around me. Ever hear of that?"

"No. Michael, what's happening?"

"I'm on my way home, Rowan. Now just imagine it, honey, a white light around me protecting me from everything bad in this world until I get there. You see what I'm saying? Ryan's arranged a plane for me. I'll be leaving within the hour."

"Michael, what's going on?"

Was she crying?

"Do it, Rowan, about the white light. Just trust me on this. Work on protecting me."

"A white light," she whispered. "All around you."

"Yeah. A white light. I love you, honey. I'm coming home."

Forty-five

"OH, THIS IS the very worst winter," said Beatrice. "You know they're even saying we might have snow?" She stood up and put her wineglass on the cart. "Well, darling, you've been very patient. And I was so worried. Now that I see you're all right, and that this great big house is so deliciously warm and cheerful, I'll be going."

"It was nothing, Bea," said Rowan, merely repeating what she had already explained. "Just depressed because Michael has been gone so long."

"And what time do you expect him?"

"Ryan said before morning. He was supposed to leave an hour ago but San Francisco International is fogged in."

"Winter, I hate it!" she said.

Rowan didn't bother to explain that San Francisco International was often fogged in during the summer. She simply watched Beatrice put on her cashmere cape, drawing the graceful hood up over her beautifully groomed gray hair.

She walked Beatrice to the door.

"Well, don't retreat in your shell like this, it worries us too much. Call me when you're down, I'll cheer you up."

"You're wonderful," said Rowan.

"We just don't want you to be frightened here. Why, I should have come over before now."

"I'm not frightened. I love it. Don't worry. I'll call you sometime tomorrow. Soon as Michael gets in, everything will be fine. We'll decorate the tree together. You must come and see it, of course."

She watched Beatrice go down the marble steps, and out the gate, the cold air gusting into the hallway. Then she shut the front door.

She stood quiet for a long time, her head bowed, letting the warmth seep around her, and then she walked back in the parlor and stared at the enormous green tree. Just beyond the arch it stood, touching the ceiling. A more perfectly triangular Christmas tree she'd never seen. It filled the whole window to the side porch. And only a small sprinkling of needles lay beneath it on the polished floor. Wild, it looked, primitive, like part of the woods come inside.

She went to the fireplace, knelt down, and placed another small log on the blaze.

"Why have you tried to hurt Michael?" she whispered, staring into the flames.

"I have not tried to hurt him."

"You are lying to me. Have you tried to hurt Aaron too?"

"I do as you command me to do, Rowan." The voice was soft and deep as always. "My world is pleasing you."

She rested back on her heels, arms folded, eyes misting, so that the flames were softened into a great flickering blur.

"He is not to suspect anything, do you hear me?" she whispered.

"I always hear you, Rowan."

"He is to believe everything is as it was."

"That is my wish, Rowan. We are in accord. I dread his enmity because it will make you unhappy. I will do only as you wish."

But it couldn't go on forever, and suddenly the fear that gripped her was so total that she couldn't speak or move. She couldn't attempt to disguise her feelings. She could not retreat into an inner sanctum of her mind as Aaron had told her to do. She sat there, shivering, staring at the flames.

"How will it end, Lasher? I don't know how to do what you want of me."

"You know, Rowan."

"It will take years of study. Without a deeper understanding of you, I can't hope to begin."

"Oh, but you know all about me, Rowan. And you seek to deceive me. You love me but you do not love me. You would lure me into the flesh if you knew how in order to destroy me."

"Would I?"

"Yes. It is an agony to feel your fear and your hatred, when I know what happiness waits for both of us. When I can see so far."

"What would you have? The body of a man already alive? With consciousness knocked out of him through some sort of trauma, so that you could begin your fusion unimpeded by his mind? That's murder, Lasher."

Silence.

"Is that what you want? For me to commit murder? Because we both know it could be done that way."

Silence.

"And I won't commit that crime for you. I won't kill one single living being so that you can live."

She closed her eyes. She could actually hear him gathering, hear the pressure building, hear the draperies rustling as he moved against them, writhing and filling the room around her, and brushing against her cheeks and her hair.

"No. Let me alone," she sighed. "I want to wait for Michael."

"He will not be enough for you now, Rowan. It causes me pain to see you weep. But I am speaking the truth."

"God, I hate you," she whispered. She wiped at her eyes with the back of her hand. Through the blur of her tears she looked at the huge green tree.

"Ah, but you don't hate me, Rowan," he said. Fingers caressing her hair, stroking it back away from her forehead, tiny fingers stroking her neck.

"Leave me alone now, Lasher," she pleaded. "If you love me, leave me alone."

Leiden. She knew it was the dream again and she wanted to wake up. Also the baby needed her. She could hear it crying. I want to leave the dream. But they were all gathered at the windows, horrified by what was happening to Jan van Abel, the mob tearing him limb from limb.

"It wasn't kept secret," said Lemle. "It's impossible for ignorant people to understand the importance of experimentation. What you do when you keep it secret is merely take the responsibility on yourself."

"In other words, protecting them," said Larkin.

He pointed to the body on the table. How patiently the man lay there, with his eyes open and all the tiny budlike organs shivering inside. Such little arms and legs.

"I can't think with the baby crying."

"You have to see the larger picture, the greater gain."

"Where is Petyr? Petyr must be frantic after what's happened to Jan van Abel."

"The Talamasca will take care of him. We're waiting for you to begin."

Impossible. She stared at the little man with the truncated arms and legs and the tiny organs. Only the head was normal. That is a normal-sized head.

"One fourth of the size of the body, to be exact."

Yes, the familiar proportion, she thought. Then the horror seized her as she stared down at it. But they were breaking the windows. The mob was streaming into the corridors of the University of Leiden, and Petyr was running towards her.

"No, Rowan. Don't do it."

She woke up with a start. Footsteps on the stairs.

She climbed out of the bed. "Michael?"

"I'm here, honey."

Just a big shadow in the darkness, smelling of the winter cold, and then his warm trembling hands on her. Roughened and tender, and his face pressed against her.

"Oh, God, Michael, it's been forever. Why did you leave me?"

"Rowan, honey . . ."

"Why?" She was sobbing. "Don't let me go, Michael, please. Don't let me go."

He cradled her in his arms.

"You shouldn't have gone, Michael. You shouldn't have." She was crying and she knew he couldn't even understand what she was saying, and that she shouldn't say it, and finally she just covered him with kisses, savoring the saltiness and roughness of his skin, and the clumsy gentleness of his hands.

"Tell me what's the matter, what's really the matter?"

"That I love you. That when you're not here, it's . . . it's like you aren't real."

She was half awake when he slipped away. She didn't want that dream to come back. She'd been lying next to him, snuggled against his chest, spoon fashion, holding tight to his arm, and now as he got out of bed, she watched almost furtively as he pulled on his jeans, and brought the tight long-sleeved rugby shirt down over his head.

"Stay here," she whispered.

"It's the doorbell," he said. "My little surprise. No, don't get up. It's nothing really, just something that I brought with me from San Francisco. Why don't you go on and sleep?"

He bent to kiss her, and she tugged at his hair. She brought him down close to her with insistent fingers, until she could smell the warm skin of his forehead, and kiss him on that smoothness, the bone underneath like a hard stone. She didn't know why that felt so good to her, his skin so moist and warm and real. She kissed him hard on the mouth.

Even before his lips left her, the dream returned.

I don't want to see that manikin on the table. "What is it? It can't be alive."

Lemle was gowned and masked and gloved for the surgery. He peered at her from under his mossy eyebrows. "You're not even sterile. Get scrubbed, I need you." The lights were like two merciless eyes trained on the table.

That thing with its tiny organs and its big eyes.

Lemle held something in his tongs. And the little body split open in the steaming incubator beside the table was a fetus, slumbering on with its chest gaping. That was a heart in the tongs, wasn't it? You monster, that you would do that. "We're going to have to work fast while the tissue is at its optimum . . ."

"It's very hard for us to come through," said the woman.

"But who are you?" she asked.

Rembrandt was sitting by the window, so tired in his old age, his nose rounded, his hair in wisps. He looked up at her sleepily when she asked him what he thought, and then he took her hand in his fingers, and he placed it on her own breast.

"I know that painting," she said, "the young bride."

She woke up. The clock had struck two. She had waited in her sleep, thinking there would be more chimes, perhaps ten in number, which meant she'd slept late; but two? That was so late.

She heard music from far away. A harpsichord was playing and a low voice was singing, a slow mournful carol, an old Celtic carol about a child laid in the manger. Smell of the Christmas tree, sweetly fragrant, and of the fire burning. Delicious in the warmth.

She was lying on her side, looking at the window, at the crust of frost forming on the panes. Very slowly a figure began to take shape—a man, with his back to the glass and his arms folded.

She narrowed her eyes, observing the process—the darkly tanned face coming into focus, billions of tiny cells forming it, and the deep glistening green eyes. The perfect replica of jeans and a shirt. Detailed like a Richard Avedon photograph in which every hair of the head is distinct and shining. He relaxed his arms and came toward her. She could hear and see the movement of his garments. As he bent over her, she saw the pores in his skin.

So we are jealous, are we? She touched his cheek, touched

his forehead the way she had touched Michael, and felt a throb beneath it, like a body really there.

"Lie to him," he said in a low voice, the lips barely moving. "If you love him, lie to him."

She could almost feel breath against her face. Then she realized she was seeing through the face, seeing the window behind it.

"No, don't let go," she said. "Hold on."

But the whole image convulsed; then it wavered like a paper cutout caught in a draft. She felt his panic in spasms of heat.

She reached out to take his wrist, but her hand closed on nothing. The hot draft swept over her and over the bed, and the draperies ballooned for a moment, and the frost rose and turned white on the panes.

"Kiss me," she whispered, closing her eyes. Like wisps of hair across her face and her lips. "No. That's not enough. Kiss me." Only slowly did the density increase, and the touch become more palpable. He was tired from the materialization. Tired and slightly frightened. His cells and the other cells had almost undergone a molecular fusion. There must be a residue somewhere, or the minuscule bits of matter had been scattered so finely that they had penetrated the walls and the ceiling the same way he penetrated them. "Kiss me!" she demanded. She felt him struggling. And only now did he make invisible lips with which to do it, pushing an unseen tongue into her mouth.

Lie to him.

Yes, of course. I love you both, don't I?

He didn't hear her come down the steps. The draperies were all closed and the hallway was dark and hushed and warm. The fire was lighted in the front fireplace of the parlor. And the only other illumination came from the tree, which was now strung with countless tiny, twinkling lights.

She stood in the doorway watching him as he sat on the very top of the ladder, making some little adjustment, and whistling softly to himself with the recording of the old Irish Christmas song.

So mournful. It made her think of a deep, ancient wood in winter. And his whistling was such a small, easy, almost unconscious sound. She'd known that carol once. She had some dim memory of listening to it with Ellie, and it had made Ellie cry.

She leaned against the door frame, merely looking at the immense tree, all speckled with its tiny lights like stars, and breathing its deep woodsy perfume.

"Ah, there she is, my sleeping beauty," he said. He gave her one of those utterly loving and protective smiles that made her feel like rushing into his arms. But she didn't move. She watched as he came down off the ladder with quick easy movements, and approached her. "Feel better now, my princess?" he asked.

"Oh, it's so very beautiful," she said. "And that song is so sad."

She put her arm around his waist and leaned her head on his shoulder as she looked up at the tree. "You've done a perfect job."

"Ah, but now comes the fun part," he said, giving her a peck on the cheek and drawing her into the room and towards the small table by the windows. A cardboard box stood open, and he gestured for her to look inside.

"Aren't they lovely!" She picked up a small white bisque angel with the faintest blush to its cheeks, and gilded wings. And here was the most beautiful detailed little Father Christmas, a tiny china doll dressed in real red velvet. "Oh, they're exquisite. Wherever did they come from?" She lifted the golden apple, and a lovely five-pointed star.

"Oh, I've had them for years. I was a college kid when I started collecting them. I never knew they were for this tree and this room, but they were. Here, you choose the first one. I've been waiting for you. I thought we'd do it together."

"The angel," she said. She lifted it by the hook and brought it close to the tree, the better to see it in the soft light. It held a tiny gilded harp in its hands, and even its little face was correctly painted with a fine reddened mouth and blue eyes. She lifted it as high as she could reach and slipped the curved hook over the thick part of the shivering branch. The angel quivered, the hook nearly invisible in the darkness, and hung suspended, as if poised like a hummingbird in flight.

"Do you think they do that, angels, they stop in midair like hummingbirds?" she asked in a whisper.

"Yeah, probably," he said. "You know angels. They're probably show-offs, and they can do anything they want." He stood behind her, kissing her hair.

"What did I ever do without you here?" she said. As his arms went around her waist she clasped them with her hands, loving the sinewy muscles, the large strong fingers holding her so tight.

For a moment the fullness of the tree and the lovely play of twinkling light in the deep shadowy green branches utterly filled her vision. And the sad music of the carol filled her ears. The moment was suspended, like the delicate angel. There was no future, no past.

"I'm so glad you're back," she whispered closing her eyes.

"It was unbearable here without you. Nothing makes any sense without you. I never want to be without you again." A deep throb of pain passed through her—a fierce terrible quaking that she locked inside her, as she turned to lay her head once more on his chest.

Forty-six

DECEMBER 23. HARD freeze tonight. Lovely, when all the Mayfairs were expected for cocktails and carol singing. Think of all those cars sliding on the icy streets. But it was wonderful to have this clean cold weather for Christmas. And they were predicting snow.

"A white Christmas, can you imagine?" he said to her. He was looking out of the front bedroom window as he put on his sweater and his leather jacket. "It might even snow tonight."

"That would be wonderful for the party," she said, "wonderful for Christmas."

She was snuggled up in the chair by the gas fire, a quilt over her shoulders, and her cheeks were ruddy and she was just a little bit softer and rounder all over. You could see it, a woman with a baby inside her, positively radiant, as if she'd absorbed the glow of the fire.

She had never seemed more relaxed and cheerful. "It would be another gift to us, Michael," she said.

"Yes, another gift," he said, looking out the window. "And you know they're saying it's going to happen. And I'll tell you something else, Rowan. It was a white Christmas the year I left."

He took the wool scarf out of the dresser drawer and fitted it inside his coat collar. Then he picked up the thick, wool-lined gloves.

"I'll never forget it," he said. "It was the first time I ever saw snow. And I went walking right down here, on First Street, and when I got home I found out my dad was dead."

"How did it happen?" How sympathetic she looked, eyes puckering slightly. Her face was so smooth that when the slightest distress came, it fell like a shadow over her.

"A warehouse fire on Tchoupitoulas," he said. "I never did know the details. Seems the chief had told them to get clear of the roof, that it was about to go. One guy fell down or something and my dad doubled back to get him, and that's when the roof began to buckle. They said it just rolled like an ocean wave, and then it fell in. Whole place just exploded. They lost three fire fighters that day, actually, and I was walking out there in the Garden District, just enjoying the snow. That's why we went out to California. All the Currys were gone—all those aunts and uncles. Everyone buried out in St. Joseph's Cemetery. All buried from Lonigan and Sons. Every one."

"That must have been so awful for you."

He shook his head. "The awful part was being so glad we were going to California, and knowing that we'd never have been able to go if he hadn't died."

"Here, come sit down and drink your chocolate, it's getting cold. Bea and Cecilia will be here any minute."

"I have to get on the road. Too many errands. Got to get to the shop, see if the boxes have arrived. Oh, I have to confirm with the caterers . . . I forgot to call them."

"No need. Ryan's taken care of it. He says you do too many things for yourself. He says he would have sent a plumber to wrap all the pipes."

"I like doing those things," he said. "Those pipes are going to freeze anyway. Hell. This is supposed to be the worst winter in a hundred years."

"Ryan says you have to think of him more as a personal manager. He told the caterers to come at six. That way if anyone is early . . ."

"Good idea. I'll be back before then. OK. I'll call you later from the store sometime. If you need me to pick up anything . . ."

"Hey, you can't walk out of this room without kissing me."

" 'Course not." He bent down and smothered her in kisses, roughly and hastily, making her laugh softly, and then he kissed her belly. "Good-bye, Little Chris," he whispered. "It's almost Christmas, Little Chris."

At the door, he stopped to pull on his heavy gloves, and then he blew her another kiss.

Like a picture she looked in the high-back wing chair, with her feet tucked under her. Even her lips had a soft rich color to them. And when she smiled he saw the dimples in her cheeks.

His breath made steam in the air when he stepped outside. It was years since he'd felt cold like this, so crisp. And the sky

was such a shining blue. They were going to lose the banana
trees and he hated it, but the beautiful camellias and azalea
were holding their own. The gardeners had put in winter grass
and the lawn looked like velvet.

He stared at the barren crepe myrtle for a moment. Was he
hearing those Mardi Gras drums again in his ears?

He let the van warm up for a couple of minutes before he
started. Then he headed straight for the bridge. It would take
him forty-five minutes to reach Oak Haven if he could make
good time on the river road.

Forty-seven

"WHAT WAS THE pact and the promise?" she asked.
She stood in the attic bedroom, so clean and sterile
with its white walls, its windows looking out on the rooftops.
No trace of Julien anymore. All the old books gone.

"Those things are not important now," he answered her. "The
prophecy is on the verge of fulfillment and you are the door."

"I want to know. What was the pact?"

"These are words passed on from human lips through gener
ation after generation."

"Yes, but what do they mean?"

"It was the covenant between me and my witch—that I should
obey her smallest command if she should but bear a female child
to inherit her power and the power to command and see me. I
should bring all riches to her; I should grant all favors. I should
look into the future so she might know the future. I should avenge
all slights and injuries. And in exchange the witch would strive
to bear a female child whom I might love and serve as I had the
witch, and that child would love and see me."

"And that child should be stronger than the mother, and mov
ing towards the thirteen."

"Yes, in time I came to see the thirteen."

"Not from the beginning?"

"No. In time I saw it. I saw the power accumulating, and
perfecting itself, I saw it fed through the strong men of the
family. I saw Julien with power so great that he outshone his

976

sister, Katherine. I saw Cortland. I saw the path to the doorway. And now you are here.''

"When did you tell your witches about the thirteen?''

"In the time of Angélique. But you must realize how simple was my own understanding of what I saw. I could scarce explain. Words were wholly new to me. The process of thinking in time was new. And so the prophecy was veiled in obscurity, not by design, but by accident. Yet it is now on the verge of being fulfilled.''

"You promised *only* your service over the centuries?''

"Is this not enough? Can't you see what my service had wrought? You stand in the house which was created by me and my service. You dream of hospitals you will build by means of the riches brought to you by me. You yourself told Aaron that I was the creator of the Mayfair Witches. You spoke the truth to Aaron. Look at the many branches of this family. All of their wealth has come from me. My generosity has fed and clothed countless men and women of the same name, who know nothing of me. It is sufficient that *you* know me.''

"You promised nothing more?''

"What more can I give? When I am in the flesh, I shall be your servant as I am now. I shall be your lover and your confidant, your pupil. No one can prevail against you when you have me.''

"Saved. What had being saved to do with it—the old saying that when the door was opened the witches would be saved?''

"Again, you bring me tired words, and old fragments.''

"Ah, but you remember everything. Trace down for me the origin of this idea—that the witches would be saved.''

Silence.

"The thirteen witches would be upheld in that moment of my final triumph. In the reward of Lasher, their faithful servant, the persecution of Suzanne and Deborah would be avenged. When Lasher steps through the doorway, Suzanne shall not have died in vain. Deborah shall not have died in vain.''

"This was the complete meaning of the word 'saved'?''

"You have now the full explanation.''

"And how is it to be done? You tell me that when I know, you will know, and I tell you I don't:''

"Remember your communication to Aaron—that I am living and of life, and that my cells can be merged with the cells of the fleshly, and that it is through mutation, and through surrender.''

"Ah, but that's the key. You are afraid of that surrender. You are afraid of being locked in a form from which you can't escape. You do realize, don't you, what it means to be flesh and blood? That you may lose your immortality? That even in the transmutation, you could be destroyed?"

"No. I will lose nothing. And when I am created in my new form, I shall open the way for you to a new form. You've always known. You knew when you first heard the old legend from your kinsmen. You knew why there were twelve crypts and one door."

"You are saying that I can be immortal."

"Yes."

"This is what you see?"

"This is what I have always seen. You are my perfect companion. You are the witch of all witches. You have Julien's strength and Mary Beth's strength. You have the beauty of Deborah and Suzanne. All the souls of the dead are in your soul. Traveling through the mystery of the cells, they have come down to you, shaping you and perfecting you. You shine as bright as Charlotte. You are more beautiful than Marie Claudette or Angélique. You have a fire in you that is hotter than Marguerite or my poor doomed Stella; you have a vision far greater than ever my lovely Antha or Deirdre. You are the one."

"Are the souls of the dead in this house?"

"The souls of the dead are gone from the earth."

"Then what did Michael see in this room?"

"He saw the impressions left behind by the dead ones. These impressions sprang to life for him from the objects that he touched. They are like unto the grooves of a phonograph record. Put the needle into the groove and the voice sings. But the singer is not there."

"But why did they crowd around him when he touched the dolls?"

"As I have said, these were impressions. Then the imagination of Michael took them up and worked them as if they were puppets. All their animation came from him."

"Why did the witches keep the dolls, then?"

"To play the same game. As if you kept a photograph of your mother, and when you held it to the light, the eyes seemed to fire with being. And to believe perhaps that the dead soul could be reached somehow, that beyond this earth lies a realm of eternity. I see no such eternity with my eyes. I see only the stars."

"I think they called to the souls of the dead through the dolls."

"Like praying, as I told you. And to be warm with the impressions. Anything more is not possible. The souls of the dead are not here. The soul of my Suzanne went past me, upwards. The soul of my Deborah rose as if on wings when her tender body fell from the battlements of the church. The dolls are keepsakes, nothing more. But don't you see? None of this matters now. The dolls, the emeralds, they are emblems. We are passing out of this realm of emblems and keepsakes and prophecies. We go to a new existence. Envision the doorway if you will. We shall pass through it, out of this house and into the world.''

"And the transmutation can be replicated. That is what you're leading me to believe?''

"That is what you know, Rowan. I read the book of life over your shoulder. All living cells replicate. In manly form I shall replicate. And my cells can be grafted to your cells, Rowan. There are possibilities of which we have not yet begun to dream.''

"And I shall become immortal.''

"Yes. My companion. And my lover. Immortal like me.''

"When is it to happen?''

"When you know I shall know. And you will know very soon.''

"You are so sure of me, aren't you? I don't know how to do it. I've told you.''

"What do your dreams tell you?''

"They are nightmares. They're full of images I don't understand. I don't know where the body on the table comes from. I don't know why Lemle is there. I don't understand what they want of me, and I don't want to see Jan van Abel struck down again. The place is meaningless to me.''

"Calm yourself, Rowan. Let me calm you. The dreams tell you. But more truly, you will tell yourself finally. Out of the caldron of your own mind will come the truth.''

"No, back away from me. Just talk to me. That's what I want of you now.''

Silence.

"You are the doorway, my beloved. I hunger for the flesh. I am weary of my loneliness. Don't you know the time is almost at hand? My mother, my beautiful one . . . This is the season for me to be reborn.''

She closed her eyes, feeling his lips on the back of her neck, feeling his fingers tracing the length of her spine. There came the pressure of a warm hand clasping her sex, fingers slipping inside her, lips against her lips. Fingers pinched her nipples hurtfully and deliciously.

"Let me wrap my arms around you," he whispered. "Others will come. And you will belong to them for hours, and I must hover hungrily at a distance, watching you, catching the words that fall from your lips as though they were drops of water to slake my thirst. Let me enfold you now. Give me these hours my beautiful Rowan . . ."

She felt herself being lifted, her feet no longer touching the floor; the darkness was swirling around her, strong hands turning her, and stroking her all over. There was no gravity any longer; she felt his strength increasing, the heat of it increasing.

The cold wind rattled the panes of the window. The great empty house seemed full of whispers. She was floating in the air. She turned over, groping in the shadowy tangle of arms supporting her, feeling her legs forced apart and her mouth opened. Yes, do it.

"How can the time be nearly at hand?" she whispered.

"Soon, my darling."

"I can't do it."

"Oh, yes you will be able to, my beauty. You know. You shall see . . ."

Forty-eight

THE DAY WAS darkening and the wind was bitter as he got out of the car, but the plantation house looked cheerful and inviting, with all its windows filled with a warm yellow light.

Aaron was waiting at the door for him, layered with wool under his gray cardigan, neck wrapped in a cashmere scarf.

"Here, this is for you," Michael said. "Merry Christmas, my friend." He placed a small bottle, wrapped in green Christmas paper, in Aaron's hands. "It's not a very big surprise, I'm afraid. But it is the best brandy I could find."

"That was very thoughtful of you," Aaron said with a little smile. "I'm going to enjoy it immensely. Every drop of it. Come in out of the cold. I have a little something for you, too. I'll show you later. Come on, inside."

The warm air was delicious. And there was quite a large and full tree set up in the living room, and very splendidly decorated with gold and silver ornaments, all of which surprised Michael because he hadn't known how the Talamasca would celebrate such a feast, if they celebrated such things at all. Even the man-els were decorated with holly. And a good fire was blazing on the large living room hearth.

"It's an old old feast, Michael," said Aaron, anticipating his question with a little smile. He set the gift on the table. "Goes back long before Christ. The winter solstice—a time when all the forces of the earth are at their strongest. That's probably why the Son of God chose it as a time to be born."

"Yeah, well, I could use a little belief in the Son of God right now," said Michael. "A little belief in the forces of the earth."

It did feel good in here. It had the nice cozy feel of a country place after First Street—with its lower ceilings and simpler crown moldings, and the large deep fireplace, built not for coal but for real raging log fire.

Michael took off his leather coat and his gloves, gave them over to Aaron gratefully, and stretched out his hands to warm them over the fire. There was no one else in the main rooms as far as he could tell, though he could hear faint sounds coming from the back kitchen. The wind beat against the French windows. Rimmed in frost, they were nevertheless filled with the pale green of landscape beyond.

The tray with the coffee was waiting and Aaron gestured for Michael to take the chair to the left of the hearth.

As soon as he sat down, he felt the knot inside him loosen. He felt he was going to bawl. He took a deep breath, eyes moving back and forth over everything and nothing, and then without preamble he began.

"It's happening," he said, his voice shaky. He could scarcely believe that it had come to this, that he was talking about her this way, yet he went on. "She's lying to me. He's there with her, and she's lying. She's been lying to me night and day since I came home."

"Tell me what's happened," said Aaron, his face sober and full of immediate sympathy.

"She didn't even ask why I came back so quickly from San Francisco. Never even brought it up. It was as if she knew. And I was frantic when I called her from the hotel out there. God-damn it, I told you on the phone what happened. I thought that thing was trying to kill me. She never even asked me what went down."

"Describe it to me again, all of it."

"Christ, Aaron, I know now it was Julien and Deborah that I saw in my vision. I don't have any doubt anymore. I don't know what the pact means or the promise. But I know that Julien and Deborah are on my side. I saw Julien. I saw him looking at me through the bus window, and it was the strangest thing, Aaron, it was as if he wanted to speak and to move and he couldn't. . was as if it was hard for him to come through.''

Aaron didn't say anything. He was sitting with his elbow o the arm of the chair, and his finger curled beneath his lower lip He looked cautious, alert, and thoughtful.

"Go on," he said.

"But the point is that this particular flash was enough to brin it all back. Not that I remembered everything that was said. Bu I recaptured the feeling. They want me to intervene. They sai something to me about 'the age-old human tools at my com mand.' I heard those words again. I heard Deborah speaking t me. It was Deborah. Only she didn't look like that pictur Aaron. Aaron, I'll tell you the most convincing piece of ev dence.''

"Yes . . .''

"What Llewellyn said to you. Remember. He said he sa Julien in a dream, and Julien wasn't the same as Julien in lif Remember? Well, you see, that's the key. In the vision Debora was a different being. And on that damn street corner in Sa Francisco, I felt both of them, and they were as I remembere them—wise and good, and knowing things, Aaron. Knowin that Rowan was in terrible danger and that I had to interven God, when I think of Julien's expression through that window It was so . . . urgent yet tranquil. I don't have words to describ it. It was concerned and yet so untroubled . . .''

"I think I know what you're trying to say."

"Go home, they said, go home. That's where you're neede Aaron, why didn't he look directly at me on the street?''

"There could be a lot of reasons. It revolves around what yo said. If they exist somewhere, it's difficult for them to com through. It isn't difficult for Lasher. And that is crucial to o understanding of what's going on. But I'll come back to tha Go on . . .''

"You can guess, can't you? I come home, private plane, lim whole number all arranged by Cousin Ryan, as if I'm a go damned rock star, and she doesn't even ask me what's bee happening. Because she's not Rowan. She's Rowan caught i something, Rowan smiling and pretending and staring at m with those great big sad gray eyes. Aaron, the worst part is . . .''

"Tell me, Michael."

"She loves me, Aaron. And it's like she's silently pleadin with me not to confront her. She knows I can see through th deception. God, when I touch her I feel it! She knows I can fe it. And silently, she's pleading with me not to force her into corner, not to make her lie. It's like she's begging me, Aaron. She's desperate. I could swear she's even afraid."

"Yes. She's in the thick of it. She's spoken to me about it. Some sort of communication apparently started when you left. Possibly even before you left."

"You knew this? Why the hell didn't you tell me?"

"Michael, we're dealing with something that knows what we're saying to each other even now."

"Oh, God!"

"There isn't any place we can hide from this being," said Aaron. "Except perhaps in the sanctuary of our own minds. Rowan said many things to me. But the crux of it is that this entire battle is now in Rowan's hands."

"Aaron, there must be something we can do. We knew it would happen; we knew it would come to this. You knew before you ever laid eyes on me that it would come to this."

"Michael, that's just the point. She is the only one who can do anything. And in loving her, and staying close to her, you are using the age-old tools at your command."

"That can't be enough!" He could hardly stand this. He stood up, paced for a minute, and then wound up with his hands on the mantel, staring down into the fire. "You should have called me, Aaron. You should have told me."

"Look, take your anger out on me if it makes you feel better, but the fact is, she forbade my contacting you with a threat. She was full of threats. Some of these threats were made in the guise of warnings—that her invisible companion wanted to kill me and would soon do it—but they were genuine threats."

"Christ, when did this happen?"

"Doesn't matter. She told me to go back to England while I still had time."

"She told you this? What else did she tell you?"

"I chose not to do it. But what more I can do here, I don't honestly know. I know that she wanted you to remain in California because she felt you were safe there. But you see, this situation has become too complicated for simple or literal interpretation of the things she said."

"I don't know what you mean. What is a literal interpretation? What other kind of interpretation is there? I don't get it."

"Michael, she talked in riddles. It wasn't communication so much as a demonstration of a struggle. Again, I have to remind you, this being, if he chooses, can be here with us in this room. We have no safe place in which we can plot aloud against him. Imagine a boxing match if you can, in which the opponents can

983

read each other's minds. Imagine a war, where every conceivable strategy is known telepathically from the start."

"It ups the stakes, ups the excitement, but it isn't impossible."

"I agree with you, but it serves no purpose for me to tell you everything that Rowan said to me. Suffice it to say, Rowan is the most able opponent this being has ever had."

"Aaron, you warned her long ago not to let this thing take her away from us. You warned her that it would seek to divide her from those she loved."

"I did. And I am sure she remembers it, Michael. Rowan is a human being upon whom almost nothing is lost. And believe me, I have argued with her since. I have told her in the plainest language why she must not allow this being to mutate. But the decision is in her hands."

"You're saying in effect that we have to just wait and let her fight this alone."

"I'm saying in effect that you're doing what you were meant to do. Love her. Stay near her. Remind her by your very presence of what is natural and inherently good. This is a struggle between the natural and the unnatural, Michael. No matter what that being is made of, no matter what he comes from—it's a struggle between normal life and aberration. Between evolution on the one hand and disastrous intervention on the other. And both have their mysteries and their miracles, and nobody knows that better than Rowan herself."

He stood up and put his hand on Michael's shoulder. "Sit down and listen to what I'm saying," he said.

"I have been listening," said Michael crossly. But he obeyed. He sat on the edge of the chair, and he couldn't stop himself from making his right hand into a fist and grinding it into his left palm.

"All her life, Rowan has confronted this split between the natural and the aberrant," said Aaron. "Rowan is essentially a conservative human being. And creatures like Lasher don't change one's basic nature. They can only work upon the traits which are already there. No one wanted that lovely white-dress wedding more than Rowan did. No one wants the family more than Rowan. No one wants that child inside her more than she."

"She doesn't even talk about the baby, Aaron. She hasn't even mentioned its existence since I came home. I wanted to tell the family tonight at the party, but she doesn't want me to do it. She says she's not ready. And this party, I know it's an agony for her. She's just going through the motions. Beatrice put her up to it."

"Yes, I know."

"I talk about the baby all the time. I kiss her and call it Little Chris, the name I gave it, and she smiles, and it's like she's not Rowan. Aaron, I'm going to lose her and the baby if she loses her battle with him. I can't think past that. I don't know anything about mutations and monsters and . . . and ghosts that want to be alive."

"Go home, and stay there with her. Stay near her. That's what they told you to do."

"And don't confront her? That's what you're saying?"

"You'll only force her to lie, if you do that. Or worse."

"What if you and I were to go back there together and try to reason with her, try to get her to turn her back on it?"

Aaron shook his head. "She and I have had our little show-down, Michael. That's why I made my excuses for this evening to Bea. I'd be challenging her and her sinister companion if I came there. But if I thought it would do any good, I'd come. I'd risk anything if I thought I could help. But I can't."

"But Aaron, what makes you so certain?"

"I'm not one of the players now, Michael. I didn't see the visions. You saw them. Julien and Deborah spoke to you. Rowan loves you."

"I don't know if I can stand this."

"I think you can. Do what you have to do to stand it. And remain close to her. Tell her in some way—silent or otherwise—that you are there for her."

Michael nodded. "All right," he said. "You know it's like she's being unfaithful."

"You mustn't see it like that. You mustn't become angry."

"I keep telling myself the same thing."

"There's something else I have to say to you. It probably won't matter in the final analysis. But I want to pass it along. If anything happens to me, well, it's something that I'd like you to know for what it's worth."

"You don't think anything is going to happen?"

"I don't honestly know. But listen to what I have to say. For centuries, we've puzzled over the nature of these seeming discarnate entities. There isn't a culture on earth which doesn't recognize their existence. But nobody knows what they really are. The Catholic Church sees them as demons. They have elaborate theological explanations for their existence. And they see them all as evil and out to destroy. Now all that would be easy to dismiss, except the Catholic Church is very wise about the behavior and the weaknesses of these beings. But I'm straying from the point.

985

"The point is, that we in the Talamasca have always assumed that these beings were very similar to the spirits of the earthbound dead. We believed or took for granted that both were essentially bodiless, possessed of intelligence, and locked in some sort of realm around the living."

"And Lasher could be a ghost, that's what you're saying."

"Yes. But more significantly, Rowan seems to have made some sort of breakthrough in discovering what these beings are. She claims that Lasher possesses a cellular structure, and that the basic components of all organic life are present in him."

"Then he's just some sort of bizarre creature, that's what you're saying."

"I don't know. But what has occurred to me is that maybe the so-called spirits of the dead are made of the same components. Maybe the intelligent part of us, when it leaves the body, takes some living portion with it. Maybe we undergo a metamorphosis, rather than a physical death. And all the age-old words—etheric body, astral body, spirit—are just terms for this fine cellular structure that persists when the flesh is gone."

"It's over my head, Aaron."

"Yes, I am being rather theoretical, aren't I? I suppose the point I'm trying to make is . . . that whatever this being can do, maybe the dead can also do. Or perhaps, even more important—even if Lasher possesses this structure, he could still be a malevolent spirit of someone who once lived."

"That's for your library in London, Aaron. Some day, maybe, we can sit by the fire in London and talk about it together. Right now I'm going to go home, and I'm going to stay with her. I'm going to do what you've told me to do, and what they've told me to do. Because that's the best thing I can do for her. And for you. I can't believe she's going to let that thing hurt you, or hurt me, or hurt anyone. But like you said, the best thing I can do is be near at hand."

"Yes, you're right," Aaron said. "But I can't stop thinking about what those old men said. About being saved. Such a strange legend."

"They were wrong about that part. She's the doorway. I knew it somehow or other when I saw that family tomb."

Aaron only sighed and shook his head. Michael could see that he was dissatisfied, that there were more things he wanted to consider. But what did they matter now? Rowan was alone in that house with that being, and the being was stealing her away from Michael, and Rowan knew all the answers now, didn't she? The being was telling her the meaning of everything, and Michael had to go home to her.

He watched anxiously as Aaron rose, a little stiffly, and went to the closet for Michael's coat and gloves.

Michael stood in the entranceway staring at the Christmas tree, with its lights burning brightly even in the light of the day.

"Why did it have to begin so soon?" he whispered. "Why now, at this time of year?" But he knew the answer. Everything that was happening was connected, somehow. All these gifts were connected with some final dénouement, and even his powerlessness was connected.

"Please be very careful," said Aaron.

"Yeah, I'll be thinking of you tomorrow night. You know, to me Christmas Eve has always been like New Year's Eve. I don't know why. Must be the Irish blood."

"The Catholic blood," said Aaron. "But I understand."

"If you break open that brandy tomorrow night, hoist one for me."

"I will. You can count on it. And Michael . . . if for any reason under God you and Rowan want to come here, you know that the door is open. Night or day. Think of this as your refuge."

"Thank you, Aaron."

"And one more thing. If you need me, if you really want me to come and believe that I should, well, then, I shall."

Michael was about to protest, to say that this was the best place for Aaron, but Aaron's eyes had moved away; his expression had brightened, and suddenly Aaron pointed to the fanlight window over the front door.

"It's snowing, Michael, look, it's really snowing. I can't believe it. It isn't even snowing in London, and look, it's snowing here."

He opened the door and they walked out on the deep front veranda together. The snow was falling in large flakes, drifting with impossible slowness and grace, down through the windless air towards the earth. It was drifting down onto the black branches of the oaks, coating them with a thick shining layer of whiteness, and making a deep white path between the two rows of trees, all the way to the road.

It was falling on the fields which were already blanketed in the same whiteness, and the sky above was shining and colorless, and seemed to be dissolving into the falling snow.

"And the day before Christmas Eve, Aaron," said Michael. He tried to see the entire spectacle—this venerable and famous avenue of old trees raising their dark knotted arms into the tumbling and gently whirling flakes of snow. "What a little miracle, that it should come now. Oh, God, it would all be so wonderful if . . ."

"May all our miracles be little ones, Michael."

"Yes, the little miracles are the best, aren't they? Look at it, it's not melting when it hits the ground. It's really staying there. It's going to be a white Christmas, no doubt about it."

"But wait a minute," said Aaron, "I almost forgot. Your Christmas present, and I have it right here." He reached inside the pocket of his sweater and he took out a very small flat package. No bigger than a half dollar. "Open it. I know we're both freezing, but I'd like it if you'd open it."

Michael tore the thin gold paper, and saw immediately that it was an old silver medal on a chain. "It's St. Michael, the archangel," he said, smiling. "Aaron, that's perfect. You're speaking to my superstitious Irish soul."

"Driving the devil into hell," said Aaron. "I found it in a little shop on Magazine Street while you were gone. I thought of you. I thought you might like to have it."

"Thank you, old buddy." Michael studied the crude image. It was worn like an old coin. But he could see the winged Michael with his trident over the horned devil who lay on his back in the flames. He lifted the chain, which was long so that he didn't have to unclasp it, and he put it over his head, and let the medal drop down under his sweater.

He stared at Aaron for a moment, and then he put his arms around him, and held him close.

"Be careful, Michael. Call me very soon."

Forty-nine

THE CEMETERY WAS closed for the night but it didn't matter. The darkness and the cold didn't matter. At the side gate the lock would be broken, and it would be very simple for her to push the gate back, and then shut it behind her, and move along the snow-covered path.

She was cold but that didn't matter either. The snow was so beautiful. She wanted to see the tomb covered with snow.

"You'll find it for me, won't you?" she whispered. It was

988

almost full darkness now and they would be coming soon, and he didn't have much time.

You know where it is, Rowan, he said in that fine subtle voice inside her head.

And she did. That was true. She was standing in front of the tomb, and the wind was chilling her, passing right through her thin shirt. There were twelve neat little headstones, one for each vault, and above was the carving of the keyhole door.

"Never to die."

That is the promise, Rowan, that is the pact that exists between you and me. We are almost at the moment of beginning . . .

"Never to die, but what did you promise the others? You promised them something. You're lying."

Oh, no, my beloved, no one matters now but you. They're all dead.

All their bones lying underneath in the frozen blackness. And the body of Deirdre, perfect still, shot full of chemicals, cold inside the satin-lined box. Cold and dead.

"Mother."

She can't hear you, beautiful one, she's gone. You and I are here.

"How can I be the doorway? Was it always meant that I would be the doorway?"

Always, my darling, and the time has almost come. One more night you'll spend with your angel of flesh and blood, and then you'll be mine forever. The stars are moving in the heavens. They are shifting into the perfect pattern.

"I can't see them. All I can see is the snow falling."

Ah, but they are there. It is the very deepest part of winter, when all that would be reborn sleeps safe in the snow.

The marble felt like ice. She put her fingers into the letters, DEIRDRE MAYFAIR. She couldn't reach the engraving of the keyhole door.

Come now, darling, come back to the house and the warmth. It's almost time. They're all coming—my children, the great clan of Mayfair, all my progeny—grown rich in the warm shadow of my wing. Back to the hearth now, beloved, but tomorrow, tomorrow, you and I shall be alone in the house. And you must drive your archangel away.

"And you'll show me how to be the doorway?"

You know, my darling. In your dreams and in your heart you've always known.

She walked swiftly over the snow, her feet wet, but it didn't matter. The streets were empty and shining in the gray dusk.

The snow was so light now it seemed a mirage. They'd be com
ing soon.

Was the tiny baby inside her cold?

Lemle had said, "There are thousands of them—millions
chucked like garbage down the drains of the world—all those
tiny brains and organs lost."

Dark and all of them coming. Essential to pretend that every
thing was normal. She was walking as fast as she could. Her
throat burned. But the cold air felt so good to her, icing her all
over, cooling the fever inside her.

And there was the house dark and waiting. She had come back
in time. She had the key in her hand.

"What if I can't get him to go tomorrow?" she whispered
She stood at the gate looking up at the empty windows. Like
that first night when Carlotta had said, Come to me. *Choose.*

But you must make him leave. By dark tomorrow, my darling
Or I'll kill him.

"No, you must never never do that. You mustn't even say it
Do you hear me? Nothing must happen to him, ever. Do you
hear me?"

She stood on the porch talking aloud to no one. And all around
her the snow came down. Snow in paradise, pelting the frozen
banana leaves, drifting past the high thick stems of bamboo. But
what would paradise have been without the beauty of snow?

"You understand me, don't you? You cannot hurt him. You
absolutely cannot hurt him. Promise me. Make the pact with
me. No harm comes to Michael."

As you wish, my darling. I do love him. But he cannot come
between us on the night of all nights. The stars are moving into
the perfect configuration. They are my eternal witnesses, old as
I am, and I would have them shine down upon me at the perfect
moment. The moment of my choosing. If you would save your
mortal lover from my wrath, see that he is gone from my sight

Fifty

IT WAS TWO in the morning before they all left. He had never seen so many happy people completely oblivious to what was really going on.

But what was really going on? It was a great warm house, full of laughter and singing, with its many fires burning, and outside the snow floating down, covering the trees and the shrubbery and the paths with luminous whiteness. And why shouldn't they all be having a wonderful time?

How they'd laughed as they slipped on the snow-covered flagstones, and crunched through the ice in the gutters. There had been enough snow even for the children to make snowballs. In their caps and mittens they had skittered along the frozen crust that covered the lawn.

Even Aunt Viv had loved the snow. She had drunk too much sherry, and in those moments reminded him frighteningly of his mother, though Bea and Lily, who had become her dearest friends, did not seem to care.

Rowan had been perfect all evening, singing carols with them at the piano, posing for the pictures before the tree.

And this was his dream, wasn't it, full of radiant faces and ringing voices, people who knew how to appreciate this moment—glasses clinked together in toasts, lips pressed to cheeks, and the melancholy sound of the old songs.

"So sweet of you to do this so soon after the wedding . . ."

". . . All gathered like in the old days."

"Christmas the way it ought to be."

And they had so admired his precious ornaments, and though they had been cautioned not to, they piled their little presents beneath the tree.

There were moments when he couldn't stand it. He'd gone upstairs to the third floor and climbed out on the roof of the north bedroom and stood near the parapet wall, looking towards downtown and the city lights. Snow on the rooftop, snow etching windowsills and gables and chimneys, and snow falling thin and beautiful, as far as he could see.

It was everything he'd ever wanted, as full and rich as the wedding, and he had never been more unhappy. It was as if that thing had its hand around his throat. He could have put his fist through a wall in his anxiety. It was bitter, bitter as grief is bitter.

And it seemed in the pockets of quiet through which he wandered, upstairs away from them, that he could feel that thing. That when he laid his naked fingers on the door frames and the doorknobs, he caught great raging glimpses of it in the shadows.

"You're here, Lasher. I know you're here."

Something stepped back for him in the shadows, playing with him, sliding up the dark walls away from him, and then dispersing so that he found himself in the upper hallway, in the dim light, alone.

Anyone spying on him would have thought he was a madman. He laughed. Is that how Daniel McIntyre had seemed in his drunken, wandering old age? What about all the other eunuch husbands who sensed the secret? They went off to mistresses—and certain death, it seemed—or drifted into irrelevance. What the hell was going to happen to him?

But this wasn't the finish. This was only the beginning, and she had to be playing for time. He had to believe that behind her silent pleas her love waited to reveal itself in truth again.

At last they'd gone.

The very last invitations to Christmas dinner had been tactfully refused, and promises had been made for future get-togethers. Aunt Viv would dine with Bea on Christmas Eve and they weren't to worry about her. They could have this Christmas to themselves.

Polaroid pictures had been exchanged and sleeping children gathered up from couches, and last-minute hugs given, and then out they all went into the clean bright cold.

Weary of the strain and sick with worry, he'd taken his time locking up. No need to smile now. No need to pretend anything. And God, what had the strain been like for her?

He dreaded going up the stairs. He went through the house checking windows, checking the little green tiny pinpoints of light on the alarm panel, and turning on the faucets to save the pipes from the freeze.

Finally he stood in the parlor, in front of his beautiful lighted tree.

Had there ever been a Christmas as bitter and lonely as this one? He would have been in a rage if it had served any purpose.

For a while he lay on the sofa, letting the fire burn itself out in the fireplace, and talking silently to Julien and Deborah, asking them as he had a thousand times tonight, what was he meant to do?

At last he climbed the stairs. The bedroom was hushed and dark. She was covered with blankets, so he saw only her hair against the pillow, her face turned away.

How many times this evening had he tried to catch her eye, and failed? Had anyone noticed that they spoke not a single syllable to each other? Everyone was too certain of their happiness. Just as he'd been so certain.

He walked silently to the front window and pulled back the heavy damask drape so that he might look at the falling snow for the last time. It was well after midnight—Christmas Eve already. And tonight would come that magic moment when he would take stock of his life and his accomplishments, when he would shape in dreams and plans the coming year.

Rowan, it's not going to end like this. It's only a skirmish. We knew at the beginning, so much more than the others . . .

He turned and saw her hand on the pillow, slender and beautiful, fingers lightly curled.

Silently he drew close to her. He wanted to touch her hand, to feel its warmth against his fingers, to grab hold of her as if she were floating away from him in some dark perilous sea. But he didn't dare.

His heart was tripping and he felt that warm pain in his chest as he looked back out into the snowfall. And then his eyes settled on her face.

Her eyes were open. She was staring at him in the darkness. And her lips slowly spread in a long, vicious smile.

He was petrified. Her face was white in the dim light from outside, and hard as marble, and the smile was frozen and the eyes gleamed like pieces of glass. His heart quickened and the warm pain spread through his chest. He continued to stare at her, unable to take his eyes off her, and then his hand shot out before he could stop it and he grabbed her wrist.

Her entire body twisted, and the vicious mask of her face crumpled completely and she sat up suddenly, anxious and confused. "What is it, Michael?" She stared at her wrist, and slowly he let her go. "I'm glad you woke me," she whispered. Her eyes were wide and her lip trembled. "I was having the most terrible dream."

"What did you dream, Rowan?"

She sat still, peering before her, and then she clasped her hands as if tearing at one with the other. And he was vaguely aware that he'd once seen her in that desperate gesture before.

"I don't know," she whispered. "I don't know what it was.

It was this place . . . centuries ago, and these doctors were gathered together. And the body lying on the table was so small.'' Her voice was low and full of agony and suddenly the tears spilled down as she looked up at him.

"Rowan."

She put up her hand. As he sank down on the side of the bed, she pressed her fingers against his lips.

"Don't say it, Michael, please. Don't say it. Don't speak a word.''

She shook her head frantically.

And sick with relief and hurt, he merely slipped his fingers around her neck, and as she bowed her head, he tried not to break down himself.

You know I love you, you know all the things I want to say.

When she was calmer, he took both of her hands and squeezed them tightly and he closed his eyes.

Trust me, Michael.

"OK, honey," he whispered. "OK." Clumsily, he stripped off his clothes, and he climbed in under the covers beside her, catching the warm clean fragrance of her flesh, and he lay there, eyes open, thinking that he would never rest, feeling her shiver against him, and then gradually as the hours ticked by, as her body softened and he saw that her eyes were closed, he slipped into uneasy sleep.

It was afternoon when he woke. He was alone, and the bedroom was suffocatingly warm. He showered and dressed and went downstairs. He couldn't find her. The lights of the tree were burning, but the house was empty.

He went through the rooms one by one.

He went outside in the coldness and walked all through the frozen garden, where the snow had become a hard glistening layer of ice over the walks and the grass. Back around the oak tree, he searched for her, but she was nowhere to be found.

And finally, he put on his heavy coat and he went out for a walk.

The sky was a deep still blue. And the neighborhood was magnificent, all dressed in white, exactly as it had been that long-ago Christmas, the last one that he was ever here.

A panic rose in him.

It was Christmas Eve and they had made no preparations. He had his little gift for her, hidden away in the pantry, a silver hand mirror which he'd found in his shop in San Francisco, and carefully wrapped long before he left, but what did it matter when she had all those jewels and all that gold, and all those riches beyond imagination? And he was alone. His thoughts were going round in circles.

Christmas Eve and the hours were melting away.

He went into the market on Washington Avenue, which was jammed with last-minute shoppers, and in a daze he bought the turkey and the other makings, rummaging in his pockets for the bills he needed, like a drunk searching for every last penny for a bottle he couldn't afford. People were laughing and chatting about the snowfall. White Christmas in New Orleans. He found himself staring at them as if they were strange animals. And all their funny noises only made him feel small and alone. He hefted the heavy sack into one arm, and started for home.

He'd walked only a few steps when he saw the firehouse where his dad had once worked. It was all done over; he scarcely recognized it now except that it was in the same place and there was the enormous archway through which the engine had roared out into the street when he was a boy. He and his dad had sat together in straight-back chairs out there on the sidewalk.

He must have looked like a drunk now, for sure stranded there, staring at the firehouse, with all the fire fighters having sense enough to be inside where it was warm. All those years ago, at Christmas, his father dying in that fire.

When he looked up at the sky, he realized it was the color of slate now, and the daylight was dying. Christmas Eve and absolutely everything had gone wrong.

No one answered his call when he came in the door. Only the tree gave off a soft glow in the parlor. He wiped his feet on the mat and walked back through the long hallway, his hands and face hurting from the cold. He unpacked the bag and put the turkey out, thinking that he would go through with all the steps, he'd do it the way he'd always done it—and tonight, at midnight, the feast would be ready, just at that hour when in the old days they'd be crowded into the church for Midnight Mass.

It wasn't Holy Communion, but it was their meal together, and this was Christmas and the house wasn't haunted and ruined and dark.

Go through the motions.

Like a priest who's sold his soul to the devil, going to the altar of God to say Mass.

He put the packages in the cupboard. It wasn't too soon to begin. He laid out the candles. Have to find the candlesticks for them. And surely she was around here somewhere. She'd gone out walking too perhaps and now she was home.

The kitchen was dark. The snow was falling again. He wanted

to turn on the lights. In fact, he wanted to turn them on everywhere, to fill the house with light. But he didn't move. He stood very still in the kitchen, looking out through the French doors over the back garden, watching the snow melt as it struck the surface of the pool. A rim of ice had formed around the edges of the blue water. He saw it glistening and he thought how cold that water must be, so awfully hurtfully cold.

Cold like the Pacific on that summer Sunday when he'd been standing there, empty and slightly afraid. The path from that moment seemed infinitely long. And it was as if all energy or will had left him now, and the cold room held him prisoner, and he could not move a finger to make himself comfortable or safe or warm.

A long time passed. He sat down at the table, lighted a cigarette and watched the darkness come down. The snow had stopped, but the ground was covered in a fresh clean whiteness again.

Time to do something, time to begin the dinner. He knew it, yet he couldn't move. He smoked another cigarette, comforted by the sight of the tiny burning red flame, and then as he crushed it out, he merely sat still, doing nothing, the way he had for hours in his room on Liberty Street, drifting in and out of a silent panic, unable to think or move.

He didn't know how long he sat there. But at some time or other, the pool lights came on, shining brilliantly up through the blackness of the night, making a great piece of blue glass of the pool. The dark foliage came alive around it, spattered with the whiteness. And the ground took on a ghostly lunar glow.

He wasn't alone. He knew it, and as the knowledge penetrated, he realized he had only to turn his head and see her standing there, in the far doorway to the pantry, with her arms folded, her head and shoulders outlined against the pale cabinets behind her, her breath making only the smallest, the most subtle sound.

This was the purest dread he'd ever known. He stood up, slipped the pack of cigarettes into his pocket, and when he looked up she was gone.

He went after her, moving swiftly through the darkened dining room and into the hallway again, and then he saw her all the way at the far end, in the light from the tree, standing against the high white front door.

He saw the keyhole shape perfect and distinct around her, and how small she looked in it, and as he came closer and closer, her stillness shocked him. He was terrified of what he'd see when he finally drew close enough to make out the features of her face in the airy dark.

But it wasn't that awful marble face he'd seen last night. She was merely looking at him, and the soft colored illumination from the tree filled her eyes with dim reflected light.

"I was going to fix our supper. I bought everything. It's back there." How uncertain he sounded. How miserable. He tried to pull himself together. He took a deep breath and hooked his thumbs in the pockets of his jeans. "Look, I can start it now. It's just a small turkey. It will be done in a few hours, and I have everything. It's all there. We'll set the table with the pretty china. We've never used any of the china. We've never had a meal on the table. This is . . . this is Christmas Eve."

"You have to go," she said.

"I . . . I don't understand you."

"You have to get out of here now."

"Rowan?"

"You have to leave, Michael. I have to be alone here now."

"Honey, I don't understand what you're telling me."

"Get out, Michael." Her voice dropped lower, becoming harder. "I want you to go."

"It's Christmas Eve, Rowan. I don't want to go."

"It's my house, Michael, I'm telling you to leave it. I'm telling you to get out."

He stared at her for a moment, stared at the way her face was changing, at the twist of her drawn lips, at the way her eyes had narrowed and she had lowered her head slightly and was looking up at him from under her brows.

"You . . . you're not making any sense, Rowan. Do you realize what you're saying?"

She took several steps towards him. He braced himself, refusing to be frightened. In fact his fear was alchemizing into anger.

"Get out, Michael," she hissed at him. "Get out of this house and leave me here to do what I must do."

Suddenly her hand swung up and forward, and before he realized what was happening, he felt the shocking slap across his face.

The pain stung him. The anger crested; but it was more bitter and painful than any anger he'd ever felt. Shocked and in a fury, he stared at her.

"It's not you, Rowan!" he said. He reached out for her, and the hand came up and as he went to block it, he felt her shove him backwards against the wall. In rage and confusion, he looked at her. She came closer, her eyes firing in the glow from the parlor.

"Get out of here," she whispered. "Do you hear what I'm saying?"

Stunned, he watched as her fingers dug into his arm. She shoved him to the left, towards the front door. Her strength was shocking to him, but physical strength had nothing to do with it. It was the malice emanating from her; it was the old mask of hate again covering her features.

"Get out of this house now, I'm ordering you out," she said, her fingers releasing him, and grabbing at the doorknob and turning it and opening the door on the cold wind.

"How can you do this to me!" he asked her. "Rowan, answer me. How can you do it?"

In desperation, he reached for her and this time nothing stopped him. He caught her and shook her, and her head fell to the side for an instant and then she turned back, merely staring at him, daring him to continue, silently forcing him to let her go.

"What good are you to me dead, Michael?" she whispered. "If you love me, leave now. Come back when I call you. I must do this alone."

"I can't. I won't do it."

She turned her back on him and walked down the hall, and he went after her.

"Rowan, I'm not going, do you hear me? I don't care what happens, I'm not leaving you. You can't ask me to do that."

"I knew you wouldn't," she said softly as he followed her into the dark library. The heavy velvet drapes were closed and he could barely see her figure as she moved towards the desk.

"Rowan, we can't go on not talking about it. It's destroying us. Rowan, listen to me."

"Michael, my beautiful angel, my archangel," she said, with her back turned to him, her words muffled. "You'd rather die, wouldn't you, than trust in me?"

"Rowan, I'll fight him with my bare hands if I have to." He came towards her. Where were the lamps in this room? He reached out, trying to find the brass lamp beside the chair, and then she wheeled around and bore down on him.

He saw the syringe raised.

"No, Rowan!"

The needle sank into his arm in the same instant.

"Christ, what have you done to me!" But he was already falling to the side, just as if he had no legs, and then the lamp went over on the floor, and he was lying beside it, staring right at the pale sharp spike of the broken bulb.

He tried to say her name, but his lips wouldn't move.

"Sleep, my darling," she said. "I love you. I love you with my whole soul."

Far far away he heard the sound of buttons on a phone. Her voice was so faint and the words . . . what was she saying? She was talking to Aaron. Yes, Aaron . . .

And when they lifted him, he said Aaron's name.

"You're going to Aaron, Michael," she whispered. "He's going to take care of you."

Not without you, Rowan, he tried to say, but he was sinking down again, and the car was moving, and he heard a man's voice: "You'll be OK, Mr. Curry. We're taking you to your friend. You just lie still back there. Dr. Mayfair said you're going to be fine."

Fine, fine, fine . . .

Hirelings. You don't understand. She's a witch, and she's put me under a spell with her poison, the way Charlotte did it to Petyr, and she's told you a damnable lie.

Fifty-one

ONLY THE TREE was lighted, and the whole house slumbered in warm darkness, except for that soft wreath of light. The cold tapped at the glass but couldn't come inside.

She sat in the middle of the sofa, her legs crossed, her arms folded, staring down the length of the room at the long mirror, barely able to see the pale glow of the chandelier.

The hands of the grandfather clock moved slowly towards midnight.

And this was the night that meant so much to you, Michael. The night when you wanted us to be together. You couldn't be farther from me now if you were on the other side of the world. All such simple and graceful things are far from me, and it is like that Christmas Eve when Lemle took me through door after door into his darkened and secret laboratory. What have such horrors to do with you, my darling?

All her life, if her life was long or short, or almost over—all her life—she'd remember Michael's face when she slapped him; she'd remember the sound of his voice when he pleaded with

999

her; she'd remember the look of shock when she'd jabbed th
needle into his arm.

So why was there no emotion? Why only this emptiness an
this shriveling stillness inside her? Her feet were bare, and th
soft flannel nightgown hung loose around her, and the silky Ch
nese rug beneath her feet was warm. Yet she felt naked an
isolated, as if nothing of warmth or comfort could ever touc
her.

Something moved in the center of the room. All the limbs o
the tree shivered, and the tiny silver bells gave off a faint barel
perceptible music in the stillness. The tiny angels with the
gilded wings danced on their long threads of gold.

A darkness was gathering and thickening.

"We are close to the hour, my beloved. To the time of m
choosing."

"Ah, but you have a poet's soul," she said, listening to th
faint echo of her own voice in this big room.

"My poetry I have learned from humans, beloved. From thos
who, for thousands of years, have loved this night of all nights.

"And now you mean to teach me science, for I don't kno
how to bring you across."

"Don't you? Haven't you always understood?"

She didn't answer. It seemed the film of her dreams thickene
about her, images catching hold and then letting go, so that he
coldness and her aloneness grew harder and more nearly ur
bearable.

The darkness grew denser. It collected itself into a shape, an
in the swirling density, she thought she saw the outline of huma
bones. The bones appeared to be dancing, gathering themselve
together, and then came the flesh over them, like the light fro
the tree pouring down over the skeleton, and the brilliant gree
eyes were suddenly peering at her from his face.

"The time is almost at hand, Rowan," he said.

In amazement she watched the lips moving. She saw the glin
mer of his teeth. She realized she'd risen to her feet and she wa
standing very close to him, and the sheer beauty of his fac
stunned her. He looked down at her, his eyes darkening slightl
and the blond eyelashes golden in the light.

"It's nearly perfect," she whispered.

She touched his face, slowly, running her finger down the ski
and stopping on the firmness of the jawbone. She placed her le
hand very gently against his chest. She closed her eyes, listenin
to the heart beat. She could see the organ inside, or was it th
replica of an organ? Shutting her eyes tighter she envisioned i

1000

s arteries and valves, and the blood rushing through it, and
pursing through the limbs.

"All you need to do is surrender!" She stood, staring at him,
seeing his lips spread in a smile. "Let go," she said. "Don't
you see, you've done it!"

"Have I?" he asked, the face working perfectly, the fine muscles flexing and releasing, the eyes growing narrow as the eyes
of any human in their concentration. "You think this is a body?
This is a replica! It's a sculpture, a statue. It's nothing, and you
now it. You think you can lure me into this shell of minuscule
feless particles so you can have me at your command? A robot?
So that you can destroy me?"

"What are you saying?" She stepped backwards. "I can't
help you. I don't know what you want of me."

"Where are you going, my darling?" he asked, eyebrows lifting ever so slightly. "You think you can flee from me? Look at
the face of the clock, my beautiful Rowan. You know what I
want. It is Christmas Eve, my darling. The witching hour is at
hand, Rowan, when Christ was born into this world, when the
Word was finally made flesh, and I would be born, too, my
beautiful witch, I am done with waiting."

He lunged forward, his right hand locking on her shoulder,
the other on her belly, a searing shimmer of warmth penetrating
her, sickening her, even as he held her.

"Get away from me!" she whispered. "I can't do it." She
called upon her anger and her will, eyes boring into those of the
thing in front of her. "You can't make me do what I won't do!"
he said. "And you can't do it without me."

"You know what I want and what I have always wanted. No
more shells, Rowan, no more coarse illusions. The living flesh
aside you. What other flesh in all the world is ready for me,
lastic, and adaptable and swarming with millions upon millions
of tiny cells which it will not use in its perfection, what other
organism has grown to a thousand times its size in the first few
weeks of its beginning, and is ready now to unfurl and lengthen
and swell as my cells merge with it!"

"Get away from me. Get away from my child! You're a stupid,
crazed thing. You won't touch my child! You won't touch me!"
She was trembling as if her anger was too great to be contained;
she could feel it boiling in her veins. Her feet were wet and
slippery on the boards as she backed away, drawing on her anger, struggling to direct it against him.

"Did you think you could trick me, Rowan?" he said in that
ow, patient, beautiful voice, his handsome image holding.
With your little performance before Aaron and Michael? Did

you think I couldn't see into the depths of your soul? I mad
your soul. I chose the genes that went into you. I chose you
parents, I chose your ancestors, I bred you, Rowan. I kno
where flesh and mind meet in you. I know your strength as n
one else knows it. And you have always known what I wante
of you. You knew when you read the history. You saw Lemle
fetus slumbering in that little bed of tubes and chemicals. Yo
knew! You knew when you ran from the laboratory what you
brilliance and courage could have done even then without me
without the knowledge that I waited for you, that I love
you, that I had the greatest gift to bestow on you. Myself, Rowar
You will help me, or that tiny simmering child will die when
go into it! And that you will never allow.''

"God. God help me!'' she whispered, her hands moving dow
over her belly, in a crisscross as if to ward off a blow, eyes fixe
on him. *Die, you son of a bitch, die!*

The hands of the clock made their tiny click as they shifte
the little hand straight up in line with the big hand. And the fir
chime of the hour sounded.

"Christ is born, Rowan,'' he cried out, his voice huge as th
image of the man dissolved in a great boiling cloud of darknes
obscuring the clock, rising to the ceiling, turning in on itself lik
a funnel. She screamed, struggling backwards against the wal
A shock ran through the rafters, through the plaster. She cou
hear it like the roar of an earthquake.

"No, God, no!'' In sheer panic, she screamed. She turne
and ran through the parlor door into the hallway. She reache
out for the knob of the front door. "God help me. Michae
Aaron!''

Somebody had to hear her screams. They were deafening
her own ears. They were ripping her apart.

But the rumbling grew louder. She felt his invisible hands o
her shoulders. She was thrown forward, hard against the doo
her hand slipping off the knob as she fell to her knees, pai
shooting up her thighs. The darkness was rising all around he
the heat was rising.

"No, not my child, I'll destroy you, with my last breath, I'
destroy you.'' She turned in one last desperate fury, facing th
darkness, spitting at it in hate, willing it to die, as the arm
wound around her and dragged her down on the floor.

The back of her head scraped the wood of the door, and the
banged against the floorboards, as her legs were wrenched for
ward. She was staring upwards, struggling to rise, her arms flai
ing, the darkness bubbling over her.

"Damn you, damn you in hell, Lasher, die. Die like that old woman! Die!" she screamed.

"Yes, Rowan, your child, and Michael's child!"

The voice surrounded her like the darkness and the heat. Her head was forced back again, slammed down again, and her arms pinned, wide and helpless.

"You my mother and Michael my father! It is the witching hour, Rowan. The clock is striking. I will be flesh. I will be born."

The darkness furled again, it coiled in upon itself and it shot downward. It shot into her, raping her, splitting her apart. Like a giant fist it shot upwards inside her womb, and her body convulsed as the pain caught her in a great lashing circle that she could see, shining bright, against her closed eyes.

The heat was unbearable. The pain came again, shock after shock of it, and she could feel the blood gushing out of her, and the water from her womb, gushing onto the floor.

"You've killed it, you damnable evil thing, you've killed my baby, damn you! God help me! God, take it back to hell!" Her hands knocked against the wall, struggled against the slimy wet floor. And the heat sickened her, caught her lungs now as she gasped for breath.

The house was burning. It had to be burning. She was burning. The heat was throbbing inside of her, and she thought she saw the flames rising, but it was only a great lurid blast of red light. And somehow she had managed to climb up on her hands and knees, again, and she knew her body was empty, her child was gone, and she was struggling now only to escape, reaching out once more, desperately and in her fierce relentless pain, for the knob of the door.

"Michael, Michael help me! Oh God, I tried to trick it, I tried to kill it. Michael, it's in the child." Another shock of pain caught her, and a fresh gush of blood poured out of her.

Sobbing, she sank down, dizzy, unable to command her arms or legs, the heat blasting her, and a great raw crying filled her ears. It was a baby's crying. It was that same awful sound she'd heard over and over in her dream. A baby's mewling cry. She struggled to cover her ears, unable to bear it, wailing for it to stop, the heat suffocating her.

"Let me die," she whispered. "Let the fire burn me. Take me to hell. Let me die."

Rowan, help me. I am in the flesh. Help me or I will die. Rowan, you cannot turn your back on me.

She tightened the grip on her ears, but she couldn't shut out the little telepathic voice that rose and fell with the baby's sobs.

Her hand slipped in the blood and her face fell down in it, stick
and wet under her, and she rolled over on her back, seeing agai
the shimmer of the heat, the baby's screams louder and loude
as though it was starving or in agony.

*Rowan, help me! I am your child! Michael's child. Rowan,
need you.*

She knew what she would see even before she looked. Throug
her tears and through the waves of heat, she saw the mani
kin, the monster. *Not out of my body, not born from me.
didn't. . . .*

On its back it lay, its man-sized head turning from side to sid
with its cries, its thin arms elongating even as she watched it
tiny fingers splayed and groping and growing, tiny feet kicking
as a baby's feet kick, working the air, the calves stretching, th
blood and mucus sliding off it, sliding down its chubby cheeks
and off its slick dark hair. All those tiny organs like buds inside
All those millions of cells dividing, merging with his cells, like
a nuclear explosion going on inside this flesh and blood thing
this mutant thing, this child that had come out of her.

*Rowan, I am alive, do not let me die. Do not let me die
Rowan. Yours is the power of saving life, and I live. Help me.*

She struggled towards it, her body still throbbing with shar
bursts of pain, her hand out for that tiny slippery leg, that little
foot pumping the air, and then as her hand closed on that soft
slick baby flesh, the darkness came down on her, and agains
her closed eyelids she saw the anatomy, saw the path of the cells
saw the evolving organs, and the age-old miracle of the cell
coming together, forming corpuscles and subcutaneous tissue
and bone tissue, and the fibers of the lungs and the liver and the
stomach, and fused with his cells, his power, the DNA merging
and the tiny chains of chromosomes whipping and swimming a
the nuclei merged, and all guided by her, all the knowledge
inside her like the knowledge of the symphony inside the com
poser, note after note and bar after bar, and crescendo following
upon crescendo.

Its flesh throbbed under her fingers, living, breathing throug
its pores. Its cries grew hoarser, deeper, echoing as she dropped
down out of consciousness and rose up again, her other hand
groping in the dark and finding his forehead, finding the thick
mass of manly curls, finding his eyes fluttering under her palm
finding his mouth now half closed with the sobs coming out of
it, finding his chest, and the heart beneath it and the long muscular arms flopping against the boards, yes, this thing so big
now that she could lay her head on its pumping chest, and the
cock between his legs, yes, and the thighs, yes, and struggling

wards, she lay on top of him, both hands on him, feeling the
se and fall of his breath beneath her, the lungs enlarging, fill-
g, the heart pumping, and dark silky hair sprouting around his
ck, and then it was a web again, a web shining in the dark-
ss, full of chemistry and mystery and certainty, and she sank
wn into the blackness, into the quiet.

A voice was talking to her, intimate and soft.

"Stop the blood."

She couldn't answer.

"You're bleeding. Stop the blood."

"I don't want to live," she said. Surely the house was burn-
g. Come, old woman, with your lamp. Light the drapes.

Lemle said, "I never said it wasn't possible, you know. The
ing is that once an advance has been envisioned, it is inevita-
e. Millions of cells. The embryo is the key to immortality."

"You can still kill him," said Petyr. He was standing over
r, looking down at her.

"They're figments of your imagination, of your conscience."

"Am I dying?"

"No." He laughed. Such a soft silky laugh. "Can you hear
e? I am laughing, Rowan. I can laugh now."

Take me to hell now. Let me die.

"No, my darling, my precious beautiful darling, stop the
eeding."

The sunlight waked her. She lay on the living room floor, on
e soft Chinese rug, and her first thought was the house had
t burned. The awful heat had not consumed it. Somehow it
d been saved.

For a moment she didn't understand what she was seeing.

A man was sitting beside her, looking down at her, and he
d the smooth unblemished skin of a baby—over the structure
 a man's face, but it resembled her face. She had never seen
human being who looked this much like her. But there were
finite differences. His eyes were large and blue and fringed
ith black lashes, and his hair was black like Michael's hair. It
as Michael's hair. Michael's hair and Michael's eyes. But he
as slender like her. His smooth hairless chest was narrow as
r chest had been in childhood, with two shining pink nipples,
d his arms were narrow, though finely muscled, and the del-
ate fingers of his hand, with which he stroked his lip thought-
lly as he looked at her, were narrow and like her fingers.

But he was bigger than she was, as big as a man. And the
ied mucus and blood was all over him, like a dark ruby red
ap covering him.

She felt a moan coming up out of her throat, pushing again her lips. Her whole body moved with it, and suddenly s screamed. Rising off the boards, she screamed. Louder, longe more wildly than she had ever screamed last night in all her fea She was this scream, leaving herself, leaving everything she seen and remembered in total horror.

His hand came down over her mouth, pushing her flat again the rug. She couldn't move. The scream was turning arou inside, like vomit that could choke her. A deep convulsion pain moved through her. She lay limp, silent.

He leaned over her. "Don't do it," he whispered. The o voice. Of course, his voice, with his unmistakable inflection.

His smooth face looked perfectly innocent, a picture of asto ishment with its flawless and radiant cheeks, and its smoo narrow nose, and the great blue eyes blinking at her. Snappi open and closed like the eyes of the manikin on the table in h dreams. He smiled. "I need you," he said. "I love you. A I'm your child."

After a while, he took his hand away.

She sat up. Her nightgown was soaked with blood and d and stiff with it. The smell of blood was everywhere. Like t smell of the Emergency Room.

She scooted back on the rug and sat forward, her kn crooked, peering at him.

Nipples, perfect, yes, cock perfect, yes, though the real te would come when it was hard. Hair perfect, yes, but what abo inside? What about every precise little interlocking part?

She drew closer, staring at his shoulders, watching the ri and fall of his chest with his breath, then looking into his eye not seeing him look back, not caring if he did, just studying t texture of the flesh and the lips.

She laid her hand on his chest and listened. A strong, stea rhythm coming from him.

He didn't move to stop her as she laid her hands on both sid of his skull. Soft, like a baby's skull, able to heal after blo that would kill a man of twenty-five. God, but how long was going to be that way?

She put her finger against his lower lip, opening his mou and staring at his tongue. Then she sat back, her hands lyi limp on her folded legs.

"Are you hurting?" he asked her. His voice was very tende He narrowed his eyes, and for just a second there was a litt bit of mature expression in the face, and then it returned to ba wonder. "You lost so much blood."

For a long moment she stared at him in silence.

He waited, merely watching her.

"No, I'm not hurt," she murmured. Again she stared at him for the longest time. "I need things," she said finally. "I need a microscope. I need to take blood samples. I need to see what the tissues really are now! God, I need all these things! I need a fully equipped laboratory. And we've got to leave here."

"Yes," he said, nodding. "That should be the very next thing that we do. Leave here."

"Can you stand up?"

"I don't know."

"Well, you're going to try," She climbed to her knees, and then grasping the edge of the marble mantel, climbed to her feet.

She took his hand, nice tight grip. "Come on, stand up, don't think about it, just do it, call on your body to know, the musculature is there, that's what differentiates you completely from a newborn, you have the skeleton and musculature of a man."

"All right, I'll try," he said. He looked frightened and also strangely delighted. Shuddering, he struggled to his knees first, as she had done, and then to his feet, only to tumble backwards, catching himself from falling with one hasty back step after another.

"Ooooh . . ." He sang it out. "I'm walking, I am, I'm walking . . ."

She rushed towards him and wrapped her arm around him and let him cling to her. He grew quiet looking down at her, and then raised his hand and stroked her cheek, the gesture imperfectly coordinated, rather like a drunken gesture, but the fingers silky and tingling.

"My beautiful Rowan," he said. "Look, the tears are rising in my eyes. Real tears. Oh, Rowan."

He tried to stand freely and to bend down to kiss her. She caught him and steadied him as his lips closed over hers, and that same powerful sensual shock passed through her that had always come with his touch.

"Rowan," he moaned aloud, crushing her against him, then slipping backwards until she brought him up short again in her arms.

"Come, we haven't much time," she said. "We have to find some place safe, some place completely unknown . . ."

"Yes, darling, yes . . . but you see it's all so new and so beautiful. Let me hold you again, let me kiss you . . ."

"There isn't time," she said, but the silken baby lips had clamped on hers again, and she felt his cock pressing against her sex, pressing into the soreness. She pulled away, drawing him after her.

"That's it," she said, watching his feet, "don't think about it. Just look at me and walk."

For one second, as she found herself in the doorway, as she was conscious of its keyhole shape, and the old discussions of its significance, all the misery and beauty of her life passed before her eyes, all her struggles and all former vows.

But this was a new door all right. It was the door she'd glimpsed a million years ago in her girlhood when she'd first opened the magical volumes of scientific lore. And it was open now, quite beyond the horrors of Lemle's laboratory, and the Dutchmen gathered around the table in a mythical Leiden.

She guided him slowly through the door and up the stairs, walking patiently, step by step, at his side.

Fifty-two

HE WAS TRYING to wake up, but every time he came near the surface, he went down again, heavy and drowsy and sinking into the soft feathery covers of the bed. The desperation would grip him and then it would go away.

It was the sickness that finally woke him. It seemed forever that he sat on the bathroom floor, against the door, vomiting so violently that a pain locked around his ribs each time he retched. Then there was nothing more to heave up, and the nausea just lay on him with no promise of relief.

The room was tilting. They had finally got the lock off the door, and they were picking him up. He wanted to say that he was sorry he'd locked it, reflex action, and he had been trying to get to the knob to open the door, but he couldn't make the words come out.

Midnight. He saw the dial of the clock on the dresser. Midnight of Christmas Eve. And he struggled to say there was a meaning to it, but it was impossible to do more than think of that thing standing behind the crib in the sanctuary. And he was sinking again, as his head hit the pillow.

When next he opened his eyes, the doctor was talking to him again, but he couldn't recall just when he'd seen the doctor before. "Mr. Curry, do you have any idea what might have been in the injection?"

No. I thought she was killing me. I thought I was going to die. Just trying to move his lips made him sick. He only shook his head, and that too made him sick. He could see the blackness of night still beyond the frost on the windows.

". . . at least another eight hours," said the doctor.

"Sleep, Michael. Don't worry now. Sleep."

"Everything else normal. Clear liquids if he should ask for something to drink. If there's the slightest change . . ."

Treacherous witch. Everything destroyed. The man smiling at him from above the crib. Of course it had been the time. The very time. He knew that he had lost her forever. Midnight Mass was over. His mother was crying because his father was dead. Nothing will ever be the same now.

"Just sleep it off. We're here with you."

I've failed. I didn't stop him. I've lost her forever.

"How long have I been here?"

"Since yesterday evening."

Christmas morning. He was staring out the window, afraid to move for fear of being sick again. "It's not snowing anymore, is it?" he said. He barely heard the answer, that it had stopped some time before daybreak.

He forced himself to sit up. Nothing as bad as before. A headache yes, and a little blur to his vision. Nothing worse than a hangover.

"Wait, Mr. Curry. Please. Let me call Aaron. The doctor will want to see you."

"Yeah, that would be fine, but I'm getting dressed."

All his clothes were in the closet. Nice little traveler's kit under plastic on the bathroom vanity. He showered, fighting an occasional bout of dizziness, shaved recklessly and fast with the little throwaway, and then came out of the bathroom. He wanted to sink down into the bed again, no doubt about it, but he said:

"I gotta go back there, find out what went down."

"I'm begging you to wait," said Aaron, "to take some food, see how you feel."

"Doesn't matter how I feel. Can you give me a car? I'll hitch if you can't."

He looked out the window. Snow still on the ground. Roads would be dangerous. Had to go now.

"Look, I can't thank you enough for taking care of me like this."

"What do you mean to do? You don't have any idea what

you'll find. Last night she told me that if I cared about you, to see that you didn't come back.''

''Hell with what she said. I'm going.''

''Then I'm going too.''

''No, you stay here. This is between me and her. Get me a car, now, I'm leaving.''

It was a big bulky gray Lincoln Town Car, hardly his choice though the soft leather seat felt good, and the thing really cruised when he finally reached the interstate highway. Up until that point, Aaron had been following in the limo. But there was no sight of him now, as Michael passed one car after another.

The snow was dirty at the sides of the road. But the ice was gone. And the sky above was that faultless mocking blue which made everything look clean and wide open. The headache gripped him, throwing a curve of dizziness and nausea at him every fifteen minutes. He just shook it off, and kept his foot on the gas pedal.

He was going ninety when he cruised into New Orleans, going up past the cemeteries of Metairie and through the rooftops and then past the ludicrous surreal spectacle of the Superdome amphitheater, like a space saucer just touching down amid sky-scrapers and church steeples.

He braked too fast, nearly skidding as he took the St. Charles Avenue turnoff. Traffic crawled amid the frozen strips of soiled snow.

Within five minutes, he made the left turn onto First, and then the car skidded dangerously again. He braked and crept his way over the slick asphalt, until he saw the house rising up like a somber fortress on its dark, shady snow-covered corner.

The gate was open. He put his key into the front door and let himself in.

For a moment, he stood stock-still. There was blood all over the floor, smeared and streaked, and the bloody print of a hand on the door frame. Something that looked like soot covered the walls, thinning out to a pale grime as it reached the ceiling.

The smell was foul, like the smell of the sickroom in which Deirdre died.

Smears of blood on the doorway to the living room. Tracks of bare feet. Blood all over the Chinese carpet, and some viscous mucuslike substance smeared on the boards, and the Christmas tree with all its lights burning, like an oblivious sentinel at the end of the room, a blind and dumb witness who could testify to nothing.

The ache was exploding in his head, but it was nothing compared to the pain in his chest, and the rapid knocking in his heart. The adrenaline was flooding his veins. And his right hand was curling convulsively into a fist.

He turned around, went out of the parlor and into the hall, and headed towards the dining room.

Without a sound, a figure stepped into the high keyhole door, peering at him, one slender hand moving up on the door frame.

It was a strange gesture. Something distinctly unsteady about the figure as if it too were reeling from shocks, and as it came forward into the light from the sun porch, Michael stopped, studying it, straining to understand what he was seeing.

This was a man, clothed in loose disheveled pants and shirt, but Michael had never seen a man like him. The man was very tall, maybe six feet two inches in height and disproportionately slender. The pants were too large, and apparently cinched tight at the waist, and the shirt was Michael's shirt, an old sweatshirt. It hung like a tunic on the slender frame. He had rich black curly hair and very large blue eyes, but otherwise he resembled Rowan. It was like looking at a male twin of Rowan! The skin was like Rowan's smooth and youthful skin, only even more youthful than that, stretching over Rowan's cheekbones, and this was almost Rowan's mouth, just a little fuller, and more sensuous. And the eyes, though large and blue, had Rowan in them, and there was Rowan in the man's sudden thin, cold smile.

He took another step towards Michael, and Michael could see he was unsteady on his feet. A radiance emanated from him. And Michael realized what it was, contradicting reason and experience, but perfectly obvious in a hideous sort of way, that the thing looked newborn, that it had the soft resilient brilliance of a baby. Its long thin hands were baby smooth, and its neck was baby smooth, and the face had no stamp of character whatsoever.

Yet the expression on its face was no baby's expression. It was filled with wonder, and seeming love, and a terrible mockery.

Michael lunged at it, catching it by surprise. He held its thin powerful arms in his hands, and was astonished and horrified by the riff of soft virile laughter that broke from it.

Lasher, alive before, alive again, back into the flesh, defeating you! Your child, your genes, your flesh and her flesh, love you, defeated you, used you, thank you, my chosen father.

In blind rage, Michael stood, unable to move, his hands clutching the arms of the being, as it struggled to free itself, pulling loose suddenly with a great arching gesture, like a bird drawing back, made of rubber and steel and flexing and preening.

1011

A low shuddering roar came out of Michael.

"You killed my child! Rowan, you gave him our child!" His cry was guttural and anguished, the words rushing together in his own ears like noise. "Rowan!"

Away from him the creature dashed, crashing awkwardly against the dining room wall, again throwing up its hands and laughing. It thrust its arm out, its huge smooth hand slamming Michael in the chest with ease and throwing him over the dining room table.

"I am your child, Father, step back. Look at me!"

Michael scrambled back onto his feet.

"Look at you? I'll kill you!"

He flew at the creature, but it danced back into the pantry, arching its back and extending its hands as if to tease. It waltzed backwards through the kitchen door. Its legs tangled, then straightened as if it were a straw man. Again its laughter rose, rich and deep and full of crazy merriment. The laughter was crazed like the eyes of the being, full of mad and uncaring delight.

"Oh, come on, Michael, don't you want to know your own child! You can't kill me! You can't kill your own flesh and blood! I have your genes in me, Michael. I am you, I am Rowan. I am your son."

Lunging again, Michael caught it and hurled it back against the French doors, rattling the panes. High up on the front of the house, the alarm sounded as the glass protectors tripped, adding its maddening peal to the mayhem.

The creature flung its long gangly arms up, gazing down at Michael in astonishment as his hands closed on its throat. Then it lifted its two hands in fists and slammed them into Michael's jaw.

Michael's feet went out from under him, but hitting the floor he rolled over at once on his hands and knees. The French door was open, the alarm still screaming, and the creature was dancing, pivoting, and frolicking with a hideous grace towards the pool.

As he went after it, he saw Rowan coming in the corner of his eye, rushing down the kitchen stairs. He heard her scream.

"Michael, stay away from him!"

"You did that, Rowan, you gave him our child! He's in our child!" He turned, his arm raised, but he couldn't hit her. Frozen, he stared at her. She was the very image of terror, her face blanched and her mouth wet and quivering. Helpless, shuddering, the pain squeezing in his chest like a bellows, he turned and glared at the thing.

It was skipping back and forth on the snow covered flagstones beside the rippling blue water, pitching its head forward and placing its hands on its knees, and then pointing to Michael. Its voice, loud and distinct, rose over the shrilling of the alarm.

"You'll get over it, as mortals say, you'll see the light, as mortals say! You've created quite a child, Michael. Michael, I am your handiwork. I love you. I have always loved you. Love has been the definition of my ambition, they are one and the same with me, I present myself to you in love."

He went out the door as Rowan rushed towards him. He went straight for the thing, sliding on the frozen snow, tearing loose from her as she tried to stop him. She went down on the ground as if she were made of paper, and a whipping pain stung his neck. She had caught the St. Michael medal by its chain, and he had the broken chain now in her hands, and the medal fell into the snow. She was sobbing and begging him to stop.

No time for her. He spun round and his powerful left hook went up, bashing into the side of the creature's head. It gave another peal of laughter even as the red blood spurted from the ruptured flesh. It tipped and spun around, slipping on the ice and careening into the iron chairs and knocking them askew.

"Oh, now look what you've done, oh, you can't imagine how that feels! Oh, I have lived for this moment, this extraordinary moment!"

With a sudden pivot, it dove for Michael's right arm, catching it and twisting it painfully back, its eyebrows raised, lips drawn back in a smile, pearly teeth flashing white against its pink tongue. All new, all shining, all pristine, like a baby.

Michael drove another left into its chest, feeling the crunch of bones.

"Yeah, you like it, you evil thing, you greedy son of a bitch, die!" He spit at it, driving his left fist into it again, even as it clung to his right wrist, like an unfurling flag tied to him. The blood squirted out of its mouth. "Yeah! You're in the flesh—now die in it!"

"I'm losing patience with you!" the creature howled, glaring down at the blood dripping from its lip all over its shirt. "Oooh, look what you've done, you angry father, you righteous parent!" It jerked Michael forward, off balance, its grip on his wrist like iron.

"You like it?" Michael cried. "You like your bleeding flesh," he roared, "my child's flesh, my flesh!" Wringing his right hand and unable to free it, he closed his left fingers around the thing's smooth throat, jabbing his thumb into its windpipe while his knee rammed into its scrotum. "Oh, she made you really complete, didn't she, right down to the outdoor plumbing!"

In a flash he saw Rowan again, but it was the thing that knocked her down this time as it let go of Michael at last. She fell against the balustrade.

The thing was shrieking in pain, the blue eyes rolling in its head. Before Rowan could get to her feet, it shot backwards, shoulders rising like wings, and then lowering its head, it cried "You are teaching me, Father. Oh yes, you're teaching me well!" A growl overrode the words, and it ran at Michael, butting him in the chest with its head, striking him one fine blow that hurled him off his feet and out over the swimming pool.

Rowan gave a deafening cry, far louder and more shrill than the siren of the alarm.

But Michael had crashed into the icy water. He sank down, down, into the deep end, the blue surface glittering high above him. The freezing temperature shocked the breath out of him. He was motionless, scalded by the cold, unable even to move his arms, until he felt his body scrape along the bottom.

Then in a desperate convulsion he started for the top, his clothes like fingers grabbing him and holding him down. And as his head passed through the surface into the blinding light, he felt another thudding blow and sank again, rising, only to be held under, his hands up in the air, free in the air, clawing futilely at the thing that held him, his mouth swallowing gulp after gulp of cold water.

Happening again, drowning again, this cold cold water. No, not like this, not again. He tried to close his mouth, but the exploding pain in his chest was too great and the water poured into his lungs. His hands could feel nothing above; and he could no longer see either color or light, or even sense up from down. And in a flash he saw the Pacific again, endless and gray, and the lights of the Cliff House dimming and vanishing as the waves rose around him.

Suddenly his body relaxed; he wasn't struggling desperately to breathe or to rise, not clawing at anything. In fact, he wasn't in his body at all. He knew this feeling, this weightlessness, this sublime freedom.

Only he wasn't traveling upward, not rising buoyant and free the way he had that long-ago day, right up into the leaden gray sky and the clouds, from which he could see all the earth down there below with its millions upon millions of tiny beings.

He was in a tunnel this time, and he was being sucked down, and it was dark and close and there seemed no end to the jour ney. In a great rush of silence, he plummeted, completely without will, and full of vague wonder.

At last a great splashing red light surrounded him. He had fallen into a familiar place. Yes, the drums, he heard the drums, the old familiar Mardi Gras cadence of marching drums, the sound of the Comus parade moving swiftly through the winter dark on the tired dreary edge of Mardi Gras night, and the flicker of the flames was the flicker of the flambeaux beneath the twisted elbows of the oaks, and his fear was the all-knowing little boy's fear of long ago, and it was all here, everything he'd feared, happening at last, not a mere glimpse on the edge of dream, or with Deirdre's nightgown in his hands, but here, around him.

His feet had struck the steaming ground, and as he tried to stand up, he saw the branches of the oaks had gone right up through the plaster roof of the parlor, catching the chandelier in a tangle of leaves, and brushing past the high mirrors. And this was really the house. Countless bodies writhed in the dark. He was stepping on them! Gray, naked shapes fornicating and twisting in the flames and in the shadows, the smoke billowing up to obscure the faces of all those surrounding him and looking at him. But he knew who they were. Taffeta skirts, cloth brushing him. He stumbled and tried to get his balance but his hand just passed right through the burning rock, his feet went down into the steaming muck.

In a circle the nuns were coming, tall black-robed figures with stiff white wimples, nuns whose names and faces he knew from childhood, rosaries rattling, their feet pounding on the heart pine floor as they came, and they closed the circle around him. Stella stepped through the circle, eyes flashing, her marcelled hair shining with pomade, and suddenly reached for him and tugged him towards her.

"Let him alone, he can climb up on his own," said Julien. And there he was, the man himself with his curling white hair and his small glittering black eyes, his clothes immaculate and fine, and his hand rising as he smiled and beckoned:

"Come on, Michael, get up," he said, with the sharp French accent. "You're with us now, it's quite finished, and stop fighting at once."

"Yes, get up, Michael," said Mary Beth, her dark taffeta skirt brushing his face, a tall stately woman, hair shot through and through with gray.

"You're with us now, Michael." It was Charlotte with her radiant blond hair, bosom bulging over her taffeta décolletage, lifting him, though he struggled to get away. His hand went right through her breast.

1015

"Stop it, get away from me!" he cried. "Get away."

Stella was naked except for the little chemise falling off her shoulder, the whole side of her head dripping with blood from the bullet.

"Come on, Michael darling, you're here now, to stay, don't you see, it's finished, darling. Job well done."

The drums were thudding closer and closer, battering at the keening song of a Dixieland band, and the coffin lay open at the end of the room, with the candles around it. The candles were going to catch the drapes and burn the place down!

"Illusion, lies," he cried. "It's a trick." He tried to stand up straight, to find some direction in which to run, but everywhere he looked he saw the nine-paned windows, the keyhole doors, the oak branches piercing the ceiling and the walls and the whole house like a great monstrous trap re-forming around the struggling gnarled trees, flames reflected in the high narrow mirrors, couches and chairs overgrown with ivy and blossoming camellias. The bougainvillea swept over the ceiling, curling down by the marble mantels, tiny purple petals fluttering into the smoking flames.

The nun's hand suddenly came down like a board against the side of his face, the pain shocking him and maddening him. "What do you say, boy! Of course you're here, stand up!" That bellowing coarse voice. "Answer me, boy!"

"Get away from me!" He shoved at her in panic, but his hand passed through her.

Julien was standing there with his hands clasped behind his back, shaking his head. And behind Julien stood handsome Cortland, with his father's same expression and his father's same mocking smile.

"Michael, it should be perfectly obvious to you that you have performed superbly," said Cortland, "that you bedded her, brought her back, and got her with child, which is exactly what we wanted you to do."

"We don't want to fight," said Marguerite, her haglike hair veiling her face as she reached out for him. "We're all on the same side, *mon cher*. Stand up, please, come to us."

"Come now, Michael, you're making all this confusion yourself," said Suzanne, her big simpleton eyes flashing and snapping as she helped him to his feet, her breasts poking through the filthy rags.

"Yes, you did it, my son," said Julien. "*Eh bien*, you have been marvelous, both of you, you and Rowan, you have done precisely what you were born to do."

"And now you can go back through with us," said Deborah.

She raised her hands for the others to step aside, the flames rising behind her, the smoke curling over her head. The emerald glimmered and winked against her dark blue velvet gown. The girl of Rembrandt's painting, so beautiful with her ruddy cheeks and her blue eyes, as beautiful as the emerald. "Don't you see? That was the pact. Now that he's gone through, we're all going to go back through! Rowan knows how to bring us back through, the same way that she brought him through. No, Michael, don't struggle. You want to be with us, earthbound here, to wait your turn, otherwise you'll simply be dead forever."

"We're all saved now, Michael," said fragile Antha, standing like a little girl in her simple flowered dress, blood pouring down her face on both sides from the bashed-in wound on the back of her head. "And you can't imagine how long we've been waiting. One loses track of time here . . ."

"Yes, saved," said Marie Claudette. She was sitting in a big four-poster bed, with Marguerite beside her, the flames twining around the posts, eating at the canopy. Lestan and Maurice stood behind the bed, looking on with vaguely bored expressions, the light glimmering on their brass buttons, flames licking at the edges of their flared coats.

"They burned us out in Saint-Dominigue," said Charlotte, holding the folds of her lovely skirt daintily. "And the river took our old plantation."

"But this house will stand forever," said Maurice gravely, eyes sweeping the ceiling, the medallions, the listing chandeliers, "thanks to your fine efforts at restoration, and we have this safe and marvelous place in which to wait our turn to become flesh again."

"We're so glad to have you, darling," said Stella, with the same bored air, shifting her weight suddenly so that her left hip poked out the silk chemise. "Surely you don't want to pass up an opportunity like this."

"I don't believe you! You're lies, figments!" Michael spun round, head crashing through the peach-colored plaster wall. The potted fern went over on the floor. Couples writhing before him snarled as his foot went through them—through the back of the man and the belly of the woman.

Stella giggled and sprinted across the floor, pitching herself back into the satin-lined coffin and reaching out for her glass of champagne. The drums were growing louder and louder. Why doesn't everything catch fire, why doesn't it all burn?

"Because this is hell, son," said the nun, who raised her hand to slap him again. "And it just burns and burns."

"Stop it, let me go!"

He crashed into Julien, falling forward, the flames flashing upward in a heated blast into his face.

But the nun had him by his collar. She had the St. Michael medal in her hand. "You dropped this, didn't you? And I told you to take care of it, didn't I? And where did I find it? I found it lying on the ground, that's where I found it!" And wham, the slap struck him again, fierce and hurtful, and he seethed with rage. She shook him as he slipped onto his knees, hands struggling to shove her away.

"All you can do now is be with us, and go back through!" said Deborah. "Don't you understand? The doorway is open; it's just a matter of time. Lasher and Rowan will bring us through, Suzanne first, then I shall go and then—"

"No, wait a minute now, I never agreed to any such order," said Charlotte.

"Neither did I," said Julien.

"Who said anything about order!" roared Marie Claudette, kicking the quilt off her legs as she sat forward in the bed.

"Why are you being so foolish!" said Mary Beth, with a bored, matter-of-fact air. "My God, everything has been fulfilled. And there is no limit to how many times the transmutation can be effected, and you can imagine, can't you, the superior quality of the mutated flesh and the mutated genes. This is actually a scientific advance of stunning brilliance."

"All natural, Michael, and to understand that is to understand the essence of the world, that things are—hmmmm, more or less predetermined," said Cortland. "Don't you know you were in our hands from the very beginning?"

"That is the crucial point for you to understand," said Mary Beth reasonably.

"The fire that killed your father," said Cortland, "that was no accident . . ."

"Don't say these things to me!" roared Michael. "You didn't do that. I don't believe it. I don't accept it!"

". . . to position you exactly, and see to it that you had the desired combination of sophistication and charm, so as to command her attention and cause her to let down her guard . . ."

"Don't bother talking to him," the tall nun snapped, her rosary beads jangling together as they hung from her thick leather belt. "He's incorrigible. You just leave him to me. I'll slap the fire out of him."

"It isn't true," he said, trying to shield his eyes from the glare of the flames, the drums pounding through his temples. "This is not the explanation," he cried. "This is not the final meaning." He outshouted the drums.

"Michael, I warned you," came the piteous little voice of Sister Bridget Marie, who peeped around the side of the mean nun. "I told you there were witches in those dark streets."

"Come here at once, and have some champagne," said Stella. "And stop creating all these hellish images. Don't you see, when you're earthbound you create your surroundings."

"Yes, you are making it so ugly here!" said Antha.

"There are no flames here," said Stella. "That's in your head. Come, let's dance to the drums, oh, I have grown so to love this music. I do like your drums, your crazy Mardi Gras drums!"

He thrashed with both his arms, his lungs burning, his chest about to burst. "I won't believe it. You're all his little joke, his trick, his connivance—"

"No, *mon cher*," said Julien, "we are the final answer and the meaning."

Mary Beth shook her head sadly, looking at him. "We always were."

"The hell you are!"

He was on his feet at last. He twisted loose from the nun, ducking her next slap, and gliding through her, and now he sped through Julien's thickening form, blind for a moment, but emerging free, ignoring the laughter, and the drums.

The nuns closed ranks but he went through. Nothing was going to stop him. He could see the way out, he could see the light pouring through the keyhole door. "I will not, I will not believe . . ."

"Darling, think back to the first drowning," said Deborah, suddenly beside him, trying to capture his hand. "It was what we explained to you before when you were dead, that we needed you, and you did agree, but of course we knew you were just bargaining for your life, lying to us, you see, and we knew that if we didn't make you forget, you would never never fulfill—"

"Lies! Lasher's lies!" He pulled free of her.

Only a few more feet to the door, and he could make it. He pitched forward, stumbling again over the bodies that littered the floor, stepping on backs and shoulders and heads, smoke stinging his eyes. But he was getting closer to the light.

And there was a figure in the doorway, and he knew that helmet, that long mantle, he knew that garb. Yes, knew it, very familiar to him.

"I'm coming," he cried out.

But his lips had barely moved.

He was lying on his back.

His body was shot through and through with pain, and the

frozen silence closed around him. And the sky high above was that dizzying blue.

He heard the voice of the man over him saying, "That's right, son, breathe!"

Yes, knew that helmet and that mantle, because it was a fire fighter's garb, and he was lying by the pool, sprawled on the icy cold flagstones, his chest burning, his arms and legs aching, and it was a fireman bending over him, clapping the plastic oxygen mask to his face and squeezing the bag beside him, a fireman with a face just like his dad's face, and the man said again: "That's it, son, breathe!"

The other firemen stood over him, great shadowy shapes against the moving clouds, all familiar by virtue of their helmets and their coats, as they cheered him on with voices so like his father's voice.

Each breath he took was a raw throb of pain, but he drew the air down into his lungs, and as they lifted him, he closed his eyes.

"I'm here, Michael," Aaron said. "I'm at your side."

The pain in his chest was enormous and pressing against his lungs, and his arms were numb. But the darkness was clean and quiet and the stretcher felt as if it were flying as they wheeled him along.

Argument, talk, the crackle of those walkie-talkie things. But none of it mattered. He opened his eyes and saw the sky flashing overhead. Ice dripping from the frozen withered bougainvillea, as they went past, all its blossoms dead. Out the gate, wheels bouncing on the uneven flagstones.

Somebody pressed the little mask hard over his face as they lifted him into the ambulance. "Cardiac emergency, coming in now, requesting . . ." Blankets all around him.

Aaron's voice again, and then another:

"He's fibrillating again! Damn it! Go!"

The doors of the ambulance slammed, his body rocking to the side slightly as they pulled away from the curb.

The fist came down on his chest, once, twice, again. Oxygen pumping into him through the plastic mask, like a cold tongue.

The alarm was still going, or was it their siren singing like that, a faraway cry, like the cries of those desperate birds in the early morning, crows cawing in the big oaks, as if scratching at the rosy sky, at the dark deep moss-covered silence.

EPILOGUE

Fifty-three

SOME TIME BEFORE nightfall, he understood he was in the critical care unit, that his heart had stopped in the pool, and again on the way in, and a third time in the Emergency Room. They were regulating his pulse now with a powerful drug called lidocaine, which was why he was in a mental fog, unable to hang on to any complete thought.

Aaron was allowed in to see him for five minutes during every hour. At some point Aunt Vivian was there too. And then Ryan came.

Various faces appeared over his bed; different voices spoke to him. It was daylight again when the doctor explained that the weakness he felt was to be expected. The good news was that he had sustained relatively little damage to the heart muscle; in fact he was already recovering. They would keep him on the regulating drugs, and the blood thinners, and the drugs that dissolved the cholesterol. Rest and heal were the last words he heard as he went under again.

It must have been New Year's Eve that they finally explained things to him. By then the medication had been reduced and he was able to follow what they were saying.

There'd been no one on the premises when the fire engine arrived. Just the alarm screaming. Not only had the glass protectors gone off, but somebody had pushed the auxiliary buttons for fire, police, and medical emergency. Rushing through the gate and back the side path, the fire fighters had immediately spotted the broken glass outside the open French doors, the overturned furniture on the veranda, and the blood on the flagstones. Then they spotted the dark shape floating just beneath the surface of the swimming pool.

Aaron had arrived about the time they were bringing Michael around. So had the police. They had searched the house, but could find no one. There was unexplained blood in the house,

and evidence of some sort of fire. Closets and drawers were ope
upstairs, and a half-packed suitcase was open on the bed. B
there was no other evidence of a struggle.

It was Ryan who determined, later that same afternoon, tha
Rowan's Mercedes convertible was gone, and that her purse an
any and all identification were also gone. No one could find he
medical bag, though the cousins were sure they had seen such
thing.

In the absence of any coherent explanation of what had hap
pened, the family was thrown into a panic. It was too soon t
report Rowan as a missing person, nevertheless police began a
unofficial search. Her car was found in the airport parking ga
rage before midnight, and it was soon confirmed that she ha
purchased two tickets to New York earlier that afternoon, an
that her plane had safely landed on schedule. A clerk remem
bered her, and that she'd been traveling with a tall man. Th
stewardesses remembered both parties, and that they were talk
ing and drinking during the entire flight. There was no evidenc
of coercion or foul play. The family could do nothing but wa
for Rowan to contact them, or for Michael to explain what ha
happened.

Three days later, on December 29, a wire had been receive
from Rowan from Switzerland, in which she explained that sh
would be in Europe for some time and instructions regardin
her personal affairs would follow. The wire contained one of
series of code words known only to the designee of the legac
and the firm of Mayfair and Mayfair. And this confirmed to th
satisfaction of everyone involved that the wire had indeed com
from Rowan. Instructions were received the same day for a sub
stantial transfer of funds to a bank in Zurich. Once again th
correct code words were used. Mayfair and Mayfair had n
grounds for questioning Rowan's instructions.

On January 6, when Michael was moved out of the critica
care unit into a regular private room, Ryan came to visit, ap
parently extremely confused and uncomfortable about th
messages he had to relay. He was as tactful as possible.

Rowan would be gone "indefinitely." Her specific where
abouts were not known, but she had been in frequent touch wit
Mayfair and Mayfair through a law firm in Paris.

Complete ownership of the First Street house was to be give
to Michael. No one in the family was to challenge his full an
exclusive right to the property. It was to remain in his hands
and his hands only, until the day he died, at which time it woul
revert—according to law—to the legacy.

As for Michael's living expenses, he was to have carte blanche to the full extent that Rowan's resources allowed. In other words, he was to have all the money he wanted or ever asked for, without specified limit.

Michael said nothing when he heard this.

Ryan assured him that he was there to see to Michael's smallest wish, that Rowan's instructions were lengthy and explicit, and that Mayfair and Mayfair was prepared to carry them out to the smallest detail. Whenever Michael was ready to go home, every preparation would be made for his comfort.

He didn't even hear most of what Ryan was saying to him. There was no need really to explain to Ryan, or anyone else, the full irony of this turn of events, or how his thoughts were running, day in and day out, in a druggy haze, over all the events and turns of his life from the time of his earliest memories.

When he closed his eyes, he saw them all again, in the flames and the smoke, the Mayfair Witches. He heard the beat of the drums, and he smelled the stench of the flames, and he heard Stella's piercing laughter.

Then it would slip away.

The quiet would return, and he would be back in his early childhood, walking up First Street that long-ago Mardi Gras night with his mother, thinking, Ah, what a beautiful house.

Some time later, when Ryan had stopped talking and sat patiently in the room merely studying Michael, a load of questions obviously crowding Ryan's brain, all of which he was afraid to voice, Michael asked if the family hated his being in the house. If they wanted him to relinquish it.

Ryan explained that they did not hate it at all. That they hoped Michael would live in the house. That they hoped Rowan would return, that some sort of reconciliation could be effected. And then Ryan seemed at a loss. Embarrassed and obviously deeply distressed, he said in a raw voice that the family "just couldn't understand what had happened."

A number of possible responses ran through Michael's mind. From a cool distance, he imagined himself making mysterious remarks that would richly feed the old family legends; obscure allusions to the thirteen and to the door, and to "the man"; remarks that would be discussed for years to come perhaps, on lawns and at dinners, and in funeral parlors. But it was really unthinkable to do that. In fact, it was absolutely crucial to remain silent.

Then he heard himself say, with extraordinary conviction, "Rowan will come back." And he didn't say anything after that.

Early the next day, when Ryan came again, Michael did make one request—that his Aunt Vivian move into the house, if she wanted to. He didn't see any reason now for her to be alone i her apartment on the avenue. And if Aaron could be his gue at the house, that too would make him happy.

Ryan went into a long-drawn-out lawyerly confirmation th; the house was Michael's house, and that Michael need ask n one's permission or approval to implement his smallest or grea est wish with regard to things at First Street. To this Ryan adde his own deepest concern that Michael call upon him for "ab solutely anything."

Finally in the silence which ensued, Ryan broke down. H said he couldn't understand where he and the family had faile Rowan. Rowan had begun shifting enormous sums of money ot of their hands. The plans for Mayfair Medical had been put o hold. He simply couldn't understand what had happened.

Michael said, "It wasn't your fault. You had nothing to d with it." And after a long time, during which Ryan sat there apparently ashamed of his outburst, and looking confused an defeated, Michael said again: "She'll come back. You wait an see. It isn't over."

On February 10, Michael was released from the hospital. H was still very weak, which was frustrating to him, but his hea muscle had showed remarkable improvement. His overall healt was good. He rode uptown in a black limousine with Aaron.

The driver of the car was a pale-skinned black man name Henri, who would be living in the back *garçonnière* behin Deirdre's oak, and taking care of everything for Michael.

The day was clear and warm. There had been a bitter freez again right after Christmas, and several inundating rains, but th weather was now like spring, and the pink and red azaleas wer blooming all over the property. The sweet olive had regained a of its beautiful green leaves in the aftermath of the freeze, an a new bright color was coming out on the oak trees.

Everybody was happy, explained Henri, because Mardi Gra was "just around the corner." The parades would be startin any day now.

Michael took a walk around the garden. All the dead tropica plants had been cleared away, but the new banana trees wer already springing up from the dark freeze-killed stumps, an even the gardenias were coming back, dropping their shrivele brown leaves and breaking out in dark glossy new foliage. Th bony white crepe myrtle trees were still bare, but that was to b expected. All along the front fence the camellias were covere with dark red blossoms. And the tulip magnolias had only jus ropped their great saucerlike blooms; the flagstones were lit-red with their large pink petals.

The house itself was shining clean and in perfect order.

Aunt Vivian had taken the bedroom which had belonged to arlotta, and Eugenia was still at the very far end of the second oor, near the kitchen stairway. Aaron slept in the second bed-oom in the front, the room that had once belonged to Millie ear.

Michael did not want to return to the front room, and they ad readied the old northside master bedroom for him. It was uite inviting—even with the high-backed wooden bed in which eirdre had died, now heaped with white down comforters and illows. He liked in particular the small northside front porch n which he could go out and sit at the iron table and look out ver the corner.

For days there was a procession of visitors. Bea came with ily, and then Cecilia and Clancy and Pierce, and Randall came y with Ryan who had various papers to be signed, and others ropped in, whose names he had trouble remembering. Some-mes he talked to them; sometimes he didn't. Aaron was very ood at taking care of things for him. Aunt Vivian was very roficient at receiving people as well.

But he could see how deeply the cousins were troubled. They ere chastened, restrained, and above all, bewildered. They vere uneasy in the house, even at times a little jumpy.

Not so Michael. The house was empty, and clean as far as he vas concerned. And he knew every little repair that had been one; every shade of paint that had been used; every bit of re-cored plaster or woodwork. It was his greatest accomplishment, ght up to the new copper gutters, and down to the heart pine oors he'd stripped and stained himself. He felt just fine here.

"I'm glad to see you're not wearing those awful gloves any-more," Beatrice said. It was Sunday, and the second time she ad come, and they were sitting in the bedroom.

"No, I don't need them now," said Michael. "It's the strang-st thing, but after the accident in the pool, my hands went back o normal."

"You don't see things anymore?"

"No," he said. "Maybe I never used the power right. Maybe didn't use it in time. And so it was taken away from me."

"Sounds like a blessing," said Bea, trying to conceal her onfusion.

"Doesn't matter now," said Michael.

Aaron saw Beatrice to the door. Only by chance did Michael vander past the head of the steps, and happen to hear her saying

to Aaron, "He looks ten years older." Bea was crying, actuall[y]
She was begging Aaron to tell her how this tragedy had com[e]
about. "I could believe it," she said, "that this house is curse[d.]
It's full of evil. They should never have planned to live in th[is]
house. We should have stopped them. You should make him g[o]
away from here."

Michael went back into the bedroom and shut the door behi[nd]
him.

When he looked into the mirror of Deirdre's old dresser, [he]
decided that Bea was right. He did look older. He hadn't notic[ed]
the gray hair at his temples. There was a little sparkle of gra[y]
mixed in with all the rest too. And he had perhaps a few mo[re]
lines in his face than he'd had before. Maybe even a lot of them
Especially around his eyes.

Suddenly he smiled. He hadn't even noticed what he put o[n]
this afternoon. Now he saw that it was a dark satin smokin[g]
jacket, with velvet lapels, which Bea had sent to him at th[e]
hospital. Aunt Viv had laid it out for him. Imagine, Micha[el]
Curry, the Irish Channel boy, wearing a thing like that, [he]
thought. It ought to belong to Maxim de Winter at Manderle[y.]
He gave a melancholy smile at his image, with one eyebro[w]
raised. And the gray at his temples making him look, wha[t.]
Distinguished.

"*Eh bien,* Monsieur," he said, striving to sound to himse[lf]
like the voice of Julien he'd heard on the street in San Francisc[o.]
Even his expression had changed somewhat. He felt he had [a]
touch of Julien's resignation.

Of course this was his Julien, the Julien he had seen on th[e]
bus, and whom Richard Llewellyn had once seen in a dream
Not the playful smiling Julien of his portraits, or the menacin[g]
laughing Julien of the dark hellish place full of smoke and fir[e.]
That place hadn't really existed.

He went downstairs, slowly, the way the doctor recom
mended, and went into the library. There had never been any
thing in the desk since it was cleaned out after Carlotta's deat[h,]
and so he had made it his, and he kept his notebook there. H[is]
diary.

It was the same diary he'd started to keep on his first visit [to]
Oak Haven. And he continued to write in it—making entrie[s]
almost every day, because it was the only place that he coul[d]
express what he really felt about what had happened.

Of course he had told Aaron everything. And Aaron was th[e]
only person he would ever tell.

But he needed this quiet, contemplative relationship with th[e]
blank page in which to voice his soul completely. It was beau[-]

ful to sit here, only now and then looking up through the lace
urtains at the passersby who were headed up to St. Charles
venue to see the Venus parade. Only two more days until Mardi
ras.

But the one thing he didn't like was that he could sometimes
ear the drums in the quiet. That had happened yesterday, and
e hated it.

When he was tired of writing, he took his copy of *Great Ex-
ectations* off the shelf, sat down at the end of the leather couch
earest the fireplace, and started reading. In a little while, Eu-
enia or Henri would come, he figured, and bring him some-
ing to eat. And maybe he'd eat it and maybe he wouldn't.

Fifty-four

TUESDAY, FEBRUARY 27, Mardi Gras Night.
"I will never believe that what I saw the second time
vas a true vision. I maintain now and always will that it was
_asher's doing. Those weren't the Mayfair Witches, because they
re not here, earthbound and waiting to pass through the door,
hough that might have been a lie he told them during their
ndividual lives, and part of the pact which he used to gain their
:ooperation.

"I believe that as each one of them died, he or she either
:eased to exist or attained a greater wisdom. And there was no
ntent to cooperate with any plan on this earth. If anything,
attempts were made to thwart it.

"Such an attempt was made when Deborah and Julien came
o me the first time. They told me about the plan and that I had
o intervene, to subvert Rowan so that Rowan could not be se-
luced by Lasher and his deceptions. And in San Francisco, when
hey told me to go home, they were trying to get me to intervene
again.

"I believe this because there is no other sensible explanation.
I would never have agreed to do anything so evil as father the
child by which that greedy monster could come through. And if
I had even been privy to such a horror, I would have awakened

not with a sense of zeal and purpose, but in an utter panic, and with a deep revulsion against those who tried to use me.

"No. It was all Lasher's doing, that last hallucinatory vision of hellish earthbound souls and their ugly, ignorant morality. And the tip-off, of course, and I don't know why Aaron can't see it, was the appearance of the nuns in the vision. For the nuns most certainly didn't belong there. And the drums of Comus—they didn't belong there either. They were from my childhood fears.

"The whole hellish spectacle was drawn from my childhood fears and dreads; and Lasher tumbled them all up with the Mayfair Witches, to create a hell for me that would keep me dead and drowned and in despair.

"If his plan had worked, I would have really died, of course, and his vision of hell would have vanished, and maybe, just maybe, in some life after I would have found the true explanation.

"It's difficult to think about that last part, however. Because I didn't die. And what I have now, for what it's worth, is a second chance to stop Lasher, simply by being alive, and being here.

"After all, Rowan knows I'm here, and I can't believe that every vestige of love for me in Rowan is dead. It doesn't check with the evidence of my senses.

"On the contrary, Rowan not only knows I'm waiting, she wants me to wait, and that is why she's given the house to me. In her own way she has asked me to remain here and continue to believe in her.

"My worst fear, however, is now that that greedy thing is in the flesh, it will hurt Rowan. It will reach some point where it doesn't need her anymore, and it will try to get rid of her. I can only hope and pray that she destroys it before that time comes, though the more I think things over, the more I come to realize how hard it will be for her to do that.

"Rowan always tried to warn me that she had a propensity for evil that I didn't have. Of course I'm not the innocent that she supposed. And she isn't really evil. But what she is—is brilliant and purely scientific. She's in love with the cells of that thing, I know she is, from a purely scientific point of view, and she's studying them. She's studying the whole organism and how it performs and how it moves through the world, and concentrating on whether or not it is indeed an improved version of a human being, and if so, what that improvement means, and how it can eventually be used for good.

"Why Aaron can't accept that, I don't know either. He is so

sympathetic but so persistently noncommittal. The Talamasca really are a bunch of monks, and though he keeps pleading with me to go to England, it's just not possible. I could never live with them; they are too passive; and much too theoretical.

"Besides, it is absolutely essential that I wait here for Rowan. After all, only two months have passed, and it may be years before Rowan can finally resolve this. Rowan is only thirty years old, and that is really young in this day and age.

"And knowing her as I do, being the only one who knows her at all, I am convinced that Rowan will move eventually towards true wisdom.

"So that is my take on what happened. The Mayfair Witches as an earthbound coven don't exist and never did, and the pact was a lie; and my initial visions were of good beings who sent me here in the hopes of ending a reign of evil.

"Are they angry with me now? Have they turned away from me in my failure? Or do they accept that I tried, using the only tools I had, and do they see perhaps, what I see, that Rowan will return and that the story isn't finished?

"I can't know. But I do know that there is no evil lurking in this house, no souls hanging about in its rooms. On the contrary, it feels wonderfully clean and bright, just the way I intended it to be.

"I've been slowly going through the attics, finding interesting things. I've found all of Antha's short stories, and they are fascinating. I sit upstairs in that third-floor room and read them by the sunlight coming in the windows, and I feel Antha all around me—not a ghost, but the living presence of the woman who wrote those delicate sentences, trying to voice her agony and her struggle, and her joy at being free for such a short time in New York.

"Who knows what else I'll find up there. Maybe Julien's autobiography is tucked behind a beam.

"If only I had more energy, if only I didn't have to take things so slowly, and a walk around the place wasn't such a chore.

"Of course it is the most exquisite place for walking imaginable. I always knew that.

"The old rose garden is coming back, gorgeously, in these warm days, and just yesterday, Aunt Viv told me that she had always dreamed of having roses to tend in her old age, and that she would care for them from now on, that the gardener only needed to give her a little assistance. Seems he remembered 'old Miss Belle' who had taken care of these roses in the past, and he's been filling her head with the names of the various species.

"I think it's marvelous, that she is so happy here.

"I myself prefer the wilder, less tended flowers. Last week, after they had put the screens back up on Deirdre's old porch and I had gotten a new rocking chair for it, I noticed that the honeysuckle was crawling over the new wooden railing in full force, and on up the cast iron, just the way it was when we first came here.

"And outside, in the flower beds, beneath the fancy camellias, the wild four o'clocks are coming back, and so is the little lantana that we called bacon and eggs with its orange and brown flowers. I told the gardeners not to touch those things. To let it have its old wild look again. After all, the patterns are too dominant at the moment.

"I feel as if I'm moving from diamonds to rectangles to squares when I walk around, and I want it softened, obscured, drenched in green, the way the Garden District always was in my memory.

"Also it isn't private enough. Today of all days, when people were trooping through the streets, heading for the parade route on St. Charles to see Rex pass, or just to wander in their carnival costumes, too many heads turned to peer through the fence. It ought to be more secretive.

"In fact, regarding that very question, the strangest thing happened tonight.

"But let me briefly review the day, being that it was Mardi Gras, and the day of days.

"The Mayfair Five Hundred were here early, as the Rex parade passes on St. Charles Avenue at about eleven o'clock. Ryan had seen to all the arrangements, with a big buffet breakfast set out at nine, followed by lunch at noon, and an open bar with coffee and tea all day.

"Perfect, especially since I didn't have to do a damned thing but now and then come down in the elevator, shake a few hands, kiss a few cheeks, and then plead fatigue, which was no lie, and go back upstairs to rest.

"My idea of how to run this place exactly. Especially with Aaron there to help, and Aunt Vivian enjoying every minute of it.

"From the upstairs porches, I watched the children running back and forth from here to the avenue, playing on the lawn outside, and even swimming, on account of its being just a perfectly lovely day. I wouldn't go near that pool for love nor money, but it's fun to see them splashing in it, it really is.

"Wonderful to realize that the house makes all this possible, whether Rowan is here or not. Whether I am here or not.

"But around five o'clock, when things were winding down,

and some of the children were napping, and everyone was waiting for Comus, my lovely peace and quiet came to an end.

"I looked up from *War and Peace* to see Aaron and Aunt Viv standing there before me, and I knew before they spoke what they were going to say.

"I ought to put on clothes, I ought to eat something, I ought to at least sample the salt-free dishes Henri had so carefully prepared for me. I ought to come downstairs.

"And I ought to at least walk up to the avenue to see Comus, said Aunt Viv, the very last parade of Mardi Gras night.

"As if I didn't know.

"Aaron stood quiet all this time saying nothing, and then he ventured that maybe it would be good for me to see the parade after all these years, and sort of dispel the mystique which had built up around it and of course he would be there with me the whole time.

"I don't know what got into me but I said yes.

"I dressed in a dark suit, tie, the works, combed my hair, thrilling at the sight of the gray, and feeling uncomfortable and constrained after weeks of robes and pajamas, I went downstairs. Lots of hugs and kisses, and warm greetings from the dozens of Mayfair lolling about everywhere. And didn't I look good? And didn't I look much better? And all those tiresome but well-intentioned remarks.

"Michael, the cardiac cripple. I was out of breath from simply coming down the stairs!

"Whatever the case, by six-thirty I started walking slowly towards the avenue with Aaron, Aunt Viv having gone ahead with Bea and Ryan and a legion of others, and there came those drums all right, that fierce diabolical cadence as if accompanying a convicted witch in a tumbrel to be burned at the stake.

"I hated it with all my heart, and I hated the sight of the lights up there, but I knew Aaron was right. I ought to see it. And besides, I wasn't really afraid. Hate is one thing. Fear is another. How completely calm I felt in my hate.

"The crowds were sparse since it was the very end of the day and the whole season, and there was no problem at all finding a comfortable place to stand on the neutral ground, in all the beaten-down grass and litter from the day-long mayhem, and I wound up leaning against a trolley line pole, hands behind my back, as the first floats came into view.

"Ghastly, ghastly as it had been in childhood, these mammoth quivering papier-mâché structures rolling slowly down the avenue beyond the heads of the jubilant crowds.

"I remembered my dad bawling me out when I was seven.

'Michael, you're not scared of anything real, you know it? But you gotta get over your crazy fear of those parades.' And he was right of course. By that time, I had had a terrible fear of them, and been a real crybaby about it, ruining Mardi Gras for him and my mother, that was true. I got over it soon enough. Or at least I learned to hide it as the years passed.

"Well, what was I seeing now, as the flambeau carriers came marching and prancing along, with those beautiful stinking torches, and the sound of the drums grew louder with the approach of the first of the big proud high school bands?

"Just a mad, pretty spectacle, wasn't it? It was all much more brightly lighted for one thing, with the high-powered street lamps, and the old flambeaux were included for old times' sake only, not for illumination, and the young boys and girls playing the drums were just handsome and bright-faced young boys and girls.

"Then came the king's float, amid cheering and screaming, a great paper throne, high and ornate and splendidly decorated, with the man himself quite fine in his jeweled crown, mask, and long curling wig. What extravagance, all that velvet. And of course he waved his golden cup with such perfect composure, as if this wasn't one of the most bizarre sights in the world.

"Harmless, all of it harmless. Not dark and terrible and no one about to be executed. Little Mona Mayfair tugged at my hand suddenly. She wanted to know if I would hold her on my shoulders. Her daddy had said he was tired.

"Of course, I told her. The hard part was getting her on and then standing back up, not so good for the old ticker—I almost died!—but I did it, and she had a great time screaming for throws and reaching for the junk beads and plastic cups raining upon us from the passing floats.

"And what pretty old-fashioned floats they were. Like the floats in our childhood, Bea explained, with none of the new mechanical or electric gimmicks. Just lovely intricate confections of delicate trembling trees and flowers and birds, trimmed exquisitely in sparkling foil. The men of the krewe, masked and costumed in satin, worked hard pitching their trinkets and junk into the sea of upthrust hands.

"At last it was finished. Mardi Gras was over. Ryan helped Mona down off my shoulders, scolding her for bothering me, and I protested that it had been fun.

"We walked back slowly, Aaron and I falling behind the others, and then as the party went on inside with champagne and music, this strange thing happened, which was as follows:

"I took my usual walk around the dark garden, enjoying the

beautiful white azaleas that were blooming all over, and the pretty petunias and other annual flowers which the gardeners had put into the beds. When I reached the big crepe myrtle at the back of the lawn, I realized for the first time that it was finally coming back into leaf. Tiny little green leaves covered it all over, though in the light of the moon it still looked bony and bare.

"I stood under the tree for a few minutes, looking towards First Street, and watching the last stragglers from the avenue pass the iron fence. I think I was wondering if I could chance a cigarette out here with no one to catch me and stop me, and then I realized that of course I didn't have any, that Aaron and Aunt Viv, on the doctor's orders, had thrown them all away.

"Whatever the case, I was drifting in my thoughts and loving the spring warmth, when I realized that a mother and child were rushing by out there, and that the child, seeing me under the tree, had pointed and said something to the mother about 'that man.'

" 'That man.'

"It hit me with a sudden jolt of hilarity. I was 'that man.' I had switched places with Lasher. I had become the man in the garden. I had now taken up his old station and his old role. I was without question the dark-haired man of First Street, and the pattern of it and the irony of it made me laugh and laugh.

"No wonder the son of a bitch said he loved me. He should. He stole my child, my wife and my lover, and he left me here, planted in his place. He took my life from me, and gave me his haunting ground in exchange. Why wouldn't he love me for all that?

"I don't know how long I stood there smiling to myself, and laughing quietly in the darkness, but gradually I got tired. Just being on my feet for any length of time tires me out.

"And then a brokenhearted sort of sadness came over me, because the pattern seemed to have significance, and I thought maybe I've been wrong all along, and there *are* real witches. And we are all damned.

"But I don't believe that.

"I went on with my nocturnal wanderings, and later said good-bye to all the lovely Mayfairs, promising to visit, yes, when I felt better, and assuring them we'd have another big party here on St. Patrick's Day in just a very few weeks.

"The night grew quiet and empty like any other night in the Garden District finally, and the Comus parade, in retrospect, became ever more unreal in its prettiness and gaudiness, like something that couldn't have taken place with all that pomp and seriousness in a grown-up world.

"Yes, conquered that old beast I did by going. Silenced those drums forever, I hope and pray.

"And I don't believe that it was all patterned and planned and destined. I don't.

"Maybe Aaron in his passivity and his dogmatic open-mindedness can entertain the idea that it was planned—that even my father's death was part of it, and that I was destined just to be a stud for Rowan, and a father for Lasher. But accept this I do not.

"And it isn't only that I don't believe it. I can't.

"I can't believe it because my reason tells me that such a system, in which anyone dictates our every move—be it a god, or a devil, or our subconscious mind, or our tyrannical genes— is simply impossible.

"Life itself must be founded upon the infinite possibility for choice and accident. And if we cannot prove that it is, we must believe that it is. We must believe that we can change, that we can control, that we can direct our own destinies.

"Things could have gone differently. Rowan could have refused to help that thing. She could have killed it. And she may kill it yet. And behind her actions may lie the tragic possibility that once it had come into the flesh, she couldn't bring herself to destroy it.

"I refuse to judge Rowan. The rage I felt against her is now gone.

"And I choose of my own free will to stay here, waiting for her, and believing in her.

"That belief in her is the first tenet of my credo. And no matter how enormous and intricate this web of events seems, no matter how much it is like all the patterns of flags and balustrades and repetitive cast iron that dominate this little plot of earth, I maintain my credo.

"I believe in Free Will, the Force Almighty by which we conduct ourselves as if we were the sons and daughters of a just and wise God, even if there is no such Supreme Being. And by free will, we can choose to do good on this earth, no matter that we all die, and do not know where we go when we die, or if a justice or explanation awaits us.

"I believe that we can through our reason know what good is, and in the communion of men and women, in which the forgiveness of wrongs will always be more significant than the avenging of them, and that in the beautiful natural world that surrounds us, we represent the best and the finest of beings, for

1036

we alone can see that natural beauty, appreciate it, learn from it, weep for it, and seek to conserve it and protect it.

"I believe finally that we are the only true moral force in the physical world, the makers of ethics and moral ideas, and that we must be as good as the gods we've created in the past to guide us.

"I believe that through our finest efforts, we will succeed finally in creating heaven on earth, and we do it every time that we love, every time that we embrace, every time that we commit to create rather than destroy, every time that we place life over death, and the natural over what is unnatural, insofar as we are able to define it.

"And I suppose I do believe in the final analysis that a peace of mind can be obtained in the face of the worst horrors and the worst losses. It can be obtained by faith in change and in will and in accident; and by faith in ourselves, that we will do the right thing, more often than not, in the face of adversity.

"For ours is the power and the glory, because we are capable of visions and ideas which are ultimately stronger and more enduring than we are.

"That is my credo. That is why I believe in my interpretation of the story of the Mayfair Witches.

"Probably wouldn't stand up against the philosophers of the Talamasca. Maybe won't even go into the file. But it's my belief, for what it's worth, and it sustains me. And if I were to die right now, I wouldn't be afraid. Because I can't believe that horror or chaos awaits us.

"If any revelation awaits us at all, it must be as good as our ideals and our best philosophy. For surely nature must embrace the visible *and* the invisible, and it couldn't fall short of us. The thing that makes the flowers open and the snowflakes fall must contain a wisdom and a final secret as intricate and beautiful as the blooming camellia or the clouds gathering above, so white and pure in the blackness.

"If that isn't so, then we are in the grip of a staggering irony. And all the spooks of hell might as well dance in the parlor. There could be a devil. People who burn other people to death are fine. There could be anything.

"But the world is simply too beautiful for that.

"At least it seems that way to me as I sit here now on the screened porch, in the rocking chair, with all the Mardi Gras noise having long ago died away, writing by the light from the distant parlor lamp behind me.

"Only our capacity for goodness is as fine as this silken breeze coming from the south, as fine as the scent of the rain just beginning to fall, with a faint roar as it strikes the shimmering leaves, so gentle, gentle as the vision of the rain itself strung like silver through the fabric of the embracing darkness.

"Come home, Rowan. I'm waiting."

ABOUT THE AUTHOR

Anne Rice was born in New Orleans, where she now lives with her husband, the poet Stan Rice, and their son, Christopher.